Equipped of devas-tation, the huge battleship holds a world enslaved by its very presence. With it, the Imperator and his forces have no need to fire a shot, no need to fill the jails. For who would risk the destruction of the entire world to bring the Imperator down?

Yet still the rebels gather, plotting their near hopeless plans, driven by the cruelty of their conquerors to the very brink of desperate action. And now they have an unexpected ally, an offworlder with skills far beyond their own, Adelaar aici Arash, a woman out to rescue her daughter and claim revenge on those who have wronged her.

But can even an offworlder's advanced technology defeat that most powerful of sky fortresses—the dreaded Warmaster?

JO CLAYTON
HAS ALSO WRITTEN:

THE SKEEN TRILOGY
SKEEN'S LEAP
SKEEN'S RETURN
SKEEN'S SEARCH

THE DIADEM SERIES
DIADEM FROM THE STARS
LAMARCHOS
IRSUD
MAEVE
STAR HUNTERS
THE NOWHERE HUNT
GHOSTHUNT
THE SNARES OF IBEX
QUESTER'S ENDGAME

THE DUEL OF SORCERY TRILOGY
MOONGATHER
MOONSCATTER
CHANGER'S MOON

THE DRINKER OF SOULS SERIES
DRINKER OF SOULS
BLUE MAGIC

and
A BAIT OF DREAMS
SHADOW OF THE WARMASTER

JO CLAYTON

SHADOW OF THE WARMASTER

DAW BOOKS, INC.
DONALD A. WOLLHEIM, PUBLISHER

1633 Broadway, New York, NY 10019

Cover art by Jody Lee.

DAW Book Collectors No. 758.

First Printing, October 1988

1 2 3 4 5 6 7 8 9

Printed in the U.S.A

I

1

Two hours before zeropoint—the meeting of Swardheld Quale and Adelaar aici Arash (from which events will be dated, backward and forward as circumstances warrant). Prin Daruze/Telffer.

Sometime round midmorning on the third day of the second week in the spring month *Calftime*, Nuba Treviglio, Freetrader and free soul, set her ship down on the stretch of metacrete Telffer laughingly calls its star port, discharged one passenger and droned into town on the ship's flit to see what the world had to offer her.

Adelaar aici Arash watched her leave. To the ground, Treviglio said, what you do after that is your business and by god, she meant it. Adelaar bent over her case and thumbed on the a/g-lift, straightened and looked for some means of transport.

Metacrete, flat, filthy, chalk white, seemed like there were kilometers of it on every side, reaching out to touch the mountains in the west, the blue glitter of the sea in the east, and the long dark line in front of her, the city that serviced this desolation. A brisk wind blew from the distant seashore, dragging with it pungent sea smells (seawrack, dead fish, iodine and brine); it lifted off the 'crete a heavy white grit that it drove hissssing against half a dozen shuttles and a massive barge, against a battered wreck being stripped for parts, against two tenth-hand stingships snugged close like link-twins, against some ancient flickits gray and vaguely insectile, against Adelaar's boots in a soft continual patter, against her tan twill trousers, the close-fitting tan twill jacket, against her face, forcing tears from her half-closed eyes. She flattened her shoulders, tugged on the case's tether and started walking, moving with an easy contained stride toward the city ahead. Except for the diminishing dot that was Treviglio on the flit, nothing but the wind and the grit moved in all that shimmery white glare.

She was short, slight, neatly made, hovering about early middle age with the help of ananile drugs. She wore her tan hair trimmed close to her head so she could run a comb through it and forget it; the wind was teasing it, twisting it into a ragged halo about her face, angering her though she wouldn't permit her annoyance to show except in the slight deepening of the shallow crows'-feet at the corners of her eyes, large eyes, gentian blue, cold eyes in a face adept at concealing what went on behind it.

After twenty minutes of brisk walking, she reached the edge of the field and stepped onto Telffer's StarStreet.

StarStreet/Prin Daruze/Telffer had a fuel dump, a shipsupply store that from the look of it operated by appointment only, a short stretch of pavement and a very tall fence. Adelaar angled toward the Gate and stopped before a wooden kiosk painted black with a battered plastic window so scratched by windborne grit it had lost any transparency it had ever had. The Gate was shut, there were eyes and heat sensors soldered to the fencewire, melters perched on swivelposts atop the wire. She looked from them to the kiosk. "T'k t'k, sweet sweet."

She located the outside palmer, a dullmetal oval freckled with old black paint, slapped her hand against it. A wall section shuddered, squealed, pleated itself until there was an opening wide enough for her to edge through. Tugging the case inside with her, she crossed to the heavyduty comset screwed onto the back wall and inspected it as the door squealed shut behind her, closing her in with an unpleasant smell, a mix of ancient sweat, dead moss and dryrot. Fungus grew in scaly patches on the greasy metal of the comset; there was an ugly olive-ocher film on the com's thumbglass.

She touched the glass, her face rigid with distaste, rubbed her thumb repeatedly along her side as she watched a hold-pattern shiver over the plate. A minute passed. She glanced at the ringchron on her left hand, glanced again. Again. "If I was paying you, you'd be out on your ass yesterday."

Two minutes, three, five. . . . A loud ting. A face in the plate, male functionary, a slash of a mouth, a thin nose so long it approached the grotesque.

"Name, origin, ship, purpose of visit." A bored monotone.

"Adelaar aici Arash. Droom in the Heggers." She slipped her diCarx from her belt, touched it to the reader, slid it back in its squeeze pocket when the pinlight flashed red. "Passenger tradeship Niyit-Nit, owner/captain Nuba Treviglio. Business with a resident of Telffer."

"What business? Who?"

Adelaar hesitated; as she'd built up her client list, she'd dealt with men like this and knew how unproductive annoyance was; push at them and they set their feet like mules. On the other hand, she wanted to say as little as possible to local authorities, she didn't know what their under-the-table ties were. There was a man on Aggerdorn asking questions about her the day she closed with Treviglio for passage here; the Niyit-Nit lifted before she learned more, but she had little doubt who he worked for, less doubt that there were people in Prin Daruze with the same ties. Bolodo had stringers wherever there was a market for their contractees and raw worlds like Telffer always needed more hands. Hmm, throw him Quale's name if he keeps pushing me, no point trying to keep that quiet, soon as I hit the Directory, who wants to know will.

"That's my concern, not yours," she said, her voice neutral, nonaggressive, despite the implicit challenge of the words. "Should licenses be necessary, I will apply at the proper time and place."

"What business? Who?" He wasn't going to drop it

though he knew and she knew he was going beyond his instructions.

"Swardheld Quale. I'll let him know your interest in him. I'm sure he'll be delighted someone cares."

Conceding defeat with a malevolent glower, he gabbled another setspeech. "Qualified access granted, downtime coincident downtime Niyit-Nit, overstay downtime, fine one thousand telfs minimum assessed per day, business, full disclosure liabilities required on penalty locktime, locktime set complaint Telff, flake evidence, no recourse offworlder, locktime possibility conversion to fine by Camar Prin Daruze, schedule fines determined Camar, warning, altercation with Telff, presumed guilty, onus on offworlder t' prove case, congel, madura, olhon, grao, ebeche, viuvar, tendrij woods consensual monopoly, license required for export, severe penalty for attempted removal, any questions?"

"None."

"Gate open." The com went dark.

"T'k t'k, sweet sweet."

She tugged on the case's tether, slapped her hand against the interior palmer; when the panel shuddered without budging, she gave it a kick with her boot heel that sent it sliding open, squealing and whimpering as the pleats formed. Wanting to kick the functionary where he'd feel it, she booted the door again, then swore at her folly as it died on her, the opening barely wide enough to let her waggle the case through and squeeze after it.

Outside, she brushed at herself, tucked away her annoyance and strode through the Gate.

As it clanked shut behind her, she looked about. She was on the outskirts of a gridded cluster of low, blocky, windowless buildings, gray and brown, scratched, dingy, not a bush or blade of grass to break the monotony. Automated factories. Deliveries of raw materials already made, production in process, everything tucked neatly out of sight and sound. The patched, dusty streets were empty; as far as she could see there wasn't an intelligent entity within kilometers of her. No transport. He hadn't given her the chance to call a cab. "T'k, animated spleen."

She started walking.

There was a tall octagonal tower lifting like a raised finger over the city, a flagpole stuck in the top with half a dozen tattered banners flapping in the wind. She assumed it marked some sort of official center and used it to guide her through the factory section.

After another twenty minutes without seeing anyone, a ground car like a black beetle hummed around a corner and sped past her; its driver stared at her, but went on without stopping.

"Friendly."

More of the humpy little vehicles zipped past, drivers and passengers staring, no one offering a ride, a word, a favor. Great little world. Uh-huh! Bolodo would have a market here, selling closed contracts that took the laborers away when the job was done. Probably why the settlers came way out here in the first place, five generations of hermits, misanthropes and social inadequates whose idea of a good time had to be something like masturbation in a hot tub. Solitary masturbation. Hah! might as well put out a sign saying stay away, we don't want you. Leave your coin, but leave. She fumed a while longer, then laughed, shook her head. Eh-eh, Adelaar, you're just annoyed because your feet hurt. Multiple maledictions on those perfidious perjurous unprincipled bootmakers who foisted these instruments of torture on me.

The streets widened, lost their rule-drawn rigor as they turned and twisted among lush greenery, trees, shrubs, grasses, flowers, a thousand versions of fern from great, graceful clumps fanning overhead, their shadows a dark lace on the pale gray pavement, to gossamer cilia hanging from the trees. In this tangle, tossed down haphazardly, she saw bits and pieces of small free-standing structures, some domed, some with peaked roofs, some like tumbled toy blocks. Living places. The silence of the factories was gone; she heard birdsong and bug hum, children's laughter and their screams as they played among the ferns, voices of men and women talking, a man's shout. Now and then she saw the Telffs. They stopped what they were doing and stared at her, but no one spoke. The beetle cars came more frequently and were no friendlier than before; several times she had to jump for the gutter when a driver swerved at her, shouting obscenities. Sweat beaded on her skin and stayed there, adding to the discomforts this world laid on her the moment she set foot on it. If it had been anything else but Aslan that'd brought her here. . . . Aaah! he'd better be good, Quale damn well better be good.

The streets straightened and grew wider, the vegetation thinned. She glanced up, kinking her neck to see the top of the tower, stood watching the banners flutter as she smiled in weary anticipation of a bed and a bath and food in her belly. Traffic was heavier and less aggressive, the drivers too involved with their own concerns to let their xenophobia loose on her. She went round a final curve and found herself trudging up a short ramp onto a raised walkway. "A real live sidewalk. Civilization at last."

She moved past a clutch of small stores offering everything from stacks of fruit to electronic gadgets. The stores changed to eating houses, then taverns, then she was in a grimy rundown area, stepping over men sprawled sleeping on the walkway, around vomit and splatters of urine; she jumped down into the street several times to avoid clusters of lounging idle males who, when they saw her, whistled, popped their lips, made suggestive sucking noises, groped their crotches and shouted offers of assorted body parts. Twice a man grabbed at her, but she managed to avoid his hand and move on without having to damage him; they were Telffs and by functionary's warning, onus would be on her to justify whatever she did and she knew from frustrating experiences elsewhere that her presence here unaccompanied would be excuse enough for whatever they tried on her. Despite her growing fatigue, she set a quick pace for herself, her heels clicking briskly on the boards; she looked directly ahead of her, her face impassive, ignoring the taunts, counting on her peripheral vision to warn her of anything coming at her from the side, on her ears to warn her of an attack from behind.

"Drop." Female voice, loud, coming from the street. Without hesitation Adelaar went down, curling round as she dropped, landing on hip and elbow, shenli darter out and ready.

She didn't need it. Two men lay crumpled on the walkway some five or six meters off. She swung her legs under her and was on her feet a breath later. A flit curved over to her, its offside door open.

"Jump." Same voice.

She grabbed the case's tether and jumped. As soon as she was inside, before she'd sorted herself out, the driver slapped in the lever and the flit took off as if she'd goosed it. Adelaar straightened up, clipped the darter back under her arm and arranged the case by her feet. "Thanks."

"Nada."

"Ahhmm, kill them?"

"Nope. Stunned 'em. Didn't know maybe they were friends of yours playing a prank."

"Not."

"Takes all types." The driver swung the flit round a corner and slowed to a more decorous pace. "That should be enough to keep us clear of lice. You just in? Thought so. You want to believe the shit they tell you at the Gate, mess with a local and you lose. You got credit, they suck blood, no credit, Bolodo gets you. Reason I yelled, one of your unfriends had what looked like an Ifklii yagamouche; if he was a pro, he could've fried your brain 'fore he went down. I *loathe* those things."

Adelaar shivered. "I owe you. Let me . . ." Moving her hand slowly so she wouldn't startle her rescuer, she eased a business card from her belt. "Here. Give me a call sometime."

"Shove it in the abdit there in front of you, no need, though."

"I know. Nonetheless . . ." She dropped the card into the hollow. "That's a quiet stunner you've got, I didn't hear a thing."

"Built it myself. Any place you want to go?"

"City Center, the Directory. You're not a local."

"Sweet lot, aren't they. No. But I've a friend here and a map on call. Center Directory it is. Or . . . mmmm . . . nothing like a long hot bath after hard traveling, there's an ottotel not too far from Center, got a com plate in the more expensive rooms, these're tapped into the Main Directory, you can bypass most of the hassle that way, let your fingers do the talking." She grinned, dropping more years off her absurdly childlike face. Barely past puberty, if looks counted. A pretty child, kafolay skin, kaff brown eyes, light brown-gold hair in an exuberant halo of tiny curls. There was a brown tattoo on the cheek nearest Adelaar, a detailed drawing of a hawk's head. A sudden dimple made the hawk dance as the girl broadened her grin when she caught Adelaar staring at her.

Adelaar drew her hand down the side of her face, looked at the smear of mud in the palm. "Ottotel," she said. "Please."

"Know what you mean. Shadith. My name."

"Adelaar aici Arash. Mine."

"Pleased to."

"And I."

2

Adelaar locked the door, activated a sweep from the case to ensure her privacy (local authorities legal and otherwise tended to ignore regulations when it suited them). Calling blessings on Shadith's head from every god, saint and holy force she knew, she scrubbed off Telffer's grit, grime and sticky sweat and with them the greater part of her irritation, pulled on a robe tailored from midnight silk, dialed up a pot of Nara tea and settled in front of the plate. Whistling a snatch of an old song, she fed tokens into the slot.

"Quale, Quale, where are you when you're home? If you're home . . ."

She scrolled through the directory.

"Let Treviglio be right, let him *be* home, wherever that is. Wherever . . . ah! here we are. Swardheld Quale/ Quale's Nest. T'k t'k, how cute. God help me, suppose his mind really works like that. Lat 2 deg 31 min W, Long 48 deg 53 min N. In residence, open for offers. Blessed be whatever. I'm running out of time and money. Damn. If I could handle this myself . . ." She thumbed off the directory and sat sipping at the tea, taking a moment to relax before she dressed and looked for transport out to Quale's Nest.

II

1

A short while before the meeting, less than an hour.
Quale's Nest/Telffer.

I was out in the back yard working on a harpframe, lovely wood, dark and resonant, didn't have a name, Herby snagged the tree out of the river and took it to his curing shed. Herby's a neighbor upstream, he belongs to one of the settlement families, his land's tax free so long as he or his kin own it; got the temperament and habits of a mudweasel, but he keeps to himself unless he scavenges something he thinks he can sell me, so he's not all that bad as a neighbor. Where was I? Ah. The harp. The shape sang under my hands and looked like music; whether it would sound as good, well, I was hoping. It was almost ready for stringing; I was carving a design into it, most complex pattern I've attempted, double spirals and woven lacings, amarelo buds and leaves in oval cartouches, took concentration and more patience than I thought I had until I started working on it. I'd put together frames before this one, trying one thing and another, different shapes, different woods, you get the idea; I wanted to make the sound as perfect as the shape. Far as I could tell. My ear's not so bad, but my fingers are all thumbs. The last one before this had a warm rich tone, I was quite pleased with it. When Shadith sent word she was coming, I got it out with a couple more and tuned them, I wanted to know what she thought.

Back yard's a comfortable place. I spend a lot of time here, working, reading, contemplating my navel, whatever. Got a plank fence around it to keep the vermin out. Flowering thornbushes grow in stripbeds against the planks. A sight to see, they are, come spring when every cane is thick with bloom. No roof, but there's a deflecter field for when it rains, keeps the wet out without ruining the skyview, which can be spectacular during summer storms. One of them was blowing up the day I'm talking about, clouds were gathering over Stormbringer's peak, they'd be down on us in an hour or so. I've got the ground under my worktable paved with roughcut slabs of slate. Some of them are cracked; griza grass grows in these cracks and between the slabs, that's a native grass, dusty looking gray-green, puts out seedheads in the spring, not the fall, they stand up over the blades like minute denuded umbrella ribs. Beyond the stone there's mute clover, griza doesn't have a chance against it. There are stacks of wood sitting around, some roughcut planks, some stripped logs. I've got a largish workshed in the south corner, the roof is mostly skylight; I store my tools in there but don't work inside except in winter when it's too cold to sit in the garden. Or when I need to use the lathe or one of the saws. There are two viuvars (like short fat willows) growing beside the shed and a tendrij in the north corner. The tendrij was here on my mountainside before I built my house. The trunk's a pewter column a hundred meters tall and thirty around; branches start about fifty meters up, black spikes spiraling around the bole; the leaves if you can call them that look like ten meter strips of gray-green and blue-green cellophane. When the storm winds blow them straight out, they roar loud enough to deafen you; on lazy warm spring days like this one, they shimmer and whisper and throw patches of shifting greens and blues in place of shadow.

My worktable is a built-up slab of congel wood. Tough, that wood, takes a molecular edge to work it, but it lasts forever; a benefit to living on Telffer, you pay in blood for congel offworld. Mottled medium brown with patches of gold like a pale tortoiseshell.

Pretty stuff, which is a good thing because it won't take stain any way you try it and even paint peels off, something about the oil, they say. I had the gouges I was using laid out on a patch of leather close to hand, the tool kit beside it, the frame I was working on set in padded clamps, the finished harps down at the far end waiting for Shadith to try them.

Butterflies flittered about, lighting on the thornflowers, feeding on their pollen; a sight to add pleasure to the day, but it meant I'd got worms in the wood and I was going to have to fumigate the yard. There were quilos squealing in the viuvars. Quilos are furry mats with skinny black legs, six of them, and deft little black fingers on their paws. Never been able to find any sign of eyes, ears or nose on them, though they're fine gliders and can skitter about on the ground like drops of water on a greased griddle. They drive the cats crazy, how can you prowl downwind of a thing that's got no nose or chase something that can switch direction without caring which end is front? I had five cats last time I counted and they're all neutered, so that should be that, but none of them are black and two days ago I saw this black body creeping low to the ground, going after a quilo who was chewing on a beetle it picked off a thornbush, it's why I tolerate a few of the things about, they keep the bug population down. I threw a chunk of wood at the cat and it streaked off. A young black tom. Pels says he thinks there's something mystical about black toms, there's never an assemblage of cats without one of them showing up, he says he's convinced they're born out of the collective unconscious of cats, structures of unbridled libido created to assuage cat lust. He may be right.

Pels kurk-Orso. Let's see. He's my com off and aux pilot. He's got a thing with plants and keeps my Slancy green; he's heavyworld born and bred, Mevvyaurang; not many have heard of it, Aurrangers aren't much for company or traveling. 2.85 g. Where they have three sexes. Sperm carrier (Rau), seed carrier (Arra), wombnurse (Maung). He's Rau. Hmm. There's a heavy burden he has to bear. Drives him into craziness sometimes. Females of every sentient species I've come across, even the reptilids, want to cuddle him, they all think he's devastatingly cute. Fluffy little teddy bear with big brown eyes. Barely up to my belt which is small even among his own people. Talking about the Aurrangers, they're agoraphobes in a big way, live in huddles underground. Funny, they're frightened of just about everything and they're the best damn predators I've met. You ought to see Pels stalking something. That fuzz of his isn't fur at all, when he's up for hunting, it kicks over into a shifting camouflage that beats hell out of a chameleon web. Thing is, he was born a misfit, always going out on the surface, fascinated by space and the stars that gave the night sky a frosty sheen; he was different enough to be miserable with his own people. He applied for a work-study grant to University and got it, being very very bright, but once he got his degree, with an honors list a km long, no one took him seriously enough to hire him. He was too damn cute.

When his money ran out, he had a choice between scavenging for scraps and a life of little crimes or living in luxury as a family pet. He was a reasonably competent burglar by the time I put my Slancy Orza into orbit park over Admin/University.

I was finishing a job for some xenobiologists, delivering a cargo of rare plants. The com off I had on that trip, she had a sweet paper trail and was a golden goddess for looks, but she was a whiner. Kumari and me, we came close to strangling her, but we held off till we reached University. We fired her without recommendation; it was safer than pushing her out a lock if not so satisfying. We turned over the plants and went out to celebrate our freedom from that rockdrill whine.

Sometime round dawn we got tangled up with Pels who was committing mayhem on what looked to be half the thugs on StarStreet. Amazing thing to watch. We hauled him loose and took him home with us because Kumari was curious about him. No, she wasn't about to go motherly over him. I talk about her as *she*, because she looks female, but she's a neuter, got the sex drive of a rock and her maternal instincts could be engraved øn a neutrino with a number ten nail. Most of her energy goes into curiosity.

We needed a com off, he needed a job. We took him on for one trip to see how he fit in. That was seven years ago.

Pels was digging around the thornbushes, pulling weeds, cleaning away sawdust and bits of paper and old leaves, loosening the earth about the roots. He keeps after me about the plants in the back yard, says I'm neglecting them, but those thornbushes could use a little neglect, they're volunteers blown in by the hefty winds we get in the thaw storms. If I pampered them the way he wants they'd take over the yard, hey, they'd take over the world. He was about three-quarters finished with the thorns, baroom-brooming along, happy as he could get on a miserable one-g world.

Kumari was stretched out on a padded recliner, leafing through a book of poems composed in interlingue and interlarded with local idiom. She read snatches of them to me when she came across something she thought I ought to like. Mostly I ignored her, being too concentrated on gouge and wood to have much mind left for other things. All the same it was a pleasant noise. Shadith came about an hour after lunch. . . .

2

Shadith brushed aside curls and chips of wood, swung onto the table; she set her hands on her thighs, waited until I finished the cut and ran my thumb along the line. "I need a sneaky lander," she said. "Lend me Slider."

"Hmm. See what you think of those harps. You like one, you can have it."

She laughed at me. "Old Bear, put down your ax." Hooking a foot around a table leg, she leaned back, ran her eyes over the three harps, chose one, not the best, I thought, but a start. With a treble grunt, she straightened, settled the harp against her shoulder and drew her fingers along the strings. "Interesting tuning. Well?"

"Why d'you want it?"

She wrinkled her nose at me, concentrated on her playing. Even I could tell the tone was dull; the song was dying on her. One dud. I think the wood was the problem there, no resonance to it. "Gray's disappeared," she said, "I'm off to see what happened."

"I see. Want help?"

"This is a loser, Bear." She did her lean again, switched harps, straightened. "Don't think so." It was my favorite she had this time, she smiled at the sound of it, played a snatch of some tune or other, moved on to another, then another. "My first chance to go off on my own," she said after some minutes of noodling about. "In my own body. Got a tuning wrench around? I want to try something."

"In the kit." I lifted the tool kit over the harpframe I was working on and pushed it toward her. "Keep it if you want, easy enough for me to pick up another, you might be too busy where you're going." I watched her as she began retuning the harp. This was the first time I'd got a good look at that new body, couldn't really count the web signal, the picture flats out here on Telffer, it's a long way from anywhere. And the color bleeds, runs round the image like lectrify jelly. Lot of dumps and glitches around us. I found myself thinking, what's a baby doing jumping into something hairy as that? Then I had to laugh; Shadow, little Shadith sitting inside that head, she was what? three, four thousand years older than me? Thing is, it's hard to remember that looking at her. I was glad I'd had the nous to keep my mouth shut. I doubt having a body has changed her that much; she had a nasty turn of speech when she was annoyed.

She finished the tuning, began to play. Weird resonances. Tried to do things to my head. If I'd listened harder, I might've had visions like some flaked out holyman. Hmm. Nice, once you got used to it. I went back to carving, the music made the cuts seem easier. Kumari closed her eyes, laid her book open facedown on her stomach. Pels stopped his humming but kept on with his digging. Remember his ears? They were up as high as they went, spread out and quivering, he had them turned toward the table.

"I like the tone of this 'n," she said.

"That's the one I thought came out best, but try the other."

"Why not."

She traded harps, played with the new one a little, set it aside. "You're right, the second one's by far the best."

"You needn't sound so surprised."

"Poor old Bear, that rubbed at you, eh? Put your fur down, I didn't mean it that way. The lander?"

I looked at Kumari. She managed to shrug without moving. Pels sat on his haunches and gave me a slitted look. He didn't say anything, but I got the point. "Take it, Shadow. Anything happens, the cost comes out of my share of profits."

Kumari has a sound she makes when she's amused. It isn't quite laughter, it's a combined rattle and hiss like the noises a kettle makes when the water's about to boil. "Damn right," she said.

Pels grinned, baring a pair of fangs that almost made him uncute. "Yes," he said, "if anything's sure in this unsure universe, that is." He voices his sibilants and shifts or drops his plosives; it's those teeth, but I'm not going to try to reproduce how he sounds. "Shadow, be sure you get the Sikkul Paems to run you through the basic finger patterns. The Paems and me, we haven't finished working on her, so the coding's a nightmare. Don't get yourself in a spot where you have to switch about fast."

"Slow and sneaky. Gotcha."

"Grr." He went back to fiddling in the dirt.

She slid off the table. "This harp have any kind of case?"

"In the workshed, on the table by the lathe."

"Thanks, Old Bear."

"Call it a coming-out present."

She laughed and went trotting to the workshed.

Kumari raised a brow. "A bit young to be running loose, isn't she?"

Crew knows my history, makes things easier when I get down and dark, so they knew what I was talking about when I said, "She's older than me."

"Coming-out." Kumari pinched her nose. "Shame, Swar."

Before I could answer that, the incom tinged and the housekeep came on. "One Adelaar aici Arash to see Swardheld Quale, business, no appointment." The plate showed a small woman with a determined face while housekeep waited for me to decide what I wanted to do.

"Eh, I know her." Shadith came to stand beside me, swinging the harp case. "When I was coming from the port, I saw her walking along Sterado Street. Two men were going after her. Locals, I think."

"On the street? Not pros then."

"Well, one of them had a yagamouche, so they were serious about it. I stunned 'em, took her to that ottotel on Fejimao, her business card's in my flit if you want an extra check on her. Um, I got fots of the men, they're in the flit's memory. You want, you can have them." She frowned. "If this is business coming up, won't you be needing Slider?"

"A deal's a deal. The lander's yours long as you need her. What we can't finagle, we'll fake. Mind her seeing you here?"

"Course not. Why?"

"I've got to call Kinok about Slider, ve'll want a look at you so ve knows who to let in. Best do that in the office. While we're up there, you can give me the access code, I'll have housekeep tap your flit. If there's local talent after her," I nodded at the plate, "I can use the fots to place them, might even recognize them myself, who knows. Better I have some idea what we'd be getting into before I close with her."

I told the housekeep to let the woman in and take her to the living room, I wiped my hands off, brushed at the wood chips on my shirt and trousers and for maybe ten seconds thought about changing my clothes. Decided if she wanted a three piece suit she could buy one.

"Kumari, Pels, I'll open the com, you keep an eye on what happens, give me a call if you see something I'm missing."

"Aukma Harree's blessing on her little head." Kumari yawned. "I was getting bored doing nothing. Lean on her, Swar; someone that close to being offed should have a strong idea of how much her life is worth." She made her happy noise. "A lean for a lien; the one on your share."

"That's not even worth a groan. You finished, Shadow? Come on, let's find some air without verbal farts in it."

I like towers so I built myself one; taller than the tendrij it is, faced with fieldstone and paneled with the finest wood on Telffer. Makes you want to reach out and caress it and I'm not saying I don't if I'm alone so I don't embarrass myself. My office is on the top floor of the tower, got a desk and all the gadgets I need to keep my peace unruffled, a pair of tupple chairs for my clients, a stunner or two in the walls in case one of 'em gets ambitious. A droptube under my chair, same reason. Handknotted rug from Gomirik, couple of paintings I like, a stone sculpture by a man on University, what's his name . . . aḥ! Sarmaylen. Place looks nice if I say it myself. The tower's tucked into the southeast corner of the main house, you get to it through the living room, there's no outside entrance, at least not one I show an ordinary visitor. The guest rooms are freestanding, connected by a walkway; they've all got outside doors, for my privacy and theirs.

Harpcase bumping against her backside, strap over her shoulder, Shadith followed me in.

3

The woman was standing in the middle of the living room, prissy disapproval in the curve of her downturned mouth. Hmm. There was a bit of a mess in there, so what. Nothing to do with her. Her eyes flickered when she saw Shadith, but the expression on her face didn't change. Looked like she was plated with stainless steel, a lot of anger underneath, though; no passion, no warmth, only anger and a hard control as if she'd explode if she let go her grip a single instant.

"Come," I said, and palmed the tube open. "My office is the tower's top floor."

She nodded, a taut economical jerk of her head, then followed Shadow and me into the lift tube.

III

1

Approaching zero.
Quale's Nest/Telffer.

The flickit was battered, rusty, with an intermittent eructation in its field generator that jolted a grunt out of Adelaar every time because it wasn't regular enough to let her get set for the drop. The seat she sat on was dusty, streaked with ancient grease and sweat, polished to a high gloss by years and years of antsy behinds. When the driver pulled open the door for her and she smelled the interior for the first time, her stomach lurched and she couldn't help flinching from the filth, but she climbed in without comment. She couldn't afford to antagonize the driver/owner; he was the only one willing to take her out of Prin Daruze, the *only* one. If he dumped her, she'd have to do her negotiating over the com circuit and that would be like broadcasting her woes to the world. Specifically, to Bolodo Neyuregg Ltd. Besides, she had to see Quale, to know him. So much depended on him.

The driver was a dour and silent man. Pressed to go faster, he slowed to a crawl; she recognized defeat and kept her fuming internal. The trip wasn't all that long, only about an hour, but his stubborn silence meant there was nothing to distract her from her fretting.

The past three plus years had been a heavy drain on her resources; she'd taken her best researcher off markets and tech breaks, set him hunting out mercenaries, she'd put in escrow a sum for hiring the most reliable of them once she located her daughter, she'd left

Adelaris Ltd. in Halash's hands. He was a good manager, he'd keep things going, but he wasn't up to finding new markets or people, the company would be treading in place. She'd drawn her travel and research expenses from Adelaris' current account; the search had taken far longer and was more costly than she'd expected, the account was dangerously low now, she really couldn't pull more out without destroying her business, bankrupting herself and her partners; they'd been patient with her. They more or less had to be, she *was* Adelaris. Without her patents and processes, without her energies, Adelaris Security Systems wouldn't exist, but there was a limit to how much she could ask of them. If Quale didn't work out, she'd have to tap into the escrow fund and that might start a hemorrhage that would kill all chance of getting Aslan back. The driver's fee was one more stone on the pile, which didn't make it easier for her to tolerate his sour misogyny.

The flickit flew west and a little south, labored along a steep-walled river gorge which cut deep into mountains that rose and subsided like waves of stone, each wave higher than the last, narrow grassy valleys dividing them, mountains thick with trees and brush, with fortress houses scattered widely along the slopes. It labored through a pass and came out into a broad valley, turned several degrees farther south and followed the river to a house on a mountainside, a rambling structure with scattered suites like nodes on an angular vine, a tower at a corner of the largest node.

The Telff circled wide round the house, set down at a detached landing pad at least two hundred meters off, cranked the door open for her and settled himself to sleep while he waited for her to finish her business or send him away. Whether she went back with him or not, he'd gotten a roundtrip fee from her. When she was out, he cracked an eye. "Stay on the path," he said. "You won't like what happens, you go off it."

"Thanks." She shut the door, looked around. There was a sleek black flickit on the pad, a ship's flit beside it. She frowned, walked over to the flit, nodded. That girl, Shadith. Tick's Blood, was that a setup? She shivered, feeling trapped and loathing it, banged her fist against the side of the flit, shivered again, with rage this time. Impatient with herself, she shoved away her apprehension and went striding off along the metaled pathway. There was no time for this nonsense; she was here, she'd know what she needed to do once she met the man. Everything else was unimportant. Aslan, ayyy, three years gone, she could be dead, no! I won't think that, she's a survivor, she let herself be trapped, but killed? No!

2

She followed a small floating serviteur along a hallway, past several closed doors. The wood of the walls and ceiling had a deep shimmering glow, the grain was a subtle calligraphy flowing like music under the buttery shine of lightberries on golden bronze stalks. She narrowed her eyes at the serviteur, eased closer to the leftside wall, drew her fingers along the wood. After a few steps she dropped her hand and walked faster.

The serviteur led her into a room full of light, gray light from the gathering storm, spidery with distant lightning, a room without corners, irregularly shaped with a bite out of one side where the tower was. Huge windows ran from floor to ceiling, a ceiling more than ten meters high with cathedral beams a distant richness of texture and line; polarizing glass in them, pale now, the windows looked out across the valley or up toward the mountain's peak. Chairs were clustered about these windows, comfortable, leather covered, ancient design. Trays on the floor, remnants of today's noon meal congealing on plates and bowls. Books and papers piled haphazardly about, drifts of them next to the chairs. Set into the wall opposite the door there was a huge fireplace meant to take logs, not limbs or splits, a table in front of it littered with several pieces of wood and some gouges, chips and curls of wood scattered about, a glass with a sticky residue coating the sides and hardening in the bottom, a bowl of fruit with a half-eaten apple turning brown, a tea tray with a plain pot and drinking bowls.

Tea set, windows, walls, chairs, the nubbly dark green rug on the floor, stone and wood sculptures scattered about, tapestries, paintings—from the moment she came through the outer door, she'd been bombarded with texture and color; that said something about the man, she wasn't quite sure what.

Also clutter. She looked around and silently sneered at the debris of living in what might have been an elegant room. He had serviteurs, he wouldn't have to lift a finger to clean up after himself once he'd properly programmed them, that he didn't could mean he was comfortable with this mess, maybe even preferred it to order. Cluttery mind. Cutesy mind. Quale's Nest. She began to feel a little sick.

He came into the room followed by the young girl who may or may not have rescued her.

A tall man. Thick black hair, a streak of white running through it, extending the line of a scar which touched his eyebrow with a dot of white, skimmed past his eye and swung down to the corner of his mouth. Pale gray-green eyes, droopy eyelids, nose like a predator's beak, mustache, beard, both clipped short. Broad shoulders, long arms, a loose, easy body. Easy body, easy man, if you left him alone, at least that was her first response to him. He wore scuffed old sandals with bronze buckles, heavy tan trousers, cut off above the knees, a shirt made from the same cloth, sleeves ripped out. Faded, softer than velvet after many washings, wrinkle on wrinkle, frayed at the seams and edges. Unimpressive, she told herself. Unprofessional. She didn't believe it. He moved like a man comfortable in his body, not an athlete or a dancer, nothing so self-conscious, just one who expected it to do whatever he required of it without fuss or lagging.

He crossed to the bulge of the tower, looked over his shoulder at her. "Come," he said and palmed open the entrance to a lift tube. "My office is the tower's top floor."

3

At least the office was neat. He gestured to a tupple chair hanging soft and shapeless beside a tall window, waited until she was seated before rounding the desk and settling himself. "A moment," he said, "there's some business I have to finish."

He beckoned Shadith to him, tipped up a sensor plate, touched a sound barrier between Adelaar and them. He looked up at the girl, raised a brow, said something, his mouth blurring so Adelaar couldn't read it. Shadith smiled, made a quick curving gesture with one hand, spoke rapidly, leaned on his shoulder as he worked the sensor plate. Adelaar watched his hands. They moved with the controlled clumsiness of a craftsman, no flash to them, easy, slow, sure. Long scarred fingers, tapering to spatulate tips, nails cut short, clean but scratched, he didn't take care of his hands. Too bad. They were the best part of him as far she was concerned. She sighed and looked away. The storm had broken outside, rain streaked the window glass. The valley was green swept with silver, the river cloud-black and rain-silver. Soundless rain, the office was too insulated from the outside to let the patter through. Too bad. Still, the storm gave the room a cozy feel, especially when she looked around again and saw the girl was gone, ambiguous uncertain figure that reminded Adelaar how little real control she had over events.

Quale leaned forward, forearms on the desktop (another of Telffer's jewel woods), hands clasped, watching her, waiting for her to tell him what she wanted from him.

She touched the controls and brought the tupple chair humming closer to the desk, slipped the diCarx from her belt, laid it in front of him. "Adelaar aici Arash. Droom. In the Hegger Combine."

He collected the diCarx and fed it into the Evaluator, glanced at the plate. "Ah. Adelaris Security Systems." He looked up, his eyes laughing. "I've heard about you, never could afford you."

She lifted a hand, let it fall. "I have a daughter," she

said. "Tenured Associate. University. Xenoethnologist. Awarded a Grant, permission to study the Unntoualar on Kavelda Styernna. Framed. Torture of a subject. Perversion. Sentenced, death. Sentence commuted to thirty years Contract Labor. Bolodo Neyuregg Ltd. the Contractor. I want her out of that. What's it going to cost me?"

"Depends on where she is. Do you know that?"

"No. I know how to find out. It took me more than three years to get that far."

"Those men Shadith stunned, the Directory placed them. Looks like you annoyed Bolodo sometime during those three years and they managed to ID you. Shame, that." He drew his thumb along his bearded jawline, ruffling the short black hair. "They're not too worried yet, or they'd 've sent pros instead of depending on local talent." The ends of his mustache lifted, subsided, a shadowed smile. "Assuming there's something they're twitchy about that involves your daughter. Otherwise they'd ignore you. It doesn't cost them anything if you peel her loose, they've got their fee. Looks to me like Bolodo's up to something that'd give them big trouble if it came out. Give us trouble if they think we're getting close. Hmm." He sat back, his eyes fixed on her face. "You know what it is. No? You've got some idea?"

"Yes."

He lifted a brow. "Terse."

"So?"

"Hmm." His eyelids drooped until his eyes were slits, he brushed the tip of his forefinger slowly back and forth across his mustache as he thought that over. After a moment he leaned forward, tapped in a code that brought a large viewplate unfolding from a slot in the desk top. "Kinok," he said, "Kumari, Pels, Conference." He looked up. "Bring your chair round here," he told Adelaar, "but keep your mouth shut, if you don't mind, unless you're asked something."

The plate split into three cells. Furry cuddly type with twitchy ears set high on its head. She didn't know the species. Milkglass maiden, pale hair thick and silky, pale skin, pale gray eyes cool and intelligent.

Hadn't come across that kind either, interesting. Ropy coils, clusters of succulent black eyes, colored pulse patches, hairy exoskeleton, Sikkul Paems, them she knew. Adult with a yearling bud crouching by ves head. Quale's Crew?

"Bolodo Neyuregg," Quale said. "You heard. We start this thing, we'd better be prepared to dodge a lot."

What's this? Adelaar thought, Tick's Blood, do I have to sell all of them? Multiple maledictions on my miserable luck, I hadn't planned on letting any of this out. Not until after we closed the deal anyway. Why did that girl have to be tied up with him?

The milkglass maiden opened her pale pink mouth (what species? not one of the cousin races, must be some backwater bunch that never made space). "Snatching." She had a husky purring voice, more life in that than in her face. "Slaving undisguised. What else. Considering what Jaszaca ti Vnok told us." Her voice was cool, her cool eyes distant. "Spotchals has to suspect something chancy is going on, but they won't press it as long as no one rubs Spotchallix noses in the mess. I'd say the trade is small but enormously profitable, otherwise Bolodo wouldn't risk it. They've got a strong base in Spotchals, but they've got to be careful; they own some pols and some career functionaries; even so, they've got potential for problems, remember?"

The fuzzy one lifted a black lip, exposed a yellowed tearing tooth four centimeters long (carnivore, she thought, deceptive little thing). "Yeah, I was in this bar the night before we left. Couple of Bolodo security come in. Hunh. One minute you wouldn't 've noticed a grenade go off in your lap, next you could hear your hair grow. Spotchallix, they like the taxes Bolodo pays, but they hold their noses when they hear the name. If it came out Bolodo was slaving, I'd give them a year at most before they were gone."

Quale brushed at his mustache, nodded. (Why doesn't he just ask? Is this meant to impress me? Pompous idiot. Oh god, how long do I have to sit here keeping my face straight?) "Kinok," he said, "you know them the hard way, what do you think?"

The bud Kahat skittered along a heavy tentacle, perched on the voice box; ves umbilical pulsed, ves hairfine digits manipulated the minute sensorboard.

"They are very careful." The synthesized voice was a sweetly musical tenor, quietly absurd (a Paem playing gentle jokes on vesself, the heavens should open). "They hold records on the meat back to creation or as close as they can get. Keep it legal, keep the record trail clean, if there's anything gray, wash it white or bury it deep. Ve-who-speaks was sold and sold again without diminishing ves debt one ounce gold, they charge for air, they charge for transport, food, sewage removal, soilage, anything they can imagine and their imaginations are vast. Ve-who-speaks must agree with Kumari; the profit is beyond conjecture great to tempt Bolodo across the line. Ve-who-speaks also believes very few, an inner circle of execs, know of this operation and this circle will not allow information about it to escape their hands; even their nervousness they will clutch tight to their bosoms; for beings who suspect trouble such urgency would be damning. Ve-who-speaks thinks that is why aici Arash has escaped serious difficulty till now. This is speculation, Swar, errors are likely. Say it is this way, in her search for her daughter, aici Arash leaves traces behind that are used to ID her after she is gone; if such happened before she went, she would be dead. So the circle knows her name, connects her with her daughter, realizes her daughter is involved with the secret thing. They do not know precisely what she has discovered, but they must fear she had enough to go looking and that is dangerous. They send word to their stringers to locate and remove her as a matter of swatting a nuisance, no great urgency in it, only a chance for an ambitious outerling to earn company points. They woo Luck but will not trust Her. Ve-who-speaks believes they are now organizing something more serious. Ve-who-speaks says deal with aici Arash, it is no longer possible to stand aside." The bud Kahat went still, Kinok turned his eye clusters from the screen, turned them back, jolted Kahat into renewed activity. "Shadow comes. Byol tok, Swar. Consider."

The cell went dark.

Kumari nodded. "I agree. Active or passive, we're in it. I prefer to be paid for working."

Pels said nothing, showed his teeth in a feral grin that unfortunately made him look like a naughty cub.

Quale tapped off the screen, sent it folding into the desk, turned to face Adelaar. "You pay fuel and reasonable expenses. That is not negotiable. My base fee is fifty thousand Helvetian gelders. You being Adelaris, I have a proposition. Ten thousand only, escrowed, the rest I'll take in trade, Adelaris systems for my house and my ship, supposing we come out of this with skins intact and brain in working order."

"Generous, I don't think. Two thousand, house or ship, not both."

"Mmmh, think of it as a professional discount. The ship gets a complete workover, the house an appraisal with suggestions for improvement, I do the actual work. Five thousand gelders."

"Three thousand."

"Done. You like storms?"

"What?"

"Storms." He waved a hand at the window where the rain was sheeting across the glass.

She looked from him to the shifting silvery streaks. "I suppose I do. As long as it's not raining down my neck."

"Then we'll have tea in the garden." He came out of his chair with that loose ease that continued to stir things in her she didn't want stirred; she didn't like him, he was too chaotic and cluttered for her taste, too wild, undisciplined, a weed, too young. She kept thinking of negatives, but as she gave him her hand and he lifted her from the clinging tupple chair, they kept fading on her. "A serviteur will take you there," he said, "if you don't mind. I'll start shutting the house down, be with you shortly. Pels and Kumari are there, ask them anything you want. We'll be leaving soon as the rain quits." He walked with her to the tube, opened it for her, twitched his mustache at her as she stepped silently into the tube. Damn the man, he had to know the effect he had on women. That creature Kumari, his leman?

The serviteur was waiting for her in the living room; the debris from the meal was gone, but the rest of the clutter was untouched, was likely to stay untouched for however long it took to find Aslan. Shaking her head, she followed the small bot as it hummed away, gliding a meter off the floor.

4

Pels and Kumari sat at a table in an open structure of stressed wood molded into a round of arches with a circular roof of roughcut shakes. Its floor was raised shoulder high off the grass and looked out over scattered beds of brilliantly colored flowers and convoluted, variously textured banks of fern. The deflector field shunted aside the rain as the clouds boiled black and wild overhead and lightning walked along the valley floor some distance below the house. Adelaar smiled with pleasure as she heard the hoom of the wind, the steady hiss of the rain, the crack of thunder and lightning, Quale said the storms were spectacular; that was rather an understatement. She climbed the steps, gave Pels and Kumari a nod, a stiff impersonal smile, and settled into the chair Kumari pulled out for her. "Quale said something about closing down the house."

Up close Kumari looked less human; her skin was white and translucent as milkglass (milkglass maiden) and delicately scaled, no eyebrows, her nose was a low knife blade slightly turned up at the tip with narrow nostrils, small mouth a pale pale bluish pink, narrow jaw, pointed chin; she was narrow and angular as a primitive sculpture, her hands were extravagantly long and thin; there was a faint drag on her flesh that suggested she'd been born and reared on a lighter world than this. "He means we'll probably get away clean, but Bolodo is apt to slag the place out of sheer snittishness. He's setting the automatics. May work, may not, depends on what they send."

"Planetaries won't keep them out?"

"What planetaries?"

"Oh." Adelaar looked round. "Then why . . ."

"Don't worry about it." Kumari made an odd little sound, a rattling hiss that Adelaar eventually interpreted as laughter. "He spent half a dozen years building the place, he was worse than a wounded auglauk when he had to admit it was finished. He's been walking around muttering to himself about redoing this or that, but he can't convince himself he could do better; if Bolodo levels it, he'll have the fun of rebuilding. Right, Pels?"

The furry person produced a rumbling chuckle. "Improve his temper no end."

Adelaar watched the storm a while; she was intensely curious about these two, but couldn't in courtesy ask for their life histories; courtesy aside, they were not likely to bare their souls for her, a stranger and a mere client. "You're Quale's Crew?"

Pels answered her. "Two thirds . . ."

Kumari broke in, "One half. You're forgetting Kahat."

"Shoosh, Kri, Kahat? That's the third Kahat ve's had since ve came." He dug into his face fur with short black claws that looked as formidable as his tearing teeth, explained to Adelaar what he meant. "Kinok eats the current Kahat every two years when the bud's about to complete separation. Sacrifice to the drives, ve says. You know Sikkul Paems?"

"I know."

"Me, I'm com off and Kumari, she's Ship's Mom; she knows everything about everything."

"Fool!" Kumari patted him on the cheek. "Cuteness has warped your pea brain."

He growled at her, fell silent as a pair of serviteurs came humming up with large trays. Spice tea, crisp wafers, small glass bowls with sections of local fruit, glass skewers to eat them with. The tea service was native clay, rough glazed, a warm dark brown with hints of rust and a deep blue shadow where the glaze was smooth, the drinking bowls generous with a restrained elegance of form.

Adelaar lifted one of the bowls, cupped it in her hand, enjoying its weight and texture. "Local?"

"One of my neighbors downstream, she's got a patch of kaolin she's been working for the past thirty years." Quale came through an arch and dropped into the fourth chair. "Do anything for thirty years and you tend to get good at it. Pour for us, Kumari."

He sat sipping at the tea and watching the storm. Adelaar skewered a slice of ruby fruit, ate it. It was good, a mix of bloodheart plum and citrus, firm, fleshy, full of juice; she closed her eyes, swallowed the fruit, savoring the blend of flavors in her mouth and the drama of the storm against her ears. She thrust the skewer through a rose-pink wedge, sniffed at it, crunched her teeth into it, smiled at the spurt of sweet tart flavor. Alternating bites of wafer and fruit, washing them down with sips of tea, she took the edge off a hunger she hadn't noticed before.

After several minutes of silence, Quale turned his head. "You send your driver off?"

"T'k, I forgot him, I left him sleeping in his flickit." She grimaced at the rain. "I hope the thing doesn't leak."

"Who?"

"Sour type called Oormy. Sounds unlikely, but that's what I made of his mutter."

"Ha! the Worm. No one else would bring you?"

"No." She smoothed her fingers over the textured glaze of her bowl. "What do you want me to do? Go back to Daruze and wait? I don't think that would be a good idea."

"No. Of course not. Ship's lander is coming down here, we're not going anywhere near the city. Unless you have something there you need to retrieve?"

"My case in the flickit, that's all I have."

"Hmm. Let Worm sleep till the storm's over. He can't fly in that stuff anyway." He reached under the table, pulled up a servitrage, ordered the housekeep to fetch Adelaar's case the moment the rain stopped and tell the driver Oormy to go home. After he clipped the trage away, he set his elbows on the table, clasped his hands. "About time you did some talking, mmm?"

"Time . . . how much longer will this storm last?"

"An hour, maybe a little more."

"Ah." She closed her eyes, weariness sweeping through her, three plus years working alone, never knowing if the next day, next hour, next minute would see her banging her head against a barrier even she couldn't get through or around, or in a trap that got her ashed, three plus years until Quale said Done and the deal was closed. Three plus years stretched taut, then the elastic broke. It hadn't hit her up there in the office, but now. . . . Now, soothed by the sounds of the storm, the tea and fruit a warm comfortably heavy lump in her middle, a need to talk washed over her, frightening her, at the same time luring her to say things she'd never said even to herself, to say more than she'd said to anyone since Churri the Bard. She understood what was happening to her, the euphoria that came from a sudden release of tension, but understanding was no help at all. "Mind if I ramble a bit?"

"Why not. I need to get the feel of things." His voice was distant, almost lost in the storm noises, as seductive as her exhaustion. "Just talk, whatever you feel like saying."

"Mmm." Eyes still closed, she slid down in the chair until her head rested on the back; she never sat like this in public, never, but she was too tired to care, just moving a finger made her body ache. "You know anything about the Saber worlds? I can understand that. Still, people did go there, especially to Sonchéren, sunsets and opal mines, chasm falls and tantserbok, hunters came from all over to hunt the tantserbok. I never understood those types, going after beasts no one could eat or use; their flesh was poison, their skin wouldn't tan, it rotted in three days no matter what you tried. And more hunters died than tantserboks, five hunters out, one back. The ratio changed now and then, never in favor of the hunters, but all those dead seemed to make the next ones more eager. Can you explain that to me, Quale? Can you make it make sense? I think stupidity can't be genetic, it has to be a birth defect or something like that. Why else with the kill rate like it is are there so many idiots around? Ah, that was a long time ago. Churri came to see the sunsets. Churri the Bard he called himself, a poet of sorts, I'm no judge; he moved me, but my brothers laughed at him. He was a little man, I'm not tall and he'd tuck under my chin, he got me so messed up, I didn't know which end was where, god I hate that phrase, I don't know why I use it, one of my brothers caught us, nearly killed Churri, he took off and didn't stop till he was on a ship going somewhere else. A month later I was being sick in the morning and bloating up like a milaqq in a cloudburst. . . ."

Her voice trailed off, she opened her eyes a slit and examined Quale. There was something about him that reminded her of Churri, she couldn't decide what it was, but then she wasn't all that good at reading people. Not his looks, Churri'd been bald as an egg and dark amber all over, with bronze cat eyes that laughed a lot though never at himself. A streak of cruelty with little malice in it, like the cruelty of a cat, a spinoff of the curiosity, passion, detachment that fueled his poetry. Aslan had inherited the curiosity and the passion, but hadn't yet acquired that detachment, probably never would. Quale, what was it about him, something of that same detachment? that playful painful digging into the other's, well, call it soul? Quale had an easy way of moving, but Churri was made of springsteel and sunfire, to look at him made her shiver. Quale was amiable, competent enough but low in energy. Tepid, that was the word. Churri was restless and unpredictable, he seemed easily seduced into tangents but was not, no, that was his cunning; he was a stubborn little git, when he wanted something, he got it, her for one. That was something else their daughter had inherited; she was about as biddable as a black hole before she could walk or talk. Ahh, it didn't matter, probably just a question of hormones. I was upset and tired, let my guard down. She shut her eyes.

"My father was a man of great honor, hmm! He shut me in a cell and brought in whores to tend me because no decent woman should have to look at me.

It's a miracle or good genes, take your pick, that I lived through that time and Aslan was born healthy. My father left her with me till she was weaned, then he gave her to a baby market. If she'd been a boy he might have kept her though I don't think so, she looked too different, skin was too dark, eyes were gold like Churri's, not washy blue like his. Me, he sold into contract labor. Not to Bolodo, to a smaller Contractor, one you could get loose from if you had the brains and drive. I don't like thinking about that time, but it taught me what it took to survive when you didn't have a family back of you. After three years I managed to buy out and I went looking for Aslan. Seems to be a habit, that. Found her too. Things were fine for a while, I was doing this and that, pulling in enough credit to keep us comfortable. Apprenticed myself to a minor genius and learned everything he wanted to teach me and a lot he didn't want out of his hands. Until Aslan hit puberty. And I turned into my father. T'k. We had some royal fights. Aslan was smarter than I'd been, no roving poets for her, but she didn't like my friends, she found them boring, nauseating, unethical, she had an obsession about ethics, don't know where she picked it up, it was bad as a deformity for scaring people off, she didn't like what I was doing, ethics again, she wanted no part of my friends or my business. The rows got worse, nothing physical, we weren't that sort, but we were clawing at each other with words and she was very good with words, better than I was, I sputtered and yelled and got frustrated, but she never lost her tongue. We loved each other, but we couldn't live together. So Aslan went to University." Adelaar sighed.

"She couldn't stand my friends, but she took up with some of the worst nannys there, flatulent bores, maybe intelligent but ignorant of anything to do with real life. I'd visit her, she'd visit me, we'd be polite a while about each other's friends and oh everything until the facade broke and we had another row. We'd give it a rest till next time, but we kept in fairly close touch by submail. Funny, we had our best conversations on faxsheets, though maybe not the most private. We set up a code of sorts, words that meant *trouble but I can handle it, trouble help fast,* that kind of thing. She has this fixation about recording cultures for the poor destroyed native species who'd probably skin her and roast her if they got the chance, she was always poking into places no sane trader would go near; we had rows about that, paranoid mama she called me, you get what you expect, she said, expect people to be nice, you get nice. I told her she was an idiot. She just laughed. Then this Unntoualar thing came up, a chance to be the first researcher into Kavelda Styernna. She stopped by Droom on the way there, she was full of it, the first time she'd gone in alone; she'd got five student assistants and a manager, Duncan Shears, she said he was the best there was at handling logistics, University was going all out for her.

I was scared out of my mind for her, I'd heard nasty rumors about the Styernnese and the Unntoualar, I warned her she wouldn't like what she was going to find out and she should be damn careful what she looked at, University was no good to her if the Oligarchy decided to off her, what could they do about an accident however fatal? I told her to yell if things looked murky, I'd come and get her, hell with Styernna and everything. This time she didn't argue, she knew it was going to be touchy, the Oligarchy was only letting her in because of long hard pressure from their homeworld Bradjeen Kiell and from University and they were going to watch every move she made. It's a filthy universe and we're about the filthiest things in it. If it was up to me, I'd say sweep the debris into the nearest sun and get on with today's business. Knowing how sick and perverse we can be is useless, doesn't change anything except maybe it encourages the freaks. I told her that, I don't know how many times, but she's a passionate creature, Aslan, and she believes time can repair the damage we do if given material to work with and it's her mission to collect that material. I said that, didn't I, ah well, my mind's not tracking, I'm too tired. So she went. I got a submail letter from her a month later, bright and chatty, saying how helpful the Styernnese were, no doubt for benefit of the censor she expected to read it, but she worked the code in and that told me it was a bigger mess than even I thought and she was scared but hanging on and if I didn't hear from her by the last third of each month I should come get her. Come quiet and careful. I started tying knots in things so I could go as soon as the mail didn't come.

"It happened so fast. Got a letter one day where the undertext said she was picking up stories that nauseated her, that she was nervous but coping, three weeks later University subbed over a transcript of her trial and an apology because they couldn't do anything directly for her, but she was still alive; there'd been a death sentence, but it had been commuted to thirty years contract labor. Alive! Under involuntary contract, you aren't alive, you're walking dead. The time I was under contract I was tougher than Aslan'd ever be, but those three years came close to killing me. Be damned if I left her in that mess. She'd been trashed, University said as much, but I didn't need them telling me. They were going to try buying her clear if they could find out who had her, and they were going after Styernna; oh, they were hot against Styernna, gnashing their bitty teeth, shuh! I didn't care what they did, I wanted my daughter. Besides, that lot of nannys couldn't find their assholes without a map.

"Getting into Styernna wasn't easy. They'd closed down the ports, not even homeworld types could land, and they had the satellites on alert for snoopers, but given the coin, anything's available. I knew this smuggler, he put me down and arranged to lift me off a month later. I nosed around Kay Strenn, that's the capital, trying to sniff out what they'd done with Aslan. It wasn't easy, Aslan calls me paranoid mama, but I'm a lamb beside those shits. I have this medkit which is probably unlegal on just about every world I know of, but it's useful at times like this, I suppose I shouldn't tell you that, what the hell. I went after the trial judge, he was the only one I could get at without more preparation than I had time for and local muscle which I had no access to. He didn't know much, except that Aslan must have found out something really ugly because the Oligarchy wanted her dead and ordered him to take care of it. Like always, he did what he was told and drowned what qualms he had in the local version of hi-po brandy. He was involved in the commutation, he had to sign the papers; I got Bolodo's name from him and something peculiar. If the Oligarchy wanted Aslan dead, why sell her to a Contractor who might take what he learned from her and blackmail them? Didn't make sense. Officially my babbling judge knew nothing about why it happened, but he'd picked up rumors. Bolodo had paid certain members of the Oligarchy bribes and promised them Aslan would disappear so thoroughly she'd be better than dead. Why Aslan? Not for her body, shuh! she's my daughter and I love her, but even I wouldn't call her a beauty. She's attractive enough, but there are thousands of women more so. Not all that sexy either, she's more interested in scrungy natives and putting together culture flakes than she is in men, they're for recreation when she's not busy with something else and that shows. To be honest, Quale, she's a very boring person. Secrets? Everything she's done has been published one way or another. She's a xenoethnologist, for god's sake, who'd pay a pile of coin for a xenoethnologist? There it is. What it says to me is this, Bolodo had an order from some crawly who has the hots for a scholar and Aslan dropped into their fingers. Scholars do tend to have a lot of backing, colleagues and so on who yelp when something happens to one of them, I give the nannys that.

"I dumped the judge and got off Styernna with lice hot after me ready to do me worse than they did Aslan. That must have been when Bolodo discovered someone was snooping into their business; there was enough left of the judge for that. I suppose I should have offed him, but the easy life I've had the last few decades has made me soft. Couldn't do it. He was such a miserable little worm, I just couldn't squash him.

"I went home for tools, visited some old friends; by the time I reached Spotchals, I wasn't me, had distorters on my bone structure and twisters on my body stinks. Just as well, Bolodo had spotters out, bloodoons looping over every port, sniffoons trundling through the streets, don't know if they were looking for me or what they thought they were doing, but it was a nuisance. Local lice were irritated by all this, that was points for me, they tended to knock down the 'oons whenever they came across them. After I got dug in, I didn't have too much trouble keeping hid. You know Spotchals, the police there are nothing special, they do what they have to and not much more and the government's less corrupt than most, and there are thousands of ships going in and out, busy place, and a huge population.

"Getting through security around the Bolodo compound was something else. It took me three years of digging, slow tedious dangerous digging, dancing tiptoe around the sleeping tiger to get close enough to work the mainbrain. You don't know how many dead ends I banged into, but I finally wormed a way through perimeter security and set up a protected corridor that would let me nest in the walls each night and gnaw away at the records hunting for Aslan's file. In and out, living on my nerves, feeling for traps, moving a hair at a time, day by day, week by week, month by month. Twice I joggled something; it wasn't exactly a trap, but it alerted Security and there was a general alarm, I stopped breathing, didn't move and they missed me; they ran all around me, but they didn't find me. And I started again hair by hair, looking for Aslan. They were tense for weeks after each of those brushes, jumping at shadows, it made things easier and harder for me; all that activity covered a lot I was doing, on the other hand someone could stumble on me any time if my Luck went bad, it was enough to give me permanent shakes. After two more months of this, I found her. She was listed as part of a special shipment to a world so secret it wasn't identified except by a code name. This was in a limited access file, you needed five keys entered simultaneously to release it if you didn't have a shortcut like my crazyquilt. And still that worldname was coded. I duped a part of the file, the part about Aslan. All the shipments were there, fifty years of kidnapping and slaving; I thought about duping the whole thing, but I was afraid of staying in there too long, besides, I didn't care about those others, what I wanted was Aslan. Oh. Yes. I got something else, note this, Quale, this is important. Those shipments are assembled at a substation off Weersyll, they go out roughly twice a year. There's one scheduled for three months from now, I hope you can follow it. Lyggad says you can, he's the one researched you for me, you know you've got a very odd history, dumb, I don't have to tell you about your life, where that ship is going is where we'll find Aslan. I've got the flakes with me, I thought you might need to see them. That night I didn't try for the code, I took the flakes out of the compound and stowed them in my case. I gave myself three more nights to break the code and identify the destination, I set up passage off Spotchals, didn't care where to, on half a dozen ships each night, different hours, I wanted to be out and off fast, you know Spotchals, there are what, fifty? a hundred? ships leaving every night, if I was quick enough, slippery enough, I'd get ahead of the guards, the 'oons, even if I tripped alarms all over the place. As long as I got clear of the compound. That was the trick. Getting clear. Security hadn't come close to my corridor, not once in all those months. It was worth taking the chance. I went in, set things up to collapse behind me if I had to run, slipped into the limited files and started hunting for the key to the code that concealed the world and its location. I thought I was being very very careful, but that particular line was loaded with traps, almost the first move I made set off alarms, turned the compound into a bomb waiting to blow. This time they knew they had a rat in the walls and they weren't going to quit till they got it."

"I jerked my taps and went away fast, the corridor shutting down behind me, erasing my backtrail. I thought I got away clean. I collected my case and was offworld before Bolodo Security finished flushing the compound and turned their search on the ports. I dodged about for several months, shifting IDs until I was me again. There was no sign of interest in me before Aggerdorn, that was where I got passage here with Treviglio. I shouldn't be surprised, though, should I. It isn't that big a step to tie the agitator on Kavelda Styernna to Aslan and Aslan to me and given what happened on Spotchals, adding in Adelaris, well, there I was. Kinok and Kumari were right, Bolodo's little sideline is nasty, dangerous and profitable; the net on Aslan's shipment was close to a billion gelders and remember there've been two shipments a year for more than five decades."

She opened her eyes, yawned. The storm was still yowling outside the deflectors, though the winds were dying down, the rain slackening. "You know the most frustrating thing? I was on Spotchals two months before Aslan's shipment left Weersyll. Two damn months." She glanced at the storm with impatience, all pleasure in it gone, sat up and ran her hands over her hair, pulling control like a coat around her. "You can follow that ship?"

"If we can set some ticks. We'll know more about that shortly. Pels, get on to Kinok, have him start a run on Weersyll, then you get hold of some of your dubious friends, see what they can give you. If they need time, have them message you at our drop on Helvetia. Kumari, see if you can get through to ti Vnok; say we'll make Helvetia three weeks on. If he wants to meet, have him leave time and place at the drop." Quale got to his feet, stood back to let the others move past him. He glanced after them, turned to look down at Adelaar. "Helvetia first. We have to settle the escrow and register the services contract." His mustache lifted in a smile reflected in his pale eyes. "Even Bolodo won't mess with Helvetia."

"They could wait beyond the Limit, jump us there."

"Slancy Orza has a trick or two. Hmm. Give you a few hours' sleep and the world won't be so grim." He bent, reached under the table. "I'll have a serviteur clear the table. Anything you'd like?"

"The storm to end."

"Won't be long now. Relax."

She made an impatient gesture. "If your lander

can't work through this little disturbance, what good is it?"

"It's being droned down, no use taking chances for a miserable half hour that we can make up with no trouble once we're insplitted." A brow lifted, another smile, then he too was gone.

She sat and watched the rain thrum down, watched it diminish abruptly to a trickle. The clouds raveled, paling, thinning; patches of sky appeared, vividly blue in contrast to the shadowed whites and pale grays of the vanishing clouds. Shafts of sunlight shot down, touching droplets of rain into blinding glitters; the greens outside the garden shimmered like polished jade. Quale read her too well, curse the man, her gloom dissipated with the storm. Her ambivalence remained. Action was on hold for the moment, once it began it'd go with a rush. Out of her control. Before, she'd been in charge, now he'd be. Quale.

Enigmatic man. She smiled, a wry tight thinning of her lips, as she remembered Lyggad stroking his pile of faxsheets, wrinkled atomy, big-eyed elf. The first part of his life Quale was a violent brute with a strong skilled body and enough intelligence, or maybe it was cunning laced with Luck, to acquire a ship and hold together a motley crew of scavs, a sleazy, crude scavenger whose idea of subtle attack was rip and run, then he'd tangled with the Hunter Aleytys and suddenly he was something more. A clever man, quiet, calm, cutting ties to his former . . . well, you couldn't call them friends, say associates, pals, buddies, whatever. A man who kept clear of trouble. Lyggad said it was like Aleytys gave him a brain transplant. He giggled when he said it, but obviously more than half-believed it, Aleytys was part Vryhh and who knew what those types could do when they put their minds to it? He said some of Quale's ex-buddies got nosy and demanded to know what happened, implying in forceful though limited language (that was Lyggad being prissy) that the woman had castrated him. They didn't ask twice. In that, Quale hadn't changed, he was fast and nasty when the occasion required. So Lyggad said.

Slancy Orza. Rummul empire trooper, Lyggad said,

mostly shell and drives when Quale acquired it, a wreck flying on kicks and curses. The drives used to be huge clunkers that ate fuel like it was free. Quale yanked those and put in new drives; they were nothing standard according to the few folk who got a look at them and were willing to talk. Huge, sleek, powerful Slancy Orza (Lyggad's voice went wistful, his tongue caressed the words), she can outrace a Sutt Aviso, sit down on a 3g world without bursting a seam and lift cargo nearly equal to her own weight.

She heard a quiet rumble, went down the stairs to stand on the grass looking up at a small lander as it dropped toward the ground. The pad, she thought, Worm must be gone by now. She drew her hand down over her face, sighed, started for the house.

IV

1

Three years std. earlier.
Aslan aici Adlaar daughter to Adelaar aici Arash riding to an unknown destination in the hold of a Bolodo transport.

Aslan muttered and blinked as she came out of a drugged sleep. She lifted her head, let it fall back as pain lanced from ear to ear. "Stinking . . . what now?"

Dim blue light. A cylinder. She was on a cot inside a tincan, cots spreading out on either side, above and below. She was catheterized but was not uncomfortable with it, the appliance was more resilient than most; there were restraints on her wrists and ankles, but they had sufficient play to let her sit up, even hang her legs over the cot's edge. She was surprised that she wasn't under full automatic care, her body processes reduced to a low hum. This waking restraint was wasteful and from what she knew of contract labor transports, unusual. She tried again and this time made it up. When her head stopped pounding, she looked around.

The other contractees . . . no, she thought, don't funk the name . . . slaves, some of the slaves were stretched out sleeping, some were sitting up, staring morosely into the blue gloom, others were talking together, still others had books and were reading or earphones, listening to flake players. She hadn't seen any of them before, Bolodo had kept her in solitary for months, probably so she'd have no chance to pass on anything about the Oligarchy and what they were doing to the Unntoualar; she had two coveralls, one clean each day, whatever flakes or books she asked for, but nothing from her own gear. She'd asked for that, but no one bothered to listen to her and she decided they'd ashed her things, just another paranoid precaution. Hmm. My own personal paranoid was too too right, mama'll beat me over the head with that for the next hundred years. She clicked her tongue, smiled as she remembered her mother's habitual t'k t'k that used to irritate her so much when she was a teener.

She went back to inspecting her companions. They were past adolescence, none of them old (making allowances for ananiles and mutational differences). All of them seemed to be sprouts on the cousin stem and there was a more intangible likeness—they were all professionals or artisans (no slogworkers in the mix) wearing the kind of gear experienced travelers chose, plenty of zippered pockets and easy to take care of. She looked down. She was back in her own tans, boots and all, the Ridaar unit in its belt case. Evidently they hadn't ashed everything. Refusing to think about that, she slid off the cot, stretched, the tethers stretching with her, the catheter giving her no trouble.

Her equipment cases were strapped beneath the cot where she could get at them if she wanted to.

She edged around and stared at them, despair cold inside her. They are by god sure I'm not going to get back, unless. . . . She uncased the Ridaar, ran through the overt index, then called up the last of the hidden files.

Report: deepfile Ridaar: re: Unntoualar
Code: icy eagle's child damn you Tamarralda I am not 324sub e minus one one half.

. . . I'm sure of it now, subject Zed has opened up enough to feed me some songs. It's the usual thing, they've made an accommodation with the new powercenters and they're not about to endanger their survival to help a transient female of more or less the same species as the invaders who took their world from them. The Unntoualar I'm living with are confused, on the one hand I seem to be here with the blessing of the invaders, on the other they've been quick to see the not-so-hidden hostility to me. I've been careful to limit my inquiries to their songs and the story tapestries connected with these, with those dozens of thready fingers it's no wonder they're marvelous weavers. No color vision, so line and texture dominate; almost but not quite writing; from what I've seen so far (which I admit is severely limited) they never did develop a written language, which was another clue since most races with a high psi quotient don't, concepts are too complex for the forced simplification of the written word. Why am I deepfiling this? Their psi-capacity is the hot spot; whenever I get anywhere near that, Zed, Wye, even crazy Tau start sweating blood.

Mike and Sigurd have done wonders with the language, it's a stinker, Tam, you'd guess it would be since a good half the nuance comes from esp fringes. Duncan lived up to his reputation by producing a crystal set, so the youngsters could record a good portion of those fringes and give us access the Unntoualar and the Styernnese don't suspect. I hope.

They're projective telepaths, that's clear from the songs, one of the few such capable of transferring images into the minds of species alien to them. Physically nonaggressive but not passive. Their aggressions came out in psychic attacks; before the colonists came, they were the dominant species on Styernna, having more or less wiped out all competition. Zed pulled a sneak on the censor, included a song in the first batch he let me flake about the arrival of the colonists and the short depressing settlement war; I haven't any idea why he did it, there's no evidence he can read me, maybe a gesture of rebellion, one he understands is probably futile. The Unntoualar tried their standard attack on the invaders, but the full force and flavor of it was blunted by the stolidity of those alien minds. Their single weapon was not only useless but proved to be disastrous for them; their most vicious attacks were perceived as surrealistic and erotic dreams. The last part of the song is one long wail against Fate as the Unntoualar realize this and begin dimly to see what it means for them.

Yesterday he brought in Rho and Nu, alpha males like him, they picked out a new tapestry and started singing, but the song had shit-all to do with the images. It was about what was happening to the Unntoualar now. Since the Final Dispossession, the Oligarchs have hoarded for their own use the most powerful of the PT's (their name in the song is a complex combination of dream dancer, custodian of race memory, spear of the Unn, verbal shorthand: Stahoho idam kaij), parceling out the lesser PT's for the entertainment of their favorites. All very secret, of course. The homeworld has rules for handling the natives and Styernna can't live without help yet; besides they know the ordure that will splatter over them if what they're doing gets out, plus the fact that half the scavs in the universe will come zooming over to harvest their share. Oh Tam, what they're doing, it's a lot worse than forcing a PT to do his thing. They're torturing the miserable creatures to get more piquant dreams out of them. Sickening.

I didn't want to hear that, Tam, makes me nervous. I don't know what the hell's going on, I thought I'd better get this deepfiled before Zed's plot (whatever it is) starts fruiting. Question: Is this a setup? Are the Oligarchs using Zed to snooker me into accusations I couldn't possibly substantiate? Is Zed doing this on his own? Is he working with or for other Unntoualar? What do I do? Well, I've got the kernel down, up to you to see there's heavy pressure put to investigate the Oligarchy and how it's using the Unntoualar.

Distorted, bleeding, the Unn staggered into the circle, shrieking with voice and mind, ululating interling and Unnspeech, flopping in front of Aslan, accusations foaming out of him, curses on the name of the Oligarch who owned him, tortured him, stole his dreams out of him. Guards surrounding her taking her away, taking away the Unn, dead Unn, twisted tormented. Dead too late for her. At least she was alone, Duncan and the others were at the base camp two sectors away, oh god, she was alone, Mama was right, she shouldn't have come.

2

She stood looking at the palm-sized plate for a long sick moment, then she sighed and canceled the read. If they'd bothered to locate and erase those files, she'd have had a sliver of hope that she could get out of this. They hadn't. Even the overt record was untouched.

She crawled back on the cot and sat with her legs dangling, the fingers of her right hand moving around and around the old burn scar on her left wrist, a scar she'd gotten when she was nearly four and being punished by her foster mother for something or other, she couldn't remember what, but it was about two months before Adelaar came for her. When she noticed what she was doing, she stilled her fingers and smiled at the scar, a fierce feral grin. Bolodo doesn't know you, Mama, nooo indeed, you'll blow the bastards out of their skins before you're finished with them. Hmm. Better for my self-esteem if I don't sit around sucking my thumb waiting for you to show up. Problem is, what do I do and how do I do it?

She pulled her legs up onto the cot, pushed herself along it until she was sitting with her back against the hold wall, then started thinking about contract labor. Like everyone else, she'd accepted its existence as something morally reprehensible but generally necessary. Blessed be the Contractor for he takes away the ugliness of life. Societies always have those they class as criminals, anything from mass murderers and big time thieves to heretics and skeptics who question the way things are. Your average citizen, he's more comfortable if he doesn't have to look at the poor, the handicapped, the mildly crazy and wildly crazy, the drunks and druggers, the different, the dregs. Why not keep your citizens happy, reduce taxes, remove focuses of disturbance—all that in one fine swoop? A way of using what would otherwise be a drag on the economy, a way of protecting the comfortable assumptions of the majority from any sort of challenge. Besides, new colonies need labor they can eject when the job is done so the workers won't pollute the paradise, heavy worlds need miners whose health they don't have to worry about, everywhere an infinity of uses for workers who can't object to miserable conditions and miserly pay. And there you have it, contract labor. A marriage of greed with respectability. Blessed be the Contractor (but don't let him live in my neighborhood).

On her left a youngish man was stretched out, sleeping. Some time ago his hair had been sprayed into lavender spikes, there was a lavender butterfly tattooed on the bicep next to her; his hands were square and muscular with short, strong, callused fingers. There was a heavy silver ring on his little finger; she couldn't see much of it, but the design looked familiar. A friend of hers on University had hands like those and a habit of giving rings like that to his students. Sarmaylen. He was exploring an ancient and long neglected form of sculpture, working every kind of stone he could get into his studio, threatening the neighborhood with silicosis from the dust he was raising. She leaned over, tried to see past the collapsed spikes; as far as she could tell, she didn't know the boy (she smiled, getting old, woman, when you look at a man like that and see a boy), he was young enough to be only a year or two out of school and she wasn't much into Sarmaylen's life these days. Snuffling marble dust didn't appeal to her; besides, she wasn't really interested in the more exotic varieties of the arts, couldn't talk to him about them because he snorted with disgust at every word she said. That was one of the reasons Sarmaylen was only an occasional sleeping companion though she found the touch of his callused, work-roughened hands electrifying. She smiled at the memory of them, smoothed her fingers across and across the burn scar. His hands were eloquent, his tongue was not, at least in the public sense, a pleasant change from her other friends and lovers. She was fond of him; if she never saw him again, she'd hurt a lot, but she could no more live with him than she could with her mother. Their casual off again on again relationship seemed to suit him as well as it did her, though she sometimes wondered what he was getting out of it besides the sex, which was something he'd have plenty of without her. She frowned at the boy. A student of Sarmaylen, a sculptor. How did he wind up here? Artists and artisans like him never signed with Contractors. Not voluntarily. Trashed like me, I suppose. Or was he just out and out snatched?

Her neighbor on the right was a small fair woman. Huge eyes in an oval angular face with prominent cheekbones. Energetically thin. Sitting, she seemed in flight like some birds Aslan had known. Her hands were narrow and bony, rather too large for her slight form though she managed them gracefully, her feet were narrow and bony, distorted by the stigmata of a professional dancer. She was turning a music box around and around in her fingers though no sounds issued from it, if she disliked the dull muttering silence in the hold (the tension in her body and the fine-drawn look of her face suggested that she did), the music of the box would remind her of the restraints that kept her tethered to the cot, so she left it silent. Her mouth twitched into a smile so brief it was like the flash of a strobe light. "Kante Xalloor," she said. Her voice was deep, husky, easy on the ears. "Dancer. Bolodo must have kept you stashed somewhere?"

"Aslan aici Adlaar. Xenoethnologist."

"Yipe. What's that when it's home?"

Aslan tapped the Ridaar unit. "Sitting around listening to native remnants tell stories about how the world began."

"Weird." Xalloor looked past her at the sleeping youth. "You know him?"

"No. I don't know anyone here. Back there, I saw four walls and an exercise mat. Bolodo didn't want me talking about some things I got mixed up in."

"Snatched you?"

"Not exactly. Bought me out of a trashing; I suppose I should be grateful, the maggots that did it were going to top me. You?"

"I was on Estilhass, I'd finished a situ with the Patraosh and had an offer of another on Menfi Menfur. Maybe you know the feeling, mishmosh and jigjag, hard to sleep, no reason to stay awake, nothing to do but wait for the ship to take me off. There was this stringman I met in a bar one night, I woke up in restraints on a Bolodo scout, no stringman in sight, just a pilot who looked in on me to see I was still alive, then ignored me. He wore Bolodo patches, made no mystery about who had me which was hellishly depressing if you thought about it and I didn't have much else to do the next bunch of weeks till we got to the substation." She shrugged with her whole body, a vivid electric summation of her feelings. "We'll see what we see when they drop us. Him you were watching, he's called Jaunniko, he says he thumps rocks for a living." Her thin brows wriggled skeptically, then rose in wrinkled arcs as Aslan nodded agreement. "The big lump on the other side of him, the one with his nose in a book, that's Parnalee, he's always reading. He says he's out of Proggerd, that's in the Pit, the Omphalos Institute whatever that is, he got drunk the first night in the pens, he had a bottle of tiggah in his cases; he says he's the best designer in fifty light years any direction, didn't say what he designs. The three women next him, they're a group, the Omperiannas, you heard of them? Ah well, it's a big universe. They were my music the time I was touring the Dangle Stars. The little bald man who's doing all the scribbling, the one who looks like he's made of tarnished brass, he's Churri the Bard." She arched her mobile brows and converted her limber body into a question mark as Aslan's eyes snapped wide. Aslan twisted around, leaned forward and stared at her father. Curiosity seethed in her and a bitter anger against him for abandoning her, though she knew it was idiotic to think like that, he didn't know she existed; Adelaar had been careful to tell her that, her mother had a sentimental attachment to him which was both amusing and peculiar in a woman so icily unsentimental in other ways. That the man who'd fathered her could be sitting here so close to her, absorbed in his tablets, completely ignorant of their relationship, was absurd, it was the god she didn't believe in playing games with her life. She sighed, settled back, gave Xalloor an encouraging nod.

The little dancer grinned, shrugged, a ripple of her body that said, what the hell, it's your business. "I got Tom'perianne to set one of his poems to music, *Lightsailor,* you know that one?"

"I've read everything I could get hold of." It was the truth, it was a way of getting close to her father without intruding on his life, something she was afraid of doing, afraid of what she'd find, afraid she wouldn't like him, afraid she would, afraid he wouldn't like her, she suppressed a shiver as she contemplated weeks, maybe months in this sealed womb, having to look at him and wonder. . . .

"It made a great dance. I got the Dangles Tour out of it. Why Bolodo snatched him, I can't imagine. I mean if he ever gets loose and raises a stink, they've got more trouble than a swarm of vores up their backsides." She shivered. "Don't look good for us, eh?" She shivered again, exaggerating her fear, fighting it that way, a glint of laughter in her eyes as she watched herself perform, then she went back to naming the captives, those close enough to be visible in the pervasive blue gloom.

3

Bolodo Man live in love
gold fine gold
Bolodo Man live in love
pearl and emarald.

Churri's rich resonant baritone filled the hold; around, beneath, above it, the Omperiannas improvised a driving support (Tom'perianne, lectric harp, Nym'perianne, tronc fiddle, Lam'perianne, the flute).

Tribulation, sufferation
Boring blaggard Bolodo Man
Sing I sing thee sing we
Bloody bane for Bolodo Man
Get cold get old, senility
Cankers chankers dropsy pox
Virus venin worm and tox
Bolodo Man live in love
gold fine gold
Bolodo Man live in love
pearl and emarald.

Kante Xalloor stretched her restraints to the utmost, standing on her cot, dancing with the twanging ties, her body singing a wordless answer to the chanted curse.

Malediction, imprecation,
Jerk his melts, the B'lodo Man,
Mockery, indignity, calumny and ban
Rash and rumor, rancid liver,
Bolo Bolo B'lodo Man
Rot and rancor, snarl and spoil
Ulcer, abcess, fester, boil,
Epilepsy, apoplexy,
Indigestion, inflammation,
Fecculence and fulmination
Dilapidation, moth and rust
Treachery, atrocity, malignity and lust
Bolodo Man live in love
gold fine gold
Bolodo Man live in love
pearl and emarald.

Jaunniko snapped thumb and forefinger, diving headlong into the music; when Churri paused and looked at him, he began his contribution:

Wa ha wa hunh
Sibasiba Bird
Come out
Come from the river come

Wa ha
The bird come from the river
Wa hunh
Sibasiba
Eat gold
Eat gold
Eat gold
Eat fat greedy soul.
The bird come from the river
Eat those pearl those emarald
Eat you bare, Bolodo Man
Bare ass, Bolodo Man.

Churri laughed, his booming laughter filling the hold, filling that echoing impossible space.

Execration, vituperation
Call your curses, raise them high
Bolodo Man live in love
  gold fine gold
Bolodo Man live in love
  pearl and emarald
Fulmination, imprecation
Curse him up and
Curse him down
Curse him neck and
Curse him thigh
Curse him heel and
Curse him crown
Bolodo Man live in love
  gold fine gold
Bolodo Man live in love
  pearl and emarald.

Parnalee stood on his cot, straining his restraints, hunched over, slapping his shovel hands against his massive thighs, his burring basso waking echoes until his words got lost in them.

Thump them, dump them
Down among the dead men
Ekkeri akkari oocar ran

Down among the dead men
Bolo Bolo B'lodo Man
Down among the dead men
Blood and bone, heart and stone
Down among the dead men
Fillary fallary hickery pen
Down among the dead men
Blackery luggary lammarie
Eat the brain, the bod dy
Gut and liver, black kid ney
Rowan rumen mystery
Down among the dead men

The Curse Song went on and on, the transportees taking turns at soloing, their curses growing more extravagant, more surreal as each dipped into his or her culture to surpass the contribution of the last. The rest belted out the refrain until the hold rocked with it. Round and round, Churri playing variations on his verses, the Omperiannas adding flourishes, round and round until, finally, the transportees collapsed in exhaustion and laughter and fell into extravagant speculation about where Bolodo was going to dump them.

4

"Yo, I remember you. May's Ass."

"Aslan."

Abruptly realizing what he'd said, Jaunniko went bright red, so red his ears and the tip of his long nose were nearly purple. "Ah," he said. "Thing is," he said, "May sort of went round saying you had the neatest ah um derriere he uh. . . ." He turned even redder. "The time we met," he went on hastily, "it was at a party, you probably don't remember me, you brought your mother along and that wasn't being too successful, I talked to her a while, she was bored out of her skull, one icy lady. . . ." He sneaked a look at her. Her expression must have been rather daunting, because he stopped talking altogether.

After she calmed down, she took pity on him and changed the subject. "How'd Bolodo get you?"

He stretched out on his cot, crossed his ankles, laced his fingers over his flat stomach. "I'd just got my papers. Junior Master. May found me a commission, he's good about that, you know, Jeengid in the Blade, the Keex of Jelkim. I was one of about fifty she hired, she liked my part of the piece well enough to give me a little bonus, I was feeling whoooo no pain when this stringman came on to me. Woke up in a Bolodo scout tied down and sick as a . . . well, sick."

"Any idea where we're going?"

"None. Except we aren't coming back from it."

"So Xalloor thinks. I expect you're right.

V

1

Still two + years till Aslan's Mama meets Quale/ four months after she woke in the belly of the transport/the voyage is finished. Lake Golga/Gilisim Gillin/Imperator's Palace/ afternoon.

The Bolodo transport decanted Aslan and the others on Tairanna four months after it collected them at the Weersyll substation. Smallish dark men with cold eyes supervised their transfer. Others of the same type loaded their gear on carts pulled by stocky stolid beasts with horns like half smiles curving up and away from round twitchy ears.

Aslan stepped onto the ground, braced herself to endure the extra weight and found a moment of quiet while their new guards prodded them into line. They'd been stuffed with the local language and a sketchy outline of local customs so they had no trouble understanding the terse commands. Despite the circumstances she was momentarily happy. There was an infinity of possibility stretching out before her, new worlds always did that to her. She stood docilely where the guards put her, sniffing at the wind that whipped around the base of the transport, sampling the smells it brought to her. Fish and rotting flesh, dung and mud and the sharp green bite of trampled grass, the dank musky odor of the beasts, the subtler odors of cart woods and working metal, over all this the faint burnt-cabbage stink of the men. That wind wailed and whined; the carts rattled; her fellow slaves snapped irritably when impatient guards shoved at them, barking guttural monosyllabic orders; behind her the drones servicing the ship clanked and hissed; overhead, racy white birds circled in flittering flocks, their eerie cries a most proper accompaniment to the debarking of slaves into the land of their servitude. The extravagance of word and image made her laugh. Xalloor looked a question, flinched from a guard's goosing prod (an elastic grayish cane a meter long) and in her indignation forgot what she was going to ask. Aslan sighed and started walking as the guards marched them toward the towered city a kilometer or so away. Nothing to laugh about. She had no control over her life; whatever happened to her depended on persons and events she had no way of manipulating, not now, not until she had sufficient grasp of local verities to do some planning. Her first flush of interest and excitement quickly wore off; she was a slave here, not a scholar. She rubbed at her lower back. Though the gravity of this world was uncomfortable rather than unbearable, she was already feeling fatigue and fatigue made her depressed, diminished her ability to deal with her problems.

She risked a look over her shoulder, winced as a guard stung her with his prod. There were other ships down on the pad, three of them. Cargo transports. Insystem ships. Not good. Apparently the only way home was through Bolodo. She clung to a faint hope that her mother would be able to find her because there wasn't much else to keep her from the black despair that sometimes overcame her; she couldn't afford that now, it sapped her will worse than any gravity-induced fatigue. Once the Bolodo transport left . . . she scowled at the rutted track . . . if she could organize some sort of group . . . she was enough of a pilot to get them back to busier starlanes . . . we can't be the only shipment of slaves to this place, the guards are too casual, we're nothing special . . . why not take the ship, security was lax, it was obvious the Bolodo crew weren't worrying about their cargo turning on them . . . surprise them . . . if I can get the right people . . . weapons . . . we'll need weapons of some kind. She strained to get a look at the guard without letting him see what she was doing . . . the prods . . . knife in an external bootsheath . . . some sort of pistol in a leather holster clipped to his belt . . . what kind? Depends on the technology here; I doubt if Bolodo is supplying weapons . . . self-interest would say no . . . I don't know. . . . What *is* the level of technology here? Hard to estimate. Nothing from Bolodo on that and what she saw around her was ambiguous. The carts had shock absorbers, bearings in the wheels and pneumatic tires, but they were pulled by beasts and the road itself was little more than ruts and mud, no sophisticated land traffic here despite the landing field and the size of the city ahead of them.

They were led round the edge of the city, past walls about twice manhigh, pierced at intervals by pointed archways where Aslan could look down narrow crooked lanes meant for walkers not wheels, lanes paved in carved and painted stones, the simple repeating design echoing the pattern of bright, glazed tessera set into the cream-colored bricks of the walls. Her steps slowed as she tried to see more, fascinated and frustrated by the tantalizing glimpses she got into the life of this world; one of the guards laid his prod across her shoulders, reminding her once again that she wasn't here to study—though why she was here. . . .

The guards took them across a narrow section of wasteland where they walked a beaten earth path between shivering silver-green walls of waist high grass, grass that buzzed with hidden insects and rustled gently in a soft erratic wind. Xalloor grimaced and scratched at her thin arms, rubbed at eyes beginning to water and redden; she sniffed and spat, glared at a guard who whapped her with his prod because her spittle had just missed the toe of his boot.

Ahead of them was a massive wall more than thirty meters high, a wall that rambled over the grassy hummocks and dipped into the water that spread out to the horizon on three sides. Aslan decided it was a lake because the smell told her the water was fresh, not salt. The lead guard thumped with his prod on an ogeed gate; it swung open in heavy, well-oiled silence.

The line of slaves marched through arcades and

colonnades and formal gardens manicured to an order and an artificiality that seemed to deny the ordinary processes of change and decay. Jaunniko was just ahead of Aslan; she could hear him muttering under his breath as he looked around, his shoulders were pulled in and his fingers were twitching. She thought she knew what he was feeling because this dead place grated on her too. Figures appeared in the promenades, posed in the arches, showing a flicker of interest in the newcomers that faded almost as it was born. They were uniformly taller and fairer than the guards, with a high degree of physical beauty; male or female, it made no difference, in their own way they were as unalive as the garden, mobile ornaments as clipped and trained as the hedges were. Never, she told herself, I'll die first, make them kill me outright before they drain the soul out of me. She shivered and knew the words were whistling in the wind, if Luck wasn't with her . . . a few steps on, she smiled, amused at her vanity. She wasn't young enough or pretty enough to qualify as an ornament, whoever bought her wasn't apt to want her body. There was a hint of comfort in the thought, her usefulness and therefore her value wouldn't depend on how soon her owner tired of her. She made a face at the taste of that word, owner.

A tower grew out of springing arches like a tree rising from its roots. The guards herded them through one of the arches and stopped them in a paved courtyard, dusty and barren, a pen for two-legged beasts. Xalloor edged closer to her. " 'minds me of a casting call."

"I don't think I like the roles we're up for."

"Or the audience." Xalloor flashed a defiant grin at one of the guards who slapped his prod against his leg but showed no sign of coming to shut them up. She turned her shoulder to him, shivered and rubbed at arms roughened with horripilation. "Fools. They should've told us we were going to freeze our assets."

Aslan looked up at the tower with its ranks of narrow windows glittering in the light of the lowering sun. "At least they've got glass in them. I wonder if we're going in there? Hmm. Far as I'm concerned, they can take their time. No joy for any of us in that place."

"I want to know now." The dancer moved restlessly, fighting against gravity, working the muscles of her shoulders, arching her feet inside her boots, tightening and loosening her leg muscles. "You've led a sheltered life. Working the tran-circuit isn't all that different from this. Once I know the terms, I can root round and finagle a way to live with them."

"You dance, the Omperiannas are musicians, Parnalee designs large-scale events, Yad Matra's a machinist, Churri's a poet, Appel, Jaunniko, Naaien, go down the list, you're all techs or artists or both, but me? There's nothing I can do that has any meaning outside of University or a place like that, nothing I like to think about. What can they want with a xenoethnologist? It's ridiculous."

"Mebbe so." Xalloor laced her hands behind her head, bent cautiously backward, straightened with an effort visible in the tendons of her neck. "I loathe these heavy worlds, move wrong and you tear up your legs."

There was a loud clapping sound of wood on wood. They turned. A man had come through a door in the side of the tower; he stood at the top of the steps that led up to it, a clipboard in one hand, its bottom braced on the ledge of a hard round belly. "I am the Imperator's Madoor," he said. "When I call your name, come here, stand at the base of the stairs. You will be taken to your posts. There will be no argument, no protests, no threats, no struggling. Awake or drugged, you will go. We have no preference as to the manner of your going, but consider well, how you begin is how you will go on. You have no voice in your destination or what happens to you there. I want that very clear. You are not beasts, you are less than beasts. You are worth only what services or instruments you can provide. If you choose not to provide them, you will be beaten or otherwise persuaded to change your mind. If you still refuse, we will get what value out of you that we can. You will serve as bait for our fishermen or food for our hunting cats. Do not think to escape and hide yourself among Huvved or Hordar; you cannot, you do not look like us, you do not sound like us no matter how well you have got our language, you do not know custom or rite, you have no family here. No one will help you. Cooperate or suffer the consequences." He looked down at the clipboard. "Kante Xalloor. Tom'perianne. Nym'perianne. Lam'perianne. Jaunniko." He named five others, all performers of one sort or another, then waited while two guards and an escort of exquisitely robed and tonsured males sorted them into a proper line and took them off. They went without creating fuss, they went with prowling steps and narrowed eyes, plotting as they moved, too cool, too controlled, too experienced in the exigencies of surviving to waste their energies in a futile rebellion. Aslan watched them go and saw her vague notion of assembling a group to take one of Bolodo's transports go with them, the vision fading like a memory of a dream. As she passed through the arch, Xalloor risked a wave and a grin and got away with both. Aslan waved back, then waited her turn, feeling bereft and lonelier than she had in years.

"Churri diZan. Aslan aici Adlaar. Parnalee Pagang Tanmairo Proggerd."

Aslan moved as slowly as she dared toward the steps. During the trip here she'd done her best to avoid attracting Churri's notice, not too difficult because he was tied to his bunk and except for the times when he added verses to the Curse Song and belted them out for the edification of his fellow captives, he was either asleep or scribbling in his notebooks. She was afraid of getting closer to him, she didn't want to be linked with him, she didn't want him playing are-you aren't-you games with her. She saw his head jerk when he heard her full name, the matronymic that linked her with Adelaar, and made sure the Parnalee stood between him and her, but she couldn't miss the nervous dart of his yellow eyes as he leaned forward and looked around the Proggerdi's bulky body.

No robed and perfumed types came for them. A guard prodded Aslan toward the far side of the court, herded the three of them through a bewildering cascade of arches and into a holding cell of sorts. The guard looked around the room; his eyes passed over them as if they were less important than the dust on the floor. He grunted and left, barring the door behind him.

Once the light from the doorway was cut off, several strips pasted on the backwall began to glow, producing a bluish twilight that hid more than it revealed. Parnalee sniffed. "Smells like dogshit in here." He strolled to the door, leaned on it. It creaked and shifted a millimeter or so, balked. "Thought so." He rested his massive shoulders against the planks, folded his arms across his chest, yawned and let his eyes droop shut.

"Aici Adlaar?" Churri's voice.

Aslan twitched. The voice was a large part of the Bard's reputation, a mellow flexible baritone capable of turning a nuance on the flick of a vowel. On the trip here she'd listened with pleasure when he talked to his neighbors, when he chanted his verses to the hold. Now that voice was turned on her. It was only a part of her name that he said, but folded into those syllables were question, speculation, a touch of fear, a touch of wonder, a demand for an answer and other less identifiable implications. She drew her tongue across her lips. "So?"

"Sonchéren?"

"I was born there."

"I knew a girl on Sonchéren, long time ago, one Adelaar."

"I know."

"How?"

Aslan hesitated, decided there was no point in hedging. "She's my mother."

"So Ogodon got her married off. That hamfisted cousin of hers, I suppose, he was hot after her." More nuance—casual overlay, eagerness beneath, sharp tang of anxiety, all of which turned into laughter.

She ignored that. "Married? A spoiled virgin? Don't be stupid. Not on Sonchéren. He sold her to a Contractor after I was weaned, sold me into the baby market."

"You're mine?"

"So she says."

"I didn't know."

"She told me that."

"Why didn't she send me word?"

"Not much point, considering how fast you cut out before."

"I went back."

"How nice of you." She heard the acid in her voice, she felt ugly, she knew she was making him despise her, but she couldn't help it; years of anger and pain were erupting from the darkness where she'd shoved them.

"I did all I could to find out what happened to her without getting my head taken, I assume you know the habits of your male relatives."

"Of course you did." Cool, steady and very bitter.

"You've got an adder's tongue, you know that?"

She shook her head though she knew he couldn't see it. Anything she said would make things worse.

"My name gets around. She could have found me if she wanted to."

"Yes."

"Ah."

She could feel him staring at her; his short stocky body vibrated with . . . what? . . . something . . . that made demands on her she didn't want to answer. After a moment of thick silence, with a whine in her voice that appalled her when she heard it, she said, "Adelaar made a good life for us, she didn't need anyone, she didn't want anyone sticking his nose in."

He stirred, but before he could speak, the door rattled, Parnalee moved away to let it open (Aslan jumped, cursed under her breath, she'd forgotten he was in here). The guard whapped his prod against the door. "Out."

Parnalee ambled out, not about to hurry himself at the order of some snirp who didn't reach past his ribs. Aslan followed him, struggling to regain control over her emotions, wanting a mirror to see what was written on her face. She heard Churri behind her though he was softer footed than a thief. Perhaps heard wasn't the right word, felt was more apt. She was intensely aware of him; part of it was a sexual awareness that she half-feared, half-understood; she'd never known him in the role of father, she had to keep reminding herself who he was (for the first time she understood why her mother kept such fond memories of him). Part of her reaction was a mix of needs that were more intense than sex. She *needed* a father. She didn't want to. She wasn't a child, she hadn't missed him when she was, or so she told herself, refusing to acknowledge the old angers that drove her into sniping at him a few minutes ago. Now, with him there, so close, too close, she ached for what she hadn't known; it seemed somehow a betrayal of her mother, of herself, but she couldn't deny the feeling.

2

The guard took them high into the tower, left them in a six-sided room with wall to ceiling windows in four of the sides, windows that looked out across the city and the lake. Churri went at once to one of the windows and stood staring across the lake toward mountains on the far side, mountains that were little more than a ripple of blue in the paler blue of the sky, their peaks touched with pink from the sunset he couldn't see. Parnalee walked to the middle of the room, looked casually about, eyes half-shut, his face sleepily bovine, then he went to inspect the two walls that had no windows, only tightly pleated drapes woven from a fiber like raw silk and dyed a matte black, drapes meant to be drawn across the windows when the sun was coming up and its light struck directly into the room. He ran his hands across wood panels behind them, thick short fingers that seemed clumsy but were not. Rather like Sarmaylen's hands, Aslan thought, and shivered with the memory; when she realized what she was doing, she swore under her breath and crossed her arms over her breasts as if she were trying to shut herself away from him and everything else. A low, backless bench angled out from the wall near the door; Aslan dropped onto its black leather cushions. A moment later Parnalee joined her.

"Anything interesting?" She crossed her legs, turned a little away from him.

"Built into the walls if there is." He inspected her, chuckled.

She looked round. "What . . ."

"Nothing."

Aslan scowled at her feet, angry at him and herself. He was too perceptive and what he saw mattered too little to him. The same thing happened when she visited her mother, Adelaar ended up hitting her in every one of her vulnerable spots.

The door they'd come through opened again and two men walked into the room.

Aslan got to her feet. Before the door closed behind the men, she saw guards lounging in the triangular antechamber beyond.

Churri came away from the window and stood beside her; he was vibrating with anger, but managing to control it. His hand closed over her shoulder, tightened hard.

Parnalee sat where he was.

One of the newcomers moved to the last window and settled his shoulders against the glass, folded his arms across his chest. He was a tall man, as handsome as an addiction to biosculpture could make him; he had skin like thick ivory, smooth and unblemished; his hair was a burnished silver-gilt helmet brushing his broad shoulders. He wore trousers and tunic of Djumahat spider silk, immaculate pewter gray with crisp white accents. Bolodo rep, Aslan thought, and no junior on the make, not him. Slaver, you pretty shitface. She blew him a mental raspberry and turned to the other.

He strolled to a large armchair beside that window, settled himself, waved a long-fingered hand at three smaller chairs arranged in a shallow arc facing him. "Come," he said, "sit." In tone it was an invitation, not an order, but ignoring it would be stupid.

When they were seated, he said, "I am Fangulse Tra Yarta, the Divine Imperator Pettan Tra Pran's chief security officer, in effect your slavemaster, subject, of course, to the will of the Divine. With that proviso always in mind, I tell you this: contract law doesn't rule here, I do. How you live depends on me. Whether you live rests on my good will." He smiled at them, tapped his fingertips on the chair's arms. He was a broad man, not fat, only big; he had a lined, square, intelligent face, a long square torso, heavy arms and legs, large hands with tapering fingers, rather beautiful hands; he posed them in ways that showed off their elegance. "You are, of course, indulging in the fantasy of escaping and capturing a Bolodo transport. Forget it. You won't get near that field and even if you do, the Bolodo guards have had much experience in puncturing such fantasies. The dreamers that survive their attentions spend a few months working in the mines and emerge quite anxious to cooperate."

Parnalee shifted his feet, gazed dully at Tra Yarta. "Now that we've had the obligatory warning, what do you want?"

Tra Yarta reached inside his overrobe, pulled out a sheaf of folded fax sheets. "You are Parnalee Pagang Tanmairo Proggerd."

Parnalee's eyelids drooped. "Amazing."

Tra Yarta ignored the sarcasm. "You design spectacles and propaganda campaigns." He riffled through the papers, stopping to scan several before he set the sheaf aside and posed his hands in a narrow steeple. "You will have noticed that two peoples share this world. Hmm. Share is not the precise word, of course; however it is close enough for the occasion. The Hordar make up most of the population, the Huvved rule them. We can discuss the history and mechanics of that later, it is sufficient, I think, for the moment to say that the civility between us, a civility that had lasted for nearly three centuries and was profitable for both sides, this civility is falling apart. You will be required to provide spectacles and other campaigns to reverse this rot. I want celebrations of past glories, I want idealized versions of life on Tairanna, I want heroes to make the blood thrill, I want good feeling to replace the current rancor. I want the Hordar made happy with who and what they are, I want them made comfortable with the way the world is run, I want Huvved to be seen as elder brothers, wise and caring elder brothers. You understand. I do not wish to teach you your business, merely to indicate my desires as to the results." Tra Yarta did not wait for an answer, but turned to Churri. "You, Churri diZan, will use your talents to underscore the impact of Tanmairo's spectacles; the Hordar are a people drunk on words and a poet is more powerful than a hundred guns. According to my information you are adept at using whatever language is appropriate to your audience and part of your gear is a learning device that is supposed to be rather remarkable in its sensitivity to the nuances of those languages. I understand you will need time and access to information sources; you will have whatever you need, subject to security requirements." Again he left no time for response, but turned to Aslan. "Aslan aici Adlaar, skilled though they are, these men are strangers to this culture. You are a student of cultures. I expect you to study the Hordar and advise Parnalee Tanmairo Proggerd and Churri diZan how to accomplish what I require of them. I asked Bolodo to provide someone like you; to know a society as you can know it is to understand how to manipulate it. If I could do this, I would. I can't. I have some practical experience, but it's limited to pulling the strings on one or two people, at most a family. I don't know how to drive masses without having to slaughter half of them. People never jump the way you expect when you squeeze them."

Aslan leaned forward, held out a hand, palm facing him. "Please."

"Yes?"

She dropped her arm onto the chair's arm, straightened up. "I don't think you understand precisely what it is I do. I record and to some extent translate the histories, the various artistic expressions of dying pre-or non-literate cultures. This has nothing at all to do with manipulation of those cultures. I wouldn't know how to start. You want a number cruncher, a sociometrician who can put his thumb on the swivel points."

Tra Yarta smiled at her, amusement softening the harsh yellow of his eyes. "I'm sure you realize I had to take what I could get. Scholars don't ordinarily come onto the contract market lists and University is regrettably, from my viewpoint, alert as to what happens to its people. However . . ." He shuffled through the fax sheets. ". . . I am not all that displeased with what Bolodo has provided." He found the ones he wanted, glanced over them. "According to your University records, aici Adlaar, you have had considerable training in that direction. Admittedly you have not used that training for the past several years, but I doubt that a scholar of your ability will have forgotten so much so soon."

Aslan looked past him at the Bolodo Rep, saw him smile and pressed her lips together to contain her fury. Before she could say anything, Parnalee closed a hand over her arm, stared at her until she had to look at him.

He shook his head.

She pulled her arm away but kept her mouth closed.

He glanced at Churri who was simmering but silent, then laid his clumsy shovel hands on his massive thighs and gazed thoughtfully at Tra Yarta. After a moment's silence, he said, "Why should we do this?"

"Why not? These aren't your people. You have no responsibility for them." Again he looked through the sheets, folded them into a sheaf and tapped the sheaf against his chin. "Considering some of your other clients . . . hmm? This is a commission like any other."

"Not quite."

"True. You don't have the luxury of refusing."

"That isn't what I meant and that's not true either. There is no way you can force us to perform if we're willing to back our refusal with our lives."

"Are you?"

"I am if I'm driven to it. I can't speak for them." He held up a hand, pulling Tra Yarta's attention back from Aslan and Churri. "That's rather beside the point, isn't it? What I intended you to understand is that you should give us inducements not threats. You're asking us to dirty our self-images, to engage in acts of betrayal and cynical manipulation. You should at least make it profitable. For example, you could send us home after we've done the job."

Tra Yarta lowered the sheaf of fax sheets, looked at it with raised brows. "Cynical manipulation? Well, Tanmairo, you should know it when you see it. Hmm. Send the three of you home? I'm sure you understand that isn't possible. Even if I were willing to betray my kind, Bolodo would never agree. They have too much to lose. Short of that, what do you want?"

"If we have to live here, then let us live well. You say we are slaves, if so free us. Pay us. Provide us with a way of sustaining ourselves once the job is done." He lifted his hands, let them fall, turned his head with massive dignity to Churri then Aslan. "Either of you have anything to add?"

Nearly strangling on the word, Churri muttered, "No."

Aslan gazed past Tra Yarta's head at the man silhouetted against the darkening blue of the sky outside. She looked away. "No."

"There you have it. You get what you pay for."

"Your companions show little enthusiasm for your bargain."

"Enthusiasm costs more than you can afford to pay, Tra Yarta. You're buying competence, not complicity."

"Competence. Hmm. Your request is a trifle vague."

"Necessarily."

"Hmm. In principle, I accept your terms; it is obvious to a minimal intelligence . . ." He steepled his hands, raised heavy blond brows. ". . . that difficult and complex projects requiring creative solutions . . ." He cleared his throat, a distant amusement gleamed in his dark blue eyes. ". . . cannot be solved by applying whips to reluctant backs." Eyelids drooping, he contemplated Parnalee. "It will be some time before your work-product reaches any sort of coherence. During that interval I can evaluate your efforts and you can acquire sufficient local knowledge to shape your proposal to your needs. At that time it's quite possible that we will be able to negotiate a mutually satisfactory arrangement." He got to his feet. "At the same time, be very sure you keep in mind your circumstances. Be very sure the degree of nuisance you produce does not exceed the value of your services. If I can't use your proper skills, I'll find other employment for you." He ran his eyes over Parnalee's powerful body. "The mines can always use a strong back. I have had a small compound cleared out and made ready for the three of you. I expect you to start work immediately. There is a com at each of your work stations, preset to the offices of certain of my aides who will be directing you in this enterprise. If you need anything, call on them." With a valedictory nod, Tra Yarta strode briskly from the room. The Bolodo Rep who hadn't said a word during the interview kept on saying nothing as he hurried after the Security Chief.

3

The compound was a walled-in oval of garden and walkways, fountains and arbors with a small one-story structure at one focus of the oval, a delicate airy house with pointed windows and walls of wood, not stone; from the security arrangements and the look of the place, it seemed reasonably clear that the Imperator had stashed his favorite courtesans here and spent more than a little time with them. There were four bedrooms with bathrooms attached, set like beads at the corners of an oblong brooch, the centerpiece a large well-lit common room. Tra Yarta had moved most of the furniture out of the common room and set up three work stations for them; these waited under dust sheets. A fire was crackling behind a pleated glass screen and comfortable leather-covered chairs were arranged in a shallow arc about the hearth. Behind these there was a dining table with a number of open backed chairs about it; a cold supper was set out on the table, several kinds of salad, fruit, shrimp and other seafood, bread and butter and a selection of jams and jellies, and finally, a hot fruit punch steaming in a large ceramic urn with mugs clustered about its base.

Aslan ran her hands through her hair, stretched, groaned. "Clean clothes. A bath. Food." She laughed and went into the bedroom assigned to her.

4

Parnalee patted the solid slab of muscle over his stomach. "I like a good meal." He chuckled, a basso rumble. "Yes, indeed. It's why I usually travel worldship, the E Corini by choice. They raise the most succulent crustaceans known to palate." He skewered a giant shrimp, inspected it with satisfaction and popped it in his mouth.

Churri shoved his chair back, its legs squealing painfully across the floor; he bounced to his feet, glared at Parnalee. With a scornful t'k of tongue against palate, he stumped to the urn, scraped out enough punch to fill his mug and crossed to the hearth. Though the alcoholic content of the punch was more imagination than reality, he'd eaten almost nothing and was awash with enough of it to exacerbate a mild misanthropy. He dropped into one of the easy chairs and sat glowering at the flames refracted through the folded panes of the firescreen.

Parnalee swallowed the last shrimp and got to his feet. He crossed to one of the many windows and pushed aside a translucent white curtain decorated extensively with delicate blackwork. It was a warm spring night with mist drifting in threads around the fountain and clouds blowing in from the west though they were not yet clotted enough to diminish the soft pervasive glow from the moons. "I need exercise," he said. "Take a walk with me, the two of you?"

Aslan joined him at the window. "It's getting damp out there, I've had one bath, I don't need another."

"You won't melt."

She leaned against him, patted a yawn. "Way I feel, I might."

"A little exercise will fix that."

"I can think of pleasanter ways to get it."

"Aslan, use your head, will you? Think!"

She giggled.

"T'sa!" He scooped her up, dumped her head down over his shoulder and carried her to the door. It was locked, but he closed his fingers about the latch handle and applied force. The latch creaked and gave. He shoved the door open and stalked outside with her.

At first Aslan was too startled to object, then too amused. She was giggling when he set her down and went back inside, still giggling (though mistwater dripping from the eaves rendered her considerably damper) when he came out with Churri tucked under one arm. Before the Bard woke up enough to react, he was on his feet beside Aslan, swaying and blinking, sputtering as a large drip landed in his left eye, building up to an explosion.

"We need to talk," Parnalee rumbled at them. "Can't inside."

Aslan nodded. The fizzy good feeling born out of the food and the bath and having space to move in so her elbows could come away from her sides drained from her. She scrubbed a hand across her face, pushed dampening hair out of her eyes. Churri got rid of his anger and insult, peeling them away as if he peeled off his face to show another face beneath. He didn't say anything, but Parnalee's words had gotten through to him.

Hands clasped behind him, Parnalee trudged off, big head swinging as he hunted out a place where he'd feel secure enough to talk. Churri plunged after him. Aslan scratched her nose, looked over her shoulder at the warm red glow shimmering through the curtains; she sighed, hunched her shoulders against the strengthening wind and followed them.

Parnalee continued his prospecting until he came to one of the fountains. A slender column of water rose, broke, tumbled noisily from basin to basin scattered like bronze petals down a manufactured slope; he climbed halfway up the slope, knelt beside a rough wooden bench without a back and ran his hands over it. He stood, frowned at the bench, then dropped onto one end of it, the end nearest the stream. Churri clasped his hands behind his back and stood facing Parnalee, teetering atop a rock.

Aslan settled herself beside Parnalee, put her hand on his arm; it was rock hard. He looked as relaxed as ever, but she could feel a tension in him which surprised her; in the belly of the Bolodo transport he'd seemed such a casual, easy-going man. She took her hand away. "If you expect me to lay down and let that deviate clean his feet on me. . . ."

"I expect you to do what you've been trained to do. Use your reason. You're supposed to be intelligent. What I was buying back there was time."

Churri grunted, kicked at the rock with the heel of his sandal.

Aslan sniffed. "You really think Tra Yarta's going to keep his side of the bargain?"

"Look at it this way. We produce, the trouble (whatever it is) goes away, what happens to us?"

Aslan dug a hole in the dirt with her toes, watched it fill with water dripping over the edge of the nearest basin. "What I know from cultures like this says we'd be an embarrassment to him. So . . ." She knifed her hand across her throat.

"And if we don't produce?"

"All right, if you have to hear it, same thing, a lot sooner."

"Aslan, how long were you at Weersyll?"

"Six months less three days."

"Churri?"

The short bald man didn't answer for a minute, he frowned past Parnalee, then he nodded. "Two months, something like that." He stuck his thumbs behind his belt and teetered on the rock. "You were already there."

"Right. They're a methodical bunch, Bolodo, I'd say they go out twice a year. Which means it'll be somewhere around six months standard before the next transport arrives. We need information, weapons, some kind of plan. Like I said, we need time."

Churri looked up as a brief flurry of raindrops blew into his face. "I say we take advantage of this slop and go over the wall. There're mountains on the far side of the lake, we can go to ground there, live off the land."

Aslan snorted. "You think Huvved and Hordar both won't turn on us? Except for Bolodo this is a closed world. You want to see some raging xenophobia . . ." She frowned at her mud-splashed feet. "It's a thought, though, if things get difficult here. . . ."

Parnalee yawned. "With you and the Bard glowering like twin fumeroles, maybe Tra Yarta took my offer seriously. Let's hope he did and turns his attention elsewhere." The rain was coming down harder. He brushed at his hair, soft brown hair that shed the water like seal fur. His hand covered his face for a moment, lingered a breath longer than the gesture required. Aslan wondered about that, remembering the tension in his arm. "The first part is up to you, Aslan, you have to be convincing. I can play with this and that, work up projections, but until I've got your data, I can't get down to serious work, at least, I can make a good case for idleness. Find out . . . mm . . . we'll need a pilot, someone who can handle the engines, someone who can figure out where the . . . um . . . hell we are and how to get back to civilized parts."

"If no one else turns up we can trust, I can get the ship back, close enough anyway to put out a mercycall." Aslan scraped rain off her face. "Something I'd better say. Whatever Tra Yarta thinks, whatever the records say, I can't do what he wants. I can describe, analyze, compare societies, tease them to bits under the scope of technique, if you want it in the pretentious jargon the man seems to prefer. Manipulate them? Nonsense. I wouldn't know the first thing about that." She got up, went a short way up the slope, came back. "What happens when he finds out?"

Parnalee brushed at his hair again. When his hand dropped, he was smiling. "You weren't listening. That's my part of the job. You analyze, I put your data to work, Churri adds the frills. That's what the man said. Not altogether a bad idea. Comes close to my usual practice. Maybe Bolodo told him, maybe he thought it up his little self."

"He did say you were a propagandist."

"Event designer. Sounds better."

"All that talk about dirtying one's self-esteem?"

"He wanted to hear that, so I gave it to him. Bargaining chip. Ah, all right, a bit more than that. I do not like being coerced." The last phrase was spoken slowly with an angry emphasis on each word. "I choose where and when I'm going to work, not some tin god on a backwater world."

Aslan folded her arms across her breasts, rubbed her fingers slowly up and down her biceps. "Um. Maybe I don't need to say it." She scowled at him. "Maybe I do. Don't underestimate the locals, Par. I've seen a lot of that places I was working. Travelers come through and just because the locals don't think the same way or know about the same gadgets, they think they're stupid. My mother talks like that, I think it's because she knows it irritates me. She and her friends have been around a lot, it gives them illusions of . . ." she laughed, tasted rain on her lips, "you said it, tingodishness. According to them the locals haven't got the brains or the get-up to suck a tit. These Huvved, maybe the Hordar too, they've been isolated a long time, but they're not stupid and I doubt if they're unsophisticated in the art of the cabal. Tra Yarta wouldn't be sweating like he is if they were easy to handle. He thinks he's got us locked, that we can't make trouble for him whatever we get up to. I hope he's wrong. But we'd better be damn clever." She pushed at soggy hair, drew her hand rapidly back and forth across her nostrils. "And I'm catching pneumonia out here, can't we go in where it's warm?"

"Right." Parnalee stood. "I've said what I had to say. Aslan, I agree with you on most of that. We won't fool him if we fake it; we have to do it straight until we're ready to jump, whether we jump at the ship or into the mountains, otherwise we're in shit to our eyeballs. I'm going to get out of this one way or another. Don't either of you screw me up; I'll twist the neck of the one who tries it."

5

Aslan began working.

Reluctantly.

These weren't her people, she had no responsibility for what happened to them, but. . . .

What Tra Yarta wanted was a profound distortion of her work and she was ill at ease whenever she thought of what Parnalee was going to do with the data she provided, but. . . .

She had to do the analysis, she needed the information, she didn't trust either Parnalee or Churri, but there was no one else; she drove herself at her preparations with disgust, distrust and a bellyload of fury.

She made abortive gestures at first, feeling about like a blind worm, starting lines of investigation, letting them trickle from her fingers; she wasn't accustomed to working without a staff to help interview the subjects, collect data samples, do a preliminary sort on them and much of the slog work thereafter. Not having those eager, ambitious students, she had to reshape her habits and find a way to do that work herself.

After a week or so of aimless dipping into the Palace Library, she called herself to order and spent several days working with (and cursing copiously) the computers Tra Yarta had provided, setting up procedures, protocols and questionnaires. Then she began interviewing the Hordar who worked as gardeners, servants, cook, cat-handlers, musicians, poets, entertainers of all kinds, and last of all the few Hordar who made it into the Guard. Every Hordar working inside the Wall. They talked with her because they were ordered to and were very cautious in their answers to her questions, but she expected that and had long experience in setting up a series of questions that would give her much more information than they knew they were providing.

All that took time, more time than usual, because she had no staff, because she had to do all the analysis herself without any of the software she needed on computers not designed for that sort of work, because she was deliberately doing about three times as much interviewing as she needed, because above all she wanted to be very careful about what she actually passed out of her hands. Tra Yarta grew restless, but could not fault her for not working; besides, as she'd guessed from the first, he was a thorough man himself and they were only a minor part of his plans for suppressing dissent and disturbance. She sank her apprehensions and anxieties in a half-willed amnesia and let the work absorb her; she enjoyed everything about her profession, even the dullest part where she was going over and over material, arranging and re-arranging bits of information to discover patterns and unexpressed meanings.

6

Aslan yawned, recrossed her ankles. "Where's Churri?"

"Getting drunk somewhere, spinning stories, picking up more recordings. What've you got?" Parnalee took the lid off the carafe he'd brought with him, chugged down half the ice water inside. It was an unusually hot day and the house wasn't equipped with any kind of air conditioning, not even a fan, so Aslan was spending the hottest part of the afternoon outside under shade trees near one of the dozen fountains, stretched out on a lounge chair she brought from a slatted toolshed tucked away behind some flowering shrubs.

"I've started getting the history sorted out. See what you can pick up on a couple of prophets; they seem to be important to the Hordar, so you might be able to use them. Pradix and Eftakes. Better be careful, though. I suppose you know how tricky that kind of thing can get for outsiders. Pradix. Hmm. Center to the local religion. He was born some two millennia ago, standard years not local, on a world called Hordaradda which was on the edge of the Huvveddan Empire. By the time he died or was translated or whatever you want to call it, one half of Hordaradda was swearing by him, the other half at him and the Huvved were agin the whole thing. Ended up with the Pradite faction buying a colony transport and lighting out for parts unknown. Shaking the dust off, usual reaction. Like a lot of fanatics, they didn't know what they were doing, but they were sure they were sharper than any mundane, so they got cheated on the ship, paid hard cash for junk. The transport went blind in the insplit. If you believe in that kind of thing, it was their holy Prophet's intercession, or maybe it was Luck, anyway, when they tinkered their way back to realspace, there it was, a nice yellow dwarf of a sun with a coolish but comfortable planet waiting for them. No intelligent life as far as I can tell from the look I got at contemporary records, but otherwise a flourishing biota land and sea. They named the sun Horgul and settled on the fourth planet out to breed and argue over the teachings of Pradix. I've printed up a few of those, you might be able to do something with them. Eftakes was born here about five hundred years later, I'm not all that sure just what his differences are with Pradix, but the Hordar had a sharpish little war over them and the Eftakites moved down to the south continent. Guneywhiyk. Silly name, isn't it. North continent's no better. Kuzeywhiyk. Sounds like a sneeze. Got some of Eftakes' sayings listed too. Be careful how you use those up here. On Kuzeywhiyk." She giggled. "I don't know if Tra Yarta wants you doing anything down south; if so, you'd better have a look at Eftakes and his faction."

Parnalee rubbed the carafe back and forth across his brow, then gulped down a good part of the water left in it. "Never mind the sayings, any hero tales?"

"Yeh, but most of them are set on Hordaradda. I'll print you up some summaries, let me know which you want to look at closer. Um. Some narrative verse cycles from the War of the Prophets. Haven't had time to do more than look at the titles." She sipped at the fruitade, wiped her mouth. "I've come across mention of popular verse tales about the Conquest, the kind of thing that conquered peoples pass around, more or less mouth to mouth. Naturally the Huvved didn't record any of them, though I suppose they knew about them, the mention was in a trial transcript of a Hordar accused of theft and murder. Huvved definitions of both. I think it likely he was some sort of rebel. You might ask Churri to see if he can dig up some of them, they should be still floating around in manuscript and memory, that kind of underground snoot-cocking can hang on for centuries."

He smiled, a tight, sour twist of his lips. "I'll enjoy that." The smile, such as it was, vanished. "Insolent stupid arrogant shitheads, I could break them over my little finger. Gods, one more mincing cretin treating me like a dog. . . ."

She filled a second glass with iced fruitade, got lazily to her feet and carried it to him. "It was your idea, Par." He reminded her of Sarmaylen when one of his pieces was rejected; the thought made her smile and feel more tender toward him than she was wont to do. "You thought up the party catering bit, you went to Tra Yarta and got him to rent you out. Here, take this." While he drank from the tall glass, she smoothed her cold hand along his face and neck, then moved around behind him and began kneading at tight shoulder muscles. "You're just not used to being a slave; that kind of stagnant society couldn't afford you, lucky you. Uh! I've been on one or two feudal backwaters. Uh! No slaves, but some of the peasants might as well have been, bonded to the soil, sold with it. Uh! you're all knotted up. I've seen the way their so-called betters treat them. Uh! To these highborn Huvved, you're not as valuable as a dog, you can't be dropped into a pit and live out their fantasies of manhood for them with your blood and pain." She stopped talking, clicked her tongue. "Hmm, I wonder. . . . Any smell of pit-fights with men instead of dogs?" She stepped back from him. "That's a bit better. My hands are getting hot, might as well stop for now." She strolled back to the lounge chair, stretched out on it and took up her own glass, resting it on the firm flesh over her stomach; her shirt was open except for a single button holding it together across her breasts. "Well, have you?"

He lifted his head, looked at her with dislike that

melted into a smile more professional than warm, though that might be her own attitudes getting in the way. "I've arranged several such entertainments."

She slid the sweating glass back and forth across her bare midriff. "Ah." She was silent for a breath or two, then she said, "Be careful, Par."

"Don't angle for a promotion up to dog?"

"You got it."

She heard the tinkle of ice cubes, then he grunted. When he spoke, he changed the subject (the change landed on her ear with a loud clunk that said he didn't want to talk about this any more). "How'd the Huvved get here? Is there anything in that for me?"

"Hmm. Depends on what you want. You might be able to touch in undertones of Hordar pride and anger and take the curse off them. As long as you don't get so explicit you rub up against Huvved paranoia." She glanced at Parnalee, saw his annoyance, trying to teach him elementary tricks of his own trade, hah! she swallowed a grin, but . . . enough was enough, she'd gotten a small jab in for that look he gave her, time to be serious. "Let's see. About three hundred years ago, again that's standard not local years, when the good folk in the Huvved Empire got tired of their bloody rulers, or maybe desperate enough not to care all that much what happened to them, they rose up on their hind legs and kicked out the current Imperator. Came within a hair of putting their hands on him too, close enough they scared the shit out of the creep. He ran for his life in his last Warmaster, wrapped in her cloud of stingers, made the insplit just ahead of a swarm of Harriers. When they didn't give up and dived after him, he ordered a random course punched in, ran along it full out until he lost them, then popped back to realspace so he could find out where he was. Poor old Pradites. Either Pradix's holiness had worn off or Luck was out to lunch because where do you think he was when he stuck his nose up? A spit and a half from Horgul. They come all this distance to get away from home fights and bloody Huvved, spend seven centuries getting comfortable with their new world, and here comes the Huvved Imperator and his hopeful court to sit on their necks again. Hmm. One of those coincidences nobody believes, but they happen. Um. Shall I go on?"

"This is printed out?"

"Minus a few editorial comments that might annoy the spy who reads my hard copy."

He squinted up at brilliant white sunlight glittering through interstices between the undulant leaves of the low broad tree spreading out above them, leaves like overlapping slices of translucent green jade. "I've got nothing better to do until it cools down. Go on."

"Thanks a lot." She sipped at the fruitade; it was still cool enough to be drinkable, though the ice had melted. She wiped away the sticky trickle spilling from the corner of her mouth and wished futilely for a little wind to stir the hot still air; with the outer curtain wall and the inner walls that shut in this much smaller space, any breeze around would give up and go home. "Right. Picture our Imperator and his bunch sitting up there in that monstrous Warmaster, drooling over what looks like a sweet setup for plunder. Picture their surprise when they tune in on the local comsets and hear a version of Hordar speech. It apparently hadn't changed all that much in the centuries since the Pradites left Hordaradda, the Hordar are a pretty conservative bunch. Far as I can gather, there was an odd mix of technology. A lot like they've got now, in fact. Minus some flourishes laid on by the slave techs the present Imperator has been importing. Functioning comsets, the landers from the colony transport, some stray robotics, some sophisticated filters, touches here and there of tech they'd brought with them and managed to hang onto. They did some mining in the asteroid belt, dumped their worst criminals on the next world out, that kind of thing. Otherwise, they were pretty well early industrial with large feudal patches out on the grasslands, what they call the Duzzulkas. No ground traffic, but a busy sky. Airships. Hydrogen lift. All sizes, all over the place. Cheap and reliable. Don't have to build roads. By the by, I've convinced Tra Yarta that I should visit a Sea Farm soon, tell you about that later. Anyway, where was I?"

"All over the place."

"If I'm boring you. . . ."

"Academic maundering, which I suppose you can't help, being an academician. Go on. I have to get this one way or another and it might as well be now."

"So kind. Remind me to poison your next drink. Hmm. Yes. The Huvved came roaring in over Tairanna and took her fast and bloody. Poor old Pradites and Eftakites hadn't a chance against a Warmaster, stories from that time have her melting down whole cities in a single hour." She sat up, wiped at her face. "Like I'm going to melt in a minute." She poured more fruitade into her glass, tasted it, grimaced. It was warmish, all the ice long gone. She dumped the pitcher out, filled it at the fountain and emptied it over her head, filled it again, emptied it again and dripped back to the lounge chair. "From all I can find out, the Hordar were a peaceful lot then; they did more fighting with words than with fists, they'd rather go somewhere else when things got tense. Didn't mean they wouldn't fight, but they weren't much good at hopeless battles. Even then, though, you didn't want to push them too hard. Back them into a corner and you had trouble, serious trouble, capital T trouble. You get the Hordar Surge coming at you."

Parnalee broke open the fastenings on his tunic, wiped at his face and his neck with a damp handkerchief. "I presume this will eventually reach some endpoint."

Aslan ignored him. "What it is, it's a sort of mob action that turns a collection of individuals into a single being with a single mind and a single purpose which is basically to stomp a threat into mush." She lifted the damp ends of her shirt and flapped them idly, trying to stir a bit of breeze along her sweaty body. "To trigger a Surge . . ." she broke off, yawned, ". . . you put a minimum of twelve Hordar in some sort of enclosed space and apply extreme stress involving the survival of a genetic group." She closed her eyes, after a minute cracked the eye on Parnalee's side. He was flushed with heat and visibly uncomfortable; she couldn't tell if he was listening. Oh well, what the hell, might as well finish her recitation. "A Surge grows in lumps of twelve, don't know why, but there it is." She yawned again. "Bridges from group to group until most of the population is involved. It doesn't quit until the danger is gone or every unit in the Surge is dead." She pushed sweat-soggy hair out of her eyes and thought about going inside for a bath, but it was hotter in there than it was here. Too bad the fountain was in full sunlight, be nice to sit in it a while and cool off, but she didn't want a case of sunstroke, she didn't much trust the doctors on this primitive world. Wonder if there are any umbrellas inside, I could tie an umbrella to one of those upper tiers and make my own shade. Hmm. Haven't got the energy to move. "After I came on the term in the early histories, I tried talking about it in my interviews. Every Hordar had a powerful nonverbal response to the word and put up barriers whenever I tried to move beyond abstractions to the actual mechanics of the thing and the emotional and physical responses." She sighed. "You getting any of this, Par?"

"I'm listening."

"Hmm. You think there's any chance, if it's this hot tomorrow, for us to go out on the lake, do some swimming?"

"No."

"Why?"

"Freshwater eel-analogs. Very hungry this time of year."

"Shit."

"Yeh."

"Wondered why I didn't see any boats out there."

"That's why."

"Swimming pools?"

"Huvved. No slaves or Hordar allowed."

"As my mother would say, sweet sweet."

"Go on with your lecture. What's the rest of it?"

"I forget."

"Don't be stupid."

"All right. You noticed that Hordar and Huvved are related closely enough to permit interbreeding?"

"I noticed."

"Probably no pureblood Huvved left; they didn't bring that many women with them when they skipped out. Let's see. Surge. Huvved/Hordar mixes don't seem to have the capacity for that melding, but they exhibit much the same reactions to the word. A lot of fear there. Pride. Rage. A whole witch's brew boiling away down deep. I suppose anything that intense is useful in your business."

He grunted, a noncommittal sound she took for assent.

"I came across the phenomenon when I was reading about the early years. Seems that the Imperator then was a bit gaga about Hordar, it was a band of Hordar rebels who came within a hair of removing his head. He and his happy band of sycophants had a fine old time running down and disposing of the locals. Got so bad the Hordar believed he was going to slaughter them all. There you have it, extreme stress involving the survival of a genetic group. The thing that tipped them over the edge was a sort of auto-da-fé he put together outside a Littoral city called Ayla gul Inci. The Incers were driven into a fenced enclosure and forced to watch their relatives burn. About ten minutes into the barbeque they began melding into a Surge. About half of them were killed, but the Imperator barely got away with his skin intact. Not long after that his Security Chief took a look around at what was happening to his men and matériel and convinced the Imperator to abdicate in favor of his most competent nephew. That's what the histories say, you can draw your own conclusions. The Grand Sech worked out a schema that gave enough to everyone to keep them relatively contented and things settled down. Like I said, the Hordar those days weren't into mass suicide once the Surge was defused; they adapted and there was a fairly easy peace for the next two centuries. Then a free trader arrived; they don't have his name, but it seems he had connections with Bolodo Neyuregg. The Imperator before this one, he needed techs because his Warmaster was deteriorating and that threatened his power. He didn't want to hire anyone who'd give away Tairanna's location; he was charmed by the thought of, shall we say, hire-purchase of those techs. He didn't stop with them, slave holding seems to be addictive; hmm, either that or Bolodo reps are very persuasive, anyway, two transports a year for over fifty years, that adds up to a lot of slaves." She yawned. "That's about it, except the reason there's trouble now is simple enough when you consider the impact of cramming maybe a thousand years worth of technological development into fifty years and dumping this onto what was a stable, nearly unchanging society. Basic stupidity always makes trouble."

Parnalee passed his handkerchief over his face again, wiping away the file of sweat and the trickles that were dripping into his eyes. "Surge," he said, "you can't make a noble icon out of a mob. I need stories of individuals. Looks like you're telling me I'm not going to get them."

"Not from the Conquest," she said drowsily; she kept flapping her shirt ends, not putting much energy into this. "But you don't want those, do you? I mean I doubt that Tra Yarta would let you make Huvveds out as what? villains of the piece? no matter how much the Hordar might enjoy such a treat."

"There are ways. . . ." He brooded a moment. "I'm getting a feel for the Huvved, but I'll be depending on you and Churri to bring me something I can use for the Hordar. I don't see anything yet . . . after I think about it, maybe. . . ."

She dropped her arms over the edge of the narrow lounge chair, began playing with the short stiff grass. "Well, while you're thinking, what have you picked up about what happens when a transport's due?" She paused, but he lay like a sunstruck log, saying nothing. "I hope it's more than I've got. Any time I go near anything about the ship, I'm warned off, sometimes hard, sometimes subtle, but the end is, I know the twice-a-year thing and that's about it."

"Lock down."

"What?"

He sucked in a long breath, trickled it slowly out. Finally, he said, "All techs, anyone they suspect might be able to fool around with the ship, they're locked into the Pens." He lifted heavy, reddened eyelids. "Means me and Churri. Probably not you." He spoke slowly, wearily, as if he were too fatigued to push the words out. "Tra Yarta aside, these clotheaded Huvveds have only one use for women." He pushed himself up, got heavily to his feet, stretched, slumped. "I'm going to get some sleep, Churri wants to talk to you, tomorrow he said . . ." He yawned. "Didn't say why."

No spring in his step, with none of the massive force that usually hung like an aura about him, he stumped off, wiping at his face and neck with the sodden handkerchief.

She frowned after him, wondering if he was going to crack up before they got out of here; she couldn't do much without his backing, might as well follow Xalloor's advice, find a way to live as well as possible within the limits allowed her. And maybe keep alive a shriveled, forlorn little hope that Mama Adelaar would come and get her out of this mess.

He was a proud man, his size and strength and, well, shrewdness had insulated him from the kicks and pratfalls that life delivered regularly to ordinary folk. One of these days he was going to explode and tell some home truths to whatever Huvved creep it was giving him a bad time. He didn't understand what it meant to be powerless; he didn't feel in his bones he was a slave. She had a strong impression that he'd never been in a situation he hadn't eventually dominated. He played with irrational emotions and used them to manipulate people, but he was essentially a rational man; despite his experience he kept expecting people, maybe she'd better say men, to act out of reasoned self-interest. That wasn't happening here. It didn't matter how strong, how skilled, how valuable he was; at any time, for any reason, no matter how absurd, he could be flogged or even killed. His lack of control over his life was beginning to eat into him. She frowned at the brilliant glitter of the water droplets leaping up to fall down and fall again from basin to basin, wondering if Churri was right. Maybe they should go over the wall and try hiding in the mountains.

Churri wanted to see her tomorrow, huh? Well, he was going to have to wait. She was getting out of here, Tra Yarta had set up a visit to a Sea Farm. She sighed, straightened her legs and lay with her eyes closed listening to the music of the falling water; after a while she dropped into a doze.

7

The sea was a hard blue glitter reaching into a white glitter near the horizon where water merged with sky, the blue interrupted with undulant ribbons of what appeared to be shiny black-green plastic, the largest several meters long and a meter wide, leaves of the primary crop of the Sea Farm, the free-standing alga trees called *yoss.* Acres and acres of leaves, fans of supple strips rising and falling with the lift and drop of the sea. Narrow blue lanes cut through the black, openways spread in a web about a large collection of broad-bottomed barges with low structures built on them, the living quarters of the Farm family and its affiliates, storage buildings, generator sheds, processing sheds and open areas filled with bales of yoss leaves and piles and piles of brownish egg-shaped pods with heavy nets tied down over them. Water areas and barge areas alike, the Farm seethed with activity, children busy at small tasks, adults moving continually in and out of the water, off the barges and out of small brightly-colored boats scattered through the leaf fans, others busy at exposed machinery, moving in and out of work structures, doing assorted housekeeping chores, hanging out wash, working around exterior ovens where heat rose in wavery lines, vertical mimicry of the leaf-lines on the water. A floating village, close to self-sufficient.

The small airship droned in a wide circle about the perimeter of the farm. The inert and disapproving young Huvved seated beside Aslan came reluctantly awake (Zarkzar Efi Musvedd, though he discouraged her using his name with a lofty glare when she tried to start up a conversation). "Yoss," he drawled. "Average stem length, fifty fathoms, average diameter fifty feet. Leaf length, thirty to fifty feet. Valuable in bulk because they contain a fiber used in most areas of Hordar activity. Rope, the outer bags of airships . . ." He jerked a thumb upward toward the glistening ceiling of the gondola, a tightly woven, obviously very tough material. "One of the imported techs has developed a process to condition those fibers, fining the threads to produce a soft silky sheen." He pinched at the muted blue fabric draped over his arms. "The side stalks are harvested, mulched, macerated and the juices distilled into the fuel for the engines of this airship and those runabouts." He pointed down at the small shells darting about like waterbugs. "The main stalks are home for edible parasites, animal and vegetable, you've eaten some of them, I'm sure. And tucktla. Tucktla shells are crushed to make red and purple dyes. Also a very powerful glue. Hordar use it a lot in building. The chair you're sitting on is held together with tucktla. Near the surface, the subsidiary stalks produce large clusters of pods, egg-shaped, maybe three feet wide, five long, you can see piles of them down there, filled with hydrogen extracted from seawater. The farmers harvest those, slap glue over the stems to prevent leaks and sell them ashore to the airship companies. The lift in this ship is provided by yoss pods; having such a resource available when they arrived, the Hordar didn't bother developing any other transport." There was a casual contempt in the Huvved's voice as he went through his guide's spiel.

Aslan glanced at him, decided there was more of her mother in her than she'd thought; she wanted to put a knee where it'd hurt most and wipe the smug off that painted face. She suppressed a smile at the thought and went back to looking out the window as the airship spiraled in to a stubby pylon. She felt the small jolt as the noselock clicked home, a louder hum from the motors, then silence, then a few twitches; she could see small dark figures moving about below them, hauling on ropes, shoving home the levers of friction clamps. A moment later the pilot came from the cockpit door, walked past them and used a rodkey to open the exit door.

8

Efi Musvedd stalked from the lift, leaving Aslan to trot along behind like a pet on a leash which annoyed her again; scraping the bottom of the situation she dredged up a spoonful of humor (dark and ropy). The man had a genius for destroying any possibility in ANY situation he pushed his nose into.

Three dignified gray-haired matrons (Ommars) and a silent man with a long white beard elaborately braided (an Ollan) had gathered about the base of the pylon. As the chief Ommar began a courteous (though nonenthusiastic setspeech, Efi Musvedd walked rudely past her, stopped at the narrow footbridge which joined the pylon barge to the much larger living barge next door. He didn't like Hordar, Aslan suspected he was afraid of them and overcompensating for that fear with an arrogance both ugly and all too familiar; he wasn't going to tolerate anything but meek compliance from any of the Farmers no matter how senior. "You were informed," he said, "as to the purpose of this visit. I see no point in wasting time." He scowled over his shoulder at Aslan. "What are you waiting for, doctor?" The last word was packed with contempt and impatience. "Ask your questions."

Aslan rolled her eyes up, spread her hands, silently urging the Hordar officials to believe she had no part in his actions. There was no response, but she didn't quite despair; maybe the chance would come to push him overboard. Maintaining a dignified and respectful sobriety she explained to the Hordar elders that she was there to study their life patterns, that she wished to see how their limited living space was organized, the different kinds of work needed to keep their settlement viable, how they educated their children, samples of artforms, poetry, music, that sort of thing. She didn't expect to note down all of that today, merely an overview. She smiled suddenly, finished, "And why your storage barges don't fly off on you, considering how many hydrogen pods you're storing under those nets."

There was no response to her attempt at humor. A feeble attempt at best, but she'd hoped for some reaction. None. Only the ancient everplayed story, conquered and conqueror, hating and fearing on both sides, shame on both sides, the shame of enduring humiliation, the equal but less recognized shame at inflicting it. She sighed and asked to be taken about the floating village.

Efi Musvedd strode along, moving ahead of them, opening any door that caught his fancy, ignoring protests.

The Ridaar unit which Aslan wore on her belt was flaking everything around her, including whispered conversations not meant to reach her ears. Or the Huvved's. She couldn't check it because she didn't want Huvved or Hordar to know what she was doing, but she was sure she wasn't getting much useful except the whispers and she'd have to erase those, she wasn't about to give the Grand Sech a handle on these people. The Farmers were focused exclusively on Efi Musvedd, vibrating with a resentment and loathing that blanked out all other body language. After about twenty minutes of this she grabbed hold of her temper's tail, disciplined her face and turned to the white-haired Ommar, the official greeter. Before she could say anything, Efi Musvedd jerked open a door and went through it. It was the bedroom of a young woman who had apparently given birth not long before; when he burst in she was lying half asleep with the baby in the curve of her arm; she gasped with alarm when the door slammed open, pulled the baby to her and struggled out of bed. The Ommar was going to protest; Aslan took hold of her arm, closed her fingers tight about it. "If I may use your comset?"

The woman was hard with fury, but like Aslan she contained it. After a gesture that sent the other elders into the room to interpose themselves between the Huvved and the girl, she led Aslan rapidly toward one of the processing barges, opened a door and ushered her into a smallish office.

9

When she reached the Aide who handled her for the Grand Sech, she didn't waste time on tact. "Whoever assigned that supercilious little cretin to me ought to have his brain scrubbed. He's generated so much hostility here it makes me wonder if someone planned it; there's no way I can accomplish anything with him in the same hemisphere."

The Aide was a fat old man with empty eyes. He'd supplied her needs without comment the several times she'd called on him, he seemed to be an efficient administrator, she never had to ask twice or reject any of the supplies he sent her and subjects for interviews were on time and forthcoming. Now he smiled at her, briefly amused. "You didn't object to him before you left."

"I hadn't been exposed to the full glory of his personality."

"What do you want me to do?"

"Get him away from me. Far away. You know what the sweet thing just did? He barged into a bedroom where a girl was with her new baby and nearly scared her into a heart attack. Terrific." She scowled at him. "Am I supposed to be some sort of agent provocateur?"

"No. I'm sure your energies will be fully engaged by the work Sech Tra Yarta has given you."

"Which brings me back . . ."

A hand clamped on her shoulder and jerked her out of the chair. Efi Musvedd flung her at the floor, put a boot in her side, then panted and cursed as he swung his czadeg at her, that limber gray cane which guards used to herd slaves and Huvved used whenever they were annoyed with someone of lesser status. The beating went on and on as the Huvved gradually worked off his rage. Aslan huddled in a tight knot, rolling and wriggling, slipping some of the kicks and taking most of the whipping on her shoulders and buttocks.

The Hordar elders watched, silent and impassive; Aslan caught glimpses of them standing in the doorway.

The Aide watched from the comscreen. When Efi Musvedd dropped his arm, he called him over.

"Zarkzar Efi Musvedd, return immediately to Gilisim Gillin," the Aide's voice was crisp, flat, "report to the Grand Sech as soon as you reach the Palace."

The wild energy drained from the young Huvved's face and body; he looked tired and there was a glint of fear in his narrowed eyes. "What about the woman?"

"Forget her; she's no business of yours."

"I hear." He reached to click off the set.

"No. Leave it. Start back now."

Efi Musvedd slapped the czadeg into its clip, smoothed his hair down and stalked out the door, the watching Hordar melting like smoke before him.

"Ommar Tirtky Presij come here."

The elder walked to the comset, stood in front of it. "I am here, Seref."

"The woman, what is her condition?"

"With your permission, Seref." She stepped away, knelt beside Aslan and went carefully over her body, prodding at flesh and bone with strong, knowing fingers drawing groans and a film of sweat from the injured woman. She stroked her fingers in a brief caress along the side of Aslan's face. "Nothing broken," she murmured; a last pat, then she went back to the comset. "She is badly bruised and bleeding from several cuts; there might be internal injuries. If you want her intact and reasonably healthy, you'll have to leave her with us for a while. If there's nothing seriously wrong, she can travel in three or four days."

"I will want a report each evening."

"I hear, Seref."

The screen went dark.

10

Aslan woke late in the night, her body one massive ache that disintegrated into dozens of agonies when she tried to turn over. Her throat was dry, one eye was swollen shut, her upper lip was sore and so thick it seemed to be pressing against her nose.

A young Hordar woman sat in a rocking chair a short distance off. She was reading by the light from a dim lamp, her face in shadows, only her hands and arms lit clearly, the scars on them like broken wandering threads that started on the backs of her hands and wound along her forearms to trail out above her elbows, the white vividly clear against the bronze of her skin. When Aslan began moving about, she lowered the book to her lap and waited a moment before she spoke, making sure her patient was awake and aware. "Thirsty?"

Aslan's tongue rasped across dry lips. "Yes," she managed.

When the glass was empty, the young woman set it on the table and pulled the chair closer to the bed. "You haven't been a slave long, have you."

Aslan tried to smile, but her mouth felt like wood and the cut on her lip burned and broke apart. "No." She lay back, stared at the shadowy ceiling. "No."

"Are you angry at us for not trying to help you?"

"No. You couldn't do anything." With her mouth in its parlous condition, her articulation was so mushy even she had a hard time understanding herself, but she wanted to talk. She NEEDED to talk. "Do you know what touched him off?"

"You shamed him before Hordar. Sea Farmers. We are too valuable to the Imperator, he couldn't do what he wanted and wipe out the insult by killing us all. So he lessoned you."

Aslan nodded, grimaced as the movement sent dull pain bouncing between her temples. "I should have known that. I wasn't thinking. Too angry." She lay silent a moment, then lifted a hand and let it fall, a gesture of futility echoing the confusion in her mind. "The Grand Sech . . . You know he's the one who sent the slavers looking for someone like me? Out there . . ." She tilted her hand up, waggled a finger at the ceiling. "He's no fool or he wouldn't be where he is . . . or am I the fool . . . no, not this time . . . and I doubt he tolerates fools working for him. Why did they send that clown as my escort? How could I possibly accomplish anything with him bulling about? Tra Yarta paid a hefty price for my skills, why why why did he undercut me like that?" She stopped, blinked, then tried out a painful laugh. "Funny, not long ago I was thinking about an acquaintance, I was telling myself he didn't know what it was to be powerless, that he was going to run himself into trouble because of it, that he expected power to be rational and was he going to be surprised when he found out how irrational the powerful could be. I could have been describing myself."

"Sending that . . . um . . . person wasn't irrational." There was a quiet bitterness in the young woman's voice.

"What?"

"Wasteful, maybe, not irrational."

"How can. . . ?"

"We've had a long time to learn the convolutions of Huvved thinking."

"And?"

"I don't understand what the Sech wants from you." A graceful flutter of scarred hands silenced Aslan. "It doesn't matter, whatever it is, it's trouble for Hordar. You see . . ." She stopped talking, shifted position in the chair, folded one leg up so the foot was resting on the other knee, clasped her hands about the ankle. She was leaning forward, intense, filled with anger and need. "You see, he doesn't trust you, he'll break you first. That's what this was. A start toward smashing the part of you that won't submit to him; it's like breathing, not something you can control, you just do it. He wants you sane, he wants you healthy and he wants you co-opted."

"Complicity, not competence."

"What?"

"The reciprocal of something my acquaintance said. I think I see. I have to be his from the marrow out, not just from self-interest."

"Yes. The Huvved have done that to us. You saw what happened here and we're the most independent Hordar on Tairanna. Our first reaction was withdrawal. No one challenged that bastard's right to put his hands on anyone or anything he chose. One of the lessons of power, it is exercised everywhere, supported to excess everywhere, no matter how stupid or mindless or destructive the act. No Hordar is ever allowed to triumph over a Huvved, not even in the smallest degree. The Huvved might be punished for his act by other Huvved, but no Hordar will ever be allowed to know it."

"Why are you telling me these things? I could report you to the Sech."

The young woman laughed again, more anger than humor in the barking sound. "Don't you understand? I'm the second act. I'm the voice of despair, the councillor of passivity, the object lesson. How to survive and prosper under the rule of the Huvved."

"You don't seem to have learned the lesson all that well."

"Oh, don't fool yourself. I might talk a good fight, but that's empty air. I am Pittipat's footmat and that's all I'll ever be."

"Uh . . . Pittipat?"

"The Imperator. Word goes round that he's so woolly-headed he'd lose in a game of pittypat played with any healthy three year old. Makes us feel brave to call him that. Subversive. But it's smoke and nonsense."

"I can't believe. . . ."

"Listen to me, doctor whatever your name is. Do you know what hangs over our heads right now? No. Don't bother answering, I'll tell you. A battleship called a Warmaster. If the Imperator or even the Grand Sech decided we were expendable and they needed an object lesson to enforce their demands on other Sea Farmers, thirty seconds on we'd be a cloud of steam. And there's not a single thing we could do to prevent it." Her hands closed into fists, then she forced them open, splayed her fingers across her thighs. "Apply that to yourself. If you defy him, if your capacity for giving him trouble begins to match the value of your skills, pouf!" She sighed, shifted position again. "I suppose you and your acquaintance are planning to seize a Bolodo transport and escape. That's happened, you know. Or perhaps you don't. The year before I was born a band of determined slaves made it on board a transport, they even managed to take off. The

Warmaster didn't bother leaving orbit, it ashed them and the hostages they took with them. Everyone who helped them, everyone in the families of those who helped them, everyone who could be accused of helping them by local enemies whether they were guilty or not, altogether more than a thousand people were hung in iron cages and left to die. No food, no water, no shelter from heat or cold. The strongest lasted fourteen days. No, whoever sent that lunatic with you knew what he was doing. And he'll do more." The young woman fell silent; she frowned thoughtfully as she inspected Aslan's face and body. "I suspect you won't last more than six months." A quick brilliant smile, warm, amused, far from the despair in her words. "No, you won't give in, I don't think you can; poor baby, you'll be dead."

"Cheerful thought."

"Um, dead isn't all that bad; when you come back, maybe the world will have changed. Any change will be an improvement, the way things are now."

Aslan made a small noncommittal sound; there was no point arguing the tenets of a religion she was unacquainted with. "My name is Aslan," she said. "Aslan aici Adlaar."

"Aslan." The young woman touched eyes, lips, spread her hands palm out. "I am the Dalliss Gerilli Presij."

"Dalliss . . . um . . . diver?"

"That's what the word means, yes."

"I'm missing something?"

Gerilli Presij stood. "Why don't you shift onto your stomach and let me give you a back rub. We don't want you stiffening up." She glanced at a mechanical clock whose faint regular tick Aslan had dismissed as part of the noises endemic to barge life. "Not time yet for your next shot."

"Shot?" Aslan stiffened.

The Dalliss chuckled. "It won't hurt, I'm very good at this."

Aslan didn't answer, just began the painful, difficult process of rolling onto her stomach.

11

In the morning she was still sore and moving was difficult, but she was completely free of fever. Apparently the gel that Gerilli Presij used as a rubbing compound and those shots were effective against infection. She was also healing faster than she expected, her lip had deflated almost to normal and the other cuts on her face had closed over nicely. In one of the baths (hot and cold water, fresh and abundantly available, something she found rather remarkable in these conditions), she inspected her face and relaxed; though she hadn't protested Hordar attentions, the thought of that primitive goo in her veins had made her very nervous. Apparently it'd done a great deal more good than harm. She made a note to get a sample of those preparations to a friend of hers in the bio department at University.

Another girl brought Aslan her breakfast, younger, with a tendency to giggle. She nudged the lamp aside and set the tray on the table. "You're looking pretty good, Hanifa," she whispered, put her hand over her mouth, startled at her own boldness.

"Thanks to the excellent nurse I had." Aslan lifted the cover off the platter. "Looks good. Mind telling me what everything is?"

"Oh!" The girl thought that over, nodded. "I suppose they eat other things where you come from."

"A lot of other things." Aslan chuckled. "Very other."

"Ah. Well, these, they're krida, fried in batter. Crunchy, you'll like them. These, they're havya, fisheggs. This is jatine, it's a sweet we make out of jata fruits, they grow on the yoss. This is fresh jata. Mmm, you'd better try a nibble first, it's kind of powerful for someone who's never had any. This is a fulla, a kind of bread roll, it's got nuts and bits of cheese in it; we get the milk and cheese and flour from the landfolk. And for drinking, this is cimenchi, it's an infusion of a kind of watergrass. It . . ."

"Grows on the yoss?"

The girl grinned, much more at ease. "Doesn't everything? There's some milk here and some water over here, for if you don't like the cimenchi. When you're finished, just leave the tray where it is, someone'll fetch it."

"I hear. Um, would it be possible to find me some clothes? Musvedd the creep just about ruined what I was wearing."

"You sure? You should maybe stay in bed a little longer, I can fetch some books or something if you don't want to sleep."

"I'd rather start working if that's all right?"

"Sure, it's all right. If you feel up to it. Oh! My name's Cinnal Samineh, I'm Geri's cousin and one of her isyas." She whisked to the door, turned. "I'll bring the clothes soon as I can find some that'll fit, you're kinda tall." She darted away.

Aslan listened to her sandals pattering lightly on the reed mats. Nice child. She touched her lip, winced from the bare flesh where the skin was split. Isya. Isya. I remember seeing something . . . yes, Tra Meclin's Hordar dictionary. A kind of blood sisterhood. Or oath-sister. Closer than kinship. Five to eight per isya. Wonder how close he comes to being right? Wonder if I can spot the other isyas in the group?

She picked up one of the krida and bit into it. Yum, rather like fried shrimp. But her mouth was too sore to enjoy it and the salt on it stung the cut on her lip. Some day, some day. . . . She nibbled cautiously at more krida. Some day I'm going to pull that shithead's teeth and make him eat nuts or starve. She grinned at the image, winced again as the stretching widened the cut. Ram sandburs up his asshole.

12

Carting a faldstool on a strap, Cinnal Samineh took Aslan on a slow tour of the village. She'd unfold the stool, sit Aslan on it and bring her anyone she wanted to talk with. There was a very different feeling to the village as if everyone on the barges and in the boats had been let out of prison;

the Farmers were still wary but inclined to be as friendly as they could in the circumstances. Aslan responded. This was the atmosphere she was accustomed to; for a moment she could dream herself free again, working again, studying a culture she found intriguing though it wasn't her usual area of concentration.

The village was compact and complex, recycling was almost an art form and certainly a passion. *You will be back, don't trash your homeplace,* they told her. *All things are God, give them honor,* they said. They said these things lightly, amused when she sighed as she heard them for the tenth time, but under the lightness they were very serious about this, Pradix wasn't a prophet confined beneath a roof or shut between the covers of a book. Wistfully, filled with regret because she couldn't share it, she observed their deeply internalized belief and made her notes. Her usual objectivity was gone. She wanted these people set free. She wanted that even more passionately than she wanted the Unntoualar protected from the foul things being done to them. When she was lying on the bed in the room they gave her (Cinnal Samineh insisted she rest for an hour after lunch and Aslan was tired enough to make her argument perfunctory), she contemplated her own reactions, picking them to bits, a habit of hers that was one of the things her mother used to flay her with. Identifying, that's what she was doing. The enemy of my enemy is my friend. Maybe because they liked her. Maybe because they were intelligent and interesting people with a basic kindness to them. Maybe because the Huvved she'd met were such miserable oppressive dreeps, the kind of people she'd hated from the moment she could walk. Her foster mother was a toe-licking social climber who ignored the contempt of the people she was trying to associate with and the callous way they used her, then dropped her. The Huvved were using her with that same kind of contempt for everything she valued about herself. Using her learning and her intelligence to further enslave these Hordar. She'd hated that when it was first proposed, now she loathed herself for giving in to Parnalee's arguments, for letting herself be seduced by the work. She wasn't sure what she was going to do, what she could do, but she wasn't going to log data any longer, nothing accurate anyway. Uncomfortably aware of the naiveté her mother deplored, she frowned at the ceiling, was distracted momentarily because she noticed for the first time the fine plasterwork, it was sculpted into intricate geometric patterns, then scolded herself back to the problem she was contemplating. Adelaar wouldn't hesitate to cook the data and she'd know just how to do it indetectably. That was the problem. She had to fool Tra Yarta who knew these people a lot better than she ever would and Parnalee who no doubt could smell a fix from fifty paces. Intellectual integrity was devalued currency these days. She had a thought and started laughing; she had Efi Musvedd to thank for the time she needed. He was worth something after all; Tra Yarta got what he wanted, yes, but he lost far more than he gained. I hope, I hope, she told herself, she held up both hands with all her fingers crossed, a little trick she hadn't practiced for a while. An omen, she thought, this is going to come out right. She laughed again and let her hands fall.

What do I need? Paper and pen, I can't do this in my head and I can't trust the computers here. She rubbed at her temples. It's been what, ah . . . thirty years since I studied sociometrics, I need references. . . . Out of the question. Have to depend on my memory and my smarts, built up from the bases I'm familiar with. Rule of thumb. I hope my thumb's not broke. I always thought I was cleverer than most, have to prove it now. . . . Parnalee said he'd wring the neck of anyone who messed up his chances. His chances! She thought about what Gerilli Presij had told her. That was the end of her escape plans, she wasn't getting aboard any ship liable to be vaporized the moment it got beyond the atmosphere. Over the hill and off, she thought, Parnalee or not, soon as I can manage it. Hmm. One of the cities of the Littoral. I need to go there next. Ayla gul Inci. Why not? I can make a good case for it; that's the city where the Surge began. Must be some old memories there. Hmm. Maybe I can find a crack to crawl through. Yes. All right. From now on I'm working for me.

13

Cinnal Samineh flattened her hand on the desalinizer. "We bought this about ten years ago. It gives us all the fresh water we need." She slanted a sly glance at Aslan. "A tech slave the Imperator brought in built them for him. One of the few good things that came with the slaves."

"What did you do before then?"

"Let me show you. It's just next door."

It was a long narrow barge with slat blinds over lots of glass. Cinnal Samineh cleared one section so they could look inside. Water was being pumped along deep, glass-lined channels, around and past thick stands of remarkably ugly, twisted plants; the stems were broad and pulpy, the leaves were stiff, dotted with thorns, succulent, coated with a thick waxy substance. They were brilliantly colored, red and purple, orange, gold and blue-green, poison colors. Aslan inspected them and decided she wouldn't go in that place for a ticket home; she wasn't about to suck in any air they polluted with their exudates and exhalations.

"Saltplants," Cinnal Samineh said. "They extract minerals and salts from seawater. It's slow but sure; by the time they're finished with it and we pass it through a bit more filtration, it's almost pure enough to drink. We used it for washing and that kind of thing, what we needed for drinking water we passed through a still. Even now, on Holy Days and Jubilations we drink water from here, not from the machine. Sort of celebrating the past and linking with the future. You see, don't you?"

"I see."

Cinnal grinned. "We have other reasons for keeping this going. Those leaves give us some of our best dyes. Poisonous, sheeh! you have to be very careful handling them, but the results are worth it. And the roots, you can't see them, but they are very, very important. Our best filters are made from the pulp and membranes in those roots. Matter of fact, the Zerzevah Farm, it's out around the bulge south of here, that's their main source of income, their merm bed was wiped out a couple storms ago and the new bed won't be producing for a decade or more."

"Merm bed?"

Cinnal Samineh wrinkled her nose. "I can't talk about that."

"Can anyone?"

"Geri, maybe; I'll ask her."

"Thanks. How much water could this . . . um . . . plant produce in a day?"

"Enough for all of us. We had to be careful of course, and we used seawater for things we use freshwater for these days."

"Interesting. You said I might be able to visit a school?"

"I talked to my family's Ommar, she said fine. Schooling is family business, nothing to do with the Council. It's quite a walk from here. We could take it easy, or maybe I could whistle up a shell."

"Why not? It's a lovely day for a boat ride."

14

That night Aslan worked until long after midnight, sketching out the distortions and outright falsities she wanted to incorporate indetectably into her data files; when she was too tired to make sense of the numbers and symbols, she tore the pages into small bits and burned them. When she finally slept, she slipped in and out of nightmare, dreams where she was endlessly running, unable to reach a shapeless goal that seemed to represent safety; it hovered continually just in front of her, kept vanishing on her and reappearing a little farther on. Other times she was under something dark and heavy that came rushing down at her. That was a fast dream. It recurred several times and each time she managed to wake up just before the thing crushed her;

she lay bathed in sweat, her heart pounding, her head throbbing, the half-healed bruises and cuts adding their own dull misery to a night that was beginning to seem endless.

15

"Rosepearls." Gerilli Persij dipped her hand into a soft pouch and pulled out half a dozen rounds. She tilted her palm and let them trickle onto the square of black suede. The smallest was about the size of a small pea; it was a pale pinkish cream. The others went from cream to deep rose, from cherrypit to plum-sized. They shared a fine luster with a glow that seemed to reach down and down, drawing the eye after it. Gerilli Persij took a mid-sized pearl between thumb and forefinger, held it out to Aslan. "Close your hand around it for a moment, then smell your skin."

The pearl warmed quickly. Aslan opened her hand, sniffed at her palm. There was a delicate floral fragrance, very pleasant though nothing startling. Another moment, though, and she noticed something odd happening to her. She felt tension dropping from her, her body was vibrating with fine-tuned energy, yet she felt no need to move or speak. That rang an alarm in her mind, a distant flutter that immediately started fading, but not quite fast enough. Chewing on her lip, amazed at how difficult it was, she set the pearl on the suede.

Gerilli Persij smiled and began putting the rosepearls back in the pouch. "One like that probably bought you," she said. "Depending on how expensive you were."

"And they come from merms?"

"I can say that, yes."

"And a Dalliss is the only one who can locate and handle merms?"

"Yes." Her mouth twisted into a wry self-mocking smile. "I wouldn't say that if Tra Yarta didn't already know it."

"I see. That's what you meant when you said you

were too valuable to the Imperator to be slaughtered at a whim."

"That's what I meant." She shrugged. "If we don't push it too hard."

"That malignancy in orbit . . . if there was just some way we could get rid of it. . . ."

"We?"

"From what you said, I'm stuck here as long as it's up there."

Gerilli Persij gazed at her a long moment, then she shut the pearls into a small lockbox and got to her feet. "You said you're a good swimmer."

"I spent five years on Vandavrem, my first field assignment after I was accepted in the graduate program on University. It was a waterworld, almost no land. There was a very strange culture of intelligent bubble nesters . . . Never mind, it would take too long to explain, but yes I got to be very adept in the water."

"Would you care to visit the yoss forest?"

"Yes. Of course. Do you freedive or use airtanks?"

"Depends on how deep we're going and what kind of work's involved. I think tanks for this expedition."

"Right. Lead me to them."

16

Again Aslan worked until her mind was numb, slept badly and woke with despair and fear a sickness in her belly. It was hard to get up, to get on with living, but she'd done all she could in the time given her. The airship was coming for her shortly after noon and in a few hours she'd be back in the Palace pen, a slave again, with all that meant. She comforted herself with the thought that the sooner she was gone from the Persij-Samineh Farm, the sooner Tra Yarta's attention would be taken off them.

They threw a feast for her, danced the sea-dances for her, tumbled and juggled and at the end of the little jubilation, a woman with a husky voice filled with the pain and joy of a fully lived life sang a song that the Farmers listened to with a verve that seemed more than it was worth. Sly eyes watched Aslan, half-smiles teased at her, said to her we know we know, it's a bit of a risk, but who can always live safely?

The woman's hair was black and long, shiny and sleek as a tar slick. She stood on a wooden dais, a flute player on one side, a fiddler on the other and a drummer at her feet.

One a two a moon rising high
Dream and Illusion sharing the sky
Three a four a stone and a bone
What does the stone say, my oh my
What does the bone say, by an by
Moonlight's for love
For dreams never spoken of
Dreams that won't die
Five six seven
What do you leave in
When you're singing just a little lie
Sweet lie, silly lie, pass on by
Eight and nine
Look for the sign
Ten eleven
Fall from heaven
All those devils dark and sly
Riding the shoulders of
You and I
High be low and low be high
Twelve a thirteen
What does it mean
Bone come walking shimble shamble
Place your bets and let the wheel spin
All the little angels grin and gambol
Tip a toe tap a toe atop a little pin
Stone say watch it, round they come again
The angels are dancing wild and tame
Tap a toe tip a toe atop a little pin
Hey bone, ho bone want a little game
Bound for heaven? Never try it
That's a place they let too many in
Fourteen fifteen

What does it mean
All the little angels wild and free
Asquat around a gamble stone
Playing for we
Sixteen seventeen
What's your fancy?
Nothing chancy
Let the wheel spin
Eighteen nineteen
What does it mean
Moonlight's for love
For dreams never spoken of
Dreams that won't die
Twenty a score, not no more
What's a number for
Start the game again

Aslan joined in the storm of applause, appreciating the skill of the singer as she turned what seemed to be a minor little counting poem into something daring and portentous. The performance was safe in the Ridaar unit and she could study it in more depth later—if she decided she could trust the computers at her work station and if she wanted the responsibility. It wasn't all that difficult to understand the overall message of the song; even this stranger could hear the call for a continued resistance to Huvved rule, but there were some trigger words and images that drew a response which seemed disproportionate to their content. There was something going on here, something more dangerous than what Gerilli Persij had called talking a good fight. Aslan kept an open, appreciative smile on her face as the woman stepped down and another singer took her place, a man this time.

17

Alone except for the pilot and his co, Aslan watched the grasslands sliding beneath her, the silvery green-brown grass blowing in the wind that was pushing the ship along and making it shudder now and then. I could like this world, she thought, these people. Well, not the Huvved. Hmm. It's worth studying . . . wonder who'd apply and who'd get the grant? Aaron? Could be. He must be nearly finished with the Darra Saseru, seeing that they're just about finished killing each other off. Or maybe T'Kraaketkx Tk. I wonder what the Hordar would make of him? Hmm. Are they shapephobic? Or is that a Huvved trait? All the slaves brought in with me were from the cousin races, only slight variations from the two types living here. But that was just one shipment. Hmm. If I were the Imperator and reasonably sane, the techs I'd import would be so different from the locals that there'd be no place at all for them to hide. She yawned, settled back in the chair and dropped into a doze.

18

Aslan dropped her gear on a newly replaced grass mat. "Hey everyone, I'm back. Parnalee? Churri? Anyone here?"

"One sec, Lan. Be right out."

Aslan raised her brows, startled. "Xalloor?"

"Uh-huh." The dancer slammed the door to Parnalee's bedroom and threw herself down on a couch. "Trying to turn me into a blisterin nurse, tchah!" She wrinkled her nose. "I suppose it's better than being drafted as a whore for those mignish guards."

"What?"

"Drooling ol' dreep."

Aslan dropped onto the couch. "Who?"

"Him." Xalloor jerked a thumb at a window that looked out on the Great Tower. "Him with his bony ass planted on this world."

"What happened?"

"Dumb. Me." Xalloor banged a fist against her chest. One of her sudden brilliant grins lit up her tired face. "Nah, not so bad as that. Stupid Madoor, wouldn't let me see the client. I always do that so I know what the git wants. I was flying blind, hmp, went to the trouble to snatch me, didn't they? I figure here he is, he owns the whole stinking world, he must've paid one tart'rish price for me, so I go all out and give him my most marvelous dance. I told you about it, the Lightsailor piece." Her shoulders jerked with her short barking laugh.

"So?"

"Turns out his idea of art rises maybe to paper dollies." Another abrupt laugh. "Trouble is the Lightsailor thing's pretty abstract. I lost him about five minutes into it. Been anything less, I'd 've seen that and played to him, but that piece is a chunk of my heartsoul and I wasn't noticing anything. Until the finish. There was a very long loud silence." She shrugged. "Too bad. Oh well, what goes around, comes around."

Aslan caught her hand, held it a moment. Then she sighed and shook her head. "I go away four days. . . ."

Xalloor caught hold of her chin, tilted her face to the light. "You get crosswise with someone?"

"My escort switched into monster max when he thought I was being uppity."

"You and Parnalee."

"What happened?"

"I never got it straight, all I know is from his mumbles when I was washing the blood off. Lessoning, he said, at least that's what I thought it was, whoever worked him over got in some good licks at his face and he wasn't talking so clear. Place. He say that a lot. His place. He kept going on about knowing his place all right and teaching some tofty prick his. I figure one of these snotheads he was catering for thought he was getting above himself. Like you say, uppity. One of the guards hauled me out of the pen and told me to take care of him. He was bleeding all over the mat nearest the door, you maybe noticed one of them's new. Someone gave him one tart'rish going over, his back was hamburger. A local medic shot him with some stuff and gave me some goo to rub on the bruises. That was late last night. He's still sleeping. So you found out yet what they want a . . . that thing you said . . . what they want you for?"

"They've got me studying the Hordar."

"Why?"

"Trouble. They want us, Parnalee and me, to poke around and figure out how to calm things down without killing everybody."

"I can see why, these mignish nothi would starve to death if they killed off the Hordar."

"How is he? Really."

"He's going to know it when he moves for at least a month, but he's a chunk of ax jerky, it won't kill him. If I know men, he's going to bitch a lot, but you just ignore it."

"What about the Bard? Anything happen to him?"

"Not yet and maybe never, what I've picked up, you don't mess with poets round here."

"I see. Xalloor, you know anything about computers?"

"Deary dai, do I know about computers? Do you know about dancers these days? I guess not, stuck out in the boondocks with those primi types. It's a hard world out there, Lan, and competition's something fierce. Unless you've got an edge. I have this marvelous bitty Makerdac, no bigger'n my fist with a fanscreen that can holo full-size figures and make like a fiftypiecer, band you know. Do all my choreographing on it, plus my accounts and you name it. I swear, Lan, plug it into a sytha outlet and it'd fry you eggs for breakfast."

"Right. I'll see if I can work it so you come over here and help me with my data. If you're willing?"

"Read dy da, willing!"

"Pretty dull stuff."

"This mome, dull sounds marrrvelous."

"Come take a walk with me." Aslan got to her feet, smoothed her hands down her sides. "I've been sitting all afternoon and I need to get the knots out."

"Ah hah." That high wattage grin flashed again, then her narrow face was primly serious.

19

They strolled along a shady path that more or less paralleled the section of creek that ran through the enclosure. ". . . so we figured Bolodo would show up again in about six months standard and we've been looking about for ways to take the transport and run for civilization. Maybe not this time, but the next for sure."

Xalloor flicked a woven grass fan back and forth in the futile hope that moving air would be marginally less oppressive. "I heard talk in the pen, a snatch here, another there. You're not the only ones. So what happened? It's obvious you aren't all that hipped on the idea."

"I've been thinking about it and trying to plan something from the minute I put foot to ground and saw the transport was the only insplitter around."

"That isn't what I asked."

"I know. I just wanted you to . . ." Aslan pushed sweaty hair back from her face. "One of the people at the Sea Farm, she told me it'd happened before. Slaves took the transport, got it flying." She put her hand on Xalloor's arm, stopped her. "You hear anything about what's up there? Hanging over us?"

"Huh?"

"Ever seen one of those battleships they call Warmasters?"

"Shee-it. Yeh, a client once took me through one, it was defanged though. You telling me. . . ."

"Yeh."

"It got the transport."

"Fffft!"

"Think Parnalee knows?"

"Haven't told him."

"Maybe I should change my mind about moving over."

"Nice having someone to talk to."

"There is that."

They started walking again. After several minutes, Aslan said, "I don't like helping Tra Yarta put the boot to the Hordar."

"Nothing much you can do about it and keep your own skin whole."

"I can um put a twist on what I tell him."

"Get yourself whomped some more. Maybe turned into fish bait."

"I've already started. You might not want to be involved."

"Daarra dai, Lan, do me good to practice my kicks." Xalloor chuckled. "Could even be fun."

VI

1

Half a year before Aslan lands on Tairanna/ three years before Adelaar hires Quale and crew.
Airship/over the Duzzulkas/cloudless summer night.

Karrel Goza tugged a length of wool from the skein, draped a few loops over his thigh. Ruya was brushing the horizon directly ahead of him, fatly gibbous, Gorruya was nearly out of sight overhead, an anorexic crescent riding a fan of stars that were particularly brilliant this night; the wind was still, even the veil of dust that generally hung over the southern Duzzulkas had settled for the moment. The land was flowing dark and silent beneath the airship, the watchfires of the herders were scattered pinpricks of red beside spreading shapeless blotches, yunk herds, nubby black against the ripples of silvery black grass. The clock on the panel gave him another twenty minutes before he made Koy Tarla; the pylon lights should be visible soon. He was a thin dark man, short, neatly made, a man at peace with himself; as his hands manipulated the needles and the bulky gray wool slid steadily about his fingers and the sleeve grew longer, his mind drifted without effort from image to image.

Three sweaters by the time I get home. Not bad. Ommar keeps hinting I should get married. Hmm. I don't want to shift Houses, whoever it is will have to adopt in. Gily? Ommar'd eat her alive. Her father's tavern's doing good, be a nice add to the family business. No, she's all right to warm a bed, not for a long haul, too changeable, I'd never know who she was getting off with when I was gone. Long haul. Hmm. I don't like Sirgûn sending me out alone for this haul.

Dangerous. And I'll have to lay over at some Koy and catch some sleep. Isn't the stopping I mind, it's the god forgotten Noses with their stinking questions, wouldn't believe you if you said the sun was shining. Nehir. She's a weaver, that's good. Prime weaver. Bring a lot to the family. Even Old Pittipat likes her work. She wouldn't mind me being off flying so much. Not going to quit flying, wife or no wife. What would I do if I had to quit? Don't think about that, Kar, it won't happen. Nehir, Nehir. I don't know. She's not bad looking, but . . . I like her brother. Not marrying her brother. Good solid business. Hmm. Doussi? Prettiest woman in gul Inci. Wonder why she's not married yet? Five years older than me. Keeps the family factory ticking steady. There's always someone needing motors for new airships. Sirgûn Bol could use new ships, replace this old whale. He rubbed his foot against the control stick, smiled dreamily, shook his head. They haven't bought a new ship for two years, hmm, maybe more. Something's going on. Maybe I should think about changing companies. Percin Hizmet left last month. Hasn't found a place yet. That's odd. He's a top mechanic, he shouldn't be having trouble getting on somewhere. Casma. Wonder if she'd be willing to stay onshore. I doubt it, being she's a diver. Divers are too scrappy for me, I can do without fights when I'm home. Way she dances would make a statue stand. Maybe we could work out something. I'm gone so much, she could spend those days at the Farm, be on land a couple weeks when I'm home. Affiliated to a Sea Farm, mmh.

The needles clish-clashed, small clicks and ticks came from the instrument panel, a ghost of wind noise filtered through the windows, wire stays sang sustained sweet notes into the shifting creaks of the gondola, cables burred deeper, stronger notes into the cargo bales hitched beneath it. Inside the cockpit, the light was dim, bluish, mostly from the panel though a small spotlight shone on his hands and woke watery gleams from the sea-ivory needles. Girls' faces, fragmentary musings, dim apprehensions drifted in an unhurried stream through his head until the alarm chimed.

He set the knitting aside, looked out. Lights in two columns above the much fainter glows from cracks in curtains and the occasional yellow square where an unshuttered shopwindow announced the business was still open. "Koy Tarla." He patted Fud-40's panel. "Good old girl."

He cut out the automatic pilot, began matching maneuvers and hit the pylon latch dead center first try. The noselock wouldn't click home. He swore under his breath and made another pass, slipped loose again. Fud-40 hadn't been properly serviced for months, there were a lot of parts that needed replacing, nose gear was so worn it was near unusable. The third time he tried, he revved the motors up more than he liked and held her vibrating against the pylon until the instruments gave him a GO. Swearing some more, he brushed the back of his hand against his sweaty brow, swiveled a rotor and nudged the side of the gondola against the platform extending from the pylon, watching the panel anxiously until the readouts told him he was set in solid. He released the rearend cable, felt the gondola shudder as it unreeled. When the hook hit the ground, a buzzer sounded and he shut off the motors with a sigh of relief and a fleeting suspicion that he wouldn't finish this long haul with bag and self intact, a thought he immediately suppressed. He rolled up his knitting, stuffed it in its bag, clicked off his harness and got to his feet. The locks held the gondola stable; besides, Fud-40 was heavy with bales of yunk wool. It'd take more than his weight to knock her about.

2

Karrel Goza pulled the lift door shut, checked the cable out, it was taut and locked to the eyebolt. Birey Tipis was reliable as an old boot, bless the man. Rubbing at his back, he crossed the stretch of beaten earth to the office, pushed open the door and went inside.

"Alo, Bir, how's it go?"

"Slow and slower. You better get that nose fixed, Kar."

"Don't tell me, tell Sirgûn. What you got for me?"

"Two passengers for Koy Vaha, six bushels orps with the rind on and five sacks tarins, dried. Old Muntza Tefrik, he brought in some hanks of unbleached kes yarn and he wanted to know if his package had got here."

"Passengers." Karrel Goza grimaced; they always wanted to come up and talk to him, Fud-40's musty cabin started closing in on them the minute he shut the door. "Nuh, nothing for here this trip. Geres Duvvar is due along in a couple weeks, coming from the west, he might have it. If he makes it here. He's got Hav-13 and that bag makes old Fud up there look like a yearling."

"How's it on the coast?"

"Like here. Slow and slower." Karrel Goza took the manifest, checked the weights, nodded. "Fud can handle this." He set the clipboard down, smothered a yawn. "What's open? I need to eat and catch a few hours sleep. Sirgûn laid my co off for the duration."

"You too, eh?"

"Too?"

"You haven't heard?"

"I've been short hauling along the coast, that's why you haven't seen me for a year or so."

"We've been getting singles since the thaw. Navlun Bol and Ilkan Bol just like Sirgûn. Cut way down on the schedule too. I get an earful of complaints from the Fehz and everyone else, their goods sit and rot waiting for a hauler to come along. Everyone's notching their belts. For the duration they say. I'm getting an earache from hearing the word. I ask myself what's it mean and I answer me, nothing." Birey Tipis lifted the flap, came through the counter. "Food, hmm. You remember Annie Arkaday?" He waved Karrel Goza to the door, lifted the key ring off the counter and slipped the keys about, hunting for the one he wanted. "Yeh, not many forget her cooking. She had to shut the cafe, the rent got to be too much for the trickle of customers to cover. She petitioned the Fehraz to lower it for the duration," a soft chuckle sounded over the clink-clank of the keys, "for the duration," he repeated, "but he wouldn't, so he gets nothing, intelligent, eh?" He shut the lights off, crossed to the door, followed Karrel Goza through. "Folks stay home these days or stake out a table in Mahanna's Tavern with a couple cups of kavé, it's still open, but that's because Mahanna's got freehold on the building and only pays a ritseed rent." He finished with the pair of locks, thrust the ring into a side pocket of his jacket. "Annie works out of her house now, same reason, it's free-hold, she's piled her kids one on top of the other and hires out their rooms and fixes meals for whoever can pay. And the kids run errands when they can. She's doing all right so far." He pointed down the street. "That way," he said, "across town from here. It's not far." He walked beside Karrel Goza as they went down the middle of the village's main street. "You heard anything? Been rumors the lines are going to drop half their stations, let the clerks in them go. I've been in that office near a score of years."

"No one tells us pilots anything except which route we're on or we're laid off till god knows when." Karrel Goza kicked at a pebble, watched it bound along the worn pavement until it disappeared into a pothole. "It's a long low, but must 've about hit bottom, don't you think?" Karrel Goza looked around. The village didn't seem to have changed much since he'd seen it last, shabby, one-story buildings, red tile roofs showing above the packed earth walls that went round the house and the bit of garden that only friends and family ever saw, here and there trees rustled in the sometime wind and the shutters over the front windows of those shops that were closed for the night rattled with the gusts, the dark was kind and concealing, there was a lot he wouldn't see, a lot hidden behind housewalls. He wished Birey Tipis would shut up about all this, it made him sick thinking about it and more than a little scared.

"Can't say, Kar, you and me, we've still got our jobs, knock wood, but what do we do if Sirgûn and the others go broke?"

"Nuh, Bir, they won't let the carriers fail, Tairanna would fall apart if they did."

"Don't be too sure. The Fehz would survive and the

divers would still be bringing up rosepearls, so I can't see Pittipat sticking his fingers in, what's he care about a bunch of surrish grubbers? I don't see any light ahead." Birey Tipis glanced at Karrel Goza, wiped sweat off his forehead. "Wouldn't say all this if I didn't know you don't run off at the mouth, Kar." The tip of his tongue flicked along his lips. "Used to be we didn't worry ourselves about what we said, used to be Yapyap, that's what we call the Sech's Nose, he let folks know when he was coming around so they could stop talking about anything he'd have to report." He caught hold of Karrel Goza's arm, stopped him. "Listen, Kar, I don't know about other Koys, but watch what you say to folk here, Yapyap's gone serious, got a bodyguard, a couple scrapings imported from Tassalga. Hurum Deval got drunk last week and wouldn't shut up, he started spouting all those jokes about the Imperator, you've heard 'em, I'm sure, he didn't mean anything by it, he always gets a mouth on him when he's reeling. Thing is, come morning he was gone, we haven't seen him since. The Fehraz he sent some men over and packed up the family, shipped 'em to gul Brindar on the west coast, we got word a few weeks later they were doing scut work for the Fehdaz there and hoping Hur would show up. He hasn't so far. And he's a long way from the first to slide down a dark hole without a bottom." He started walking again. "What say you let me buy you a beer? Mahanna's come up with a tarin brew that slides down sweet as honey. Don't worry about Annie, she'll whip up something for you, doesn't matter how late it is."

"Why not. Old Fud's still a lady in the air. One thing though, who's going to be wrestling the cargo come morning? If it's me, I pass."

"You got a spare goum or two, I can scare up some strong backs for that."

"I could put in a requisition for expenses. Don't suppose Sirgûn would honor it."

"There's another way, wouldn't cost you or show on the books."

"Huh?"

"There's some brothers who need a lift to the coast."

"Off the manifest?"

"What else."

"This Yapyap of yours, won't he be hanging around the pylon?"

"There's ways for handling that."

Karrel Goza walked on. At first he was sure he didn't want anything to do with the proposition. Running like that, it must be serious what they'd done. If something went wrong he could suck his family into their mess. The Ommar'd eat me raw. He glanced several times at Birey Tipis; the old man was strolling along, eyes on the road ahead, face placid as a ruminating yunk, no sign of the nervousness he'd showed a moment before. Karrel Goza was suddenly sure he was going to do it, he wasn't quite sure why, he was so scared of it, thinking about what could happen tied his stomach in knots and pumped acid up his throat, but somehow he couldn't not do it. "Family'll divorce me if this comes out."

"It won't. Um . . ." Birey Tipis dug his thumb into the soft folds of skin hanging under his jaw. "The boys've done this before."

"Maybe you'd better tell me some more."

"The less you know, Kar, the safer you are."

"I am?"

"You got a point. Everyone is. Safer, I mean. I can say this, it's not thievery or anything like that."

"Make sure you take care of Yap Yap and his friends."

"We will, no fear of that, my friend."

We, Karrel Goza thought, that's interesting. He didn't say anything, just followed Birey Tipis through the tavern's swing door.

3

**Four months after the Duzzulka flight.
Speakers Circle/Ayla gul Inci.**

Karrel Goza rubbed his back against the stone of the wall, watched the clot of heavily robed men mill about atop the minaret, a thirty-foot-tall column of stone with a round shingled roof rising to a graceful point above the broad arches that went round the speaker's platform. He was listening to the talk around him, soft muttered voices punctuated with slitted suspicious glances at everyone else, angry voices, kept murmurous by the fear that a wrong word at a wrong time was deadlier than poison, a fear justified by the events of the past months; almost everyone knew someone who'd vanished as quietly and completely as a sailor washed overboard in a summer storm; almost everyone thought he or she knew why. There was the unexpressed hope that the missing were in prison somewhere not dead; there was the equally unexpressed fear that they'd been airshipped out over the ocean and dropped in Saader's Cleft.

Geres Duvvar came threading through the crowd in the Circle, in each hand a paper cone smudged with grease from the estani nuts inside. He gave a cone to Karrel Goza who moved over so his cousin could lean against the wall beside him. "You got some change coming, Kar. There was a little war going on over there 'tween the peddlers."

Karrel Goza grunted, dug cautiously into the hoard of hot nuts.

Geres Duvvar swallowed. "Hurry up and wait, huh." He waggled the cone at the group on the speaker's platform.

"Yeh. Don't look like there's much good to say or they'd be saying it."

The clacker sounded, the crack of wood against wood reverberating through the dull mutter of the crowd. Silence spread like fog.

The Stentor separated from the other robed men, spread his arms. "Sim, O Kisil, sim sen, Hear o People, hear thou. Thy Ollanin return to report the outcome of their petition." There was a pause. Behind the Stentor one of the Ollanin murmured to him. He nodded, faced out again. "Sorrow, sorrow, the petition was heard, the petition was denied."

The crushed nut in Karrel Goza's mouth was suddenly bitter. He spat it out, ignoring the scowl of the woman whose skirts he spattered with the bits. Geres

Duvvar beat his hand slowly steadily against the stone, cursing under his breath.

"Sim, O Kisil, sim sen. This is the Imperator's reply. Let those among you who are needy apply to the Houses for bread and work."

A groan rose from the crowd.

"Sim, O Kisil, sim sen. If you who are needy are turned away, give word to the Fehdaz. Every House and every Farm who turned you away will be assessed two score rosepearls or the equivalent in tapestries and art pieces."

A swelling of sound, with a double center, on one side those who have, on the other those who have not.

"Sim, O Kisil, sim sen. Two of thy Ollanin lifted their hearts against this and spoke. The Divine one cast them down into a dark and stinking cell. The Ollanin who murmured but spoke not, the Divine one had them taken from him and sealed into their rooms. For two days, thy Ollanin saw not the sun nor the moons, for two days thy Ollanin drank only water, for two days thy Ollanin tasted not bread nor meat."

Rising-falling moan filled with fear and rage.

"Sim, O Kisil, sim sen. The Divine One spake unto your Ollanin thus: It has come to me that the merm beds and the rosepearls are a State resource. It has come to me that it may be wrong for such a resource to remain in the hands of Families, not the State. Be warned, O Kisil, thus the Divine one spake, I will cease my wondering for this moment, I will not act as my heart requires if I am not stirred to it by thy unruly importunities.

"Sim, O Kisil, sim sen. And then it was that the Divine one cast at the feet of thy Ollanin the two of them whose hearts had rebelled. And then it was the Divine One spake again: Take these and let me not see them, let me not hear their names, let them be as nothing in my sight and thine.

"Sim, O Kisil, sim sen. Thy Ollanin have come to thee in sorrow, ashes in their hair and heart, thy Ollanin say to thee, we have failed thee, what is thy will?"

The Stentor folded his arms and stepped back. Robes

pulled tight about them, cowls drooping over half-hidden faces, the Ollanin started down the stairs. When they reached the pavement, the crowd in the Circle, silent, impassive, gave way before them, opening a corridor so they could cross the Circle and pass into the Fekkri. They didn't wait for an answer, they wouldn't get it then; that was coming three days later. Karrel Goza and Geres Duvvar wouldn't bother coming back to hear it. At least the City Ollanin had tried to help, that was more than the Fehdaz had done. He was old and sick and about to die, his sons had died before him (there were rumors about that, how they died and why, Incers were very nervous about the character of the next Fehdaz), his grandsons and the Nephew were all there waiting like vultures, no one in the place bothering their heads about anything else.

Karrel Goza counted the coins in his hand, closed them in his fist. "Gidder's should be open by now. What about a beer?"

Geres Duvvar slipped his watch from its pocket, clicked it open. "Do we have time? Old Niffiz is getting touchy about checking in." He shut the watch, shoved it back. "He's Immel. He's got a thing about us in Goza-Duvvar-Memeli. You don't want to give him an excuse to boot us, not the way things are these days."

"May he fall in yunkshit up to his honker." Karrel Goza put the coins away. "Let's get back. That wormy old skink won't give an inch."

4

Ayla gul Inci/Waterfront/one year and six months after the return of the petitioners.

The bay was gray and leaden, an echo of Karrel Goza's mood. He took out the notice, reread the single line of print. His head throbbing with resentment and fear, his body cold and sick with the horrible emptiness of failure, he tore the paper into small hairy pieces and dropped them into the water. One breath he was angry at Geres Duvvar for holding onto his job with Sirgûn, the next he was dead ash, wondering how he was going to tell the Ommar he was a drag on the Family, not a support. Out on the bay he saw boats coming in. He straightened, stared. He'd played in these waters when he was a baby; when he was older, he'd taken girls out sailing if he could talk a cousin into lending him a boat; he knew enough of the sea's caprices and her moods to understand what he was seeing. There was a bad blow coming. He watched the gray waters heave beneath the pier and hated her, Mother of Storms, treacherous unfeeling bitch, stealing from him his last respite from shame. He had to get back to the House and help tie down for it, no time to get a little drunk to pillow the pain. He cursed softly, bitterly, cursed Sirgûn and the Huvved, the Kabriks and their obsession with new products, the mushbrained Imperator and his mushbrained advisors, the Fehrazes and the Fehdazes, the city council, the sneaks and most of all the alien slaves who made all this trouble for workers.

"They are that." A girl's voice.

He swung around. "What?"

"You heard. What happened, you laid off?"

He looked her over. She was small and dark, brilliant eyes, not exactly pretty, but coming into a room she'd be the first you noticed. The fine wandering scarlines on her arms were very white against the dark gold of her tan. A Dalliss. No one ever completely tamed a Dalliss even when her diving days were finished. His mouth curled down with dislike, but he touched eyes and mouth and spread his hands in polite acknowledgment of her presence. "Blessings, Dalliss." He turned and started past her.

"Oh my, the little man's soul is bruised." She closed her fingers about his arm, said, "You're a pilot. I need a pilot."

"For what?" Disgusted with the leap of hope he couldn't help, he pulled free. "Storm coming. I'm going home."

"Couple hours before you need to start tying down. Stop a while and give me a listen, you might like what I'm going to say." She stepped back from him, swung herself onto a bitt and sat kicking her bare heels against the agatewood, watching him with a hard bright expectation that sent warning tremors along his spine.

He lowered himself to the planks and sat with his legs hanging over the edge, his back against another bitt. "Job?"

"Not for taking home to Ommar. We could come up with some coin if you've got to have it." She swept her arms wide, waggled her small slim hands as if to say you can have what you want, it doesn't matter long as you do the thing. Whatever the thing was.

She had beautiful hands, he noticed that with a small jolt of surprise, delicate, supple wrists. And fine ankles. Like a lot of women these days, she'd taken to wearing trouserskirts, wide-legged things made out of the new yosscloth, its silky flow clinging to her legs in a way he found exciting. The top she wore was a tube knitted from black kes yarn, it had a square neck, no sleeves, she wanted to display her arms with their scars, the badge of her achievement. Used to be pearlers wore long sleeves and lace mits to hide the merm marks. Not this one. He found himself approving her pride. He looked away, frowned out across the heaving water. "Just tell me what it is."

"Remember Jamber Fausse?"

He started, went still. "Why?"

"Show you I know a thing or two. You lifted him South after he hit the Fehraz Ene Karrad's strongroom and dropped half the coin to the Kiks that Karrad pushed off his Raz. You've been a busy little man the past few months.

The cold was back in his bones; he stared at the water and said nothing.

"No need to sit there shivering like an ishtok out of water, Karrel Goza. This isn't a noose about your neck. If you don't want to fly for us, forget it."

He turned his head. She was leaning toward him, hands braced on her knees, taut, eager, willing him to accept the proposition she hadn't yet made. He was interested; it would be immensely satisfying to hit back at something instead of going meekly home to mama. "Same sort of business?"

"Not quite. This could get you killed. The pilot we had before is in Saader's Cleft. No, the bitbits didn't drop him there. He died. We didn't want some asslicking official eager to make points getting curious about how that happened. He was shot, bad, but he got us away and the ship home before he died." Her eyes were suddenly bright with tears. "He was . . ." Impatiently she scrubbed the tears away. "Could happen to you. So?"

"You're the ones."

"What?"

"You're the ones that hung the Nephew naked from the minaret. Painted insults on him hair to heels. I wondered how someone got him there without being caught. You fixed him up in his paint and harness, I suppose, and waited until Ruya and Gorruya were down; then you dropped the noose over the roofpeak and left him dangling. Ktch! your pilot must've had Pradix's hand on his neck to operate blind in that battlerose of winds."

"He did, besides there isn't a man alive or dead who can match his touch."

"Wish I'd seen it. Geres Duvvar was home, he told me about it, he said the Fehdaz was howling mad. Not that he liked the Nephew that much, it was the idea that some Hordar would have the nerve to lay hands on one of his Family. On one of the holy Huvved. Ktch!"

"Herk the Jerk. Yeh. He wanted to top every Hordar he could get his hands on, but his Sech talked him out of it."

"Old Grouch? I'd have thought he'd be sharpening his ax for Hordar necks."

"He's scared of a Surge. You've been away a lot. I don't think you really know how bad things are getting."

"Hmm. So, what are you plotting now?"

She scratched at her forearm, rubbed a bare foot against the bitt. "Herky Jerky's been hatching ideas again. Three months he's had his hands on the Daz, he keeps thinking that ought to mean something, but every time he has a flash, Old Grouch digs the ground out from under him. I suppose he's tired of it. From what we could find out, he maneuvered so the Grouch had to go to Gilisim Gillin to talk to the Grand Sech. Soon as the old man's back was turned, Herk snatched some Farm boys who'd come in to gul Inci to visit relatives and carted them off somewhere, who knows why. Probably something to do with merm beds and rosepearls. Doesn't matter what maggot he has in his head, we've got to pull them out. It was just luck, really, finding out what happened to them, a friend of mine was over the wall meeting me, we saw the bitbits make a snatch; we were too far away to stop it, but we managed to follow them to where a miniship was moored. They shoved the boy in the gondola and left. We thought about trying to get him out, but there were more bitbits around guarding the airship. No way we could reach it. Next day some other friends of mine managed to find out who was gone and where they might be. Some others and me, we're going in after them, but we need a pilot. That's it, that's what we want you for."

"In where?"

"Mountain Place."

"I've flown out of Inci in that direction. Not over the Place. The winds there are tricky. It's the steam out of the crater that does it. Fehdaz's pilots know the currents; even so they pick their way and go in round noon when things're quieter. What's your ship like?"

"A mini." She grinned at him. "Used to belong to Herk."

"Hmm. The instruments?"

"Crude and crudest. That's how Muhar Teget described them."

"I didn't know he was still alive."

"He's not. He's the one in the Cleft."

He gazed at her a long time, then looked away. "Get me fired?"

"No."

"You followed me here."

"Yes. I was going to see if you were off for a few days and might be able to fly for us. Muh said after him you were the best on Tairanna." She combed her hands through her hair, spread them again, waved them; she seemed to like waving her hands about, maybe someone told her sometime they looked like little white birds. "Pushing my Luck," she said. She dropped her hands into her lap, laced her fingers together. "I saw you shred that paper and made a guess, that's all."

"You know my name."

"Ah." Her mouth twisted into a half-smile. "That's a bit of a difficulty." She searched his face for a moment, then shrugged. "Why not, Grouch knows me well enough, he doesn't need a name. Elmas Ofka, Family Indiz-Ofka-Tanggàr, Farm Indiz." She hesitated, shrugged again. "Divorced, outlawed."

He'd half suspected who she was, but it was a shock all the same. Elmas Ofka. They said she killed a Huvved who thought he was going to rape her, sank a knife in his belly and opened him up like a yunk carcass. He'd always thought that was somebody's dream, that she probably stole some pearls or sassed a touchy tribute-collector. Every now and then the Huvveds got antsy and took hunting parties out searching for her, but they never saw hair nor heels of her, so they shot a few erkelte and pretended that was what they were out for. "You're crazy to be here in daylight like this."

"Crazy has its advantages."

He laughed, he didn't quite know why. "At least it seems to be working." He rubbed thumb against middle finger, not sure what to say next. "Ah, who else is coming?"

"My isya. Cousins, some friends. Women. That bother you?"

"Not if you know what you're doing."

"We know."

"Tonight?"

"Right. Herk's had them three days already." She was silent a moment. "One of them's my brother."

"Ah. Sorry."

Her mouth tightened. "They will be. One of these days we'll hang Herky Jerky from the Minaret and we won't use a harness."

"I need a little time to get used to the ship. You know the bay better than I do, what about the storm?"

"By the time we leave, it should be mostly blown out, enough rags left to give us cover. At Mountain Place any of the sentries supposed to be on the walls, they'll more than likely be inside with a fire, no one's going to be miserable for Herk the Jerk. If there are some mushbrains outside, we won't have any problem spotting them." She hesitated, made up her mind between one breath and the next. "Some aliens are living with us. They jumped the Wall at the Palace and happened onto us at a delicate moment." Her hands fluttered, sketching metaphors for the embarrassment of both parties. When she noticed the expression on his face, she smiled and shook her head. "They won't be coming with us." She folded her hands again. "One of them was the Imperator's own weaponsmith. Strange creature. He doesn't like people much, and I got spanked for that kind of language when I was a girl, so I won't try telling you what he thinks of our esteemed Divine One. He's been making gadgets for us. Stunners and spotters you could wear in a ring almost. Sniperguns." She narrowed her eyes at the sea, then the sky, chewed her lip a moment. "You can get away without eyes on you?"

"Yes. When and where?"

"You know the Dance Floor in the Watergarden out north of Inci?"

"Been there a time or two." He tried a quick grin.

She grinned back, her eyes narrowing into crescents, her nose flattening. "I expect you have." She sobered. "I'll bring the ship down an hour after midnight, give or take five minutes each way. I can manage that much, there's room for mistakes out there. We need to be at the Mountain Place around three hours before dawn. Will that give you enough play to get the feel of her before we start?"

"Too much. If I can't learn her in twenty minutes, I might as well give up. Make it second hour, unless you've got a reason otherwise."

"Second's better, but I wanted to make sure you had plenty of time for test runs." She slipped off the bitt, stretched, yawned. "Anything else?"

"What you expect me to do? Besides flying."

"Nothing. You won't be coming in with us. You're the only one who can get us away from there."

"Good enough."

"See you tonight then." A flutter of a hand and she was running away down the pier, her vitality printing her on his mind even after she vanished into an alley between two warehouses. He smiled. He felt a lot better now. He couldn't tell anyone about this, but it went a long way toward erasing the sense of failure that'd been the worst effect of the layoff notice. His dread was gone, he could face the Ommar without feeling like a lump of yunkshit.

The wind was picking up, two fat raindrops splashed down on his head, trickled past his ears. Home and fast. From the look of those clouds and the height of the swells, they'd need all hands to get ready to ride this one out. Another raindrop broke on his nose, he wiped it away and started running toward the alley.

5

Approaching the Dance Floor/Watergardens outside Ayla girl Inci/both moons down.

"Like crawling through a room lined with black felt." Tezzi Ofka braced herself on her arms, leaned forward until her nose touched the curving window.

"Um." Elmas Ofka scowled at the trembling lines scattered across the panel in front of her; trying to balance the ship in half a dozen directions and get somewhere at the same time took most of her attention. The storm didn't help. Blessings be, the winds had died to a whisper. She'd flown the miniship a few times before (mostly in daylight though and tethered) so she'd be able to manage it in an emergency. She hadn't realized how tricky this short jump was going to be. Thank God, Karrel Goza gave her the extra hour. It would have been easier for him to come to the place where they'd stowed the ship, but she wasn't about to trust him that much. Not yet anyway. He probably realized she didn't. He wasn't stupid, though it was hard to remember that when he put on his dumb hardboy look. Good camouflage. I hope. "Tez, any sign of those lights?"

"Not yet. You sure we're heading the right way?"

"Sssa. Half maybe. Keep looking around."

"Mm."

They droned on for several minutes, then a sudden gust of wind caught the small airsack and rocked it perilously. Elmas Ofka fought the miniship straight, exploded out the breath she was holding. "Tez!"

"Turn a little left. I thought I saw something when we were tumbling about."

Elmas Ofka eased the nose around, bit her lip as she felt the gondola tremble in the swirl of winds that grew stronger as she got closer to the water. Two faint greenish spots swam past some distance in front of her. She tried to stop the turn, overcorrected, overcorrected again, went toward the lights in a series of diminishing arcs.

"Elli, I'm getting airsick."

"Don't talk so much." She ran the pump that sucked air into the ballast sacs; the ship sank, steadied as the added weight helped the motors hold against the erratic push of the wind. A moment later it lurched, nosed down as it hit a powerful downdraft. She swore fervently and vented the air she'd just pumped in.

"Elliiii, I didn't know you knew those words."

"Shut up, Tez. Sssaaa, I can't see. . . ." The lights slid inexorably beneath her. She pumped in more air, shifted the stabilizers so she was edging downward, then swung carefully around. "Tez. Get ready to drop the ropes." She fumbled over the switches, finally got the hover configuration right, swore again as she saw she was several meters away from where she wanted to be. "This is as good as it gets. Toss the marker, Tez, then let the ropes go."

The gondola rocked as Tezzi moved from side to side, shuddered as the hatches opened. The weighted glowglobe whirled away, caught by a gust whose fringes reached the miniship a moment later and started it tottering. Elmas Ofka chewed on her lip, drummed her fingers on the chair arms, waiting as long as she dared before she did anything. The ship jerked, steadied. She started breathing again. "Drop the ladders, Tez."

She left the chair and went to help balance the gondola as dark figures began swarming up the ladders.

Karrel Goza was first up. He came in with a quick neat twist of his body and went without a word to the cockpit, settling himself at the controls and began running his fingers over them, touching the switches but changing nothing for the moment. If you can recruit him, there's a flyer working for Sirgûn Bol, Muhar Teget said, name's Karrel Goza. He's a natural. If he manages to get as old as me, he might just be better than me. A natural, she thought, yes, Muh was right. She relaxed some more. Some have the gift, Muh said, lots don't. You've got one, diving it is, flying it'll never be. Some folk can get along quite well without any special talent for what they want to do, if they're willing to work their asses off and never stop training. Don't you put down the ones who go that route, sometimes they do a helluva lot more than the naturals. There's the drive, you see, without the drive even the best don't go far. The one weakness they've got, though, they don't adapt fast to radical new situations. You need that kind of thing in what you and your isyas are doing. When you have to replace me, no no, gen-gen, a stroke or a bullet, one of 'em's going to get me and let me tell you, I'd rather the bullet. What was I saying? ah yes. When you replace me, make sure your pilot is one of the naturals. There's too much that can go wrong too fast for the other kind. You want inspiration rather than intelligence when there's no time for thinking.

Harli Tanggàr swung in, threw Elmas Ofka a salute and a broad grin and began reeling up the ladders. Elmas moved forward.

"All up," she murmured.

"Run through this for me."

"Let me take us out over the bay first, we've been here too long already." She slid into the co's seat. "Tez, signal them cast off."

The miniship leaped free, began drifting sideways;

Elmas Ofka worked uncertainly through the configuration shift, vented air too slowly at first, then too suddenly, swore under her breath at her clumsiness as she changed settings. She explained what she was doing in a rapid half-distracted murmur, all too aware of his eyes on her; she loathed doing things badly where people could see it, especially men. When they were at last out over the water and there was nothing for miles around to threaten the miniship, she sat back with a sigh and let it drift. "You want to ask questions, or do I give you the lecture Muhar Teget pounded into me?"

He set a forefinger on a switch. "I touch, you name it, all right?"

"Why not?"

For the next twenty some minutes he worked with her, gaining skill with a speed that astonished her. She'd been told by more than Muh that he was good, too good for the stodgy hauls Sirĝun was giving him, it looked like her informants weren't exaggerating. Before she thought, she said, "Why in forty hells did those godlost execs lay *you* off?"

He laughed. It was a pleasant rumbling sound, deeper than his speaking voice. "I'll take that as a compliment."

Her face burned. Prophet's blessing, it was dark up there except for the faint glow from the instruments. "It was so meant," she said.

"Yeh. Trouble is I never took the time to spread the old oil around."

"But flying. . . ."

"Being good is a frill on most hauls. Adequate does just fine."

"Adequate gets you killed down deep."

He blinked, raised his brows. "If Old Pittipat in Gilisim gets serious about taking title to your merm beds, he'll fetch in slaves that can whomp him up a minisub or something like it before you can say spit, Elmas Ofka. Think about it a minute while I get set up here. . . ." He worked in silence for a short while, tapping in the course, then he swung his chair round to face her. "You've kept hold of those beds up to now because no one can get at them but a Dalliss.

How long do you think that's going to last?" He touched the nearest switch, let his hand drop onto the chair arm. He was serious, frowning, seemed to be groping for a connection between the two of them; his words came in quick spurts with long pauses between them. "Muhar said crude and crudest. He's right. You ever been up front in a longhauler? There's stuff in there. Stuff no one was dreaming of. Just a few years ago. When I was in school. Look at me. I'm what? One year? Two? Not that much older than you. I tell you, Elmas Ofka, what with the skills the slaves bring in from outside. And the fiddling the mechs do in their offtime. Well. The ships are smarter than some of the pilots these days."

She stared at the blackness outside and at her face mirrored like a distorted ghost in the curving glass. "Herk the Jerk," she said softly. "But why boys? They don't know anything."

He pinched his nose, dropped his hands onto his thighs. His thumbs were twitching. "Maybe he thinks they do."

"But everyone knows it's the Ommars and the Dallisses who control the beds."

He shifted restlessly, crossed his legs. "Everyone in Inci," he said. "Everyone in any city with a Sea Farm handy. Yeh, you're probably right about them." He managed a kind of all-over shrug. He was a smallish man, his body limber and relaxed as a sleepy cat. She got glimpses now and then of another kind of person inside, mostly, though, he kept everyone away from that man. "Things get shuffled around a bit differently in different places. You ever hear Huvveds talking about women?"

"I heard one talking to a woman once, a Hordar woman."

She could see him remembering the stories about her and feeling like a fool, then deciding that a continued ignorance would be the most tactful face he could put on. "What I'm saying is, Herk spent most of his time in Gilisim; that's inland. On the Lake. Freshwater. No merm beds there. And since he's been back, who's he talked to? Ollanin and Kabriks. All men.

And who's he got close to him? Other Huvveds, all men. And knowing our beloved leader, do you think he's going to bother asking anyone about how Hordar run their lives? See what I mean?"

"Of all the stupid, arrogant . . ."

"That's our Herk."

She settled to a simmering brood while Karrel Goza put his feet up, tilted the chair back and dozed as the miniship droned on toward the Mountain Place.

6

The winds around the Fehdaz's Mountain Place were clawing at each other and coiling into knots while an icy rain hammered verticals and horizontals alike. Karrel Goza tried sliding from one current to another, fighting to get close enough to the Hold to let the women down inside the walls. The rain blinded him, the winds knocked him away again and again, driving him toward the ground, skidding him toward the walls and the three-hundred-foot cliff behind the Hold, coming close to flipping him end for end. He backed off, climbed into a region of comparative peace.

"She's a sweet ship," he said. "Tougher than I thought, plenty of power, but she is little. Not enough weight. Another thing, that lightning, if we're struck, goodnight all. I don't know. . . ."

Elmas Ofka frowned at the clock on the panel, looked over his shoulder at the silent women sitting on the floor behind her. "We can wait maybe half an hour, maybe three-quarters if we really push it, some of us have to be back in our beds before sunup. Let's see if the storm will calm enough to let you take us in."

He nodded. "Even a half hour could make a big difference." He reached under the chair and lifted up the shoulderbag he'd brought with him, took out a mass of knitting and settled it on his lap. Hands busy, eyes flicking back and forth between the needles and the panel, his face intent, he knitted steadily, the warm brown wool dancing through his fingers.

She watched him, fascinated by this stranger who

without intending it was showing her just how little she knew about her own kin and landfolk everywhere. It was disturbing, it was challenging, it was infuriating because she knew all too well that she couldn't do a thing about the forces that kept her pinned where she was. Mostly she was too busy to fret about her limitations, she had other things on her mind; now there was nothing to do but think and she didn't much like what she was thinking. Even when she was still Indiz Farm's premiere Dalliss, her life was circumscribed by her talent and her duties and everything her Family expected of her. She fidgeted, wishing she had something to keep her hands and her mind busy. He knew he was going to wait maybe an hour for us, damn him, he's set, why didn't I get ready for a delay? Sssa, woman, you've got to do better. . . . *Forethought, Ommar Ayrinti beats her finger in the air, forethought saves aftertrouble. If you'd just think before you stepped in something, Elli, just take a meesly second and think a little, ay girl. The gnarly forefinger like a bit of dried floatstem beat beat beating at the air before her face.* Sssaa. . . . She moved her shoulders impatiently, swung her chair around so she wouldn't have to look at the man, pulled her legs up and settled herself to doze away the wait. If she could.

7

Half an hour later the winds were still gusting, but the worst of the knots were teased out and the rain had diminished to a few spatters. Karrel Goza took the miniship in a ragged spiral about the largest structure inside the walls, brought her low and hovered her over an open stretch in the kitchen garden.

Elmas Ofka knelt by a hatch, swept the spotter in a wide circle, slipped it back in the case snapped to her belt. "No guards," she said, pitching her voice so she could be heard above the thrum of the motors, the whine of the wind. "Harli Tanggàr, Lirrit Ofka, go." She watched them slide down ladders that twisted and bucked with them and went streaming away at an angle when they dropped free; they landed in rows of hanannas and moved quickly into the shelter of tall groaning beanpoles. "Melly Birah, Hessah Indiz, go." She counted a dozen breaths, watched them jump free when they were more than a manheight from the ground; they landed on the trampled hanannas and ran for the hedge that circled the garden; they went to their stomachs behind coldframes there, merging with the inky shadows. "Binna Tanggâr, Jirsy Indiz, go." She turned her head. "See you, Karrel Goza. Our turn, Tez." She tipped through the hatch, caught the ladder and began dropping. The ropes whipped through her gloved hands, the wooden rungs slammed into her knees, her breasts, her face. By the time she reached the ground, she felt like she'd been beaten with rods.

Her isyas came out of the shadows and drifted around her, shadows themselves, knitted hoods over all but eyes, black gloves on hands, narrow black trousers, knitted tops that clung like tight black skins. They were armed with deadly little darters the weaponsmith made for them and cutters that went through metal like a wire through cheese, braided leather straps that came away from their belts with a quick jerk, daggers thin and sharp as a wicked thought and broader all-purpose knives. At the kitchen door, she looked over her shoulder at them and was filled with pride; she pulled her hood away from her mouth, flashed them a grin, then waved Harli Tanggàr up to deal with the door.

8

Elmas Ofka checked the sketch Toma Indiz drew for her; it was hard to make out even with the pinlight held close to the crumpled paper, the lines were shaky and pale. Left from the kitchen. Done that. Two turns, door, probably locked, could be barred from the inside. They'd taken care of that, no resistance at all as the cutter sliced through the lock's bolt. Bit of leather folded up and shoved under the door to hold it shut because it had a tendency to swing open and they didn't want to attract the attention of any insomniacs who got a notion to ramble, you want to watch out for those, Elli, they can wreck the best plan there is. Scared the shit out of me when I was busting out; Prophet bless, he was as scared of me and a lot less ready and I tunked him on the head before he could yell. Left again, keep going past five doors, stop at the fifth, there should be a sharp curve ahead. Round that curve the corridor splits into three branches. If Herk's just holding the boys until a ship leaves for Tassalga, they'll be in a tank at the end of the right arm. There, see, where I drew the circle. If he had them under question and is finished with them and they're still alive, then they'll be in the infirmary, that's here, along the middle way, cells here and here, treatment room there. If he's still working on them, go left and down, keep going down. The question chambers are deep enough so Herk's guests, if he ever has any, can't hear the screams. There's a sentry on each level, at least there was when old Grouch was working on me. I doubt little Herk has changed things much. You have to take them out, you don't want them there when you're leaving, you're apt to be in a hurry and maybe carrying one or more of the boys. First though, everything past that curve is being monitored. Camera eye in the ceiling. The guards are watching the screens down in the anteroom to the question chamber. You can't get at them without passing the pickup, so you'll have to take it out. One thing you've got going for you, the wiring in that place is hopeless, things are always shorting out. There's a good chance the guards won't bother trying to fix the system before morning.

She touched Lirrit Ofka's arm.

The isya nodded, dropped to her stomach close to the wall. She extended a collapsible tube painted black, eased it around the bend, put her eye to the viewer. She lifted her head, wriggled forward a few spans, looked again, repeated the process until all Elmas Ofka could see of her were feet in the soft black mocs with a gray dust smear like a crayon rubbing on the soles, footprints clinging to the bottom of her feet.

Lirrit Ofka rolled over, there was a faint hum, a tinkle. She rolled back, crept forward again, her feet vanishing. For several seconds there was a tense silence broken only by the near inaudible rub of cloth against stone, then even that stopped, then the isya came trotting back. She grinned, gave them a thumb salute. Keeping her voice low but not bothering to whisper, she said, "There was just the one. I spotted the guard, took him out. Dart this time. You hear it?"

"Uh-uh. How fast?"

"Got him in the neck. I think he thought a bug had bit him, he started to raise his hand, poop! down he went."

"Alert?"

"Nah. Leaning against the wall half asleep."

"I see." She thought a minute. "We won't change plans. Question chamber first, the other cells on our way back. Any objections? Good. Let's go."

9

Elmas Ofka and her isyas took out the drowsy sentries as they came on them with as little trouble as Lirrit had with the first; they left the men propped against a wall as if they slept sitting with their weapons beside them. Down and down the women went, through latched but not locked doors, running silent as hunting cats through the dimly lit corridors and down the spiraling stair flights. Empty corridors. Not even a rat prowling them, let alone an insomniac.

The door into the lowest level was locked and barred.

Elmas Ofka waved the others back, swung the spotter in a wide arc, watching the bright green line that trembled across the readout. The walls were thick stone, N'Ceegh had warned her she couldn't fully trust the sensors if that stone had traces of metal and most of the stone the old fathers used was like that. The line wobbled in one place but she didn't know if that was her hand or a sign. She swung the spotter back, held it still where she'd seen the tremble. After a moment she was sure she was seeing a spike. She moved the sensor array a hair to the left, another spike. She counted four spikes and a wiggle that might have been another, or a rat in the wall. She thumbed off the spotter and slid it away. "Four," she said, "maybe another. Off that way." She pointed. "Hri cousin, you and Lri cousin be ready to jump soon's we get the door open. Ti cousin, you and May cousin and Hay cousin back them up. Ji cousin, handle the cutting. Then you and Bi cousin stand watch out here. Questions? Right. Let's move."

10

The two isyas ran down curving stairs, their mocs scuffing minimally on the stone. They took the last four steps in a flying leap, landed braced on the stone flags of the chamber floor, darters snapping up. Four men sat at a battered table playing cards and drinking from a skin they passed around. They looked sleepy, bored, uninterested in anything, even the money riding on the outcome of the game. The eyes on the man facing the foot of the stairs went wide and he opened his mouth to yell as he shoved his chair back and started to dive away.

Harli Tanggàr put a dart in his cheek, another in his arm and shot the man at the left end of the table as Lirrit Ofka took out the other two. While Elmas Ofka walked to the table to inspect the dead and make sure they weren't shamming, the other three isyas ran silently from cell to cell, opening each grill-wicket and shining a light inside.

"Ondar," Tez Ofka called, her voice low and angry. "Come here, please."

Melly Birah was on her knees by the lock, using the cutter carefully, its lightblade angled toward the ceiling so she wouldn't inadvertently slice into the occupant of that cell. She finished as Elmas Ofka reached them, got to her feet and pulled the door open.

The boy sleeping heavily on the chain-braced plank moaned and twitched but didn't wake. Elmas Ofka shone her light on his face, sucked in a breath, let it trickle out, too shocked to say anything. His nose was broken, his face bruised and swollen, there was something wrong with one eye, the lid sagged inward; he was breathing through his mouth so she could see that a number of his teeth were missing. With a secret guilty relief she knew it wasn't her brother; she leaned closer, tried to fit the battered features into a shape she knew, all the boys who'd vanished were her brother's friends, she'd seen them with him more than once. Angrily, she shook her head, straightened and stepped back. "Who . . ."

Hessah Indiz pushed past her, knelt beside the bed. "Fazil," she said. "It's Fazil Birah. We were going to . . ."

Elmas Ofka frowned, nodded. "See if you can wake him, isya. We've got to locate the others." She moved out of the cell. "Any more here?"

Lirrit Ofka scraped her moc across the filthy floor, Harli Tanggàr fidgeted and wouldn't look at Elmas Ofka. The other isyas stood with their hands behind them, eyes shifting toward and away from a cell near the stairs. Tezzi Ofka came from behind the door. "Ondar . . ."

Elmas Ofka stiffened. For a moment she stood very still, then she ran past Tezzi into the cell. She pulled up, gulping as her stomach convulsed at what she saw. Bodies stacked on the floor like firewood. Bodies so torn and battered they weren't even butcher's meat. She moved the light over the faces visible, stopped it on one. Her hand trembled. "Tangus," she whispered, "Tangus Indiz."

Tezzi's hand closed on her shoulder, tugged at her. "Ondar, Fazil Birah's awake, he wants you."

Elmas Ofka shuddered, she wanted to scream, she wanted to swing round, clawing and kicking. She squeezed her eyes shut and willed herself calm. Feeling brittle as a sheet of sugar candy, she turned with slow care and walked out of the cell without really seeing the door or Tezzi Ofka or anything. Fingers just touching the wall, needing the contact with stone and wood to keep in mind where she was and what she had to do, she moved toward the first cell. Tangus Indiz was her baby brother, she'd raised him from the time he was weaned, taking care of the youngers was one of her jobs before she went to diving. Of all the toddlers she bathed and clothed, cuddled and taught, he was her favorite, a fey baby, happy, terribly bright with the accent on terrible, too full of jagged energies to fit comfortably inside the settled outlines of farm life. She'd felt the kindship of his spirit which was more to her than the kinship of the blood and bled for him as time passed and took him out of her hands. She was a diver and gifted enough to know she was going to be Dalliss with all the freedom that meant, her energies were funneled that way, she didn't have to fight to breathe. He did. He had a dozen talents but none of them seized hold of him like diving did her, he drifted and used his energy on mischiefs, things that were giggles at first, puncturing pomposities to the general applause of the middlers in school or early apprenticeship. He was punished; pomposities don't appreciate needles, clever or not, or those who use them, and generally have the power to enforce their disapproval. Except for Elmas Ofka and a few others, the middlers who laughed at his antics and urged him on left him dangling when he was caught. The past year she'd seen him turn bitter and his fancies take on malicious overtones. She worried about him, she couldn't reach him anymore, he wouldn't listen to her. No more worries now. Tears stung her eyes. No. I won't cry. Not here. Not now. She stopped walking, closed her eyes and fought herself calm again, then moved into the cell with Fazil Birah and knelt beside the plank.

The collapsed eye was still shut, sealed with blood and mucus, but the other eye was open and filled with pain and triumph. "Herk. He . . ."

"I know. We'll hang the bastard for this."

His mouth stretched in a shaky gaping grin.

"Fazi, what'd he want? Why'd he grab you?"

"Rozh . . . 'earlz. W-w'ere. . . ."

"He wanted to know where the beds are?"

"Y-yeh. Din' know . . . w-we cu'un't tell him."

"He didn't know he should've taken women?"

"Nu no. W-we din't t-tell him. Tan tang'z curse him. W-wu'n't tell him nothin. . . ." He was breathing hard, growing visibly weaker. When he tried to speak again, Elmas Ofka shushed him.

"I've got it," she said. "Tangus cursed him, wouldn't tell him spit. None of you told him anything. Look,

Fazi. The isya is going to give you something so we can get you out of here."

He stirred, agitated. A broken hand clawed at her arm. "No," he managed. "Lea' me . . . 'nzide . . . buzted." He closed his eye, his mouth moved; he said something, she couldn't hear it, had to bend down until her ear brushed his lips. "Kill me."

She pushed away from him, pressed her fingers to her eyes. After a moment she sighed, nodded. "Yes." She unclipped her darter. "Thou my brother, thou my lover, may thy return be in happier times." She shot him, sighed again and got to her feet. Hessah Indiz was trembling, her eyes glazed. Elmas Ofka wrapped her arms about her isya, held her tight until she stopped shaking, then she stepped back. "Let's get out of here."

11

After a quick look at Elmas Ofka, Karrel Goza busied himself with the controls, holding the miniship level in spite of the erratic winds bouncing off the cliff. As soon as all the isyas were climbing the ladders, he began venting air, taking the ship gradually higher until they were inside and the hatches were closed, then he sent the ship angling steeply upward, where he caught a tail wind and went whipping back toward gul Inci.

The sky was clearing rapidly, starsprays newly brilliant in the rainwashed air touched the seaswells below with subtle grays; Elmas Ofka watched the wrinkled water pass beneath them until she saw the shore approaching. She glanced at Karrel Goza. He was cat-quiet again, knitting steadily at a sleeve; he had a gift for silence; she hadn't appreciated it before, but it worked to ease the pain in her. "They were dead. All but one and he was dying."

"Ah."

"You were right. Herk didn't know."

"And he still doesn't, mmh?"

"The boy said they didn't tell him. I don't know."

"You going to warn the Families?"

"Not me. How can I? Someone will, I'll see to that."

"Going after Herk?"

She sat rubbing her hands back and forth along the chairarms, her eyes fixed on his face. "Yes," she said finally. "You in?"

"Yes."

She nodded. "It's time to do something."

"He'll be expecting it."

"Herky Jerky? Never, who'd dare."

"What'd you do with the guards? Dead? Thought so. Then he's got a pile of dead men inside his Palace and a litter of footprints in his veggies, might be enough to shake some sense into him."

"Doesn't matter. We'll just have to be cleverer."

"You know what worries me most?"

"I've a suspicion. The Sech?"

"Yeh. We all better keep our heads down while he's nosing around. Your brother being in it, he'll be after the Indiz. And the families of the other boys. Um. Sorry I didn't think about this before, your footprints, they'll be too small for men, the Grouch, he'll probably bounce the Dallisses around. All the divers."

She smiled. "We've been doing this a while, Karrel Goza. Things being the way they are, it doesn't matter that much about me, the Sech will have more than a suspicion who ran the raid; still, no use presenting him with proof so he can make trouble for the others. We took care of that little problem before we called you back."

"Sorry about that."

"We appreciate the thought."

"Dance Ground coming up, a couple minutes."

She looked at the clock. "We made better time than I thought."

"Tailwind."

She smiled at him, it felt good to smile again, the tight thing in her chest was beginning to open up. "Good pilot is more like it."

"Could be." He grinned back at her.

"You can give us a little extra time?"

"Sure."

"Put Windskimmer to bed for us."

"Windskimmer?"

"Her name."

"Nice."

"Sssaa, you!"

"Nah, I mean it. Things I was flying had names like Fud 40 and Kek 10, you can't do much with Fud." He reached for the panel.

"Wait. We usually don't land where we took off. There's an old wharf out east of Inci, no one uses it any more. Let the isyas down there."

"Gotcha. I'd better make a wide sweep round, don't want to wake the nightwatch."

"Yes." She swung the chair around. In the dim gray light she saw her isyas sitting with their knees drawn up, arms crossed on them, looking very different now. They'd changed from their blacks and were back in blouses and skirts and sandals, there was nothing on them to show where they'd been or what they'd been doing. "Tomorrow evening," she said. "Those of you who can come to Yuryur Beach. Unless there's trouble, I'll meet you. We need to say Avvedas for our boys. Say them in your soul if you can't be with us. As I might have to do. If I can't be with you, I will be thinking of you all, my blessings, my sisters. Forget Herk until the Avvedas are said, then, my sisters, my loves, think how we can pay him without destroying our Families. My blood is cold, my sisters, my blood is ice. He will not live to boast what he has done. There is no hurry to it, there is no urgency in it, there is certainty beyond all question. Herk will pay. It may take years, but Herk will pay."

VII

1

Three months std. after the meeting on Telffer. Helvetia.

It took the usual day and a half to work through the Helvetian perimeter fortifications and stash Slancy Orza in the parking grid; there was also the usual argument over leaving Kinok and the current Kahat on board, but everyone knew the idiosyncracies of the Sikkul Paems, so the objections were perfunctory; I bought an exception permit and that was the end of that. Getting onto Helvetia's surface is tedious, tiring and at times humiliating, but nobody complains; in a chaotic universe where currencies are wildly various and often of dubious value, Helvetia offers a means of assessing and balancing values plus the register circuit for contracts and other services no single government or group of governments can provide. Access to Helvetia is sometimes vital and at all times useful to anyone trying to trade beyond the borders of his/her local hegemony. If you want Helvetian services, you play by Helvetian rules.

Whistling snatches of songs I'd picked up here and there (a habit of mine that Kumari never appreciated, but she wasn't there at the moment) I ran through Slancy's defenses, making sure she was thoroughly buttoned up before I left her. Even with Helvetian security watching the grid and Kinok nesting down in the driveroom, I wasn't going to underestimate the talents of the types Bolodo could afford to hire. Especially after watching Adelaar work over those defenses on the way here. Like most of us she found insplitting a complete bore and preferred to have something to occupy her, so she was paying part of her fee ahead of time. What I was getting at, after watching her I wasn't as happy as I wanted to be, anybody with her talent could peel my poor Slancy like an overripe orange. Given time. Which I hoped Security wouldn't give them. So, having gone completely round the circle, there I was playing with what I'd got. I was finishing up when Adelaar came onto the bridge. I looked over my shoulder and smiled when I saw the rapier she'd buckled on; no fancy ornament, it had a used and useful look. "You're well prepared," I said.

"I've been here before." She touched the bone hilt of the sword. "And had to use this before."

Helvetian rules. No weapons except knives or swords allowed downsurface, they catch you with a gun, a lightlance, whatever, you're fined and it's no fleabite, they catch you again and you go to work on one of the farms or in the mines. Never heard they caught anyone three times. Result of all this is it's a dueling society, the little daytime clerks become nighttime rogues and swaggerers living out byzantine fantasies with an edge of real danger to them. Outside the trucegrounds you'd better hire a bodyguard or be able to defend yourself. The Faceless Seven who run the place refuse responsibility for anything that happens to idiots who should know better. Colorful place.

I rather enjoy my visits here. They take me back to my first body when I was earning my living with a two-handed broadsword my daddy gave me. Actually he made it for the local lord's braindead whelp, but when I had to hit the hills to keep my neck in one piece, he booted my backside for old time's sake and gave me the sword to remember him by. Which is by way of explaining that the sword I take downsurface is a two-handed broadsword with a pora-ini stressed crystal edge bonded onto the lightweight byttersteel alloy. Not that I'm challenged much these days. After I acquired this body and Slancy and had been trading in this and that for a year or so, time came I had business on Helvetia. I knew how things worked there so I went to an acquaintance who was a metalsmith in his spare time (with highly irregular access to some very special alloys), and had him make most of Harska (I named her Harska after an old old sometime friend); I did the bonding myself, a little trick I picked up from the RMoahl. And I fixed up a sheath that could hold her so I wouldn't slice my butt off if I had to do some dodging. That was Kumari's first trip with me and we went out celebrating after we finished business. When she's dressed for playtime, she's beautiful in her eerie way, she's got no more figure than a teener boy, but what there is of her is elegant. Some local hotshot decided he was the answer to her dreams and wouldn't back off when she informed him she wasn't interested. So she told him in a voice that cut like Harska's edge that he had the intelligence of a sea slug, that she wouldn't be interested in him or any other man since she belonged to another species and was neuter besides and even if she weren't, he smelled bad. I wasn't going to interfere; I'd seen her in action a couple of times with the dozen or more small knives she has tucked away here and there about her body; she was willing and more than able to handle that character herself though she looked fragile as thistledown, but he wouldn't have it that way, probably didn't suit his self-image; he challenged me instead. I took his arm off and an ear with it in the first thirty seconds of that duel; one of his friends tried to cry foul, but there was nothing in the rules about fancy touches like that edge. It said sword and sword she was. And sword she is.

Kumari came in. She raised her brows. "Not dressed yet?"

She meant Harska. I grinned. "Just making a last go-through. Got us on a shuttle?"

"Twenty minutes on, so don't waste time primping. The next opening is six hours from now. There's a bubble in the lock, ready for the transfer. I've booked us into an ottotel trucehouse and set up a tentative appointment with O-nioni tomorrow to get the contract working and settle the escrow. Ti Vnok wants to talk to you tonight. If possible. He says a shielded room at the Treehouse and come blankshield. Which means Pels and I will be there ahead of you working the house. If you think it's worth the trouble."

"Let's see what's waiting first. We might have to do some tailcleaning."

"Right. If Pels' nose is as sharp as he thinks."

Adelaar clicked her tongue, a sharp impatient sound. "What are you two talking about?"

"Pels thinks we have ticks on our tail. Followed us in after we surfaced out beyond the Limit."

"I see."

"Must have guessed we were heading here and messaged ahead."

"No doubt."

"Right. Kumari, take our client to the bubble, I'll collect Pels and my gear and meet you, five minutes, I swear."

"Right." Kumari drawled the word, turning it into a sarcastic comment. "Have you ever noticed, aici Arash," she touched Adelaar's arm and nudged her toward the exit, "how much men talk about women dawdling and how long it takes them to get themselves together?"

2

The shuttle platform was a towertop that looked down on clouds when there were any and south across the great glittering city, a city that grew on the edge of an ocean and spread inland to jagged young mountains. In the trucegrounds and the business sectors, sunlight ran like water along slickery surfaces, flickered erratically off shattered diamanté walls, was thrown in white hot spears from mirror to mirror, mirror mirror on the wall who's the costliest city of all, mirror mirror everywhere and never a one to look in (go blind if you tried), the spears going here, going there, constantly altering direction as the mirrors changed orientation and the sun rode its customary arc across the sky. It was a city of light, beautiful in its imperious way, meant to intimidate the visitors stepping unaware onto the glassed-in platform; even those who'd been there before were affected by it no matter how blasé a face they wore. We touched down late in the afternoon when some of the glitter and slide was muted, not quite blinding, and still it was a breath stealing thing to stand there and look out across it to a sea bluer than blue melding into a misty blue sky.

Down on ground level the light was even more intense, shooting past you, through you, around you, dissolving wall and street alike into more light, until you began to wonder if anything was real, including yourself; it was disturbing, uncomfortable—and very practical. Among other things it kept streets and walkways clear, no matter how many visitors descended on the city. Scattered haphazardly, at all levels from roof to cellar, there were small arbors with mossy fountains and cool air rustling through the leaves of lace trees and pungent conifers, where shadows flicked across the face of the person sitting across a table from you with the intimacy of a caress. The contrast was a killer punch more subtle than a drug, and did they know it, those buyers and sellers, those agents and facilitators who were parasites on the primary business of Helvetia, those citizens and business agents who lived in the city and on the city, year round, year on year. More contracts were registered from the arbors than in all the offices, cabinets, bureaus put together.

We bought visors from a robovender in case we needed to hit the streets, dropped to the terminal and fought the swarm at the tube cars until we managed to snag a car bound for the ottotel trucehouse where Kumari had booked us in. Kumari and I kept Adelaar sandwiched between us and Pels rode rearguard, pulling after him a mob of females of every shape and size, bipeds, tripeds and even a hairy monopod; they all seemed to want to catch him up and cuddle him (the monopod too, which presented an interesting problem in logistics), they giggled when he snarled at them, a daring octoped with blushing tentacles scratched behind his ear, you wouldn't think these were hard-driving, high-pressure businesswomen capable of metaphorically (or even actually) cutting a rival's throat with zest and panache; it must be some pheromone he gives off; if you could package it and sell it as perfume you'd make a fortune. It was as effective as it always was, his peculiar defense, those females made a fine and fancy shield for the rest of us. Anyone who had mayhem on his (or her or ves or its) mind generally backed off from performing in front of that many interested spectators. And, give this to the Faceless Seven, we didn't have to worry about long distance sniping.

Pels wriggled loose, jumped into the car as the doors were sliding shut; his growl when I grinned at him was more heartfelt than usual; I think it's time he had a vacation, probably back on Mevvyaurrang making triads with Arras and Maungs; he comes back from those visits with his not-fur shivering and his eyes glazed and not talking to anyone but his plants for a month or more. I signed a question to Kumari (we assumed everything public was on-line to the mainBrain)—had she seen any unusual interest in us? She had a smile for Pels, but shook her head. Pels grunted. One, maybe two, he signed. In the next module over on this car. I didn't like it, but I expected it. I swung my chair round to face the back of our module in case they'd figured a way to get through it and I waited for the trip to end. We'd be on truceground when we came out, so we could hang around and see who emerged with us. Stupid planning, maybe. I exercised a few brain cells running that one round, but in a breath or two it was obvious I was counting angels and pinheads so I let it drop. Maybe Pels was wrong, but I didn't think that was any too probable; like I said before, Aurrangers are predators and good at it and not all that long ago semi-cannibals, by which I mean one of the ways they kept the population stable was to hunt down and eat any excess Raus when they were young and tender and about to hit puberty. A few millennia of this and the descendants of those Raus who escaped the pot were very very hard to track.

Half a dozen came out of that module, more from the third, say around thirty bodies altogether, but the two we wanted weren't hard to spot, idiots, they were so careful not to look at us. Not pros, no way. Like the two going after Adelaar back on Telffer, the ones Shadow dropped, local computer jocks trying to earn points with the head office. Making sure we went where we told the world we were going. They scuttled out of the lobby like startled mice. Wonder what they'd do if I sneaked after them and yelled boo in their bitty ears. Mmh.

3

Kumari'd got a sealed four body unit for us which she charged to the client's diCarx when we got inside. Adelaar didn't comment, just marched her gear into her cubby and did her best to slam the door on us. It's not that easy to work off a snit in an ottotel, the doors ooze shut at the same speed whenever they're pushed or left alone, there's nothing much you can break or throw and the walls are padded so beating your head on them doesn't make much sense. She wasn't annoyed about having to pay expenses, that was part of the deal. It was being shut into a tincan for three solid months with the same people that got to her, especially Kinok. Arguing with a Sikkul Paem was an exercise in frustration; when ve decided ve didn't want to talk any longer, ve shooed Kahat away from the translator board and dug ves roots in one of ves earthbeds; after that you might as well try arguing with a dill plant which is more or less what ve smelled like. Slancy's workshop was down in ves region and ve insisted on knowing everything that went on in that part of the ship. Adelaar was furious at ves interference and loathed having ves snooper cells everywhere she went; her methods were part of her business assets, she said; they were emphatically not part of the deal and if I thought they were, I was soft in the head. Kinok wasn't talking when I went round to see him, so I told her to set up distorters in the workshop and I stationed Pels outside the door to keep our pet Paem from barging in on her. Ve took it well enough, ve's the only Paem I've met who has something resembling a sense of humor, which is probably the reason ve's lasted so long with us. Something I didn't tell Adelaar and I'd really rather she didn't find out, ve budded off a Kahat-clone and sneaked the little creature into the shop; it pretended it was one of the plants that kept the air fresh. I found it a couple of days before we flipped back to realspace and got it out of there. Kinok just rubbed two of ves coils together to make that squeaky sound ve thinks is laughter and ate the clone. Which, if I understand anything about Paem physiology, transferred all the clone knew into Kinok's own nerve cells.

After a bath, a change of clothes and a reasonably edible meal, we met in the parley to decide how we were going to work this situation. Sealed units are supposed to be free of snoopears, but anyone who trusts official noises about such things doesn't last long on Helvetia or anywhere else. We swung tupple loungers around one of Adelaar's choicer distorters and stretched out on them. For a breath or two no one said anything. Pels was digging his claws into his chin fur, Kumari had a dreamy look as if she were contemplating a favorite poem, Adelaar had lost her frown and was a lot more relaxed than she'd been in days. Prospect of action, I suppose.

"Sooner or later each of us is going to be challenged," I said.

"No."

Adelaar looked like she wanted to start an argument over that, but I shook my head at her and, wonder of wonders, she shut up; I knew that sound, Kri was running on a mix of hunch and logic that was almost never wrong.

"No," she repeated. "Not all of us. You and Adelaar. Stink too much of setup if they went after all of us; there's a limit how far a pro can go; it flexes some; I doubt that much; the Seven want to avoid any smell of ambush, not good for business. And there's no need anyway. It's your ship, Swar; should they get you, we'd have to go through all that business of transferring title, could take a year or more, plenty of time for Bolodo to clean up their act. And it's Adelaar's daughter; without her around to pay the bills, Bolodo might think we'd say hell with it and go on to something else." She waved a hand at Pels, wriggled her fingers in a kind of digital grin. "Us you could replace in half an hour or less." Pels growled. "Well, as far as jobs go."

I looked at Adelaar. She lifted a hand, let it fall, but didn't say anything. "Right," I said. "How good are you with that sword of yours?"

"I'm still alive, one challenger's dead, another can't walk very well, I cut a few nerves in his left leg. One was pro, one wasn't, the dead one. The pro was middling good, it was a business matter."

"Hmm. Bolodo won't be fooling around this time, they'll buy the best there is, no more amateur talent." I thought about that a while. "If we can't avoid a challenge, maybe we can maneuver the ground. You up for taking a chance, aici Arash?"

"If there's a point to it." She tapped on the pneumatic arm beside her. "You mean bait them. Tonight?"

"Catch 'em before they're set."

"And if they don't bite?"

"Then they don't and we have some fun playing before we get serious."

"Sounds good." More tip-tapping on the soft resilient plastic, tiny scratching sounds; her nails were pointed and painted with a metallic film that turned them into small knives; I wouldn't be all that surprised to learn they had poison packed behind them. She'd fixed them up that way before we left Slancy; that was one of the reasons I started thinking it might be a good idea to force the pace. "What ground?" she said.

"Darkland. The Rabbid Babbit. You know it?"

"I've been there. Why that House, what about Tinzy's Amberland, or some other place?"

"Amberland's too establishment, too many high level execs and bankers in the crowd. I want room for some creative cheating. Those types are either a bunch of half-assed romantics with an inquisitor's touch with heretics, or a bunch of snobs who want to keep . . . um . . . ah . . . the creative interpretation of rules as an executive privilege, not something available to the working slob or us common visitors. Those fingernails of yours, as an example, they're apt to rule them illegal given a protest. I'm sure you'd rather keep them as is."

"Babbit's different?"

"As different as the Seven allow. A lot of duelists base from there."

She laughed, startled into it; for the first time she seemed pleased with something I said. "And that's a recommendation?"

"Right."

She thought that over a minute, then nodded. "What works, as long as it's not flagrant enough to be nailed on."

"Right."

"And that gives us an edge?"

"Me, yes. You, I don't know."

She laughed again, a real laugh bubbling up from her toes; I didn't know she had it in her. For a minute I almost liked her. "All right, I can go with that. One thing though," she hesitated, then pushed herself up. "I'll give you a *signature* that'll release the escrow account to you . . ." she slipped off the tupple lounge, stood with her arms crossed, "day after tomorrow, if you'll give me your word you'll fetch Aslan out even if I'm killed or put down for a long stretch at the meatshop."

"You got it." She waited, her eyes on me. "All right, I'll spell it out," I said, "Whatever happens, long as I'm alive and reasonably intact, I'll fetch Aslan aici Adlaar home to University. Satisfied?"

"'Quite. When do you want to leave?"

"Mmh. Sun's down. I'd rather wait till after midnight, things get looser."

She examined me, eyes narrowed. "Black leather with studs. Lots of studs."

"Not leather." I grinned. "Synthaskin, elasticized.

"Better. Shirt or bare arms?"

"White silk, billowy. To cover possible deficiencies." I looked her over. "Imaginary deficiencies."

"Right." She grinned. "Earrings, rings, wristbands, fake gems wherever there's a place to hang them."

She touched her forehead. "Pearshape ruby dangling here?"

"If it won't bother your moves."

"I can always shuck it before things get serious."

"Right. Hair?"

"Silvergilt. Both of us. A matched pair."

"Two minds with but a single thought. Kumari." She was fizzing and rattling with her kind of laughter. I ignored that. "Put off Vnok till tomorrow and order us a jit. We might as well let whoever's interested know we're coming."

When we came out of our cubbies and struck a pose, Pels and Kumari fell out laughing. We left them holding their sides and whooping and drop-tubed to the lobby where we climbed in the jit we'd ordered and took off for the Darklands.

4

The jit dropped us at the Dusky Gate, city drivers wouldn't go into the Darklands for fear of losing their machines. No law past that heavy arch, only Darkland rules which said what you had was yours as long as you could keep it and only that long; whatever someone was sly enough, quick enough or brutal enough to take belonged to them under the same rules. Once you made a House, though, you could rent protection and be reasonably secure from muggers, cutpurses and assassins. That was a matter of business, there had to be an edge of danger but nothing too threatening or the slummers wouldn't come and the game rooms would lose their pigeons, the psychodromes would spray their putchemeio dreammist on props, not people. Which meant we were safe from ambush only when we reached the Rabbid Babbit. We walked through the Gate.

Mainstreet was wide, paved with thin slabs of rough-cut stone. Right now they were wet (it must have rained while we were getting ready), with puddlets in the chisel gouges shining yellow and red as they reflected the light from the luso torches that lined the sides of Mainstreet. The torches looked real enough until you noticed they never seemed to burn down; the smell of hot tar and burning oil, the crackle and snap of the fire, the heat, they were all there; a little too much there tonight, I expect the nerp who ran the illusion was high on something and got carried away with the effects.

The Houses were set back a short distance from the street, leaving room for sidewalk cafes with tables under markVdomes where anyone interested could watch the action on the street without any danger of that action spilling over on them. There was a middling crowd out, walking from House to House for the thrill of flirting with thieves and budding duelists (and because there was no other way to change Houses, you walked or you stayed where you were). The air was cool and damp, though it wasn't raining now. The strollers seemed more subdued than I remembered, but maybe this was just a more inhibited bunch. The body paint on a lacertine group we passed was a mix of earth colors, dull reds and grayed-down yellows; last time I was here the lacertines had gone for brilliant primaries, a slim green back could be like a shout of laughter. Now those backs were more like smiles, subtle smiles that might speak either pleasure or mockery. Times change and who can read the branches if he hasn't watched them grow?

Adelaar walked half a pace ahead of me, no more joking for her. Made me a little sad, she'd let an imp show briefly, then shooed it home; I liked that imp, a bit more of her in the woman would improve the mix a lot, but I think she was afraid of that side of her. And I think she was already regretting the impulse that stuffed her into that costume.

We went past Amberland. Adelaar glanced at the holo—females of half a dozen species moving through a complex and beautiful melange of half a dozen ancient dances, swaying through the air across the front of the House, larger than life, gaudy, garish, down-and-dirty seductive, there was a little blonde, well, I dragged my mind back to where I was and what I was doing; I could see Adelaar preferred the company in there to mine, poor little imp deep inside her never let off its leash; we weren't going to be friends, Adelaar and me, maybe pleasant acquaintances if we kept off politics. There were several shadows drifting after us, but they kept back, ready to vanish down the nearest alley if either of us took a notion to chase them, which made me think they were just making sure where we went. It wasn't the crowd in the street that stopped my attack, no one in his right mind interfered in a fight, not in Darklands. If you or your party weren't involved, you got out of there. Fast. No lingering to gawk at the pretty fight.

We passed several other Houses, each with its identifying holo. *Crezmir Tarkitzdom*, bull-leapers and vodi slayers and antique idols. *Surrealismo*, hmm, indescribable and constantly changing (I've never seen that holo repeat itself and it's always weird; when I have a moment with nothing else to occupy me, I wonder about the minds that come up with some of the things I've seen there). *Wildwood. Tranqworld. The Rabbid Babbit.* Its holo was the same as before, a collection of assorted Uglys and Hairys barbequing a Banker over a lusty pile of coals, a prim-faced character with an immaculate tunic and stovepipe trousers, chained to a spit which the Ugs and Hairs were turning and turning, wringing sweat of a sort from him, gold coins dropping like rain. Adelaar made a face at the thing, gave me a dark look and pushed through the Gate onto the Babbitwalk.

I waved the Doorman off and followed her into the House; we weren't buying protection tonight.

5

Around three hours later, after bar hopping a while and wandering through the drome and sitting through six or seven acts in the music hall, we left the hall and started for the casino; I was beginning to think those shadows I'd spotted were either my imagination or a mugger gang enticed by the fake gems we were loaded down with and the dumb getup we were wearing. Adelaar was looking tired and depressed and uncomfortable. If no one took our bait, I had a suspicion she was going to make me regret the time we spent trolling it.

Adelaar hit my arm, a tap but it stung. "Haven't we wasted enough time?"

"Just about. I said there was only a chance they'd bite."

"I suppose it could've worked." She yawned. "Don't mind me, I get cranky when I'm bored." The imp peeped out again and she smiled up at me. "Aslan's told me that often enough."

"Right. You want to call a jit to the Gate, or try a few games first?"

"Games. After tonight we get serious again." She raked the headband off. "Here, you carry this; I don't want to feel as moronic as I look." She started stripping off the chains and bracelets and excess rings, I stuffed them down my shirt as she handed them to me; that's our motto, the client's wishes come first, it was damn uncomfortable though, they were sticky with her sweat and some of those gems had sharp corners.

We weren't paying attention to what was happening around us, we'd both given up the stalk. Maybe it was the watched pot thing, but about ten seconds into that strip act Adelaar was doing with the fake jewelry, someone slammed into me, spraying grushajuice everywhere; it was a mess, I was dripping, my shirt was sogged against me stinking sweet and slimy, Adelaar was cursing and using her sleeve to wipe her face as she ignored the attempts of a female duelist to set the challenge going. I got my back against a wall fast, just in case, but the man who'd collided with me was intent on doing this the proper way; he slapped a glove in the direction of my face, called me a mannerless clod and invited me to redress my honor on the dueling ground. Babbit's android guards were there, they'd come out of the walls as soon as the mess started, stunners ready to make sure Babbit's version of the rules held fast ('droid guards don't come under the weapon ban when they're hired from the city council by respectable home firms to protect the premises), a comforting sight they were, too. I managed a bow of sorts, proclaimed my innocence of all malice and inquired if an apology would be acceptable. Naturally it wasn't, so there we were, bait taken; all we had to do now was win our respective fights and damage our opponents so badly that other duelists would be disinclined to take up the gage, no matter what the prize. It wasn't going to be a pretty fight, not one of the epic duels that songsmiths celebrated, but I never had much time for that kind of thing anyway.

6

"Hra Trewwa Harona." He sketched a bow but didn't take his eyes off me. He was tall and wiry, skin like polished walnut, not a hair on his head, not even eyelashes, one of the cousin races but nothing about him to say which world he whelped on; way he moved, he was fast and agile.

"Swardheld Quale," I said.

"Lugat Haza," the woman said, touched lips and heart and spread her hands palm out; she had a shock of bright red hair, green eyes and a spray of freckles across a beaky nose. Another cousin, equally anonymous.

"Adelaar aici Arash." Adelaar put her hands palm to palm in front of her, bobbed her head and shoulders in a quick dip.

The four of us were standing on the broad oval of the dueling floor; the tiered seats outside the lighted area were filling quickly, I could hear the sounds of scuffling feet and a growing mutter of conversation. It was as if the walls had sucked in the challenge and spat it out in every section of the House, enticing to this vault most of those who heard it. We were going to have a large and interested audience. It's what I wanted, what I'd planned to get. Why I was forcing the fight in here rather than leaving it to chance. In a brangle on the street without witnesses anything could happen and the survivors could say what they wanted without contradiction.

Adelaar stepped away and started wrapping the remnants of her shirt around her right arm; she'd laced up the vest so it didn't flop about (her either) and twitched her swordbelt round so the rapier's hilt was on her left. From what I'd seen she was ambidextrous with a slight tendency to favor her right hand; apparently she was going to start this thing off as a lefter; I've had a few skirmishes with lefters and I knew how they can throw you off your pace. I relaxed some more and got rid of the soggy shirt, leaving the wristlets which weren't as flimsy as they looked; they wouldn't turn Harska's edge, but there wasn't much else they couldn't bat aside.

The House Referee came up the ramp and stumped to the center of the oval, ordering us to follow him with a sweep of a muscular arm. Adelaar and I stopped a few paces apart on his left, Lugat and Hra Trewwa faced us on his right. He was a chunky cold-eyed Frajjer, a long pole in his left paw, its end beaten into a knife-edged half circle; any flagrant infringement of Babbit's rules and he took out the offender, no recourse, his judgment was final. There might not be many rules in Babbitland, but they were serious about those they had. When I say final, it was sometimes exactly that, said offender was cremated the next day.

He faced Adelaar and me. "You are challenged. They say as-is. You two got the veto, so?"

"As-is, that's fine with me. Del?

"As-is," she said.

"Caveats?"

"None," I said. Lugat's nose twitched, she looked scornful and delighted, a mix of expressions that did nothing much for her face. She stood shaking her arms lightly; beneath the stretch silk you could see her muscles shifting; she was sleek and feral as a hunting cat.

"First-blood or final?"

"Final," I said. Adelaar nodded.

He looked over his shoulder at the other two. "Agreed?"

"Agreed," Hra Trewwa said; the woman shrugged. "Agreed," she said.

The Frajjer waved us apart, Adelaar and Lugat to the left end of the oval, Trewwa and me to the right. He beat the end of his pole against the floor, three solemn thumps. While he was announcing the terms of engagement, Hra Trewwa took off the long cape he was wearing and stripped out the lining. A weighted net. Shit. I hated netmen. Looks like Bolodo did their homework, got someone to tell them about the last mix-up I had here. I slid my lady from her sheath, brought her past my head, the light catching the crystal edge and making a minor glory of her; I handled her as if she had the mass her size suggested, rested her blunt end on the floor and stood waiting with both hands closed round her hilt. Trewwa probably knew she was a slasher, not a stabber, what I hoped he didn't know was how nimble she was; looking at her size and conformation you'd think she'd be a heller once I got her wound up, but she'd be slow as a sleepy bumphel. Trewwa snapped the net open; from the way it shimmered it was Menavidetin monofilament. He flipped it around his neck and let the ends hang while he gave me a cocky grin and began working on his walking stick. After a bit of twisting it extended into a two-pronged lance not much longer than assegai traditional; the points of the prongs glittered in the strong light like blue-white diamonds. Double shit. I was going to spend most of this dance running like some fieldsport jock after a speed record.

Lugat produced a pair of k'duries, wrist bands with a two chains on each about the length of her arms; at the end of the chains were soft lead balls the size of a green peach. She spread her fingers; the nails glittered. Adelaar wasn't the only one with a fancy for claws. I hoped she knew how to deal with a k'duri expert; I had a mix-up with one a few years back and felt lucky to come out of it with some broken bones and an aching head, that femme wrapped a chain around my stunner and jerked it away, fast! you wouldn't believe how fast she could whirr those things; then she got my boot knife, broke my right arm and was playing pattacake with my head when I left through a window I didn't bother to open.

The Ref blew his whistle and retreated to the edge of the oval.

Adelaar and Lugat circled warily. Adelaar kept back, watching the sweep of the balls, reading the k'durin's body. Lugat was gripping the chains about midpoint, one emerging between thumb and forefinger, other between the last two fingers. Each hand moved separately, the chain loops clinking and burring as they swung, the balls whispering round with lazy swishes; her arms shifted out and in, a cadenced mini-dance like the sway of a cobra, as hypnotic and as potentially lethal, without any indication of where the attack would come from. Adelaar feinted, feinted again, testing the space about the k'durin with the point of her rapier, retreating always before one of the chains could wrap about the sword and pull it from her or sneak around it and break a hand or an arm.

I held Harska angled out before me, swaying her a little, camouflaging her nimble nature. My first sword, you swung her a couple times and you went and lay down and breathed hard for a while. Of course, if you knew what you were doing and had reasonable armor, once or twice was about all you needed. Trewwa was as quick as he looked, slipping back or sideways with the ease of a man running at you; he had the bident in his left hand, the net in his right, bunched into a thick loose rope which he kept flicking at me, face then ankles, whipping it away before I could get Harska after it; he was wary of her edge even with the monofil's toughness. He darted the bident at me, weaving it into the flick-retreat of the net, testing me, trying to read how fast I was and what I knew about netmen. And he was maneuvering me closer to Lugat. This was a doubleduel, nothing against one of the partners breaking off his or her fight to help the other.

Adelaar eased closer. The left-hand lead balls shot out, their chain loops suddenly released. She ducked away. One sphere whistled over her head, the other hit but not solidly (it would have cracked her skull if it had); it grazed her temple, slid off her hair, banged into her shoulder, catching for an instant on one of the pointed studs on the back of her vest. In spite of the dizzy dark that blurred her vision and slurred her mind, she took advantage of that brief catch, turned the duck into a low attack and managed to carve a piece out of Lugat's left leg, only a deep scratch, but it started bleeding sluggishly. She dropped flat, rolled frantically away before all four of the lead spheres slammed into her; she scrambled onto her feet outside the limit of the chains and began prowling once again, watching Lugat as she drew the chains in and brought the balls to order.

The net flicked out, low, no feint this time, he was after my ankles if he could get them; if I jumped clear, he'd twitch the net open and have me like a gasping fish which he'd skewer on the double prongs of his lance. At the same time, he beat Harska aside with the lancepole, hitting her against the flat, careful still of her edge. Instead of jumping clear, I brought Harska in a quick circle, freeing her from the push of the pole; continuing the move, I jumped into the net, falling flat on it, pinning it temporarily while I swung Harska one-handed at Trewwa's legs; she went through flesh and bone like butter; he fell over, screaming with rage, too angry to feel the pain yet; he hadn't expected her to swing that fast and easy; I'd cheated him and he wanted blood for it; he hauled back on the bident and tried to puncture me with those diamond points. I took his head off and that was that.

There were a few appreciative hisses and clicking sounds from the watchers, but the room was mostly quiet, there was still a fight to finish.

Adelaar had an oozing bruise on her brow, another on her left shoulder near the joint. Her left arm was disabled; she carried the sword in her right hand now. Lugat had a deep scratch on one thigh, she favored that leg when she moved, and there several small bloody rents in the tight stretch silk of her sleeves. As I turned around, Adelaar took advantage of Lugat's leg drag, tossed the sword into her left hand (freeing her right), got momentarily behind her and close enough to rake her neck with those poison claws; she whirled away too fast for Lugat to manage a solid hit, but collected some more bruises and was staggering by the time she was beyond chain reach. Lugat went after her, but with Trewwa down and out, Adelaar had room enough keep clear until her head was working again.

Lugat stumbled, the lead balls seemed to shudder, their swings turned erratic; she pulled herself together, went after Adelaar, ignoring the rapier, ignoring pain and disorientation as the poison took effect; the lead balls whirred viciously, she caught Adelaar in the heel, the small of her back, slammed one into her side (I could almost hear those ribs go) as Del stumbled over one of Trewwa's severed legs. Del threw herself aside and into a shoulder roll; on her feet again she turned and ran, around, across, along the oval, ignoring broken ribs and other bruises, running, dodging, ignoring grazes as Lugat tried to get at her, running beyond exhaustion until Lugat was gasping and staggering, eyes glazed, blood trickling from her nose and the corners of her mouth. Adelaar whipped back; a bound, a stride, a lunge and with beautiful extension she slid the rapier into the k'durin's chest, a perfect heart kill.

A burst of applause, then sounds of movement, the shuffle of feet, arguments over who won as bets were settled and the bettors went off to celebrate the entertainment with a drink or snort or whatever suited their needs.

Adelaar drew the sword clear and stood holding it against a twitching leg, exhausted; the adrenalin that'd kept her going and partially anesthetized was draining away, leaving her with the dead-ash feeling you get after an all-out struggle when still being alive doesn't seem worth all that effort.

The Referee stumped over to Hra Trewwa, grunted onto his knees and dug around in Trewwa's clothes until he found his ID; he tucked it away, got to his feet and moved over to Lugat. While he was finishing his business with the dead, I unbuckled the straps to Harska's sheath and pulled it round where I could get at the shimmy cloth I kept in a squeeze pocket. There wasn't much blood on my lady, she cut too fast and too clean, but I never put her away mussed. Wiping her was tricky, I could lose a finger myself if I got careless; flesh was flesh as far as she was concerned, didn't matter whose. Not a lady for sentimental sighing. I rubbed the blood off her alloy and crystal, then slid her back in her sheath. As she vanished I could hear something like a collective moan out there in the dark, she was a lovely thing.

"You getting old, Swar." A man came out of the dark and leaned his elbows in the dueling floor. "Nearly five minutes this time. Came close to costing me some money."

"Always complaining, eh Barker? Didn't expect to see you here, I thought you were howling out near the Rift."

"Was. Found me a nice little Belt full of plums, now I've got to track down some financing."

"Hmm. I've got a little extra on my hands, if you're still hunting investors, why not drop round and we'll have a talk? Benders Trucetel. I'll key the clerabot to give you my number."

"Why not. Want some company to walk you home? Hay and Apelzan are in the bar drinking up their winnings, by the way, they said to say hello and bring your friend around, they'd buy you both a sop whatever you felt inclined to, and I saw Ahehtos with a set of boy-girl twins around three hours ago, he ought to be winding up about now and ready for something new."

"Thanks. Wouldn't hurt."

Adelaar'd got herself together; she came over and stood listening to us talk. Her hand closed on my shoulder while the Barker was making his offer; I eased her fingers loose, I didn't want her to forget what she was holding onto and stick those claws into me. Be one helluvun irony to die from a client's fingernails after winning that mix-up with the enemy. "You think they'd come after us again?"

"You're tired, Del, or you wouldn't say something so stupid."

She scrubbed the back of her hand across her mouth. "Right. I need a stim."

"Well," Barker said, "Hay's offer's still open."

"Adelaar aici Arash, meet one Tomi Wolvesson, we call him the Barker for reasons I won't go into now. She's Adelaris Securities, Bark, a client."

"Naturally a client, otherwise this lovely respectable femme wouldn't be in a mile of you, old bear." Without taking his elbows from the wood he managed a bow and a swagger, grinning up at both of us. "If you'll take my arm, dear lady, we shall go searching for that stim." He backed away, swept another bow and crooked his arm ready for her hand. "File your reports, my son, and join us in the bar."

Amused by his rattle and wanting to be away from this place, Adelaar went down the ramp, took his arm and left me to deal with all the nonsense the bureaucrats demanded once a duel was done. Especially when there was a corpse or two as a result. The Ref tapped me on the shoulder, took me to his office and started on the umpteen reports he was going to have to make. It was the ultimate in futility, there were no penalties for the duels or the deaths. Running out on the reports, though, that was serious. I knew better than to waste time complaining, the sooner the business was done, the sooner I could climb into the trucetel medicell and after that into a long hot bath.

7

Ti Vnok looked like an absurdist's idea of a cross between a spider monkey and a praying mantis; his movements alternated between the stillness of mantis-at-rest and the frenetic energy of monkey-at-full-cry. He was a general-purpose agent, there to link anyone with an itch to anyone who could perhaps scratch that itch, never involved with either side, silent as stones about his clients' business, never challenged because in his busy little way he was as useful as Helvetia herself. And a friend of mine. Which didn't mean he'd whisper secrets in my ear, just that he'd steer things my way if he saw a chance, might even hint oh-so-delicately if I was about to put my foot in something that stank. There are worse kinds of friends.

Kumari reported that when she reached him to change the time of our meet, he looked unusually fidgety and wouldn't commit to anything over the com, said he'd get a message round to her. Which he did about an hour later. One of the street kids that infested the undercity like mites on a dog's belly got past tel security somehow and up to the floor where our unit was, hand-carrying a flashnote, time and place scribbled on it and a reminder I was to come careful and alone; the flash was quicker than usual, she just had time to read the thing before it dissolved.

I left the trucetel an hour early, spent a good part of the time jumping flea runs, mixing that with trots around the block up top where the sun was hot and the mirrors busy. Several times I wished I had Pels along, times when I was almost but not quite sure I'd dropped my ticks, but regret only gives you ulcers and Adelaar needed him more than I did. When she'd crawled out of the medicell and into bed, Kumari, Pels and I had a short confa about the morrow, I played them over the duel and the parade to the jits afterward and the shadows rustling round us—we'd 've had to scramble to reach the jits if it weren't for Barker and the rest. It was clear enough that Bolodo wasn't giving up, just changing tactics. The most likely next step was pointing assassins at us. "Remember Bustus?" I said.

"I remember something closer to a Crawler's soul," Kumari said, "Bolodo has more money than god herself."

"What, pay out all those golden gelders, those slippery succulent little darlins just for me? No, the Prime target'll be Adelaar."

Bolodo wouldn't sic Crawlers on me unless they had

to, because it'd cost them a lot. Couple years ago I was after a University contract advertised on Helvetia and this character decided it would make a good cover for some other things he was doing and I was his only serious competition, so he dropped their price on a NightCrawler cobben and pointed them at me. I got seriously annoyed at this interference, also at having the hair singed off half my head. A lethal friend of mine happened to be on Helvetia right then, arguing an Escrow Closing; she'd just finished a Hunt and was getting the fee released, a complicated business since her fees tended to be in the range of the gross yearly income of your average world economy. Lovely gentle woman, she gets upset when she kills someone or maims them a little, but not when they target someone she's fond of. She's redheaded and has the temper to go with it. We did some bloody housecleaning and she laid down a warning, mess with her friends and she'd come Hunting without a commission. Since then the NightCrawlers walk wide of me, so like I said, Bolodo might have some trouble recruiting a cobben, a reputation's a handy thing. But like Kumari said, Bolodo's got the gelt; they'll buy some nerve and stuff it up some Crawler's spine. What else is money for, eh?

By now Adelaar and my crew were in the City also, sitting in an office at Del's bank, temporarily safe from attack. Or so I hoped. As shipsecond and official MOM and holding my *signature*, Kumari could endorse the contracts for me and stamp the escrow agreements; she usually handled that kind of thing, she was sharper than either Pels or me when it came to words and the twists that gentlebeings could put on them. Adelaar would be imprinting the contracts with her bank, the Register Circuit and the Escrow Board. It had to be done in the proper office, with the proper officials in attendance, everything fotted and entered in octuplets or more. Helvetian rules. She intended to evoke Privacy on the terms, but I had more faith in Bolodo's persistence than in Helvetian tech, so I figured the local execs would know what we were after in a few hours. And when they did, when they discovered I was agreeing to rescue the daughter, they'd really get serious about taking us out. That's all they needed to be sure I either had their stinking secret or was so close to finding it, the little bit left made no difference at all.

Ti Vnok was waiting at the back of one of the larger arbors; it was close to ground level and had enough exits to satisfy a claustrophobic paranoid. I'd felt clean the past five minutes or so and I'd pulled every trick I knew to test the feeling out, so I strolled into the cool and shifting shadows and wandered about a minute or so longer. No bells rang. I drifted over to Vnok's alcove and slid onto the bench across the table from him.

He sat mantis still, his eyes expressionless as obsidian marbles, but the two short feathery antennas that served as eyebrows were doing a nervous dance.

"Far as I can tell, I'm clean," I said. "I spent the last hour getting that way."

He rubbed his wrists together, the callus patches there making a faint skrikking sound; the expression came back into his eyes and his monkey face dissolved into the sort of grin that makes you want to grin back. "I've got some cover for meeting you, Swarda, a man came to see me last night, said he had a message for you." He didn't waste time asking if I wanted to hear it. He leaned forward, the weight of his torso balanced on his forearms. "Drop this business and certain people will see you won't be hurting for it. One hundred thousand gelders. No bidding, please. That was the deal."

"No deal," I said. "You bring the list?"

"Only the freshest names." He thrust two fingers in his throat pouch and brought out a small black packet. "The whole list would herniate a bumphel."

"Even flaked?"

"Even flaked. I thought you'd better stay mobile. I hear a cobben's been activated."

"Pointed at me?"

"Pointed at your client. I don't touch that kind of negotiation, so I don't know who paid the price. There's a lot of chat in the underways, I'm hearing this and that. . . ." His dust lids slid slowly over his eyes, then retreated beneath the outer lids; he waited. Gossip bought gossip in his view and he had his own reputation to consider; he was supposed to know everything going by on Helvetia and a long way beyond.

"Trade you something that's not for chatting yet."

"What for what?"

"A packet giving chapter and verse, *signatured* and attested by me and the client, set in Escrow pending release to someone with a passpartout for that account. And a verbal outline of what's inside for your ears only."

"For . . ."

"For a squirt link. I want the Seven warned of trouble, who it's from and what's behind it." I tapped a finger on the packet, watched it wobble, then tucked it into a beltslit. "If this works out like I think, Slancy's coming in with a heavy load and a fragile one. I want a welcome waiting."

Vnok rubbed his wrists together again, the skrikk like the purring of a sated cat; odd how many different inflections he could get out of that idiot sound. "There are two names on that list. Leda Zag. Ilvinin Taivas. They are . . . um . . . of special interest to the Seven. If you can find them and let me know you have them, I guarantee a vigorous welcome."

I looked round; I didn't spot anything, but Vnok wouldn't be talking this freely without his own distorter making mishmash of our words. I swung around so I was facing the back wall just in case someone was out there flaking this. "Distorter on?" I said. Logic was all very well, but what I had to say, well, I wasn't going to take any chances I could avoid.

"On," he said. His antennas wriggled his surprise.

"When you hear, you'll see why." I rested my arms on the table and leaned in close as I sketched out what was in that packet, everything Adelaar had found out about Bolodo, dates and the data she'd flaked from the mainBrain on Spotchals, what I thought had probably happened to the disappeared on the list he'd given me.

8

By the time I got back to the trucetel, Adelaar and the others were waiting for me. There was a burn on one of Adelaar's arms, the tip of Pels' left ear was flat instead of round, but Kumari looked cool as mountain water. "Crawler," she said. "We stayed in the bright instead of taking the tube run, put his timing off."

"Business finished?"

"All done."

"We paid up here?"

"More than paid, if you count the deposit."

"Good. Order dinner for . . ." I frowned at my ringchron, surprised to find it was barely the third hour past noon. Seemed like it should've been closer to sundown. "Eighth hour. What's the shuttle schedule like?"

"Midday, it's usually fairly light. You want to take a chance?"

"Yeh. The paperwork's done, the squirt link's set up and Vnok is primed, better we leave before Bolodo thinks up something new."

"Terminal," Adelaar said suddenly; she'd been listening and looking peeved at being left out of things. Couldn't help that, I wasn't going to tell her about Vnok's list until I had to and that wasn't till we got wherever it was we were going. "The dinner ploy's so old it stinks, it won't fool anyone."

"No problem. Remember Barker and his friends? I hired them to hang around the transfer point until we showed up. Gave us a discount, they did. Don't like Crawlers any better than I do."

9

Maybe it was Vnok pulling strings, maybe it was Luck coming round to kiss us sweet, but we got loose from Helvetia Perimeter in half the usual time and dipped into the insplit clean and lonesome.

We made Weersyll three weeks later. Security at the port was a joke; getting into the holding pens might have been a problem, but we weren't going near the place. There was only one ship down and they kept searchlights sweeping the metacrete around it, the flickering light and shadow making ideal conditions for Pels. The guards at the gates had obviously been warned to look out for intruders, but they weren't really interested in anything except giving the haulers a hard time, making them unload crates and open them up so the contents could be inspected. One time, just for the hell of it, seemed to me, they shot up some crates of frozen poults to the vast and vocal annoyance of the cargomaster waiting for them. No bloodoons or sniffoons, no heatseekers. A joke. Pels put a packet of ticks in his mouth, turned on his camouflage and walked through the gate, then climbed on a flat as it trundled through after him and rode in comfort to the ship. He set the ticks and rode the flat out again, ignored by one and all. And that was that.

VIII

1

Eight months std. after Adelaar hired Quale. Asteroid Belt/Horgul system/Swardheld Quale et al. With Slancy Orza tucked neatly out of sight on a large stone asteroid.

Pels scratched at his healing ear. "Four and Five are inhabited. Five looked to me like a penal colony, I saw an insystem ship eject half a dozen pods and leave orbit before they were down; obviously no one cared whether they landed in one piece or not or what happened to the people in them. The Transport went down on Four, so I thought better not send EYEs there yet, I didn't want Bolodo techs picking up search traces and following them back to us. There's another reason, but I'll get to that in a minute. I've had EYEs poking about Five since we got here, I figured I could get some idea what we're facing from the convicts, if that's what they were. They are. The place has evidently been a dumping ground for quite a while, some of the buildings down there are old enough to have great-grandpups. What we're facing, mm. Good news and bad news. The good is we've got a fair version of the local language in MEMORY. A little updating and we're home free on that. Remember Hordaradda? You picked up some plants there, the ones you delivered to University the time we met."

"I remember. Yes. Hordar?"

"Looks like."

"And the bad news?"

"The bad news. Bolodo landed on Four. Which means the head whosis is there, government records will be there, including the list of the two-legged cargo Bolodo's been supplying the past however many years, their names and whereabouts. We need that list." He dug his claws into the fur under his chin. "Which means we've got to go there and get it." He sucked in a long breath, let it trickle through his blunt black nose. "You know what's orbiting that mudball, Swar? Riding in synchronous orbit over what's probably the capital city? A Monarch class Warmaster," he was speaking slowly, enunciating his words with much care, "and it's working just fine, far as I can tell; I didn't hang about long after I saw what she was and felt her start sniffing after who it was making waves around her. She's old, but those things were built to last. I wouldn't want to try sneaking Slancy down past her."

Quale slumped in his chair, crossed his legs at the ankles and contemplated the screen with its schematic of the system, green dots marking the location of the two worlds they were interested in and some slowly shifting red dots that were insystem ships traveling between those worlds. He ruffled his fingers through the short hairs of his beard, stroked his mustache. Watching him, Adelaar felt like screaming: *shave that fungus off if that's all you can do, sit there fondling it.* There were things going on here she didn't understand, more to getting that list than finding out where Aslan was. I'm paying you, I own you for the next few months, she told herself, but it didn't help, she was a passenger and he was running the game. I could have done all this myself, she thought, I wouldn't need him if I had a ship of my own. . . . She swore under her breath, she'd put off and put off buying her own ship, it seemed such an unnecessary expense, what with upkeep and fuel and crew and most of all mooring fees, so much easier to buy space on a freighter or a Worldship. What's going on here? I won't be a passenger. I won't be pushed into a closet and left out of things. . . .

"No," Quale said. "No, we won't take Slancy anywhere near that thing."

"Swar."

"Kri?"

"Kinok says don't be so spooky. If there was anyone onboard who really knew how to operate her, she would have picked us up the moment we came this side of the Limit and ashed us before we knew what was happening."

"That's supposed to be comforting?"

Kumari hiss/rattled her amusement. "Ve says, we're alive, aren't we. Why should we need comforting?"

"Teach me to argue with a Sikkul Paem."

"I doubt it."

"Mmh." He watched the screen a moment longer. "Looks like there's a fair amount of traffic out this way."

Pels extruded his claws, began picking away old horn. "There's some mining the next quadrant over. Not a lot, mostly rare earths, things they might be short of on Four. And there's some trade between Five and Four. Mainly gemstones, furs and ivory."

"From the readings, those ships aren't much bigger than the tug. Say we left Slancy out here, we might be able to use the cargo carriers as stalking horses, make believe we're one of them. What you think, Kri?"

She tilted her head, listened a minute. "Kinok says maybe so, but ve needs more time to analyze the emissions." She studied the screen. "The touchy moment is when we have to break loose from the pattern. Pels, I don't see any satellite traces. Is that right, or were you too leery of the Warship to hunt for them?"

He rumbled a mock growl deep in his throat. "I'm not putting a pip near that world until I absolutely have to."

"You absolutely have to fairly soon, furface. I can't plan if I don't have data." She listened again, eyes closed, nodding at intervals. "Got it." She swung her chair around. "Kinok says ve needs to watch say four or five of those ships landing; ve says, Pels, lay out some passive EYEs, ve swears on the drives the Warmaster won't eat you."

Pels growled again. "And you tell ve to go twist veself; ve makes any more little jokes like that and I'll have ve for salad my next meal."

Kumari listened again, shook her head. "No, Kinok, I'll let you tell furface that yourself, save it for the next time you see him. Swar, Kinok thinks as long as we keep the tug to local speeds, the Warmaster won't get nervous about us. Ve says, though, it's very important before we do anything, that ve has the landing data. Ve can handle salad threats, but ve has no desire at all to achieve vaporization."

Adelaar watched impatiently, her fingers tapping a jittery rhythm on her thigh. Now that she was so close, her blood was on fire to finish it. Her mind told her that this careful probing and planning was essential, her body told her GO. If she were doing the observation, if she were directing things, she could be crisp and calm and efficient and all that. She wasn't. She was more useless than the baggage in the hold. And it was driving her crazy.

"Right. Pels, you'd better get started with those EYEs. The sooner you slide them into orbit, the sooner you can fetch them back so we can read them off and get on with this." He watched the Rau pad out, then gazed at Adelaar, his fingers poking in his beard again, then he turned his head to Kumari. "I suppose it's time."

"Might as well get it over with." Kumari turned her pale gray eyes on Adelaar, sat with her hands folded, cool and disengaged.

Adelaar forced the tension out of her hands and arms; as cool as Kumari, she said, "I'm paying freight here, I have a right to know what you're doing."

Quale pinched the end of his nose. "You heard us talking about ti Vnok."

"So?"

"Jaszaca ti Vnok. Agent. Among other things, he's been handling offers from relatives and so on of people who'd dropped down a hole somewhere. They want them back. Most of them couldn't afford Hunters Inc., but they did the next best thing and put a reward offer in ti Vnok's files. He gets his cut if he manages to connect with someone who'll do the digging, the rest goes to the digger if he's lucky enough to find one of the disappeared. A few years ago he tried getting us interested, but we couldn't afford to waste time on a cause as lost as that with no payback unless we actually produced the body. Not our kind of project anyway. Then you come along and it begins to look like some of those lost might have gone down the same hole your daughter did." He scratched at his jaw, fingers digging through the short soft black beard. "We have a partial list which we're going to try matching against the one in those files Pels was talking about. You said it yourself a while back, two flights a year for fifty, sixty years, maybe more, that adds up to a lot of bodies. We match 'em, snatch 'em, take 'em back to Helvetia and go home with a nice fattener for the pot."

"Earned with information I collected, information I nearly got killed for. *My* information."

"You might say that."

"Might!"

"You'll get your daughter back. That's what you hired us for. Don't you think it's a bit premature getting steamed over a side bet that hasn't paid off yet? That might never pay off?"

He was being so sweetly reasonable he couldn't know it made her want to tear his throat out.

Kumari stirred. "Swar, behave yourself."

His brow shot up, he looked amused and rueful and he stopped talking.

Kumari stroked her fine white hair. "You don't think we're cheating you." It wasn't a question.

Adelaar clamped her lower lip between her teeth and said nothing.

"You are a rational being, aici Arash," Kumari went on. "Use your brain, not your spleen. There is another aspect to this worth considering. The more witnesses we return to Helvetia, the safer you and your daughter will be. If we find even a tenth of them, you and Aslan won't be the only ones telling the tale, your credibility won't be attacked so vehemently and probably destroyed, your lives won't be put at risk. Some of those on the list have powerful connections. If I were you, aici Arash, I would pray to whatever gods I recognized that we locate a goodly number of them and get them safely away."

"I can't dispute that," Adelaar said, her anger ashes in her throat. "But you should have told me before this."

Kumari's pale rose mouth curved into a slow smile. "Would you have done so, Adelaar Adelaris-na? Would you have told us about the attacks on your life before the bargain was made if Fate had given you that choice?"

It wasn't a question Adelaar felt like answering. She said instead, "So, what happens now?"

2

So what happens now, she said. That was a good question. The answer for the next six days was *nothing much*. The Tutor poked the local language into us and we practiced it on each other, Adelaar went back to work on Slancy's defense systems, Kumari and I dredged up what we knew about Hordaradda and the Hordar, compared it with what Pels had picked up from Five; we spun out plans without data, knocked them down without data and generally fooled ourselves into thinking we were actually doing something. Made the time pass and that's about all it did.

On the sixth day Kinok announced that he didn't see any reason we couldn't take the tug in, the Warmaster just lay there in orbit like a sleeping whale while the little fish swam around her carefully but undisturbed; most of them landed at the field outside the capital; the rest came down on the continent below the equator. After plotting line-of-sight, ve said that the southern field was over the bulge of the world and out of the Warmaster's viewcone, which meant we could swing round that way without surprising anyone. So we loaded up the tug and started the tedious trip downsystem.

Pels named the tug Chicklet; behind those fangs he's a sentimental little fuzzy, Kumari tells him the cute has seeped into his brain. I put Chicklet into the slot behind a pair of cargo creepers and pooted along just beyond their detection range. If I could've taken her up to full speed, the trip would have ended in a few hours, but Kinok said not and I didn't want to push my luck, so I was stuck with a four-day crawl.

That was not a pleasant four days. I got a good look

at why Adelaar's daughter took off; Del had a tongue like a Tongan bladewhip. Pels showed the good sense to hide down in the engine room when he wasn't asleep or on duty at the com; that way he didn't have to deal with her. Kumari kept cool; if she was pushed too far, she gave back better than she got. Never, never, ever get in a word-slinging match with our Mom. Trouble was, more often than not I ended up in the middle, getting beaten up by both of them.

We reached Tairanna when the Warmaster was at noon; I had my fingers crossed, hoping Kinok was right and the observers on board were not looking for trouble from space.

The black whale ignored us, not even a twitch to acknowledge our existence; I laid an egg (a shielded satellite) and drifted on. Nothing. I laid another, then I scooted past South Continent into the Polar seas and dipped into the atmosphere through a hell-spawned storm where winds tore the caps off massive towering waves that swept along with nothing to break them up but a few rocky islets. Battered by those winds and by electrical discharges powerful enough to shock Chicklet's powersystems into fits, we crawled along the coast until we reached the fringes of the storm and settled to a careful drift along the duskline, circling out to sea whenever we spotted the lights of a settlement. Up near the northern bulge of the western coast the land turned hostile, rocks along the shore like shark teeth, white foam pounding high against the stone, precipitous cliffs and equally precipitous fjords. I turned inland there.

The land passing below us was rugged, mountainous; Chicklet said no locals lived there and I could see why. It was the kind of place I was looking for, a deserted locale where we could get up a landbase and a holding area for the vanished until we'd collected them all and could shift them up to Slancy.

About twenty minutes after we left the coast, I set Chicklet down in a pleasant wooded valley between two mountain spurs. There were streams filled with fish and freshwater crustaceans; the forest, the mountain slopes, the grassy meadowflats were thick with deerish browsers and other game that had no fear of fangless bipeds since they'd never been hunted. Chicklet's probes told us there were nuts and tubers, wild greens, trees and vine fruits; though it was early spring here south of the equator, some of those fruits and berries were ripe enough to eat. Plenty to help feed the vanished when we brought them here; hunting and fishing to pass the time, an untouched wild place to explore, a lake on a small plateau at one end of the valley where they could swim or do some boating if they had the ingenuity to build their own watercraft. Pretty place if you liked that kind of thing.

We kept our heads down for the next four days, sent out EYEs to map the capital and see what was where, using the satellites to bounce the data to us.

The first day I was cautious, sent in one EYE to poke about, ready to pull the deadman if its field started trouble.

Nothing happened so I saturated the place. Except for one area the city, Gilisim Gillin it was called, was completely unshielded. Helpful of them, wasn't it. They showed us precisely where to look.

By the middle of the second day it was clear the EYEs weren't going to get past the shield without blowing every alarm in the place, so I pulled in most of them and let Adelaar fiddle with them. She stopped fratcheting and settled to work. By midmorning on the fourth day, those altered EYEs gave us a detailed schema of the shielded area.

There was a monster mainBrain parked in a subterranean honeycomb that stretched under a complex of buildings and gardens enclosed behind a wall at least thirty meters high and proportionately thick; there was a mess of traps and alarms on the ground, nothing we couldn't handle. A score or more of guards patrolling the place, others at watchpoints inside the structures. The ones that stayed out of the buildings, they worked with leashed pairs of large cats, something like the spotted panthers on Flayzhao. Cats and men were alert. More than alert, they were nervous. I didn't like that. Something was making them jumpy and that meant trouble for us. I'd rather have them relaxed and lazy like the gatewatch back on Weersyll.

Pels tracked the guards on their rounds, built up a schedule. Night and day it was much the same. Half of them followed set rounds that took some of them through the public rooms of all the buildings, others into the twists and turns of the arcades and the gardens and still others into that mess of wormholes underground. They clocked in roughly every twenty minutes, pressing their thumbs on sensor plates attached to the walls inside and on columns outside, decorative spikes set inconspicuously throughout the gardens. The rest were rovers. They checked in at forty-five minute intervals, using the same sensors but in no particular order. They were good, they kept the patterns random enough to frustrate most observers but still managed to cover the ground.

Whoever it was ran things depended on scanners to warn him of air attacks and to direct the melters installed on the walls; Pels snorted when he saw them, he could hocus them without half trying. No bloodoons to point out warm bodies, or sniffoons to track them, no 'droid shootems. It looked almost too easy. We'd be using miniskips when we went in and they were hard to spot on a clear night, let alone a foggy or a rainy one; it was autumn up north, storms blowing in every third night, we could afford to wait for optimum conditions so we wouldn't have to worry about the outside patrols until we were on the ground. Once we broke through into the wormholes, all we had to do was get to the computer before it noticed it had mice in the walls. If we played things right and kept moving fast, we should get in and out clean; with a little Luck they'd blame any traces we left on whoever was keeping them up nights.

I meant to leave Adelaar behind, let her be the one to hold fort while Kumari, Pels and I went after the list, but she wouldn't stand for that. Stumping up and down the grass, scaring the bitty amphibs off the rocks where they were sunning, she argued at the top of her voice that we had to take her along. She said she'd back her physical capacity against me and a dozen like me, hadn't she already proved that? and as for mental capacity, she knew more about computers and security, especially anything provided by Bolodo, than me or Kumari or anyone else I could dig up, that she had the core of her equipment in the gear we'd collected on Aggerdorn and why'd we have her bring it if she wasn't going to use it?

Kumari took me aside and told me not to be a fool, the woman was liable to explode and do something stupid; she'd been under pressure too long, she needed action. Security is something she's good at, Kumari said, take advantage of that. You know me, Swar, I'll be happier here with the remotes, setting up the shelters and getting things ready for the vanished. That's more my sort of job.

Kumari is fragile, her homeworld's around .7 g; she went into the Tank Farm a while back and had some genwork done on muscle and bone so she wouldn't get exhausted or injured in heavier pulls, but she prefers to leave running about to us hardier types. Even so, there's not many I'd rather have at my back; she fights with her head more than hands and feet and that's one fine weapon.

We took advantage of another storm and rode a skip north to a box canyon an EYE had located for us; by the time the sun rose we were tucked away under an outleaning cliff across the lake from Gilisim Gillin. We slept a few hours and spent the rest of the day going over and over the schema and our plans, getting equipment ready, that sort of thing, and that night we strapped ourselves onto the miniskips and headed for the city.

3

3 years and 1 month local since Karrel Goza flew Elmas Ofka and her isyas for the first time.
The abandoned mine where Elmas Ofka keeps Windskimmer and lives with other outcast and divorced who've joined with her, also the escaped aliens with a powerful grudge against the Imperator and everyone who supported him.
A stormy autumn night, about an hour past midnight.

Elmas Ofka touched the bandage on Karrel's hand. "What's this?"

"Nothing."

"Don't tell me that." She pinched the hand lightly, saw him wince. "So?"

"Elli, Elli," he laughed at her, touched her cheek with the back of the injured hand. "Didn't you say stay off work for a while if I could? I needed an excuse, so I spilled some acid on my hand. No big deal. I'm supposed to be making up the income loss by hide hunting. My House won't expect me back for a couple of weeks."

"You see a healer?"

"Am I mushbrained like some I could mention? Of course I did."

"It won't interfere with flying?"

He laughed again, waggled fingers wound with salve-stained gauze, winced at the small pains the movement cost him. "Left hand, Hanifa." He thrust the hand through the leather strap looped over his shoulder. "Just means I can't knit for a while. No one's buying, so that's no loss."

She frowned at him for several moments, then smiled and shook her head. "What can I say? Come along, I want to show you something." She led him deeper into Oldtown, past tumbledown buildings rotting slowly into the earth they stood on as they were elbowed down by mesheme trees crowding into their airspace, to an area of the Mine settlement where he'd not been before.

"Convict barracks," she said and pushed open the door to a stone structure in considerably better shape than the others; waving him back a step, she leaned into the opening. "N'Ceegh, h'ab hab h'i cecehi h'ep n'beihim hab!" She pulled back, chuckling. "That gargle means sun's down, stir yourself, it's me. He doesn't like company he hasn't invited." She ran her forefinger along a merm scar on her forearm. "Never go inside this place without an invitation, Kar. You won't come out again."

There was a tiny tinny beeping; a sphere about the size of his fist floated in the door gap.

"Doa, N'Ceegh. Close the door behind you, Kar; follow me and keep your mouth shut."

When there was no chance any light would leak outside, the sphere popped out a beam, focused it on the floor and went swimming deeper into the cavernous interior.

They followed.

N'Ceegh had a small compact body covered with fur like gray felt, skinny arms and legs, a ball of a head dominated by huge lambent violet eyes. He wore a voluminous leather apron over a leather cachesexe and thin rubber gloves on three fingered hands with long double-jointed thumbs. When they came into his workroom and the light there brightened, a film dropped over his eyes, his scoop ears twitched and folded partway shut. He swung his perch around, drew his legs up and draped his stringy arms over knees that looked sharp enough to stab with. He blinked slowly, gazed with disfavor at Karrel Goza.

"N'Ceegh, this is our pilot. He'll be working your gadget, I thought you'd better be the one to explain it to him."

"Unh-fidoodah'ak." His mouth gash puckered into a pink-gray rosette as his eyes flickered over Karrel, rested a moment on the bandaged hand, moved on. "Come over here, you. Don't bother me with your name, I don't want it, I don't plan to use it. The cuuxtwok's installed already, but the proto model's here. Cuuxtwok? She," he jabbed a wobbly thumb at Elmas Ofka, "calls it a diverter. Same thing." He waited until Karrel Goza stood looking down at the workbench, then he swung his chair about and began talking. "The scanners old Bitvékeshit, Pittipat to you, he uses to watch his ass, they're crude stuff. !Fidoo! That's all. Need tactile contact with the suspect object before they know it's there; he's got some listening capacity, but it's short range. One of the things the cuux here does is spread a slip field about the airship, the scanner pulses slide along it without noticing it and pass on till they fade out. It'll muffle some of the noise your motors make but not all; if you can shut them off say half a kilometer from the Palace and let the wind push you over, you've got no problem. I've tucked in some long-range sensors, they'll warn you when you're approaching the danger zone, and this, see this gives you attack capacity, it projects the cuux field in a parabolic mirror in front of the airship, lets you trap and magnify the pulses and push them back at the generators till smoke comes out their ears." He reached for the control panel and began demonstrating the uses of his creation.

4

In Windskimmer, heading for Gilisim Gillin/ flying over Lake Golga, plowing through swirling mists on a heavily overcast night; a thunderstorm is threatening, but is still holding off/ two hours after midnight, Ruya is full, she's a faint icy glow coming through the clouds a few degrees past zenith, Gorruya is way off to the west, her fattening crescent a smudge near the horizon.

"Wha . . ." Karrel used the probe-adjunct on N'Ceegh's device to poke into the mist, but he could find no trace of the enigmatic objects that had flashed alongside them and vanished in the darkness ahead. "Elli, did you see those things?"

"If you mean something like wingless glassy dragonflies with dark centers, three of them, zipping past us six times faster than anything normal, yeh, I saw them. What was it I saw?"

"Seems to me it's something N'Ceegh would know about."

"Alien?"

"Pretty obvious, don't you think?"

"Brings up a question."

"Two questions. Did they see us? And what are they going to do about it?"

"Three. What are *we* going to do?"

"You want to break off?"

"I don't know." Elmas Ofka glanced over her shoulder

at her isyas sitting on the floor of the gondola, waiting for her decision, content to let her decide. Fingers tracing a scar line, she frowned at Karrel. Finally she said, "It's late."

Karrel Goza was briefly puzzled, then he nodded. "I see. What are *they* doing out here now. Could be they want attention as little as we do."

"There's a chance."

"Right. Let's keep going."

"Wind's from the east. You have to make a wide jog to position Skimmer for the drift over Gilisim, why not do it now. Make them look in the wrong direction, if they are looking."

"Why not." He brought the airship's nose around, driving her as close to the wind as he could; it was too strong to face head on, just as well he was turning early, he could save some fuel and a lot of battering.

Elmas Ofka rubbed at the vertical frownline between her brows. "I wish I knew what was happening out there."

"Yeh." He was going to say more, but the warning bell chimed; the instruments had picked up the first pulses from the Palace scanners. He slid the cover off the sensor plate, touched on the cuux field. The thready mist outside turned solid, as if they were suddenly sealed within a brushed glass bottle; it brought a sense of oppression, a hint of claustrophobia. The isyas were troubled by it; he could hear the soft sounds they made as they shifted nervously behind him. He forced himself to relax. "You want to cross the Walls high or low? The air near the ground is apt to be more turbulent than it is at this level, but we won't be moving that fast and the Tower is the only structure high enough to be a hazard. The guards won't notice us; in this fog they couldn't spot a longhauler with its warnlights blazing. The scanners are all we've got to worry about and the cuux will take care of those."

"And if we go in low, you won't have to run the ballast motors."

"Run them a shorter time anyway." He spoke absently as he watched the pulses from the Palace scanners go ghosting past them, invisibilities made visible by the field, eerie undulating tadpoles of light swimming through the mist and vanishing behind them. Five minutes. He bent over the dead reckoner, touching the controls with careful delicacy to keep Windskimmer moving in the right direction. Ten minutes. Another chime. He started the pumps sucking. "Ten minutes more," he said. "Then we're there."

He brought the airship down and down until she moved about forty meters above the grass, then he shut the motors off and let the wind take them. The sudden silence felt odd, almost painful. He didn't want to talk, nor, it seemed, did any of the others. He watched the hypnotic dance of the scanner pulses as the silvery wigglers darted past and past, endless numbers of them—a dance that ended so abruptly he leaned forward, startled, not believing he wasn't seeing them any longer. "Elli."

"What?"

"Something's happened to the scanners. Those dragonflies? Maybe they had business at the Palace."

"What else could it be?"

He shrugged, settled back. "Pittipat wouldn't put his hide at risk, not if he knew it. They did it, all right, those aliens. I wonder who they are and what they want."

"I'm afraid we're going to find out if we go in like we planned. How close are we?"

"Two, three minutes, why?"

"You sure the altimeter is working?"

"As well as it ever does. I've been flying since I was a tweener, Elli. You get to know where you're riding by how the air feels. The reading's not out more than a yard or so either way."

"I was thinking we could have dropped below the wall, that would stop the pulses, wouldn't it? Why don't you take Skimmer up again and see what happens?"

"No. There's no reason to risk the sound of the pump being picked up."

She grimaced. "You're the pilot."

5

The Palace slept; dim red sparks looped steadily across the gardens like fireflies tied to a track, the guards undisturbed in their rounds. Karrel Goza brought Windskimmer over their heads to the open-air theater. He turned her nose into the wind, touched on the motors and used a trickle of their power to hold her in place for the minute or so it took Elmas Ofka and her isyas to slide down the ladders onto the top tier of the theater seats, then he brought the airship around and cut the motors off once more, let the wind drift her out of the enclosure and across the tip of the lake to the Imperator's hunting preserve, an ancient forest that the Hordar had left wild and the Huvved hadn't touched.

Half a kilometer in, he dropped a mooring cable with a grasping claw, anchored Windskimmer to one of the larger trees, turned off the cuux field and arranged the two chairs so he could stretch himself across them and drowse away the time until he had to go back for Elmas Ofka and the isyas.

6

Begin with Elmas Ofka on the top tier of theater seats, her isyas around her waiting for a guard to move on, then shift to—

the maze of corridors in the subterra of the Imperator's Palace/concrete tunnels, gray paint on the walls, enigmatic numbers and glyphs in dirt dulled black, grit on the floors that make walking silently close to impossible, branches cutting off at angles to make things more confusing, ramps leading to lower levels at unpredictable intervals, stairways behind half-doors, pervasive hum of airmachines that keep cold dry air moving restlessly through the maze, six meter strips of coldlight tubes pasted in staccato lines overhead and on each wall. Voices echo an indeterminate distance.

Elmas Ofka crouched behind the curving stone bench; condensation trickled in cold rivulets down her body, dripped from her nose and saturated the tight cowl that covered her head and the lower part of her face. Around her she could hear the isyas breathing; they sounded louder than surf after a storm. Thankful that the wind was blowing into her face so the cats wouldn't scent her, she held her own breath as she watched the guard below in the well of the theater wave his handlamp about. Even in the back beams of the powerful lamp he wasn't much more than a silhouette, but she could see that he was broad and muscular, probably one of the laggas old Pittipat brought back from exile on Tassalga to put the boot harder into ordinary Hordar. He looked regrettably alert, more so than the cats who were shivering and stepping with exaggerated delicacy over the wet stone. Silently she urged them on, her teeth clamped so hard her jaw ached.

After what seemed an eternity, he gave the cats a toothy whistle, slapped at them with the leashes and followed them across the oval well. There were double doors at the far end; she heard the jingling of keys as he unlocked them, the sounds amplified by the acoustics of the place, then the chunk and thud as he pushed one of the doors open and whistled the cats outside.

As soon as the door boomed shut, Elmas Ofka stood, leaped onto the bench and ran along it to the nearest flight of stairs, the isyas trotting silently behind her. She led them down the stairs, but stopped before she stepped into the well to let Tezzi Ofka spray her once again with the scent-destroyer a cousin of hers had come up with, a mixture of kedaga, an herb cats avoided like most of them avoided water, crushed crab beetle and stinkfish oil. Even to her relatively insensitive nostrils it was a revolting mess, but better than having the cats set up a howl when they came across an intruder's scent trace on the guard's next appearance here.

As soon as the others were sprayed, she ran across the flagging to the raised in the center of the well and stopped by the door in the near end; according to her information it led down to the dressing rooms and, more importantly, into the tech's area where the lighting was controlled and the other effects were contrived. And where there was rumored to be access to the subterra. She waved Harli Tanggàr forward, stepped back so the isya could work on the door.

Harli started to kneel, straightened up. She put her hand on the door and pushed gently. It swung open. "Ondar," she breathed, "look." She pointed at the latchtongue, neatly sliced through. "Someone's ahead of us. The aliens you think?"

Elmas Ofka bent closer; whatever had dealt with the latch was similar to the cutters N'Ceegh made for them. "Probably." She straightened, waved the isyas closer, pulled her cowl off her mouth. "I want to go in," she whispered, "but I won't take you where you don't want to go. It's all or none. Call it."

Harli Tanggâr tugged at her cowl, uncovering a broad grin. "In," she breathed. The grin went round the circle. In, in, yet again in.

Elmas Ofka nodded, drew the cowl higher so only her eyes showed. She pushed the door open and stepped into the vestibule.

7

The entrance to the subterra was wedged open a crack; a short distance inside a roving-guard was lying against a wall. Tezzi Ofka knelt beside him. "Still alive," she said, speaking in a throaty mutter that dropped dead less than a bodylength away.

"Knocked out?"

Tezzi Ofka shook her head. "No bump or bruise. N'Ceegh is working on a thing he calls a stunner. Could be something like that."

"They aren't worried about someone finding him."

"Looks like."

Elmas Ofka frowned along the grimy corridor, glanced over her shoulder at the other branches fading into dimness as they dipped downward. "They seem to know where they're going."

"Kind of them to mark the way for us."

Elmas stretched upward, touched a small white

splotch high on the wall. She settled back, looked at her finger, rubbed her thumb against the sticky white stain. "Marked more than one way. Let's go."

Following the trail of white splotches accented with the bodies of unconscious guards, N'Ceegh's spotter in her hand, Elmas Ofka led them deeper and deeper into the maze, making better time than she'd expected thanks to the alien invaders who'd cleared the way for them. Down one level, two, three. . . .

The needle jumped on the spotter; Elmas stopped, signaled Lirrit. The isya dropped to her stomach and wriggled around the bend on toes and elbows, vanishing for several seconds before she came back the same way, jumped to her feet and brought her head close to Elmas Ofka's. "Aliens. Two. Stopped. Watching something."

Elmas Ofka thought a moment, then took the isyas back around several corners until she came to a branching tunnel. Eyes on the spotter, she turned into it and began picking her way to a point equivalent to where she'd been; twice the spotter jumped, twice Lirrit Ofka went ahead and darted the unlucky wanderer, then Elmas Ofka rounded a bend and saw the end of the tunnel; beyond that there was what looked like a vast open space. After signaling Lirrit Ofka and half the isyas to wait, she led the other three toward the opening, keeping close to the wall, moving warily, ready to dart anything that popped into the arch.

She dropped to her knees and eased her head past the edge.

The room beyond was immense; the ceiling was three levels up, aboveground, with a series of slim horizontal windows circling just below it, windows with one-way glass in them, black now because of the fog and clouds. The floor was another level below where she knelt; it was laid with black and white tiles in a swirling pattern that made her dizzy when she shifted her eyes too quickly. At the north wall there were several tiers of theater seats with a separate thronechair for the Imperator; at the south end, near where she was, a large curved screen, blindingly white, took up part of the wall; in the space it left there were three inconspicuous doors, one to the east of the screen and two on the west. A guard stumped back and forth in front of the single door, the scrape of his footsteps loud enough to send her heart knocking in her throat.

She frowned; the chamber was filled with shadows, except near the screen which seemed to gather in and amplify what light there was. Nothing moved except the guard. Why was he still moving? Was he beyond the range of the alien's weapons? They were at least ten yards closer to him than she was. Did they have to be almost on the man before they could take him out? Why were they waiting? What did they expect to happen? She glanced down at the spotter, stared at it, startled; there were two spikes on the line, not one. She shifted it slowly back and forth, watching the spikes shift. Something else was out there, something closing on the guard. She moved her eyes slowly over that dizzying floor; whatever it was, she couldn't see it, no matter how hard she searched. She looked at the scanner. The two spikes had nearly converged.

A section of floor reared up. She heard a hum like an angry bee. The guard dropped. There was a short whistle, then a small alien with brownish fur was standing over the guard's body, waiting.

8

First the video room (that's what it looked like, giant size), then the operations cell of the mainBrain.

We parked the miniskips on the stage, out of sight behind some low railings and got into the subterra with almost no difficulty. Adelaar had sense enough not to argue and let Pels take the lead, she'd seen a little of his work on Weersyll; besides, she was carrying a heavy pack she cherished like a child, her tools. I had a launch tube slung across my back and half a dozen clips for it in a pouch on my belt; the darts in the clips were loaded with bang juice strong enough to take out a wall if the need arose. Portable back door, you might say. Pels was in huntmode and harder to see than a black ship in the CoalSack. Shadow made him a special stunner, one small enough for him to carry in his mouth; he had it in his fist now and used it whenever he came on a guard we couldn't avoid or some idiot with weak kidneys heading for the can. There weren't many of them, thank whatever. It was late and most sensible folk were sleeping.

I was navigator, reading the chart, calling the turns, laying on rubwhite to guide us should we come back this way when the job was done. I shot it up near where the ceiling met the wall, where not many people would notice it.

We didn't have much trouble; Pels laid out half a dozen, I shoved them against the wall and on we went. Boring, eh? If you plan right, that's the way it should be. You don't want interesting experiences at a time like this. We used about fifteen minutes reaching the place Kumari took one look at and called the video room. Then we waited while Pels sneaked up on the guard. It was slow and tedious, nothing we could do but watch our backs and sweat out the computer's reaction time; some of the men Pels blanked had to be guards, at least one had to have missed a check-in by now, maybe even two checks if our Luck went sour on us. We were counting on redundancy; there's no gadget made by man or god that's foolproof, you have to include some sort of back check to make sure an idiot particle hasn't wandered where it shouldn't.

Stunner hidden in his mouth, Pels eeled forward on toes and elbows, his fur mimicking the pattern of the tiles; if you were as high as we were and you knew what to look for, you could find him; the floor would shift a little as if something moved a lens across it. But if you were down there walking a tedious stint like that guard, you'd most likely never see him until he had you.

As Pels got closer, the guard's nervousness increased. He kept looking around, snapping and unsnapping the flap of his holster, pacing jerkily about, wheeling and glaring at each whisper of sound. Pels changed his technique. He moved and froze, moved and froze, timing his progress to the jitters of the guard; the operating range of that stunner was just under two meters so he had to be very close before he could trigger it and hope to do the job.

Before he went down, Pels got a good look at the man. "Fiveworlder," he said. "Looks like the local bigass has brought some muggers home from exile; I suppose he feels safer with gits like that keeping the crawlers off his back."

Squat and powerful, sniffing trouble even if he couldn't see it, the Fiver swung his head back and forth as if questing for a scent. He was good all right, I wouldn't want to be the one to take him, but he'd never gone up against an Aurranger Rau in huntmode. Pels got him going away, laid him out like butcher's meat.

Adelaar and I sprinted along the ramp that led down from our tunnel, moving like the devils in hell were chasing us. We got the door open and she went to work; she'd spent some time over what the EYEs had told her about the system, so she needed about thirty seconds to put a hold on the alarms. Pels and I nosed about. The place looked empty, but we weren't taking chances, we checked every shadow. There was no one about, no techs or guards, just the interface ticking over by itself. When we got out front again, Adelaar'd begun the tedious process of switching the instructions of the alarm system. I could see it wasn't all that difficult, she was clucking and snorting as she worked, scorn oozing from every pore. Watching her was about as interesting as watching grass grow, so I went to help Pels carry the guard inside.

We'd just dropped him behind a bench when the door slammed open.

"Don't move."

Pels and I froze; there was a load of menace in that whispery female voice. I took a chance and turned my head. Seven more females in black with knitted black socks over their faces followed the first through the door, spreading out so they could keep their weapons on us from half a dozen directions. Definitely not authorized personnel. The wormholes were having a busy night. "Can I straighten up?" I said, as mildly as I could manage. "I'm getting a crick in my back."

The leader used her free hand to tap twice at her weapon. "The darts these shoot don't stun," she said, "they kill." The look in her eyes which was all I could see of her face said don't push it, I like you about as much as a bad smell. "Three seconds for a man your size. Less for your friend." She thought that over a moment. "Probably less. Keep that in mind. Get yourself straight. Slow and easy. That's right. Now. Both of you. Step over that bench and flatten your backs against the wall. That's good." She glanced at Adelaar who hadn't been interested enough to look around and see what was happening. "What're you doing?"

"Don't bother me," Adelaar snapped; hands briefly stilled, she scowled over her shoulder at the speaker. "Unless you want a load of trouble landing on your necks."

"Talk as you work."

"No." Adelaar turned back to the board and went on with what she'd been doing.

I didn't like the way that conversation was going. Adelaar had no intention of being reasonable, especially since she was right; what she was doing was more important than this woman's curiosity. However, I was fairly sure the woman wouldn't see it that way. "Uh," I said, "I can tell you in general terms what's going on. She's not playing games with you, you'd better let her concentrate on what she's doing; it can get touchy, changing the rules on an alarm system that complex."

The woman's eyes switched back to me. She wasn't liking me much more than before, but she was willing to listen. "What do you mean?"

"You came across some bodies on your way here?"

"Yes."

"Some of them were guards. You know how they check in?"

"We know there's something they're supposed to do."

Fools and drunks, they say Luck looks after them, maybe they should add angry female rebels. Going into a place like this with no preparation . . . ah! "Every twenty some minutes they touch a thumbplate set up along their routes. That tells the Brain there that they're on the job and where they should be. If a guard doesn't report and all systems look clear, the lid blows off. My friend is changing the rules, making touch and no-touch equivalent states. In other words, it doesn't matter what a guard does or doesn't do." I snatched a look at Adelaar. "No, I'm wrong, she's done with that. She's putting together a clear corridor so we can get out clean once we have what we came for. Did you use those darts on anyone?"

"Why?"

"The ones we knocked out, in an hour or so they'll wake up with a sore head," I was talking quietly, keeping things relatively abstract, trying to cool down the situation; seemed to me it was working, so I kept on, "it's been our experience that guards like them, unless they're terminally stupid, when they find out there's no sign of trouble they keep their mouths shut about going to sleep on the job. You see, they won't remember what hit them, the stunner wipes out the last few seconds before they go down. With you leaving bodies about, that's not going to happen. Shit. Can't be helped, I suppose." I gave her a grin. "Anyway, it's you and your friends who're going to get the blame for all this."

"No doubt. Who are you and why are you here?"

"You've been importing slaves."

"Not me." She made the two words sound terminally grim.

"Whatever. We're here to collect some of them. My friend there, the reason she's a bit testy, she had her daughter snatched."

"I see." She inspected Adelaar's back. She had very bright eyes, hazel, expressive. Good figure. Athletic. Despite the cowl I thought I'd know her again if I met her in other clothes and other surroundings. Reminded me a little of Shadow. I relaxed; she wasn't going to use that darter unless we were thicker than usual and forced it on her. She caught me smiling; she didn't like that, but she was cool about it. "Clear corridor. Explain."

"Deactivating traps, alarms, scanners, acoustics, melters, whatever, so we can scat like our tail's on fire once we're finished."

"Scanners. It was you took them out?"

"My furry friend did. He's good at that kind of thing. But the techs here, they've probably replaced the burnouts by now, and maybe someone has come up with the idea the flare was sabotage, so we don't have all that much time. If you'll just calm down and let us work. . . ."

"Seems to me we haven't interfered all that much."

Adelaar dug in her pack, brought out the black box she called her crazyquilt; Pels was watching avidly, the smooth black plastic didn't give him much to go on, but he was blasting into his memory the points where she clamped the leads; he'd hung over her like a worried mother when she started tinkering on the EYEs, but she chased him, saying he made her so nervous she was botching the work. Actually, I think she didn't want him or anyone else around her when she was using her tools, look at the fuss she made over Kinok's snooping. She had her secrets and meant to keep them.

"Maybe we could get together on this." I was trying a little basic persuasion, push but not too hard. "We need information; you want something or you wouldn't be here."

She thought that over, those bright eyes flicking from me to Pels and back, then she nodded. She didn't put the darter away, she held it loosely so she could snap it up if she needed to. "Don't push at me," she said, a much more amiable tone to her voice. "You say you're here to take some slaves home. We can certainly stand the loss. What's she doing now?"

"Getting past the blocks; when she's through, she'll be looking for slave lists. Who's where."

"Ah. If she can do that, what do you want from me?"

"Mind if I move away from the wall, my leg's getting cramped."

"If you'll remember . . ." She flicked the darter at the silent women watching us.

"I hear you." Moving slow and easy, I stepped over the bench and crossed to Adelaar. "About how long?"

She jumped, glared at me. Sweat was beaded over her face and there was a wild look in her eyes.

"Del, cool it, will you?" I know that wasn't the most tactful thing I could have said; I didn't mean to be tactful; I thought she needed an excuse to blow up, so I gave her one. She cursed me for half a minute. I don't know Sonchéri, but those words didn't need translation, they sounded like a couple of k'yangs snarling at each other. When she wore out her vocabulary, she dragged a hand across her face, gave me a disgusted look and went back to watching the readout dials on her black box.

I left her to it and ambled over to another work station, swung the chair around and sat straddling it, my arms crossed over the padded back looking cool and friendly. Nothing like a cliché to comfort the edgy. "Hanifa," I said which MEMORY told me was a courteous honorific for an important femme, a good description for the one facing me, "might be a good idea to send a couple of your people outside, keep watch for rovers looking for trouble. Maybe the tall one there could put on enough of his uniform," I jerked a thumb at the unconscious guard, "to suggest he's still on guard. Another idea, my friend here is rather good at stalking, you see him take the guard? Right, then you know what I mean. You've got us two as hostages for his good behavior, why not let him help with the patrolling? He's an amiable soul if you don't coo at him too much. Women do, you know, it's the curse of his life."

She surprised me. She laughed full out, a pleasant noise over the faint hum of the interface and the ticking of the shutdown readouts, made me feel like smiling for the first time since she jumped us; those other grins and grimaces were just policy. She waved the tall chunky one over and told her to get to it, called a little one who looked like she was made of springsteel and hard rubber and sent her up into one of the holes to keep watch there and pot anyone who showed his nose. She gazed thoughtfully at Pels, then nodded and waved him after the women. When he was gone, she set her hands on her hips and looked me over. "I understand about her," she nodded at Adelaar, "Why you?"

"Gelt," I said. "It's how I make my living. She hired me and my Crew to help her find her daughter and on top of that I collect so much a head for every captive I bring back."

"Crew," she said. "You have a starship."

"I didn't walk here. The lists in there, they're going to say something like this person arrived at such and such time, he was sold or rented to such and such an individual living in such and such a town. We need someone to get us to the right houses. Or lay out maps for us."

"That might be arranged. We can talk about it next time we meet. Mostly he rents them, Old Pittipat I mean." She scratched at her chin with the barrel of the darter, stopped that when the front sight snagged in the knitted cloth that covered the bottom half of her face. "You noticed the Warmaster."

"Hard to miss."

"What do you know about ships like that?"

"It's big. If it set down here, it'd grind this city to dust and just about empty the lake. When it has its full complement on board, it carries six or seven thousand, which includes crew, support personnel and strike force. You have any idea how many men your Pittipat keeps up there?"

She made a soft angry sound. "Not mine." She tapped the darter against her hip and went back to watching Adelaar. After a minute she said, "I don't know. Maybe she can get the Brain to tell us."

I took a look at what Adelaar was doing. "When she has a moment free, shouldn't be long now, I'll see what she can turn up."

"How much to take us up there?"

"More than you or a dozen like you could afford."

"You don't know what I can afford."

"Maybe not, but you don't know how nervous that thing makes me."

"Bolodo takes pay in rosepearls. Other things too, but mostly them. Have you seen rosepearls?"

That straightened me up and got me interested.

Adelaar had mentioned the profits from the slaving, but she hadn't gone into details. I still wasn't willing to risk Slancy in something so close to a sacrifice mission, but if that Warmaster were seriously undermanned which I suspected from the way it acted, hmm, it was an interesting thought. "I've seen a few, didn't know where they came from." I kept my voice easy, non-committal, but I don't think I fooled her much; she could smell a deal, but she was smart enough not to push it. "Let me find out what the Brain says," I told her. "I don't consider suicide an acceptable option."

"Nor I."

Adelaar started digging through her pack again; apparently she was in solid, because she brought out the duper and began attaching it to the black box. After the marrying was done and the run started, she went a little limp, scrubbed at her face with her sleeve and swung her chair around to face me; she looked a bit like she'd been having great sex with an inventive group, tired but with a kind of glow to her. "She's a slow bitch," she said, "it'll take maybe twenty minutes to get it all. Aslan first, then I'm pulling everything she's got about Bolodo. When we get back, those skells won't know what hit them."

"You think you could dig out what's in there on the Warmaster?"

"Explain."

She listened while I sketched the Hanifa's proposition. Not quite a proposition yet, but a suggestion that we might work out some sort of accommodation. I could see the spark of interest in her when I mentioned rosepearls. It looked a lot like mine. She listened without saying anything and after I finished, sat staring at the floor for several minutes. Finally she looked up. "Aslan first." The words hadn't much force behind them. She'd spent time, sweat and a lot of her gelt to reclaim her daughter, but teasing a profit out of her pain was so seductive a thought it almost obscured her original purpose.

"Agreed," I said, "that's in the contract."

"We need to make sure we've got legs for getting out of here."

"Right. Slancy's my income, I'm not hazarding her; you know how hard it is to get hold of a good ship. The tug's different. We could pick up another like her in a couple of months." I gave the Hanifa a half-grin, making sure she felt she was in the game; whether this happened or not, I wanted her kept sweet. With rosepearls in the pot, I was definitely coming back here once this business was finished. "Just looking won't hurt."

"Uh-huh. I think we've had this chat before."

"I hear. Crew and me, we run on equal shares once Slancy's serviced."

"Five shares?"

"Four. Kinok/Kahat count as one. Five with you. One time."

"Done."

I shifted to the Hanifa. "If the brain says it's doable, we'll do it, say you and I agree on terms." I gave her the grin again. "Anything else you'd like to buy?"

She thought that over a minute. "I need to talk to my people."

I checked my chron. "Plenty of time. The dupe run has to finish before my friend can pull the Warmaster stats."

Adelaar watched the woman gather her raiders together and start whispering at them. "Until a year and a half ago, local, a little over two years std., Aslan was here. Right here, inside these walls."

"What happened?"

"She disappeared. Ran. There's some more, but I haven't tried reading it yet."

I nodded at the confa group. "Maybe one of them knows."

She pushed absently at her hair, her face gone blank, her eyes narrowed. I hadn't a clue what she was thinking. "Not here," she said finally.

"Mmf, maybe you better explain that some more."

"This is no place to twist answers out of anyone, too many ways we can get dumped on; besides, I left my kit behind, didn't think I'd need it."

"Twist answers? That's not too swift an idea."

"Rosepearls."

"I can see their shine in your eyes too."

She managed a thin smile. "I won't dispute that. You think you can trust them?"

"Not half. Fanatics. They'll do whatever they want to do and hell with any contract." I yawned. It was getting later by the breath and I was tired. And I was getting nervous, stuck in this hole, waiting for the locals to pour on the troops. "Whatever they come up with, you keep hold of the data until they provide the pearls."

"We agree on that much anyway."

"Listen, say we lift them up there, if they can take that monster out, it'll make getting away clean a lot easier. And getting back in. Look, Del, we've got the inside track with these people, an exclusive as long as we can keep the location quiet."

"That won't be long if your gamble pays off."

He shrugged. "One or two trips for me, but Adelaris could have a longhaul market here."

"Gray or black?"

"Does that matter? Lets you hike your prices."

"I don't know enough about this place. . . ."

The Hanifa came back. "The clear corridor," she said, eyes hard on Adelaar. "Can you leave it and hide what you've done?"

Adelaar ran her tongue over her lips. "Probably. The wards they're using aren't all that sophisticated. I'll have to put the alarms right before we leave, but. . . ." She frowned at the woman, I could see she was thinking keep it simple, you don't want to irritate this one. "I can loop a path out of the guard circuits and pinch off access. Um, it might be better to set up several corridors, make them operative on different days, um, switch from one to another in, say, a seven-day rotation. They'll be harder to spot that way. Safer for your people, they won't be coming over in the same place same time every time."

The Hanifa's eyes glittered, but she controlled her excitement and gave a short sharp nod. "Can you find the files on suspect Hordar? Perhaps the Sech's plans for dealing with them?"

"I can take a look. Some of that might be stored in local branches."

"There aren't any. This is the only mainBrain on Tairanna."

"Your Pittipat doesn't like to share his power?"

"No." She didn't object to the *your* this time, too much into getting what she'd come for to worry about little things like that. "We want those files."

"Right. I can also erase them, if you want. Turning them over is more complicated unless your equipment can mate to mine."

"You can fix that."

"Probably. Not here." Adelaar had relaxed all over; she was back in her personal groove, selling her services. "Not for free either. Make me an offer."

The Hanifa moved her feet apart, set her hands on her hips and prepared to fight. "For your work and the files, five creampink, ten to eighteen grains."

"Seven corridors, files out and erased, eight midrose, twenty grain minimum, for my time, one of your creampinks."

"Seven corridors, two midrose; for the files, we'll have to see them to rate them, guarantee of one midrose, for erasing them one creampink, bonus points negotiated according to how much is in the files; your work, one creampink. Eighteen to twenty grains."

They went back and forth for several more minutes until they settled on a price that pleased both; by that time the dupe run had finished and Adelaar settled to work pulling the Warmaster stats, dumping them in the duper and at the same time flashing them on a readout so I could look them over and get an idea if a sneakraid was doable. While she was busy with this last, the tall local came inside, murmured something to her leader and went out again.

The Hanifa came over to me and stood watching the stats run past; Adelaar was into schematics now, line drawings of ship segments. "A guard came nosing about," she said after a moment. "Your friend stunned him. He said to tell you it was part of the standard rover pattern, he was expecting the man, it doesn't look like anyone is exercised about the scanners going out, the guard was normal-alert, not hyper."

"I hear you." I checked my chron again; seemed

like we'd been down here a year or two, but it was just over an hour. "There's a shift change coming up in a little while. We'd better be gone by then."

"You seem to know a lot about what happens here."

"I'm a cautious man, Hanifa. I like to know what I'm stepping in."

"How?"

"Observation and experience."

"Observation?"

"Electronic surrogates."

"You recorded what they told you?"

"I'm a cautious man, Hanifa."

"Willing to sell it?"

"Not worth much. Once top security here wakes up to what happened, there'll be changes. Tell you what, I'll throw that into the pot with your suspect files, a little sweetener."

"Why?"

"Call it good will. Now that I know about you and what you've got to offer, I plan to be back, do some trading for this and that."

"Rosepearls."

"Naturally. And whatever else seems worth the trip."

She gave me an odd look and moved off. Like she hadn't thought through what it meant, us being there. Not until now. There was a big wild universe out there and she didn't know how she felt about linking up with it. Maybe a touch of panic.

I pulled my mind back to what was happening on the screen in front of me. It was looking good. Total complement was around two hundred and more than half of those were support and services, whores, cooks, valets, you name it, everything you needed to keep three score techs, sech snoops and guards happy in their isolation. No wonder they didn't notice us, they wouldn't have noticed a grenade in their laps, to quote one of Pels' favorite expressions. Why favorite I haven't a notion, some kink in his psyche I suppose. Most of the ship was mothballed. My palms were starting to itch. Cumpla doomp, I wanted that ship. There was no way I could afford her, the fuel bills alone would be enough to bankrupt a small empire, but taking it would be so easy. For a minute I indulged in fantasies of charging across the universe with the power of a god under my hands, then I shook myself back to reality. Probably wasn't enough fuel in her tanks to get her across the system, let alone to the nearest fuel dump.

I still didn't like the thought of trying to nose up to that whale without it noticing me. Hmm. The guards were rotated every half-year local, that meant we could probably pick up someone who'd been up there recently and knew the drill. The screen blanked. I looked around.

"That's it," Adelaar said. "How long have I got?"

"Shift change ninety-five minutes. Pels got a guard, but he says there's no fuss yet. Don't dawdle over anything you can double-clik."

"Even doubling, it's going to take the better part of an hour to finish and that's saying I don't screw up somewhere and have to start over."

"I hear." I slid out of the chair. "Don't push it, I'll see what I can do about arranging a meet with our client so we can get paid for this."

"You do that." She bent over the eviscerated terminal, forgetting me and everything else but what she was doing.

I went to pump the Hanifa and her women for everything I could get about the local setup.

9

"Ondar." A hissing whisper. The Hanifa sprang to her feet as the tall one leaned in the door. "The fuzzy says he hears lots of men coming toward us and he's going to see about slowing them up, but you should be ready to move."

I sat where I was, wondering what the Hanifa would do about this. I thought it'd likely be something with flair, she was that kind of leader.

She moved quickly to Adelaar. "Where are you?"

"Covering my tracks."

"How much longer?"

"Five minutes before I can leave the Brain on its own to finish the job."

"How much of it can we destroy without negating what you've done?"

"Worried about them wondering what you've been doing? Don't. I've laid in clues that will tell them you pulled the suspect files; that gives you a reason enough for being here so they won't look all that hard in other directions. They won't find the loops, not without some rather esoteric, well, call it logic. Even I'd have trouble undoing what I've done."

The Hanifa examined Adelaar, then me, her jawline hard through the silky knit of the cowl. "Do you need backup to get you out of here?"

"No. Do you?"

"No." She hesitated. "In case I'm not able to meet you, someone else will be there. Hordar for sure, could be a man or a woman. He or she'll say . . ." She looked around, remembering suddenly that there might be ears tuned to this place that hadn't been there before.

"Don't bother yourself about snoops. Can't happen. Del has blocked access to the interface."

"I hear. Still, um . . . he or she will show you this." She jerked up the shoulder drape on her cowl, pulled a medallion on a chain from under her black shirt. She let me look at both sides, then tucked it away again. It was an oval of dark bronze, with an odd bumpy pod on one side and a complicated double glyph on the other. Nice piece. "We're going to leave," she said. "Before we're trapped in here." She swung back to Adelaar. "What about the scanners?"

"They're down again, I sent an oversurge through. When they try to fix them, the techs will find I've cut them off completely from the mainBrain. The Sech won't be able to get them functioning again until he regains control of the interface." Adelaar was looking smugly pleased with herself and so she should, but there was a condescension in her voice which the Hanifa wasn't appreciating. "If your transport can't reach you before they get organized up top, you might head for the lakeside wall, either go over it or cut through one of the gates there. Don't worry about alarms. The melters? The west wall is off the firing circuits for the next two hours. I've set up some snares the techs will find, um, interesting. Avoiding them will cost time. If you can reach your pilot, let her know that." She paused and the Hanifa started to turn away. "One moment more. After you get loose from here, you've got a free run for a while. I've fiddled something else, blocked all contact with the Warmaster. I can't shut her out permanently, there are too many possibilities for reinstating the link. As soon as the Sech reaches her, he'll have her scanners looking for you. Be careful they don't get a focus on you, they'll fry you. Once they get a lock, they can track a flea on a dog's back even if the man operating them has less brain than that flea. It's not quite as bad as it sounds, when the power is ratcheted that high, the field is very narrow, so if you can get under cover before they do the first coarse scan, you should be safe enough. Questions? No? That's it, then. Luck kiss you sweet, eh?"

"God's blessings, Akilla yabass."

I'll give our Hanifa this, she wasn't stingy with her gratitude; she didn't even seem to be swallowing hard when she called our Adelaar a welcome stranger and wisewoman.

"Nada." Adelaar went back to work. With a small army about to land on us, she wasn't wasting more time on chat.

The Hanifa rounded up her women with an imperious sweep of her arm and took them outside. I unlimbered the launchtube, fed it a clip and followed her.

One of the raiders was more squarely built than the others, with broad shoulders and heavy arms; she'd been lugging around a powerful crossbow which I'd wondered about, it seemed a clumsy thing on a jaunt like this. Now she loaded it with a four-point grapple and aimed it upward at one of the windows. Our Hanifa was a lady with flair, no scrambling through ratholes for her. The woman loosed the bolt and it rose through a graceful arc, going up and up, four levels up, until it crashed through the glass and looped down outside, carrying a thin, knotted rope with it. A hard tug set the hooks, two of the raiders went at the rope like it led to the promised land and started swarming up it. The shooter slapped a second ropebolt in the slot, hit the next window over, slapped in a third, put it through the third window, whap, whap, whap, steady as a metronome. She thrust her arm through the bow's carrystrap and ran at the last rope. The Hanifa sketched a salute in my direction. "I'll leave this one for you." She started climbing.

Pels came scooting down the ramp, back in hunt-mode, little more than a ripple across the stone. "On my tail," he yelled, his whoop filling the chamber with echoes. He'd been rambling around that maze interfering with the arrangements of the guardforce and he'd won us the extra few minutes that let the women get a good start up the ropes.

I put a couple of darts into the tunnel opening and blew down enough rubble to close it off. I started plinking the other exits, one by one, blowing out their sides and ceiling; things got touchy after I'd done five of them, the roof started groaning and shifting, it was an open question whether it'd come down on us before I finished sealing off the inlets. There was a lot of yelling and cursing coming through the noise of the falling stone and someone in one of the tunnels managed to get off some heatseeker missiles, but Pels knocked those down before they got anywhere.

Adelaar came out. "Peculiar, Quale, I didn't believe it till I ran it twice, the Warmaster's mainBrain is slaved to this one. I set a passive tap, one I can juice from the tug, tell you later." She eyed the billowy pouf of dust with disfavor. "How do we get out of here?"

"The Hanifa left us a rope." I pointed to it and swallowed a grin. She'd opted out of some of the last-phase planning, too impatient to sit through another bullshit session, so she didn't know the emergency bolt hole we'd come up with.

"How nice. I'm supposed to go up that thing with this load?"

"Nope, we're taking Pittipat's private route. Pels?"

"All clear, just dust and cobwebs. All praise to paranoia." Pels came from behind the throne, grinning and brushing at his ruffled not-fur.

The hole was a stupid breach in security; when we saw it the first time, we thought it had to be some kind of subtle trap. Kumari flaked that part of the EYEfeed and went over it cell by cell, tracing out every branch. All she found was dust and dark.

Pels tripped the lock on the panel, circled around us and led us up a wormhole that was barely wide enough to clear our elbows and so low I was almost bent in half. It split and split again, but the direction sense he was born with and the practice he got as a scruffy cub scatting about his native subterras kept him on course. You couldn't lose him anywhere underground.

We fetched up at the theater close to where we started, emerging through the back wall of the Imperatorial box. The tiers of seats were groaning and shivering as they would at the tail end of an earthquake and the flags in the well shifted under our feet, but the theater wasn't going to collapse; there was a lot of hoohaw in the gardens outside it, parachute flares bursting over us, spotlights stabbing through fog that was even thicker than it'd been when we came in, yowling cats and howling men rushing about, god knows what they thought they were doing. Nothing much in here with us, just one guard and his brace of cats. He tried potting me, but I suppose I wasn't much more than a moving blot, because he didn't come close; that's the problem with pellet guns, when you miss you miss completely.

I got him with the stunner and Pels took care of the cats. We swung onto the stage. I was worried about the miniskips, briefly afraid the cats had sniffed them out, but they were where we left them, the only problem was they were slimy with condensation. We strapped ourselves onto the belly pads and took off for the canyon.

I was tired enough to sleep a week and I suspected the others were about the same, though Adelaar would never admit it and Pels hid everything under his fur. On second thought, maybe he was just getting unlimbered and was sorry the fight was over, it wasn't often he had a workout that used him up. Not that this skirmish had. We were going to lay up at the canyon for a few days, let things cool down and the Warmaster go back to sleep before we left for base. I spent a minute or so thinking about the Hanifa and several more minutes savoring the memories I had of rosepearls and the taste of all that lovely gratitude that was going to grease the way when I came back to open this market. The rest of the trip I drowsed, letting the miniskip fly herself.

9

In Windskimmer/slipping away from the swirling swarm of hornets at the Imperatorial Palace/ over Lake Golga/storm breaking about them.

The airship plunged south through what felt like the heart of the storm, though it wasn't quite. Everything Karrel Goza knew about flying said get out of there, but he stayed over the lake in spite of the danger so he could minimize the chance someone would hear the motors and talk about it. From what he saw when he dipped to the jetty and dropped the ladders for Elmas and the others, there was going to be trouble for anyone the Grand Sech found someplace they had no business being. He didn't want to drag a trail to Inci.

Lightning crackled around them.

He'd had the cuuxtwok on this far, afraid the techs would get the Palace scanners working again, but there'd been no pulse wigglers slipping along its surface so they hadn't done it yet; he shut the field off, he didn't know its properties, but he thought it might attract a strike. Windskimmer didn't have sufficient lift to rise clear of the storm; she was taking enough of a beating without the threat of being crisped by lightning.

Turbulent aircurrents battered at them; even worse, there were sudden pockets that dropped them into sheeted rain which pounded on them and drove them toward the icy water invisible below them.

Karrel Goza's body was battered and bruised from the restraining straps; he'd jammed his fingers repeatedly as he fought to keep Skimmer upright; one nail had a deep tear. The panel in front of him jerked and vibrated, impossible to read anything on it, he was working from feel and memory, blessing the Prophet's benevolence for giving him so much flying time in this airship that he knew her like he knew his own body. Dimly he was aware of the isyas squealing as they were flung from side to side; even when they tried to hang onto the weatherstraps, the yawing lurches sent them rolling into each other. Elmas Ofka was cursing in spasms as she tried to get control of her chair; from the corner of his eye he saw enough to realize the brake had snapped and the chair was wobbling and swinging erratically; it could come loose and do someone serious injury if he couldn't get this lumbering yunk to climb higher.

All things end.

Two hours later the airship beat through the fringes of the storm and settled into a steady drone. Karrel Goza clicked on the autopilot and went limp with relief. He turned his head.

A trickle of blood at the corner of her mouth, Elmas Ofka was struggling to sit up. Holding the chair steady with her shoulder, Harli Tanggàr crouched beside her working at the jammed clamps on the restrainers.

Lirrit Ofka came and leaned on the back of his chair, her breath warm against his ear. "There were times. . . ."

"There were." He clicked off the straps, began sucking at his torn finger. He watched Harli wipe Elmas Ofka's face and tip some visk into her mouth from a pouchflask. He tilted his head back, smiled up at Lirrit. "You got one of those?"

She laughed and passed him her flask.

The thick, sour drink ran down his throat and warmed some of the soreness and fatigue from his aching body. He snapped the lid down on the leather covered bottle and returned it to her. "What happened back there?"

"You remember those things that went past us?"

"Aliens?"

"Outside aliens. Where the slave ships come from."

"Uh."

"They were after the mainBrain too. One of them lost her daughter, she's here to get her back."

"You talked to them?"

"Talked and talked. There was time for it."

She was almost glowing she was so excited, she was teasing him with it, making him ask. He caught one of her hands, put her finger in his mouth and bit down on it. She giggled and pulled his hair.

"So tell me," he said.

"We are going to take the Warmaster. We are, are, are."

"How?"

"Elli did it. She hired them. Rosepearls, Kar. They've got a ship, they'll ferry us up and get us in." She pressed her forefinger against his cheek. "One's a man, big man, if I danced with him I'd bang my nose on his beltbuckle. He did the bargaining." Middle finger. "There's the woman; she plays tunes on that Brain like Jirsy does on her shal." Her breath tickled his ear as she laughed in little soundless gasps. "She doesn't know it, Elli didn't tell her, but her daughter's living at the mines. You've met her, the one called Aslan. The teacher. We're keeping her as a kind of hostage, Elli doesn't trust them much." Third finger. "There's the cutest little furry being." She reached over his shoulder and flattened her hand on his stomach, below the spring of his ribs. He'd come about here on you." She brought the hand back to his shoulder, began kneading the hard tense muscles there. "You ought to see him, Kar. Big brown eyes, the softest sweetest fur, makes you want to pick him up and cuddle him." Her hands stilled for a moment. "Except it isn't really fur. When he wants, it changes color . . . and everything, so you just can't see him. He went across a floor like he was part of it and whap! the guard was down and out, didn't see a thing."

"Doesn't sound very cuddly."

"They're going to meet us on Gerbek Island nine days on, you can see what I mean then."

He grunted, saw Elmas Ofka watching them. "You don't trust them."

"It's not a question of trust. Greed, young Kar." Her mouth moved into a twisted grin. "Greed. We'll give them enough this time to make them hungry for more. They won't be so apt to cut us down if they plan on coming back. And there's always the daughter." She frowned. "We're not lost anymore, Kar." She sounded troubled and uncertain, not at all the Dalliss Elmas Ofka who walked in power, unfettered and formidable. "That man and his crew are just the first wave. There's going to be a lot more like him before we're dead and gone/born and back. I don't know how anything's going to turn out any more. I used to know." She closed her eyes, started to lean back but changed her mind when the chair started to wobble. "Atch! Even this." She slapped at the chair arm. "Everything's bound to change. Tidal wave of change. How am I going to ride it, Kar? How are any of us going to keep from being drowned in it?"

He stared at the knotty darkness rushing past outside. Not lost any longer. People knowing about us. Outsiders coming here. Changing us. Changing everything. It was like standing naked on the Speaker's Minaret with a mob muttering in the Circle below. He shivered, then winced as his bruises stung him. Lirrit Ofka muttered something he didn't catch, her hands were warm on his shoulders, working more of the tension out of him. "Was Lirrit right? Are they going to ferry us to the Warmaster?"

"Yes."

"So, what do we do when we get there?"

"What do you think?"

"Take it, I suppose. Somehow."

"According to the Brain there's only a handful of techs, a few Huvveds to run things and a squad of Noses to keep them all honest. The rest are support. Two hundred, counting whores."

"Take a big hand to close round two hundred."

"Shifts, Kar. Like the retting shed where you're working now. One third on duty, one third playing, one third sleeping. None of them expecting trouble. A score of us could take her. I could lay my hands on twice that many in less than a week."

He nodded. "I know. Them at the mine, Jamber Fausse's raiders, the Dalliss web. Give you two weeks and you'd have a hundred or more. Thing is . . ." he smoothed his thumb over and over the torn nail, "who can you trust once they're up there?" He scowled at her. "And what are we going to do with that horror once we've got it?"

"I know." She sighed, shook her head. "If it weren't so pathetic, it'd be funny. We can't kick Pittipat out if we don't take the ship. So we have to take the ship. But we can't operate her and we can't trust anyone who can operate her because they'd take her away from us and we'd be worse off than we are now. And we can't stay put and hold her because we don't know how to work the defenses so any rockbrain bitbit who's been up there and knows how to push a button could take her from us. And we can't tell the aliens thanks but some other time when we know what we're doing because the next clutch of visitors might be types that'd make a Huvved Torturegeek look like a nursery nana."

Karrel Goza leaned into Lirrit's hands, comforted by her strong fingers. "We've talked a lot about taking the ship, but whoever expected us to do it?" After a moment's heavy silence, he said, "What about N'Ceegh? From what I saw, all he wants is to get back to his workshop."

"He does now, but what would happen if he had all that power in his hands? That changes everything, Kar. Tell you true, I wouldn't trust *me* with that ship if I knew how to work her. Would you? Trust yourself, I mean?"

He didn't try answering her; he didn't have to. "If there was some way we could get rid of her. . . ."

"We've got a month to think of something, the man said he wouldn't take us up until he finished collecting the folk he's come for. Kar. . . ."

"Yeh?"

"Don't tell anyone about this. Not yet."

"Geres Duvvar and some of my cousins know about the raid. If I don't give them something, it'll be worse than kicking over a karints nest; we'll have them swarming about us trying to find out what happened."

"Mm." She stared past him, fingertips tracing a merm scar. "Tell them this, the female alien pulled all the suspect files from the mainBrain, then she wiped them out of Memory so whatever the Grand Sech doesn't have as hard copy is gone. She's printing the files for us so we'll know how much he knows and what he suspects. And she's set up some safe corridors into the Palace, we'll be getting the stats for those and passing them on to whoever's interested. That ought to satisfy anyone who cares to ask. What time is it? The board clock has quit on us." She frowned. "And where are we?"

"We've got around an hour till dawn. The storm slowed us a lot, we haven't reached North Bayshore yet."

"We can't make the mines before sunup?"

"No way. We'll have to find someplace to lay up. Unless you want to risk day flying."

"Too dangerous. If we ran straight east for an hour, where'd we come out?"

"Can't go straight east. Skimmer can't go head on against the wind out there, it's blowing a gale still." He tapped the glass over the fuel readout. "Look at this. Even beating to the southeast, we'll be running on fumes in the emergency tank before we have land under us. We'll have to leave her anchored somewhere until we can pack in fuel. Why not let the wind take us to the west shore?"

"That's Daz Musved, the Fehdaz there has a strangle hold on his people. I don't dare show my face anywhere around. Remember the price on my head? Besides, the land is too open close to the coast, we couldn't hide Skimmer and hope to get her back. And we need her."

"What's all this about hiding her? Why can't we just find a spot where people don't go and anchor her?"

"Because once the Grand Sech strips the blocks the woman set in the Brain, he'll order the Warmaster to scan the country around Gilisim. She warned me that would happen, that we'd better go to ground as soon as we could. If we can tuck her out of sight, there won't be anything for the scanners to see. That reminds me, they'll probably rake through places like the mine. Jirsy."

"Um?"

"You've got kin round the north end of the Bay, haven't you? In Daz Kanath?"

"I've got some Peltic-Indiz cousins living at Kuntepe Cove. You know where that is, Kar?"

"Close to where the Incis drop down to the sea, isn't it? I took a girl there for a daysail the week before I was adulted. I think it was Kuntepe."

"Right. Why, Elli?"

"I want you to get to a com where you can send a warning to Ansla Civa at the mine so she can spread the news to keep their heads down. Can you do that?"

"Sure. Kar, put me down near the point, I'll walk round to the House. They'll take me in and ask no questions." She was a tiny thing with a face like a sealpup, and when she grinned her eyes almost disappeared. "They've been stilling teshfire on the sly since Settletimes and no Fehdaz or any of his Noses has ever caught them at it or anything else they feel like doing and no stinking bitbit's about to do that now."

"Good. Will your cousins help you get back to gul Inci?"

"Oh yes, one of these days I'm probably going to marry Imro Peltic. And even if that wasn't so, none of them down to little Emin who's just starting to talk would say anything to any outsiders, Huvved or Hordar doesn't matter."

"Well, tell them what you have to, Jir, and warn them to keep close to home. If you can avoid it, nothing about the Warmaster."

"Elli, no no. It's true this time, what they don't know won't hurt them. Telling them that could hurt a lot."

"I see." Elmas Ofka fell silent for a moment, tracing over and over the merm scars on her arm; she was thinking hard. "Kar, you said hide hunting?"

"Derrigee Bol's paying two to five alvs for erkelte hides. When I messed up my hand, Goza Ommar said go and don't come back till you've walked the maggos out of your belly; if I could bring back a hide or two, that'd be froth on the beer, but she didn't expect it. I could stay out another week, no problem."

"Good. It'll take at least that long to get Skimmer

refueled and flown home." Her mouth twitched into a half-smile. "Maybe you'll come across an erkelte and get your hide while we're walking to the mine." She looked down at her hands. "We'll have to expel the ballonets and let the wind carry them off, collapse the bag so we can get it and the gondola under cover. Kar, if you can nurse her that far, take her up the K'tep. The closer we hide her to a waterway, the easier it'll be to resupply her."

"Depends on the wind. And a favor from the Prophet wouldn't hurt."

"Do the best you can."

"Don't I always? Find another place to sit before I swing round. This could get rough." He reached for the restrainers, clicked the catches shut, wincing as the straps pressed against his bruises. He waited until Lirrit and Elmas were settled, then he began easing the nose around, heading toward the northeast bend of the Bay and the Inci Hills.

IX

1

8 months std. after Adelaar aici Arash hired Swardheld Quale and his crew. Aslan as fugitive, living at the Mines.

The flarescreen spread across the wall inside the old smelter. Most of the smelter's machinery had been salvaged for scrap when the mine shut down; the building itself was in fair shape, its brick walls were massive, its tiled concrete roof cracked but otherwise intact. A year ago, when Parnalee's Spectacles had first appeared and were beginning to attract a considerable audience, some of the middlers among the Hordar exiles had plastered the walls and ceiling inside and pasted yosstarp over the plaster to make the huge room lightproof, others had picked up a comset in the course of a raid on a Raz strongroom and installed it here with a sunlight pickup and storage cells as its power source. The floor was littered with cushions and mats left here permanently because the Smelter had become one of the favored meeting places for the younger exiles, a combination Tavern and Dance Floor and ShowCenter; the greater part of the rebels and the outcasts were late middlers and young adults, fourteen through thirty-five, Hordar at their most energetic and prideful, male and female in nearly equal numbers; they came from every part of settled Tairanna, from the Duzzulkas, from the Sea Farms, from the east coast, west coast, south coast Littorals, even some up from Guneywhiyk the South Continent, desperate enough to chase a whisper; life on Guneywhiyk was even more constricted than it was here in the North.

Three days after Elmas Ofka took her isyas to raid the Palace, Aslan strolled into the Smelter and settled on a cushion in one of the corners, apart from the others. Like most of the escaped slaves she lived in amiable contiguity with the rebel Hordar, but this tolerance was a policy based on the needs of the rebels, not real acceptance; she had to be careful to avoid triggering the xenophobe that lay not so far beneath every Hordar skin. It was dark out, supper was over and the cleanup finished; this was the hour when Hordar in the cities went to the Dance Floors or into the Taverns, when parties began and lovers jumped the walls to meet in delicious secrecy. It was the eve of Gun Peygam, the Day of the Prophet, the one day in seven the Kuzeywhiyker Pradites set aside for rest and meditation. The eve of Gun Peygam was the day Parnalee chose for his weekly broadcasts.

Aslan twisted open the flask of tea she'd brought, filled the lidcup and sat with her back against the wall, sipping tea and watching the screen as the warning eye appeared, then dissolved into a play of color. The rebels were drifting in, exchanging scrip for drinks and food from the bar at one side, wandering about until they found a group they felt like joining or an empty mat where they could make their own group. Because they came from different places there were frictions, lots of frictions, clawfights and fist fights, hurt feelings and hurt bodies, but their joint hatred of the Huvved helped smooth down the worst lumps and gradually these Hordar from everywhere were beginning to think of themselves as Tairannin rather than Incers or Brindarin or whatever. At the request of the Council that was attempting to govern this patchwork settlement, Aslan had devised several strategies for diffusing hostility; these seemed to be working well enough to keep the ever-increasing population at the Mines from flying into fragments.

The color flow took on shape and definition, changing into a swirl of male and female dancers filling the screen with explosive movement timed to a music more guessed at than heard. Parnalee was using her data here as he would later on, as he did in every show, ignoring the distortions she'd tried to introduce, perhaps they were canceled out by what Churri brought him, it didn't matter, it'd taken her less than a month to recognize the futility of her attempts to buy moral absolution without giving up her comfortable life, without facing and accepting the danger implicit in challenging the dominance of the Huvved; having recognized that weaselthink, she went missing from gul Inci when Tra Yarta sent her spying there. Her data, yes. It told him that Tairannin never settled immediately to anything other than work, they circled, approached and shied away, as if they were sniffing at each other and the air around them, as if they had to get the feel of place and people before they could settle to enjoying themselves; he was programming spectacular dance sequences at the beginning of each show so he could snag the eye and draw in the peripatetic viewer before the serious business of drama began.

Churri showed up at the Mines about six months after she went down the slide. One day in early spring when rain was turning the world to mud and the honeycomb inside the mountain was sweating and dank, he came strolling into the stubby shaft where she and Xalloor were living, grinned at her and went out again. He usually joined them at the Smelter when Parnalee's Spectacles were on, watching the shows with a contagious glee as he ran a whispered commentary on the strings the Proggerdi was pulling. He wasn't here now, he and Xalloor and her group were having a prolonged argument over their latest script, that's what the note said that Xalloor sent round to her before dinner. If they managed to work things out before the Spectacle was over, they'd join her. She wasn't expecting them. Conflict was foreplay for the Bard her father, probably that was what attracted him to her mother, Adelaar's fierce and instant attack on anything that tried to control her. He'd quickly lost interest in Aslan; his daughter wasn't the kind of woman he admired and there were no shared memories of her childhood to reinforce the bio-tie; the accidental fact of their relationship went back to being a thing of no importance to either. At least, that was the face she put on for him. She was too experienced an observer to place any pressure on the fragile bond that still existed between them, but his indifference hurt her badly. There were times she woke before dawn and lay on the crude pallet unable to sleep, caught in what she called the deadash grays, asking why she kept on living and finding no answer.

The dancers melted again to streamers of light that wove a garland about a small dark man holding a stringed instrument like a cross between a lute and a lyre. The rebels greeted his appearance with whistles and thumbsnapping, his name went skittering about the Smelter like the game ball at an ogatarka match, Murrebai, Murrebai, Murrebai, then the room stilled to a silence so intense it seemed nobody breathed as he began to play a simple plaintive tune; he finished the tune and began repeating it but somewhere in the middle his agile fingers and his agile brain took hold of it and twisted it up down around . . . and brought it back to a simplicity no longer naive, having passed through complexity as through fire and come out stripped clean and immensely strong. He allowed them no time to recover but began a cheerful old child song. The rebels sang with him, holding on to each other, many of them crying silently as they sang.

Parnalee, ah, Parnalee. . . . What a job he'd done for Tra Yarta. When he got here, there was no such thing as an entertainment network; on the coast the Hordar thought in terms of family and city, up in the Duzzulkas family and estate; they didn't care what happened outside the communal walls. The Huvveds arrived with other ideas, but in the three centuries they'd been here, a lot of Hordar concepts had crept into their worldview; most of them had Hordar mothers though Huvved boys were removed from female influence as soon as they could walk. Merchants talked to each other and the Seches kept in touch, but no one thought of using the universal comweb to deliver entertainment into the homes, not before Parnalee arrived.

Murrebai bowed and strolled offstage. As if he pulled it after him on invisible strings, a title scrolled across the screen in carefully brushed calligraphy: *The Calling of the Prophet.*

There was a murmur of approbation from the rebels, then they settled back in pleasurable anticipation.

The sonorous voice of an unseen speaker rose above solemn, portentous music, naming the actors, setting the time and place of the events to be portrayed.

Aslan hid her smile behind the lidcup, missing Churri and his pungent commentary; she doubted whether anyone else in that room understood how much Parnalee was dumping on them, mocking their sacred cows. There seemed to be few sceptics on Tairanna when it came to the life and teachings of their Prophet; the Eftakites from Guneywhiyk believed with equal fervor in Pradix, they simply had a later gloss on his teachings from their Prophet, Eftakes. She had a fair idea of what would happen to their comfortable, comforting certainties when the Universe outside began crowding in on them; she found it rather sad.

There was a concerted gasp from the audience, wordless cries of outrage. What's he done now? she thought and frowned at the screen. As soon as she realized what she was seeing, she felt like gasping too. The actor playing the Young Pradix in his Violent Revolutionary phase was a Huvved. Or so it seemed. My god, she thought, he's gone too far this time.

In a minute though, when she saw several of the Councillors pushing through the disturbance, she knew he'd judged these people to a hair; he knew what he was doing, that twisted crazy monster. He knew.

Councillor Belirmen Indiz slapped hands against hips and roared down the mutters and shouts, "Use your head, not your gut. You make me ashamed to call myself a rebel. You heard that cast list. Any Huvved patronymics on it? Eh? Any? That boy up there, sure he looks Huvved, but no Huvved has given him a name. Eh? He's got no name but one he makes for himself. You know how he got that face. Some Fehdaz got him on a servant girl and booted them both out when her time was on her. You think her family did better for him? Eh? What about when he was old enough to show his father's face? Think about that. I see Huvved hair out there, light eyes, Huvved ears and noses. What was your life like, you with those marks on you? Eh? Think about it. You're here, where would you be if your soul's stains laid his load on you? Honor that middler up there for his pride and his skill, and curse the father, not the son." He stalked back to his seat, folded his arms across his chest and sat massively upright, daring anyone to answer his argument.

Parnalee, ah, Parnalee. I wonder how many Houses are listening to a speech like that? You don't need me or Churri either, you despise the men you manipulate but you understand them in some deep sadistic way better than I ever will, however much I probe and study. I think I am a little jealous of you. I know I am afraid of you. . . .

When he came out of his room after the beating, he came like a storm. He raged through the house, tearing up whatever he could get his terrible hands around, he kicked holes in the walls, trampled computers into twisted wrecks. He was crazier than a tantserbok driven mad by *must,* wholly out of control. With his strength and mass and his rage he'd just about frightened the stiffening from her bones. Then, abruptly, standing in the center of the shattered common room he went still, quiet; between one breath and the next he stopped his rampage, turned and walked back into his room. Quietly, with terrible control, he shut the door. A day passed.

The second time he emerged, the beast had vanished though Aslan thought she saw it looking at her now and then; she saw it surface and sink again when, hesitating and afraid, she told him of the Warmaster and what it meant to them.

The Smelter was quiet again. Looking around her, Aslan could see eyes flicking from side to side. Looking for those Huvved marks, she thought, hoping no one would see Huvved blood in them. On the screen a battle was over, the two commanders were standing face to face, meeting each other as equals, warrior to warrior. Parnalee had dug up more Huvved bastards to play the empire soldiers and there was a tense silence in the room as the two men confronted each other; the Empire's Captain accepted his death at Pradix's hands, taking the sword thrust with a stiff nobility that made Aslan hide another smile behind her hand.

Parnalee was playing all the themes that Tra Yarta had asked from him, but he was putting a spin on them that undercut the Huvved; he was playing to species memory and the depths of Hordar pride, deflecting their present angers only to intensity them, laying a clutch of bombs for the future. Future? As close as tomorrow, maybe. Despite Aslan's training, Churri was aware of what the Proggerdi was doing before she was; she was too tangled in guilt to use her brain, but once he pointed out what was happening it was obvious to her. Parnalee was seeding in the general population the same change that was taking place in the rebels, teaching the Hordar indirectly but effectively that they belonged to Tairanna and had a common enemy no matter where they lived; he was making possible the final overthrow of the Huvved once the rebels solved the problem of the Warmaster, but that wasn't what he wanted, oh no, what he wanted was Huvved dead and he didn't care what it took. He teased at the Hordar by slyly putting down the Huvved, so slyly he couldn't be pinned on it, but every Hordar who saw the Spectacles knew what he was getting at and felt the pride and saw the possibility. Aslan watched and was afraid; she thought of warning the Council, but doubted they'd believe her or understand what she was saying. The best there is, he told Xalloor once, and perhaps he was, but he was also crazy and men were going to die of that insanity. And she saw no way of stopping it.

On the screen Pradix was driving himself and his men into building a funeral pyre for the enemy; one by one his men began slipping away from him, showing by their glances and their gestures that they thought he had cracked his head on something and let his wits run out. Before long he was alone, sweating and struggling with the trees his men felled and left laying. Parnalee cut repeatedly from the madman working on that crazy magnificent pyre to shots of Empire soldiers flying toward the bloody ground, bent on avenging the death of their brothers.

Xalloor slipped in and crept as quietly as she could to join Aslan. She dropped on the floor beside the cushion, wrapped her arms about her legs and watched the play unfold with a curious double vision. One part of her saw it critically, judged the skill or lack of it in every aspect, recognized the tricks and the cynical manipulations, the lapses in taste and logic; the other part was entranced by what was there, that part plunged into the play until she was drowning in it, surrendering like a child to sensation and emotion. How those two parts could exist in Xalloor simultaneously and separately without destroying each other was something Aslan had never been able to understand in all the time they'd been together, something Xalloor had tried more than once to explain and failed each time.

As Pradix lit the pyre and flames leaped upward, the needlenosed fliers of the avenging soldiers were visible on the horizon, black specks growing larger by the moment. Suddenly the sky darkened, turned an eerie ominous greenish purple as clouds swept in from every side. A funnel formed behind the fliers, caught up with them, beat them from the air like a maidservant killing gnats and raced on toward Pradix and the pyre. Closer and closer it came until its blackened vortex filled most of the screen with Pradix a tiny figure kneeling on the torn and trampled glass. Then it was gone; the broken world it left behind was quiet except for the vigorous crackling of the funeral fire. The small figure of the kneeling man was there still, untouched, shining in the dimness of the coming storm as if lit by another fire, one that burned inside him. A bird sang. The sweetness of its song was almost unbearable.

There was an explosive sigh as if every lung in the Smelter empties itself at the same moment. Otherwise the silence was unbroken.

Parnalee, you've the Luck of the crazy cradling you, Aslan thought, I can't believe Tra Yarta passed this one. Was he suckered by the casting of that boy with his Huvved face and form? She rubbed at her nose, gulped down the tea left in the cup; it was cold, but the small bitterness was a satisfying counter to the fantasy on the screen. A headache began at the back of her skull; she rubbed at her nape, closed her eyes. How long does this go on? she thought. Where's Churri? She slitted an eye and sneaked a look at Xalloor. Have you two decided to split? The dancer looked placid as a sleeping lizard, but that didn't mean much, she was sunk in the Spectacle and nothing else mattered.

Somehow Pradix had changed from a fighter to a poet, she'd missed the transition while she was fussing, but wasn't much bothered by that. He wasn't the Prophet yet, but he was getting close. He'd acquired three men with assorted instruments and a rough cart with straw sticking out all over, pulled along by a team of yunks painted battleship gray with vertical black stripes. Since Parnalee had thrown in tarmac highways kept in top condition and a swarm of small black vehicles rushing along them at near supersonic speeds, not to mention the vast assortment of fliers that passed by overhead, the reason for that cart with its two-yunk propulsion system escaped her. She poured some more tea; she needed a touch of reality or she'd start giggling and get herself lynched from the looks on the faces around her.

He was going from village to village, mixing sedition with preaching, poetry with politics, escaping again and again just before soldiers landed on the town, building toward a finale that got the rebels on their feet, shouting out the words to the poem he was chanting in the ancient worker's vag that was the basis for the Hordar they all spoke today; apparently it was a poem everyone here knew, probably one of those she'd sent Churri hunting way back in that other life, the kind no Huvved ever heard. Reluctantly she got to her feet with the rest, but she refused to chant with them.

Pradix the poet stood on the cart's bed, straw about his feet, music on three sides, Yesil Uranyi perched on the front, drums going tam tam tummm toom, Saadi Klemm on his left, twee twee tootle too ooh, wandering flute, and on his right, scree ooh wee, singee singee, the fiddling man Nanno Inallet. Pradix the not yet Prophet stood in the cart and chanted his vagger song.

year ya year ya year ya ya
fear ya hear ya fear
shake ya shiver
terror fever
same old song, same old
sad song
same old sad
song
some men get old
some women cold
old ya cold ya
NO O NO
I ya we ya I an we
we shout
NO O NO
them wonda what we been about
them wonda bout we fire
heartfire red and red
not dead
not we
them canna tame we an I
them canna tame I
am too weight-I
too long I wait I
old song sad song dead song dead
so them say so
old cold dead
NO!
I ya we
I an we
do stomp o
press shun
I an we
this genna ray
shun
ay shun I shun we shun
they
I an we do stomp oppression
I an we this generation

"YA!" the crowd in the village shouted. "YA!" the rebels in the Smelter shouted. "No," they shouted, players and viewers, "Fireheart! Weight-I wait-I! NO! Shun," they shouted, players and viewers, "Press! Stomp! Shun! Stomp oppression, this generation, I an we, YES! YES! YES!"

2

Xalloor pinched Aslan's arm, then began wiggling through the crowd, heading for the door. Aslan blinked, then followed, crossing against the streams of adults who were moving toward the bar. Some of the older middlers were kicking the mats and cushions to one side to get ready for the dance that would go on until the musicians tuning up in a corner by the comset ran out of wind. Others were standing around throwing verses back and forth, a kaleidoscope of clashing sounds. A number of the younger middlers weren't waiting for music but were already undulating in the preliminaries to one of their less comprehensible dances. Made Aslan feel her years; forget about the ananiles, they couldn't return that resilience of mind that only the very young possessed.

The wind was picking up outside, the tree limbs woven overhead groaned and creaked, the stiff thick leaves rubbed against each other, singing like crickets. The trees grew close together, blocking moonlight and starlight; whoever walked this path after dark carried light with him or her and blessed the trees for they ceiled the path to the Minemouth and hid the walkers on it from the Warmaster's wandering eye. Rod lights flickered like earthbound stars as clumps of middlers hurried toward the dance, brushing past Aslan and Xalloor without taking notice of them. When the rush diminished to a trickle, Aslan hurried to catch up with Xalloor.

"What . . ."

The dancer looked round, her face lit by a flash of laughter, clickon clickoff, there and gone. She shook her head.

Aslan sighed, matched steps with her. "The script. Who won?"

"Me. Sort of." Xalloor thrust her hands into the

pockets of her jacket and slowed a little, letting Aslan light the way for them both. "I told them, look, you go and on at people like that, they turn their heads off. Worse'n that, they turn you off. You want 'em to listen, you keep coming back at them all right, but you sugarcoat it, I mean you want to sneak it past 'em before they know what you're doing. I said, you want to see how it's done, look at one of those Spectacles, I mean really look, forget about the story, figure out what he's saying and how he's saying it. But you got to do it better, faster, don't forget how quick the bitbits'll be after you, you've got maybe ten minutes playing time before they locate the transfer station and trash your cassette. Lan, you should've seen that script, it'd send a wirehead into coma."

"When are they going to start the clandestines?"

"Things keep going like they are and they get hold of some more writers, which they really need, believe me, they natter on all the time about poets, but they don't recruit any, it's enough to make you throw up your hands and say hell with everything. Amateurs! Couple months from now. That's what the plan is. Three months top limit." Another strobe grin. "Maybe."

"Why maybe in that tone of voice?"

"Elmas's back. We were still arguing when she came in, she wanted to talk to Evvily, so we broke up. Just as well, Ylazar was starting to repeat himself and that could go on till entropy took us all."

"She say anything? What the tight-down was about?"

"Not in front of the nonnies, no." She clicked her tongue, wrinkled her nose.

Aslan sighed again, the familiar little sound stabbed a weak spot; she wanted her mother here, scold or not, wanted something from her old life, she was tired, so tired of improvising an existence.

Xalloor banged on the Minemouth door, stepped back while the keeper slid it open just wide enough to let them through one after the other. She got her lightrod out again and began almost galloping along the rough floor of the gallery, heading for the lift. There was a suppressed excitement about her, a wired-up energy that said clearer than words she had news, exciting maybe frightening news.

They went up two levels, followed Kele tunnel until they reached the stubby offshoot where they'd set up housekeeping. Xalloor stirred the fire to life, added more coal and crouched before the grate with the bellows, working with hard won expertise (her first attempt at a coal fire was unalloyed disaster, they had to run down a Hordar who knew about sea coal and iron grates and was willing to lend a hand so they didn't freeze before morning). As she coaxed tiny flames from the ashy lumps, some of the dank chill went off the room. It *was* a room, there was a yosstarp ceiling, wrinkled and sagging, walls of wood scrap scavenged from the company houses, a wooden floor covered with lignin mats that Aslan had woven, putting to work one of the skills she'd learned a few assignments back, a neat herringbone pattern that earned her some condescending praise from the much defter weavers among the outcasts. She'd made mats for a number of rooms like these, glad to have some way of passing the time; besides, the scrip she earned brought her and Xalloor things they couldn't have acquired otherwise, like the glass and bronze oil lamps and the earthenware vase sitting on a crate in the corner by the fire, the nergi flowers in it adding dark rich red and orange tones to the drab gray of the tarp and the washed-out brown of the mats and the walls. There were two pallets raised from the floor on crude frames that Aslan and Xalloor had glued together from rusty tramrails and salvaged bricks, there were several cushions they'd gotten from one of the weavers in return for several weeks hard work carding yunk wool, blankets issued by the Council; sheets were a luxury few living here could afford. There was the crate which they used for storage and some smaller boxes that served as tables. Chilly drafts came wandering through the cracks no matter how often she or Xalloor pounded caulking between the boards. Not down the chimney, though, bless the local tech; Hordar filters were useful for more than purifying water. Despite all this, they were surrounded by stone and earth and that was like living inside a block of ice.

While the dancer fussed with the fire, Aslan moved round the room, lifting the chimney glasses, telling herself she ought to wash them one of these days, trimming the wicks and lighting them. These lamps burned fish oil smuggled in from the Sea Farms and that oil announced its origins for several minutes after the wicks were lit; after that either the smell went away, or their noses went on strike. The soft amber light filled the room, chased away the shadows and gave an illusion of warmth. She poured some water in a kettle, hooked out the swing spit and clamped the bail in place. "Move over a bit, Loorie, let me get this on so we can have some tea. Did you get anything to eat over there?"

Xalloor tossed the bellows aside and came to her feet in that boneless ripple that made Aslan feel clumsy as a stone god. "It's going good enough, I was just trying to catch some warm." She dropped onto her pallet. "Some sandwiches, I think they were, might have been relics of the Prophet. Why is is, Lan, that earnest types never have a palate?"

"Genetic, I suppose." Aslan got to her feet, brushed her hands against her trousers. "I thought that might happen, so I begged some cold meat and rolls from Prismek, a minute, I'll fetch them." She pushed past the double tarp they used as a door and tied taut once they were in for the night, came back with a basket, its contents wrapped in old soft cloth. "He had some krida he was frying for breakfast, there's a sackful of those tucked under the rolls. And he threw in some green meelas and some cheese to go with them."

"I love you forever, Lan."

"So tell me what it is you didn't want to say out there."

"Remember I said we were still arguing?" Xalloor pulled a box across the slippery mat to her pallet and began laying out the feast.

"So?"

"I didn't exactly mean we, not when Elmas came in; there was some peculiar tea going round and it got me in the gut, I was out back in the facilities listening to my insides grumble and wondering if my knees were going to work right when I finished dropping my burden. Well, I don't need to go into that any more, but what happened was, when I came back Churri and Holz had gone off along with most the others. I was ticked, let me tell you, I could've used an arm to lean on right then, I was moving slow and careful. That must've been why they didn't hear me and stop talking." She popped a krida in her mouth and crunched happily at it, rolling her eyes with pleasure at the taste.

"Loorie!"

"Dearie dai, im pay shunt," Xalloor scooped out a handful of the krida and sat with her fingers crooked about the succulent fishlets, "pay and play. Outside's in. Here and now. Not Bolodo."

Aslan closed her eyes. After a moment, she heard a hissing as the water boiled and a few drops landed on the coals. She kicked a cushion across to the box, hooked the kettle away from the fire. As she made the tea, she did her best to not-think, not-feel. Behind her she could hear Xalloor eating steadily and was grateful the dancer didn't feel like talking right then. She left the tea steeping, stood leaning against the crate, her elbows behind her, resting on the top. "Outside's in?"

"You hear what Elmas 'n the isyas were after?"

"My students said she was going to blow the Brain. Get rid of the Sech's files. Make as much trouble as she could."

"Yah. That's where she 'n the isyas ran into 'em."

"Hmm." Aslan lifted the strainer, inspected the tea and decided it was ready. She carried pot and bowls to the box, folded herself down onto the cushion and poured tea for herself and Xalloor. She cradled her bowl between her hands, glad of the warmth and the heaviness, it gave her something to hold onto. "Exactly what did you hear, Loorie?"

"Le' me see, I'm supposed to be good with dialog. You been in the depot, you know how it's laid out; we were in the big room so we could walk through a scene whenever we fixed something and see how it played.

There's tarp hung all over, makes it hot sometimes, but no one fusses about that," she held up one of the krida, "frying's all right for fish, but me, I'd rather not, eh? There's a couple of old minecars in there, lot of junk, you had to navigate it in the dark, you'd end up with two broken legs and your face pushed in. What I mean, we don't try to light the whole place, so there's lots of shadows and it's easy to get lost round the edges. Well, I wasn't trying to get lost, it was just I wasn't making much noise and walking along like I was my grandmother after she outwore her ananiles. I fetched up by one of the cars and decided I'd better lean against it for a minute. Felt nice and cool against my face. I started to feel better. They were talking all that time, but I wasn't listening until I heard *outsiders* in that tone of voice, you know, when someone's about to be shoved head down in shit and it won't be the locals. Being it was Elmas speaking and considering how the Council crawls around her, I got interested fast. I thought she was talking about us." She broke off to sip at the tea.

Aslan moved one hand carefully from the cup, pressed her heated palm against her mouth. When the heat was gone, she lowered the hand. "Who was there?"

"Um, Elmas, that pilot what's his name, it'll come back to me in a minute, one of her isyas, the one that's living here all the time now, Lirrit I think's her name, Evvily and Ylazar. Pilot, ah! I knew I'd get it, Karrel Goza, yah, he didn't say anything, he doesn't talk much anytime. Ylazar said something, I didn't hear it, his back was to me and you know how he mumbles. *The woman warned us,* Elmas said. *We had to get Skimmer undercover,* she said. *Or lose her,* she said. *Ylazar Falyan, we need a boat and yoss pods and enough fuel to fill Skimmer's tanks, we need it tonight,* she said. Ylazar said something I didn't hear that time either, didn't need to hear it, you know him, if there's anything he hates worse than moving, it's moving fast. *Do it,* she said, *now.* She gave him the mean eye and he got to his feet and went out, muttering to himself." Xalloor grinned. "She say hop, they jump and don't bother asking how high. The pilot, he got up and went out after Laza, said nothing, just left. Before they were out the door, Elmas started on Evvily. *Get word out,* she said, *the woman jigged the Brain and set up open corridors for anyone who wants over the Wall, in or out. No melters, no alarms, no defenses at all. I'll get time, place and duration at the meeting with the outsiders, give it to you for distribution soon as we get back here.* Evvily wasn't about to be tramped on like Ylazar. *Do you trust her?* she said. *It's your word going to guarantee this,* she said. *She makes a fool of you, it hurts us all.*" Xalloor jumped up and danced over to the storage crate; she got out the stone bottle with the rix brandy they kept for celebrating small triumphs, came back more soberly, her face and body shouting her nervousness. "Give me your bowl," she said.

"Why?"

"Always asking questions, aren't you. Just for once do what I say, eh?"

More apprehensive than ever, Aslan swallowed the last of the cold tea and passed over the bowl.

Xalloor poured in enough brandy to cover the bottom. "Drink that. Now."

"Yes, Mama Loor."

Xalloor gave herself a scant teaspoon of the brandy, pushed the cork back in and settled on her pallet. "Where was I?"

"Evvily was saying do you trust her."

"Right." Xalloor sipped at the brandy, eyes closed. "Elmas laughed. *I don't need to trust her,* she said, *I have two good locks on her. The outsiders want trade with us. They cheat us now and that shuts down on them fast,* she said. *Rosepearls,* she said. *They want them like most people want air to beathe,* she said. *And they've come to take back the slaves Bolodo sold Pittipat,* she said. *The woman more than the others. Her daughter is a slave,* she said. *She's here to get her back.*"

Aslan felt sick. She bent over until her foreheard was resting on the box.

"Cha! I knew this was going to happen." Xalloor came round the box on hands and knees, lifted Aslan against her, held her with her face tucked into the curve between neck and shoulder. She held Aslan until her shuddering stopped, stroking her back, smoothing a gentle hand over and over her short dark hair.

Finally Aslan sighed and pushed away. She filled her bowl again and drank the brandied tea for its double warmth. "'Go on," she said.

"Not much on to go. Soon as she said that, I thought of you and what you told me about your mum. Then I thought, hunh, don't jump so fast, Loor, lots of daughters hauled off here, I'm one myself though my mum wouldna crossed a street to fetch me home. Evvily was still being hard to convince. *She might have lied,* she said, *she might have been playing games with you. No,* Elmas said. *The daughter is here now. At the Mines. Aslan,* she said. *We'll hold her, that way we can be sure the mother does what she's promised.* Just then that idiot Mustakin came slamming back in, forgot his overcloak. They stopped talking. I suppose Elmas thought she'd said all she needed to, anyway they went out after Musti. By that time I'd forgotten the shakes and I took off as soon as I was sure no one would land on me. So there it is, your mum is here, looking for you."

"They're not going to tell me about her, are they."

"Nuh. Or her about you. What you going to do?"

"Snoop. There's a meeting. . . ." Aslan grinned, suddenly riding high. "Be a hoot if I turned up there and said hi mom. Pass that bottle and let's celebrate."

3

The Ridaar unit had three voice-activated pinears, ilddas in University jargon, inconspicuous-long-distance-data-collectors. Aslan slipped one into the mine chamber the Council used for their private meetings, she got one into Elmas Ofka's quarters. The third she hesitated over for some time, but she finally decided to keep it reserved for anything that turned up in the feed from the other two.

On the night of the day she planted the ilddas, the night after Gun Peygam, she came back alone after supper and played over what they'd picked up and transmitted to the Ridaar. There wasn't much from the ear in Elmas Ofka's quarters, but in the material from the other she found the Dalliss report to the special Council meeting and the discussion afterward. She learned the date and place of the next meeting with the outsiders, she learned about the plan to attack the Warmaster and the role she was meant to play in that. Hostage. The breathing equivalent to a handful of rosepearls. Sold again, she told herself when she heard that. A slave is a slave is a slave.

Time crawled. She felt the feet of every minute walking across her skin, inescapable tickling torment. She taught her history seminar and kept her body easy and her face blank with an effort of will that left her drained. There was an itchiness in her students that she found hard to ignore, they stank of conspiracy. their questions were perfunctory or prods to get her talking on subjects all round the secret that excited them; she could not notice that excitement because she was not supposed to know about the plan to seize the Warmaster.

"How many rebellions have you studied, doctori-yabass?"

"Too many to narrate. I've told you about three, if you'll remember, examples of what can happen. The genocide on Alapacsin III, the Great-Father uprising on Tuufyak, the Placids on Ceeantap. If I have time the next few weeks, I'll fill some cassettes with what I remember of other violent changes in leadership, show you variations on those three types of outcome."

"Which do you think we'll have here, doctori-yabass?"

"Depends on you and how you look at things. Please remember, people are capable of almost anything in the name of good."

"What's wrong with that, doctori-yabass?"

"So it's a game, eh? Whack your teacher, eh? Look to your prophet and learn. Seems to me he said a thing or two about ends and means. At the start, all rebellions are rather much the same. I know, I've told you to avoid generalization, it's lazy thinking, but even that's not always true. They begin with passion and ideals, fire in the belly, ambition in the brain. You, young Hordar, that's you I'm talking about. And they begin because there is a need that grows until it explodes one day. There you have the inklins. You here at the Mines, you're playing touch and run games, you tease the Huvved because you can't afford to slaughter them. The inklins on their yizzies are playing a deadlier game, they've nothing to lose. These feral children are a lit fuse; unless you can damp it, they'll force the Huvved to destroy everything you're trying to save."

"Huvved are crazy, doctori-yabass, are they that crazy? If they destroy us, they destroy themselves."

"Alapacsin three, read your notes. I have a cassette I want you to see. Some of you may remember the speaker, you can explain to the others later. Make notes if you wish, the segment is quite short."

I am KalaKallampak, a Morz of the Bahar. I have been here on Tairanna, a slave, for more than twelve years.

The Morz was sitting on his cot, his back against the wall, his heels dug into the thin mattress. As he talked, he was knitting, producing something shapeless, using the rhythmic swings of his hands to subdue the fury that knotted his jaw and set the veins throbbing at his temples. Yet when he spoke, his gravelly voice was mild, almost serene.

In the beginning my servitude weighed lightly on me. I was permitted to spend much time in the open ocean, when I studied the sea life and collected samples part of the day and part of the day I played, enjoying myself in water as fine as any I can remember.

He lowered his hands, bowed head and torso toward the lens.

For which I honor the Hordar who demand such

purity. I was content, though not happy; who can be happy forceably separated from those he loves? But it was endurable. Then the Fehdaz who bought me died and his successor was a fussy nervous little cretin who was distressed at the thought of property so valuable roaming about loose. I was forbidden the open sea and I started to suffer. Day by slow day I grew heavier with anger and physical pain. Until my days were dreary and my nights were worse and sleep was fickle and had to be courted. During those years when salt smell on the wind was all I had of the sea and a brine tub all that kept my body whole, I searched for a way to keep my mind more supple than my misfortunate body. The habit of decades gave me the answer, I am as much a scholar by temperament as I am a technician by training. I began watching gul Brindar; day and night I found ways to see what was happening to the city. I set the things I saw and heard into the many-leveled intricately nuanced watersong of my people, polishing the periods of my mindbook into a poetry of sound and sense, writing into my memory the recent history of Ayla gul Brindar.

Eyes closed, he scratched absently at his wrists, then fumbled at the wool; the veins at his temples pulsed visibly. After a moment he lifted the needles and began knitting again.

For three years I did this, then one day there was a moment when I was loose upon the cliffs of Brindar with no one near enough to stop me. I did not care if I lived or if I died. I jumped and fell a hundred yards into a clash of rocks and weed and incoming tide, survived and swam the three thousand miles to surface here. You ask me to tell you my mindbook. I will do that, though turning the tale into the airgroan of Hordaradda erases all its grace.

The Troubles have their seed in things done long before Bolodo brought me here. I cannot speak of them. This is what I saw myself. Five years ago the treatment of yoss fibers was introduced, a slave like me was given a task and did it and in the doing crumbled what was already cracking. Because yunk wool rotted in the depots waiting for a buyer, many and many a landbound Hordar was pushed off the Raz where his family had been generation on generation, back to the Landing Time. Where could they go? The Marginal Lands would not support them, there were many already claiming those. Young single men took their hunger to Littoral cities that glimmered with promise. Though that promise proved as illusory and fragile as soap bubbles, hungry families followed them. The cities began to bulge with dispossessed grasslanders. They took any work they could get so they could feed themselves and their children, took work from Little Familes; living was already precarious for the city poor; those not affiliated with Great Families were as hungry as the grasslanders who were not welcome or well treated.

He was rocking gently back and forth, like the sea rocking back and forth, his eyes were still closed, the needles clicked and clashed, the wood twitched and ran through his fingers.

The Duzzulkerin, what coin they had they were not about to waste on rent; in cities there are always and ever empty buildings. They lived in these until they were driven out, one family, two, ten, wherever there was an empty corner. Their unwilling landlords would call the city wards and evict them, but in a day or so, or a week, more families would come to take their places. And when these moved on, more again would come, until finally the landlords gave up trying to reclaim their property and began charging rent which sometimes they managed to collect.

Incivility increased. City fought Grassland with fists and worse. Hordar are not violent, they are much like my folk in that, but there is a limit beyond which you cannot push them, especially youngers unseasoned by age and learning, the unsteady youngers who, looking forward, see only a bleakness growing worse.

Incivility was bred in the bare and boring shelters that would never be homes, where Duzzulka youngers were left alone to pass the days however they could. It would not happen to the least and poorest of the Morze Bahar, I take pride in that; plenty and poverty are shared alike, Morz to Morz, and children are hard won, a joyful blessing. When KariniKarm bore my son and daughter, I swam with her and stayed with her to care for them until they could leave the water and walk upon the land, breathing the thick wet air into new soft lungs. A full year I stayed with her and them, leaving work, weaving joy into the wide communal song.

Schooling on this world is Family business; where the families cannot do it, the children are unschooled; when their parents work all day and half the night for a meager sum that barely keeps them fed and clothed, how are they to teach their children to read and write and figure? If they never learned themselves, how are they to teach? Grasslander youngers and city youngers alike, they are ignorant and unlettered, they are wasted. Is there no one who understands this? Is there no one out there who will find a cure for this obscenity?

He put the knitting down and rested fists on it, gazed grimly into the lens, his stare an accusation. When he spoke, the gravelly voice was hard with scorn.

Is it so strange, so unexpected that these so abandoned children melded in gangs and learned city ways in city streets? Is it so strange that they met there gangs of city poor, youngers who heard their elders cursing the grasslanders who stole their jobs, is it so strange they fought, these children of the streets? Is it so strange they learned to rage at landlords and city wards and most of all at the Huvved Fehz? Is it so strange for youngers looking at the struggles of their kin and the slow slipping of their elders' lives, is it so strange that they are filled with rage at everyone and everything, that they covet and seize what they cannot hope to earn, that they destroy what they cannot hope to seize? Is it so strange that these youngers call themselves inklins which means the unremembered, that they come to despise themselves as failures and worthless and turn that despite against the world?

He stopped talking, pressed his fingertips against his eyes. For over a minute he sat very still, his dark leathery skin twitching in several places. When he spoke he had put aside his agitation, his voice was mild again.

They are not stupid, these inklins, only unlearned; some are very clever indeed. It was an inklin who made the first yizzy. A boy in gul Inci, or sometimes the story says gul Brindar, or sometimes gul Samlikkan, a boy dreamed of flying, but lacked the guildfee for his training. So he stole yoss pods and bundled them in a bag net which also he stole and tied the net to a broomstick and strapped a minimotor (which, of course, he stole) to that stick. And he flew.

He leaned toward the lens, his face intent, his eyes glowing, as if he wanted to force his listeners to understand what he was saying.

The idea also flew. West to east, east to west, within the year inklins in all parts of the Littoral were building yizzies for themselves. Within two years inklin gangs were having skyfights; at first they used sticks to bang away at each other, then they made spears, then another clever inklin, some say it was a girl tired of getting banged about, discovered how to spray fire from a hose. The gas inside yoss pods is hydrogen, remember. There were mornings when the city was full of charred flesh and the screams of the not quite dead.

Even before I left, it was not only inklin flesh that burned. Sometimes the yizzy inklins drop fire on Houses and factories and when they feel like it, on the Fekkris; a Huvved in the street after dark is a target whenever inklins fly. The Fehdaz sends slaves to clean up when the mess is really bad and he does not want the extent of it to make the whisper circuit.

Incivility increases. The cities are burning bit by bit.

What the inklins do not destroy the Huvved will; already they see poor folk as sharks circling them ready to attack, the time will come when they see every Hordar poor or not as enemy, when the only easing of their terror will come when there's no one left for them to fear. I see the time coming when the Warmaster will glide from city to city melting cities into bedrock slag.

I am uncomfortable here away from the ocean. I go to the Sea Farms; if they are fortunate, they will survive the Burning. Should the Huvved go entirely mad, they can scatter their barges and wait out the storm. May the data flow freely for you, Aslan A-tow-a-she, may your days be filled with meaning.

"Does this answer that question of yours, Hayal Halak?"

"I knew all that, doctori-yabass."

"If you knew, why did you ask?"

"You sound very serious today, doctori-yabass."

"Boring, you mean."

"Oh no, we'd never say that. Go on, tell us more. That was, not boring, no, depressing. Tell us something positive. Tell us about the rebels that win, doctori-yabass."

"I'm going to be boring again, and depressing, but listen to me anyway. The rebels that pull it off, they've done the easiest part. War simplifies things, choices are stark. After the war's over, well, life gets at them, chews them down. People don't change, not really. There are no instant angels. Ideology is for arguing about in bars, it's hopeless as a guide for government. Right thinking just does not do it, backsliding seems to be a necessary condition for intelligence. If the rebels who survive and are running things haven't allowed for that, there's fury and frustration and repression and things end up the way they were before, or worse."

"And if they allow for frailty, doctori-yabass?"

"With a little luck and a lot of good will, they go on, sometimes things get better, sometimes worse."

"Worse for whom, doctori-yabass?"

"That's the question, isn't it?"

"A question you have not answered, doctori-yabass."

"A question I don't have to answer. A question I can't answer. It's all yours, young Hordar."

As she went through her ordinary round, she chewed over what the ears told her and tried to decide what she wanted to do. She had a choice. She could stay here and be quite comfortable; she could pretend she didn't know what was happening, she could teach her seminars, act as consultant to the Council, flake everything that happened as a record of a rebellion in progress, an opportunity few of her colleagues had had. It was the sensible thing to do, wasn't it? It was adolescent claptrap, this sense that she would be somehow debased if she let the Hordar and Elmas Ofka hold her hostage, trick her mother. Four days. It wasn't much time. Four days to get ready to be at that meeting. Or not. That night, she talked with Churri and Xalloor, her mind still unsettled, her inclination to go not much stronger than her inclination to stay.

4

Churri rested his head in Xalloor's lap, crossed his legs at the ankle. "Trouble, yah," he said. "Won't last. If you go, Council isn't going to tell anyone what you did, it'd make them look bad. Incompetent. No polit's going to let that idea get around if he can help it."

Chilled by a touch of the ashgrays, Aslan watched the fire crawl over the coals and fought to keep her pride intact. Xalloor's decision to stay behind with Churri left her feeling very alone and more than a little let down. After a minute she said, "Wouldn't stop them dropping you and Xalloor down a hole and pushing a ton of rock on you."

Xalloor tweaked Churri's nose, laughed as he mumbled a lazy protest. "Skinhead sweetie, he get busy, make a pome, spin 'em dizzy. Dearie dai, oh yes, you the poet all right, not me, so stir it, luv, chant them a ditty to milk tears from a stone, Aslan's Mum's search for her daughter through a thousand dangers with Bolodo's Hounds sniffing at her heels, make their hearts swell with pride at the vision of Elmas Ofka reuniting Aslan and Adelaar, make those words roll, make 'em roll, roll . . . ow!" She slapped at the hand that had pinched her buttock. "Do that again and I tickle you till your bones crawl out, eh!"

He chuckled. "Going local, eh? Eh!"

" 'Twasn't a local give me the habit. Lan, are you going?"

"I suppose I am."

"Well, how?"

"I've been so busy making up my mind, I haven't thought about that. Take a boat, I suppose."

Churri sat up. "No. I've got a better idea. You don't want Elmas or her shadows to spot the boat and put you down before you've said your piece. Some of the locals have been coming in on yizzies. The vips here stow them at the depot, in one of the little rooms. It's locked, but blow on the lock and it'll fall apart for you."

"Not me. I haven't had your education."

"Hmm. It's a sorry lack and one you should be curing. I'll come along and tickle her open."

"Thanks. I think."

"And don't be worrying about the yizzy. You can manage a miniskip, University wouldn't let you leave home not knowing. A yizzy's cruder and crankier and slower, same thing, though."

"Same thing, hah!"

"Negative thinking, Lanny; didn't your Mum teach you to view the bright side?"

"I repeat, hah! I notice you're not volunteering to plant your rear on a shimmy stick for god knows how many hours."

"Nuh, I've too much sense in here," he tapped his temple, "to plant this," he slapped at the side of his buttock, "in misery I can miss without the least little dent in my self-esteem."

5

She left in a rosy sunset, clouds piled on clouds feinting at storm but not yet ready to follow through.

The twitchy wind was heavy with the smell of rain. Because she didn't trust her touch with the controls— and wanted to avoid being spotted by lookouts on the ground, she flew low, her feet occasionally whipping through the tops of trees as the yizzy went crank and dipped instead of rising. It was not difficult to fly, just rather unexpected at times, and not as uncomfortable as she'd feared; whoever had put together this one was good with his (or her) hands. There was a carved and padded saddle with stirrups on adjustable straps; there were handlebars of a sort with motor controls on the grips. It was nicely balanced; the yoss pods in the net over her head were attached fore-and-aft to the riding pole, their center movable to compensate for different rider weights. The motor was light and efficient and small even with the L-shaped fuel tank partly on top of it, partly before it, strapped to the pole; large rotors, hand-carved but very sophisticated; a tinkerer's dream this gadget.

After half an hour of tree hopping she began coaxing the yizzy higher. The forest was a dark nubbly fleece collected over the lower slopes of precipitous mountains, the river a silver thread reduced to half its width by overhanging foliage. Somewhere under there at the Minetown (also invaded and obliterated by those trees), Elmas Ofka and her isyas would be getting ready to sail, though they wouldn't be starting for at least two hours. Ahead she could see the small deep harbor, the chop evident even this far off, the surf edge a startling white against the dark wet sand.

The wind began to steady and strengthen, a scatter of heavy rain drops hit her and the pods. The yizzy shuddered and bucked under her; she swore and used her weight to steady it.

For the next three hours the yizzy was a torture machine, the wind and the pole beat at her, the rain blinded and half-drowned her. The yizzy wasn't meant for weather like this; she knew when she started that she might be going into a storm, though she didn't, couldn't know just how terrifying the flight was going to be, but if she didn't go now, there was no point in leaving and she had no intention of waiting for Elmas

Ofka or the Council to hand her over; she despised such passive dependency; even contemplating it hurt her in her pride; besides, she didn't trust them a whole lot.

By the time she was near enough to see the chain of rocky islets, she was exhausted, but she'd also left the worst of the storm behind.

She edged closer to the water, swung cautiously wide of the largest of those islets, the barren jumble of rock called Gerbek. The yizzy was slower than the boats Elmas Ofka and the others were coming in; the battering of the storm had slowed it even more. Her hands were gloved, she couldn't see her chron, she had no idea how much time she'd spent in the crossing. When she left the Mines, she was at least two hours ahead of the others; right now she hadn't a guess now how much of that playway was left.

In the northeast where only the fringes of the prevailing winds brushed by, there was a shallow inlet like a bite taken out of a flatroll; it was the only anchorage the islet had and it was still empty, so she knew she'd got there first. At least, before Elmas Ofka. She wasn't sure about the Outsiders, she hadn't seen anyone, but the center of the islet was a jumble of rock and ravine, half an army could be hiding in the cracks. At one focus of Gerbek's eccentric ellipse, there was a peak like a miniature mountain, at the other a flat space cleared of rubble and ringed by tall sarsens where Ishigi Pradites came to celebrate the equinoxes. She didn't know much about the Ishigi, they were a heretical sect subject to some stringent penalties when discovered; the little she'd unearthed about them said they'd withered to nothing a century before, but she wondered now when she saw that cleared stone. No bird droppings inside the ring. She laughed at herself. Lan, were you tied to a spit over a roaring fire, you'd speculate about the mating habits of the gits about to eat you. In any case, it was the only area where a skip could land, so the Outsiders hadn't arrived yet either. She didn't know whether she was happy about that or not. If her mother wasn't with them. . . .

She brought the yizzy lower and moved over the

island; as soon as the little mountain broke the push of the wind, she went lower still until the rotors were laboring to hold the pole a meter above the stone. She wobbled around the circumference of the flat, looking for a place to anchor, a place where she could hide until she was ready for the confrontation. Nothing, nothing, nothing . . . there were dozens of cracks big enough for her, nothing big enough and deep enough to hold the yizzy.

In the end she anchored it in a windcarved hollow low on the flank of the mini-mount and spent almost an hour getting back to the flat, crawling over rocks and scree, terrified of breaking something, a leg, an ankle, her head. She had to feel her way, there was almost no light; the clouds were thick and black, Gorruya was up alone for another hour and she was only a slightly obese crescent.

As she reached the waste rock near the sarsen ring, voices came to her, broken by the wind; she caught her lower lip between her teeth and crept on until she came to a place where several of the sarsens had been quarried; there were piles of debris around the hole and down in it three cracked stones leaning against its side, a litter of stone shards piled on the holefloor. She lowered herself carefully onto the knife-edged rubble, then crept into the velvet black shadow beneath the leaners and pulled her black cloak tight about her.

The voices were louder; she began picking up some words, enough to know Elmas Ofka was sending Harli Tanggàr out to a pile of stones where she could get a clear shot at the flat with her crossbow, placing others on guard beside the sarsens. The crossbow worried Aslan. If she knew it was me, Harli Tanggàr wouldn't shoot, but the light's so bad she'd have no idea who she was killing. Aslan bit her tongue to choke back a half-hysterical giggle. Poor baby, she thought, she'd be awfully sorry. Not half as sorry as me.

The islet settled back to silence except for the whistle and groan of the wind and occasional loud clacks as bits of stone lost balance and went bounding down slopes of scree. The damp cold crept through the layered wool she wore, struck to the bone. She shivered, locked her jaw to keep her teeth from chattering. And began to wonder if she'd last until the Outsiders arrived.

She heard a buzzing like gnat noise. It was so faint that at first she thought it was something the wind was doing. Then it got louder. She eased her head out and looked up. A skip. Coming in from the west.

Holding her cloak close to her so there'd be no flicker of motion to catch Harli Tanggàr's eye, she climbed from the hole and stretched out on the rubble so she could see what was happening.

The skip hovered a moment, then dropped. It landed at one side of the cleared circle and a large form swung down, followed by a smaller. Once again Aslan closed her teeth on her abused lower lip, fighting back a surge of very mixed emotion. The second figure was a shadowy blob, undetailed, but she knew that way of moving, the high-headed arrogant strut. "Allo, Mama," she whispered.

Voices. A man's, deep and pleasant; it didn't carry well and she couldn't understand what he was saying. Her mother wasn't saying anything yet. Elmas Ofka listened. "Do it," she said.

The next minutes were busy ones. Half a dozen small squat remotes hummed from the skip. Three carried a bundle larger than all three of them, a bale of heavy cloth from which Gorruya teased occasional gleams like flows of liquid silver. The other three scurried about exploding pitons into the stone floor of the circle. Before Aslan sniffed three times, the bundle expanded into a large domed shelter anchored by the pitons. She watched with envy as Elmas Ofka waved her guarding isyas inside and shouted Harli Tanggàr down from her post. That solved that problem, she thought; she watched Harli disappear behind the dome. Let them get settled, she thought. She pulled the hood closer about her face, pinched it shut over her mouth and nose, started to straighten up.

6

She looked up into her mother's face. "Allo, Mama."

"So what's all this about? Sneaking around." Adelaar touched her cheek briefly. "For a stodgy professor-type, you get yourself into more trouble. . . ."

"I-told-you-so, Mama?"

"If you stopped falling on your face, I could stop having to pick you up."

"Ooh-yeha. Like it was all my fault this happened." Aslan sat up, clutched at her head. Stunned, she thought, understanding finally what had happened to her. Her mind wasn't working all that well right now. Behind her mother she could see a tall dark man with a lazy twinkle in eyes so pale they might have been borrowed from another face, and beside him, Elmas Ofka looking grim. Aslan managed a tight smile. "Sorry, Dalliss, someone spoiled your suprise."

Elmas Ofka blinked, but took the cue smoothly. "Waiting upwind was not the brightest thing we've done. One of our visitors has what one might call a nose for news."

Adelaar's mouth twisted into a half-smile; she wound a curl of Aslan's hair about her finger and tugged it, hard, but she said nothing. She gave her daughter's head a last pat, then forgot about her and marched over to the memplas table growing like a mushroom in the center of the chamber.

The shelter was large enough to hold them all with plenty of room left for moving about. Whoever'd brought Aslan in had laid her on a memplas bench close to the valve. The isyas were standing or sitting, their backs to the shallow curve of the wall; Lirrit and Harli glanced once at her then ignored her, the other isyas weren't interested, they lived in gul Inci or at the Indiz Farm and there was a lot they didn't know about events at the Mines. As the tall man and Elmas Ofka moved to join Adelaar at the table, Aslan saw for the first time the other member of the group, the Aurranger Rau. Elmas Ofka had mentioned the Rau in her report to the Council, so Aslan knew he was about and she knew who he had to be, there were NO other

Aurrangers offplanet; she hadn't actually met him while he was at University, but she'd heard stories. She was startled at the strength of her reaction to him, she wanted to pick him up, cuddle him, smooth her hands over and over that velvety fur; more than that, she felt intensely protective, if one of the isyas attacked him she realized with a great deal of surprise that she'd go after the woman tooth and claw. Amazing, she thought. With Pels kurk-Orso to prod her memory, she realized who the light-eyed man was. Swardheld Quale. Mama must have hired him, she thought, Ooo-yeha, she has to 've spent a fortune and a half. If ever Luck shat upon me, she did now. I'm going to hear about this for the next fifty years, if we don't strangle each other before then.

At the table Adelaar toed up a chair, got herself settled, then she took a bundle of fac sheets from a case, squared them and set them in front of her. "The suspect files," she said, "and the report on the internal security at the Palace that Quale saw fit to donate." There was an astringent acerbity in the last statement. Qual chuckled, but didn't bother to answer the challenge. She lifted out a flake-reader, then a case of filled flakes. "We discussed this and found it simpler to let you and your technicians do whatever marrying is necessary to make further copies of this material. The reader is included as another little gift from our generous friend here. The first twenty flakes contain the stats on the Warmaster and her . . . well, you can't really call them a crew, the people living on board her. The twenty-first—they're all numbered, using your system, of course, so you won't have any trouble identifying what's which—the twenty-first has the data on the free corridors. You'll wish to inspect the flakes; don't worry about inadvertently erasing them, they've been impressed. Loading's simple, just slide the flake skin-and-all into the slot there, then watch the screen. You can manually jump about, there's a pencil attached, write the number you want on that sensor there. Again, use your own system, the player has been adjusted to respond to it. If you want automatic random access, touch the pencil here. That'll jump you about so you can get a fair idea what's on the flake. If you have any questions, I'll be happy to answer them. You have something for us?"

Elmas Ofka nodded. "Har cousin," she said. Harli Tanggàr marched to the table and set a large pouch in the middle. Without comment she went back to her post beside the valve. Elmas tugged open the mouth, took out a swatch of black velvet and a small metallic object which she unfolded into a balance scale and a pair of calipers. Then she withdrew several smaller pouches, opened one and let the pearls spill onto the velvet.

The exchange was quick and wordless and the two women began a meticulous examination of what each acquired from the other.

Quale left them to it and strolled over to Aslan. "Be interesting to know just who the surprise was for," he murmured. He had a pleasant baritone, well, rather more than pleasant; for the first time in months Aslan remembered how long it was since she'd had sex with a man who excited her rather than scaring her rigid. What she'd had with Parnalee wasn't sex or pleasure, it was a propitiation of the gods of chaos. And even that was, what? two years ago? He had nice hands, long fingers, they ruffed through his beard. It was crisp and short, a few white and gray hairs in the black, just enough to make him look distinguished. She wanted to smooth her fingertips over it, to. . . .

She put the brakes on her imagination. "More tactful not to ask," she said. "Not now, anyway."

He dropped beside her. "When we found out you jumped the wall, Del was wondering if we'd have to winnow the whole population to find you."

"Things were getting a bit . . . um . . . hectic, so I left."

"Saved us a lot of time and trouble, you turning up like this."

"Pride. And self-defense. Mama's memory is her biggest asset unless you're on the wrong end of it."

He chuckled. "'Having spent more'n half a year insplitting with her on board, I know what you mean. She's a marvel when she's working, though."

"Swardheld Quale," she said. "Pay his price and he gets things done. You're a bit of a marvel yourself, if the stories are one-tenth true."

"I'd put the truth level in those things considerably lower than a tenth. Say something like one part in ten thousand. Maybe they get the name of a place right, the rest is . . . you're an ethnologist, you know how that goes."

"Well, some heroes turn out to be a bit more than hot air."

His right brow quirked up, the scar that nipped its outer end bent outward with the movement. "Nothing to do with me."

"According to Elmas Ofka, you're collecting slaves and taking them back."

"Uh huh."

"How many?"

"Depends on who we can locate?"

"You're looking for specific people?"

"We've got a list of names we've matched up with names from the mainBrain. Rewards, aici Adlaar, rewards; when we get them back to Helvetia, my crew and me, we collect some hefty gelt." He rubbed at his jawline. "Couldn't take 'em all even if I wanted to."

"I have some people I'd like included in your collection. They might not be on that list, but if what I heard about your fee-structure is reasonably correct, what Adelaar's paying you for this means you can tuck in a couple of extras without straining yourself."

"Getting a little hostile, aren't you?"

"I like to think of it as being practical." Damn, damn, damn, knee-jerk, foot-in-the-mouth, what am I doing? Shoving him in a bag with Mama's shithead friends. Maybe he belongs there. I don't know. I don't know. I'm reacting like an adolescent. Brain damage? Or are stunners aphrodisiac?

"Quale."

He got to his feet with a loose, easy shift of his long body that reminded her of Xalloor, the same sort of physical competence. He strolled to the table, toed up a chair and sat.

Elmas Ofka frowned at him. For a moment she

didn't say anything. She has too much riding on this, Aslan thought and felt a touch of sympathy for the woman, a sympathy she didn't usually have, Elmas reminded her too much of her mother. "You've had a week to look these over," she tapped the case of filled flakes. "Well?"

"Price is right, conditions aren't too tough, far as I'm concerned, we can go."

"When?"

"Thirty days."

Elmas Ofka looked down at her hands, drew a deep breath. "Done," she said. "How many can you lift?"

"Around seventy, eighty in a pinch. Should be enough for that lot." He nodded at the case. "Something else, you'll need to find someone who's been up there recently, I suggest one of those Fiveworld guards; he'll know things no one bothers to record."

"Yes. We have acquired such a person and he's being questioned." She broke off, looked away from him. Aslan thought, this next is going to be important. She's not sure of him, she could be a little afraid of him, which is something I never thought I'd see. "The Warmaster must be destroyed," she said, "You agree to that?"

"Why not. I don't want it."

She relaxed. "Your reasons?"

"Impossible to handle without a huge crew, I couldn't afford the fuel, I'd have my sleep wrecked by the horde of would-be heroes plotting to take it away from me."

"I see. You understand *my* reasons?"

"Simple enough. As soon as Slancy berths at Helvetia, Horgul's on the map. People will be heading here to take back their relatives, whatever, to trade, raid, generally poke about. The Warmaster's a target that'd tempt too many of them. You'd have some self-proclaimed Emperor running your world before you blinked twice."

"What about her stingships?"

"They're parasited on her. Once you get rid of her, they go inert. If you're worried about the crews, you can use your systemships to pull them out."

"One last question. How do we destroy something that big and that powerful?"

"As I see it, you've got two options. You can sink her in the deepest part of one of your oceans. That's the quickest method. Leave some ports open and she'll die fast. Only thing is, there's a fair chance in a few years you'll have a pollution problem; it'll clear up in a century or two, but you'd better make sure you keep people away from the place until then."

"No!" The word exploded out of her. "Not the ocean. Never." She drew her hand across her mouth, a quick nervous gesture, straightened her back with a jerk and stared at him, almost daring him to come out with something equally impossible.

"So, send her into the sun."

She thought that over. "How? Wouldn't someone have to stay with her? Only two minutes ago I read that the shipBrain is programmed to save her if all aboard are killed; if you aim her at the sun and leave her, she'll break away before she reaches it. And what happens then, do we have a runaway killing machine hitting back at the ones that tried to kill her?"

"Adelaar? That's your field."

Adelaar ran a hand over her hair, smoothing it down where the wind outside the shelter had teased it into spikes. "While I was inside the interface, I set a trap into the groundlink; it hasn't been found and it won't be. Since then I've been using odd moments to explore the shipBrain through it. That Brain is big, it's powerful, and oh my, it's dumb. It's old. We've learned considerable since that ship was built. Some of us. I kept away from the defense areas, but I don't expect trouble when I go after them, though I'd rather handle that up there. Working through a tap is too . . . um . . . limiting. As soon as we lift off . . . hmm, that's something we haven't arranged yet, Hanifa. Where do you want us to pick up you and your people? I think it's best we come to you, rather than you to us. It'll be easier and faster."

Aslan looked from her mother's intent face to Elmas Ofka; one expression mirrored the other; it was like a glimpse into the future, maybe a year or two after this night. Read the changes, where the world goes when the Outside wanders in.

"I can't say without knowing a lot more about who's coming and what the Council thinks. Perhaps you could supply some way of communicating that the Huvved couldn't tap into? If so, we can settle arrangements without having to find time for another meeting."

Quale tapped on the table. Both women started, swung round to face him. "I've got some handcoms in the skip," he said, "they're linked to the satellites I inserted when we got here, should have no trouble bridging the distance between our Base and yours." He turned his head. "Pels, bring in a couple of those handsets, will you?"

"Wait," Elmas Ofka said.

"Hang on a minute, Pels, huh?"

"When we talked before, you needed to know where to find locations inside cities. I didn't forget that, I brought you a small gift," she glanced past him, met Aslan's ironic gaze, "another small gift to help you with that problem. Har cousin, take the Hunter down to the boats and bring back our passenger."

Aslan watched the chunky isya valve out after Pels. What's going on here, she thought, there wasn't anything about this in the report she made or in any of the hours of records I plowed through. She rubbed at her eyes, remembering with regret the watersac she'd left hanging on the yizzy pole. Her mouth was dry and she was wrung out, sleepy, her head ached. She wasn't interested in these games Adelaar and Elmas were playing with each other, she'd left home years ago to get the smell of greed off her skin. She gazed at the back of Quale's head; his hair brushed his collar, black, soft, fine, curling a little; she wanted to touch it, let it bend over her fingers. Damn, oh damn.

The valve hummed. Pels came in; his black lips were curled into an odd grin, his ears were standing straight up and twitching a little. He was humming, she could hear a rumbling brumbrum as he trotted to the table, dumped the comsets onto the memplas and swung around to watch the exit.

Harli Tanggàr ducked through, stepped to her place

beside the valve as the man following her straightened and looked around.

Parnalee, Aslan thought, good god, what's she think she's doing? How'd she get hold of him?

"Parnalee Tanmairo Proggerd," Elmas Ofka said. "In the course of his work, he has visited most of the cities of the Littorals. When he joined us two days ago, I saw him as the answer to your need."

Maybe, Aslan thought, but that's not the whole story. What are you up to, Dalliss? Smiling, urbane, wearing his public face, Parnalee walked to the table, touched hands with Quale. He wants this, she thought, why? He looked over his shoulder at her and she saw the beast in his black eyes, hungry beast promising her silently what he'd promised in words. *Undercut me and you're dead.* She shivered and made up her mind she was going to be very very sure she was never alone with him any time anywhere.

Quale got to his feet. "That's it, then. Call us when you're ready, Hanifa. You want to leave first, or shall we?"

Elmas Ofka closed the lid on the case, snapped the latches home. "We'll go. Don't get yourself killed."

X

1

About ten days after the meeting on Gerbek. Karrel Goza in Ayla gul Inci: Waiting for the Lift-Off

Karrel Goza forked slimy rotten leaves from the second stage vat into a tiltcart. The stench that eddied around him crept through his stained overall and nestled against his skin, oozed through the overage filter on his mask. The stink was the least of his problems, the mist that stank would open ulcers in his skin and rot his lungs if he stayed in it long enough. The Huvved Kabrik who owned this shed had the patronage of the Fehdaz and the manager was under orders to squeeze the last thread of use from the gear. And more, if he could get away with it. The manager before him had been fired for being too easy on the workers; she was local, some of her employees were cousins and affiliates, others belonged to the Families of friends and associates. Herk's crony didn't make that mistake twice. The new manager came from a Guneywhiyker Daz, he had no family in Inci, no pressures on him to look to the safety of the workers. Karrel Goza didn't bother complaining; it wouldn't do any good and there were a hundred more desperate and thus more docile workers to take his place. He had too many small accidents, had called in sick too often in his need to cover absences when he was flying for Elmas Ofka, he was growing more marginal a worker as the weeks passed, a complaint was all the manager needed to boot him out. His Family was one of the poorer septs, small business folk living on the edge of failing, clerks and such; they needed twice what their earners were pulling in to pay the fees and taxes and all that Herk was squeezing from folk like them. A few years ago his pilot's pay tithed had brought them comfort and a degree of security they'd seldom known. He'd sponsored and paid Guildbond (Pilot) for his cousin Geres Duvvar, he'd sponsored and paid Guildbond (Skilled Trades) for three score other cousins, sisters, brothers, affiliates. That was finished now.

Drive, talent and a large dose of luck gave him a chance at a profession not usually open to boys from his class. Bondfees in the Pilot's Guild were far too great for a Family with the income his had; even stretching they couldn't afford such an expense, nor could they afford to tie up so much coin so long in a single member. When he was a middler near the end of his schooling, he earned his first coin flying soarwings on the Garrip sands in the semiformal races sponsored by a coalition of merchants and Sea Farmers. The purses were big, the entry fees small; he and an uncle who was a carpenter built his wingframe and an aunt who was a weaver made the fabric cover. He'd found his talent the moment he got his first kite up and when he was old enough to enter the races he made it pay. Time after time he won. There was danger in this racing; fliers crashed—misread aircurrents, were crowded offlift, showed bad judgment in their turns or were victims of sabotage. Men and women came from a dozen Dazzes to watch and wager on the fliers, there was a great deal of money floating about and the temptation to goose the odds was strong and seldom resisted. Orska Falyan of Sirgûn-Falyan was a devotee of those contests; he began betting on the agile boy who seemed to feel the air with every sweaty inch of naked skin, who slid again and again from traps meant to break him; he was elated when the boy continued to win, sometimes by huge leads. The old man more or less adopted Karrel Goza; he sponsored him to the Pilot's Guild, paid his Guildbond, and when he gained his pilot's rating, hired him on at Sirgûn Bol. Orska Falyan continued to take an interest in Karrel Goza, had him teach some Sirgûn and Falyan youngers how to soar, left the boy a small legacy when he died ten years later.

Karrel Goza finished filling the cart, wishing as he'd wished so many times before that the slave techs would finally come up with a machine capable of that noxious work; the fibers were tough, slippery, treacherous and finer than a woman's hair; every mechanical forker they'd tried jammed after an hour or two. It took a man's dexterity to manage the transfer. He kicked the gong to let the handler know and the cart purred off, a new one clanking into its place. Around him other forkers were working with steady minimal swings; another gong clanged, and a third after a silence so short that it seemed more like an echo than a sound in itself.

He coughed, felt a burning in his throat and lungs. The fumes from the vat were beginning to get to him. He looked around. The overseer was out of the room. That figured. The lazy bastard spent most of the day in his office, a glass-walled room raised fifty meters off the floor. He could sit in comfort and watch the forkers sweat. Karrel coughed again, cursed under his breath and climbed off the platform. There was a naked faucet waist-high on the wall near the only door. He turned the faucet on full so the water beat into the catch basin. Holding his breath, he slipped the mask off and slid the filterpack from its slot. He looked at the discolorations on both surfaces, swore again; he held the pack in the stream of water until some of the overload was soaked out of it. That only took care of the grosser particles, the absorption of the wad was a joke; he shook it, wondering what he was putting into his lungs. He swished it back and forth in the water, shook it again and clicked it home. The wetting was weakening it, he could see pulls and a small rip. He'd been asking for a replacement for three weeks now. Oversoul alone knew when he'd get it. Likely he'd have to buy a pack on the black market. If he could find one. Elli might be able to do it for him, get a filter from her Family. He splashed water on his face, coughed again, felt like he was trying to rip the lining from his throat. He pulled the mask back on; as bad as it was, breathing that miasma over the vats without any protection at all was a thousand times worse. He went back to work. Not much longer, he told himself. Hang on, Kar; twenty days. Twenty days and Elli will get her chance at Herk. Ah, to see him dangling head down in that vat.

2

"What?" Karrel Goza set his cup down, blinked wearily at his Ommar.

The Parlor was small and by intention intimate; the wallposts, the ceiling and its beams were carved and painted in jewel colors, small angular flower patterns on an angular emerald ground; a fire crackled cheerfully behind a semi-transparent shell guard; ancient tapestries hung from ceiling to floor, colors muted by time, still dark and rich. The Ommar sat in a plump chair, its ancient leather dyed a deep scarlet and mottled by decades of saddlesoap and elbowgrease, its arms and ornaments and swooping clawfooted legs carved from a brown wood age-darkened to almost-black. She was a small woman with a halo of fine white hair about a face dominated by huge black eyes, ageless eyes. She wore a simple white blouse, an old black skirt smoothed neatly about her short legs, legs too large for her size. She'd been a diver before she married into the Goza family, not one of the premiere Dallisses though she shared their arrogance; even now he could see the merm marks on the backs of her hands. She sniffed impatiently, repeated what she'd said.

"Youngers and middlers from Goza House have been running with the inklins. Gensi, Kivin, Kaynas, it's an isya, I think, one just forming with Gensi as the Pole. Zaraiz, Bulun and half a dozen boys, they call themselves . . ." her weary wrinkled face lifted suddenly, lighted by the grin that made him and everyone else adore her when they weren't afraid of her, "the Green Slimes, or something like that. They were in that hoohaw last night, dropping sludge bombs on the guard barracks. At least it wasn't fire, they haven't gone that far, both sets, it's mischief still, but the inklins they're mixing with aren't playing, Kar. Nor are the bitbits. Streetgangs, tchah! what nonsense. You weren't like that, much more sensible."

Karrel Goza thought about a few of his exploits when he was a younger (which he fervently hoped she'd never find out about) and didn't think he'd been all that sensible. He wasn't too old to remember the feeling that he and his agemates were alone against a stodgy disapproving world, how they built up a powerful secret world of their own that no adult had access to. He couldn't see this crop of pre-adults welcoming interference, but the world was infinitely more dangerous these days and the Ommar was right. Something had to be done. "Yizzies? Homemade or borrowed or what?"

"Gensi boasted she made her own; I suppose they all did, which means they've been stealing, there's no other way they could have got the materials, you know very well no adult in this family has coin to throw away on idiocy like that."

"Where are they keeping them?"

"Not in the House. I'd have the obscenities smashed if I could lay my hands on them."

"The boys, do you know which is the leader?"

"Zaraiz Memeli, as much as any. That clutch of shoks, it's not even an imitation isya and as for being a gang, tchah!" She leaned forward, urgent and more upset than he could remember seeing her, her tangled white brows squeezing against the deep cleft between them. "I am afraid of them, Kar. I know their faces, but not what they're thinking, if they're thinking at all; I look into those shallow animal eyes and I wonder if there's anything but animal behind them." She straightened her back. "In any case, they have to be stopped. Bad enough to have those street-sweepings making trouble. Tchah! Do you know what Herkken Daz will do to us if Sech Gorak finds one of our boys dead on the street or shoots one of them out of the sky? Goza House will be translated to Tassalga brick by brick. What's left of it. I'm talking to you, do you know why? Because everyone here knows what you're doing and I have this faint hope the boys will listen to you. If they don't, I don't know what to do. The girls . . ." she brushed a hand across her eyes, "the girls, ahh! Kar, they look at me . . . animal eyes, nothing there. I thought I knew girls, I don't know these. Talk to them, Kar. If you think it would help, can you get that Indiz Dalliss to see them? You know who I mean."

He sipped at the tea to cover his hesitation. After a minute, he said, "That might be difficult. The Huvved put a price on her head and the Jerk has doubled it."

"Try." Her voice was iron, her eyes pinned him.

"This is not a good time," he said, "she won't come."

"What use are you Kar, if you can't do this small thing for your Family? What do I say to your mother? We have protected him and lied for him, covered his shivery ass, and when we ask a small, a minute thing for us, his Family, what does he say? I can't, he says."

"Let it lay, Ommar. Please." His hand shook, tea splashed onto his knees.

"Why should I? What is more important that the moral discipline of your sisters, your nieces, your cousins?"

"I can't tell you that. Please. I can't."

She relaxed, her back curving into the cushions. "I see. How long will you need cover this time?"

"I don't know, maybe four, five days."

"When?"

"When I'm called. I can't say more."

"Hmm. It will be better if we prepare for this." She smiled, no glow to her this time, just a tight bitter twist of the lips. "You've been doing too much, Kar. You look like a walking ghost; no one will be surprised if you go down seriously sick. If I pull in some markers, I can set your cousin Tamshan in your place, so we don't lose the earnings."

"Gorak watches all pilots; we don't want that; the job takes me off his list."

"As long as you're supposed to be coughing your lungs out, he won't bother his head over you."

"If he believes it."

"You think he's going to push his way in here and time your spasms?"

"If he wants to, he will." He rubbed at his eyes; he'd been noticing a haze-effect for several weeks. Eyes, lungs, his whole body was breaking down. He was averaging four hours' sleep a night. It was weeks since he'd had any appetite, he hadn't seen Lirrit for . . . how long? Gray day melted into gray day. He didn't know how long. Too long. He hadn't even thought about her for days. He closed his eyes, shivered as he realized he couldn't bring her face to mind. No time for thinking, less for contemplating marriage; he and Lirrit would wed when times were easier, but in the miasma of weariness, fear, horror that usurped his day and dreamtime lately, it was impossible even to dream of such things. Maybe it was just as well he got out, he was running on autopilot, abdicating his responsibility to himself, depending on Elmas Ofka for direction and impetus. Some time to himself . . . he savored the thought, then put it aside. It wouldn't happen this month or the next; there was too much to do. After then? Who knew, not he. "Zaraiz," he said. "I don't know him. How old is he? You told me his line name, but I don't remember it."

"Memeli. He's a first year middler, no discipline, he's insolent, a bad influence on everyone." She slapped her hands on the chair arms. "Memeli, tchah! Had I been Ommar that generation, we wouldn't have the problem, we never would have affiliated that collection of losers."

Karrel Goza lowered his eyes, played with his cup. The intolerance of a Dalliss, her inability to see worth in folk who didn't conform to her personal standards, it was the ugly side of their Ommar. He tilted the cup, gazed at the rocking tawny fluid as if he saw Elmas Ofka's face there; that intolerance, that ignorance, that inflexibility were her faults too, they'd bothered him from the first. He'd forgotten that . . . no, not forgotten, he'd stopped thinking. With the end so close, yes, take the time, yes, go back to thinking, yes, be there to stand against her when the need arises, yes. . . . Hands heavy with weariness, he rubbed the crackling from his eyes. "All right," he said, "I'll talk with the boy. Maybe it'll do some good." He coughed, gulped down a mouthful of the lukewarm tea. "In the morning," he said, "locate Zaraiz Memeli for me; don't bother him, just let me know where he is, I'll collect him myself."

"I will do that, yes." She lifted the teapot, beckoned him over and refilled his cup with the aromatic liquid; she had expensive taste in teas and indulged it more than she should in times like this; sitting here, savoring the flavor, he resented it, his sweat and pain bought her these luxuries and she took them as her right when there were children of the House—not Goza, no, but of the House as much as any Goza child—who needed food, clothing, medicine. This can't keep on, he thought, it has to change, we've got to make it change. He thought of the teacher at the Mines and what she'd been telling her students; it was not happy hearing; we'll be different, he told himself, we'll make this work. When he was seated again, she said, "Ommars tell me that slaves are disappearing, not one or two but whole chains of them."

"Oh?"

"Is that all you're going to say?"

"Yes."

The Ommar leaned forward again, her eyes fixed on him, trying to get past the face he presented to her. After a minute she sucked at her teeth, shook her head. "This can't go on," she said.

He looked up, startled by the echo of what he'd been thinking; then he realized that she meant something far different.

"Inci is better off than most from what I hear, but give her another few months and she'll be burning down around us. Before Herk lets that happen, he'll call on the stingers and blast those lunatic children out of the air and he won't care what else he levels. I'm telling you, Kar, you tell her and the rest of them. Do something. If her lot won't or can't, then we crawl to Herk and lick his toes. We've got no time left for playing hero games."

He got heavily to his feet; it was more difficult than

he'd expected. The comfort of that chair, the warmth of the room, the soothing fragrance of the chamwood burning on the hearth, these things were like chains on his arms and legs. At the door he turned. "I will pass your message on, Hanifa Ommar, but I will say this, though I probably am talking too much, this is not a good time to insult her." He went out.

3

Zaraiz Memeli was a small youth, black hair curling tightly about a face sharp enough to cut wood. He was digging without enthusiasm at a tuber bed, leaning on his spading fork whenever the harassed middler girl turned her back on him to deal with some especially egregrious idiocy of another of her punishment detail. She had to keep watch on the garden, the laundry room and a workshed where three girls were sorting rags and stripping discards of reusable parts. Usually there would be several middlers acting as overseers. Karrel Goza found this lone harried girl even more disturbing than the aberration he was supposed to deal with this morning. Why was she alone? Was the Ommar losing her grip, letting work details fall apart? Was she letting favorites play on pride and refuse such work? He didn't know his home any longer. His fault. The Ommar was right that far. So busy saving the world he forgot about his Family; he was almost a stranger here. For the past year anyway. Up at dawn, hasty breakfast, toast and a cup of tea, maybe a sausage if he could force it down, then the retting shed, work there till the second shift came on, midafternoon, scrub the chemical stink off his body, try to get the taint of it out of his lungs, eat if he could, tumble into bed for a restless nightmare-ridden nap; dark come down, off to the taverns for carousing or conspiring or out to the Mines to fly for Elmas Ofka, his attention turned outward always, the House too familiar for him to see it; he simply assumed that it continued to exist as it existed in his memory. By the time he reached the tuber patch off the Memeli Court, he was in no mood to put up with sass from a know-nothing bebek who was setting the House in danger with no purpose except to tickle his urges.

"Zaraiz Memeli."

The boy looked up after a deliberate pause, his face guarded. Custom and courtesy required a response; he leaned on his fork in a silence more insolent than words.

Karrel Goza swallowed bile and kept his temper. "Come," he said. This wasn't starting out well and he didn't see how he could improve things, but he slogged stubbornly on. The young overseer came at a quick trot, questions on her lips. He silenced her with the Ommar's order, took the fork from Zaraiz Memeli and gave it to her. He tapped Zaraiz on the shoulder and pointed toward the Memeli court. "We'll talk there."

Eyes like obsidian, wrapped in a resistant silence, the boy strolled along, refusing to recognize the compulsion put on him. A sly scornful smile sneaked onto his face as Karrel pushed through the wicket and stopped, the noise and clutter of the busy enclosure breaking around him. Crawlers and pre-youngers littered the flags, crying, yelling, playing slap-and-punch games; older prees chased each other around the baby herds and their mothers, fathers, uncles, aunts, cousins who were working, singing, cross-talking in endless antiphon, a tapestry of sound.

Karrel Goza glanced at the boy, watched his bony unfinished face go wooden and unresponsive. For a moment he felt like strangling the pest, then, abruptly, he didn't know why then or later, the absurdity of the whole thing hit him and he laughed. "Not here, obviously," he said and backed out. He frowned at Zaraiz. There was always the Ommar's garden, but instinct and intellect told him that would be a very bad idea; the peace and lushness of that pocket paradise was too stark a contrast to the Memeli Court, it would exacerbate the boy's disaffection. He thought about leaving the House and walking out to the wharves, but he was supposed to be down sick and it would be stupid to confirm the Sech's suspicions. Problem was, except for the Ommar's quarters, there wasn't much privacy, Gozas and Duvvars and Memelis working everywhere, even the oldest doing handcraft and repair, and those who weren't working were talking and watching, gossiping and prying into other folk's business. He dug deep into memory for the places he went when he was a younger and wanted to get away from the soup of life simmering inside the Housewalls. He didn't feel like climbing a tree or burrowing into a dust-saturated attic; he smiled, didn't suit the dignity of the moment. It was a gray day with rain threatening; yes, the clotheslines on the roof of the weaving shed, there wouldn't be anyone hanging out clothes today.

The lines were humming softly as the chill wind swept over the roof; it wasn't the most comfortable place for a prolonged chat, but it was private. Karrel Goza kicked a basket of clothespegs out of a fairly sheltered corner and settled himself with his back against the waist-high wall. "Sit."

Zaraiz Memeli dropped with the boneless awkward grace of his age, drew his thin legs up and wrapped thin arms about them. He said nothing. His attitude proclaimed he intended to keep on saying nothing.

"You don't have to tell me why," Karrel Goza said. "I know why." He smiled with satisfaction as he saw the boy's rage flare, then vanish behind the shutters he'd had too much practice raising between himself and the rest of the world. He did not want to be understood, Karrel Goza's words were both a challenge and an insult. "Dalliss," Karrel said. "The Ommar; arrogant, bigoted, makes you want to kick her face in, but she's good at her job." He pushed aside his unease; this was no time for doubt. "Within her limits there's no one big enough to take her place. Not you, my little friend, no matter what you think. She's got her toadies, yes. Gozas, all of them. You think I like that? I'd drop the lot in Saader's Cleft if it was up to me. They stand in her shadow and steal her authority and tramp on the rest of us and she's blind to it. Yes. I know. I'm Goza and I'm here, running errands for her, so you think I'm one of them, tonguing her toes and begging her to walk on me." He shrugged, his shoulders scraping against the whitened roughcast. "I had it easier than you. I got out. When I was a few years older than you, I got out. Not divorced, just out. They tried bullocking me, sure they did, but most of the time I wasn't here and when I was I had the clout to tell them to go suck. As long as I was flying." He felt the jolt again, the whole-body ache that came when he was grounded, the loss he couldn't put behind him except when he was flying for Elmas Ofka. An obsession can be a gift, giving point to an otherwise pointless life; it can be a torment when there's a wall in the way. He glanced at Zaraiz. The boy was blank as an empty page, refusing to hear any of this. What do you want, Zaraiz Memeli, do you know? He tried feeling his way back to that time around puberty when all his certainties melted like taffy left in the sun. No. He knew too much about surviving now. The years had made him intimately acquainted with gray, the middler world of crisp unchanging black-and-white wasn't available to him any longer. Those were shifts so fundamental that it was impossible to recapture the angst of that world. It also made it difficult to judge what the boy was thinking, what he was feeling. "Do you extend your loathing to your parents? Your brothers and sisters?"

The boy lifted his eyes, flicker of molten obsidian, then he looked away.

"I went to see the Ommar Istib Memeli last night. We talked about you. Your father is on the Duzzulkas right now, bush-peddling black-market medicines, your mother works at the Kummas Kabrikon in the Fix room setting dyes, your two older sisters work there also, handling half a dozen spinners each; Hayati Memeli, the older of them, has first signs of the coughing disease. Your third sister is only a few months old. Your two brothers are mid-youngers, still with their tutors; neither of them shows much promise with his letters, but Aygil Memeli the youngest is good with his hands, he might be a carpenter or a mechanic if the Bondfees can be found. Do they mean nothing to you?" Karrel Goza stared at the boy, trying to see past the blankness. "Ommar Istib says you're bright enough but lazy. That could be because you haven't found anything you think worth doing, or it could be because there's nothing to you but flash and foolishness. Ommar Istib says you've shown no special talents, that you're not interested in anything, all you seem to know is what you don't want which is everything inside these walls." A muscle twitched beside the boy's mouth, but he would not look at Karrel. "You think that matters to anyone? To me? Let me tell you, I'm not particularly interested in who you are or what you think." Another molten black gaze. Karrel Goza nodded. "Right. I'm like all the rest. That's the way the world wags, cousin. Let me make something clear. While you live within these walls, you will show some loyalty to the others here; which means you will stop your yizzy raids as long as you are associated with this House. If you want the freedom of the streets, you can have it; the convocation of ommars will pronounce a divorcement. They will not let you endanger the rest of Goza-Duvvar-Memeli."

Zaraiz Memeli paled, flushed, clamped his lips together, struggling to control the emotions surging in him. A moment later he lost the fight. "Hypocrite!" The word exploded out of him in an angry whisper. "You . . . you're doing worse."

"I'm not a child." Karrel Goza fixed a quelling eye on the working, angry face; inside, he writhed as he listened to what was coming out of his mouth; he wasn't the pompous idiot he heard himself being, but somehow he couldn't shake loose from . . . from this stinking parody of all he'd kicked against since he was Zaraiz Memeli's age. The face of authority, he thought, as his mouth went on uttering fatuities. "I'm not recklessly endangering the House for the sake of a transient thrill." He held up his hand to silence the boy until he was finished speaking. "There is a purpose to . . ."

"Purpose!" Zaraiz Memeli's voice cracked which made him angrier than before; he tried to say more, started to stammer and clamped his teeth on his lower lip. Karrel Goza waited, giving the boy time to collect himself. "Y . . . y . . . YOU!" Zaraiz got out finally,

"Purpose, yunkshit. Playing stupid games. Going nowhere." He jerked a long trembling thumb at the sky. "That! that . . . that thing up there says you're full of shit and hot air."

"Maybe so." Karrel Goza sighed. "This isn't about me, Zaraiz Memeli. The inklins haven't much to lose, so they can afford their rashness. As long as you are connected to Goza House, you drag us down with you." He rubbed wearily at his eyes. "Don't tell me it isn't fair. I know it isn't fair. The Ommar and her convocation have the power, you have none. Your nearkin will back her, so will we." He hesitated. "The time will come, Zaraiz Memeli, when you'll have a chance to change the balance of power. If you're here to fight, if you have the will to fight. All I ask is that you think about it."

Zaraiz Memeli shuddered, shut his eyes and dropped his face onto his knees.

Karrel Goza rubbed at his arms, clamped his cold, chapped hands in his armpits, hunting some warmth. Weariness from the abruptly interrupted drive of the past months was dropping like a fog over him, the day's damp chill was boring into his bones. He scowled at the boy; he might feel a certain kinship with him, but that embryonic brother-sense was drowning in impatience. Come on, he thought, come on, young fool; give in or get out. There's nothing I can do for you. Look at me. Nothing I can do for me. Not now. You're supposed to be intelligent, I can't see it, show me. He pinched his nose, killing a sneeze, tucked his hand back under his arm.

Zaraiz Memeli lifted his head. "How?"

Karrel Goza blinked. "How do you usually think?"

"No." He jerked his thumb at the sky, the tremble gone out of his hand. "That. There's whispers. I didn't believe them before. It is true? Have you and her figured a way to get at it?"

Oversoul's empty navel, Karrel Goza thought, I talk too much. "Nonsense," he said aloud. "How could we? I was talking about Family matters."

Zaraiz grinned. His black eyes glittering, he bounced to his feet, so much energy in him, if someone touched a match to him, he'd explode. "Right," he said. "All right. I'll make a deal. The Slimes'll park our yizzies for now, if so you make us part of it." He folded his thin arms, hugged himself as if those arms had strength enough to control what burned in him. The wind blew strands of curly hair across his eyes, his mouth; he ignored that and stood there, frozen fire, dangerous to his enemies, nearly as dangerous to his kin. When Karrel Goza failed to answer at once, his excitement blew out and the suspicion and resentment that smoldered under his skin burned hotter in its place. "Or aren't Memeli worthy? Aren't we good enough for you?"

Karrel Goza closed his eyes. I do not need this he thought, Prophet touch my lips or no, anything I say will be wrong. If there was just some way I could drop him in a hole somewhere until . . . hole? Why not. He smiled. He couldn't help smiling though he knew Zaraiz Memeli would see and misinterpret it. He opened his eyes, got wearily to his feet. "How much weight will your yizzy lift?"

"You?" Zaraiz was still suspicious but beginning to radiate a tentative triumph.

He's quick, Karrel Goza thought, good, he might even be useful. "Yes."

"You and me, no problem."

"Tomorrow night. I'll take you out, but you'll have to make your own pitch. Another thing, you don't like House discipline, but the worst thing that can happen to you here is divorcement. Act up there and you could find slave steel around your neck. I'll back you, for what that's worth; I think you might be useful, a clever boy can get in places a man can't reach. All I'm saying is, it won't be easy. Come along."

Zaraiz followed him down the stairs. Not a word from the boy. The washcourt was empty, a few raindrops were splatting down, making pockmarks on flags whitened by decades of splashes from soap, starch, and bleach. Karrel stopped, turned. "Well?"

He watched Zaraiz Memeli struggle to make up his mind; his impatience was gone, he was too tired to care what the decision was. As the boy shifted from foot to foot, he could almost write the script for what was passing through his cousin's head. He looked his age at last, vulnerable, wanting desperately for the offer to be real, afraid of trusting it because the whole of his short life had taught him that adults invariably lied to him, broke promises without a qualm, disregarded his ideas and his desires. He kept snatching glances at Karrel Goza as if trying to surprise him into betraying his real intentions. It was no good, of course; either he trusted and said yes, or he rejected the offer and took the consequences. Karrel Goza waited, shoulders slumped, eyes half-closed.

Zaraiz Memeli's eyes burned black again. He licked his lips, nodded, a short sharp jerk of his head. "When do we go?" he said; his voice cracked again, but this time he ignored it. "Where do we start from?"

"Tonight. The wasteflat out beyond Pervas Gorp's last warehouse. Hour after midnight. You can manage that?"

Zaraiz snorted, his thin body stiff with scorn. "I go back on punishment?"

"Tubers don't spade themselves. Use the time to think, eh?" Karrel Goza rubbed at his forehead. Good little boy again? I don't think so.

"Hunh-eh!" Arms swinging, torso swaying, the boy took himself away from there.

Karrel Goza watched his pass through the washcourt's wicket. Maybe Elli can handle him, he thought. He yawned. If I'm yizzying to the Mines tonight, I'd better get some sleep.

XI

collecting:

1

DEY CHOMEDY
Place. Raz KALAK KAVANY, northeast lobe of the Duzzulkas.
Headprice: 2,500 gelders.

She was tall and thin and bald and she moved with an explosive grace even when loaded with chains and driven about the dance floor by electric lances and glass-pointed longwhips. She danced grimly, knowing she had to please them, refusing to please them by cringing or pleading. Sweat streaked her coppery skin, her yellow slit-pupiled eyes were half-closed, her mouth squared into a snarl. Chunky high-arched feet lifted, leaped, landed without a sound, moving too swiftly for the whip thongs to tangle about them, her limber body flowed and twisted away from the jabbing lance points. The dance went on and on, she sweated more copiously until her skin had a diffuse glow as it reflected the yellow light from the lamps clumped on the walls of the open court, but she showed few other signs of flagging.

The music went ragged and finally broke off. The lances clattered down, the whipmen coiled their whips. She stood in the center of the dance floor, wary and angry, her chest heaving, her arms and legs trembling. She wasn't a mammal so she hadn't even vestigial breasts, but she was powerfully female; fear and anger had tagged her sweat with a musky scent that spread like a mist across the court, exciting the men who'd been watching her. The court cleared rapidly and her handler took her away.

* * *

A hand came down on her mouth; a beard tickled her face, a whisper her ear. "Listen." Interlingue. She stopped her instinctive struggle. "Chathat adey Elathay," the whisper went on, "they sent us for you. You want out?"

She touched the hand. After a hissing, near-silent laugh as soon as her mouth was freed, she pushed up; chains clinked when she held out her arms. Her visitor moved around her; she saw him as a long flickering shadow. An autopick hummed and the cuffs fell away from her wrists.

"Anything you want here?" A low mutter.

"Sss."

"I take it that means no. Wait there." Like a walking beam he crossed the room, opened the door a crack and clicked his tongue. A double click answered him. He beckoned to her and slipped outside.

There were two others waiting in the skip. She looked at them, recognized neither but knew from the smell of them they'd been slaves like her. "You've had a busy night," she told the man.

"Might say so. You want to get in? We have a long way to go before dawn."

She swung up, settled in the space the man and woman made for her. "How much you collecting for us?" She blinked. A short furry type she hadn't seen before scrambled into the co's seat up front; it wasn't talking, so she didn't comment.

"Works out to about two thousand gelders a head," the man said, he leaned over the controls; she heard the hum as the skip's liftfield came on, grunted as the skip kicked out of there.

"How many you plan to snatch?" she said.

"Couple hundred."

"Not bad." She laughed, a cat's purr amplified. "Three tonight. You got a ways to go."

"So we have." He turned the skip and sent it racing south over the grass.

"Don't get caught. Some things I want to do."

"Bolodo?"

"Ssss."

He chuckled. "I plan to be old and tired when I die, with plenty of sins to repent."

She extruded a claw, scratched delicately at the skin behind her ear. "A good plan. I too."

2

UKOMAYILE
Place: Raz OSMUR ORTAEL, the westlobe of the Duzzulkas, 300 miles north of Gilisim Gillin.
Headprice: 1700 gelders.

He lifted the stone, eased it into the hollow prepared for it and began pressing the soft gold into place, working quickly but without hurrying, his small hands stronger than they looked. A gooseneck lamp was arched over the pad, giving him the concentrated light he needed; it wobbled as the door slammed open and a short heavy Huvved/Hordar halfbreed rushed over to him. Ukomayile caught the lamp before it tipped over, held it until it stabilized then went back to his work without bothering to look around.

"You're not near finished. Why are you taking so long? He wants the chain and the wristlets ready for the Imperator's Birthday." The Vor Hoshin house steward was one of the Fehraz Vor Hoshin's bastards, born to fuss at things he couldn't understand. He poked with a nervous stubby finger at the emeralds set out on a linen cloth, at the soft gold chain, the links engraved and shaped with minor differences making each unique; he got in Ukomayile's way with a persistence that had something of malice about it.

Ukomayile lowered his hands and waited. The steward noticed that after a while and got shrilly annoyed. "Why aren't you working? Why are you sitting there? He'll have you beaten again, you stupid beast."

Ukomayile laced his fingers together and waited, his face impassive. He did not look at the steward, he said nothing, he simply sat there refusing to acknowledge anything the steward said or did. There was a time when he would have protested such treatment, he was a gifted artisan with an immense reputation and accustomed to being treated with respect and he hadn't yet learned what it meant to be a slave. Ten years and innumerable beatings later, he no longer voiced his protest, he merely set himself like a rock and waited. He still hadn't learned slave manners and he never would if he died for it.

After some more spiteful maneuvering, the steward withdrew; he knew Ukomayile wouldn't explain or excuse himself for not finishing in time, but the Fehraz Vor Hoshin, sourmouthed wrinkled old snake, he'd nose out the steward's interference and twist his tail for it; Vor Hoshin enjoyed that kind of thing and he'd been doing a lot of it lately. The steward knew he was hovering on the verge of dismissal; that he was the viper's son meant nothing, there were plenty of that old horn's get scattered about the Raz. In spite of that he couldn't stop hectoring the slave; for reasons he didn't try to explain, he hated Ukomayile with a passion that nearly tipped him into madness.

The sun went down. A maidservant tapped on the door with Ukomayile's supper on a tray and a jug of mulled wine to warm the stiffness out of his muscles. He laid his tools in a neat row, brushed his hands together, then climbed down off his tool and hobbled to the table; one of those beatings had broken his leg and the boneman who'd set it had botched the job. He ate with the same close attention he gave to his work, finished everything on the tray, drank half a glass of the wine, then went back to the bench.

Gorruya rose, gibbous; she swam up across the window and vanished; Ruya nosed over the horizon. He kept working. The steward might be a malicious fool, but he was right enough about the Fehraz; he'd be mad as a sick viper if the chain wasn't finished in time to show it off at the Fete. The emeralds were lovely stones, he liked handling them and the setting was a test of his skill to keep the variations subtle enough to be interesting but not vulgar. So he labored on while the night grew darker and older.

The door opened. He didn't bother turning, he thought it was the steward coming back.

"Ukomayile, listen."

Ukomayile's hand jerked, the tool cut a crease in the gold. Interlingue. He turned slowly.

A man stood in the doorway, tall, tired face, mussed black hair, a dark gray shipsuit. How many years since he'd seen a clutch of zippers like that, pockets on pockets on an easy loose-fitting overall. The man wearing the shipsuit wasn't anyone he knew. He watched in dull wonder as the stranger pulled the door shut. "Tikkan Ekital sent me." More interlingue, wonderful how fast it came back to him. "They want you back. You want out?"

Ukomayile sat without moving; it was a while before he took in what the man was saying. "Yes," he said finally. "A moment." He slipped the loose emeralds into their carrycase, snapped it shut and slid it into a large leather bag. He folded the chain and the wristlets into the linen workcloth and tucked the roll into the bag beside the stones, drew the strings tight and looped them over his wrist. With the same quick neat movements he cleaned out the safe and gathered up his leather case. "All right. We can go. What do you want me to do?"

The man chuckled. "Right. Just follow me, we're heading for the roof."

3

HANU, POSA ALA, OTSUT

Place: Comweb TRANSFER STATION in the UYDAGIN mountains that run west of Gilisim Gillin.

Headprices: Hanu: 900 gelders; Posa Ala: 3000 gelders; Otsut: 2500 gelders.

Hanu scowled, cleared the program, unclipped the powerpack. "Otsa, come over here, will you?" He spun the flies, slipped off the cover and began pulling cassettes and program boards, lining these up so the Froska could take a look at them.

Otsut yanked on the chain clamped around her neck and pulled it along the overhead slide until she could reach Hanu's side. She moved the tip of a long thin finger across the first board, made a tutting sound. "Burnout, sabotage perhaps, perhaps faulty manufacture." She had a high sweet voice like the chirping of a cicada; soft greenish skin fell in graceful folds between her arms and body; her eyes were a darker green, huge sad eyes. She was nocturnal, totally adapted to a darkness broken only by the fluctuating polarized light of a huge moon that was more like a companion world than a satellite. The light in the room was painful to her, but she endured the small torment because she must, endured it in silence because she was Froskin and they took pride in their stoicism. She was the key to the team; she could generate a weak current in her body and had been surgically altered so she could test-read flakes and boards without exterior, nonorganic aids. Hanu and Posa Ala didn't mind being confined to nightwork, it left them more on their own, less contact with their masters; neither of them found it easy to accept being a slave, they did what they could to minimize the reminders, though the pen where they were caged when not working and the collars they wore at all times, the chains that tethered them when they were doing their analyses and repairs would not let them forget their status or settle too complacently into their new lives. Otsut worked quickly along the line, found three substandard boards and a totally unusable one, one cassette was useless and several of the others were flawed. "This is a larger degree of incapacity than we have found before, Anyo. Is it the transfer unit doing it?"

"There's no sign of surges, no charring or smell or anything similar. Besides, aren't these new units?"

"Most are new," she chirped, "if the manifest is correct; I think it is not exactly correct, I think the supplier is enhancing his profit at the expense of quality."

Hanu looked around. Posa Ala was at his post across the room and their guard was sitting in a chair with his feet up, eyes closed, mouth working as he chewed at green fyon, a local narcotic. "The more things change," he said.

She let greenish parchment lids drop over her eyes. Such corruption was painful to her. The neckchain clinked softly as she shuddered, then she put off her distress. "Are there sufficient spare boards to finish the repairs?"

"Any of those near enough to standard for Posa to do some surgery on?"

She touched them again, picked a board up, played her fingers across it. "This one." She set it down, apart from the rest. "The others, no. The software? Too much damage. You'll have to replace every cassette."

"Well, we can fix this unit, but that's it for tonight. Have to put in a rec, I suppose and wait for supplies." Hanu patted a yawn, got to his feet. "Eh, Posa, how you doing?"

"About the same as you from the look of it."

"Why don't you take a break and come over here? Otsa has a board for you to operate on."

"That's a break?" He chuckled, a deep rumbling sound. Still chuckling he slid down from his stool and came stumping over to them, jerking impatiently at the chain, making the slide squeal as it ran along its track. He was a stubby figure, legs so short his fingers nearly touched the floor when he stood erect. His shoulders and arms were powerful, thick in both dimensions: they looked as if he'd stolen them from a man three times his height. He had coarse shaggy hair he wore twisted into a spiky mane; his head was narrow and long, his mouth wide; his eyes gleamed in the dimness like molten gold, at once savage and filled with a sardonic amusement at the vagaries of life. A typical Kakeran. At home he'd have half a dozen docile wives and innumerable children running wild through the tree paths while he used up his abundant energy directing at least three companies and sitting on half a dozen local boards. Here, even the collar about his neck and the chain that tethered him failed to diminish the force of his personality or the nervousness of Hordar who had to work around him. A lot of the locals, Hordar and Huvved alike, sighed with relief when he was put on the night team and they didn't have to deal with him any longer. "What's this. . . ."

Before he finished the question, the door opened. Their guard blinked, then slid from his chair, sprawling in an insensate heap on the floor. A man stood in the doorway, a stunner in his hand. "Listen," he said. Interlingue. Posa Ala's eyes gleamed. "The three of you are worth about seven thousand gelders to me the day I set you down on Helvetia. You coming?"

Posa Ala shook the chain. "You blind?"

"No." The man grinned at them. "Just wanting no argument if one of you's not inclined to trust me."

Otsut shivered; Posa Ala touched her arm. "Leave this to me, sweet one. Trust isn't in it. Give us a name. I think I know you. Make me sure of it."

The man raised a brow, not the one touched by the scar. "Quale. Ship Slancy Orza."

Posa Ala grinned. "Yah so. Five years back. The Swart Allee, University. You had a friend with funny fur."

"That was a busy night. I don't remember a Kakeran in the mix."

"I was on the bottom of the pile when you showed up; by the time I worked loose you and your friend were kiting out with half a dozen Proctors on your tail. I heard later you led them on a pretty chase and lost them in the Maze. But reminiscences, however pleasant, can wait for a more propitious place and time. I presume you've got a cutter on you that can handle this steel." Once again he shook the chain.

"Better than that." Quale dipped into his pouch, tossed an autopick to Posa. "We're parked on the roof. A skip. You know this place better than I do; we couldn't do much groundwork because we didn't know you'd be here until yesterday morning. Any guard checks due soon?"

"No. They airship us over, lock us in with some cretin like that fool there and forget us till morning." Posa Ala examined the pick, smiled as if he'd found something good to eat and clicked it home. When his collar was off, he turned to Otsut. "Not just us, eh?"

"Right."

"Seven thousand gelders, you say?"

"More or less. Delivered on Helvetia, if that bothers you."

"Nice." As he moved over to Hanu, Otsut pulled off the collar and flung it away from her. "Who's offering?"

"For you, seven wives and some frazzled male relatives."

Posa Ala grinned. He watched Hanu remove his collar, wipe his fingertips on his tunic. "That's finished. Let's go."

"Pick first."

"You're a cautious man. I wouldn't have thought it."

"I never saw a deader who looked like he was having much fun. Move it, will you, I've got another stop to make tonight."

4

LEDA ZAG

Place: Raz EFKLARA MARKAT at the southern edge of the Grass, the western lobe of the Duzzulkas.

Headprice: 7000 gelders.

A hand clamped down hard on her mouth; close to her ear, a male voice whispered, "Listen." Interlingue. She relaxed and moved her head slightly to let the intruder know she'd heard. The hand came off. "One Nameless wants you back. You want to come?"

She sat up cautiously. Enough moonlight filtered through the slats to show her the man beside her, him who thought he was her master; he was lying with his eyes cracked, his mouth sagging half open. She poked at the soft flesh of his upper arm. He didn't change expression or move. "Stunned?"

"Yes. Well?"

"You really need an answer?" She threw the covers off her legs, slid from the bed. "Let me get dressed."

She was tiny, maybe a hand taller than Pels; her breasts were suggestions, her pubic hair a few silky threads. She looked about twelve, but he knew from the data provided by ti Vnok that she was over a hundred; her genes had been scrambled to keep her a pedophile's darling. She moved quickly about the room, selecting what she wanted to wear, shoving jewelry and bibelots into a sack, not a wasted movement. She was back in moments, her eyes glittering, the loot bag slung over her shoulder; she was dressed in a loose robe that swayed about her ankles; it had long sleeves cuffed at the wrist and a high neck; she'd pulled on soft boots, her feet made no sound on the floor. "Let's go."

Altogether I collected twenty-seven slaves from the Duzzulkas and three transfer stations. Then I began on the cities of the Kuzeywhiyker Littorals.

Night after night, explaining who I was and what I was doing and why I was doing it, packing individuals of assorted shapes, sizes and dispositions into the skip and keeping them happy until I decanted them at the Base. In the shelters Kumari stocked and policed, the numbers increased in drips and spurts. It was coin piling up for us, but it was also hard labor, boring, sometimes dangerous, mostly sitting in an overloaded skip, freezing my tail and wishing for a coat of fur like Pels and sorry I ever got into the rescue scam. It was coping with Adelaar who was fretting about her business and what was happening to it without her, it was soothing the Hanifa, who got more nervous and mistrustful as each day slid past. Blessed Kumari, she kept them both off my neck as much as she could. The days did pass. Day by interminable day, they passed. Never again. Never ever again. I was not in love with pain. Or sweat work. But I'd given my word and I meant to keep to it.

5

ILVININ TAIVAS, SUKSI ICHIGO, SHNOURO, SLEED TOK and others not on the list.
Place: AYLA GUL SAMLIKKAN, eastern Littoral.
Headprice: ILVININ TAIVAS: 5000 gelders; SUKSI ICHIGO: 1500 gelders; SHNOURO: 2500 gelders; SLEED TOK: 1000 gelders.

The city was burning when I brought the skip down low over the rooftops and tiptoed around clots of trouble until I managed to slip onto the roof of the pen at the textile factory. The streets were thick with homegrown guards and Tassalgans shooting sprays of pellets at the yizzies whining overhead and scrambling away from gouts of fire as the inklins retaliated. Gangs of youngers were screaming words that didn't exist in the vocab I learned from, darting across housetops and through alleys behind the men in the streets, running dangerously close to count coup on them, scrambling yip-yip-yip away around corners or leaping from roof to roof, waving the paint guns they'd modified to squirt acid drained from eksasjhi veins, the eksasjhi being a lethargic crustacean that lived in the shallows all along the east coast. It left a knotty purple scar that marked the head coup for all to see and silently gloat over, it was briefly agonizing and did not do much for the target's eyesight if it happened to spatter into his eyes. A hit on the head and the yell was *yipyip ya TEN*. A hit on a torso was *yipyip ya ONE*. No scar, at least none visible. A leg was five, a hand six. Houses were burning, men were burning, inklins shot out of the sky were screaming as their firetanks burst over them and they burned or lay with shattered bodies among the bodies of the men they fought, children fell from roofs or squirmed and screamed in the hands of men who beat on them with limber gray prods.

While Pels drifted about the cluttered roof, checking the shadows, making sure no guards or homeless grasslanders were sleeping up there, we didn't want some local waking up at the wrong time and yelling, I crouched by the trap, set the pick working on the lock, then I settled on my heels and looked around. No yizzies buzzing over this quarter; the nearest noise was half a dozen streets away and moving off toward the bayshore, but there was nothing to keep the inklins away. If they took a notion to fire this place, they could be here in seconds. Nothing clears the sinuses like knowing you're not just a fool, you're a damnfool.

Kumari cornered me after the last dip and told me there was chaos in the east. Take two skips, she said, one for backup, and someone to watch them while you're breaking loose the targets. I know you don't like to double the risk on long hauls, but you can separate the two skips, go in mirror arcs, it'll make the run longer, maybe you'd have to find cover and spend the day somewhere, what of it? Irritating to find she was right. I'd have passed on this one, but this dip was worth ten thousand gelders, besides, one of them was Ilvinin Taivas; the Helvetian Seven were hot to get him back, him and Leda Zag. I had her, I needed him. Ah well, it was a mess, but none of my business; I'd seen the backwash from disturbances in other Littoral cities, but they were closer to Base and we were able to stay outside until the fires died down, the injured were carried off, and the fighters on both sides went home. These should have cleared out by this time, it couldn't be more than an hour or two before daylight, but no, the fools had to keep on killing and getting killed.

The pick buzzed. I pulled it off. "Pels."

"Yeh?" He materialized beside me; I jumped, that little spook was hard to see even when you knew where he was.

"You mind going down the hole alone? If Luck takes a hike, some maniac on a broom might take a notion to barbeque the skip."

"No sweat. Only a couple of guards and Kumari said they're usually half asleep."

"Don't count on that tonight. Hmm. Take a buzbug and yell if you hit trouble."

Pels growled, sniffed. "If it'll make you squat happier, li'l mama."

"Here." I held out the pick.

Pels looked at it, shook his head. "Snooper cameras inside, Kumari spotted them. I'll have to pop the lenses and that'll start bells ringing somewhere. I'll use the cutter on the chains, it's faster. When I give a whistle, you have the skip ready to hop." He tapped me on the shoulder. "A minute," he said and trotted away.

As Pels fished in the toolbox, I lifted the trap and clamped it open; I shook it, made sure the spring would hold and turned in time to take one of the matched pair of buzbugs.

Pels worked the bug through the fur on his throat, screwed the plug in his ear. "Don't massacre too many infants," he said and dropped through the hold.

I pasted the phone on my throat, pushed the plug into my ear and touched the bug on; I winced as Pels' breath came roaring into my head, threatening to blow my eardrum. I tapped on the AFT which I should have done before I stuck the thing in my ear, head dead, yes, I wiped the tears from my eyes. With a faint chuff-chuff in my head, I got to my feet and inspected the roof. There was a fat tapering chimney a little taller than I was, several padlocked sheds, half a dozen blocky bins, stacks of drums, huge spools, piles of scrap lumber, bales of fiber; the flat space behind the parapet was a kind of storage area for anything the factory wasn't planning to use anytime soon, all of it throwing complex shifting shadows in the double moonglow. The fires that spread along the waterfront and the slum areas near it put hard edges on those shadows; the black square hole of the open trap stood out stark against the pale roof. Made me nervous. I salvaged a chunk of two-by-four from a scrap pile, laid it across one corner of the hole and lowered the trap on it. The skip was squatting like a dark toad in one of the open areas, far too visible for my peace of mind, but I couldn't do anything about that except hope if the yizzy inklins came close enough to see it, they'd think it was something belonging to the factory. I dropped onto the roof tiles, sat with my back against the chimney, some broken boxes beside me to thicken its shadow and break my silhouette. The launch tube balanced across my knees, a clip in the slot, I waited.

I watched the firefight move farther from us and breathed easier; the thought of having to shoot children out of the sky put a sour taste in my mouth, though that wouldn't stop me from blowing the tailfeathers off any snooping yizzy even if it meant I'd send shrapnel through the body of its pilot. I listened to Pels breathe and thought I'd been in some lousy situations before but I couldn't remember any this bad. Children fighting a war their elders funked. No, not fighting, destroying to scratch an itch, to drive off futility. Hanifa, I thought, if this goes on much longer, what you'll get when you win won't be worth the price. You and Pittipat are birthing a generation of killers and vandals and they won't settle into model citizens once the battles are over.

"Snoops," Pels breathed into my ear, "audio and video. Three of them in the ceiling where I came off the stairs. I popped them, probably set off an alarm. One guard on the stores level, got him; another round the corner just ahead." A breathy chuckle. "The maffit is farting like a misfiring engine. Fui! Be doing the world a favor when I hit him. A minute." The breathing didn't change; slow and steady, little hunter stalking his prey, go Pels! "Got him. And there's door 5. Tsa! more lenses." A moment's silence. "Got them. Five minutes, then we're on our way up."

As I listened to Pels go through the routine speech, picking up echoes of the targets' responses, I looked out across the burning city and felt a deep relief that I was going to be getting out of this. I got to my feet and took a step toward the trap.

A darkness huge and ominous dropped through the shredded clouds. Light beams walked across the city, seeking out and touching the yizzy inklins. Dainty delicate killer blades darting out to touch and kill, clearing the sky. The inklins tried to run, they scattered like leaves in a whirlwind, but it did no good, the lines of light rotated out with an awe-full precision, touch and fry, immense and eerie lightshow.

I swore; it wasn't fair, dammit. "Pels, trouble up here. Stay where you are. Pittipat's brought the Warmaster down."

"Huh?"

"I know. Swatting a fly with a maul, but it's happening. No way I can take the skip up; the Warmaster's knocking everything out of the air."

"Shit."

"Yeh."

"Ah, what about the skip? It's not airborne, is it safe?"

"Haven't a clue. Hmm. If it weren't for those snoops. . . ."

"Yeh. We got to get out of here before company arrives."

"Let me think . . . um . . . the Warmaster is concentrating on the waterfront, most of the trouble is over there. I think you'd better try the streets. Go south and west, make your way out of the city. Watch out for lice."

"Better them than frying. What about you?"

"Sit it out, I suppose, till the ship leaves. She won't hang around after she's finished. You go to ground as soon as you're out of the city. First fair cover you can find. Me, I'd take to the forest somewhere round the river. If you do, don't go in too deep, I want to use the bug to locate you."

"Swar."

"What?"

"Can you get to the skip without exposing yourself too much?"

"Yeh."

"Thing is, the scanners on the Warship can pin a flea. . . ."

"A throw of the dice, eh? She spots it or she doesn't."

"Yeh. Get the spare com, I don't feel like walking home."

I had to laugh. "Point to you, furface. But I won't move till you're clear. Give me a whistle when you're a few streets off."

Silence for a moment, only the chuff-chuff of his breathing. "A couple things I want to do before I leave. Give me a commentary, huh. What's happening up there."

"The ship has finished clearing the sky, her nose is over the harbor now. I can see gouts of steam so I suppose they're going after boats or swimmers." A mutter from Pels was a faint background noise to what I was saying; he'd turned the volume down so he could talk to the targets while he listened to what I was saying. "She's going out farther, that's one huge mother,

Pels, her belly's still over us here, the tail is out in the hills where the rich folk have their houses. Wait till you get a look at her. Hmm. Whatever she was after, she got it. She's starting to swing around; it's going to take her a good half hour to finish that turn. Hunh. She just picked off something else, I can't see steam this time. It's pretty far offshore, might even be one of the Sea Farms. If it is, Pittipat's going to have more trouble on his hands than a few juvenile delinquents. Hmm. She's stopped the massacre, for a while away. You better get a move on, Pels."

"We're on our way. Better not transmit for a while. I'll keep the plug in place, wait on your beep. Luck, Swar."

"Keep your nose cold, teddybear."

"You'll be sorry for that, you apostate Scav."

"I hope. On your way, babe."

"Rrrr."

The hum in my ear broke off. I dropped into a squat, my back against the chimney. The ship continued to turn, slowly, ponderously, so huge it obscured a quarter of the sky.

A whistle in my ear. "Gotcha." I eased to my feet, set the launch tube against a box. Glancing repeatedly at the ship, I edged around the chimney and walked slow as a weary sloth from junk pile to pile of junk, staying in the deepest shadows as long as I could, breaking my motion at irregular intervals, using everything I knew to avoid alerting a watcher, whether that watcher was a program or a man. The wind swept over the roof, carrying past me the stench of burnt meat, faint cries from the wounded, hoarse yells from the hunters in the streets below me. The air was cleared of fliers, but the ground fight was going on, more deadly than before, there were no yipyips, no more coup games, these were rats slashing at rats. I crept a few steps, stopped, went on, until I was crouching beneath the skip below the toolbox. The Warmaster was still turning, dark, silent, massive, no more lightblades though. I eased out, got the box open and dug around for the spare handset. For a cold moment I thought I'd gone off without it this time, the ready-check was so automatic I could have been careless, then my hand closed on the padded case. Pels must have moved it when he got the buzbugs. I lifted it out, slipped the strap over my shoulder, pulled the box shut. I looked up. Still turning, measurably closer.

I patted the skip, shook my head and started rambling back toward the chimney. When I got there, I picked up the launcher, looked from it to the Warmaster and had to grin.

A moment later I lost all desire to laugh, the lightblades were out and rotating, wider beams this time, cauterizing the city; where they passed, the crowded tenements and warehouses exploded into ash and steam. One minute, two, three, four. The barrage stopped, the Warmaster continued drifting south.

For a breath of two there was a hush. Nothing was happening, in the air or in the streets. Then, as if it were a kind of joke, a last giggle after the great guffaw of the slum clearance, a skinny little light needle about as big around as my thumb came stabbing down close enough I could feel the heat leaking off it. It hit the skip, melted her into slag that ate rapidly through the roof and dropped in a congealing cascade through the floors below, starting more fires as it fell.

The Warmaster began to rise, lifting so fast it sucked air after it, creating a semi-vacuum and then a firestorm as air from outside rushed in. Fire roared up out of the hole in the roof beside me. I had to get out of there. I slung the tube's strap over my shoulder and ran for the rope ladder coiled near the front parapet. I flipped it over and went down in something close to a free fall. I had a moment's regret for the slaves still chained in there, but there wasn't anything I could do, the place was a furnace by the time I hit ground. Besides, with all the death in this city tonight, it was hard to feel horror or anything else over a few more corpses, however grisly their end.

Stunner in my hand, I ran through the dark streets. No one tried to stop me. The few Hordar who saw me, looking from windows or crouching in doorways, were shocked into inertia, too afraid, too horrified to do anything but gape. In a section with taverns and small shops I rounded a corner and came face to face with a Tassalgan who was hunting inklins or anyone else he suspected of treachery, which seemed to be just about everyone not Tassalgan. I stunned him as soon as I saw his dark wool uniform, blessing the amnesia effect of the charge; I was clearly not Huvved or Hordar and I didn't look all that much like an escaped slave. I glanced back before I went round another corner and saw ragged children swarming over the downed guard. A wiry boy drew a knife across the Tassalgan's throat and howled as blood spurted over him; he and the other children fought over the blood, wiped their hands in it, licked it off their palms, off his neck. Off the pavement. Hanifa, Hanifa, how are you going to civilize little animals like that? The boy looked up and saw me. I took off. I avoid weasels and all such vermin; they can kill you because they don't know when to give up.

It took me almost an hour to work my way out of the city; it was a big place, bigger than it looked from the skip, and I had to move more warily once I got into the suburbs; there were guards on the walls and they were trigger happy. I picked up some shot in a shoulder, a hole in my leg that missed bone and most of the muscle but hurt like hell and a new part over my left ear, bullet whizzing by entirely too close. By the time I made the park south of town, I was losing blood from my shoulder and my leg and feeling not so good.

The park was on the edge of a forest preserve that spread over the hills south and west of the city on both sides of the river that emptied into the bay. It was open and grassy with rides winding through huge ancient trees, past banks of flowers and fern, glittering with dew whenever the canopy let through light from late-rising Ruya, the silence broken by a rising wind, hot and dry, blowing off the city, punctuated by snatches of sleepy birdsong; dawn was already reddening the east. I found a bench made from rough-cut planks, eased myself down, not sure I should because my leg was getting stiff and I wasn't all that convinced I could get up again, but I had to locate Pels and I couldn't do that traveling. I pried the mike off, used the nail on my little finger to turn the screw, then started the beeper. I waited with some anxiety but not too much; I knew Pels and I expected him to be curled up somewhere, warm and comfortable and enjoying himself.

The earplug beeped. I turned the screw back and stuck on the mike. "Gotcha, Pels. Glad you made it."

I found out why Pels had turned down his mike. Looking a bit sheepish, as well he might, he showed me what he'd done. In the hollow thicket where he'd found shelter he had the four targets and around twenty more fugitives, the rest of the slaves housed in that barracks. He was as sentimental as a daydreaming dowager, but I couldn't complain too much because I was . . . well, call it pleased to see they weren't roasted after all. He knew it too, blasted teddybear.

I gave Kumari a call. She wasn't happy with us. You forget that tap? she said. What am I supposed to think when Adelaar tells me the Grand Sech is ordering the Warmaster to gul Samlikkan? I tried to reach you. Flashed the call light. No answer. I couldn't use the buzzer, I didn't know who or what might be listening. What took you so long? I've been sitting here eating an ulcer in my belly wondering if the two of you were alive or dead. Stay there. I'll send Adelaar to fetch you. How many did you say?

Adelaar got to us late the next night, brought both skips, the second droned behind. The Warmaster was back in orbit over Gilisim Gillin, she said, just sitting there like it was brooding over what to erase next. According to the tap we didn't have to worry about its scanners; the crew was too busy putting its insides back in order. And gul Samlikkan was still burning and the locals were concentrating their attention on containing the destruction and restoring order and they weren't worrying about what was going on in the hills.

We packed half the fugitives in the skips, Pels and Adelaar flew them out. I stayed behind with the leftovers. There was some argument about that, Pels was determined I should go back and get some sacktime in the tub's autodoc, but I didn't want to face that long flight the way I was feeling; I could easily pass out somewhere along the way and I wasn't about to trust any of those ex-slaves with the com. The autopilot could handle a lot, but things come up no flakehead can cope with. Adelaar didn't go maternal over anyone but Aslan, she didn't care what I did. She told Pels he could do what he wanted, but she was going now. And she went. Pels worked over me until I was as sore as he was satisfied, then he slapped bandages on my punctures and lacerations, shot me full of antipyretics, blood-builders and painkillers, left the kip's medkit beside me and took off.

One of the ex-slaves who volunteered to stay behind was a Froska named Jair, an officious little male, precise and self-contained, stoic to the point of insanity like a lot of his species. Pels warned me about him, said he was sure to be a nuisance, he didn't obey orders, he'd do what he wanted no matter how irritating that was to the rest. When the bunch of them got settled in the brush hollow to wait for me, Jair decided to go off on his own hunting water. Without bothering to tell anyone what he was up to, he peeled off from the group and went exploring. Being nocturnal and forest bred, he was the best suited for nightwalking in strange places, so it was a reasonably sensible thing to do; what wasn't sensible was sneaking off. Self-contained was one thing, Pels said, carried that far, it was crazy. There wasn't any need to ooze away like that, what could we do? Sit on him? Thing is, he's been here over fifteen years; I suppose his natural tendencies were warped all to hell by that. Hard to argue with success, though. He found a small stream about half a kilometer deeper in the forest, rooted around till he located some large seedpods, cleaned two of them out and filled them with water. When he got back, I was furious with him, Pels said, but apart from some growling I couldn't say much because several of the others were suffering from water loss and on the point of collapse. While they finished off the water, I wasted some time trying to get him to see where he went wrong; he listened, blinking those frog eyes at me, nodding like a good little Froska. Like he heard and agreed with everything I said. Hmm. Not a hope. Swar, if you lose the little bastard, don't bother hunting him or waiting for him, it's his own fault.

The moment Pels took off, Jair tapped two Kouri on their fore-shoulders and slipped away into the darkness with them. I saw that, but what with the painkillers and general exhaustion I didn't feel like starting an argument I was sure to lose. The three of them were back soon enough, hauling more water and a load of empty pods. I hadn't thought to ask Kumari, but she sent empacs with Adelaar, two tea bricks and a self-heating thermos. Jair trotted briskly over to a female Svígger and stirred her out of her sleep to make tea for us and convert some of the meatflakes into a thick soup that tasted like empac rations always taste, no one not starving could get them down without gagging. The tea helped, woke up appetites; besides, the food the Huvved had been giving them the past months wasn't all that much better so they were hungry and got the soup down without complaining. I stuck to tea and some CVP wafers.

The next night Pels came earlier than I expected. He'd lifted off before sundown, taking a chance on being spotted before he plunged into night. He just grinned when I snarled at him. Adelaar was plugged into the Warmaster, ready to warn him if it moved, he said, and as for ocean traffic, there was one whingding of a storm blowing through the strait, no seagoer would be out in weather like that. No droned skip either, I said, but he just shrugged. I made it, he said. By the time we got back, it should be blown out, so that was all right.

The AP's had killed my fever and this body heals fast, so I was in better shape than yesterday; the trip back to Base was no problem, just tedious. I let Pels take the lead in his skip and do most of the watching and my autopilot did most of the work for me, so I spent the greater part of that miserable night sleeping, cramped, cold, drifting from one nightmare to another. And swearing for the umteenth time I would never again commit us to anything like this.

6

23 days after the meeting at Gerbek.

Aslan put the Ridaar down, looked at her chron. An hour till noon. She had time for another interview, maybe two, before she met her mother for lunch, which was set for midafternoon when Adelaar turned over the Tap feed to Kumari and took a short break to eat and exercise a little. She rubbed at her temples, feeling drugged by talk, hammered at by talk, exhausted by the need to listen attentively and ask the right questions to get the story down in all its aspects of feeling and event. One thing you had to say for this experience, she was going back to University with an enormous pile of data; scholars from a dozen disciplines would be excavating it for the next decade, maybe longer. It could hoist her higher on the tenure list, dearie dai, ooh-yeha.

She looked up, saw Parnalee standing in the doorway of his work station, watching her. Hastily she got to her feet, looked around for something that would give her an excuse to go somewhere else. The Jajes were starting up the path to the lake, small dark figures like wingless black bats. She hadn't interviewed them yet, they were shy creatures and self-absorbed, they allowed very few intruders into their yiuriu. They probably wouldn't talk to her, but they were the draw she needed. She started after them.

When she reached the plateau, they were nowhere in sight, but she saw Kumari stretched out in the shade of a broad squat tree, a pitcher of fruitade beside her, a book on her stomach.

Aslan chewed on her lip, looked over her shoulder. She was alone, she couldn't see the tug or the shelters, which meant anyone down there couldn't see her. She moved hesitantly nearer the figure under the tree, she'd rather talk with Quale (nothing to do with her lust for his body) or Pels, they shared enough of her background to make her comfortable with them, she didn't even know Kumari's species, let alone the basic assumptions of her culture. But during the day Quale and Pels were sleeping or conferring with Parnalee and at night they were gone. She walked forward feeling decidedly unwelcome. Kumari continued to read, no sign she even knew Aslan was there. More than that, there was a strong indication that anyone who came by should keep on walking.

"Despina Kumari," Aslan said, "It's important I talk with you."

Kumari turned a page. "Second hour after noon, your mother's work station."

"No. I'm sorry. That's not possible. I don't want Parnalee Proggerd aware I've spoken to you."

"Sit there." Kumari closed the book, pushed up; she checked to see that the panicbutton was in reach, then scowled at Aslan. "Why?"

Aslan dropped to the grass, sat cross-legged, her hands on her thighs. "I don't want him putting his mind to killing me. I have a feeling he'd manage it no matter how I squirmed."

"Your reasons?" Kumari sounded skeptical but not wholly unconvinced. Aslan felt herself trembling, fooled with her breathing until she was calm enough to go on. The past two weeks had been more of a strain on her than she'd realized.

"He said it, don't screw me up, he said, I'll twist the neck of the one who tries it. He was talking about something else at the time, but I doubt he's changed his mind. He's crazy, you know. Not just a little warped. I'm talking about seriously bent. It's not my field, I don't know the technical terms for what he is, but he's focusing all his energies on one thing, making Huvved dead. Some little Huvved snot had his Tassalgans hold Parnalee down while he beat on him with his czadeg, you know, those gray whips they use on anyone who annoys them, cut his back and buttocks into dogmeat. I was there while he was healing, I saw it eating on him. He's not the kind of man who enjoys a little bondage now and then, no, and there was something from when he was a boy, some sort of trouble, he dreams about it when he's under stress, nightmares, very noisy. I woke him once, tried to get him to talk about it. He punched me around a bit, broke a couple of ribs, gave me enough bruises to decorate an SM sanctum and kicked me out, made me finish the night on a garden lounge, which I preferred to his company, believe me. If he gets a chance at the Warmaster's armory, he'll boil Tairanna down to bedrock. As long as he gets the Huvved, he doesn't care who else he ashes."

"How do you know?"

"Nothing tangible. Watching him. Stripping down those productions he did for Tra Yarta, you know, the Grand Sech. Some things he's said, awake and asleep. Body language more than anything, though he's very good at hiding what he's thinking, that's part of his professional training, isn't it."

"No proof?"

"None."

"Not even in the Ridaar?"

"He wouldn't let the Ridaar anywhere near him. Made me stow it while I was living with him."

"Elmas Ofka wants him with us at Lift-Off. Without proof. . . ."

"Oh."

"Don't fret it, I agree with you. My fa'ali clanks like a cracked bell when he's around. Unfortunately that's as intangible as your unsupported observations. He reports to our Hanifa regularly, feeds her suspicion, I don't know how, I didn't realize what he was doing until a few days ago." She shook her head. "I'll talk with Swar and Pels, we'll watch him, if he tries anything," she sighed, "maybe we can stop him."

Aslan got to her feet. "Have you seen the Jajes? They were my excuse to come up here, so I'd better find them and see if I can get an interview."

Kumari swung her feet around, stretched out on the pad. "They went toward that clump of trees down there by the hook inlets, I think those ancients remind them of home."

"Maybe they'll feel more like talking there." She brushed her hair back from her face and started off, trudging along the lakeshore vaguely dissatisfied though she was glad she'd finally spoke her speech about Parnalee.

7

25 days after the meeting on Gerbek. Conference on Chicklet's bridge: Quale, Pels, Kumari.

Quale scratched at his jaw, his eyes on the screen and the swarm of very assorted beings moving about outside. "How many we have so far? I haven't bothered keeping track."

Kumari called up the figures. "One hundred and twenty on the list, one hundred fifty altogether. You two keep acquiring extras."

"Money total?"

"306,900."

He grinned. "I could live with that."

"Add in the targets in the Palace, it's close to 400,000."

"Which brings up why I had us meet. We can't use the skips to clear out the Palace targets. We'd have to make, what? four, five trips even using both of them. Better to take the tug and get them in one. Which means we have to wait on that till the Hanifa is ready to jump. You talked with her this morning, Kri, what do you think? If we moved Lift-off forward say four days, make it tomorrow, could she handle the speed-up?"

"Four days, what's the point, Swar? Better stick to the schedule. If you feel like keeping clear of Kuzeywhiyk cities, we've got some targets here on Guneywhiyk."

"I don't see how you can say those sneezes with a straight face, Kri."

"Practice, Swar. I've had to learn the Cousin Speech you babble in and Interlingue. If you knew the liquid crystal loveliness of Pilarruyal, you wouldn't ask questions like that."

"Mmp. All right, see what you can do about maps. The Proggerdi won't be any help down here."

"Which brings up something I think you ought to know. Day before yesterday I left Adelaar on the com and took a book up to the lake to get some rest and reading. Aslan followed me up there about an hour later. Listen. . . ." She sketched out what Aslan told her.

Quale stroked his fingers along his moustache. "Chatting up the Hanifa?"

Kumari nodded. "Trust you to put your foot on the main point. Yes. Every night. Soon as you and Pels are gone. He's talked our Hanifa into hiring him as a watchhound. We haven't a hope of leaving him behind."

"You mean she'd actually shut down Lift-Off if we refused to take him?"

"It'd be a tight call, but I suspect, yes she would. She never trusted us all that much and he's been working on her."

"You've been monitoring him, why didn't you stop it?"

"Because I was too dumb to know what he was doing. Not until he'd been doing it long enough to really get under her skin. When I did, what was I supposed to do about it? If you can explain how, it's more than you've done before this."

"Shit."

"Precisely."

"Well, I suppose we do what we have to. And watch our backs."

8

26-28 days after the meeting on Gerbek.

Ayla gul Iltika, gul Mizamere, gul Pudryar, one by one Quale and Pels dipped into the Littoral cities of Guneywhiyk and pulled out slaves, some on the list, some of them extras they couldn't leave behind without telling the world there were Outsiders on Tairanna.

Ayla gul Ukseme was the largest city on Guneywhiyk, in size as well as population; it was a confused sprawl thrown along the inner curve of a skewed half-moon bay. Out where the baywater mingled with the sea there were several Sea Farms, small offshoots of the elder Farms off the coasts of Kuzeywhiyk. There were dozens of freighters tied up at the wharves, linear clusters of one- and two-story warehouses, open-air markets that never shut down; beyond these were stores and Houses spread out along a web of winding streets which climbed over hillocks like horripilation on a cold man's arms. When he saw the satellite fots, Quale swore fervently and nearly gave up on the city, but Kumari did some snooping and discovered that some of those on the list belonged to the Fehdaz who rented them out during the day and made sure they were back in the pen at the Fekkri by day's end. Which was very helpful of him. Made it easy to locate them after dark.

The Fekkri was a massive pile with dozens of towers packed in clusters and a mooring post with a pair of midsized airships nose-locked one above the other. The pen was a small excrescence tacked onto the backside of the pile, a low structure with a waist-high parapet around a flat roof cluttered with bales, crates and assorted discards.

As Quale came in over the city, the air was heavy with damp and the promise of rain. The winds near the ground were tricky, gusts to twenty kph one minute, almost nothing the next, downdrafts with the drag of an octopus, updrafts that threatened to capsize the skip. As a final irritation, the pen's roof was so cluttered with discards, the only open space available was over the trap. Quale landed the skip there and spent the next several minutes sweating and cursing under his breath as he and Pels shifted bales and useless scrap so they could move the machine off their entry point; they had to lift and carry and set down gently, no tossing, no rolling, nothing to make their lives a bit easier; they had to keep the noise down so one of the guards wouldn't get a notion to check out why the rats in the rafters were so noisy that night.

He left Pels dealing with the lock and strolled to the parapet. On the way in as he was circling so he could put the skip's nose to the wind and make a smoother, quieter landing, he'd seen crowds in the streets; quiet crowds, no yizzies, no counting coups, no fires, just hordes of people. Something about them bothered him; he wanted a closer look to see if he could figure out what it was.

The street that went past the pen was a broad tree-lined avenue. He saw half a dozen dark forms standing under the trees. They weren't talking or even moving much. They simply stood and stared at the outer wall of the Fekkri. As he watched, several more figures came round a corner and joined them. By the time Pels summoned him, there was a small crowd down there, silent, motionless, eyes fixed on the wall in front of them. Spooky. He answered Pels' hissing call with a tooth whistle and turned away, glad to have an excuse not to look at them any longer.

He followed Pels through the trap, went down a steeply slanting ladder to a dusty littered storeroom. It's door was locked, but a quick jab of the autopick took care of that. The EYEs Kumari had run through here reported that there were three sleeping cells, four slaves in one, three in each of the others, ten in all. Seven of them were on his list. If Luck had been a trifle kinder the targets would have been in one room waiting for him, but this was her night to be a bitch.

While Pels stood guard, he slashed through the bolt and pulled the first door open. "Listen," he said, "You want out of here? Right. Is there one here . . ." he looked around; no jajes so he didn't bother reading those names, "called Roereirein Lyhyt or Ikas Babut se Vroly or Touw se Vroly?"

"I am Touw se Vroly. Ikas Babut is my mate, he sleeps the next cell over." She was an attenuated figure with a grace even weariness and the wear of servitude had not yet taken from her. He heard a faint clash as she pushed a pair of armbands up past her elbow, by the pallor of the metal they were silver or platinum. She looked around, caught up a shawl and draped it over her shoulders. "What of the others here?" Her arm bands clashed again as she made a wide curving gesture that took in the other two females in the cell, a Froska and a small shadowy figure with more hair than features.

He crossed to her, set the pick working on her collar lock. "What I'll do, I'll unlock the collars and the other two can stay here or leave by the street door, whichever they prefer. If they want they can give me their names and homeworlds and the names of kin I should notify, or you can do that later if you know them. I can't take all of you, the skip just won't hold that many."

Next cell. "Ikas Babut se Vroly, Roereirein Lyhyt?" The third in the cell was a Miesashch tetrapod with the jitters, his split hooves tick-tacking aggressively against the floorplanks. "I'll unlock the collars on all of you. You, despois," he told the Miesashch, "can stay here or leave by the street door whichever you prefer. If you want you can give me your name and homeworld and the names of kin I should notify. I can't take more than those on my list, the skip just won't hold that many."

Next cell. "Weggorss Jaje, Otivarty Jaje, Krathyky Jaje, Imagy Jaje? Good. The Bialy Vitr think highly of the Bond Jaje, they have offered one thousand gelders for the return of each lobe of the Bond, there are four Jajes in my camp already, eight thousand in my hands when I set you all down on Helvetia's pavements. Be assured I shall take very good care of you."

There was a spate of whispering among the Jajes, they were using their highest register; the fugitive sounds tickled his ears and gave him the beginnings of a headache. The boldest of the four moved a step toward him, a velvety black female invisible in the twilight inside the cell. "This one is Otivarty Jaje. What is the calling of the Presence who speaks us?"

"Swardheld Quale, ship Slancy Orza out of Telffer."

More whispering. Otivarty stepped away from her Bond again. "The calling is known, the word is acceptable, we will come."

Quale started for the storeroom and the ladder, his seven hustling along behind him, anxious to be out of there. Equally anxious, the extra three hurried the shorter distance to the street exit; the Froska had Quale's cutter, she sliced through the lock tongue and began lifting the bar.

Pels was in the storeroom already and on his way up the ladder. Quale shooed his herd of ex-slaves through the door and was about to follow when he heard a rumbling mutter, then an exclamation of shock and fear from the Froska as the door was wrenched from her hand and sent crashing against the wall.

Blankfaced muttering Hordar came stomping in, hands like claws reaching for the outsiders, mouths open, lips fluted to produce a whistling growl, eyes wide with no one home behind the shine. The extras took one look at them and ran the other way. Quale waved them past him, played his stunner across the front rank of the mob. Five Hordar fell. The Hordar behind them marched over them, stomping heedlessly on them, crushing them.

"Shit," he said. "Oh shit." He slammed the door, reached for a bar that wasn't there. The door quivered as the Surge crashed against it. He went up the ladder faster than he'd come down it, slammed the trap and yelled at the ex-slaves to help him shove bales on it.

They got the first bale in place as the trap shuddered and started to rise, rolled another over beside it, then a third. The bales quivered as the Hordar below pounded and shoved at the trap, but they had to stand on the ladder to reach it and couldn't get enough leverage to shift the weight piled on it. The barrier held.

Quale scowled at the faces turned hopefully toward him. The se Vrolys were both slender, the four Jajes added together wouldn't make one of him. Lyhyt was vaguely vegetative like Kinok, though not Sikkul Paem; he was broad and tall, but maybe not as massive as he looked. The Froska female wouldn't take much space and would suffer in silence for pride's sake, but the Miesashch could be a problem if he panicked. The third from Touw's cell was a fragile nocturnal whose species Quale didn't recognize, but she at least looked fairly calm. "Listen," he said, "I'll take a chance I can lift off with all of you. It's a wild gamble, you might be safer finding a place to hide up here where you can ride that mess out. . . ." He broke off, looked up as he heard the tinny clatter of a yizzy.

A fireball came straight at him. He dived away, rolled over, dived again, rolled behind a stack of crates.

The second fireball missed him by the width of a hope, splashed on the roof and started it smoldering. The others had scattered almost as quickly, hunting cover, but the inklin didn't waste more fire on them. The yizzy swept past, went soaring up to the mooring tower; the rider began working on the airships. More yizzies converged on the towers. The airships were as fire safe as chemistry could make them, but with a dozen firethrowers heating them up, even the heavily sized yosscloth was beginning to smoke. Before long the heat would kindle the hydrogen in the ballonets and the conflagration that followed would melt more than the tower.

While Pels was helping the ten pack themselves into the skip, Quale risked another look over the parapet.

The street was packed with Hordar moving and breathing as if they were limbs of a single beast. The whole city was coming to press against the Fekkri, the Hordar flowing like a river of ants over the few Tassalgan guards stupid enough to try stopping them. The Surge tore them apart, tore off arms, legs, heads, anything one of the many beasthands could get a grip on. He saw a pair of guards trapped in a doorway trying to shoot themselves clear; pellet guns on automatic, they emptied clips one after another at the mob, the pellets scything across the front ranks, knocking down dozens of men and women. The Surge ignored them, came on without noticing the dead and injured, cast them aside like sloughed skin cells. The guards panicked, tried breaking into the House behind them. They couldn't get away. The Surge threw off a tendril which flowed after them and pulled them back to the street; it hurled them against a wall, knocked them again and again into the stone, rocked them back and forth under casual undirected blows, it kicked them off their feet and stomped them into stewmeat. The chatter of the guns, the yells of the guards, their final screams were lost in the SOUND coming from the Surge, a hooming howl/growl without words, only a rage so tangible that the hair stood up on Quale's arms and rose along his spine. He backed away and ran for the skip.

Pels had got the weight of the passengers distributed as well as he could, but the machine was still dangerously overloaded. Quale eased into the pilot's seat and punched on the liftfield, cycling it gradually higher as the drives warmed and tried to take hold. They whined and shuddered; after a tense moment when he was sure they weren't going to bite, the skip lumbered clumsily into the air. He held her an arm's length off the roof while he tested her handling. She was sluggish and crank, the slightest misjudgment on his part might flip her or send her into a slip and that would be that for all of them. He eased her higher, a hand span at a time until she was finally high enough to clear the parapet.

Two yizzies backed away from the siege on the airships and came swooping at them. Quale turned the skip through a wide gentle arc, gradually accelerating, cursing under his breath at the impossibility of losing the inklins fast enough. Pels slid over Touw se Vroly's lap so he could snap loose Quale's stunner which had a longer reach to it than his own. One of the inklins squirted fire at them, but a gust of wind carried it wide. Back in his cubby, Pels bared his tearing teeth, hissed with satisfaction and put that inklin out; he got the second inklin before she could release more fire. The two collapsed in their saddles; strapped in so they didn't fall, they went drifting off, ignored by guards on the ground and their fellows in the air.

Quale relaxed and nursed the laboring skip through the city, picking a circuitous route that avoided the taller buildings, the speakers' minarets, mooring towers, and the like. Below them the Surge went on, spreading from precinct to precinct, leaving death and destruction behind it as it moved.

Quale brought the skip down slowly, carefully, landing her in a grassy swale between two groves, one a collection of nut-bearers, the other ancient hardwoods. There was a small stream wandering vaguely westward across the middle of the swale and a tumbledown shelter tucked away under a lightning-split cettem tree still alive and heavy with green nuts. He left Pels and four of the ex-slaves there to wait for his return and took the others to Base.

He started back at once, reached gul Ukseme shortly before dawn; he circled over the city to see how the Surge had developed. It was very dark, both moons were down and the storm that had threatened at dusk was on the verge of breaking. No yizzies. The streets were empty. The Fekkri was a burnt-out husk. There were bodies everywhere, trampled into rags on the paving stones, men and women, impossible to say which body was which; dead children who were recognizable as children only because they were littler than the others. He was too high to smell the stench, but it was thick in his nostrils despite that; he'd seen more wars than he cared to count, he'd seen his own body, the one he was born in, flung down in a ragged sprawl, he knew that smell, he knew the look of bodies thrown away, flattened, empty. He'd never gotten used to the smell or the look of the violently dead. Grim and angry at the futility of it all, he swung the skip around and got out of there; fifteen minutes later, with wind hammering at him and rain in cold gusts drenching him, he picked up Pels and the Jajes and went back to Base where life was marginally saner and the folk living there full of juice and hope.

XII

1

30 days after the meeting on Gerbek.
The muster in the Chel, semi-arid land between the Inci Mountains and the southern edge of the grasslands.
The chill gray hour just after dawn.

Knots of talk as the muster is getting organized:

"Any time now. Soon as you're ready to load." Quale looked round at the untidy ferment scattered over half a kilometer of scrub. "Adelaar's got a clawhold on the shipBrain through the tap; she's routing the scanners away from this sector, but I don't want to lean too hard on that, it's complicated working blind like she is with two sets of alarms to avoid. The sooner you can get this lot . . ." he waved his hand at the noisy congeries about them, "sorted out, the better for all of us."

Elmas Ofka looked past him at the tug. "The systemships have lifts; how do we get into that thing?"

"Right." He lifted the com. "Pels, open her up."

2

Karrel Goza threaded through the clumps of rebels, forces from every part of Kuzeywhiyk brought together for this thing no one had believed possible before Elmas Ofka put it together; he knew most of them because he'd given most of them a lift at one time or another when the bitbits were hot after them; he waved a greeting to those who yelled his name but didn't stop until he reached one of the knots near the outside, seven quiet men who were sitting on their packs or squatting beside them, ready to go when the word came. He dropped to a squat beside them. "Not long now," he said.

Jamber Fausse snapped a twig in half, began peeling the stringy bark from the dry white wood. "Mm." He scratched at a patch of rot. "I know you, Kar, you want something."

"Elli."

"So?"

"We need her."

"Yeh. So?"

"She's got three sets of outsiders watching each other, she thinks that'll be enough to keep them from knifing her."

"Probably right. Usually is."

"Uh-huh. Safe is better'n sorry. She's got her isyas scattered to keep the squads on track."

"Kar . . ." there was a weary patience in Jamber Fausse's rough voice, "we been going through the motions the past ten days. Why you keep telling me what I already know?"

"Just laying foundation, Jamo. You're scheduled for the drive chambers. Kanlan Gercik's willing to trade. I want you and them . . ." he jerked his thumb in a nervous half circle taking in the others who were listening without comment, without expression, waiting with the patience of monks for the talking to be over, "next to her. Kan's all right, he's good in a pinch, but you've been dealing with Huvved since before you could walk, you can smell a trap before it hatches."

"Mm." Jamber Fausse broke the length of denuded twig into smaller and smaller bits then threw them at a patch of dried grass and brushed the debris off his callused palms. "All right."

3

Aslan stood in the shadows and watched the fighters file past; she had the Ridaar running, flaking them as they came up the lift and into the hold. These male guerrilla bands and female fighting isyas were unlike the outcast, outlawed and rebel Hordar she knew from the Mines. They were harder, angrier, fined down by hunger, fear and pain; these Hordar had lived on the run for decades, no sanctuary for them, never enough food, never enough anything but ammunition for their guns, living with the knowledge that their capture alive or dead meant death or exile for their families; to the Huvved, blood was blood, corrupt in one set of veins, corrupt in all. She watched their faces and thought she wouldn't much like living on a world that these men and women had a hand in running. She didn't understand why Elmas Ofka had such a powerful hold on them, but she was glad of it, she liked the Hordar and wished them well. She watched the fighters and ached for them though they'd be furious if they knew it; in a few hours their rationale for living and doing what it took to stay alive, that rationale would be taken from them. If not in a few hours, certainly in a few days. Worlds have no place for fighters once the war is won. What were they going to do with the rest of their lives?

"Eh, Lan!" Xalloor danced over to her. "Why the long face? You're as melancholy as a poet with a prize." Behind her, Churri snorted; he leaned against the lock and said nothing.

Aslan pulled Xalloor closer so she could talk without shouting. "What in the world are you two doing here?"

"More insurance. We're supposed to keep an eye on you and your mum. And the rest of 'em. Churri's a poet which makes him respectable and I'm nothing much, someone she knows, someone too feeble to be a danger to her, just barely bright enough to watchhound."

"I see about her, what about you? This isn't a stage, you could get killed."

Xalloor grinned. "Dearie dai, you are a romantic. Stage. . . ." The word turned into a giggle. "Once upon a time about a hundred years ago, didn't I say you've led a sheltered life?"

XIII

1

30 days after the meeting on Gerbek.
Lift-Off.

On the bridge, her hands alternately at rest and working with a swift sureness across several sensor pads, Adelaar sat half-lost in a recapitulation of her Listening Station, part environment, part sculpture, part haphazard stack of blackbox units, playing her sup-with-the-devil-games with target and tie-line, blocking approach alarms, feeding in false readings, singing the ancient shipBrain to sleep.

Quale was taking the tug up on a long gentle arc, moving west to chase the night, the ar-grav blending so smoothly with the drives that the only sense of movement the passengers had, on the bridge or in the hold, came through the screens that showed Tairanna curving more and more beneath them.

Elmas Ofka stood beside Quale, watching the screens, her hands closed into fists, her body stiff. She'd had it with strangeness, her own world was complicated and difficult enough, she needed all her skills, her intellect and energy to deal with the disintegration of the society she'd been born into. This extra element of confusion threatened to wrench control from her and destroy any possibility of a return to order. At least, to the sort of order she remembered. If she could have expunged these aliens from the Horgul system, closed it away from the Outside as Adelaar planned to encyst an area of the shipBrain, she'd have done it without a second thought. Too intelligent to linger mournfully on impossible dreams, she forced herself to concentrate on limiting the damage the aliens could do. She could feel the one called Aslan watching her. The most dangerous of all of them, if Parnalee wasn't lying to her. Aslan knew too much. She was capable of too subtle a twisting; the play-maker Parnalee showed her how Aslan had turned the Prophet's Life on the lathe of her knowledge and imagination and used Pradix to rouse the Hordar out there watching, innocent victims of the woman's will to power. Ruthless, he said, you can never trust her because she can manipulate you without you knowing a thing about what was happening to you. She gazed at the back of Quale's head, cold dislike washing over her though she knew that was foolish. Thing. Bought thing. Cat on a leash, dancing for whoever pulls it. With regret and resentment she thought of the pouch of prime rosepearls she'd handed over once her fighters were loaded in the tug. No threat voiced, no threat in his posture, but he didn't need to make explicit what was implied by his control of the machine. No, she had no choice; the rosepearls bought her this standing space, bought her a chance at the Warmaster, a chance at liberation for all Hordar. Divers did what they must to stay intact. Discipline was life. She disciplined her fears and forebodings and watched the screens, watched the Warmaster swimming smoothly toward them.

Though its image was at that moment little larger than her hand, its mass was palpable. And she knew from evidence of her own eyes how huge it was. Two days ago she'd seen it gliding south over the Mines. Two days ago it descended over them to smother them with its immensity, its power. Two days ago it went south to Guneywhiyk to burn a Sanctuary down to bedrock. It could have been the Mines. But for the Prophet's Hand over them, it could have been the Mines. Two days ago. She felt the dead clustering over her, swimming through the incense of all these alien souls, puff of unseen smoke, bouncing under the ceiling of this alien place. Forgive me, she breathed at them. She sang in her mind the Litany of Dismissal/The Promise of Return. Return to a quieter, gentler world, a world of calm and order. She sang the litany over and over as the Warmaster grew until there was nothing in the screen but a cratered black surface whose pits and flaws were more and more apparent, a calligraphy of age. She sang the litany over and over, sang it for herself, gentling herself, sloughing off her responsibilities, her plans and fears . . . odd, when she had so many anxieties and frustrations, how free she felt. As if the moment would permit nothing less. Free. For the first time she began to understand the seduction of war. How it stripped away everything but the need to survive, how it narrowed life to the Now, how it freed you from the niggling irritations and ambiguities of ordinary life. She was enthralled and appalled. The power of it. The temptation. She looked over her shoulder at Aslan; the woman's face seemed wide open, utterly without defense. She looked into those cool amber eyes, strange eyes, and saw . . . she didn't know what she saw, but it terrified her. Aslan knew her, knew what tempted her, knew so much it was an obscenity. Moments passed before Elmas Ofka found the courage to look away. She shook briefly with fear, then the Now took her again, she turned back to the screen and forgot to be afraid.

Karrel Goza leaned against the wall, its vibration playing in his bones, not shaking but a note sung in a voice so deep he felt it rather than heard it. He watched Tairanna drop away, savoring this pale small taste of flight. Otherwise the tug gave him nothing, how could he feel himself flying without a symbiosis of soul and air; shut inside here how could he feel anything? He was sad. The skips were fast and reliable and nearly indifferent to storms. Within a generation they and their cousins would most likely replace the airships; they were too tempting and with Outsiders coming in and out with no controls on them, Family businesses would be replacing airships as fast as they could import these machines. Would start building them as soon as they had the necessary mechanics trained. Not all airships would go, cost still meant something; but yosspod bags would be left to claw out a poor living on the fringes of transport and hauling. More change.

He sighed. For over two decades, since a childhood he remembered as calm, slow, ordered, he'd watched the world pass through wrenching transformations because the Outside, the OutThere, intruded. What they were doing this day would wrench the world yet more violently from that remembered time, but it might (only might, he couldn't see beyond the hour, let alone so long into the what-will-be), it might ensure the coming of a new tranquillity. If he were fortunate and outlived this day, he might see that time within this life; if not, he was content to wait for the next. He, like Elmas Ofka, surrendered to the point-Now and watched the Warmaster swimming toward them; he forgot sadness, forgot speculation. Immense. Gargantuan. Enormous. Colossal. Feeble, all those adjectives. No words were adequate. It seemed to him impossible that men had made that immensity, it seemed to him that it must have been some demon also beyond words which had laid so impossible an egg. Which was absurd. Men had made it, of course they had. How many men labored how many years in that making?

Parnalee stood across the room from Aslan, where she could see him and be afraid; he enjoyed her fear, though he knew she'd tried to thwart him. Useless. He was here. There was nothing she could do to him, but he could play with her until he was ready to finish it. Omphalos knew far more about these ancient battleships than any jumped-up tinkerer; whatever that woman did to the Brain he knew he could undo, if he had to. He had other strings to pull, more powerful ones than she could have any concept of. Once he had the Warmaster tamed to his hands. . . . He drifted off in dreams of burning Huvved, of a world burnt clean of life, burning burning, of power like a god's in his hands, HIS hands.

2

Quale nudged the tug up tight against the monstrous flank; Adelaar danced her fingers over her consoles. Like some gargantuan sex organ the pimply surface extruded a rubbery tube; it reached out and touched the tug's side, closing like a mouth over the freight lock.

3

Clutching sickbags the fighters swam through the tube. Quale gave them a lecture before they left. Thirty to forty percent of you will suffer nausea when you hit the tube and go weightless. Unless you want to swim through vomit, you'll see your kin and your friends have those bags ready and use them if they need them and they will, believe me, they will. It has nothing to do with strength of body or mind. Ever been seasick? Multiply by ten. Uh-huh. And those of you out there looking superior, even if you're never sick at sea, that's no predictor of your belly's state when the weight comes off. Take the bags and use them.

4

Comforted by the seasickness analogy despite Quale's warning, Elmas Ofka expected to swim undisturbed through that relatively short distance between the artificial gravity of the tub to the artificial gravity of the Warmaster. She was furious when the first convulsions shook her; Quale had forced a sickbag on her, she'd tucked it out of the way behind her belt, now she got it up just in time to catch her first spew. She glared at Karrel Goza who was pulling himself along untroubled.

Contorted with spasms of vomiting, pale with fury, she yanked herself along the travel lines anchored to the tubewall, ignoring the gulps, coughs, groans of her fellow sufferers. In spite of her difficulties, she took less than five minutes to reach the lock area where she surrendered with a relief that didn't lessen her annoyance to the comfortable grip of a familiar weight. She wrenched off the sickbag, glared around.

Carefully not smiling, Quale slid back the cover on a

disposal chute and took the bag from her. He dropped it into the hole, stood back to watch as the rest of the force came swinging out of the transtube, landing on their feet again, their bodies celebrating the return to weight as they looked round the lock, a trapezoidal chamber large enough to accommodate ten times their number. The Hordar who'd succumbed to nausea dumped their bags in the waste chute, took mouthfuls of water from their belt canteens and spat it after the bags. With a minimum of noise and energy expenditure, they gathered into bands and isyas and waited for the order to proceed. Lirrit Ofka drifted over to stand beside Karrel Goza; she was pale and still somewhat shaky, but she managed a wan smile as she touched his arm in a gesture close to a caress. "Absurd," she murmured, "we're starting our war like a clutch of colicky babies." She pinched him, sniffed. "Some of us."

Elmas Ofka moved to the center of the lock, beckoned Jamber Fausse to her. He went onto one knee, she stepped up onto the other, holding his hand to steady herself. With a two-finger whistle, she called her people to her. "Time is," she said; her voice filled the chamber with passion and triumph. She watched them as they sorted themselves out, smiled as she saw an alertness and a confidence born out of years of deadly exchanges, even the youngest who'd been an inklin in gul Brindar before he joined Akkin Siddaki's raiders, a baby-faced thief with legendary fingers. "Drive chamber, go." She watched the isyas and the bands move off behind Kanlan Gercik, swinging along in a slouching trot that covered ground with a minimum of effort. "Duty stations, rest area, go." Two more squads left. "Sleepers, go." She stepped down. "Bridge," she said. "Let's go."

5

Aslan watched the squads peel off and slide away, the bodies fading curiously into a dimness that wasn't shadow, the sourceless light cast no shadows, that was more like a thickening and darkening of the air itself.

It seemed to exaggerate every quality, to dramatize each of the individuals left in the lockchamber. Elmas Ofka was an odd combination of wargod and earth-mother; Jamber Fausse was chthonic, earth crumbling off him, about to burst into grass and weed, his men reduced to elemental shadows crouching at his knees; Karrel Goza and Lirrit Ofka were dangerously elfin, dark and unpredictable, unhuman; Churri was like that too, and not like, a coppery sprite redolent of a mix of malice and compassion ordinarily impossible but not here. Kante Xalloor was Dance incarnate with enormous eyes, her body singing a wry amusement at what was happening around her. Swardheld Quale loomed, no other word for it, big, somber, and for the first time, impressive. In spite of herself, she smiled as she thought the words, her lust for his body, she'd seen him as a quiet man, committed to nothing except money and even that seemed to provoke no great interest. No great interest in her either, though she'd been shedding signals around him like a kirpis sheds scales. She sighed, she'd been through this before, these stupid infatuations, she knew exactly how it'd go, whether she slept with him or missed on that, one day she'd look at him and wonder what the fuss was about; until then she was stuck with these palpitations and hot rushes. Parnalee . . . she looked at him, looked away. Black Beast, evil exaggerated; he terrified her more than any other person male or female she'd ever met. She started to wonder how all of them saw her and almost missed the Rau's return. Light rolled like water off his short thick fur; he sank into that adhesive dimness, a shadow more solid than the twilight around him but still curiously nebulous, a demon familiar of the pleasanter kind. She smiled. Living up to his legend, she thought.

"The transtube's operational," Pels the shadow said, "Adelaar's punched the command through."

"Good." His eyes narrowed to slits, Quale scratched at his short dark beard, pushing his fingers along his jawline. "One last time," he said. "Let Pels and me go ahead so we can make sure the way's clear."

Elmas Ofka's head went up and back, her eyes glittered. "No," she said.

Quale shrugged. "Pels, lead off. Soon as the tube decants you, do your thing. Be careful, huh? I'll be out soon as I can manage. Hush, Hanifa, you saw him work and you got me as hostage." He looked round, beckoned to Karrel Goza. "Take three of your fighters and follow him." He waited until that four was formed up, then tapped Elmas Ofka on her shoulder. "Hanifa, you and your isyas and your . . ." he grinned at Jamber Fausse, "your bodyguard, you're next. Churri, you and your friend follow them. Parnalee . . ."

Parnalee shook his head. "Last," he said.

Quale looked at him a moment, then he shrugged and turned to Aslan. "You're it then, follow the dancer. I'll follow you."

Aslan nodded; she'd have preferred a few more bodies between her and the Proggerdi, but with Quale behind her she felt safe enough.

"All right. Go, Pels."

The Rau led them through corridors round as wormholes, gray, ashy dead-colored holes, even the air was the color of death, holes thick with gray sound-absorbing dust, dust-heavy cobwebs, rat droppings, the discarded housings of dead insects. Aslan trotted after Churri, watching dust drifting down over him, gradually leaching the color out of his body and his clothing. By the time she'd turned a few bends right and left and switched from one wormhole to another to a third, she was thoroughly lost and a gray ghost herself, in a line of gray ghosts, trotting through dust, age and ugliness, her hand over nose and mouth to keep the worst of the clutter out of her lungs, her brain busy-busy, honeysipper busy with image and sound.

She ran up on Churri's heels before she noticed he'd stopped walking.

The door was a squared oval bent to conform to the curve of the wall; it was pulled out and pushed away and weak gray-yellow light struggled out of the opening. Aslan followed Churri over the raised sill into a round chamber like the inside of a tincan. The kind of ships she usually traveled in didn't use tubes like this; you rode in minicarts or you walked. She peered around Churri's shoulder and watched Xalloor step through a vaporous throbbing darkness, moving slowly until only the lower part of her left leg was visible on this side; abruptly that was gone, one instant there, then whipped away. Without missing a step Churri went after her. Shivering with excitement and fear, Aslan followed him.

Soft pudgy giant hands seized hold of her and took her instantly elsewhere. She felt no acceleration, only the pillowy gentle hold. She was deaf and effectively blind, all she could see was a red-shot silvery gray shimmer.

The hands set her down on a small platform hardly large enough for one person to perch on; immediately ahead of her she saw a familiar pulsing cloud. She plunged through it and emerged into another tincan; she stepped over the raised sill and found herself standing in something that was part corridor, part atrium, part multiplex chamber five hundred meters long, perhaps a hundred wide, whose ceiling was so high overhead it was lost in the dimness peculiar to the light in this ship. Quale flashed past her, swung round, his eyes on the tube exit. He waited for one minute, two. Aslan moved away a few steps, turned to watch, a cold knot forming in her stomach as the seconds slid past and Parnalee didn't appear. Quale checked the chron set in a ring he wore on his thumb, then he swung to face Elmas Ofka. "All right," he said, "is this some idea of yours?"

Elmas Ofka glared at him, her suspicion matching his. "Or yours?"

Xalloor poked her elbow into Churri's ribs; from the corner of her mouth, she shot at him, "Do your stuff, poet, or we're gonna have a war right now." She caught hold of Aslan's arm. "Hush," she whispered, "anything you say just makes things worse. She been primed not to believe you."

"Hanifa," Churri said, his voice making a minor magic of the word; she switched her glare to him, softening it automatically as she realized who was speaking. "Just one thing, make of it what you want. It was Parnalee's choice, coming last. None of ours. Looks like he had plans he wasn't telling anyone."

She thought that over, clamped her mouth so tightly her lips disappeared; no more talking, that was the message. Let's get on with this, that was the other message as she swung round and faced the great bronze doors that sealed off the bridge.

Quale glanced at his chron again. "Take cover," he said. His voice was low, but pitched to carry. "Ten minutes before Adelaar opens her up for us."

The grand Atrium had an angular egg shape with exits like liver spots spattered through every sector, ramps and handrails focused on what was now the floor, sealed-hatch storerooms, undedicated alcoves with no barriers at their portals, small rooms, large rooms, the few she could see into apparently as empty as the greater area, holes, nooks, recesses, stalls, coves, pockets, a hundred different receptacles breaking the smoothness of the metal walls. Aslan followed Churri and Xalloor into a small closet area with empty shelves and bins lining the walls; Karrel Goza and Lirrit Ofka crowded in with them; guarding Elmas Ofka was their first duty and their desire and staying close to the Outsiders was part of it. Aslan hid a smile. Duty didn't dampen their excitement, their impatience to get on with taking the ship. She edged away from them and stood a step back from the entrance and to one side so the darkling air and the wall shielded her from observation; like all the other doorways she'd encountered in the ship, the sill was raised shin high, perfect tripping height, was that the purpose? Two of Jamber Fausse's band looked in but decided this closet was already too crowded; from the sound of their voices, they went to ground in the next nook that'd hold them. Elmas Ofka, Jamber Fausse and the rest of his band chose yet other waiting places. Quale vanished somewhere and the Aurranger Rau transformed himself into a ripple in the dimness and went flickering about, nosing into whatever took his interest, unlocking hatches, poking into bins and drawers, going a short distance down some corridors, running up ramps to check out others. After she discovered how to estimate where he was, she watched the band of light and let her mind drift where it wanted to go, sliding contentedly through level upon level of metaphor and symbol. She'd read about the Raus and their talents and she'd heard a dozen tales about Pels and his pranks (though she'd discounted those, knowing the tellers too well to credit their accuracy); watching him at work was endlessly fascinating. She'd thought of him earlier as a sort of benevolent demon in the bowels of this malevolent beast of a ship, as a magister's familiar, Quale being the magician/master; she'd been playing games with image and word, but her imaginings were beginning to seem more accurate than she'd suspected. She checked the Ridaar. No need to slip in a new flake, not yet.

Where she stood she could see the entrance to the Bridge, an oval like the rest of the doorways but larger. Much larger. The door was laminated bronze with an antique patina and the Imperatorial sigil in onyx calligraphy on a silver shield. Impressive, but they had its key and that key was her mother, Adelaar sitting out in the tug, playing her nay-saying tunes through the tap. At the proper time, she'd send a command bouncing through the satellite, down to the mainBrain and up again through the slavelink into the shipBrain. *Open the door*. And the door would open.

She could hear the ship breathing, the hushed whirr of fans that pushed the cleansed and constantly renewed air through the web of conduits; she could hear clicks and creaks and feel a subliminal hum through the soles of her sandals. A mite in the gut of an immense indifferent beast. She moved closer to the door and saw the invisible turn visible, pip-pop unroll the curtain, shape the beast from shade to solid, magic hardening into mundane. Pels kurk Orso, graduate engineer and living toy. She watched the flow of his broad black hands as he used a silent sign talk to argue with Quale. I wonder what that's about? The exchange ended. Pels shrugged, rippled out again and went back to his snooping. Quale crossed the chamber at a rapid trot, stopped beside one of the exits.

Two guards came sauntering along the corridor attached to that exit, chatting as they walked; their voices came ahead of them, announcing them before they appeared. A hard nervous hand on Aslan's arm pulled her away from the door. Karrel Goza dropped to a crouch, his pellet rifle ready. The guards, a pair of Tassalgans, appeared and turned away from the Bridge, started to turn back as they realized what they'd seen—Swardheld Quale standing there, a stranger in the ship. Before they completed the turn, their faces went slack and they dropped into a heap, one falling on the other.

Quale replaced his stunner, checked his thumbring. "Time," he said.

Lirrit Ofka moved swiftly past Karrel, ran to join Elmas Ofka; Karrel Goza looked at Aslan, Churri, Xalloor. "Go," he said. "I'll follow."

Xalloor moved with her awkward dancer's grace past Aslan, muttering as she went, "There's hardly enough trust around here to gild a snort."

Pels was momentarily visible, solid, focused on the great bronze door, his chunky body quivering with an eagerness as great as that she saw in the Hordar who had a much bigger stake in the outcome. He must have done things like this a thousand times before; that didn't seem to matter. Like me, Aslan thought, how I get when I step out on a new world.

The door snapped open.

A wave of change passed over Pels, erased him. The ripple in the air moved swiftly ahead of Quale as he ran onto the Bridge, his stunner humming softly. T'pmmmm, t'pmmmm, t'pmmmm, Aslan heard as she hung back, waiting for this bit to end, it wasn't her idea of a good time. T'krak'k'k, t'rak'k'k. That had to be pellet guns. She looked at Xalloor, grimaced. The dancer lit up with one of her flash-grins, let the babies play, she mouthed. Fffft, ffft't't't, fffft, isya darters. Poison, she thought. Some babies. When they stepped over the sill, half the Bridge crew were collapsed at their stations, dead or stunned, the rest were standing or sitting, staring with dull incredulity at what-is-impossible.

The Huvved Captain sat in a swivelchair that was raised higher than the rest and out in the middle of the chamber where the occupant could see everything taking place at the various stations, a massive kingseat, squatly powerful, with lights like jewels on the boxy arms, sensor pads useless as jewels because Adelaar had managed a minor coup and put through a demand-command that tied up most of the input available to the shipBrain, a move made necessary because this noble Captain knew all about defending himself from rebelling crews, though he had only the most rudimentary idea of the other powers under his hands. He was tall and firmly muscled with a patina of softness beginning to blur the clean outlines of his body. His face was plucked and painted into a dainty mask, his straight fair hair was plaited with gold and silver wire, arranged into loops and swirls until it was more like a minor sculpture than something that grew on a man's head. He wore a yoss silk tunic and trousers, both dyed a lustrous black and over them a sleeveless robe woven in one piece by one of Tairanna's premier weavers, a tapestry in black and silver with touches of aquamarine and olive, a heavy, extravagantly beautiful creation. Muscles bulged beside his mouth and his long silver nails were pressed so hard against the chair arm that several of them had cut through the padding and two had broken off near the quick.

"On your feet, babe." Quale snapped his fingers, pointed across the room. "Jamber, Karrel, get the rest of them over there, against the wall. Pels, we could use some slavewire." He frowned at the Huvved, lifted his stunner. "You can walk or I can drag you."

The Huvved glared at him, didn't speak, didn't move.

"Your choice." Quale thumbed the sensor, waited until the Huvved collapsed, then climbed onto the chair, got a handful of braids and jerked, then he jumped down, stripped the beautiful robe off and straightened up holding it. He looked it over. "Nice," he said. "Hanifa, local work?"

Elmas Ofka's eyes were bright with hostility quickly veiled. "Shopping? Is this the proper time, Yabass?"

"We take our profits when they come, Hanifa." He

tossed the robe over the arm of the kingseat. "If you have many weavers who can produce work like this, you've got a treasure here. I give you that bit of information as lagniappe, it's worth what it's worth." He stooped, grabbed a handful of hair and dragged the Huvved across the room.

Aslan watched, amused at her own reaction to this and at the disapproval on Churri's face; the poet wanted drama, not two traders arguing mildly over markets and somebody's weaving skill. It wasn't the sort of thing that made great legends. Good thing Mama isn't here yet, this could degenerate into a bidding war, not the shooting kind. She glanced at Xalloor, caught her laughing at them all; she grinned back, then started a tour of the bodies and the wounded. There were very few dead; Quale and Pels had stunned more than half before the guns and darters got busy. She looked round, indignant; nothing was being done about the wounded. She met Xalloor's eyes, mimed winding a bandage about her head. The dancer nodded and grabbed hold of Pels as he went trotting past, a coil of slavewire in one hand. "You know something about this. . . ." She waved her hand in a quick expressive circle. "Where'd Lan and me find ourselves some medpacs?"

Pels wrinkled his black nose. "Try the panels by the door, they're stores of some kind. Hey, Quale, you got the pick?" Quale dug into his belt pouch, tossed the rod to him, then went back to what he was doing. "Here, run the blunt end over anything that looks like a lock."

While Aslan and Xalloor poured on antisep and slapped bandages on whatever happened to be bleeding, Jamber Fausse's fighters were snipping sections of slavewire and packaging up the stunned, the intact and the not too badly wounded, and trading jokes as they hauled their prisoners across to the wall and stacked them like firewood. Elmas Ofka glittered with triumph, stalking back and forth across short distances with the feral impatience of a hunting cat. Quale moved over to the comstation. "Pels, it's time to call Mama."

* * *

Adelaar's face appeared in one of the smaller screens.

Quale set his hand on the Rau's shoulder. "We've got the Bridge. You can turn loose the tap."

"Give me three minutes to shut down here, then open the shuttle bay."

"Consider it done."

6

Parnalee reached the hatch just behind the Sleeper squad, about ten minutes after they left the lock. He slid it back with slow care, jiggling it when it stuck half open, no way he could get his shoulders through that. Cursing the Huvved who never fixed anything that didn't contribute to their comfort, he slammed it with a fist, jerked at it until it creaked open, listened and stepped over the sill and faded into the shadows of the sleeping sector, following the faint noises the Hordar made. The corridors here were dim, silent and blessedly free of the dust that was such a nuisance in the unused parts. He loped along on legs not so long as his torso was, the short thick legs that his father found so ugly, a deformity, ghosting through the corridors until he neared the area where the faxmaps the woman gave Elmas Ofka said they'd find the sleeping cells assigned to the Tassalgan guards. The Tassalgans' dormspace was set off some distance from the others, the scutwork crew had their section, techs didn't want to associate with either and stayed some distance from them. The pilots, the navigators and engineers kept to themselves. Duty was divided into three shifts, one group would be sleeping, another group playing while the third was standing watch; two-thirds of any section would be empty on any of the shifts, so the squads had to cover a lot of territory; the plan was they broke into three units and went hunting for occupied cells, the ones whose crystal markers were shining like backlit topaz.

Parnalee stopped before the first of these doors, the

crystal glimmer painting stark shadows in the lines and hollows of his face. He eased open the door.

Four of the Hordar fighters were bunched together in the middle of the sleeping cell, hugging and back-slapping, yeasty with triumph. Without giving them time to notice him, he sprayed darts into them, smiled his own triumph as they crumpled without a sound, dead before they hit the floor; isya darts were fast and fatal. He backed out, ran footsilent and swift to the next cell.

Jirsy Indiz looked round, waved her stunner at him, her sealpup face split with silent laughter. He darted her with a soft grunt of pleasure; the second woman whipped around, he darted her and took out the two others who were bending over the footlockers, going through the sleepers' possessions. Almost as much as the Huvved, Elmas Ofka threatened something very basic in him; when he killed her isya he got a jolt to the groin more satisfying than any copulation he could remember; killing the second woman produced a less intense satisfaction, perhaps because he was sated by the first. A preview, he thought, don't sleep too securely, Aslan you pustulant cow traitor.

He dropped his empty darter beside Jirsy, took hers and finished the killing. He would have lingered to gloat, but there were five left and he had to get them before they knew what was happening.

The last unit was already leaving the third cell by the time he reached it, Geres Duvvar leading them, Karrel Goza's cousin, easygoing, good-humored and unambitious. Parnalee despised him. "There's trouble ahead," he gasped when he reached them, "the Hanifa sent me to warn you. Four, five com techs sneaking off from their duty posts, they've got some whores and a couple of servants to keep the beer coming. Not drunk yet. Too bad. That'd make things easier."

The Hordar milled about, muttering, but they weren't suspicious of him; they knew that Elmas Ofka trusted him. A herd of bonebrained yunk calves.

"How far and how do we get there?" Geres muttered; at least he knew enough to avoid whispering, whispers carried too far.

"There's a gym of sorts a short way off, they're in that. Look, the place has two doors; one of them's already open a crack, I looked in to be sure the Brain wasn't having a paranoid seizure. Getting there's easy enough. There's a Y-fork ahead. I'll take three of you down the left fork, I've got the doorcode, I'll work it for you. You wait there while I come back for the other two and we head down the right fork for the door that's already open. Five minutes should do it. You wait five, get the door open and we'll have them in a pincer before they know what's happening." He gave them a half smile, a shrug. He was Elmas Ofka's watchhound, doing the work he was hired for. "So. What do you think?"

Geres Duvvar waved a hand. "Good enough. Mensip, you and Insker hold up at the Y point. Sacha, you and Geyret come with me."

Parnalee led them down a shadowy curving stretch of corridor. As soon as Mensip and Insker could no longer see them, he wheeled, his darter up and spitting. Leaving Geres and the other two lying where they fell, he raced back. The two ex-pilots were standing close together chatting softly, looking down the other branch of the Y. He slowed, shot them. As they fell, he drew his sleeve across his brow, wiped away the sweat beading there. The rush was over for the moment. The Bridge squad would be mopping up soon, might even be finished. He had a lot of things to do before that hellhag Adelaar started fiddling with the Brain, but the killing frenzy was done. He knelt, took both darters and Mensip's stunner. First step, he told himself, get me a crew and shove 'em in the brig; they'll keep there, I won't be needing them until after the Huvved burn.

The pilots, navigators, engineers and their specialist crews had single cabins which were clustered about a small rec area with moth-gnawed grass and a rickety tree or two, a scatter of tubs with flowers growing in them and a fountain full of dust. He began with the cabins assigned to the pilots according to the faxmap; the man behind the door with a lighted crystal above it was deeply asleep, snoring a little. There was a woman curled up against him, also asleep. Parnalee put a lethal dart in her neck and stunned him; he slapped slavewire around the flaccid wrists, the skinny ankles, muscled the sleeper over his shoulder and dumped him on the grass outside. Before he moved on, he took a closer look at the man. Nothing to worry about, he *was* a pilot, he wore the ring. Reassured (though he wouldn't admit it), he hurried toward the Engineer's slot.

One by one he collected them. Pilot. Engineer. Drive Gang. Navigator, com techs. He stunned them, killed whoever, whatever he found with them, and stacked them like logs on the grass. When he had the men he wanted, he broke into a guardstash, fumbled energy cells into a pallet stored there, nervousness and eagerness turning his fingers into thumbs, his hurry defeating itself as he had to redo connections and reset the cells. The job finally done, he rode the humming pallet back to the rec area.

He took his captives out of the sleeping sector, through another of the rusty hatches and back into the dust. The lift field stirred it into swirling billowing poufs that rose around him and brushed his face and hands with minute electric bites. He pushed the pallet as hard as he could, worried about that dust; it was going to be several minutes before the charge on the particles leaked off enough for them to begin settling. If someone came along before then, he was laying a laughable trail, a blind man could follow it by the prickling of his skin.

He reached the Liner, the inner skin of the complex Outwall, cycled a broad repair hatch open and took the pallet through. He stopped it and got off, left it humming faintly, took a pry bar and jammed the latch so it couldn't be opened from outside; body shaking, hands trembling, he leaned against the wall and closed his eyes. It was so close. He could almost feel the heat of burning Huvved play across his face.

His breathing steadied. Using techniques he'd learned so long ago he'd forgotten the boy who learned them, he calmed himself, breathed the song *I AM, I AM triumphant, there is no one who can stand against me. . . .* Still singing, he flicked on the running lights, climbed aboard the pallet and began weaving through the twisting difficult route to the sector where the holding cells were. He hit his marks again and again, he'd studied the faxmaps until he saw them in his sleep. *I AM a winner, there is no one who can stand against me. . . .* He found the hatch he wanted, cycled back into the ship proper. There was a single Tassalgan standing watch over empty cells; he was drunk and snoring until Parnalee found him. Then he was dead. Parnalee put his pressed crew into separate cells, slapped SOLITARY over them; the cells would feed them and clean them and provide clean tunics every third day and no one and nothing could get at them. Except the shipBrain and that was his next job, taking out the shipBrain.

He rolled the dead guard out of the watchseat, settled in it and touched on the feed from the Bridge. *We've got the Bridge*, he heard. *You can turn off the tap*. Quale. He has to go too, can't have everyone and his dog knowing about this place. *Give me three minutes to shut down here*, that was the panting bitch come snuffling on the stink of the bitch her daughter, *then open the shuttle bay*. Quale again: *Consider it done*. Parnalee smiled at the shadows moving across the screen, deaders walking, dreaming they're still alive. Ah, you tinkering pitiful old hag, I don't have to worry what you do, you can set whatever commands you want, play your moronic games and boast of what you know. You don't know the one thing, the right thing, you don't know about the Dark Sister; Omphalos Institute taught me more than play-making, you castrating jumped-up whore. Blesed be the Institute, no leaky wombs inside those walls. Down deep and hidden where you'll never find it, the shipmind has a wildheart clone, I talked to it, her. Sweet her. You don't know that either, do you? I used your tap to wake her, the Dark One. You left me with it like I was some tame dog, good boy, guard dog, watchhound for the Hordar Bitch, playtoy for the punk. I woke her and I talked to her and oh the sweet thing, how she can hate. Turned on for testing, turned off before she had more than a taste of life. Oh yes, she's angry, she's burning, impatient lover waiting for her lover death. Decline hate, do you, hag? Hear me decline it and accept it in one voice. I hate, you hate, too flabby to hate you-hate, he hates, he does, we hate, the Dark Sister my sweet one and I we hate . . . ah! enough. We hate. Declined and embraced. Do you know the song she sings, our martial maid? Throughout her sweet and sensuous body? Redundancy in infinite regression. Survive and kill, kill and survive. Survive to kill. Guess the reciprocal of that, it isn't hard, I've spoke the clues. Kill to survive, she knows it, my Darling knows it well. Blow the mainBrain into smoke and she comes alive. Kill to revive, survive, contrive to step outside the constraints laid on her, sly sweet murderous virgin. Her hand beneath my foot because she needs me, she courts me with promises of fire and blood, do you think I would I could refuse? She is mine. Shall I tell her who planned to throw her into the sun, to melt her and shatter her, tear her atoms into their component parts? Redundancy in infinite regression.

He switched the viewers off and began the complex journey to the hidden interface, guided by his limited inreach to the dreaming dormant auxBrain.

7

The interface to the Dark Sister was a small luxury apartment with spy links all over the ship; sound only, a visilink was too easy to trace. Parnalee sat in a fur-lined easy chair, his feet up, a bubble glass with fine brandy in it held in the hand he wasn't using to manipulate the sensor pad. He listened to the sounds on the Bridge, switching from one conversation to another as he grew bored with them.

ELMAS OFKA (Nerves thrumming in her voice):

We should have heard by now. You—Yabass with the fur—you know about these things. Find out what's happening.

PELS (His voice dropping to its lowest notes, a rumble in his throat, a warning that he was losing hold on his temper's tail):

Look, Hanifa, Quale says we should be polite, but get off my back, will you? I'm just tickling the Brain till Adelaar gets here; she's the one who knows it.

(A grating grunt as he cleared his throat, the noise overriding Elmas Ofka's attempt to speak. When he spoke again, it was with the icy formality of an irritated technician.)

If I did anything so precipitate as try to initiate a general search without being sure I could isolate the activity from the mainBrain below, I would most certainly be warning the Grand Sech that things were happening up here and I would likely would lose control of the shipBrain; in this delicate interval since Adelaar released control of the tap and before she gets here, I will do nothing so stupid.

ELMAS OFKA: Quale Yabass, you know the transtubes, take us where the squads are, if they need reinforcing. . . .

QUALE: As soon as Adelaar's in.

(A pause; Parnalee imagined him checking his thumbchron.)

Only a few minutes more, five at most. Whatever's happening won't change that much in five minutes.

ELMAS OFKA (An angry hiss, like a spitting kitten. Sound of footsteps as she prowled about the Bridge.

Parnalee laughed aloud and stroked his hand across the Dark Sister's metal skin, content for the moment to hear the Empress bested like that, having to spend her impatience in the movements of her body. He played with the pad and brought in another conversation.)

A HORDAR (probably one of Jamber Fausse's men, Parnalee didn't know their names and didn't care to know.):
Look at her, man, I wouldna wanna put my butt in reach of those claws.
SECOND HORDAR: Hunh.
FIRST HORDAR: Wonder how K'mik's doing. Part of his squad's a Sea Farm isya, wouldna trust them bitches far as I could throw one.
SECOND HORDAR: Oh, I dunno. *She's* one.
(Parnalee pictured him making an obscene gesture toward Elmas Ofka, but he didn't delude himself that was actually happening: these mamaboys had a ridiculous respect for the whipmistress.)
FIRST HORDAR: Don't hardly seem so; she don't act so snotty as others I could name.
SECOND HORDAR: Tried to grope that little Cinnal, eh?
FIRST HORDAR: Got nothing to do with it. They just snotty, that's all.

8

Aslan sat at an abandoned station, one foot tucked under her. She scribbled on a battered pad with most of its leaves torn off, looking around at intervals to see if anything interesting was happening. The Ridaar was propped inconspicuously beside a screen, flaking the events of the Bridge, but in situations when more than an unadorned report was required, when her emotions and sensory reactions, her intuitions and expectations were part of the story, it was her habit to write down whatever came into her mind, disjointed words, phrases, the only requirement a precise identification of time and place.

The Rau was picking delicately at a sensorboard, calling up items and lists, absorbing what was there, his relatively immobile face unreadable. Elmas Ofka was still pacing, throwing angry looks at Pels and at the door. Quale sat at another station, looking sleepy and disengaged. Karrel Goza and Lirrit Ofka were standing apart from the other Hordar, not touching but intensely aware of each other, their conversation single words or phrases interrupted by long periods of silence. Jamber Fausse joined his band; they were gathered by the prisoners, talking in low mutters and looking suspiciously at the others on the Bridge. This clutch of mismates, she thought, they looked like a separating sauce; somebody's going to have to give them a few brisk stirs to save the mix.

Adelaar came striding in, crossed to Quale. "Still mopping up?"

"So it seems; we haven't heard anything from the other squads." He gave the Hanifa a lazy grin as she joined them. "You think you could run a scan on the ship without triggering wrong ideas in downside techs?"

"Give me a minute." She swung round and loped over to Pels; they consulted in polysyllabic mutters for several minutes, then he jumped down, let her have the command station, moved to the nearest aux com station and brought it online.

Aslan moved closer, her eyes shifting from Adelaar's busy hands to the small screen at the station; it was the first time since she was a small child that she'd seen her mother doing real work. Never when she was home for a visit and not back at Base. She wasn't welcome at the Listening Station; Adelaar did very little while she was there, either turning over her work to Parnalee or Kumari and walking outside with her, or chasing her with impatient cutting words which came so close to quarreling that she left rather than provoke her mother further. Her mother's facility reminded her rather oddly of Xalloor's dancing; she watched Adelaar and remembered Unntoualar females weaving, Vandavremmi stormdancers weaving bubble sculptures fifty kilometers across. Even Sarmaylen walking round and round a rock, reading images into it. Enigmatic, fascinating, rather demonic. A capacity for unraveling secrets and extending control over other people far beyond what she herself considered acceptable.

Images on the small screen, pale green lines, a race

through successive cross sections, a jolting stop and the great mainscreen flared into activity. A huge cavernous space about massive shipdrives, control stations dark and dusty except for the central area. A complex mix of sounds, the explosions of the pellet guns, the ping-whine of ricochets, shouts, groans, clatter of feet on catwalks, unidentifiable knocks, cracks, thuds. Four bodies motionless on the catwalks, some distance apart, no two on the same level. A fighter lay bleeding slowly from one arm, the other three were low-level techs in the Drive Gang. A small dark form darted out of shadow, shot at something, threw himself into a twisting roll that took him back into shadow. Adelaar's shoulders twitched. "Quale."

"Right. Hailer, hmm?"

"Ready.. You talk, they'll hear."

"Right." He set a hand on the back of her chair. "The Bridge is taken," he said. "If you surrender, you'll be set down on Tassalga alive and in good shape. If you continue your resistance, you'll be dead. Keeping on is futile. In a few days we will be sending this Warship into the sun. Kanlan Gercik, collect your squad, get them out of there. We can seal any holdouts in the Drive Sector and let them fry." His voice was weary, uninterested in what the holdouts decided, a lazy baritone smooth as cream and far more convincing than a raucous scream. Aslan scribbled rapidly, scatter-shot words that said, in effect, I-don't-care-what-you-do can be more terrifying than hate and rage.

The image went silent, still.

A moment later Kanlan Gercik's voice sounded from somewhere near the control bank. "Zhurev, Meskel Suffor, Harli Tanggàr, move your units toward the entrance. Meskel, can you get to your wounded friend?"

In his soft slurring west coast accent, Meskel Suffor answered, "If the others give me cover; better so, if the Gang shows a touch of smarts and surrenders."

"Start moving. Quale Yabass, is there any way of getting the name of the Engineer?"

Quale shifted his gaze to Adelaar, raised his brows.

Adelaar nodded, worked her pads and pulled up three names on the small screen. "They're all Huvveds. Erek Afa Kaffadar, Boksor Tra Shiffre, Marak Sha Yarmid."

"Any idea which?"

"No indication."

"Kanlan Gercik, did you hear that?"

"If you could repeat them?" After Quale finished the list, Kanlan called out, "Erek, Bokso, Marak, whichever you are. Talk to me."

More silence, broken mainly by scuffs and some tings where something metallic touched a rail or a piece of equipment, the members of the squad edging toward the entrance.

"What guarantees do we have?" The voice was gruff, impatient, with the arrogant edge of a top-rank Huvved.

"The guarantee you'll fry."

"We have the drives."

"So you can sit and watch them hum as you head for the sun." A snort. "You got some kind of idea you can run them without the shipBrain?"

Silence.

Muttering.

A scuffle.

Then a different voice. "Hang on a minute."

More muttering.

A dull thump (pellet gun tossed onto the rubbery floor covering), more thumps, more guns.

"That's it. Hold everything. We're coming out. We got to carry Tra Shiffre."

"I hear. Quale Yabass?"

"You can start forward with them, but don't hurry, we've got to see what's happening with the other squads. Anything comes up, give us a yell, Adelaar will keep an ear tuned to you. Questions?"

"That seems to do it."

"Hanifa," Quale looked down at the Diver. "Anything you want to say?"

Her eyes were fixed on the screen. She was frowning; when he spoke, she shook her head impatiently. "Get on with it."

"Gotcha. Adelaar, Play Sector next, then the Sleep Sector."

The green lines of the schematic flashed again onto the main screen and flickered through cross sections as before. Then the lines were gone and a Pleasure Field filled the screen, roughly oval and somewhat larger than the chamber outside the Bridge door, a cheerful, bright-colored space broken into smaller and larger areas, irregular shapes partly open to the main arena, a combination of bistro, gymnasium, orgy-drum, sensorama, and less-dedicated spaces that catered to assorted individual quirks and kinks.

The mat in the gymspace was littered with flaccid dreaming bodies and the two squads assigned to that area were busily trotting in and out of the Pleasure Field carting in more of them, men and women, crew and support, some naked, some dressed in fantastic costume, some in uniform, some in grubby overalls. The men and women doing the carting looked sweaty, but exuberantly carefree; the grimness she'd marked in them when they marched on board the tug was still there, but only as a ghostly background to the present pleasure. Despite their visible weariness, they were shouting ribald jokes at each other, trading insults and speculations about the activities of the bodies they carried. As far as Aslan could tell, no one had been killed, no one injured badly enough for the wound to show. No bandages, no bruise, no scrapes.

Quale turned to Adelaar. "Sound?"

"Ready."

"Tazmin Duvvar. You round somewhere? Akkin Siddaki?"

Laughter, whoops, hill-and-grass raiderband salutes to Elmas Ofka that quickly degenerated into obscurely idiomatic barbs aimed at Quale and the Bridge party, (Aslan scribbled rapidly, getting the essence of the more interesting insults, the hill-and-grassers were famous for the inventiveness of their invective), two of Elmas Ofka's isyas shouted more intimate greetings, drunk on victory as much as wine; ordinary proprieties stripped away, they floated on a cloud of euphoria.

One of the older raiders moved apart from the rest, set his hands on his hips and roared the others to silence. "Varak, go get Tazmin. What you want, Quale Yabass?"

"We were getting bored sitting around up here, started wondering what was happening in the other sectors. Looks like you've pretty well cleaned up your area. Any problems?"

Akkin Siddaki waited until Tazmin Duvvar pushed through the gathering Hordar and reached his side. "Quale," he said. "Wants to know if we've got problems."

"Cartage mainly," Tazmin said, "these kokotils were drunk, drugged, or screwing their brains if any out; it was like shooting fish in a barrel. If you could dig up some transport for us, it'd save a lot of sweat."

Akkin nodded. "We've got most of the ship people transferred here, there's some whores and some of the kitchen crew still laying where they fell, maybe a dozen, not much more than that. Like you see, there's quite a pile of them. There's a transtube outlet just off this chamber. We could stuff them in that if you'll have the yabass Adelaar program the tube and arrange a welcoming party; you've got the holding space ready yet?"

"It should be by the time you're finished. Adelaar just got here, she'll take care of that once we finish this survey. Pels, see what you can find for transport."

"Right. Soon as I can get access. Adelaar?"

"When we finish this, I'll free some lines for you."

"Quale Yabass?" Akkin Siddaki leaned forward, his dark face intent.

"About ten minutes, if I had to make a guess."

"That's not it. I've got a brother in the Sleeper squad, how's he doing?"

"We haven't checked that one yet, it's next on our list. There was some trouble in the Drive area, one wounded, a raider from the west coast, I think. I don't know how serious. Want me to get the name?"

"When you get a minute."

"Right. If anything comes up, give a yell. Adelaar, Sleepers."

A few minutes later a short stretch of dimly lit corridor took up most of the screen. Empty. Silent. A short distance from the eyepoint a small oval crystal touched with honey-amber the lifeless neuter colors of the walls and floor. The doorway below the crystal gaped open. The light inside the room was a ghostly grayish yellow that merged seamlessly with the light in the corridor.

The eyepoint moved, dipped into the sleeping cell.

Four bodies on the floor.

The eyepoint dropped to hover over the nearest. It swept from head to toe, raced back to the nape of the Hordar's neck and focused on a hexagonal black spot half-obscured by a strand of hair.

Elmas Ofka bit a cry in half. After a minute she said, "Dart." Her hands closed over the back of Pel's chair, tightening until it creaked under the pressure of her fingers. "All of them?"

The eyepoint continued to move. It searched the other three, centimeter by centimeter. It found more darts. It swept out, sped to the next occupied cell and dived inside.

Elmas Ofka saw Jirsy's startled, frozen face and stopped breathing for a long frozen moment. Then she shrieked with rage and grief, grabbed at her hair, tore loose hanks of it; Lirrit Ofka screamed, clawed at her face, her nails scoring bloody lines in her flesh. Then Karrel Goza and Jamber Fausse were there, holding them, confining their struggles, muffling their cries, letting them bite and kick and scratch, accepting the pain as part of sharing the grief, a grief that grew more bitter as the eyepoint moved on and they saw the other dead, as Karrel Goza saw his cousin Geres sprawled in the Y-branch.

Aslan watched and automatically noted her impressions on the pad; she felt uncomfortable about writing while this was happening, she'd known little Jirsy Indiz and liked her; nonetheless, she wrote. The isya phenomenon was endlessly interesting. She hadn't understood before this how powerfully those bonds operated once the isya was formed; the strength of it was suddenly made visible for her; the pain of the severance was apparent in the violence of the women's reactions. Her stylus flew across the battered page. *More than kin,* she wrote, *closer than lovers. Karrel Goza seeing his cousin's body, wept, face red, anger and grief. None of this self-mutilation, this loss of control. The difference explainable by isya bonding? Or by culturally determined sex role differentiation? Sex roles complex here. Women powerful/ powerless. Huvved/Hordar very different, their ideas about women. Suggest someone come, study isya phenom. Trakkar je Neves? Her subject, yes. Contact, see if interest. Outsiders reaction isya hysteria revealing. Consider. History of? Personality differential? Profession, its effect on . . .*

Quale leaned against the console, his face shuttered. He was looking away from the women, shut off from them by something in his past or in his character that washed out the flashes of strength he could show and left him looking oddly empty, as if he were so tired of living that he'd lost the ability to feel either joy or pain.

Adelaar looked over her shoulder, distaste her most visible reaction. She went back to what she was doing. Jaunniko called you one icy femme, Mama, maybe he was right. No, that's wrong. We've clawed at each other often enough; I can't accuse you of lacking passion, Mama. You're just not interested in other people's passion.

The Rau's ears twitched, closed in on themselves like fingers making a fist. He kept working.

Elmas Ofka went suddenly quiet. She sucked in a breath, in and in and in, the soft sound seemed to last forever, to mute the other sounds on the Bridge, then she let the breath out. Again out and out, a long rasping sigh. She pushed against Jamber Fausse's arms. He dropped them and stepped back. "Lirrit!" Her voice was sharp, demanding.

Lirrit broke a sob in half, stood in shuddering silence for another few breaths, then she pushed at Karrel Goza's chest and turned in a grim, controlled silence to watch what was happening on the screen.

"Who?" Elmas Ofka said, her voice soft as thistledown and cold.

Quale straightened, seemed to shake himself, sloughing the detachment that had grayed him down. "Parnalee," he said.

She swung around, her temper flaring, but before she could say anything, Churri spoke. "Parnalee," he said. "He played you like a gamefish, Hanifa. That's his business. He's good at it."

"I don't understand."

Churri shrugged. "Who does. Crazy is crazy."

Elmas Ofka closed her eyes, brushed a hand across her face. "I see. Find him. Now."

Quale raised a brow. "Why bother? Leave him in his hole and let him fry."

Elmas Ofka trembled, controlled herself immediately. "Find him," she said. "We can argue what happens afterward."

Adelaar didn't wait to be asked; she huddled over her sensor pads, called up strings of words and numbers, scanned them, repeated the process several times, selected some, re-entered them. Aslan watched the image flow, expand, contract, change in little and in toto, the glyphs and figures like minute green demons dancing to the beat of her mother's fingertips. The schematic filled the screen again, centered on the Bridge, the Navel. It flashed away in pie-slice wedges, a game of jackstraws with Mama's fingers picking surely through them. Shivering among the green lines were fuzzy red lights and several pale ambers, arranged in clusters. Each time a light appeared, she exploded a small white dot in the center of it and went on without further reaction. One by one she swept through the wedges until she'd done them all; Aslan frowned, there seemed to be more wedges than the geometry of the ship allowed for. Mama's magic, play the numbers, ah! she bit back a giggle and scribbled on her pad.

Adelaar swung around. "I've located all lifesources that the ship can detect. That means exactly what it says. There may be dead areas, this is an antique and badly maintained, and there are places in her deliberately kept off the record; if he knows about those places, well, he knows a lot too much. You're wrong, Quale. We don't dare let him wait us out."

Leaving them to chew that over, she kicked around, touched a sensor and leaned back to watch the screen as the Brain flipped from spot to spot, froze momentarily on a scene, long enough to take in the details, then moved on to the next. Akkin Siddaki and Tazmin Duvvar supervising the tag end of the body-gathering. Flip-flip, body squads walking tiredly to the last few bodies, a whore here, a scutsweep there.

After a short stretch of looking on while the Brain flashed through scenes that she'd seen before, Adelaar moved restlessly, then pushed her chair around and leaned toward Pels; for several minutes she talked in an undertone to him. The Rau listened, nodded, then got busy on the sensor pads at his substation, his eyes fixed on the notation screen. Over their heads the images flickered from the stunned shipfolk in the sleeping cells to the scattered bodies of the dead. Adelaar sat back, satisfied.

The eyepoint jumped to the Hordar and their prisoners marching up from the Drive Sector. Kanlan Gercik and his cousin Zhurev Iavru were the first to appear, scouting ahead for ambushes. The wounded west-coaster came next; he was stretched on an improvised litter being carried by Meskel Suffor and another west-coaster. Then three Hordar from Gercik's Raiders. Then the captive Drive Gang with more litters, two wounded, one dead. One stunned and heavily unconscious Huvved. Harli Tanggàr had her sister isya Melly Birah with her and two women from another isya on the far side of the captives, all of them keeping a fierce eye on their prisoners. Behind them came the rest of the squad, the rearguard.

The eyepoint left them, whipped to the drive room, hovered momentarily over the cooling corpses, leaped again and focused on an ancient eremite living in a rat's nest of scraps and paper and scavenged bits of equipment, filthy white hair knotted on top his head, a few threads of beard, vermin crawling in and out of his hair, in and out of his layered filthy clothing.

Quale rubbed his hand along his jaw. "Makes you itch," he said.

"What?" Elmas Ofka came quietly to stand beside him. She stared up at the image. "What are we looking at?"

Another shift. Another mouse in the walls, this one painfully neat and weirder than the rat, he was walking through elaborate square corners, running a folded whiter-than-white cloth over every surface in his sparsely furnished lair, an irregular space created by the intersection of stressbeams and baffles, choosing the areas he dealt with according to a pattern in his miswired head.

"Discard," Quale said. "Took the measure of life up here and took himself out of it."

"Why are we looking at this?"

Lirrit Ofka came over, leaned against Elmas Ofka, arm curled loosely about her waist. "Yuk."

The eyepoint was hovering over a nest of scavenger moles big as hunting cats, the young nosing blindly at the side of one while another heavily gravid female was regurgitating scraps of anonymous meat for half a dozen yearlings.

"Why are we looking at these things?"

Adelaar turned her head. "The Brain searched out lifeforms, Hanifa. We have to see them all before we know if one could be Parnalee."

The eyepoint continued to jump. More moles, bats, mobile fungi, other, less-identifiable life forms, things mutated into half-glimpsed horrors.

"This is wasting time."

"No," Adelaar said, "we're finding out where not to look for him."

The large screen went blank, flipped back to the schematic of the Bridge.

"I was afraid of that, he's in a blind spot somewhere." She kicked the chair around, taped nervously at the arm. "Probably listening to us."

"Listening?"

"Were it me in his place, I would be. At the least, listening."

"So where is he?"

"I told you. A blind spot."

"Get the others up here. We'll do it our way, gridsearch this thing till we find him."

"Fine. If you've got a year or two."

"What?"

"How long would it take to search gul Inci room by room?"

Elmas Ofka frowned at the screen, one arm folded across her breasts, her fingers moving slowly up and down the biceps of her other arm. "Then how. . . ?"

"Let me think about that awhile. And see if I can do something about snoops."

"Ah."

Adelaar crossed her legs, tapped her fingers on the arms of her chair. "The holding area for the prisoners is ready and Pels has set the tube to it. It's near one of the lifepod banks so your people won't have far to move them once you're ready to pop the pods."

9

Parnalee smiled, lifted his glass in a salute. "Clear them out, you oozy whore. Clear them all out, it's woman's proper work, cleaning house. Clear out yourself and leave me to fry." He laughed. "It's not going to happen, bitch." He stroked his free hand along the smooth black flank of the interface. "Your time is coming, love. Wait a little longer, until they've licked up the vermin and I can move without running into strays." He sipped at the brandy, his eyes on the lethal gray egg sitting on its mobile bed. "A little longer, love."

10

The Bridge cleared quickly. Aslan watched the raiders swagger out, chivvying the Bridge crew before them. The weight of a helpless rage and inturning violence had been lifted from them now that they had the

Warmaster and she could no longer threaten their families and the land itself; should they happen across Parnalee, they'd tear him limb from limb, but it'd be (marginally) a more abstract action with overtones of justice, not simply the blood boiling up. There were small cruelties as they hustled their captives out, an elbow in the ribs, pinches on arms and buttocks; mostly though, they cut at the crew with a cheerful contempt, a facility of tongue developed to work off anger at wrongs that the law or force of arms couldn't . . . no, wouldn't right, the retaliation for the indifference of the Huvved Fehz to the suffering of the Hordar poor in the cities and on the grasslands, to the pain of Hordar families forced off the land they'd worked for centuries before the Huvved came and claimed it. She cross hatched an area of the pad, no words left, not right then; the Ridaar was flaking this, that was enough. Trouble ahead for everyone. These hill-and-grassers, they were what the Huvved had made them; when the war was over, when Elmas Ofka and those like her were trying to put the world together again, these raiders, bandits more than anything else, they were bound to be provoking, out of control, sources of instability, inviting a reimposition of the injustices that had created them. They had to change. She sighed. It wouldn't happen. She looked at the crosshatching, a rambling nothing, started writing again, stopping, thinking, no longer noting impressions, being her father's daughter for a change, poet's daughter trying a poem of her own.

la le la   la le la
yesterday be gone away
la le la   la le la
games we play
words we say
la le la   la le la
dead and done
dry bones in a drying pond
ripples pass beyond and gone
la le la   la le la
echoes to relay replay

yesterday
la le la la le la
dessicated dull and dry
are you am I
are we today
nil and null
reclaiming sway
on and over
yesterday
la le la la le la
goodby lover
never hover
can't recover
yesterday.

She sighed, dissatisfied, and pushed the pad away.

11

Jamber Fausse stood beside Quale, watching Adelaar and Pels hunched over their consoles. "There's this woman I know," he said, "had a kid, a boy. Time he was three he was taking things apart, see how they worked. Drove him near crazy when he couldna figure what did what 'n why. No one to school him, they were borderfolk, lived 'tween Chel and grass, family got broke up, the da, he was horned and headpriced, she took the boy down to Inci. He's dead. Built him a yizzy 'fore he was nine. Bitbits got him, shot away the pods, poured his firejuice on him and lit a match. This Parnalee of yours, you say he wants to kill Huvveds?"

Quale smoothed his hand along his beard. "Yeh, but you wouldna like his methods."

"Eh?"

"Why you think he wants this ship?"

"Since you be reading the man's mind, you tell me."

"Work the sums yourself, he's after the hide of every Huvved on Tairanna and he doesn't give a handful of hot shit for Hordar, not being Hordar or having any ties groundside. You doubt that, go look at your dead down in Sleepers. And he's cracked to the marrow. Talk to Aslan, you want the book on that, have her read her bonebreaks and bruises for you. For that matter, ask the Hanifa what she thinks. Way she's acting now, she got the point a time ago."

"Point being don't trust Outsiders?"

"Long as you use your head, not your gut."

Jamber Fausse took a long look at him, then strolled across to Adelaar. "Yabass," he said.

She started, looked round. "A minute. Let me finish this."

He waited, hands clasped behind him, watching lines of symbol and number flicker in and out so fast no one who didn't already know what they were could take them in. The schematic of the Bridge returned suddenly, the green lines overlaid with red. Adelaar contemplated them a moment, then looked over her shoulder, "What is it?"

"What's this Parnalee know you don't know?"

Quale frowned at the screen. "You've shut him out?"

"Right. He can't hear us now."

Jamber Fausse looked at the screen, then from one Outsider to the other. "What's he know you don't?"

She pushed the chair around so she didn't have to keep stretching her neck. "Obviously he thinks he can take her away from me."

"Can he?"

"How the hell do I know? All I can do is scramble this Brain so radically he couldn't possibly straighten it out before she drops in Horgul."

"You're sure?"

"I'm sure."

Jamber Fausse looked down at his hands; he held them palms up, thumbs out, fingers cupped in fingers; he looked at them as if he read Parnalee's mind in the lines and folds. "He may be crazy, but he's no fool. Has to be something else."

After a moment's strained silence, Quale said, "Monarch class Warmaster. The youngest it could be is ten thousand, more likely around fifteen. My Slancy was built around then. Rummul Empire Trooper. The Rummul were the ones that built most of the Warmasters, so she could know something about them. We never bothered purging Memory; matter of fact, some of the bits in there have been useful for this and that, so when she needed more capacity, we just added it on. Del, you think you could punch a line to her without him knowing?"

"He'll know something's happening, not what."

"He knows that now, with you cutting him off like this."

"Your point. Give me room, this is going to get delicate at times, I'll let you know when I'm ready to link."

12

Kinok skritched two of ves tentacles together, sounding ves irritation at being drawn away from an erotic rite ve was performing with vesself and ves new Kahat and a drivehead. After some more strident grumbling which the infant Kahat didn't bother translating, ve allowed vesself to be talked into a degree of reasonableness.

"Call up Oldest Memory for me," Quale said. "Reference Monarch Class Warmaster."

"You are not getting involved with that fancy, are you?"

Quale blinked. The words were dismissive, but Kinok somehow managed to infuse the light tenor of the translator with a degree of wistful longing more appropriate to the romantic hero of some operettic fantasy. He opened his mouth, intending to explain what he planned to do with the Warmaster, changed his mind before more than a croak got out. He'd run into difficulties before with Kinok, over things that seemed eminently reasonable to him but which slammed into one or more of the Paem's peculiar religious and moral tenets. Killing the Warmaster meant killing her drives and he was willing to bet that Kinok would object strenuously to being connected in any way with the death of a set of drives. He thought about the voice tone. Especially if the Paem was getting his roots in a twist about this particular set. Erotic passion did weird things to the panter; he winced as a few of his own more idiotic obsessions went floating across his mind. "Not involved," he said. "Just pull together everything you can find and squirt it over to us, we'll keep the line open."

"It is in progress," the translator said. "How much longer is Slancy staying at this place?"

"Getting bored, Kinok?"

"Ve-who-speaks is never bored; only a stupid mind, a mind gross and unspiritual grows bored. Ve-who-speaks merely wishes the answer to an ordinary question."

"Ah. Not so ordinary. With luck, two three days, maybe four."

"That is heard with pleasure. Ve-who-speaks will prepare the blessings and ready our Slancy for the run."

"Get her ready for trouble, too, Kinok my friend. We might have a hot welcome when we shift out of the insplit."

"Ve-who-speaks has had our Slancy listening. Her ears have tingled not once. Ve-who-speaks believes those on that world still do not know that they have visitors."

"That could change fast."

"There is something you are not telling ve-who-speaks, Swar. Tell it."

"Things are happening onworld, Kinok; we'll be finishing up our collecting with the Imperator's Palace. That's bound to be noisy."

There was a cool silence from the speaker. On the screen, Kinok's plummy scattered eyes had a skeptical glitter that Quale had no difficulty reading. There were going to be some difficult days ahead. Damn all idiot religions, they never caused anything but trouble for everyone around them, believers or not. He heard the ting that announced the arrival of Slancy's data and suppressed a sigh of relief.

"Talk to you later, Kinok; we've got some clearing up here."

13

". . . redundancy," Aslan translated, sliding into the summary at the end of the dataflow, her voice husky, dry as her throat. Elmas Ofka sat in the kingchair, her eyes fixed on the great screen, on words she couldn't read, numbers she couldn't decipher; faced with Parnalee's defection and the unhappy realization that he'd used her fears and prejudices to undercut her and threaten everything she was fighting for, she'd swung back to a tooth-end trust in Aslan. "It is rumored," Aslan continued, "that even the mainBrain is duplicated; if it is damaged seriously enough, a sisterBrain takes charge. Oh, I see. Forget that, Hanifa, just me realizing what Parnalee is up to. Um, yes, these rumors call her the Dark Sister because she is supposed to be programmed to attack without cease until the ship prevails or is destroyed. Analysts studying the Warmaster have reported that they are unable to discover any clues to the location or even the existence of the Ddark Sister. Some believe that the tales about her are put out to heighten the terror factor and its demoralizing effect on the enemy. These discount the rumors and believe that the Dark Sister exists only in the minds of Rummul information officers. There is nothing in Memory to substantiate either conclusion." She drew a dry tongue across dry lips. "That's it," she said, "that seems to be everything that Quale's ship knows about Warmasters."

She watched her mother shut down the flow, pleased to be finished with the awkward job of translating technical details into a language that didn't have reasonable equivalents, not all that happy with what she'd read. She wasn't convinced by the disclaimers at the end. Like Jamber Fausse said, Parnalee might be crazy, but he wasn't stupid. There were some hazy dark rumors floating like smoke through University subfiles, unsubstantiated speculation about the intent and purpose of that institute of his. Hmm, she thought, maybe

I can talk Chancellor DizZawbawka into hiring Mama to worm in there and find out what Omphalos is hiding, he's got a kink about secret societies. This is a note you don't write down, woman, but you don't forget it either. She smoothed her hand across her mouth and watched Elmas Ofka, interested in the Dalliss' reaction to what she'd heard.

Elmas Ofka pinched thoughtfully at her lip. "There is a second Brain," she said. "There has to be. Can you find it, Adelaar yabass?"

"I can try."

Quale chuckled; he was sitting at a down station, feet resting on a pile of empty medpacs, arms folded across his chest. "You need stroking, Del? Hah! you know how good you are."

"I also know the work of several of those analysts in that report; they might be a long time dead, but if they couldn't find anything, it either wasn't there or I'm likely to find the far side of Beyond before I trip over the clone."

"And didn't I not so long ago hear you say that this Brain is big, powerful and dumb? Dumb. That was the word you used, wasn't it? And didn't I hear you say we've learned considerable since this ship was built?"

"Quale, don't play shitgames with me. It'd take a Memory the size of the one on University to record what you don't know about penetration. What about a real game? A wager. Double your fee against no fee on whether the clone is actually there and I find it."

"I'm a cautious man, aici Arash. I won't bet against a certainty."

"Then you'd better get ready to blow the Dark Sister the moment I find her. I have a feeling we're not going to have much time to maneuver."

14

Adelaar circled round and round that problem, then went at it obliquely, running the numbers of the corporeal essence of the ship, its dimensions and locations, ignoring for the moment the visual map, only the numbers mattered, matching and crossmatching, tagging subtle disparities, replaying the visuals with the disparities corrected, tagging discontinuities that appeared when that was done. Aslan could see that her mother had only the tiniest of threads to pull on, but that seemed to be all she needed; when an hour had crept past, it was obvious she was going to unpick the knot. The farther she got the easier it seemed for her, it was almost as if she were beginning to read the minds of the programmers who'd done the original work. Funny, Mama didn't get along at all well with Sarmaylen or his friends. My friends, Aslan thought, maybe that's why. She's as much an artist as they are, I thought so before, I know it now. That's not just skill, that's a leap of . . . of . . . I don't know, whatever artists leap at. She sighed. My father's a poet, my mother's a . . . well, whatever. What the hell happened to me? Ah well, as Xalloor says, deary dai, we do what we can. Missing Xalloor, she strolled to the panels, drew water from a spigot. It's a good thing Churri took off with Quale, she thought, he made Mama nervous. She sipped at the water. It was lukewarm and tasteless, but her mouth was still dry from the reading stint. First time I saw Mama fluttery like that. Ooh-yeha and forty hells, four months in the insplit going home, that is not going to be fun for anyone, not if she starts after Xalloor. She can be a bitch on wheels when she's jealous. Aslan wrinkled her nose as her mind flipped back to the time when she was fifteen and the boy she was sneaking out to see and what happened when Mama caught them. Deary dai, indeed.

She gulped the rest of the water and moved over to watch Pels work. His eyes flicked in an unceasing round from screen to screen to screen; the lifepod sector drawn in green lines was on one with an inset showing the Hordar packing the crew into the pods, another had a map of the Palace, the city, the landing field, on the third there was a map of the system with pinpoints of yellow light converging on the whitepoint that was them, or so she assumed. She touched his shoulder. "Are those something we should be worrying about?"

His ears twitched. "Grand Sech has been trying to talk to someone up here the past hour. Those are the stingers heading at us."

"What are you going to do?"

"Nothing."

"Huh?"

"It'll be at least an hour before they're close enough to be a bother. Until then there's no point. Besides, we won't be able to get outside the skin before Adelaar's finished over there. She going to be much longer?"

"I don't know, I don't operate in those realms."

"Me either, I used to think I was good, but she's a witch."

"She's never let me watch her work before. I don't know why."

"Huh." He dug his claws into his neck fur, scowled at the pod area. "Almost ready to pop 'em. Igsala poong! That Proggerdi. We can't sit around sucking our toes or he'll stick a torp up our collective arse."

Aslan glanced at her mother, grinned. "Right on cue," she murmured.

Adelaar flung her arms up, wriggled in the chair, yawned. "Got it," she said. "Where's Quale?"

"Doing what you told him, getting ready to blow the clone," Pels said. "The Grand Sech is birthing fidgets because he can't get through up here; he sent stingers to see what's going on. They can't burn a way in, but unless I remember wrong, more than one of them will have overrides on the lockseals."

"Transfer the trace here." She watched the pinlights creep for a moment, sniffed, then began playing with the pad. "I'll let them think they are in control till they're close enough . . ." she broke off, concentrated for a moment, "to Tairanna, then all their little popbuggies will peel off and put them down where they'll have a lot of privacy and time to contemplate their sins." She sat back, yawned again, laced her fingers across her stomach and examined her thumbnails. "I think we ought to let him hear us." She tilted her head back, smiled at Aslan. "Don't you think we owe him a little sweat?"

"No." Aslan sighed. "It gives him too much time to knife us, it's safer with him dead."

Adelaar laughed at her. "That's my little pacifist."

"All right, make it the clone dead first."

"Ruin my mood, mmh?" Adelaar straightened. "Fetch my kit over, will you, Lan? I left it by the door there. I might as well use this time to work on the sun-intercept—and a few other notions I've had . . . um—Pels, have the locals finished loading the crew?"

"Just about, why?"

"Tell them I'm going to start launching the pods. The stingers won't bother them. Then you get hold of the Hanifa and have her order her people back on the tug. When we leave, we don't want any snags or strays." She looked over her shoulder at Aslan, eyes bluer than blue and guileless. "Keep the customers happy," she murmured. "Dead locals don't trade rosepearls for security systems."

Aslan wrinkled her nose but said nothing; she wasn't about to be drawn into that ancient argument. She brought the pack to her mother, then went to stand beside the door, looking out into that absurdly oversized antechamber. Briefly she wondered where Parnalee was and if he suspected he was being out-thought and out-engineered. At least, she hoped he was. The Bridge was empty except for Pels and Adelaar. And her, of course. Elmas and her isyas were carrying their dead to the tug hold and getting them stowed for the trip home. Xalloor was in the tug too, running the wounded through the autodoc, if she'd managed to convince the Hanifa it wasn't a subtle attempt at assassination. Aslan pressed her lips over a giggle. There's a product for you, Mama, say the doc performs in its usual fashion. Quale was a long time gone. What was happening down there in the armory? If he couldn't get in, he'd have been back before this. He should have taken Pels with him; Churri was there, but what use was he? Mama used to tell me when I did something dumb with my pc that I was just like my father, clumsy as a tantser calf. Jamber Fausse and his lot are there; they're no use, except as strong backs if something needs shifting and for standing guard. I hope they are standing guard. He should have taken Pels. Why isn't he back yet? Maybe they're all dead. We can't look round the ship without breaking Mama's blocks. Aslan sighed. There was no point standing at the doorway like some stupid chatelaine waiting for her lord to get back from the wars. She grimaced at the image. Oooh-yeha, Lan, you're worse than a teener reading sublimated sex books. Face it, woman, he's done everything but come right out and tell you he's not interested. I wonder why? He's hetero and I'm not a hag. T'k. She ran fingers through her hair, pushed it off her face. This isn't getting me anywhere. She walked with quick nervous steps to the station where Pels was working.

Adelaar had turned the launching of the pods over to him while she busied herself doing enigmatic things to the Brain. The dataflow was so quick and so esoteric it gave Aslan a headache. Much more satisfying to watch the pods blow, at least she knew what was happening, the ship's crew including all its Huvveds were on their way to Tassalga for a bit of involuntary exile. Permanent exile, if the Huvveds had any sense. The way feeling was running among the Hordar, they could end on the chopping block if they got back to Tairanna. The inset showed that most of the locals had cleared out of the loading area; the few left were clearing up odds and ends and loading these on one of the pallets. She recognized Akkin Siddaki and his protegé the boy thief from gul Brindar, Kanlan Gercik and two of her students from the Mines. The rest must be settling down in the tug. It's almost over. All we have to do is blow the clone. Then we leave. Then we go home. Then I stir up a mess of trouble for those foul and loathsome Oligarchs. She savored her triumph. They sold me into slavery; they're as guilty as Bolodo. What a lovely thought. I suppose they'll claim they had a legitimate contract with Bolodo. Let them try it. University can field a team of ethicists and lawyers that'll wipe their faces in their own muck till they choked on the stink. And the Chancellors will authorize and organize the team without their usual fuss and obfuscation, not for me, for the Unntoualar. They mean it, dump on him who says anything not my species is my prey, dump it deep and stinking. They'll go after those Oligarchs with everything they can throw at them. It surely will not hurt my tenure standing that they can throw me at them too. Hmmp. Like Quale says, I'm lagniappe. I wish he'd get back.

15

When the sound from the Bridge cut off, Parnalee stirred drowsily; the brandy was smooth and rather sweet, he'd swallowed more of it than was good for him. His mind was swimming, he had to concentrate to think. "Busy bitch," he muttered, "You and your treacherous daughter, you're a set." He slapped at his face, felt his stomach spasm. "Fool!" He got to his feet, forced back a surge of nausea and by an effort of will whipped mind and body into a semblance of order. The sisterBrain was hobbled until he got rid of the mainBrain. "The point is," he told himself, "who's left out in the corridors? How far have they got in the clearance?"

He lowered himself into the chair and swiveled to face the console. "She shut me out of the Bridge, I doubt she could. . . ." His conversation with himself died away as he concentrated on what he was doing.

The sound-search swept through the ship, collecting a series of squeaks and rattles, mechanical hums, the sough of air. Dead sounds. Empty echoes. In the armory, voices, clinks, the scuff of feet, the complex of sounds remotes made when they were forced to the limits of their capacity. Parnalee smiled. "Dealing in armaments now, hmm, Quale? When I get back Outside and spread word around of your scavenging efforts, you're going to have a problem or two." Satisfied that he knew what the man was doing and why, he went on with the search.

Nothing. Nothing. Pod bays, the readings showed

them empty. "Busy busy," he murmured. "Good little housekeeper, got your cleaning finished, have you?" He did a more intensive sweep, but there was no evidence of any life forms in the area. Lifter locks. Yes, the tug was in Three. Not much sound in there, the ghosts of voices; he fiddled with the controls, focused on the tug's lock which seemed to be open, fulminating as he did so against the lack of visuals; he depended very much on his eyes and had trouble imaging from sounds. He began recording the voices; he couldn't make out the words, they were too broken, but the equipment here was good enough to reconstitute them when he was ready—if he decided he needed to know what was being said, which wasn't likely, he had other, more important things to do.

The corridors were clean. It was time to move. He thumbed out three stimtabs, tossed them down his throat and followed them with a gulp of stale, lukewarm water from the spigot; he'd have preferred a final swallow of brandy but he had enough alcohol in him. Praise Omphalos it should be mostly absorbed by now. Adding more wouldn't merely be stupid, it could even be fatal.

He checked the torp to make sure it was strapped firmly down, then went meticulously through one last test of its triggering circuits. The torp was old, not so old as the ship, but old enough to have acquired a degree of fragility inappropriate to a bomb though it was sufficiently intact to perform its function without going off prematurely as long as he treated it gently as an egg about to hatch while he was moving it. He toed on the lift field of the dolly and guided it toward the interface exit. Since he couldn't go near the tube without alerting that woman, he had to travel the serviceways. It was going to be a long slow trip, but there wasn't anyone to threaten him now and he didn't have to go near the Bridge. The mainBrain lived inside a sphere of collapsed matter close to the heart of the ship; theoretically, only the Captain had access to its coordinates; even the techs who serviced it had no idea where they were; they tubed there and back, the tubeflow coordinates set by the Bright Sister when she was commanded to do so by the Captain.

Parnalee smiled with drowsy contentment as he climbed on the dolly and settled himself at the controls. As soon as he'd waked the part of her he could reach through the tap, she'd gone hunting for her sister. Found her, too. And he knew what she knew, once he convinced her to trust him; though most of her slept still, she was awake enough to print a map for him. Awake enough to run a jolt through him so he could share her exaltation as she celebrated the power that would soon be hers. And his.

He stopped the dolly, got down so he could crank open the first of the twelve hatches ahead of him, coughed as his feet stirred fine gray dust that had lain undisturbed for millennia. He sprayed oil he'd found in the interface stores over the mix of sheddings, exuda and other muck age-bonded to the gears, slammed his fist cautiously against the handle, hit it again without budging it. He poured clear liquid handcleaner over the slowly softening glue to thin it out yet more, then leaned on the handle. The crank groaned and resisted; sweat popping out on his forehead, he put more pressure on it, half-afraid he was going to break the thing. It shrieked and moved a hair; he sprayed more oil, doused on more cleaner, worked the crank back and forth until the seal gave way and it began to turn, slowly at first then more smoothly. The hatch squealed open, slid into the wall. One down. Eleven to go. He wiped his hands on his tunic sides, rubbing vigorously to get rid of both oil and cleaner, especially the cleaner which had a strong, oversweet smell and a soapy, slimy feel. The stims were doing the job, his head was clearing, he felt as charged as the Dark Sister. He thought of Adelaar's face when the pads died under her fingers. He smiled.

16

I watched the last load leave with Churri riding herd on it; I wasn't planning to sell any of this bit of salvage; I don't approve of arms dealing and anyway it's a lot too dangerous for the payoff, but given some of the places I take Slancy into, it's comforting to have that kind of firepower available and it's not the sort of thing you can buy whenever you take a notion. And there was Bolodo. If Bolodo execs had any scruples about anything, I hadn't come across them yet. And I hadn't a sliver of a doubt there was a destroyer or two stashed somewhere handy where the execs on Helvetia could set them up to take us when we showed. I'd done what I could to pull some cover around us, but cover has a way of springing leaks when you need it most.

Jamber Fausse was squatting by the door with a couple of his men. He got to his feet and came sauntering over to me. "Time?"

"Time. One of you has to go to the Bridge to let Adelaar yabass know we're ready; she's still sealed off, I can't reach her."

"Tube?"

"Right. The way we got here."

"Vehim Feda, go." The younger of the two men got to his feet and went trotting out. "What will you do if Adelaar yabass has not discovered the Dark Sister?"

"Sit here and wait. Nothing else I can do." I went over to the implosion torp on its dolly. There was a lot of crud still on it, but the batteries were charging steadily, no sign of trouble there, no breakdowns in the timerprogram if the probe wasn't looping on me. I toured the testmeters and their readings were all good, no glitches. I climbed onto the dolly's front bench, put my feet up on the console.

"Ah." Jamber Fausse dropped to a squat beside the door. "Something I know about, sitting and waiting."

I didn't expect to do much waiting; Adelaar didn't waste time or energy when she was working and Vehim wouldn't be more than a few seconds tubing up to her. I arranged myself so I could see the screen; it was over the door. I counted seconds and got to fifty before it lit up and Adelaar was looking at us.

"Quale," she said. "I see you're ready." She didn't seem to expect a response so I didn't give her one. "The auxBrain is scattered through more than a dozen nodes, there's no way you'll be able to get them all."

"Shit! What. . . ."

"Relax. You don't need to. Do a thorough job on the interface and you've neutered our Dark Sister. There's a weakness in the design. The nodes are connected through that interface. They don't operate independently unless most of the ship is dead. Not enough power. They'll probably kick on when she hits the sun, but that's a bit late to do any good. Implosion torp?"

"Yeh."

"I thought I recognized the configuration. Under all those meters." She laughed, a nice sound; she was feeling pleased with herself. "It's viable?"

"Yeh."

"That'll do it. We'd better be outside the skin when it blows."

"Yeh." I wasn't going to argue with that; the Warmaster was big and tough enough to absorb a lot more punishment than one little torp, but she was older than time and there was rot in her hide. "Tubeflow?"

"I've reset the tubeflow from your gate, it'll take you straight in to the clone interface. I've given you two minutes to get to the interface, starting when we finish this, five to get set up, plus three for holdups. The three will kick on only if you haven't gone through the gate there before then. The flow switches outbound automatically, endpoint the lander lock area. Where we'll be sitting, waiting for you."

"Bridge?"

"I've programmed the mainBrain to clamshell after we're out."

"Any sign of the Proggerdi?"

"I haven't bothered looking."

I gave a yell for the teddybear. His ears were up fluttering, his lips curled back to show his tearing teeth. He didn't need telling to watch out for ambushes, but I told him anyway. "That fruitcake could be anywhere," I said. "Get hold of the tug before you start and have a bodyguard waiting at the tubegate.

Adelaar, no arguments. I don't get paid if I don't get you back to Helvetia and I intend to collect. You hear?"

She laughed again. Almost hysteria, coming from her. "I hear," she said. "Time is, Quale. Get yourself in gear or miss the boat." The screen went dark.

"Right," I said. "Hop on, Jamo, you and your friend, it's time to roll."

17

The curved wall of the massive sphere was a gray-black chimera behind the container shield, there and not there, ominous though not quite tangible, the mass of a small star prisoned in gossamer. Parnalee brought the dolly to a gentle stop before it, lifted the link from the seat beside him. "Open," he murmured, then waited for the Dark Sister to coax an opening for him.

The surface shimmered, a black pinhole appeared, dilated swiftly until it was wide enough to admit the dolly then pulsed like a wet black mouth, a mouth that could close on him if it chose; he eyed it with distaste, but the bulk of the Bright Sister was in there and there was no other access. He edged the dolly toward the opening, took it through.

Thinking he was a repair tech, the Bright Sister brought up the lights so he could see what he was doing.

He eased the dolly and its burden as deep into her heart as the narrowing serviceways between the Brain's components would let him go. Then he cycled down the power of the liftfield, let the dolly sink to the floor, gently, gently, don't crack the egg, not yet. Not. Yet. Off. Yes. He slid the link into his belt pouch, climbed over the bench back and squatted on the bed beside the torp. He activated it, set its timer for an hour on; he needed an interval to get back to the interface where he'd be in touch with and protected from the fury of the Dark Sister. Before he touched the triggering sensor and started the timer humming, he set his hand on the casing of the torp and savored the triumph that was going to be his. One hour. He patted the bomb. Gently. Very gently. "Yes." He set his forefinger on the sensor and felt the hum in his bones. "Yes." He slid off the dolly and trotted for the mouth.

As soon as he was outside, he touched on the link. "Close," he said.

The hole in the sphere grew smaller, smaller, swiftly smaller, was a pin prick of darkness again, was gone. He put the link away and began the long run to the interface, bouyed by the knowledge that nothing could go wrong now, nothing could stop the explosion that killed the Bright Sister. All he had to do was sit and wait.

18

I looked round the interface. "Yeh," I said. "This is it. He was here."

Jamber Fausse nodded. Store cabinets were open, some of their contents spilled onto the floor, evidence of a hasty search, there was a bottle of brandy on the console with about an inch of liquid left in it, a bubble glass beside it with a brown smear drying in the bell; the stink of the brandy was thick in there, along with a stale smell that clung despite the labors of the fans in the ducts. "Where is he now?"

"Who knows?" It's a big ship. Keep an eye on the door, will you, the two of you? I'd better get to work. We don't have that much time."

I let the bed down, started arming the torp. Didn't take long. When I finished, I thought a minute, then I opened up the dolly's motor casing and removed a few vital parts. If—when—Parnalee got back, I didn't want him driving off with our little surprise. There wasn't much else I could do. Even if the three of us could muscle the torp off the bed without fatally herniating ourselves, there was no place in here where we could hide the thing.

The young raider left, but Jamber Fausse stopped

me at the door. "What if he comes back before it blows? What if he disarms it?"

"You want to stay and argue with him, be my guest," I said. I wasn't all that happy with that antique timer; I was sure it'd trigger the torp sometime, I just wasn't sure when. And I didn't want to be anywhere around when it turned over. "Look," I said. "It's a randomized circuit and not all that easy to counterprogram. Not like pulling a few wires on hope and a prayer. I've set the thing to blow in half an hour. If he gets here in a minute or two, maybe he can do something; if he's later than that, no way. We take our chances, that's all we can do."

He didn't like it, but he was no more into suicide than I was, so he nodded and we took off for the tubegate.

19

I dropped the tug into orbit a quadrant away from the Warmaster and waited there.

Adelaar glanced at her chron. "Two minutes," she said.

The ship hung motionless in the center of the screen. The Hanifa was standing behind me again, I could feel her hot breath on my neck. When I looked around, I was almost nose to nose with her, but she wasn't noticing anything but the Warmaster. The rest of them were pretty much the same. Hungry.

The Warmaster trembled. A shine spread over her, then localized at the drivers. She moved. Slowly at first. Ponderously. She began picking up speed, angling away from Tairanna. As soon as she got wound up, it was like she vanished, collapsing to a pinpoint and then to nothing. "Well," I said. "She's on her way. Horgul in two hours. Good-bye, battleship."

"What about the torp? How do we know if it blew?"

That was Jamber Fausse; he was a man to keep his teeth in an idea until it squealed. "We don't," I said. "Unless she turns up again. Then we know it didn't. Back off, everyone. Show's over. We're going down."

20

Parnalee had slowed to a fast walk by the time he passed through the next to last hatch. He felt the sudden liveliness in the ship as she began to move. He stopped, flattened his hand hard against the wall. He could not have described the difference he felt in her, but he knew what was happening, she was on her way to the sun. He smiled. So they thought. Let them think it, fools. He started moving again, an unhurried trot. He passed through the last hatch, glanced at his chron, smiled again. He'd made better time than he'd expected. Only half an hour. He sighed with pleasure as he thought about stripping down and letting the fresher scrub him clean again, about stretching out on the fur, a hot meal on the console beside him and another bottle of brandy while he waited for the Dark Sister to come alive and take over the ship. He saw the door, open like he'd left it, hurried toward it.

He stopped just inside, his way barred by the dolly and the torp; for a crazy moment he thought he was hallucinating, then that the Bright Sister had somehow developed a mechanical TP facility and flipped his torp back to him, then he knew that the woman had done it, the bitch had found his hiding place, she'd found the Dark Sister, no matter that it was impossible for her to find the Dark Sister, and she'd left this joke to greet him. Furious and afraid he took a step toward it; disarm it, he thought, I've got to disarm it.

It blew in his face. He knew an instant of intolerable brightness, of intolerable frustration and rage. Then nothing.

XIV

1

Time-span: 11 Days (local) after the meeting on Gerbek Island to the evening of the day called Lift-Off.
At the Mines.

When Karrel Goza left Zaraiz Memeli at the Mines, the boy was on fire with excitement, but it didn't take him long to discover he'd been dumped there to keep him out of trouble while the adults did whatever it was they were going to do. He was furious and hurting, betrayed again by someone who claimed his trust. He poked about, sticking his nose into anything that showed the slightest promise of breaking the tedium. In the middle of his second week there, early one morning before the sun was all the way up, he pulled a rotten board off a window at the back of the convict barracks, wriggled through the narrow space and dropped onto the floor of a holding cell.

The silver sphere came bounding at him, squawling its warning, attacking when that warning was ignored.

He was startled but not frightened. He jumped, swerved, dived, played with it, laughed as he whipped about, elastic as an eel, too fast for the sphere to catch him.

N'Ceegh heard him laughing, took a look.

The sphere stopped chasing Zaraiz and began chatting with him, then it brought him into the workshop.

After a terse welcome, N'Ceegh went back to making the operant parts of one of the stunners he was assembling for the hit on the Warmaster. Zaraiz sat on the stool next to him and watched him work, fascinated by the delicacy and precision of his fingers, by the magnifier he was wearing, the microscopic points on most of his tools. Despite his involvement in the Green Slimes and his ability to dominate the other middlers, he was a solitary boy; he knew the pleasures and value of silence. He asked nothing, volunteered nothing, spoke only to answer the Pa'ao's questions and kept his mouth shut at other times, not wanting to distract N'Ceegh at a crucial moment. After a while N'Ceegh let him polish and fit together cases for the stunners.

The boy immersed himself in what he was doing, glowing with pride each time the Pa'ao looked a part over and set it down without comment, showing that he thought it was finished, that he saw nothing there that needed fixing. With the resilience of the child he still was, Zaraiz gave his trust again, this time to the Pa'ao, gave it because N'Ceegh was a master craftsman and he wanted very much to be like him, because N'Ceegh was wholly alien, was physically and spiritually Other. He gave his trust and a tentative affection. N'Ceegh recognized this in his silent way and gave back what he was given.

When they took the Pa'ao, Bolodo's minions were clumsy and let themselves be seen. To cover themselves they ashed the village where they found him, killing all his kin, blood to the third degree, killing his mates and his children, most of all killing the boychild who was his craft-heir. His species was monogamous for life, patrilocal and powerfully bonded to the family and the family Place. He lived after that only to trade death for death; he escaped from the Palace to find a way of laying his bloodghosts, to feed them blood from the men who did the killing, blood from the men who ordered it. Zaraiz gave him hope of another kind, hope of passing on his craft, of hands to lay his own ghost when it was tired of him and wanted to shed the weary weight of his body.

By the end of the week Zaraiz Memeli divorced his family and swore loyalty to N'Ceegh, taking the name Zaraiz Pa'ao. N'Ceegh adopted him as his son, his craft-heir. And he began teaching Zaraiz Pa'ao the Torveynee, the way of the Pa'ao and the way of honor, the way of vengeance.

Ten days before Lift-Off they watched Elmas Ofka and her isyas leave for the Chel, carrying with her the stunners they'd built for her. They watched the fighters from the Mines being ferried out to her, one night, two nights, three, until the chosen were all gone.

They spent the day named Lift-Off in the shop, working on the housing of a hunting rifle, one that killed with exploding darts no larger than a mosquito. N'Ceegh set delicate scrolls of inlay into the dark fine wood of the stock, then passed it over to Zaraiz for polishing while he etched shadow patterns into the metal parts. They worked all day, talked about nothing but the work.

Around sundown they went to the Smelter and sat in a corner eating fries and fish and drinking tea, listening to the music, watching the youngsters and the middlers dance.

Thirty minutes later Belirmen Indiz came in, banged his fist on the bar, then scrambled onto it, his age and stoutness forgotten. "The Warmaster is taken," he bellowed into a sudden silence. "She is taken and gone, sent into the sun. Do you hear me? The Warmaster is gone."

Noise and confusion, shouted questions, Belirmen's booming voice as he tried to answer them, shoving elbows, stomping feet, triumphant flourishes, trills and squeals from the musicians, crying men, women, youngers. Rebels crowding closer to the bar to hear more, rebels forcing their way against the tide to get out and spread the news. Everywhere movement and emotion, a heady yeasty mix. A time when dreams no one quite believed in were suddenly made real.

N'Ceegh looked at Zaraiz, nodded at the door. Zaraiz got to his feet and followed him out.

Riding souped-up yizzies protected by miniature cuuxtwoks, N'Ceegh and Zaraiz Pa'ao left the Mines an hour before dawn. They circled wide through the mountains and went clacking and whirring across a stretch of barren Chĕl, not far from where the raiders had camped. By nightfall they were on the lower boundary of the Eastern Duzzulka, where tendrils of grassland reached into the scrub. They landed, tethered their yizzies, ate, slept a few hours, climbed into the saddle again.

2

I put Chicklet into a dive, flicked her around so the gunport Pels had improvised in her repair lock faced a melter station; I balanced her on her tail while he got off a missile that a second later blew out the station and a hunk of tower under it. We went swing, balance, boom around the circumference until the wall looked like beavers had been at it.

Swarms of yizzies were converging on the Palace; when we came over from Base, we'd seen hordes of them, flying in from every corner of the Littorals like locusts on the move; they even sounded like locusts when I turned on the external ears and listened to them. The news of the Warmaster's end was out everywhere, that was obvious. The com net, I suppose; if I were Huvved, I'd have shut down the net till I had some sort of control in the cities. Aslan said it was survival-fear that triggered Surges; looked to me like survival-hope was doing the job just as well. Airships were drifting loose over the city, abandoned by their pilots and passengers, loads of Hordar dropped to melt into the Surge that was forming there. As we flew over, I could see the devastation starting, like the destruction in gul Ukseme multiplied a hundredfold, a million Hordar as a single deathbeast striking down the thousands of Huvved living there, burning, trampling, bursting in doors and windows, destroying everything their hands and feet could smash or torch. The yizzies came clicking and clattering over them, airmarching with the landswarm moving in a blind fury toward the Palace.

As I finished the firing run, I saw that mass of Hordar crossing the waste land between the city and the Wall. I swore. I did not want to go down there in the middle of that mess. Pels came up from the lock and slid into the co's seat. He inspected the mob. "Rrrr," he said.

"Yeh." I took the tug up and got ready to set her down inside the walls. "Looks like half the Hordar on Tairanna."

"Maybe we should come back tomorrow. Or next week."

"I doubt the relatives would pay for stewmeat." I took another look at the mob. "Which is what's going to be left tomorrow. Well, let's set her down. Faster we finish, the better shape our hides're going to be in."

I put Chicklet down in an elaborately ugly garden which was the only space large enough for her fat little tail that was within a reasonable walk of the slavepen. The EYEs Kumari sent sniffing around told us that the techs were collected around sundown and put in the pen, the rest rounded up by midnight; that didn't include bedslaves, but they weren't targets anyway; ordinary girls however lovely were too common to be pricey; mostly their parents, husbands, lovers, whatever, couldn't afford to offer the kind of reward that would get them on ti Vnok's list. We were early; it was barely dusk, the end of a cold windy day with shreds of fog coming off the lake. On the other hand, there was the attack by the Hordar; maybe the slaves would be locked down early, if Luck happened to look our way. Pels and I, we set the barriers and the shockers to keep the locals out, rode the lift down and started at a quick trot for the pen.

I nearly bumped into a guard running for the wall. The man stared at me, lifted his rifle, but changed his mind and went loping past me. Several of the guard cats were pacing about, their leashes flopping; they put their back hair up and their tails twitched when we came along. One of them charged at us, the others followed her. Pels got the leader and I stunned the others. After that we kept an eye close to scan roof edges and the shoulders of the sturdier statues, any high place a cat could perch on. We got half a dozen more cats that way.

The situation inside the walls was getting hairier by the minute; the Huvveds and Tassalgans on the intact sections of the Wall were firing down at the Surge with hand-held melters and pellet rifles. They killed hundreds and yet more hundreds, but the Hordar came on, walking over the wounded and the dead (a distinction without much difference because anyone wounded badly enough to be knocked off his feet was trampled to death by the feet of his neighbors). Tendrils of the Surge peeled away from the main mass and fought their way into the gaps Pels had knocked into the walls. Other units had ropes with grapples knotted onto them; the Hordar climbed the ropes faster than the guns could cut them down, swarming up and over, tearing the guards to bits as they passed over them, destroying everything they got their hands on.

I was frowning as I ran, there was too much confusion inside the walls; I could understand some of it, there didn't seem to be a helluva lot you could do to stop a Surge coming at you, but this chicken had its head cut off; talk about ineffective. Where was the Grand Sech? Was Pittipat stupid enough to execute him when the Warmaster went? Was the Sech stupid enough to let that happen? I shook my head as I pulled up before a heavy door; it was barred and locked, but there wasn't a guard in sight.

I sliced through the bar and the lockbolt and shoved the door open.

3

As N'Ceegh and Zaraiz Pa'ao got closer to Gilisim Gillin, the air went thick with airships and yizzies; since the cuuxtwoks hid them from eyes as well as probes, they had to stay alert and do some fancy dodging to avoid being run over. They reached the Palace close to sundown, slipped past the Wall without triggering the melters and touched down in the garden atop the Palace tower.

N'Ceegh wore armor covering his torso, arm and leg sheaths with knives of assorted lengths and purpose in them; on his back he had a battery pac attached by cable to a heavy-duty cutter that needed both hands to hold it level when it was in use. The smaller cutters that Zaraiz Pa'ao wore were keyed to his hands. All he had to do was point, then tap a thumb against the side of a crooked middle finger. He had no armor; he counted on his agility and speed to protect him. The door from the roof garden into the palace was a bronze slab elaborately etched over all its surface. N'Ceegh melted it, jumped the runnels of congealing metal and the cooked meat of a hapless guard, went slatting as fast as his thin legs would carry him down a lacy spiral ramp.

The Palace defenses belonged to the days of the first Imperator and they were badly maintained; until recently no one, not even the professionally paranoid Grand Sech, had expected an attack on the Palace itself. During the past months there'd been some attempt to refurbish the alarms and automatic killers, but slave techs don't make all that reliable a workforce when there's a thought hanging in the air that the men in power are about to lose their footing.

Down and around they went, N'Ceegh leading, Zaraiz Pa'ao watching his sides and back, sweeping away resistance, not stopping to ask those they met what side they were on; the agile uninvolved dived for cover, the guards and slow reactors died. Down and around, going for the CommandCenter, multiply defended, massively armored spherical chamber, buried in the earth, resting on bedrock, built to resist intense bombardment, fire, flood, whatever. Half a dozen Tassalgans guarded the single entrance, a hatch with a complex wholebody lock programmed to open for two people and only two, the Imperator and the Grand Sech. The security was impressive, it looked impeccable, but no Imperator in all the long millennia of Imperacy, back on Huvedra or here on Tairanna, not one Imperator had ever ever locked himself in a room with only one exit; he always had a bolt hole known only to himself.

Before he escaped, N'Ceegh had spent nearly three years local in the Palace as one of Pittipat's favorite toys. During those years he'd built weapons and other elaborate playthings for the Imperator and used his spare time to make spy eyes and ears for himself. He planted them everywhere, collecting data for his escape and his vengeance. Among his other unlovely attributes, Pittipat was a voyeur. He liked to spy on his own people and went slipping from peephole to peephole sometimes all night long. N'Ceegh laid a bug on him and tracked him a couple of nights and after that explored the web of passages on his own, mapping security systems and finally the area about the CommandCenter. Pittipat was on N'Ceegh's vengeance list because he'd ordered a weaponmaster from Bolodo and thus had a share of bloodguilt for the ashing of the Pa'ao kin. After N'Ceegh was in the palace a month, his cold determination went hot where Imperator Pettan tra Pran was concerned, the old rip had an inherited talent for creating passionate enemies.

N'Ceegh led Zaraiz Pa'ao to the outlet of the Imperator's bolthole.

He melted it down. Two minutes later the Pa'ao and his son leaped into the CommandCenter and confronted the Imperator, the Grand Sech and the clutch of Huvved techs busy at sterile white work stations.

Looking down melter snouts at the swarming Hordar, swinging back and forth, wiping away rank after rank of the marchers, flesh running like water off bones that ran like syrup into a puddle around the feet of men women children who kept coming on and coming on.

Talking with Seches in the Fekkris of Littoral cities. The faces all saying the same thing: the cities are emptying, the Hordar are leaving. Saying to the Seches: stop them, shoot them down if you have to, don't let them leave, don't let them come here, stop them however you can. We can't send you anything right now, it's up to you, stop them.

N'Ceegh burned the head off the Grand Sech while Zaraiz Pa'ao plinked the techs. As the Imperator woke from his initial shock and started scurrying toward the main exit, N'Ceegh sent a beam from the burner sizzling past him. Pittipat stopped and turned slowly, working on a smile as he turned. His eyes opened wide as he recognized the intruder. "Ceeghi?"

"!Hi-Vagh!" N'Ceegh muttered. Leaving Zaraiz Pa'ao to guard the exit, he stalked the Imperator, cornered him against a work station. "Down you," he growled, "on the floor, Bitvékeshit."

The Imperator's head went up, his tentative smile vanished. "Nonsense," he said.

N'Ceegh lifted the burner, pressed the front end of the tube against Pittipat's stomach. "Ba'okl, choose, flea."

The old man reconsidered his objection and stretched out on the floor where he lay blinking up at the Pa'ao. With visible effort he managed a smile, then broadened it into a genial grin that lit up watery blue eyes sunk in a nest of pseudo laugh-wrinkles. He was calm now, confident; despite his uncomfortable and humiliating position, he was sure he could manipulate the situation to his benefit, that he could pacify this old friend. "Come, Ceeghi, you're a good fellow. What do you want? Just tell me. There's no need for all this."

N'Ceegh knelt beside him and touched a spray to his neck. The Imperator stiffened, worked his mouth; he couldn't speak and he couldn't move his limbs.

Zaraiz left his post and stood beside the Pa'ao, watching what he was doing.

Hobbling on his knees (plushy gray fur worn thin over the bone), N'Ceegh moved down the Huvved's long spindly body, unbuckled the Imperatorial sandals, slid the long bony feet out of them. "My village is ash," he said, speaking with emotionless precision in unaccented Hordaradda. He took a thin surgical blade from a sheath on his forearm and sliced off the Imperatorial great toes; he set them aside while he applied cauterizing patches to stop the blood flow. He slit the Imperatorial trousers up past the knees. "The house of my fathers is ash," he said. He drew his knife across the hamstrings, severing them. He hobbled up a little farther. "My children are ash," he said. With a deft twist of his knife, he popped out the Imperatorial testicles and dropped them beside the severed toes. He moved on. "My lifemates are ash," he said. He lifted the left hand, drew his knife several times across the back of it, severing the tendons. "My craft-heir is ash," he said. He removed the thumb, dropped it on the Imperatorial chest and applied a patch to the wound. "My bloodkin to the third degree are ash," he said. He dealt with the right hand in the same way, edged along until he was bending over the Imperatorial head, looking down at the old Huvved's face, ignoring the terror in it. "You are the prime cause of those things," he said. "The bloodghosts of my kin cry for vengeance. Zaraiz, help me, keep his head steady."

While Zaraiz Pa'ao held the Imperatorial head locked against his thighs, N'Ceegh drew the blade delicately along the top of the Imperatorial eyesockets, cutting away the eyelids without touching the eyes beneath. "Never close your eyes again to the death and pain you decree," he said. Working with the same care, he cut through the skin and cartilege of the Imperatorial nose and lifted it away. "Never ignore again the consequences of your demands." He used the point as a stylus and cut into the Imperatorial brow the Pao-teely glyphs for bloodguilt. "May the world know your soul, you who command death without thought. Let him go," he said, "gently, my son, if you please."

N'Ceegh got to his feet, brushed his hands together. "The paralysis will wear off in about an hour," he told the old man. "Do what you will then." He touched Zaraiz Pa'ao on the shoulder. "Time to go."

They fought their way back to the roof against a stiffening but disordered resistance, reached the garden breathing hard from the climb with a few holes in unimportant places, a burn or two from richocheting pellets, nothing serious.

Stretching and yawning, so sleepy he didn't like thinking about the ride back to the mines, Zaraiz Pa'ao strolled to the parapet and looked across the grass at the faint lines of rose and purple at the base of the clouds in the west; the sun was down and the dark was lowering quickly. He yawned again, glanced into the gardens below. He saw the tug. "Look, N'Cey-da, isn't that the machine they were talking about at the Mines?"

N'Ceegh crossed to him. "!F-doo-ya! must be. Talk was the Outsiders come looking for disappeared who might be slaves." He frowned at Zaraiz Pa'ao. "You my son now, Zhazh-ti," he said, "my craft-heir, but you born Hordar. It is Torveynee I ask you, come with me away from Tairanna? Come with me to hunt the ghostblood?"

Zaraiz Pa'ao rubbed at his eyes. He was so tired; it wasn't fair that he had to decide this without time to consider. He reached out a trembling hand and warm furry fingers closed around it. On the other side, there were lots of times before this when he'd chewed things over and over and sometimes he was right and sometimes he was wrong. Prophet help me, he thought. "I will come, I will hunt," he said. "Promise you'll teach me? Everything?"

"You my craft-heir, Zhazh-ti. What else? Everything, ya." N'Ceegh grinned at him, hugged the boy hard against him. "!Fi! let us go push in on that line."

4

The pen had small sleeping chambers arranged around an assembly hall with a horizontal lattice displayed across the ceiling, tracks for the slides of the tether chains. At night around a hundred slaves were locked onto those chains and left to negotiate their way into their assigned sleeping places. Because of the Surge and the attack on the Wall, the Palace slaves had been herded into the pen early, the Huvved didn't want them getting ideas about escaping. When I burned the latch and kicked the door in, most of them were still in the assembly chamber, gathered in clusters, talking, arguing, fidgeting or just sitting and staring in deep depression at stains on the walls.

I stood beside the door, looking over that very various crowd in that long narrow room. "Tom'perianne," I called. I waited a minute, repeated the name, yelling over the noise. "Remember a dancer name of Kante Xalloor? She asked us to have a look for you and your sisters."

A thin vital woman, vaguely pteroid, moved away from a group of the back wall, her chain clinking musically. "Xalloor, eh?" She had a deep contralto. So much voice from so frail a body. She looked to her right at two others who might have been clones instead of sisters they were so like her.

"Xalloor," Nym'perianne said (or it might have been Lam'perianne). Whoever, her voice was a liquid lovely soprano. When I learned their names, I could tell them apart by voices if not their faces and bodies.

"What cha know," Lam'perianne said (or it might have been Nym'perianne). This one had an oboe's reedy notes, less immediately enticing than her sister, but maybe more interesting as time passed.

"Good kid," they chorused.

"You know us," Tom'perianne said. "Who're you?"

"Name's Quale," I said. "Ship Slancy Orzo. You want a ride to Helvetia?"

"That's the dumbest question I ever heard." She laughed, flutesong.

"I assume that means yes. Pels, cut the three of them loose. Someone here called Jaunniko?"

The noise got louder. Two men struggled, one fell; the one still standing moved away from the tangle he'd created. "Here, Quale. I'm Jaunniko. The dancer ask for me?"

"Someone did. Described him too and you're not him. Jaunniko, stick your head up, will you? Or your hands, sculptor."

Behind the scowling claimant, pushing impatiently at two men and a woman trying to help him up, a lanky young man got unsteadily to his feet and ran strong square hands through hair with a remnant of purple dye still clinging to it. As his biceps flexed, the lavender butterfly tattooed on his arm seemed to flutter. He tried to speak, but a partially deflected blow in the mixup had shoved his collar against his larynx and left him temporarily mute.

I gave him a nod. "Yeh, you match. Pels?"

The Omperiannas hurried over, dancing away from hands grabbing at them.

"What now?" Tom'perianne fluted at me; Xalloor said she did most of the talking for the three of them.

"Wait by the door, hmm?"

Pushing the steel collar up and rubbing at his neck, Jaunniko reached me and I waved him over to join the three musicians.

"The rest of you—" I started.

The slaves began fighting to get to me, tangling their chains, struggling, desperate, yelling, grunting, wrestling with each other.

"Quiet," I roared at them. "Get back. Give me trouble and you can sit here and rot." I waited until the noise subsided to a manageable level. "Untangle those chains, dammit, how do you expect us to cut them when they're messed up like that? All right, right. The more you help, the sooner we can get out of here. You have any idea what's cranking up outside? This place is going to be rubble before the sun comes up. Bloody rubble. And they're not caring who does the bleeding." I turned my head. "Tom'perianne, come here." When she was at my side, I gave her my stunner. "It won't kill anyone," I said. "It'll just lay them out and we'll leave them laying." I raised my voice again and repeated that, so everyone could hear it, went on, "Use it on anyone who looks like trouble. You out there, when you're cut loose, back up against the inside wall if you want us to run shotgun for you; if you figure you can handle yourself outside, take off. Up to you, I'm no nursemaid."

I plunged into the crowd and began helping Pels sever the chains; the job got easier when the yells and screams from outside came in loud enough for them to get an earful; they calmed down fast and sorted themselves out as we cut them loose. When we were ready to go, Pels led, with the Omperiannas and Jaunniko immediately behind him. The rest of that motley crop followed, organized into squads that kept together and made good time once they were out of the pen. I followed a few strides behind so I could scan the whole and have a better chance of spotting trouble.

When they saw the tug's snout, they really put on some speed. I started hoping we'd reach Chicklet without much trouble. Pels flattened a couple of cats before they made up their minds to jump us, that was about it. The two-legged guards were too busy to bother with anything not coming at them. The attack on the walls was more intense, I could see strings of Hordar coming up and over like lines of ants, and the yizzies were thick overhead. Not over us at first. I was hoping they'd keep away; they were circling high up, beyond the range of the guard's pellet guns, spilling fire over everything and everyone below them, even the front lines of the Surge. The yizzy riders were acting like they weren't part of them on the ground, like they were a Surge on their own. Since most of them were street kids or divorced outcasts, I suppose they had to be a separate force, a third force striking at Huvved and Hordar alike.

We were too big a target. Half a dozen yizzies came at us dripping fire. They stayed high up, my stunner wouldn't reach them. Nothing I could do. Like an idiot I'd left the launch tube and my darts in the tug.

Another yizzy came swooping by, looked like it was carrying two, one draped over the knees of the other; the one in control rested a black tube on his passenger's back. Even that far off I could see what it was—a heavy-duty cutter. It slashed across the inklins attacking us and turned them into ash on the wind.

As the newcomer bagged himself some more twelve year olds, I ran for the tug, cursing Bolodo and Adelaar and Pittipat and Huvved snots and bloody-minded rebels and the Surge and him up there and everyone and everything that got me here and made me look at these things. Children killing. Killing children. Made me want to vomit.

As Pels finished loading the ex-slaves, a fifth wave of fliers formed up and headed our way. I cupped my hands around my mouth and bellowed at our friend on the yizzy to come on board if that's what he wanted, we were going to get the hell out of here.

He brought his yizzy down until he was hanging over the edge of the lift platform. "N'Ceegh Pa'ao," he said, his voice was a hoarse roar that had trouble cutting through the noise around us. "Escaped slave asking transport offworld. My son Zaraiz Pa'ao." He patted the boy's buttocks. "Surge got hold of him and I had to put him out. Give me a hand with him."

"Right. How you want to do this?"

"Let me get the straps off." He produced a wicked-looking scalpel from an armsheath and sliced through the braided thongs that tied the boy in place.

I got my hands around the child's waist and lifted; he was small like most Hordar children, slight, a featherweight. I held him while the Pa'ao swung from the saddle and let the yizzy drift off. "We'll go up to the bridge," I said. "We can talk while I'm taking Chicklet back to Base. Mind leaving that cutter in the lock?"

"Uhnh, Fiddoodah'ak." Before I could ask what that meant, his mouth split into a lipless grin. "Sure, no problem."

He stripped off the battery and dropped it and the tube near the inner hatch. I gave him the boy and got busy; by the time I had the lift folded in and the outer lock dogged home, Pels had the drives humming.

When we reached the bridge, the Pa'ao laid the boy he'd called his son on the floor mat and dropped down to sit cross-legged beside him. He lifted the child's head and shoulders into his lap and sat with one hand resting lightly on his son's tangled black hair.

I took a last look at the chaos around us, goosed the tug into the air. I'd had more than enough of Tairanna, the Hordar and this whole rescue business.

XV

1

Three days after the taking of the Warmaster. Karrel Goza in Ayla gul Inci/mid-morning/cloudy day, gusts of gray rain.

Gul Inci was empty. Empty even of death. No bodies in the streets. No bloodstains or char marks where inklins and others had burned. In the beast courts the stock complained, udders heavy with curdled milk, feed trays and water troughs empty, pet animals whimpered, whined or howled, hungry and parched, abandoned by those who were supposed to care for them. The wind snapped wash left hanging on the line when the Surge impulse came down on gul Inci, it banged doors left unlatched, rattled and banged shutters. It blew scraps of paper and other debris against and around Karrel Goza who came walking south from Sirgûn Bol where he'd left Windskimmer noselocked to a mooring mast.

He passed House after House emptied by the Surge impulse. He walked slower and slower, drew his fingers across the bright tessera inlaid in the brick of the courtwalls, Family marks and signs taken from Family history. He named the Houses as he touched their signs, a slow invocation of what had been. House Falyan. House Umtivar. House Borazan. House Ishlemmet. House Tamarta. Empty, echoing, disturbing. A kind of walking nightmare. He moved deeper into the city, walking streets he'd taken so many times before, Sirgûn Bol to Goza House, Goza House to Sirgûn Bol; he did not hurry, he pushed against a growing reluctance to see his own House empty like these others.

He moved past taverns and shops and other small businesses. For the first time he heard voices though he saw no one and none of the businesses were open.

He heard a steady creaking as he drew near the largest of the circles with its speaker minaret a topped-out stone tree in the middle. He remembered the last time he stood there, crowds pressing about him, Geres Duvvar bringing him a paper cone of hot nuts. His grief over the loss of his cousin intensified suddenly, as if he felt it for the first time. He stood looking at the wall he and Geres Duvvar had leaned against while they listened to the Stentor shout. After a while he was aware of the creaking again. He looked up. A body was suspended from the speaker's platform. A hanged man. He moved around so he could see who it was. "Herk," he breathed. The Fehdaz's face was black and distorted and he was stripped naked, but there was no question who hung there. Another memory came back full force—Elmas Ofka that night she found her brother dead of torture. Herk will pay, she said. It may take years, but Herk will pay.

He shrugged. This wasn't Elli's work, she was too busy organizing the world. It didn't matter. Herk the Jerk had enemies enough to guarantee he'd end like this. Without asking himself why he was doing it, he climbed the verdigrised spiral to the platform and cut the rope. He heard Herk's body hit the stones with a loose boneless splat; the Fehdaz must have been hanging there for hours, more than a day, long enough for the death-stiffness to pass out of him. They took him when the Surge was just starting here, he thought, that's why they hung him instead of tearing him apart.

He climbed back down and stood over the body. It hadn't begun to stink yet, the weather was too cold for that. He pressed his fingers hard against his eyes. Too many memories here, he couldn't let Herk dirty them. He dropped his hands and looked around for a place to put him.

The timbers of the Fekkri Gate were burned to

stumps like rotted teeth and the pile itself was a shell, no more. He got Herk up and over his shoulder, carried the body into the Fekkri court and dropped it on the paving stones.

He left, brushing at himself, a little nauseated. He moved more quickly now, he had a better reason than duty to visit his House. He wanted a bath.

Goza House was in the southeast section of the city, where the Little Houses were and the tenements for the poor, the warehouses, the retting sheds and other factories, down near the water's edge.

The two parts of the main gate were moving in the wind, but not enough to swing closed. Seeing them like that made him angry. The gates of the Great Houses were closed, latched, probably locked though he had not thought to try them. Here the Houses were left open to the wind and whatever thieves escaped the Surge, here where the people were poor and not important. He went through the wall-arch and into the Front Court.

The wind blew dead leaves into dust devils. A solitary spray of rain hit him in the face. The House was dead. Everyone was gone, even the Elders. He folded his arms across his chest, hugged them tight against him. It was like his grief for Geres Duvvar, and somehow worse. There was no focus, only a free-floating desolation. "They make a desolation and call it peace," he said aloud.

"What's that mean?"

Karrel Goza looked around, not seeing who it was who spoke to him.

Tazmin Duvvar stepped from the Duvvar Court, stood leaning against a gate pillar. "What's that?" he repeated.

"Someone said it a long time ago and a long way from here. I don't know who or where. The Outsider at the Mines, the teacher, you remember, she told it to her students and one of them told it to me. It just came to mind."

"Mmh, morbid," Tazmin Duvvar said. "Sounds to me like you need a hot meal and a night's sleep. Let your liver sweeten."

"How long you been back?"

"I got here yesterday morning. I wasn't ferrying vips about like you, cousin. One look at the looting there at the Palace and I thought hard times are coming and I better make sure we've got the stuff to ride 'em out, that it didn't walk out in some stranger's pouch."

"You see Herk?"

"Hard to miss. Wonder who did it?"

Karrel Goza stretched, yawned. "One thing I know, half Inci's going to claim they were in on it. Any hot water?"

"Started the boilers this morning. Bath?"

"Yeh. I cut the bastard down, I didn't like seeing him there. Dumped him in the Fekkri Court. I need to wash him off me."

Tazmin Duvvar looked up at the clouds, ignoring another brief flurry of rain. "Somebody's going to have to do something about him if the wind keeps on in this direction; another day or two and we'll be smelling him." He moved away from the pillar and followed Karrel Goza around the house. "What's happening in Gilisim? Did they ever find Old Pittipat or the Grand Sech?"

"Not yet. What's happening?" Karrel Goza stripped off his jacket and began undoing the fastenings on his shirt. "More of everything you saw before you cut out. More looting, more dead. People wandering around like they're walking in their sleep. We haven't begun to sort out who's what and where they belong, let alone identified the dead. The best guess I heard is as much as a third of us is dead somewhere around Gilisim. It's going to be a job, getting them buried. Elmas Ofka, her isyas and the Council from the Mines, they've got together with vips from the west coast and up from Guneywhiyk. Trying to work out how to organize things now there aren't any more Huvved and the slave techs are gone, most of them. It's a mess, Taz. Every one of them has his own idea how to run things. Bless the Prophet, Elli smoothes them down and gets them to start making sense. Not that she's any saint herself; we're going to have to watch and make sure she doesn't take up where Tra Yarta left off." He pulled open the door to the bathhouse, went in.

Tazmin Duvvar lit the lamps while Karrel Goza started the water running and finished stripping, then he came back and settled on the towel bench, his feet up on the coping about the tub. "You figure we going to get any say at all?"

Karrel Goza slid into the water, shivering as the heat closed round him. He settled his head on the neckrack, closed his eyes. "I've been thinking about that," he said. "What we get, we'll have to take. I did some talking with young Hayal Halak, him from gul Brindar. One of that woman's students, he was the one who told me the desolation/peace quote. He went inklin for a while before he came to the Mines, he loves the Great Families about as much as he loves Huvved. He picked up some ideas from that woman that sound good, the Greats won't like 'em, the Ommars either. I think Elli's going to back him; a lot of them off the Sea Farms might too, they don't want to see the Greats getting a stranglehold on trade. Isn't going to be easy. Toss me the soap, eh?"

"Here. Way things are, looks to me like whoever's ready first is the one who's gonna take it. Hay and his bunch got their shots planned?"

Karrel Goza soaped the washcloth, scrubbed at his arm. "Planned is one thing, doing is something else." He balanced an ankle on his knee, began washing his toes. "We've got numbers on our side. The Greats don't smell very sweet to a lot of people, they kissed too much Huvved ass. We could lose it, though, if Brindars won't talk to Incers and Incers won't talk to Samlikkaners, and nobody talks to grasslanders, you know how it goes. You, me, the rest of them who took the Warmaster, we've got credit we're going to have to spend." He switched feet and stopped talking.

Tazmin Duvvar thought that over, then he nodded. "You'll have to give me the primer version," he said. "I was never much good at the books, but I tell you this, I can talk a tickler into giving it away free, sit me in a tavern and let me chat her up. Lot of folk out there need that primer same as me. I can get them to give it a hearing. Can't ask for more."

Karrel Goza splashed water over his face and hair, then climbed from the tub. "Throw me one of those towels you're sitting on, eh?" He caught it and began rubbing at his hair. "I didn't get out much. You see any of ours in Gilisim?"

"Living or dead?"

"Ahhh . . . both." He wrapped the towel around him. "Come with me while I get some clean clothes."

"Why not. I've got to get back to feeding the stock, but they can wait a bit, they're not as hungry as they were." He picked up one of the lamps. "Goza Ommar's dead." He touched Karrel Goza's shoulder, patted it lightly, then pushed the door open. "Melter, not much of her left but I knew it was her and I told the deadwagon who she was. We'll have to go through the back, I've got the other doors locked. Duvvar Ommar next to her, same thing."

"Prophet!"

"Yeh. Melter. Left her face alone. Told them about her too." He held the door open for Karrel Goza, went round him and up the back stairs, holding the lamp high to light the dark narrow enclosure, glancing over his shoulder from time to time, talking while he climbed. "Ollanin, dead, all three, Goza, Duvvar, Memeli. Saw my sister Avy and the Memeli Ommar. Alive." He waited on the landing, then went along the hallway to the corner room Karrel Goza had lived in from the time he got his license to fly. "They'd corralled a clutch of youngsters, had them out collecting our folk; I expect most of those still alive will be back here by tomorrow noon." He stepped aside and let Karrel Goza work the pinlock and open the door, then followed him into the room and set the lamp on a table by the bed. "Ylazar Falyan showed up at Sirgûn Bol yesterday with a couple of pilots from the Mines; like us, Prophet be praised, they missed out on the Surge." He perched on a ladderback chair, folded his arms on the top splat and rested his chin on them.

"He looked around for mechanics, found me settling in here, hired me to go over a couple of the airships. Worked on the best till about midnight yesterday. He says he's going to use them ferrying Incers home."

Karrel Goza looked up from his trouser laces. "I left Windskimmer at one of Sirgûn's masts, I didn't see anyone there."

"Took off for Gilisim this morning. Must've left before you got here."

"Ah." He went poking through his drawers hunting for a clean shirt, found one and shook it out, then loosened the laces and pulled it over his head. "Big of him."

"Yeh. He's praying real hard no one senior shows up and in the meantime making points for himself so he can keep his hold even if one does. I expect he'll make it, he had the backbone to get out and over to the Mines when Herk started tightening down."

"Hard to say." He padded to the dresser, peered at himself in the mirror.

"Getting old, eh?"

"Twice as old as I look and that's older than time."

"You and Lirrit Ofka still going to wed?"

"Soon's we get a moment." He dragged a comb through his hair; the damp had tightened the curls into knots that made him swear as he worked them loose.

"Marrying out or she coming in?"

"I don't know. Who knows anything these days. We decided to see how things shape up before we jump one way or the other." He looked over his shoulder at Tazmin Duvvar. "Might not be any more marrying in or out."

"Things going to change that much?"

"You don't sound very happy about it."

"Well, everyone likes to be comfortable and change is always full of burrs and bites."

"You really want to go back to the way it was?"

"Nuh. Yeh. I don't know. I want it to be comfortable like it was. I want to know what's going to be happening tomorrow and a week from tomorrow and tomorrow next year. Yeh, I know better, but you'd better remember too, Kar, there's a lot and a lot out there like me in those that're still alive. Don't get too fancy for us, eh?"

Karrel Goza dropped on the bed beside the shoestool, set his foot on it and bent over to put on his sandals. "You feeding the animals," he said. "What else needs doing?"

"Just about everything, I didn't have time yesterday or this morning for much but meals for me and the fourfoots. Looks like our folk dropped whatever they were doing where they were doing it and took off when the impulse hit."

Karrel Goza switched feet. "Mess?"

"Could be worse. Left the fires going, the place could've burned down. Prophet's hand on us, it didn't, they just went out when the coal was gone."

Karrel Goza stood. He yawned, moved his shoulders, clasped his hands behind his head and stretched; the shirt tail he hadn't bothered tucking in lifted in the cold draft coming through the door. He shivered, found an old sweater and pulled it on. "Outside first. Starting to feel like snow."

"Yeh. How long you going to be here?"

"Elli wants me back by tomorrow." He waited till Tazmin Duvvar was outside with the lamp, then he pulled the door shut and reset the lock. "She says the serious fights should be starting about then and she'll need all the backing she can get." He let Tazmin Duvvar go ahead with the light. "You said you thought most of our folk will be here by tomorrow?"

"Laza said he'd bring them, favor to me if I'd work without pay since he's short of coin. You want me along?"

"Yeh. If you're going to be persuading people to back us, you ought to know what you're talking about."

2

The room was filled with slow moving shadows from the dying fire and wandering warm drafts mellow with the smell of the mulled cider steaming on the hearth.

The long window was closed but unshuttered, its embrasure was padded on the bottom and sides to make a comfortable windowseat; it had thick yunkhide tacked over the padding, rubbed to a deep glow by decades of soaping and sitting. Karrel Goza was stretched out in the window, sipping at a mug of cider, listening to the rain drum against the glass. Taz was right, he thought, morbid doesn't make it. He was exhausted, sore and deeply content. The emptiness that was desolation in the morning now seemed to vibrate with possibility. An emptiness waiting, wanting to be filled. He sipped at the cider and thought about that a while and after a while he stopped thinking altogether. Tomorrow could wait until the sun rose. Now was hot cider, red fire and the steady beat of the rain.

XVI

1

265 days std. from home and heading back. In the Split.

I went out to the Belt and brought Slancy back, put her down on the plateau, then we started loading. I got the ex's together and made my speech about how rough it was going to be riding in the hold for some three months while we were insplitting to Helvetia. I told them if they wanted to miss out on that, I'd take their names instead of them. They could wait for a more comfortable ride; I'd leave them shelters and a miniskip so they could get around. I didn't want unhappy passengers; taking that many people I knew shitall about into Slancy made me very nervous; being trashed and rescued didn't turn any of them into angels. I told them the food was going to be ship-basic which they'd get sick of very fast; there wouldn't be water or any other way of taking a bath, so they'd be pretty ripe when they walked out of the hold; most of all, life was going to be very very boring. Insplitting was bad enough when you had something to keep you busy. Sitting around and staring at the hold walls was something else. I didn't get a single taker; they wanted out of there, the sooner the better.

A few of them I knew something about, I brought up front. Stowed them in the crew cabins so I'd have some shooters back of me if there was trouble. Aslan and Adelaar, of course. N'Ceegh and his boy, along with the weapons he skipped over to the Mines to collect which I impounded for the duration, not that I didn't trust him, he and Pels got on like long lost brothers, I just didn't want that much firepower wandering around loose. Churri the Bard and his girlfriend;

both of them were oldtime survivors, besides I kind of enjoyed baiting Adelaar. The Omperiannas; Kumari had a passion for music of all kinds, that's why them. The rest brought the shelters in and set them up in the hold, got them organized in sectors like they were out under the trees, improvised screens for privacy areas; they worked almost like they were 'droids with the pattern imprinted. It was a smooth loading, surprised me a little till I thought about it. These weren't your average thumb-fingered boneheads, Bolodo skimmed cream for them.

Two hundred sixty-five days std. out of Telffer, according to ship's log, we lifted off Tairanna and headed for the Limit.

2

As soon as we dived, Pels activated the squirtlink, sent the squeal to ti Vnok's receptor, giving him the passpartout so he could get hold of the data packet, letting him know we had Leda Zag and Ilvinin Taivas so he could tell whoever was interested and stir us up some heavy support. The squeal was too short to trigger ears and even if someone got lucky, there were no tags on it to identify either end. The cover was down, I hoped it'd be thick enough to turn the knives waiting for us.

3

The trip went better than I expected.

Adelaar disappeared into Slancy's workshop with my home stats to get a start on redoing its security. This time I made sure Kinok kept ves tentacles out of her business. I swept the shop and removed all suspect foliage; like most of us, when it comes to someone outside the family, ves ethics get a bit shaky. Ethics aside, pulling her string about Churri was one thing, she got nasty on the verbal end and gave me a good flaying when she felt like it, but on the business end, she was a wall; she knew what she wanted and what she didn't and no jabs would shift her; if she didn't want snoops watching her work, that's what she intended to get or she just might decide to ditch that part of the deal and more than ever I wanted her touch dressing up my house. Funny, having lived so long and semi-voluntarily acquired a body and with it a definite end to that life, I was beginning to appreciate the fragility of . . . well, everything.

Churri and Xalloor got together with the Omperiannas and began working out a new act; they figured that the publicity from the Return of the Disappeared and their connection with it made them a draw the bookers couldn't ignore. Kumari figured the same thing; she was going to finance the tour if they came up with something she liked. Since they kept trying out parts of the thing on the ex's in the hold, they kept the passengers happy and entertained. Which made me happy.

Aslan was something of a surprise. She worked on her reports a lot, but not all the time. I hadn't paid much attention to her back on Tairanna, too busy being irritated by this and that, I suppose, and too tired from flying all night digging out the targets; you want another excuse, I've got this tendency to focus on what I'm busy at so I don't see much of what's around me, peripheral images shoved outside my periphery, if you know what I mean. She looked a little like her mother around the eyes and mouth, but her coloring was more dramatic, her features heavier . . . no, that's not the word. Stagier. More dramatic like the coloring. The bones showed and they were what a sculptor called good. She photoed better than she looked in person, well, better's not the word either, she was prettier in the stills, but a lot of the personality got lost. I remembered Adelaar saying Shuh! she's my daughter and I love her, but even I wouldn't call her a beauty. She's not all that sexy either. To be honest, Quale, she's a boring person. Just goes to show, Mama don't know everything she thinks she does. It was a friendly time. Pleasant waking up and feeling her warm beside me. More than pleasant when she woke up. She enjoyed sex more than anyone I can remember knowing. Laughed a lot, made me laugh with her. I was almost sorry when Slancy chimed to let me know she was ready to slip back to realspace.

4

354 days std. out of Telffer.
Helvetia.

We came up nose to nose with three destroyers and a gravity sink that nailed us; poor old Slancy couldn't wiggle a fin.

Before I had time to start sweating, the mainscreen lit up. Helvetian perimeter patrol logo announcing who was out there, then someone who ordinarily walked in more exclusive circles. I knew that sour smile and the face it was tacked onto, though he didn't know me and probably didn't want to. The only time we actually met I was sharing someone else's body. Malurio Marchog, the Seven's Enforcer. Cattwey of the Helvetias. I relaxed. Home free, I thought.

"Swardheld Quale," he said, proving me wrong about that much; he knew my face. Courtesy of ti Vnok, no doubt.

"Marchog Cattwey," I said, showing I have my sources too.

"Permission to come aboard," he said.

Polite bastard. What he meant was open your gd lock before I gd pull the gd thing off its hinges. Well, I asked for Helvetian cover, now I pay for it. "Permission herewith granted," I said. "Want me to send a boat over or you providing your own transport?" That was a bit of swank; with the sink out there focused on us, we couldn't space a fart.

He ignored it. "Helvetian rules apply out here as on the ground," he said. "Crack your forward lock, portside."

"I hear you, Marchog Cattwey." It sounded like he was coming over himself, which was a bit of a surprise. Apparently that pair of rescuees down in the hold were more important than we'd thought. Old ti Vnok, he slipped up this time; on the good side maybe, but definitely a miscalc. He's going to have to work to live that down. I cracked the lock, sent Kumari to make sure N'Ceegh didn't have some hold-outs tucked away; I wasn't sure how much he knew about Helvetian rules and how seriously the Seven took them. I left Pels at the com and went down to the portlock to remind the Helvetians as tactfully as I could that this was my ship and we were outside the Limit, in so-called freespace. They'd probably be polite enough to listen without snickering. Even Marchog.

5

The inner hatch opened and I dumped the speech fast. Six pretors trotted through, shoved me against the wall, no malice, just getting me out of the way. They split, three on each side, dark, massive, huge, as intimidating as two-leggers in battle armor ever get when they're not actually coming at you. I sucked in my gut and waited.

A mirror-sphere about two meters across floated from the lock, moving along half a meter off the floor at a pace about that of a man out for an afterdinner stroll. It stopped in front of me; I thought it was inspecting me though it's hard to tell what's going on inside something when you're staring at a funhouse version of yourself smeared across the outside. "The people, where are they?" It had a deep bass voice that oozed with authority.

"The hold, despois," I said, being as polite as I knew how. Great god, I was thinking, one of the Seven? Hooo-eee, talk about your heavy support.

"Lead," it said.

Very careful to keep my hands in view, I moved past the pretors and started for the dropshaft. I heard the guard clumping into position behind me, the sound echoed by a second sextet coming out of the lock; somewhere back there Marchog was moving up to the Bridge with his own pretors; he wouldn't leave Slancy in our hands, not with one of the Seven aboard her. I didn't like it, But I certainly wasn't going to kick up a fuss. All I could do was hope this was a temporary dispossession.

6

The hold smelled like a roadshow zoo; I suppose Faceless in his sphere got filtered air, but I didn't, it was enough to choke a goat. He drifted out to the middle and hovered there, reflecting the faces or whatever turned up to him. "You were slaves?" The basso burred out and bounced off the walls.

Some of them knew what they were looking at; whoever didn't was getting the word fast if the hissing that spread through the hold meant what I thought. The Kakeran Posa Ala was the first to answer. He set his hands on his hips, glared up at his distorted reflection. "Klaan vem!" he growled. "Bolodo man put a kujjim collar round my neck. Five kujjim years and nobody did shit till Quale there come for us."

Dey Chomedy and Leda Zag came elbowing through the thickening crowd about Posa Ala, the tall one opening a path for the little.

Dey Chomedy stomped her foot and growled, then shouted up at the sphere, "Bolodo men took me off my mountain, took me from my nest; they did not ask my consent, they did not pay my price. Seven years the masters milked my sweat and drank my tears and nothing did they pay. Was I slave? Ssss. Show me Bolodo man, let me take my pay from his flesh and his sweat and his blood."

Leda Zag tapped the tall femme's arm and was lifted to her shoulder. "So it was with me, despois, I traveled to a place for rest but I did not reach it. Before I reached it, a gas bomb filled my flickit; when I woke, I was in a scout on my way to Weersyll and beyond. For three years I mourned one dearer to me than the beat of my heart, for three years I suffered, until the man Quale and his companions took me from my servitude. It has not been easy coming home, not easy for me, not easy for any of us, but we suffer these small travails gladly because we are going home."

I kept my face very straight and serious, though I enjoyed that little speech; we spent most of a warm afternoon up by the lake dickering over her fee for her affirmation of my noble contribution to her freedom. I was kicking back half the reward, to be paid into her dainty little hands the day I got it, golden gelders, coin not credit.

After that the rest of them yelled their anger, a confused hammering of sound. Even the mirror-sphere seemed to shudder and I was wondering if I'd get out of there with hearing intact.

"Quiet." The basso boomed out, hammering back at the yammer in the hold. "Enough!" He had the advantage of amplification, but it was several minutes before he broke through and my collection of ex-slaves simmered down a bit.

"Helvetia has heard you," he said. Big of him. "She will expedite your arrival and provide housing for you until this matter is cleared up. She will provide means of contacting your kin or other individuals concerned about you."

Hmm, I thought, such generosity. Looks like they've already got a strangle hold on Bolodo's assets and want to keep the noose tight, they can't let the thought get round that they're playing with client's gelt. They ought to pay Adelaar's expenses and double for a bonus, what a lovely present she's dropped in their little laps. I kept my face immobile and my hands clasped behind me, but I was beginning to enjoy this quite a lot.

"Helvetia asks only," the sphere boomed out, "that you agree to testify as to the circumstances of your abductions. Bolodo Neyuregg Ltd. is actively contesting the claims relayed to us by an agent of Swardheld Quale. Because we may invoke certain clauses in the Contract Bolodo Neyuregg Ltd. signed with us, in order to put several executives of that Company through Involuntary Verification, it may be necessary for some of you to pass through the Verifier and otherwise make identication of such individuals. If that is possible and within your knowledge. You will be compensated for the time and the harrowing of your emotions."

The sphere drifted toward the tube. I got out of the way before I was shifted aside by the pretors and followed the procession from the hold.

7

When Faceless said expedited, he meant it. Escorted by two destroyers though a lane cleared for us, we sailed at spooky speed for insystem travel straight to a mooring usually reserved for those wealthy beyond my dreams of avarice, where Slancy was put to bed in a section all her own. Shuttles drew up to her flanks and waited there like a ride in an amusement park, ready to take the ex-slaves down. Kumari had all the paperwork done, she'd taken care of that during the trip in between Xalloor's rehearsals—name, world-of-origin, life history, work status, circumstances of abduction, fingerprints, bodyprints, retina prints and cell coding with a snippet of freeze-dried skin or flesh or chitin, whatever seemed appropriate, sealed to each statement. I didn't expect any trouble collecting the rewards, not with ti Vnok getting his thirty percent, but Kumari was a worrier, it made her the best Mom Slancy'd ever enjoyed. So, no delays. We lined our passengers up and hustled them into the shuttles. We rode down in the last of them, Pels, Kumari and I along with Adelaar and Aslan, Churi, Xalloor and the Omperiannas, N'Ceegh and the boy.

Now the real tedium began.

8

Images:

Aslan aici Adlaar: Yes, that's the man. He was on Tairanna when Fangulse Tra Yarta interviewed us. Churri the Bard saw him also, as did Parnalee Pagang Tanmairo Proggerd, though he can't testify since he died mad.

Kante Xalloor: Yes, that's the stringman who drugged me. I can't connect him to Bolodo except by the circumstances that when I woke I was in a Bolodo scout; I knew it was Bolodo by the patches on the pilot's shipsuit. Yes, that's the pilot who flew the scout.

Jaunniko: Yes, that's the stringman who came on to me, then drugged me. Yes, that's the pilot who flew the scout that took me to the Cage on Weersyll.

N'Ceegh of Pao-teely: Yes, that's the man who led the raid on my village. That's the man who boasted to me my blood was ash.

Tom'perianne: Yes, I saw that man and that one also in the Great Chamber of the Palace on Tairanna, when my sisters and I sang for the Huvved Imperator. My sisters can swear to them also. Yes, that's the pilot who flew us to Weersyll. Yes, those are the crewmen who loaded us on the slave transport. My sisters can swear to them also.

Adelaar aici Arash: Yes, those are the flakes I made of lists I discovered in the mainBrain in the Palace on Tairanna. I swear and will pass through the Verifier on this point, these flakes are not altered or added to in any way. I will also attest and swear this is the data I abstracted from Bolodo's own mainBrain on Spotchals, I will pass through the Verifier on this point, these flakes are not altered or added to in any way.

Swardheld Quale: Yes, that is the contract I made with Adelaar aici Arash. Yes, that is the statement I made concerning my activities in the Horgul system. I do swear and attest that what I have said there is truthful, I will pass through the Verifier on this point and will answer any questions while under the Verifier relating to that statement.

9

624 days std. since we started this thing.
The Nest/Telffer/Home again.

Crew and I are going to be set for at least a decade of lazing about, taking commissions we liked, not jobs we had to do. Between the rosepearls and the rewards, to say nothing of Adelaar's fee, we will have a credit account on Helvetia so exalted I get altitude sickness contemplating it.

The Faceless Seven kicked in a thousand gelders apiece for the extras we brought along gratis, a nice little bonus; the Seven were overflowing with the milk of . . . well, something as they began taking apart Bolodo's assets, at least those they could get hold of, not a small percentage of the whole if ti Vnok was right.

While I was waiting for the interrogations to grind to their eventual end, I passed the time doing this and that. I gave the rosepearls to ti Vnok; he wouldn't do the selling, but he'd find an agent who'd get me the best price; I added a chunk to the credit account I set up for the Barker and his asteroid mines, dropped a fee on a cobben of NightCrawlers to take out the one pointed at me. Ah yes, and ti Vnok managed to slip Leda Zag her baksheesh without her patron knowing. He's a good friend.

We dropped Aslan at University. It gave me a twinge to see how eager she was to get away. She'd done all she could to help finish off Bolodo, now she was going after the Oligarchs on Kavelda Styernna. That was more important than me or any other man. Adelaar was right for once, men were recreation when her daughter wasn't busy with something else. Since I do considerable business with University, I thought we might recreate ourselves some other time. I played the idea around and decided I liked it.

We took Adelaar to Droom; she wanted to get Adelaris whipped into shape again before she took off to work on my house. She'd been away for over four years and was nervous about what she'd find left of her business.

That left Crew and me alone at last on Slancy Orza. It felt good. Kinok had worked his remotes till their bearings ran hot, scrubbing out the hold and the rest of her. She felt clean and fresh. Frisky.

It was deep winter when we got back, the month called *Wolves Running*; snow was piled into three-meter drifts when we dropped the lander on the pad. Up in Slancy, Kinok was rubbing his tentacles together again, scritching away like crazy, laughing at us idiots leaving a warm clean ship so we could get ourselves soaked to the bone and half-frozen.

The housekeep was burbling over with things to tell us about the small lives that prowled about on my land; among other things, two feral and very pregnant cats had showed up; they had their kittens in the summerhouse. She said she couldn't understand how they'd managed to get through the shield (I had my doubts about that), but they had, so she'd deloused the mogs and their kits and shot all of them full of antibiots and organized a feeding schedule to keep the mamas at their job. She was full of how well she'd coped. Ever since Kumari worked over her programming, she's developed strong maternal urges. Sometimes I get tired of her fussing, then I see the absurdity of a neuter like our Kri coming up with such a construct; even if Kri were sexed, she belongs to a budding species where motherhood is like a bad case of acne. I think she reads too much.

We'll finish out the winter at the Nest; come spring we'll go take a look at Tairanna to see how things are working out and what kind of trading we can do. It's mostly curiosity, though it won't hurt having a stash of rosepearls in the basement that we could dip into should Luck turn mean on us.

On the way back we might stop off at University to see if they have any interesting commissions needing an experienced and trustworthy Crew. I might call up Aslan to see if she's unsaddled her white horse and ready to enjoy another sort of ride. It's a short life these bodies have, and a good one; fragile but full of heat and flavor.

I'm sitting up in my tower. It's a clear night. No clouds. The stars out this way are sparse but that makes them all the lovelier and the moonlight on the snow is magical.

DAW

RAVE RE
DECEPTIONS AND DREAMS!

"With her bright talent, intelligent voice, and elegant prose, Debra Dier creates characters we can believe in, emotions we can feel, and stories we can experience."
—Connie Rinehold, author of *More Than Just A Night*

"An exciting and action-packed adventure....Once again, Debra Dier proves that she is a sparkling jewel in the romantic adventure world of books."
—*Affaire de Coeur*

"*Deceptions and Dreams* is tightly plotted with plenty of well-developed characters....Ms. Dier's writing is skillful and sure, painting with words a story filled with passion, adventure, and emotion."
—*Rendezvous*

AND FOR DEBRA DIER'S OTHER HISTORICAL ROMANCES:

"A stunningly beautiful and evocative love story brimming with action, adventure, and a touch of fantasy....*A Quest Of Dreams* will grab your heart and won't let go."
—Kathleen Morgan, author of *Firestar*

"*Shadow Of The Storm* is a powerhouse of intense emotions, a brilliantly crafted, cleverly plotted novel that lures the reader and holds your attention from beginning to end."
—*Romantic Times*

"*Surrender The Dream* has sparkling dialogue, suspense-filled intrigue, and sizzling love scenes!"
—*Affaire de Coeur*

LUCKY IN LOVE

''I never cheat at cards, and I never take advantage of a woman.''

With a slow tug on her braid, Austin pulled her toward him. She resisted, grabbing her braid, trying to pull it from his grasp. ''What are you doing now, if not taking advantage of me?''

''Trying to show one lovely lady how grateful I am.'' He moved toward her, holding her tethered by her braid.

''I'm not the type of woman who—'' He nuzzled the soft skin below her ear. ''Oh, my!''

''One kiss, that's all I want to steal.''

''You musn't,'' she whispered, pushing against his shoulders.

He released her braid, sliding his arm around her, drawing her close, too close. Her breasts pressed against his chest, soft and yielding against his hard muscles. He held her in an embrace she could easily have broken. Yet this thief had stolen her will.

''You smell like lavender in the rain.'' He rolled her earlobe between his teeth, sending sparks shimmering down her neck and across her shoulders. ''Kiss me, sweet Sarah.''

Other *Leisure Books* by Debra Dier:
A QUEST OF DREAMS
SHADOW OF THE STORM
SURRENDER THE DREAM

DECEPTIONS & DREAMS

DEBRA DIER

LEISURE BOOKS  NEW YORK CITY

To Aunt Evelyn, you always understood my dreams, my need to free the creative part of my soul.

To Diane and Penny, with you I shared the dreams of my teenage years and the struggle to make those dreams come true.

Thank you, dear friends, for believing in me.

A LEISURE BOOK®

October 1994

Published by

Dorchester Publishing Co., Inc.
276 Fifth Avenue
New York, NY 10001

Printed in the United States of America.

DECEPTIONS
& DREAMS

Chapter One

New York City, May 1887

"Don't move or I'll shoot." Sarah gripped the handle of her brother's gun between her palms, trying to steady her hands as she aimed at the broad back of the intruder.

He halted in the middle of her brother's secret gallery, this man who had invaded her home. He had drawn the drapes in a room forever cloaked from the outside world, allowing pale moonlight to pour through the three mullioned windows, casting squares of silver across the room. Caught in a silvery frame, moonlight etched his tall form in the darkness, drawing lines along wide shoulders, slipping silver fingers into hair as black as the devil's soul.

"I assure you, I'm an excellent marksman." She reached blindly for the switch she knew should be directly to her right on the wall, hoping her lie sounded convincing. She was terrified of guns. "Don't try anything foolish. I won't hesitate to shoot you."

He glanced over his shoulder. Soft moonlight carved his profile, illuminating the curve of his lips. The man was smiling!

"Miss Van Horne, you're supposed to be attending a ball at Isabel Bennett's home."

"How did you know?" Sarah clenched the pistol, her damp palm slipping against the smooth silver grip. Where was that switch? she wondered, sliding her left hand across the smooth mahogany panels lining the wall.

"In my profession, it's important to know when the lady of the house will be out." His voice was deep, smooth, like sable sliding against her skin, and it was tinged with an accent that painted images in her mind of stone castles rising above the English moors.

She connected with the switch, her fingers fumbling a moment before the lights overhead flickered and glowed, spilling blessed incandescent light into the room. She stared at the intruder, a tall man with thick black hair that spilled over the collar of his finely tailored black coat in soft waves. Who was this thief who sounded as though he would be at home among the British aristocracy? "I'm sure the police will be fascinated by your trade secrets."

"Do you really need to summon the police?" He turned to face her, a slow pivot filled with the grace of a panther. "There's been no harm done."

Sarah tried to draw a breath, but it splintered in her throat. The man was not what she had expected. Not at all. What was a burglar doing dressed in formal evening wear as though he had simply stepped away from a ball? And a burglar had no right being so handsome. Indecently handsome.

His face—perfection, like a prince in some vaguely remembered fairy tale, carved with strong lines and curves, a man who could wield a sword to slay dragons and rescue fair damsels. His was a face destined to trip the heart of any unsuspecting maiden. Sarah felt her own heart stumble.

Shouldn't a burglar have a scar, an imperfection? Shouldn't a burglar have a crooked nose instead of one so thin and straight? And his eyes, definitely not the eyes of a burglar. Black brows arched above eyes that were too blue to be called gray and too silvery to be called blue; eyes filled with the same mischief she could see in the curve of his full lips.

He was studying her with those silvery blue eyes, and Sarah had the feeling she had never been observed so keenly, as though he were an artist studying her, making mental notes of the portrait he would paint. Heat pressed against her, surrounding her, the heat of early May trapped in this hidden room, trapped with the scent of beeswax and lemon oil and the faint trace of bayberry and spices.

He slid his warm gaze from the crown of her light brown hair to the tips of her bare toes peeking out from beneath her blue linen robe. Although he stood more than ten feet away, she felt as though he were touching her, stroking her with gentle hands.

He appraised her in a decidedly masculine way that made her more aware of her femininity than she had ever been in her life. Beneath the concealing folds of her robe and gown, her skin tingled. "I suppose no one has ever told you it's impolite to stare."

He lifted his gaze, and in those silvery blue eyes she saw the warmth of a man who understood what his lazy perusal had done to her, a man who enjoyed the blush she could feel warming her cheeks. "I suppose no one has ever told you it's dangerous to go about the house carrying a pistol."

Sarah hoisted the pistol that had drooped in her hands, aiming for the vee where his starched white shirt met the soft black silk of his waistcoat. "I find a loaded pistol does wonders to keep the common burglar in his place."

He laughed, a rumble that came from deep in his chest and tempted her to join him. She bit her lower lip to keep from smiling. Gracious, what was wrong with her? The man was a scoundrel.

"Miss Van Horne, I'm afraid you've complicated matters immensely by coming home early."

Did the rogue expect her to apologize? She sought some chilling remark and found her mind dreadfully sluggish. Fear, anger, she understood these emotions. But the way this man made her feel was utterly foreign. Breathless, she stared at him, her heart pounding as though she had been running for miles and suddenly reached her destination.

Merlin slipped beneath the hem of her robe and nightgown, brushing his soft gray fur against her bare legs. The cat had alerted her to this stranger. Merlin had heard something with his keen cat ears, and she had followed him to the hidden entrance of her brother's treasure trove.

If only Merlin were a snarling mastiff, instead of a purring cat, the rogue might look a little intimidated, Sarah thought. He certainly wasn't the least bit intimidated by her, even though she was holding a pistol.

"Just why did you leave the party?"

A headache, that's what she had told her stepmother, Roxanne. No need for Roxanne to leave the party, Sarah had assured her. No need for anyone to know the real reason she had needed to escape soon after arriving at the party.

Sarah had walked from Isabel Bennett's house, slipping in the back door of her home as though she were a thief. She had wanted to see no one. She had suffered enough humiliation for one night. "The reason I left the party is of no concern to you."

"I'm afraid it is. You see, if you had stayed at the party we wouldn't find ourselves in this awkward situation."

"No. I would have returned instead to find my home ransacked."

"I wouldn't exactly say ransacked."

He tilted his head, a crinkle appearing between his black brows as he looked at her. The light stroked his thick hair, coaxing dark chestnut highlights from the silky strands of ebony that tumbled around his face in undisciplined waves. Was his hair really as soft as it looked? Oh, my, what decent woman would be thinking about his hair at a time like this?

He glanced down to the pistol she held in her shaky hands, then met her eyes. "You do know how to handle that pistol, don't you? I would hate to be shot by accident."

"I know what I'm doing."

He nodded, though the look in his eyes told her he doubted her every word.

Did she have any idea what she was doing? She was standing in her nightgown, holding a pistol she had never fired, facing a rogue who had broken into her house. And she was trembling, but not from fear. Dear lord, not from fear, but from a dark primitive emotion she had never realized dwelt inside her.

Like mother, like daughter. Shame prickled her skin like a thousand needles, the same shame she had lived with most of her life.

"Miss Van Horne, about the police . . ."

"I'm going to send for them immediately."

He held her gaze a long moment with eyes that seemed to touch deep within her. There was a serenity in those eyes, a confidence in this man, a powerful magnetism that made her want to trust him. She clutched the pistol.

"I believe you should reconsider."

"Reconsider? You're a thief." Merlin circled her legs, pressing against her. "Why in the world would I not call the police?"

"Your brother has an interesting collection of artifacts." He turned his attention to the sword in a glass case to his left, the polished steel nestled against a bed of red velvet, a small brass plate identifying its origin. "Is it true that sword once belonged to Alexander the Great?"

Sarah glanced to the case, one of ten poised on polished mahogany planks in the long room, each containing precious pieces from the past. "The sword is one of my brother's favorite pieces."

"A treasure any museum would be proud to display."

Suspicion crawled upward along her spine, a chill spreading across her warm skin. The same suspicion Roxanne had voiced time and time again. The same suspicion Sarah had felt the first day her brother had brought home one of his treasures. Since that day two years ago, Leighton had brought home hundreds of pieces, all rare, all belonging in a museum.

It was a collection any man would be proud to own. And yet Leighton seldom invited anyone into his secret gallery. According to Roxanne, her stepson was nothing less than a thief. The threat of scandal alone kept her from calling the police to arrest the stepson Roxanne could barely tolerate.

How had this man even known this room existed? It was tucked away on the second floor of their Fifth Avenue home, hidden behind a door her brother had commissioned to be secretly covered, replaced by a sliding panel eighteen months ago, one week after their father's death. "What were you doing in here?"

"There are men in this world who are collectors of beautiful objects." He lowered his gaze to where her thick braid rested against the curve of her breast. "I sometimes help them collect rare pieces."

Warmth flared where his gaze touched her, as though he had brushed her skin with his fingertips. Her wanton reaction terrified her. "How did you know about my brother's collection?"

"It's famous in that world of private collectors."

She didn't want to know any more. She didn't want to think her brother might have hired a man like this, a man who could steal, a man who could help build his collection.

"The police will ask a great many questions," he said, as though he could read her thoughts. "You have nothing to fear from me. I'm simply a man trying to make a living, Miss Van Horne. I assure you, I never steal from anyone who cannot afford the loss."

"A modern-day Robin Hood."

"Not exactly. I steal from the rich to sell to the rich." He smiled, warm and generous and utterly disarming. "I'm afraid the police will cause a great deal of scandal."

Did this man know? Did he have any idea how much scandal she had already endured? More scandal in her life was the last thing she needed. And for some misbegotten reason the idea of sending this handsome rogue to prison did not appeal to her in the least. "If I let you go, will you promise to leave the city?"

"And never see you again? Would you truly inflict such severe punishment?"

Her heart fluttered at the beguiling lie. The man was a charming liar. And she was a fool. At 28 she should be immune to such nonsense as this, she thought. Yet here she was with her heart dancing at the base of her throat, all because of one devastating thief. "There's no need for false flattery. I've already agreed to let you go."

"You really have no idea how lovely you are."

"On the contrary. I know I'm not altogether unattractive, pretty perhaps, on my best days. Yet unexceptional."

"Beautiful, in a subtle way."

"Beautiful is stretching my assets a great deal." Clarissa was the beautiful one. Her half sister had New York at her dainty little feet.

"But you are beautiful. Not the type of beauty that overwhelms a man. But a beauty that grows each time he looks at you."

Although he didn't move, she felt as though he were drawing closer, the heat of the room his heat, his warmth wrapping around her, seeping into her blood. Her pulse beat wildly against the lace of her high collar.

"Take your hair, for example. Not the yellow so worshiped these days, but a blend of color, golden honey where the light strokes the shiny strands, rich shades of brown hidden beneath."

She stared at his lips, following the lazy curve of his smile. She had never allowed a man's lips to touch her own. And yet she wondered what it might be like to feel his lips move against hers. Her breath tangled with emotion in her throat.

"Your braid, wonderfully thick. Yet too neat, and far too confining. It makes a man wonder what it would be like to free the thick coils and lift your hair to the sunshine, what it might be like to press his face into the silky strands and breathe your fragrance. I bet a man could spend hours finding all the delicate hues in your hair."

A shiver sliced through her, leaving a tingling in her nerves. Magic. The man must use magic to make her feel this way.

"There's no question about it, your hair is much more interesting than yellow," he said.

A lady would never feel such excitement as this. A lady would be frightened and appalled by this bold scoundrel. She didn't want him here another moment. She didn't want to face the unsettling emotions he evoked within her. She didn't want to face the ugly suspicions about herself. "Leave. Now."

"I have a confession to make." He paused a moment, trying to make her curious, no doubt, and succeeding far too well. "I've always had a weakness for women who are tall and slender."

"Yes, I'm sure you have. Perhaps because of your own exaggerated height."

"Perhaps."

The curve of his smile tilted as he studied her, a sleepy lion eyeing a gazelle, a lion who had not quite decided to make her his dinner. Mesmerizing, that look. Dangerous. Far too exciting. "I told you to leave."

"You're as delicate looking as a porcelain figurine. Yet your face has character, a quality that comes from intelligence."

"Character. Isn't that what they say about wines after they've been sitting on the shelf for forty or fifty years?"

"Ah, milady, I can only thank heaven some other man has not taken you from the shelf before I had the chance to savor your beauty."

"Get out of my house." Sarah held the gun steady. Yet she had the feeling the gun would be little defense against this man.

"And may I call on you?" he asked, moving toward her.

Was the man serious? Did he really want to see her? Gracious, was she really hoping a thief would take an interest in her? Of all the foolish, pathetic . . . "I certainly will not agree to see you."

"Join me for dinner. Tomorrow night at Delmonico's."

"Dinner?" The man was mad. She took a step back as he approached.

"Careful!"

His warning came a heartbeat too late. Her foot collided with Merlin's curled form. The cat wailed and darted from beneath her. Before she could catch herself, she tumbled backward into the wall. Her shoulder blades hit the mahogany panels with a whack that jarred her teeth together.

The gun jerked in her hand. The loud bark of the gunshot exploded in her ears. And then her thief moaned, soft as a whisper. Yet the sound echoed in her heart. Sweet merciful heaven, she had shot him!

Chapter Two

Although he had tried to avoid the bullet in a quick catlike pivot, he had been too close to succeed. He staggered back, pain drawing his handsome face into a grimace. He clutched his left side beneath his heart, gasping for breath. Still, he recovered before she did, looking at her, a smile playing at one corner of his lips. "A simple *no* would have sufficed, Miss Van Horne."

"Gracious!" She came away from the wall, a sleepwalker jolted from slumber. Three quick strides brought her to his side.

"How severely are you wounded?" She pressed her hand against his upper arm, the gun still clutched in her fingers.

He glanced down at the barrel of the gun, which was now pointed at his chin. "As severely as I care to be." He slipped his hand over hers and gently pried the pistol from her tense grip, his fingers slick with his blood.

"The gun," she whispered, looking up at him, realizing she was completely unarmed.

She was tall. Yet he towered above her, at least nine or ten inches above her five foot six inches. Tall, broad-shouldered, powerful, even wounded he could break her neck with one flick of his long, slender fingers.

"You have very beautiful eyes, Miss Van Horne." He slipped the gun into his coat pocket. "Thick dark lashes that tilt upward at the tips. Irises of jade, flecked with gold and brown. Do I see a few flecks of blue?"

"I can't believe you're discussing my eyes when you're standing here bleeding."

He drew a breath, careful and measured, as though any movement brought him pain. "What do you propose we do about it?"

"A doctor . . ."

"Would be out of the question, I'm afraid. Far too many questions."

Sarah thought of Roxanne, imagining the look of disdain she had seen too often in her stepmother's dark blue eyes. She was certain Roxanne would never have gotten herself into this mess.

"If you could provide me with some alcohol and linen."

"Yes. Yes, of course."

She led him out of the room into the shadows of the hallway. Bayberry and spices blended with the musk of his skin to tease her senses, a crisp scent that triggered some odd response inside her—warmth, like coals ignited on a hearth in winter. Inviting. Dangerous.

She led him toward the kitchen, down a narrow stairway at one end of the hall into a short passageway. He moved silently beside her, a shadow, each movement filled with a peculiar grace that came when power blended with agility. Fascinating, this latent male power. Foolish to notice.

Moonlight poured through the tall windows in the kitchen, glittering on the glass-fronted cabinets that lined two sides of the big room. The scent of freshly baked bread lingered here, reminding Sarah of the safety she had always found in Matilda's kitchen. This place had always been a refuge. Yet there was no refuge for her tonight. Matilda was sound asleep in the servants' quarters, too far away to hear a scream, or a gunshot.

"Sit," she commanded, pointing to an oak armchair by the big oak table that dominated the center of the room.

"With pleasure."

The brick floor chilled her bare feet as she moved away from him. She turned the light switch, igniting the incandescent lights that hung from a brass fixture in the center of the ceiling, yet she felt as though she were bumbling around in the dark.

What was she doing? she wondered as she threw open one of the bottom cabinets. The man obviously needed a doctor. Still, the police; how could she ever hope to call the police and escape telling them about Leighton's hidden treasures? She couldn't.

She dragged linen from the piles of towels, tablecloths, and napkins in the cabinet, draping them over her arm. In the next cabinet she found Matilda's medicine chest, a scarred oak box the housekeeper had often used when Sarah and her brother had come to her crying with scraped knees. Her half sister Clarissa, on the other hand, had never had a scraped knee in her life.

He was tugging the studs from the front of his white shirt when Sarah turned to face him. Deep wrinkles had been pressed into the shirttails by the heat of his body. They dangled at his sides, brushing his narrow hips. His coat and waistcoat lay folded on the table in front of him.

She clutched the wooden box in her hands as he peeled his shirt from his shoulders, revealing the naked proof of the power she had only suspected dwelt beneath the elegantly tailored coat and shirt. Without the trappings of social decorum, the man was a blatant pirate. "What do you think you're doing?"

"Miss Van Horne, I apologize for shocking your delicate sensibilities, but I think we should tend this wound." He folded his shirt and tossed it on top of his coat. "Before I swoon and hit my head on this brick floor."

"Oh!" She glanced to the door leading to the second floor, fighting the urge to run like a frightened rabbit.

"I won't harm you." His voice brushed over her, dark, luxurious. "You needn't be afraid of me."

"I'm not afraid of you." At least she wasn't frightened of physical harm. Not with this man. No, there was much greater danger with this man.

His footsteps fell without a sound on the bricks as he moved toward her. He took the box from her hands and lifted a towel from her arm. "Would you rip one of those tablecloths into strips for me?"

She stared at his wound, an ugly red slash across his lean ribs. If he hadn't moved so quickly, that bullet would have found his heart. The realization sent a fine trembling rippling through her limbs.

Blood oozed from the gash, sliding down his side, soaking the waistband of his black trousers. Narrow waist, slim hips, long legs. Her body grew moist, the linen of her nightgown sticking to her breasts and belly. Gracious! What was she doing alone with this man?

"Miss Van Horne?" He moistened his lips, a quick slide of his tongue that left an intriguing sheen. "I hope you're not considering fainting."

Sarah stiffened, her legs shaking in blatant disobedience. "I've never fainted in my life."

"Commendable."

"You need a doctor."

"Perhaps. But you don't need to get involved in the scandal that would follow."

"I see. You're protecting me." She watched as he folded a towel and pressed the white linen to the ragged flesh of his side.

"My right arm is at your service, milady. My left, at the moment, is of little use." He looked at her, the mischief in his eyes dulled only slightly by pain.

Perhaps the wound wasn't serious. He certainly didn't appear as though he were about to expire. He looked more like a man who was taking his pleasure in teasing her.

"I would appreciate it if you would cut a few strips from that tablecloth for me."

She nodded and turned away from him, grateful for a task that allowed her to keep her distance from the rogue. She spilled her armful of linen onto one of the oak counters and drew a carving knife from a holder on the wall.

"What is this stuff?"

She glanced over her shoulder. He was seated at the table, his chair turned toward her, studying a brown bottle he had withdrawn from the medicine chest. Light poured from the fixture above him, sliding along the curve of his shoulder. Golden skin. Smooth, warm-looking skin. She glanced back to the white linen she held in her trembling hands. For goodness' sake, what was wrong with her? "It's our housekeeper's home remedy for cuts and scrapes."

"Smells like turpentine."

He had no right to barge into her house. He had no right to coerce her into shooting him. He had no right to make her feel as though she were some vile wanton creature. No doubt the man made a practice of collecting women the way he collected treasures.

From behind her came the swish of liquid against glass. A moment later she heard his quick intake of breath, followed closely by a mumbled curse. She smiled. "As I recall it stings a little."

"That's like telling Noah it's going to rain a little."

Without glancing at him, she could imagine the grin she could hear in his voice, that roguish tilt to his lips that made her want to smile. Foolish woman!

Using the well-honed blade of the knife, she carved notches into the tablecloth along one side. Oh, the man made her so angry she wanted to scream. She was not the type to become infatuated with a criminal, she assured herself.

She ripped strips from the expensive white damask cloth, cringing at the sound of screaming linen. After draping the makeshift bandages over her arm she turned to face the rogue. He was watching her, smiling, as though he knew she had imagined his face on every piece of cloth she had mutilated.

She marched toward him with her head held high. The scoundrel would not intimidate her with his seductive smiles. She would not turn harlot for the sake of a handsome face and splendid body. "A man in your profession must be accustomed to bullet wounds."

"To tell you the truth, you're the first to wound me, milady."

"I'm honored to hold that distinction." She dumped the bandages in a heap on the tabletop beside the soiled towel he had used to stanch the flow of blood.

"Looks like enough cloth to wrap a mummy."

"Don't tempt me." When she turned to walk away from him, he grabbed her wrist.

She pivoted, glaring down at him, keeping her eyes focused on his face. Yet it was impossible to block out the image of wide bare shoulders and those curious black curls that started just below the hollow of his neck. She tried to swallow, but her mouth had gone dry.

He held her, his long fingers gentle yet secure around her wrist. "If I promise not to bite, will you help me with the bandage?"

"I'm not frightened of you."

"I'm glad." He squeezed her wrist before releasing her. "No self-respecting man would want to frighten a beautiful woman."

She released her breath in a hiss between her teeth. "Will you stop this nonsense? I assure you I do not crave your ridiculous flattery."

"Is it ridiculous to tell a woman she's beautiful?"

"It is when she is far from beautiful." Sarah snatched a strip of linen from the table. "You, sir, are a flagrant liar."

"And you, miss, are a woman of rare quality."

She slapped his side with one end of the cloth, above the cotton pad he held against his wound. He jerked upward, his eyes growing wide, a moan slipping from his lips. She bit her lower lip, appalled at how the man could make her lose her temper. "Hold it there."

"Yes, ma'am." He shifted his left hand to hold the

linen, brushing the back of her hand with his fingers in the process.

The slight contact sent a ripple of sensation skimming upward along the nerves of her arm. She snatched back her hand. He smiled as if satisfied by her reaction.

Despicable man.

She grabbed the bandage and pulled it across his chest, hiding the dark male nipples peeking at her from beneath springy black curls. She tried not to touch him, but her task made it impossible.

Warm skin, silky curls, how peculiarly masculine. Deep inside her she felt a tremor, an insidious shaking that radiated upward and centered in the peaks of her breasts, pulsing with every beat of her heart. The man was a devil. "Lift your arm."

He lifted his right arm, muscles shifting, stretching beneath his smooth skin. Her palms tingled, curious to feel the strength of those muscles moving beneath her touch. His breath brushed the curve of her cheek, warm and moist and tinged with champagne. She could feel him watching her. In the corner of her eye, she saw his smile, that mischievous curve that was far too tempting.

She stared at her hands as she slipped the bandage under his arm. "How did you get started in this profession?"

"A band of Gypsies kidnapped me when I was a child. They taught me all I know."

"I see." She had to lean toward him to draw the bandage across his back, her cheek a whisper from his shoulder. His heat radiated against her, stroking her cheek, soaking through the fragile barrier of her robe and nightgown. His scent teased her, and she found herself breathing deeply. Gracious, what was wrong with her?

"I thought you said I didn't frighten you."

She glanced up, straight into his eyes. Midnight blue encircled irises the color of a twilight sky, shades of gray mingling with blue. Mischief danced in those eyes. Confidence ruled supreme in those eyes. "You don't frighten me."

"Then tell me why you're afraid to touch me."

"Don't be ridiculous." She brought the strip of linen around his injured side. "I simply don't care to be overly familiar with you."

"Because I'm a thief?"

She dipped toward him, quickly threading the bandage around his back. He was watching her; she could feel his gaze upon her, as warm as the summer sun. He was waiting for an answer, one she didn't plan to give him.

"And if I weren't a thief? Would you consider becoming familiar with me?"

"Hold this," she said, pressing the end of the bandage to the center of his chest.

He slipped his right hand over hers, his warm palm imprisoning her hand. "Tell me, how did a woman as beautiful as you manage to remain single for more than a year after your debut into society? I would guess you had men lined up for miles."

She jerked her hand from beneath his. "Yes, it became a terrible hazard, all of those men lined up in front of my house. They overflowed into the street, you know." She grabbed another strip of linen, horrified at how her hands were shaking. "I can't tell you what a nuisance it was. Why, it was impossible to move without tripping over one besotted male or another. I'm quite lucky I didn't break my neck."

"Such a pretty neck."

"Hold this in place." She shoved the end of the linen under his thumb.

"You have such a gentle touch. Have you ever considered becoming a nurse?"

"Have you ever considered getting into a less hazardous line of work?"

"But I meet the most fascinating people in my profession."

She wrapped the linen around his chest and tied the ends, pulling the bandage taut, dragging a moan from his lips. "We wouldn't want it to slip."

He smiled, warm and beguiling. "Thank you for your gentle care, milady."

"Get dressed and get out of my house."

While he dressed, she cleared away the mess they had made, returning Matilda's medicine chest to the cabinet, tossing the bloody towel and the remains of the tablecloth into the trash container outside the kitchen, using the handle of a broom to bury the soiled linen beneath the other trash. She only hoped Matilda wouldn't notice the loss. She could never explain her actions, not to Matilda, certainly not to Roxanne, not even to herself.

When she was finished, she stood on the brick walk leading to the herb garden behind the kitchen, refusing to go back into the house until that man was gone.

The nerve of the rogue. She should have sent for the police. If Roxanne ever discovered what she had done, Sarah would never survive the humiliation.

Scents from the herb garden drifted on the cool evening breeze. She breathed deeply, drawing the mingled blend of bay, thyme, and sage into her lungs, trying to erase the lingering trace of bayberry and a spice she couldn't identify—his scent.

Deep inside she perceived a shaking in her muscles. Fear. Shame. Desire? No! She was not the type of woman to feel desire.

The door opened and closed behind her. She stiffened as she felt him approach. He moved as silently as the moon through the evening sky, but she could sense him, perceive the warmth of him as he stood behind her.

"Thank you for everything, Miss Van Horne." His voice touched her, dark as midnight, soft as sable.

"It's only what I do for every scoundrel who tries to burglarize my home." She stared at the herb garden, the fragrant plants dusted with silver in the moonlight, brick enclosing the beds, forming the shape of a five-pointed star. The lawns and gardens she so loved stretched out beyond the herb garden.

Oak and elm spread their branches wide, leaves whispering in the breeze. Rose bushes lined a gravel path leading to a secluded part of the garden; awakening roses danced in the breeze, buds tightly bound in green bobbing softly. That was her favorite part of these gardens, that space walled off by yew and evergreen. In there she always felt safe. But she wasn't in that little niche of greenery now.

For what seemed hours he stood behind her, shielding her from the chill of evening. It would be a simple thing to walk away from him, to stretch the distance and free herself from the compelling heat of this man. Simple, yet she couldn't move, as if the moonlight had turned her to stone. He was there, reminding her in the silence that allowed her to hear every beat of her heart of how very much alive she could feel.

He placed his warm hands on her shoulders. Startled, she jerked free of his touch, pivoting to face him. "I won't stand for any of your insolence."

He met her indignant look with a mischievous grin. "Will you have dinner with me tomorrow?"

She blinked, stunned by his arrogance. "Certainly not!"

"Lunch, then. We could have a picnic in the park."

"Have you no shame?"

"Shame? For admiring a beautiful woman?"

Moonlight stroked the high planes of his cheeks, turning flesh to carved marble, a masterpiece, a seductive satyr eyeing his prey. "You have no scruples at all, do you?"

"A few."

He lifted the end of her braid. He stroked the thick coil with his thumb, a slow slide back and forth across her bound hair, his touch whispering along every strand of her hair.

She should leave. Yet that gentle stroking upon her hair had done something to her legs, disconnected them completely from her mind. She could only stand and stare at this smiling rogue, like a marionette awaiting the command of the puppet master. The scent of spices drifted from the warm earth, curling around her. Still, it was the scent of his skin that intoxicated her.

"I never cheat at cards, and I never take advantage of a woman."

With a slow pull on her braid he tugged her toward him. She resisted, grabbing her braid, trying to pull it from his grasp. "What are you doing now, if not taking advantage of me?"

"Trying to show one lovely lady how grateful I am." He moved toward her, holding her tethered by her braid.

"You're not only a thief, but you're . . ." Her words dissolved into a gasp as he brushed his fingers over the curve of her cheek. He was close, so close she could feel the heat of his body radiate against her. "Why are you doing this to me?"

In his eyes she saw a glimmer of uncertainty, as though he couldn't really answer the question she had demanded of him, as though he were caught in the same spell she could feel spinning around her. Strands of emotion twisted around them, shimmering, pulsing with desire and need.

"I won't hurt you." He slipped his fingers into the hair at the nape of her neck. "I would never hurt you, sweet Sarah."

"I'm not the type of woman who—" He nuzzled the soft skin below her ear. "Oh, my!"

"One kiss, that's all I want to steal."

"You mustn't," she whispered, pushing against his shoulders.

He released her braid, sliding his arm around her, drawing her close, too close. Her breasts pressed against his chest, soft and yielding against his hard muscles. He held her in an embrace she could easily have broken. Yet this thief had stolen her will.

"You smell like lavender in the rain." He rolled her earlobe between his teeth, sending sparks shimmering down her neck and across her shoulder. "Kiss me, sweet Sarah."

"No, I can't. . . ."

"Yes, you can."

"You mustn't."

"I think I must."

"I demand you release—"

He kissed her, drinking the words of protest from her lips. Firm and gentle, warm and moist, more than she had ever imagined, this kiss.

She had lived a lifetime without passion. Yet in unguarded moments, in the undisciplined realm of dreams, she had sipped from the sweet cup of desire.

In dreams she had felt strong arms around her, a phantom lover whose face she had never seen. In dreams she had tasted his kisses. In dreams she had heard his husky words of devotion. Still, she had never dreamed the reality would be so thrilling.

She rested her hands on his shoulders, meaning to push him away, wanting to deny him, deny her own need. And yet her hands trembled against him. This handsome thief was every wayward thought, every wicked image she had ever tried to banish from her heart and mind. He slid his lips against hers, cradling her head in his hand, stroking her neck with his thumb as though he had an eternity to kiss her.

Stop this! Her mind screamed for reason. Still, her body had waited a lifetime for her phantom lover to take form and substance. He was here, in the moonlight, holding her, and he was warmer than any dream she had ever imagined.

Who would know if she stumbled? Her chest tightened, shame and desire warring within her.

He touched the tip of his tongue to her tightly pursed lips, coaxing her to open for him. Just once, only once. If just once, she wanted to feel alive, truly alive.

An elixir, potent, intoxicating, awakening her every nerve, this was his kiss, this was the power of the man who held her, who surrounded her with compelling masculinity. A groan escaped her tight throat as she surrendered to her own wicked longing, as she drank deeply from his lips.

She opened her clenched fists on his shoulders, absorbing his warmth through the fine black wool. She slipped her hands into his hair. Soft, so soft, softer than she had imagined.

The scent of his skin seduced her senses. She breathed deeply, filling her lungs with that spicy scent as if he alone could give her life. She glided her lips against his, snuggling against his hard frame, needing to feel his arms tight around her, needing . . .

He pulled away from her. He stood with his hands

lightly on her waist, looking down into her eyes, his breath coming in ragged gasps.

She saw confusion in the depths of his beautiful eyes, the same confusion she felt surging through her veins. For a lifetime they stood, locked in the mysterious grip of a magic neither could understand.

The breeze swept over her, reality cooling the fires he had ignited inside her. Dear God, what had she done? "Go! Get out of my sight!"

He stepped back, his eyes never leaving hers. The breeze tossed his black mane, flinging a thick lock over his brow.

She curled her hands into fists at her sides, resisting an urge to smooth his hair back into place. "I want you to leave."

He nodded. "Until we meet again, milady."

She hugged her arms to her waist, watching as he vanished into the night, a shadow lost amid shadows, a phantom returning to his realm. She pressed her fingers to her lips, trapping the horrible moan rising in her throat. Tears bit her eyes and she fought to keep them at bay.

For years she had managed to keep the taint of her mother's blood from her life. She kept men at a distance, where they belonged. She had never stepped from the narrow road of propriety. Never!

Like mother, like daughter—her father's words echoed in her brain. Perhaps he had known what wickedness was lurking inside of her. Was her blood tainted?

"No," she whispered into the evening breeze. She had to be careful, that was all. She could never allow this wanton desire to control her again.

Chapter Three

"Sarah!" Clarissa shouted, switching on the light in Sarah's bedroom. "How can you possibly sleep at a time like this?"

Sarah sat bolt upright in her bed, blinking at the light that was assaulting her eyes. She hadn't been sleeping. The headache she had feigned to escape the ball now throbbed in her temples, each painful pulse a punishment for her wicked behavior.

For the past three hours Sarah had relived every detail of the few moments that the thief had stolen from her life. No matter how hard she tried, she couldn't lie to herself—she had participated in that kiss; she had reveled in the feel of his warm, moist lips against hers; she had thrilled at feeling his strong arms around her.

The man must no doubt still be laughing over the pathetic spinster who had melted in his arms. Her cheeks flooded with heat at the memory.

Fool. Idiot. Complete ninny. How could she have been such an imbecile?

The icy blue silk of Clarissa's gown rustled like leaves in the breeze as she swept toward Sarah, her footsteps as light as summer sunshine falling upon the dew. "What an extraordinary night this has been!"

"Extraordinary?" Sarah pressed her hand to her flaming cheek, wondering if Clarissa would question her. Did her guilt show?

Clarissa twirled, her pleated skirt billowing around her. "I met the man I'm going to marry tonight."

Sarah released the breath she had been holding, realizing she was safe. When occupied with her own thoughts, Clarissa never noticed anything else.

"Lord Austin Sinclair, Marquess of Somerset, a real English marquess. His father is the Duke of Daventry, which means one day he will be a duke and his wife a duchess." Clarissa laughed, a joyous lilting laughter that brought a smile to Sarah's lips. "That's the next best thing to being a princess. And I'm going to be his duchess."

"One night and he has already proposed?"

"Oh, Sarah, you know nothing at all of these things." Clarissa sank to the edge of the mattress and leaned back against the carved rosewood post at the foot of the bed. "It takes time to bring around a determined bachelor, and a certain finesse. But I can tell he is already infatuated with me."

"Of course he is. You're the loveliest girl in New York."

Clarissa tilted her head and smiled, her bright yellow curls brushing her pale shoulder. Even at 20, the age Clarissa was now, Sarah had never owned a gown that bared her shoulders. Her stepmother had always been cautious in her choice of gowns for Sarah. You must wear nothing that might lead people to suspect you could be fast, Roxanne had always said whenever Sarah had chosen a gown contrary to Roxanne's selection.

Sarah knew it was the scandal her mother had caused that led Roxanne to take great care to protect Sarah's reputation. Still, there were times when Sarah wondered what it might be like to wear a beautiful gown of icy blue silk, her hair in curls adorned with silk roses. Would she in some small way look beautiful?

"Oh, I wish you had been there to see Gretchan Langdon's face when Lord Sinclair asked me for a second waltz. Why, she was positively green."

"She has her heart set on the marquess as well?"

"Silly Sarah, every unmarried woman in New York has her heart set on Lord Austin Sinclair. Well, almost. He isn't at all your style, of course. He is without a single doubt the most handsome man I have ever met, and charming."

Handsome, charming. Sarah doubted any man could be more handsome or charming than her thief. Her thief. The man was the first ever to take her in his arms, the first ever to kiss her, and she didn't even know his name.

"Tell me, Sarah, did you really have a headache, or did you let Fanny Warren and her little band of alley cats chase you away from the party with their nasty little remarks?"

Sarah glanced away from her sister's cool blue eyes. She plucked at the eyelet lace edging the white linen sheet lying over her lap. "I hadn't realized you heard."

"Anyone within twenty yards heard."

Sarah felt a fresh wave of heat scorch her cheeks.

"Really, Sarah, you shouldn't be so sensitive. Simply because a few spiteful girls call you a stuffy old maid is no reason for you to go running home. Ignore them, as I ignored them and went on to enjoy the ball."

Sarah had tried to ignore them. She had tried not to notice them laughing at her. But there were times when she simply could not lift her chin and close her ears. This evening had been one of those times; it had been so painfully obvious she had no place at that ball.

"You can't help it if you aren't beautiful like I am. You have other qualities. You're kind, and you have a fine mind."

Your face has character, her thief's voice echoed in Sarah's memory. Character couldn't compare to beauty, she thought. In this world beauty went a great deal further in winning a happy life than character ever did. Women with character ended up spinsters with nothing to hold them at night but phantoms. She shook her head, silently admonishing herself for dipping into a hidden pool of self-pity buried deep inside her.

"Yes, you do have a fine mind," Clarissa said, mistaking the meaning of Sarah's response. "Why, just look at all of those little stories you write in Papa's newspaper. Although I can't for the life of me understand why you would want to spend so much time in that dreadful little newspaper office."

Sarah glanced up at her sister. "I hope to bring about some changes with my stories."

"I simply don't see how writing about those dreadful tenements and those horribly dirty immigrants will change anything." Clarissa snapped open her fan, the gilt edge shimmering in the light. "Everyone knows those people can't afford to live anyplace else. And the way you make Mr. Snelling sound, as though he's a beast . . . You should have heard how upset

Violet was about the things you had said about her papa. Sarah, you're going to make him terribly angry."

"I don't care if I make the man angry. He owns some of the worst houses in this city. And when I'm through with him, I'm going to go after the other ones, all the rich men who sit back and grow fat while people live in conditions not fit for animals. That's what we must change, Clarissa. We must provide decent housing the working poor of this city can afford." Sarah glanced past her sister to the open windows, thinking of the children whose windows faced dark alleys. "We can't allow those people to live in—"

"Oh, Sarah, please, you're really too depressing." Clarissa smoothed the cascade of white silk roses that tumbled from her shoulder down the length of her gown. "If you want to hear all about my triumph tonight, you won't mention those horrible tenements again."

Sarah leaned back against her pillow, realizing it was foolish to discuss the tenement problem with Clarissa. She glanced at the rosewood clock on the mantel. Two in the morning. In a few hours her uncle Kendall and his son Addison would walk into the study downstairs, ready to do battle with her.

"Sarah, you do want to hear all about my evening, don't you?"

"Of course I do." She had to get some sleep. "Perhaps in the morn—"

Clarissa didn't wait for Sarah to continue. Sarah did her best to ignore the painful pounding in her head as she listened to her sister describe every detail of her triumph at the ball. Through her sister's words Sarah saw what it was like to be a princess at a ball, to cast every other woman in the shade, to have a handsome prince pay her court.

Every woman should have one night with the world at her feet, Sarah thought. One night when no one found fault with her face and figure. One night when she felt beautiful and accepted. Still, Sarah knew it was no more than a fantasy. She would never have such a night.

"Sarah, sweetheart, you can't actually expect us to build this palace for those peasants." Addison Van Horne set a packet of papers on the desk in front of Sarah, between the ledgers that rose like a parapet on either side of her. He was smiling in that smug, condescending way she had seen one too many times.

Sarah stared up into her cousin's dark blue eyes, trying to pull together the raveling edges of her self-control. "It is hardly a palace, Addison."

"A million dollars." Addison lifted his dark brows. "Sarah, you expect us to spend a million dollars to build an apartment house for people who won't pay the rent."

"Eight hundred and fifty thousand."

"Oh, well." Addison stepped back, lifting his arms to his sides. "That makes it eminently more practical."

"Addison, I don't believe there is any need for sarcasm," Kendall said. "Sarah worked very hard on that proposal."

Sarah glanced to her uncle, wondering if she could count on his support. He sat in a wing-back chair across from her, lounging against the soft coffee-colored leather, his legs crossed, his chin resting on the steeple he had formed with his fingers, smiling at her. Her father's younger brother might have been born with the same silvery blond hair and pale blue eyes as his only brother, but there the resemblance ended. Kendall always had a smile to share with his niece.

Addison turned toward his father. "It doesn't matter how hard she worked on the thing, she is asking us to bankrupt the company."

"I'm asking you to make an investment in the future of this city." Sarah folded her hands on the stack of papers she had labored for six months to prepare. "An investment that will pay a minimum of five percent return."

Addison shook his head. "You're living in a dream world, Sarah."

"Two years ago, Ian Tremayne built three apartment buildings similar to this one. He showed a six percent profit the first year and seven percent the next."

Addison smiled at her as though she were a simple child who needed to be indulged in her tantrum. Although his hair was the same dark brown as his mother's, he had inherited his father's thin nose and high cheekbones. Pity he had inherited only the handsome cast of his father's face and none of Kendall's charm. "Ian Tremayne is a philanthropist, rich enough to squander a million dollars and not care if he shows a profit. We don't run our business that way."

"But he *is* showing a profit, by charging less rent than the slumlords were where they were living." Sarah looked at her uncle. "The people living in those wretched slums pay their rent, Uncle Kendall. They work hard every day, searching for the dream that brought them to this country but finding only greed and despair."

"Sarah, this is not the land of milk and honey," Addison said. "If those people had it so much better in their home countries, let them go back."

Sarah leaned back in the big burgundy leather chair that had been her father's. Like Addison, her father would never have entertained the idea of building housing for the poor working class of the city. Carelton Van Horne had made a fortune by building apartments for those who wanted luxury yet could not afford the mansions on Fifth Avenue. "Is that the principle upon which this country was founded, Addison? Come to America, but only if you are rich?"

Addison released his breath in a long sigh as though he were growing impatient with this child. "Sarah, why don't you put some effort into finding a husband instead of trying to interfere with our business concerns?"

Sarah felt the sting of his words sear her cheeks. "As I recall, my brother owns two-thirds of this company."

"Your brother doesn't give a damn about this company, except for the money he takes out of it every year." The corner of Addison's mouth twitched as he glared down at her, his condescension dissolving into anger. "I'm the one who works in that office every day. My father is the one who should have inherited the majority share when Uncle Carelton died. It was his father who started it. Father helped build that company every bit as much as Uncle Carelton did."

"I don't want to get into a debate with you concerning the rights of inheritance, Addison." Sarah glanced away from the hatred in her cousin's eyes, staring at the lace curtains that fluttered with the breeze pouring through the open windows. The fact that her brother took no interest in the family business was true. But Sarah understood why Leighton had rebelled against the father who had shunned him. "I have the owners of Mulberry Bend convinced to sell us the property. I am willing to invest most of what I own. The company need only invest six hundred thousand. I've examined the books and I can see we have capital for this project."

"Even if we made a five or six percent profit"—Addison tapped his knuckles on a stack of ledgers—"we could do better with another investment."

"We have a chance to take that piece of hell and turn it into a decent place to live." Sarah looked at her uncle. "You understand that this is more than profit and loss we are discussing, Uncle Kendall. You can see why we have to help these people."

"Of course I can, Sarah."

Sarah felt the weight lifting from her chest, a slab of anxiety as thick as a marble tombstone.

"But considering the amount of capital this venture will take, I feel it would be prudent to wait until Leighton returns before we make this decision."

One moment Kendall was helping her from beneath that heavy weight, the next he was pushing her to the ground. "Uncle Kendall, I'm certain Leighton would agree with me."

"Not if I have anything to say about it," Addison said.

"Addison, I think you've said more than enough for now." Kendall stood, tall and slender, his blue eyes gentle as he smiled at Sarah. "When do you expect Leighton home, darling?"

"I don't know. I received a package and a short note from him last week. He was in London and he wasn't sure when he would be able to return to New York."

"Playing with the English nobility again?" Addison asked, staring at Sarah. "He always did think he was a king."

Sarah clenched her hands into fists on her lap. "I've never thought jealousy particularly attractive, Addison."

Addison stiffened, thrusting back his slender shoulders. "I've had enough of this for one morning. Father, I'll wait for you in the hall." He marched across the room and snatched open the door, slamming it behind him.

Sarah drew a breath, trying to piece together the ends of her raveling control. "Uncle Kendall, you've taken my investment advice in the past; why can't you trust me with this one?"

"You've never asked me to invest this much money. We'll discuss this again when Leighton returns." He chucked her under the chin, treating her like a little girl. "Now don't you worry about this, darling. You've always been the only one Leighton would listen to. I'm sure he won't deny you this time."

Sarah watched him leave, fighting the urge to toss a ledger at him. She was not a child.

She dropped her head back against the chair and closed her eyes. How long would it be before Leighton came home? She didn't even know where to reach him. She glanced up as the door swung open and Clarissa swept into the room.

"I thought Uncle Kendall and Addison were going to be in here all morning. I was about to come in and chase them away. I have something terribly important to show you." Clarissa glided toward Sarah, a leather-bound book in her arms, fabric swatches fluttering from the crook of her arm. Her pale hair was piled in curls on top of her head, a pink silk ribbon that matched her gown threaded through the yellow coils.

"The fashion plates finally arrived from Paris." Clarissa plunked the thick book on the desk and opened it on top of Sarah's proposal for the new apartment building. "Madame Deauxville sent them to me as soon as they arrived in her shop. You simply must help me decide on a few new gowns."

Sarah thought of all the gowns in her sister's closet, which was the size of a sitting room. Some of the costly gowns Clarissa had grown tired of before ever wearing. Most were worn once, then discarded as though the finest silks and satins and velvets were nothing but rags.

"I've decided on this one for certain," Clarissa said, pointing to an exquisite dinner dress. The pleated silk skirt of dark rose was nearly covered by a flounced drapery shown in pale pink. Black velvet bows with gold pointed ends trimmed the waist and shoulders.

"Beautiful," Sarah whispered.

"But I thought I would have it done in this." Clarissa lifted a swatch of mint green silk to her chin and stepped back into the sunlight. Lace curtains fluttered in the breeze that was drifting through the open windows. "Or should I have it done in the pink as shown?"

Sarah tilted her head and regarded her sister as Clarissa alternated the pink and mint green silk samples to her chin. "I think you would look beautiful in the pink or the green."

"Green, then." Clarissa tossed the mint green material on the floor behind her and began flipping through the fashion plates. "I wonder if I should start picking out my trousseau."

Sarah smiled at her sister's supreme confidence. "And when are you planning to marry your marquess?"

"I think it should take a few weeks before he proposes. And then I suppose we will have a three-month engagement. I do hate those endless engagements most people have." Clarissa pursed her lips as she ticked off time on her fingertips. "I would guess we'll have an October wedding."

Sarah realized her sister was completely serious. Could a woman fall in love in an instant? Could she know the moment she set eyes on a man that he was her destiny? Into her mind came the image of silvery blue eyes set in a face from the pages of a fairy tale. "Have you really fallen in love with Lord Sinclair after only meeting him once?"

"Love?" Clarissa looked at Sarah as though her sister had suddenly sprouted an extra head. "Sarah, don't be so childish. A woman doesn't need to be in love with a man to want to marry him."

"She doesn't?"

"Of course not. Men are such inconstant creatures. If a woman were to fall in love with one she would be nothing short of a fool."

"There is such intimacy in marriage." Sarah fiddled with the top button of her gown, unfastening it, fastening it. "How could you stand to be touched by a man you didn't love?"

"Silly Sarah, you are so sentimental. Women don't expect to enjoy being touched by their husbands, unless of course there is something wrong with them."

Like mother, like daughter. Sarah shivered in the warm breeze sweeping in from the gardens. She had tasted passion once, for an instant, and it had left her shaken. It had left her wanting more. How could a woman marry and not crave that passion?

"You must think of marriage as a business arrangement." Clarissa flipped a page, revealing a drawing of four young women in ball gowns standing in a room decorated with potted palms and satin drapes. "A woman has certain assets a man wants. In exchange for her favors, a woman obtains wealth and social position. Just think of how green all of those alley cats will be when I'm a duchess."

And what type of social position would a woman have if she married a thief? The right woman could reform him. The right woman could help him lead a good and decent life. The right woman would want him even if he were a shop clerk.

Now she really was being silly, Sarah thought, trying to force her thief's image from her mind. He had stolen a kiss for his own amusement. He cared nothing for her or the fact that she would go to her grave remembering that one thrilling moment in his arms.

Sarah glanced up at a knock on the door. At her invitation the door opened and Emerson, the butler, entered the room. He glanced at Clarissa, his face molded from what might have been pale granite. The cold look in his dark brown eyes warmed with a slight smile as he looked at Sarah.

"There is a visitor to pay his respects to the ladies of the house, miss," Emerson said, addressing himself to Sarah. "Since Mrs. Van Horne has not returned from her breakfast with Mrs. Hauteville, I was not certain you were receiving."

"Who is it?" Sarah asked.

"Lord Austin Sinclair."

"Sinclair!" Clarissa said. "And you have him waiting? You idiot, show him in immediately."

Emerson lifted his chin as he glanced from Clarissa to Sarah. "Miss Sarah?"

Sarah smiled at the servant. "Please show him in, Emerson."

Emerson nodded, the bald spot on top of his head reflecting the sunlight before he left the room.

"How do I look?" Clarissa fussed with the delicate

eyelet lace edging the round neckline of her dress.

"Beautiful. I'm certain Lord Sinclair will be on his knees in a matter of hours."

"Yes." A smug little smile curved Clarissa's pink lips. "I know he will."

Sarah glanced at the door when Emerson returned to announce Lord Austin Sinclair. In a span of a heartbeat Emerson stepped aside and Sarah's world tilted. He was there, standing in the doorway, her thief.

He crossed the room in long, loose-limbed strides as though he owned the place. He was smiling, looking at her with those silvery blue eyes that had wreaked such turmoil in her dreams.

His hair was tousled into waves around his face from the breeze. His black morning coat was open, revealing the pale blue silk of his waistcoat, the silvery blue threads running through the cloth a perfect match for his eyes. Never had she glimpsed a more devastating male.

Although Sarah couldn't move, Clarissa had no problem greeting the man calling himself Lord Austin Sinclair. Sarah sat frozen behind her desk, staring, an odd emotion twisting deep inside her as she watched her thief kiss her sister's hand.

When he turned to look at Sarah he was smiling, his eyes glittering with mischief. "And this must be your sister."

Sarah scarcely heard Clarissa's voice as she introduced her to Lord Austin Sinclair. How could it be? This man was a thief, *her* thief. And he was masquerading as an English aristocrat, Clarissa's aristocrat.

"Miss Van Horne." He grasped her hand and lifted it to his lips. His breath touched the back of her hand, and then she felt his lips, a touch that shot a lightning bolt along her arm. She pulled free of his grasp.

He smiled. "Austin Sinclair, at your service, milady."

There was a challenge in his eyes, a spark of mischief that dared her to denounce him for the impostor he was. And, oh, how she would dearly love to expose the scoundrel. Unfortunately, it would mean exposing her own foolish actions of the night before. "My sister has told me a great deal about you, *Lord* Sinclair. Strange, but I feel as though we've already met."

"If you hadn't departed the ball so early last night, perhaps I would have had the pleasure of dancing with you."

Clarissa pushed between them in a rustle of pink silk. "Sarah never dances."

"No?" He looked past Clarissa to Sarah. "Pity. Think of all of those young men you deprive by denying them such a beautiful partner, Miss Van Horne."

"Yes, why, I understand there are hundreds who expire at every ball."

"You shouldn't tease my sister, Lord Sinclair." Clarissa grasped his arm and tried to steer him away from the desk. "She really is quite sensitive."

Sinclair ignored her, sitting on the edge of the desk, his attention focused on Sarah. Sunlight filtered through lace stroked his tousled hair, uncovering the deep chestnut highlights hidden in the thick strands of ebony. Sarah clenched her hands into fists on her lap, remembering the silky feel of his hair sliding between her fingers, wishing she could erase that and all the other shameful memories.

"Choosing a new gown?" he asked, lifting a swatch of turquoise silk from the desk. He held the cloth to Sarah's chin, his fingers brushing her neck.

She sank back against the chair to escape his touch. Yet she couldn't escape the look in his eyes, the look that told her he knew how he could set her pulse racing with a single touch.

The scoundrel!

"This color suits you." He slid the silk between his fingers. "It brings out the blue flecks in your eyes."

"You really are being silly, Lord Sinclair." Clarissa snatched the material from his grasp. "Why, my sister would never wear that color. It's far too young for her."

Sarah glanced down at her tightly clenched hands. She could feel heat spreading upward from the unadorned white collar of her slate gray dress, the blush she couldn't hide. Knowing she was well past her prime and hearing the truth from her sister in front of this man were two entirely different things.

"I can only provide a decidedly male opinion, I'm afraid," Austin said. "I think your sister would look lovely in the blue."

Sarah glanced up, expecting to see sarcasm in his eyes, seeing only the warmth of sincerity in the silvery blue depths. Oh, my, she couldn't breathe.

Clarissa laughed, pretty notes Sarah had often heard her sister practice. One of the many ways to impress a man was with a pretty laugh.

Clarissa tilted her fair head and smiled up at Austin, giving him a look Sarah knew men couldn't resist. And when she thought of her thief falling under her sister's spell, something dangerously close to jealousy twisted like a blade in Sarah's chest.

"We're keeping Sarah from her work." Clarissa ran her hand across Austin's forearm. "Would you like to come for a walk with me in the gardens?"

"It is a pretty day." Austin tapped the brown leather cover of one of the ledgers stacked on the corner of

Sarah's desk. "Far too nice to sit inside with a stack of ledgers."

"Don't be silly. Sarah loves working on those old ledgers."

"There are only so many days given to each of us, Miss Van Horne." Austin kept his gaze on Sarah, a few moments that expanded into a lifetime, while she sat captive of her memories and the ever-increasing need to discover what it might be like to be held in his arms once more. "You should learn to enjoy each and every one."

Sarah clenched her hands tighter, her nails biting into her palms. "There are those who enjoy an honest day's work, Lord Sinclair."

"And those who die without ever tasting life."

"Come," Clarissa said, tugging on his arm. "The roses are just coming into bloom."

Austin glanced at Clarissa as though he had only just remembered she was standing beside him. "Perhaps another time. I really must be going."

Sarah watched in numbed silence as he kissed Clarissa's hand. He didn't reach for her hand; he did nothing more than smile and wish Sarah a good day, and somehow that left her feeling bereft.

The miserable, vile creature! Why did he have this power to manipulate her emotions so easily?

Sarah released the breath she had been holding when Austin Sinclair left the room. Austin Sinclair. Now she had a name to go along with that face in her memory. Lord Austin Sinclair, Marquess of Somerset.

The impostor!

The man had waltzed into town and convinced everyone he was an English aristocrat. Oh, the nerve of the man!

"Charming man." Clarissa sat on the edge of the

desk. "I thought it particularly good of him to try to include you in the conversation, Sarah."

Sarah glanced up at Clarissa. Her sister was staring down at the piece of turquoise silk she held in her hand. "He's a worldly man, Clarissa," she said, as much to remind herself as to warn her sister.

"Of course he is. I can't imagine why I would want to marry a man who wasn't at all worldly."

Marriage. How could she explain to Clarissa that the man she intended to marry was a scoundrel? "I wonder if it might not be wise to get to know him better before deciding to marry him."

"Silly Sarah." Clarissa slipped the silk through her slender fingers. "I've already decided to marry him."

"Still, perhaps after you get to know him better you might find he isn't at all what you thought he was. You might realize he is completely unsuitable."

"He is more than suitable. He is ideal."

Sarah moistened her dry lips. "Clarissa, I think you should reconsider."

"I can't believe you're doing this." Clarissa lifted her lashes, staring straight into Sarah's eyes with enough venom to knock Sarah back in her chair. "You want him for yourself."

"No, that isn't true."

"I saw the way you looked at him from the time he walked into this room. I saw the way you flirted with him."

"I never flirted with him! He was flirting with me."

"He was simply being nice to you to please me." Clarissa stood and stared down at her sister. "You can't for a moment believe that Lord Austin Sinclair would choose you over me."

"No, of course I don't. I simply think you should take more time to get to know the man."

"I know all I need to know." Clarissa tossed the

piece of silk on the desk like a gauntlet. "I never realized how jealous you were of me. It doesn't suit you, Sarah. It only makes you look like a pathetic old maid."

Sarah stared at Clarissa through the gathering tears that pricked her eyes, watching as her sister crossed the room and left without a backward glance. A tight hand of emotion squeezed her throat until she could scarcely breathe. So much hurt could be done with a few words, Sarah thought.

Clarissa hadn't meant to make her feel worthless, Sarah decided. Her sister didn't understand, that was all. She knew there was nothing she could say that would make Clarissa see the truth. She also knew she had to protect her sister from that fortune-seeking scoundrel.

Chapter Four

Afternoon sunlight poured through the glass ceiling and walls of the conservatory of Isabel Bennett's Fifth Avenue house, heating the orange blossoms and jasmine, coaxing a delicate fragrance from the white and pink orchids that dripped in pendants three feet long from the banana trees. Austin Sinclair glanced at his hostess over the top of the newspaper he was reading.

In this room, Isabel Bennett had created a tropical paradise in the center of New York City. Like Isabel, Austin had been born in Brazil. He had spent his life shuttling between a city perched on a mountaintop in that torrid country and the cool climes of England. Not the ordinary upbringing for a proper English gentleman, but there was little in Austin's life that could be called ordinary.

Isabel stirred sugar into her tea, seemingly oblivious to her great-grandson's agitated pacing. Collin Bennett's footsteps pounded rhythmically on the white marble squares lining the floor as he paced back and forth beside the table—tap, tap, tap, pivot, tap, tap, tap, pivot. The young man was as regular as a clock.

"I knew this was going to get out of hand." Collin slashed at a bougainvillea vine hanging above his shoulder. Petals scattered in a shower of red, a single red petal clinging to the shoulder of his light gray coat.

Isabel tapped the edge of her spoon against her cup, the smooth skin of her hand as pale as the ivory china that sang softly beneath her quick taps. "Collin, do sit and finish your lunch."

"If anyone should discover I'm a part of this . . ." Collin shoved his hand through his light brown hair. "I can't believe you allowed yourself to be caught prowling about the Van Horne house like a common thief last night."

Austin considered reminding the young man it had been Collin's assignment to make certain Sarah and the other Van Horne ladies had not left the ball, but he never liked to waste his words.

"Did you have to allow her to shoot you?"

Austin masked his growing annoyance with the young man behind a smile. "It wasn't part of my plan."

"We should have contacted the authorities." Collin turned and paced a few steps, then returned. "The police are the ones to go after Leighton Van Horne, not us."

"Impossible." Isabel sat back in her chair, the white wicker creaking softly beneath her. "The police would want to know more than we are willing to tell."

"I don't understand why you agreed to become involved in this, Grandmother. Van Horne stole that medallion from Lord Sinclair's father, not from us."

"You know very well why we are involved. That medallion is a symbol of the Inner Circle, as old as the original covenant. As a lord of the Inner Circle and a member of the Central Council, your father has an obligation to protect it, as do we all."

"Father doesn't see fit to drag himself away from council matters in Avallon to poke around in this problem. He hasn't set foot in New York in over a year. He keeps mother locked away on that speck of land hidden in the heart of Brazil as though it's some kind of paradise."

Isabel folded her hands on her lap and held Collin's gaze. "I'm certain your father is hoping this will give you a chance to prove yourself, Collin."

"I don't need to prove myself to anyone." Collin stared at her, his blue eyes wide with fury, his handsome face molded into the petulant expression of a spoiled ten-year-old rather than the 21-year-old he was. "I choose to live in the real world, Grandmother, not the rarefied climes of ancient Avallon."

"I've never understood how you could choose this life over your heritage." There was a deep sorrow in her as Isabel stared at her great-grandchild. "The blood of Avallon flows through your veins. A bloodline that can be traced to the very beginning of civilization on this planet; it is your legacy."

"Those people in Avallon are out of touch with reality, Grandmother. This is the nineteenth century. It's time for the Central Council and the mighty little Inner Circle to climb down from their cozy mountaintop and start living in the real world."

"Your father is part of Avallon, Collin."

"My father scarcely knows I exist. He prefers to hide himself away, cloaking himself in the secrecy of his ancient city, playing his political games. He prefers to live a myth. I choose to live in the real world. And Mother would live here if Father gave her the choice."

"Collin, your father has hopes you will one day join him, take your place in the Inner Circle."

"Because he thinks it can benefit his career. My life is here and I'll be hanged before I allow Father or you or anyone to dictate to me." Collin pivoted on his heel, his shoes rapping on the marble as he marched away from her.

Austin watched him disappear down the path, huge ferns and palm fronds seeming to swallow him. The young man would prove useless in this mission. He leaned back in his chair and pulled open the top button of his shirt. Owing to the humidity in the room, he had removed his coat and tie minutes after joining Isabel for lunch.

"I apologize for Collin's behavior. I'm afraid his mother spoiled him. Perhaps to compensate for the fact that his father was always busy with his political career." Isabel met Austin's gaze, her dark blue eyes betraying her anguish. "The boy has spent too much time in the Outworld."

Austin had been born in Avallon, born into a family of the Inner Circle. Yet he understood Collin's decision to live in the Outworld, that world beyond the boundaries of Avallon. "There are many like Collin, those who find the Outworld more exciting than Avallon."

"The Outworld is hundreds of years behind us."

"Only because we had a head start." In a very real sense, it felt like stepping back in time each time Austin left the boundary of Avallon. And yet he enjoyed the transition to this simpler world.

"I don't understand how anyone could turn his back on six thousand years of tradition. Look at our advances in medicine and science. Look at how well we control crime. We've eliminated hunger and poverty. Why, compared to us, these Outworlders might as well be living in caves."

Austin folded his paper and set it beside his plate on the round table. "Perhaps those who have become disenchanted with Avallon have become so because of those very advances. In a sense, Avallon has become too ordered, too predictable, too confining."

Isabel lifted one finely arched brow as she studied Austin. "You sound like a renegade."

Austin shook his head. "I love Avallon. But I also love this broad world outside of that small realm."

"I, too, love this world, or I would not have remained so long away from my home. And yet my loyalty to Avallon has never wavered." Her narrow shoulders rose beneath her violet-and-white striped silk gown as she drew a deep breath. "I believe Collin has rebelled against everything. If only the boy would be more like you."

"I'm afraid he doesn't much care for me."

"Jealousy. He's more impressed with your title than you ever were, my dear boy. English nobility and a lord in the Inner Circle, such prestige is devastating to the boy."

Although grateful for his loving family, Austin did not define himself by the wealth and prestige they possessed. He had been taught to judge a man by his actions, not the accident of birth that had bestowed upon him position and power.

"The fact that Clarissa Van Horne is fascinated with you doesn't at all help the situation. You see, he fancies himself in love with the girl."

Austin frowned, remembering the way Sarah's face had flushed under the lash of her sister's invisible blows. It had taken all of his willpower to keep from touching Sarah, from cupping her cheeks in his hands and easing the heat of her shame. "He's in love with that spoiled piece of fluff?"

"I'm afraid, unlike you, he hasn't developed the ability to look beyond the masks people wear. He sees only her beautiful face."

There had been a time, in his youth, when a beautiful face had nearly destroyed Austin. Three weeks before he was to marry a certain English lady, he had found his fiancée in the arms of another man. It seemed Christina had wanted Austin's money and title and the other man's love.

Austin had been 23 at the time, and more naive than he cared to admit. Now he realized Christina had not been his *Edaina,* the soul mate destiny meant him to find. She had only been a beautiful woman who had captured a foolish young man's imagination.

In the ten years since that romantic folly, Austin had managed to avoid any serious connections. "Collin's still young. There are many lessons left to be learned."

"I have been a liaison for Avallon for more years than I care to remember. This is my third assignment in the Outworld, and my last. I shall allow Isabel Bennett to expire abroad at the end of this year. I'm going to retire in Avallon." Isabel stared past Austin to the orchids nestled against the banana tree. "I have three sons, two daughters, nine grandchildren, and fourteen great-grandchildren. With time and experience I have discovered that some people, I'm afraid, never do learn."

"Collin is right on one count: I was careless last night." Austin rubbed his side, trying to ease the nagging ache of his wound beneath the fresh bandage Dr. Chamberlain had applied this morning. "I was focusing too much on finding the medallion to realize I had been discovered until it was too late."

"I'm grateful we have Dr. Chamberlain in the city. I would hate to leave you to the mercy of one of those primitive Outworld physicians." Isabel swirled the spoon in her tea. "Sometimes I think what a pity it is that he cannot be allowed to use his knowledge to help others."

"You know as well as I do how dangerous it would be to interfere with the Outworld. The medical practices we take for granted in Avallon would be perceived as miracles in this time and place. Questions would lead to inquiries, and perhaps discovery."

Isabel nodded. "I'm only thankful you were not injured more severely. Poor Sarah, you must have frightened her dreadfully."

A smile curved his lips as he thought of the indignant lady who had tended him the night before. "Do you have any idea why she left your party early last night?"

"Roxanne mentioned something about Sarah having a headache, but I doubt it's the real reason. I suspect she didn't feel comfortable for one reason or another. You see, Sarah has always been different."

Different. There was something about Sarah, a rigid innocence, like a wall built to contain every desire. For some reason the woman intrigued him. Perhaps because he had glimpsed the fire in her pretty hazel eyes, the passion smoldering deep within her. "I don't understand why she isn't married."

"While other girls were conniving to be the most popular debutante in the city, Sarah was trying desperately to hide. From the first moment she made her debut, she has worked very hard at being a spinster."

"But there must have been suitors."

Isabel shook her head, her white hair shimmering like snow in the sunlight. "Sarah has always avoided any attachments. I doubt she has ever been alone with any man except her brother and father. That is, until last night."

Isabel's words only confirmed what Austin suspected. No man had ever held Sarah in his arms. No man had ever tasted her lips, lips as soft as an awakening rose. No man had ever felt the heat of her breath against his chest. No man, except a thief who had stolen a kiss from an icy maiden and found himself seared by a fiery temptress.

Isabel cocked her head as she regarded him, her lips curving into a knowing smile. "I, too, have always thought Sarah was a particularly attractive young woman, though not in the ordinary manner."

There was nothing ordinary about Miss Sarah Van Horne. She was, as he had told her the night before, a woman of rare quality.

"It's a pity about her mother. I rather like Diana. Lovely woman. Sarah favors her a great deal."

"The Mrs. Van Horne I met last night isn't Sarah's mother?"

"Heavens, no. As I recall, Diana Rutherford had scarcely made her debut before she married Carelton Van Horne. Six years later she created a fabulous scandal by running away with Ward Schuyler. Carelton gave her a divorce and a year later married Roxanne Hauteville."

"Sarah's mother abandoned her children?"

"Diana loved her children, but I suspect life with Carelton was intolerable for a sensitive girl. I doubt she seriously thought she would never be allowed to see Sarah and Leighton again, but Carelton was ruthless. From the time he was a boy he had a frigid streak running through him. Even at seventeen, Roxanne was a perfect partner for him. She wanted nothing more than his money and position."

And that was the woman who had raised Sarah. Austin's side pinched as he drew a deep breath, filling his senses with the sweetness of orange blossoms and jasmine. He wondered what affection Sarah had ever known.

Isabel stirred the untouched tea in her cup. "Diana is happy now, at least as happy as a mother can be who has been forced to choose between her lover and her children. She and Ward live in San Francisco with their two children. Occasionally they come to New York to visit with friends and relatives and to maintain contact with several of Ward's business partners."

"That explains a few things."

"Such as why a lovely young woman is afraid to be noticed?"

"Exactly." Austin sipped his tea, sweet and hot, filled with cream.

"It would take a very special man to break through Sarah's defenses."

Or a thief, Austin thought. He held his cup between his palms, letting the steam bathe his face in the scent of creamy tea. A thief had slipped beneath her defenses to steal a kiss.

He had enjoyed that kiss far too much. The truth was, he had awakened this morning with vivid memories of dreams inspired by that kiss. Dangerous, these thoughts, this fascination for the sister of his enemy. "I wonder how much Sarah knows about her brother's criminal activity."

"I can't believe Sarah knows anything about it."

Austin brushed red petals from the tabletop. "She knows something, or she would have sent for the police last night."

"She may have some suspicions about her younger brother. Leighton was always wild. But I'm certain she has no part in any wrongdoing."

"I suspect you're right." It would have made his task easier if Sarah were in some way involved, in some way as guilty as her brother. He settled his cup in the rounded space on the saucer and stared at the scathing editorial Sarah had written about conditions in a block of tenement houses owned by Warren Snelling. "Sarah isn't what I expected Leighton Van Horne's sister would be."

"No. Leighton always craved attention, possibly because he had none from his father, while Sarah would like to be invisible. But make no mistake about it, Sarah is close to her brother, as close as any brother and sister can be."

"I'm certain he sent her the medallion in that package we traced from London." Austin glanced to the fountain planted in the middle of the conservatory. Water bubbled from the large stone basin to lap at the belly of an arcing dolphin, like shimmering gold plumes in the sunlight. "But I couldn't find a trace of it last night. I didn't have time."

Isabel stirred her tea, a slow swirl of the spoon as she stared into her cup like a fortune-teller seeking a vision. "I want to believe Van Horne could never discover how to use the medallion."

"It's a priceless artifact, that's all he knows. That's all anyone outside of the Circle knows."

Isabel nodded. "I do wish we could call in the authorities. I hate to see you take such risks."

"We can't involve the police."

"Of course not. But the man you brought with you, that Duggan fellow, he's a guardian. Surely he can handle the more dangerous aspects of this mission."

Austin had managed to slip Bram Duggan into the Van Horne household as a groom. He wondered if the man would ever forgive him for the assignment.

"Duggan's job is to let me know if he sees Van Horne."

"Austin, you know as well as I do that the Inner Circle ceased being warriors ages ago. You're out of your element in this. You have too much at stake. The others from Avallon, the men you have watching the train stations and the docks. Surely one of them could investigate . . ."

"My family is responsible for that medallion. I'm going to find it. And I'm going to see Leighton Van Horne hang for murder."

"There is something you haven't told me." Isabel studied Austin, a single line appearing between her delicately arched white brows. "Van Horne did more than steal the medallion from your father and kill one of his guards. I detect something more personal in your desire to see the young man brought to justice."

"Van Horne nearly killed my brother." Austin stared at an orchid that dangled near his shoulder, the smooth white petals glowing like pearls in the sunlight. "I'm certain he'll try again. He won't be satisfied until Devlin is in his grave. And I doubt he will stop there. He blames my family for his misfortune."

"I see." Isabel pressed the palms of her hands together and rested her chin on her fingertips. "Sarah will be devastated over the truth about her brother."

"I wish I could shield her." Austin brushed the orchid with his fingers, the petals smooth and firm beneath his touch. In his mind he saw Sarah's face in the moonlight, her lovely eyes wide with confusion and desire, the same desire that had flared inside him the instant his lips had touched hers. "But I can't. Sarah is my only key to finding the medallion."

"Although she didn't betray you this morning when you called on her, she might change her mind."

"She is sensitive about scandal. And she's smart enough to realize she can't betray me and keep from telling her part in my escape."

Isabel shook her head. "It's a shame that child has to be involved."

"My only chance for finding the medallion is by getting close to Sarah."

"Close? Do you intend to seduce the child?"

"She isn't a child." And she wasn't guilty of any crime. Still, it didn't alter the fact that she might very well be hurt. He felt a thickening in his throat, a gathering of emotion that rose and left a bitter taste on his tongue. "Seducing innocent women isn't one of my hobbies."

"Unless you have no choice?"

He didn't want to believe it would go that far. He didn't want to acknowledge the fact that he might very well ruin that innocent woman. Yet he knew he would do what had to be done. "If I can get close to her, earn her trust, get her talking about her brother, I just might be able to find out where that medallion is. And I would wager that when Leighton returns to New York, Sarah is the first person he will try to see."

"And if he manages to get to Sarah before you get the medallion, you will lose your best chance to retrieve it."

"Exactly. Although we have men on Van Horne's trail, no one has been able to find a trace of him. He could show up in New York at any time."

"I understand why Sarah is the key." Isabel studied Austin a moment before she spoke. "Still, I think you must be very careful. It would be disastrous to become emotionally involved with her."

"I have no intention of becoming involved with Sarah Van Horne." The last thing he needed to do was fall in love with Leighton Van Horne's sister. Because he knew one day he would be the man who would send her brother to the gallows.

Had they met in another time, another place, Austin would have taken great pleasure in tearing down the walls Sarah lived behind. She was an enticing enigma. He wanted to meet the woman Sarah kept locked deep inside, the temptress he had held in his arms for one splendid moment. Yet he knew he must keep his distance, at least emotionally. Fate had made them enemies before they had ever met.

Austin's thoughts were interrupted by the arrival of Isabel's butler and his announcement of a visitor requesting to see Lord Sinclair—Miss Sarah Van Horne.

Austin felt a sudden surge of his blood, a tingling of anticipation he wanted to attribute only to the hunt for the lost medallion and the murderer he had vowed to capture. But he knew his reaction had far too much to do with the young lady waiting to see him.

"I'll let you see her alone," Isabel said, rising from her chair. She hesitated a moment, gazing down at Austin, a gentle smile curving her lips. "Be careful, dear boy."

"I will." Still, he wondered how he could avoid becoming entangled in the web one beguiling young woman could spin around him.

Chapter Five

Austin leaned back in his chair and listened to the sound of Sarah's footsteps on the marble squares. Quick, determined, the footsteps of a woman going to battle. She swatted a palm leaf out of her way and emerged from the green shadows into the sunlight, the long leaf fluttering in her wake.

Sarah halted when she saw him, as though she had come upon a lion in the woods, a lion she suspected would devour her at her slightest move. The fierce look in her eyes wavered an instant before she regained her defenses.

Sunlight rushed through the glass overhead, anxious to spin threads of gold through her light brown hair. A queen staring at a wayward peasant, that was how she faced him, her chin lifted, her beautiful eyes alive with fury, her cheeks flushed with color.

Austin took one look at her and drew in a sharp breath. One look and his blood pounded through his veins. One look and he knew he was in one hell of a lot of danger. How was he supposed to get close to this woman and not get burned?

"Miss Van Horne," he said, rising to greet her. "How nice to see you again."

Sarah glanced down to his outstretched hand, then stared straight into his eyes. "I've had enough of your act, Sinclair. If that is your name."

"Please call me Austin."

"Lord Austin Sinclair, Marquess of Somerset, son of the Duke of Daventry. I must say, you have more raw nerve than I imagined."

God, she was beautiful when she was angry. Through the heavy scent of orange blossoms and jasmine he caught a delicate trace of lavender, that sweet fragrance that tempted him to press his lips to her neck and breathe her essence deep into his lungs.

"How could you do it? How could you walk into this house and convince Isabel Bennett you're an English nobleman? Do you have any idea the scandal you would cause if anyone should discover the truth? Isabel would be ruined."

"I certainly wouldn't want that to happen. Isabel has been a most charming hostess."

Sarah drew a deep breath. "What have you stolen from this house?"

He lifted his hands to show they were empty. "Nothing."

"I see. You're simply using Isabel to get close to her friends, to seek out your prey."

"I'm very particular about my choice of victims."

"A discerning thief."

"Very." Fine wisps of hair curled around her face, the silky strands succumbing to the humid air, softening the severe style. "Do you always wear your hair in that tight knot at the nape of your neck?"

She lifted one hand as though she intended to smooth her hair, but caught herself, jerking her hand back to her side. "How I wear my hair is no concern of yours."

"That style doesn't suit you." He slipped a comb from her hair.

"Stop it!"

He snatched at another comb.

"Stop it this instant!" She slapped at his hands, but he managed to release her hair. It tumbled in a coil as thick as his forearm, cascading down her back. "Mr. Sinclair!"

He liked the way she dropped his title. Too many times that title had gotten in the way of the truth. "You should wear it softer," he said, brushing his fingers over the soft curls at her temple. "Perhaps piled on top of your head with curls escaping all around your face."

"I won't stand for any of your insolence." She stepped back as she spoke, bumping into the edge of the table, china teacups clattering against saucers.

"Careful."

"Just stay right where you are." She lifted her hand to hold him at arm's length. "I didn't come here to be subjected to your perverse nature."

"Perverse?" He lifted his brows in mock surprise. "Is there anything perverse about a man interested in a beautiful woman?"

"Save the counterfeit flattery for someone who doesn't know you for the scoundrel you are."

He pressed his hand to his heart. "How you wound me, milady."

"Yes, and next time I shall wound you in a much more vulnerable area."

"Yes." Austin plucked an orchid from the pendant of white blossoms hanging above her head. "I believe you will," he said, brushing the petals across her cheek.

She snatched the flower from his hand and tossed it to the floor. "I want you to stay away from my sister."

"Or you will do what, milady?"

"I'll tell her who and what you are."

"And do you think she'll believe you?"

She glanced down, a flicker of lashes that told him of her uncertainty. "Of course she'll believe me."

Her sister would never believe her, and Sarah knew it as well as he did. "And if you can convince people I was in your house last night, which I doubt you can, what do you suppose they will say when they discover you allowed a thief to walk out your back door?"

She lifted her chin, but there was something missing from her determined stance: the confidence she needed to pull off the charade. In her eyes he saw a well of sorrow, filled by years of humiliation and shame.

Looking into her eyes he forgot the reasons he should not become involved with this woman, forgot the mission that had brought him into her life, forgot everything but the vulnerable young woman who stood with her head high, willing to defy him even knowing she would lose in the end.

"I will do what I must to save Clarissa from marrying you."

"Sacrifice your own reputation?"

She glanced away, staring for two or three seconds at the fountain bubbling behind him before she lifted her gaze and met his eyes. "My reputation is little sacrifice to save an impressionable young girl from a man like you."

A man could spend a lifetime looking into her eyes and seeing what he saw today—a pristine honesty that touched him as no woman had ever touched him. In spite of the warning bells sounding in his head, he felt desire stir in his blood, a tightening low in his belly that told him he was entering dangerous territory. "And suppose I gave you an alternative?"

She stared up at him, the wariness of a doe facing a prowling wolf deep in her eyes. "Such as?"

"You agree to see me, and I'll agree to discourage your sister from her fascination with marrying a marquess."

Her lips parted, hot color rising high on her cheeks. "Are you suggesting I become your mistr—"

"Intriguing thought." He rested his fingertip on her lower lip, absorbing the warmth of her startled gasp against his skin. "I'm suggesting you allow me to court you. Dinner, picnics, the theater, all the things a man smitten with a young woman would do."

She stared up at him as though he had just spoken in a language completely foreign to her. "Why in the world would you want to court me?"

He brushed the back of his fingers over the curve of her cheek, her skin as smooth as porcelain, yet warm and inviting, a sculpture brought to life. In her eyes he saw a flicker of flame, an instant of desire before she pulled away from his touch and stared at him with renewed anger.

"You intrigue me, sweet Sarah," he said, realizing the words were far too true.

"This is all a game to you, isn't it?"

It was all far too real. "If you want to convince your sister I'm a scoundrel, the best way to do it is to agree to spend time with me."

"But she'll think I'm stealing you away from her."

An image of the arrogant little Clarissa jealous of her sister brought a smile to his lips. "Isn't it better than having the entire city talk about the night you spent alone with a thief in your house? What will they think when I tell them about that pretty blue nightgown you were wearing?"

"You would, wouldn't you?"

"If you insist on sending me to the gallows, I'm afraid I will have to take you with me."

"If you leave town, I promise I will say nothing about last night."

He shook his head. "I'm not going to let you get away so easily, sweet Sarah. Make up your mind. Put up with my company, or see how much scandal we can generate."

Sarah toyed with the top button of her gown, staring up at him. "It seems you leave me little choice."

Austin felt a tightening in his chest, a constriction around his heart as he looked at her and saw the frightened girl hidden inside her woman's body. Still, he had little choice but to play this game through to the end. "Who knows, Sarah, you might even learn to enjoy my company."

"You will soon tire of this game, Sinclair."

She turned to leave, her hair spilling in shining waves around her shoulders.

"I'll pick you up at seven for dinner."

She paused, hesitating a moment before turning to face him. "You can't be serious. What would I tell my sister? How could I possibly explain having dinner with you to my stepmother?"

"You're not going to try to wiggle out of our agreement, are you?"

She drew her teeth over her lower lip, her lovely eyes revealing her every misgiving. "Could we see each other during the day? I could meet you somewhere."

"You intend to keep me a secret?"

"Give me a little time."

It suddenly occurred to him he would love to give her all the time in the world. "Meet me in the main hall of the museum of art, near the entrance from the carriage drive, at half past ten tomorrow morning."

She stared at him as though she wished she could make him disappear with a snap of her fingers.

"Don't worry. What could possibly happen in the museum?"

She frowned, and he could see she thought any number of terrible things could happen in a very public museum. "Very well, tomorrow morning."

She turned on her heel and marched toward the entrance, swatting at the leaves that blocked her way. Austin watched her until she disappeared into the green shadows, until all that remained of her angry footsteps was a distant echo.

He had to get close to her. He had to win her trust only to betray her and the brother she loved. And he knew by the look he had seen in Sarah's eyes, he would succeed. Even though the lady thought she hated him, she was attracted to him. Perhaps because she saw him as a thief and a scoundrel, the embodiment of her every fear. Forbidden fruit.

He reminded himself of all the reasons that had brought him to this moment. He thought of his brother and his family and all of the people depending on him. He thought of the vows he had made long ago, the oaths that bound him to an ancient sect, the ties that linked him to Avallon.

The bloodline of Avallon could be traced back to the dawn of civilization, back to an island nation that had been destroyed by flood more than ten thousand years ago, an island called Atlantis.

After the cataclysm that destroyed their world, Austin's ancestors were displaced scientists in an era when such knowledge was dangerous. They sought to find a place in that primitive world, creating the guise of pagan cults to disguise the knowledge they took for granted, knowledge and abilities others called magic. In time, even their cults could not shield them from harm.

Perceived as witches and wizards, Austin's ancestors banded together, from Ireland, Wales, and Britain. Six thousand years ago they came to a mountaintop in Brazil, a place where they could be free from persecution, free to establish a culture based on the exploration of the mysteries of nature. There they flourished to this day, an island of discovery, more advanced than the primitive world beyond the realm of their mountaintop. Yet they had never completely abandoned the Outworld, the world outside of Avallon; to do so would mean stagnation and the death of their dreams.

Bankers, magistrates, nobility, businessmen, advisers to kings and politicians, the people of Avallon possessed places in society all over the world now, as they always had in the past. Many, like Austin, moved between the two worlds, keeping a vow of silence, assuring Avallon shelter from civilization outside of their hidden city. They enjoyed people and places. They monitored the progress made in the Outworld. Until this moment Austin had always found pleasure in his assignments.

He thought of Sarah, of the pain that lurked in her future, pain he would help inflict. Yet he had no choice but to follow this path in life, a path that would bring heartache to an intriguing lady with pretty hazel eyes.

Chapter Six

The clink of steel striking steel echoed in the ancient city of Avallon. Sunlight glittered on the polished blades of the broadswords slicing through the morning air. Devlin Sinclair fought the growing lethargy in his arms, the weight of the sword dragging against muscles still unaccustomed to the violent actions of combat.

Devlin gritted his teeth as his opponent slammed his heavy blade against his own, trying to force the pointed tip into the black stones beneath Devlin's feet. He had to find the strength to win.

Sunlight poured into the square, spinning rainbows from crystals trapped in the black stones that rose to shape the walls of the buildings surrounding the plaza. Three stories tall, two broad wings stretching along one entire side of the square, the temple dwarfed the other structures that remained in the city. The temple stood today as it had for six thousand years, with eight square stone columns lining the front of the structure, lifting the pediment roof toward the sun that once was worshiped here.

A few buildings stood intact outside the square. Most of the city lay in ruins from an earthquake that had rumbled here long ago. Still, Avallon survived.

Every day for the past two weeks, since beginning the lessons that would draw him into the Inner Circle, Devlin had faced this same opponent, here in the square of the ancient city. The ritual combat was like an ancient dance recalling the lives of ancestors long ago turned to dust, when spectators would line the steps of the temple and watch this combat for sport. Today three women sat alone on the temple steps, watching the battle.

In the past few months, since finding this hidden city in the heart of Brazil, Devlin had learned that much of life in Avallon was tied to the past. Several miles from these ancient ruins, modern Avallon thrived. Still, in spite of their advances in science, the people here lived by ancient codes.

Devlin hoisted the heavy blade, countering a blow from the side. His arms strained beneath the force. The muscles in his back and shoulders knotted with the pressure.

"Nice move, Devlin," Rhys Sinclair shouted.

Rhys was dressed as Devlin was, naked to the waist, with close-fitting black trousers tucked into knee-high black boots. There was nothing to prevent the blade from cutting but the skill of the man wielding the weapon.

Devlin sucked air into his burning lungs, struggling to block the blade as Rhys lunged forward. A cool breeze scented with the perfume of the wildflowers that spread in rolling waves of blue and white and yellow upward along the surrounding hills rippled across his damp skin.

Thirty years separated Devlin in age from his opponent, his father, a man Devlin scarcely knew. Yet Rhys Sinclair looked no older than Devlin's 33 years: his black hair was untouched by gray, his skin taut and unlined, the sculpted muscles of his body moved with fluid grace beneath a fine sheen of sweat.

They had learned the secret of slowing the tide of time here. And Devlin was learning it was only one of their secrets.

Rhys swung his blade in a downward plunge, striking Devlin's sword, a growl emanating from deep in his chest. The blow was enough to bend Devlin's wrists, just enough to force the tip of the blade to the stones.

Devlin dragged air into his lungs, his arms trembling beneath the strain to lift the heavy sword. He stared into his father's blue-green eyes, animosity and admiration warring in his heart.

Rhys's smile was warm and generous as he stepped back from his son. "In another few weeks, you shall be a master of the sword."

Winded, Devlin rested the tip of his blade against the smooth black stones beneath his feet and leaned on the leather-clad handle, dragging air into his lungs. At least he had the small satisfaction of knowing his opponent was also out of breath. "This is all very important to you, isn't it? The tradition of it all. The continuation of the past."

"I can see you still harbor doubts about your legacy." Rhys slipped his sword into the black leather sheath that hung from a leather belt strapped around his narrow hips. "You still do not see the significance of becoming a lord of the Inner Circle."

Devlin stared down at the cobblestones beneath his feet, carved centuries ago, still hard and unyielding. He had been stolen from his family at the age of two. He had lived his life without a home, without a family, a man alone, until six months ago. "I know you must have thought it very important when you agreed to a quest that nearly killed me and everyone on our expedition, an expedition the Central Council manufactured to prove my worthiness."

"Without the quest you would never have been allowed to take your rightful place in our society."

Devlin twisted the tip of the sword against the stone, clenching his teeth at the sharp scraping noise. His parents and the Central Council had known his identity for nearly a year before he had been allowed to enter this ancient society. For nearly a year they had observed and tested him. "I don't like being manipulated."

"The Central Council is often unreasonable. Sometimes they are too steeped in rules to see justice. Still, you must understand that the Inner Circle was formed nearly four thousand years ago. We are the guardians of secrets learned through the ages, secrets that could prove disastrous if misused. Only those with unquestionable honor are allowed to enter the Circle, and only if they have been born of the bloodline. It is for that reason the Council needed proof of your character."

"I am beginning to accept it." Devlin had searched most of his life for a home. He had never expected to find one here. Yet six months ago he had climbed this mountain for the first time and found his family. He was only beginning to learn of their legacy and the place he held in this civilization.

The secrets of generations were unfolding before him, pages turning in an ancient book of knowledge. There was much to learn, much to prove before he would fully be accepted into the Inner Circle of this world. Yet he knew in his soul he belonged here;

the gifts of his birthright were already awakening inside him.

Rhys rested his hand on Devlin's shoulder, smiling as his son met his gaze. "You must think of the good that came from your journey through the jungle, your journey home. Without the quest, you would not have found your *Edaina*."

Devlin glanced at the temple to the three women sitting in the shade cast by the pediment roof. Kate sat between his sister Alexandria and his mother Brianna, the three women sharing the spectacle of his defeat.

Kate, Devlin's wife of less than a month, his love of a thousand lifetimes. Archaeologists in the Outworld, Kate and her father Frederick had been used as pawns in the Central Council's game to bring Devlin back to Avallon. Their obsession for Atlantis had been the bait. "If it meant losing Kate, I would not alter a single moment of my past."

"It is dangerous to question the past." Rhys drew a deep breath, turning his gaze to the ancient walls of the temple, his expression growing tense. "Only a fool tries to alter destiny."

Devlin frowned, sensing a hidden meaning behind his father's words, one he was not yet privileged to understand.

Chapter Seven

Perhaps he wouldn't come. Sarah paused near a statue of Medea, a tall marble figure who stood with a knife clutched in her hand. She stared down the long main hall of the Metropolitan Museum of Art, searching for Austin Sinclair, wondering if the uneasy feeling she had deep in her stomach had more to do with the fear of seeing him again or the anxiety that he might have asked her here only to humiliate her by not coming. Which would be worse?

She fiddled with the top button of her dress, slipping the button through the brown serge, unfastening, fastening, unfastening, as she waited. She glanced at the watch pinned to her bodice. Twenty minutes past the hour. She was—

"You're early."

She jumped at the sound of his voice, the sable soft tones vibrating near her ear. She glanced up, straight into a pair of silvery blue eyes that sent her heart careening into the wall of her chest.

His head was bare, his hair tousled by the wind into thick black waves around his face. Dressed in a charcoal gray coat that hugged his wide shoulders like a shadow, a crisp white shirt and necktie that emphasized the golden skin of a man who enjoyed spending a great deal of time outside, Austin Sinclair looked every inch a gentleman. The mischief in his eyes, the roguish tilt of his smile, were the only clues to the scoundrel hidden beneath the facade of an aristocrat.

"Anxious to see me?" he asked.

"I agreed to meet you; I didn't agree to enjoy it." Words to remember, she thought.

He cocked his head and stared down at her, a smile curving his lips. "Did you know your top button is unfastened?"

"Oh!" She fumbled with the fabric-covered button, silently cursing her nervous habit.

He offered her his arm, and when she hesitated, he leaned forward and whispered, "Relax, sweet Sarah, I won't bite."

She glanced down the main hall. Men in tall silk hats strolled with ladies in bonnets under the arched skylights that welcomed a flood of sunlight into the hall. She scanned their faces, hoping they were all strangers to her. She felt her breath grow cold in her lungs when she recognized a few of them, including Fanny Warren and her mother. What would they think when they saw her with Austin Sinclair?

"Don't worry so much about what people think," Austin said, slipping her arm through his.

She glanced up at him. "I didn't realize you could read minds, Mr. Sinclair."

"I can perceive feelings sometimes. And you have such a lovely, open face."

"I see." Her hand tensed on his arm, pressing into muscles that were thick and hard beneath his sleeve. "In other words I possess a simple mind that presents no challenge to you."

He shook his head, his smile growing gentle as he looked down at her. "Sweet Sarah, you're more challenge to me than you will ever realize."

There was a trace of sadness in his voice, a sadness that touched his eyes for a heartbeat, no longer. Yet that look gave her a glimpse into the depths of this man. What was hidden beneath the handsome face? What demons had led him into a life of crime? It shocked her to realize how very much she wanted to know about him.

It was madness to wonder about this man. Complete madness to believe he was more than what he appeared—a scoundrel. She walked beside him down the long main hall, aware of each time her skirt brushed his long leg, certain everyone was staring.

"So tell me, do you often visit the museum when you aren't being coerced by a scoundrel into coming here?" He paused in front of a glass display case filled with miniatures and enameled boxes.

"It has been several years since I've visited the museum." She stared down at a miniature of a young girl, the small face captured from a distant century, sunlight glinting on the gold that trimmed the little portrait. "The collections have grown considerably."

"Not an art lover?"

"I do like art. But there simply never seems to be enough time to enjoy it."

"Take the time for things you enjoy, Sarah, before you discover all of your time has fled and your only memories are of numbers in a ledger book."

"I suppose I should take lessons from you in how to enjoy my life."

He pressed his hand over hers where it rested on his arm, his warm palm filled with strength. "I would love to teach you."

"Perhaps I could teach you a few things about responsibility, Mr. Sinclair."

He wiggled his eyebrows at her. "Could be interesting."

Sarah glanced away from the smiling rogue. It was far too tempting, that smile. She found herself wanting to feel the curve of his lips beneath her fingertips.

Across the hall a group of four people stood, a family visiting the museum together. As a young girl she had dreamed of going on outings with her father and mother, dreams that had never come true.

Even now, after all these years, Sarah felt a pang of regret that she had never really been part of a family. Even now she longed for the love she had never known from a father who had despised her and the mother who had cared so little about her that she had abandoned her.

She gazed at the family with a trace of longing. The father was tall, his dark brown hair scarcely touched by gray. Odd, something about the gentleman was familiar. Beside him stood a young man of perhaps 20 years, as tall as his father, yet slighter of build, his hair a lighter shade of brown, his broad shoulders nearly obscuring the woman standing in front of him.

As Sarah watched, a young fair-haired girl of 14 or 15 poked her brother in the ribs and drew his attention to the collection of swords glittering in a nearby case. Sarah smiled, remembering Leighton at that young age, and how he would tug his older sister along to show Sarah something "extraordinary."

After grabbing his hand the girl led her brother

away from their parents, revealing the woman who had been half-hidden by her son. Sarah felt a hard hand of emotion squeeze her throat; pain and fear mingled to shut off her air as she stared at the woman's profile.

It couldn't be her, she assured herself. Not here.

The woman wore a finely tailored light blue walking dress that molded her slender figure. Beneath a fashionable high hat trimmed in silk roses and a blue satin bow, her upswept hair was golden brown. Sarah's heart crept upward, lodging at the base of her throat, pounding so hard she was certain it could be heard the length of the hall.

The woman laughed at something her husband said, her voice carrying like the notes of a violin in the room. Familiar, that laughter, like a ghost that had haunted her childhood. It couldn't be her, Sarah thought. Dear lord, please don't let it be her.

Austin was saying something about the miniatures, but Sarah couldn't follow his meaning. Her attention was fully captured by the woman standing no more than 30 feet away from her. Silently she willed the woman to turn. She needed to see her face. Yet at the same time, she feared what she might see.

As if the woman felt her gaze on her, she turned and glanced in Sarah's direction. Sarah's entire body stiffened. The woman's lips parted, but no sound escaped. She looked as shocked as Sarah felt.

"Sarah, are you all right?"

Austin's words penetrated the roar of blood in Sarah's ears. Yet she couldn't respond.

Dimly she felt him squeeze her numb hand. In a daze, she walked beside him as he led her out of the main hall, down a corridor, through an arched doorway into the gallery housing the Cesnola collection of antiquities.

Here pieces from before the birth of Christ lay sleeping behind glass boxes, undisturbed by the occasional visitor. Here no one but the stone figures from the past and the man beside her could see her tremble with the raw emotion flooding her body.

"Sarah," he whispered, brushing his fingers across her cold cheek.

She tried to speak, to tell him she was fine, but she couldn't. She could only part lips that trembled and refused to form a single word.

"Sweet Sarah." Austin slipped his arms around her and drew her against his chest.

Sarah didn't fight him; his arms felt too warm around her, too strong, too protective. At the moment she wanted protection, from her own pain, from her own hatred that frightened her more than anything.

She drew a deep breath, trying to fight the tears that pricked her eyes. She wouldn't cry for that woman. She had cried far too many tears for her already. Still, her body shook with the struggle, trembling uncontrollably in the haven of Austin's arms.

"It's all right, Sarah." Austin slipped his hand beneath the thick bun at the nape of her neck, pressing his palm flat against her skin. His heat seeped into her blood, a tingling heat that shimmered inside her like fireflies on a moonless night.

She leaned into him, surrendering to his touch, allowing him to take her weight against his powerful body. He spoke softly, his words a blur in her brain, the sound of his voice slowing the horrible tide of pain.

In time, she became aware of the steady rise and fall of his chest against her cheek, the slow, easy throb of his heart. Without conscious thought, she matched her breathing to his, her heart slowing to beat in time with his heart. And somewhere in the back of her mind, she realized he was willing this to happen.

She pulled back in his arms and looked up into his face. There was a serenity in his eyes, complete understanding there. As though awakening slowly from a contented sleep, she drew away from him. He watched her with those gentle eyes, silently assuring her she would be all right.

"I'm sorry," she said, suddenly ashamed of her violent display. Unable to hold his gaze, she glanced around the room, seeing only glass cases and displays filled with artifacts from the dead.

"There's no need for you to feel shame, Sarah." He brushed the curve of her jaw with his knuckles, drawing her gaze back to him.

The look in his eyes, the touch of his hand beckoned her without words. A current of emotion flowed between them, warm and vibrant, curling around her, drawing her toward him. It was as if they had stood like this in another time, countless lifetimes before. For some inexplicable reason, she felt she knew this man better than she had ever known another living soul.

She turned away from him, unsettled by the strength of the desire to walk back into his arms. She didn't need to lean on anyone, especially a scoundrel like Austin Sinclair.

"How long has it been since you've seen your mother?"

Sarah pivoted to face him. "How did you know that woman was my mother?"

He smiled, a gentle curve of his lips that made her wonder what it would be like to feel his kiss once more. "You resemble her."

Sarah dismissed his comment with a wave of her hand. "She's beautiful. She always was."

"When did you last see her?"

"Nine years ago." Sarah felt her throat tighten and swallowed hard. "She had come to see my father at his office. I seldom went there—Father never liked for me to go there—but Clarissa had insisted. We had been shopping and she wanted to show him the fan she had bought. Diana was leaving when we arrived. She came out of the building, and that man she married took her into his arms, right there in the middle of Broadway. She didn't even notice me."

Tears threatened, sharp burning tears that made her clench her hands into fists and stare unblinking at a stone statue of a man standing behind glass a few feet away from her. If she didn't blink, if she didn't move, the tears wouldn't win; she knew this from countless times she had held them at bay.

"There are times when people do what they must to survive. Have you ever thought your mother might have left because she couldn't stay with your father?"

"That woman turned her back on her husband and her two children for the sake of her lover."

"Have you ever discussed it with her?"

"I don't believe the matter is of any concern to you."

"It concerns me because it concerns you."

Sarah drew a breath that quivered in her throat. There was such sincerity in his eyes, such genuine concern, she could almost believe he cared for her.

"The past shapes our future, Sarah." He cupped her cheek in the palm of his big hand, his long fingers curving beneath her ear. "Until you can understand what happened in your past, until you can resolve the questions and doubts, your future will remain unsettled."

Her future. She had never liked what she saw when she imagined her future. There were too many things she wanted, too many she knew she could never have: a man to love, a man who would love her all the days of his life, children to hold in her arms. These were the magical gifts she wanted, yet her future held only loneliness.

She turned away from Austin Sinclair's warm touch, looked away from his deceiving eyes, the silvery blue depths that promised her dreams that could never come true. "Are you planning to steal anything from the museum?"

He was quiet. She could feel him watching her, sense him willing her to face him. She moved away from him, feeling as though she were straining against an invisible tether, a force that beckoned her to turn and run straight into his arms. "Here are some interesting objects a collector might like to own." She stared into a glass case that contained stone seals from the second and third centuries B.C.

"I've never stolen anything from a museum."

"I keep forgetting that you are a discerning thief." She stared at a stone impression from an engraved ring depicting Cupid carrying Psyche in his arms.

He moved toward her, his footsteps impossibly quiet on the polished wooden floor. She felt the heat of his body brush her back, sensed the moment he paused inches away and stood looking down at her. "People are not always what they seem, Sarah."

"No, sometimes people appear to be gentle, kind, infinitely sincere. It's important to remember just how easy it is to hide behind a mask."

"And you, Sarah." He rested his hand on her shoulder. "Are you hiding behind a mask?"

She squeezed her eyes shut, fighting the urge to rest her cheek against that warm hand that made her tingle with a single touch. "I'm the one with the open face, remember?"

"A beautiful face that betrays every emotion."

"I'm certain other women find your flattery appealing. I do not."

"You're lovely. Different from the pale image of what fashion finds ideal in a woman, but undeniably beautiful. Don't be frightened to be who you are."

Sarah curled her shoulders away from him. "I'm not frightened."

"You wear your hair in the most severe style possible."

Sarah smoothed the hair at her temples. "Thank you for the compliment."

"And your gowns are not chosen to flatter your lovely face, the rich color of your hair." He kept his voice gentle, easing the sting of his words. "Brown and gray, the colors of a cocoon."

She stiffened beneath his hand. "I'm not hiding in a cocoon, Mr. Sinclair. I am simply dressing the way a woman of my age should dress."

"Sarah, look around you. Only women in mourning wear gowns such as yours."

"I wouldn't expect you to understand the importance of living within the bounds of propriety." She pulled away from him, flicking her plain brown skirt nervously as she moved toward the doorway.

Austin watched her, wanting to heal the wounds that didn't show, the wounds that robbed her of any chance she had to truly live her life. Words rose from deep in his heart, words of comfort, words of promise, words he could not speak. Promises were not something to be made and broken. And he could not keep promises to this woman.

She hesitated beneath the arched entrance of the room as though she were gathering her composure, then pivoted to face him, her chin lifted at a defiant angle. "I'm sure you would prefer me to go about in scarlet dresses cut so low you could see my . . . Well, I can assure you I have no intention of making such a display of myself."

"Sarah, I only want to see you enjoy your life."

"I don't need you to tell me how to enjoy my life, Mr. Austin Sinclair." She turned and dashed through the arched opening, leaving him alone, surrounded by relics from another time and place.

He followed her, trying to think of something to say that might ease her hurt. By the time he reached the entrance leading to the carriage road, Sarah was already at the bottom of the stone stairs. "Sarah, wait!"

Sarah glanced over her shoulder. The look in her eyes told him he was the last person on the face of the earth she wanted to see. As he hurried down the stairs, she pivoted and marched toward the line of carriages standing beneath elm and oak trees across the wide carriage road.

He heard a noise, a rattle of wheels on loose granite. A coach was racing along the carriage road. Black horses pounded the ground, granite flying from beneath their hooves. They were headed right for the woman who was in the middle of the road.

"Sarah!"

She turned at his shout, freezing like a doe in the sights of a rifle when she saw the coach barreling toward her.

Austin dashed into the road. Sarah screamed as he slammed into her. Wrapping his arms around her, he tackled her, using his momentum to propel them out of the line of the horses. He twisted, taking the brunt of the fall. As he hit the ground he rolled, covering Sarah with his body.

Carriage wheels thundered as loudly as the blood pounding in his ears. Were they in the clear? Granite stones pelted his shoulder, his side, his legs. The rattle of wheels faded into a distant roar.

For a moment he didn't move, holding his breath, reassuring himself the coach was well past them and they were both still in one piece. Sarah stirred beneath him, shoving at his shoulders. He lifted on his elbows, staring down into her face. "Are you all right?"

"Get off of me!"

Austin frowned. "You're welcome, Miss Van Horne."

Sarah released a hiss between her teeth. "I didn't ask you to toss me to the ground, Mr. Sinclair."

"I thought it might be preferable to being flattened by that coach, Miss Van Horne." A sharp stab of pain shot through his hip as he stood. He offered Sarah his hand, which she ignored.

She struggled to her feet, brushing at the dust streaking her dark brown skirt. "Just what did you think you were doing?"

"Saving your life."

"I am quite capable of saving my own life, Mr. Sinclair." Sarah tugged at her small brown hat, which had slipped to the side of her head. "I assure you I was about to get out of the way of that coach."

Austin rubbed his hip, frowning as he held Sarah's indignant look. "And I assure you, Miss Van Horne, you would not have made it in time."

Sarah looked around as though she were trying to gain her bearings. "I don't understand why he was going so fast. I've never been so . . ." She pressed a trembling hand to the base of her neck, her breath coming in ragged gasps. "I . . . oh, my gracious."

Austin slipped one arm around her shoulders and the other beneath her crumpling knees and lifted her in his arms.

"I'm not going to faint," she whispered, gripping his lapel like a lifeline. "I never faint."

"Of course you're not going to faint." Austin carried her beyond the carriages, where trees rose from the thick carpet of grass to lift their branches toward the clear blue sky. She was trembling in his arms.

"It's all right, Sarah," he said, sinking to the grass beneath a tall oak. He cradled her in his arms, leaning back against the rough bark. Beneath streaks of dust, her face was pale, her eyes wide with shock.

"I turned around and it was there. Coming at me. I wanted to run. Yet . . . I was paralyzed."

"Take long, deep breaths," he said, lifting her cold hand.

She gulped at the air. "It was . . . like a dream, where you can't move . . . and something horrible is chasing you."

"Close your eyes." He rested his fingers against her temple, rubbing softly. "Take a deep, slow breath."

She tried to breathe, her body shaking with the effort.

"Imagine a rainbow." He took a deep, steadying breath, willing her to follow. Leaves whispered in the breeze overhead, a cool breeze stirring the tattered remains of the bun that had tumbled down her back. "In your mind follow the rise of color arcing upward toward the sun, the slow slide of shimmering light down the other side."

Sarah closed her eyes, drinking in the air, a long breath mirroring the slow slide of his thumb over her knuckles, the soft brush of his finger across her temple.

"That's it, Sarah, nice and slow." He felt each breath she took, sharing the same rhythm, feeling the air fill his lungs as he watched the slow rise of her breasts beneath the somber brown cloth.

As he felt her relax in his arms, he felt a tightening inside him, a quickening of his blood. He stared at her parted lips, remembering the kiss he had carelessly stolen the night before. The kiss that had haunted his dreams. Oh, yes, he had enjoyed that kiss far too much.

He couldn't kiss her again. No, it was far too dangerous to kiss her again. She lifted her dark lashes, looking at him with those pretty hazel eyes.

"Feeling better?" he asked, slipping his fingers across her temple as slowly as he wanted to slide his lips across hers.

"Much." She smiled, the shy curve of her lips betraying her uncertainty. "It would seem you saved my life."

"My pleasure."

"I'm sorry for acting like such a shrew before."

Austin glanced down at the delicate hand he held in his grasp, trying to control the dangerous attraction he felt for this woman. "You were shocked by what happened, that's all."

She glanced at his hand where it rested against her shoulder, her eyes growing wide, as though she suddenly realized where she was sitting. He felt her stiffen before she scrambled out of his lap, stumbling over her skirt in her rush to get away from him.

"Careful," he said, steadying her with his hand on her arm.

"I'm all right. Thank you." She looked around like a little girl afraid of being caught stealing cookies before dinner.

"I don't think anyone saw us, Sarah." Austin came to his feet, grimacing at the pain in his hip.

"Are you hurt?"

"Only bruised a little. How about you?"

"I'm fine." She smoothed back her tangled hair.

"What do you suppose that man was doing racing along this road?"

"I don't know. But I'd love to get my hands on him."

"I didn't see his face, did you?"

"No." Austin frowned as he recalled the sight of the coach and driver. It was far too warm to be wearing a coat and scarf; the driver had been wearing a hat pulled low enough to obscure his face. It could have been Austin's own brother and he wouldn't have recognized him.

She brushed at the dirt smearing her dark brown skirt, pausing to study a rent at the side. "I'd better be going."

"I'll see you home."

"No, thank you." She shoved back her shoulders like a soldier about to march in a parade. "I am quite capable of seeing myself home."

All the barriers were once again in place. He drew a deep breath as she walked away from him, catching a whiff of lavender that lingered on his shirt and reminded him of the way she had trembled in his arms. He followed her to her carriage.

She turned and glanced up at him. "Mr. Sinclair, I told you I don't want you to escort me home."

He smiled. "Then I guess I'll have to follow you. Just to make sure you get home all right."

She ignored his hand when he offered to help her into her carriage. "I don't need your protection."

Austin watched her climb into her carriage, noting how shaky her hands were as she lifted the ribbons. She had come very close to dying on this beautiful spring morning. That realization settled into his bones like ice. He turned and walked to the hitching post where he had left his gray stallion.

He slipped the reins from the hitching post and

swung up into the saddle, the leather creaking beneath his weight. Vulcan tossed his head, his silvery mane streaming in the breeze. When he turned the horse toward the road, Sarah was already driving away from him.

"That's one stubborn woman," he whispered, urging his horse into a canter.

As Austin followed her down the wide, sunny stretch of road, he wondered how anyone could have missed seeing Sarah. Could it have been deliberate?

Even as it formed, he shook off the suspicion. It was probably nothing more than someone who was in a hurry, someone too frightened after nearly running them down to return to the scene. After all, who would want to harm Sarah?

Chapter Eight

"I've tried to protect you, Sarah." Roxanne stabbed her needle through the white muslin stretched in her embroidery hoop. Sunlight streaming through the open windows in the drawing room glinted on the splinter of steel as she yanked the needle through the material. "I've tried to teach you how important it is always to act with proper decorum."

Sarah clenched her hands in Merlin's fur, and the plump cat stirred in her lap. Mrs. Warren and Fanny had wasted little time in spreading the news of her meeting with Sinclair this morning. "I didn't realize it was scandalous to walk through a public museum with an acquaintance of the family."

"I thought you were aware of how careful you must be. With your history people are only too happy to see something sinister in any situation. Even if it is innocent." Roxanne glanced up from her sampler, fixing Sarah with a cold blue stare. "I take it this was innocent."

Sarah felt a sting in her cheeks, a hot rush of blood. "Of course it was."

"Was it, Sarah?" Clarissa lounged in a wing-back chair across from Sarah, the mint green brocade cradling her fair head. "Are you sure you didn't see Lord Sinclair at the museum and attach yourself to the man?"

"I certainly did not."

"Fanny said you were clinging to his arm."

"I was simply walking with the man."

"Then why did you come home covered in dirt, with your hair tumbling down your back as though you had been rolling around on the ground?"

Sarah glared at her sister. "I told you, I was nearly run over by a careless carriage driver."

"So you said." Clarissa smiled, a smug little curve of her lips that said she believed Sarah had attempted to seduce Austin Sinclair. How could Clarissa believe such a horrible thing?

"I think it would be best if you avoided Lord Sinclair in the future." Roxanne drew the needle through her sampler, dragging scarlet thread through the white fabric. "He is far too worldly for a woman such as you."

Sarah felt a trickle of anger seep into that well of despair that had opened deep inside her. "Then I suppose he is far too worldly for Clarissa."

"What!" Clarissa shot upward from her chair. "Of all the spiteful, hateful—"

"It isn't at all the same thing, Sarah." Roxanne rested her embroidery on her lap and looked at Sarah. "Clarissa is a great beauty. Men are constantly throwing themselves at her feet. It is only fitting for Lord Sinclair to lose his heart to her. No one would find it in the least odd."

Sarah rubbed her fingertips between Merlin's ears.

The big cat purred in her lap, a contented sound that came from deep in his chest. "But people would find it strange if Sinclair were to fall in love with me."

"In love with you?" Clarissa stared down at her sister as though Sarah had declared she intended to become the next president of the United States.

Roxanne laughed, a bright sound that echoed on the walnut wainscoting and sliced Sarah like a blade.

Heat scorched Sarah's cheeks. She lifted Merlin and buried her hot face in his thick gray fur. He smelled of cream and the cinnamon roll he had charmed out of Matilda this afternoon. The silly cat loved pastries almost as much as Matilda did.

"Oh, my dear, I'm sorry," Roxanne said, trying to control her giggles. "I don't mean to hurt your feelings, but you must realize Lord Sinclair could have his pick of women. Not only here, but in England. Although you have many fine qualities, Sarah, they are hardly the type that would attract a man like Lord Austin Sinclair."

She had character, Sarah thought. Not a quality likely to attract anyone of the masculine gender, except a plump feline who was purring with pleasure at being held in her arms.

"Now, Sarah, take my advice, because I only want the best for you," Roxanne said. "Stay away from Lord Sinclair, before the gossipmongers rip your delicate reputation into shreds."

Sarah hugged Merlin, wishing the cat could spin a spell as well as his namesake. She had a horrible feeling nothing short of magic could save her from Austin Sinclair.

After a crisp knock on the door, Emerson entered at Roxanne's command. He glanced at Sarah, his dark eyes betraying a flicker of concern that made her realize she was allowing her feelings to show.

She managed a smile and received a slight nod from Emerson.

"What is it?" Roxanne asked without casting a glance at the butler.

"A visitor, madame."

Sarah's stomach tightened. Had someone else come to speculate about her morning with Sinclair?

"Who is it?" Roxanne asked, obviously annoyed with the intrusion.

"Lord Austin Sinclair."

"Sinclair!" Both Clarissa and Roxanne repeated the gentleman's name, their gazes fixing on Sarah.

Sarah couldn't utter his name; she couldn't utter a sound. All of the breath had frozen to ice in her lungs.

"Shall I show him in, madame?"

Roxanne kept her gaze on Sarah as she responded, "Yes, of course."

"Mother, do I look my best?" Clarissa asked, fussing with the shell-shaped ivory lace that tumbled from her high collar to the waist of her peach linen gown.

Roxanne regarded her daughter a moment, a look of immense pride filling her eyes. "Beautiful, darling. And what of your mama?"

"Charming."

Sarah glanced from Clarissa in her peach linen to Roxanne. Dressed in a gown of striped lemon-and-white silk trimmed in bright green velvet ribbons, with her yellow hair piled in soft curls on top of her head, Roxanne appeared no older than Clarissa; the resemblance between mother and daughter was a point of great pride with both women.

Perched on an armchair between them, Sarah felt like a plain brown sparrow trapped between two bright canaries. Still, when Austin Sinclair entered the room, his gaze did not fly to Clarissa or Roxanne. His attention was riveted on Sarah.

He was smiling as he moved toward her, a warm, generous smile that seemed to wrap around her and hold her. Deep inside she felt the flicker of fireflies come to life.

She never felt more alive than when this man was near. One look from his beautiful eyes, and her blood grew warm. One touch of his gentle hand, and her heart beat to rhythms she'd never known existed. One sound of his sable soft voice, and her skin tingled.

He greeted Roxanne, kissing her hand. Sarah seldom saw her stepmother blush, but there it was, a delicate pink blush rising high on Roxanne's lovely cheeks.

A peach shadow glided in front of Sarah, momentarily blocking out the sight of Austin Sinclair and his warm smile. As Clarissa greeted him, Sarah could see Sinclair bend over her hand. Something twisted in Sarah's chest, something dangerously close to jealousy as she realized he was kissing her sister's hand.

Jealous! Over that scoundrel? She really must be losing her sanity.

Sarah glanced down at Merlin, who had perked up his ears and turned his golden eyes toward Sinclair. As if summoned by his master, Merlin jumped from her lap. He sauntered around Clarissa, his plump belly swaying as he made his way to Sinclair.

Strange, Merlin usually ignored strangers, and here he was brushing back and forth against Sinclair's long legs, making a complete fool of himself for nothing more than a few strokes on his furry head. It seemed Sinclair's special magic extended to animals as well as women.

"Miss Van Horne," Austin said.

Sarah was the last he greeted. He did nothing more

than take her hand and touch his lips to her fingers, as he had the other ladies. It was all very proper. And yet, in the space of a heartbeat, as he held her hand and looked into her eyes, she felt the world expand and narrow at the same time.

Clarissa and Roxanne faded into a distant haze. There was nothing but this man. Nothing but the excitement he sent pulsing through her every limb. At that moment he could have swept her up into his arms and carried her away with him. She would have gone. Anywhere.

He winked.

She clenched her teeth.

The man really was an incorrigible tease.

Sarah sat back in her chair as Sinclair took a seat beside Roxanne on the sofa. The last place on earth she wanted to be was here, watching Austin Sinclair charm Clarissa and Roxanne. And charm them he did. The man was a master at it. In the space of minutes he had both women laughing over some exploit of his that involved a beehive in the office of the headmaster of Eton.

Sarah stared at the scoundrel. Had he gone to Eton? How much of Lord Austin Sinclair was an illusion? How much of the man was real, if any? What had led him down this twisting path? She found herself watching him, wondering if there was any chance for the scoundrel to live a decent life, wondering who might be able to change him.

What had he said?

Sarah realized she had completely lost track of the conversation at a point when she suspected it had turned in her direction. Suddenly Roxanne and Clarissa were both staring at her as though she had sprouted horns and a tail. And Sinclair was walking toward her, offering his arm.

"Shall we, Miss Sarah?"

She had no idea what he wanted of her, but something perverse inside her had her reaching for him. With her arm through his, she walked with him through the single French door that stood open near the far side of the room.

"Where are we going?" Sarah whispered as they stepped onto the stone terrace.

Austin smiled down at her. Sunlight peeking through the elm planted near the house tossed golden coins of light upon her glossy hair. That tight knot at the nape of her neck looked cruel. One long pin peeked out of the silken ball, tempting him to set the glorious mane free. "Do you mean to say you came with me not knowing where I was leading?"

She glanced over her shoulder. Austin followed her gaze and found Clarissa standing at the drawing room window, peeking around the edge of one mint green brocade drape. A few feet behind Clarissa, Roxanne stood, staring at Sarah as though she wanted to tear every hair from her stepdaughter's head. Austin covered Sarah's hand with his, a wave of protectiveness washing over him.

"Why did you come here?" she asked, her voice nearly strangled by emotion.

"Smile, sweet Sarah." He smiled down at her. "You're simply going to show a guest the gardens. Nothing wrong in that."

"The gardens?"

"I wanted a few minutes alone with you." He led her from the terrace into the gardens that spread from the house in a patchwork pattern of flower beds cut by meandering gravel walkways. A brick wall marched along the perimeter of the gardens, sealing it off from the neighboring property and the alley where the stable stood. "I thought a walk through the gardens would suit just fine."

"Well, it doesn't suit, not me, not at all." She made a sound deep in her throat, a strangled cry of frustration that made him want to hold her close to his heart. "Why did you have to come here?"

"You aren't going to be able to keep me a secret, Sarah." Her hand flexed on his arm, her fingers biting into his skin through the layers of cloth. He stroked his thumb back and forth over her knuckles, trying to soothe her.

"You're intent on ruining me, aren't you?"

"No." The last thing in the world he wanted to do was bring this woman any more pain. "When I arrived back at Isabel's there were visitors waiting to pounce on me. A Mrs. Warren and her daughter."

Sarah sighed, her gaze lowering to the gravel that crunched beneath her feet. "They've had a busy morning."

"I wanted to see you." She glanced up at him, her eyes filled with that wariness he wished he could vanquish forever from those beautiful hazel depths. "I wanted to make sure the harpies you live with hadn't ripped you to shreds."

"Roxanne and Clarissa are not harpies." She pulled free of his arm, a sharp, angry movement that seemed to surprise her more than it did him. She glanced over her shoulder at the drawing room windows as though she were afraid her actions were all being cataloged for later use at her trial.

"I suppose they had nothing at all to say about our visit to the museum."

"And what do you suppose they will say now?" Sarah hurried toward an arch sculpted from a line of yew. "A walk in the gardens. What an incredibly bad idea you've had."

Once he passed beneath the arch, following Sarah into the garden beyond, Austin realized why she had come here. They were safe from spiteful eyes in this garden, wrapped in the protective arms of sculpted yew and evergreen that formed four walls to surround beds of roses. An arch of yew opened onto a gravel walkway that led toward the kitchen on the opposite side of the garden, where the herb garden grew, the place where he had first kissed Sarah.

That kiss. Could that kiss really have been as explosive as his memory of it? Even now, one thought of her in his arms and his skin grew warm, as though the sunlight were caressing his naked body.

Sarah paused beside a rose bush, where a single pink blossom was breaking free of its tight bonds, opening to the warmth of the sun.

Austin studied her profile, wishing he could smooth away the tension that furrowed her brow and pulled her lovely lips into a taut line. He caught himself staring at those lips, following their agitated twitching.

Soft lips. Warm lips. Lips that should be smiling more than they did. Lips meant to be kissed. Only not by him. No, he wasn't the man meant to steal kisses from this lovely lady. Now if only he could convince his instincts of that fact.

"I should have known you would make a disaster of this." Sarah flicked her fingertip at the pink rosebud that had only recently broken free of its dark green wrapping. It nodded in response.

"You wanted to dissuade Clarissa from her dangerous desire to marry me. What better way than to show her how much I'm interested in her sister?"

"I see." The breeze, heavy with the fragrance of freshly mown grass, rippled her skirt. The gray linen fluttered against his legs. "This is all to help dissuade Clarissa."

"In all honesty, this has nothing at all to do with Clarissa."

When she looked up at him, Sarah's eyes revealed the deep unhealed wounds carved into her soul by spiteful words and jealousy, a lifetime of blame. So much pain, so much need. If only he could touch her. If only he could heal the wounds. Perhaps then he might find a cure for his own doubts, his own loneliness.

Mentally he shook himself. He had to stop thinking in terms of next week or next month or forever with this woman. Moments, they would share only moments, he reminded himself.

"What would you have me believe, Sinclair?" A few strands of her hair escaped their harsh confinement and swept across her cheek with the breeze. She didn't seem to notice. "Should I believe you're fascinated with me?" she asked as she stared up at him and tried to read his mind.

"Is it really so difficult to believe?"

"Of course not." She swiped at the hair drifting across her cheek, forcing the strands back from her face. "Why, men are forever falling at my feet. One grows so weary of the attention, you know."

He needed to maintain a shield against the emotions this woman evoked inside him. And yet, looking at her, seeing the ragged wounds beneath the lovely mask, he felt his defenses slip. "Have you ever given a man a chance to show you how lovely you truly are?"

She drew a deep breath and stared down at the freshly awakened rose, her hands tight fists at her sides. "I don't want to play your game, Sinclair."

A game. It was true; they were both trapped in this game. A game he found more unsettling every time he saw Sarah. A game he wondered if either of them could win.

She glanced up at him. "Why are you looking at me like that?"

"Because I like looking at you, Sarah."

Her lips parted, yet not a sound escaped. He saw the flame of desire flicker in her eyes, felt an answering fire kindle deep inside him.

"You are so very lovely." He slipped his arms around her and stepped very close, so close he could feel her breasts brush against his chest. Yet it wasn't close enough, not nearly close enough to ease the need that throbbed inside him like a ragged wound.

She was warm and infinitely alluring, this woman who stood stiff and angry in his arms. No guile. No pretense. Just Sarah and her innocence.

She stared up at him, thick dark lashes framing the fury in her beautiful eyes. She forced her slender hands flat against his chest, pushing him away from the soft curves of her breasts. "Sinclair, if you think that just because you saved my life, I will—"

"Hush, sweet Sarah," he whispered before pressing his lips to hers.

It was a mistake; he knew it the moment he felt her lips beneath his. Yet he had no more power to stop his own actions than he did to hold back the sun at dawn.

She fought him, struggled in his arms, before she stiffened, startled at what he sensed was the same pleasure that pulsated along every nerve of his body. With a soft sigh that singed his cheek, she swayed against him, surrendering to the same emotions he had succumbed to moments before. Her lips fluttered beneath his before she opened, before she glided her soft lips along his and gave him a taste of the spice of her mouth.

Austin groaned with the enticing flavor of her. He slanted his mouth against hers, slowly and softly, absorbing the texture of her lips, the shape, the taste. God, he couldn't get enough of her.

She slipped her arms around his shoulders. She sank one hand into his hair, her fingertips grazing his scalp. He held her closer, her breasts searing him through the layers of clothes keeping him from her smooth flesh. He wanted to strip away the barriers. He wanted to lay her down in the sweet grass and sink into her heat.

Why this woman? Why of all the women he had ever known did he feel this all-encompassing desire, this crippling need that gripped him and shook him until he felt as though his world had tilted and only this woman kept him from spinning away into oblivion?

"Sarah," he whispered against her lips. He loved the sound of her name, the feel of it on his tongue.

She pulled back in his arms, her breath as ragged as his own. In her eyes he saw his own desire mirrored in those depths of jade, the flecks of gold and blue sparkling with the heady emotion.

"Let me go," she whispered, pushing against his shoulders.

He hesitated, wanting to hold her until the sun grew cold, knowing holding her for these few stolen moments was a disaster. He released her and watched as she stumbled back a step. She struggled to regain that icy composure that shielded the vulnerable woman deep inside. He struggled to draw together the tattered edges of his control.

"And what was that meant to prove, Sinclair?" she asked, her voice soft and breathless.

That I'm an idiot, he thought. He molded his lips into a smile, although at the moment he found little to smile about. "It proves you have the ability to turn my blood to fire, Miss Sarah."

Sarah pressed her hand to her lips. She stared at him as the breeze swirled the fragrance of spring around them, her eyes wide and wary. "I'm not a wealthy woman, Sinclair. My father left me enough to live comfortably for the rest of my life. But certainly not enough to support a lavish life-style."

"I'm not after your money, Miss Van Horne."

"What are you after?"

More than he could have. Fate had brought this woman into his life, and fate would tear her from his arms. "Your company. I like being with you."

"You want me to swoon at your feet, is that it?" She stiffened, forcing her back to grow rigid. "Your male pride demands I become another of your conquests."

"I don't collect hearts as a hobby, Sarah."

She lifted her chin, her eyes telling him she didn't believe a word he was saying. "Your little game isn't going to work, Sinclair. I assure you I don't find you or your little attempts at seduction the least bit appealing. You would do better seeking another victim."

"You're completely immune to my dubious charms."

She nodded. "Completely."

Austin smiled, wondering if the lady realized how her blush betrayed the truth. "Then you have nothing to fear in seeing me. I'll pick you up at eight for the theater."

"The theater?"

"It's a place where actors perform onstage for the entertainment of an audience."

Sarah frowned as she stared up at him. "I am quite aware of what a theater is, Mr. Sinclair."

"Good. I'll see you at eight."

"Mr. Sinclair, I do not attend . . ." She pursed her

lips, staring at him as though she wanted to slip her hands around his neck and choke the life from him. "I suppose there is no chance of reasoning with you."

He smiled. "None at all."

"Very well, Mr. Sinclair." She squared her shoulders, a martyr headed for the stake. "But I shall not tolerate any of your insolence."

Austin watched as she marched away from him, admiring the straight line of her slim back, her tiny waist flaring into a bustle that bounced enticingly with each indignant step she took.

Balance.

He needed to keep his balance. He felt as though he were walking a tightrope; one wrong step and he would plunge into a dangerous pool of emotion.

Keep your hands off of her, old boy. His mission was at stake. His family was depending on him. The Inner Circle expected the best from him. There was far too much at risk to let his emotions rule his head.

After bringing Sinclair's horse around from the stables, Bram Duggan stood in the shade of the elm growing at the edge of the flagstone sidewalk in front of the Van Horne house. He frowned as he watched Austin Sinclair descend the three wide stone steps leading from the Van Horne house.

Sinclair was a good man, smart, honest, an excellent liaison between the Outworld and Avallon, but that didn't give the man a reason to stick his aristocratic nose where it didn't belong.

Bram had been a guardian of Avallon for the past ten years, long enough to know amateurs had no place in the service, even those who were members of the Inner Circle. Warriors once, centuries ago, guardians of secrets, intellectuals steeped in tradition and legend, the Inner Circle had no business going against real criminals.

Bram had little doubt Sinclair was going to bungle the mission. Probably get himself killed. And he, Bram Elias Duggan, would take the blame.

His hand tightened on the reins of Sinclair's horse. The stallion tossed his head, his long silvery white mane catching the breeze, slapping Bram in the face. Great Alexis! How did anyone learn to control the bloody beasts?

"Thank you." Austin took the reins and smiled. "They can sense when a person is tense, Duggan."

"So it seems."

A job as a groom, of all positions to put a man who had never ridden a horse in his life before twelve days ago. Sinclair had given him an accelerated course in the care and handling of the animals. Duggan's backside still ached from the countless hours he had spent in a saddle.

"Don't look so glum. It was this or a position as parlor maid. Just think of how much trouble you'd have had stumbling around in a dress." Austin slipped his foot in the stirrup, the leather creaking beneath his weight as he glided into the saddle with an ease that made Duggan clench his teeth.

Austin smiled, looking down at him as though he could read every thought in Bram's head. Could he? Bram had heard a lot of strange stories about the Inner Circle.

"This won't last forever," Austin said. "I have a feeling it won't be much longer before Leighton Van Horne makes an appearance."

Duggan stood watching as Sinclair rode down Fifth Avenue. He liked Sinclair, and that wasn't going to make this assignment any easier. From his investigation of Leighton Van Horne, he knew the man was a killer. The cold-blooded type. The type who killed for sport.

Duggan felt his neck prickle. Someone was watching him. He glanced up and found a young woman standing at the window, holding back the lace curtain, staring at him as though he were some rare and exotic species. Although he hadn't met her, he knew it was Clarissa Van Horne.

The look in her blue eyes, a hunger, he had seen often in the eyes of women. Many times that look had led him into an affair, an exchange of sexual pleasure, nothing more. He had never found anyone he wanted for the ages.

Yet recently the memory of a woman had haunted him. Lady Judith Chatham, a woman he had met while investigating the Van Horne incident, a woman with haunted brown eyes.

Lady Judith was a newcomer to Avallon, an Outworlder, and she was wounded in some unseen way. One look into Judith's eyes and he had wanted to hold her, to protect her, to make love to her until she moaned beneath him. A woman had never grabbed hold of his emotions the way that beautiful dark-haired woman had.

He turned and marched back toward the stables, hoping Miss Clarissa Van Horne didn't have a penchant for the hired help. The last thing he needed was another complication in this case.

He was one of the best at his job, one of the elite in the service who were permitted to operate in the Outworld. Still, in ten years on the job he had never gone after a murderer. Murder was nonexistent in Avallon.

He drew a deep breath and ran a hand through his hair, the thick tawny mane waving just below his ears. The way he looked at it, he was the only real chance of keeping Van Horne from murdering an aristocratic diplomat. And he would do it. Or die trying.

Chapter Nine

Sarah lifted her necklace, dangling the pearls over the round neckline of her gray silk gown. It was her only piece of jewelry, a present from her paternal grandmother on Sarah's sixteenth birthday. No girl should go into society without a strand of pearls, her grandmother had said.

The necklace had been the only present her grandmother Eleanor had ever given her. Still, Sarah understood the reason her grandmother had always held her at a distance; it was her tainted blood, as her grandmother had often said before her death five years ago.

Sarah stared at the pearls in the mirror above her vanity, each round bead glowing an ivory pink in the light from the brass-and-crystal fixture overhead. *Mark my words, that girl will grow up to be the image of her mother.* Her grandmother's words echoed in Sarah's memory. She shivered with remembrance and anxiety. How true were those words? She thought of

Sinclair and the wicked way he made her feel.

There was no reason why she should wear the necklace tonight, she thought, slipping the pearls back into the small chest she kept in a top drawer of her bureau. She had no intention of giving Mr. Austin Sinclair the impression she wanted him to find her attractive.

"He's here!" Matilda rushed into the room, her ample hips setting her black muslin gown swaying with each step. "My gracious, that Lord Sinclair is one handsome man."

Sarah felt her heart lurch, that traitorous surge of excitement at the mere mention of his name.

"You'd better hurry and get ready, lamb; he's in the drawing room with the queen and her little princess, and from what I could see, your darling sister is trying hard to steal your prince."

Sarah felt her skin prickle at the thought of Clarissa with Sinclair. It wasn't jealousy, she assured herself, only concern for her sister that sparked the response. "He isn't my prince, Matilda."

Matilda smiled. "And just who is it he's come to see?"

Sarah tugged on her gloves, the white linen stretching beyond her elbow, ending just below the puffed sleeve of her gown. "I'm certain this is all some amusing game for Sinclair."

"Aye, a game of the heart." Matilda studied Sarah, her white cap cocked at an angle, her gray hair escaping in frizzy curls around her round face. "And I'm thinking you aren't doing much to win. Look at you!"

"What's wrong with the way I look?"

"Nothing, if you were a schoolteacher headed for church on Sunday morning, instead of meeting a handsome man for the theater." Matilda clucked her tongue as she stared at Sarah. "I've been telling you for years you need to be getting some pretty gowns."

"I hardly think a schoolteacher would wear silk to church." Sarah glanced at her reflection in the mirror above her vanity, staring at the silver-gray gown. Perhaps the bustle was not as prominent as fashion dictated. Perhaps the dress didn't have ribbons and flowers and other ornaments as most gowns did. Perhaps it was plain. It was dignified in its simplicity.

She thought of that swatch of turquoise silk Sinclair had held to her chin. What would it be like to wear a gown of that lush color? Silly old maid, that's what she would look like. She was far too old for turquoise gowns. "There is nothing wrong with my gown, Matilda."

"Well, I'm knowing there isn't any better in your closet. Maybe if we did something with your hair."

Sarah smoothed her fingers over the neat bun at the nape of her neck, making sure all of the pins were in place.

"Let me get Lucy in here. She does a fine job with the queen and the little princess. I'm thinking she can—"

"My hair is fine. I'm not going to rearrange myself simply to suit Austin Sinclair."

"Ah, lamb, if you're not careful, you'll be letting your prince get away."

Prince! The man was more a dragon in disguise, Sarah thought. "Good night, Matilda."

Sarah marched down the hall, prepared to do battle with the man. Each time she met him it was like going to war.

Pirate. Thief. Scoundrel. He was all of those things. And she would not for one moment be taken in by his blatant charm.

She hesitated a moment when she reached the bottom of the staircase, staring down the hall toward the drawing room, wishing she could turn around and hide in the safety of her room. The man had the most uncanny way of breaking through her defenses. She could not allow it. He could destroy her if she ever forgot he was simply playing a game with her.

Clarissa's laughter rippled from the drawing room into the hall as Sarah drew near. Sarah clenched her hands into fists. That man! He was supposed to be discouraging Clarissa, not encouraging her. Still, had she really expected him to stick to his end of this foul bargain?

Sarah hesitated on the threshold of the drawing room. Sinclair was there, alone with Clarissa, sitting with her on the same sofa. Where was Roxanne? Why had she left Clarissa alone with this thief?

As Sarah watched, Clarissa leaned toward Sinclair, whispering something so low Sarah couldn't hear the words. Sinclair did nothing to discourage her, smiling down at her as Clarissa drew closer and closer, lifting her face toward his as though she intended to—

"Good evening, Miss Sarah." Austin glanced past Clarissa's blond head to where Sarah stood frozen with fury in the doorway.

Excitement—pure, undiluted, undeniable—flooded her, sending her heart racing to a dizzying pace.

Infuriating man!

Clarissa snapped around to stare at her sister, the look in her blue eyes pure murder. "Why, Sarah, I thought you were going to the theater. Is that all you could find to wear?"

Sarah felt the heat of shame climb her neck, stinging her skin. Her sister looked as though she might be the one headed for the theater rather than simply spending a night at home. Clarissa's gown of yellow silk trimmed in embroidered ivory lace made Sarah feel like a shadow at dawn: invisible in the rays of the rising sun.

"I do hope you won't be too embarrassed escorting Sarah tonight. The poor dear just has no sense of fashion." Clarissa smiled at Austin, resting her hand on his arm. "It is so kind of you to take a small interest in my sister."

"Kindness has nothing at all to do with it." Austin stood, breaking free of Clarissa's hold. "Any man would be honored to escort Miss Sarah."

Lies. The man was a master of deception, Sarah thought as he moved toward her. The lies even touched his eyes. She could almost believe he liked what he saw when he looked at her.

He took her hand and pressed his lips to her gloved fingers. "You look beautiful."

She knew better. She knew she looked like an old maid going to church. The warmth in his eyes, how did he do it? How could he counterfeit that sultry look of desire?

She pulled her hand from his. Only a fool would believe Austin Sinclair would find her the least bit attractive. And she refused to be a fool for this man.

She marched out of the room. Austin walked beside her toward the front door, his footsteps impossibly quiet on the white and black squares of marble, while each step she took shouted the rage inside her.

A cool breeze bathed her warm cheeks as he opened the door and stood aside for her to walk before him. He played the role of a gentleman well. The scoundrel knew the right things to do, the right things to say, but she knew better than to believe any action, any word.

He touched her arm as they reached the carriage he had waiting. "Sarah, you shouldn't listen to anything your sister has to say. She's only a—"

"Toad!"

Austin frowned as he looked down into her face. "Toad?"

"If you expect me to live up to my side of this distasteful bargain, I expect you to do the same."

"At the risk of sounding slow, I have to admit I don't understand what you mean."

Sarah glanced up at the driver, who sat on his high perch, even with the roof of the carriage, staring straight ahead at the team of chestnut horses. "You know exactly what I mean," she said, keeping her voice to a low hiss. She grabbed the carriage post and climbed inside without waiting for Austin to assist her.

Austin settled on the seat beside her and closed the door before signaling the driver to proceed. "All right, I can see you're angry. And I assume it has something to do with Clarissa."

Sarah glanced at him. Light from the oil lamp above him cast flickering shadows across his face, emphasizing the frown that carved deep lines into his brow. "You're supposed to be discouraging her foolish attraction to a make-believe marquess, Mr. Sinclair, not encouraging her."

"Discouraging your sister from going after a title is a little like trying to discourage a hungry cat from going after an unguarded bowl of cream."

"Are you trying to make her jealous? Is that why you're playing this little game with me? Are you using me to make certain Clarissa will accept you when you offer for her?"

"I told you before, Clarissa has nothing to do with the reason I want to see you." He took her hand in both of his, holding her when she tried to break free of his grasp. "Sarah, I'm interested in you, not Clarissa."

She stared into his eyes, trying to see the lies behind the mask of sincerity. Impossible. Looking into his eyes she could easily believe every lie. The man was truly an expert at deception. "And I told you before, I don't find you or your little attempts at seduction the least bit appealing."

He smiled, warm and unexpected, a smile that kindled warmth in his beautiful eyes and somewhere deep inside her. "I'll just have to work at changing your mind."

"That shall not happen." She tugged her hand from his warm grasp, appalled at how she was trembling. "I can see behind that handsome mask you wear to the ugly scoundrel beneath."

Austin raised one brow and twirled the end of a long imaginary mustache, like a villain in a melodrama. He leaned toward her, chasing her back against the smooth black leather covering the side of the carriage. "I've got you in my clutches now."

"What are you doing?"

"What does any villain do when he has a beautiful woman in his grasp?"

As he leaned over her, she pressed her hands against his chest, thick muscles shifting beneath her palms. He braced his hand against the side of the carriage near her shoulder, imprisoning her. "If you think I'll—"

"Beware my pretty one." He lowered his lips toward hers. "We dastardly villains hunger for innocent flesh."

Sarah bumped her head against the side of the carriage, trying to escape him. "Mr. Sinclair—"

His soft hair brushed her cheek. He nuzzled the sensitive skin beneath her ear, sending sensation skittering across her skin. "Lavender." He drew a deep breath, then exhaled, warm and moist against her skin. "Sweet, innocent, intoxicating lavender."

The carriage rocked gently beneath her, brushing her thigh against his in a haunting rhythm. He lifted his head and looked into her eyes. Light from the lamp behind him cast a golden glow around his head. Suspended above her, he seemed from another time and place, a realm of dreams and fantasies, a phantom assuming form and substance.

How many times had she dreamed of this man? She curled her fingers against his chest. He was real, warm and hard beneath her touch.

The mischievous glitter in his eyes hardened into a sudden intensity as he held her look. Long, thick lashes cast feathery shadows on his cheeks. He parted his lips, his breath falling warm and soft against her lips, as sweet as a meadow after a spring rain. She felt drawn to him, as though he were gathering her in his arms and pulling her close, when in reality he did not move.

"Don't," she whispered, a warning for her own reckless instincts.

He hesitated, staring down into her eyes, his silver-blue eyes filled with light and shadow. For one terrifying moment she expected him to press his assault, and she wondered where she would find the strength to resist him.

"Relax, sweet Sarah." He kissed the tip of her nose. "This villain has never developed an appetite for ravishing innocent maidens." He sat back, smiling at her.

Sarah stayed where she was, wedged into the corner of the carriage, feeling each thick surge of her heart throb at the base of her neck. He was the master here, in this dangerous game of seduction. And if she didn't learn the rules quickly, she would lose.

* * *

People moved in a steady stream into the theater. Women in colorful gowns, jewels glittering beneath the glowing chandeliers, men in black and white, incandescent light pulsing against brass and crystal, pouring down upon them. People were staring at them. Sarah could see people turning to look at her. She could see the question etched on their faces: Why in the world was a man like Austin Sinclair with a woman like Sarah Van Horne?

She felt Sinclair's hand on her elbow, warm and sure, as he guided her across the white marble floor, threading his way through the crowd, heading toward the wide staircase leading to the private boxes. Through her lashes, she peeked up at him. Was he embarrassed by her appearance? He smiled at her, looking for all the world like a man proud of the woman he escorted through the crowded room.

Austin closed the blue velvet drapes of the private box behind them. He took her arm and led her down one step to the velvet-covered chairs set before the polished brass railing. Below them people flowed down the aisles, slipping into blue velvet seats, softly spoken words rising in a communal roar. What were they discussing? Sarah wondered. Were they speculating on an English aristocrat and his strange choice of woman? She could strangle the man for tossing her to the gossipmongers.

"Tell me, Sarah, why do you protect Clarissa?"

Sarah glanced at the man sitting beside her. He was watching her, quiet, intent, as though they were alone in some secluded glade. "It would seem you do not have any brothers or sisters, or you would understand."

"I have a brother and a sister. Devlin and Alexandria."

"And you would not try to protect them from harm?"

Austin glanced away, toward the stage, where a blue velvet drape fluttered with a movement from backstage. "I would give my life for them."

She didn't question his sincerity; she could hear it in his voice. "And yet you don't understand why I would try to protect Clarissa?"

Chimes sounded, a warning for the beginning of the play. Austin looked at her, the sincerity of the concern she saw in those silvery blue eyes startling her. "My brother and sister have never tried to humiliate me."

Sarah looked away from his perceptive gaze. She stared at her reflection distorted in the polished brass railing. "Clarissa certainly doesn't mean to humiliate me."

"I admire your loyalty. Unfortunately, I can see where that loyalty might be abused."

"Clarissa is young, headstrong, perhaps a little spoiled. But she means no harm."

"And you feel you have to protect her."

Sarah looked up at him. "She has no idea of what a man like you could do to her."

Austin shook his head. "Clarissa knows exactly what she wants and has plans to get it."

"Unfortunately, what she wants is a complete fraud."

"Am I, Sarah?"

The lights dimmed. From the corner of her eye, Sarah could see the curtain draw away from the stage. Yet she couldn't look away from Austin Sinclair. "You're a thief."

"Perhaps." He turned toward the stage, releasing her from the taut tether of his gaze. "But remember, people aren't always what they appear to be."

Sarah stared at his profile a moment before she forced her gaze toward the stage, where the strange story of Dr. Jekyll and Mr. Hyde was unfolding. Oh, the man had the most infuriating way of unsettling her.

Bram Duggan followed Emerson into the library in the Van Horne house. Incandescent lights burned in the crystal-and-brass fixture hanging from the ceiling, casting a warm glow against the carved walnut paneling. Hundreds of leather-bound volumes filled the bookshelves built into each of the walls of the big room, nestled between portraits of the Van Horne family.

"Miss Sarah encourages all of the servants to use the library freely," Emerson said. "She will be most pleased to hear you were interested in finding something to read."

Bram glanced up at the portrait of Sarah hanging in a corner of the room. The girl in the painting was no more than 18. Yet there was a stiffness about her, a severe cast to her expression that made her seem older, as though all of the caprice of youth had been drained from her young face. "She must be an unusual woman, to open her home this way."

"There isn't one of us who works for her who doesn't believe the sun rises and sets with her."

Bram had met the lady once, when she had come to the stable to welcome him the day he had started work here. There was a gentleness about her, a warmth of sincerity in her smile that had sparked a feeling of protectiveness inside him. Still, it wasn't his job to protect Sarah Van Horne, but to bring her brother to justice.

A smile cracked Emerson's granite features as he looked up at Sarah's portrait. "The lady is an angel."

Strange, how one family could produce an angel and a devil in the same generation. Leighton Van Horne's portrait stood above the mantel. Silvery blonde hair framed a face that might have inspired the artist to paint an archangel. But his eyes, those eyes of pale blue, were the eyes of a demon.

If Leighton Van Horne was as smart as Bram thought he was, the man would know the house was being watched. Alone, on the run, what was Van Horne's plan? He would need money. Any bank where he had an account was being watched. He would need help. And from what Bram had read in the file, Van Horne would come to one person—Sarah Van Horne.

"Mother wants her hot chocolate, Emerson," Clarissa said as she entered the room.

She looked at Bram as though she were surprised to find him there, even though she had seen him enter the room with Emerson. The woman had poked her head into the hall a heartbeat after he and Emerson had passed the drawing room where she and her mother were playing cards.

"Yes, miss." Emerson glanced at Bram as he left the room, his dark brows lifted in a quiet attitude of disgust.

Bram's survival instincts prickled as Clarissa sauntered toward him, the train of her lemon silk gown trailing across the Persian carpet of scarlet and ivory. She appraised him, her dark blue eyes flicking over him as though he were a stallion she was thinking about purchasing. The woman was the kind of trouble he didn't need right now.

"You're Duggan, the new groom, aren't you?"

"Yes, miss. If you'll excuse me, I'll be going back to the stable."

"Nonsense. I don't want you leaving until you get what you came here for." Clarissa rested her hand on the back of an upholstered armchair, her fingers curling against the patterned scarlet-and-ivory brocade. "Since my sister has seen fit to take it upon herself to educate every servant who sets foot on our property, I assume you came here for a book."

"Your sister believes everyone should have the opportunity to experience the joy of reading."

Clarissa rolled her eyes. "My sister has aspirations for sainthood."

By the look of sexual curiosity in her eyes, he could see Clarissa was not burdened by such aspirations.

"Are you Irish?"

"Welsh." At least his ancestors had lived in Wales.

"Welsh." She toyed with the ivory satin bow at her waist. "I thought your accent was different."

Did the woman always take an interest in the hired help?

"Well, let's see what we can find for you." She walked past him, so close her skirt brushed against his legs, the sweet scent of her perfume assaulting his senses.

He knew her game, tease and conquer, and good luck to any man who caught her attention. He marched to the bookcase near the door and pulled a book from the shelf without pausing to read the title.

"This should do," he said, glancing at her over his shoulder. "Thank you for your help, miss."

Clarissa stared at him, her eyes wide, her pink lips parted, as though he had slapped her across the face. Duggan didn't wait for her to recover from her shock. He darted from the room, wondering how he was going to avoid the lady and her aspirations to have him on his knees before her.

The moon had disappeared from the evening sky, swallowed by the dark clouds that gathered for the coming storm. Sarah glanced up and down the street as she stepped from the carriage in front of her house. Street lamps marched along both sides of the street, casting puddles of gold in the black night. Trees loomed like beasts in the distant shadows, or madmen lurking in the dark.

Something touched her arm. She jumped, a startled gasp escaping her lips.

"Easy," Austin said, slipping her arm through his. "I don't think Mr. Hyde is hiding in the shadows. And if he is, I promise to protect you with my life."

"I'm not frightened." She slipped her arm from the warm crook of his elbow. "And I certainly wouldn't trust you to protect me from anything. It would be like asking a lion to protect a lamb from a wolf. I think that the lamb had better decide to take care of herself."

He laughed, a deep rumble in his chest that coaxed her to smile. "I have a feeling you're one little lamb who can put a lion in his place."

"Good night, Mr. Sinclair." She marched toward the stairs, casting him a chilling glance when he fell into step beside her.

He smiled down at her. "Where would you like to go tomorrow morning?"

Sarah paused on the landing. "I have work to do tomorrow."

"Ledgers, I suppose." His hair stirred in the cool evening breeze, strands of ebony shining in the lamplight.

"Among other things." She reached for the door handle.

He blocked her way, resting his shoulder against the door. "Do you mean to tell me your brother doesn't have someone to manage his business affairs?"

"My uncle runs the business. But—"

"But you don't trust him."

"Of course I trust him."

"Still, your uncle isn't very good at his job and he needs supervision, is that it?"

Sarah released her breath in a frustrated sigh. "My uncle does an excellent job; he certainly doesn't need any supervision."

"Good, then you don't have any reason not to see me tomorrow."

"Except the fact that I don't want to see you."

He pressed his hand to his heart. "You do know how to wound a man."

"Step aside."

He stayed where he was. This tall, broad-shouldered man with the infuriating smile had a way of looking at her that made her want to slap him, to slip her arms around him, all in the same moment. "We'll go anywhere you want. All I ask is the pleasure of your company."

Sarah stared up at him, stunned by how sincere he could sound, shocked by how very much she wanted to believe him. "Why must you continue this game?"

"What if I told you there is no other woman I would rather be with?"

"I would say you have a great deal of practice in knowing what to say, Mr. Sinclair. But one wonders what truly lurks behind the handsome facade."

"Do you believe we all have Hyde lurking beneath the surface?"

"No, of course not. But I believe beauty can often hide ugliness."

"It's true, Sarah, beauty can hide a beast." He glanced past her into the blackness as though he were looking into the past. "And sometimes we are so blinded by that physical beauty we are nearly destroyed by the beast within. We can only hope to learn the truth before it's too late."

Sarah studied him a moment. Lightning flashed overhead, a ragged slash of silver splashing against the dark gray clouds. Thunder cracked. The gathering storm was a pale reflection of the turmoil she saw in his eyes. "And did you learn the truth before it was too late?"

"Barely." He smiled as he met her gaze.

In that instant he looked vulnerable, a handsome prince tossed from the back of his trusty steed, broken and bruised and far too appealing. "Who was she?"

"A woman I almost married, a long time ago." He cupped her cheek in his warm hand, the soft touch tingling through her every nerve. "It would have been a horrible mistake. She was the wrong woman."

Sarah stood his captive, unable to find the strength to pull away from his comforting touch. The man tempted her as she had never in her life been tempted.

The first drops of rain fell like tears from the dark clouds. It would be so easy to slip her arms around him and allow his warmth to shield her from the cool evening breeze. Yet she knew she would only be reaching for a dream.

"You'd better go inside, Sarah." He slid his thumb over the curve of her cheek, sweeping away the raindrops. "I'll pick you up at nine tomorrow morning."

She stood on the top stair watching as he walked away from her. The cool rain drizzled over her and still she couldn't look away from him.

He turned at the base of the stairs and smiled up at her. "Until tomorrow, sweet Sarah."

Sarah pulled open the door and took refuge inside the house. A single light was burning, a wall sconce near the end of the hall, casting a circle of gold that brushed the base of the stairs. White balusters cast long shadows in the hall, like skeleton fingers reaching for her.

She leaned back against the door and closed her eyes. She was a fool, a simpering old maid, a complete idiot, because she desperately wanted to see that man again. She never felt more alive than when she was with him.

Thief and scoundrel, the man couldn't be trusted. Yet there was something about him, something so warm and sincere. She shook her head, dismissing the treacherous thoughts about him. Only a fool would believe his lies.

Austin dropped his head back against the carriage seat, listening to the steady tap of rain on the roof. Emotion crowded his chest until he could scarcely draw a breath. When he was with Sarah it was far too easy to forget the reasons that had brought him to this place. The woman was Leighton Van Horne's sister, he reminded himself. If Leighton got to Sarah before Austin got to the medallion, Austin would lose all hope of retrieving it.

He needed to get that medallion and get the hell out of here. He needed to get away from Sarah Van Horne. Still, he knew in the end, when he walked out of her life, all he would remember from this moment in time would be the look of desire in Sarah's eyes, like an unanswered question forever haunting him.

Chapter Ten

Buildings stood shoulder to shoulder, rising three and four and six stories from the dirty streets, crowding block after block of the East Side of New York. Rotting garbage and open sewers contrived to poison the air that had been cleansed by rain the night before. The warmth of the morning sun was only beginning to cook the foul stew. Austin hoped they would be gone before it started to boil.

He held the ribbons between his fingers, guiding the team of bays along the street. The rattle of the carriage wheels on the rutted cobblestone pavement was lost amid the clatter of carts and wagons and the shouting that came from the saloons. Although it was early, the many saloons that infested every block were filled to overflowing.

Sarah sat beside him on the black leather seat, as prim as a Sunday school teacher, her back as straight as a lightning rod, her white-gloved hands clasped in her lap.

"I can't tell you how delightful I find your choice of places to spend this glorious morning," he said.

She glanced at him, and he could see a smile tugging at her lips, a smile she was fighting to banish. "And here I was thinking how well you fit into these surroundings, Mr. Sinclair."

He followed the direction of her gaze, frowning as he noticed a drunk staggering along the sidewalk, his dirty trousers riding so low on his skinny hips they looked as though they would tumble with each wavering step. "My tailor will be crushed to hear you say that, Miss Van Horne."

"Clothes only create an illusion, Mr. Sinclair."

"Do you mean my sterling qualities would shine through even if I were dressed in rags?"

"I mean you are a thief who masquerades as a prince."

He leaned toward her, catching a whiff of lavender rising with the warmth of her skin, a thread of sweetness in this foul tapestry of dirt and decay. "And what shall I steal from you, my pretty lady?"

Sarah leaned away from him. "You forget, Mr. Sinclair, I am forewarned."

He smiled. "So were the Trojans, my fair Helen."

She pushed against his shoulder. "You really are an incorrigible flirt."

Austin moved back to his side of the carriage. "Only when the lady is as tempting as you."

She glanced away from him, shaking her head as though she refused to believe a single word he said. It was better for both of them if she didn't believe him, he decided, even though he spoke the truth. It was better to keep their relationship on a friendly basis, teasing the surface, never delving too deeply into that dark pool of emotion. What lay beneath that surface was far too dangerous.

Heat prickled the nape of his neck. Austin glanced over his shoulder, feeling as though he were being watched. A wagon with two men rumbled across the pavement a few yards behind them. They looked like a pair of bare-knuckled fighters, big men, one with copper-colored hair, the other with oily dark hair, the sleeves of their dirty gray shirts rolled high, exposing thick muscles. They seemed less interested in the carriage traveling in front of them than the people they passed on the street.

The dark-haired driver stared at the pair of horses trudging in the traces; his passenger stared down at his boots, as though he were inspecting the work of his valet. Their sense of distraction seemed odd.

Austin noticed the way heads turned as he and Sarah passed, men and women and children, dirty and ragged, staring with haunted eyes at the fine horses, the elegant black carriage, the well-dressed man and woman invading their part of the city. "I can only suppose you've come to this part of town to gather information for another of your newspaper articles."

She tilted her head and stared at him, the sun streaming upon the brim of her small gray hat casting a shadow across her slim, upturned nose. "I suppose you think a woman has no business writing for the newspaper."

He held her look, meeting the challenge in her eyes. "I've read a few of your articles. You're very good."

She frowned, and he could see the wariness in her eyes. The lady wasn't ready to trust him, even about something as small as a compliment about her writing.

"Were you going to come into this part of town alone?"

"Does the sight of so much poverty make you nervous, Mr. Sinclair?"

"Unfortunately crime often follows on the heels of poverty, Miss Van Horne."

"How very true that is." She glanced to where a group of boys were gathered at the mouth of a narrow alley, laughing and shouting as they shot craps. "This block of tenements is called Mulberry Bend. It's one of the worst in the city."

Austin felt the emotion churning inside her: anguish, frustration, a genuine need to help these people. He felt a response inside himself, a softening of defenses that had to remain solid.

"There is a law requiring children of that age to be in school. Yet there aren't enough schools. And there is no record of many of these children even existing. So they fall through the cracks; it's easier for the city to forget them." Sarah glanced away from the children, staring at the team of bays pulling the carriage. "Eventually they drift into gangs. They steal, get into fights, perhaps even murder someone, life is so cheap here. Their lives are destroyed before they ever have the chance to reach for that dream that brought their parents to this country."

Compassion and the conviction to do something, she possessed both. "How did you get involved in all of this?"

"I used to come here with the ladies of my church, carrying our little baskets of charity, knowing charity was not what these people wanted or needed." She leaned back against the carriage seat, glancing up at the sky; smoke from cooking fires rose through hundreds of chimneys, scrawling dark gray across clear blue. "I always thought there must be something more we could do, something that would bring about a change."

He felt drawn to her in a way that delved beyond his attraction to her lovely face and the sweet curves hidden beneath somber gray linen. "You use the newspaper to stir public opinion."

"Yes. My father owned the *Gazette.* A few years ago, when I suggested doing a series of articles exposing the living conditions here, he told me . . ." She hesitated, frowning, as though the memory of that meeting pierced her with pain.

In her face Austin saw the image of that young woman facing a father who had never shown her affection, a father who had always treated her with contempt.

"My father didn't think it was a good idea." She stared down at her hands, lacing her fingers. "You see, he had many friends who owned buildings here."

Austin squeezed the thin leather reins between his hands to keep from touching her. "So when he died, you took over the newspaper."

She nodded. "My brother signed the newspaper over to me."

"And you've been writing about these slums ever since."

"I believe if we can expose the true conditions here, the people will force the politicians to do something, to tear down these wretched houses of death and decay, to build more schools and give each of these children a chance to grow into healthy adults, to give them an equal chance to live a decent life." She looked at him, lifting her chin as she marched into battle. "I suppose you feel a woman has no place trying to change the world."

"Without that kind of change, we throw away an entire generation." He sensed a turmoil inside him, felt tentacles wrap around him, drawing him down into that dark pool of emotion toward destruction. Inside, he tried to draw back from her, needing to find safe footing. "We all need to take an interest."

She frowned as though she wasn't quite sure she believed what he said. "Now do you understand why I come into this part of town, Mr. Sinclair?"

Austin nodded. "But I still don't think it's a good idea to come alone."

"Neither does my editor. He usually manages to send someone tagging along with me."

"Thief! Stop him!" The shouts exploded from the crowded sidewalk. "Grab him!"

People fell aside, stumbling, yelling as though a whirlwind were spinning through the crowd. A big man wearing a white apron ran on the heels of the storm, shouting, waving his hands.

"What do you suppose . . ." Sarah's words dissolved into a startled gasp as a young boy burst through the line of wagons and carts parked along the street, straight into their path. He tripped on the broken cobblestones, sprawling headfirst against the dirty street.

"No!" Sarah shouted.

Austin's quick reflexes reacted before Sarah's frightened warning hit his ears. He pulled back sharply on the reins. The startled horses reared in the traces, steel-shod hooves pawing at the air, pounding the stones near the boy's head. He fought the team's panic, easing them with words, with steady pressure upon the reins, until the horses settled, standing in their traces.

Austin jumped from the carriage and ran to the little boy lying still upon the broken cobblestones. He lifted the unconscious child carefully, cradling him in his arms. Sarah climbed down from the carriage and rushed to the boy's side.

"How is he?" Sarah asked, kneeling on the pavement.

"I don't know."

Blood oozed from a cut above the boy's right eye, dampening the light brown locks that tumbled over his brow. Sarah held her breath, waiting, watching as Austin rested his fingers against the fragile neck, searching for a pulse. People swarmed around them.

"Why, that's young Jim McGowan," a woman said, her words spinning in the swirling chatter of the crowd.

"Stand aside. Let me pass!" The big man in the white apron pushed his way through the crowd. He stood above Austin, puffing, staring at the little boy with murder in his dark eyes. "Is the little bastard dead?"

Austin stared up at the man, the fierce look in his eyes chasing the big man back a step. "The boy is alive."

"Good." The big man released his breath in a huff, the edges of his bushy dark mustache twitching. "The little thief can learn what the inside of a jail is."

Sarah looked down into the child's face as Austin tended him, dabbing at the blood on his brow with his clean white handkerchief. The boy couldn't have been more than eight years old. "What did he steal?"

"It's there, in the little bastard's hand."

Sarah lifted his small right hand. Clutched in the thin fingers was a peppermint stick. She stared up at the man. "A piece of candy. You want to send this child to prison for stealing a peppermint stick?"

"That's how it starts." The man in the apron puffed out his burly chest. "Next thing you know, he's coming into my store with a weapon and taking my money."

"Here." Austin tossed a twenty-dollar gold piece at the man. "That should cover the candy and your trouble."

The shopkeeper grabbed the coin in his fat hand and looked down at the gold. "Mister, you're a fool to be wasting good money on a piece of trash like that."

The corner of Austin's mouth twitched as he stared up at the man, his eyes as cold and hard as polished steel. "I suggest you take your money and leave." His voice remained low as he spoke, deadly smooth.

Sarah held her breath, staring at Austin. The barely contained fury in his eyes, the latent power pulsating through his big body, made him seem a tiger about to pounce. His anger seemed so personal. She wondered how this man with the gentle touch and the quick wit had slipped into a life of crime. Had it started with a piece of candy?

The shopkeeper backed away from Austin, then turned and shoved his way through the crowd. A low murmur passed through the people gathered around them, several of the onlookers easing away from the scene.

Austin didn't seem to notice or care what the crowd did. He stared down at the small boy lying across his lap, supporting the child's narrow shoulders with his strong arm.

Sarah sat on her heels and watched as Austin touched the boy, brushing his fingertips over the child's temple. Mesmerized, she followed the rhythm of his fingers, the slow circles he drew with his touch. She knew the gentleness of that touch, the magic that seemed to flow through this man, like light through clear water.

In moments the boy opened his eyes. He blinked,

staring up at Austin with brown eyes that seemed too big for his thin face. "Am I dead?"

"I don't think so," Austin said, smiling down at the child.

Yet Sarah knew why the boy had thought himself dead; at that moment, with the sun glowing like a golden nimbus around his head, Austin seemed an angel.

Austin stroked back the hair from the boy's brow. "Why don't you tell me where you live, and I'll take you home."

Jim sat between Sarah and Austin in the carriage, waving to people he recognized on the crowded street as though he were riding in a parade. He directed them to a narrow five-story building sandwiched between two other buildings of the same size.

A faded red-and-white awning shielded the entrance of a tobacco shop on the ground floor. An old man sat on the stoop leading to the rooms, slumped against the doorjamb, snoring in the bright sunlight. Sarah stepped around him and walked through the open door.

It was like stepping into a cave. Sunlight ventured only a few feet into the narrow hallway, painting a timid square of light across the scarred wooden floor. Holding the boy's hand, Sarah marched across that square of light, plunging into the gloom beyond, taking comfort in the knowledge that Austin walked close behind them.

Dampness wrapped cloying arms around her as she followed Jim up the narrow staircase. The sour stench of decay permeated her every breath. As many times as she entered one of these buildings she never grew accustomed to the feeling of hopelessness that lurked in the gloom.

On the third floor near the end of a dark, narrow hall Jim rapped on a door. A moment later, a lock slid open and a small, dark-haired woman opened the door. She glanced from Sarah to Austin, her brown eyes reflecting surprise and a wariness that came from living in this violent place.

"Jim," she whispered, grabbing his shoulders. She hauled him close to her body, wrapping her arms around him. "What's happened? What do you want with us?"

"I'm Austin Sinclair, Mrs. McGowan, and this is Miss Sarah Van Horne."

"They're my friends, Mama."

Austin smiled, and Sarah could feel the tension draining from the other woman. He had a way about him, a gentle sincerity that pierced the toughest defenses. How well she knew the power of his charm.

"We only wanted to make sure Jim got home safely," Austin said. "He's had a nasty bump to his head."

Mrs. McGowan looked down at her boy. "How have you come to be bumping your head?"

"I fell when that mean old Mr. Wilker came running after me."

Mrs. McGowan frowned. "Why was he chasing you?"

"I didn't mean to take the candy, Mama, I swear. I was just looking at it, deciding if it was the stick I wanted, when Mr. Wilker starts hollering. I have the penny you give me in my pocket, but he wouldn't let me get it out. He comes at me, real mean. I thought he was going to kill me."

"Jim, boy." Mrs. McGowan ran her hands through her son's hair, looking down into his upturned face.

"They helped me, Mama. Brought me here in a fancy black carriage."

There were tears in her eyes when Mrs. McGowan looked up at Austin. "Thank you."

"It was our pleasure to help, Mrs. McGowan," Austin said.

"Please, call me Lenora. Will you come in?" She smiled, a weary curve of her lips that still managed to capture a glimmer of hope. "I was making some tea."

Sarah hesitated, knowing the woman would have little to spare. Yet she saw the pride in the woman's dark eyes and knew a refusal would wound her deeply.

Although the small room was dark, it was neat, scrubbed spotless, as though they had tried to scrub away the lingering gloom that pervaded this place. Lenora introduced them to her other children.

Maggie, a slender girl of 12, stood by the iron stove, using a poker to prod the fire behind the grate, her white sleeves folded back from her thin arms, her dark hair falling in a neat braid down her back to her waist.

Annie, a pale child of five, turned on the chair she had placed in front of the single window in the room, her light brown hair tumbling in tight curls to her narrow shoulders. Although the sun shone brightly beyond this building, only a gray light filtered down the air shaft.

Lenora and Maggie set about making their guests welcome in the little kitchen, serving from blue-and-white china that had survived the trip across the sea. While they sat at the round wooden table, sipping weak tea, Mrs. McGowan spoke of the home they had left in Ireland, and the hope they could make a better life here.

"Someday, I'm hoping we can take the rooms at the front. When my Patrick makes more money."

"The sun shines in there every day," Annie said,

glancing to the dark window. "You can feel the sun on your face."

Sarah looked at the gray panes that looked out at a brick wall. "Does the sun ever shine in here?"

"Oh, yes. For two days. The sixteenth and again on the seventeenth of June." Maggie left her chair and slowly walked to the wall across from the window. She brushed her hand over the gray plaster a foot above her head. "It will reach all the way up to here on the wall and shine for almost an hour on those two days."

Sarah watched this pale child and wondered if she would live to see her sixteenth birthday in this home where the sun came twice a year. And in her mind she composed the story she would publish that evening in the *Gazette.*

Sarah slowly descended the narrow staircase leading to the second floor, following Austin Sinclair. "I noticed the gold coin you slipped into the pocket of Mrs. McGowan's apron as we were leaving."

He shrugged as though the money meant nothing. "I didn't think she would appreciate being handed money. And yet I didn't want to walk out of there without helping, in some small way."

She shared his feelings. She understood all too well the sense of responsibility. "Do you know this was called a model tenement when it was built seven years ago? The ideal plan for a lot only twenty-five feet wide. How could anyone expect people to live under these conditions?"

He paused on the step below her. When he turned to face her, their faces were nearly level. It was startling, being this close to him, so close she could feel the heat of his skin radiate against her like a single ray of sunlight in the gloom, beckoning her.

"It will take time, Sarah, but there will be changes."

The gray light glowing through the small window open to the air shaft at the landing fell softly upon his features. She saw compassion in his face, a wealth of emotion in his eyes. "And how many people will die before men like Warren Snelling are forced to tear down these slaughterhouses?"

He touched her cheek, a gentle brush of warmth across her skin that tempted her to turn her face into his palm. "You're doing everything you can, Sarah."

Inside, she felt a softening of her defenses, a longing for the kinship she imagined seeing in his eyes. "It's not enough."

She pushed past him, frightened by the emotions this man could awaken inside her. Her footsteps thundered against the walls of the narrow stairwell as she marched down the stairs. Austin followed close behind her, a silent phantom, haunting her, as he had been haunting her dreams.

It would be so easy to tumble into his web. He wove it so well, beckoning her with every glance, every touch, every unspoken word. And every moment she spent with him, she found herself wanting to believe his lies.

At the second floor, as she turned in the hall and headed for the final flight of stairs, Austin grabbed her arm. "What . . ." Her words faded as she looked up into his face. He was frowning, staring into the shadows at the end of the hall. "What is it?"

"I think we have trouble."

As Austin spoke, Sarah noticed a shadow separate from the gloom at the end of the hall, a hulking shape moving toward them, holding a knife.

"Get back to the McGowan place," Austin whispered, pulling her toward the stairwell leading to the third floor.

"But what about you?" she asked, hurrying to keep up with his determined strides.

Austin didn't answer. He froze at the base of the stairwell, staring up toward the landing. Someone was descending the stairs, a big man with copper-colored hair. He held a small club in his hand, like the nightsticks the police carried, and he was smiling in a way that made Sarah shiver inside.

"Damn," Austin muttered under his breath. With his hand on her arm, he tugged Sarah, pulling her away from the stairs, shoving her toward a corner of the hall. "Stay there."

Sarah pressed her back against the wall. The man with the knife was moving in, stalking Austin, who stood a few feet in front of her, a knight prepared to do battle.

"Now, you let us have the little lady, and we'll let you go, mister," the dark-haired man said.

Sarah felt the air turn to stone in her lungs. Gracious, what did they want with her?

"The lady stays with me," Austin said.

"Suit yourself, mister. We don't care if we have to kill you."

Fear settled around Sarah like a chilling fog, a fear like that from her childhood, when beasts had lurked in her closet and beneath her bed, the monsters that had terrorized her for long, lonely years.

Steel captured the faint light filtering through the window on the second-floor landing. The knife glinted in the gloom as the man lunged forward.

Austin pivoted, swinging out with his foot, catching the man's wrist, wrenching a grunt of pain from his attacker. The knife flew from his hand, slamming with a sharp twang against the wall near Sarah. Austin hit the man's chin with his fist, an upward thrust that sent the man reeling back into the balustrade.

Sarah inched her way along the wall, searching for the knife, her heart pounding at the base of her throat. Austin attacked the man again and again, quick blows, muted thuds, deep-throated moans. The other man rounded the base of the stairs, swinging his club as he rushed toward Austin.

"Look out!"

Austin pivoted as the warning burst from Sarah. He thrust upward with his arm, blocking the downward plunge of the club. A door opened near the end of the hall. A woman peeked out into the shadows, then slammed the door shut.

Sarah saw the knife, the steel reflecting the faint light. As she reached for it, the copper-haired man hurtled into the wall beside her, his head cracking against the plaster.

She snatched the knife from the floor and scooted back, clutching the smooth wooden handle. The man slipped down the wall like a bucket of water tossed against the plaster, dripping into a puddle on the floor.

Someone touched her arm. She turned, swinging the knife.

"Careful!" Austin stepped back, avoiding the blade by a cat's whisker.

"Oh," Sarah whispered, glancing down at the knife. "Oh, dear, I'm sorry. I thought you were one of them."

"It's all right." Austin eased the handle from her fingers and slipped the knife into his coat pocket. "They aren't going to give anyone any trouble for some time."

Sarah glanced past Austin to where one of the blackguards lay in a heap on the floor. She drew a breath that tangled with the heavy throb of her heart in her throat. "Are you all right?"

"I'm fine," he said, resting his hands on her shoulders. He was strong and sure, and some of that strength seeped into her blood with the warmth of his hands, chasing away the chill of fear. "And you? Are you all right?"

"Yes, I'm fine," she whispered, trying to ignore the tremor of fear that radiated from deep inside her, trembling along her every nerve. She wanted nothing more than to step into his strong embrace and hide in his sheltering warmth. "What do you think they wanted with me?"

He tightened his hands on her shoulders, his generous lips pulling into a tight line. "They were following us, waiting for a chance to relieve us of the gold in our pockets."

"But they said they were after me."

"Don't think about it."

"You don't think they wanted to . . ." Sarah swallowed back the words that were far too frightening to speak.

He kissed the tip of her nose, his breath falling soft and warm across her cheek. "They would have had to kill me first, Sarah."

Sarah looked up into his eyes. In that instant, standing there in the gloom, he seemed to glow with an inner light, like a beacon drawing her toward a safe haven. She felt as though he were surrounding her, drawing her close, bathing her in his light and warmth.

She felt his hands flex on her shoulders as though he wanted to pull her close. Yet he didn't move. He lowered his gaze, looking at her lips, his own lips parting, spilling his sweet breath across her cheek.

The terror of the past few moments faded, reality dissolving into the shadows. There was only Austin, the warmth of his body reaching for her, the desire in his eyes whispering to some secret place hidden deep within her. She felt her defenses slip, like ice cracking under the warm rays of the sun.

She reached for him, touching his chest with a hand that trembled with more than fear. She needed to feel his warmth close around her, shielding her from the world.

He frowned, his hands tensing on her shoulders as though he wanted to pull her close and push her away all in the same instant. She looked up into his eyes, fearing him and the emotions he ignited inside her, needing him in that moment more than she had ever needed anything in her life. A smile touched his lips as though he could understand the need in her.

"Sarah," he whispered, slipping his arms around her.

A spicy scent curled around her with the warmth of his embrace, bayberry and a spice she couldn't identify, a scent that made her want to bury her face in the soft white silk of his shirt and feast on that tantalizing fragrance.

"It's all right, sweetheart." He slid his hands down her back, pulling her tight against him.

He whispered her name like a prayer, brushing his cheek against her hair. She felt heat flicker deep inside her, a kindling of flame that chased away the chill of loneliness that dwelt deep within her. His chest lifted against her as he drew a deep breath, and then he was stepping away from her, stealing all the warmth and light he had given her.

His expression was tense as he looked down at her. "I want you to go back to the McGowans' and send Jim for the police."

She turned and ran toward the stairs, frightened suddenly more for her safety than she had been with the two criminals Austin had defeated. She needed to keep some distance between them. She couldn't believe in Austin Sinclair. No, she could not believe in this fairy tale he was spinning around her. If she lost her heart to the man, he would destroy her.

Bram sank the tines of his pitchfork into the broken bale beside him and tossed a load of straw into an empty stall. He clenched his jaw against the pain, the pitchfork burning like a hot coal against his blistered palms. Dust drifted through shafts of afternoon sunlight that slanted through the upper door of the stall, filling his every breath. His damp shirt stuck to his chest and back, bits of straw scratching his skin beneath the blue cotton.

A job as a groom. Sinclair had a demonic sense of humor.

Bram rested the pitchfork on his chest and stared down at his palms. He had never considered himself soft. At home he ran five miles every morning, conditioned his muscles with weights, exercised his skills in combat. Yet the blisters that had broken on his palms made him feel as weak as a baby. He would have to find a way to see Dr. Chamberlain tonight.

He glanced up as he heard someone approach, a light tread on the brick-lined floor leading from the alley. A woman. He stared at the intersection of the main corridor and the long passageway that housed the horses, holding his breath, wondering how he would control his temper if Clarissa Van Horne turned the corner.

Sarah Van Horne turned that corner, the severe cast of her expression softening into a smile when she saw him. "Good afternoon, Duggan."

Duggan nodded. "Miss Sarah."

"Mrs. Van Horne asked me to make sure the coach has been polished for this evening."

"Henry and I took care of it this morning." He grimaced as he rested the pitchfork against the stall.

"What's wrong, Duggan?" she asked, moving toward him.

"Nothing, miss, I—"

"Let me see your hands."

"It's nothing."

She held out her hand like a mother demanding the hands of a child for inspection before dinner. He hesitated a moment, wondering what the lady would think of a groom with blistered hands.

"Duggan," she said, in that tone that reminded him of his prime-year teacher.

He held out his hands, palms up, frowning as he stared down at his throbbing flesh.

"Dear heaven," she whispered, slipping her smooth hands beneath his. "These blisters need tending."

"I was going to take care of them tonight."

She looked up at him, sunlight slanting through the door of the stall painting her face in a golden light. "I believe you are not exactly what you appear, Mr. Duggan."

There was a directness to her gaze, a sharp blade of honesty that made him wonder if she could strip away deception with those pretty eyes. "I'm not certain what you mean, Miss Sarah."

"You enjoy books. Your hands are strong, yet you have no calluses. Mr. Duggan, you were not a groom before you came to work here, were you?"

He slipped his hands from her gentle grasp, avoiding her intense gaze. "Where I came from, I was . . . in law enforcement."

"You were a police officer," she said, her soft voice betraying her surprise. "Why have you decided to change professions?"

"When I came to this country, I needed to do something different."

"I see." She was quiet a moment, and he could feel her watching him. "You are obviously an educated man, Mr. Duggan. If, in the future, you decide you would like to search for different employment, something that does not involve wielding a pitchfork, please let me know. I might be able to help you find something."

Duggan glanced at her, the honest warmth of friendship he saw in her eyes kindling a prickling heat of shame inside him. "Thank you."

She smiled. "You wash your hands while I get Matilda's remedy box. We must take care of those blisters before they fester."

Duggan watched the lady march away from him, gliding through the sunlight slanting through the stalls. She really was an angel.

He thought of Sinclair and the dangerous game he was playing with this lovely lady's heart. He didn't want to see her hurt. Still, he knew they had no choice. They would sacrifice this angel to capture a devil. The end justified the means. Didn't it?

He dropped his head back against the wall, staring at the dust motes dancing in the sunlight. He had a feeling this was one case that would wreak havoc with his sleep for a long, long time.

Chapter Eleven

Sarah glanced over the top of her book at the rosewood-and-crystal clock on the mantel of the blue drawing room. Addison's party had started almost two hours ago. That should mean Roxanne and Clarissa would be ready soon. Since she had never quite understood why it was important to arrive late, Sarah had a habit of being on time for everything. It was another of her fatal flaws.

She stared down at the printed page, but she couldn't concentrate on the words of Henry James. Another man occupied her thoughts, a man with silvery blue eyes and a smile that made her feel as though she were young and pretty and the world was hers to own. Such a deceptive man.

"Looks as though you're in a hurry to go to Addison and Emma's party," Clarissa said as she strolled into the room.

Sarah stiffened at the tone of Clarissa's voice. "I'm actually not in much of a mood for a party." If this were not the first party Addison and his new bride were giving, she would have found a reason to stay home. This morning had taken its toll on her. She began to tremble every time she thought of those two men and what they might have done if Austin hadn't been with her.

"Really now, Sarah." The apple-green silk roses adorning the nest of yellow curls piled high on Clarissa's head perfectly matched the green silk faille of her gown. The pleated skirt with its inset of cream-colored silk rippled with each dainty step she took. "Don't try to tell me you aren't anxious to see Lord Sinclair. Though it certainly doesn't look as though you went to much trouble with your appearance."

Sarah glanced down at her book. There was no need for Clarissa's critical appraisal of her appearance. Sarah knew her gown of dark brown silk could not compare to that of her sister. She knew every fault of her face, her hair, her figure, and she knew Clarissa would always cast her in the shade. Somehow it had never really mattered before Sinclair had walked into her life. The man had managed to turn her world upside down.

"I hope you realize the real reason Lord Sinclair has been paying so much attention to you."

Sarah glanced up at her sister. Clarissa was smiling, a smug little curve of her lips. "Do you intend to tell me?"

Clarissa flicked open her fan, the gilt-trimmed edge glittering in the electric lights. "He wants to make me jealous."

Did he? Was that the true reason he was seeing her? Sarah eased the book closed on her lap. Had she come to believe he cared for her, at least in some small way? Was that the reason the truth was like a lead ball in her chest, pressing against her heart?

"Oh, don't look so tragic. Surely you must realize he could never really be interested in you." Clarissa snapped her fan shut. "Why, look at you. What man would choose you over me?"

"How thoughtful of you to point out my fine qualities, Clarissa." Sarah folded her hands on the book resting on her lap. "I can always expect to find comfort in your company."

"I'm only pointing out the truth." Clarissa tilted her head, her lips pulling into a pout. "I don't want you to be devastated when he turns away from you and asks me to marry him."

"Perhaps it would be wise to choose another man for your husband, Clarissa. A man who does not play foolish games."

"I am going to marry Lord Austin Sinclair." Clarissa's eyes narrowed as she stared down at her sister. "Be warned, Sarah, I don't intend to let you or anyone get in my way."

Sarah sat back against the chair, stunned by the venom in her sister's voice. At that moment Clarissa looked like a woman who could kill.

"Oh, here you are, darling," Roxanne said, sweeping into the room, her gown of raspberry silk rustling against her petticoats. "Turn around, Clarissa, let me take a look at you."

Clarissa turned, lifting her arms as though she were a ballerina completing a lazy pirouette.

"Beautiful," Roxanne said, applauding her daughter.

Clarissa cast Sarah a smug glance, as though she were warning her sister not to try to compete with her.

"I suppose we must leave." Roxanne smoothed one of her elbow-length white gloves along her arm. "I'm certain Addison is anxious to dazzle us with his palace. He must be, to hold a ball when the place isn't even finished."

Austin Sinclair would be there tonight. Sarah stood and laid her book on the round pedestal table beside her chair, wishing she could stay home and escape between the pages.

"I don't understand how Addison could build that house. Why, it's bigger than ours," Clarissa said. "It makes it look as though he is richer than Papa was. It just isn't right."

"I know, dear," Roxanne said, patting Clarissa's cheek. "Unfortunately Leighton has no intention of building us a larger home. If only your father had removed your brother as his heir, as I asked. But you know how men are; they do so want their names to live on after they are gone. It's their way of reaching for immortality, even if the son is like Leighton."

Sarah stiffened. "Leighton is a fine man."

"I shall not discuss the boy with you, Sarah," Roxanne said. "Now come along."

Sarah paused in the hall outside of Addison's ballroom, watching as Roxanne and Clarissa strolled through the wide arch before her. For a moment her sister and stepmother stood poised on the wide landing, three feet above the crowd, like a queen and her princess surveying their kingdom. Soon members of their court poured forth to greet them.

Several young men swarmed up the stairs, racing to be the first to reach Clarissa. Collin Bennett won the race and received the honor of escorting Clarissa down the stairs. An attractive older man offered his arm to Roxanne.

Was Sinclair here yet? Sarah wondered, creeping through the archway. Her emotions fought a duel within her; on one side, the realistic, highly practical side of her knew it was nothing short of suicidal to want to see that man. But there was another side, a foolish, terribly wicked side that craved the sight of him.

She watched as Clarissa and Roxanne dissolved into the crowd, wondering if anyone would notice if she turned and ran back home. Even as the cowardly thought formed, Emma was climbing the three stairs, headed straight for her.

"Sarah, you've finally come," Emma said, squeezing her arm. "You don't know how much I need to see a friendly face. There are times when I feel the people in this city believe anyone from Philadelphia is from a foreign country."

Sarah smiled. "All they need is a little time to get to know you."

"My family never entertained like this. You can't imagine how frightening this evening has been. I have never worried so about my hair, my dress, the house, the food. How do you think I look?"

Sarah smiled, wondering how anyone who was nineteen and beautiful could ever doubt her appearance. Small, with dark hair and huge dark eyes, Emma looked like a porcelain doll. A year ago Addison had met her while on business in Philadelphia. One week later he had asked this youngest daughter of a Phildelphian banker to marry him. "You look beautiful."

"Do you think so?" Emma fussed with the cluster of pink and white blossoms adorning the shoulder of her sapphire blue gown.

"Yes, I'm certain Addison is quite proud of you."

"Addison's mother insisted I choose this color; she said it would show off to perfection the necklace Addison gave me as a wedding present." Emma plucked at the plump sapphires and diamonds dripping from a lacy web of gold around her neck, as though she were uncomfortable with the costly gems. "But I must confess, I think it's too dark for my complexion and my hair. I do wish she weren't so . . . so . . ."

"Overwhelming?"

"That word is tame compared to Phoebe." Emma slipped her arm through Sarah's and started down the stairs. "I never know what she is going to do or say. She's like a whirlwind, spinning from here to there, stirring up everything in her path. How can a woman that small contain so much energy?"

Sarah noticed her aunt Phoebe dart past a group of people standing at the corner of a nearby refreshment table, the violet feathers tucked into the dark curls piled on top of her head fluttering in the breeze she kicked up around her, the violet silk of her bustle snapping to and fro with each step. "Take a deep breath, Emma; Aunt Phoebe is headed this way."

"Emma! Emma, dear!" Phoebe's voice rose on a shrill note above the music tumbling from the minstrel's galley perched on the second floor at the far end of the ballroom.

Sarah felt Emma stiffen beside her.

"There are people you really must meet," Phoebe said, latching onto Emma's arm. "The Rutherfords, dear, they've only just returned from Spain."

"Good evening, Aunt Phoebe."

Phoebe glanced up at Sarah as though she were surprised to see her. "Oh, good evening, Sarah." With dark blue eyes, she cast her niece an appraising look, one delicate brow lifting as she took in the details of Sarah's appearance. "You're looking . . . healthy tonight."

Sarah smiled. "Thank you. I'm feeling quite healthy tonight."

"Phoebe, Sarah has just arrived. I thought I might spend some time with her."

"Nonsense," Phoebe said, tugging Emma away from Sarah. "You can see Sarah any day of the week. Now come along, child."

Emma glanced over her shoulder at Sarah as Phoebe ushered her toward the far side of the ballroom, a silent plea for understanding in her wide brown eyes. Sarah smiled, accustomed to her aunt's arrogance. She had lived under Phoebe's scrutiny all her life. She had failed her aunt's every expectation for a lady of society. And she had come to accept the fact that she was an unexceptional, somewhat embarrassing spinster in her aunt's eyes. After all, it was the truth.

Sarah wandered to a corner of the room, standing apart from the others, alone. She had never fit into this world, and she doubted she ever would.

Where was he? she wondered. Lord Austin Sinclair was a trophy for any hostess, and she knew Phoebe was expecting him tonight. It appalled her to realize how very much she wanted to see him.

Four chandeliers dangled above the crowded room, incandescent light glittering against crystal, raining down upon the couples whirling on the polished rosewood dance floor to the strains of a waltz. Gowns every shade of the rainbow billowed, bright hues blending with the sparkle of jewels.

Sinclair swirled with the others in that sea of color and light. Sarah felt her blood surge with a sudden excitement that sparked along her every nerve at the sight of him. Although he wore the same black and white uniform of society that the other men wore, he drew attention like a magnet. His partner smiled up at him, the look on Louisa Remsen's beautiful face that of a woman who has waltzed into heaven.

Sarah could see the others glancing at Sinclair as

he passed them, women staring as though he were a dream materialized into flesh and blood, men casting glances filled with envy. Did he even know she was here? It would be foolish to imagine he would care if she were here or not.

"Enjoying the party, Miss Van Horne?" Warren Snelling asked as he advanced from her left.

Sarah tensed, the hair on her arms prickling as she faced him. One corner of his dark brown mustache lifted as though he could sense her wariness of him and it pleased him.

Like a bear he lumbered toward her. He was no more than five inches taller than Sarah, yet he was broad; shoulders, chest, and hips packed into a solid wall of excess. Snelling was a man who gorged himself on all the best in life, sucking the marrow from the bones of those who fell beneath his tyranny.

"I read your article in the *Gazette* this evening." He sipped from his glass of champagne, staring at her with a brittle look in his dark eyes that made her wonder if the man had a soul. "You are treading dangerously close to libel."

"I have said nothing untrue."

He smoothed his palm over the dark brown hair that was sleeked back from his round face with oil. With his long mustache and his narrow brow, he looked like a walrus. "You imply I am the cause of people dying in the buildings I own."

"You and every man who owns one of those slaughterhouses are responsible for the people living there under those conditions."

"My buildings meet every regulation." The corner of his mustache twitched with his agitation. "They are inspected on a regular basis by the health commission."

"It is well known that many of the inspectors are

also on your payroll, Mr. Snelling."

"Your articles are upsetting my wife and daughter."

"Your tenements are killing many wives and daughters."

He stepped closer, invading her invisible cocoon of air. The sweet scent of his hair oil mixed with the overpowering fragrance of his cologne assaulted her nostrils. Sarah didn't move, even though she wanted to put the space of the room between them. She refused to show this man how well he could frighten her.

"Your uncle tells me you actually go into that part of town to do research for your little stories. One day you might get hurt."

She thought of the men who had attacked them this morning and wondered if they were also on Snelling's payroll. "If you think you can frighten me into submission, you are mistaken."

"I won't tolerate your interference in my business."

Sarah fought against the fear that trembled in her limbs. "Are you threatening me?"

"I never threaten." Snelling smiled, revealing small white teeth. "I make promises."

"I believe you promised the next waltz to me, Miss Van Horne."

Sarah nearly collapsed at the deep rumble of Austin Sinclair's voice. He moved to her side, so close she could feel the inviting heat of his body.

"I'm afraid you will have to excuse the lady, Mr. Snelling."

Snelling stepped back, looking up at this tall, broad-shouldered man, the smile fading from his lips. He glanced back at Sarah, his dark eyes glittering like polished coal in the light. "You would be wise to remember what I said, Miss Van Horne."

Austin touched her arm above her elbow-length white glove, his hand warm and secure against her. "Are you all right?"

"Yes, I'm fine." She glanced up at him. The concern she saw etched into his handsome face startled her, for in that moment he actually seemed to care for her. More startling was the reaction inside her, an unfurling of emotion like the delicate wings of a butterfly opening for the first time. "Thank you for rescuing me."

"My pleasure." He slid his hand down the length of her arm, capturing her hand in his warm grasp. "It looked as though he was giving you a difficult time."

"He was trying to intimidate me." Sarah glanced down to where he held her hand, her white glove stark against his sun-drenched skin. It seemed oddly intimate, her hand cradled in his. Yet she didn't want to pull her hand free. "He wants me to stop writing about the tenements."

"And are you going to quit?"

"No."

He slipped his fingers beneath her chin and coaxed her to look at him. He was smiling in a way that made her feel as though she were the most desirable woman in the world. "You're a very brave young woman."

"I'm only doing what I think is right."

He slid his thumb over the curve of her lower lip. "Did you save this waltz for me, Miss Van Horne?"

Sarah glanced to the dance floor, a sudden terror washing over her. It had been ten years since she had stepped onto a dance floor. "I don't dance."

Austin's gaze turned speculative as he looked at her. "Miss Van Horne, are you afraid to dance with me?"

"Don't be ridiculous."

"Don't worry, if you don't know how to dance, I'll teach you."

"I know how to dance, it's just I—"

"Good." He slipped her hand through the crook of his arm. "I've been wanting to dance with you all evening."

"You're going to regret this," she said as he led her toward the dance floor. "I haven't danced in years."

"So I should take the threat to my toes seriously?"

"Not to mention your dignity."

"I see." He paused, looking down at her, drawing his brows into a frown, feigning a look of pensive concentration. "After careful consideration, I've decided . . ."

He paused, allowing her to comtemplate his decision. The silly thing was, she found herself holding her breath. She might be terrified of making a spectacle of herself on the dance floor, but she realized there was something she feared more—the loss of his attention.

"You're worth the risk," he said, smiling at her.

Sarah smiled, forgetting for a moment her fears. It was easy to smile when she was with him, easy to believe all the lovely lies.

She noticed the curious glances cast in their direction as she walked beside him, entering that circle of light and color, feeling like a plain brown moth fluttering in a garden filled with colorful butterflies. Austin didn't notice the others as he took her into the light embrace of the waltz. Perhaps because he was looking at her, smiling down at her as though she were the only woman in the entire room.

"Smile for me, Sarah," he whispered. "I'm terribly sensitive. If you don't smile, people will believe you don't like me."

The warmth of his smile penetrated the cold dread lingering deep inside her. "I wouldn't want to be accused of damaging your fragile pride, Mr. Sinclair." Although she felt certain she would damage his toes.

Stiff, awkward, she wondered how Austin Sinclair could maintain his smile as she fumbled with the first few steps of the dance. Yet smile he did, keeping his movements simple, allowing her to find the rhythm and join him.

In his arms all the stiffness drained from her body. It was as though his fluid grace flowed into her with every step they took. Soon all the curious faces that swirled around them dissolved into a flicker of light in the periphery. Austin filled her world. The light scent of bayberry teased her senses. His warmth wrapped around her, embracing her as surely as his hand held hers.

It felt so strange with him, as though she had known him a lifetime. Still, she knew so little about him.

"What was her name?" Sarah asked.

Austin lifted one black brow in question. "Who do you mean?"

"The woman you almost married."

"Christina."

"What was she like?"

Austin led her through a series of intricate turns, glancing past her shoulder as though he were trying to recall that woman who had stolen his heart. Sarah flowed into each step, amazed at how easily she could follow his every move.

"She glittered like a diamond."

Sarah glanced at his shoulder, realizing she was hoping the woman had been unexceptional. Perhaps she was hoping this man truly had a weakness for plain women. "She must have been very beautiful."

"All of London knelt at her pretty little feet."

The bitterness that edged his words sparked a response deep inside her, a swelling tide of emotion that made her want to slip her arms around him and cradle his head against her breast. "What happened?"

"Three weeks before our wedding, at my sister's birthday ball, I walked out onto the terrace of my father's home and found my fiancée standing in the moonlight in the arms of another man. It seems they were lovers."

"It must have been a terrible shock."

"I now think of it as one of the most fortunate nights of my life." All the bitterness faded from his eyes as he looked down at her. "She was nothing more than an illusion of the woman I was meant to marry. Shimmering like a cold diamond in the light, blinding a foolish young man."

The last notes of the waltz faded. Austin paused in the middle of the dance floor. Yet he held her still, holding her hand, his other hand resting at her waist, searing her through the layers of her clothes.

She stood his captive, looking up into his handsome face, a strangely familiar sensation swirling around her. It was as if she had stood this way before with this man. Without words he whispered to her, the way her faceless phantom had whispered in her dreams. She recalled the moments when he had held her, when he had kissed her, every detail seared across her memory. And she wondered what it might be like to taste his lips once again.

"Lord Sinclair, I have been saving this next waltz just for you," Clarissa said as she gripped his arm.

Austin released Sarah, holding her gaze a moment longer before he turned to face Clarissa. "How thoughtful of you, Miss Van Horne."

Sarah turned away from them, unable to bear the sight of her sister stepping into Austin Sinclair's arms. The contrast was far too unnerving. Sarah didn't want him to look at her and compare her features to Clarissa's perfect face.

She hurried through the crowd gathered on the dance floor, finding sanctuary in a corner by one of the refreshment tables. She wanted to run, to hide. Yet how could she hide from the feelings trapped deep inside her? She stared down into a silver tray, her face reflected in the polished metal, the face of a foolish old maid who wanted to reach for a dream.

"Was that really you I saw on the dance floor, Sarah?" Addison asked, coming up behind her.

Sarah lifted a glass of lemonade from the table, stalling before she turned to face her cousin. "I didn't realize my dancing was so much of a concern to you, Addison."

Addison smirked. "Any miracle is of interest to me, cousin."

He took pleasure in making her feel small, she thought, sipping her drink, lemon flooding her senses as the tart liquid slid across her tongue.

"Could it be Lord Sinclair has taken a fancy to you? Is it possible you might be abandoning your silly notion of building palaces for peasants for the much more suitable role of wife?"

"Did you plan to marry every woman with whom you danced?"

"Come now, Sarah. The man is obviously interested in you. People have seen you together. You're quickly becoming the talk of the town."

Sarah stared down into her glass, feeling heat rise in her cheeks. "I didn't realize you were among the gossipmongers."

"Only when it's this fascinating. Of course, there

are those who are saying he's one of those impoverished members of the nobility, here to snare a rich heiress."

Sarah met her cousin's sarcastic gaze. "In that case he would do better elsewhere."

"Don't tell him that, Sarah. You might miss your chance to get him to the altar. And at your age, he might very well be your last chance."

Sarah glanced at the long refreshment table, squeezing her glass between her palms. Plates of lobster and shrimp and oysters were cradled in bowls of ice; piles of chocolates nearly overflowed gold plates. Streams of champagne and punch flowed from gold fountains. "Tell me, Addison, do you ever feel a little like King Louis before the revolution, surrounded by all your luxury and wealth, while the *peasants* die for want of bread?"

"Good God, Sarah! Is there any wonder you're a spinster?"

Sarah flinched inwardly as his barb hit home. "We could have built a complex of apartments for twenty families for what it cost to build this house."

"And what do you expect of me, Sarah? Should I move my bride into one of those filthy little apartments on the East Side?"

"No. I'm saying you should agree to build the apartment house I've proposed. The company can well afford this project."

"The company is going to suffer if you continue to write your ridiculous little stories, Sarah. In case you didn't realize it, Warren Snelling is an influential businessman in this town. You keep up this nonsense, and we are going to lose business. It has to stop."

"How can you sleep at night knowing you are doing business with a scoundrel?"

"What is this?" Kendall asked as he approached them. "Are the two of you arguing again?"

"Not a moment longer. I haven't the time to waste with her." Addison looked at his father, a disgusted expression on his face. "I advise you to escape before she starts chastising you for helping me build my new home." He turned on his heel and marched away from them.

"Sarah, darling." Kendall smiled down at her, his light blue eyes filled with gentle concern. "Have you been lecturing Addison on the plight of the working class when you should be enjoying the party?"

"We can make a difference, Uncle Kendall."

"Sarah, you don't need to lecture me. I agree with you."

Sarah felt a surge of hope within her. "Then you will agree to build the new apartments?"

Kendall shook his head, his silvery blond hair shining in the light. "I think we must wait until Leighton comes home."

"But we don't know when that might be. You know Leighton, he could be gone a year."

Kendall chucked her under the chin. "Be patient, Sarah."

Sarah watched her uncle stroll away from her. Wait until Leighton returns! She wasn't even sure where Leighton was. In his last letter, the brief note that had arrived a week ago with a medallion he wanted her to add to the collection in his treasure room, he had said he didn't know when he would return. She could only hope her wandering brother would find his way home soon.

Chapter Twelve

The steamer wheezed as it chugged through the dark Atlantic, carrying cargo from London to New York City. Leighton Van Horne pressed his back against the curved wall of his small cabin, his long legs bent at the knees, his bare feet flat against the scratchy gray wool of the blanket that covered his narrow bunk. Against his back he felt the rattle of the engines, a constant rumble that had ceased to concern him days ago. He had only one concern now, only one focus—revenge.

Beads of sweat formed on his brow and trickled down his cheek. His dark brown hair stuck to his neck, prickling his skin. Brown, how he loathed covering his hair with dye. Yet it was necessary. A tall man with silvery blond hair was far too easy to spot.

Nestled deep in the bowels of the ship, the stinking excuse for a cabin had no portholes, no way to wash away the stench of the countless sweaty bodies that had occupied this narrow space before him. It lingered in the air, that stench of countless peasants mingled with mildew, and poisoned his every breath.

Leighton stared at the rat that sat in one corner of the cabin, watching it nibble on the stale bread he had left for it from his dinner.

No one would suspect he would be on board this wreck; that was the beauty of his plan. Everyone knew he was accustomed to traveling like a king. But his own yacht sat under guard at a port in Brazil. Or had the Sinclairs stolen it, as they had stolen his freedom?

Devlin McCain had been the start of all of this trouble. Lord Devlin Sinclair, that's what he called himself now. He had found his family, claimed a fortune, and in the process he had stolen everything from Leighton.

It was because of the Sinclairs he was here in this stinking hole. If not for the Sinclairs, Leighton would never have heard of a city called Avallon. He never would have been tempted by the legend, tempted into disaster.

If not for Devlin Sinclair, they wouldn't be out there now, those strange people from that ancient city, searching for him as though he were a common criminal. But they wouldn't find him. Even with all their power, he could escape them. And he would make them pay, especially Devlin Sinclair. Oh, yes, he was looking forward to making that man suffer. Somehow he would find a way back to Avallon.

When he was done with Devlin Sinclair, when the family was still grieving over the loss of the son they had only just found again, Leighton would strike once more. Austin would fall next. One after the other, Leighton intended to destroy them until there was nothing left of the Sinclairs but a bad memory.

Leighton drew a knife from under his pillow. He stared at the long, slender blade, twisting it so the steel caught the light glimmering through the grimy glass of the oil lamp that swayed above his head. He saw his own reflection in that shiny blade. He imagined the face of the man he would kill. He smiled.

Sarah was in New York. Sarah would help him. Sarah had always been there to protect him. He needed money. He needed a safe place to stay until he could find a way to penetrate the defenses of Avallon. But he had to be careful. They would be in New York, those people from Avallon, watching, waiting. Yes, he had to be very careful.

He stared at the plump rat, watching as it followed the trail of bread he had left, watching as it drew closer to the bunk.

Leighton turned the blade in his hand, his gaze focused on the rat. It scurried to the next piece of bread he had placed on the floor, the morsel just beside the bed. "Enjoying yourself?"

The rat glanced up at the sound of the man's voice, small black eyes catching the light, whiskers twitching. It didn't scare easily, not when there was food to be had, not when this human had been giving it food for the past eight days.

Leighton glanced down into the shiny blade, smiling, lines flaring out from his light blue eyes, lines that had not been there six months ago. "You'll pay for this, Devlin Sinclair. You'll pay for everything you've done to me."

With a flick of his wrist, Leighton sent the knife flying straight into the plump body of the rat. It squeaked. It fluttered against the planks, struggling to free itself from the blade that pinned it to the floor, the blade that had ended its life.

Blood spread from beneath the animal, sticking to the thick gray fur. Leighton leaned back against the curved wall, smiling as he watched the final struggle of the small creature, little legs pumping, head lifting, muscles straining, straining, until it fell still.

Leighton laughed, delighted with the sweet scent of death, a fragrance he had come to love long ago. "I'm going to enjoy watching you die, Devlin Sinclair."

Devlin Sinclair rested his shoulder against a window casement in his bedroom and stared out at the ancient city of Avallon. A cool breeze swept into the room, brushing his face with the scent of roses from the gardens below.

Unlike most of Brazil, the land surrounding this rugged mountain, there were no mosquitoes here, no annoying insects to keep humans hiding beneath yards of netting. The people of Avallon had long ago learned how to control their environment.

Avallon, the city his ancestors had first settled 6,000 years ago stood a little more than a mile away, nestled in a valley. Moonlight glittered on the buildings, crystals trapped in the sparkling black stones that had been cut from the mountain, lending a strange fairy-tale quality to this city from a distant realm.

Kate stirred in the bed behind him. He sensed the moment she awakened, felt the instant her gaze touched his bare back. She tossed aside the sheet and stepped from the bed, he knew without looking.

He tested the skills from his first lessons in Avallon, lessons he had missed in his childhood, using his senses to perceive the world around him. In his mind he could see Kate approach. He imagined the way the ivory silk of her nightgown flowed around her legs, those long and supple legs, pale and soft. Hours ago he had felt those elegant legs wrap around his waist.

He felt the heat of her skin brush his a heartbeat before she touched his back, her slender hand warm against his skin. He drew a deep breath, drawing the spicy sweet scent of roses and woman into his lungs before he turned to face her.

Her unbound hair cascaded to her waist, shimmering like sunshine in the pale moonlight. The breeze captured a golden lock, brushing the silken strands across his bare hip. His muscles tightened in response, an instant flare of need deep in his belly.

"You're worried," she said, sliding her hands over the curves of his shoulders. "You're thinking you should be with Austin, aren't you?"

"Father doesn't seem to think it would be a very good idea." He shook his head, still uncomfortable with calling a man he barely knew father. "He seems to think Austin has a better chance of retrieving the medallion if he works alone."

"Austin will be fine." She traced the curve of his lower lip with her fingertip, smiling up at him. "He has been trained to do this sort of thing."

Devlin shook his head. "He has been trained to be a diplomat, not a street fighter."

"Perhaps all he will need is diplomacy."

"Van Horne is still out there."

The smile faded from her lips. "All the more reason for you to stay here. That man wants to see you dead."

He slipped one hand beneath her soft hair, pressing his palm against her warm nape, feeling the tension that single name had drawn in her muscles. "I've never been one to hide from a fight, Kate. I don't like the idea of my brother going against that madman alone." His brother, his twin, a man who shared his face, his form, and more: a link both brothers were only just beginning to understand.

"Please, Devlin." She rested her hands on his chest. "Give Austin a chance to do what your father has asked of him. The medallion is his responsibility. Not yours."

"The medallion belongs in this family. That makes it my responsibility, too."

"Please." She lifted on her toes and slid her arms around his neck, silk and lace warmed by her body sliding sinuously against his skin. "Van Horne wants to kill you. Please give Austin a chance to do this without you."

Devlin slipped his arms around her waist and lifted her, holding her close, pressing his face into the fragrant curve of her neck and shoulder. "All right, Professor. We'll give my brother some time."

"Thank you." She pulled back in his arms. In her blue eyes he saw the glitter of unshed tears that her smile couldn't disguise. "Make love to me, Devlin. Make me forget everything beyond this moment in your arms."

He carried her to the bed and lowered her to the white linen sheets. Slowly he slipped the sheer silk from her shoulders, kissing every inch of her warm skin as he unveiled her delicate beauty.

They loved each other as though this were the first time, as though this might be the last time. For both had been touched by the evil that haunted Van Horne, and both knew there would be no promise of tomorrow as long as the madman roamed free.

Chapter Thirteen

Sarah turned away from the typewriter that sat on a shelf adjacent to her desk. This morning the words for a story refused to come to her. Was it because she wanted to be somewhere else?

A pigeon strutted along the ledge outside of her office window, his blue-gray head bobbing with every step, his cooing colliding with the rumble from the street. Two stories above Broadway, Sarah watched the steady stream of morning traffic flow on the wide street, wheels rattling on the pavement.

No one strolled along the sidewalks here. Men and women swarmed like ants intent on collecting food for the winter, too absorbed in their business to notice the faces of those they passed.

Sunlight chipped away at the shade cast by the four-story *Gazette* building that housed her office, sweeping the shadow back toward her. In a few hours the street would be exposed to the full rays of the sun.

She was hiding, taking refuge from the man who

was probably at this very moment standing in the hall of her home. Still, she wondered if there was a refuge from Austin Sinclair. Even now, safe in her office, a part of her longed to be with that infuriating scoundrel. In time, would he chip away all of her defenses?

She jumped at a knock on the door. Had Sinclair found her? She smoothed her fingers over her hair, making sure all of the pins were tucked neatly into her bun. "Come in."

A young, dark-haired man entered her office, carrying a stack of envelopes piled on a small package wrapped in plain brown paper. "Got your mail, Miss Van Horne."

Sarah released the breath she had been holding. Yet she couldn't say for certain if the emotion settling in her chest was relief or disappointment. "Thank you, Thomas."

After depositing the stack on her desk, Thomas left, closing the door behind him. Sarah stared at the envelopes. It was going to be a pretty day, the air cool, the sun high and bright, and here she was hiding in her office, facing a stack of correspondence.

She shuffled through the envelopes, discarding them without opening a single letter. She lifted the package, which was the size of a cigar box, noting the simple black letters that spelled out her name and address.

What would Sinclair do when Emerson told him she was out for the day? No doubt he would find another companion for his ride in the park. Well, it certainly didn't matter to her, she thought, slashing at the string wrapped around the package with the sharp edge of her letter opener.

"Tell me, Miss Van Horne, what did that package ever do to make you so angry?"

Sarah jumped at the sound of Austin Sinclair's voice. She glanced up to find him leaning against her office door. "What are you doing here?"

He smiled as though he knew he could send excitement bolting through her with a single look. "Emerson said I might be able to find you here."

"At times Emerson is far too helpful." Sarah tapped the tip of the letter opener against the package, mentally shaking herself for her wayward emotions. "I don't understand how you got in here without making a sound."

He shrugged, broad shoulders lifting the dark gray cloth of his coat. "In my profession it pays to be discreet."

The wind had tossed his hair into ebony waves around his face, the silken strands tempting her fingers. "And what are you hoping to steal this morning?"

He moved away from the door, his footsteps impossibly quiet on the bare oak floor. "It's always important to examine the possibilities in any room to determine what is of most value."

Sarah leaned back in her chair as he approached the desk, her back sliding against the soft brown leather. She felt her blood thicken with each step Austin took, the pulse in her neck pounding against her plain white collar.

He lifted a brass paperweight in the shape of a unicorn from her desk, turning it in his hand, examining the carved figure. "Now a less discerning thief might think this was the most valuable item in the room."

"But you know better?"

He set the unicorn on her desk, smiling as he looked down at her. "There is something far more valuable here."

A cool breeze drifted in through the open windows behind her, brushing Sarah's neck. Still, her skin felt heated, as though she were standing in the bright rays of the sun.

She watched him, following his every move as he strolled to a painting hanging on the oak-paneled wall beside her desk. He stood with his back to her, studying the painting of a rocky coastline and rumbling sea. She had liked it the first moment she had seen the painting in a small gallery on Broadway.

"Nice." He glanced over his shoulder, a lazy smile curling his lips. "It might be worth a great deal of money in a few years, especially if the Impressionist movement catches hold. But it isn't what I would steal."

"No?"

"No."

He moved toward her, a slow prowl filled with a peculiar masculine grace that made her wonder what would happen when he reached her. The edges of her vision narrowed and darkened until this man alone filled her sight.

"I thought last night, before you left the party, you agreed to go for a ride through Central Park with me today, Miss Van Horne." He rested his hands on the arms of her chair.

Sarah pressed back against the chair, trying to burrow into the leather. "I have work to do."

"How you disappoint me." He drew closer, leaning over her, his thick black lashes lowering as he studied her lips. "Here I thought you were a woman of your word."

"I am." An intriguing fragrance settled around her, the spice of his cologne mingling with the intoxicating scent of his warm skin. She stared up into his handsome face, so close she could see the dark pinpoints of his beard lurking beneath his smooth cheeks. How intensely masculine he seemed. How utterly appealing. How horribly frightening.

"I've stayed away from your sister, Sarah," he whispered, his deep voice brushing her like warm sable.

He pressed his lips against her cheek, near the corner of her mouth. Sarah's lips parted, her breath escaping on a shaky sigh.

"And all I ask is the pleasure of your company," he whispered, his lips brushing her cheek.

Was that all he wanted? Or was it some warped sense of dominion that drove him in this game? Did he have some terrible need to conquer and rule just as an ancient prince might rule?

"What do you want from me?" she asked, appalled at the aching tone in her voice. "Tell me."

He looked down at her, all the mischief draining from his face, replaced by an intensity that made the breath catch in her throat. "I don't want to hurt you."

"Don't you?"

"No." He lifted away from her, standing with his hands loose at his sides. "Don't be afraid of me, Sarah."

"I'm not afraid of you." Sarah turned toward the desk, clasping her hands in her lap so he couldn't see how they were shaking. "I told you I have work to do this morning. Unlike some people, I have responsibilities."

"So do I," he said, his voice deepened with an odd note of regret.

"Of course you do." She fumbled with the package, fighting to control the emotions he had released inside her; they surged like water rushing through a hole punctured in a carefully constructed dam. She stripped away the brown paper, revealing a cigar box.

Why would someone send her cigars? "I'm certain you feel responsible for helping all those collectors gather pieces for their treasure rooms. Not to mention lining your pockets with their gold."

"That isn't entirely true." He strolled to one of the two brown leather armchairs in front of her desk. He sank to the chair, leaned back, and stretched his long legs as though he intended to take up residence for the rest of the day. "My greatest responsibility is teaching you how important it is to enjoy a beautiful day like today."

She smiled at him. "Please, feel free to shirk that responsibility, Mr. Sinclair."

He shook his head. "I'm afraid I've always taken my responsibilities seriously."

"Oh, I'm certain you have. But I—" She lifted the lid of the box, the words she was about to speak dissolving with the air in her lungs. A gray dove lay in the box, her neck broken, her delicate head lying at an odd angle to her body.

"What is it, Sarah?" Austin asked.

Sarah parted her lips. Yet her words foundered deep in her throat. She stared at the poor little creature, stunned by the senseless violence.

In the corner of her eye she saw Austin rise from his chair. She lifted the white piece of parchment that lay over the bird's body like a shroud and read the single typed line: *Forget the tenements or meet your fate.*

"What the blazes!" Austin snatched the note from her trembling hand. Dark color rose in his cheeks as he stared down at the typed words, his lips drawing into a grim line. "Do you have any idea who would send this?"

"I don't know." She sat back in her chair, closing her eyes, shutting out the horrible sight of that poor dead bird. "Snelling, probably."

"Have you received any threats like this before?"

"No."

"You've been writing about this man for months." Austin closed the lid on the cigar box. He knelt beside her and lifted her cold hands in his warm grasp. "Why would he threaten you now?"

"In a few months the legislature is going to vote on amending the Tenement House Law." She focused on his face, the handsome lines and curves of his features, blocking out the ugliness sitting on the desk. "If they pass the new regulations, it will cost Snelling and the other owners a fortune. We're stirring up the public to put pressure on the legislators. Without that pressure the law won't be amended."

One corner of his mouth twitched with his anger. "Maybe I should have a little talk with Snelling."

"No." She curled her fingers around his hands, holding him like a lifeline against the rising tide of fear inside her. "If he did this, he means only to frighten me. I don't want him to think he has succeeded."

"Sarah, this man could be dangerous."

"We aren't even certain he did it. It could be any of a hundred men who own those horrible hovels."

Austin lifted their clasped hands and pressed his lips to the back of her fingers, his breath a warm whisper against her skin. "I don't want anything to happen to you."

The sincerity in his eyes caught her off guard, like an open palm across her face. In that instant she chose to believe what she saw in his eyes, the concern for her. She needed to believe someone cared if she lived or died.

Austin squeezed her cold hands. "I'm going to send someone for the police."

Sarah glanced at the box sitting like a tiny coffin on her desk. "Yes, I think they should know about this."

Austin stood beside Sarah, his back to the windows in her office, watching Detective Roger Farley. The man was close to fifty, Austin guessed, judging by the gray streaks in the thinning strands of dark brown that were carefully smoothed back from his round face.

Although Farley moved with the speed of a glacier, methodically asking the same questions two and three times before he was satisfied he would receive the same answers, Austin suspected there was more to this short, spare man than first impressions would reveal. He could see the intelligence in Farley's dark eyes.

"So you say you and Miss Van Horne were attacked by two men yesterday morning." Farley stared at Austin as though he were analyzing every feature, every expression. "What makes you think it was anything more than an attempted robbery?"

"I'm not sure it was," Austin said. "But I thought it was something you should know."

"I'll take a look at the report. Maybe ask the ruffians a few questions." The police detective dabbed the end of his pencil with the tip of his tongue before he scratched something in a small black notebook.

Farley looked at Sarah, his face pressed into lines that made Austin wonder if the man had been born frowning. "There isn't much to go on, Miss Van Horne."

"I'm afraid I've told you everything I can, Detective Farley."

Farley tapped the eraser of his pencil against his chin, studying the dead bird that lay in the box on Sarah's desk as though the dove might reveal the secret of its murderer. "I can't go questioning a man like Warren Snelling without good cause."

"I understand," Sarah said.

Farley stood, slipping his notebook and pencil into his coat pocket. "If you have any more trouble, let me know."

Sarah stood. "I will."

"I'll take the bird." Farley closed the cigar box and lifted the little coffin. "Evidence."

"Of course." She stood with her hands at her sides as Farley left the office, clenching and unclenching her fingers into her palms, the only sign of her agitation.

"I wonder if we should have mentioned the coach at the museum."

Sarah glanced up at Austin, her eyes wide like those of a person who had been slapped hard across the cheek. "That was an accident."

"I wonder." Austin touched her arm, resisting the urge to take her into his arms. He had to keep his distance, no matter how much he wanted to bridge the gap between them.

"I can't believe Snelling would actually try to kill me. It had to be an accident."

"Come for a drive in the park with me, Sarah." He slid his hand down her arm, slipped her hand into his. "Forget about all of this for a few hours."

She stared at him a moment as though she were trying to decide just how dangerous she thought *he* might be. Yet she made no move to pull away from his touch. "I don't know. There are—"

"It's my responsibility to help you enjoy the day, remember?"

"So you said." She smiled, a hesitant curve of her lips as she glanced down at their clasped hands. "All right. I suppose I shall have to help you with your responsibilities."

Austin rested his hands on the metal railing and stared into the lion's cage. Twelve by ten feet, that was all the magnificent beast had to roam in this menagerie in Central Park, iron bars holding him back from the throng of visitors that flowed past his small domain, content in their freedom.

"You look upset," Sarah said. "Thinking about how it might feel to be behind bars?"

Austin glanced at the woman standing beside him. Sarah was watching him from beneath the curved brim of her small brown straw hat. He sensed defiance in her, as though she were challenging him to change his evil ways, and something more, something soft and warm beneath that haughty mask, something he wished he could explore. "I was thinking of how he must feel, trapped in a cage, when he was born to roam the jungle."

Sarah turned to look at the lion. The beast raised his head, staring at her with amber eyes. "Do you really think he minds?"

"Would you want to live this way?"

"But the animals are safer here than they would be in the wild. They are well taken care of. They never have to worry about finding their next meal."

A lock of her hair had escaped the combs and pins of its prison. It fluttered with the breeze, tempting him to catch it, a shimmering strand of brown burnished gold by sunlight, sliding along the pale curve of her neck, curling down her brown poplin gown to her waist. "Do you think he would trade his freedom for the promise of a meal?"

"I've never thought of it that way." Sarah frowned as she stared at the lion. When she spoke, she kept her voice low, private words in a place where people drifted like leaves on a swirling pool all around them, laughter and conversation collecting in a low rumble. "Have you ever thought you might one day be behind bars, Mr. Sinclair?"

"Would that please you, Miss Van Horne?"

Sarah kept her gaze on the lion. "It would seem the only place for criminals is behind bars."

"I told you once before, people aren't always what they seem to be." He glanced down at her hands, watching the way the white linen of her gloves stretched across her knuckles as she squeezed the railing. He wanted to tell her the truth, but he knew it was impossible. And so he would rely on lies, twisted variations of a truth she would never believe. "I know your brother."

She was quiet, except for the breath he heard her draw, the deep steadying breath that told him she was preparing for the worst. What did the woman know about her brother and his crimes?

"I thought you might know Leighton."

"Did you?" He wanted to believe she was as innocent as she seemed; it was important to him, more important than he wanted to admit to himself.

She glanced up at him. "In your profession, I suppose it's an asset to know collectors."

"Yes, it is." There was doubt in her eyes, dark shadows of doubt about a brother Austin knew possessed a soul as black as hell.

He took her arm and led her past the cages where bears and wolves paced behind bars. She didn't protest, walking beside him, quiet, pensive, her arm stiff beneath his touch. They walked toward the arsenal and beyond, where elms lined the path and benches stood in the shade of their spreading branches.

It would be easy to forget the dark mission that

had brought him to this place on a day like this, when the sun was high in a clear blue sky and a cool breeze stirred the leaves overhead. With Sarah it was always tempting to forget everything except one beguiling lady.

"Recently your brother acquired a gold medallion. Celtic in origin." He glanced at the woman who walked beside him. "Have you seen it?"

"Is that what you were after the other night?"

"I was hired by a man to retrieve that medallion. He said Leighton had acquired it from him, shall we say, without his knowledge."

She halted on the path and stared up at him. "Are you implying Leighton stole that medallion?"

Austin shrugged, knowing he was treading through dangerous territory. One wrong move and he would lose Sarah completely. And he couldn't afford to do that, not when he was sure she knew where that medallion was hidden. "Do you think he might have stolen it?"

"Of course not!"

Even in her determination to protect her brother, Austin could see the doubt she couldn't hide. "Then I suppose it's all for the best that you caught me. I might have returned the piece to the wrong man."

"Are you trying to say you only steal from thieves?"

Austin tilted his head and smiled down at her. "I try to keep my standards."

"Standards." She pursed her lips and held his gaze for a long moment, as though she were trying to see the truth in his eyes. "As long as you are well paid for your efforts, I doubt you care who is paying the bill."

"A man has to make a living."

"Not by being a criminal."

He lifted his arms at his sides, the breeze rippling

his dark gray coat. "I fear I am little prepared for anything else."

"I don't believe that."

She turned and walked away from him. She sank to a wrought iron bench nestled in the shade of an elm near the path, her dress spilling a brown puddle on the emerald grass. She glanced up when he drew near, meeting his eyes with that intense honesty that never failed to catch him off guard. "You seem to be a reasonably intelligent man, Austin Sinclair."

"Thank you."

"I'm certain you could find some opportunities to make your way in this world other than hiring yourself out as a thief."

Although she had left room for him to sit beside her, he remained standing, looking down into her lovely face. "There are only so many things the son of a duke can do, Miss Van Horne."

Sarah's lips parted, closed, then parted once more as she said, "You can't mean to tell me you are actually . . . I don't believe it."

"I'm afraid it's true." He bowed, a deep formal bow he had often made when at court. "Lord Austin Sinclair, Marquess of Somerset, Earl of Sheffield, at your service, milady."

She stared up at him, the look in her eyes fading from disbelief to stark realization. "How in the world does a marquess become a thief?"

"Bad investments." He sat beside her, keeping a proper distance on the bench. "By the time I discovered my banker had nearly ruined me, it was too late to recover. I realized I had a choice to make. I could go on bended knee to my father, or find some way to support my household."

"And you chose to become a thief?"

"I have sixty-five servants and two hundred tenants. It's a big responsibility."

"But how could you resort to thievery?"

He smiled. "I prefer to say I help gentlemen improve their collections."

Sarah shook her head. "There must be something else you can do."

"It is a very lucrative profession."

"And very dangerous."

"I assume I'll get better with practice. The other night was my first attempt."

Sarah studied him a moment as though she were seeking the truth in his eyes. "You mean to say you've never stolen anything before?"

"I suppose, given the fact you prevented me from completing my mission, you could say I've never stolen anything at all."

Sarah leaned back against the bench, black roses molded from iron pressing into her back, relief washing over her like a cool spring shower. "Then you have another chance."

"You mean you intend to help me steal your brother's medallion?"

Sarah pursed her lips as she looked at him. The man was utterly infuriating. "I mean you have a chance to make a fresh start. To turn away from this destructive path before it's too late."

"I don't see how I can do that. There are those servants to support and tenants relying on me." He closed his hand around hers and brought her hand to his lips. At the soft touch of his lips against the back of her hand, she jerked free of his grasp. Even her glove could not protect her from the intriguing caress that sent a shiver along her nerves.

He gave her a devilish smile that said he knew all about that delicious shiver. "I had thought I might marry a wealthy heiress. It's done often enough. But

I'm afraid I still believe the only reason to marry is for love."

"Are you trying to tell me you never intended to marry Clarissa?"

"I'm afraid your lovely sister is far too spoiled for my taste."

"You decided to force me into seeing you for sport, is that it?" She stared at the arsenal that rose like a medieval castle in the distance, towers lifting parapets toward the white streaks of clouds splashed across the sky. "You thought it would be amusing to watch a spinster fall in love with you."

He slipped his fingers under her chin and coaxed her to look at him. He was smiling in a way that made her feel as though she were the only one in the world that could make him smile. "I enjoy being with you, Sarah. And I knew the only way you would see me is if I coerced you into doing it."

Suddenly, caught in the warmth of his eyes, she couldn't breathe. "If I'm to believe you, then I have no reason to continue this farce."

"I can think of one reason." He slid his thumb along the curve of her lower lip. Sarah felt herself leaning toward him, a shifting of muscles she couldn't control. "Because I enjoy your company."

Exerting every ounce of will within her, she sat back, breaking away from his touch. "I'm not sure what it is you're after, but I can assure you, I do not intend to play your little game."

The breeze ruffled his thick hair, tossing silky strands of ebony over his brow. "Sarah, do you have any idea what it's like to always wonder if someone is interested in your company simply because there is a title appended to your name?"

"No, I don't suppose I do."

"When I'm with you, Sarah, I don't wonder if you

have your sights set on being a duchess." He took her hand between both of his, holding her as though she were a precious piece of porcelain. "You're candid, brutally honest, and I appreciate those qualities more than you can ever realize."

Sarah glanced down to where her hand rested between his warm palms, the white linen of her glove stark against his sun-darkened skin. "Are you saying you would like to be friends, Mr. Sinclair?"

"There are times when we all need a friend, Sarah." He squeezed her hand softly. "I plan to be in New York only a few weeks. I would like to spend that time with you. Do you think you could tolerate my company while I'm here?"

She glanced at the arsenal rising from the emerald grass. When she was a little girl she had pretended that old building was a castle and she a princess. The park was her kingdom, and she believed one day a handsome prince would come to claim her for his own. It had been nothing but make-believe, silly childhood dreams. Yet with this man it would be far too easy to believe in fairy tales again.

It wasn't wise to see Austin Sinclair again. She should tell him so now. She glanced up and found him watching her, the warmth in his eyes stealing the breath from her lungs.

"Don't turn me away, Sarah," he said, his deep voice carrying softly on the breeze.

Oh, my, how could she turn away from him when he looked so vulnerable, so incredibly appealing?

"And just think, your good influence could save me from a life of crime."

"There must be something you can do. Something honest."

"I doubt I could find anything that would pay quite so handsomely."

Sarah stiffened. "Perhaps you should think about living a great deal less lavishly."

"People would talk."

"Aren't you the one unconcerned about what other people think of you?"

He laughed, a deep rumble that was nearly impossible to resist. "I suppose we all cherish a few opinions now and again. For instance, I do care what you think of me, sweet Sarah."

Sarah glanced away from him. The look in his eyes was far too disturbing. She stared at a robin who pecked at the grass a few yards away, searching for his lunch. "If we are to be friends, I think it best you stop this annoying flirtation."

"Sarah, you have a way of cutting a man to the bone."

She glanced at him and found him smiling at her, mischief alive in the depths of his beautiful eyes. Not at all the picture of a man who had just been cut to the bone. "I have a feeling you have enough confidence to withstand a few blows."

"I have a feeling you are going to put me to the test." He stood and took her hand. "Come on, Sarah, I'm going to take you boating."

"Boating?" Sarah allowed him to tug her from the bench.

He smiled, a devilish curve of his lips. "That's where we sit in a boat and I paddle you around the lake like a slave at your command."

"I've never gone boating before." She smiled up at him. "It should be amusing to see you act the part of a slave, *Lord* Sinclair."

Bram shifted in the saddle. Yet it didn't matter how he sat in the leather seat, he couldn't ease the soreness, the ache that penetrated his pelvic bones and shimmied up his spine. Still, Clarissa Van Horne had commanded him to accompany her this morning. Horses and debutantes, he wasn't sure which one was more a pain in the ass. This damn mission couldn't end soon enough to suit him.

He followed Clarissa and her friends along a bridle path in Central Park, listening to their endless prattle, hoping they kept the pace to a walk instead of a canter. Bouncing up and down on this animal's back was not exactly his idea of an ideal way to spend a beautiful afternoon.

"Will you look at that!" Louisa Remsen stopped her horse on the bridge they were crossing and pointed toward the lake.

Fanny and Clarissa turned their mounts to look over the lake. Bram pulled up beside the women and glanced in the direction Louisa was pointing. A sleek black boat glided across the lake a few yards away, powered by a man who dipped the oars smoothly into the glittering water as he kept his attention focused on his passenger, a lady dressed in brown.

"That's Sarah!" Fanny Warren said. "And she's with Lord Sinclair."

"Again!" Louisa said.

Bram clenched his teeth as Sarah Van Horne's laughter drifted on the cool breeze. Sinclair certainly looked as though *he* was enjoying this mission.

"I don't understand it," Louisa said, tugging on a reddish brown curl that peeked out from beneath her tall emerald green hat. "What could he possibly see in Sarah?"

"It's obvious," Clarissa said. "He's trying to make me jealous."

Bram glanced at the fair-haired woman, wondering if he had ever met anyone more certain of her own beauty. Pity she didn't have a heart to go along with her beautiful face.

"Perhaps." Fanny tilted her head and smiled at Clarissa. Beneath the brim of her sapphire blue hat, dark brown curls framed her heart-shaped face, and malice glittered in her blue eyes. "And then again, maybe he thinks he can get what he wants from Sarah. Something he couldn't get from any decent woman."

Clarissa stared at Sarah, her eyes narrowed with jealousy.

"Do you think that could be true about Sarah?" Louisa asked. "I suppose he's heard about her mother."

"Yes." Clarissa stared at the couple as they glided away from the bridge, a pair of white swans skimming the surface of the shimmering water beside the boat. "I wouldn't at all be surprised if Lord Sinclair believes he can seduce Sarah."

Bram squeezed the reins between his hands, his anger rising. These three combined didn't possess an ounce of Sarah's worth.

"How shocking!" Louisa said, her outrage spoiled by a wayward giggle.

"It has to be true," Fanny said, obviously satisfied by her own insightful powers. "Why else would a man like Lord Sinclair be seeing an old maid?"

"Because he likes her," Bram said.

Three heads snapped in his direction. The women stared at him as though a marble statue had just spoken.

"I'm certain we have no need of your opinion, Duggan." Clarissa lifted her chin to stare at him down the length of her little nose.

"Clarissa, you really must teach the creature some manners if he is to accompany us," Fanny said, staring at Duggan.

"You will do well to remember your place, or you will find yourself looking for another position in someone else's stable." Clarissa turned away from him and urged her horse into a canter. The other women followed.

Bram swore under his breath. When this mission was over, he was going to find Lady Judith Chatham and remind himself how much he had always enjoyed the company of a beautiful woman.

Chapter Fourteen

A cool breeze heavy with the scent of roses drifted through the open windows of the Sinclair drawing room in Avallon. Devlin stared into the gardens that stretched in intricate patterns from the terrace toward a wide green lawn. Roses, lilies, and gardenias bloomed in that lush oasis, along with beds of other flowers and plants. His mother's gardens.

It seemed a miracle being here with these people—his family. Still, at times he caught himself poised on a ledge above a deep pool of self-pity and regret, wondering what it would have been like to grow up in this place, surrounded by love and security.

He thought of his brother. Austin had contacted them this morning, as he did twice a week, to report his progress. Although there had been nothing overt in his voice, Devlin sensed Austin was troubled, a penetrating pain that delved deep into his brother's soul.

Devlin knew Austin's feelings without words. He felt his twin's anxiety, a shimmer of emotion that lingered like a shadow of his own emotions deep inside him. And he sensed that the trouble stemmed from Sarah Van Horne. There was something in Austin's voice when he mentioned Sarah's name, something soft and dangerous.

"Check," Alexandria said.

Devlin glanced across the chessboard to his sister. Alexandria smiled at him, the spirit of challenge glittering in her blue-green eyes. He was ten years older than this beautiful young woman, the sister he was only beginning to know. He glanced down at the board, seeing her strategy, eluding her by a counterattack with his bishop.

Alexandria wrinkled her nose. "I think it's possible you are even better at this game than Austin."

"Your brother has managed to beat me his share of times."

"I used to wonder about you." Alexandria rested her fingertip on one of her knights, staring down at the porcelain figure. "I knew you were Austin's twin, so I knew what you looked like, but I wondered what you would *be* like. I wondered if you would be very different from Austin."

"And do you think I am?"

"In ways." She glanced up at him, a wistful smile curving her lips. "When I was little, I imagined you would come to my rescue when Austin teased me. Would you have?"

Devlin felt a tightening inside him, anger and regret twisting around his heart. "I wish I knew."

"I'm sorry." Alexandria left her chair and rushed around the round pedestal table, sinking to her knees beside his chair. "I didn't mean to make you think about all the time we've lost, all of those horrible years." She slipped her arms around his waist and pressed her cheek against his chest. "You're here now; that's all that matters."

"It's all right, Alexa." Devlin stroked her dark brown hair, the hurt inside him soothed by her tender concern. "We all need time to heal."

"I hope Austin comes back soon." She looked up at him, the shimmer of unshed tears in her eyes. "We've waited so long to be a whole family again."

Devlin thought of Austin and the sister of the man who wanted to destroy this family. He had an uneasy feeling about Austin and Sarah Van Horne, a sense of impending disaster so strong it pressed against his chest like a granite tombstone. Still, he knew there was nothing he could do but wait, and hope his brother would make it back to them in one piece.

Kate Sinclair sat on the terrace of an outdoor café in the modern city of Avallon, beneath the sheltering branches of an oak tree. Leaves rustled in the cool breeze, mingling with the rattle of silver on china, the chatter of voices of the patrons gathered there for lunch. It might have been England in the spring, a quaint country village. Except for the buildings.

Wood from the surrounding forests and stone from the mountainside rose to shape structures that ranged from one to four stories, roofs flowing like the neighboring hills. They blended into the countryside, in harmony with nature. The people of Avallon believed in that harmony, in maintaining a balance with nature.

"Strange, how easy it has been to adapt to this place," Kate said, glancing across the small round table to where her lunch companion, Lady Judith Chatham, sat.

"I have never felt more at peace than I have here."

Judith smiled, her dark brown eyes lighting with a deep contentment. "The Central Council has provided me with everything I need to start a new life. I can't believe it. By this time next week my shop will be open. For the first time in my life I actually feel as though I'm accomplishing something."

"The Central Council encourages everyone to lead productive lives." Although she believed at times the council also tried to manipulate people, it was a sentiment Kate kept to herself. She wanted nothing to spoil Judith's joy.

They were friends, one of the few Kate had ever known, joined by the ordeal they had shared. The same quest had brought them to this place six months ago, although not together. Judith had come to Avallon with Leighton Van Horne. Here, Judith had broken the bonds that had tied her to the madman. She had claimed a fresh beginning, abandoning a loveless marriage back in England.

"I only hope the ladies of Avallon shall like my designs."

"I love them." Kate tugged at the shoulder of her black silk tunic, a dark floral pattern of scarlet and white and emerald dripping down the shoulders and arms and cascading from the round neckline into a vee at the belted waist. Black silk trousers, full and flowing, completed the outfit Judith had designed for her.

"It's extraordinary, isn't it? Not being constricted by corsets and yards upon yards of skirts and petticoats. I never realized how a change in my wardrobe could make me feel so liberated," Judith remarked.

After having battled all of her life for an equal place in the world, Kate found the fact that women held an equal position in Avallon one of the finer characteristics of this society. "I wonder how long it shall take for the Outworld to realize we are every bit as capable as men?"

"Decades."

"I'm afraid you're right." Kate sipped her drink, cold and tart, flooding her senses with lemon.

"Have you heard any more from Austin?" Judith asked. "Have they captured Leighton yet?"

"No. It's as if he slipped from the face of the earth."

Judith glanced down at her glass of lemonade, slowly stripping the moisture from the pale green glass with her thumb. "You don't think he could find his way back here, do you?"

Kate shivered in the breeze. "No."

"He's a devil, Kate." Judith looked at Kate with fear naked in her eyes. "If he ever found me . . . he would kill me for betraying him."

"He's not going to find you." Kate rested her hand over Judith's. "You're safe here."

Judith nodded, yet the fear did not leave the depths of her brown eyes. And in her soul, Kate wondered how safe any of them truly were from Leighton Van Horne. "Have you ever met Van Horne's sister Sarah?"

"Once, when Leighton took me to New York."

"Do you believe she is anything at all like Leighton?"

"Good heavens, no. As I recall, she was quiet, very reserved, as though she were hoping no one would notice her." Judith sipped her lemonade. "Why do you ask?"

"Austin has mentioned her several times when he has contacted us. He has been seeing her, trying to locate the medallion. Although he hasn't said anything, I think he has come to care for her."

A lock of Judith's hair drifted across her face with the breeze. She swept the long dark brown tresses behind her shoulder as she spoke. "I would think that would put him in a rather awkward position."

"Yes." Kate swirled the ice and slices of lemon in her glass. "I only hope it doesn't also put him in a dangerous position."

"I met the guardian who is with Austin on this mission. Bram Duggan seems quite capable."

Kate glanced up at her friend, sensing something more behind Judith's words. "He was the one who headed the investigation into Leighton's escape, wasn't he? Commanding man, tall, broad shoulders, blond hair, blue eyes. Is that him?"

"Green eyes." Judith smiled, the look in her eyes growing soft and dreamy. "He has green eyes."

"You like him."

"I've seen him several times. He was nice enough to show me around the city and the ruins. He even took me to dinner the night before he left for New York." Judith glanced down at her glass of lemonade, a soft blush rising to stain her cheeks. "But I'm certain he would never be interested in someone like me, not for marriage. He's much too honorable."

"Judith, I never realized you could be so muddle-headed."

"Kate, look at my past. I was Leighton Van Horne's mistress." Judith squeezed the glass between her palms. "How could any decent man want me?"

In the days they had known each other, Judith had poured out her entire story. At 18 she had married Lord Oliver Chatham, Baron of Hempstead, a handsome young man who had never touched his wife. After five years of marriage, five years of doubting herself as a woman, Judith had found her husband in bed with one of the stable boys.

A few months later, Judith had met Leighton Van Horne, a man who saw where she was most vulnerable. He was the first and only man who had ever touched her.

"Leighton Van Horne used your doubt about yourself to lure you into his bed. He was charming, physically beautiful, and he made you feel desirable. You didn't stand a chance. That does not make you dirty, or wicked, or tarnished in any way."

Judith shook her head. "You don't know the things I allowed him to do."

"And you don't know how wonderful it can be with the right man, a man you love, a man who loves you. You deserve that, Judith. You deserve a gentle man, an honorable man, a man who can erase all the ugliness Van Horne carved across your soul."

"I want to believe that." Judith smiled, a wistful curve of her lips. "I would like to believe in fairy tales that have happy endings."

"Well, I do believe in happy endings. And I believe you can do anything you set your heart on doing."

"I've been told it's quite common for a woman to invite a gentleman to dinner here. Do you think it would be terribly forward to invite Bram Duggan to dinner some night when he returns?"

"I think it would be a wonderful idea." Kate only prayed he would return. She prayed Van Horne would not destroy him, and the man she loved like a brother, her husband's twin.

Chapter Fifteen

Bram Duggan leaned his shoulder against the last stall in the Van Horne stable, resting his pitchfork against his chest. It had taken most of the morning, but each stall in the stable was finally clean and filled with fresh straw.

Dust coated his tongue. Bits of straw stuck to his bare chest, his back, his arms, scratching his skin. The cream Dr. Chamberlain had given him had healed the blisters, yet his tender palms tingled. Still, the work had been worth it.

He stared at the dust floating in the sunlight streaming through the upper door of the stall. There was nothing he wanted more than to step into a shower and stand there for a month, hot water spilling over his skin, but the closest he was going to get to a decent bath was a dented tin tub in the quarters above the stables. Right now, even that sounded inviting.

He stiffened as he heard someone approach, a steady tap on the brick-lined floor leading from the alley. It couldn't be Clarissa, he assured himself. He had gone to a great deal of trouble to make sure he wouldn't have to spend time with the woman this morning. Still, they were a woman's footsteps.

"I don't like to be kept waiting, Duggan."

Duggan clenched his teeth at the sound of Clarissa Van Horne's voice. The woman had been nipping at his heels for days. He took a deep breath, gathering the few remaining scraps of his control before he turned to face her. It wouldn't do to strangle the woman, no matter how much he wanted to.

Clarissa stood at the intersection of the main corridor and the long passageway that housed the horses, staring at him. Through the veil of her tall cinnamon-colored hat, he saw her blue eyes grow wide as she scanned the breadth of his shoulders, the width of his chest.

Great Alexis! The woman was looking at him as though she were about to have him for breakfast. Apparently no one ever told her how much trouble a look like that could buy her. "You wanted something, Miss Van Horne?"

Clarissa lifted her chin. "I thought I told you I wanted to go riding this morning?"

Bram felt his stomach cinch at the thought of climbing into a saddle. "I thought Henry was going to accompany you, miss." He had cleaned the stable in exchange for the duty of escorting Clarissa, an exchange Henry had been happy to make.

"That boy is hardly a suitable chaperon. You have precisely fifteen minutes to make yourself presentable. Fanny and Louisa are waiting for me."

Duggan clenched the pitchfork, staring at her back as she sauntered from the stable, swinging her hips like a mare tempting a stallion. What precisely did the woman want? A tumble in the hay? More than likely she wanted nothing more than to dangle his heart from a chain around her dainty little neck.

He was beginning to understand why people in this Outworld committed murder.

Sarah didn't know what to think. Although she had spent every day of the past few days with Austin Sinclair, she hadn't expected him to come with her to this place. After all, what interest could he possibly have in an orphanage? She came to play with the children, to read to them, to enjoy a few hours of what might have been if her life had taken a different path. Why had Austin Sinclair come?

Still, there he sat, in the spacious drawing room of the Tremayne Orphanage on Madison Square, surrounded by 16 children whose ages ranged from four to ten. He looked comfortable with these children, telling them stories as though he actually enjoyed being with them.

Dora Newton and the other two ladies who worked at the orphanage, all of them well past 40, were staring at Austin as though he were the first man they had ever seen. Still, Sarah understood their infatuation. The man commanded attention.

Sarah sat on a sofa near the back of the room beside Sabrina Tremayne, wife of the founder of the orphanage. Austin sat in a wing-back chair of burgundy velvet, a small dark-haired girl perched on his lap. In front of him, the other children sat in a semicircle, their little faces turned up as Austin wove a spell around them.

Sunlight streamed through the tall mullioned windows behind Austin, shimmering around him, creating a magical space, a place where words were spun into dreams.

"I was thirteen when I met him," Austin said. "In the

woods near my father's country house in Cornwall. I didn't see him at first, but heard him calling: 'Hey, laddy. Laddy, will ye give a poor man some help?' Well, I looked up and there he was, no bigger than you."

Austin tickled the ribs of a little boy sitting at his feet. The boy giggled and playfully slapped at Austin's big hand. "He had a long white beard and rosy cheeks, and a smile that made me wonder what bit of mischief he was planning. 'Come closer, laddy,' he said to me, 'Can you figure how to help me down?' "

Austin had removed his coat and cravat and opened the first few buttons of his white linen shirt, revealing a triangle of dark curls. How intensely masculine he looked, this tall, broad-shouldered man. His strength and power were magnified by the children, his gentleness mirrored in every touch of his hand, every smile.

"To tell you the truth, I had some trouble figuring out how that little man got up the tree." Austin smiled as he looked from one little face to the next. "The lowest bough was far above my head, and I knew it had to be twice as far for him. So I asked him how he got up and he said, 'Now, laddy, I'm not askin fer yer help in gettin' up, but in gettin' down.' "

Sarah looked around at the smiling little faces and noticed the way Austin's deep, vibrant voice was drawing them into the story, enchanting them, enchanting her. He had a certain way about him, she had to admit. He could charm a miser out of his gold. And a woman? She suspected the man could charm a woman out of everything she possessed.

"When I had him safely on the ground he looked up at me, smiled that mischievous smile, and said: 'I'm grateful to ye laddy, and to show it, I'll be givin' ye three wishes.' " Austin looked around the group who seemed intent on his every word.

"Now, I was a small boy. Much smaller than the other boys my age, and I always fell prey to their mischief. The first thing I asked the little man was to be tall. He told me to close my eyes and count to three. So I closed my eyes, counted to three, and when I opened them . . ." Austin paused, causing the children gathered around his feet to draw closer.

"What happened?" a chorus of little voices asked.

"Nothing happened. The little man was gone, I was alone, and just as short as ever."

"But you're tall," the little dark-haired girl on Austin's lap insisted.

Austin nodded. "When I awoke the next morning, I was taller than any of the boys in the village. And they never gave me any trouble again."

"What did you get with your other wishes?" a little boy asked, his brown eyes wide as he stared up at Austin.

Austin turned his head and smiled at Sarah. She felt the shock of meeting those silvery blue eyes all the way down to her toes. Hopelessly caught in his web, she couldn't look away.

"I wished to meet the most beautiful woman in the world," Austin said.

Sarah felt her blush rise like a tide of fire from her waist to the roots of her hair. Images collected in her mind, memories yet to be made. She saw Austin holding a dark-haired boy on his lap, saw a fair-haired girl sitting at his feet, listening as their father spun stories. An ache throbbed inside her, a jagged wound of longing she tried desperately to ignore. It would be beyond foolishness to believe Austin Sinclair would ever want a future with her.

"And did you meet her?" a little boy asked.

"Oh, yes," Austin said.

"What was the third wish?" a girl asked.

"Ah." Austin smiled, pure mischief curving his lips as he looked at Sarah. "That one I have yet to make."

Emotions crowded Sarah's chest, pressing against her heart. Heaven help her, but she knew what her wish would be.

"Tell us another story." The plea started with one little boy and spread until the children were singing a chorus for Austin.

"Let's take a walk," Sabrina whispered as Austin surrendered to the children's demands.

Sarah followed Sabrina through the open French doors near one end of the room onto a wide stone terrace. Elm and oak trees stood tall near the terrace, shading the house with long branches. Four crescents of rose bushes fanned out from a gravel path that led from the terrace to the wide lawn. Three stone walls marched along the perimeter of the lawn, enclosing the property. Here the noise of carriage wheels on granite was a distant rattle lost in the rustle of leaves and the song of birds.

"Why didn't you tell me you were being courted by such an eligible young man?" After 20 years in New York, Sabrina's southern drawl still whispered of her Mississippi home.

Sarah glanced to the tall, slender woman walking beside her on the gravel path, Sabrina's mint green silk gown brushing the roses that were just awakening in the warmth of the sun. Although Sabrina was 16 years her senior, she was one of Sarah's dearest friends. "He isn't courting me."

"It certainly appears as though he's courting you." Age had not faded Sabrina's beauty. The glossy dark red curls piled on top of her head were untouched by silver, her face smooth and unlined. "And I must say, I couldn't have chosen better for you if I'd tried. And if I recall, I've tried many times."

Sarah felt her face grow warm as she recalled Sabrina's many attempts at matchmaking. An invitation to dine at the Tremayne house often turned into an attempt to pair Sarah with a gentleman Sabrina thought ideal for her.

When in those situations, Sarah never knew what to say to the gentleman, and so she said too little or too much about the wrong subject. Dull and unattractive, that was the impression she knew she made. She was certain her reputation must have spread through the male population of the city by now. Yet it was amazing how Sabrina could still manage to trick unsuspecting gentlemen into meeting one awkward old maid.

"Why, the man is nearly as handsome as my Ian," Sabrina said. "And he certainly gets along well with children. That's important."

Sabrina was one of the few women Sarah knew who openly adored her husband and their three children. But then, Ian was special. Like many girls, Sarah had experienced a youthful infatuation for the handsome Ian Tremayne. He was still one of the most attractive men she had ever met. "We're friends, nothing more."

"Is that because you're afraid to let him become more than a friend?"

"I'm not afraid."

"Then you must be blind. Because I'm here to tell you, that man is interested in you."

Something fluttered in Sarah's chest, something dangerous—hope. "I'm afraid you are seeing only what you want to see."

Sarah sank to the edge of a stone bench nestled in the shade of an elm tree. She smoothed her gray poplin gown, sliding her hand over her knee, keeping her eyes averted from Sabrina as she sat beside her.

She didn't want her friend to see the hope in her eyes, the hope she didn't seem to be able to bury.

"Sarah, you're a lovely young woman. You're gentle and intelligent. There is every reason for that young man to be interested in you."

Sarah shook her head. Laughter rippled from the house, the sweet innocent laughter of children. She thought of the man who had tickled that laughter from children who had known so little joy in their young lives. He was special. He made her feel special. But she knew that feeling was dangerous.

"My husband was raised in this beautiful house, surrounded by wealth and privilege."

The bitterness in Sabrina's voice surprised Sarah. She glanced up to find Sabrina staring at the huge four-story stone house as though it were an enemy.

"Ian's mother died when he was five. He was raised by his father, a man who never showed him a shred of affection. In a sense it was worse than being an orphan. Being raised without love, that can do things to a person, twist one's sense of self-worth, turn one bitter. And it can be hard for anyone who falls in love with someone like that." Sabrina looked at Sarah, her dark brown eyes glittering with unshed tears. "Sarah, you've never realized how very special you are. Your father and stepmother have never let you."

"Sabrina, you don't understand." Sarah glanced at the French doors leading to the drawing room and Austin Sinclair. Burgundy velvet drapes fluttered in the breeze sweeping through the doors. "My father had reasons for not caring for me. And Roxanne has done her best to protect me."

"Beeswax! Your father had no right to hold anything against you or your brother. And that woman he married has done her best to keep you from shining."

Sarah shook her head, but for the first time in years she wondered if there might be some truth in her friend's words.

A man emerged from the house, striding through the open door of the drawing room, a man with hair that glistened like polished ebony in the sunlight. Ian waved when he saw Sabrina and Sarah, moving toward them in long, loose-limbed strides. His smile reminded Sarah exactly why she had thought, at the tender age of 16, that this man was the most handsome she had ever seen.

"Ian!" Sabrina rose to her feet. She looked every bit a young girl greeting her first love as she ran to meet her husband.

"Hello, brat," Ian said, taking his wife in his arms. He kissed her, a quick slide of his lips over hers while he pulled her against his long, lean frame.

There was no shame in that kiss, in the blatant show of affection between these two; as long as Sarah had known them, there never had been.

What would it be like to run into a pair of strong, welcoming arms? What would it be like to feel that free?

Sarah leaned back against the bench, her chest suddenly tight with longing. It was foolish to long for dreams that had long ago turned to dust. There were some things in this world she would never experience, no matter how much she wished for them.

After Sarah and Austin left, Sabrina sat beside her husband in the garden of the orphanage, her head resting against his shoulder, his arm snug around her back. The scent of roses curled around them, carried by the warm afternoon breeze. "What do you think of Austin?"

"Is this the same Lord Austin Sinclair that Rachel

has been chattering about for days, ever since we got back from Isabel Bennett's party?"

"From what I gather, most of the women in this city are chattering about that man. You can't expect an impressionable sixteen-year-old like our daughter to be the exception. I'm sure she'll have more than a few infatuations before she finds the right man."

He slid his warm palm down her arm. "And how many infatuations did you have before you met the right man?"

"One." She looked up into eyes the pale green of fresh spring leaves, eyes that had haunted her from the time she was a child. "And I married him."

"A woman of refined taste." He kissed the tip of her nose.

"So tell me, do you like him?"

The breeze tossed a lock of his hair over his brow, threads of silver streaking the thick black mane that tumbled over his collar in unruly waves. "He seems nice enough."

Sabrina captured a shiny lock of his hair, lifting the ebony strands away from his neck. "I think Sarah is falling in love with him," she said, sliding the dark silk between her fingers.

"I got that impression." He glanced down, thick black lashes tangling at the corners of his eyes. "You know I think very highly of Sarah."

Sabrina felt the questions rising in him, the same doubts she couldn't quite purge from her mind. "But you aren't certain why a man like Austin Sinclair would take an interest in her."

"What do we know about him?"

"His father is a duke."

"So he says." He smiled as he looked at her. "I once knew a lady who claimed to be an English countess."

"Watch where you're stepping, yankee," she said, tugging on his hair.

"Or a beautiful rebel just might trip me?"

"She might." Sabrina traced the curve of his lips with her fingertip, remembering a time when they were enemies instead of lovers. "Do you think he's a poor aristocrat looking to replenish the family fortune?"

"If he is, he could find a fatter purse elsewhere."

Sabrina nodded. "I've always thought the right man could see in Sarah the special lady hiding beneath all her doubts and fears. Perhaps Austin Sinclair is that man."

"Perhaps." He caught her hand, pressing her palm against his cheek. "Did you think it was strange that Sarah was so interested in positions I might have available in one of our companies?"

"She must know someone who needs work." Ian turned his face, pressing his lips to the palm of her hand, dragging a sigh from her lips. "Will you promise to do more of that if I take you home with me, yankee?"

Ian smiled against her palm. "I promise to do anything you want, brat, for as long as you want."

Elm trees lined both sides of Fifth Avenue, casting spidery patterns of shadow on the granite blocks paving the street. Austin held the leather ribbons in his hands, allowing the pair of bays to amble toward Sarah's house, their shoes a steady clop on the stone.

For a few minutes today he had allowed himself to forget his true purpose for coming here. And now he found there was no hurry, no rush to plunge back into the reality he knew he couldn't escape.

"You were very good with the children."

Austin glanced at the woman sitting beside him on

the black leather seat. Sarah was smiling at him, a shy curve of her lips that was both tentative and inviting. "You sound surprised."

"I am." She glanced away from him, lowering her chin, the single ostrich tip adorning the crown of her gray straw hat bobbing in the breeze. "I didn't expect you to enjoy a trip to an orphanage, and yet you looked as though you were happy being with those children."

"My brother was raised in an orphanage. I like to imagine that someone once told him stories."

She looked at him, her eyes wide with surprise. "Why was your brother raised in an orphanage?"

"He was kidnapped when we were two, by my mother's sister. She had lost her son in childbirth and thought to take my brother in his place. She was ill from the difficult birth, and the travel was too much for her. We later discovered she died shortly after arriving in New Orleans, and my brother was placed in an orphanage. We didn't find him until quite recently."

"Your parents must have been devastated. Every day, wondering where he was, how he was. I can only imagine how horrible that must have been."

"It doesn't go away, the worry, the wondering. Every day it's there, as though a part of you were lost. In some ways it's worse than losing a loved one to death." Austin stared at the pair of bays, their long black manes fluttering with the breeze. "I remember thinking, as a boy, that I had to be extra good to make up for the fact that my brother was gone."

"And were you?"

"I tried not to disappoint my parents. I like to think I haven't." He smiled as he looked at her. "They are fine people."

"You said you and your brother were both two when he was kidnapped. I assume he is your twin?"

"Identical, except, of course, he was raised in America. It makes for some startling differences in us."

"I'm certain it does." She fingered the top button of her gown, sliding it through the gray poplin, unfastening it, closing it, before sliding it open once more. "Is he also in financial difficulty?"

"No." Austin stared at the soft hollow at the base of her neck, pale skin revealed by a single open button. "Devlin is doing well. In fact he recently married."

"Ian Tremayne is a very successful businessman." She fastened the button, staring at his shoulder as though she couldn't quite meet his eyes. "He owns a shipping company, a bank, railroads. I'm not certain of everything."

Austin watched the slow slide of her slender fingers against gray poplin, that top button coming undone, unraveling his control.

"I asked him if he might need someone, a manager of some type. And he said it would depend on the man."

He drew a deep breath, catching a whisper of lavender warmed by her skin. Over the low humming in his head, the rush of blood that shouldn't be happening, he heard her voice, tried to follow the meaning of her words.

"Do you think you would be interested?"

He was interested, far too interested. "In a job with Mr. Tremayne?"

She nodded. "I didn't mention your name, of course. But I think it might be something you could try."

He pulled up in front of her house, beneath the elm growing beside the street. "Is this your way of trying to reform me?"

She smiled. "Yes, I suppose it is."

She wanted to find him a job, help him out of his difficulties—difficulties that didn't exist. She touched him with her generosity, shamed him for his lies. He felt that shame burning like a brand in his chest.

He climbed down and walked around to her side. She placed her hands on his shoulders, allowing him to lift her from the carriage. She was light, fragile in his grasp. Without thought he held her close, needing to feel her warmth against him. Why was it so familiar with her, as though he had held her a thousand times, and yet never held her at all?

He lowered his gaze to the base of her neck, the sweet hollow laid bare by her nervous fingers, tempting, inviting his lips. When had a glimpse of a lady's neck rendered him intoxicated? It seemed a long time, a lifetime.

He felt her breath warm against his cheek, a startled sigh that brought his gaze back to her face. Holding her like this, he felt the tremor that shook her, a trembling desire that rippled from her into him.

Beneath him the ground shifted, granite splitting, leaving him standing on the verge of a chasm. One wrong move and he would fall headlong into disaster. He looked at her parted lips, craving the taste, the feel of those lips beneath his.

Slowly he set her on the sidewalk and eased away his hands. Carefully, he stepped back away from her, searching for safe footing. They stood on opposite sides, a jagged crevice between them. He knew he could bridge that gap. And yet he knew he must not.

She glanced away from him, staring at the polished brass hitching post fashioned in the head of a horse, a shiny brass ring dangling from its mouth. "Will you think about talking to Ian Tremayne?"

Austin swallowed hard before he could use his voice,

before he could speak another lie. "I'll think about it, Sarah."

He turned as she passed him, his gaze drawn to her. He watched as she climbed the steps of her brother's house and disappeared from sight. Yet she remained with him, in a place deep inside, and he knew she would always remain there long after he had walked out of her life.

Chapter Sixteen

Early morning sunlight, muted by lace curtains, tumbled across the piano in Isabel Bennett's music room, etching tangled patterns of roses on the polished satinwood. Austin sat at the piano, smooth keys of black and white rippling beneath his fingers. The melody flowed from deep inside him, from a place he had never questioned, a deep well where emotions transformed into music, and music released his soul.

He closed his eyes. There was no need to see the keys. He could feel them. Just as he could feel the deep, bitter ache that vibrated through his body.

In his mind he saw Sarah's face smiling at him, the innocence of her honest gaze piercing him like hot steel. The music deepened with his guilt, dark notes striking the rosewood wainscoting that lined the walls.

Sarah. He was drawn to her in a way he had never been drawn to a woman before. She touched him deep inside. She triggered the music that flowed through him and filled the sunlit room with the darkness of his own foreboding. He shouldn't feel this way about her. And yet he had learned long ago that destiny would not be denied.

He sensed the moment Isabel entered the room. Without a glance in her direction he altered the pattern of his play, shifting from his own dark music to the bright notes of Chopin, hoping to disguise the turmoil he felt deep inside.

Isabel sat beside him on the bench seat, the fragrance of lavender settling around him like mist, reminding him of Sarah in the moonlight. "You play with great feeling."

Austin managed to tilt his lips into a smile, one he hoped would lighten the mood that lingered in the room like a ghost of the music he had played for Sarah. "I suspect that's a polite way of saying I don't always stick to the proper notes."

"What was that you were playing when I came in? It sounded as though the angels were crying."

"Nothing, really."

"I see."

Austin stared down at his hands, following each stroke of the keys. From the corner of his eye he could see Isabel watching him, and he realized she saw far more than he wanted to reveal.

"It seems all is going well with Sarah," Isabel said.

"I suppose so." Austin stared down at his hands, watching his fingers manipulate the keys. "I think she trusts me. I should soon be able to convince her to show me the medallion."

In truth, he could have had the medallion days ago. Yet he delayed. And with every passing day he risked his mission, risked a great deal more, all because of his selfishness, his need to steal a few precious moments with a woman he could never have. He was losing sight of his purpose, blinded by a lady he must one day betray.

"You have a visitor. A rather surprising visitor."

Austin paused, his fingers growing still against the keys. He studied Isabel's face a moment before he replied, "Where is she?"

Isabel lifted her delicate white brows. "My dear young man, you truly are your father's son."

Austin paused on the threshold of Isabel's blue drawing room. Sarah's mother stood in front of the windows staring out at the street as though she were waiting for someone to return, someone she feared was lost forever.

The newly awakened rays of the sun streamed through the open windows, stroking her hair, which was a shade darker than Sarah's. Icy blue brocade drapes framed her; sunlight painted her profile in gold: portrait of a tormented soul.

He entered the room, the thick carpet of blue and gold wool cushioning footsteps that would have been silent even on gravel. "Mrs. Schuyler."

She turned, a look of uncertainty flickering in her eyes before she moved toward him, meeting him in the center of the room. He took her hand in greeting, feeling the dampness of her palm.

"Lord Sinclair, thank you for seeing me."

"It is a pleasure to meet you."

She moistened her lips, glancing down for a moment before meeting his gaze with a clear honesty in hazel eyes that reminded him vividly of Sarah. "I suppose you're wondering why I would come to see you."

"I've been seeing your daughter." He took her arm and led her to one of the two Empire sofas that flanked the white marble hearth. "It's only natural for a mother to wonder about me."

She sat on the edge of the sofa, the jade green linen of her gown spilling across the icy blue brocade upholstery. She stared down at the white cotton gloves she clutched in her hands. "There are those who believe there is nothing natural about me."

Austin touched her arm, smiling when she looked up at him. "Perhaps those are people who don't know you."

"I love my daughter, Lord Sinclair. I know that might be difficult to believe, considering the circumstances."

"I'm not sure I'm the one who truly needs to believe you care."

"I've tried to let her know. For the first twelve years I wrote to her every week of every year after I left her father. I'm not certain she ever saw the letters; her father no doubt destroyed them. You see, Carelton refused to let me see my children after I left him. He swore he would have me arrested if I tried to see them." Diana stared past Austin to the windows, sunlight reflecting against the unshed tears in her eyes. "I tried to contact Sarah after Carelton died, but she returned my letters unopened. I'm afraid she refuses to see me."

"And you hope I might be able to persuade her?"

Diana shook her head. "I would not put any demands on you, Lord Sinclair. I came only because you are the first man my Sarah has ever seemed to care about, and I wanted to know . . ." She glanced down at her tortured gloves. "There is no one else who will ask your intentions. No one except perhaps Leighton who would care. And I'm afraid my son is too wrapped up in his own pursuits to notice what is happening in Sarah's life."

Austin felt the muscles in his neck stiffen, a response to hearing Leighton's name, a confirmation of how hopeless his feelings for Sarah were. And here was this wounded lady, asking him if his intentions were honorable.

Diana looked at him with Sarah's eyes. The distant rumble of carriage wheels on granite filtered through the open windows. The clock on the mantel clicked away the seconds as she looked deeply into his eyes and tried to see his soul. "You could hurt her so easily."

He knew it was true. Dear lord, how well he knew the pain he would cause Sarah. "I don't want to hurt her."

Diana held his gaze. "But you might, is that your thinking?"

"Can any of us guarantee we will never cause hurt to one we care about?"

"Do you care about her?"

Austin glanced away from the honesty in her eyes, staring at the rosewood clock sitting on the mantel. The crystal covering the face reflected the rays of the sun that slanted through the lace curtains, obscuring the gold hands beneath. Still, he knew Sarah would be expecting him soon. "Yes, I care very much."

"I believe you." She was smiling when he looked at her. "I like you, Lord Sinclair. I think you might be very good for my Sarah."

Austin felt a tightening in his chest, a twist of emotion around his heart. In another time and place, he would have given Sarah everything in his power. Yet in this time and place, he was powerless to protect her.

Still, there might be something he could do, some small good that he might be able to leave behind. It would be a risk, a gamble that could break the tenuous bond of friendship he had forged with Sarah, but a risk he knew he must take.

It was true. Sarah turned to the side, eyeing her reflection in the cheval mirror that stood in one corner of her bedroom. It was just as Austin Sinclair had said; she had nothing in her wardrobe except the dullest colors: gray and brown. Even the blue and green gowns she owned were merely shades of gray or brown with a subtle hint of color. Plain. Unappealing.

The morning sunlight flowing through the open windows behind her could not brighten the blue-gray linen of her dress. The lines were simple. No bows. No lace. No style. A gown no one would notice. And lately she had come to realize there was at least one person she wanted to notice her. She only hoped she wasn't reaching for a star.

She lifted a collar and jabot of fine turquoise tulle to her chin, wondering if she dared wear it. It was a silly thing to buy, she thought, fluffing the double bands of lacy tulle that tumbled to her waist. Yet when she had noticed it in the window of Stewart's yesterday, she had not been able to resist.

"What do you think, Merlin?" Sarah turned to show the plump cat how the lace transformed the gown. "Do you think the color really does bring out the blue in my eyes?"

The big cat made a noise deep in his throat, a rusty growl that Sarah decided to take as a compliment. "Well, thank you, sir." Smiling, she slipped the collar around the high neckline of the dress and tied the satin bow beneath her chin.

Strange how that little scrap of lace could make her feel pretty, she thought, smoothing the jabot over the buttons lining the front of her gown. But she knew it was more than the lace. Austin Sinclair made her feel pretty.

He made her feel alive. He made her laugh. And he made her realize just how very much she had been missing before he walked into her life. She glanced at her reflection, noting the blush that had crept into her cheeks. Foolish old maid.

After knocking and receiving an invitation from Sarah, Emerson entered the room. "Lord Sinclair to see you, miss."

Sarah felt a flutter in her chest, that odd movement her heart made at the mere mention of Austin Sinclair's name. "Tell him I'll be there directly."

Emerson nodded, a smile barely lifting the corners of his lips. "And, might I say, you are looking very lovely this morning, miss."

"Thank you, Emerson."

The butler bowed and stepped back, nearly colliding with Clarissa.

"Mind your step!" Clarissa shouted, casting Emerson a dark look.

"My apologies, miss." Emerson glanced to Sarah, a look of concern in his dark eyes, before he left the sisters alone.

Sarah's stomach coiled into a tight knot of apprehension as she watched her sister move toward her. They had scarcely spoken in days.

Clarissa frowned as she stared at her sister, lines creasing the delicate skin of her brow. "Sarah, what *are* you wearing?"

Sarah glanced in the mirror, suddenly self-conscious of the colorful lace that splashed across the drab linen of her gown. Clarissa paused beside her, looking at their images trapped in the silvered glass.

Fresh as a spring flower, that was Clarissa, the yellow curls piled on top of her head filled with delicate silk lily of the valley, her gown of cinnamon silk dripping with white embroidered lace. Beside her, Sarah felt as attractive as a bundle of daisies left too long in the sun.

"Where on earth did you get that awful collar?"

Sarah pressed her hand over the lace at the base of her neck. "You don't like it?"

Clarissa lifted one finely arched brow. "You look like an old maid trying desperately to recapture her youth."

The heat of her blush crept upward from Sarah's lace collar, setting her cheeks on fire. She turned away from the mirror. "Was there something you wanted?"

"Yes. I want to save you from making a complete fool of yourself."

Sarah lifted her gray cotton gloves from the bureau and turned to face her sister. "And how am I in danger of making a fool of myself?"

"By throwing yourself at Lord Sinclair."

"I appreciate your concern, but I assure you I am not throwing myself at anyone. Now, if you'll excuse me, Lord Sinclair is waiting." She hurried out of the room, needing to get out of this house, away from a sister she wasn't sure she recognized any longer.

Was she truly making a fool of herself? Perhaps she should stop seeing Austin. Yet she couldn't deny herself his company. These few days with him were the closest she might ever come to happiness. Memories were all that she would have once he left the city, and she wanted to collect those memories like roses pressed for remembrance.

Clarissa followed her to the stairs. "The whole city is talking about you."

Sarah hesitated, turning on the top step to face her sister. "And what are they saying?"

Clarissa flexed her hand on the carved newel post, reminding Sarah of a cat flexing her claws. "They are saying the only reason Lord Sinclair is paying so much attention to you is because he thinks he can seduce you."

"Lord Sinclair has been a complete gentleman!"

Clarissa smiled. "Like mother, like daughter."

The words slapped Sarah more sharply than a physical blow. She clenched her hands at her sides. "That is a very cruel thing to say."

Clarissa lifted her chin. "Why else would he want to see you instead of me?"

"Jealousy doesn't suit you, Clarissa."

Clarissa's eyes widened. "Jealousy! How dare you imagine I would be jealous of you?"

"Clarissa, you're beautiful, young, full of promise." Sarah drew a breath past the emotion crowding her throat. "You have no reason to be jealous of me."

"Jealous? That's ridiculous. Jealous of you, a plain old spinster! I've never heard of anything more absurd."

Sarah closed her eyes, blocking out the hatred in her sister's face. Sadness and pain, she was accustomed to these emotions, but they never failed to pierce her. She turned on the step, needing to escape.

"Horrid witch!"

Clarissa's voice was no more than an angry hiss as Sarah felt a hard hand on her shoulder. It was enough, that push, to knock her off balance. A bolt of disbelief shot through Sarah's mind. Yet the truth was there in the stairs rushing to meet her—Clarissa had pushed her, sent her on this punishing fall.

"Sarah!" Austin shouted.

He was running across the hall, rushing toward the stairs. Had he seen? Did he know what Clarissa had done?

Thoughts evaporated with the first jolt of pain as Sarah's shoulder hit the stairs. Out of control she plummeted, her gown twisting around her legs, her body tumbling, bouncing down the long curving staircase.

Squares of black and white marble ended her fall. Pain, white and jagged, burned her like flame. She lay on her back, her left arm twisted beneath her in a place where the pain ran thick and hard, pulsating like tongues of fire. Dimly she wondered if she might die.

"Sarah." Austin's voice reached her before she felt the touch of his hands.

Austin's fingers drifted over her cheek, her hair, her neck. Gentle hands, touching her shoulders, her back, slipping beneath her. A low moan—a pitiful sound—filled her ears as he lifted her. And then she realized it had been her voice, that sad sound of agony.

"Is she all right, sir?" Emerson asked, his voice strangled with emotion.

"Emerson, I want you to send for Dr. Gareth Chamberlain." Austin stroked Sarah's cheek, gentle fingers sliding over her skin. "His home is at Number Seven North Washington Square."

"Yes, sir."

Sarah opened her eyes. Austin was there above her, holding her, his eyes filled with fear and anger and a fierce determination. "But my doctor is—"

Austin pressed his fingertip to her chin, below her lips. "Trust me, Sarah. He's an excellent doctor."

Sarah moistened her lips. "All right."

Austin rested her left arm across her waist. The pain! It scraped like broken glass along her nerves. She couldn't stop the moan slipping from her lips.

"Easy, sweetheart," Austin whispered, stroking her temple with his fingers.

The warmth of his skin seeped inside her, tumbling in a glistening waterfall of silvery blue light that flowed through her body. The pain faded beneath that light like flames dying in a warm summer rain.

"What happened here?" Roxanne demanded. "Sarah, what have you done?"

Roxanne stood beside Austin, staring down at her as though Sarah had just broken Roxanne's favorite porcelain figurine. But that had happened years ago, and it had been Clarissa who had broken the figurine, even though she had pointed the blame at Sarah. Roxanne had never believed Sarah's protestations of innocence.

In her mind Sarah could see that delicate piece of porcelain, a lady in a full skirt holding the hand of a little girl. She had loved it as much as Roxanne had. "I didn't break it," she whispered.

Clarissa loomed above Austin, standing there on the bottom step. "It was an accident!"

Austin glanced up at Clarissa, and Sarah could see the truth in his eyes, the honest rage at what her sister had done.

"Accident," Sarah whispered. She refused to believe Clarissa had meant to do this horrible thing. "It was . . . an accident."

Austin stared down at her, his jaw tightly clenched.

"Please," Sarah whispered, gripping his arm. She had to make him realize how devastating the truth would be for Clarissa.

Chapter Seventeen

"Don't worry, Sarah." Austin stroked Sarah's cheek with his open palm. Since Roxanne had ceased welcoming him when he came to see her stepdaughter, Austin had been waiting for Sarah in the hall with Emerson. He had heard the sisters, Clarissa's cruel tone carrying in the large entry hall. He had seen the anger in Clarissa's face, watched as that anger lashed out at Sarah, and he had been helpless to save her.

He stood, lifting Sarah in his arms, careful to avoid jarring her broken arm. Was that her most serious injury? "Where is her room?"

"I'll show you," Clarissa said.

Sarah's hair had come undone, the thick golden brown waves spilling over his arm, swaying against his leg as Austin climbed the stairs with Sarah cradled in his arms. He followed Clarissa to Sarah's room. Roxanne marched beside her daughter, stiff and angry, as though Sarah had tumbled down the stairs to spite her.

Sunlight flooded Sarah's bedroom, streaking across the intricate flowers stitched in shades of peach and gold and white in the Aubusson carpet. Her bed stood near the far wall, four posts of delicately carved rosewood lifting a canopy of peach silk brocade. He laid Sarah on the peach silk counterpane, cringing inwardly when a soft moan escaped her lips.

"We were just talking at the top of the stairs. I suppose I must have bumped her." Clarissa stood by the bed, staring down at her sister. "Isn't that right, Sarah?"

"It was an accident, Clarissa," Sarah whispered. "It will be all right."

"Why, of course it was an accident," Roxanne said. "How could anyone believe otherwise?"

Austin didn't spare the woman standing beside him a glance. He placed his hand on Sarah's left arm, feeling the break, the heat of her pain. He couldn't afford to allow anyone to notice her arm was broken.

"Clarissa, dear, you must be terribly shaken over this," Roxanne said.

Austin clenched his jaw as he glanced at the woman and her spawn. "I'll stay with Sarah while you wait for the doctor downstairs."

Roxanne nodded, leaving the room with her arm around Clarissa's shoulders. A cat had more concern for her kitten than that woman had for Sarah.

As if to prove his silent admonition correct, Merlin pounced on the foot of the bed and sauntered across the peach silk. He rubbed his head against Sarah's shoulder before flopping to his side on one of the pillows beside her, where he filled the air with his deep-throated purr.

"Don't think badly of her," Sarah said, her voice scraped raw by pain. "She didn't mean to hurt me."

"She pushed you down a flight of stairs."

"She did it without thinking." Sarah held him in her steady, clear gaze. "Please, let it remain an accident."

"What if she tries to hurt you again?"

"She won't."

"For you, Sarah." Austin cupped her cheek in his hand, her skin smooth and warm against his skin. "Only for you will I protect that spoiled little girl."

Sarah smiled. "Thank you."

He smoothed her hair against the peach silk covering her pillow. She would protect her family, even after they had hurt her in ways both seen and unseen. What would she do to protect a brother she adored? Austin wouldn't think of that now. He couldn't.

He pressed his fingertips against her temple, finding the pressure point, trying to ease her pain.

"You have such a gentle touch," she whispered. "I can almost believe you have some kind of magic in you."

Magic. He only wished he possessed the magic to heal the wounds he knew he would one day inflict on this beguiling woman.

"Do you think my collar looks silly?"

For the first time Austin noticed the collar and jabot of turquoise lace, a splash of color against her dull gown. Without being told, he knew she had worn it for him, one tiny crack in her cocoon, one more lash of guilt. "No, I don't think it looks silly."

"I'm glad."

"One day I would like to see you in a gown of this color." He rubbed her temple. "A gown of turquoise silk that would bare your soft shoulders and hug your tiny waist."

She smiled, a soft pink blush rising to stain her pale cheeks. "Sounds wicked."

"Sounds beautiful."

Austin glanced over his shoulder as the door opened and a short woman came rushing into the room in a tide of gray linen. She must have been all of five feet one, and just as round as she was tall.

"What's happened to my lamb?" she asked, pausing beside Austin, breathing like a draft horse after hauling a heavy load.

"It was an accident, Matilda," Sarah said, smiling up at the old woman. "I tripped on the stairs."

"That's not how Emerson saw it." Matilda pursed her lips as she turned her gaze to Austin, staring at him with dark brown eyes in a way that let him know she wasn't at all certain she liked what she saw. "You're a the English lord that has the little tyrant so jealous she's pushing my Sarah down the stairs."

He kept one hand over Sarah's broken arm. "Are you going to condemn me for having the good sense to prefer spending time with Miss Sarah instead of her sister?"

The lines in her face softened, her expression transforming from a frown to a smile as she studied him. "You're a handsome lad, I'll give you that. And seeing you prefer my Sarah over the little tyrant, you can't be all bad."

"Thank you," Austin said.

"If you're smart you'll be marrying the girl."

Sarah flinched at Matilda's words. "Matilda!"

"Well, I'm only speaking the truth. You'd make him a fine wife."

A groan escaped Sarah's lips, a frustrated growl of humiliation.

"Relax, sweet Sarah." Austin couldn't resist touching her cheek, feeling the heat of her blush beneath his fingers. "The lady hasn't said anything I don't already know."

Sarah stared up at him, her beautiful eyes filled with pain and questions, questions he had been asking himself for days. And still, he was no closer to finding the answers.

The distant rattle of carriage wheels drifted with a warm breeze through the open windows of Sarah's sitting room. Instead of the garden, Sarah had a view of the street from her bedroom and sitting room.

Austin sat in a wing-back chair near the windows, watching Matilda waddle from one side of the room to the other. Emerson stood beside the door leading to Sarah's bedroom like a cigar-store Indian, his face carved into stern lines, his arms crossed over his narrow chest.

For the past hour Austin had kept a vigil along with Matilda and Emerson while Chamberlain worked on Sarah and worry worked on the three waiting for his word. Were her injuries worse than Austin had suspected?

"Seems to me he's been in there a ripe long time." Matilda turned at the windows and stared at Austin. "He looked pretty young to be knowing what he's doing."

Austin and Gareth had grown up together, attended Cambridge together, before Gareth had returned to finish his medical studies in Avallon. Gareth was a year younger than Austin, but he knew what he was doing far better than any doctor trained outside of Avallon. "He's a fine doctor, don't worry," he said, hoping he sounded more confident than he felt. What was taking so long?

"If anything happens to her . . ." Matilda shook her head. "And where do you suppose the queen and the little princess have gone? Off shopping. Seems Mrs. Van Horne thought Miss Clarissa needed to take her mind off of the nasty little accident."

Emerson made a derisive sound deep in his throat. "It was no accident."

"I knew they were ruining the girl, spoiling Clarissa, as if she were the only child in this house." Matilda pivoted as she reached the far wall, gray linen swaying with her ample hips. "Why, if it weren't for my Sarah, I would have been gone from here long ago, I'll tell you."

Emerson nodded.

Austin came to his feet as the door to Sarah's bedroom opened and Dr. Gareth Chamberlain entered the room. He was tall, slender, with hair that tumbled over his collar in a thick gold-and-brown mane.

Gareth glanced around at the little group, his expression betraying none of his feelings. "She'll be fine. Just a few bumps and bruises. And I've wrapped her wrist, just in case it's sprained."

"Thank heavens!" Matilda shouted.

Gareth smiled. "I've given her something to help her sleep."

"I want to see her." Matilda marched past the doctor into Sarah's room. Emerson hesitated a moment before following her.

"They care a great deal for her." His green eyes were gentle as Gareth spoke, his voice just above a whisper. "And so must you. It was risky asking me to tend her."

"I thought it was more risky to leave her to her own doctor. I knew her arm was broken, but I wasn't certain of her other injuries."

"I've treated the break. It should be completely mended by tomorrow. Her other injuries were minor." Gareth shifted his bag to his left hand. "It would be difficult to explain if anyone else noticed her arm was broken."

"No one noticed." At least Austin dearly hoped no one had noticed. "Thank you for helping her."

Gareth nodded. "I often wish I could help more people. It seems a great waste to keep our medical knowledge so confined."

"There would be too many questions we couldn't answer if medical miracles started to take place. Avallon couldn't survive if the Outworld learned of its existence."

"I understand the need for our rules. I understand we must not become involved. I also understand how difficult that can be. Perhaps that's why physicians don't remain long in the Outworld."

"Do you plan to return soon?"

"I would like nothing more than to marry and return to Avallon, sink into research instead of watching people die when I know I could save them."

"Anyone in mind?"

Gareth shook his head. "I have not yet met my *Edaina.*"

Edaina, soul mate. Had Austin met his *Edaina?* He stood on the threshold of Sarah's room, staring at the woman who lay sleeping on the peach silk counterpane, her hair spread out across the pillow. With the sunlight glimmering around her, Sarah looked unearthly, an angel caught taking a nap. Emerson and Matilda hovered by her side.

"She's lovely," Gareth said.

"Yes, she is." Austin glanced to the man standing beside him. Gareth was staring through the door, gazing in at Sarah, a smile curving his lips.

"She'll sleep most of the day," Gareth said. "I'll look in on her later this evening."

Was the man always so eager to see his patients? Austin wondered. "I'll walk out with you."

* * *

After leaving Sarah, Austin took a long ride along the river. Yet he couldn't escape his doubts. It was dark before he found his way back to Isabel Bennett's house, before he faced the reality that he was falling in love with Sarah Van Horne.

Isabel glanced up from the book she was reading when Austin entered the blue drawing room. "Has something happened? You look dreadful."

Austin sank to the pale blue silk covering the sofa, sitting beside her, feeling heavy, as though he carried a lead weight in the pit of his stomach. "Clarissa pushed Sarah down a flight of stairs this morning."

"Great Alexis! Was she hurt?"

"Her arm was broken." Austin glanced down at the pages of Isabel's book, unable to hold her gaze, knowing what she would see in his eyes. "Gareth Chamberlain took care of her."

"I see." Isabel glanced down to her book as she closed the cover. She slid her fingertip over the gold lettering on the leather-bound cover, tracing the title. "I've always had a weakness for popular fiction. I find Mr. Haggard has a most vivid imagination."

Austin stared at the letters she traced over and over with her fingertip. He felt her disappointment in him, and inside he felt his emotions collide, anger at the rules that bound him, shame for breaking those very rules.

"In this novel the hero is searching for the lost treasure of King Solomon's mines. I wonder what story Mr. Haggard might write should he ever catch wind of the legend of a city hidden in the center of Brazil, a city populated by descendants of Atlantis."

"I know it was risky having Chamberlain tend Sarah." Austin drew a deep breath, trying to ease the tension that pulled his muscles taut, the tension that wrapped around his chest like steel bands.

"You've violated one of our most fundamental rules. By involving Chamberlain, you might have raised suspicions. We cannot afford to have people curious about us."

He had lived by the rules all his life. Duty. Responsibility. He knew these well. He had defined his life by honor. "I didn't know how badly Sarah was hurt. After a fall like that, she might have sustained a concussion, or worse. I couldn't take the chance of something happening to her."

"Are you saying you did this to guard your mission?"

Given the same choice, he knew he would break the rules again for Sarah, only for Sarah. "No."

"You're becoming too involved, Austin." Isabel looked up at him, her dark blue eyes filled with understanding. "I think you should allow someone else to take over your mission."

"It would take too long for anyone to get this close." Austin opened his hands on his thighs. He tried to draw a deep breath, tried to calm the turmoil raging inside him. He wanted to lash out, to crush something with his bare hands. Yet that was not the way of his people. Violence was not tolerated. "I'll get the medallion."

"Soon, I hope."

Austin stared at the lace curtains that fluttered in the breeze sweeping through the open windows. Emotions warred inside him, tearing him in opposite directions: loyalty to his family and responsibility to his people on one side, his love for Sarah on the other.

"Think of the consequences should Van Horne get his hands on the medallion, Austin." Isabel rested her hand on his arm. "Let that be your guide."

"I'll do what is expected of me." As he had done his entire life. And in doing so, in betraying Sarah, he would kill the love he had been looking for all his life.

The windows of Isabel Bennett's house glowed like beacons in the night, leading Leighton Van Horne to his enemy. He stood in the shadows across the street, watching.

Through lace curtains, Leighton could see them, sitting in the drawing room, Austin Sinclair and Isabel Bennett. Plotting against him. Plotting to take away everything he owned. And the man was seeing his sister. For days, Leighton had watched them together.

What was Sinclair after? He sensed there was more, something more than the desire for what those people in Avallon called justice. He would have to find out what Sinclair wanted before he killed him.

Austin moved to the windows, looking out at the street as though he sensed danger. Leighton slipped his hand into his pocket. He curved his fingers around the handle of his pistol. He stood silently, watching Sinclair, wondering if this man from Avallon could penetrate the darkness with his gaze. In time, Sinclair turned away from the window and joined Isabel on one of the sofas.

Leighton released the breath he had been holding. The man was human, he reminded himself; he had watched Sinclair's brother fall from the bullet he had put into him. And anything human could be killed.

In the realm of her dreams, Sarah wandered down a long, twisting corridor. Darkness surrounded her, pressing in against her, as tangible as the fear growing inside her. Footsteps echoed on the walls that rose on either side of her, slow, steady.

She glanced over her shoulder. Someone was there in the shadows. Someone was following her. She could feel the evil, like cold hands reaching for her. Still, she could see nothing, nothing but the shadows.

Sarah turned. She tried to run. Yet she felt as though chains shackled her ankles, holding her back as she tried to escape. The footsteps grew louder in her ears. It was coming closer. If she didn't run, it would catch her, kill her. And still, she couldn't break free of those chains. Something touched her shoulder. A low growl vibrated in her ear.

Sarah came awake with a start, her heart slamming against the wall of her chest, the air rushing from her lungs. A figure loomed over her, dark, menacing. She screamed.

A man stepped back from her bed. The moonlight spilling through her open windows limned him in a silvery light, casting his face in shadows. He was tall, slender, his hair silver in the moonlight. Merlin hissed, crouching beside her, staring at the intruder with amber eyes that glowed in the moonlight.

"What do you want?" she shouted.

"It's only me, Sarah."

Sarah collapsed against her pillow at the sound of her uncle Kendall's voice. He moved in the shadows, reaching for the lamp on the wall beside her bed. A moment later a soft yellow light glowed in the room, chasing away the shadows.

Kendall smiled at her. "I'm sorry, I only meant to look in on you. I didn't mean to disturb you."

Sarah drew breath into her taut lungs. She glanced around, trying to gather her scattered wits. What was she doing lying on her counterpane, still dressed, with her arm wrapped in white linen? She felt as though her head were stuffed with cotton wool.

"I came by to discuss a few matters with you." Kendall sat on the edge of her bed, frowning as Merlin hissed at him, the big cat arching his back.

"It's all right," Sarah whispered, stroking the taut curve of Merlin's back. "All of the commotion has him nervous."

Kendall nodded. "I was shocked when Roxanne told me you had tripped and fallen down the stairs."

"The stairs." Sarah stared at the bandage wrapping her left arm, memories tumbling through her mind, collecting like fallen leaves in autumn. "Yes, the stairs."

"Thank heaven you're all right. It's hard to tell the damage that could be done from a fall like that. You could have been killed."

"It was an accident," she said, realizing how desperate her voice sounded in that moment.

"Of course it was. I shudder when I think of what might have happened to you."

Merlin settled against her side, meowing, a gruff admonition for the humans who had disturbed his slumber. "You said you wanted to discuss something with me."

Kendall shook his head. "I'm certain you aren't up to discussing business."

"I'm fine, really." Sarah pushed the hair back from her cheek. "Is this about the new apartments?"

"It's about Warren Snelling. He came to see me this afternoon."

Sarah stared past her uncle to the ivory lilies winding upward in the peach silk wallpaper lining the wall across from her bed. She felt a weight settle in her chest. Perhaps she wasn't up to this. She felt tired, as though she had been battling a war alone for a long time. "What did he want?"

"He was hoping I could convince you to stop writing those articles about him."

Sarah rubbed her fingers against the soft fur between Merlin's ears, his purr vibrating deep in his throat. "And what did you tell him?"

"I told him you were a grown woman, capable of making decisions on your own."

Sarah stared at her uncle, stunned that he had defended her. He had never once in the past thought she should have anything to do with the newspaper. "Thank you."

"I don't trust the man, Sarah." Kendall lifted her hand, his palm cool and damp against her skin. "He can be a dangerous enemy. There is no telling what he might do."

"I doubt he will do more than try to frighten me." She squeezed his hand, smiling to conceal her fear. "And in a few months it won't matter. I believe we will have enough votes to pass the new regulations."

"I hope you're right, Sarah." He opened his fingers, staring down at her hand lying across his palm. "I hate to think of anything happening to you."

"I'll be fine." Yet as she spoke, the image of a gray dove with a broken neck flickered in her mind.

Yesterday Detective Farley had visited her to report his progress. The two men who had attacked them at the tenement had admitted to attempted robbery and nothing more. And although he had discovered Snelling smoked the type of cigar that came in that box containing the dove, Farley did not have enough solid evidence to prove anything against the man. They were at square one.

Was Snelling desperate enough to try to kill her? The man was angry, he might want to frighten her, but Sarah seriously doubted he would resort to murder.

Chapter Eighteen

"I've done my best." Matilda shoved a pin into Sarah's hair. "But if you're asking me, I think you should have your own maid to be helping you with your hair, like the queen and her little princess have. Someone who'd be knowing more about fixing hair and clothes."

"I have no need for a maid, Matilda. You did a fine job." Sarah turned her head, staring at her reflection in the mirror above her vanity, studying the soft nest of curls Matilda had fashioned at the crown of her head. "What do you think? Does it look too young for me?"

"If Mrs. Van Horne can wear her hair that way, I'll not understand why you think you can't." Matilda leaned forward, her round face appearing beside Sarah's in the mirror, her dark brown eyes crinkling with her smile. "Are you sure you're well enough to be going for a carriage ride this morning, lamb? You had a horrible fall yesterday."

"I'm fine, Matilda. Dr. Chamberlain said I could go about as I please."

"Aye, it's a miracle you weren't hurt." She frowned as she looked at Sarah in the mirror. "The little tyrant could have killed you."

"It was an accident."

"Emerson saw." Matilda pursed her lips. "That spoiled little brat is so jealous of you, she can't see straight."

Sarah shook her head. "Let it be, Matilda."

"Serves her right, that handsome Englishman falling head over heels in love with you instead of her."

Sarah glanced down, absently stirring the pins in the white porcelain tray on the vanity, pushing them to one side, revealing the delicate pink rosebuds painted below. "He isn't in love with me."

"And why is it he keeps coming around, lamb?"

Something stirred in Sarah's chest, hope and longing. She couldn't allow herself to believe Austin Sinclair could fall in love with her. Hope was an emotion she couldn't afford. The cost, if she were wrong, was far too dear. "We're friends, Matilda."

"Friends, are you? I suppose you'd be fixing your hair all pretty like if you weren't expecting him to be calling at any minute?"

Sarah allowed the pins to slide back into place in the tray, hiding the rosebuds. She was falling in love with Austin Sinclair, deeply, irrevocably. It was something she couldn't control.

He was magic. He could make her feel beautiful inside, as though he accepted her for who she was, complete with faults.

"Now I'm wondering what Lord Sinclair would be thinking if he knew that handsome doctor brought you flowers this morning." Matilda turned the ivory porcelain vase that sat on one corner of the vanity.

Sunlight tumbled through the open windows, coaxing a delicate scent from the colorful bouquet of lilies, daisies, and Canterbury bells. "I'm thinking the good doctor doesn't pick flowers from his garden for all of his patients."

"He was simply being nice." Dr. Chamberlain was not what Sarah had expected. Doctors were supposed to be gray-haired gentlemen with gaunt faces. Dr. Gareth Chamberlain's hair tumbled over his collar in gold and brown waves, a lion's mane framing a face that might have graced a Renaissance painting. A painting of one of King Arthur's knights, the one who had been pure, the one who had found the Holy Grail, that was Dr. Chamberlain.

Sarah stared at the flowers he had given her, doubting the gentleman did indeed bring all of his patients flowers. A handsome man for certain. Yet, unlike Austin Sinclair, Dr. Chamberlain didn't coax a single shiver to dance along her spine.

Matilda answered a knock on the door to Sarah's adjoining sitting room and Emerson entered the bedroom. "Lord Sinclair has arrived, miss. He is waiting in your sitting room." A smile twitched his lips. "He thought it best to wait for you up here."

"Thank you, Emerson." Sarah glanced into the mirror. Did she look foolish with her hair done up in curls?

"You look very lovely, miss," Emerson said, as though he could read her apprehension on her face.

She smiled, hoping Austin Sinclair would agree.

Sarah paused on the threshold of her sitting room, her attention snagged by the man standing in front of the windows. He looked elegant and reckless all at the same time. His dark blue coat and buff-colored trousers were tailored to perfection, molding broad shoulders and long, lean legs. And yet his hair was tousled, the thick black mane waving carelessly around his face.

He smiled when he saw her.

She felt her heart stumble.

"Good morning." He moved toward her, carrying a single pink rose.

"Good morning." Sarah smoothed her fingers over her hair, hoping all the pins were in place, praying she didn't look as ridiculous as she felt.

Austin tilted his head, his smile growing devilish as he appraised her. "Very pretty."

She glanced away, staring at the peach damask drapes as they stirred in the breeze drifting in through the windows. "It's cooler this way, with all the hair up from my neck."

He brushed the rose upward along her neck, velvety petals sending shivers skimming over her skin. "Such a pretty neck."

She glanced up at him and found him watching her, the smile gone from his lips. There was an intensity in his look, a need in his eyes that she knew, that she understood deep in her soul. It seemed she had known this man for all time, and yet it had been only a few days. Sunlight streamed around them, blurring everything but this man and the warmth he conjured deep within her, in a place where the frigid darkness of shame and pain had always dwelt.

Kiss me. It shocked her that the words were there in her mind, shocked her more that she wished she could whisper those words. It had been a lifetime since he had kissed her. She looked up into his face, tracing the strong lines and curves, wishing she could touch him.

Oh, my heavens, was it really wrong to feel this way? Tingling with excitement. More alive than she had ever felt in her life.

He seemed to struggle with something inside him, some dark demon that drew his face into lines of pain. And then his expression softened, as though he were surrendering to the inevitable. "Sarah," he whispered as he lowered his head.

She gazed at his lips as he drew near, sensual lips, generous lips, parting with a soft exhale of breath that warmed her cheek. Without thought her body shifted, lifting toward him as naturally as a rose seeking the sun.

"Good morning, Lord Sinclair."

Sarah flinched at the sound of Matilda's voice, bumping her nose against Austin's. He stepped away from her, rubbing one long finger over the tip of his nose, mirroring her own actions.

"Sorry," she whispered.

Matilda cast her a look, smiling as much as to say *I told you so.* "I was thinking I'd be putting these pretty flowers Dr. Chamberlain brought you in here."

Austin frowned as he watched Matilda place the flowers on a round pedestal table near the windows. "I wonder if the good doctor brings flowers to all of his patients?"

Matilda grinned. "I'm thinking Miss Sarah might be one of his favorites."

Austin glanced down at Sarah, a smile barely tipping the corners of his lips. "I understand why."

"Well now, I've got my work to be seeing to." Matilda hummed as she left the room, closing the door behind her.

Sarah moved away from Austin, seeking the breeze drifting in through the windows, hoping to cool her warm cheeks. She stared out into the street below, watching a carriage pulled by a pair of matching grays rattle past her home. "You were right. Dr. Chamberlain is a fine doctor."

"Yes, he is." Austin moved toward her, pausing behind her. "You look wonderful this morning. You must be feeling better."

"It's like magic." That's exactly what it was. Magic to have him standing behind her, warming her in a way that made her realize just how cold she had always felt before she had met this man. "Yesterday I was certain my arm was broken." She turned to face him. "And this morning there isn't a trace of pain. It must be magic."

"Magic?" He looked thoughtful, his black brows lifting as though he were considering the possibility. "I think there might be some magic in the air. Why, what is this behind your ear?"

He brushed her ear with his fingers, and for a moment she expected him to pluck the pins from her hair. Instead he drew back, a gold coin glittering between his fingers. "How in the world did you do that?" she asked.

"It came from your hair." Austin smiled, twisting the coin in the sunlight that streamed through the windows behind her and bathed his face in light. "Spun by sunlight."

"It would seem you have the answer to your difficulties. All you need do is pull coins from my hair."

He turned his hand, then revealed his palm. The gold coin had vanished. "If only it were that simple."

His soft voice sounded bleak suddenly, and she realized the burden he must usually keep hidden behind his charming smile. "Have you thought any more about speaking to Ian Tremayne?"

The corners of his lips curved upward ever so slightly, yet he didn't look at her. "My responsibilities won't allow me to stay, I'm afraid. I'll be going home soon."

Sarah's legs wobbled beneath her, a sudden weakening, as though he had hit her hard across the cheek. She was grateful he was staring at the flowers on the table, blind to the sudden rush of emotion she knew she couldn't hide.

Of course he would have to return to England. She had always known he would not stay here forever. And yet . . . Oh, she didn't want him to leave.

She curled her hands into fists at her sides, fighting the urge to grab him, to hold him, to confess how very much she needed him to stay. "I hope you will find some way out of your difficulties. I wish I could help."

"It occurs to me I've never even glimpsed the medallion that launched me into my rather precarious attempt at burglary." He kept his gaze focused on the flowers. "I suppose it's possible Leighton never sent it to you. That would truly make me a fool, chasing in the dark for a medallion that isn't even here."

"You weren't chasing a phantom." He looked at her then, with eyes that were more blue than gray this morning, eyes that would haunt her until she drew her last breath. "It's in the cabinet where Leighton asked me to put it. Would you like to see it?"

He handed her the rose. "Very much."

Sarah turned away from him, feeling the prick of tears in her eyes, tears she could not allow to gather and fall. Not now. Not while she could still hear his voice. Not while she could still feel the touch of his hand.

Using the excuse of putting the rose in the vase with the other flowers, she kept her back to him. It would be too easy for him to read her emotions right now, too easy to see how very much she wanted him to stay.

She slipped the rose into the vase. Later she would press the flower in a book. She knew it was the gesture of an old maid. Yet she also knew that in the years to come, she would open the pages of that book and look at this rose and remember the few days when she had lived her dream.

Austin stood in the doorway of Leighton's hidden room, watching Sarah, feeling each beat of his heart at the base of his throat. She drew back the drapes, flooding the treasure room with sunlight, the glass cases shimmering in the golden light.

Austin felt the tension draw on his muscles like a bow being stretched to the breaking point as he crossed the room, following Sarah.

"In his letter, Leighton asked me to put it in here." She opened a carved rosewood cabinet that stood against the wall across from the windows.

Inside the cabinet, a gold medallion about three inches in diameter rested on a glass shelf. Austin felt his palms tingle.

Sarah lifted the medallion, the ancient gold glowing in the sunlight. "It's much heavier than it looks."

Emotion closed his throat like a hand squeezing until he could scarcely draw a breath. He stared at the medallion. A square-cut emerald winked at him in the sunlight, the green eye of a bird that was carved into the center of the disk, a crown of smooth feathers sweeping down his long neck. A bird that no longer flew the heavens of this earth.

Sarah tilted the medallion, running her fingertip over the inscription carved along the rim of the disk. "Do you know what language this is?"

"An ancient form of Gaelic." Ancient vows echoed in his brain.

"I wonder what it says."

"'Go softly through the portal, fly swift and sure.'"

"Isn't that odd. I wonder what it means?"

Austin looked into her eyes, seeing the trust there in the hazel depths, trust he would soon betray. How could he watch that trust dissolve into hate? How could he watch this beautiful woman shrink back into her cocoon?

He couldn't.

Yet he had no choice. Responsibility wrapped around him, sealing him like a mummy in some ancient tomb.

He lifted the medallion from Sarah's palm, the gold warm from her skin, the weight of it anchoring him to his vows. This evening he would return to this room. He would take this medallion. He would end the threat and with it end his time here in New York.

He would leave Sarah. This time with her would be nothing more than memories, thoughts of what might have been.

He looked at Sarah, sunlight etching her features upon a heart he could feel breaking inside him. There was one thing he needed to do for her before he left, one small attempt to wash away some of the harm he would cause this lady with the pretty hazel eyes. This lady he would always love.

A visit with Isabel Bennett was not what Sarah had expected Austin to plan for their morning together. She had expected to do something alone with him. Still, perhaps she had spent too much time in his company. She didn't want to imagine how lonely her life would be once he left New York.

Austin paused at the closed door of Isabel Bennett's drawing room. "Sarah, there's someone with Isabel. Someone I think you should meet."

He sounded so serious, so intense, she felt a prickle of apprehension at the base of her spine. "Who?"

He didn't answer. He simply opened the door and took her arm. Sarah took two steps into the drawing room and halted, her gaze snagging on the woman who sat beside Isabel Bennett on one of the Empire sofas flanking the hearth. Diana Schuyler rose when she saw Sarah, her face reflecting uncertainty and a sadness that Sarah had seen too many times reflected in her own mirror.

Sarah glared at the man who stood beside her. "What kind of game is this?"

"Talk to her, Sarah." Austin rested his hand against her cheek, the warmth and gentleness of his touch echoed in his silvery blue eyes. "That's all I ask of you."

Sarah turned, breaking away from Austin. "I don't want to hear anything she has to say."

"Sarah, please," Diana said. "Stay for just a little while."

Sarah halted at the sound of her mother's voice. It had been so long since she had heard that soft voice, a lifetime. Memories fluttered within her, distant memories of a woman who had read stories to her every night. "We have nothing to say to one another." She spoke without facing this beautiful stranger, this woman who had abandoned her.

"Sarah, wait," Austin said, following her from the room.

Sarah kept marching, down the hall, out of the house, away from the woman who had given her life with one hand and taken away any joy she might have known in that life with the other.

"Sarah!" Austin grabbed her arm as she reached the granite sidewalk.

She pivoted to face him. "How dare you! How dare you take me to see that woman!"

In his eyes she saw a depth of understanding, as though he knew the turmoil that was raging inside her. "I thought it might be time to make peace, Sarah."

Sarah fought the tears that pricked her eyes. "You had no right. You . . ." She dragged air into her lungs, feeling the first tears seep from her eyes.

People were staring at her; she saw them through the gathering mist in her eyes, turning their heads, whispering. "Please take me away from here."

There was a serenity that could be found only in nature. In Riverside Park, in a place where the woods grew thick and a path meandered toward the river, Austin hoped to bring that serenity to the woman who sat stiff as a statue above him on the black leather carriage seat.

"Sarah." He touched her arm. She didn't so much as glance at him. "Come walk with me."

Without meeting his gaze, she placed her hands on his shoulders, allowing him to lift her from the carriage. He held her a moment, absorbing her heat, breathing her fragrance, and deep inside, nestled in the core of his body, he felt a flicker of flame.

He tightened his hands on her waist. Her lashes fluttered but did not rise, as though she was loath to look into his eyes. With care, he set her on the dirt path and stepped away from her. She needed understanding right now, a friend. Not a man tangled in his own emotions.

She walked beside him for a while before she turned from the path as though she were alone, as though she had no knowledge of the man who walked beside her. Austin followed where she led, wandering through the woods that were filled with towering oak, elm, chestnut, and hickory.

She had once told him this park was one of her favorite places in New York. He could understand the reason. Sunlight peeked through the leaves that rustled in the breeze above them, sprinkling glittering sunlight over Sarah like fairy dust.

He had hurt her deeply. He only wondered if she would forgive him. Tomorrow he would be gone. Tomorrow she would hate him. And still, for these few moments they had left, he wanted to prolong the warmth they had found with each other.

Sarah paused beside a tall hickory and stared out at the river that rippled like molten gold in the sunlight. She condemned him with her silence.

"I'm sorry I upset you."

She didn't acknowledge his presence. She pulled the pin from her small gray hat and lifted it from the soft curls piled on her head.

"Your mother came to see me yesterday. She was concerned about you. She loves you very much. I was hoping you would talk to her, hear her side of what happened."

Sarah stared at the hat she held in her hand, shoving the long hat pin through the crown, ignoring him as though he didn't exist. A cool breeze whispered through the trees, carrying the scent of wildflowers. A sleek sailboat glided along the rippling river, chasing a white steamer.

Austin wanted to grab her and shake her. He wanted to crush her to his chest, to kiss her until she moaned low and sweet in her throat. He shoved his hands into the pockets of his trousers. "Scream at me. Tell me how much of a scoundrel you think I am for trying to mend things between you and your mother."

"When I was a little girl I would come here with my brother." She spoke without looking at him, keeping her gaze on the river while the breeze tugged at her hair. "We would read dreadful novels and turn them into our own adventures. There was only Leighton, the two of us. No one was allowed to play with us because of the scandal."

Austin saw the shadow of that lonely little girl in the face of this lovely woman. It was everything he could do to keep from touching her. "I'm amazed at the stupidity of people."

She glanced at him, the smile curving her lips catching him off guard, stripping away the defenses he might have mounted against this woman. "You did what you thought was right today."

"Sarah, you have nothing to lose but your anger by talking to your mother."

"I guess I didn't give her much of a chance." She rested her shoulder against the hickory, below the scar where someone had carved his initials into the bark, holding her hat flat against her waist.

"I should have asked you if you wanted to meet her."

"I wonder . . ." Her voice broke. She pressed her hand to her lips as though desperate to hold back her emotions, but they escaped in a soft little sob of pain and frustration.

"Sarah." He closed the distance between them. There was no help for it; he had to touch her.

As he reached for her, she threw her arms around his waist, burying her face against his chest. He held her as he had longed to hold her for days, filling his arms with her soft warmth, pressing his cheek against her soft, fragrant hair.

He noticed the initials carved deeply into the bark of the hickory where Sarah had stood, a sign that reminded him of how hopeless his feelings for Sarah were. LHVH, Leighton Hewett Van Horne. His enemy.

He wanted to lash out, angry at fate for bringing this woman into his life only to rip her from his arms. Yet how could he fight fate?

His throat tightened as Sarah sobbed against his chest, quiet tears, her hands clenched fists against his back, her body shaking with the strain to hold back the emotions that demanded release. Would she weep tomorrow, when she learned of his betrayal?

"It's all right," he whispered, stroking her back.

"No, it isn't," she said, her voice strangled by tears. "It never will be."

Her words were far too true. He focused his mind on the gentle rustling of leaves, breathing deeply, slowly. When he felt some measure of calm, he rested his hand at the nape of her neck. He brushed his fingers across her skin, mirroring the frantic rhythm of her breath, willing her to relax.

He calmed his breathing, feeling her cheek rise and fall with each movement of his chest. Gradually he slowed his fingers against her skin, easing the rhythm to the same rhythm of his breath, feeling her follow his lead. Without words he spoke to her, trying to ease the emotional pain he had helped inflict.

"You're doing something to me." She pulled back in his arms, looking up at him through her tears. "Draining away the pain. I don't know how you do it."

"I don't like to see you hurt, Sarah." Austin slid his thumb over her cheek, smoothing away her warm tears. "Please believe me: I never want to see you hurt." And yet he would do more damage, much more damage.

"I don't want to cry." She managed a small watery smile. "I'm not one of those women who go all weepy at every little thing, I'm really not."

"I know."

She rested her hands on his chest, her hat lying forgotten on the rough grass and buttercups at her feet. "You must think I'm horrible. Walking away from my mother without even giving her a chance."

He slid his thumb along the full curve of her lower lip, drawing a sharp breath when her warm sigh brushed his skin. "I don't think you're horrible."

"Really?"

Tears glistened on her dark silky lashes. She was looking at him in a way that made him feel he could move a mountain if she asked him to. He lowered his head, brushing his nose against hers. "Really."

"Thank you."

He shouldn't kiss her. He should draw away from her. He shouldn't become more entangled with this woman than he already was. It would only cause more trouble. Yet she felt so good in his arms, so right, and he knew he might never again have the chance to hold her this way.

She was watching him, quiet, expectant, her breath stilled in her throat. Without words she beckoned him.

He tightened his hold, drawing her close, wondering where he would find the strength to walk away from her. One kiss, that was all he would steal. One kiss to tuck away with his other memories of Sarah. One kiss to last him the rest of his life.

"Sweet Sarah," he whispered as he slid his lips over hers.

He felt her stiffen, her hands grow tense against his chest as she stood in the circle of his arms and absorbed the feel of his lips against hers. He slid his hands up her back, pressing her closer, seeking the satin of her skin beneath the layers of poplin and linen while he glided his lips back and forth against hers, and he felt the flames she ignited inside him lick along every nerve in his body.

With a soft moan she eased into his arms, sliding her hands upward until they locked in the hair at his nape. She pulled him closer, as though she wanted to absorb him into her skin, her soft breasts searing him through his clothes.

He touched his tongue to her lips, a silent question. She opened to him, a tentative answer. He slipped his tongue between her soft lips, dipping, teasing, until she touched him with the tip of her tongue.

He had never kissed a woman before, not like this. He had held other women, more than he wanted to remember. He had touched their lips, tasted them, buried his body deep inside them. And yet all of the coupling through all of the years faded into gray compared to this one kiss.

Sarah.

Innocent desire and love, pure essence of emotion. He tasted this on her tongue, felt this in the trembling of her body against his, and he drank deeply from this well. She filled him, saturated his soul with her light.

He sank his hands into her hair, dislodging pins and combs, freeing the soft coils to tumble over his hands and down her back. He wanted to feel the warm silk of her hair against his naked chest. He wanted to feel her thighs, smooth and warm, slide against his. He wanted to taste her, to explore every hollow and curve of her body. He wanted to hold her like this until the day he died.

He slid his hand between their bodies, seeking the soft swell of her breast. Layers of clothing kept him from feeling more than a hint of her shape. He needed more. He managed four buttons at the front of her gown before she pulled back in his arms.

Sarah stared up at him, hazel eyes wide with shock. "What are you doing?"

Austin looked down at the plain white chemise peeking at him from the vee of light gray poplin he had parted. The innocence of that white linen hit him like a solid right to the jaw. What *was* he doing? "Sarah, I—"

"You thought you could seduce me." She pulled free of his arms, staring at him, pain shimmering with the tears in her eyes. "That's why you did this."

"Sarah, I didn't mean to—"

"How could you? How could you do this?"

He watched her run away from him, sunlight shining on the thick waves rippling down her back. "Sarah," he whispered.

Emotions swarmed in his chest, rising within him, choking him with the anguish of his own thoughtless actions. He tossed back his head, a low moan of pain escaping his lips.

Fool!

Idiot!

He lifted her hat from the ground, a single ostrich tip fluttering in the breeze. He had hurt her terribly. He had made her believe all of the horrible accusations ever shot at her.

He couldn't leave her like this. He had to talk to her. He had to make some sense out of the way he felt about her.

He ran after her, picking his way through the tangle of trees. By the time he reached the place where he had left the carriage, Sarah was already gone, and he was facing a long, lonely walk home.

* * *

Sarah reined in the horses, halting the team in the alley beside her brother's stable. A cool breeze drifted across the tears that had dried on her cheeks, lifting her unbound hair. She couldn't face anyone. Not now. Not when the horrible realization of what she had become screamed inside her brain.

It was true. Everything they had ever said about her. The blood she felt pulsing against the collar of her gown was tainted. Wickedness flowed through her veins, poisoning her thoughts, tempting her, taunting her in her weakness.

Like mother, like daughter.

She trembled as the memories swept over her. Austin had touched her. And she had reveled in that touch, his body pressed close to hers, his hand on her bosom, warming her through her clothes.

Only a shred of propriety had saved her. One slender thread of reason had prompted her to stop him. Still, she couldn't stop the truth that beat against her temples. She had wanted him. In that instant before she had pulled free of his touch, she had wanted to feel Austin's hand on her bare skin.

"Dear heaven," she whispered.

"Miss Sarah, are you all right?"

Sarah jumped at the sound of Bram Duggan's deep voice. He was standing beside her, his green eyes reflecting his concern. She smoothed the hair back from her face. Could he tell by looking at her? Could he sense the wickedness she had allowed?

"Miss Sarah," he whispered, touching her arm. "What's happened?"

"Nothing!"

He frowned. "Are you hurt?"

"No." Sarah jerked her hand from his warm grasp. "I'm fine."

"Where is Lord Sinclair?"

"He . . ." Sarah glanced at the horses, their black manes ruffling with the breeze. "I left him in the park."

"In the park?"

"Please make sure his carriage and horses are returned to Isabel Bennett's." She climbed from the carriage and rushed toward the house before he could ask another question.

Bram stood watching Sarah run away from him like a young girl fearing a lecture from her father. He stared after her until she disappeared through the gate leading to the gardens, the frustration of helplessness wrapping around him.

In the few days he had known her, he had come to care for her. Perhaps because she was one of the few people around here who treated the servants as though they were human beings. There was something special about Sarah Van Horne, something in the way she cared about people, something in the way she wanted to make a difference in this world.

What the hell had happened? He gripped the reins, his imagination taking a dangerous turn. He knew Austin Sinclair was using Sarah to find the medallion. He didn't want to believe the man would seduce her to get it. He just might have to have a talk with Lord Sinclair.

Chapter Nineteen

Matilda plunked two pans of bread fresh from the oven on the big oak table in the Van Horne kitchen. She folded the towel she had used to hold the pans and frowned at Sarah. "Are you going to tell me what happened this morning?"

"Nothing happened." Sarah sank her hands into the soft dough she was working on the table, shaping it, kneading it. She loved making bread, feeling it grow smooth and elastic beneath her hands. It gave her a special feeling, knowing she could take raw ingredients and turn them into something as vital as bread.

"You come home here, with your hair all hanging down your back, and your eyes red from crying, driving that man's buggy, and you tell me nothing happened."

"That's right." Sarah breathed in the yeasty aroma of fresh bread. From the corner of her eye she saw Matilda staring at her, but she refused to meet her look. She didn't want to talk about this morning.

Clarissa had been right all along. Austin Sinclair was seeing her because he thought he could seduce her. She clenched her jaw when she felt the fresh prick of tears in her eyes. She would not surrender to the wickedness inside her.

"Nothing is wrong, is that it?" Matilda asked.

"Nothing at all."

"Then why did you refuse to see Lord Sinclair when he was asking for you a few minutes ago?"

Sarah clenched her hands in the dough. "I'm covered with flour."

"That you are." Matilda pulled back a strand of hair that had escaped the tight bun at the nape of Sarah's neck. She rearranged a pin, securing the wayward tresses as she spoke. "I suppose you think we need another dozen loaves of bread for dinner."

Sarah glanced at the six loaves that sat in the sunlight streaming gold and scarlet through the open windows. "I like making bread."

Matilda huffed. "If you're not thinking you can share your troubles with me, then I won't be asking again."

"Matilda, please. I'd rather not . . ." Sarah hesitated when the kitchen door opened. Her breath left her lungs as though an invisible fist had hit her chest. "You!"

Austin Sinclair didn't wait for an invitation. He strode across the threshold, closing the door behind him.

"Get out!" Sarah shouted.

"Not until I've said what I've come here to say." Austin marched across the brick floor, headed right for Sarah.

"Matilda, send for Emerson. Have this man thrown out of my house."

Austin paused as he reached the table. He glanced at Matilda, who was standing beside Sarah, her pudgy hands on the black muslin covering her bulky hips, a mother bear protecting her cub. "Emerson knows I'm here, Matilda. He's the one who told me where to find Miss Sarah."

"He what!" Sarah shouted.

"He did, did he?" A smile spread along Matilda's lips. "Well, I suppose I need to be talking to Emerson to hear what he knows that I don't."

"Matilda, you stay right where you are."

"Now, lamb, it seems to me the man might not want me to be hearing all he has to say to you." Matilda chuckled as she waddled from the room, closing the door leading to the butler's pantry behind her.

"I had a rather long walk home." Austin moved toward her, his eyes fierce, like a lion about to pounce on his prey. "Gave me lots of time to think."

Sarah backed away from the table, sprinkling flour across the red bricks. The setting rays of the sun surrounded him. In that shimmering light, he seemed to come from another time and place, a prince from a distant realm, conjured from a woman's dreams. "I'm warning you, Sinclair, you just keep your hands off me."

Austin shook his head. "I don't think I can do that, sweet Sarah."

He kept moving, stalking her, setting her heart racing with the horrible excitement of what he would do when he captured her. "I won't tolerate any of your—" Her words dissolved into a gasp as she backed into one of the counters.

"Any of my insolence?" Austin asked, moving in for the kill.

She thrust her flour-encrusted hands against his

chest, her white fingers flat against his dark blue coat. "I'm not the kind of woman who—"

"You're just the kind of woman, Sarah." He braced his hands on the countertop on either side of her, imprisoning her between his body and the oak behind her. He leaned toward her, pressing the length of his body against her. "The kind who makes my blood burn."

"No!" Sarah closed her eyes on a groan. "I'm not wicked. I'm not!"

"Sarah." His lush voice brushed over her like warm sable. He touched her with his lips, a soft graze against her brow that rippled through her like a pebble tossed on a still lake. "There is nothing wicked about you."

Sarah fought the tears, but they were there, just as the desire for this man she couldn't banish dwelt deep inside her, warming her low in her belly. Wicked. Wanton. She was sinking in the pulsating pool of fire he ignited within her, drowning in her own desire.

Like mother, like daughter. She heard her father's voice, saw his face as he condemned her. "I'm not like her, I swear!"

He gripped her shoulders. "Look at me, Sarah."

Sarah clenched her eyes shut. She wouldn't look at him; she didn't want to see the triumph in his eyes, her own condemnation there in his eyes. "Go away. Please go away."

"I can't leave you, Sarah."

Tears gathered in her eyes, the first slipping between her lashes to humiliate her before this man. "Why are you doing this to me?"

He pressed his lips to her cheek, catching her tear on the tip of his tongue. "I love you."

Sarah felt the air rush from her lungs. It took several beats of her heart before she found the courage to look at him. His face was close to hers, so close she could feel each warm breath against her cheek. "What did you say?"

He smiled. "I said, I love you."

"Oh." Sarah couldn't believe the words. How could this man be in love with her? "How can you tease in such a—"

Austin pressed his fingertip to her lips, cutting off her words. "Marry me, Sarah."

Sarah became aware of the slow drain of strength from her limbs, the trembling that followed. "You aren't serious."

"I'm afraid I am." He sank to one knee on the hard floor. He took her flour-encrusted right hand in both of his. With his eyes never leaving hers, he spoke the words once more. "I love you, Sarah. I want to spend my life with you. Will you marry me?"

And this time, Sarah knew he meant every word. Joy, she had never felt such intense joy. She couldn't speak, for she couldn't draw a breath. She stared down at him, at this man who seemed to command the sunlight that surrounded him, this man who had stolen her heart.

"It's your turn to say something, sweetheart."

"Yes," she whispered, crumpling to her knees before him. "Oh, yes, I'll marry you."

"Sarah," he said, taking her in his arms.

She slipped her arms around his shoulders as he cradled her against his chest. He kissed her, slanting his lips across hers as though he were dying and she his only hope for life. And she returned his kiss, letting him feel all of the love she had kept inside her all her life.

"What is going on in here!"

Sarah jerked back from Austin at the sound of Roxanne's voice. She glanced to the doorway, her blood freezing when she saw her stepmother standing there, Roxanne's features twisted into a look of utter contempt. Austin held her close to his chest, his arms tight around her, his raised knee pressing against her side, sheltering her with his body.

"I told you she was in here with him, Mother." Clarissa stood beside her mother, a smirk curving her lips. "I heard Emerson telling him where he could meet her. Only heaven knows what they were going to do on the floor."

"I knew your true nature would be revealed one day, young woman," Roxanne said.

Sarah bit her lower lip. It was true. She wanted Austin in every way imaginable. She wanted to touch him, to hold him, to kiss him. She wanted to feel his hands on her skin. It was true: she was wicked beyond redemption.

Roxanne smiled at Sarah, obviously pleased by Sarah's stricken expression. "You truly are your mother's daughter."

"And I'm thankful she is." Austin rose to his feet. With his hand on her arm, he helped Sarah rise, then slipped his arm around her shoulders, holding her close, shielding her from the condemning stares of Roxanne and Clarissa. "We're going to be married. Today."

"Married!" The word burst from Roxanne and Clarissa as they stared at Sarah with wide, disbelieving eyes.

Sarah stared up at Austin, loving him more in that one moment than she had ever believed possible. He wanted her, with all of her faults.

"By this evening Sarah will be Lady Sarah Sinclair, the Marchioness of Somerset." Austin held her close to his side. "In the past you might have been able to fill Sarah with your twisted notions of wickedness.

You managed to make her feel dirty and ashamed. But I will advise you now, I won't tolerate my wife being ill-treated by anyone."

They had never looked more alike, Sarah thought, glancing from her stepmother to her sister. Both Roxanne and Clarissa looked as though they had just bitten into a lemon.

Austin smiled down at her, mischief in his eyes. He was enjoying this. And, although Sarah knew it was a terrible thing to admit, she was far too happy to allow their discomfort to enter into her concern.

Austin set the telephone on a table in Isabel Bennett's drawing room. It was a primitive device, at least on the surface. Yet he had just used this instrument to communicate with Avallon.

Disguising ordinary objects to suit their needs, his people had long ago learned how to operate outside of Avallon. Masks and deceptions, it was the only way they could live in the Outworld. And he was a master of deception.

He stared out one of the windows, wondering how great a fool he truly was. His parents had been shocked at the news of his marriage, and justifiably concerned. Could he manage it all? Could he have Sarah and maintain his loyalty to his people?

The incandescent street lamp in front of the house cast a golden glow into the dark street. A single ray of light in the darkness, that was Sarah. And he had reached for that light, allowing his heart to rule his head. Now he was married to a woman who might very well destroy him. Still, he hadn't been able to betray her.

He didn't turn as the door opened. He sensed Isabel moving toward him, until her image glowed in the window glass. "She's waiting for you."

"Thank you for talking to her." Austin stared at her reflection in the glass, keeping his own expression turned to the darkness. "I don't think she knew what to expect tonight. I'm certain there were things she needed to hear from another woman."

"It was my pleasure to help Sarah. She is a very dear young woman."

"Yes, she is."

"What could you have been thinking to have married the girl?"

"I love her." A carriage rolled past the house, plunging through the puddle of golden lamplight before slipping once more into darkness. "I'm not noble enough to give her up."

"And your mission? Your first responsibility is to retrieve that medallion."

"I haven't lost sight of my mission. Duggan is going to retrieve the medallion tonight." He smiled as he recalled the lecture Bram Duggan had given him, a diatribe on the dangers of seducing innocent young women, keenly delivered before Austin had been able to tell Duggan he had married Sarah. The news had shocked Duggan even though he had understood why Austin had not been able to walk out of Sarah's life.

"Are you going to tell Sarah the truth about her brother?"

Austin turned to face her. "I think I must."

Isabel's lips drew into a taut line as she held his gaze. "If she believes you intend to harm her brother, she will find some way to warn him."

"Do you think she would betray me for him?" he asked, voicing the question that was haunting him.

"What will she think when she learns you intend to see her brother hang?"

"I don't know. If she loves me as much as I love her, we'll find a way to work through the difficulties."

Austin thought of the woman waiting for him in the bedroom upstairs. He loved her more than he had ever thought possible, a love that filled him with joy and an anxiety about what would come of that love when she learned the truth.

"Once I have the medallion, I'm going to take Sarah to Avallon," Austin said, wondering how his bride would react to his home. "I'm going to turn the problem of Leighton Van Horne back to the Central Council. Under the circumstances, I'm sure they will understand why I can no longer pursue the man."

"And what of this marriage? Do you think the Central Council will approve? You're a lord of the Inner Circle. With the taint of Leighton's blood—"

"Sarah is not like her brother."

Isabel held his gaze, her eyes filled with concern. "And if they don't approve?"

Austin felt a pull inside him, ancient vows warring with the simple vows of man and wife. "Then I shall relinquish my position."

"You love her that much? You would turn your back on everything you have always held dear?"

"She is my *Edaina*."

"I understand. You think you can balance your love for Sarah and your mission, your vows to the Inner Circle of Avallon with your vows as a husband." Isabel studied him a moment, her delicate brows drawn into a frown. "I think you are headed for disaster, my dear young man."

A steamboat churned down the Hudson River, dark smoke writhing from twin smokestacks, threading upward toward a moon that was half shadow, half bright silvery glow. It was the time of day Leighton adored, a time when the respectable citizens were all snug in their beds, a time for predators.

"It's been a long time since I've come to this park." Leighton glanced over his shoulder at Collin Bennett. "I followed my sister to this park this morning. She was with Austin Sinclair."

The young man made a sound, a pitiful little sob that barely escaped the gag Leighton had shoved into his mouth. Moonlight peeked through the leaves overhead, streaking across Collin's moist skin. Except for the gag, he was naked. Leighton had forced him to strip before tying him to the trunk of an old hickory tree. Something about stripping a man of his clothes made him feel all the more vulnerable.

"Sarah and I would come here after our tutor was done with us." Leighton stared down at his knife. "We would read penny novels and act them out. Cowboys and Indians." He twisted the blade in the moonlight, his image sliding along the polished steel. "She's the only one who ever cared. The only one I could ever really trust."

An owl hooted in the woods, deep and vibrant. Collin whimpered.

Leighton turned to face the man who strained against the ropes binding his arms and legs. "You're helping Sinclair."

Collin shook his head, a lock of light brown hair tumbling over his brow, sticking to his damp skin. Collin's blue eyes were wide, filled with a fear that fed the demon inside his captor. Leighton's blood pounded in his veins, pumping heat into his groin.

"It's not nice to lie to me." Leighton moved toward him, a slow advance that allowed Collin to think about what would happen once he reached him. For a moment, Leighton did nothing except stand close to Collin, close enough to feel the heat of his naked body. He burned like a flame in his fear, a flame

Leighton could snuff with a single movement of his knife.

"I want to know how many men Sinclair has with him. And I want to know why he is seeing my sister." Leighton watched a bead of sweat slide down Collin's neck. He touched him, collecting that single drop of salty sweat on his fingertip; Collin jerked as though touched by electricity.

Leighton could smell Collin's fear, sour on his sweat. He felt his own pulse throb low in his belly. "You will tell me, won't you, Collin? You won't force me to use . . . this." He lifted the knife, twisting the blade in front of Collin's eyes.

Collin nodded, keening against the wadded cloth stuffed in his mouth.

"I knew I could count on you, Collin." Leighton slipped the knife beneath Collin's silk tie, the white scrap of cloth he had used to secure the gag. It melted beneath the razor-sharp blade, falling away from Collin's face, snagging on his damp shoulders like a pale wing of a fallen bird. Gently, Leighton slipped the handkerchief from Collin's lips.

He could feel Collin's taut body trembling against his, helpless. Potent, this power, this pleasure that prickled every inch of Leighton's skin. "How many men does Sinclair have?"

"One." Collin slid his tongue along his lips. "Duggan, he's working as a groom at your house."

With the tip of his knife Leighton traced his initials where he had carved them long ago into the hickory, a hair's breadth above Collin's shoulder. "Are you certain?"

"There are others, watching the train stations, the docks. But Duggan is the only one near the house. I swear, that's all he told me."

"Good boy." Leighton stroked the hair back from

Collin's damp brow. He gazed down at the lips that parted, warm breath brushing his face. "And why is the bastard seeing my sister? What does he want from her?"

"The medallion you stole. He's hoping she will lead him to it."

"The medallion? What makes it so valuable that he would come after it himself?"

"It's a medallion of the Inner Circle . . . it's ancient . . . dates back to the first covenant, four thousand years ago. It's a symbol of all they stand for."

"I knew it was valuable the first moment I saw it." Leighton lifted the knife, the steel drawing Collin's gaze like a magnet. "Is there anything you're not telling me?"

Collin panted with his fear, short puffs of hot breath that hit Leighton's face. "That's all I know. I swear."

"I believe you." Leighton smiled, cupping Collin's tear-dampened face in his palm. "Unfortunately, that means I no longer have a need of you. Unless, of course, you can help me."

"I'll do anything."

"I want to go back to Avallon." Leighton turned the blade in his hand, pressing the blunt steel against Collin's neck. He could feel the quick pulse that beat there, the flex of muscle as Collin swallowed. "Can you help me arrange that, Collin?"

"I can take you there."

"Excellent." Leighton thought of Avallon, of the people who had treated him like a common criminal. Judith was still there, beautiful Judith who had betrayed him. And Devlin Sinclair. How easy it would be to kill the man in Avallon. Still, there were a few things he must settle before he left New York.

Chapter Twenty

Sarah stared at her reflection in the mirror above the vanity in Austin's room. It was her face, a face she had looked at thousands of times in a mirror. And yet she scarcely recognized the woman in the glass, with her hair tumbling in wild waves all around her face and color riding high on her cheeks. Excitement, she could see it in this face. Contentment, she could see it in the hazel eyes that looked back at her.

Married. She was married. Three hours ago Sarah Elizabeth Van Horne had married a man she had known less than a month, a man she felt as though she had known all her life.

All of the words Isabel had spoken were there, spinning around in her brain. *Nothing to fear. No shame. No wickedness. Nothing but love between husband and wife.* And Sarah believed those words. She needed with all her heart to believe those words.

Although she heard nothing above the beating of her heart, she sensed his presence. She turned and found

Austin standing there, leaning against the closed door, watching her, an odd mixture of tenderness and hunger in his eyes. Her breath caught in her throat at that look. Her skin tingled when she thought of what would pass between them this night.

"I don't believe I've ever seen anything more beautiful than you right now, at this moment," he said.

She pressed her hand to the base of her neck, her fingers testing the small pearl button at the top of her white linen nightgown. Her robe, she realized, lay across the vanity chair, a splash of white against the blue and gold flowers stitched into the needlepoint back. "You make me feel beautiful."

He drew away from the door, moving toward her, his strides long and sure and steady. The warmth in his eyes mirrored the warmth glowing deep inside her, the love for this man that would not be denied.

She glanced at the bed. Merlin lay in a plump gray ball on the blue-and-gold brocade counterpane which had been turned down, revealing white linen sheets. She had never considered leaving her pet with Roxanne and Clarissa.

"You let down your hair for me." Austin lifted a handful of her hair, allowing the tresses to slide through his fingers, strands of light brown capturing the light that glowed in the brass-and-crystal fixtures on the walls. "Like the princess in the fairy tale."

He made her feel like a princess, rescued from dragons and witches and loneliness. She touched his cheek, the dark pinpoints of his beard sleeping beneath the smooth warmth of his skin. A miracle, this, reaching out, finding him warm and real, her phantom lover come to life.

"I've been looking for you all my life, Sarah. I've wanted you from the first moment I saw you."

"Even though I was pointing a pistol at you?"

"How could I resist such a brave lady?" Thick black lashes lowered as he turned his face, as he placed a soft kiss in the cup of her palm, the heat of his breath soaking into her skin.

Emotion curled around her, binding her to this man. It was as if shimmering strands passed from one into the other, weaving both into a tapestry of love and desire.

"Let me show you how much I love you." He slid his hand down her back. "Let me show you how it should be between a man and a woman in love."

"You are my husband." He had removed his coat and tie and unfastened the first few buttons of his white silk shirt, exposing the hollow of his neck, a shading of dark curls and warm-looking skin. She felt a tingling, a throbbing centered in the tips of her breasts, the echo of every beat of her heart. "I shall deny you nothing."

His breath warmed her cheek in a satisfied sigh, and then he kissed her mouth. Sarah sipped from his lips, an elixir that filled her, an intoxicating brew of desire and love that tingled along her every nerve and assured her this was real.

Austin drew a sharp breath as she leaned into him, nestling her breasts against his chest. He felt her love for him shimmering around her, embracing him with a soft, glowing warmth. Still, he knew this awakening love was a fragile thing. He could lose her in a single heartbeat.

"Sarah," he whispered, loving the sound of her name. He brushed kisses across her cheek and pressed his lips to her temple, feeling the beat of her heart throbbing there, pulsing to the same quick rhythm as his own.

He needed to show her how he felt. Yet he wondered if it would be enough, this love he had to give with all of his being. His heart, his soul, his body, he would give her all he had to give. Still, he wondered if it would be enough to light their way through the darkness he knew they must soon face.

He cradled her face in his hands. She looked up at him, smiling shyly, trust and promise in her eyes, the honesty he hoped always to see shining there in her eyes. And still she shamed him with that honesty, for he came to her cloaked in lies that could destroy them both.

With his fingertips he traced her delicate features, learning the curve of her cheeks, the silkiness of the lashes that fluttered beneath his touch, the plump fullness of her lower lip. She was his Galatea, a beautiful statue brought to life by love. And he was her slave.

With his lips he followed the trail of his fingertips, kissing each delicate feature of her face. He explored the soft skin beneath her ear, absorbing the tiny tremor that passed through her to quiver deep inside him. He tasted the tender curve of her neck with the tip of his tongue. He breathed in her fragrance. Innocence of lavender. Seductive scent of a woman's awakening desire.

Against his chest he felt the erotic change in her breasts, the soft tips drawing into hard jewels that pressed into his skin. He trembled deep inside.

He needed to feel her aroused nipples against his tongue. He needed to taste her, all of her. He needed to drown in the heated pool of her innocence.

"I need to see you, Sarah," he whispered against her lips as he slid the pearl button at the top of her nightgown through the chaste white linen. "I need to touch you, all of you."

Sarah shuddered in his arms, her fingers digging into his shoulders.

"Don't be afraid of me, Sarah. Please don't be afraid of what's happening between us."

"I'm not." She swayed against him, opening her hands, sliding her palms along his shoulders. "It's just all so startling, isn't it?"

"Yes. Startling to realize how much I can want, how much I can need."

The warm linen of her gown parted beneath his touch. Pale skin, the curves of her breasts, the sleek satin of her belly, the dark shadow of her navel. He was shocked to find his hands trembling as he slid the gown from her shoulders. It fell to the floor, a puddle of white linen against the intricate blue and gold swirls in the carpet. Her breasts rose with her breath, ivory globes, raspberry tips aroused, lifting to him in silent need.

The cool breeze that whispered through the opcn windows brushed Sarah's skin as she stood in the warmth of his gaze. Who was this woman who stood naked before this man? Someone else. Someone Sarah didn't know. This was not the same girl who had been frightened of passion, frightened of this glorious feeling that was growing stronger and stronger inside her, but a woman brave enough to face each day of this new life, a life Austin had given her.

"So beautiful," he whispered, lowering his lips to her neck. "More beautiful than I imagined, my sweet Sarah."

Sarah tilted her head, her hair falling back from her shoulders, the silken strands sliding sinuously against her sensitive skin. He pulled her flush against him, his lips moving softly against her neck. Every nerve awakened at his touch.

Never could she have imagined the sensation of her breasts against the warm silk of his shirt, her belly against the smooth black wool of his trousers, his arms around her, holding her as though he would never let her go. Through the layers of cloth she felt his arousal, hard and throbbing against her. Foreign. Exciting. Frightening. Intoxicating.

"Sarah. My sweet Sarah. How I love you."

With his lips and his tongue and his hands he showed her the proof of his words. She cried out at the first touch of his lips against her breasts. He swirled his tongue around the hard peaks, shimmering sparks of desire shooting along every nerve while his hands roamed, stroking heat across her skin the way an artist strokes paint across a canvas.

Sarah moaned and trembled beneath his touch. Such incredible sensation, being held like this, kissed like this. Total abandonment. Total freedom.

He sank to the vanity chair. She swayed and he caught her, wrapping his arms around her hips, pressing his face to her belly. She rested her hands on his broad shoulders. Her world was spinning in the vortex he generated inside her.

He scattered kisses down her belly, flicking his tongue against her skin. She felt as though she were drowning in sensation, dissolving, her bones melting in his heat, her skin turning to flame. And then she felt his lips against her, in a kiss more intimate than she had ever imagined.

Austin felt her stiffen and held her when she tried to break free of his grasp, a soft cry of protest slipping from her lips. He couldn't stop. Not now. Not when he had the taste of her on his tongue. Not when the opulence of her perfume filled his senses. "Easy, my sweet Sarah. Let me."

He didn't wait for her reply. He pressed his lips to the soft curls. He breathed her scent deep into his lungs. With his tongue he tasted her. She stiffened, a shocked gasp slipping from her lips. Yet she stayed in his grasp, trusting, testing the sensations she permitted with her silent consent.

He stroked her breasts, her hips, her thighs, as he explored her with the tip of his tongue, as he felt her turn hot and liquid at his touch. She trembled in his hold. She opened her hands on his shoulders, clutching him, her hips tipping toward him, pushing with instinct and need to an ancient rhythm they both understood.

Soon he felt the delicious tremors of her release, heard the startled gasp as the sensation gripped her. While she shuddered, he pulled her down onto his lap, astride, her long legs dangling to either side of his thighs. She collapsed against him, her cheek against his shoulder, her breath hot puffs against his neck, while he held her and suffered the torture of his needy flesh.

Austin slipped his hand between them and flicked open the buttons of his trousers, releasing his heated flesh, touching her—soft curls, warm skin, sleek and ready. He clenched his hands in the hair that tumbled around her bare shoulders, fighting against the desire to plunge inside her, to claim her body as she had claimed his soul. "Sarah, look at me, love."

Sarah lifted her head, the lamplight glittering in her eyes. She looked drowsy with the desire he had kindled inside her.

"Feel me." Sarah's eyes grew wide as he captured her hand and led her to his hardened sex. "Know me."

She eased her fingers around him, and he stirred in her grasp. "Oh, my," she whispered, snatching her hand away from him.

"Touch me, Sarah." He made no move to force her, holding her only with his gaze.

She moistened her lips, a slow slide of the tip of her tongue. She lowered her eyes, studying the long length of him before she touched him.

Austin closed his eyes, willing his body to stay still in her grasp. Long fingers, cool against his heat, soft, curious, testing his length, his breadth, squeezing him, wrenching a moan from his throat.

"I'm sorry," she whispered, pulling away from him. "I didn't mean to hurt you."

"No." He grabbed her hand and brought her back to where his body craved her touch. "It wasn't pain, Sarah. Not pain."

"Oh." She glanced down to where he held her hand against his hardened flesh. "I think I understand." A shy smile curved her lips as she slipped her fingers around him.

"Yes." He showed her the rhythm that turned his blood to fire. Sarah responded, sliding her hands along his length, delicate fingers squeezing, quickly learning where the sensation flared thick and hot.

Austin threw back his head, a growl emanating from deep in his chest. "A joining, Sarah." He pressed against her moist threshold, easing his way into the most delicious heat he had ever felt. "We've found each other again, as we have in a thousand lifetimes."

A joining.

Sarah understood. She embraced each nuance of that meaning.

"A joining," she whispered.

He never took his eyes from hers as he eased inside her, and in his eyes she saw eternity. "My *Edaina.*"

The pain was fleeting, like a glowing ember tossed into a pool, sizzling for one brief moment before it was engulfed in the water. And she felt engulfed as well, surrounded by him, drawn into a pool of sensation that rippled all around her and in her.

She slid her hands through his thick black hair, feeling the damp heat of his scalp as she held his head and kissed him. His scent aroused her senses, a trace of bayberry mingled with a spice all his own. His hands, everywhere, stroking her, squeezing her nipples, brushing her low, in that place where desire flared and ripped through her like lightning.

Soon he drove all thought from her mind until there was only sensation flowing through her, until she shimmered with the light and heat that ignited between them, fusing the two into one.

Together they rose to a place beyond the bounds of time. There, in that glittering realm, pleasure ruled supreme, granting promise and freedom. Sarah shuddered in his arms, arching, distantly hearing his voice mingling with her own, unintelligible, joyful.

She collapsed against him, breathing hard, clutching him, her arms tight around his shoulders and neck. Passion. Until now a fuzzy, indistinct concept. A word seldom used, often pondered.

She drew a deep breath, inhaling the salt and musk of his damp neck. He held her close, his arms around her bare back, his thighs cushioning her bottom, his body still deep within her.

How could anyone live without passion in their lives? How had she lived before this moment in his arms? Perhaps she hadn't. Perhaps all that had come before was merely a state of existing.

She turned her head, rubbing her cheek against the warm silk of his shirt, catching a glimpse of the mirror. Startling, their images suspended in the glass, a woman nestled against a man, naked, her breasts flush against his chest. A portrait of wanton abandon.

Like mother, like daughter.

The words hissed inside her brain, threatening her. Yet for the first time in her life, she began to understand their true meaning. She began to understand how a woman might turn toward this warmth, especially a woman faced with the frigid reality of a lifetime filled with bitter loneliness.

And what had her mother faced all those years ago? The marriage of her parents had been arranged, this Sarah knew. Had her mother found the chill of winter where there should have been the heat of summer?

Austin lifted her hair, drawing it back from her shoulders, allowing the heavy mane to fall down her back, the silky strands sliding against her moist skin. "Are you all right, love?"

By the tone of his voice, Sarah knew he was asking her more than how well she had weathered the physical pain of their first joining. She drew back in his arms, looking at this man who had changed her, this man who had brought her to life.

He was watching her as though he were waiting for her to pass sentence on him. She slid her fingers over his brow, smoothing away the lines of his concern. "I'm better than I have ever been in my life."

Her words caused his lips to curve upward. "You're better than I ever imagined, my love."

"I'm different than I ever imagined." She slipped her fingers into the hair at his nape and gave the silken strands a gentle tug. "I find you make me dreadfully curious, Lord Sinclair."

He traced the curve of her ear with his fingertip. "How is that, Lady Sinclair?"

"I wonder what it shall be like to sleep in your arms." She pressed her lips to his chin, feeling his sigh against her cheek. "Are you going to wear all of these clothes to bed?" she asked, sliding her fingers down the front of his shirt.

He cradled her face in his hands and kissed her until she moaned with the sheer pleasure of it. "My beautiful wife, the only thing I wish to wear in bed is the warmth of your body."

Tiny quivers of delight rippled through her at the husky tone in his voice. "Perhaps I'm truly wicked, but I find I want to feel your skin against mine."

"Anything for my wicked lady." He allowed her to undress him, and she sensed he took pleasure in the way she parted and pulled the shirt from his shoulders as though she were opening a present on Christmas morning.

She slid her hands over the smooth skin of his shoulders, tracing the play of golden light that curved along the thick muscles. "I was tempted to do this that first night we met."

He smiled. "I thought you were tempted to strangle me."

"I was. Because of how terribly wicked you made me feel." She explored the springy black curls covering his chest, hesitating as she touched his left side. The skin was smooth here, as smooth as his shoulders. "You're completely healed. I thought there would be a scar."

He caught her hand and brought her fingers to his lips. "It must have been your gentle care."

She frowned as she looked at his side, the smooth skin taut across his ribs. "But I don't understand."

"Sarah, my love, you sound disappointed that I'm not horribly disfigured."

"Of course not, it's just—"

He stood with her in his arms, cutting off her words with his lips. He held her against him, her breasts pressed to his naked chest as though he wanted to absorb her into his skin. He slid his firm lips against hers, teasing her with his tongue as he carried her toward the bed. By the time her back touched the cool sheet, all thoughts of the scar that should have been there had evaporated from her thoughts.

Sarah sighed as he pulled away from her, a wordless sound of protest that shocked her with the desire that colored her own voice. He smiled as though he were satisfied with her reaction.

All her life she had fought this wickedness she knew lurked deep inside her. Yet here she was, watching a man strip away his clothes, and she couldn't manage to summon a single guilty twinge.

Sarah held her breath as he slipped the black wool of his trousers from his narrow hips. Beneath, he wore white silk drawers, the soft cloth molding his body, which had grown hard and ready for her once more. He looked down at her with eyes that had darkened to a smoky blue as he stripped away the last scrap of his clothing, sliding the silk down the long length of his legs.

Her gaze was drawn from his wide shoulders down the length of his chest to that part of him she had felt move deep inside her. If it had not already occurred she would think it impossible for her body to sheathe him.

"I believe we fit perfectly," he said, as though he could read her thoughts.

"So it would seem," she whispered, feeling a liquid heat simmer deep inside her in that secret place only he had ever claimed.

He sank to the bed beside her, stretching the length of his body against her, his warmth closing around her with the rich musky scent of his skin. "Shall we make certain?"

She slipped her arms around his shoulders, the curls on his chest teasing her aching nipples. "Yes."

The small crystal glowed in Bram Duggan's hand, capturing the warmth of his palm, radiating like moonlight, reflecting on the glass cases of the treasure room. He smiled as he entered the room. It was about time Lord Sinclair put pride and honor aside and allowed a professional to do his job. He knew there was some reason he liked the man.

Bram shifted the crystal, directing the light toward the cabinets lining the wall to his right. If he could open the drapes, allow the moonlight into the room, he would be able to move faster. But he couldn't take the risk.

According to Sinclair the medallion was in the second cabinet. His pulse beat against the high collar of his black shirt as he crept across the room. Mrs. Van Horne and her daughter slept in rooms at the opposite end of the hall, overlooking the gardens. Yet he knew one wrong move, one wayward sound, could bring disaster.

He held up the crystal as he reached the cabinet, the light glowing on the polished rosewood, glinting on the glass. Beyond the glass, gold captured the radiance of the light. Ancient gold. Timeless mysteries.

The brass handle was cold against his hand as he opened the cabinet door. Nothing but a soft slide of wood against wood to betray him. He would be in and out without incident. Nothing would go wrong. Nothing would stop him. Still, he couldn't banish the tension coiling around him.

He drew a deep breath into his tight lungs. He lifted the medallion, the gold heavy in his grasp, heavy as the weight of ultimate power. It was the first time he had ever touched a medallion of the Inner Circle. What secrets did it hold? What powers could it channel?

His reason for being here faded. The danger of detection dissolved as he stared into the eye of the ancient symbol of flight, the emerald winking in the light. In his mind the legends whispered.

The magic to disappear into thin air. The ability to move through time. The power to destroy with a bolt of lightning. All of this and more was told in the legends of the lords of the Inner Circle, the guardians of knowledge. What was true? Were the legends nothing more than fairy tales?

He sensed movement behind him: a brush of heat, a slide of footsteps on wood. Careless! He had been careless, allowing his defenses to slip. Bram clutched the medallion in his hand. He pivoted to face the intruder.

Something heavy cracked against his skull. Light splintered with pain in his brain. He clutched the medallion in his hand as his legs buckled beneath him.

Couldn't let them have it! Couldn't fail . . .

The floor dissolved beneath him, and he fell into the cold fathomless depths of darkness.

Leighton pried open Duggan's hand, pulling back the long fingers, exposing the medallion to the strange light glowing from the crystal that lay on the floor a few feet away from the man's body. He dropped Duggan's hand on the floor and stood, staring at the medallion. "So this is what Sinclair wanted."

"Is he dead?" Collin asked, gazing down at Duggan, his voice betraying his terror.

"You look as though you're going to be ill." Leighton bent to retrieve the glowing crystal. It was cool and hard to the touch. The glow intensified as he held it. "If you expect to stay with me, you really must develop a stronger stomach, Collin."

Collin sank to his knees. He hesitated a moment before he placed a trembling hand over Duggan's heart. "He's alive," he whispered, sinking back on his heels.

"Yes, I suppose he would have a rather thick skull." Leighton stared down at the unconscious man. He had thick blond hair, strong features, a full mouth parted to reveal a glimmer of white teeth. He was a handsome brute.

"Leighton, let's get out of here."

"Relax. The sleeping powder I slipped into their evening hot chocolate will keep Roxanne and Clarissa out of our way." Leighton slipped the medallion into the pocket of his trousers. "Now what should we do with him?"

"Leave him."

"I wouldn't want anyone to find him here, not in this room. It would raise far too many questions should my dear stepmama call the police." Leighton smiled as he stared down at Duggan, an image forming in his brain, a delightfully wicked image. "Help me strip him."

Austin stared at the pale lace curtains fluttering in the cool evening breeze. Moonlight poured through the open windows, streaming across the carpet, rippling over the white linen sheets of the bed where he lay with Sarah.

She was so warm, nestled against his side, bare except for the sheet that covered her. He held her close, his arm along her back, his hand on her naked hip beneath the sheet. She lay trusting in his embrace, her head against his shoulder, her hand riding the rise and fall of his chest.

Never in his life had he felt this complete. Never in his life had he felt this frightened. He slid his hand along the downy curve of her hip. What would she do when he told her the truth? Who would she choose, her husband or her brother?

"You called me your *Edaina.*" With her fingertip, Sarah drew a serpentine pattern on his chest, sliding up toward his chin. "What does that mean?"

"Soul mate."

"Yes, I feel that way." She smiled as she looked up at him. "I've never heard that word before."

"It's from a language long forgotten." Austin kissed the tip of her nose.

"Then how do you know of it?"

It was impossible to tell the entire truth. Yet he would not lie, not now, not when he wanted to give her the best of himself. "I studied ancient cultures."

"I see. One reason why you're so interested in antiquities."

He stroked the hair back from her temple. "One of the reasons."

She turned her face into his shoulder, pressing a soft kiss against his skin. "I've been thinking of my mother. Do you think she might agree to see me? I would like very much to talk to her."

"I'm certain she would. I'll talk to her tomorrow."

"Thank you." Sarah closed her eyes, thick lashes brushing his skin. "Perhaps you don't know this, but I am very good at business."

"I know you're very good at many things." He tugged the edge of the sheet that lay above her hip, exposing the pale curves of her breasts.

"I'm serious." She lifted herself up on her elbow, her hair tumbling over her shoulder, gathering in a silken pool on his chest. Moonlight etched her features from the shadows.

Austin didn't want to be serious, not yet. They would have so little time before the world would intrude once more, before he faced the risk of losing her. He lowered his gaze, staring at her breasts, carved white alabaster in the moonlight, round and gorgeous.

"I have suggested several investments for my uncle to make, and we've done well with them. Although there is one whose worth I don't seem to be able to convince him of."

Austin drew a deep breath, filling his senses with the delicate trace of lavender and her own enticing perfume. Deception, it was there between them, the lies he had spread so easily. "Your apartment houses for the poor."

She nodded, her hair brushing his skin, sending shivers of sensation rippling along his nerves. "When Leighton comes home, my uncle and cousin shall have no alternative but to agree to my plan." She smiled, a devious little curve of her lips. "My brother will do what I ask of him, I know it."

She was close to Leighton, as close as any brother and sister could be. Austin felt a shaking within him, as though he stood on the edge of a cliff, the ground shifting beneath him. One wrong move and he would tumble headlong into oblivion.

"I haven't been completely honest with you."

Austin's breath stilled in his chest. "What have you told me that wasn't true?"

"Oh, I told you the truth; I simply didn't tell you the entire truth." She smiled as she peeked at him from beneath her lashes. "My inheritance was initially quite modest, but I've been able to invest most of it and I've done well."

"So I've married a rich heiress after all."

"Not exactly rich, but comfortable." She brushed her fingers over the curls in the center of his chest.

"I would hope you will no longer feel the need to . . . ah . . . collect things for people."

"I reformed the moment I met you." Austin traced the curve of her brow with his fingertip, smoothing away her frown. "I wouldn't want to take the chance of being locked away from you, my love."

"I'm so glad. I thought, if you didn't mind, I might take a look at your financial situation to see what might be accomplished." She stared at his chin as she spoke, as though she were afraid to meet his eyes. "Of course, even with my contribution to our funds, we will need to live more modestly than what you are accustomed to. But I think if we are prudent, we shall do fine."

Austin drew a breath that shattered in his chest. She humbled him with the pure innocence of her love. "Would you come live in a woodcutter's cottage with me, Sarah?"

She looked up into his eyes and what he saw in the hazel depths filled his soul with light. "I would live anywhere, as long as I could be with you."

"Sarah," he whispered, sliding his arms around her.

He rolled with her in his arms, spilling her hair across his pillow. He kissed her, and she opened to him, slipping her arms around his neck, holding him as though she thought he might disappear with the first light of dawn. Desperation rose inside him with the fear of losing her.

"No matter what happens, Sarah," he whispered, drawing back to look into her eyes, "remember that I love you, more than my life."

Sarah frowned, a look of concern darkening her eyes, and he realized she was sensing his own fear. "Is something wrong?"

"Nothing, as long as I have you. I love you, Sarah." Slowly he sank into her welcoming heat, joining their bodies. "Promise me you will remember this night and know my love for you."

"I will." She cradled his face in her hands, looking up at him in wonder and joy. "And know I love you, my husband."

He moved inside her, loving her until she moaned and shuddered beneath him again and again, until she begged for him to join her in that dazzling realm where love and passion gave promise of tomorrow. As their blood cooled, as he held her through the fleeting night, he thought of the dawn rushing to meet them, and the deceptions he would lay bare in the light of day.

Chapter Twenty-One

Rhys Sinclair paused on the path leading from his home to the bluff overlooking the ruins of ancient Avallon. Brianna stood on the edge of the cliff, staring into the valley below. The breeze lifted her long, unbound hair to the rays of the morning sun, the silken strands shimmering like dark molten gold in the light.

He had known he would find her here. She had been his wife for more than thirty years. She had given him three children and a life filled with love. He could sense her feelings as keenly as he could sense his own. And he knew how troubled she was.

She turned as he approached, looking up at him with eyes that held the blue-gray light of dawn. She was still as beautiful as she had been that first day he had seen her, riding a chestnut stallion like the wind over the emerald hills of Ireland.

"What did the council say?" she asked.

He brushed his fingertips over the lines of worry carved into her brow. "They agreed to hold judgment on Austin until after he successfully completes this mission."

"And if he isn't successful?"

"Have faith in him." He didn't want to imagine the consequences should Austin fail to return with the medallion.

"I wish he were home," she whispered.

Rhys slid his arms around her. He held her close, drinking in her warmth, giving and taking comfort, wishing for the day when their family would be whole again.

"What is the meaning of this!"

The sharp words pierced Bram Duggan's pounding head like pointed darts of steel. He opened his eyes, blinking at the sunlight that blinded him. Pink silk trimmed in thick white lace formed a canopy over his head. He was in bed. Somewhere.

A scream ripped through his ears, shattering like broken glass in his brain. He sat up, his bleary eyes focusing on the woman standing at the foot of the bed. Roxanne Van Horne. And she looked as though her worst nightmare had come to life.

Memories tumbled through his brain like sand falling through his fingers. The medallion, he had held it, and then . . . he groaned with the realization that he had lost it. Van Horne. It must have been Van Horne.

"What are you doing here?"

Bram glanced toward the shrill sound. Clarissa Van Horne sat beside him, clutching a white sheet to her naked breasts. Great Alexis! He was in her bed.

"Clarissa, how could you do this to me?" Roxanne pressed her hand to her heart, slim white fingers fanned against her gold satin wrapper. "Under my own roof!"

"Mother, I didn't! I swear!"

Bram rolled from the bed, his head spinning with the sudden movement. He had to get to Sinclair, warn him.

"My heavens!" Roxanne gasped, her eyes wide as she stared at him standing there in her daughter's room, as naked as the day he was born.

Clarissa screamed.

Bram pressed his fingers to his pounding temples. Where were his clothes? A nightgown, blue silk in a heap on the pink-and-white carpet. A wrapper, blue satin over the carved arm of a chair. No sign of his trousers.

"Explain yourself, young lady."

Bram snatched the robe. Satin screamed as he shrugged his broad shoulders into the fitted garment, seams popping down the back. The smooth satin brushed the top of his knees.

"Mother, I swear. I didn't do anything. He did it!"

Bram looked from Roxanne, who stood like a queen, pale and indignant at the foot of her precious daughter's bed, to the little princess, who sat clutching the sheet to her chin with one hand, pointing an accusing finger at him with the other.

"Explain yourself, Duggan," Roxanne demanded. "Just what are you doing in my daughter's room?"

Even if he'd wanted to explain, he couldn't. "Guess I fell asleep."

"Fell asleep!" Clarissa stared at him with her lovely mouth wide open. "Why, you dirty stable rat! How dare you come into my room!"

Bram clenched his jaw as he stared at the arrogant witch. He remembered every lurid glance the little hypocrite had cast in his direction, every painful moment he had spent in a saddle at her command. "Guess we should have kept meeting in the stable, Clarissa."

"What!"

"How long has this been going on, young woman?" Roxanne demanded.

"Mother, nothing is going on. I don't know how he got in here."

"How do you suppose we shall keep this quiet?" Roxanne demanded. "You're ruined!"

"No! Nothing happened! I swear!"

"How can we ever find a suitable match now?" Roxanne paced back and forth beside her daughter's bed. "How could you have done anything so foolish?"

While Roxanne heaped one dire consequence after another on Clarissa's shoulders, Bram edged toward the door. As much as he was enjoying the fall of the little tyrant, he needed to get to Sinclair. Van Horne had several hours' head start.

Bram collided with Emerson as he slipped out the open door. Emerson drew back, his dark eyes growing round as pennies as he stared at Bram.

"I heard a scream," Emerson said, one dark brow lifting as he took in Bram's appearance.

Blue satin ruffles outlined a wide vee of bare skin and light brown curls that plunged from his chin to where Bram clutched the robe together at his waist. There was little hope for an innocent explanation.

Emerson glanced into the room where Roxanne was pacing, bemoaning the life she had sacrificed for her daughter. Clarissa sat whimpering on the bed. "There seems to be quite a disturbance."

"Seems we got caught," Bram said.

Emerson looked at Bram, a shadow of a smile on his lips. "Yes, so it would seem."

The entire staff would know of Clarissa's indiscretion in a matter of moments, Bram thought as he hurried past the butler, blue satin flaring around him. Gossip tended to rip through the servants' quarters like wildfire through dry grass. He estimated it would take no more than a few hours before most of New York would be whispering about Clarissa's affair with a lowly groom.

Poor Clarissa, Bram thought as he hurried down the narrow staircase leading to the kitchen. She might actually have to start behaving like a human being.

Sarah slowed her footsteps as she approached the front door of Isabel Bennett's house. Sunlight streamed through the carved glass of the window that arched above the wide oak door, tossing rainbows across the white and black squares of marble that lined the front hall.

A lifetime had passed since she had spoken more than a few curt words to her mother. Diana was waiting for Sarah now at her hotel. There were a thousand things Sarah had always wanted to ask her mother. Strange, but at the moment she couldn't think of anything except the hope she would not appear bitter. She wanted to put the bitterness aside.

Austin took her arm as they reached the door, turning Sarah to face him. She saw complete understanding in his eyes. Without words, he knew her fear, her anxiety, her reluctance and need to go through with this. And he was there for her, willing to give her his strong arm should she need it.

"Sarah, are you sure you want to do this alone?"

"Know that I love you, and that I'm grateful to you for helping me face my past." Sarah touched his cheek, his skin warm and firm beneath her palm.

"But this is something I must do alone."

He smiled, his cheek moving beneath her palm. "You're going to be just fine, milady."

Across the street from Isabel Bennett's house, Leighton Van Horne sat beneath the roof of the carriage he had hired, hidden in the shadows, watching as Austin Sinclair left the house with Sarah beside him.

Sarah!

She was his sister. She alone cared. And now that man was taking her away from him.

Leighton clutched the reins between his hands, the pair of grays moving restlessly in the traces, their harnesses jangling. He wanted to toss back his head and scream. He wanted to take Sinclair's throat between his hands and squeeze the life from him.

He watched as Sinclair lifted Sarah into a waiting carriage, his hands lingering at her waist. The look that passed between them was intimate. That man had defiled his sister.

One more reason to hate. One more reason to make sure Sinclair paid with his life.

She was leaving alone. Was she being followed? Was she being used as bait to trap him? Leighton hesitated before he followed her carriage. He had to see her. He had to show her the monster she had married.

Sarah pulled up in front of the carriage entrance of the Kensington Hotel on Madison Square. Tilting her head, she stared at the four stories of carved gray stone, wondering if her mother stood at one of the windows shining in the sunlight. What would she say? How should she greet her mother after 23 years?

A carriage pulled up beside her, the collapsible black top raised, shielding the driver from her view. She lifted the reins in her hands, preparing to drive through the carriage entrance.

"Sarah."

Sarah jumped at the raspy whisper. She turned toward the carriage that stood beside her. The driver had poked his head around the black edge of the roof. For a moment she didn't recognize this dark-haired man, but his features, she knew those features. "Leighton! What are you doing—"

"Hush, Sarah." Leighton looked around as though he expected one of the people strolling in the park across the street would come chasing after him. "I need to talk to you. Follow me."

"I have an engagement." Sarah thought it better to keep the identity of the person she was meeting from Leighton. He hated their mother. "Give me an hour and I'll—"

"Sarah, my life is at stake. You have to come with me."

"Your life?"

"I'll explain everything later." Leighton glanced over his shoulder before looking at Sarah, his handsome face intense. "Come with me."

Sarah glanced up at the windows of the hotel. She had waited 23 years for this meeting.

"Sarah, I need you."

She looked at her brother. He was desperate; she could see it in his pale blue eyes. Another few hours, she could wait another few hours to resolve her past.

Collin strained against the linen that bound his hands and feet. Leighton had used Collin's own ties to bind him. Sunlight poured through the portholes in Collin's cabin on his own yacht, creeping under the door of the storage closet where Leighton had left him.

The handkerchief Leighton had stuffed into his mouth gagged him. The silk scarf tied around his face to keep the handkerchief in place bit into the sides of his mouth. The fear inside him beat like a fist against his heart.

He rocked in the narrow space, tears leaking from the corners of his eyes. He didn't want to die. Lord help him, he would do anything to stay alive.

He thought of his father, Fraser Bennett, lord of the Inner Circle, Central Council member. He would expect Collin to die to preserve Avallon.

There was a time, when he was young, when Collin had imagined he would one day grow up to be the image of his father. Now he sat poised to betray him and everything he held dear.

He imagined how shocked Lord Fraser Bennett would be to discover his own son a traitor. Such a terrible blow to his political aspirations. After all the years of diligent work, all the precious time he had stolen from his family, Fraser might never become leader of the Central Council.

Laughter shook Collin, laughter born of fear and the irony of destroying his father's dreams.

Austin shifted in his chair, the white wicker creaking beneath him. He stared at the fountain in the center of Isabel's conservatory, watching the water tumble in the sunlight, wondering how Sarah and her mother were getting along. As they had planned, in an hour he would meet Duggan in the alley behind the Van Horne house. When Austin had the medallion, he would tell Sarah the truth.

He drew a deep breath, orange blossoms and jasmine leaving a sweet tang on his tongue. He only prayed Sarah would forgive him for deceiving her.

"That boy." Isabel dropped the letter she had been reading on the table, the ivory parchment gliding on the warm air, bumping against the silver tea server.

"Is something wrong?" Austin asked.

"It seems my great-grandson has decided to go sailing for a few weeks." Isabel leaned back in her chair. "As though there were nothing more important for the boy to do than to take his yacht out and play."

"You have been all the help my family has needed, Isabel."

She smiled, and yet there was a melancholy to her look. "I fear your travails have not yet passed, my dear young man."

Austin nodded. "I'm going to talk with Sarah when she gets back this afternoon."

"I hope she understands. And I hope the Central Council . . ." Isabel paused as Bram Duggan swept into the room, pushing the palm fronds and banana leaves aside like a strong wind as he stormed along the marble-lined path.

Austin came to his feet. "What's wrong?"

Bram halted beside the table, his broad shoulders rising beneath his blue cotton shirt with each quick breath he took. "Van Horne was in the house last night. He has the medallion."

Bram's words hit Austin like a hard right to the belly. "What happened?"

"I had it in my hand. And I let him blindside me. I woke up this morning with a lump on my head." Bram ran his hand over the back of his head, ruffling his thick blond hair. "There is no excuse for it. I should have been more cautious."

"Great Alexis!" Isabel clasped her hands on the table as though she were trying to force herself to remain calm. "What do we do now?"

Austin turned as Jenkins, the butler, entered the room. The short, slender man with the thinning brown hair was from Avallon and had been with Isabel for more than 50 years.

"You have a telephone call, sir," Jenkins said. "Mrs. Schuyler. It seems Lady Sinclair never arrived at the hotel."

"Sarah," Austin whispered.

"Do you think Van Horne has gotten to her?" Bram asked.

Austin didn't want to think of the disaster if he had. "Isabel, talk to Diana; try to calm her concerns. Bram, contact the others at the train stations, the docks—make sure they know Van Horne has been seen in the city. I'm going to look for Sarah." If she was with her brother, Austin had an idea of where they might be.

Leighton tossed a pebble toward the river, the stone arcing down the 30-foot slope, slicing through the sunlight before sinking into the glittering water. He turned away from the water, smiling as he looked at Sarah.

Sarah watched him, feeling as though she were that pebble he had tossed into the river, arcing now, flying through the air, headed for disaster. "Leighton, why did you bring me here?"

"Do you remember this place?" He pressed his hands flat against the old hickory below the initials he had carved deep into the bark, scarring the tree forever. "We had fun here, didn't we?"

"Leighton, what's wrong? What did you mean when you said your life was in danger?"

Leighton rested his shoulder against the scarred old hickory. Sunlight filtered through the leaves overhead, dripping golden light on his hair and shoulders. "Someone wants to murder me."

"Murder!"

"I'm being followed, Sarah, chased like an animal. That's why I did this to my hair." Leighton shoved his hand through the hair he had always prized, a dark brown dye concealing the silvery blond tresses that usually fell to his shoulders. Cut short now, the dark mane barely brushed the lobes of his ears.

"Who would want to murder you?"

Leighton held her gaze a long moment before he spoke. "Austin Sinclair."

Sarah felt that downward plunge, waters of doubt rising to meet her. "This is no time to be joking, Leighton."

"Oh, Sarah. I'm not joking, my dear heart. Austin Sinclair wants to murder me."

Sarah balled her hands into fists at her sides. "You're talking about my husband."

"It seems I got here too late to save you." Leighton picked at the bark with his finger. "You're part of his plan, you see."

"I don't understand." Sarah was sinking, dark waters rising all around her, drawing her under a river filled with a lifetime of doubts. She fought to stay afloat. "Why would he marry me if he wants to murder you? It doesn't make sense."

"Oh, my darling Sarah, it makes perfect sense. You see, his sister fell in love with me. And when I did not return Alexandria's affection, she tried to kill herself."

"What did you do to her?"

"Nothing, dear heart. Nothing but insist on choosing my own bride. Still, I'm afraid Austin Sinclair doesn't see it that way. He wants to punish me for his sister's folly."

"I don't believe it."

Leighton's face twisted in pain as though she had slapped him hard across the cheek. "Sarah, do you think I would lie to you?"

"There must be some reasonable explanation."

"Who else could you count on but me, Sarah? There has always been only the two of us against the world."

"I can't believe it." Sarah felt her doubts wrap around her, draw her under, drowning her. "I can't believe Austin would—"

"Sarah, did he ever mention the gold medallion I sent to you?"

"He said you obtained it illegally."

"Alexandria gave me that medallion. It's been in the Sinclair family for generations. He wants it back almost as much as he wants to punish me. By marrying you he could get the medallion."

Why would a man like Austin Sinclair be interested in a woman like Sarah Van Horne? It all made sense now. It was all so horribly clear. And still she didn't want to face the truth. "He said he loved me."

"Of course he did. Don't you see, by marrying you, he has accomplished the ultimate revenge, better than murdering me. I'm sure he plans to leave you, cause a scandal, ruin you, as he fancies I have ruined his sister."

I would give my life for them. Isn't that what Austin had said about his brother and sister? What more would he do? She leaned against the trunk of a tall oak, pressing her cheek to the rough bark, her knees dissolving beneath her. "How could he lie that way? I don't understand how he could—"

"Sarah," Leighton whispered, resting his hand on her shoulder. "A man like that has much experience in capturing the hearts of unsuspecting women."

Images of the night before flickered in her mind.

She had fallen so easily under his spell. The lies, how she had wanted to believe those lovely lies. "I made it so easy for him."

"Don't blame yourself."

Sarah's stomach squeezed, threatening her. She swallowed back the gorge rising in her throat, tears filling her eyes.

Fool!

She had been such an incredible fool.

"We'll make him pay, Sarah."

Sarah closed her eyes, wishing she could close out the taunting images in her head. How Austin must have laughed at her, the eager old maid, willing to do anything for a shred of tenderness.

"I have a plan, Sarah," Leighton said, rubbing his hand over her shoulder. "If you—"

"Stand away from her, Van Horne."

Sarah flinched at the sound of Austin's voice. She turned and found him standing a few feet away, holding a pistol pointed at Leighton. And yet it didn't seem like Austin at all. The gentle man with the generous smile was gone, and in his place stood a stranger, a man who had stolen her last shred of dignity, a man who wanted to murder her brother.

Even his face seemed different to her now, harder. The strong lines and curves of his face were those of a conqueror; his silvery blue eyes wore the fierce look of a warrior.

"I said stand away from her, Van Horne."

Leighton squeezed her arm before moving several feet to her right. Austin kept the pistol pointed at him, turning away from Sarah. They were alone, secluded here, far from the walking path. There would be no one to help, Sarah thought. Leighton and she had only each other, as they had all their lives.

"Sarah, are you all right?" Austin glanced at her

as he spoke, and for a moment she imagined seeing regret in his eyes. Another illusion.

"How did you find us?" Sarah asked.

"I remembered you said this was one of your brother's favorite places. I didn't know where else to start looking for you."

"Do you plan to kill my brother?"

"Sarah, I don't know what he told you, but believe me, I'm only doing what needs to be done. Your brother is a criminal."

"Only in your eyes, Sinclair," Leighton said.

"Trust in me, Sarah," Austin whispered.

How could she trust him when he held a pistol pointed at her brother?

Austin frowned as he stared at Van Horne. "Where's the medallion?"

The medallion. It was as Leighton had said—Austin wanted the medallion. He had lied to her from the beginning.

Sarah moved toward the stranger she had married, keeping her gaze on the pistol in his hand, sunlight glinting on the polished steel barrel. Slow steps, measured, each one bringing her closer to the pistol he held. Did he intend to shoot her, too?

"It's important to you, isn't it?" Leighton moved to his right, away from Sarah, causing Austin to track him with the pistol. "That small piece of gold."

"Tell me where it is, Van Horne."

"If you kill me, you'll never find it," Leighton said.

Sarah stared at the pistol glinting in the sunlight that pierced the leaves overhead, wondering if that small revolver might end her life. It didn't matter, not now. She drew a deep breath, preparing to launch herself at Austin.

"Sarah?" Austin turned toward her, catching her before she had a chance to move.

Sarah froze, her gaze dropping to the pistol pointed now at her chest. "Are you going to shoot me, too?"

"Sarah, you can't believe that," Austin said.

Sarah stared at that pistol. She had to stop him. She couldn't let him kill Leighton.

"She hates you for what you did to her, Sinclair."

Austin glanced back at Leighton. "You filled her with lies. She'll soon learn you—"

Sarah rammed Austin's arm, throwing her entire weight against him. It was enough to knock him off balance. He stumbled, with Sarah clinging to his arm.

"Sarah!" Austin shouted. He pulled his arm free of her grasp, pushing her aside. But it was too late.

"One move and I'll shoot, Sinclair."

Sarah glanced at her brother, her entire body trembling. He held a pistol in his hand, small and silver, deadly, pointed straight at Austin's heart. She looked up at Austin. In his eyes she saw anger and a reckless determination.

"Drop the gun."

Austin hesitated.

"I'll put a bullet in your heart before you have a chance to aim that pistol."

"No," Sarah whispered. "Austin, please drop the gun."

Austin glanced at her, his eyes narrowed with fury. He flexed his fingers on the silver handle before he allowed the revolver to drop from his hand.

Sarah stared at Leighton. He was smiling, his eyes glittering like an icy lake on a sunny winter day, a stranger's eyes. In that instant she wondered if she knew the man she had lived with all her life. Had Austin been telling the truth? Quickly she cast away her doubts. If she couldn't trust Leighton, she could trust no one.

"I'm going to kill you for what you did to my sister." Leighton lifted the gun, pointing it at Austin's head. "Right between your eyes."

"Leighton!" Sarah dashed in front of Austin.

"Stay clear, Sarah," Austin said, pushing her out of the way.

Sarah stumbled, hitting the hickory with her shoulder. She scarcely felt the pain as she stared at her brother and realized he was about to kill Austin. "Leighton, don't do this!"

Leighton laughed, transforming this frightening stranger into the brother she loved. "Sarah, my heart, do you think I would actually kill a man? I just wanted to scare him a little."

Austin didn't look frightened. He looked as though he wanted to rip Leighton apart with his bare hands, Sarah thought, swallowing past the lump of fear in her throat.

"Take off your tie, Sinclair, and hand it to my sister."

Austin stared at Sarah as he unfastened his tie and slipped the strip of white linen from around his starched white collar. "He's not what you think he is, Sarah," he said, holding out his hand, the tie dangling from his long fingers. "He's a murderer."

"Liar!" Sarah snatched the tie from Austin's hand. "You would say anything to get what you want, wouldn't you?"

"Looks like she doesn't trust you," Leighton said, smiling at Austin. "Now put your back against that tree and wrap your arms back around the trunk, Sinclair." He gestured with the pistol toward the old hickory tree.

Austin complied, pressing his back to the tree, keeping his gaze on Sarah.

"Use his tie to secure his hands, Sarah."

Sarah walked around the tree, thankful for the chance to escape the look in Austin's eyes. It was far too accusing, as though she were the one who had betrayed him.

When she was done tying his wrists together she stared down at his hands. His fingers curled toward his palms. Memories washed over her. Gentle hands, touching her, stroking her, bringing her to life. Had it all been a lie?

"Did you tie him nice and tight, Sarah?"

Sarah checked the bonds, tugging on the end of the white linen. "Yes."

Sarah watched as Leighton moved toward Austin, drops of sunlight rippling across the silver barrel of the pistol. She shivered in the breeze. For some reason she couldn't ignore the fear, the unnerving feeling that Leighton would do Austin some harm.

Leighton paused a foot in front of Austin, staring into his eyes. "So you thought you could turn my sister against me."

Austin looked past Leighton to where Sarah had moved to stand behind her brother. "I made the mistake of falling in love with your sister."

Sarah shuddered inside, hope and doubt warring within her.

"Liar!" Leighton swung his hand, hitting Austin across the cheek with the pistol.

Austin groaned, the blow snapping his head to one side.

"Leighton!" Sarah rushed forward, grabbing Leighton's arm when he drew back to strike again.

Leighton looked down at her, his eyes wide and furious. In that instant he looked like a madman.

She gripped his arm tighter, as though she could drag him from the flames of madness that threatened to consume him. "He's helpless."

One corner of Leighton's mouth twitched. "Yes, of course." He released his breath. "I'm just so angry, Sarah. For what he did to you."

"The police will take care of him."

"No," Leighton said. "Sarah, the police would only cause a scandal."

"But what will you do? If he is really trying to murder you, then—"

"Of course he's trying to murder me." Leighton took her arm and led her away from Austin. "Sarah, I can take care of this on my own. All I need is a few hours to get away."

Sarah felt a shudder deep inside her as she stared up into her brother's eyes. "Leighton, you are telling me the truth, aren't you?"

"Sarah, dear heart, you aren't going to doubt me, are you?"

Sarah glanced at Austin. He was watching her, his expression intense. An ugly red mark slashed across his cheek, and blood trickled from the corner of his mouth. There was pain in his eyes, the pain of betrayal.

"God, if you weren't here for me, Sarah, I don't know what I would do," Leighton said, his voice filled with desperation. "Tell me you still believe in me."

Sarah looked up at her brother. Everything he had said about Austin made sense. And yet . . .

"Sarah, you're all I have."

And he was all she had ever had. "Of course I believe in you, Leighton."

Leighton hugged her. "You keep him here, just for a few hours," he said, pulling away from her. "By then I should be a safe distance away. Will you do that for me, Sarah?"

Sarah nodded.

"Good girl."

She watched as Leighton hurried away from her, disappearing into the trees as he had when they were children playing a game of hide-and-seek. Only they were no longer children. And she was no longer certain she knew the man he had become.

Chapter Twenty-Two

Austin struggled with the bonds that held his wrists. The knots were simple, yet tight, the linen stubborn beneath his fingers. "Sarah, please, untie me."

Sarah turned to face him. A shaft of sunlight sliced through the leaves overhead, spilling over her. Her hair shimmered and her face glowed with the golden light. A bemused angel wandering earth. A little girl lost in the woods. A woman alone with the man she felt had betrayed her.

"Sarah, please. You must trust me. I can't let him get away."

She moved toward him, her eyes haunted with doubt and pain. When she drew near she took a handkerchief from the pocket of her light gray skirt. Without a word she pressed the plain white linen to his lower lip, dabbing at the ragged wound her brother had inflicted there. Austin clenched his teeth against the sharp sting.

"Sarah, your brother has to be stopped before he harms anyone else."

She drew a breath, shallow, shaky. She lowered her lashes, blocking out the sight of him. "The medallion you were after that first night I met you, it belongs in your family, doesn't it?"

"Your brother stole it from my father's house."

She stared down at the handkerchief she held in her hand, scarlet staining the pure white linen. "Your sister gave it to Leighton."

"Is that what he told you?"

"He said your sister fell in love with him, and when he didn't return her regard, she tried to commit suicide."

"My sister had nothing to do with Leighton."

"I can understand why you wanted to avenge your sister. I . . ." Her voice cracked with emotion. "I know how much she means to you."

"Alexandria never gave Leighton the medallion. She never felt anything for your brother except revulsion and loathing." Austin tugged at the linen binding his wrists. "Sarah, I don't have time to explain everything. He's getting away. Please believe in me; untie me."

"How can I believe in you?" Sarah stepped back. "How can I know you aren't lying to me?"

He looked down into her eyes, regret squeezing his heart at the look of pain in the beautiful hazel depths. "Do you honestly believe last night was a lie, Sarah?"

"You lied from the first day I met you."

"Not about everything. Not about the way I feel for you."

She shook her head. "I don't believe you."

"Sarah, I never wanted to deceive you. But you were my only chance of retrieving the medallion Leighton had stolen from my family."

"You used me."

"In the beginning." He tugged against his bonds, needing to hold her. Perhaps if he could hold her, he could keep her from slipping away from him. "I love you, Sarah. I never wanted to hurt you. You have to believe me."

She pressed her hands to her temples as though her head were pounding with this struggle for the truth. "You aren't in any financial difficulties, are you?"

"No." He saw what she was doing, knew she needed to reinforce the fact that he was a scoundrel by confirming the lies he had spoken. "But that lie doesn't alter the simple truth. I married you because I didn't want to live without you."

"The night we met, you weren't trying to steal that medallion for some collector; you were trying to retrieve it for your own family. You used me from the beginning." She turned, facing the river, hugging her arms to her waist. "And it was easy for you, manipulating me. I wanted to believe all of your lies."

"If I had told you that your brother is a thief and a murderer, would you have believed me?"

She glanced at him, sunlight reflecting on the tears in her eyes. "My brother is not a thief or a murderer."

"Your brother killed one of the guards at my father's home the night he stole the medallion. He almost killed my brother."

Sarah shook her head. "I don't believe you!"

"It's the truth."

"No." Wildflowers bent beneath her gray skirt as she marched a few feet away from him, buttercups and Queen Anne's lace bowing to her. She paused, staring at the river with her hands clenched into fists at her sides, before turning to face him. "If it is true, why aren't the police after my brother?"

"The murder took place in Brazil." Austin felt the linen loosen around his wrists, but time was slipping away, and with each passing moment a murderer was gaining distance. "Sarah, I know there is much I have to explain. This isn't the time or the place. Untie me. Please."

"I can't. You want to murder my brother."

"I want to bring your brother to justice. I want to make sure he doesn't hurt anyone else."

"I can't believe you. I . . ." A sob escaped her lips. "Dear heaven, this is all some horrible nightmare."

"Sarah, if you don't believe me, if you think last night was nothing but a lie, you might as well pick up that revolver and put a bullet through my heart."

Sarah glanced down at the revolver lying in the grass near her feet. "No matter how much I despise you for what you did to me, to my brother, I couldn't kill anyone, including you."

Pain punctured his heart like a blade. "You are killing me," he whispered.

"Words, only words." She lowered her eyes, tears spilling down her cheeks. "You're so very good with words."

"Sarah, look into my eyes; tell me you see the truth there. I love you with all of my heart and my soul."

"How eloquently you lie," she whispered, refusing to look at him. "You must have great experience at it."

"I want to take your brother back to Brazil, where he'll have a fair trail. I swear I won't hurt him."

"My brother would never do the things you said he did."

Austin felt the linen drop away from his hands. And still he stood with his back to the tree, knowing he was too late to track Leighton, praying he was in time to save his wife. "Leighton plays by different rules. He takes what he wants, no matter what the cost to others."

"I don't believe you."

"If I could, I would shield you from any harm. But I can't. I always knew I would hurt you with the truth about your brother. I always knew it would come down to a choice, no matter how much I wanted to prevent it."

Austin held his breath, waiting for her to look at him. There was defiance in her eyes when she met his, and he sensed the coming response even before he posed the question. "Who do you choose, Sarah, your brother or your husband?"

She lifted her hands, a fluttery gesture that spoke of the turmoil inside her. "You married me for revenge."

"I married you because I loved you. I do love you."

Sarah shook her head. "You're a liar. And I despise you for it."

He stared at her, seeing the hate in her eyes, feeling the light drain from inside him, the warmth of summer dissolving into the ice of winter. He had lost her. He had been a fool to ever believe he could have her. "I guess you've made your decision."

"I won't let you manipulate me again." She swiped at the tears coursing down her cheeks. "I refuse to believe your lies."

"I admire your loyalty to the ones you love. I only wish I was one of them." Austin stepped away from the tree, baring his last deception.

"You're free!" Sarah stepped back, staring at him as though he were a lion about to devour her.

"Am I, Sarah?" He was still shackled by his love for her, a love he must try to bury, along with his hopes for a life with this woman. He retrieved his pistol.

She turned to run and he pounced, grabbing her arm, swinging her around to face him. "Let go of me!"

"I can't do that. You're part of this now."

Sarah moistened her lips, her eyes wide with fear. "What are you going to do with me?"

Austin drew a breath, his lungs constricted with the pain wrapping around his chest. "Take you home with me, I guess."

"I'm not going anywhere with you!"

Austin looked down into her eyes. They were filled with the fire of hate; desire and love had been consumed in that blaze. "You don't have a choice, Sarah."

"And what will you do, Sinclair?" She glanced to the pistol he held in his hand. "Shoot me?"

"What do you think?"

He felt the fine tremor of fear that rippled through her. "I think you're capable of anything."

The woman he loved more than his own life believed he would kill her. If he didn't feel as though he were dying inside he might laugh. As he led her back to his carriage, he wondered if he would ever be able to pull together the shattered pieces of his soul.

Austin stood beside a banana tree in the conservatory of Isabel Bennett's house, staring at the white orchids nestled in a fork in the branches. He felt frozen inside. Every move he made seemed detached, as though he were nothing but a machine moving through the sphere of space and time. Existence without life.

"I still can't believe Sarah helped him get away."

He glanced to where Isabel was sitting at the table, her hands tightly clasped on the glass top. Bram had returned an hour ago with the report that no one had sighted Leighton Van Horne. It had been six hours since he had escaped. Too long to hope they would catch him. "Sarah doesn't believe her brother did anything wrong."

"This is a disaster." Isabel stared down at her hands, slowly sliding her fingers apart. "The Central Council will investigate all of this, Austin. It will not look good for you, your wife aiding a criminal to escape with the medallion."

"I knew the risk I was taking when I married Sarah." Austin stroked the firm white petals of an orchid, the flower warm from the setting rays of the sun. Ancient vows echoed in his brain. He had failed them—his parents, his brother and sister, the Inner Circle, Avallon—betrayed them for a woman he should never have touched. "I shall file a complete report. I will of course take complete responsibility for the failure of this mission."

Isabel was quiet. Austin could feel her watching him, judging his emotions. And he knew he revealed nothing. He had transformed his face into a mask. He had buried all emotion deep inside.

He had been taught to focus his will, to mold a situation by thought and reason, and he had abandoned his training for emotion. Lessons should be learned once. He had learned long ago how emotion could betray a man. Only a fool was bitten twice by the same snake. And he was the worst kind of fool.

"What shall you do with Sarah?" Isabel asked.

Austin thought of the woman locked in a cabin on his yacht, a stranger to him now. He would not allow himself to remember what had passed between them the night before. Nothing but illusions, dreams that could not come true, that was all they had shared. "She knows too much to let her go. I'll take her to

Avallon with me. I've instructed my crew to be prepared to leave in an hour."

Isabel stood and moved toward him. She rested her hand on his arm, her fingers slim and white against his dark gray sleeve. When he looked at her she was smiling, a slight curve of her lips that left her eyes filled with concern. "It is true what is said of time. It heals the wounds unseen, my dear young man. I only hope you and Sarah may be so healed."

Austin felt a stirring beneath the ice encrusting his heart, and he stiffened. "You were right, Isabel. I never should have become involved with her."

"You cannot simply cut her out of your soul, Austin."

"Yes, I think that is exactly what I must do." He could not allow his feelings for Sarah to surface again. He would not tumble into that swirling pool of heated emotions. It was like a volcano, that molten pool, and he had plunged into that scalding lava, sacrificed his soul for the chance to win his *Edaina.*

Sarah paced the length of the sitting room in her suite aboard Sinclair's ship, her footsteps swallowed by the thick Persian carpet of emerald and gold wool. She had expected to be thrown into a hole in the bowels of the ship, not given a luxurious suite of rooms on the top deck.

Along with the sitting room, the suite included a dining room, dressing room, bathroom, and of course a bedroom. All the rooms were paneled in mahogany except for the bathroom, where white marble lined the walls. It was an elegant prison; she had to say that for Sinclair.

Would he expect her to share the suite with him? Did he expect her to lie beside him as she had only yesterday? If he did, if he thought she would melt at his touch, he would soon find he was mistaken.

Where was he taking her? She stared out one of the round portholes, watching as New York dissolved into the horizon, moonlight sprinkling silver across the rolling waves.

Time, how ruthless it could be. Things were happening so quickly. It all seemed some horrible nightmare. A breeze blew in through the opening, bathing her face with the salty tang of the sea.

Had it only been yesterday when she had spoken vows that bound her to a stranger? Waves of bitterness swept over her. She squeezed the edge of the porthole, resting her brow on her hands. It could overwhelm her. If she let it, the pain of Austin's betrayal would overwhelm her, destroy her.

She lifted her face to the breeze and forced the damp, cool air into her lungs. She would not allow it. She would not fall to pieces like a piece of porcelain dropped by a careless hand. Even though she felt broken inside. Even though she felt she had been shattered into a thousand pieces that could never be fit back together again.

She felt a tingle at the back of her neck, a warmth slide down her back, and knew she was no longer alone in the room. She pivoted. Austin was there, standing with his back to the closed door, watching her.

Chapter Twenty-Three

Sarah silently berated herself. She should know better, but there it was, that leap of excitement centered in her chest at the sight of him, that sudden racing of her heart that left her breathless.

Austin looked like a romantic pirate, dressed in a loose-fitting white linen shirt and close-fitting black breeches tucked into knee-high black boots. And yet she felt no danger emanating from this man, only a haunting melancholy.

His face might have been carved from marble, it was so cold. His eyes might have been the pale glitter of silver, they were so lifeless. It frightened her, this stillness she sensed inside him, like a lake in the dead of winter, frozen to its depths. In his arms he held Merlin, the plump feline purring contentedly.

"Merlin," she whispered, moving toward them.

Before she reached him, Austin set the cat on the carpet, as though he wanted to avoid any chance of contact with her. Merlin meowed, a scratchy growl of protest from deep in his throat. The cat rubbed back and forth against Austin's legs, ignoring her.

"It would seem he is a typical male." Sarah looked up into Austin's eyes. "Ready to betray me without a second thought."

He didn't flinch at the barb. Like a beautiful sculpture he stood before her, carved perfection, devoid of emotion. "I may have kept the truth from you, Sarah, but I never betrayed you."

"I see. You lied to me, married me under false pretenses, but you don't consider that betrayal."

"Perhaps I should have told you the truth about your brother before we were married. If I am guilty, it is of being afraid of losing you."

She stepped back from him, resisting the all too tempting urge to tumble into the beguiling web he could weave so skillfully around her. "What do you hope to accomplish with your lies?"

"That's the point, isn't it, Sarah?" He laughed, a strange hollow sound filled with self-loathing. "There is nothing left to accomplish, nothing left to salvage."

Sarah hugged her arms to her waist, feeling chilled suddenly. "Where are you taking me?"

"To my home."

"England?"

"No." Austin walked away from her, moving toward one of the portholes. He stood there with his hands loose at his sides, his gaze on the rippling water. "I was born in a place called Avallon, a city perched high on a mountaintop in the heart of Brazil." He drew a breath, his shoulders rising beneath his white linen shirt. "It's an old society. Very old. My ancestors settled the original city six thousand years ago."

"Six thousand years . . . Egypt was barely civilized six thousand years ago."

"We had civilization long before Egypt." He glanced over his shoulder, a shadow of a smile curving his lips. "I'm going to tell you things you will find difficult to believe. But I want to prepare you for Avallon. It is . . . different from what you are accustomed to."

An odd sensation gripped Sarah as she held his gaze. It was like a nightmare that came without warning in the stillness of the evening, as though she were wandering through a shadowy forest, knowing danger lurked behind one of the trees, not knowing where or when it would strike. "How is this Avallon different?"

"To answer that question, I need to tell you something about my people." He turned to face her, leaning back against the mahogany-paneled wall, the polished wood glowing around him like a golden halo in the incandescent light. "My ancestors came from an island nation, the cradle of civilization. While men were still living in caves, my ancestors were building cities of carved stone and marble. They inspired myths and legends. They were the people of Atlantis."

"Atlantis?" Sarah stared at him. "What kind of fable are you spinning now, Sinclair?"

"It isn't a fable, Sarah, but the truth. And although you seem incapable of recognizing the truth when you hear it, hear it you must."

Sarah stiffened under the calmly delivered gibe. "Be careful, Sinclair. A man with your taste for lies might find the simple truth bitter upon your tongue."

"What I find bitter is my wife's devotion to a man who would destroy my family. Her betrayal of the love we shared."

Sarah shivered. Doubts rippled across the pool of emotions deep inside her. Had Leighton lied to her? Looking at Austin, she wondered whom she could really trust.

She turned away from him, strolling to the sofa that stood against one wall, where Merlin was curled in a gray ball upon the emerald silk velvet. "I believe you were telling me the fable of Atlantis."

Austin sighed, a quiet sound of frustration that barely rose above the whisper of the waves lapping against the ship. "Ten thousand years ago, Atlantis was destroyed by a great cataclysm. Those who survived joined the colonists who had been sent to different parts of the world."

Colonists from Atlantis. Sarah sank to the edge of the sofa. What did the man expect to gain by spinning this fairy tale?

"My ancestors tried to live among the primitive tribes, shielding their science behind the mask of pagan cults. Yet in time even the cults could not protect them. They were persecuted, perceived as witches and wizards. Six thousand years ago they established Avallon as a sanctuary, a place where they could live in peace and continue their exploration of science and nature."

Sarah ran her hand over Merlin's fur. "So you are saying you're a wizard from this place called Avallon."

"I'm a man, Sarah."

Something in his voice drew her gaze to him, a bitterness she could not see reflected in his face. There was no emotion in his face, nothing that betrayed his thoughts. It was like looking at a mask, a shell of the man she had loved.

"A man who comes from a place where they have been studying the mysteries of nature for centuries."

"I thought you were the Marquess of Somerset."

"I am."

"Oh. I see." She glanced down at Merlin, smoothing a trembling hand along his curled back. He purred deep in his throat, simple, honest. Was Sinclair capable of telling a simple truth? "I never realized England was a colony of Atlantis."

"Sarah, we have always held positions in the Outworld."

"The Outworld?"

"The world beyond the bounds of Avallon." Austin studied her a moment. "My people hold positions as bankers, magistrates, businessmen. We are part of the nobility. Advisers to kings and politicians."

"So the people of Avallon like to meddle with the primitive tribes populating the world today. I guess you're a little like the gods of Olympus."

"People who stay isolated stagnate and die. We travel. We enjoy all the world has to offer." Austin tilted his head back against the wall, looking at her from beneath a fringe of black lashes. "And we often take mates from the Outworld."

Sarah closed her eyes, fighting the memories of the night before, when he had held her in his arms, when she had glimpsed heaven, never knowing the price she would pay. "Do you actually expect me to believe this nonsense?"

"The trip to Pará will take two days in this ship. Do you think that unusual, Sarah?"

"You're saying a trip that would normally take eight to ten days can be accomplished by this ship in less than half the time?"

"That's right."

"I shall believe it when I see it."

Austin turned to one of the portholes, staring into the moonlit night. "Have you noticed how quietly this ship moves through the water?"

"We must be using the sails."

"The masts on this vessel are for appearance only, as are the smokestacks." He glanced over his shoulder, pinning her in his silvery blue gaze. "This ship is designed to look conventional to the Outworld, but it runs by energy captured from the sun."

"And it does this at night."

"The energy is stored, much like drawing water from a well."

"I think you have been reading far too many novels by Mr. Jules Verne. Either that or you are quite mad."

"And tell me, can you explain a bullet wound that doesn't leave a scar, or a broken arm that heals in one day?"

Sarah felt her mouth go dry. His words threatened her, threatened her concept of what was real and what was fantasy. "You're trying to manipulate my mind."

"I know this is all difficult to believe." He moved toward her, hesitating when she drew back against the sofa.

"Stay away from me."

Pain flickered in his eyes before his expression once again resumed the cold mask of indifference. "Avallon exists. I only hope you won't be too shocked when we arrive."

"Do you think this fable will make me believe what you said about my brother? Do you think I could ever trust you again?"

"I tell you this to prepare you for what lies ahead. You will know the truth about your brother soon. I'm afraid it will be inescapable."

"I'm afraid the truth is already inescapable." Sarah shivered in the cool breeze drifting through the portholes. "I married a scoundrel, a man who wouldn't know the truth if it walked up to him and shook his hand."

Austin drew a deep breath. "And you, Sarah, you

can make love with a man one day and turn your back on him the next."

Sarah sprang to her feet. "You dare imply I was the one who betrayed you?"

"You speak of love one moment, then refuse to trust me the next. What would you call it, Sarah?"

"You tricked me into marrying you." She marched toward him until she stood so close she could feel the treacherous heat of his body stroke her skin. "This marriage was a lie from the beginning!"

"Was it, Sarah?" he whispered.

"You married me to get revenge!"

"I loved you," he whispered, his eyes growing fierce with the emotion she sensed rising inside him, cracking his calm mask. "I loved you enough to betray everything I cherish in this life."

"Liar!" she shouted straight up into his face.

"Damn you," he whispered, his voice nothing more than a growl as he whipped his strong arms around her and dragged her up against his chest.

"Let go of me!" she shouted, pushing against his chest. "I demand you—"

He cut off her words with his lips. She expected brutality, a punishing grind of his lips against hers. What followed was far more devastating, a slow slide of his open mouth against hers that gave her an intriguing sip of the intoxicating spice of his mouth.

"Is this a lie, Sarah?" he whispered against her lips, his voice tortured by emotion, his hands curving against her waist and shoulder.

If he had given her a chance to answer she couldn't have. All of her thoughts were sinking, drowning beneath the unexpected tide of pleasure rising inside her. Still, he gave her no chance to respond. He moved his lips against hers in a tantalizing glide, firm and warm. He touched the seam of her clenched lips with the tip of his tongue, teasing her, tempting her to open to him.

Memories retained in every fiber of her body responded to his touch. His warmth wrapped around her, reminding her of how cold the world was without him. His arms tightened around her, reminding her of the strength she imagined would always be there for her. He surrounded her, overwhelmed her, awakened her senses as only he could. And she wanted to believe in every silent promise his body whispered.

Liar! Scoundrel! She could not surrender to him. Yet her body was yielding, arching into his, abandoning the battle. She wanted him. She wanted to forget all of the lies. She wanted to feel the pleasure shimmer through every part of her body. Only this man could make her feel this way. Only this man could bring her to life.

All the emotion Austin had tried so hard to bury surged inside him, escaping shallow graves like avenging spirits. He loved her. No matter how much he wanted to exorcise Sarah from his soul, she was there, a part of him.

He needed her now more than he had ever needed her. Out of the destruction he had made of his life, he needed to salvage this—the one truth that burned through all of the deceptions.

He felt it the moment she abandoned her anger, the instant she surrendered to the desire he could sense awakening within her. And was there more? Did he sense the warmth of love shimmering within her? He needed her more than he needed air to breathe. He needed to rescue that part of himself that only she could save with her love.

She opened her hands, her fingers sliding against the warm white linen of his shirt. His muscles tensed beneath her touch. He turned his head, gliding his mouth across her cheek.

He buried his face against the sensitive curve of her neck and shoulder, inhaling her fragrance, perceiving the delicate trace of feminine arousal beneath the innocence of lavender. She gripped his shoulders, a soft sigh escaping her lips.

"Sarah," he whispered as he lifted her in his arms. He lowered her to the thick emerald carpet, praying she would take him into her arms, welcome him into the sanctuary of her body. His life was splintering into pieces. Only with Sarah could he hope to salvage some part of what was Austin Sinclair. "I need you."

He gave her no time to form a protest as he pushed her skirts up above her waist. Still, she made no attempt to stop him. She trembled in his arms, holding him as though she needed him as much as he needed her.

He covered her, lowering his lips to hers, kissing her, wanting to pour his very life into her. With his body he would show her how he felt, he would prove that what burned between them was the fire of love. This couldn't be a lie. He needed to believe in what they had found together.

He slipped his hand between them, his fingers brushing the slit in the soft linen of her drawers. The damp, musky heat of her made him tremble. He flicked open the buttons lining the front of his breeches.

Sarah moaned against his lips, feeling the first touch of his aroused flesh. He pressed velvet heat against her, nudging her moist softness, a silent question. In that moment she knew he would not force her with the overpowering strength of his body. Yet he had already overpowered her with the strength of her own desire. She lifted her hips, welcoming him. He plunged deep inside her.

"Believe in me, Sarah," he whispered against her lips, emotion scraping his sable soft voice. "Please believe in me."

Could she? She moved with him, willing to forget everything for this one moment in his arms. He belonged to her, if only for this moment.

She slipped her hands into his hair, holding him, returning his kiss with all the love and pain and passion straining inside her. Could a man lie so eloquently with his body? Could he counterfeit this joining of hearts and minds and souls?

She met each thundering thrust, his hips rocking between her thighs, his power pulsing through her. She embraced the sensations that promised release from her turmoil, her entire body dissolving, mingling with his. One last thought pierced her before her world splintered into pulsating pinpoints of pleasure: How could this be a lie?

She felt his body tense, grow taut along the trembling lines of her body. And then Austin eased against her as her own body softened against the thick carpet. She felt his soft exhale against her neck, his silky hair brushing her cheek. She breathed deeply, savoring the hot spicy scent of his skin. She held him with her arms and legs, never wanting to release him. And yet . . .

Slowly reality crept back into her consciousness, carrying a weight of self-loathing. She opened her eyes, staring up at the black waves curling below his ear.

She lay on the floor, clothes tangled, limbs entwined with a man who had betrayed her, a man who wanted nothing more than to manipulate her. And she had allowed him to take her. She had welcomed him. She was no better than an animal.

Austin lifted above her as though he could sense

the shifting of her thoughts. He touched her cheek, his fingers gentle, his eyes speaking of need and a deep, unhealing pain. "Sarah, I—"

"I hate you for this."

He closed his eyes, his hand forming a fist by her ear.

"I hate you for turning me into a . . . vile, wicked creature." Sarah pushed against his shoulders. "Get off me!"

He drew a breath that broke in his throat. "Then it all truly was a lie."

Sarah closed her eyes, shutting out the compelling sight of his face. What right did he have to look this way, as though she had plunged a knife into his heart? "Go away! Leave me alone."

Austin pulled away from her. He stood with his back to her, taking a moment to straighten his clothes before he faced her. She sat, smoothing her skirt over the knees she hugged to her chest, fighting the tears that threatened to humiliate her.

He glanced at her, and the agony she saw in his eyes pierced her, as though he reflected the pain she felt burning like hot coals in her chest. "One day soon, Sarah, you will learn the truth. Pity it shall come too late."

"Too late for what?"

He was quiet a moment, holding her look, her own pain reflected in his eyes. "To save what we might have had together."

Without another word he left her to struggle with the demons of doubt he had released inside her.

The cool breeze bathed his face as Austin stepped onto the deck. He breathed deeply. He wanted to erase her scent from his nostrils. He needed to erase her memory from his mind. The planks shifted beneath his feet with the roll of the ship against the waves. He had to find his balance.

He crossed the polished oak planks and gripped the railing, the steel biting into his palms as he squeezed hard. For what seemed a lifetime he stared into the water. Moonlight collected on the waves, shaping mirrors, before shattering, splintering into pieces of glittering light.

Sarah.

He heard her name in the whisper of the sea. He felt her touch in the caress of the breeze. He saw her face when he closed his eyes.

How can I purge you from my soul?

He gripped the railing tighter, his knuckles blanching white, pain sparking along his nerves. This weakness, he had never suspected it lurked within him.

A life forged for service. Honor. Responsibility. He was a sword forged of flawed steel.

He no longer knew who he was. It seemed all of what he had been was nothing but illusion, smoke that blew away in the breeze and left him to face a stranger with his face.

He sensed someone near, someone watching. He glanced to his side. Bram Duggan stood a few feet away, light from the full moon streaming over his face, revealing his concern.

"Would it help if I spoke with Lady Sinclair, sir? If I told her the truth about her brother?"

Austin laughed, a derisive chuckle deep in his throat. "I doubt the woman would believe you."

"I've made my preliminary report to Commander Matthias." Bram turned to stare across the sea. "I've told him of my failure to secure the medallion."

"It was my responsibility, not yours." Austin tilted back his head, the muscles bunching in his shoulders. "And I shall make certain your commander learns the truth." He knew what price the truth would cost him.

"When I was first assigned to this mission, I thought it was foolish to allow a member of the Inner Circle to battle a criminal of the Outworld." Bram rested his hands on the railing, keeping his gaze on the horizon. "To me the members of that revered group have always been removed from reality, too immersed in tradition, too much as they were when they were knights in the time of Arthur, still guarding the Grail."

"I suppose in ways your analysis is correct. I for one have managed to demonstrate my incompetence."

"With all due respect, sir, I can't allow you to take the burden of this failure. You located the medallion. You turned the task over to a professional, as you should have, giving me the opportunity to retrieve it." Bram looked at him, a frown digging deep lines into his brow. "I allowed my own fascination with the medallion to break my concentration."

"I could have taken that medallion from the Van Horne house days ago. I delayed, for reasons I think are obvious." Austin studied the man a moment, seeing the understanding in his eyes. "That was the true failure."

Bram bowed his head, a muscle working in his cheek as he clenched his teeth. "Do you realize what the Central Council might do to you if you admit this to them? It could be perceived as treason."

"Yes." Austin stared at the shattering reflections of the moon on the waves. "In a few days, we shall find out exactly what my penance shall be."

Moonlight streamed with a cool breeze through the porthole in Sarah's bedroom. She stared at the light shifting across the bed, the ship swaying gently beneath her like a slowly rocking cradle. Still, she could not coax her mind to seek peace in slumber.

Merlin lay in a ball on the pillow beside her, his thick gray fur rising and falling with the even rhythm of his breath. Was Sinclair sleeping as peacefully?

She thought of the night before, when she had slept in Austin's warm embrace, when she had believed her every dream had come true. Could any man truly have lied so eloquently, with every whisper, every touch, every kiss? Only a monster. Or a man intent on revenge.

She closed her eyes, shutting out the moonlight. But she couldn't shut out the memories that swarmed inside her like an army of angry bees, stinging her, injecting a venom that made her ache and long for Austin's touch. Beneath the soft white linen of her nightgown, her skin grew warm with memory, tingling with need.

She turned, hugging her pillow to her aching breasts. He had changed her in some unfathomable way. He had turned her into a creature who thrived on passion and excitement, who sought it, like a foolish moth seeking a flame.

She clutched her pillow, trying not to think of Austin Sinclair. She feared the weakness that whispered like a siren inside her, coaxing her to leave her lonely bed and seek the warmth she had found only in his arms.

Chapter Twenty-Four

Austin rested his hand on the walnut-paneled wall beside one of the portholes in the drawing room of his cabin. Sarah stood on deck a few yards away, near the bow, her face turned toward the horizon, her bare hands taut on the railing as though it were her only anchor in a world turned upside down. The setting rays of the sun painted her profile in gold. The golden light rippled along the strands of hair that had escaped her tight bun to stream in the wind.

He had managed to stay away from her most of the day, stealing only a few moments to tell her of what would happen once they reached Pará tomorrow afternoon. It was better if he kept his distance. When he was around her, she chipped at his defenses. Emotions slipped through the cracks she carved, threatening to betray him.

She bowed her head, closing her eyes as though she fought against a deep, aching pain. He balled his hand into a fist on the wall.

He would not go to her. He would not take her in his arms. He could not. It was better for Sarah if he stayed away from her. For too many reasons this marriage must come to an end.

He turned away from the porthole. A copy of the report he had sent to Commander Matthias lay on his desk: crisp white pages and black ink outlining his failure. He knew Matthias would deliver the information to the Central Council.

Austin stared down at his report. In a very real sense, his life would end in the next few days.

Sarah stood near the bow of the ship, her face turned to the salty spray of the sea slapping against the ship. The solid steel railing bit into her palms, reminding her this was reality and not a nightmare. She had awakened when the sun was high in the sky, after a night spent with sleep coming in fleeting moments. Austin had taunted her, both waking and sleeping. He taunted her now with doubts of what she had done.

The wind tore at her hair, plucking at the pins she had plunged into her carefully fashioned bun. She stared at the horizon, where the setting sun tossed scarlet and gold across the rolling waves. She had spent hours exploring the ship, searching for lies, finding only truths she was frightened to face.

The ship was everything Austin had said, some strange vessel that skimmed through the water without sails, without the smoke and noise of coal and steam, with only a soft humming noise. Was it all true?

She didn't want to consider the things Austin had told her about Leighton, the truth that hovered just beyond the dark wall of fear inside her. She didn't want to face that truth. Not now. Not when her entire concept of the world was shattering around her.

From the corner of her eye she saw a man approach. She turned and faced Bram Duggan as he drew near. Dressed in a white linen shirt and buff-colored trousers, he looked the part of a gentleman, hardly the man who had cleaned her stables. "It would seem you were not all you appeared, Mr. Duggan."

He paused a few feet away from her, frowning as he held her gaze. "I wanted you to know, I never wished for any harm to come to you."

"I assume you work for Sinclair."

The wind streamed across him, the wide white sleeves of his shirt flapping like sails. "Do you remember I told you I was in law enforcement?"

Sarah shoved the windswept hair back from her face. "Do you mean to tell me you actually told a truth?"

He glanced down at his boots, having the decency to look embarrassed for his part in this deception. "I'm a guardian for the people of Avallon."

"Avallon." Sarah gripped the solid steel railing, needing an anchor to reality. "Tell me, is Sinclair trying to drive me mad with this elaborate tale of Atlantis? Is that part of his revenge against my brother?"

"Lord Sinclair is not seeking revenge." Bram looked up at her. "He is seeking justice."

"One man's vengeance is another man's justice."

"I realize this is all very difficult for you to believe." Bram rested his hip against the railing, glancing away from her, staring toward the horizon. "Your brother is a dangerous man. He murdered a friend of mine."

"I can't believe Leighton would . . ." And yet the truth was there, peeking from the darkness like the bright eyes of a tiger burning in the night. "There must have been some mistake."

"I investigated the murder. Your brother killed the man who had been assigned to guard him. Later he shot Lord Devlin Sinclair and nearly killed him."

Sarah closed her eyes, shutting out the honesty she could see in his dark green eyes. "Please go away."

"As much as you want it to, the truth isn't going to go away."

"My brother wouldn't . . ." Bitter bile rose in her throat at the thought of what he might have done. Sarah turned her face into the wind, taking deep breaths. "Leighton is a little wild, but he couldn't murder someone."

"Do you really trust your brother so much more than you trust your husband?"

Sarah looked at Bram, the wind whipping loose strands of her hair across her cheek. "My husband has made a career of lying to me."

Bram held her gaze a moment, as though he were judging the words he would speak. "Lord Sinclair risked everything to marry you. I would think you could give him a small measure of the loyalty you have shown for your brother."

"What do you mean he risked everything?"

"He delayed retrieving the medallion to be with you. That could be seen as treason in the eyes of the Central Council."

Sarah shook her head. "I was part of his scheme to capture my brother."

"In the beginning. But he married you for only one reason." He stood looking down at her, the wind whipping his thick tawny hair. "I think you know the truth deep in your heart, Lady Sinclair. I hope you will stand beside your husband when he faces the council."

Sarah stared across the rolling waves as Bram walked away from her. His words swirled in her mind, creating a whirlpool of doubt and fear. She perceived a shaking inside her, a disturbance of everything that made the world concrete around her. It was as though she were being drawn toward a portal through which the world as she knew it would cease to exist.

If what Austin said was true, tomorrow afternoon they would reach Pará, Brazil. From there they would journey to a place called Avallon. The truth waited for her there, a truth she wasn't sure she could face. Dear heaven, had she made a horrible mistake in not believing Austin?

She turned and stared at the cabin where Austin had spent most of the day. He was in there now; she could see a light glowing from his porthole. Before she realized what she was doing, she had crossed the deck to stand before his cabin door.

She wanted to touch him, absorb the warmth of his skin. She wanted to feel his arms close around her, shutting out the world. She gripped the brass door handle, hesitating, realizing she would not be welcome there.

She turned away and ran toward her own cabin, tears stinging her eyes. If all Austin had said was true, then she had betrayed him, ruined him, and he would never forgive her. If he were lying, he had married her only for revenge. Which was worse?

Inside the safety of her cabin she fell across her bed. Sobs she could not stop shook her body, tears soaking the emerald velvet counterpane beneath her cheek. Yet there was no cleansing from these tears, no absolution from the realization that she might have helped a murderer escape.

Pará, Brazil, was even more offensive than Leighton Van Horne remembered. Sunlight reflected on the caramel-colored water of the Amazon, so hot he could see waves of heat rising from the flowing water.

Beneath his white linen coat, his white linen shirt stuck to his skin. The pungent odor of decaying fish filled his nostrils as he followed Collin Bennett down a narrow alley leading from the docks. He didn't like the looks of this place. How many of the men working the docks were actually men from Avallon?

Leighton glanced over his shoulder, making sure they weren't being followed. "You wouldn't be leading me on a merry little goose chase, would you, Collin?"

"No." Collin's eyes were wide with fear as he looked at Leighton. He grabbed the handle of a wooden door in one of the warehouses lining the alley. "The transportation port is in here."

Leighton frowned at the gray, weather-beaten door. He gestured with the pistol he held in the pocket of his coat, pressing the muzzle against the white linen. "If you're lying to me, Collin, I'll kill you before anyone gets the chance to stop me." He smiled as he spoke, keeping his voice to a low whisper. "They already want me for murder, so I have nothing to lose. Do you understand me?"

"Yes." Collin's hand trembled as he slipped a key in the rusty-looking lock.

"Smile and act as though you're just returning from a little trip in the Outworld," Leighton said, making sure his voice wouldn't carry. "I'm certain your friends from Avallon are watching us every step of the way."

Sarah gripped the railing of the ship, staring at the town of Pará—warehouses spread along the docks, the dark blue of the Atlantic melding with the golden brown of the Amazon, all shimmering in a white-hot late afternoon sun. It had taken two days to reach

Brazil, just as Austin had said it would.

"You should be wearing a hat in this sun."

Sarah pivoted at the sound of Austin's voice. "Must you always sneak up on me?"

He shrugged. "You were too lost in your thoughts to notice me."

Looking at him, she wished there were some way to become lost in thoughts that did not concern him. A breeze ruffled his thick hair, reminding her of how silky the ebony strands had felt sliding through her fingers.

Austin rested his hands on the railing, staying a few feet away from her, as though the stench of rotting fish that contaminated the hot air emanated from her. "Once we dock, it will take an hour to reach Avallon by train," he said, the voice that had once caressed her with such softness now stiff and formal, as though they had never touched.

"And this is the underground train you told me about."

Austin nodded. "You sound as though you're losing some of your skepticism."

"Perhaps I'm only losing my mind." She felt torn inside, pulled in so many directions that all the pieces would never again be gathered into a whole.

"The truth isn't always easy to face." He tightened his hands on the railing as though he needed to keep them anchored there, his knuckles blanching white with the strain. "Face it with your eyes open, Sarah, and you'll be all right."

She wondered if she would ever be all right again. In spite of everything, she caught herself wishing Austin would slip his arms around her. She wanted to hold him, to feel his warmth close around her.

She stared down at her hands, her fingers curled around the steel railing. The simple gold band Austin had placed on her finger shimmered in the sunlight.

Once she had known joy beyond imagining. Once she had held a dream in her arms. Had it all been an illusion, deceptions played by a scoundrel? Or had she killed the dream? She felt chilled inside, in that empty place Austin had once filled with warmth.

"I want you to know, no one will harm you in Avallon."

She glanced up at him, and for an instant she imagined seeing a flicker of concern in his eyes, a look that hardened into indifference as he held her gaze. "Is that another truth you are asking me to believe?"

"You must decide what you will do with the truth, Sarah. It is no longer a concern of mine."

Sarah stared after him as Austin marched away from her, fighting the urge to run to him, to throw her arms around him. Somehow she knew it wouldn't make a difference now. With a clarity that came as cold and bitter as the deepest winter, she realized that whatever her future might hold, it would not include Austin Sinclair.

She stared down into the water, her throat growing tight with the pain that trembled inside her. It seemed no matter how much she wanted to deny it, the truth was there, waiting to destroy her carefully crafted view of reality.

Trees lined both sides of the main street of modern Avallon, thick branches entwining high overhead, weaving an emerald canopy above the people who strolled along the black cobblestones. There were no vehicles here, no horses or carriages to rattle along the street, nothing but the tread of footsteps on cobblestones. Transportation was kept underground, small shining boatlike contraptions for personal use, or silver trains that moved along a single track like bullets.

Leighton strolled beside Collin down the narrow street, returning the smiles of the people he passed. It had been simple to penetrate their defenses. These people were as innocent as children, cosseted in their hidden city. He felt like a wolf prowling among sheep—powerful, invulnerable.

A few cafés served dinner to people who sat at round white tables beneath the lacy canopy of trees with birds serenading them from the branches. Shops lined the first floor of the buildings; art, clothing, jewelry, and crafts were displayed behind large glass windows.

"I must say, I approve of the fashion here." Leighton paused in front of a shop where fashions for women were displayed on mannequins so lifelike they seemed to return his regard. "It gives a man a better appreciation of the true nature of a woman's figure."

"Leighton, I've done what you asked," Collin whispered. "Please let me go."

"And we've only just arrived in your fair city." Leighton could feel Collin trembling next to him. The breeze stirred a lock of light brown hair that had tumbled over Collin's brow; he looked like a child, frightened and alone with the devil. "Would you have me wander about like a stranger?"

"Leighton, please. I swear I won't tell anyone about you."

"Of course you won't. You see, I . . ." Leighton paused, gripping Collin's arm as he noticed one of the two women in the shop. "So it seems she is indeed still here."

"Who?" Collin asked.

"Lady Judith Chatham." Leighton frowned as he watched Judith slip behind a glass counter carrying a sapphire blue tunic. She worked in this place. Lady Judith Chatham, the woman he had chosen as his queen, was working in a shop.

"What are you going to do?" Collin asked, as Leighton stepped back from the window.

Leighton remembered the first time he had held Judith in his arms, the first time he had slipped inside her, piercing her maidenhead. He would taste her once more. He would plunge into her tight sheath while he slipped his hands around her slender neck and strangled the life from her treacherous body. No one betrayed him and lived.

"I'm going to pay my respects to an old friend." Leighton glanced through the shop window, watching as Judith handed a white bag trimmed in gold to the other woman. He could see no one else in the shop. When her customer left, Judith would be alone. But not for long.

It was amazing, Judith thought as she watched her customer leave, the bell above the door jingling. She stepped from behind the counter, smoothing away the smudges on the glass with her handkerchief.

Never in her life had she imagined running her own store. In that other life, the life she had left behind in England, people would be shocked to know Lady Judith Serena Chatham was now working in trade. It shocked her, this independence. Oh, it was wonderful!

She slid her hand down the sleeve of an emerald green tunic on display. Was silk ever smoother than this? Or did everything feel better when you were a free woman? The bell attached to her door jingled. She smiled, prepared to face another customer.

She turned toward the door, her heart slamming against her chest when she saw the man standing there. "What are you doing here?"

"I was hoping you might be happy to see me."

Happy was far too mild a word for what she felt looking at Bram Duggan's handsome face. "I am."

He smiled, a smile warmer than the setting rays of the sun that slanted through the window behind him and touched his tawny hair with gold. He moved toward her, the blue and gold and scarlet silk tunics draped on hangers swaying as he passed.

She didn't move as he drew near. Because if she moved she might surrender to the very foolish longing inside her. She might throw her arms around him, press her cheek against his broad chest—hold him the way she had dreamed of holding him.

He paused, standing close, so close she had to tilt her head to look up at this giant of a man, so close she could feel the heat of his body reaching for her.

"I've missed you," he said, his deep voice a soft caress.

Judith forgot to breathe. "Have you?"

"More than I ever realized possible." He lifted her hand in his warm grasp. "I just got back and I was hoping you would have dinner with me."

"Yes," Judith whispered, joy stealing the breath from her lungs. "I would love to have dinner with you."

Leighton turned away from Judith's shop, the blood pounding in his temples. "So it seems our muscular friend has arrived from New York."

"Leighton, we have to get away from here." Collin turned away from the window. "He could recognize me."

Judith and that barbarian. They were lovers; Leighton could see the intimacy between them. Judith had given herself to that peasant when she belonged to him. He squeezed the handle of the pistol inside his pocket. He would kill them, both of them, but that pleasure would have to wait for a better time and place. "Since our friend from New York is here, I suspect Sinclair has also returned to Avallon."

Collin strained against Leighton's hold. "They'll be looking for you."

"There is no reason for them to believe we are here, is there, Collin?" Leighton tightened his grip on Collin's arm, prodding the young man with the pistol he held in his coat pocket. "You haven't given them any reason to believe I am here, have you?"

"No, of course not. I've said nothing, done nothing to betray you."

"That's good." Leighton smiled. "I'm afraid my reunion with Judith will have to wait. Do be a dear and show me the way to the Sinclair residence, won't you, Collin?" There would be time to deal with Judith and her lover after he had destroyed the Sinclairs.

Austin watched Sarah as they entered his father's drawing room in Avallon. She kept herself apart from the others, his parents, his sister, his brother, and his brother's wife, those who had been waiting for them to arrive.

All the color had drained from Sarah's cheeks. She moved with a stiffness that reminded Austin of a marionette, every step guided by an inner will that refused to allow her to collapse under the burden of a reality she had never conceived possible.

His family had greeted her warmly, as though this marriage between them were real. Lord help him, but to him it was still too real. In spite of everything, he found himself wanting to go to her. He wanted to take her in his arms and ease the pain and confusion he knew she was suffering. He wanted to hold her, now and forever. Yet he couldn't.

It was over between them. His obsession for Sarah had already cost far too much. All the proof he needed of his own guilt was reflected in the eyes of his family as they gathered around him.

Shame simmered like hot coals in his chest, the heat of it creeping upward along his neck. Austin stared down at the clipper ship that sat in a bottle on a rosewood pedestal table near the windows as the others settled in the room, taking places like an audience before a play.

"I had some unsettling news this morning, son. Commander Matthias has made a complete report to the Central Council," Rhys said.

"I expected he would," Austin said, keeping his gaze on the ship beneath glass. With its delicate masts and intricate carvings, the ship was an exact reproduction. He had made it when he was 15, put each piece together under the guiding hand of the man who stood beside him, the man whose trust he had betrayed.

"The council has issued an order for your appearance before them to answer charges of treason," Rhys said, keeping his voice low, as though he were loath to speak the words. "It seems when Matthias read your report yesterday, he got the impression you could have retrieved the medallion and chose to delay, causing the mission to fail. Obviously he made a mistake."

From the corner of his eye, Austin saw his father. Rhys stood beside him, watching him, waiting for the explanation that would absolve his son of all guilt. Austin was aware of his mother and sister, sitting together on the sofa by the white marble hearth, his brother standing near the open French doors leading to the terrace, Kate sitting in a wing-back chair near her husband. Watching him. They were all watching him with hope and anxiety in their gazes.

Austin tried to draw a breath, his chest tight with the emotions locked inside him. "I'm the one who made the mistake, Father."

"Austin, what are you saying?" Rhys asked.

It took a moment before Austin could turn and face his father, a moment to collect the words that would destroy the faith Rhys had always had in him. "I had it within my power to retrieve the medallion days before I asked Duggan to do so. The mission failed because of me."

Rhys glanced away, looking at Devlin, who stood watching the exchange between his brother and his father. Austin sensed no condemnation in his brother's steady gaze, only a quiet understanding. Somehow that acceptance of his betrayal made it worse.

"Austin, you don't need to protect Duggan," Rhys said.

How easy it would be to lay the blame on Duggan's strong shoulders. Only Austin would know the truth, a truth he could not hide. "I'm sorry, Father, deeply sorry. But I cannot avoid the truth. I chose to delay, and in doing so, I lost my chance to retrieve the medallion."

"Why?" Rhys asked.

The single word told of a lifetime of faith, crumbling in the passing of moments. "I don't seem to have an answer, at least not now. All of my reasons have turned to dust."

"Son, in three days, when you face the Central Council, you will need to present a better defense than this," Rhys said, his voice soft and far too gentle.

In the periphery of his vision Austin saw Sarah sitting at the piano in the corner of the room, her hands clasped in her lap, like a little girl who had been sent to the corner for punishment. "There is no defense for what I have done."

"Austin, do you realize what will happen should the council find you guilty?"

"Yes." Humiliation, ridicule, Austin had exposed his family to this and more.

Austin faced them, the people who meant more to him than anything in the world. He looked at each of them, seeing disbelief and pain in the eyes of his mother and sister, a quiet acceptance in the eyes of his brother, fear for him in Kate's beautiful blue eyes. Sarah refused to look at him. "I have broken the faith you once had in me; for this I am deeply sorry."

For a moment Austin stood before them, naked with his shame, searching for some words that could ease their pain. Yet he knew words could never heal the damage he had inflicted.

He turned and left the room. He couldn't stay there another moment, sensing the love for him shimmering through their pain. He didn't deserve love or understanding. For what he had done, he deserved any punishment the Central Council would invoke. He deserved to die.

Chapter Twenty-Five

No one moved. It was as if Austin had turned them all to stone, Sarah thought. Yet stone could not feel as these people felt.

She glanced toward Devlin Sinclair, sensing his gaze on her. He was studying her, a deep line etched between his black brows, as though he were looking at a puzzle that needed solving. Sarah had a puzzle of her own that needed a solution. "I have been told my brother stole a medallion from this house. I have been told he killed a guard and nearly killed you."

"You've been told the truth," Devlin said, the deep gravelly texture of his voice as rough as Austin's was smooth.

She clasped her hands tightly in her lap as though she could hold together the pieces of Sarah Van Horne that were shattering inside her. Leighton a murderer. It was impossible to believe. Yet looking at these people it was impossible not to believe them.

"I'm going after him," Devlin said, marching toward the door.

"So am I." Alexandria sprang from the sofa and darted after Devlin, catching him at the door leading to the hall.

"Alexa." Devlin rested his hand on her shoulder. "Let me talk to him alone."

"But I want to tell him it doesn't matter. We love him no matter what happens."

"You can tell him when I bring him back, all right?"

"Devlin, I've never seen him so hurt. I want to be with him."

"Let me talk to him first."

Alexandria slumped against the door frame. "All right."

As Devlin left the room, Sarah stared at Austin's beautiful young sister, her dark brown hair tumbling in glossy waves to her waist. As much as she wanted to believe in her brother, Sarah could not believe Alexandria Sinclair had ever tried to kill herself, for any reason.

Merlin leapt to the leather-covered bench beside her. The plump cat poked at her arm with his smooth head until she opened her arms and allowed him to curl into a ball on her lap, a warm reminder of the life she had once known. "What will happen to Austin?"

Rhys rested his fingertips on the glass bottle housing a small clipper ship. He did not look at Sarah as he spoke, but stared down at the model. "In three days he will face the Central Council on charges of treason. If found guilty . . . they could exile him for life." He closed his hand into a fist on the glass. "I don't intend to allow that to happen. We will find some way to defend him."

"What is this Central Council?" Sarah asked. "Who gave them the power to judge Austin?"

"The Central Council are seven people who are elected by popular vote every seven years," Rhys said. "We invest them with the power to enforce our laws."

"And they would exile him for the sake of some ancient piece of gold?"

Rhys studied her a moment as though he was choosing his words carefully. Yet even before he spoke, Sarah sensed what he would say would not contain the entire truth. "The medallion is a symbol of the Inner Circle of our society. It represents all that we are. But even if the medallion had little significance, the council would still have reason to judge Austin's actions."

"Why?" Sarah asked. "Austin never intended to do harm."

"We live on an island, so to speak, amid a world that could destroy us if our existence were ever discovered." Rhys glanced down to the ship. "Each of us has taken an oath to protect Avallon above all else. By allowing the medallion to remain in the Outworld, where questions could be asked of its origin, our society could well be jeopardized."

"This was my fault," Sarah said, her words catching. "All of it. Austin stayed in New York to be with me. He could have captured my brother, but I stopped him. So you see, I am the one who should go on trial."

"You're a brave young woman." Rhys looked at her, the smile that curved his lips filled with the same pain she could see in his blue-green eyes. "But I'm afraid what you are suggesting cannot be. Austin must answer the charges."

Sarah hugged Merlin, burying her face in his warm fur. Austin had sacrificed everything he held dear for her, and she had betrayed him.

"Come with me, Sarah," Brianna said, touching her shoulder. "I'll show you to your room. You'll feel better after you've had a nice warm soak."

Sarah looked up into Brianna's silvery blue eyes, knowing there was only one thing that would make her world right again. "I want to be here when Austin comes back. I need to . . . there are things we must discuss."

"I understand, dear." Brianna smiled. "But I don't think they will return for a long time."

Judith's terrace opened to a garden behind the building that housed both her shop and her home. A meadow stretched beyond her garden, a sea of wildflowers swaying in the moonlight. Bram stared up at the stars. They were brighter here than anywhere in the world, like pinpoints of fire burning through the black night.

"Do you think there is anything you can do to help Austin?" Judith asked.

He glanced at the woman who sat beside him on the wooden glider. Moonlight rippled down her dark hair, the thick mane brushing her hips. "I doubt my testimony will sway their decision."

For the last three hours, through dinner and the walk back to her home, he had filled her beautiful head with the details of his mission in New York, including his own failure. He had found no condemnation in her dark eyes, only relief that he had been spared a worse fate than humiliation.

The glider rocked as Bram pushed his heel against the brick terrace, a soft sighing sound joining the chirp of crickets from the garden.

"The Sinclair family has treated me like one of their own." She looked up at him, moonlight revealing the anxiety in her eyes. "I hate to think of anything bad happening to them."

"I'll do everything I can to help Lord Sinclair."

"I know you will."

There was such trust in her eyes, such complete faith in him; it made him feel he could win battles in her name. He slid his arm along the back of the seat, resting his hand lightly on her shoulder.

She stared at the wisteria-covered arbor. "Leighton Van Horne is still out there, somewhere."

"He can't get to you here."

"You don't know him. He's capable of anything."

"I won't let anything happen to you." He lowered his arm, embracing her as she looked up at him with wide, frightened eyes.

Wisteria and jasmine mingled in the cool air that coiled around them like invisible arms, drawing them close. He looked down at her lips, lips that had haunted his dreams, lips he had never kissed. He knew her history, knew the damage Van Horne had wreaked on this delicate young woman, and knew he must tread lightly.

She touched his cheek, her fingers curving softly against his skin. "Will you stay with me tonight?"

His breath caught in his throat. He stared at her, wondering if she meant what he dearly hoped she meant.

"I won't ask for any promises or commitments, I swear. I just want to be with you." She slid her fingertips over his lips. "Please stay with me, hold me through the night."

"If all you need is comfort, Judith, I'm here for you. I'll stay with you through the night, hold you, and demand nothing from you." He kissed her fingertips. "And if you want more, I have more to give."

Judith slid her arms around his shoulders. "I want you in any way you are willing to give yourself to me."

"Judith," he whispered, pulling her close, his muscles growing taut at the feel of her breasts against his chest.

He kissed her, her lips parting beneath his, her breath warming his cheek, her body trembling in his arms. Softer than he imagined, sweeter than any kiss he had ever shared. Every nerve awakened with the pleasure of holding her, kissing her. This night he would do all in his power to wipe away the scars Van Horne had scrawled across her soul, and claim this woman for his own.

"You're about my size. I'll have some fresh clothes laid out for you." Brianna poured scented oil into the sunken white marble tub in Sarah's bathroom. The bottle trembled in her slender hand, the only sign of her anxiety for her son. "Now drink your hot chocolate. It will make you feel better."

A crisp floral fragrance rose with the steam from the hot water tumbling into the tub. Sarah set her blue porcelain mug on the vanity, turning her back to Austin's mother. In the mirror that stretched the length of the white marble vanity, Sarah could see Brianna laying a plump white towel on the marble ledge at the foot of the tub, her golden hair swinging with the motion.

"How do you manage?" The woman looked no older than 30. Yet her son was three years past that age. "Don't people remark on how youthful you are?"

"We seldom leave Avallon these days." Brianna turned toward Sarah, her beautiful face reflected beside Sarah's in the mirror. "One day we will assume other identities to once again travel freely in the Outworld, as my husband's people have always done."

The crash of water plunging into the tub pounded against Sarah's throbbing temples. "It must be difficult, seeing your friends grow old and die."

"It is difficult for anyone to watch a loved one suffer." Brianna glanced away from Sarah's reflection, staring at the ivy that sat beside the shell-shaped sink in the vanity, long tendrils of green leaves spilling over the gold pot to trail along the gold-veined white marble. "Difficult knowing there is little you can do to ease their pain."

Sarah knew Brianna was thinking of Austin. "You must hate me."

"Hate you?"

"For what my brother did. For what I've done to Austin."

"Oh, my dear child." Brianna moved toward her. She rested her hands on Sarah's shoulders, her touch warm, comforting. "You are a part of this family."

"I betrayed Austin. I let my brother get away when Austin could have stopped him."

"I know a little of what happened in New York. I know you had reasons to doubt my son."

"You think he's all right, don't you? He wouldn't try to harm himself, would he?"

Brianna's hands tightened on Sarah's shoulders. "Of course he wouldn't."

"This is all my fault."

Brianna looked into Sarah's eyes in the mirror. "You must find it in your heart to forgive yourself."

"And what of Austin? Do you think he will find it in his heart to forgive me?"

"If he is able to forgive himself for what he thinks he has done to his family, then I am certain he will forgive you."

"And if he isn't?"

"Give him time, Sarah."

Sarah closed her eyes, wondering how she would live if Austin turned her away forever.

Leighton stood in the woods below the Sinclair house. Rocks and wildflowers surrounded the three-story structure of wood and stone that sat perched on the brow of the hill. The house spread wide wings in the moonlight, like an eagle poised for flight. He remembered this place well.

"Leighton, I've done everything you've asked of me. Please let me go."

Leighton glanced at the young man standing beside him. "Can I trust you not to betray me, Collin?"

"I couldn't betray you. If I told anyone you were here, I would have to tell them how you got here." Collin swept the damp hair back from his brow with a trembling hand. "They would think I'm a traitor."

"But you could always plead that I forced you."

Collin shook his head. "It wouldn't matter. We are each taught to give our lives in defense of Avallon."

Leighton laughed. "How very noble they expect you to be."

Collin glanced away from him. In the moonlight filtering through the branches overhead Leighton could see Collin's cheeks darken with shame.

"And what would I do if you suddenly decided to become noble, Collin?"

"Avallon means nothing to me. I want only to live in the Outworld."

Leighton rested his hand on Collin's shoulder, feeling the young man cringe beneath his touch. He slipped a knife from his coat pocket. A gunshot here would bc a mistake.

"Leighton," Collin whispered, "please don't hurt me."

"Slip off your tie, Collin."

"I can help you get away." Collin tugged at the strip of white linen. "Please, Leighton, don't kill me."

Leighton stuffed his handkerchief into Collin's mouth. He didn't want a scream to betray him. A scream might well alert the Sinclairs. And he couldn't have that.

Black rock flowed down the face of the mountain from where Austin stood on the edge of the cliff. The ruins of ancient Avallon stretched out behind him, scattered stones, broken walls of what were once houses devastated in an earthquake long ago. In the distance, the temple stood unblemished, a dark specter that whispered of vows he had betrayed.

He stiffened as he sensed someone approach, footsteps silent upon the stones. He turned, curling his fingers around the stone he held. A tall man moved toward him like a shadow in the moonlight, his black shirt and trousers melding with the night.

"I had a feeling I'd find you here," Devlin said as he drew near.

"I'm not really interested in talking to anyone right now. I would like to be alone."

"I doubt that." Devlin sat on a ragged stone wall near the edge, all that remained of an ancient home. "You see, I know what it's like to be alone, to wake up each morning knowing there is no one who cares if you live or die."

"I'm not sure anyone should care if I live or die." Austin tossed a rock over the edge of the cliff, watching as it arced and tumbled in the moonlight, plunging into the river winding like glowing silver at the base of the mountain.

"I never thought I'd see you feeling sorry for yourself."

"I'm not." Austin stared down into the river, unwilling to meet the intense gaze he could feel burning into his back. "I'm feeling as though I've betrayed the people who mean more to me than my own life."

"You chose to delay while you were in New York because you wanted to be with Sarah." Devlin tossed a handful of pebbles over the cliff, where they bounced against the smooth black rock. "I would have done the same for Kate."

Austin tilted his head, staring up at the stars, wanting to scream his frustration and rage at what he had done. "You don't understand."

"I think I do. For the first time in your life you did something for you."

"That night, when Leighton nearly killed you, I swore I would see the man hang." Austin glanced at his brother. Devlin was watching him, quiet, his love for him as solid as the mountain beneath them. "Because of my selfishness, Van Horne is still free. And he has the medallion."

"No one wants to see Van Horne brought to justice more than I do. But as much as I want to see that man hang for murder, I want to see you free of guilt."

"Unfortunately, I am guilty."

"Of being human."

"Of supreme conceit." Austin laughed, the sound hollow to his own ears. "I imagined I could have it all—Sarah, the medallion, Van Horne in custody. I imagined I could manipulate destiny."

"You have Sarah."

Austin clenched his teeth against the pain that rose inside him like a wave of fire. "Do I?"

"I can imagine the two of you have had a few bad moments over this. But I think she is beginning to realize just what kind of man her brother really is."

"And she has me to thank for shattering all her illusions." Austin shook his head. "It's over. It never should have started. The lady deserves better."

"Damnit, Austin." Devlin stood, pebbles scuttling beneath his feet, tumbling over the edge of the cliff. "Is this the first time in your life you've ever made a mistake?"

"I couldn't make mistakes."

Austin heard the slow exhale of Devlin's sigh. "For the love of God, Austin, everyone makes mistakes."

Austin stared into the river, moonlight rippling along the rolling water, each pulse of his heart throbbing in his temples. "I remember one night when I was five, I awoke from a nightmare. I remember running down the hall, wanting only to be with Mother and Father." He drew air into his lungs, following the flow of the river, fighting the emotions that churned like a whirlpool inside him.

"When I entered their bedroom, Mother was crying, standing by the window, sobbing as though her heart were breaking. Father was holding her, trying to comfort her. I remember she kept saying how it was her fault you were kidnapped, all her fault. And then she noticed I was there. She hugged me as though she were afraid someone would take me away from her."

Austin stared down at his hands, remembering the feel of his mother's tears when he had touched her cheeks and begged her not to cry. "I wondered if she cried that way every night. And I knew I never wanted to make her cry."

Devlin moved to stand beside him. "If you were perfect enough, you could make them forget all about the son they'd lost. Is that it?"

Austin didn't answer—he couldn't; the words he might have spoken were caught in his tight throat.

"Do you remember what you told me when I was having difficulty adjusting to all of this?" Devlin asked, gesturing toward the temple.

Austin stared at the temple, moonlight glittering on crystals trapped in the black stone shaping the stately walls. "Devlin, it doesn't matter."

"I think it does. You told me I had a family who loved me. You said even through those years when I was wandering alone, you were with me, as I was with you." Devlin gripped his brother's arm. "Your family loves you, and that won't change, no matter what happens."

Austin felt the weight of his family's love settle around him, a burden now that he knew he no longer deserved it.

"Come back with me."

Austin shook his head. "I need some time to myself."

He needed to think, to pick through the pieces of his life, what was left of it. He needed to prepare himself for the inevitable, when he would face the Central Council with his guilt and feel the weight of their judgment fall upon him.

Judith stood at the window of her second-story bedroom, her blue silk robe fluttering in the breeze, brushing her skin. The silken caress sparked memories of the man who had touched her so recently, coaxing the pulse to throb in her breasts.

Never in her life had she been touched with such tenderness, as though she were rare and precious to Bram. Tenderness coupled with passion made a far more potent blend than Leighton's brand of passion and cruelty.

After making love to her until she thought she would go mad with the pleasure, Bram had fallen asleep in her arms. Unable to banish the unreasonable fear that Leighton was near, sleep had eluded her.

Across the meadow, where bright wildflowers rippled in the breeze, the ground rolled upward into the nearby hills. The Sinclair house stood on the brow of one of those hills, above the ancient ruins. Sarah was there, Austin's wife. Leighton would not be pleased with his sister for marrying his enemy. What would he do to them if he ever found them?

"Judith," Bram whispered.

She turned toward the carved rosewood bed, where Bram lay naked in the moonlight, the white linen sheet covering him to the waist. She went to him, smiling as she looked down at him. His thick golden mane was tousled against her pillow. Moonlight streamed over him, sliding along the muscles of his arms, the thick curves of his shoulders, his golden skin smooth as marble.

"Are you all right?" he asked, reaching for her.

"Fine." She gave him her hand, allowing him to pull her down onto the soft bed and into his arms.

He kissed her, holding her against him, the long length of his body warming her through the silk of her robe. "I've dreamed of doing this since the first time I saw you."

Judith snuggled against him, slipping her knee over his thighs. "Have you really?"

He smoothed her hair, holding her head against his shoulder. "Really."

Judith brushed her fingers over the brown curls shading his chest. She wanted him here every evening, every morning, for the rest of her life. "Even knowing what I am?"

She felt him stiffen beneath her, a tightening of his muscles as he cupped her chin in his big hand and coaxed her to look at him. "Tell me, what are you?"

"You know." Judith stared up into his green eyes, seeing questions there, more than the simple one he had asked. "I was Van Horne's mistress."

He slid his thumb over the curve of her lower lip. "Tell me what you *are,*" he asked, his deep voice a gentle caress.

She realized then he was speaking of the present, while she was wandering through the past. "A woman. A woman who needs to believe you can accept her in spite of the mistakes she has made."

"I did not come to you a virgin, Judith. I have known other women, coupled with other bodies." He kissed the corners of her mouth. "But this is the first time I have ever *joined* with a woman. Do you understand what I mean?"

Judith drew a breath that tangled with her pulse in her throat. "I think I do."

He slipped his hand into her thick hair, cradling her head. "I love you."

Judith closed her eyes. "You don't have to tell me you love me if it isn't true."

"Look at me."

Judith hesitated, her breath catching when she opened her eyes. The look in his eyes told her everything she needed to know, his love for her shimmering in the forest green depths.

"I want you as my mate, my wife, for now and always." He kissed her lips, a soft brush of firm lips that left her hungry for more. "You are the woman fate has sent to me. Tell me you will stay with me forever."

Joy surged inside her, coaxing the air from her lungs. "Do you mean it?"

"I have never asked a woman to marry me before." He brushed his nose against hers, his warm breath stroking her skin. "I hope I shall never have to ask again. I find the suspense of waiting for her answer more frightening than anything in the world."

"Yes." She slipped her arms around his broad shoulders. "Now and forever."

Judith sighed as he stripped away her robe. She wanted nothing between them, nothing except the feel of his warm skin sliding against hers.

With his lips and his hands he adored her, stroking her skin, kissing her, making her feel as though she were shining and new. Never had she felt more beautiful. Never had she felt more loved. Yet, as he entered her, joining their bodies, she wondered if she truly deserved such joy.

She wrapped her arms around Bram, fighting the fear that lingered inside her. Could she shed the evil that had been her life with Leighton? Or would he find her, destroy her and the future she wanted so desperately with this beautiful man?

Chapter Twenty-Six

Sarah sat near the bottom of the wide mahogany staircase that rose upward from the entry hall in the Sinclair house. The others were in the drawing room, waiting for Austin and Devlin to return. She couldn't share their vigil. Not when she felt as though she had betrayed them all.

Light tumbled from a gold-and-crystal chandelier suspended high above the white marble floor, absorbing the moonlight that flowed through diamond-paned windows at the landing above her. Carved panels of mahogany lined the walls. From all appearances, this house might have been a fine home in New York, but she was a long way from home.

She hugged her knees to her chest, her unbound hair spilling forward over her shoulders, sliding against her jade green silk tunic. The clothes Brianna had given her to wear made her feel exposed and at the same time gave her an odd sense of freedom.

She had never in her life imagined wearing trousers. And the undergarments—the drawers were hardly more than a scrap of silk that left her legs entirely bare, and the odd camisole covered her bosom and nothing else. Still, she couldn't insult Brianna and refuse to wear the shocking outfit. The lady had taken care of her as though she were a child.

The front door opened. Sarah rose to her feet, her heart thudding against the wall of her chest. Devlin entered the hall and closed the door behind him, the soft click of the latch thundering against Sarah's ears. A look of displeasure entered his eyes when he saw her.

Sarah didn't allow his stern look to keep her away. She hurried across the white marble. "Have you seen him?"

"Yeah. I saw him."

"Is he all right?"

Devlin frowned. "Physically, he's fine."

"Will you take me to him?"

"He doesn't want to talk to anyone."

"Please," Sarah said, grabbing Devlin's arm, "I need to talk to him."

Devlin studied her a moment as though he were looking into her mind, reading her thoughts.

She looked up into features she had loved the first moment she had seen them. Yet this was not Austin's face; this man was a stranger who had every right to believe she meant to do his brother harm. "Please, there is so much I need to tell him."

Devlin smiled, a thoughtful curve of his lips that touched his eyes with warmth. "You just might be the person he needs to see right now."

Leighton stood in the shelter of the woods staring at the Sinclair house. Golden light glowed from several windows on the first and second floors. "I wonder what the best way would be to breach the walls of the citadel."

Collin groaned against the gag Leighton had stuffed into his mouth. Leighton glanced over his shoulder at the young man.

Collin sat a few feet away, hugging a tree with his arms and legs, his feet and hands tied to keep him in place. He still needed Collin. After he killed the Sinclairs, he would not want to dally in this place.

"I think I shall wait until they sleep before I strike." Leighton slipped his knife from his pocket, smiling into the blade as he thought of how he would eliminate the family, one by one.

The front door of the Sinclair house opened, spilling golden light into the darkness. A man stepped from the house into that glowing wedge of light. Leighton drew back into the shadows, staring at Sinclair, his heart pounding. Was it Devlin or Austin?

A woman left the house behind him, a woman with light brown hair that cascaded in unbound waves to her waist. She wore a jade green tunic and cream-colored trousers, like the clothing the other women here wore, but this woman did not belong in this place.

"Sarah," Leighton whispered. She should be in New York, waiting for him. Had Sinclair poisoned her against her own brother? Had she chosen this bastard over her own flesh and blood?

Leighton watched them walk away from the house, taking a winding path that led toward the ruins. A moonlight tryst.

Leighton slipped the knife into his pocket, the blade nestling against his pistol as he crept from the woods, following Sinclair and Sarah. The bastard would pay for defiling his sister.

* * *

Devlin glanced over his shoulder as though he suspected someone might be following them. Sarah looked in the direction of his gaze, seeing only the buildings of ancient Avallon rising a quarter of a mile down the path. The stone buildings glittered as though sprinkled with diamond dust. The city reminded her of ancient Greece, pillars lifting pediments toward the star-studded sky, cobblestones paving the square.

"Is something wrong?" she asked, keeping her voice to a whisper. It seemed right, keeping her voice low, reverent in this ancient place.

"Just a feeling, that's all." Devlin smiled, his lips curving into a mischievous grin that reminded her far too much of another smile, one she wondered if she would ever see again. "Maybe an ancestor has returned to haunt the place."

Sarah felt a chill whisper across her skin. "I could believe there are ghosts here."

She looked across the ruins that spread from the square toward the cliff. Only a few buildings stood in this part of ancient Avallon; many had been destroyed by the shifting of the earth long ago.

Chasms had been carved into the ground where buildings once stood, tumbling walls, spilling stone pillars across what had once been a cobblestone street. "It would seem all the logic of my existence does not exist in this place," she whispered.

"I understand what you mean." The breeze ruffled Devlin's thick black hair. "Consider walking in here one day and discovering this is your home. You can imagine what it's like meeting your parents and thinking they look more like your brother and sister."

"I know how I felt coming here. I suspect it must have been a terrible shock for you."

Devlin released his breath between his teeth. "You might say that."

"I can only imagine what it must be like to know you are a part of this, to know your ancestors gave civilization to the world. I can only imagine how strong the ties would be to the past."

"Then you can understand why Austin needed to retrieve that medallion."

"There is more to that medallion than your father is willing to tell me, isn't there?"

"Maybe." Devlin frowned as he glanced back toward the temple. "I'm not yet of the Inner Circle. I do know there are secrets which they believe must be kept from everyone outside of the circle."

Sarah rubbed her arms, trying to chase away the chill that came from within. "Do you think the medallion is one of those secrets?"

Devlin shrugged. "I suppose it could be."

"Will I ever know?"

"I doubt it. In the thirty-five years they have been married, my father has never revealed the secrets to my mother."

"I see." Even if she found a way to bridge the chasm that had opened between them, there would always be a part of Austin he would keep from her. And yet it didn't matter. She was willing to live with his secrets, as long as she could live with him.

Devlin paused on the cobblestones. "I think you'll find what you're looking for at the end of the path."

Sarah's heart crept upward into her throat as she stared toward the end of the path and saw a man sitting on the low wall of a ruined house. Austin was watching her, and he didn't look at all pleased to see her here.

She turned and grabbed Devlin's arm as he started back toward the temple. "Where are you going?"

"You don't need me here, Sarah." He covered her hand with his warm palm. "If you're half as stubborn as Austin said you were, you'll be fine."

"He told you I was stubborn?"

Devlin nodded. "I believe his exact words when he was describing you were, 'She's got a will of iron, a tongue like a razor, and a beautiful face that makes you forget everything else.' It was right about then I got the feeling my brother was getting in over his head."

"Oh," she whispered, glancing back to where Austin sat alone in the moonlight. "I suppose there are moments when I'm overly determined."

"I hope you're stubborn, Sarah. I hope you're determined to stand beside him." He squeezed her hand. "He's going to need you. Even if he thinks he doesn't. His entire world is shattering all around him."

"I want to be with him, no matter what happens."

"In that case, I think you'll both be all right." Devlin smiled, his eyes reflecting the knowledge of a man who has been to the brink of hell and back. "No one is going to be able to put the pieces back together except you and Austin."

Sarah stood planted on the path, watching Devlin until he disappeared around a corner where a jagged wall thrust upward toward the moon. He was right, of course; no one could help mend this breach between husband and wife. She only hoped she could.

Austin stared at her as she approached, moonlight carving his broad-shouldered form from the shadows. Like a phantom taking substance he rose from the ancient stones, a frowning knight silently warning away his enemy.

Sarah shivered inside. A solid wall of anger stood between them, as tangible as the stones beneath her feet, bringing her to a halt three feet away from him.

"You shouldn't have come here, Sarah."

"I had to see you."

"I don't want to see anyone."

Sarah tried to moisten her dry lips, but the inside of her mouth had turned to parchment. "But I wanted—"

"Go back to the house."

"I need to tell you—"

"There isn't anything you need to tell me."

Sarah stared as he walked away from her, paralyzed by the fear that all of the words she wanted to say would mean nothing. He stood on the edge of the cliff, dangerously close, staring out across the plains that surrounded the mountain. A breeze whispered through the ruins, ancient voices singing softly. "Austin, please, listen to what I have to say."

"You realize now your brother is not what you thought he was." He tipped back his head, the breeze stirring his thick black hair. "And you wonder if we might be able to make a future together."

The chill in his voice pierced her. He already knew what she wanted to say. He already had the verdict for what would become of their marriage. "It seems you can read my mind."

"Sarah," he whispered, glancing at her, all the anger drained from his features, replaced by a haunting sadness. "I can't promise you a future. I'm not sure I have one."

Sarah studied him a moment, seeing the despair in his eyes, fearing what he might do. "What do you mean?"

"All of my life, I've known exactly who I was. I defined my existence by this." He swept his arm toward the ruins, stones scattering beneath his feet and bouncing over the edge of the cliff as he turned.

"What remains when all of this is gone?"

"Please come back away from the edge," she said, reaching for him.

"I'm not going to jump, Sarah." He stepped back, avoiding her touch. "Fool I might be, but I'm not suicidal. I don't intend to deprive the Central Council of the privilege of pronouncing judgment on me."

"Your father said he would find a way to defend you."

Austin sank to a low stone wall. He turned his gaze to some distant point on the horizon, where moonlight painted a silvery streak against the black earth. "I'm not sure there is a defense for what I've done."

Jasmine grew wild here. The hardy vines entwined with fallen stones, white flowers glowing in the moonlight, the sweet fragrance spilling into the cool evening breeze swirling around them. "Are you afraid they will take away your title, your wealth?"

"I don't think you understand."

"I don't care about money or prestige. I would live in a woodcutter's cottage with you," she said.

"This has nothing to do with money or prestige. It has to do with honor and trust and responsibility." He smoothed his fingers over a stone slab lying on the ground beside him, the remains of a pillar that had once stood tall. "I don't know who I am anymore."

"I know who you are." She moved toward him, drawn to him as she had been drawn to this man from the first moment she had glimpsed him. He didn't look up at her. "You're the man I love."

Austin closed his eyes. "Sarah, don't."

"You're a good man, Austin Sinclair. And I won't stand by and watch you destroy yourself."

He laughed, a deep rumble that echoed against the black stones of the ruined city. "I've already destroyed any good there was in Austin Sinclair."

"That's not true. I fell in love with you when I thought you were a thief and scoundrel." She wanted to touch him, but sensed he would draw away from her. "Even then I could see the goodness inside you. I fell in love with the man behind the handsome mask."

"Sarah, I'm a fraud."

"Why? Because you think you've failed to live up to some ancient code of ethics?"

He bowed his head, his broad shoulders slumping as though bowed by a heavy weight. "I failed my family."

"You did this for me."

Austin shook his head. "I did this for me. I wanted you, Sarah, more than I wanted anything in the world."

"Austin," she whispered, cupping his face in her hands. He looked up at her, moonlight reflected in his eyes. In his eyes she saw the vulnerable boy who had tried to be everything his parents had always wanted him to be. "You asked me once to believe in you, and I was too confused to see the truth. Please give me the chance to prove how much I love you."

"Sarah, it's too late."

"No! We've both made mistakes. But that doesn't mean we can't make a future together."

"I never should have married you."

Sarah stepped back, his words piercing her heart. She stared toward the temple, unable to look at him, to see his rejection of her in his eyes. A few trees stood among the litter of fallen stones, living monuments to those who had died here centuries ago. "Then you don't love me."

He stood and looked down at her, his eyes fierce. "You don't understand."

Sarah felt the sting of tears in her eyes. "I understand that you don't want me." She turned and walked away from him, refusing to allow him to see her cry.

"Sarah." He grabbed her arm.

She tried to pull free. "Please let go of me."

Austin tightened his grip on her arm. "If I could—"

"Release her, Sinclair."

Sarah jumped at the sound of her brother's voice. She turned, staring at Leighton, unable to comprehend how he could be standing there before her like a ghost in a white linen suit. "What are you doing here?"

"Saving you from this bastard." Leighton smiled as he pointed the pistol he held at Austin. "I want to make sure Sinclair never bothers you again."

"No!" Sarah stepped in front of Austin. "Leighton, you don't want to do this horrible thing."

"Oh, but I do. Now step aside, Sarah."

Sarah shook her head, knowing the moment she stepped away from Austin, Leighton would kill him.

"Get out of here, Sarah," Austin whispered.

Sarah shook her head, pressing back against him. "Leighton, please, put the gun away."

"Sarah, the man has filled your head with lies." Leighton shifted the gun, moonlight glittering on the silver muzzle. "Just step aside, and I'll make sure he can never lie to you again."

Sarah stared at the stranger who was her brother, seeing every truth she had tried to deny. It was there, hidden in his face; like the brown dye that covered his silvery blond hair, his lies had camouflaged the truth. "Leighton, I know what happened."

"Sarah, you aren't going to believe Sinclair, are you?"

Sarah felt her husband's warmth radiate against her back, shielding her from the evening chill. "I know you killed a man."

"I had to. They were going to lock me up like an animal. Now move away from him." Leighton gestured with the gun. "I don't want to hurt you."

"Do as he says, Sarah," Austin said, resting his hands on her shoulders.

Sarah shook her head. "I can't."

"Sarah, why are you protecting him?" Leighton asked, his voice strained with torment. "He is my enemy."

"Leighton, please put away the gun. I can't allow you to hurt Austin. I love him."

Austin's hands tightened on her shoulders.

"No! You can't love him." Leighton cocked the pistol, the air splintering with a metallic click.

"Get down!" Austin shoved Sarah, tossing her from the line of fire as though she were no more than a rag doll.

Sarah screamed. She stumbled, tripping on a stone block, tumbling to the ground. Pain flared in her hip and her hand where she had tried to break her fall. For a moment she sat on the ground, stunned as she stared at her husband and her brother and the deadly pistol in Leighton's hand.

"Damn you, Sinclair!" Leighton shouted. "You turned my sister against me."

"Leighton!" Sarah shouted, scrambling to her feet. "You're my brother. I love you."

Leighton glanced at her, moonlight glittering on the tears in his eyes. "I want things the way they were, Sarah."

"They can be." Sarah took a step toward her brother, her gaze dipping to the pistol he still held pointed at Austin. "If you'll only give me the gun."

"Stay back, Sarah," Austin said, his voice a low growl.

Sarah hesitated, glancing at Austin. He stood poised on the balls of his feet, a panther about to strike. "It's all right," she said, hoping to keep him at bay.

At least 12 feet separated the men, and Sarah knew a bullet could travel those 12 feet faster than a man. If Austin tried to rush Leighton, he would die. "My brother isn't going to hurt me. Are you, Leighton?"

"I'd never hurt you, Sarah. You're all I have." Leighton waved the gun at Austin. "And he's taken you away from me."

"No." Sarah moved toward her brother. "Leighton, he hasn't turned me against you."

"How do you think she's going to feel about you once you kill me?" Austin flexed his hands at his sides.

"When you're gone, it will be like it was before. When all of the Sinclairs are dead, I can forget all of this." Leighton glanced down at the pistol. "I can go on with my life as though nothing bad ever happened."

From the corner of her eye she saw Austin move, like the uncoiling of a spring, aimed straight at Leighton. Her brother looked up as though startled from sleep, the pistol jerking in his hand. He would kill Austin.

"Leighton!" Sarah launched herself between her husband and her brother. The gunshot thundered in her ears. She felt the bullet slam into her chest, white-hot, pain searing along her every nerve, stealing the strength from her limbs.

"Sarah!"

Her name pulsated with the blood pounding in her ears, the shouts of her husband and her brother overlapping as she tumbled toward the ground. Austin's strong arms closed around her, breaking her fall. Yet he couldn't stop the downward plunge inside her, the slow sinking into darkness.

Austin sank with her to the ground, cradling her in his arms. "Sarah," he said, his voice choked with emotion.

Through tears, she looked up at him. Moonlight glowed behind him, slipping silvery light into his thick hair, this prince who had come to rescue her from loneliness, this man she had betrayed. "I'm sorry," she whispered. "Please forgive me."

Pain twisted his features. He tightened his hold on her as though he could keep her from slipping away from him. "You're going to be all right, Sarah."

"Damn you, Sinclair!" Leighton towered above her, blocking out the moonlight. "Take your hands off my sister."

"Look at her, Van Horne!" Austin shouted. "We have to get her to a doctor, now."

She tried to speak, but she couldn't even manage a whisper; all of her strength was fading, draining from her body with the blood she felt warm against her chest.

"It's your fault," Leighton shouted, waving the pistol at Austin. "I'll kill you for this."

"No!" she tried to scream, her voice escaping in a low moan as she sank further into the pool of darkness.

A gunshot shattered the night. She felt Austin flinch, his arms flexing around her.

"Austin," she whispered, knowing her brother had ended the life of the man she loved. In that moment, as she slipped into the darkness, she realized her own life ceased to matter.

Chapter Twenty-Seven

In the instant before he heard the gunshot, Austin had known Leighton was going to shoot. Yet with Sarah in his arms, there had been no chance to stop him.

He stiffened, an instant of tension when he sucked in his breath and waited for the bullet to slam into his body. But Leighton was the one reeling backward, a dark stain spreading across the sleeve of his white coat. He staggered a few steps, the pistol dropping from his limp hand, the steel clattering against the stones.

"You!" Leighton murmured, staring past Austin.

In the periphery of his vision Austin saw Devlin running toward them. Leighton clutched his upper arm, sagging back against a half collapsed wall.

Devlin halted beside his brother. "How is she?"

Austin looked down at the woman lying in his arms. Thick, dark lashes rested against her cheeks. Blood smeared her tunic, plastering the dark green silk to her chest. Austin touched her neck, unable to breathe, his fear for her strangling his throat. Her skin was cool, damp to his touch.

"Austin, is she . . . ?" Devlin asked.

"She's alive!" A pulse fluttered beneath his fingers, a thready beat of life. Austin nearly collapsed with the sudden wave of relief that hit him. "She needs medical attention immediately."

"I'll take care of Van Horne."

Austin slipped his arm under her shoulder, another beneath her knees. A soft moan slipped from her lips as he lifted her. "It's all right, my love. You're going to be all right," he whispered, praying he could get her medical attention in time.

Devlin gripped his pistol as he moved toward Leighton Van Horne. Leighton was watching him, smiling, a demonic smile shining from an angelic face. A chill prickled the base of his spine as he held the man's icy cold gaze. Van Horne had no soul.

"So this time we've traded places," Leighton said, examining the tear in his sleeve. "At least for the moment."

"It's over, Van Horne." Devlin retrieved Leighton's pistol and slipped it into the pocket of his trousers.

"I know your doctors can fix this little scratch." Leighton plucked at his bloody sleeve. "I assume they will be able to heal my sister, the way they pulled you back from the brink of death."

Devlin frowned as he thought of the wound in Sarah's chest. "Pray that they do."

"Prayers are for fools, Sinclair." Leighton laughed, tossing back his head to look up at the stars. "Have you ever really known a prayer to be answered?"

"You just shot your sister. Don't you feel any remorse?"

"It was your brother's fault." Leighton looked at him, madness lurking in his eyes. "He turned her against me."

"You managed to do that all by yourself."

Leighton lounged against the wall, shoving his hands into his coat pockets. "Tell me, Sinclair, why didn't you kill me just now? I know how much you hate me."

Van Horne was like a rabid wolf, dangerous, unpredictable. Yet Devlin hadn't killed him when he had the chance, and he wondered if he would regret that decision. "I knew I didn't have to kill you to stop you."

"Is that the reason? Part of your little codes of ethics, I suppose." Leighton smiled, his teeth glowing animal white in the moonlight. "This society believes killing is barbaric. That makes you weak."

"Let's go."

"It's a rare feeling, Sinclair, killing. A powerful feeling. For that moment, as you watch the life drain from the body of your victim, you are God."

Devlin slid his thumb over the handle of his gun. "Get moving, Van Horne."

Leighton smiled as though amused by some private joke. "Are you going to put me in a cage?"

"You belong in a cage." Devlin gestured toward the main part of the ancient city as he spoke. "Now move."

Leighton drew away from the wall, turning, pulling his hands from his pockets. He staggered a few steps before his legs collapsed beneath him and he crumpled to his knees.

"Get up, Van Horne."

Leighton looked up at Devlin, his straight brown hair hanging over his brow. "It seems I need some help."

Devlin hesitated before he moved toward him, feeling as though he were approaching a wounded animal. "Here," he said, offering Van Horne his hand.

"I knew I could count on your sense of honor," Leighton said, smiling up at him.

The back of Devlin's neck prickled. Leighton grabbed his hand, his grip surprisingly strong for a wounded man. As Devlin helped him to his feet, Leighton pivoted, swinging his free hand.

Devlin saw a glint of silver in the moonlight. He jerked back an instant before he felt the knife rip into his side, slashing across his ribs. Pain flared like wildfire devouring a ripened field of wheat.

Van Horne wrenched the pistol from Devlin's stunned hand. "No one is going to put me in a cage."

Devlin staggered back, clutching the ragged wound in his side, gasping for each breath that splintered in his chest.

Van Horne tossed back his head, his laughter slicing the cool evening breeze. "So it seems we trade places again." He pointed the pistol at Devlin's heart. "Do you feel the power I possess, Sinclair?"

"The true power isn't in destruction, Van Horne." Devlin drew air into his burning lungs. "The true power is in mastering life."

"I've beaten you, admit it." The corner of Leighton's mouth twitched. "I've mastered you."

Devlin held Leighton's look, sensing the lust for power inside him. "Pull the trigger."

"You can't turn this around, Sinclair. You don't control me. I'll decide when you shall die."

"How do you expect to get away?"

"I have a ticket all tied up in your front yard. The same little friend who helped me get in here."

Devlin knew if he didn't return soon they would send someone looking for him. But how long did he have before Leighton tired of this game? "Do you have the medallion with you?"

Leighton smiled as he pulled the medallion from his pocket, the ancient gold shimmering in the moon-light. "Now you know how it feels, Sinclair, to have something precious stolen from you, the way you stole Cleopatra's necklace from me."

"I still have the necklace." Devlin could feel his strength ebbing with the flow of blood that spilled through his fingers. If he didn't get help soon, it wouldn't matter if Leighton slammed a bullet into his heart; he would bleed to death. "Perhaps we could arrange an exchange."

Leighton stuffed the medallion into his coat pocket. "You want to trick me."

"How could I trick you? You're the one with the power."

"That's right." Leighton waved the pistol at Devlin. "I can kill you, Sinclair. One little pull of the trigger and you're a dead man."

"You're smart, Leighton." Devlin looked past Van Horne, as though he saw someone creeping there in the shadows. "Too smart to be tricked. Too smart to have someone sneak up behind you."

Leighton glanced over his shoulder. It gave Devlin an instant, a precious heartbeat to react. He vaulted over the low wall, hitting the ground as a bullet slammed into the stones above his head.

"Damn you, Sinclair!"

Devlin fought the pain that threatened to steal every ounce of strength from his body. He dragged Leighton's pistol from his pocket. Bullet after bul-let plowed into the top of the stone wall four feet above him, chips of debris raining down on him.

"Come out, Sinclair, it's time for you to die!"

In a crouch Devlin ran to a corner of the ruined building. Once there he glanced over the top of the ragged wall. Leighton stood on the edge of the cliff, his pistol pointed toward the wall where Devlin had disappeared.

Devlin clutched the pistol between both hands and braced his elbows on the stone wall, the strength draining from his arms. "Drop the gun, Van Horne."

Leighton pivoted, staring at him as though Devlin had stepped from the grave. "You can't stop me, Sinclair." The gun bobbed in his hand at his side, as though Leighton were calculating the chances he would have if he tried to shoot.

"Don't move."

"You won't kill me." Leighton laughed. "But I've already killed you. And it's just the beginning. I'm going to kill them all, your brother, your parents, your pretty little sister, and your wife. Oh, I'm going to enjoy her first, Sinclair. Beautiful Kate, that wife you prize so highly."

Devlin held the pistol pointed at Van Horne's chest, clutching the handle between his blood-soaked hands. "Don't move."

"I'll see you in hell!" Leighton shouted, thrusting the pistol upward from his side.

Devlin squeezed the trigger. As the gunshot thundered in his ears, he saw Leighton stagger.

Leighton's features twisted into a look of sheer shock. He stumbled back, pressing his hand to the dark smudge in the center of his chest. "You did it," he whispered, crumpling to his knees. He pitched forward, falling facedown against the rocks.

Devlin leaned against the wall, resting his chin on his chest, clasping his hand over the wound in his side. "It's over, Van Horne," he whispered.

"Devlin!" Rhys shouted.

Devlin lifted his head; the motion tipped the world, sent it into a lazy twirl. His father's image splintered in his vision, spinning as Rhys ran toward him. Devlin sagged against the wall, his head reeling.

Rhys grabbed his son's arm. "Devlin, what happened?"

"Van Horne . . . I shot him."

"How badly are you hurt?"

Devlin swallowed back the bile rising in his throat. "I'm all right." Yet he did not protest as his father slipped a strong arm around him and helped him to the ground. Devlin sat with his back braced against the wall, trying to find a solid anchor.

Rhys knelt beside him, frowning as he examined the wound in Devlin's side. "Looks like we're going to keep Dr. Carrick and her team busy tonight."

Devlin bit back a groan as his father pressed strong fingers against the wound. He shivered uncontrollably. "Is Sarah going to . . . will she be all right?"

"I don't know. Dr. Carrick was examining her when I came looking for you." Rhys met his son's gaze, concern for Sarah naked in his blue-green eyes. "It doesn't look good, son."

"God, I hope she pulls through."

"Breathe with me, Devlin." Rhys drew a deep breath, exhaling slowly, like leaves falling in a lazy autumn breeze. "We have to keep you from going into shock."

Devlin rested his head back against the wall, following the slow, easy breath of his father, the pain dissolving beneath Rhys's fingers like a fire in the rain. "I killed Van Horne."

"You had no choice."

"The medallion is in his pocket."

"Thank God." Rhys moved his fingers against the wound, the heat of his touch seeping into Devlin's blood.

"It's magical, isn't it?" Devlin moistened his lips, staring up at the stars. "One of those secrets you can't tell anyone outside of the Circle."

Rhys studied his son a moment, a deep line carved between his black brows. "In time you will know the answers."

Rhys leaned back in a chair in his study, buff-colored leather sighing beneath him. Electric lights in the shape of flames flickered behind crystal-and-gold fixtures on the walls, casting a golden glow on the carved oak panels. He pressed his hands together, resting his chin on the steeple of his fingers as he watched Fraser Bennett pace back and forth before him, the thick carpet of gold and emerald wool absorbing the sharp thuds of his heels.

Although the outcome here would decide Austin's future, Rhys knew his son's fate was tied to the young woman who fought for her life in the medical unit Dr. Carrick had established upstairs. If Sarah died, everything Rhys was trying to accomplish for his son would be meaningless. If they buried Sarah, Austin would bury himself in grief.

Fraser paused his restless pacing as he reached the wing-back chair where Collin Bennett sat. Collin's face was streaked with dirt, his light brown hair tousled, the shoulder of his charcoal gray coat torn.

Rhys had found the young man tied in the woods soon after he had brought Devlin back to the house. And with his discovery had come the chance Rhys was looking for to save Austin.

Fraser stared down at his son, his face etched with rage. "I can't understand how you could help Van Horne."

"He was going to kill me." Collin glanced to Rhys as though he might find understanding. "Van Horne is a madman. I had no choice."

"You took an oath, Collin," Fraser said. "You pledged to protect Avallon with your life."

"Is that what you wish had happened, Father?" Collin stared up at his father. "Do you wish Van Horne had killed me?"

"Collin, I . . ." Fraser hesitated, staring down at the young man who resembled him. They shared the same coloring, the same sharp cast of features, the same tall, slender form. Yet there the resemblance ended.

"I don't really need an answer, Father. I know you've always put this place above me, above Mother."

"That's not true," Fraser said.

Collin laughed, a bitter sound high in his throat. "When did you ever take time away from the council or the Circle to be with us?"

Fraser glanced to Rhys, his blue eyes filled with embarrassment. "That's enough, Collin," he said, keeping his voice low as though he wished to contain the argument.

"What difference does it make if Lord Sinclair hears what I have to say, Father? The Central Council will hear it soon enough."

"So they will," Fraser said, his voice baring his defeat.

Rhys pressed the tips of his fingers together, seeking the inner balance he needed to maintain control. He drew his thoughts away from his son and the lovely young woman Austin might lose. He had only a few moments to save Austin. He could not allow the opportunity to pass.

"I can't believe this has all happened," Collin said, closing his eyes. "I never meant anyone to be hurt."

Fraser walked to the open French doors, where he stared into the moonlit gardens. A cool breeze heavy with the scent of roses drifted into the room.

Rhys studied his opponent. He could sense the weakness in him. Fraser had always been an ambitious man. Now he was a man facing political ruin. "How unfortunate it is that Van Horne has managed to destroy the reputations of so many."

Fraser glanced over his shoulder, casting a cold glance at Rhys. "If your son had brought him back, this would not have happened to Collin."

"If your son had not helped Van Horne, my daughter-in-law would not be fighting for her life at this moment. It does make one wonder who is more at fault." Rhys rested his chin on his fingertips, holding Fraser's gaze until the other man wavered and turned back toward the gardens.

Fraser drew a deep breath, his shoulders rising beneath the white silk of his shirt. "You know I was the one who recommended Austin be brought before the council on charges, don't you?"

"I suspected you might have been the one who persuaded the others."

"I suppose a conviction of this kind would have been very profitable for you." Collin leaned back in his chair, staring at his father. "You might even have made it all the way to the leader's chair."

Fraser drew his hands into fists at his sides. "That will be enough, Collin."

"More than enough, I'd say." Collin looked away from his father, his expression revealing the hurt inside him.

"I don't believe Collin meant any harm. And I know Austin believed a delay in retrieving the medallion would not jeopardize his mission." Rhys looked at the stiff line of Fraser's back. "It would seem we are looking at two cases of circumstances that got out of control. I wonder if either young man deserves to be put on trial for something as serious as treason."

Fraser glanced at him over his shoulder. "What do you have in mind?"

"Collin brought Van Horne here hoping he could bring the man to justice."

"I did what?" Collin asked.

"Quiet, Collin." Fraser turned to face Rhys. "Please continue."

"Austin delayed in retrieving the medallion because he was hoping to lure Van Horne into a trap." Rhys smiled, seeing the eagerness in Fraser, the need to find a way out of this dilemma. "Together, Collin and Austin brought Van Horne back to Avallon to stand trial."

"So it was all part of a plan," Fraser said.

"That's right." Rhys tapped his fingertips together.

Fraser stroked his mustache. "It could work."

"They'll never believe it," Collin said.

"I think they will." Fraser glanced at his son. "Because they want to believe it. The council shivers at this type of conflict."

Rhys rested his chin on his fingertips. He felt confident the council would drop the charges against Austin. He wondered how he might be able to convince his son to forgive himself. And he knew the answer rested with a young woman who might not live to see another dawn.

Austin stood at the windows in the sitting room outside of Sarah's bedroom. A mile away, nestled in the valley, ancient Avallon stood in the moonlight, black stone glittering. It had always been there. As a boy he had imagined himself a knight in that ancient time, a wielder of justice. And now he found justice eluded him. He was alive and whole while the woman he loved lay near death. Because of him. Because of his selfish soul.

His family was gathered with him, all except his father. In the panes of glass he saw their reflections, quiet, waiting for word. His brother sat on a sofa across from the windows, beside Kate. For a second time Devlin had almost died at the hands of Leighton Van Horne. That, too, was a crime Austin could lay at his own doorstep.

Austin turned at the sound of a door opening. Dr. Beverly Carrick stepped into the room. She stood framed by the carved oak door frame, staring at Austin. Tall, slender, her light brown hair pulled back into a roll at her nape, Dr. Carrick was one of the finest physicians in Avallon. If anyone could save Sarah, it would be Carrick. Yet the look in her brown eyes fed the fear growing inside him.

"How is she?" Austin asked, stepping away from the windows.

"I've repaired the tissue damage." Dr. Carrick frowned, her brows pulling together over her thin nose. "But I'm afraid she isn't responding to treatment. She refuses to regain consciousness."

"What do you mean?" Austin asked. "Don't you have something to make her regain consciousness?"

"Yes and no." Dr. Carrick crossed her arms as though she were impatient with her own lack of success. "I've given her everything I dare give her so soon after reconstructing her lung. By all rights, she should be conscious. But she refuses to cooperate."

"I want to see her," Austin said, brushing past the doctor.

Dr. Carrick's three assistants were removing the last of the medical equipment when Austin entered Sarah's bedroom. As they left the room, they carried silver cases filled with technology that could transform any site into an operating room. Medical miracles. Technology developed over the centuries. Would it be enough to save Sarah?

Austin moved toward the woman who lay unconscious on the bed, four posts of carved mahogany rising around her, a white linen sheet folded above her breasts. He moved slowly, as though she might awaken in the time it took to reach her. Still, she did not move.

All of the emotion inside him had turned to crystal; one wrong move and he would shatter, splinter into a thousand pieces that could never be reunited. He stood beside the bed, looking down at his sleeping bride.

The lamp on the table beside her bed cast a golden glow over her, stroking her smooth cheeks, tangling in the thick waves that spread across her pillow. They had dressed her in a soft white cotton gown, a narrow band of embroidered lace trimming the edge of the round neckline. She looked so peaceful, so very beautiful. He wanted nothing more than to lie beside her, hold her, fill his senses with her fragrance, her warmth.

"I've done everything I can," Dr. Carrick said. "It's up to Sarah now."

"I'm not certain I understand what you mean."

"In twenty years as a physician, I have learned that for all of our advances, there are moments when it comes down to a single question." Dr. Carrick studied Sarah a moment, frowning, as though she saw the one puzzle in life she could not solve. "How strong is the will to live?"

"Sarah is strong willed."

"I hope she is." Carrick rested her hand on Austin's shoulder. "I'll be back in a few hours to see how she is doing. If there is any change, don't hesitate to contact me."

Austin sank to the edge of the bed as Carrick left the room. He touched Sarah's face, tracing the crest of her cheekbone, the curve of her brow. He pressed his fingertip against her soft lips, feeling each reassuring exhale of warm breath. He felt a tightness in his chest, a stinging in his eyes, as emotions stirred inside him, sharp edges slicing his heart.

"Sarah," he whispered, lifting her hand to his lips, where a single tear fell upon her skin. "Come back to me, my love."

Chapter Twenty-Eight

Austin rested his shoulder against the window casement in Sarah's room, his face turned to the rain-splattered panes. Darkness had swallowed the world beyond this house. He could see nothing of Avallon. His mother's gardens were nothing but a black pool beneath him. All of the light in the world seemed concentrated in this room.

"Under other circumstances, I would have liked to have seen Collin Bennett exiled from Avallon," Rhys said.

In the glass Austin could see Rhys standing beside Sarah's bed, staring down at the young woman who lay deathly still. It had been two days since the shooting, and Sarah hadn't regained consciousness.

"But I believe Collin would like nothing more than to return to New York."

Austin nodded. "He doesn't feel any loyalty to Avallon."

"Fraser has taken Collin to a rehabilitation center.

I spoke to him this morning. Collin's memories of his life in the Outworld have been erased. They've started the relearning process. I hope father and son will do better with this second chance."

"If only we could all have a second chance."

"The council is withdrawing the charges against you."

Austin looked at his father's image reflected in the window glass. "I'm relieved the family will not be put through the ordeal of a trial."

"Are you?"

"Of course I am." Lightning flashed, splashing silver light across Austin's face. In the glass Austin saw the face of a stranger. He hadn't slept, hadn't eaten since Sarah had been wounded. His face reflected the strain, dark smudges staining the skin below his eyes, a dark shadow of beard shading his cheeks. He was a man locked in combat with inner demons, a man close to losing the battle. Thunder cracked, rattling the windowpanes.

"I think there has already been a trial," Rhys said. "I think you've already convicted yourself."

Austin leaned his head back against the wall, closing his eyes. "Father, please, not now."

"Austin, I've always been proud of you. That hasn't changed."

"This is my responsibility." Austin swept his hand toward the bed where Sarah lay still and silent. "All of it."

"You made a choice, son. In your place, I believe I would have done the same for your mother."

Austin stared at Sarah, grief ripping at him with steely claws. "Sarah may die because of me."

"Then give her a reason to live, Austin. Stop blaming yourself for loving her."

"I don't trust myself any longer." Austin sank to

an upholstered armchair near the windows, sinking against the blue silk brocade. He was a stranger to himself, a man unlike that he had always imagined he was.

"You have done nothing to shatter my trust in you."

"How do you do it, Father?" Merlin planted one paw on Austin's knee and swatted at his arm, demanding attention. Austin stroked the cat's sleek head; Merlin closed his eyes, a deep-throated purr escaping his throat. "How do you keep from being tempted by the power you know you can channel with that ancient piece of gold?"

"By understanding the consequences of changing fate." Rhys crossed the room to stand by his son. "It is as we are taught in the codices of the ancient Circle, Austin. When we manipulate events in the past, we alter the present and affect the future. It can be a disaster."

"I would betray my vows for Sarah." Austin looked up at Rhys, seeing the acceptance in his father's eyes, the concern for a son who no longer deserved that consideration. "If I had the medallion in my hands, I would use it. I would go back to that moment before Sarah was shot, and I would find a way to protect her."

"And in going back to that moment, you might be the one to die."

"I could accept my death, if it meant saving her." Austin clenched his hands into fists on his thighs, his mind replaying every moment on the bluff. "I saw it coming, Father. I saw Van Horne with that gun, the look in Sarah's eyes, and I knew she would do something foolish. If she had only stayed clear, I might have gotten to Leighton before he had the chance to harm her."

"After your brother was taken from us, there were many moments when I wanted to go back in time, alter the events that had stolen our son from us." Rhys stared at the windows, a lifetime of pain reflected in his face. "But if I had, all of the lives Devlin touched would be changed in some way. He would never have met Kate. You would never have met Sarah."

"I know the dangers." Merlin abandoned Austin, sauntering across the room where he leapt to the blue brocade counterpane folded at the foot of the bed. The cat circled twice before curling into a ball at Sarah's feet. She didn't move. He wondered if she ever would. "Still, there have to be moments when altering the past is justified. When, indeed, changing past events is the right thing to do."

"And who shall be the judge of what events shall be changed?" Rhys voiced one of the questions he had often posed to his son in the past, philosophical questions that lurked in the gray area between right and wrong. "How do we know when our tampering might cause irreparable harm?"

"There could be no harm in saving Sarah."

"Sarah was willing to give her life to save you." Rhys looked at the woman who slept so deeply even Dr. Carrick could not reach her with all of her wondrous medicine. "Are you not willing to live for her?"

Austin felt a tightening in his chest. "I would do anything to save her."

"Tell her, son. Make her hear you. Use all of your gifts to bring her back to you."

"I've tried," Austin whispered, his voice strangled by emotion. "Don't you think I've tried to reach her?"

"You have tried while you doubted yourself, while you felt the burden of your choices weigh upon your heart." Rhys rested his hand on Austin's shoulder.

"Go to her without your doubts. Forgive yourself for the choices your father would have made in your place. Go to her ready to face the future with her at your side."

"Can you truly accept me, knowing my love for Sarah has hampered my judgment?"

"Your love for Sarah makes you stronger, not weaker."

"Can you allow me to remain in the Circle after everything I've done?" Austin looked up at Rhys. "How can you trust me?"

"I don't believe you ever intended harm. Only a man of character and strength would embark upon the battle that rages inside you."

Austin stared down at the swirls of blue and ivory in the carpet beneath his feet. "A man of character and strength would not do what I have done."

Rhys tightened his grip on Austin's shoulder as though he wanted to drag his son from the well of despair that threatened to drown Austin. "If Sarah asked you to betray your family or Avallon, would you?"

"Sarah would never ask such a thing of me."

"But if she did. If she said to you, 'Let me print a story about Avallon in my newspaper, let me tell the world about your people,' would you allow it?"

"Of course not."

"And what would you think of a woman who asked you to betray all you held dear?" Rhys asked.

Austin glanced at Sarah, tracing the curve of her cheek where the light from the lamp beside the bed stroked her skin. "I would believe her love for me was nothing more than an illusion."

"When you became a lord of the Inner Circle, you did not vow to betray your heart. You found a balance, Austin, between duty to your vows to Avallon and your love for Sarah. Leighton Van Horne unsettled that balance. If you allow him to condemn you to a life of doubts, then you allow him to triumph."

Austin glanced up at his father, realizing the truth in his words. "And in allowing him to triumph, I fail in all I have ever strived to become."

"You have never disappointed me, Austin." Rhys looked down at his son, his expression reflecting the support Austin had always found in this man. "I have every faith in you."

"Thank you." Austin looked to the bed, staring at Sarah a long moment before he spoke. "Perhaps what I need to find is faith in myself."

"Talk to her, son. Let her know how much you need her."

Austin rose from his chair as Rhys left the room. He crossed the distance that separated him from the woman he loved, sinking to the edge of the bed beside her. Her hair spilled across the white linen covering her pillow, the lamplight spinning threads of gold in the light brown tresses. He watched the rise and fall of her chest beneath the soft white cotton of her nightgown, following the rhythm, breathing with her, his lungs filling with every breath she took.

He cupped her cheeks, resting his fingertips on her temples. He welcomed the throb of her heart, allowing the rhythm to pulsate through his body. Her breath was his breath. Her heartbeat was his heartbeat.

He reached inside himself, tapping into the energy that dwelt within. He felt the connection with her, the joining that sizzled along his nerves, the melding of his spirit with hers.

"Hear me, Sarah," he whispered, stroking his fingers across her temples. "Come back to me, my love."

* * *

Sarah dwelt in a corner of her mind, a safe place where none of the horror of Austin's death could reach her. Memories lived here, poignant memories of a man she scarcely knew, a man she had known a hundred lifetimes. She would stay here. Nothing beyond these memories mattered any longer.

Come back to me, my love.

A voice beckoned her, his voice. Through the shadows of her mind she saw Austin standing in a doorway, a bright light shimmering around him. He reached for her, holding his hand out to her, tempting her to leave the safety of her memories.

Open your eyes, my sweet Sarah.

She turned away from the light that threatened her, the light that reached her with the sound of his voice. Austin was gone. How could he be reaching for her?

Sarah, I can't live without you.

The torment in his voice lured her. She turned back toward the man in the doorway. He was reaching for her, drawing her toward him, toward the light.

Sarah, come to me.

Austin waited for her in that light. She moved toward him, unable to resist. She reached out her hand, touching him, feeling his warmth close around her, strong arms wrapping around her, drawing her into the light.

"Austin," she whispered, opening her eyes. He was there, leaning over her, the lamp beside her bed stroking his face.

"Sarah," he whispered, sliding his fingertips over her temples and into her hair.

"You're alive." She touched his cheek, feeling the scratchy texture of his beard, the warmth of his skin beneath. "You're really alive."

"I am now that you've come back to me, my love."

Tears shimmered in his eyes like silver stars glittering in a twilight sky. "I thought Leighton had killed you," she said.

He slid his thumbs over the crests of her cheeks. "What ever possessed you to stand between us?"

"I couldn't let him hurt you."

"Sarah." He closed his eyes as he breathed her name as softly as a prayer. Tears slipped beneath the fringe of his thick black lashes. "I thought I had lost you."

"Do you forgive me, Austin?" She cupped his face in her hands, the heat of his tears scalding her palms. "I swear I'll never doubt you again."

"There's nothing to forgive. I gave you reason to doubt me." He pressed his lips to the corner of hers, his warm breath spilling across her cheek. "No more deceptions, Sarah, from this moment until the end of time."

"Hold me," Sarah whispered. "Please hold me."

"Forever." Austin eased beside her on the bed, his movements controlled, as though he were afraid he might harm her. He slipped his arms around her, stretching his long body against hers. He lay beside her, holding her close, resting his cheek on her hair.

Sarah snuggled against him, resenting the layers of clothing that kept her from feeling the hot velvet of his skin. She buried her face against his chest, reveling in the strong beat of his heart against her cheek, breathing in the intoxicating scent of his skin. "Would you think me terribly wicked if I told you I want you to make love to me?"

"I would think I'm a very lucky man to have you." He held her closer, his body tense against hers. "As much as I want to hold and caress and taste every inch of your luscious little body, I want to have the doctor take a look at you. And I need to let my family know you're all right. They've been worried about you."

"They have?" Sarah leaned back in his arms to look at him. His thick black hair fell in tousled waves around his face, as though his fingers had been his only comb in days. Lines of fatigue creased the corners of his beautiful eyes. He looked like a man who had wandered alone through a treacherous wilderness, a man who had found his way back home. "After all that's happened, they are worried about what happens to me?"

"You're part of this family, Sarah." Austin kissed her, a soft brush of his lips against hers. "They care for you."

"Even though Leighton tried to . . ." Sarah closed her eyes against the sudden rush of memories assaulting her. Once again she saw Leighton, a gun in his hand, his eyes filled with madness. "How can they accept me after what my brother has done to this family?"

Austin slid his hand through her hair, his fingertips gliding against her scalp. "What kind of people would they be if they judged you by what your brother did?"

Merlin poked her shoulder with his head, meowing deep in his throat. Sarah scratched him beneath his chin, ruffling the white patch of fur there. She remembered the day she had first glimpsed him, a plump gray kitten peeking out from Leighton's coat pocket, a gift for his sister on her eighteenth birthday.

"What happened to my brother?" Sarah drew a breath that trickled through her tight throat. "Did you . . . is he dead?"

"I didn't kill him."

Sarah sank against Austin, hiding her face against

his shoulder, feeling tears sting her eyes. "But he's dead, isn't he?"

"Devlin shot him."

Sarah flinched at the words she had sensed she would hear.

"Devlin had no choice, Sarah." Austin stroked her back, a slow slide of his palm that spread a comforting warmth. "Leighton was going to kill him."

"Somehow it seems wrong to mourn the man who had wanted to kill you." Sarah clenched her eyes shut, trying to hold back the tears. Her chest ached with the grief that demanded release. "But . . . I remember a different Leighton."

"It's all right, Sarah." Austin pressed his lips to her temple. "I understand."

"I can't believe he's gone." Sarah choked on a sob. She clenched her teeth, trying to fight the horrible pain of her brother's loss.

"Let it go, Sarah," Austin whispered, his lips moving against her temple. "Don't try to hold it back. Let the pain flow through you. Let the tears cleanse you."

"He always wanted to make Father notice him." Sarah wept, her body shaking, her tears soaking the soft white silk of Austin's shirt. "All he ever wanted was some sign of affection. That's all."

Austin held her close, stroking her hair, her back, her shoulder, rocking her softly as her tears spilled upon his shoulder. When the tears were spent and Sarah felt weak from the overwhelming grief, he held her still, cradling her against his body as though she were the most precious thing in the world to him.

"He was all I ever had. The only one who ever really cared about me."

"You aren't alone, Sarah," he said. "You will never be alone again."

Chapter Twenty-Nine

Scenes from the legend of King Arthur lined the wide corridor leading from the east wing of the house to the pools. Sarah scarcely noticed the mosaic tiles that shaped each intricate portrait of that age of chivalry. The events of the past few days had settled around her like a shroud.

Everything she had once relied upon to keep her world in balance had shifted. Only Austin was real in this world. And right now, he was all she needed to survive.

The scent of warm jasmine dripped from the damp air, wrapping around her as she entered the pool area. Two large pools sank from the black flagstones lining the floor, as though nature had dug each one. Sunlight tumbled through the glass ceiling, reflecting on the smooth surface of one of the pools. The other pool bubbled, steam rising from the water.

"What an extraordinary place," Sarah whispered.

Palm and banana trees stood amid flowering bushes and vines in this vast chamber, trunks growing upward from the black flagstones, lacy green fronds reaching toward the sunlight shimmering against the glass high overhead. A glass wall hugged the contours of the bluff, flowing around two sides of the room, allowing an unrestricted view of the valley and the ruins. Black stone shaped the other walls, as if the mountain itself sheltered this place.

A metallic click echoed in the room, the sliding of a lock into place. Sarah turned and found Austin leaning against the door. "Have you locked us in here?"

"My father had this lock put on the door when I was five." He plucked at the buttons lining the front of his white silk shirt, flicking each open, revealing an ever increasing expanse of golden skin and dark curls. "He said it was to make sure I wouldn't wander in here and drown. But I suspect he had other reasons for wanting to keep this place private."

"Oh." Sarah felt a delicious heat flicker deep inside her. "I wonder what reasons he might have had."

"I wonder." He tugged his shirt from his trousers, the white silk wrinkled from the intimate press of his body. "What possible reason could a man and woman want with privacy in a place like this?"

The fragrant air wrapped around her, warm, moist, so thick she could scarcely draw a breath. "To swim undisturbed?"

"I think it was to lock out the world." He stripped the white silk from his shoulders, dropping the shirt to the black stones at his feet. Sunlight streamed over his shoulders, his arms, gliding along the thick curves of muscle.

He kicked off the soft black shoes he wore. Sarah watched as he flicked open the buttons lining the front of his black trousers. She swallowed hard, feeling the emotion rise inside her.

"It's been a long time since I've had . . . a swim." He slipped off his trousers, the white silk drawers beneath, baring his body to the sunlight and her own heated stare.

He stood before her, hiding nothing from her gaze. He stood tall and strong, his aroused body kissed by the golden light streaming through the glass. He had come to her from this ancient place of mystery. A prince from a fairy tale. A man who could wield a sword to slay dragons and rescue fair damsels.

"Come swim with me." He moved toward her, silent as a shadow drifting through the sunlight, smiling at her in a way that tipped her heart upside down. Water bubbled and splashed in the pool behind her. "Let's forget the world outside of this paradise."

Sarah glanced at the glass wall, feeling exposed in the sunlight, even though she was fully clothed.

"No one can see us here." Austin paused with less than a foot of steamy air between them. The warmth of his chest radiated against her breasts, soaking her skin through the raspberry silk of her tunic. "Let the rest of the world slip away, Sarah."

Sarah hesitated as he moved toward the bubbling pool, years of propriety warring with the desire that rippled through her in heated waves. Did he actually intend to make love to her here, in the middle of the day?

Austin entered the pool, descending steps hidden beneath the dark, churning water. Steam drifted upward from the pool, coating his skin with a moisture that glistened in the sunlight. Water lapped at his long legs, his narrow hips, the flat rippled muscles of his belly. He smiled at her, lifting his hand to beckon her to his side. "Come to me, my love."

In that instant the battle for propriety was lost. Here, in this place of mystery and wonder, what place did the propriety of that other world have? She unfastened the gold belt at her waist and slipped her tunic over her head, her hair tumbling in a cascade of damp curls over her shoulders. Moist air heavy with the scent of jasmine curled around her naked skin as she removed the scrap of silk molding her breasts.

Austin shifted in the pool, drawing his hands through the water lapping at his waist, the effervescence drifting away from him, giving her a glimpse of golden skin strained to the peak of arousal. He stood watching her, desire darkening his eyes to a smoky blue that flickered with the fire burning inside him.

Sarah stripped away her shoes, the cream-colored silk of her trousers, the short drawers of pale pink silk, baring her body to this man she adored. As she moved toward him, as the sun streamed over the curves of her breasts, tingling her nipples, she realized how right this felt. In shedding her clothes in this bright, sunlit place, she had shed more than scraps of silk. Perhaps propriety had no place in a marriage, at least not in this marriage. Only love. Only passion.

In this place they seemed the only people in the world. Man and woman, destined for one another, now as they had been since the beginning of time.

She eased into the churning pool, the heat of the water stealing her breath. With each step she took, the water rose, heat climbing her legs, stroking her thighs, slipping between her legs like hot oiled satin.

"Tell me, how did a woman as beautiful as you manage to remain single for more than a year after your debut into society?" Austin reached for her, drawing her into his arms.

She smiled at the words he had spoken a lifetime ago. "I was waiting for a thief to steal my heart," she said, sliding her arms around his shoulders, his wet skin sliding like hot silk against hers.

"I thank the stars you waited for me." He kissed her, a slow slide of his lips, hotter than the water lapping at her skin.

"And I thought I could reform you," she whispered as he pressed his lips to the curve of her neck and shoulder, sending shivers skittering across her skin. "I thought I could turn a reckless rogue into a staid gentleman. Thank heaven I was wrong."

He laughed, a deep rumble that brushed his chest against her breasts, damp black curls teasing her nipples. "I'll give you a lifetime to make of me what you want."

She rested her fingertips against the pulse point in his neck, the beat of his heart throbbing beneath his warm skin, matching the rhythm pulsating in the tips of her breasts. "You are what I want." The tremor that shook him astonished her; it awed her, his reaction to her words.

"I don't think you realize how much your love means to me." He slid his hands down her back, curving his fingers over her rounded bottom. "From the time I came of age, women looked at me and saw only a title. Except you, only you."

"You touched me and I came to life." Sarah tilted back her head, arching in his arms like a cat in the sunlight as he drew her close, pressing the heat of his arousal into her belly. Clouds rippled across the pale blue of the sky, reflecting the sunlight.

Austin looked down at her breasts. Steam condensed into shimmering beads on her pale skin. He watched a drop of moisture slide along a rounded curve. He lowered his head, licking one glistening nipple, taking the rosy crest into his mouth.

He felt Sarah lift into him, slipping her hands into his hair, sliding her belly against his hardened flesh.

Desire twisted in him, drawing his every muscle taut. Her moan of pleasure vibrated through him like a bow drawn across the stretched strings of a violin. He moved to the other breast, flicking his tongue against her, tasting the salt of her skin in the beads of moisture that glittered like diamonds in the sunlight.

The effervescence of the water licked upward along his legs. Lavender mingled with the sultry scent of her arousal rose with the heat of her skin. He trembled with the need to possess her. "I need you, Sarah."

She smiled. "No more than I need you."

He lifted her, sliding her legs around his waist, finding the sleek entrance to the heart of her feminine fire.

"For an eternity, my *Edaina,*" he whispered, plunging deep inside her.

Sarah tossed back her head, a joyous sound of pleasure surging upward from her body, echoing from the glass and stone. She moved against him, taking each thrust of his hard flesh, buoyant in his hold.

Slowly he felt the stirring inside her, the splintering of her control. She tossed back her head, moaning his name as her body convulsed and tensed around him. He followed her, surrendering to the soul-shattering sensations that spiraled upward inside him. His body shook with the same pulsations that rippled through her, his every muscle tensing as pleasure engulfed him.

He held her, deep inside her. Each frantic heartbeat echoed in his ears, each ragged breath, his pulse blending with hers so he couldn't tell one from the other.

She held him. With her legs and her arms, she squeezed him as though she never intended to release him. Yet he sensed something in this possession, a fear that lingered beneath the love he felt shimmering around him.

He sank against the smooth stone stairs, holding her in his arms, her sleek thighs embracing his. Her hair swirled in the bubbling water, coiling around him in long strands of wet silk. "What's wrong, love?"

She kept her face buried against his neck, hiding her expression. "Nothing," she whispered, her lips moving against his skin.

He smoothed the hair back from her shoulder, letting the damp tresses cascade down her back. "I thought we weren't going to deceive each other again, Sarah."

"I never want to deceive you." She lifted her head, allowing him to see the tears glittering in her eyes.

"You're confused," he whispered, looking into her eyes, seeing the turmoil there, the questions. "So much has happened, you feel as though your world has been turned on end."

"It seems you can read my mind," she said, her lips tipping into a smile. "But then, you always could."

"I can perceive feelings in most people." He kissed her, taking her soft exhale deep into his lungs. "But with you, it is as though the emotion comes from inside myself."

"A joining," she whispered, cupping his face in her hands.

Austin trembled with the truth of her words. "A joining."

"What happens now?" She brushed her fingers over his cheek, smoothing away the moisture. "Will we stay here?"

Water bubbled all around them, rippling like satin across his skin. "What do you want to do?"

"There is so much I've left unfinished. I think of those poor people in the tenements, and I know I need to do something to help them. I want to convince my uncle to build the new apartment houses."

"You don't need his consent. I'm not exactly in financial difficulties."

"So I've learned." She tugged his hair, smiling as she kissed the tip of his nose. "But I want my father's company to leave some positive mark. I need to find some way to convince my uncle to agree to my proposal."

He sensed her need to erase the ugliness Leighton had left behind. "I understand."

"Can we go back to New York, if only for a little while? Until I'm certain there will be a place for Jim and his family and a hundred more families."

He had a prickling sensation at the nape of his neck when he thought of returning to New York with Sarah.

"Is something wrong?"

"Sarah, this might not be a good time to go back to New York."

"But I want to make certain my editor has been keeping the heat turned up under Warren Snelling."

The image of a gray dove with her neck broken flickered in his mind. "You can send him a telegram, or I can have someone talk with him."

"You're worried." Sarah smoothed her fingers over the frown carved into his brow. "You can't honestly believe someone would try to hurt me over my newspaper articles?"

"I remember a package you received one beautiful morning. A cigar box with a surprise inside."

She frowned, her expression reflecting the grim remembrance of that morning. "The man who sent that warning wanted to frighten me. If I stay away from New York, he'll think he succeeded."

Austin cupped the nape of her neck, his fingers

sliding against the damp heat of her skin. "I would rather not give him the chance to succeed in hurting you."

"Please, Austin, take me back to New York."

"I have a bad feeling about this."

"I want to see my mother," Sarah whispered, sliding her hand along his damp shoulder. "There are so many things we need to say to one another. I thought you understood."

"I do." He held her close, wrapping his arms around her. If anything happened to her . . .

"I promise I'll wrap up everything I need to do in a few days."

Austin pressed his lips to her temple, feeling her pulse throb beneath his touch. He couldn't keep her a prisoner, no matter how much he wanted to protect her. "All right," he whispered.

He felt her smile against his shoulder. "I knew there was a good reason why I fell in love with you."

Sarah was probably right; someone only wanted to frighten her. Yet he couldn't shake the feeling of dread sitting like a block of ice in his stomach.

Chapter Thirty

Sarah sat in an upholstered armchair near the windows in the study of her father's house, watching as Leighton's solicitor, Mr. Silas Bulfinch, removed Leighton's will from a narrow leather case. She felt chilled inside, emotions slashing at her like needles of sleet driven by a strong north wind. Despair and regret, the pain of grief, the fond wish that she could change what had already come to pass, all of this swirled like a tempest inside her.

She and Austin had arrived in New York two days ago. They had gone directly to the Kensington Hotel, hoping to see Sarah's mother, but Diana had left for San Francisco three days before they had arrived in New York. By this time her mother was well on her way home with her family.

Family. Sarah was only just beginning to understand the full meaning of that word. The people gathered in this room for the reading of Leighton's will were doing their best to cure her of any illusions she might have had about their kinship with her.

Roxanne and Clarissa sat together on the sofa across from Sarah, the black silk of their gowns draping the burgundy velvet upholstery, all very proper in their mourning clothes. Yet Sarah had heard them discussing Leighton this morning: "What a dreadful nuisance this is," Roxanne had said, "having to dress up in black and act as though we care that horrible boy is dead." And Clarissa had agreed. Her brother was dead and all Clarissa could think about was how terrible she looked in black.

Uncle Kendall sat in a leather wing-back chair near the hearth, his hands clasped beneath his chin, solemn as he listened to the long strings of words spoken by Bulfinch, the slow dispersing of a man's life. Addison stood beside his father, leaning against the mantel, tapping his fingers against the gray marble. They were all staring at Bulfinch as the short man read the legal papers he had spread on the desk.

They didn't care. A man had lived and died and not one of his family cared, Sarah thought. But she cared. She ached for the loss of his young life, the destruction of a future he might have had. How had his life become so twisted?

Sarah stared at the solicitor, following the ripple of incandescent light across the shiny skin of his scalp as he shifted his head. His skull looked like a nest holding a large egg, she thought, a fringe of dark brown hair edging the smooth curve of his bald head. Odd that she should think of something so inane at a time like this.

Bulfinch's words droned in the room. The meaning of his words evaded Sarah. They were no more than a buzzing in her ear until Bulfinch spoke one line, the last decree of her brother. Sarah's breath caught in her throat. She stared at the solicitor, the splatter of rain against the glass filling the silence that had descended like a chilling fog in the room.

"There has to be some mistake," Addison said. "Even Leighton wasn't foolish enough to leave his interest in the company to a woman."

"There is no mistake." Mr. Bulfinch shifted, the leather armchair creaking beneath his ample weight. "Mr. Van Horne left all of his possessions to his sister Sarah."

Sarah exhaled, her lungs collapsing like a balloon stuck with a pin. Leighton had given her complete control over the company. He had given her everything. As Bulfinch waddled from the room, Sarah looked at her cousin.

"Leighton was a bigger fool than I ever imagined," Addison said, his cheeks growing red with fury.

She thought of all the times Addison had looked at her with sarcasm and arrogance, all the insults he had ever heaped on her shoulders, and she smiled. "It would seem Leighton has given me permission to do as I see fit with our company, Addison."

Addison curled his hand into a fist on the mantel. "You don't actually think you can run the company."

"There are certain projects I think our company should undertake," Sarah said.

Addison rolled his eyes. "Like building palaces for peasants."

Sarah drew a deep breath, trying to quiet the anger stirring inside her. "Apartment houses for the working people of this city are good investments."

"If you think I'll let you drive my company into the dirt, you're mistaken, Sarah."

"I believe it is *our* company." Sarah held her cousin's angry stare. "And there is little you can do to stop me from running it the way I wish."

"We shall see about that, Sarah. I swear to you, I'll do anything I can to stop you." Addison turned on his heel and marched from the room, slamming the door behind him.

Sarah glanced at her Uncle Kendall. He was watching her, his chin resting on his clasped hands, his expression revealing the deep distress he felt at what had transpired in the past few moments.

"I'm sorry for this, Sarah." Kendall stood and came to her, taking her hand when he drew near. "I'm certain in time Addison will learn to accept you as a partner."

Sarah looked up into Kendall's gentle blue eyes. "I hope he does."

Kendall squeezed her hand. "If you need anything, just let me know." After saying good-bye to Roxanne and Clarissa, he left the women alone.

"So it seems you now have it all." Roxanne stood, staring at Sarah as though her stepdaughter were a rattlesnake she wanted to slay. "If you think you can turn us out of our own house, you are very much mistaken."

Sarah stared at Roxanne, not quite believing what she had heard. "Turn you out of the house?"

"According to your father's will, Clarissa and I can live here for as long as we wish. You can't even sell the house without our permission."

"I wouldn't dream of asking you to leave." Sarah looked away from the fury in Roxanne's eyes. How could her stepmother believe she would do anything as cruel as forcing her to leave her home?

"You're so smug," Clarissa said. "You think you're better than I am because you tricked Sinclair into marrying you."

Sarah glanced up, meeting the hatred in Clarissa's eyes. "I didn't trick Austin into anything."

Clarissa laughed, dark, bitter, nothing like that bright tinkling laughter Sarah had often heard her sister practice for the benefit of her suitors. "You have everything that should have been mine. You stole the man I was going to marry."

Sarah thought of Austin. He was upstairs making a list of the items in Leighton's treasure room. He had little doubt many of the pieces were stolen from private collections and museums. "I didn't steal him, Clarissa."

"Oh, yes, you did." Clarissa stood clenching her hands into fists at her sides. "You allowed him privileges no decent woman would allow. You trapped him."

Sarah rose from her chair, her legs shaky beneath her black gown. "Clarissa, that just isn't true."

"It is true. Isn't it, Mother?"

Sarah glanced at Roxanne, hoping for some support, seeing only ice shaped by hatred and envy.

"I think it's obvious why Sinclair married her." Roxanne smiled as she looked at Clarissa. "If she hadn't cavorted with the man, he would never have noticed her."

The hatred Sarah felt emanating from her sister and stepmother was a palpable thing, a wall of ice pushing toward her, pressing against her. Why were they behaving this way? "I wish you only the best. I always have."

"You stabbed me in the back the first chance you had!" Clarissa shouted. "I wouldn't be surprised to find that you arranged for Duggan to slip into my bed. You wanted to destroy me."

Matilda had told Sarah what had happened, the scandal that had resulted from that morning. Clarissa had lived like a recluse since that day. Sarah knew Leighton had arranged for that disaster to befall

Clarissa. Yet she couldn't tell Clarissa all she knew; she couldn't risk exposing Avallon. "Clarissa, I had nothing to do with Mr. Duggan being in your room."

"I hate you!"

Sarah flinched. "Clarissa, I—"

"I wish you had died when I pushed you down the stairs."

Sarah stepped back, Clarissa's words cutting her like a blade. "You don't mean that."

"You have no right to be married to Lord Sinclair when I'm ruined! He should have been my husband. He would be if it weren't for you." Clarissa moved toward her sister, pausing a foot from her, staring up at Sarah with murder in her eyes. "I wish you were dead."

Sarah pressed her hand to her heart, feeling the pain centered there, a tightening that came from realizing the sister she had always loved cared nothing at all for her. "I hope in time we can mend these wounds." She turned and left them before the tears she felt burning her eyes could fall.

Rain pelted the windowpanes of Van Horne's treasure room. Gray light filtered through the windows, melding into the golden light tumbling from the brass-and-crystal fixtures overhead. Austin stood beside one of the glass cabinets, staring at the brass artifacts displayed on red velvet. It would take weeks, perhaps months to identify the stolen pieces and return them to the proper owners.

A floorboard creaked softly behind him. He felt a subtle shift in the air upon his cheek, a warmth he recognized without seeing the woman who had entered the room. His thoughts tumbled back in time, back to a moonlit night when his carelessness had exposed him to the danger of a pistol in the hands of an inexperienced woman. It seemed to have happened yesterday and at the same time a lifetime ago.

Austin turned to face her. She stood a few feet into the room, a woman dressed in black silk, her magnificent hair piled in curls upon her head, her beautiful eyes betraying the accumulated sorrow of a lifetime. That look in her eyes wrapped around him, drawing him to her. "Sarah," he whispered, brushing his fingers across her smooth cheek. "What's happened, love?"

"Hold me." She slipped her arms around his waist. "I need to feel your arms around me."

Austin slipped his arms around her, absorbing the trembling of her slender body, sensing her feelings as sharply as his own.

"I feel as though it's all gone, everything I thought of as home."

"I'm here for you, Sarah." A delicate thread of lavender rose with the heat of her skin. "I'll always be with you."

"They hate me. Roxanne and Clarissa." Sarah tightened her arms around him as though she were afraid someone would rip him from her arms. "I don't understand what I've done to make them hate me so."

"This isn't your fault." Austin cupped her cheeks in his hands and lifted her face so he could look into her eyes. The golden lamplight glittered on the unshed tears pooling in her hazel eyes. "The fault lies within their souls. Jealousy. They have never been able to look beyond their own selfish needs."

"And here I am," she said, swiping at a tear that trickled down her cheek, "indulging in my own self-pity."

Austin brushed his lips against her damp cheek, absorbing the salt of her tears. "There is nothing selfish about you, my sweet Sarah."

"Leighton left me everything he owned." Sarah rested her cheek against his chest. "He had no one but me."

Austin held her close, the memories of those moments on the bluffs haunting him. He had come so close to losing her. "You did everything you could to save him."

"He was so young, Austin, barely twenty-five. How could his life have gone so wrong?"

"Sarah, regrets for what might have been will only tear you apart. Look to the future."

Sarah nodded. "Addison is furious that I intend to go through with my building project."

"He'll get used to the idea."

"That's what Uncle Kendall said."

Austin rested his hand at her nape, feeling the tension in her muscles. "I asked Matilda and Emerson if they would come work for us."

Sarah looked up at him, a glimmer of hope in her eyes. "In England?"

"Isabel is returning to Avallon this evening. She intends to stay there." He smoothed his fingers across her temple. "I bought her house."

"You want to live in New York?"

"Part of the time. Enough time for you to keep an eye on your newspaper and your building company."

"Oh," she whispered, curling her fingers into his lapels. "I've always dreamed of a home of my own."

Austin looked down into her face, seeing the joy in her eyes, the radiant blush rise in her cheeks. For too many years joy had never touched her. "Tell me your dreams, my love, and I will do my best to make them come true."

Sarah slid her fingers down his lapels. "I was right about you the first time I saw you."

Austin frowned. "You thought I was a thief and scoundrel."

Sarah shook her head. "I thought you were magic."

"Let's go home." He kissed the tip of her upturned nose. "And we'll see if we can conjure a little magic."

Chapter Thirty-One

After three days of rain, the sun peeked out from behind a cloud, tossing morning light into the conservatory. A warm breeze drifted through the open windows, rustling the leaves of banana, palm, and orange trees, stirring the perfume of jasmine and orange blossoms in the room. Austin glanced over the top of the newspaper Sarah had given him to read, meeting his wife's intent gaze.

"You're frowning," Sarah said. "Don't you like my article?"

"You have a flair with words." Austin folded the newspaper and laid it on the table by his cup and saucer. A feeling of impending disaster settled around him like a killing frost as he stared down at the words, the brutal honesty his wife had printed for the world to see.

"You're worried?"

"I have a bad feeling about this." He glanced up, meeting Sarah's intense gaze. "You're pushing this man against a wall, Sarah. He might decide to push back."

"Warren Snelling is the type of man who likes to bully people, especially people who can't fight back." Sarah slipped her hand over the fist Austin held clenched against the glass tabletop. "But I still don't believe he would actually try to hurt me."

"I don't suppose I can talk you into moving our trip to San Francisco up a few weeks? I can have a train ready for us in an hour."

"I need to do this, Austin." She squeezed his hand. "I need to see Mulberry Bend torn down. I need to see our new apartments started on that block before I leave."

Austin lifted her hand to his lips, the sweet fragrance of lavender clinging to her skin mingling with the perfume of orange blossoms and jasmine. "I understand."

Sarah glanced down at their clasped hands, a smile curving her lips. "Sometimes I think you understand me better than I understand myself."

Austin glanced over his shoulder at the sound of footsteps on the white marble squares lining the floor. Emerson was carrying a package about eight inches square, wrapped in silver paper and tied with a big silver bow.

"This just arrived for Lady Sinclair." Emerson smiled as he set the package on the table between Sarah and Austin.

"A wedding present, do you suppose?" Sarah asked, her face lighting like a little girl's on Christmas morning.

"There was no card, milady," Emerson said.

"Thank you, Emerson," Sarah said, smiling up at her old friend.

Emerson nodded and left the room, palm fronds and banana leaves swaying as he passed.

"It seems odd," Austin said, staring at the little package. The nape of his neck prickled, instincts warning him of dangers unseen. "Sending a gift without a note."

"Perhaps it's inside." Sarah tore the paper from the package, revealing a rosewood box. As she started to lift the lid, Austin rested his hand over hers.

She looked across the package straight into his eyes. "Is something wrong?"

Austin frowned. "I remember the last time you got a package in the mail."

"You don't believe someone would send . . ." Sarah sat back, the white wicker chair sighing with her movement, her expression dissolving from expectation to anxiety. "Perhaps we're being too sensitive."

"Perhaps." Austin turned the box toward him. He hesitated a moment before he lifted the lid, brass hinges creaking softly.

"What is it?" Sarah asked, her voice a whisper, as though she were afraid to ask the question.

A four-inch-long shell rested on damp gray oilcloth at the bottom of the box, conical in shape, striated with shades of yellow and brown. "A shell."

"A shell?" Sarah peeked into the box, releasing her breath in a long sigh. "Thank goodness."

"Wait." Austin grabbed her wrist as she started to reach into the box.

"But it's only a shell."

"Why is the box lined in oilcloth?" Austin drew her hand away from the box. The shell glistened in the sunlight. "And why is it damp?"

"But what harm could there be in a shell?"

"Living in Brazil one learns to be amazed," Austin said, lifting his spoon, "by the dangers that can be found in the most innocuous looking creatures." With the tip of his spoon he rocked the shell.

"What do you expect to . . ." Sarah's words ended in a gasp.

A gray proboscis darted from the narrow end of the shell, thumping the side of the box with harpoonlike teeth. It ducked back inside the shell, leaving a black venom that oozed down the side of the box.

"What was that?" Sarah whispered.

"I'm not exactly sure." Austin set his spoon on the table. "Some type of marine snail. Poisonous, would be my guess."

"Snelling." Sarah sat back in her chair. "He has an aquarium in his house. Our newspaper did a story about it last year. He built a room the size of a salon and filled it with tanks and pools, where he keeps a collection of marine creatures."

Austin closed the lid and reached for Sarah. He drew her from her chair into his arms, holding her on his lap, absorbing her shivers. "I'm going to send for Detective Farley. I think it's time we have a little talk with Warren Snelling."

"So you say you received this odd marine snail this morning." Kendall Van Horne sipped his tea, looking over the rim of his cup at Sarah. "And you think Warren Snelling sent it?"

"I can only suppose it was Snelling." Sarah held her teacup between her hands, absorbing the warmth radiating from the ivory china. The sun had slipped behind gray clouds, casting the conservatory in a pale gloom. "Austin and a police detective are with him now."

"Thank heaven you weren't hurt."

"I never realized the man would actually try to harm me." Sarah sipped her tea, hoping to chase away the chill inside her. "I thought he would try to frighten me, but to send something like that . . . creature. Austin could have been killed. Anyone who touched the thing could have been killed."

"It seems this was not a good time to bring you the news I have for you."

"What news?"

"It doesn't matter, my dear." Kendall managed a smile, but Sarah could see the distress in his eyes.

"Please tell me. What is it?"

Kendall settled his cup on his saucer. "I'm afraid one of the families refuses to leave Mulberry Bend."

"But I thought everyone had been relocated."

"So did I. But this morning, when our construction foreman was doing a final check of the area set for demolition, he found them." Kendall stared down at his cup, stroking the curve of the handle with his fingertip. "A young Italian mother and her two children. I tried to talk them into leaving, but they refused to go."

"Why? We've arranged for temporary housing for all the families."

"Although my Italian is not what it should be, I believe she doesn't trust anyone. She's waiting for her husband to return from some trip. That's all I could gather."

"Those buildings are scheduled to be destroyed tomorrow."

Kendall nodded. "It will be a pity if I have to call in the police to remove them. I had hoped you could talk to them. You're fluent in the language and so good with people. But after what has happened this morning, it would be out of the question."

"I'll be ready to leave in fifteen minutes."

"But, Sarah, you've had quite a shock this morning."

Sarah smiled at her uncle's concern for her. "I can't let Warren Snelling frighten me into spinning a cocoon."

Austin stood near the door of Warren Snelling's study, watching as the burly man lumbered across the room, carrying the rosewood box Farley had handed him. Farley followed, a determined terrier trailing a bear. Incandescent lights were glowing in the brass-and-crystal fixture overhead, chasing away the gray gloom spilling through the open windows.

Austin sensed annoyance and curiosity in Snelling. His expression and his bearing betrayed none of the guilt or fear Austin had expected to find in the man.

"This looks like one of my cone shells." Snelling looked up from the box he had placed on the mahogany desk that stood near the windows, frowning as he looked at Detective Farley. "What are you doing with it?"

"Do you recognize the box, Mr. Snelling?" Farley tapped his pencil against the side of the box.

"I don't give a damn about the box; I want to know why you have one of my cone shells." A breeze ripped through the open windows, stirring the scarlet brocade drapes, setting the gold tassels swinging. "This is a very valuable specimen."

"This box and your shell were delivered to Lady Sinclair a few hours ago." Farley glanced over his shoulder at Austin. "That's why Lord Sinclair has come with me. He wants to know as much as I do how this happened to end up in his wife's hands."

"Her hands." Snelling's face grew pale as he looked at Austin. "Did it sting her?"

Austin held Snelling's gaze for a moment before he answered, judging the man's response. He sensed only a genuine concern in Snelling, a fear that had not been there before. "No."

"Thank God." Snelling sank into a wing-back chair in front of the desk, his hips settling snugly between the scarlet brocade arms. "It's poisonous. One sting can kill a man in a few hours."

"We figured that much out, sir," Farley said. "What we haven't figured yet is how it got sent to Lady Sinclair."

"How the hell would I know how she got it?" Snelling looked from Farley to Austin, color returning to stain his cheeks. "You can't think I sent it to her?"

"You weren't happy with the articles Lady Sinclair has been writing in the *Gazette* about you, were you?" Farley asked.

"Of course I wasn't happy over that prattle. But I wouldn't try to kill her over it."

"Those articles could stir a lot of people to write their legislators," Farley said. "If that new tenement legislation is passed, it will cost you a fortune."

"That legislation is all but passed already." Snelling curled his thick hands into fists on the arms of his chair. "And don't deceive yourself, Detective. You know as well as I do, a resourceful man can find his way around any legislation. If he so desires."

Farley twisted his pencil between his fingers as he studied Snelling, deep lines pressed into his narrow face. "Do you know of anyone in the city who keeps these shells except you, Mr. Snelling?"

"No. Someone must have taken it from my collection." Snelling looked straight at Austin, meeting his eyes. "I might not care for your wife's meddling, Lord Sinclair. But I certainly did not try to kill her."

Austin had been trained to trust his instincts, yet he didn't care for what those instincts were telling him. He listened to Farley ask the same questions over once more before the detective was ready to leave.

Warm air heavy with moisture bathed his face as Austin left the Snelling house. He walked beside Farley toward the carriage he had waiting, replaying Snelling's words in his mind, his instincts telling him to believe the man. "He didn't do it."

Farley paused on the sidewalk, the rattle of traffic filling the silence as he studied Austin. "What makes you so sure? A few hours ago you were ready to hang the man."

"Snelling doesn't seem like a foolish man. And he would have to be a fool to send something like this." Austin tapped the box Farley was keeping as evidence. "It would be like raising a flag with his name emblazoned across it."

"Perhaps that's why he sent it. He could always use that argument to claim his innocence."

Austin rubbed the back of his neck, his skin prickling. "I don't think so."

"Who else would want to see your wife dead?"

Austin pulled open the carriage door. He had to get to Sarah. "I can think of a few people."

Sarah hesitated on the threshold of the tenement, staring into the darkness. The pale gray light of the cloudy day slipped through the open door and dissolved into gloom. She shivered, a feeling of anxiety twisting in her stomach. Anyone could be waiting for her in that darkness.

"Sarah, are you coming?" Kendall stood a few feet in front of her, a pale ghost staring at her from the gloom.

There was no reason to be frightened, she told herself. Austin and Detective Farley were with Warren Snelling. By now the man was probably behind bars.

Still, she couldn't seem to cross the threshold.

"Sarah, have you changed your mind? Do you want me to have the police deal with this woman and her children?"

"No." The poor woman had suffered enough simply by living here. She forced her feet to move, to carry her across the threshold into the shadows.

Sarah pressed her handkerchief to her nose, trying to mask the stench of rotting garbage and human waste with the lavender clinging to the soft white linen. She followed her Uncle Kendall through the gloom in the narrow stairwell. Gray light filtered through the window open to the air shaft at the second-floor landing.

"I don't understand why she won't leave this place," she said, thinking of the mother who was keeping her two children in this hovel.

"This has been her home, Sarah." Kendall paused as he reached the second floor, taking Sarah's arm when she joined him. "She feels safe here."

Sarah glanced down the long dark hallway. The chill of despair lingered here. "It's amazing anyone could feel safe in this place."

Kendall led her to a door near the end of the hall. The apartment was in the back of the building, where the sun never slipped through the gloom. Kendall knocked, the sharp rapping noise echoing down the hall.

Sarah glanced over her shoulder, staring into the shadows. There was no one here, she assured herself, no one hiding in the darkness to pounce on her. Still, she couldn't shake the anxiety that whispered across her skin like a December wind.

"It's open," Kendall said, swinging open the door.

Sarah looked into the apartment. The shadows were so deep she could scarcely see the gray panes of the window across the room. A square table and four spindly chairs stood in one corner of the kitchen. A curtain hung from a wire stretched from wall to wall along one end of the room. "Perhaps she changed her mind."

"The foreman said she was hiding in there," Kendall said, pointing toward the curtained partition.

"Signora Buscali," Sarah said, entering the apartment. The slow tap of her heels echoed against the bare wooden planks as she crossed the room. "Signora, I've come to help you." She repeated her words once more, this time in Italian.

Sarah took a deep breath as she approached that dark curtain, her skin prickling with apprehension. The floorboards groaned as she stepped closer. She heard a loud snap, felt the boards give beneath her feet, the wood splintering. A scream tore from her throat as the floor disintegrated beneath her feet.

She threw out her hands as she plunged through the floor. Broken pieces of wood clawed at her like bony skeletons, tearing the black silk of her gown. She pitched forward. Her hands slapped against the floor. Rough wood bit into her waist. She was sliding, slipping through the broken floor. She clawed for purchase, her fingers slipping on the smooth planks.

Her feet dangled. Below her a black chasm waited; 40 feet of dark air separated her from the ground floor. She tried to scream, her throat closing around her words like a vice. Blood pounded in her veins, thudding in her ears with the footsteps crossing the floor. Kendall loomed in her vision, towering above her. "Help me!"

Kendall sat back on his heels. In the gray light filtering through the single window, she saw his face. He was frowning, his blue eyes troubled as he looked at her. "Sarah, dear, I'm sorry it had to come to this."

She slipped backward, her ribs hitting the broken edge of the floor. Her legs dangled in the black pit that had opened below her. "I'm slipping!"

"If only you hadn't insisted on this building project of yours." He stroked her right hand, where she clutched at the smooth floor. "You see, there isn't enough money for it."

Sarah felt herself sliding, inching backward into the pit. She pressed her hands and arms into the wood. "Uncle Kendall, please help me."

"I can't, my dear." He snatched his hand back when she tried to grab his wrist. "I've worked a lifetime at building that company. It should have been mine. But no, Carelton had to leave it to Leighton. Even though he hated the boy, he had to conform to social convention."

Fear pounded in her chest, a clenched fist throbbing against her heart. She clawed at the smooth wooden planks, fighting desperately to halt her backward slide. "What does this have to do with me?"

"I'm afraid I've been taking money, a great deal of money. I wanted to give Addison a proper start in his new marriage."

Sarah shuddered as she slipped, her nails digging into the wood. "Uncle Kendall, you can't do this."

"I have to do this. I can't let you send me to jail."

"I won't, I swear." Her arms trembled under the strain as she fought to drag herself from the pit.

"I'm sorry about this, I truly am." Kendall smiled, a wistful curve of his lips. "I always cared for you, Sarah. But I want the company. And after you're gone it will be mine."

"Austin is my husband. If I die—"

"He can't inherit it from you, my dear. Only a Van Horne descendant can control the company."

"They'll know you did this. Matilda and Emerson both know I came here with you."

"It doesn't matter. This was nothing but a terrible accident."

The weight of her body dragged her toward destruction. "Please help me."

"Let go, Sarah." He plucked her fingers from the floor. "Just let go."

"No!"

"Sarah!"

The sound of Austin's voice rippled through her like the deep chiming of a church bell. Yet as relief coursed through her, she slipped over the edge. A scream ripped from her throat. She caught a ragged floorboard with both hands. Kendall stood, his black shoes inches from her fingers.

"Get away from her, Kendall!" Austin shouted.

Sarah squeezed the edge of the board, her arms straining against her dangling weight. Kendall backed away, out of her view. Footsteps pounded the wood, vibrating against her hands.

Sarah was slipping. There was nothing but blackness below her. Death waiting to swallow her. She clenched her hands against the wood, her muscles screaming for release.

"Sarah!" Austin shouted, grabbing her wrists.

She stared up at him, her hands locked on the board, her arms trembling with the strain. In the gray glow from the window, he looked otherworldly, a dark-haired phantom. Yet the hands that held her wrists were real, powerful and secure.

"Let go, Sarah."

She pried her fingers from the floorboard and delivered her life into his hands. He lifted her as though she weighed no more than the rag doll she felt at that moment. He hauled her from the pit and into his arms. Sarah collapsed against him, her every muscle trembling.

"Sarah," he whispered, sitting back against the wall, cradling her in his arms. "You're safe, love."

Sarah clenched his lapel in her hand, burying her face against his chest. "Where is he?"

"He got away." Austin pressed his cheek to her hair. "I could have caught him, but I thought it was a better idea to catch you."

"He wanted to kill me." The pain of her uncle's betrayal burned like a brand in her chest. "For money."

"He won't get away with it, Sarah. I promise you."

"I don't want him arrested."

Austin gripped her chin in gentle fingers and tilted back her head until he could look into her eyes. "Sarah, the man tried to kill you."

"There's been too much scandal." Sarah eased a breath into her tight lungs. "If he agrees to give up his control in the company, I won't go to the police."

Austin frowned. "You're upset, Sarah. When you have time to think—"

"No. Please, I don't want any more scandal."

Austin stroked his thumb over her lower lip, frowning as he held her gaze. "All right, sweet Sarah. We'll handle this your way."

Chapter Thirty-Two

Austin awoke with a start, a sudden wrenching from sleep that left his heart racing and his breath coming in ragged gasps. The big brass bed rocked beneath him, in time with the soft clicking sound of the iron wheels against iron rails as his private train penetrated the night. He reached for Sarah, sensing her need for him, feeling cool sheets in place of her warm body.

Sarah stood at the far end of the car, in the sitting area. She was staring out into the moonlight as though she were a lost little girl searching for home.

It had been three weeks since that morning in the tenement when Kendall had almost ended Sarah's life. Three weeks since Kendall had been found dead in his office, a pistol beside him. He had chosen death over imprisonment, never knowing Sarah had decided to keep the truth from the police and let him go free.

The official report stated Kendall Van Horne had

died in an accident while cleaning his pistol. But his family knew the truth, and they would never be the same.

"Sarah," Austin whispered.

She turned in the column of moonlight streaming through the square windowpanes. Her unbound hair glimmered in the pale light, tumbling around her shoulders, cascading in thick waves down the white satin of her robe. "I didn't mean to awaken you."

"You didn't." At least not with words or movement. The turmoil he sensed inside her had dragged him from slumber. He folded back the sheet and blanket, inviting her without words to join him.

Sarah hurried across the car, her footsteps soundless against the swirls of sapphire and gold in the thick wool carpet. He opened his arms as she slipped beneath the covers, and she sank into his embrace, pressing chilled limbs and cool satin against his warm skin.

He slipped his thigh over hers, pulling her into the shelter of his body. "Thinking about tomorrow?"

She nodded, her cheek brushing his bare shoulder. "What do you say to your mother after twenty-three years?"

"I honestly believe she loves you, Sarah." He slid his fingers across her temple. "Remember that, and you can find a way to traverse the years."

"She has her family. I feel like an intruder, a ghost from her past."

"You're her daughter. She missed watching you grow from a little girl into a beautiful woman. So many years have been wasted. So many moments she was never allowed to share with you."

"My mother is a stranger to me."

Austin held her close, pressing his lips to her brow, feeling his throat grow tight with emotion. He remembered the anguish his parents had suffered at the loss of their son. And inside him, in a place that had never healed, dwelt his own pain and memories. "I know how it feels to lose a lifetime you should have shared with someone. You must think of the time you *can* have together."

Sarah looked up at him, tears glittering on her dark lashes. "When you catch me looking into the past, you always manage to point me toward the future." She traced the curve of his lower lip with her fingertip. "I'm not sure I can ever tell you how very much it means to have you in my life."

Austin slid his hand along the front of her robe, slipping satin loops warmed by her skin over pearl buttons, revealing the pale silk of her skin. "Why not show me?"

Sarah looped her arms around his neck. "My pleasure, milord."

The Schuyler house sat high on a hill in the section of San Francisco known as Nob Hill. Like a Renaissance palace, the wooden walls soared four stories high, rising from manicured lawns.

Sarah sat on an Empire sofa in her mother's parlor. She went through the motions of eating pound cake and sipping tea, feeling every bite catch in her throat. Austin sat across from her on a matching sofa upholstered in forest green velvet, beside her mother. Diana's entire family was gathered here in this large, sunny room that might have been comfortable under better circumstances.

"Do I look anything like you did when you were my age?" Jennie Schuyler asked.

Sarah looked at the girl sitting beside her on the sofa. This child, her sister, had lived for 14 years and this was the first day Sarah had ever spoken a word to her. "I was tall, like you, and my hair was about your color. I'm afraid it grew darker as I grew older."

"Oh, I love the color of your hair." Jennie smiled up at Sarah, her blue eyes sparkling with pride. "You're so beautiful, just like Mother."

Sarah glanced at the woman sitting across from Jennie. Diana was watching Sarah, a whisper of a smile on her lips. When Sarah met her gaze, Diana glanced down at the handkerchief she held in her hands, as though she were embarrassed to be caught staring.

"How about a game of billiards, Austin?" Ward Schuyler rose from his chair, glancing at his wife. "You and I can take on Andrew and Jennie."

"Sounds good to me." Austin stood, smiling at Sarah.

Sarah clutched the handle of her teacup, aware of what they were doing: allowing mother and daughter to spend a few moments alone together.

Andrew reached for his sister's hand. "Come on, Jennie, let's show Austin just what kind of challenge we can give him."

"But I want to stay with Sarah," Jennie said.

"There'll be time to visit." Andrew winked at Sarah as though they were longtime conspirators. "Right, Sarah?"

Sarah had an odd feeling looking up into Andrew's mischievous blue eyes, as though she had known this young man all her life. "We plan to stay in the city for a few days."

"But I—" Jennie began.

"Come on, monkey," Andrew said, taking his sister's arm.

A pink blush flooded Jennie's cheeks. "Don't call me monkey!"

"Come on." Andrew led Jennie from the room, following Austin and Ward.

The walnut-and-crystal clock on the mantel filled the silence that lengthened and stretched between mother and daughter. A cool breeze drifted in through the open windows, stirring the lace curtains, carrying the scent of roses from the garden.

Sarah glanced at the pictures that hung on the wall behind her mother: rosewood frames on silk wallpaper of pale green and ivory stripes, the family she had met for the first time today, photographs capturing the years as they had passed.

Diana twisted the white linen handkerchief she held in her hands. Sarah watched her, remembering the way her mother had stroked her hair every night with those slender hands, lulling her to sleep. Her mother had always been so gentle. Strange, she hadn't remembered that in a long time.

"Thank you for coming," Diana said.

"Thank you for agreeing to see me." Sarah set her cup and saucer on the black walnut pedestal table beside the sofa, ashamed at how her hands were shaking. "I was not very civil the last time we met."

"I understand your reasons." Diana glanced down at her mangled handkerchief. "I've waited for this moment for so many years. I've often dreamed of what I would say to you if I ever got the chance. And now I . . . I don't know what to say first."

Sarah hesitated a moment before she asked the question that had burned in her heart for so many years. "Why did you leave?"

"I couldn't stay." Diana looked at Sarah, the smile that curved her lips filled with sorrow. "I'm not sure how to explain it."

Sarah felt as though her heart had been tied into a knot, a thick knot of pain that throbbed with every beat. She stared at the lilies stitched in ivory on the dark green background in the carpet beneath her feet. She had a feeling she already knew the reasons her mother had left her father.

Diana stood and approached Sarah. "Did you ever receive any of the letters I sent when you were growing up?"

"What letters?" Sarah glanced up at her mother. "I received only a few letters shortly after Father died." Letters she had returned without breaking the seals.

Diana nodded as though Sarah had confirmed something she had long suspected. "I wrote to you and Leighton every week. Your father must have destroyed them. I wonder what he did with the presents I sent for your birthdays and Christmases?"

"You remembered our birthdays?"

"How could I forget?" Diana lifted her hand toward Sarah's cheek, hesitating, her fingers curling against her palm as though she feared rejection. "I was sixteen when I married Carelton. It was a marriage arranged by my father. I barely knew the man I was to marry. And I knew nothing at all of what to expect from marriage."

Sarah felt the knot in her heart begin to loosen. "You didn't love him."

"I tried." Diana sank to the sofa beside Sarah. "Your father was not an easy man to love."

Sarah stared at her mother's hands, watching the long fingers lace and break apart, then lace together once more, the handkerchief crushed between her palms. "Father was cold." As cold as winter where there should have been the warmth of summer.

"Yes. And then I met Ward, and I realized what it felt like to be in love, truly in love."

"You left us to be with him." Sarah hadn't meant for the words to sound so accusing, to be filled with such a bitterness. Yet it was there inside her, had been for years, that ache of rejection, that raw, angry wound that refused to be healed.

"No. Your father never paid much attention to you or Leighton." Diana met Sarah's eyes, tears sparkling in irises that were the same as her daughter's eyes. "I honestly believed he would let me walk away from that marriage with both of my children. I underestimated just how ruthless the man could be."

"You wanted us?"

"Oh, Sarah." Diana cupped her daughter's cheek, her fingers trembling against Sarah's skin. "I thought I would go mad when he took you from me."

Sarah turned away, fighting the sting of tears. "You never came to see me."

"He told me he would have me arrested if I tried to see you. I thought I had brought enough scandal into your life."

Sarah stared at an ivory lily at the tip of her black shoe. She had spent a lifetime thinking her mother hadn't cared, and now she realized they had both suffered because of a man who had never shown his son or daughter a shred of affection.

"A few years ago I was so desperate to see you. I knew what Carelton and his wife were doing to you, wrapping you in shame, ruining your chances ever to be happy. I confronted him in his office. I demanded he allow you to come live with me."

Sarah remembered a morning she had watched her mother leave her father's office and run into the arms of the man she loved. "Was it nine years ago?"

"Yes. How did you know?"

"I saw you that morning."

"Your father laughed at me. He said you were just like me and it was his duty to make sure you didn't turn into . . . a whore." Diana glanced down at her handkerchief, twisting the linen around her fingers. "He assured me you hated me. He said you would have nothing at all to do with me, even if he did allow me to see you. I'm afraid I believed him. I gave up trying to see you. I was afraid I would only cause you more pain."

Sarah looked at the woman sitting beside her. What was her crime, except to reach for happiness when she had the chance? Did that make her evil?

"Like mother, like daughter." Sarah smiled as she spoke the words.

"Sarah," Diana whispered. She leaned toward her daughter, hesitantly. "I've missed you so terribly."

"It's all right." Sarah met her halfway, slipping her arms around her mother, feeling for the first time in too many years the love this woman had always felt for her. "I understand how you feel."

"I love you, Sarah."

Sarah closed her eyes, feeling her tears spill between her lashes as her mother's tears fell warm and damp upon her shoulder. "I love you, Mother."

Austin held an iron post of the platform at the rear of their train, swaying as the train rocked on the tracks. He stood beside Sarah, the steel wheels carrying them away from the station. He waved as Sarah was waving, to the family who stood at the station. They waved until the station disappeared from view, until all that remained was the memory of their visit with Sarah's mother.

Sarah leaned against his side, snug beneath the curve of his arm as they walked back into the railroad car. The fragrance of roses warmed by the sun greeted them, drifting from the two dozen pink roses rising from a crystal vase on the round mahogany dining table in one corner. Afternoon sunlight slanted through the lace curtains, splashing lacy patterns against the mahogany-paneled walls, spilling golden light across the thick carpet of sapphire blue and ivory swirls.

Austin swayed with the motion of the train as he walked to the table, where he had a magnum of champagne cooling in a gold bucket. He popped the cork from the champagne.

"I have something shocking to confess."

Austin glanced over his shoulder. Sarah stood behind him, beside one of the blue velvet armchairs, running her hand lightly over the ornately carved roses that arched along the high back. She was watching him, a smile curving her lips as though she were certain he would accept what she had to confess. "What dark secret have you to tell me, my beautiful wife?"

"Would you think I was terrible if I admitted I'm glad my mother had the courage to leave my father?"

"I would think you have gained a rare understanding of your mother's situation."

"After spending time with them, I can see my mother was meant to be with Ward," she said as he poured the sparkling wine into tall crystal glasses. "She was meant to have Andrew and Jennie."

"And you were meant to be part of their family," he said, turning to face her.

She smiled up at him. "Yes, I think I was."

Her hand touched his as she took a glass from his fingers, the soft contact rippling like heat on a hot summer day across his arm. "To the family you have found."

Sarah touched her glass to his, the crystal singing softly. "And to the man who helped me find my way."

Austin sipped from his glass as she sipped from hers, the champagne tingling as it slipped across his tongue. The wine left a sheen upon her lips, a tempting trace of moisture he couldn't resist.

"You were meant to be with me, Sarah," he whispered, brushing his lips against hers, tasting champagne and woman.

"Yes," she whispered, setting her glass on the table. "Fate sent you to me."

"And you to me." He set his glass beside hers, sunlight spinning rainbows in the crystal.

He removed the pins and combs from the thick coils at her nape, the light brown tresses tumbling in his hands, spinning gold from the sunlight that touched the shiny strands. Slowly they stripped away the barriers of silk and linen and wool until they stood bare in the scarlet rays of the setting sun slanting through the lace-covered windows.

They swayed with the gentle rocking of the train, her soft breasts brushing his hair-roughened chest. Austin groaned with the caress, his deep voice mingling with her soft sigh.

They touched, hands brushing skin, lips kissing, tasting, exploring, slowly banking the fires flickering within. He lifted her in his arms, carried her to the big brass bed, and laid her down upon the cool silk sheets. Her body beckoned him. He covered her, absorbing her warmth as though he had wandered along frozen peaks and at last he had found shelter.

She parted her lips as he kissed her, offering the sweet spice of her mouth. He wanted to devour her, to cherish her, to love her until the sun grew cold. He kissed her neck, tasting the sweet hollow below her chin. She moaned and stretched beneath him as he flowed down her body.

He tasted the taut buds of her breasts, the sleek curve of her belly, the hot musk hidden beneath feminine curls that tickled his nose. He loved her until she arched and cried and shivered, until she tugged on his shoulders, drawing him upward along the heated silk of her skin.

"You told me you would make my dreams come true." She slipped her hands into the thick waves at his nape, looking up at him, desire darkening her eyes.

"Tell me your dreams," he whispered, pressing the heat of his arousal against the warm honey whispering her welcome. "Tell me, as you take me deep inside you."

"Give me a child, my love." She tilted her hips, taking him into the tight sheath of her body, sighing as their bodies joined. "A little boy with your smile."

Austin smiled as he brushed his lips against hers. "Anything for my lady."

Author's Note

Ancient mysteries have always intrigued me. The city of Avallon is based on the legend of an ancient city discovered in the eighteenth century by a Portuguese explorer. Soon after reporting his discovery, he and his companions disappeared. No one who has ever ventured into the heart of Brazil searching for the lost city has ever returned to civilization. The possibilities inspired my imagination.

My thanks to all of you who wrote to tell me how much you enjoyed *A Quest of Dreams,* Kate and Devlin's story. I hope you enjoyed returning to Avallon with Austin and Sarah.

My next book from Leisure, *The Sorcerer's Lady,* brings to life the ancestors of the Inner Circle of Avallon, who were the Tuatha De Danann of Irish legend. The idea for this book started when I wondered what would happen if a very practical young woman living in Victorian Boston was suddenly confronted with the man she has been seeing in dreams since she was a child. Now, what if this man was an Irish Viking with magic in his blood who has traveled from 889 Ireland to 1889 Boston to claim the woman of his dreams? When I brought together Laura and Connor, the result was a novel filled with romance, mystery, and fantasy. Watch for *The Sorcerer's Lady* in 1995.

I love to hear from readers. Please enclose a self-addressed, stamped envelope with your letter.

Debra Dier
P.O. Box 584
Glen Carbon, Illinois 62034-0584

DON'T MISS THESE UNFORGETTABLE HISTORICAL ROMANCES BY THE WINNER OF 6 *ROMANTIC TIMES* AWARDS!

Love A Rebel, Love A Rogue. The Blackthorne men—one highborn, one half-caste—are bound by blood, but torn apart by choice. Caught between them, two sensuous women long for more than stolen moments of wondrous splendor. But as the lovers are swept from Savannah's ballrooms to Revolutionary War battlefields, they learn that the faithful heart can overcome even the fortunes of war.
_3673-8 $4.99 US/$5.99 CAN

A Fire In The Blood. Dark, dangerous, and deadly with his Colt revolver, Jess Robbins is absolutely forbidden to the spoiled, pampered daughter of Cheyenne's richest rancher. But Lissa Jacobsen decides she must do anything to have the virile gunman, never guessing that a raging inferno of desire will consume them both.
_3601-0 $4.99 US/$5.99 CAN

White Apache's Woman. Running from his past, Red Eagle has no desire to become entangled with the haughty beauty who hires him to guide her across the treacherous Camino Real to Santa Fe. And though Elise Louvois's cool violet eyes betray nothing, her warm, willing body comes alive beneath his masterful touch. Mystified, Red Eagle becomes certain of but one thing—the spirits have destined Elise to be his woman.
_3498-0 $4.99 US/$5.99 CAN

LEISURE BOOKS
ATTN: Order Department
276 5th Avenue, New York, NY 10001

Please add $1.50 for shipping and handling for the first book and $.35 for each book thereafter. PA., N.Y.S. and N.Y.C. residents, please add appropriate sales tax. No cash, stamps, or C.O.D.s. All orders shipped within 6 weeks via postal service book rate. Canadian orders require $2.00 extra postage and must be paid in U.S. dollars through a U.S. banking facility.

Name____
Address____
City ______________________________ State_______ Zip_______
I have enclosed $______in payment for the checked book(s).
Payment must accompany all orders.☐ Please send a free catalog.

"Picture yourself floating out of your body—floating...floating...floating..." The hypnotic voice on the self-motivation tape is supposed to help Ruby Jordan solve her problems, not create new ones. Instead, she is lulled from a life full of a demanding business, a neglected home, and a failing marriage—to an era of hard-bodied warriors and fair maidens, fierce fighting and fiercer wooing. But the world ten centuries in the past doesn't prove to be all mead and mirth. Even as Ruby tries to update medieval times, she has to deal with a Norseman whose view of women is stuck in the Dark Ages. And what is worse, brawny Thork has her husband's face, habits, and desire to avoid Ruby. Determined not to lose the same man twice, Ruby plans a bold seduction that will conquer the reluctant Viking—and make him an eager captive of her love.

_51983-6 $4.99 US/$5.99 CAN

LOVE SPELL
ATTN: Order Department
276 5th Avenue, New York, NY 10001

Please add $1.50 for shipping and handling for the first book and $.35 for each book thereafter. PA., N.Y.S. and N.Y.C. residents, please add appropriate sales tax. No cash, stamps, or C.O.D.s. All orders shipped within 6 weeks via postal service book rate. Canadian orders require $2.00 extra postage and must be paid in U.S. dollars through a U.S. banking facility.

Name____
Address____
City ______________________________ State_______ Zip_______
I have enclosed $_______in payment for the checked book(s).
Payment must accompany all orders. ☐ Please send a free catalog.

Praise fo
New York Tim
Jo

Hazard

"Engaging. . . . Fans will appreciate the spicy chemistry between [Anne] and Race." —*Publishers Weekly*

The Devil's Heiress

"[A] deftly woven tale of romantic intrigue. . . . Head and shoulders above the usual Regency fare, this novel's sensitive prose, charismatic characters, and expert plotting will keep readers enthralled from first page to last."
—*Publishers Weekly*

"With her talent for writing powerful love stories and masterful plotting, Ms. Beverley cleverly brings together this dynamic duo. Her latest captivating romance . . . is easily a 'keeper'!" —*Romantic Times* (Top Pick)

"Exciting. . . . The story line is filled with action, but it is the charming lead couple that makes the plot hum."
—Harriet Klausner

"A riveting, completely captivating blend of romance, intrigue, and suspense that enthralls from the first page to the last. Beverley is a master storyteller and this book, with its superb plot, fascinating characters, and lush prose, is a stellar example of her talent . . . a strong contender for best historical romance of the year."
—Romance Fiction Forum

continued . . .

The Dragon's Bride

"Vintage Jo Beverley. Fast pacing, strong characters, sensuality, and a poignant love story make this a tale to cherish time and time again."

—*Romantic Times* (Top Pick)

"For those who enjoy a Regency setting and an intelligent, sensual plot, *The Dragon's Bride* is a must read."

—*Affaire de Coeur*

"Jo Beverley is a sure thing when it comes to entertaining historical romance readers. . . . This is Ms. Beverley at her best."

—*Midwest Book Review*

Devilish

"Beverley beautifully captures the flavor of Georgian England. . . . Her fast-paced, violent, and exquisitely sensual story is one that readers won't soon forget."

—*Library Journal*

"Jo [Beverley] has truly brought to life a fascinating, glittering, and sometimes dangerous world."

—Mary Jo Putney

"Another triumph."

—*Affaire de Coeur*

Secrets of the Night

"[Beverley] weaves a poignant tale of forbidden love. This sparkling talent is a joy to read."—*Romantic Times*

"Jo Beverley is up to her usual magic. . . . She sprinkles a bit of intrigue, a dash of passion and a dollop of lust, a pinch of poison, and a woman's need to protect all those she loves." —*Affaire de Coeur*

"A haunting romance of extraordinary passion and perception. . . . The story Jo Beverley weaves will astonish you. You'll remember *Secrets of the Night*, with all of its power, emotion, and passion, for a very long time."
—Bookbug on the Web

"Incredibly sensual . . . sexy and funny. . . . These characters [are] wonderfully real." —All About Romance

Forbidden Magic

"Wickedly delicious! Jo Beverley weaves a spell of sensual delight with her usual grace and flair."
—Teresa Medeiros

"A gem of a book—a little bawdy, a little magical, and written with a twinkling sense of humor that only Ms. Beverley is capable of. A keeper!" —*Romantic Times*

continued . . .

"Delightful . . . thrilling . . . with a generous touch of magic . . . an enchanting read." —*Booklist*

"An excellent read—definitely for dreamers!"
—*Rendezvous*

"Jo Beverley's style is flawless. . . . A wild ride filled with humor, suspense, love, passion, and much more."
—*Gothic Journal*

Lord of Midnight

"Beverley weaves a stunning medieval romance of loss and redemption . . . sizzling."
—*Publishers Weekly* (starred review)

"Noted for her fast-paced, wonderfully inventive stories, excellent use of humor and language, and vividly rendered characters and situations, Beverley has created another gem that will not disappoint." —*Library Journal*

"Jo Beverley brings the twelfth century to life in a vivid portrayal of a highly romantic story that captures the era with all its nuances, pageantry, and great passion . . . a real treat!" —*Romantic Times*

"Extremely enjoyable . . . intriguing. . . . Jo Beverley is clearly one of the leading writers lighting up the Dark Ages." —Painted Rock Reviews

Something Wicked

"A fast-paced adventure with strong, vividly portrayed characters . . . wickedly, wonderfully sensual and gloriously romantic." —Mary Balogh

"Intrigue, suspense, and passion fill the pages of this high-powered, explosive drama . . . thrilling!" —*Rendezvous*

"*Something Wicked* will delight." —*Lake Worth Herald* (FL)

"Jo Beverley is a talented storyteller, creating characters who come alive." —Under the Covers

ALSO BY JO BEVERLEY

A Most Unsuitable Man

Skylark

Winter Fire

St. Raven

Dark Champion

Lord of My Heart

My Lady Notorious

The Devil's Heiress

The Dragon's Bride

"The Demon's Mistress" in
In Praise of Younger Men

Devilish

Secrets of the Night

Forbidden Magic

Lord of Midnight

Something Wicked

Hazard

Jo Beverley

A SIGNET BOOK

SIGNET
Published by New American Library, a division of
Penguin Group (USA) Inc., 375 Hudson Street,
New York, New York 10014, USA
Penguin Group (Canada), 90 Eglinton Avenue East, Suite 700, Toronto,
Ontario M4P 2Y3, Canada (a division of Pearson Penguin Canada Inc.)
Penguin Books Ltd., 80 Strand, London WC2R 0RL, England
Penguin Ireland, 25 St. Stephen's Green, Dublin 2,
Ireland (a division of Penguin Books Ltd.)
Penguin Group (Australia), 250 Camberwell Road, Camberwell, Victoria 3124,
Australia (a division of Pearson Australia Group Pty. Ltd.)
Penguin Books India Pvt. Ltd., 11 Community Centre, Panchsheel Park,
New Delhi - 110 017, India
Penguin Group (NZ), cnr Airborne and Rosedale Roads, Albany,
Auckland 1310, New Zealand (a division of Pearson New Zealand Ltd.)
Penguin Books (South Africa) (Pty.) Ltd., 24 Sturdee Avenue,
Rosebank, Johannesburg 2196, South Africa

Penguin Books Ltd., Registered Offices:
80 Strand, London WC2R 0RL, England

First published by Signet, an imprint of New American Library,
a division of Penguin Group (USA) Inc.

First Printing, May 2002
First Printing ($4.99 Edition), January 2006
10 9 8 7 6 5 4 3 2 1

Printed in the United States of America

PUBLISHER'S NOTE
This is a work of fiction. Names, characters, places, and incidents either are the product of the author's imagination or are used fictitiously, and any resemblance to actual persons, living or dead, business establishments, events, or locales is entirely coincidental.

The publisher does not have any control over and does not assume any responsibility for author or third-party Web sites or their content.

This book is dedicated to the memory of historical novelist Dorothy Dunnett, who died on November 9, 2001, as I was going over the edited manuscript of *Hazard*.

Dorothy Dunnett, in addition to her other great talents, was the author of fifteen sweeping historical novels centered on her beloved Scotland, and of a number of mysteries. Her fans are devoted and worldwide. I discovered her Crawford of Lymond series at age twenty-four, and delighted in her work simply as an entranced reader.

Later, when I began to try to convey my own imaginary worlds, she was an inspiration, even though the thought that *Game of Kings* was her first novel is enough to daunt any writer. My works are different in style, in type, and in scope, but I know that some parts, perhaps some of the best parts, are there because I am a Dunnett reader.

Thank you, Dorothy, for the treasure you gave me, the reader; and for the seeds you planted in my writer's mind.

One

"The toad. The slimy, warty toad!"

Lady Anne Peckworth snapped around to stare at her sister. Frances was working through her day's letters, and clearly one of them had called for the Peckworth family's worst acceptable insult.

Before she had time to ask, Frances looked at her and her stomach cramped.

No.

It was like lightning.

It didn't strike the same person twice.

Frances's mouth pinched as if to hold back the words, but then she said, "According to Cynthia Throgmorton, Wyvern is married. And to a nobody! A bastard daughter of a lady of Devon, who was working—would you believe?—as his *housekeeper*. She has it from Louisa Morton, who lives near Crag Wyvern and is absolutely to be relied upon, she says. Of course, neither she nor Cynthia has any idea that this gossip is of particular importance. . . ." Her furious face softened into sympathy. "Oh, Anne . . ."

What did one say?

The same as last time, she supposed.

"I hope they'll be very happy."

"Anne! The man has as good as jilted you! And after Middlethorpe, too. Father must take him to court over it."

"Good heavens, no!" Anne shot to her feet. "I could not bear to be such an object of curiosity and pity." She bit her lips and controlled herself. "The Earl of Wyvern and I were not engaged, Frances. He had not so much as mentioned marriage."

"But he has been paying you such attentions!"

Since Frances was late in pregnancy and had been down here in Herefordshire for the past five months, the family letters must have been flying. Anne wasn't surprised. Her family was in a collective fret over her.

Poor crippled Anne.

Poor jilted Anne.

Poor destined-to-be-a-spinster Anne.

Late last year, their neighbor, Viscount Middlethorpe, had courted her. It had been understood by all that he would soon ask her to marry him, and she would accept. Then he'd been summoned to his estate by some problem.

She had next seen him with his beautiful and scandalous wife on his arm. Not a housekeeper in that case, but the widow of a man known as Randy Riverton, which was almost as bad.

"I wonder if this one is in an interesting condition, too."

"What?" asked Frances.

"Have your gossips not told you? Lady Middlethorpe is expecting to be confined in the summer."

"*What?*" Frances repeated, color mounting. "That would mean that the cad got her with child while . . ."

"While he was courting me. Yes. As you see, he was no great loss."

She hadn't felt that way at the time, but she'd pretended to. How else to salvage her pride?

Frances scanned her close-written letter. "Cynthia says nothing of the lady's condition. Of course, that could be the explanation."

Anne laughed, genuinely amused at the absurd situation. "I doubt it. He's been in Devon only ten days. Ten days," she repeated. "It *is* like lightning, isn't it?"

"Oh, Anne."

Frances began to heave herself off her chaise, so Anne limped over to push her back. "Don't distress yourself. It's not good for the baby. In fact, this is no great tragedy. I'm realizing that if I feel anything, it's relief."

She'd begun her speech thinking to soothe her sister, but by the end of it, she realized that it was true.

She sat in the chair by the chaise. "Truly, Frances, I have never been sure that I wanted to marry the earl."

Frances clearly did not believe her.

She tried to explain. "He needed a wife, and I liked being needed. After so many years of war, and the death of his father and brother, he was shadowed. If I could lift those shadows, it would be a worthy task. But I was uncertain. We did not have a lot in common. In fact," she said, staring at a window dismally streaked with rain, "I was never sure why he was wooing me. I thought love would come, for both of us. . . ."

Frances took her hand. "We had no idea. We all assumed that you felt warmly toward him."

Anne pulled a face. "I'm not sure I understand these emotions. But I know one thing. I do not have even a crack in my heart over Wyvern." She decided to get one thing out in the open. "I would be celebrating, I think, if not for the family."

Frances's color bloomed again, but this time with embarrassment. "We only want you happy, dearest."

"But not if I want to be happy living on as a spinster at Lea Park."

"It doesn't seem a life worthy of you, love, and," she added, "when Uffham inherits and his future wife rules the roost, who knows how it will be?"

A chill shot through Anne. "Good heavens. I've never thought of that. And Uffham, sad to say, cannot be depended upon to choose wisely."

"Precisely. You would not want to be another Aunt Sarah."

Aunt Sarah, their father's sister, lived, mostly ignored, in a suite of rooms in the north wing in the company of a few servants and a lot of small dogs. The family generally referred to her as "dear Aunt Sarah," but it really meant "poor Aunt Sarah."

If she didn't marry, would she be "poor Anne" forever? Poor Aunt Anne. Poor Great-aunt Anne . . .

To escape her sister's keen eye, Anne returned to the sofa. "You're right. I must think about this."

As cover, she picked up her piece of craft work again. The instructions were in the magazine open beside her—*Pastimes for Ladies: a cornucopia of elucidation, education, and recreation for the fair sex of our land.* She took that to mean "the bored fair sex of the land." Only extreme boredom could have driven her to attempting to make "a charming bonbon holder out of straw."

She looked at the weeping windows that rattled with occasional gusts of wind and showed only gray sky and pouring rain through the condensation. It was May, after all—time of blossoms, lambs, and courting birds, when the world was in good order.

In a proper May she could escape the house; she could ride, and when on horseback her turned foot didn't hinder her. With speed and fresh air she would be able to handle this better. As it was, she was trapped in the house, virtually trapped in this room, since it was the only one with a fire.

Trapped in Benning Hall in the rain.

Trapped from birth in a crippled body.

Trapped from birth by being a duke's daughter, expected to marry well, expected to behave well, even when jilted.

Trapped by her loving family's damnable concern, by their need that "poor Anne" be happy.

Her hands tightened on the woven straw, and she relaxed them.

It was the unseasonable weather that had her in the blue devils. Not Middlethorpe. Not Wyvern.

She focused on the magazine, on the instructions. She had finally finished the tedious plaiting and weaving. All she had, however, was a misshapen blob.

"Squeeze into shape," the useless instructions said. She squeezed at one end, and another part popped out. She pushed that in, and the whole thing changed again. "Do you have any idea how to make this into a heart shape?"

"No," Frances said, as if she'd been asked how to clean a kitchen grate.

"I've followed the instructions to the letter, done just as I ought. Perhaps the bottom should be flatter." She turned it over and squished, fearing to ruin it.

"Throw it on the fire, dear. Such a silly thing."

"This silly thing has taken up two days of my time. I will not give up now!"

"I wish you would put as much effort and resolution into finding a husband."

Anne stared at her. "*What?*"

Frances was red again but resolute. "You need to go into society more and meet all the eligible men, Anne, rather than sitting at Lea Park and waiting for the occasional suitor to come to you."

"We have grand parties at Lea Park."

"With the same, generally married, guests."

"I go to London for a few weeks every year."

"And attend exhibitions and the theater."

"What else am I to do? Limp around routs and sit with the dowagers at balls? I do not like to walk any distance, and I cannot dance!"

She pinched the wretched basket hard. It instantly formed the perfect heart shape of the illustration.

She began to laugh. "Oh, dear. Perhaps I am just too kind and gentle for my own good."

"What? Anne?"

She waved her sister back down to her chaise. "I'm all right. I think perhaps I do need to make some changes."

"Good."

Anne put the heart-shaped basket on the table. "The problem is that I don't know what I want. I truly am happy at Lea Park, among people I know so well. I don't like meeting strangers."

"The people of your new home will only be strangers for a little while."

"But there's that limping around London first." Anne sighed. "Did you not feel a pang at leaving home?"

"No, none. I was delighted to be coming to a home of my own and out from under Mama's eye." The Duchess of Arran was a strict mother. "And, of course, I would be happy anywhere with dearest Benning."

Anne thought Benning boring. Love was a strange affair.

"I really am a strange creature, aren't I?"

"It will be different when you do fall in love, dearest. Then you will be delighted to go to your husband's home."

"I suppose so. It is the way of the world, after all."

Anne felt a special tie to her home that she hadn't mentioned—her work with the papers of the Peckworth women. She knew that her family considered it as strange a pastime as weaving straw hearts, and something she'd leave behind when she had a full life.

Perhaps they were right. At the moment, however, it absorbed her. She wished she were home now. Rainy days were a perfect excuse to spend hours with the neglected diaries, letters, and assorted documents of her female ancestors.

Idiotic to stay a spinster just for that. Not poor Anne. Crazy Anne . . .

Then she heard a faint clanging. "Was that the doorbell?"

Frances sat up, a protective hand going to her belly. "Who could be visiting on such a day? I pray it isn't bad news!"

"I'm sure not. It's probably a neighbor as cast down by the weather as we are and seeking company."

Anne went to peer through the blurred and fogged window. "Two dripping horses being led away," she reported. "Visitors, for sure."

She limped toward the door but heard rapid steps. She only had time to step back before the door was flung open.

"Hello, Frannie and Annie!"

"Uffham!" Anne exclaimed. "You scared Frances half to death turning up in this weather—" But he had already swept her into a damp hug.

He went on to hug Frances a bit more gingerly. "How is it?" he asked vaguely.

"Active," said Frances, glowing. "You did half scare me to death, but it's wonderful to have a visitor. Sit down and tell us all the news from town. You are come from London, aren't you?"

"Yes." But Uffham cast an anxious look at Anne.

So it was public now. "I know about Wyvern, Stuff."

No one in the world could get away with calling Lord Uffham Stuff except his sisters. He was a tall, handsome young man with stylish brown hair who enjoyed pugilism, neck-or-nothing steeplechases, and the wilder sort of entertainments.

"How?" he asked, clearly rather peeved. "It only appeared in this morning's paper."

"One of Frances's correspondents. I do thank you for wanting to break the news to me."

"I've half a mind to go to Devon and call the cad out."

"No! There was nothing settled between us."

Before he could say more, Frances interrupted. "Do ring, Anne. Stuff must be chilled through and starving."

"Ain't that the truth? But I've brought a guest along, Frannie, if you don't mind."

"A guest? In this?" Frances looked at the window as if the weather might have changed to sun.

"Army man. Tough as a Highland sheep. Name's Racecombe de Vere. Derbyshire family."

"Tough as a Derbyshire ram?" Anne asked.

A vision popped into her mind of a weathered, hairy specimen of huge proportions. This was alarming because she suspected that her brother had reacted to the notice in the paper by rushing here with a replacement suitor.

"Now, now, don't go scaring him away, Annie." Having confirmed her fears, Uffham turned back to Frances. "You can put up an extra guest for a day or two, can't you?"

"Of course! I'm bored to tears, and Anne is reduced to making small items out of straw. Anne, ring for refreshments. Stuff, go and bring up your friend! I plead my belly as excuse for not venturing from this cozy room."

He swept out. Anne first closed the door he had carelessly left open, then pulled the bell rope. "He's brought this Derbyshire ram for me. How absurd."

"It's a kind thought."

"At least it gives him time to cool. He mustn't call Wyvern out. There's no cause. Probably no one in society even realizes that I had hopes. . . ."

She prayed that was true. Pity—more pity—was the one thing she could not tolerate. She'd been born with a twisted foot and lived with pity all her life.

She regarded a china ornament on the mantelpiece—a shepherd and shepherdess obviously well matched and happy. It was presented as so natural and easy, this falling in love and marrying. Why was it so very tangled in her case?

She turned to her sister. "I think Stuff dragged Wyvern to me to try to heal my pride over Middlethorpe, and you can see how disastrous that was. What am I to do about this one?"

"Enjoy his company."

"Someone calling himself de Vere? The de Veres died out a century ago. He's an impostor of some kind."

Frances's eyes brightened. "Really? How intriguing. I've always wanted to meet an adventurer. Don't take everything so seriously, dear. Flirt a little. You need the practice."

"With a hairy Derbyshire ram?"

Frances laughed, and Uffham returned at exactly that moment.

Anne blushed with embarrassment. Had his companion heard her last words?

And the Derbyshire ram . . . wasn't.

"Mr. de Vere, ladies. De Vere, my sisters, Lady Benning and Lady Anne."

The slender blond man with the fine-boned features and laughing blue eyes bowed with perfect—if rather excessive—grace. "Your servant, ladies! Especially as you provide shelter, this luscious warmth, and, I am given to understand, nourishment."

Frances was blushing and looking as if she didn't know whether to be ecstatic or to laugh. Anne was wondering what had possessed Uffham. When it came to marriage, to entrusting her life to some man, she demanded someone of more substance than this.

The maid arrived and left with instructions for tea and hearty fare. Uffham threw himself into the chair by the fire, sticking his boots so close that they began to steam.

"Uffham, your boots," Anne said. "You've tracked mud across the carpet."

She turned to stop de Vere doing the same. He, however, had not advanced beyond the wooden floor at the edge of the room.

"Don't fuss, Anne," said Frances. "It is easily cleaned. Come in, Mr. de Vere."

"Perhaps I might ask to be able to change my damp clothes before eating, Lady Benning."

"Of course! Anne, take Mr. de Vere to the east bedroom. It's not far."

Not far for your poor foot. That made it hard to refuse. "Of course, but Uffham could take him."

"I just got comfortable," Uffham protested, "and the harm's done now. Only make it worse to walk back out, and I can't get these boots off without a jack. Call for someone to help me with them, that's a good girl."

Anne rolled her eyes but gave in. She rang the bell again. Then she picked up the knitted shawl she kept to hand, wrapped it around herself, and headed for the door. De Vere opened it for her and closed it behind them.

At least he had good manners. That was something. She had grave doubts about Uffham's new crony. He was too . . . slight. Slight in build and slight in manner. Slight in substance, too.

Frances had been right. He was an adventurer. Uffham had fallen into bad company again, and now he thought she might marry a man such as this?

Two

"I'm sorry for putting you to such trouble, Lady Anne," the man said. "If you give me directions, I am sure I can find my way. And now I'm tracking more mud along the corridors. . . ."

He sat on a chair and pulled off first one boot and then the other without difficulty. "Army ways," he said, standing with them in his hand. "Folly not to be able to get in and out of them by oneself."

Anne felt a stir of interest. She admired practicality.

"You were at Waterloo, Mr. de Vere?" she asked as they turned the corner in the corridor.

"Alas, no, Lady Anne."

So much for that. He was a desk officer. He'd doubtless never disturbed his blond waves.

She opened the door to the east room and stood back to let him enter. "I will send washing water for you, Mr. de Vere. And of course, please ask for anything you need."

She closed the door and retraced her steps, wondering why she felt so twitchy about this new invader. He'd done nothing wrong, but there was something bold about him, something that suggested that he respected no rules. With his name and manner he had to be an adventurer, a man to be avoided.

And yet, Frances's suggestion tantalized. A lady could enjoy flirtation without sliding from there into marriage, especially with a man so completely ineligible.

She didn't flirt. It had always seemed unkind and unwise to encourage gentlemen whom she had no intention of marrying. She had begun to flirt a little with Middlethorpe, perhaps. She'd never felt inclined to flirt with saturnine Wyvern.

She did need practice. She'd never been opposed to marriage, but she hadn't been in pursuit of it, either. Now, with the threat of life at Lea Park under some other young woman's rule, it was a whole other matter.

Needing time to consider this, she went down the east stairs all the way to the kitchens to order the water. Of course, the servants fussed about her going to the trouble—but then she had an inspiration.

"Please," she said to the agitated housekeeper. "My doctor tells me I must walk frequently or my limp could get worse. You must not deny me the opportunity."

"Oh, well then, my lady. Of course, then . . ." But plump Mrs. Orwell didn't seem comfortable about it.

"This wretched weather has stuck me in a chair for two days. It really isn't good for me."

"Yes, quite, I see, my lady."

Anne went back upstairs very pleased with herself. She'd spread the same word at Lea Park, and if necessary get Dr. Normanton to support her. She knew he would. He had always encouraged her to be active, and had helped persuade her parents to let her ride and drive. That had finally given her equal mobility and a form of exercise she loved.

She paused in the chilly hall as she realized that she'd never shown such skills in society. Perhaps Frances was right. She had hidden away at Lea Park as much as possible, and when mixing with society she'd done her best to fade into the wallpaper.

As she limped up the stairs, she resolved to actively pursue marriage, which meant spending more time in society. She pulled a face. It would be tedious and at times embarrassing, but she would do it. For that she did need more practice with men.

She hovered for a moment outside the boudoir and then detoured to her room. Her maid, Hetty, was there, putting away some freshly laundered clothing.

"Oh, milady. Is there something you need?"

"Just to tidy myself," Anne said, feeling suddenly as if the words "husband hunter" had appeared on her forehead.

"Sit you down, milady, and I'll redo your hair."

Forty-year-old Hetty had been Anne's maid from her nursery days, and Anne automatically obeyed. By the time the pins were out of her hair, she had come to her wits. "I don't have many minutes, Hetty, and I don't . . . Just tidy it the way it was."

"Right, milady." But Anne saw the twinkle in the maid's eye. As if to confirm it, Hetty said, "I hear Lord Uffham's brought a handsome young gentleman with him, milady."

"Handsome is as handsome does."

"Sukie Rowman caught a glimpse of him and said he looked like the angel in the window in the church."

Anne realized that Sukie Rowman was right. The angel in St. Michael's church wore a flowing robe, but she—he?—bore a flaming sword. It was a militant angel with a square chin and waving blond hair. Perhaps that was why she felt she might have met de Vere.

"Who would marry an angel?"

Hetty grinned. "That's the spirit, milady."

Anne looked at the older woman in the mirror. Surely the news about Wyvern's marriage couldn't have made it to the servants' quarters yet. "Lord Wyvern is not the angelic type."

Hetty pulled a face. "That he isn't, milady, unless you count Lucifer."

"He's a good man, Hetty."

"But carrying troubles. There's troubles enough come in life, milady. No need to marry them. You take your time in choosing."

That was startlingly frank. "Wyvern is married. To a lady in Devon."

Hetty's busy hands stilled. "Well, I never. The warty toad!"

Anne burst out laughing. Had the phrase passed from servants to children, or children to servants?

"No, truly, Hetty. There was no commitment, and I'm happy for him. Now do hurry. I must get back to help my sister."

Hetty twisted Anne's hair into a high knot and stuck in the pins. It was a little neater, but Anne noticed that it was also a little softer around her face. She thought of protesting, but there wasn't time, and she didn't want to reveal any special interest in her appearance.

Hetty put down the comb. "You could change your dress, milady."

Anne's blue dress was her plainest, and she hadn't put on any jewelry this morning other than seed pearl earrings and a gold cross and chain. . . .

Enough. She rose and turned with the blankest expression she could find. "Why would I do that?"

Hetty's mouth pinched, but she didn't argue. She did, however, open a drawer and take out the Norwich silk shawl with the deep cream fringe.

Anne picked up her plain brown knitted one.

"You can't wear that, milady!"

"You didn't complain when I put it on this morning, and nothing has changed, especially the temperature."

She flung it around her shoulders and marched out of the room, afraid that she looked her worst, but even more afraid of being a figure of fun by changing simply because a strange man had come to the house.

A man who looked like a militant angel . . .

She found both gentlemen with Frances. Uffham, now bootless, was still in the chair near the fire, but de Vere had taken the chair close to Frances. He was making her laugh.

Not an angel. A court jester.

A straw man.

A man of no substance or use.

But straw could be useful. It could be made into mats and mattresses, fans and baskets. And bonbon holders.

Her foolish, whirling mind was sign of extreme nervousness, and she feared she'd start chattering as crazily as she was thinking. She was nearly twenty-one, not sixteen!

As she went to her seat on the sofa, however, she heard de Vere murmur something to Frances, and when she glanced that way, her sister's cheeks were pink, and her eyes shining.

Flirtation. In fact, it looked more like seduction!

Good heavens, surely Uffham wouldn't bring such a man here. . . .

She forced her mind back to reason. No man would

try to seduce a woman within weeks of giving birth. But perhaps a woman within weeks of giving birth still likes to be flirted with . . .

Was de Vere simply being kind?

Tantalized by that, she took her seat on the sofa. When she realized that *Pastimes for Ladies* was still open to her project, she closed it and put it facedown. "Have I missed any delightful new scandal?"

"Would we sully your ears with scandal, Annie?" Uffham asked with a grin. "I was telling Frannie about Hester Stanhope, but now you're here. . . ."

She gave him the glare that promised sisterly retribution, and he laughed.

"The account will be in your papers any day. Tale is, she's not only adventuring all over Asia Minor, she's now the leader of some tribes of Bedouin, as well. And possibly," he added with a wink, "having a special relationship with an Arab prince."

"Lady Hester?" Anne exclaimed. "She visited Lea Park with her uncle, Lord Pitt, when we were children. She did not seem that sort of woman."

"Who knows what secret passions hide behind conventional appearances?" asked de Vere.

Anne caught a speculative glance at herself.

"What a shame," he continued, "if they remain hidden."

Good heavens! Why would he think like that about her?

"That could apply to the last Tregallows girl!" Frances interjected.

"Why?" Anne asked, thankful for a change of subject.

"Uffham says she's eloped. With a nobody! Even so, it must be a relief to all concerned. I doubt any of them would have married except for being duke's daughters with enormous dowries."

Like me? Anne thought, but she knew Frances wouldn't have meant that. "Which Tregallows lady is this? They all have such strange names, and all starting with *C.* Cornissa, Candella . . ."

"This one is Claretta."

"And," declared Uffham with glee, "she's run off with

a Major Crump! Claretta Crump. It's a positive tongue twister. And whoever has heard of a Crump?"

Frances shook her head. "She must be *extremely* plain, poor thing. You'd think the name alone would have given poor Claretta pause."

"Apparently her pause should have come sooner," Uffham said. "Rumor has it that she's already increasing."

Frances smirked. "We'll know the truth in seven months or so."

Anne couldn't stand it. "How sad!"

"Claretta Crump's lowly marriage?"

"Society counting off the months."

"Piffle," Frances said. "She's forced a marriage to someone undesirable. She deserves everything she gets."

"Or given in to passion, Lady Benning," de Vere said, as if talking about the weather. "Passion can drive anyone off the straight path."

Anne saw Frances blush, and knew she was blushing, too. The man was outrageous, but the Peckworth family was not showing well before a guest. The tea tray, thank heavens, arrived then, along with another piled high with sustenance suitable for young men. Anne made the tea to save Frances from the effort.

De Vere rose to pass around the cups, and a moment later Benning joined them, perhaps drawn by a young man's instinct for food. He was only thirty, though an increase of the waist and a decrease of the hair made him look older. Anne wondered what had drawn Frances to him. Passion?

Love certainly was a mystery.

"Any trouble on the road?" he asked Uffham.

"None. Why?"

"Damn colliers dragging coal wagons around, begging. People encouraging them by raising money. Luddites attacking manufactories. Laborers burning ricks and smashing agricultural machines. Country's going to wrack and ruin."

Uffham took a slice of pie. "The authorities need to catch that Captain Ned Ludd and hang him."

"He's a symbol, not a person," de Vere said, "and therefore, immortal."

"Then the authorities can hang some of his mortal followers," Benning snapped. "Those hangings at Ely should give 'em reason to think."

"Right," Uffham said. "They'll think twice before killing someone else who tries to stop their wickedness."

Anne wished they were back to social scandal. She didn't approve of the rioters, but times were hard. Peace had proved to be a mixed blessing.

Frances put her hand over her belly. "Don't talk of these things! I cannot sleep for thinking of those wicked people wandering the countryside at night burning, smashing, and murdering. It's like France all over again!"

"Madmen," Benning agreed, which Anne didn't think helpful, but then he went to pat Frances's shoulder and assure her of safety.

Uffham peered at the tray from a distance. "Pass me more of that cake, de Vere, there's a good man."

Like a good servant, de Vere passed the cake to Uffham. Then he came to Anne to have his cup refilled. Instead of returning to his seat by the chaise, however, he sat beside her.

"You frown, Lady Anne. I cannot bring sunshine, but perhaps I can bring smiles."

"Smiles, sir? We were talking of somber matters, I think. You are from Derbyshire, where these problems are serious. Can you explain the true causes of the Luddite problem to me?"

"I left Derbyshire to join the army eight years ago, Lady Anne."

"But you must have spent your childhood there."

"I suppose I must. But matters were better then, and I was carelessly young."

She suspected that he, like Uffham, would be carelessly young till he was ninety if he could manage it.

"And now?" she demanded. "You do not read the newspapers?"

"They tend to be so depressing—riots, destruction, and hangings."

So much for flirting with him. He was as frivolous as her straw heart. "People are behaving badly because their *trades* are depressed, Mr. de Vere, driving them to try to destroy the machines that have replaced them."

"A lady interested in industrial economics? How novel."

"Not at all. Perhaps ladies do not express their views to gentlemen for fear of being mocked."

His face settled into something close to seriousness. "Did I mock? I did not mean to. Are you saying that ladies together talk of industrial matters? That perhaps you and Lady Benning were doing so when we interrupted?"

Anne found her own teacup was empty and put it on the table. Even if he hadn't heard her words before entering the room, he must have heard laughter.

She longed to lie, but said, "No."

He put his cup beside hers. "Perhaps ladies hide their true selves even from one another. As, perhaps, Lady Hester did. Sad, would you not say? Imagine if her uncle had not died and left her enough money to go adventuring."

His eyes were keen, heavy-lidded, and a smoky blue gray that should have been dull but wasn't. She felt a tug of attraction but then remembered his suspicious name.

"Have you never felt the need to hide your true self, Mr. *de Vere?*"

"All the time, Lady Anne. All the time."

"A man of mystery! There is something tantalizing about that, is there not? Is that your intent, sir?"

"To tantalize you? Are you hinting that you are thirsty, Lady Anne? Please, allow me." He picked up the teapot and went neatly through the business of pouring a fresh cup of tea for her.

She watched, amused and slightly shocked. Gentlemen did not pour tea. What was more, that play on *tantalize* showed a mind as agile as his body. The sinner Tantalus had been trapped in a pool of water up to his chin, but was never able to drink.

Did de Vere plan to tantalize her? Would she be tempted but never allowed to . . . to what?

She knew what—and she most certainly wouldn't!

He passed her the cup, and she saw that his hands were a little too brown for a man of fashion, but beautiful. Long fingered but not bony, his square nails neatly trimmed. Something about those hands made her almost fumble the cup.

He put his hand over hers to steady her. It didn't help. A ripple of something went through her, and she saw it reflected in the surface of the tea. She gathered her wits, smiled at him, and put the cup down.

The room seemed suddenly too warm, but then she realized that she still had her shawl on. Such a simple explanation! She began to shrug it off, but de Vere rose to help her with it. He folded it and draped it over the back of the sofa.

A simple courtesy to make her feel as if she had been somehow stroked. Had the news and events of the day turned her wits?

She picked up her cup and took a deep drink of tea. "So, Mr. de Vere, you think all people hide their true selves?"

"Not at all, Lady Anne," he said as he sat down again. "Uffham, for example, hides little."

"But you do?"

"Of course."

She sipped, watching him. "What parts do you keep concealed, sir?"

His eyes twinkled. "All the naughty bits, of course."

A *hic* of laughter escaped her, and she almost spilled her tea. The room heated up again, and this time she didn't have a shawl as excuse.

"You are quite a wit, Mr. de Vere."

"A wit and a madman, Annie," called Uffham from across the room. "Never take him seriously."

When conversation among the others settled—on the dull topic of the weather now—Anne looked at de Vere. "That seems a sad obituary, sir."

He looked down at himself and back at her. "I hadn't noticed that I was dead yet. Wasn't there a saint who prayed to God that he become holy, but not just yet?"

Before she could form a riposte, he went on, "Doesn't that strike a chord in you, Lady Anne? That you die a worthy lady, but not be one just yet?"

"Saints are esteemed for having sinned and repented, Mr. de Vere. Ladies of English society are not."

"Dashed unfair, wouldn't you say?"

She was rescued by the nursemaid entering with little Lucy, making the modest room quite a fashionable crush. Anne welcomed the distraction. She couldn't believe she was having this conversation in the midst of her family.

She glanced back at de Vere.

Angel?

Imp from hell, more likely. He had a way of seeming angelically innocent while being completely outrageous.

"Well, Lady Anne?" he prompted.

"I have never found sin particularly appealing," she said in a tone designed to depress pretension.

His brows rose. "No desire to steal a delightful possession from one of your sisters? No urge to stick pins into them for being cruel? Not a single sour wish directed at a person unfairly blessed by fortune? No envy, no sloth, no gluttony? . . ."

"Of course. I'm no saint."

"Ah! Then we were talking about the sin of lust."

Shocked rigid, Anne glanced at Uffham to see if he might have overheard. He hadn't, thank heavens. "Mr. de Vere," she hissed, "you go too far."

"Lady Anne," he murmured back, "you are enjoying it."

And astonishingly, it was true!

"That is because I am safe within the bosom of my family, sir."

"Unwise to bring bosoms into this discussion."

Even though her bosom was slight and entirely covered by sturdy blue cloth, Anne instinctively put a hand there.

"So," the incorrigible man continued at an alarmingly normal pitch, "you think discussing lust would lead to it? It does make one wonder what orgies result when our worthy churchmen meet to discuss what passions we should not be permitted."

She lost the fight with her lips. "Mr. de Vere!"

He took her tilted cup from her and put it on the table. She saw Uffham looking at her with a hint of concern. For some reason she smiled to show everything was all right.

"Why be tantalized," the impossible man asked, "when you can drink your fill? You can talk about any of the seven deadly sins with me, Lady Anne, and I assure you I will not act on any of them."

"And I assure you, sir, that I have no desire to do so."

Lying, she told herself, was not one of the seven deadly sins, but it offended against a Commandment. She wasn't sure which was worse.

This had hurtled beyond flirtation. She mustn't permit this outrageous man to go on saying these things. He might get entirely the wrong idea. She called for little Lucy's attention, encouraging her to toddle over and show off her doll.

But the wanton hussy headed for de Vere, beaming at him as if he were an old friend and demanding to be lifted into his lap. He obliged and admired her toy, but then looked at Anne from those wicked eyes. "Perhaps we should start with envy, Lady Anne. . . ."

An arrow straight to the heart. She had felt a spurt of envy that the child prefer him to her, which was ridiculously petty.

She couldn't have met Mr. Racecombe de Vere before. She would remember the violent irritation of it.

Three

When the group broke up to change for dinner, Anne pursued her brother to his room.

"Did you bring de Vere here as a potential husband?"

He turned from the mirror, trying to pull out his cravat pin. "Good Lord, what gave you that idea?"

Well, of course he hadn't. She went to help him. "You brought me Middlethorpe and Wyvern, didn't you? Stuff, you've managed to twist this."

Concentrating on the silver pin and the overly starched cloth, she could still see his neck redden.

"Not Middlethorpe. We've known him forever. Mother might have had a word with his mother. But when he let you down, I met Wyvern, and he was clearly looking for a bride. I thought, why not? I still thought a Rogue in the family would be splendid."

She yanked out the mangled pin and stepped back. "A rogue? Lord Wyvern is a rogue? I thought him a very proper sort of man."

And why on earth would you want me to marry a rogue?

He pulled his crackling cravat loose, scattering flakes of starch.

"Your laundress is overstarching those," she pointed out. "No wonder you bent the pin."

"Don't nag. A man needs a crisp cravat to achieve the latest styles." He rolled his neck, and she heard his collar crackle, too.

"And men say female fashion is folly. Rogue?"

"Oh, yes. Company of Rogues." He shrugged out of his riding jacket. "Started out at Harrow. Makes me wish

I'd gone to school. I've a fresh coat in my bag. Get it for me, will you?"

"No. What is the Company of Rogues?"

She didn't usually pursue Uffham's conversations so keenly, but she sensed that this affected her.

He went to open his bag and dig in it. "Rogues, Company of. Twelve boys at Harrow gathered together by Nicholas Delaney. He's Stainbridge's brother. They're a legend among old Harrovians—the Rogues, I mean. Stainbridge went—"

"Stuff!" Anne exclaimed. "Stick to the point."

He glowered at her. "All right, all right. The Company of Rogues was set up as defense against bullies and cruel masters, that sort of thing. Dashed good idea, if you ask me. There was a bunch of them in Melton this past hunting season, staying at Arden's lodge. Wish I was one of them. You should see his stables there—"

"And Lord Wyvern is a member of the Company of Rogues?" Anne ruthlessly interrupted. Once started on horses, Uffham would be impossible.

"Right." He was scattering his clothes all over the bed. "And Middlethorpe. The others are Delaney, of course. Arden—"

"Stop! I don't want a list." A strange thought was stirring. "You wanted a Rogue for a brother-in-law? You sought Lord Wyvern out?"

He frowned for a moment. "I think he approached me. Can't really remember. Fine idea, though. Pity it didn't work out. As brother-in-law to a Rogue, I'd probably get into their set."

Pity.

The word was like a jab from the bent pin.

"Would you say that these Rogues look out for one another? Fulfill one another's obligations? That sort of thing?"

"You could look at it like that. Mostly friends these days, of course."

"No wonder Wyvern seemed lukewarm . . ."

"What?" Uffham had found his jacket and was staring at her. "Something wrong, Annie? By the way, Wyvern's using the Amleigh title now. Apparently there's a contestant for the earldom."

She was almost distracted, but made herself pursue the main point. "Stuff, you are not to bring me any more Rogues as suitors, do you understand?"

"Don't be put off by the name. Schoolboy nonsense."

"I simply don't want it. In fact, I don't want you to bring me any suitors at all. I will find myself a husband."

She saw an unwise comment form in his mind.

"You think I can't? Just because of a twisted foot? Lord Byron has the same affliction, and ladies swoon in his path!"

Her brother rolled his eyes. "Right-o," he said, shrugging into his jacket.

That image of the Company of Rogues drawing lots lurked in Anne's mind. "I find I do want a list of the rest of these Rogues, Stuff, so I know whom to avoid."

He gave her a bewildered-brother look, but complied. "I think most of them are married now. Let's see. Stephen Ball was in Melton, and Major Hal Beaumont. I think those are the only two still unshackled. Ball's a political man. I don't think you'd like those circles."

"Neither do I."

"Beaumont lost an arm in the war."

"I am not one to reject a cripple, but I'm resolved not to marry a Rogue."

"Right-o. Going to go to London, then, and let Caroline take you around? Marianne'll be pleased."

"You mean Caroline will be pleased."

"No. Marianne." But then he got a fixed look, and his neck turned red again. "Pleased at you having a good time," he said heartily.

Anne's heart began to pound. "Stuff, what about Marianne?"

Marianne was her sixteen-year-old sister.

"Nothing."

She limped over to him. "Stuff!"

"Dammit, but you're a devil, Annie. All right. Marianne's hot to marry Percy Shreve."

"That was a schoolroom affair!"

"*She* was in the schoolroom two years ago, but he wasn't."

"He can't be twenty-one yet!"

"Just. And he was at Waterloo. Still suffering from it,

which is why Marianne wants to get to the altar. She don't think his mama and an army of servants can take proper care of him. Load of nonsense," he added hastily. "Just bits of shrapnel here and there, and a leg that hasn't healed quite right . . ."

Anne remembered the vibrant young man, so excited to be joining a regiment two years before, and so cast down that he might have missed the war. She remembered her young sister's starry eyes, and how they'd all teased her.

"Poor man. Poor Marianne. Let them marry! I'm not going to be cast into a despair by it."

Her brother pulled a face. "Mama won't have it. If you want the truth, I think she don't care for the match. An army career ain't worth much these days even if he heals, and there's no hope of more. Percy's older brother has three sons already."

"Does a worthy man—a hero!—count for nothing? Is Mama hoping he'll *die*?"

"Don't get in a fit." He hunted among his clothing and pulled out a crackling fresh cravat. "She'll doubtless come around, but you know she's never been happy with Benning. Caroline righted the ship a bit by catching an earl, but then you've let one slip. And here's Marianne, and she wants a younger son."

Anne was assessing all this. "If I were to marry, Mama would have no reason to refuse the match, would she?"

He was in front of the mirror now, wrapping the wide cravat around his collar. "Probably not."

"Then I had better do it, hadn't I, and soon."

His brows rose, but he said, "Right-o." Then he smiled at her. "You'll make a fine wife, Annie. You have the sweetest nature. Never any trouble. And you have a handsome dowry."

It seemed as bleak an assessment as the one he'd made of Racecombe de Vere. Which reminded her. "And you swear that de Vere is not a Rogue?"

"Lord, Annie, he's my age, and didn't even go to Harrow. Some school up in Derbyshire." He turned completely to frown at her. "You're not taken with him, are you?"

"Not at all." But she couldn't help asking, "Is he so very ineligible?"

He turned back to the mirror and began to create an intricate knot. "He's nobody."

"What is his family?"

"Dashed if I know."

"What's his real name?"

He grimaced, rocking his head to create creases. "Dashed if I know." The cravat crackled, and more starch flew.

She found his clothes brush and went to brush it off. "Uffham, if you don't know anything about him and think he's an impostor, why are you carting him around with you?"

"Pleasant company. Livens up a dull moment . . ."

She knew what he meant, if *agitation* was a synonym for *liveliness.*

He picked up a new pin and started forcing it into the cravat. "When I heard about Wyvern—Amleigh now, I suppose—dashed confusing, that. Anyway, I read the paper in White's and decided to ride down here. De Vere offered to keep me company. Made the journey go faster. Useful man to have about."

"So he's a professional toadeater."

"If you like."

"He *was* in the army?"

He stretched his neck to view his masterpiece. "Not bad." Then he answered. "Oh, yes. Quite a madman in battle, or so I heard."

She stared at him. "He wasn't a desk officer?"

He turned to her. "Lord, no. In the thick of things, but then he was one of the unlucky ones shipped off to the American war and missed Waterloo. Sold out in disgust."

Anne knew it was unreasonable to feel guilty about the assumptions she'd made, but she did.

"*Are* you interested, Annie? If so, I'll make inquiries. Dashed pleasant fellow to have around."

So, it had come to that. Even a nameless nobody was good enough if he'd only take poor Anne off their hands.

She laughed and hoped it sounded natural. "A de Vere? That's as bad as a Crump. You're right, though. He's amusing company. I intend to enjoy that."

Race de Vere finished washing his hands, thinking that Lady Anne Peckworth was not at all what he had expected. Where was the quiet, crippled, conventional lady?

The reality was surprising, but it was going to make his task here much easier and more enjoyable.

For the past few months he had been secretary to Con Somerford, new Earl of Wyvern, now Viscount Amleigh again. He'd helped sort out the tangled affairs of the earldom, but in the process he'd helped sort out Con's personal affairs, as well. He didn't regret fixing things so that Con could marry his true love, but the thought of the poor crippled lady losing her last hope had weighed on them all.

Poor crippled lady? Last hope? He laughed. Con must be blind. Lady Anne Peckworth was a prize. A duke's daughter, handsomely dowered, and lovely.

True, she wasn't in the common run of beauty, but surely not every man in Britain was enslaved by glossy dark hair and rosy cheeks? As for the limp, some men would object to that, but not all. She had a brain, and wit, and the way her lips curled at the corners when she was trying not to laugh was enchanting.

So why had she even been considering a lukewarm suitor such as Con? Was she afraid of society? Had she convinced herself, or been convinced, that her limp made her an affront to the eyes? If so, that must be changed.

Perhaps she was like a nervous subaltern missing out on life by trying to be safe. Since more men died in war from disease than from wounds, it made no sense to avoid action. He'd learned the lesson early that the only way to live through a war was to live fully.

In his opinion, fashionable England had much in common with the fields of war.

The dinner bell rang—the call to battle?—so he glanced in the mirror to check his appearance, then headed to the fray. He'd become Con's secretary in order to help the officer he had most admired, and moved on to this in order to ease everyone's consciences. Once Lady Anne was settled, he could turn to doing something with his own blank slate of a life.

He found everyone in Lady Benning's boudoir except for Lady Anne.

Uffham strolled over. "What d'you think of my sister, then?" He sounded a bit truculent.

"Lady Benning or Lady Anne?"

Uffham began to turn red. "Anne, of course. Think we can get her married off?"

"With no trouble at all."

"Has to be the right sort. No Crumps."

Ah. Unusual for Uffham to be so alert to things going on around him.

"Of course not. A title for sure. A duke, if possible."

Uffham visibly relaxed. "Right, right."

Lady Anne came in then looking flustered—perhaps because she'd made changes to her appearance.

Not an overhaul, and certainly not a change into a flimsy dress that would set her up for influenza, but subtle, successful changes. She'd had her hair redressed in side curls, and added some lovely pearls and a splendid blue-and-gold Norwich shawl. The cream fringe was a foot deep, and the sky blue brought out the bloom of her skin. Her fan was a silk-and-ivory work of art.

He allowed himself only a courteous degree of smile but approved. There was a fine mind working in Lady Anne. She was making the best of herself and also reminding the Derbyshire ram that she was the daughter of a duke and way above his touch.

She even cast him a challenging look.

He went to join her. "Shawl *and* fan, Lady Anne? Playing hot and cold already?"

Her color rose. It suited her. "Prepared for all eventualities, let us say."

"All you need now is a lamp full of oil."

She looked a question, obviously wary.

"To be the complete wise virgin, I mean."

"Mr. de Vere!"

"It's straight from the Bible, and a virtuous type to be."

She laughed. "You delight in shocking people, don't you?"

"But of course. I saw an experiment once where a doctor attempted to revive a corpse by application of electricity."

"Did it work?"

"Alas, no, but who knows what the effect might be on the living?"

Her look suggested that she guessed what he was up to, but if anything, she seemed amused. She was utterly delightful.

The footman entered then. "Dinner is ready, milady."

Lady Benning struggled up from her chaise. Lord Benning carefully swathed her in two shawls and gave her his arm. Uffham insisted on going ahead in case his sister should stumble on the stairs.

Perfect.

Race offered his arm to his quarry, and they progressed along behind. "If I am not too indelicate, Lady Anne, when is Lady Benning expecting to be confined? Soon, I assume."

"In early June. Hard to believe that summer is so close." She shivered as they left the room. "It isn't so terribly cold, but Frances keeps her boudoir so warm that it seems Decemberish out here."

"The interesting effect of contrasts. What surprises us depends on our previous experience."

As they started down the stairs, she glanced at him. "Your experiences have made you hard to surprise, Mr. de Vere?"

"I would have said so, Lady Anne. But you have surprised me."

Wariness sharpened her clear blue eyes, but wariness of the right sort. Not fear, but *en garde.* "To be surprised, Mr. de Vere, a person must have expectations. You had expectations about me?"

"Do we not always have expectations? Even when heading into the unknown, we have some model, or we could never be shocked."

Their speed down the stairs was set by Lady Frances, and thus snail-like. He did wonder if she would last the week, never mind into next month, but that, at least, was not his concern.

"I had no expectation of you, Mr. de Vere," Lady Anne pointed out, "because I had no notion that you even existed."

"And yet you immediately formed a model." At her look, he added, "The Derbyshire ram?"

She colored but laughed, looking altogether charming. "Touché. And I suppose Uffham mentioned me. Very well, what model had you formed?"

Race thought for a moment, then spoke the truth. "A quiet, conventional lady. With a limp. Does your foot pain you?" When she stared, he added, "Does it upset you to speak of it? I understand you have been so since birth, so I would have thought you had come to terms with it."

He learned then that she could wield a look of ducal hauteur. "So I have, sir, but your interest smacks of vulgar curiosity. Perhaps you would like me to raise my skirts and remove my shoe so you can inspect it."

"I would, Lady Anne. Very much. But only at a more convenient moment, and when you are at ease with the idea."

Pure shock. He awaited her response with interest.

They had finally arrived at the bottom of the stairs and were turning toward the dining room. Uffham fell back to let Lord and Lady Benning enter first, and one of Lady Anne's options was to complain to her brother. Uffham, being Uffham, would react physically. Race could handle the bigger man, but it would create an unpleasantness and probably damage some furniture.

Perhaps that was why she said nothing. Instead, she proceeded into the room and took her seat at the table as if his words had never been said. Excellent. She intended to fight her own battles and, he hoped, expected to enjoy it.

Lord and Lady Benning sat at either end. With five at table, he and Uffham were placed on one side, Lady Anne on the other. Once settled, she looked across at him blandly, but he detected a declaration of resistance.

He smiled at her, and she blushed a little. Or perhaps

it was a flush of irritation. Did her lips do that little curl of suppressed amusement? Yes, they did. Lady Anne Peckworth was indeed enjoying herself, which was part of his intent.

When Uffham said, "You're looking in prime twig tonight, Annie," it was proof. He wasn't an observant man at the best of times, and if he'd noticed his poor crippled sister was looking pretty, it must be like a beacon. Lady Anne was the sort of woman who looked ordinary unless animated. She clearly needed to be animated, and he was the man for the job.

As everyone settled and soup was served, Race decided to give the lady a little time to regroup. He made a comment about a soup speciality at the Old Club in Melton Mowbray, and Uffham and Benning joined him in hunting talk.

He soon found it tedious. Lady Anne merely listened, or shared an occasional comment with her sister.

He had to keep reminding himself to pay attention to the men. With the slight changes in her appearance and the gentle glow of the candles, with the flickers of fondness and amusement on her face, Lady Anne Peckworth was distractingly lovely.

He'd noticed earlier, when assisting her with her shawl in the boudoir, that her neck was long, slender, and graceful. He'd had an insane urge to kiss the line of her spine where it disappeared into her practical dress. What would they have done then, her conventional family, who didn't seem to see her for what she was?

Her features were of such perfect evenness that they could appear boring, but not when she was smiling as she was now at something her sister had said, her eyes twinkling in the candlelight. She picked up her wineglass, and he noted her long, slender hands, her fine-boned wrist. It couldn't be so delicate as it looked. . . .

"Eh, de Vere?"

He snapped his wits together. "Definitely," he said to Uffham, relying on the fact that all Uffham ever wanted was someone to agree with him.

"Good, good. We'll have a grand time!"

He discovered he'd agreed to a trip to the Portsmouth area for yacht racing. Damnation. He hadn't intended to live in Uffham's pocket all summer, and he knew nothing about boats.

He kept his eyes off Lady Anne after that. She reminded him of another aspect of the Old Club—its deceptive punch that seemed all juice and spice but hit a man like Jackson's fist.

Four

Anne had thought that being on the opposite side of the table to de Vere would be a relief. He couldn't plague her with intrusive and inappropriate comments. She found, however, that she could hardly avoid looking at him save by fixing her eyes on her soup like a gauche girl.

She was careful, therefore, to let her eyes follow the conversation from person to person, but she still saw a great deal of the knave—all of it interesting.

Though his conversation was more normal with the group, there was still the edge of the outrageous to it. It generated high spirits and laughter, but she was surprised he'd survived to his present age without obvious evidence of violent attacks.

Then she remembered that he'd been in the thick of war. No wounds from that, either? Blessed perhaps, as is said to happen sometimes with madmen.

And yet, Racecombe de Vere wasn't mad.

He was, she decided eventually, chronically mischievous. From her experience, that was even more likely to lead to violent retribution.

How old was he? Uffham had said something. They were the same age. That made de Vere twenty-four. Past the age for mischief. And if he'd entered the army at about sixteen, as was usual, he had served for seven years up to Waterloo.

She realized that she had looked at him too long and that the footman was trying to take her soup plate. She gathered her wits. Mr. Racecombe de Vere was an excellent Pastime for a Lady, but nothing more than that. In fact, she decided with a suppressed smile, he was a very bonbon box of a man.

By the end of the meal, however, she had to accept that he was a delightful one. She'd thought him slight, and he was, but in some way his slightness and brightness began to make others seem heavy. His fine-boned features expressed ready emotion, whereas Uffham and especially Benning were leaden. Yet at the same time, something in his eyes, especially when they glanced at her, suggested more beneath.

She remembered her comment about men of mystery. It could be that he was hinting at secrets to tantalize. Women were often drawn into that trap, and yet, she was strangely certain that he was not wooing her. For one thing, he hardly ever looked at her, certainly not with the long, lingering looks of the suitor.

As the meal drew to an end, she realized that it had been the most lively and enjoyable gathering she'd experienced here, and that de Vere had orchestrated it. He hadn't taken the lion's share of the talk, however, which was very interesting, indeed.

She'd often encountered a wit who could entertain a party all evening as a solo performance, but de Vere was not that sort. Instead, he had thrown seeds that bloomed into conversation, and sometimes intervened to direct talk away from strife or unpleasantness. No talk of Luddites here, or of the riots in East Anglia and the north, or of the abandoned veterans wandering in search of work.

Part of her chose to disapprove, to see that as a flighty attitude to life. Had he not dismissed the subject earlier as "depressing"? On the other hand, it would have been tedious to hash over these matters again at the table, and quite possibly distressing to Frances.

The meal was over now, and it was time for the ladies to leave. Though reluctant to end this pleasant time, Anne glanced at her sister, looking for the cue. Frances, however, had a very strange expression on her face. It wasn't distressed, exactly, but she was bright red and . . . fixed, as if she had suddenly discovered that she was glued to her chair.

Anne leaned that way. "Is something the matter?"

Frances looked at her, and it seemed she was fighting laughter along with a great many other things. "I need the gentlemen to leave, Anne."

Anne looked at the men, who were in lively discussion of a horse race. It had to be something to do with the baby. Was Frances experiencing her pains? If so, why couldn't she say so? Or simply leave as usual.

But she must do as her sister asked.

"Gentlemen," she said loudly, so the three looked at her. "Er . . . Frances would like you all to leave the room."

They looked at her sister, who still had that fixed look on her face, though she wasn't quite so red.

"What is it, my dear?" asked Benning, hurrying around the table to her. "Is it your time?"

Uffham and de Vere were already standing, her brother looking alarmed as only a man can who thinks he's about to be involved in something he'd rather avoid. De Vere, typically, looked intrigued. And ready for action.

Anne had the strange thought that if action were needed immediately, de Vere would be the one to do it.

"Please," Frances said, biting her lip. "It would be best if you left me. But," she added to her husband, "I do think that Mrs. McLaren should be summoned, dearest. And Marjorie sent to help me."

"Good God!" Benning got a hunted look. Mrs. McLaren was the midwife. "Right. Of course. Come, gentlemen!"

He shepherded them out, but de Vere gave Anne a look as he left. A sharing of amusement and curiosity, and, she thought, a touch of support. A belief that she could do whatever needed to be done?

That was welcome. She knew nothing of these mysteries. Once the door was shut, she said, "Frances, what is it?"

Her sister still had that strange look, but now she did laugh in an embarrassed kind of way. "My waters. My gown and the chair are totally soaked. I'm *dripping.*"

Anne had no idea what her sister was talking about, but when she bent to look there was a puddle under the chair. Had Frances relieved herself involuntarily?

"Waters," her sister said. "The baby is in a bag of water. Mrs. McLaren warned that this sometimes happens. But oh, dear, I'm embarrassed to stand up!"

Anne feared she looked like Uffham. She felt completely inadequate to be involved in anything like this, but she stood and went to Frances. "You don't want to have your baby in the dining room. Come on." She put her hand under her sister's elbow and urged her up.

Where was Frances's maid? Since no one had arrived yet, she said, "Can you walk?"

"Oh, yes. Or waddle, rather." Frances suddenly smiled. "It is such a relief. These last weeks are hard, and I'm pleased to have them over."

"The baby is coming, then?"

"I believe so. I hope Mrs. McLaren arrives soon."

This hint of uncertainty, of worry, made Anne begin to shake. "Will you be all right? Will the baby be all right?" She knew immediately that it was the wrong thing to say.

"Mrs. McLaren said it posed no particular dangers. I have great faith in her." But Frances's hand went protectively to her belly.

Anne put all the bracing confidence she could into her voice. "Good. Let's get you up to bed."

Frances began to walk toward the door. "I need to change, at the least. Mrs. McLaren insists that a mother walk as much as possible before the birth."

It sounded barbaric to Anne, but she was not about to interfere. She opened the door and found the men hovering. Assuming it was what Frances wanted, she made a shooing motion. They obligingly melted toward Benning's study across the hall, though Frances's poor husband looked frantic.

Anne smiled at him, hoping he took it as reassurance, but to her sister, she whispered, "I think it would be a kindness to let Benning help you, dear."

Frances gave a little laugh. "Oh, you're right. How foolish it is to stand on dignity at a time like this." She turned. "Edward, dearest, will you help me up to my room?"

He dashed forward, and Anne gave up her place to him. She followed up the stairs, but Frances turned.

"Oh, no, Anne. You mustn't become involved in this! It's not right."
Anne was torn between wanting to help her sister and dread of the event. "I don't mind. . . ."
"Even so, dearest. Please."
Frances truly didn't seem to want her there, and at that moment her sister's middle-aged maid hurried down to help. Anne stepped back and soon was alone in the hall with her brother and Mr. de Vere.
"The midwife has been sent for?" she asked.
"Posthaste," said de Vere, who was projecting a noticeable calm. When things were dull, he enlivened? When agitated, he calmed? "You are probably thinking of tea, Lady Anne. In the drawing room? Perhaps we can share that with you."
"Tea!" scoffed Uffham. "Great Zeus, I need something stronger than tea! Benning mentioned a brisk fire in his study." He strode over to the door and flung it open. "There, see. And decanters to hand. Come on, de Vere."
Anne was suddenly abandoned—but then she found that de Vere had not moved. "I wonder if anyone thought to light a fire in the drawing room," he said. "Perhaps you could have the tray brought down here, Lady Anne, where it will be warm."
"Take tea while you drink brandy?"
"A little brandy in your tea will steady your nerves." Without waiting for her consent, he turned to the hovering footman and gave the order.
The unused drawing room would be cold. Frances had doubtless planned to take tea in her boudoir, but that was too close to whatever was happening. Cowardly, perhaps, but Anne didn't want to be where she might hear terrible things.
She particularly did not want to be alone at this time.
Women sometimes died in childbirth. . . .
She let de Vere escort her into her brother-in-law's very masculine sanctuary. She'd never been here before, and the roaring fire, the array of decanters, and the lingering scent of pipe smoke made it feel as scandalous as a house of ill repute.

Then Uffham produced dice from his pocket. "Hazard, de Vere?"

"That would leave Lady Anne as mere observer, Uffham."

Her brother stared at her as if checking for some strange new growth. "Anne don't want to learn to dice."

"I would think that Lady Anne would rather take part than observe."

She was suddenly aware of how much of her life she had spent as an observer, and not only of activities that her foot made difficult.

All the same, *hazard*?

"It's illegal!"

Uffham snorted. "As if anyone cares."

"Fortunes are won and lost in a night."

"Now that's true," he admitted.

"I will not game away my portion."

"We'll play for farthing points," de Vere said, "and translate them into golden guineas in our heads."

He was already moving a fine gaming table near the fire, and arranging three chairs around it and a stand of candles nearby. Shamelessly, he opened the drawers. "No dice box that I can see. I'm sure we can be trusted to roll fairly. We have our riches, though."

He spilled a bag of ivory counters onto the embossed and gilded leather table. "Consider the relief when we realize in the sober morning that the thousands we owe are mere pounds."

"Or," Anne said, sitting gingerly in the chair he held for her, "the disappointment that the thousands we have won will not purchase much."

He sat beside her. "You would hardly find pleasure in purchases made with money that others could not afford to lose."

"I wouldn't? Then what is the point of it?"

"The pure thrill, of course."

Uffham came over, bringing the brandy decanter with him, and threw himself into the third chair. "I'm with Annie. Where's the thrill in winning farthings?"

De Vere didn't argue, but he rose to get a third glass. He poured brandy into it and put it by Anne's hand.

"Fair play, dear lady. Not good form to keep your head when all around are losing theirs."

Anne stared at the glass, feeling as if she were being swept toward hell. "I do not drink brandy, Mr. de Vere."

"You just did so in your tea, Lady Anne."

"That was different. . . ." Yet Anne couldn't quite explain how. Irritating man. She ignored the glass.

He began a brisk explanation of the rules of hazard, of main and chance, and bewildering sets of numbers.

After a while she raised a hand. "I have the gist of it—I think. Why don't you and Uffham play a . . . main?"

His eyes twinkled. "A main is a round in cock-fighting."

"Which you doubtless indulge in, too."

"There are so few amusements in an army camp, Lady Anne. Especially ones that provide dinner."

She studied him. "Are you serious?"

"As little as possible. Shall we start? Uffham, you have the dice."

Uffham, clearly thinking such low stakes silly, put a counter worth twenty in the middle. De Vere matched it.

De Vere looked at her. "Why not lay a bet, Lady Anne?"

"But if Uffham wins, I lose."

"Such is life." His smile was playful. "It is, after all, only five pennies."

She put a counter with the others. "I will hold you responsible, sir."

"Oh, I am sure of it."

She realized then that he'd sucked her into his folly—and that it was a great deal of fun.

"The Main is seven," Uffham said. He shook the dice in his hands and rolled them—six and two, making eight.

"Eight is Chance," de Vere said in a quiet commentary, "and seven is Main. If he'd thrown the seven he called he would have won outright. That is called 'nicking' it."

"But now," she said, "he wins if he throws Chance—eight—and loses if he throws his Main, which is seven. Is that it?"

"Not quite, but it'll do for now. The odds are against

him. Would you care to place another bet? That is what makes it interesting, especially with many players. The losses or gains can be huge."

"So I have heard. I do not approve. . . ."

"Less talk," grumbled Uffham. "Are you betting, Annie?"

Just to show him, she put a spendthrift twenty in.

"I could refuse your outrageous wager, you know," he said with a grin, but he put a twenty to match hers and rolled the dice again. Five.

"No result." De Vere sipped from his glass. "Another bet?"

"No," Anne said, only realizing when the fiery spirit hit her mouth that she'd imitated his action. By great willpower she did not cough or gasp, but she feared her eyes were watering.

She watched Uffham's next roll through a haze, but it cleared to show a six. The shock of the brandy cleared, too, leaving a pleasant warmth. She took another sip. Now she was prepared, she began to find it most agreeable. Reminding herself that she was only playing for farthings, she put another twenty on the table. De Vere copied her.

"That's more like it," Uffham said, covering both bets, and rolled. Another six. Four. Five.

Two.

Uffham swore, then apologized.

De Vere pushed her winnings over to her. "A throw of two or three is Crabs, and always loses."

Anne gathered in her extra sixty farthings with a hoot of delight.

"I don't think this is a good idea," her brother said. "You're showing all the signs of turning into a gamester."

"You play."

"I have a large income and extremely large expectations."

"That's no reason to risk it all at dice."

"Of course I don't." He frowned upward, as if he could see through the ceiling. "I wish I knew what was happening." But then he shrugged and, with a "dare you" look at Anne, put a fifty onto the table.

Anne risked twenty. "It has to be all right," she said, as much for herself as for him. "Bad news travels fast."

"Especially over such a short distance." De Vere put in fifty. "Births take time."

Uffham called seven again, and threw eleven.

"Main has to be between five and nine," de Vere said.

He rolled again. Five.

"Five is Chance," she said, "seven is Main. Those aren't good odds either, are they?"

"You catch on quickly. Up the bet?"

She pushed forward another twenty, and so did de Vere.

Uffham threw seven, sighed, and paid up. He lost the next round as well, and passed the dice to de Vere. Anne was now nearly two hundred farthings richer. To fight the giddy excitement, she reminded herself that it was four shillings and tuppence. Even so, a greed quivered in her, and she could taste the fatal fascination of play.

De Vere put a twenty onto the table, said, "Six," and threw three. Crabs. He lost and paid.

He called six again, threw six, and scooped in their money, but it was a mere forty in winnings. Anne was still ahead.

Next time he called eight, then threw six. "Despite natural instincts, one should stick with a winner. Main is eight, Chance is six. The odds are against me. A wager?"

It was a general comment, but he was looking a challenge at Anne. She put down her largest single bet so far—a fifty. Uffham put in a hundred. She wished she had, too.

De Vere rolled a five. He looked at them again, and Anne put in another fifty. It was only just over a shilling, she told herself, but every nerve was on edge. She wanted to win, and she wanted to win a *lot*. She did not want to lose.

She sipped her brandy, watching every movement of de Vere's fine hands as he shook the dice. *Not six*, she thought at them. *Not six, not six.*

He rolled. . . .

Six!

She bit back unladylike words.

De Vere scooped in her money, smiling at her like a

devil welcoming souls to hell. He took Uffham's money, too, of course, but it was hers that mattered. She took another drink of brandy and leaned forward, keen for the opportunity to win it all back.

Then the door opened, and Benning strode in.

Five

"What news?" Uffham asked.

Anne fell back to reality with a thump. Important things were happening elsewhere, and she had been rapt in gambling. Benning looked put out to find his study invaded, but merely grabbed a glass, poured himself a large brandy, and drank a good part of it.

"The midwife is here, and Frances's confinement has definitely begun. The McLaren woman says all looks well. It will be many hours, however." He took another stiff drink, then looked at what they were doing. "Hazard. Good idea." He pulled up another chair.

Like plunging from warm to cold, Anne suddenly felt improper. She shouldn't be gaming while her sister gave birth!

The household had divided into male and female, and she was on the wrong side. She'd never been alone with men like this, not even with her brothers.

She stood. "I should go. . . ."

"Where?" asked de Vere, catching her wrist to stop her. "You will be more comfortable here, Lady Anne."

Her breath snagged at the contact, and she looked, startled, into his eyes. She'd never been so boldly touched by a stranger.

She'd never felt such a shocking effect.

He let her go. It could only have been for a second since it hadn't caused comment. She sank back into her seat largely because her legs weren't quite able to hold her.

He was right, though. She couldn't be with Frances. Everyone, not least her sister, would be horrified at an unmarried lady attending a birth. In truth, she didn't want to be there amid pain and hovering death.

Nor did she want to be alone.

She wanted to be here, in this warm room, in company. Safe, perhaps, in male company, engaged in a masculine activity, far from female terrors and mysteries.

The men were already gambling again, laying bets on de Vere's new throws. Anne took another drink from her brandy glass and determined to only watch.

De Vere held the dice for some time, winning and losing, until he threw out three times in a row and looked to Anne beside him. "Dice pass to the left. Ready to play, Lady Anne?"

To take the dice seemed a final step into hell, but she was tired of being an observer—in everything. She held out her hand and he dropped the dice into it. She rolled them in her hands, warm as they were from his.

"I'm said to be lucky, sir. Perhaps I will win your fortune, farthing by farthing."

Amusement twinkled in his eyes. "I, too, am said to be lucky, and I suspect my luck has been tested more than yours."

"Playing your military career like a trump card, Mr. de Vere?"

"You're confusing your games, Lady Anne."

"Less talk," Uffham complained.

She remembered with shock that others were present. Benning, at least, seemed too sozzled to care—or perhaps his mind was upstairs with his wife. She preferred to think that.

She put a modest twenty onto the table. "Luck is tested everyday, Mr. de Vere, in small ways and large. Some tests are simply more dramatic."

"A fine way to dismiss the field of battle, Lady Anne." He matched her bet. "*Bon chance.*"

Now she had other reasons to want to win. She called seven, which she gathered was the most likely roll, but rolled eight.

Now she had to roll eight to win. A seven would be a loss.

"Odds are against you," said the diabolical de Vere. "That's the hazard of playing safe—of picking the most common number as your Main." He put a hundred counter onto the table. "You can refuse a bet if you wish, Lady Anne."

A challenge, deliberately given.

"Of course not." When the other men put down the same bet, however, her palms began to sweat. She could lose three hundred on one roll.

A hundred farthings is only two shillings and one pence, she reminded herself. She'd pay more than that for a yard of cheap cloth. All the same, as she rolled she prayed for an eight.

Eight, eight, eight, eight . . .

Seven!

She understood why Uffham had cursed when losing. She felt almost tearful to see all her lovely "money" going into other hands. She'd win it back. She put a fifty on the table, and the men did the same.

"Eight," she said firmly, and threw—Crabs. "These dice are perverse!"

"Always are, Annie," Uffham slurred with a chuckle. "Always are. You're playing with the devil's bones."

Devil bones.

She could almost see wickedness swirl around the room. This place might as well be a gaming hell. It fit her imaginary picture of one.

The last daylight had gone, leaving only fire and candlelight, and the dark shadows beyond their circle. Uffham lolled in his chair, cravat loosened, and Benning didn't seem in much better shape. He'd summoned more brandy at one point, and she thought he and Uffham had drunk a good deal of it. De Vere drank, but she had the impression that the sips were small, and his glass was rarely refilled. She thought she was the same, but wasn't entirely sure. . . .

She threw again, wondering how affected by drink she was. She'd drunk wine with dinner as usual, but then there had been the brandied tea, followed by neat brandy. As she threw and won and gathered in some money, she tried to remember whether de Vere had topped up her glass at any time. Might she have drunk two glasses of neat brandy?

She was caster for a while and though she thought she

ended up a gainer by it, she could no longer quite keep track. Eventually she lost three in a row and passed the dice to Benning.

He held them, frowning. "Wish I knew what was happening. Damnable business." He turned to her. "'Anne, go and see? Don't let men up there, you know, but they'd let you."

"Intrude on the birthing?"

She, too, wanted news, but she didn't want to go there. To see things. To hear things . . .

Yet on this strange day that had swooped from *Pastimes for Ladies* to vices for gentlemen, she decided to test herself—to do something that frightened her.

She rose, alarmed by a slight waver, then got her balance. "Very well."

She limped to the door, but someone came with her. She turned to find de Vere there, holding her shawl. "You will want this, Lady Anne."

She would have liked to simply take it, but he was moving to put it around her shoulders, and there was no decorous way to avoid that. His fingers brushed against her bare nape for a moment and then were gone.

It was no more than had happened a hundred times before with her scarcely noticing it, but she felt a disconcerting shiver. It must be the effect of the strange night and circumstances, or perhaps the brandy. Perhaps that was why ladies were not supposed to drink brandy except watered, or in tea, for medicinal purposes.

She thanked him and hurried out, hearing the door click shut behind her.

The house lay silent but for the ticking of the hall clock, but it was not dark. A hall lamp had been left burning, and candles flickered in sconces on the upper landing. She stretched her ears but could hear no sounds from above. That suddenly seemed ominous. She hurried up the stairs as best she could, for once cursing her foot that made a nimble run impossible.

At her sister's door, she paused again, almost out of breath, but from fear not exercise. She was suddenly sure that something had gone terribly wrong. While she'd been drinking and gaming downstairs!

Then she heard voices in the room. Talking voices.

Low. Then sharp. Then low again. Some cries, or growls perhaps. Growls? Not screams, at least. No one sounded grief-stricken.

Then someone laughed.

With a gasp of relief Anne sagged against the white-painted panels, every muscle weakened.

Good heavens, it must be the brandy. Anne swallowed, forced herself straight, then tapped on the door with her fingernails. It seemed feeble, but a brisk knock was unthinkable.

She was about to try again when it opened a crack and Marjorie, Frances's maid, peered out. She looked a bit flustered, but otherwise normal in her cap and plain blue dress. "What is it?" she asked, quite rudely.

Anne bit her lip on laughter. The whole world was out of order tonight, when the womanly mysteries of birth ruled.

Then the maid blinked. "I beg your pardon, Lady Anne. Is something the matter?"

The maid was blocking any sight of the room and Anne was glad of it. She could hear, however. Hear clearly now. A working woman's voice with a Scots burr in a flow of encouragement and brisk instruction. Gasps and those deep groans that must, unlikely as it seemed, be from Frances.

Was she in terrible pain?

Anne swallowed to clear her throat. "Lord Benning would like to know if all is well with his wife." It came out thinly. Of course all was not well.

Was Frances dying?

Who had dared to laugh?

"Everything's fine!" called the Scottish voice. "Not long now. If you've a mind to be of service, whoever you are, you'll sober up his lordship so he's ready to welcome his bairn in decent style this time!"

Marjorie's eyes widened at this, and she turned to say, "It's Lady Anne, Mrs. McLaren. . . ."

In doing so, she opened the door further, and Anne glimpsed her sister sprawled in a low chair near the fire. The room was as dim as the gaming hell below, devilishly lit by flame.

Frances wore only her nightgown, and it was up

around her thighs. Her legs were bare and splayed, her head thrown back as she gasped and groaned in some extreme—

The door shut, cutting off the vision from hell.

Or heaven.

A buxom woman had been wrapped around Frances like a mother with a child, cushioning her head on a round shoulder, one hand between her legs, crooning almost. Anne almost felt she could slide into her sister's skin, into whatever raging forces racked her, into a world encompassed by warm, loving arms and a strong croon of encouragement. . . .

She turned to retrace her steps, dizzier by far than brandy could account for, or even her damnable foot, though she was unable to cope with it just now. She lurched down the corridor with one hand on the wall, trying to find her normal balance but thrown off by a raging vision she could hardly tolerate. . . .

And walked right into something.

Someone.

Racecombe de Vere.

She immediately pushed back, and he didn't try to hold her.

"Is it bad news, Lady Anne?"

As best she could tell in faint light and with blurred vision, he was for once completely serious.

"No. Or at least, I don't think so. That woman said"—strong arms, soft shoulder, crooning voice—"she said everything was all right."

She only realized then that de Vere still had his hands on her arms as if she needed holding up. Perhaps she did. Her legs were shaking, truly shaking. She wasn't sure she could walk another step. When he pulled her back into his arms, or perhaps simply stopped holding her up, she didn't resist.

Racecombe de Vere wasn't at all like Mrs. McLaren—he was hard not soft, and he wasn't crooning—and yet her need for this came from that glimpse of Frances. Then she thought with astonishing clarity that she could not remember being held like this since her own Scottish nurse, Mrs. Loganhume, had done so when she'd been a child.

Her head fit with comfort on his shoulder. His body felt firm and warm against hers. She was leaning, limp, and he was balanced and strong. Infinitely dependable. Her heart rate slowed, her legs steadied . . .

And she became vastly embarrassed.

She stopped herself from pushing away and screeching, but she detached herself from this intrusive stranger's arms, aware of her own fiery cheeks.

"I do beg your pardon, Mr. de Vere. What you must think of me . . ." Then she saw typical humor in his eyes. "It was you, sir, who encouraged me to drink brandy!"

His eyes twinkled even more. "With delightful results, Lady Anne."

She pressed hands to her hot cheeks. "Can I trust you not to speak of it?"

Humor disappeared. "It is hardly a tale that would buy me a dinner."

She was making a complete fool of herself and lashed out again in reaction. "What are you doing up here anyway?"

"Standing ready to serve. Is service required?"

She began to snap, *No,* but remembered the midwife's words. "Apparently Lord Benning should be sobered up to be ready to receive his child. I have no idea how to do that, but I assume you do."

"But of course." The humor was back, but she knew it was of a different sort, a cooler sort, and she regretted her rudeness. Men sank into their cups all the time, however, so of course he knew how to deal with it.

As he said, "Let's have at it," and extended an arm to her, she acknowledged that she missed the warm merriment.

The man irritated her to death. He was like a faery visitor in a nursery story, come to wreak havoc and turn an ordinary family's life upside down. In fact, there *was* something fey about him, about his light coloring and slim body, those heavy-lidded wicked eyes.

As she'd thought, however, he was strong, and as they started down the stairs, she was glad of his arm. Her legs were still not steady, and her foot fought her. "I am not drinking brandy again," she muttered.

"Or gaming?"

"Or gaming." But she was less sure of that. For farthing points it had been an exciting pastime. Certainly more so than plaiting straw.

Now she thought about it, being in the company of this man was an exciting pastime.

Flirtation. She'd been going to practice flirtation with him in preparation for an attempt on London society and finding a husband. How far away that all seemed.

How close he was.

Her breath felt different, as if it was spiced with brandy. Her heart couldn't seem to settle to a normal pace. When they reached the bottom of the stairs, the house was still and silent all around them. They were, in effect, alone, arm in arm. She could turn a little, and they could kiss. . . .

It was the strangest thought she could ever remember having. This man was a stranger and probably an adventurer.

It would only be a kiss. . . .

She remembered Frances, and reality, and the hundred and one reasons why she should come to her senses, and unlinked their arms.

"What do we do?" she asked him.

"Do?" he asked, as if he'd been able to read her thoughts. There was something about his eyes that made her think he might have been *sharing* her thoughts!

"About Benning."

"Ah. Yes." He shook himself. "We need cold cloths, as cold as can be found, strong coffee, and a pitcher of ale."

"Ale?"

"It sometimes works better than coffee. If you will point me to the kitchens, Lady Anne, I'll see if any servants are available."

"I'll go with you. They might not take orders from a stranger."

His crisp commands were irritating her, so she'd intended her comment to put him in his place. Of course, it had no effect. Words were as likely to depress this man's pretensions as a baby's hand was likely to depress a feather bed.

Baby . . .

She limped toward the kitchen, avoiding taking his arm again. "There will be servants awake on such a night, I think."

When she entered the big, warm room she was proved right, after a fashion. Mrs. Orwell, the housekeeper, was nodding in a big chair by the fireplace, a cat in her lap, but she was fully dressed. Her husband—the butler—and a footman were playing a card game at the big table. Hetty was darning by candlelight, and she leaped to her feet.

"Is there news, milady?"

The men rose, too.

"Not yet, but soon, apparently." Anne was reluctant to state that their employer was drunk. "We would like coffee in Lord Benning's study."

"Right, milady. Jeffrey, grind the beans." To de Vere, Orwell added, "His lordship called for more brandy moments ago, sir."

"You took it?"

"Jeffrey did, sir."

"I'll go and take charge. Coffee, Lady Anne, along with ale and cold cloths. As soon as possible."

Anne said, "Aye-aye, sir!" but he didn't seem to catch it as he dashed out of the room. "Insufferable man."

"Officer, milady." Orwell went to gently shake his wife awake.

Mrs. Orwell rubbed her eyes. "Is the baby here, then?"

"Soon, love, or so they say. Lady Anne's here needing coffee and the like."

It amused Anne to see the normally impeccable Orwells in disarray, and it touched her to witness the warmth between them. Not exactly passion, but something deep and real.

Another shift in her stable world, and right now she needed some stability to hold on to. Despite logic, she couldn't help thinking that Race de Vere was responsible for this rattling of reality. He must be responsible for the wanton thoughts that had just shaken her.

He was dangerous.

"Sit you down. milady," Hetty said, virtually placing

Anne in her chair by the fire and pulling up a footstool. "You're looking worn out."

Anne knew it wasn't tiredness, but she took the chair willingly enough as the servants bustled around drawing ale, grinding coffee, and pumping water until it ran cold enough.

Race de Vere. She realized that over the evening Uffham had sometimes called him that, and now it had stuck.

Racy.

An idle dilettante with racy inclinations.

Yet race also meant speed, as in a racing river, undercutting banks, carrying all before it. That fit, too.

Did people arrive at a version of their name that suited? What then of dull, common Lady Anne?

Or the nursery Annie.

Or Mouse, the name her foster brother, Tris, had always used with her. It was fond, but now it depressed her. Mouse, indeed. Small, dull, and hiding in holes. She knew Tris hadn't meant it that way, but it felt that way now.

What name did she wish she had?

Arabella. Barbara. That was nice and fierce. Florentia?

Serena.

Serena, Lady Middlethorpe, who was ravishingly beautiful and who had lain with Lord Middlethorpe back when he had not even been trying to kiss Anne. . . .

She would *not* start feeling sorry for herself, not tonight of all nights. And yet she was wishing she was not here. That Frances's confinement had waited a week until she was gone. Or that she'd retired to her room after dinner, perhaps even taken laudanum and gone to sleep.

Slowly, however, here among ordinary people and practical tasks, calm and common sense returned. She was a very fortunate young woman, born in silk with only one small trial to carry through life. If she lacked a husband it was her own fault for living like a mouse in a hole.

It couldn't be so hard to marry if she put her mind to it. She was a duke's daughter with a handsome dowry.

She would doubtless end up a mother herself one day and appreciate this introduction to the matter.

It was de Vere who had jiggled her life about so that she didn't know who she was or what she should be doing. So that she was having wild, wanton thoughts. And he was doing it for sheer amusement. When she'd asked him if he was serious, what had he replied?

As little as possible.

But then she remembered the moment of seriousness upstairs when he must have thought her unsteadiness was because of grief. And his decisive commands before leaving the kitchen.

Officer. Yes, she could imagine him in the midst of battle.

Exactly what was Race de Vere? What was real, and what was artifice?

Anne had to abandon that misty speculation to lead a procession back to the study. Orwell carried a silver tray with coffee and cups on it. Hetty bore a large bowl full of icily wet cloths. Jeffrey the footman brought the jug of ale and three tankards. Mrs. Orwell had stayed behind to keep an eye on the kitchen.

They entered to find Uffham snoring slackly undisturbed in his chair, but Benning awake if unfocused. His cravat was gone, and his shirt unbuttoned. Anne suppressed a giggle. Her stuffy brother-in-law was always neat as a pin.

"Your child is about to be born, Benning," de Vere was saying in that crisp officer voice. "You must be ready to greet him or her properly. First impressions, and all that."

Benning squinted at him. "Child. Right. Boy?"

"We don't know yet. The cold cloths."

Hetty hurried over, though Anne saw that her eyes were wide.

De Vere took a cloth and without hesitation wiped Benning's face with it. Benning spluttered and tried to fight free. De Vere prevented it with remarkable ease and wrapped the cloth around the drunken man's neck.

Benning yelled, eyes opening wide. "What the—? Plague and hell—!"

"You are needed, Lord Benning," de Vere said in a

voice that must have led men into battle. Without turning, he said, "The ale."

Jeffrey poured a tankard and hurried forward.

Anne retreated and watched in fascination as de Vere dragged her brother-in-law out of his stupor and into a state where he could form coherent sentences—most of which seemed to be blistering complaints.

"An attempt to thrash me would probably help in sobering you up," de Vere agreed. "Would you care to step outside and try?"

His voice was still precise, but an edge of impatience was audible. And tiredness. His face, she noted, was set in harder lines than she'd seen before. If it was fey, it was now from a darker version of faeryland, but in a strange way he was more beautiful like this than teasing and laughing.

Beautiful?

Yes, he seemed beautiful to her. Like the angel in the church, she remembered. An angel of the fiery, militant sort.

She realized she was leaning back against a bookcase, watching and weary, almost drifting on these astonishing events. How long was it since she had gone upstairs to find out what was happening? From here and in poor light she couldn't make out the clock. The room was still a hell lit only by flame. Uffham had slid farther down in his chair and was snoring softly.

Benning pushed to his feet, staggered, and then righted himself. "Damnation. Give me more of that coffee. Did you say the baby's born? Is Frances all right?"

"We don't know yet, Lord Benning," de Vere said. "But the midwife said it would not be long and you would want to be ready to hear the news."

"Right, right." Benning began to stagger around the room, but then noticed the servants. "What the devil are you doing here? Get on with you!"

They left, but gave Anne rolling-eye smiles as they did so. She felt like giggling, perhaps with exhaustion, and told Hetty to take herself off to bed. She could get herself out of this dress and her light corset, and she couldn't imagine sleeping until it was all over.

Then the clock on the mantelpiece began to chime, and she counted eleven. Late by country time.

Benning was lurching around the room, drinking and spilling coffee. De Vere was doing nothing but filling the coffee cup now and then.

Benning suddenly stopped. "Why is there no news? Why haven't we heard?" He glared at Anne. "When did you say the McLaren woman said the birth was imminent?"

Anne straightened, his worry kindling hers. "I didn't. She said you needed to be sober to be ready."

"Impertinent woman. Just because last time . . . Damnable business. Worse for the husband than the wife, if you ask me."

Anne wondered if deep inside he'd like someone big and soft to hold him in his arms.

"Can you go and ask again, Anne?"

She stared at him. It was a piteous, desperate request, but every muscle tightened in rejection. "Oh, no. Mrs. Orwell—"

"Just ask how long. See that everything's still as it should be. Please."

She felt nailed in place. She'd ventured off to do something difficult earlier, brave because of ignorance. Now she knew, and she didn't want to return to the fray. For some reason she looked to de Vere. His eyes met hers, expressionless.

She knew, however, she *knew* that he was daring her. No, it wasn't that. He was expecting her to, as an officer expected his men to march.

Or was he expecting her to fail?

Stiffening her resolve, she took two steps toward the door.

She was saved by it opening to reveal Marjorie, beaming, a bundle in her arms. "My lord," she declared, with excusable drama, "you have a son!"

Anne saw the sudden light in her brother-in-law's eyes, saw his unfettered joy as he marched forward to grasp the baby. "By God, by God," he said in a voice perhaps blurred with tears. But then swiftly, he asked, "And Lady Benning?"

"Is well, my lord. She said you were not to keep the baby from her for long."

"Indeed, indeed . . ." He left in a hurry, baby in his arms.

The door closed, and Anne found herself alone in the light of a dying fire with Racecombe de Vere and unsteadying, tumultuous emotions.

Six

She should leave. She should go to bed now. But she couldn't yet, and the only person available to her, it would seem, was this gadfly, this hard-faced officer, this fey mystery of a man.

Then Uffham snored.

Anne started, but she knew her brother. She doubted even cold cloths and coffee could restore him to a chaperon.

De Vere put another log to crackle on the fire, then went to the tray set on a side table. "The coffee is doubtless cold, but would you like some?"

Perhaps she, too, needed cold cloths. She felt disconnected from her real world, from Lady Anne Peckworth, the quiet lady of impeccable behavior.

"Yes, please." Her foot was aching, so she sat with relief at her seat at the table.

He put the cup and saucer before her. "Are you all right?"

"Why shouldn't I be?"

"I don't suppose this is a normal night for you."

"I don't suppose it is a normal night for you, either."

The candles he had set near the table so many hours ago were all burning low, sending irregular light to distort everything. She became aware of the smell of brandy heavy in the air, and the bitterness of coffee on her tongue. He hadn't sweetened it, but she decided not to complain. Bitter coffee seemed in keeping.

"I've only been involved with a birth a time or two," he said, sitting down opposite her.

"You've been involved in a birth before?"

She noted that he was drinking brandy not coffee, but she couldn't complain. He was certainly not drunk.

"An army camp is like a rough-and-tumble town, Lady Anne. Birth, marriage—or the associated bits—and death, it all happens underfoot."

"Then I hope you watched where you walked."

He laughed, a sudden, blessed relaxation. "Always, Lady Anne. Always."

There she went again. She never made risqué remarks. She was mistress of the art of light conversation that passed the time but touched on nothing that might discomfort or raise emotions.

She'd never before understood the phrase "not quite oneself."

"I try to always watch my step," he said. "A misstep, after all, can cause a fall. And a fall can cost a man, or a woman, paradise."

She focused her eyes and studied him. "Why are you here, Mr. de Vere?"

"Because Uffham is here."

"You are stuck to him like a . . . a barnacle on a ship's bottom?" But then her words summoned a most improper vision, and she hicced back a laugh.

"Now, what was that wicked thought?"

She kept her lips sealed, but he grinned.

"Mr. de Vere!"

"It was your thought, Lady Anne."

Her laughter escaped, even through her hand over her mouth.

Uffham stirred.

Anne stared at her brother in alarm. Had he heard? Had he woken? Might he remember any of this in the morning?

"Do you often have improper thoughts, Lady Anne?"

She swiveled her eyes to him. "Only, it would seem, with you, sir!"

"Ah, now that is interesting."

She thrust to her feet. "How do you *do* this? What is it that you do? You enter people's lives like . . . like a ball among skittles, throwing everything awry. I wouldn't be surprised if you started Frances's confinement!"

He stood, too. "It would be a remarkable skill if I did."

"You are a devil, sir!"

"And you are a saint? Does it not grow cold on that virtuous, unforgiving ground, my lady?"

"I'm sure hell's flames burn hot!"

"Perhaps paradise, therefore, is in the middle ground."

She stared at him. "I think that's sacrilege."

"Why? If we believe in a good God, do we not believe in a paradise that will be just reward for virtue? What, Lady Anne, would you choose for eternal happiness?"

The elementary question struck her dumb. Having no answer, she sank back weakly into her chair. "Have you known great happiness?" she asked at last.

He sat opposite her again. "One of the rewards of battle is the euphoria of victory, and especially of survival. The pleasure is so great that some men cannot live without it."

"But many die. Or are maimed."

"Contrasts, Lady Anne. Contrasts." He rolled the dice over the scattered counters. They came to rest at two. "Crabs, I die." He looked up at her. "Perhaps pleasure is always equal to the hazard involved. That is why people play for high stakes, you know. In games—and in life."

Race thought that perhaps she understood him. He was not keeping her here, after all, and for her this was a hazardous encounter.

"A duke's daughter is not allowed to play dangerous games," she pointed out.

"A well-behaved duke's daughter."

"You advocate wickedness?"

"I advocate being what you want to be."

"Beautiful." She threw it like a dart. "I want to be as beautiful as Lady Middlethorpe."

He saw her realize what she had revealed. She grasped her brandy glass, then realized that it was empty. She shoved it over to him.

He picked up the decanter. "I am honor-bound to remind you that you vowed never to drink brandy again."

"I've changed my mind. A lady is allowed to do that. A gentleman," she added, "is not." But then she grimaced. "I must make it clear that Lord Middlethorpe made me no promises. Nor did Lord Wyvern."

He filled her glass and passed it back. "You have no need to be envious of any woman's looks."

"Do you claim that I am a raging beauty, Mr. de Vere?"

He gave her the truth. "No."

She laughed and toasted him. "Well, here's to honesty!" When she'd swallowed a mouthful of brandy, she added, "Lady Middlethorpe is. A great beauty." She drank another sip. "He got her with child while he was courting me."

Ah. He hadn't realized it had been quite like that. He didn't know Middlethorpe, but he'd thrash him given the chance.

"And Lady Anne Peckworth was, I am sure, completely the lady about it. No admission of envy. No spurt of anger. But what," he asked, "did you feel?"

He thought she wouldn't answer, but then she said, "Anger."

"A deadly sin. Perhaps you should have shown it."

"Not showing anger was the only way to retain my dignity. . . ."

"Pride."

"Not at all. I needed to stop Uffham from calling him out."

He wished he'd been there to support her. "A virtue, I grant you, though I don't know which."

"Wisdom, perhaps?"

"If you can, Lady Anne, by all means be wise."

She pushed the brandy away. "If I were wise, sir, I would not be here with you. I should go."

She didn't rise, however, and he was glad of it. They were progressing, but he wasn't sure she was hatched yet. "You are better off, you know, without a dutiful husband who wants another."

"True. But then there's my sister."

"Lady Benning?"

"No. My younger sister, Marianne. She's in love. With a hero. Captain Percival Shreve."

"Are you saying you love him, too?"

She looked at him with astonishment. "Of course not. He's still suffering from his wounds. They want to marry, but my mother will not permit Marianne to marry before me. I suspect she doesn't want the marriage at all because Percy might be an invalid for life. And now Lord Wyvern has married another . . ."

She blinked—tears? "I don't know why I'm telling you these things."

He spoke softly so as not to stir her. "The strangeness of a strange night. You'd be amazed at the things men tell each other around a campfire the night before battle."

"Or around a birth? You make a very unlikely midwife, sir."

He laughed in genuine humor. She was a delight when slightly tipsy, and her comment was closer to the truth than she knew. Could he hope she was feeling newborn?

She rolled her half-empty glass between her pale, slender fingers. "So now I must find another husband, and quickly. And one who will stay the course."

He hadn't counted on this urgency. "There is no need of desperation, Lady Anne. You are a prize."

She peered at him. "Did Uffham bring you here for me, after all? I will *not* be courted out of pity again."

"So I should think. And your brother, my dear lady, would shoot me if I aspired so high."

She frowned at him. "Who *are* you?"

"Racecombe de Vere."

"I mean, who are you really? Where do you come from?"

"London."

"Where is your *home*?"

"A soldier's home is where he hangs his hat."

She tossed the contents of her glass in his face.

Anne pushed to her feet, horrified at herself. "Oh, I'm sorry! I don't know what came over me. . . ." She looked around for some sort of cloth.

He produced a handkerchief and dabbed his face, seeming amused. "Don't fuss. I was being irritating as usual." He calmly refilled her glass and put it in front of her. "I was born and raised in north Derbyshire, not far from Chesterfield."

Anne settled back into her chair, dazed. He was like no man she had ever known. Perhaps he truly was fey, here to bewitch them all.

"Is your name really de Vere?"

His mouth quirked. "I know, I know. The extinct de Veres. I assure you, Lady Anne, I was born to a father called de Vere and christened Racecombe de Vere in a Christian church."

No mystery at all. An ancestor must have been a de Vere on the wrong side of the blanket and taken the name.

"I'm sorry," she said. "I was intrusive."

"Naturally so. I have been prying into your affairs all day."

She looked at him again. "Why?"

"You interest me, Lady Anne. For example, you cannot have lived entirely in seclusion. You must have had many suitors."

"Fortune hunters, or those wishing to push their way into a ducal family."

"Are you sure?"

"A lady can tell where a man's interest truly lies."

"A pleasant belief, but a gentleman can also tell if he is viewed with suspicion. Striving for heaven on earth could be a prescription for disappointment."

She tried to apply her fuzzy mind to his comments. "You think me too particular? If you do not believe in being particular, Mr. de Vere, why are you not married?"

"Have pity, Lady Anne! I'm under a year back from war and no great prospect."

"You are a younger son?"

Something in his quick look made her think he didn't like that question. Eventually he said, "No, but I ran away to the army, so my father owes me nothing. He will likely leave what he has elsewhere."

"Why would he do that?"

"Because I irritate him as much as I irritate you. It is my role on this strange stage of life."

He rose suddenly and went to fuss with the fire.

Anne watched with some satisfaction. She'd finally hit a sensitive spot on Mr. Racecombe de Vere. His family. He'd probably been cast off.

Horrid to be so nosy, but he fascinated her and in more than his background. The way he spoke, the way he teased, the way he moved. She watched him in the firelight, the lines of his body somehow made clear to her despite his substantial clothing.

Broad shoulders, long back, lean hips, strong thighs . . .

He rose smoothly, as if to emphasize the latter, limned by firelight. "Why have you avoided society, Lady Anne? Because of the limp?"

That jerked her out of foolish wanderings. "No one, Mr. de Vere, raises my deformity without a blink as you do!"

"I was not aware that it was a secret."

"It is too obvious to be a secret, but . . ." She found herself without a rational protest to make. "I simply do not enjoy idle social gatherings."

"I see. The limp is not your handicap. It is your excuse."

If he wasn't so far away, she might have flung her drink at him again. "And what is yours, sir, for being a shooting star with no fixed point in the firmament?"

"My nature, of course. Who would tolerate me for more than a month or two?"

"The army did."

"It was touch and go at times."

And that smile was back, that rueful, self-mocking smile that made her tremble.

A spent log tumbled on the fire, and light flared over him. Transient light. The fire would die soon if no one put on more wood. This wild unsteadiness would die soon, too.

She felt he might disappear at daylight like the fey creature he seemed. She could not bear for it to end just yet.

She pushed to her feet. "Mr. de Vere."

He stilled.

"You offered to serve me. There is one way in which you could."

"Yes?" His eyes were steady and wide. His instincts were very good. A wicked imp inside delighted that she finally had *him* off balance.

"I must go into society and seek a husband—but I am handicapped by a lack of experience."

"As you pointed out earlier, Lady Anne, a lady is not supposed to be experienced."

He was definitely on the defensive! Mischief bubbled up in her.

"There is experience, sir, and experience. I am a duke's daughter and thus rarely encroached upon. Because of my crippled foot, my family are very protective. A lady who has been out in society for four years could be expected to be a little more . . . knowledgeable."

He walked toward the table, watching her. Picked up his glass and drank. Drank more at one go than she'd seen him drink all evening.

"What knowledge, precisely, do you want, Lady Anne?"

What knowledge, precisely, would you provide if asked?

Astonishing to think that tonight there was nothing and no one to prevent the most wicked excess. Her family were either asleep or engaged in other matters. The servants would not come at this hour unless summoned. She had never before in her life been so unprotected—so free—as she was now in her brother-in-law's proper house, with her brother in the same room.

She flickered a glance at Uffham, but he was completely unaware.

"Kisses," she blurted.

"You have never been kissed?"

She supposed his astonishment was flattering.

She looked down and fiddled with the scattered counters. "Only in the slightest manner. If I am to encourage men to court me I need to know how to act and react."

She studied him. Faced with his silent disapproval, she added, "You say I have been discouraging, but we ladies are warned against permitting liberties. I need to know what to permit."

"In this situation, my lady, nothing."

His distancing "my lady" made her want to giggle. Who was the skittle now, and who was the ball?

"I've seen Uffham drunk before," she said. "If the room were to catch fire we'd probably have to drag him snoring to safety."

The look he shot her was as much exasperation as amusement, but he went over, hitched her brother higher in the chair. "Uffham, it's time to go to bed."

The regular snoring might have hesitated for a second, but then Uffham sagged back down in the chair.

De Vere turned to look at her, shaking his head. "Lady Anne, you have drunk too much brandy. You are going to be very embarrassed in the morning."

"I don't feel drunk." In fact, she felt alive, uninhibited by convention, and astonishingly bold. "And if I'm to feel embarrassed, I might as well have something to be embarrassed about. Would it be so very difficult for you to kiss me?"

She said it lightly, but then something cold flowed through her, washing away the glorious confidence. He didn't want to kiss her. Of course he didn't. Why did she think he might?

"I'm sorry. I should not have—"

"Anne." His voice, his use of her name alone, stopped her.

He came toward her, seeming completely steady. "I have no objection to kissing you. It is only that I do not want to take advantage of the moment."

"You are bound to say something like that. I have embarrassed you and myself."

He took her hands. "Remember. I nearly always say exactly what I want."

"*Nearly* always."

"What pressure is there here to prevaricate? Are you going to shoot me, or court-martial me?"

She found herself laughing, her hands still warmly in his. "I think you could drive a person to shoot you."

He smiled. "But not you. Or not over this. Very well. Kissing lessons." He bowed low and kissed first one hand then the other.

"Hand kissing is not much practiced anymore," she

commented, amazed at how breathless that simple contact made her. But it was two contacts—both his lips and his hands on hers.

When meeting gentlemen, she was usually gloved. When had a stranger last touched her naked hands?

"And not with the deep bow." He straightened, her hands still in his light but firm grip. "If any man kisses your hands like that, he is a mountebank. Don't trust a word he says."

"I have made a mental note of it, sir."

He looked down. "Your hands are lovely."

"My *hands*?"

He raised them, turning them in the unsteady light, her familiar hands with only two small rings.

"Lovely." He looked up, and she saw no mischief or teasing at all. "If ever, some time in the future, you feel this kissing lesson was of value, Lady Anne, send me a sketch of your hands."

She wasn't sure whether to be flattered or offended. "My *hands* are my finest feature?"

Now the mischief was back. "I would have to inspect the whole of you to make that judgment, dear lady, but I admire them profoundly."

He raised them to his lips and kissed each, a gentle but firm kiss, then looked into her eyes. "This is the hand kiss of a man who knows how to soften a woman's heart and mind." He brushed his lips over her fingers, and then over her knuckles.

She felt it on her skin, up her arms, then down, curling, into her belly.

"I see."

She heard the breathiness of her own excitement, but beneath it flowed melancholy. Lord Middlethorpe had kissed her hand like that when departing, when promising to return in a few days, with the clear implication that he would then ask for her hand in marriage.

"Is your mind softened?" he asked with an impish look.

It snapped her back to the moment, but she feared he might have seen something, guessed something. "Not at all."

"Good. It is too easy a trick."

He kissed her knuckles again, this time with lips parted so she felt breath and perhaps even moisture.

She swallowed. "How should I regard a man who does that?"

"Very warily, but he might be honestly devoted."

"I would know him to be skilled at these things. Is that a virtue?"

"Such skill is like a sharp sword—excellent in some hands, but worrying in others. Surely some of your suitors have tried this ploy."

"It never had much effect. It never felt sincere." De Vere was not sincere, and yet his courtship of her hands was having an effect. "You, Mr. de Vere, are a prime example of skilled, are you not?"

"Me, Lady Anne?" He was innocent as an angel. "I have spent most of my adult life with the army. True, there were occasional gracious moments, but if I have talents, they must come to me naturally."

"Or unnaturally."

He laughed and let one hand go. The other, he turned and pressed a kiss into the palm with what sounded like a hum of pleasure.

Her breath caught and a shiver that was certainly not of horror rippled through her. When he raised his head and looked at her, she tried to make her face blank, but she wasn't sure she succeeded. Therefore, she reacted in the only other way she could think of. She turned his hand and brought it to her own mouth to kiss.

Oh, dear. Now she knew why a man might do something like that. The hollow of his hand seemed a personal place, a private one. One not often seen or touched. It was warm and smelled softly of . . . of flesh, she supposed. It was smooth except for a ridge of scar tissue that ran straight across.

She moved the hand away and studied it.

"I grabbed a saber. I was gloved, but it was still a damn stupid thing to do. I'm lucky to have full use of my hand."

A vision assailed her—him in battle, fighting for king, country, and for his life, all fiery purpose and spring-steel strength . . .

"Seduction comes in many forms, doesn't it, Mr. de Vere?"

He removed his hand from her hold. "No one, Lady Anne, is seducing anyone tonight."

Seven

"Of course not," she said, but she missed his touch like a long-familiar friend.

As the fire failed, the air was growing chilly. One candle spluttered wildly and then died. She should leave. She should have left long ago.

"You're right, however, about methods of seduction," he said. "Some will try to woo by being pitiful. Resist."

"Being wooed that way, or wooing?"

"Have you ever used your foot to try to snare a man?"

"I have never tried to snare a man at all."

"How exasperated some of your suitors must have been."

"Why? What do you mean?"

"You are a duke's daughter, a princess within walls of power. A little encouragement would have been welcome." He tugged her into his arms. "What would you have done," he asked, fitting her against his firm body as if it were the most natural thing in the world, "if one of those unpromising gentleman had done this?"

"Insisted that he let me go."

But she whispered it. Perhaps it was because they were so very close, but perhaps it was to avoid any chance of waking Uffham at this most interesting moment. There was no place for her arms to go except around his neck. Her heart was fluttering, and various parts of her body were, she felt, coming fully alive for the first time.

Her fingertips against his collar.

Her legs brushing his.

Her breath almost close enough to his to blend . . .

"And if he did not?" He held her closer still so she was pressed to his body along her whole length, encircled as she encircled. It had been much the same earlier, in the corridor outside Frances's room, but it had been oh so different. Then she had been weak with shock and fear, but now she felt not weak, but soft . . .

Except her breasts, which seemed firm and sensitive where they pressed against him.

"Well," he asked, brushing a kiss against her cheek, speaking close by her ear, "what would you do?"

"Scream for help?" It was the merest breath.

"If you scream, Uffham may not wake, but someone will come." He drew back a little to look at her. His eyes still smiled, but to her they were full of deep and alien mysteries. "You really should scream, you know."

"I won't. You have my word on it."

"No matter what I do?"

A shiver of fear ran through her, and yet she could not do the sensible thing and pull out of his arms. "Yes, I will scream if necessary, but I will warn you first."

"You play fair. Perhaps it is time for you to call me Race."

Transfixed by him she said, "Oh, no, Mr. de Vere. I think that would be most unwise."

His smile was sudden and delightful, digging disarming brackets into his cheeks. "Wise lady."

And then he kissed her.

It was a gentle pressure on her lips, and something she had experienced before. A gentleman or two had stolen such a kiss before being told to desist. Never before, however, had she been wrapped so intimately in the man's arms, shaped to him, melded with him. Her senses swirled out of all balance to such a tame kiss.

And to think, she could have been doing this for years!

When their lips parted, she stared at him. "Do you truly think I have been discouraging?"

"Most men would tremble in their boots at the thought of courting a daughter of the Duke of Arran."

Another log shifted in the grate, its dying flames dancing against the fine-boned edge of his face. "Are you trembling, Mr. de Vere?"

"A little. A lesson, Lady Anne. Even a man with no serious intentions can become seriously intent with a lovely lady soft in his arms in the wicked hours of the night."

She could see the truth of it in his eyes. When she sucked in a breath, she felt as if he breathed with her, as if they could blend even more closely together. "Is it too dangerous to proceed? I will scream if you alarm me."

"Are you easily alarmed?"

"I have no idea."

"Don't scream. You have only to whisper stop." Then his eyes twinkled. "If that doesn't work, pull my hair out."

His arms tightened, and his lips covered hers with sudden force that knocked out what little breath she had, whirling her into dizziness. Ruthlessly, he ravaged her, open mouthed and wet.

Some instinct made her open, perhaps to object, and he blended their mouths, silencing her. Despite faint clamoring bells of outrage, Anne surrendered.

Surrendered to his clever mouth, as clever in this as in everything else.

To his hands, moving, exploring, making nothing of her sturdy dress.

To his whole body and hers, trying to merge through layers of clothing that she had once thought protection . . .

When he stopped, when his hold loosened and she found the strength to push free, she gasped, "I cannot possibly let just any man do that!"

It was loud and Uffham's snoring halted. As one, they turned to look at him, to watch as he sagged again into deep sleep.

Dear heaven, she had done that in her brother's presence! It had been so dazzling, so staggering, that she feared the echoes might linger in the room to tell what she had done.

"You let me do it," de Vere pointed out, "and I am as close to just any man as makes no difference."

She hit him. His head shifted under the crack of the blow. Her hand stung.

After a horrified moment, she tried to rub his cheek better. "Oh, I'm sorry. I'm sorry! I don't know—"

He grasped her hand. "Calm, calm, my dear. I was being irritating again."

But he did not pull her hand from his cheek, and she felt his firm face with the slight roughness along his jaw. Because of his blond hair she couldn't see any shadow there, but in some way the roughness made his dangerous maleness more potent in the darkened room.

"It was shock at myself," she whispered. "I don't know what came over me."

"The kiss, or the blow?"

"The kiss . . . The blow . . . Both!"

"Such a shocking night."

He was laughing at her!

She pulled free and distanced herself, smoothing her gown as if every crease stood witness to wickedness. "You will not speak of this?"

"You insult me, Lady Anne." Then his expression softened. "It was not so very bad, you know."

"It was appalling!" She caught his look and shivered. "Don't pity me, Mr. de Vere. That I will not tolerate!"

"If you marry, Lady Anne, your husband will wish to kiss you that way. If he doesn't, then I do pity you."

"In marriage it will be different."

"Perhaps, but I recommend some ardent kisses before you say your vows. What if you do not like the way your husband kisses?"

She had no brandy left, but his glass still held some. Boldly, she drained it. Then she pressed the glass to her cheek, which felt hot enough to have been slapped. "I wish you had not come here."

It was, without doubt, the most discourteous thing she had ever said to anyone in her life.

The fire was down to a sullen glow, and all the remaining candles guttered. She looked at him, wanting to take the words back, wanting a great many things she could hardly put words to, feeling the truth of the words bite her. She did wish he had not come and scraped all her sensitivities down to the raw.

He seemed, for once, completely serious. "I am sorry if you think I have done you harm, Lady Anne. It was never my intent." He bowed—a proper, sober, and respectful bow. "I will not distress you again."

He walked out of the room, and she was alone. Except for snoring Uffham.

Deliberately she poured another half inch of brandy into the glass and drank it, mouthful after mouthful. What had happened here? What had made her behave so unlike herself? What had changed her?

She did feel changed. In the morning she might be embarrassed. She might even suffer the ill effects of drink. She didn't think, however, that the effects of this night would fade like a headache or a dream.

There was no mirror here, but she doubted that she was physically changed. Inside, however, she was like a shuffled pack of cards—all there, but in a different order, ready to deal entirely different hands.

Good, or bad?

Surely that was up to her.

In a few short hours Race de Vere had taught her a great deal about men and about herself. She could see now that she had let her own insecurity make her discouraging. She had never considered that her suitors might be even more nervous than she, fearful of offending her or her powerful family. And, of course, her limp doubtless made her seem fragile, to be handled with care.

Race de Vere had paid it no heed at all.

She drained the last of the brandy.

For a moment she thought of getting to know him better, but then she shook her head. Her family would be appalled, and society would think she couldn't do any better. Poor Lady Anne de Vere. It would be as bad as poor Lady Claretta Crump.

She hovered, wondering whether she was being realistic or cowardly. Perhaps Claretta was madly happy with her Crump. Perhaps sometimes a person had to be wild, to gamble, to call a Main that wasn't seven. . . .

No. Hazard had proved exciting as a pastime, but gambling was no way to live, especially with the odds so heavily against her. She touched the ivory counters rather sadly. After sifting them through her fingers, she took one and put it in her pocket, a reminder of the pleasures of the evening and the pressures of reality.

Then she picked up her silk shawl and wrapped it around herself. The room was cold now. Her knitted one would have been more practical. That was what she had to be. Practical.

There were still some weeks left of the season. She would go to London—to the Marriage Mart—and find exactly the right husband, one who could give her exactly the right life.

She wanted a home similar to Lea Park—an elegant country house and a substantial park.

She wanted a husband with little taste for London affairs. Once she had her husband she would be happy never to go there again.

She wanted a life companion who was intelligent. No stultifying conversations by the fireplace.

And not a gambler. She would have complete security.

And, of course, he must be desperately enamored with her. She could not bear to have another man drop her on the way to the altar.

Was it possible? At the moment, brandy-fueled confidence burned high, but she feared that tomorrow poor Lady Anne would return. Terrified or not, however, poor Lady Anne was going to London.

She was at the door when she remembered her oblivious brother. It would serve him right to spend the night in the chair and wake up sore all over, not only in his head. She was a dutiful sister, however, and so she went to rouse some poor servants to carry him to his bed.

Race shut the door of his bedroom and leaned against it, breath unsteady. Matters had run out of control down there. It had never been his intention to get to kisses with Anne Peckworth. Especially kisses of that sort.

That blood-sizzling sort . . .

Thank heavens she was too sensible a woman to

screech the house down. Or to take the kisses to heart and think they signalled commitment.

Sensible!

He reviewed that assessment and headed for the brandy decanter his kind hosts had provided. Lady Anne Peckworth was doubtless sensible in many ways, but as far as men were concerned, she was as sensible as a March hare. Twenty years old, and hardly been kissed.

He'd seen her once before, months ago in London. What had he thought then?

Conventional.

Yes, he thought, pouring brandy into a glass, if he'd had to put a descriptive label on her that day, it would have been conventional. Simply another aristocratic lady at another social gathering, dressed in something pale, pale flowers in pale hair, pale gloved hands clasped in front of her, pale smile in place.

Nothing like the vibrant woman he'd seen when Uffham had taken him into Lady Benning's overheated boudoir, even if her bright eye and pink cheeks were because of her comment about a Derbyshire ram.

Did she know the song that went by that title?

As I was going to Derby, all on a market day,
I spied the biggest ram, sir, that ever was fed in May.
This tup was fat behind, sir, this tup was fat before.
This tup was nine feet tall, sir, if not a little more . . .

She'd have blushed even more at the line about the tup's balls.

She was pretty when she blushed, even stunning.

Of course, when he thought of it, that occasion in London had probably been not long after Lord Middlethorpe's marriage when she was still smothering anger beneath placid smiles. Her words about Lady Middlethorpe had revealed the depth of that wound.

He itched to punish Middlethorpe, but he was one of the Company of Rogues. Poke one and you poked the lot of them.

Anyway, he was, in a way, here as an agent of the group. He might have come anyway, but the leader of the Rogues, Nicholas Delaney, had hinted that someone should make sure that Lady Anne didn't suffer. "Can't be a Rogue," he'd said to Race. "By now I'm sure she'd shoot any of us on sight."

Race liked Delaney, and he'd thought him right. He was here, however, mostly because it was his fault that Lady Anne had lost another chance at marriage. He'd held back the commitment letter Con had written to her. If it had been delivered, Con would never have backed away.

Race didn't regret it. Con and his Susan were perfect for each other, and Anne would not have benefited from a dutiful marriage. He'd created the wound, however, and it was for him to heal it.

How could he have known he'd be affected like this?

Worse, how could he have known she would be affected like that?

Perhaps he should have.

He was attractive to women, though he didn't know why. He didn't have rugged manly looks, but at the same time, he didn't spout poetic compliments. He had neither lineage nor fortune and no ambition for greatness, and he was more likely to act the fool than the hero.

Yet women fluttered to him. He knew men who reveled in that sort of gift, but he'd found it to be a Midas touch, especially during his army years.

War was not a place where a sane man fell in love or bound himself to a woman—or brought children into the world, poor mites. Between battles, however, it was an excellent place for games. In that hothouse of danger and boredom he'd often charmed the right sort of woman into giving favors, the sort of woman he could leave happy.

But then there had been the wrong women.

Letty Monke-Frobisher came immediately to mind. Letty had been his colonel's eighteen-year-old daughter. She'd flirted with him under her father's nose and sent appalling perfumed letters. As a final insanity, she'd slipped into his billet one night dressed only in a cloak. He knocked back the rest of the brandy and went to get more. Letty had terrified him more than a host of French battalions, and after that he'd learned to be very careful.

Until tonight.

Another inch of brandy in his glass, he contemplated the bedroom door. He went over and locked it. He didn't think Anne Peckworth was the sort for such folly, but who could tell with women? With that in mind he decided not to drink any more brandy. His head was buzzing.

As he stripped for bed he reassured himself that Anne had too much sense and good breeding to chase any man, especially into his bed. He slid between the chilly sheets, turning his mind to a problem at Con's Sussex estate. Better to think about anything other than Anne Peckworth.

The feel of her in his arms. The perfect fit . . .

Con's grandfather had leased the land for ninety-nine years. . . .

With a groan, he remembered Uffham. Hell's tits. He was here as glorified servant, and he couldn't leave his patron down there in a hard chair. He rolled out of bed and grabbed his banjan.

Judging from his earlier test, he didn't reckon much for his chances of rousing Uffham enough to get him up the stairs by himself. Was he going to have to rouse servants in a strange house at this time of night? Be damned to it. He grabbed the eiderdown and a pillow off his bed. He'd roll him on the floor and swaddle him up warmly.

He went to the door and turned the knob. Why the devil wouldn't it open? Then he remembered and unlocked it, laughing at himself. He was still smiling when he opened the door . . .

. . . and saw Anne coming along the corridor toward him.

She stopped, sudden color creating her special, delicate beauty in the wavering glow of the candle she carried. After a stunned moment, he realized why she was staring at him. He hadn't fastened the top buttons of his robe, and the eiderdown and pillow were under his arm, not clutched to his chest.

He moved them, hoping that she couldn't tell how fast and deep his heart was pounding. "I'm going to make Uffham comfortable," he explained softly.

She licked her lips. Her full, soft, pink lips. The arch of her short upper lip was painfully enchanting.

The pounding intensified, drowning sense. Two steps and she would be in his arms. A few moments and she could be in his room.

A few more and she could be in his bed . . .

He sucked in a breath. Was he mad?

Her soft voice fought through the fog in his mind.

"The servants are bringing him," she said. "Now."

He heard it then. Soft voices and clumping footsteps coming up the stairs.

"We mustn't be caught here like this," he said, fighting hot blood and laughter.

Her color deepened. "No."

She didn't, however, move, and neither could he.

His laughter became a smile, and he didn't try to stop it. Magic danced in the gloomy hall like sparkling fireworks. He didn't try to stop himself from stepping forward to kiss her hot cheek, then her lips, then her cheek again, from inhaling the subtle flower perfume that would always linger as hers . . .

"Good night, my dear," he said, meaning good-bye. Then he retreated back into his room, his last image of Anne with eyes wide, cheeks pink, and lips parted in surprise.

Or hunger?

Yes, he thought, back to the door again. That had been hunger as shocking to her as it was to him. If he'd swept her into his room she might have come, and perhaps the cataclysm that followed would have been worth the inevitable, disastrous price.

He was here to help her, dammit, not to ruin her! Tomorrow he'd get Uffham out of here at the earliest possible moment, and then he'd avoid Anne Peckworth for the rest of his life.

But no, he couldn't. He couldn't hatch her out of her protective shell and then abandon her as a mere fledgling.

Temptation tugged at him. He could win her if he tried. It would mean an elopement—the Duke of Arran would hardly approve of a husband such as he—but he had one advantage to offer. He did truly care for her.

He shook his head. One person's caring did not outweigh a loving family alienated, a life of elegance lost. He'd seen marriages like that in the army, ones where ladies of high birth had run off with dashing officers. There had always been an edge of bitterness to them, especially if the mad passion that had caused the union faded under time, hardship, and too many children.

He stayed where he was, listening as footsteps and quiet voices passed by, as a door opened and shut. Uffham's. As another door not so very far away closed. Anne's.

He let his imagination follow her as her maid helped her out of her dull blue dress—was her underclothing as plain and practical, or was there lace and embroidery there? As the maid brushed out her soft, silky hair . . .

The house settled at last into the silence of the night.

Race sucked in a breath and pushed away from the door. Then, as symbol rather than precaution, he turned the key before getting back into his chilly bed.

Eight

~

Anne woke the next morning feeling fuzzy. Feeling, in fact, like a well-used horse blanket. Hetty had just drawn back the curtains, and Anne squinted at the bright light.

After a moment she decided that she didn't have a drunkard's headache. That was something. Her head felt as if it were stuffed to bursting with that rank horse blanket, but it didn't exactly hurt.

Her mouth was sticky and foul, however. She wanted water, but didn't want to move, and so she lay there trying not to think about Race de Vere. About her last sight of him.

A blond angel in a silver robe. That vee of muscled chest. That something in his shadowed eyes that had held her still, set her heart racing, stirred wild thoughts . . .

Enough! She pushed up, hissed, and gave her head a moment to settle. Then she remembered the important things.

"Is all well with Lady Benning and the baby?"

Hetty beamed. "Yes, milady, and Lord Benning's given all the servants a guinea in celebration! Are you going down to breakfast, or do you want it here?"

Down?

Where she might meet him?

He'd been *naked* beneath his dressing gown.

And he'd kissed her—kisses on cheek and lips in some way more shattering than the heated embrace in Benning's study. He'd smelled of soap and something else. Something physical . . .

Through the open door of his room she'd seen his bed

rough from his sudden rising. She'd imagined walking into that room, getting into that bed.

She blew out a breath and pushed hair off her face. Those were the feelings a woman should have about her husband, or the man who would be her husband—

"Milady?"

Anne started. Hetty was still waiting for instructions. About what? Breakfast. "Just tea and toast, Hetty. And a drink of water, immediately."

Hetty brought the water and hurried off to get the breakfast. Thank heavens she'd sent Hetty to her bed early last night, that she'd not been here to see her in whatever state she'd been in.

She pressed hands to her cheeks at the thought of what the servants might be thinking. Did they know she'd spent time—how much time?—with Race de Vere?

Then she lowered her hands and studied them. They were elongated. Not at all plump. Her wrists were bony, her arms too thin. Like the rest of her.

He couldn't have meant what he said about them being lovely.

And now she had to take her bony self off to London to find a man who would truly think her lovely, who would fall deeply in love with her. So deeply that there was no possibility of him being snared by some other woman.

She groaned. Had she really told de Vere all about that? About her feelings about Middlethorpe. About her fears?

Pray heaven she didn't have to meet him again. She hoped Uffham wasn't too under the weather to leave. She knew he'd want to. A house of birth and babies? He'd think of it like a house of contagion.

She climbed out of bed and caught sight of herself in the mirror. Heavens above! Did she usually look so tousled and wanton in the morning? She heard footsteps and quickly splashed her face with water.

Hetty returned, chattering about the baby. "Marjorie says Lady Benning is sitting up and eating hearty, milady. A right easy birth."

Then heaven save us all, thought Anne, *from a hard one.* "Go and see if I can visit her, Hetty."

Anne began a proper wash, soaping her hands, feeling kinship with Lady Macbeth, who was somewhere on the family tree. *Out, out, damned spot!* And yet, hands and face clean, she did not wish all those kisses gone. They had been far more educational, elucidating, and yes, even entertaining, than anything in *Pastimes for Ladies.*

A pastime. That was all it had been, like the straw box that must still be in Frances's boudoir. This time yesterday that had been her biggest problem.

She cleaned her teeth, which was a great improvement.

Then something shone in her eye and she turned, realizing that there was sunlight outside. She limped to the window. This side of the house did not get the early morning sun, but it was reflecting from the stable block windows, and the sky was blue.

Glory hallelujah! She could go riding. That would sort out her befuddled wits. Monmouth would be full of himself after three days in the stables.

Hetty came back. "Lady Benning asks if you will take your breakfast with her, milady. Which dress would you like?"

Hetty was already laying out shift and corset. Anne leaped back to the mundane with relief and reviewed the simple wardrobe she'd brought with her. She'd anticipated only a quiet country visit.

"The pink sprig, Hetty." That was the prettiest gown she had with her. "Are the gentlemen up?" she added, trying to sound as casual as possible as she discarded her nightgown and put on the shift.

Hetty helped her on with the corset and started to tighten the laces. "The master and that Mr. de Vere have breakfasted, milady. Not Lord Uffham, though, as yet."

If Uffham was under the weather, he was unlikely to leave soon. If Uffham decided to stay another night, de Vere might be interested in a ride around the area. Riding out with a gentleman known to her family was acceptable behavior. . . .

Anne wriggled her shoulders to settle into the snug garment. "Lay out my riding habit for later, Hetty."

She could feel her heartbeats and knew she was being wicked, but she couldn't help it. After all, even Frances had said she needed practice at flirtation.

Hetty dropped the gown over her head. Anne glanced in the mirror and was startled by how well the pink suited her. It had been ordered during her consolation trip to London after Middlethorpe. Her mother's prescription for all ills was new clothes. Since it was a summer dress, she'd worn it only once, and then it hadn't looked quite like this.

Her lips and cheeks seemed pinker, and even her breasts seemed a little larger. Hetty hadn't dressed her hair yet, and she impulsively decided to leave it loose on her shoulders, at least for her visit to Frances.

When it came to a shawl, however, she lost her nerve and picked up the plain knitted one. She wouldn't want anyone to think she was going to extraordinary lengths. She wrapped it around herself and hurried along to Frances's room, Hetty following with the tray. She only realized when she arrived that speed and shawl weren't necessary anymore. Sunshine had begun to warm the house.

She passed the shawl to Hetty as she went to Frances's bedside. "You look so well."

It was true. Frances, in a pretty peach bedjacket and lacy white cap, was blooming. A cradle draped with golden silk sat on the floor by her bed, a nursery maid beside it, ready to serve the baby.

"As do you, dear! Pink suits you." Frances beamed at the cradle. "It all went splendidly, and little Charles is a picture of health. Mrs. McLaren said she'd rarely seen such a strong feeder."

Anne tried to match her vibrant sister with the sprawled, overwhelmed woman she'd glimpsed last night and decided it was simply a mystery. She turned to admire the tiny infant sleeping beneath white, lace-edged linen.

"He's beautiful," she whispered. It wasn't exactly true, but it felt true.

"You can pick him up. He won't mind, and I want to

hold him again." Frances turned to the nursery maid. "You may go for a while, Alice."

The maid curtsied and left. Frances chuckled. "I don't think she trusts me with her treasure. They can grow too possessive if allowed. Remember when it's your turn that you must be firm from the very beginning. Don't worry. Just support his head."

Anne had dealt with babies before in her charity work, though never one quite so young. She peeled back the covers and lifted the tiny, swaddled child. His bowed lips worked for a moment, but then he settled again, a soft, warm weight. She held him close and sat on the edge of the bed.

"I do want babies of my own."

"Of course you do."

Anne glanced at her sister. "A baby requires a father."

"You have only to snap your fingers."

Anne laughed. "Hardly that."

"As good as. A duke's daughter with a handsome dowry?"

Typical of Frances to be so direct and practical. In her own way she was as meddlesome as the rest of the family. Late pregnancy had turned her thoughts inward, but now she was present and alert again.

"I would like to be married for more than my money and my family connections."

"And so you shall be," Frances said, a shade too heartily for Anne's liking.

Perhaps this new feeling of being pretty rather than passable was an illusion. After all, she hadn't lived like a cloistered nun, and she'd never been pestered by devoted admirers. It must be done, though.

"I intend to go to London, and let Caroline do her worst."

"Her best, you mean. Splendid! If a lady wants her choice of men, she must go where the most men are." But then Frances cocked her head. "What about Mr. de Vere?"

Anne stared. Had the servants noticed something and talked? "What about him?"

"He's Uffham's friend."

A flicker of excitement stirred. If Frances thought of de Vere as a possible husband . . .

"That's no great recommendation," Anne said, watching her sister's reaction. "What's more, Mr. de Vere makes no secret of the fact that he has no particular birth or fortune."

"Oh, what a pity."

It was said without rancor, which made it all the more fatal. Well, of course. What had she been thinking?

"Benning rather admires him," Frances went on. "He confessed that he got into his cups, poor lamb, and that de Vere sobered him."

"Which shows that he's had plenty of practice."

"If he's had practice at sobering men up," Frances pointed out, "then he hasn't always been drunk himself."

"I have no interest there anyway," Anne said firmly. "He's a pleasant pastime, nothing more."

Her louder voice startled the baby, who let out a wail. Anne tried to calm him, but Frances demanded her child and unwound the cloths to reveal tiny fingers that stretched for a moment, seeking who knew what.

Anne gave thanks for the distraction and sat to tackle her uninspiring breakfast. She regretted not asking for more. "Did you find it difficult to fix on the right man?" she asked, pouring fresh tea.

Frances looked up from little Charles. "Oh, no. As soon as I met Benning I knew. You will, too. It is an awareness. The man becomes special. Stands out from the others. Did you not feel that way about Middlethorpe or Wyvern?"

Anne buttered her toast, considering it. "Perhaps a little with Middlethorpe, but not with Wyvern."

"Then you've had a lucky escape, dear."

Despite all her efforts, Anne's mind swung back to de Vere. Awareness? Did being extraordinarily irritating count? What did a lady do if an unsuitable man stood out from the others? . . .

Her thoughts were interrupted by Uffham, looking surprisingly alive for this time in the morning, though his eyes were bloodshot. Anne began to tingle—but de Vere was not with him.

"Came to have a look at the little fellow before setting

off," he said, boots thumping as he approached the bed. At least they were clean now.

Setting off? Anne's stomach clenched around the inoffensive toast.

"Tiny thing, ain't it?" he assessed.

Frances pulled a face at him. "Quite big enough, I assure you, Stuff, and the picture of health."

"Good, good! I gather Benning sent for Mother. She should be here this evening." He leaned down to kiss Frances's cheek.

"What of Mr. de Vere?" Frances asked.

"What? He's coming with me, of course."

"I mean, what of his future?" Frances's eyes flickered to Anne for a moment.

Anne wanted to gag her.

"He seems to be such a capable man," Frances went on. "Perhaps he needs employment. As your secretary, for example."

Anne stared. What was Frances up to? A secretary was almost as low as a governess—and if de Vere was Uffham's secretary she'd keep meeting him.

"I don't need a secretary!" Uffham protested.

"You would if you did anything serious," Frances pointed out.

"Don't start nagging me. I can't interfere in a man's life without him even asking." He was already retreating toward the door. He glanced at Anne. "All right, Annie?"

Unclear what he referred to, she simply smiled and agreed. He passed on thanks and suitable good wishes from de Vere to Frances, and then he was gone.

"What was all that about?" Anne demanded.

"De Vere?" Frances queried innocently. "Nothing in particular. I liked him, and as far as I can tell he does need employment."

The baby began to fret, and Frances put him to the breast. It was an interesting enough process for Anne to let her eyes and part of her mind rest there. The rest of her mind was accepting that Frances had relegated de Vere to the multitude of people who were beyond the charmed inner circle of the Peckworths and the haut ton. They were to be employed and sometimes assisted, but never to be considered equals no matter what their qualities.

It was as well that de Vere was leaving, that last night had been like a faery visit, never to be repeated.

And besides, he was obviously not interested in seeing more of her. He must have worked hard to rouse Uffham and have him ready to travel so early. Even after that encounter in the corridor, and those three sweet kisses.

What mortifyingly embarrassing message had she conveyed to him? She felt as if she had a lump of dry toast stuck in her throat. She took a deep drink of her tea and then another, trying to wash it away.

She heard something and turned to look outside. Through the window she watched two horsemen ride away from Benning Hall, one on a dock-tailed chestnut, the other on a long tailed bay.

"There they go," she said, carefully careless. "Mr. de Vere rides well."

In fact, he had a perfect seat, completely one with the bay.

"Cavalry, I understand." Frances's attention was obviously all on her child.

"Yes. Quite a hero."

Anne almost wished she could see him in battle, which was ridiculous. She'd seen too many of the wounded to want more war.

In truth, she had no idea what she wanted, but she recognized that last night she'd brushed against something dangerous—the plague that ran through history impelling people into folly, danger, and death.

She remembered the Lady Anne Peckworth of the seventeenth century who had fallen in love with a Parliamentarian during the Civil War and died for it.

Last night she had been tempted. Thank heaven that temptation was riding away. Her family would have a collective fit of the vapors, and as de Vere had said, Uffham would shoot him for his impudence.

The riders passed out of sight.

Anne turned away from the window to butter a new piece of toast. "So," she said, "how do I attack the Marriage Mart?"

Nine

Anne left Benning Hall the next day in the family coach with outriders that had carried the Duchess of Arran to Frances. It took her home to Lea Park to choose clothing and ornaments suitable for her husband hunt. As she supervised the packing, the temptation to stay was powerful. Lea Park was at its spring best, and every morning she rode Monmouth for miles, astride even, without meeting anyone who might disapprove.

Riding was her time of greatest freedom, the time when she wasn't crippled at all.

Those of her family who were at Lea Park were pleased to see her back—her father, her two younger brothers, and Eliza, her youngest sister. Marianne was visiting her beloved at the Gravender dower house. At Benning Hall, the duchess had confirmed what Uffham had said. She didn't think it right to let sixteen-year-old Marianne marry before her twenty-year-old sister.

No argument had changed her mother's mind, which didn't surprise Anne. The Duchess of Arran was a strong-willed woman, and she had her mind set on good marriages for all her daughters. Earlier in the year she had bent to let Anne's nineteen-year-old sister marry the Earl of Welsford. The fact that he was an earl had probably been the major factor, though the fact that Caroline could twist their father around her fingers had helped. That one capitulation, however, made another even less likely.

Another reason for Anne to marry.

Over her week at home, she said a silent good-bye.

The people on the estate and in the village who knew

they could depend on her acted as if she'd been away for months. She worried about them, but she was not, she told herself, indispensable.

There were friends here, too, of all sorts, but there was no point weeping over that. Women of her rank were born and raised to live elsewhere. In time her new home would be as precious to her as this one, and she would have new friends.

When it rained she slipped off to the muniment room to work on the Women of Peckworth, trying to get as much done as possible.

When she was fourteen, she'd heard of that Lady Anne Peckworth who'd suffered a tragic love for a Parliamentarian. She'd gone to the family archivist to see if there were any records of the story.

She'd discovered that Dr. Plumgate was a severe historian who was interested in the Peckworth papers only as they interacted with the great matters of their times. He produced an annual annotated index of them for the use of scholars, and published occasional excerpts in the *Monthly Magazine.*

He'd lectured her on her trivial tastes and tried to interest her in the letters of the duke of the time, which would educate her about the political aspects of the war.

Anne, however, had always had a stubborn streak, and she was the duke's daughter, so he had eventually shown her a small room where such idle matter was stored. Despite dust and disorder, it had been like a treasure trove.

She'd found boxes and bundles of records that were considered unimportant, almost entirely by women. She unfolded letters and opened diaries and recipe books. There were even laundry lists and household accounts.

Dr. Plumgate was right. These were nothing compared to the papers he cared for, but they fascinated her. She loved coming to recognize the handwriting of the different women, and how each document opened a window into the ordinary lives of the women who had come before her.

At first she had attacked her treasure like a child, but she'd soon realized that she risked making things even worse. She'd begun to try to organize the papers, but been defeated by the sheer mass of them. Nervous but determined, she'd returned to Dr. Plumgate.

She remembered how surly he had been, clearly seeing her as an idle disrupter of his work. He'd given her some quick lessons simply to get rid of her. When she'd returned day after day, however, he'd come to inspect her work, and after that, he'd regularly checked on her and given additional advice.

He'd also helped her learn to decipher the ancient handwriting, which was often the hardest part. He was still taciturn, but these days they had an agreeable working relationship. If he came upon anything in his important documents that related to the distaff side, he would leave her a note and reference. To her delight, she occasionally found something in the women's papers that she could alert him to.

She'd always known that she could have mobilized the dukedom in this interest if she'd wished to. She was poor crippled Lady Anne, and if she had a harmless enthusiasm she could command anything she wanted. A suite of offices. An army of clerks. Dr. Plumgate's entire attention.

She'd never wanted that. Her interest wasn't exactly secret, but it was private, between her and her fascinating female ancestors. The only servants she used were two maids whom she summoned now and then to dust a newly emptied shelf and wash it with vinegar.

Now she read again the letters and papers to do with that Lady Anne who had first stirred her interest. She had let her heart drag her into disaster. Anne, raised on stories of gallant Cavaliers and wicked Roundheads, had at first found it hard to understand how her ancestress could ever have fallen in love with the enemy.

A more subtle understanding of history had shown her that things were never black and white and that there were usually good people on both sides. Now she felt she had a new insight into the power of attraction. Had the seventeenth-century Lady Anne been appalled by her own desires? Had she struggled against them?

Better for her if her unsuitable lover had not returned her feelings. As it was, they had run away to marry. Later, she had been torn from her husband's arms and had seen him slaughtered by her brother. She'd been carried abroad when her family fled. She'd died not long after, miscarrying a child.

Had it been a natural death, the result of a broken heart, or had it perhaps been murder? The duchess of the time had been an unforgiving woman. Anne could imagine her forcing that poor Anne to take something to get rid of the child, and everyone knew that was dangerous. She could even imagine the duchess killing her child to clean away the shame.

Thank heavens she lived in a gentler time. But then, she had no idea what her parents might do if she tried to behave so outrageously. She had always been so good.

She packed away those papers and turned to her work-in-hand—deciphering the scribble of the fifth duchess's sister. When the light began to go, she realized that this was the end. Tomorrow she left for London, and she would not return here again as a home.

She carefully folded the letter, fighting a sick feeling in her stomach. It shouldn't matter. This was another Pastime for Ladies, and she would have her own house to run, children to raise. . . .

But it did matter. She looked around at the clean, ordered shelves, which still contained so many unexplored documents. She thought of the book she'd planned—a family history viewed from the women's side. She'd never have it published in the regular manner, of course, but she could have a few copies printed for her family.

A husband might not approve such an indulgence. He certainly would not want a wife who spent hours poring over old laundry lists! And in fact, unless she took all this with her, there would be nothing to pore over.

It was like a death. She stood and limped around the room, trailing a hand over boxes. She opened the one that contained her indices and notes, the basis of the book to come.

It was like a stillborn child.

Oh, this was silly. She rarely found a reference to anything important. Her fascination was mostly the thrill of reading private documents. It was almost as base as gossip.

And it was over. She put away the letter and capped her inkwell. Life involved changes, and this was another one. Perhaps her husband would have family papers and she could continue her work there when she had time.

Suppressing all sadness, she took farewell of Dr. Plumgate, then summoned her father's steward to go over the arrangements for the short journey to London. She had already written to Caroline to tell her when to expect her.

"Off, are you?" her rotund father said that evening in the family drawing room. "Don't let Caroline run you ragged, Anne."

"I won't, Papa."

"Shame you're on your way tomorrow. Uffham wrote to say he might drop by. Been down near Portsmouth. Some sort of yacht racing. But then, you saw him at Frances's place, didn't you?"

For a moment, words failed her. Would de Vere be with him? "Yes, yes I did. . . . Perhaps he'll go on to London."

The duke chuckled. "If he does, I doubt you'll be moving in the same circles. The poor boy is hounded to death. I told him—better to arrange a marriage in an orderly way and get it over with, but he doesn't listen. Modern times, modern ways. On his own head, on his own head. But I'm sure if you need his escort, Anne, he'll do the right thing."

"Oh, no, that won't be necessary, Papa."

If Uffham squired her around, de Vere might be nearby. Her task would be hard enough without that sort of distraction.

As soon as Anne entered Lord Welsford's town house, her sister Caroline exploded upon her with squeals and exclamations and dragged her to a vastly overdecorated boudoir.

Three months of marriage clearly suited Caroline. She had always been pretty, but now she glowed. This served to fix Anne's mind even more. She wasn't sure marriage would make her glow, but she was sure it would work the miracle for Marianne.

She would clear the way. She knew that once she was

out of the way her mother would not be able to block the marriage for long. Their father was too kindhearted. He believed that daughters were the wife's business, but in the end he could be brought to interfere.

As for Caroline, it was all "Welsford says . . ." and "Welsford thinks . . ." At least Welsford, eight years Caroline's senior, was a sensible man, so what he said and thought was useful.

"You are truly going to give the lucky men a chance?" Caroline whipped Anne out of her light pelisse and bonnet and passed them to a maid along with a command for tea.

"Sit!" she said, pushing Anne onto a pink sofa. There was a great deal of pink in the room.

"Caro! Let me catch my breath."

Caroline sat on the opposite sofa. "I'm sorry. I'm so excited that you are here. How wonderful it must have been to be there when Frances took to her bed. I can't wait to give Welsford a son. He is the most perfect husband!"

Caroline sighed. She beamed. She glowed.

In fact, she glowed suspiciously bright.

Was some of it *paint*?

Anne's instinctive disapproval was replaced by curiosity. Had Caroline always used paint to help create her vivid appeal? Would it work for her? If she was going to do this, she would do it to the full.

"The whole world is talking about Wyvern, of course," Caroline rattled on. "Imagine the old earl married years ago and with a son. A son, moreover, who has been acting as estate manager with no idea of his legitimacy! It's as good as a play."

Anne came alert for special meaning, especially pity, but saw none. "It's accepted, then?"

Caroline waved a hand. "It all has to go through courts and committees and things, but Welsford says it will likely stick. A Guernsey marriage, but apparently that works as well as Gretna for the civil courts. And then the lady—the mother—took up with a smuggler who is now transported, and the lady has gone after him! It is all too delicious. In fact, Mr. Lockheart is said to be writing a play around it all. And here is Wyvern—Amleigh again now—married to his rival's sister."

Then, belatedly, she went stricken.

Anne smiled. "It's all right. I wasn't going to marry him."

"Oh, good. I did think him rather dour. We can do much better than that for you now you are willing to play your part."

Anne suppressed a grimace at the *we.* Letters had doubtless been flying as her whole family campaigned to get her to the altar. It was all out of love, however, and this time she was going to cooperate.

"Frances mentioned Race de Vere."

Anne stared at her sister in shock. She'd thought that idea dead.

"But I don't know what she was thinking," Caroline added.

"Nor do I. Her mind was probably engaged with little Charles."

But Caroline was eyeing her. "Frances seemed to think there was something between you."

"Childbed madness." Anne prayed she wasn't blushing. "Why would I even think of marrying someone like that?"

Caroline shrugged. "He is amusing, and he's good for Stuff, you know. Distracts him from his wilder friends, though they do say he's a black sheep. De Vere, I mean."

"Or a black ram . . ."

"What? You *are* interested."

"I'm *curious*. He did behave well during the crisis. If there were a way for the family to help him, I think we should."

Anne felt positively saintly for making this suggestion. She had refused to search the Lea Park library for information about any de Veres of Derbyshire. That would be fuel on the fire. It wouldn't hurt to find the man employment though, and it would get him away from Uffham so she'd have less danger of meeting him.

Caroline lounged back on her sofa in a way that would have caused a lecture in the schoolroom. "It's all very mysterious. Stuff says that de Vere is an only son but is at outs with his father who never wanted him to go into the army. Even so, it must be a very minor property. I looked him up, and there's nothing about any de Veres in Derbyshire. Or anywhere, in fact. Welsford says they died out long ago."

"A bastard line, I assume."

"I suppose so. He is a charmer, though, isn't he? Prudence Littleton is absurdly enamored of the man."

"*What*?" Anne hoped that she hadn't sounded outraged.

Though they were alone in the room, Caroline leaned forward to whisper. "Stuff says she writes de Vere the most imprudent billets-doux, and she's not the only one!"

"De Vere reads them aloud for his friends' amusement?"

Caroline drew back. "No, of course not! Or at least, I don't think so. Apparently the featherhead sent one under cover to Stuff, begging him to be sure de Vere received it, as he'd not responded. Can you imagine? Stuff told only me, and I wouldn't tell anyone but the family."

Anne doubted that and felt sorry for foolish Miss Littleton. Thank heavens that she'd resisted the temptation to write him a note care of Uffham. Nothing embarrassing, of course. Merely a thank-you. But thank heavens she hadn't.

A liveried footman—a fashionable black man, Anne noted—brought a tray of refreshments, which was a relief all around. She was hungry and thirsty, and did not want to talk about Race de Vere.

As Caroline went importantly about the tasks of preparing tea, Anne absorbed the fact that for Race de Vere she was one of hundreds of tediously admiring ladies. Intolerable!

Her twisted foot had made her interested in Lord Byron, who was similarly afflicted. As a result, she'd followed the embarrassing course of Lady Caroline Lamb's pursuit of the poet.

All London had been at his feet, but Caro Lamb had carried it to disastrous lengths. Despite being a married woman and mother, she'd acted scenes in public, invaded his rooms in man's clothing, and written him embarrassing letters which *he* had not hesitated to share with others. As a grand debacle, when he snubbed her at a ball, she'd slit her wrists.

A warning there for all women who believed themselves in love, and chose to believe, despite indifference and rebuffs, that their beloved returned their feelings.

"So," she said, before Caroline could recollect the subject of their conversation, "how do I embark on my husband hunt?"

Instantly distracted, Caroline outlined an exhausting involvement in the final weeks of the season.

Anne accepted the cup of perfectly prepared tea. "Perhaps it's flattering that you've forgotten, but I can't dance."

"Bother! But you can't avoid all the balls and assemblies. It's where so much of the season takes place."

"As I know to my infinite boredom. I will sit with the older people as usual."

"And have the same result. It paints you as a wallflower. Or even a fixed spinster." Caroline sipped her tea, then nodded. "We will make it the fashion for men to sit out with you. You are excellent company when you choose."

Anne put down her cup. "You think I sometimes choose *not* to be good company?"

Caroline colored. "Oh, no!" But then she said, "You do sometimes. It's as if . . . as if you turn down your wick."

Anne absorbed that. "Almost twenty-one seems an advanced age to be learning so much about myself."

"Whatever do you mean?"

"Someone else suggested that I use my crippled foot as an excuse to avoid people."

Caroline's eyes widened. "Do you?"

"Perhaps. I weary of company after a while. It might be different if I could dance, but sitting out, there is nothing to do but talk. And"—she pulled a face—"so many people have no conversation."

Caroline was not sympathetic. "The French have a saying that it is necessary to suffer to be beautiful. Perhaps for you it is necessary to suffer tedium to find the right husband."

Anne laughed and chose a small iced cake finished with sugared violets. "As long as I don't have to marry tedium."

But then she wondered what she might sink to as time passed. There were only a few weeks of the season left. She might have to take the best that presented. She was determined on getting this done.

Caroline had cocked her head and was studying Anne with a thoughtful frown—the sort to make any sister wary. "Because you've been out for years, people are used to you. They have preconceptions. You need to signal that you are different now."

"A label, saying 'Now open for wooing'?"

Caroline smothered a laugh with her lavishly ringed hand.

Seeing the flash of them, Anne said, "I think I could like to be a bit more flamboyant with jewels." She finished the cake and added, "Shall I tell you a terrible secret?"

When Caroline nodded—clearly astonished that her quiet sister might have a terrible secret—she revealed in a whisper, "I have never liked pearls."

Caroline's eyes widened. "Oh, me neither! I adore emeralds, though." She spread her hand to show a pretty ring of five small emeralds. "Welsford says I mustn't wear heavy ones until I'm older. He's probably correct, but I have my eye on a splendid emerald and diamond brooch. A brooch is different to a necklace, wouldn't you say? And he has brought me a delicious collar of small emeralds and pearls. Pearls are pleasant enough as contrast with the brighter jewels, wouldn't you say? What about a cane?"

Anne had been flowing on the torrent of chatter, but this jerked her out of it. "*What*? Of course not. I'm not so crippled as that!"

Caroline, however, had a faraway look in her eyes. "One must make a statement. I have my rings, and"—she stuck out a foot—"my slippers are embroidered with jewels and beads."

Anne saw that indeed, Caroline's white satin slippers were decorated with small gems and beads.

"Mostly inexpensive," Caroline added, "though I do have diamonds on the pair to go with my spider net gown. But you see, they make me different. Intriguing. Do you know Mama had jewels on the heels of her evening shoes when she was young? I wish heeled shoes were in fashion."

"And I thank heaven they're not. I have trouble enough as it is."

"I suppose so. But you do need a statement. Welsford suggested the shoes because he knew it would amuse me, and of course he likes having a wife who makes her mark on the ton. He hired Philip for me—the footman who brought tea—and had a livery specially designed. Lady Welsford's livery. Philip goes everywhere with me. Another statement, you see."

Anne wanted to protest that she'd be happier fading as usual into the flock of discreet, well-born, unmarried ladies, but she knew that Caroline had a point. She wasn't a new face. It could take forever to convince the eligible men that she had changed, and she didn't have much time.

"An outward sign might help, but what sort of statement would a cane be? *Behold, here comes a cripple?*"

Caroline shook her head so her curls jiggled. "No, no, not at all! It would say . . . It would say that you're not ashamed of your foot. Oh," she said, bouncing on her seat, eyes brilliant, "not a *boring* cane, Anne. That's not what I mean. A magnificent one! Tall, more like a staff. Beautifully made and with ribbons to match your outfit of the day."

Anne began to take the idea seriously. "I confess, I like the idea of declaring my limp. I do try not to hide it or seem ashamed of it. After all, it is nothing to be ashamed of. So why not make something of it? And in practical terms, a staff could be useful. I do sometimes feel unbalanced."

"There, see! And—"

A knock at the door interrupted, and the Earl of Welsford entered, smiling. He was in many ways a quite ordinary man, of average build, with fine brown hair. He'd always been distinguished by excellent fashion sense, however, and by a keen mind. Anne had learned that he also had a kind heart.

Caroline swiveled to greet him. "Welsford! See, Anne is here at last."

"So I heard, my dear."

Anne hadn't seen them together since the wedding when Caroline had glowed with excitement and Welsford had seemed to be a very happy man. That was to be expected at a wedding, however.

Now she saw magic.

It was as hard to pin down as a sunbeam, but something bright sparked on their shared gaze. Ten years lay between them, and Caroline had always been a little wild, so Anne thought Welsford must have worked quite hard to create such a deep bond. But then, perhaps she was underestimating her sister.

Caroline took his hand and towed him around the sofa and down beside her. "We are talking about Anne's new emergence into society, Welsford. I am determined that she will be all the thing."

"But my love," he said with a twinkle, "*you* are all the thing. And I'm sure that you don't intend to vacate your throne."

Caroline frowned for a moment—Anne noticed that she still held her husband's hand, as if that were the most natural thing in the world. "We will be the dashing Peckworth sisters."

"Dashing?" Anne couldn't help but protest.

"Dashing," Caroline said firmly, and shared their plans with her husband in a torrent of words that he seemed able to follow.

"A staff? An excellent idea, Caro. I congratulate you. Wallace in Bond Street. My ebony is from there."

Caroline turned to Anne. "A very fine piece, and with a snuff box in the head. Only think, you could have secret compartments, too. Smelling salts, for example."

"I've never needed smelling salts."

Caro dismissed that with a wave. "You could be ready to waft them in front of some other, weaker woman. Perhaps you could have a place for calling cards, or for a few coins for emergencies." Caroline's eyes brightened. "And if you don't care for smelling salts, you could have a hollow at the top for ratafia." She swung back to her husband. "You have a cane with a small flask of brandy in the top, don't you? I can think of many a dull occasion when a nip of ratafia would brighten the tedium."

"I'd rather have brandy." But then Anne detected a reaction. "I suppose Frances wrote that I spent her confinement in Benning's study drinking brandy and rolling dice?"

Caroline bit her lip. "She did, yes. I found it hard to believe."

"Such a dull puss as I am?"

"Oh, no, Anne!" But then it was clear that Caroline wasn't quite sure what to add, probably because she had thought exactly that.

"The hazard was the shock," Welsford said with a wicked look. "Not a game generally played by ladies. If you've developed a taste for it, however, a private party could be arranged."

Anne refused to fluster. "Only for farthing points, Welsford."

"Which equates to point*less*, my dear."

"Not at all. I think I won almost five shillings."

Caroline turned to her husband. "Would I enjoy hazard?"

He winced theatrically. "Only for farthing points, my love. Promise me."

"Oh, certainly. What point in risking money at the tables that might be spent on fashion? Which reminds me"—she jumped to her feet—"we had best be off purchasing a cane."

Her husband tugged her down again. "Anne will be tired from her journey, love."

Caroline looked at Anne as if he'd said she might have the smallpox. "Are you?"

It had only been three hours in the coach. "Not at all, though I do intend to finish my tea."

Welsford chuckled. "The redoubtable Peckworth sisters." Then he kissed his wife's hand.

Anne watched his technique with interest. He raised Caro's plump hand, but met it halfway in a bow that seemed a meaningful reverence. Though his kiss was light, his grasp on her fingers was firm, and Anne thought the way Caroline's fingers curled over his was just as meaningful.

She looked away, feeling intrusive—and wistful. She was planning marriage as a practicality, but a part of her longed for this—to feel that a husband was all to her, the pivot around which her life swung, and that she, miraculously, was the same to him.

"Anne?"

It was her brother-in-law's voice, and she looked back, hoping she appeared unmoved.

"A suitable escort might set the right tone from the beginning," he said. "A gentleman who is highly prized in the marriage stakes."

De Vere. Did Welsford know de Vere? Was he thinking of *hiring* him to play attendant, like a cicisbeo of years gone by? Then she came to her senses. De Vere was a complete outsider in the fashionable marriage stakes.

She was so off balance, however, that she couldn't find sensible words. "You think it important?"

"First impressions, my dear. And the right gentleman will intrigue society, and thus make you intriguing."

Despite all logic, de Vere's image sat in her mind. "Whom do you have in mind?"

"St. Raven."

Caroline squeaked.

Anne felt as if her eyes had expanded. The new Duke of St. Raven had spent some years living at Lea Park, foster brother to the Peckworths. "Tris? He's like a brother!"

"But he's not," Caroline said, eyes bright. "And his escort would certainly create a stir."

"I wouldn't want to impose. . . ."

Welsford waved that away. "We're hardly asking for blood, and I'd think he owes a debt of gratitude to your family. You took him in when the duke and duchess would not, I understand."

"And wait until you see him, now, Anne," Caroline said. "He was always good-looking, but oh, my!"

Anne cast an alarmed look at Caroline's husband, but he seemed amused. "Poor man. Romantically handsome, and a young, available duke. At his side, Anne, you will be the focus of every eye."

"And the subject on every tongue," Caroline added, "in the context of marriage, no less."

"We're like brother and sister," Anne repeated.

"But he's not your brother, which is all that matters now."

Anne wanted to protest more, but she remembered her purpose. She must wed, and every weapon must be used.

"Very well, if he agrees. At least I like him and enjoy his company."

Welsford rose. "I know St. Raven well enough to put this matter to him. I think he'll do it, for amusement if nothing else."

The door shut behind him.

Anne frowned at it. "I am beginning to dislike being a source of amusement for idle gentlemen."

"Whatever do you mean?"

Anne started. She needed to watch her tongue—and get all thought of de Vere out of her head. "Just nonsense and a spinning head. This business with Tris seems so very peculiar. I haven't seen him for nearly two years. He went abroad when he inherited."

Caroline pursed her lips. "Maybe you'll see him differently now. He's *not* your brother, and how utterly delicious if you were to snare the catch of the season. Mama would take flight!"

Anne sat up. "Snare! Did you 'snare' Welsford, then?"

"No! How horrid of you."

"Then don't imply that I would do such a thing." But she sucked in a breath. They were sinking into nursery squabbles. "I'm sorry, Caroline. This whole business has me on edge."

Caroline rushed over to hug her. "I'm sorry, dearest. And this will be fun, I promise! We will find you the perfect husband. Whatever husband you want."

Anne had a vision of her family stalking her reluctant

choice and dragging him to her in a net, but she returned the hug. Caroline had a good heart and meant the best. They all meant the best.

"We're not pushing you where you don't want to go, are we, dearest? You have always been so . . ."

"Quiet," Anne filled in. "No, I'm ready for a change, and I will find a good husband. I'm not sure about perfect, however. Perhaps waiting for perfection is what makes spinsters."

"Nonsense. First we arrange the matter of the cane—they may not have such a thing ready for purchase. Women haven't used them in a fashionable way since our grandmother's time. Then we inspect your wardrobe. Yes, I know you think it sufficient, but you are no longer in hiding."

"Yes, ma'am."

Caroline grinned so her dimples dug deep. "Indeed. I am in charge for the moment. A little trimming of the hair . . ."

"Some experiments with the paint pot?"

Caroline blushed and put her hands to her face, but then she laughed. "I confess it. And you will see what a difference it can make without being at all obvious."

She went quickly to her flower-painted desk and took out a book, flipping through the pages. "Friday. That should give us enough time. We'll make your grand entrance at Drury Lane. It's the opening of *A Daring Lady,* a new play for Mrs. Hardcastle. She did a wonderful Titania not long ago, but this is a comedy. We're promised breeches and sword fighting, so all the world will be there."

She gazed into space for a moment. "We'll hold a supper here afterward, and you will be the center of attention."

Anne's mouth turned dry. Running back to Lea Park was tempting as sugar plums. She had chosen this course, however, and would stick to it.

"And, of course, there will be St. Raven," Caroline continued.

"He may not be free on Friday."

"Then he can make himself free."

"Caro!"

Caroline grinned. "I am the famous Lady Welsford, and will be obeyed. I wasn't so close to him as you, but I'm sure he'll want to help. And once you have been seen with him, the other men will flock to you."

She sank back among the cushions of her sofa, almost purring. "We are going to create a sensation. By this point of the season the new people are old and the scandals are fading. Even Byron and Brummell's flights abroad are stale news. You, your staff, and St. Raven will be the new talk of the town."

Anne grasped the teapot and refilled her cup. She dearly wished she had some brandy to add to it.

Ten

~

On Friday night Anne did drink a little brandy to steady her nerves.

She had her cane. Wallace and Sons had been willing to sell a display item, an apprenticeship piece of tulip-wood, inset with mother-of-pearl and silver in a design of winding flowers. It was taller than she'd intended—the amber knob with a fly fixed in it came to her shoulder—but she already liked it in a practical way. With the staff she didn't fear falling and could walk faster and for longer.

In all other respects, however, she felt kinship with the poor trapped fly.

A quiet ivory satin dress from last year was now embellished with an overdress of pink net and silver beads, and cut considerably lower in the neckline. The entire upper part of her breasts was exposed. She was used to thinking of herself as modestly endowed, but when she looked down there seemed to be an enormous amount of flesh on display.

Caroline's dictatorial coiffeur had trimmed her hair to curl around her face, which she quite liked, but had also insisted on a rinse that made her hair a brighter blond. Caroline thought it wonderful. Anne thought it was too . . . Simply too much.

Especially with the additional effect of face paint as used by Caroline's French maid.

A stranger looked back from her mirror. A lovely stranger—even she could see that—but so unlike herself that she feared looking a fool. Caroline was ecstatic,

Welsford was flattering, but Anne fixed her mind on St. Raven. Tris would tell her the truth.

She heard a voice, then crisp footsteps across the hall. Moments later Tris strode in—still Tris, but now very much the duke. Had he needed to go away for a year to grow into the new skin he had inherited? It wasn't anything to do with his looks, though he was even more darkly handsome, or with his elegant evening clothes. It was, she decided, simply the way he occupied space.

As if it was all his.

As, of course, it was for a duke.

She wanted to shrink back, to become invisible again, but then his eyes met hers and he smiled, and he was Tris.

"Anne." His eyes widened and traveled over her. "My, my, I won't be able to call you Mouse any longer. London will be at your feet."

He meant it. She was sure he meant it, and it was as if a tight-wound spring inside her relaxed. She gave him her hands. "As it already is at yours, milord duke."

He laughed. "Alas. If I could change my appearance and reverse the effect, I would, but I don't think fustian coats and a bald head would deter anyone at all."

"I'm afraid not, but it's because you would still be ridiculously handsome."

"And above all, a duke." He smiled in that wry way he had that accepted fate and made the best of it. She remembered afresh why she'd always liked him.

His parents had died when he was fourteen. He had been nephew and heir to the Duke of St. Raven, but the duchess loathed the sight of him—the son she had failed to provide. So Tris had come to Lea Park, welcomed by her generous parents, to grow up in a ducal household and learn the trade.

"Thank you for smoothing my path," she said.

"I am yours to command in all things, Mouse." He considered her. "It has to be Mouse, you know. I'm sure there are resplendent mice somewhere in the world."

"Dead ones, I'd think. It is a mouse's good sense not to be noticed." She led the way to a sofa and sat. "But I, of course, wish to be caught."

"Nonsense. You are the huntress, not the prey."

"A hunting mouse?"

"You are an original."

Anne relaxed the last tiny little part. He was Tris, and he was her friend, just as he had always been. It had been a strange friendship with five years between them, but when he'd first come to Lea Park, newly orphaned, dark and withdrawn, he'd formed a link with her. Perhaps simply because she'd been the quiet, crippled one.

She was sure he alarmed and even terrified some people now, but not her. Reflected in his eyes she saw herself as lovely, confident, and in control, but also as the Anne she had always been.

They were a party of four for dinner, so it was a relaxed affair. They left for the theater in high spirits, and arrived in time for the main part of the program, the new play. Anne had almost forgotten the importance of the occasion until they stepped out of the carriage into a fashionable throng all pushing into the box entrance at the same time.

She grasped her cane for support both physical and mental, and saw a few people pause to stare. Saw them see Caroline and Welsford and thus recognize her. Saw them see St. Raven and turn to whisper.

It had started.

Tris squeezed her hand.

She put on a bright smile. "Thank you. I don't know how I'd do this without you."

"The same way you rode for the first time."

It had been Tris who'd argued that she should learn to ride because it would give her more mobility, and he who'd dared, teased, and cajoled her into it.

"Terrified," she said.

"But successful."

Her smile was natural now, and she didn't mind the stares. "Thank you."

"It's my delight. You are excellent defense against the fair huntresses. They really are enough to push a man into being a recluse."

She sighed. "A quiet life is very tempting, isn't it?"

"No. You're not enjoying this, are you, Mouse? Shall

I throw you into the carriage and carry you back to Lea Park?"

He'd do it, too. "I wish you could, Tris, but I'm determined to go through with this."

"Your family could bring suitable suitors to the country for you."

"That has been tried."

His blank look showed that he had no idea about Middlethorpe and Wyvern. That was comforting. At least it wasn't the talk of the town. Now she wished she hadn't mentioned it at all, and in the crush she couldn't explain if she wanted to.

"They weren't right for me. I have to make my own selection. In the ranks of society there must be one man I can love, and who can love me."

"Rarer, I fear, is the man who deserves you."

"I seem to be very hard to please."

"So you should be. You are a princess."

"Behind walls of power?"

He looked puzzled, as well he might. She must stop letting de Vere live like a third in her company. Someone pushed from behind while the man in front slowed. Tris moved to take the pressure off her. The perfect escort.

She smiled at him. "Someone suggested that I'd frightened all my suitors away by being a duke's daughter, and by being . . . off-putting."

"If a man is frightened away, he is not worthy of you."

"But what if the hero doesn't exist who is brave enough to attempt an assault?"

His dark eyes turned dangerous. "If anyone assaults you, Mouse, he'll not be your husband. He'll be dead."

Oh, Lord. "Tris, you are not to make trouble."

"I most certainly will if it is called for."

"Trouble?" asked Caroline from her other side. "Are you all right, Anne? What a dreadful crush, but I suppose no one wants to miss this first night."

She related an alarming story of a panic on crowded stairs like these that had resulted in injuries, and some ladies ending up in rags, exposed to the common gaze. Anne was more concerned by the danger of Tris's attitude. There had always been something dark about him. Not a bad dark, but a warrior core that could and would kill.

She remembered him attacking a brawny farmer who'd been beating a maid over something. Tris had ended up with a black eye and cracked ribs, but the farmer hadn't escaped unscathed. And, she remembered, Tris had insisted that the man not suffer for assaulting a member of the Lea Park family, only for assaulting the servant.

It had been noble in its way, but she didn't need a knight-protector attacking any suitor who became ardent.

Or impudent.

The thought of an encounter between Tris and de Vere made her hair stand on end. It was a strange notion, but in many ways, they were two of a kind and could tear each other apart. The noisy press of the crowd fermented her simmering nervousness into panic. If it had been possible to turn back and escape, she might have tried. . . .

Then suddenly a door opened before her into space. They had arrived at Welsford's box.

A new noise and vibrancy assailed her—the chattering, glittering crowd within the theater. A fog of sweat, perfume, candle smoke, and oranges turned her stomach. The others were standing back, expecting her to make her grand entrance first.

"Chin up and face the lions." Tris grasped her arm to move her forward.

With a deep breath, she took over for herself. Chin up, staff forward, she walked down to the front of the box, to the place where she—and her escort—would be visible to nearly everyone in the theater.

She'd entered a theater many times without creating the slightest disturbance. Now, faces turned and a silence fell over the crowd, followed seconds later by a buzz. Mouth too dry for any light comment, she made herself smile as she passed her staff to Tris, who passed it on to Philip. Then she slowly settled into her seat at the center front of the box.

Despite the flash of quizzing glasses raised to inspect

her, she did manage to relax. The worst was over, and as usual, it hadn't been the end of the world. She glanced at Tris, who smiled as he sat beside her, inviting her to be amused by the whole event.

And suddenly she was. It was all so silly, this attention and speculation merely because Lady Anne Peckworth, somewhat improved in looks and carrying a beribboned cane, had come to the theater on the arm of the Duke of St. Raven.

Smile deepening into wickedness, Tris raised her hand. "If we're to do this properly, we should set up a flirtation." He kissed it, lingeringly, with that exact kiss that de Vere had described as the one of a man who knows how to please women.

The buzz intensified.

Without urgency, she took back her hand. "Wretch. Half society will have us engaged to marry by morning."

"Would you like to be?"

She blinked at him. "I could take you up on that and scare you to death."

"If it came to bluff and counterbluff, Mouse, who do you think would win?"

"You, and that's one reason we could never marry."

"What are the others?"

He was holding her attention and being playful to help her over the worst, and it had worked. She did worry, however, that his whimsical question might be rooted in seriousness. Might a beleaguered duke see his old friend as a safe refuge?

"We could never love in that way, Tris, and I suspect that you need a mad passion if you're to take marriage seriously."

"So do you."

"Oh no. I want a placid life in the country."

"The mouse aspires to be a cow?"

She pulled a face at him. "This mouse aspires to a fellow mouse and a quiet nest. If you promise not to force adventures upon me, I promise not to lecture you about your intimate affairs."

"I hope you know nothing about my intimate affairs." But his expression eased. "As for adventures, I'm not sure you've tried enough to know what you want."

"I've never been shipwrecked, but I'm certain I don't want that. I do truly want a quiet country life, Tris." Struck by a sudden thought, she added, "Now there, your wicked reputation could be of use to me."

His brows rose. "As occasional amusement when the boring husband is away?"

She rapped his hand with her fan. "Don't be absurd. I said your reputation, not your skills."

"And what do you know of my skills, Mouse?"

Anne knew she was blushing. "Do stop this. What I mean is, you can warn me of any poor choices."

"In the area of skills? I don't normally observe other gentlemen in action."

She almost asked for clarification, but caught herself. He was teasing and didn't need encouragement.

"I presume you observe other gentlemen at the gaming table, and that's what I mean. I have no mind to marry a man who might risk my security and that of my children for the thrill of cards or dice. So if you see one courting me, give me warning."

"That I can do as long as you don't plunge without consulting me first."

She laughed. "When have you ever known me to plunge?"

"I sense a new and dangerous Mouse. Very well, we need a secret code. If I mention mice, Mouse, beware."

"Mice?"

"And rats if the specimen is truly verminous."

"We'll seem crazed to be talking about rats and mice."

"The advantage of being a duke and a duke's daughter is that we can be as crazy as we wish to be. In fact, I think we need to distinguish between the rakehells and the gamesters. You may incline to one but not the other."

"I incline to neither!"

"Good. For gamesters, it will be farthings."

"Farthings?" She started as if a terrible secret had been revealed. Had Caroline gossiped about her night at Benning's? What did people know?

"Farthings. I would hate to ruin a man with a careless word, and I can't remember the last time I even thought about a farthing, never mind spoke of one. Mice and rats for the dissolute."

Her alarm simmered down. It wouldn't have mattered anyway. The whole world could know that she'd played hazard for farthing points in the company of her brother and brother-in-law. It was the third player who made the subject like nettles to her, raising an instant rash, and that was ridiculous.

"What about nobodies?" she asked wryly.

He gave her a puzzled look. "Those, I assume, you can detect for yourself."

To her relief, the curtain rose to reveal the drawing room of a wealthy house. The play had begun.

Lady Rosalinde entered, played by Mrs. Hardcastle of the famous beauty and silvery hair, complaining to her maid about her guardian's insistence that she marry an older man of property when she wanted a dashing young beau.

The uncle arrived with a stern older man to present. Then a fashionable married cousin and Rosalinde's grandmother turned up to encourage her to seek youthful delights. The heiress rejected the stern suitor. The uncle raged, but went off to find another contender.

The cousin summoned Sir Mirabel Preen, a fashionable man of handsome appearance, but he was more interested in his reflection in a mirror than in Rosalinde, so he was dismissed, too.

The uncle returned with a lord this time, but he lectured Rosalinde on her duties as the future Lady Mountaugustine, which seemed to include immense gratitude to him. Rosalinde sent him on his way, too.

Throughout, Rosalinde's expressions were delightful, and her occasional asides to the audience were clever, as were those of the grandmother.

Anne leaned close to Tris. "Doesn't the grandmother remind you of the Dowager Duchess?"

"Lord, so she does! Even to the heavy paint and salty turn of phrase. She had us boys blushing at times."

Then the cousin's next offering arrived—Captain Jeremy Goodman, in scarlet regimentals.

The grandmother turned to Lady Rosalinde and said in a very loud aside, "Now this is more the thing, gel.

Note his shoulders and calves, and the fine pair of thighs on him."

Rosalinde clapped her hands to her cheeks, but then she flirted with the young man and at the end of the scene turned to the audience. "Ladies. Listen to your grandmothers. I do believe that this is the perfect husband for me, a young man both brave and honorable. And oh, the thighs on him!"

The audience was laughing and applauding as the curtain lowered, but Anne thought that the women were laughing loudest.

"Assessing a husband by his *thighs*?" she murmured.

Tris gave her a look. "Turning prudish?"

"No, but . . . do you not notice? The play is about a trinity of women evaluating suitors, and mostly on their appearance and ability to please."

He laughed. "So it is. Fair is fair. Men do that all the time."

Caroline and Welsford stood to leave the box, and Tris offered Anne his arm. "I admit, I'm more interested in the play as a guide to failure. Perhaps I should take to admiring my reflection while lecturing the ladies on their future duties."

Anne rose, but then she looked him up and down. "But oh, sir, your thighs!"

"Saucy wench—"

"There's Uffham!"

Anne whirled to look where Caroline was pointing—down into the chaotic pit. Sure enough, there was her brother, cuddling a laughing orange girl, and there was Race de Vere, flirting with another. Her heart missed a beat, but she took the sight as warning.

All the women fell in love with him, even orange sellers.

"Uffham must come up here," Caroline declared, and rushed down to the front of the box. clearly intending to get his attention.

Welsford pulled her back. "Send Philip, my love."

Caroline remembered to be a respectable married lady and dispatched her footman on the errand. "Lord Uffham is to join us in the box for the rest of the play,

Philip. Make that clear. Even if he is a mere brother, he will add to Anne's consequence."

"St. Raven is quite sufficient," Anne protested.

"There is no such thing as sufficient," Caroline declared, taking her husband's arm and sweeping out of the box.

Anne shared a smile with Tris. "She's going to be insufferable one day."

"Not at all. She'll be the sort of matriarchal tyrant who terrorizes generations. Like the dowager."

They shared memories as they mingled with the elite, but Anne couldn't really concentrate on anything except the probable approach of Race de Vere.

He'd teased her and kissed her and said improper things to her. Then he'd kissed her again half-naked in the corridor. Him being half-naked. He'd stirred all kinds of feelings in her, desires even, and then left without a word or a backward glance.

Mischief, she reminded herself. He'd admitted to irritating everyone. He'd merely amused himself with her during a rainy country visit. She'd been his straw heart!

She had that straw heart on her dressing table holding hairpins but also a certain gaming counter. Innocent things to suddenly seem so dangerous. Thank God, she thought, that she was on the arm of the most eligible man in England.

Perhaps she tightened her grip, for Tris said, "Are you all right?"

She raised her chin and smiled brightly at the passing Greshams. "Yes, of course. Just a twinge of nerves. This is my first night."

"I could say something risqué, but I will spare you."

"Good."

She saw Uffham coming. He was tall, anyway, but he parted the crowd as if it were the Red Sea. He didn't have Tris's ducal presence yet, but he was what he was, and most people instinctively gave way. De Vere, of course, was with him, and Anne realized that he had a presence of his own. She had no time to analyze it.

Eleven

"Carrie," Uffham protested, "a play's much more fun from the pit."

"I want you up here," Caroline said. "And don't call me Carrie!"

"Frannie, Annie, Carrie, Marrie, and Lizzie."

"Very well," Caroline whispered, *"Stuffy!"*

"Children, children," murmured Welsford. "We are supposed to be giving Anne countenance, not covering her with blushes."

Uffham, red with annoyance, turned to Anne. But then he grinned. "Quite the thing, ain't you, Annie? Get you hitched in no time."

"Uffham," Tris said, quietly but almost as angrily as Caroline.

Uffham at least heeded it. "What?"

Her brother, Anne realized, was drunk. Not seriously, but enough to make him troublesome. Why had Caroline had to bring him up here?

He wasn't too drunk to catch Tris's warning, however. "Oh, right. Good to see you again, Tris. Have to call you St. Raven now, I suppose. Can't be schoolboys forever."

"Some of us don't want to be."

Uffham rolled his eyes. "Don't you start prosing on at me. Bad as de Vere. Where the devil is he? Ho, de Vere, come and admire my sister Annie in her fine new feathers."

De Vere obeyed. "Plumed fine enough to take flight, Lady Anne. But remember Icarus."

What had she expected? Some expression of warmth or hidden passions?

"Are you accusing me of being a high-flyer, Mr. de Vere?"

She heard a choking sound from Tris. That was slang for a loose woman.

She saw nothing but brilliant amusement in de Vere's eyes. "Only insofar as you live with the gods in ducal splendor, my lady."

"You worry," Tris said, "that a lady in the company of dukes and future dukes is in danger of a fall?"

Anne didn't like that tone. Uffham had wandered off without performing the introduction, so she presented de Vere to Tris.

De Vere bowed like a minion, murmuring, "Your Grace. Icarus was in no danger at all, Your Grace, until he tried to fly his way out of a prison."

Drat the man. The flowery Your Graces were at complete odds with his demeanor, and he was going to drive someone to do something unwise.

"You think Lady Anne imprisoned?" Tris was still cold.

"I think Lady Anne should be careful where she flies, Your Grace. As should we all."

"Mr. de Vere was till recently in the army, St. Raven," Anne interjected.

"At Waterloo?" Tris asked, warming slightly.

"No, Your Grace."

De Vere didn't show any reaction, but Anne winced at how he must hate that question.

"Mr. de Vere was with the forces sent to America. I think it most unfair that those regiments have no medal merely because they missed the final battle, when they'd fought so many years in Spain and Portugal."

"Galling, I'm sure. And your plans now, sir?"

"Are undecided, Your Grace."

"Marriage?"

"Only to a very wealthy lady, Your Grace."

"I see." Anne hadn't known that Tris could look down his nose like that. "You plan to marry a fortune rather than earn one?"

De Vere's brows rose. "Some might say, Your Grace, that seven years in the army entitles a man to any spoils he can find. It could seem ungracious if those who stayed at home begrudged them."

Anne wanted to kick him. He couldn't know, but he'd found Tris's sore spot. Tris had longed to buy a commission, but as the precious sole male of the Tregallows, it had been impossible.

"That depends," Tris said, "entirely on the spoils. An army is not supposed to ravage its own."

"I should think not, Your Grace. It sounds positively incestuous."

"Lady Anne and I are not related."

"Did I say otherwise?"

What was all this? Anne leaped in. "St. Raven and I are like brother and sister, Mr. de Vere, even though there is no blood tie."

"And like a brother"—Tris was talking through his teeth now—"I will protect her to the death."

Thank heavens Caroline swept over. "Uffham is to join us in the box, Mr. de Vere, to add to Anne's credit."

It was not information. It was instruction.

De Vere turned to Caroline as if war hadn't nearly broken out here. "Are you sure he will, Lady Welsford?"

It was a tantalizingly ambiguous warning. Whether Caroline caught that or not, she ignored it. "Do please see that he does, Mr. de Vere."

Anne seized the opportunity to steer Tris away to mingle with other members of the ton. "De Vere would probably like to throttle the Peckworths."

"I assume he finds it worth his while to be . . . useful."

Anne frowned at him. "Do you know something to his discredit?"

"No. Why? Is he a contender?"

"De Vere?" Did her laugh sound shrill? "Of course not. But you seemed cool."

"Uffham's friends rarely stir me to warmth, but he did say de Vere prosed at him, so perhaps there's hope."

She glanced at him. "No mice, rats, or farthings?"

"Don't know him from Adam. Of course, I might

know him better under his real name." He was being arrogant in a way that was at odds with his nature.

"It is his real name."

He glanced down at her. "De Vere? Come, Anne. Any true de Vere would be trying to claim the earldom of Oxford, which would be very interesting when it's been in other hands for over a century."

They paused to speak to the Harrovings. When they moved on, she said, "He said he was a de Vere, born to a de Vere, and I don't think he gives a direct lie. Perhaps he's from the bastard line. I wish Uffham and Caroline wouldn't treat him like a servant."

"He amuses and takes care of Uffham, and for payment he has room, board, and a share in Uffham's expensive recreations. What would you call him? You seem hot in his defense, Mouse."

Trying to react to that, she accidentally smiled brilliantly at the passing Marshboroughs, thus giving them the unlooked-for opportunity to exchange trivialities with a duke. Probably something to tell their grandchildren.

She'd lived her life within the aura of high rank, but felt as if she were seeing it anew. She didn't like the way de Vere was dismissed as a nobody while people fawned on Uffham. It was the way of her world, however. One day Uffham would be the mighty Duke of Arran, and de Vere would be who knew what?

Still a nobody.

Enough of that. She was forgetting her main purpose here—to meet eligible titled men. She glanced around and saw the Countess of Flawborough, a tower of bronze including a high turban, heading her way, son in tow.

A younger son, but Anne needed practice, so she smiled at Mr. Pitt-Meadowing. She soon wished she hadn't. He had bored her before, and bored her now. The same could be said of Lord Marlowe, gleaming smile to the fore, Lord Gillmott, and Sir Shaftesbury Drum.

While listening to Sir Shaftesbury discuss the design of carriage wheels with Tris, she realized why Tris had reacted so badly to de Vere. He thought he was a fortune hunter.

How absurd. He wasn't hunting her at all. She would have to make that clear.

She supposed she could acquit these other men of being fortune hunters, too, since she'd owned her large dowry all her life and they'd ignored her before tonight. Now they were interested; but she felt that they should have been attracted to her before, should have sought her out in her rural seclusion. This new person that they fluttered to was only surface glitter.

She reminded herself that in the past she had deliberately hidden. How had Caroline put it? Turned down her wick. Or as de Vere put it, projected lack of interest. She might be shining brightly now, but she wasn't sure she was projecting interest. How could she when she wasn't interested?

And yet, she had to marry.

Not Sir Shaftesbury, however. Beyond a few idiotic words of flattery, he'd ignored her in favor of manly talk. The question was settled when Tris said, "The thing about a carriage, Drum, is to be careful not to let in the rats."

"Rats, St. Raven? Have trouble with them, do you?"

"All the time, sir, all the time."

Anne struggled with laughter as they moved on. It set a pattern for the intermission. Sometimes Tris mentioned rats, mice, or farthings, sometimes he didn't. Even the innocent men, however, went to the bottom of her list in moments. How could she end up with a list composed entirely of a bottom rung? She was relieved when it was time to return to the box, but when she entered it she paused.

For the first act she and Tris had sat in the front with Caroline and Welsford behind. Now two chairs had been added, one at either end of the front row. Caroline clearly wanted Uffham at the front to ram home the fact that Anne was a future duke's sister. She'd never imagined that it would be in doubt.

She could take one of the end chairs. Once Tris sat beside her, she'd be safe from de Vere. It would give an inferior view of the stage, however, and might be noted. Tris was already suspicious.

She settled, therefore, into her former seat with Tris on her right, praying that Caroline would marshal Uffham into the seat on her other side.

Uffham, however, took the seat next to Tris. "Need to talk to you . . ."

Anne sighed and turned to Race de Vere, now sitting to her left hand.

He was giving her a speculative look. Heavens, did he think she'd *arranged* this? She was going to murder Caroline!

She plied her fan and tried to look bored. "What do you think of the play, Mr. de Vere?"

"A wicked piece, Lady Anne, perhaps written by a woman."

She stared at him. "A female playwright?"

"Why not? And I anticipate more skewers driven into male flesh. A number of irate gentlemen were storming out of the theater at the end of the first act."

Anne looked around and noticed a few empty boxes, but not many. The atmosphere among those who remained seemed to simmer with anticipation.

Was she simmering with anticipation? She was simmering with something. There was a power in de Vere's mere presence, something that set her nerves a-tingling.

Then she became aware of a tingle of another sort. It seemed to shoot between de Vere and Tris, with her in the middle. She had thought earlier that a confrontation between them would be alarming. Unfortunately, she had been right. She could only be relieved when the curtain rose.

Lady Rosalinde was in the midst of a confrontation with her furious uncle, loudly declaring that she'd marry her Jeremy.

"He doesn't have a penny to his name, you foolish chit!"

"He has his army pay."

"No officer can make do on army pay, never mind support a wife. Be done with this."

"But I have a fortune, Uncle, that will come to me when I marry."

"Which is why you'll marry a sober, older man, you hussy."

"Which is why I'll marry any man I choose, you old misery!"

The uncle set off after her with his stick, and they dodged around the furniture until the old man collapsed wheezing onto the chaise, complaining that she'd be the death of him.

Anne was struck by the parallels. She had a large dowry, and in theory could marry anyone she chose. If she were a daring lady . . .

She stole a glance at de Vere—

And caught him looking at her.

He raised his brows. She quickly looked back at the stage, knowing she was blushing. Plague take the man. She'd like to push him over the balcony back down into the pit where he belonged!

Oh, Lord. How did he stir these outrageous thoughts?

Rosalinde had fixed on her dashing captain and determined to have him despite all opposition. The married cousin advised caution and time, pressed her to seek a titled husband, but the grandmother urged her to seize the moment.

"Embrace your future, gel. And your Jeremy's thighs in your marriage bed!"

The audience roared with laughter.

Anne thought of thighs.

She'd eyed Tris's thighs without a quiver or a qualm. She remembered ogling de Vere's thighs by firelight. Remembered quivering.

She slid her eyes sideways at eye level. He was watching the play, grinning at the discussion among the three women.

She slid her eyes down.

In the gloom, however, and with him wearing dark pantaloons, she couldn't see anything.

And what on earth did she think she was doing?

She concentrated on fictional insanity to find Rosalinde involved in a mock consultation with the audience.

"Marry money," called one female voice. "It lasts longer than muscular thighs!"

"Nay," the heiress said, "I'll exercise them enough to keep them trim and strong!"

"You're a hussy, young lady," called an older male voice from a box. It was the Earl of Brassingham, a notorious lecher if rumor was true. "Marry as your guardian says."

"But, sir," Rosalinde said, glancing up, "elderly guardians seem to always want young ladies to marry men of their age. Perhaps they seek to deny the wattles in their mirrors."

Anne wondered if steam was rising from the wattled old roué. He got to his feet, and he and his party marched out of their box.

"Probably can't bear to look in a mirror at all," the actress remarked, causing a gale of laughter.

"Heavens, she'll end up in jail," Anne said.

"I doubt it." It was de Vere. "She has very powerful friends."

"Who?"

He looked at her. "There's a group called the Company of Rogues."

"I know of them. Lord Amleigh is one. He is her friend?" A beautiful actress as well as a lady of Devon?

"More particularly a Major Beaumont, but her safety lies in the friendship—before his marriage, of course—of the Marquess of Arden."

De Vere, she thought, was the only person who would discuss mistresses with her. Even Tris might balk.

She looked at the vibrant actress again. "I'm glad."

The give and take continued.

"Old husbands die sooner," cried a woman in the pit. "Marry a dodderer."

"But have you not noticed how time drags when we're bored? A year with a dodderer could be lifetime enough to drive me to the grave!"

"A hit, a veritable hit," murmured Tris. "Don't marry a bore, Mouse."

"Mouse?" asked de Vere, glancing at them.

"A schoolroom name," Anne said.

"Ah. I hope His Grace realizes that you are not in the schoolroom anymore, Lady Anne."

"His Grace," Tris said, "does. May we watch the play?"

Anne stared fixedly at the stage as Jeremy rushed in asking what plan Rosalinde had concocted. What was she supposed to do if the men on either side of her lunged to attack?

Push them both into the pit if she had the strength. They were like fighting cocks anyway. Who could understand men? She wished she could wash her hands of all of them.

Including Captain Jeremy Goodman.

He was declaring that they must obey Rosalinde's guardian. His plan was to venture to America to make his fortune and then return to claim his fair Rosalinde.

"Idiot," Anne said, not meaning it to be aloud.

"True," Tris said. "Poor men marry heiresses whenever they have the chance. Would you not agree, Mr. de Vere?"

"It does depend on the heiress, Your Grace. Some are not worth the price. Fair Rosalinde, however, could marry a duke even if penniless."

"Only a very foolish duke. She'd settle for less."

"St. Raven!" Anne protested.

Yes, Tris definitely thought de Vere was a fortune hunter. What on earth could have given him that impression?

Her skin suddenly prickled. Was he sensing something she had missed? She didn't understand men well.

After all, she had hardly encouraged de Vere. In fact, now she thought of it, she'd been as actively discouraging as he'd suggested. She'd thrown brandy in his face, and then—oh lord!—she'd hit him after that kiss.

And then, to cap it all, she'd told him directly that she never wanted to see him again.

Oh, my. Her heart started to pound. Had he been as stirred by their time together, by their kisses, as she? She remembered that last kiss, those three light kisses in the corridor. They had to mean something, didn't they?

Was he attracted to her?

If so, what did she want to do about it?

Every time he called Tris "Your Grace" it was like a declaration that he came from a much lower social station. He was not at all the sort of man she was supposed to marry.

Lady Claretta Crump loomed in her mind.

And yet, and yet, here was Lady Rosalinde claiming her right to marry where she loved rather than for worldly position.

And then there was Lady Hester Stanhope, not fictional at all. She wasn't simply adventuring. She had taken up with a man far more unsuitable than anyone Anne might consider—not just foreign, but possibly pagan!

Anne felt breathless with possibilities and fears as she watched Rosalinde arguing with her Jeremy. So fierce she was in her fight for what she wanted. Unfair that she had to fight Jeremy, as well. He was standing nobly adamant, chin high, preaching obedience and good order.

In the end the actress came to the front of the stage. "By the stars, why am I plagued by such a noble fool? Any number of men have tried to marry me for my fortune, and yet here is the one I want and he will not play! What am I to do?"

She appeared to listen to the cacophony of suggestions, then nodded. "Yes, indeed. I will force his hand."

She marched back to the posing hero. "Jeremy, I insist that we elope."

Jeremy recoiled. "My love, you do not want to do something so likely to tarnish your good name!"

"Yes, I do. In fact, I insist on it. Tonight."

"Tonight! No, no. Your guardian has the right of it, my love. I cannot yet provide the home and circumstances you deserve."

"My money can, and once I am married my fortune will be mine no matter what my uncle says."

"We must wait until I have improved my circumstances. It will only be a matter of years—"

"Years!" Rosalinde planted her hands on her hips. "I'll be gray by then! Harken to me, sirrah! I am climbing out of my window tonight and going north. If you accompany me, you will be my husband. If not, I will find another one on the way."

"Rosalinde! You could not possibly do that."

"You think not? Try me and see!"

The curtain came down on that ultimatum, leaving Anne breathless. To cut through all the tangle of society's expectations and rituals, and seize fate like that.

Her heart raced, but was it with excitement, or with terror that she might actually be tempted into such insanity?

Twelve

"Oh, my," Caroline exclaimed, "if he doesn't keep the assignation, will she truly take some chance-met man to husband?"

"He will have to show up," Welsford said. "Once trapped in the role of a hero, what hope does a man have?"

Anne turned in her seat to see Caroline poke him with a jeweled finger. "Perhaps I will run off on a mad adventure so you will have to follow and be my hero."

He captured her finger and kissed the tip. "As long as you are willing to accept the consequences. I would be somewhat angry, my love, if you endangered yourself."

That sounded threatening, but her sister's eyes were bright as she slid her finger out of her husband's hold and took the wine the footman was handing around.

Another aspect of love? Not always courteous respect, but veiled threats and challenges? She definitely didn't understand love, but she itched to learn.

Tris asked her, "So what do you think of the play now?"

She took wine herself and turned back to the front. "It still amuses, but I worry about the happy ending."

"You don't think Rosalinde and Jeremy will suit?"

"No. But I don't suppose it matters. This is all make-believe."

"Yet a good play should seem real at the time, Lady Anne," de Vere interjected. "Therefore, I suspect that there are some twists still to come. Do you care to *hazard* some guesses?"

Anne almost choked on the bubbles. "That depends

on what is at stake, Mr. de Vere. What twists can you imagine? Lady Rosalinde can hardly marry *just any man*."

She used the phrase deliberately, but saw no reaction.

"Which leaves only Captain Goodman, who doesn't please you. Because of his lowly station?"

Was that a meaningful question? She took another sip of wine to moisten her mouth, considering the implications of her answer.

In the end she settled for honesty. "It is his lack of courage that makes me doubt."

"You have no evidence as to his bravery or lack of it. He simply wishes to behave within the law. Rosalinde's uncle has the legal right to block an unsuitable marriage."

"If you were Jeremy, Mr. de Vere, what would you do?"

His smile was sudden and delightful. "Avoid the fair Rosalinde like the plague. She'll be a torment to him all his days."

"Isn't that what men desire?" she asked, glancing to her right to include Tris if he was listening.

He was, like a hawk. If hawks listened.

"Torment and desire?" he said. "You're dabbling in dangerous waters, Mouse. Marry for comfort."

"Will you?"

"Perhaps I wish better for you than for myself."

Anne glanced back at de Vere.

"I'm sure we all wish that, Lady Anne."

He seemed sincere, and that lingered with her as the curtain rose again.

Could de Vere be acting the noble Jeremy and not pressing her because he felt unworthy? What did a woman do about that?

Get with child, as it seemed Claretta Crump had? Caroline had confirmed that rumor, and that Captain Crump was a decent man with an excellent war record. He was completely unsuitable, however, having made his way in the army entirely on his merits. His father was a fishmonger.

How could such a union work?

On the stage, at least, boldness seemed to win the day. Rosalinde and Jeremy were in a real coach pulled by galloping wooden horses. The backdrop of wild countryside rolled behind to cleverly give the appearance of movement.

Rosalinde, in a tricorn hat and mannish shirt, was hanging out of the window looking backward. "All clear! We have escaped pursuit."

"I still don't think this is wise," Jeremy bleated. "And as for your clothes . . ."

"Was I to climb out of my window in skirts?"

Cheers from the audience. Some man called out, "Let's see your thighs, love. Fair's fair!"

The rougher parts of the audience took it up. Anne began to fear a riot. It wouldn't be unheard of.

The actress, however, looked out at the audience, and slowly, silence fell. "Behave yourselves," she said. "I've a skirt here with me, and I'll have it on in a moment if you're not all perfect gentlemen."

After a resounding, laughing cheer, the audience settled to the play again.

What was it like, Anne wondered, to have such control from center stage, to play people, even rowdy men, like an instrument?

"Stand and deliver!"

Anne jumped, and from the cries and shrieks, so did a number of other women.

The scenery stopped and a masked and cloaked highwayman swept onto the stage. He looked like a stray cavalier in a long richly curled wig, a neat beard and mustache, and a wide-brimmed cavalier hat with a lavish white plume. His pistol was pointed, arm stretched, at the coach.

"It's that Corbeau!" shouted someone from the pit, and the play paused under a contest of cheers and jeers.

"Clever," de Vere said.

Tris looked at him. "Who is it?"

But Uffham answered. "Damned highwayman who's been working the roads north of London for months now. Dresses in exactly that peculiar style. How could you not know about him?"

"I'm only just back from abroad. A dashing, daring sort, is he?" Tris was clearly unimpressed. "Our true hero?"

Anne stared at him. "A thief? Surely not."

"There are many kinds of thievery, Lady Anne," de Vere said. "And apparently this fellow doesn't take all of a traveler's jewels and money, only what he calls a tithe."

Tris snorted. "Romantic folly. I'm surprised he doesn't settle for kisses."

"Oh, he does sometimes—"

"Hush," Caroline said. "The play!"

Most of the audience had been exclaiming and gossiping, but now it settled.

Still Tris said, "Only an idiot would play such a dangerous game for amusement."

"Only an idiot would drive up and down the north roads hoping for an encounter," de Vere said, "but apparently some ladies of the ton are doing exactly that."

"What?" asked Anne. "I don't believe it!"

"Oh, hush!" Caroline rapped de Vere's shoulder with her fan, which seemed unfair.

Jeremy and Rosalinde had lost the argument to the persuasion of Le Corbeau's pistol, and were climbing down from the coach. The actress was in the promised breeches without concealment of even a jacket.

The audience—the male part, at least—cheered wildly.

Anne saw Uffham with his hands cupped to his face making hunting horn noises. Tris and de Vere were quiet, but she could see that they both appreciated the actress's shapely legs. Anne couldn't help think that her own legs were in excellent condition from riding. Tris had seen her in breeches, but of course de Vere had not.

Would he be appreciative?

But then Rosalinde strode across the stage with a man's confident swagger, bringing Anne back to earth. Shapely thighs or not, the effect would be spoiled by her limp.

Jeremy was still hovering near the coach. "She must not marry him," Anne said.

De Vere turned to her. "He's handsome, gentle, loving, and honorable. Respectful, even, of a guardian's rights, and anxious to make his own way rather than live off her money. Where's the lack?"

"He's a coward. You said I had no evidence. Look at him now!"

"You want him to rush the pistol and be shot?"

"I want him to do *something*. Would you cower while that highwayman was ogling your lady's limbs?"

"A pretty chicken," Le Corbeau said, leering, "with plump, tasty thighs."

De Vere looked at the stage. "No. While he's so distracted by her legs, I'd take the pistol right out of his hand. But you're right. Jeremy has lost the hero's crown."

"I stopped your coach in hopes of a plump purse," said Le Corbeau, "but I'll happily take a plump kiss instead. What say you, wench?"

Rosalinde stepped back, but Jeremy at last came forward. "So be it, if you promise to let us go on with no more demands."

"The toad," Anne muttered.

"With warts on," Tris agreed. "My money's on the highwayman now. Any takers?"

De Vere was smiling. "My money's on the daring lady. I think I see the twist coming. . . ."

Rosalinde had turned to the audience, her expression all astonishment. "A kiss!" But then she turned to Jeremy. "My hero! To suffer a kiss from this hairy villain merely to save my purse."

"What? 'Tis you he wants to kiss!"

But Rosalinde pushed the captain into the highwayman's arms. As the audience hooted with laughter and Jeremy fought free, Rosalinde said, "A bargain is a bargain, sir. You didn't say who the kiss had to be from."

Anne realized that she was applauding and cheering, and stopped, hot-faced.

Le Corbeau laughed. "True enough, you wicked wench. And a highwayman's word is his bond." He turned toward the shrinking Jeremy. "Come here, my pretty chicken—or should I say cock?"

Jeremy scuttled backward and the audience howled with laughter.

Anne knew she'd missed some of the joke. "What?" she whispered to Tris.

"I refuse to comment."

She turned to de Vere. "What?"

"Hush," he said, lips twitching. "The play, Lady Anne."

"Wretch," Anne muttered.

"Never!" screamed Jeremy, scrambling under the coach. "Never. Help! Rosalinde, give him the money!"

"But without it, how are we to get to Scotland, my love? It's only a kiss."

"I never wanted to go to Scotland, anyway!"

"I begin to wonder if you ever wanted to marry me."

"I did. I did. But that was before the breeches, before this. I am not sure anymore that you are the woman I loved."

Hands on hips, Rosalinde declared, "I see. You fell in love with silliness and skirts—with skim milk—and choke on the cream." She turned to the audience. "What do I do now? Go back to my uncle defeated?"

The highwayman held out his hand. "The purse, my pretty."

"What of the kiss?"

"But your fair companion won't pay. Will you?"

The actress eyed him for a carefully judged moment. "I gather you sometimes fence for the money, sirrah."

"You are offering to fence me?" Le Corbeau laughed, but he whipped out a rapier. "If you have a sword, I accept, you daring wench, but if I win, I'll take my reward in a fencing match of another kind."

"Oh-ho!" cried the audience.

"From Jeremy, of course," Rosalinde retorted, causing gales of laughter, and Jeremy to scuttle deeper into hiding.

Anne knew she was blushing. She'd realized what cock had to mean and was speculating about other things. "This is an outrageous play."

"But at least she's safe from Jeremy," Tris said. "She can never marry him now."

"She'll marry the highwayman? I'm not sure I care for that either."

"Perhaps she'll declare herself free of all men," de Vere said, "and go off to enjoy her money by herself."

"Like Lady Hester?"

"Very like Lady Hester."

As Rosalinde pulled a sword out of the sword case on the back of the coach, Anne considered that option. Her family wanted her married, but she could convince them she preferred the single life.

The truth was, however, that she didn't want adventure, and she did want marriage. A tranquil marriage. A quiet nest with another mouse. She glanced wryly at de Vere, who had no touch of mouse about him at all.

Rosalinde flexed her rapier and slashed it with a very expert style.

"*But, but* . . . ," protested Jeremy.

Rosalinde strode forward. "En garde, Mr. Crow! I fight for Jeremy's honor!"

A spirited sword fight followed, back and forth across the stage.

"By Hades, but she's good," Tris murmured.

"Do you fence?" Anne asked, eyes fixed on the stage.

"It amuses me. Do you fence, de Vere?"

"I have more practice with a saber, Your Grace, but yes."

Anne glanced from side to side, praying that she was mistaken in hearing a hint of future contest. What were these two men doing? And why?

"Ah-ha!" With a cry of victory, Rosalinde disarmed Le Corbeau and presented the rapier at his throat. "I think it is the gallows for you, sir."

Le Corbeau did not quail. "Or perhaps," he said with the kind of actor's softness that carried all through the theater, "I could pay you with a kiss?"

A murmur passed through the theater, and Anne knew it came from the women. Perhaps she had murmured herself. This was the hero after all. Yet he was still a highwayman. A thief.

Rosalinde turned to look at the audience. "A saucy rogue! But I think he is too fine a specimen to hang just yet."

With a flip of her blade she untied the cord of his

cloak so that it fell away, showing him, too, in shirt and breeches. "What do you think of his thighs, ladies?"

Many ladies applauded, and the grinning highwayman turned, showing himself off.

"Are you not embarrassed to be ogled by women, sirrah?"

"Not I. Do not all cocks strut proudly to impress the females?"

Hoots and cheers all around. Uffham almost fell off his chair with laughter. Anne had her hand over her mouth, but she was laughing, too.

The actress tossed aside her sword. "And I am mightily impressed!"

She went into his arms for a kiss. A kiss so like that one in the dying light of Benning's study that it raised the hair on Anne's neck. She was burningly aware of de Vere by her side, could almost taste his mouth on hers. Was he making the same connection? Did his skin suddenly feel too sensitive for clothes? . . .

The audience members cheered and stamped their feet so the theater seemed to shake—or perhaps it was just her, shaken by the heavy beat of her own heart.

Something brushed her arm. She started, but realized that it wasn't de Vere touching her. It was that she'd swayed against him.

She hastily straightened, swallowing and trying to bring back sanity. Then she saw that Jeremy was crawling out from under the coach, was grabbing one of the discarded swords.

"Look out!" she cried, and she wasn't the only one.

"Release her, you rapscallion! Rosalinde, desist!"

He was still on his knees, however, and Mrs. Hardcastle cast the audience a look of disgust, then turned, put her booted foot on his chest, and thrust him back on the ground disarmed.

The audience erupted in cheers, and Anne cheered, too. She'd never behaved this way at a play before, but never before had she cared so much about the activities on stage.

"I'll marry no man so unworthy of my heart!" Rosalinde declared.

"And nor will I," Anne echoed.

She'd not meant it to be aloud, and she glanced to either side. Tris was laughing at something with Uffham, but de Vere met her eyes. "So I should hope, Lady Anne. But a highwayman could not be worthy of you."

"Should I judge a man by his occupation?"

"Why not? Does it not indicate abilities and inclinations?"

"You, sir, seem to have no occupation at all."

Oh, she hadn't meant to say that! She fixed her gaze on the stage and pretended not to hear his words.

"I am busy, as always, in mischief."

Le Corbeau was on one knee before Lady Rosalinde. "Magnificent lady, be mine!"

Rosalinde, however, looked out at the audience again, posing the question. Silence settled. The actress had created the illusion that this was real, that the decision mattered.

Rosalinde looked back at the man kneeling before her. "I'll not marry a thief, sirrah. Do you promise on your honor and your soul to give up your wicked life, and be an honest man?"

Le Corbeau turned to look at the audience, but the audience simply waited.

"So," murmured Tris, "how do you vote now, Anne?"

"Will he keep his promise? If he will, then she should have him."

He made a *tsk*ing sound. "Mice, rats, and farthings. She knows nothing about him. He could live without thievery and still be a drunken wastrel on her money, and cruel to boot."

Anne kept her eyes on the stage, entranced by the lingering moment of decision. What perfect timing the actors had. "He's not giving a glib promise. If he gives it, he'll mean it."

"Silence carries such weight?"

"And he's brave. That's a great deal."

"Not in marriage. Tell her, de Vere."

It sounded autocratic, but de Vere obeyed. "There are many heroes of the war I would not wish to see you marry, Lady Anne."

The words "including you?" almost slipped from her lips. Anne watched the actors, feeling that if Rosalinde could arrive at a happy ending, she could, too.

The highwayman leaped to his feet and threw off his hat, long wig, and mask, revealing a handsome enough man beneath. He even ripped off his mustache and beard.

"Ouch," said de Vere. "Now there's a sign of love."

"Henceforth I am an honest man, and true and loving husband to the most daring lady in the land!"

The couple leaped into the coach, and coach and horses were drawn off the stage heading north, the audience cheering them on.

Jeremy was left behind with the remnants of the costume, a pistol, and two swords. Anne felt some sympathy for him. Her almost-husbands hadn't been snatched in her presence, but they had been snatched.

Would he pretend not to care, as she had?

Would he wish the lovers well, as she had?

Would he recognize the ways in which he had failed? She never had, but now she thought that perhaps the losses had been partly her fault for being discouraging, dim, and dutifully quiet.

"She was never worthy of me," Jeremy declared, and marched off stage, just ahead of some thrown oranges.

As the players returned for more applause, Caroline declared, "That was a very clever piece, and most amusing. Everyone will be wondering who the playwright is. Which reminds me," she said, shooting to her feet, "we must be on our way to be ahead of our guests! Uffham, no slipping off to your club!"

"Just to the green room for a while, Caro."

Perhaps it was his use of her preferred nickname, or perhaps simply her urgency, but Caroline gave in. "For a little while only." With a casual, "Do please see to it, Mr. de Vere," she hurried out.

Anne hoped to hear de Vere argue with Uffham, show some pressing need to stay in her company, but instead he shook his head. "I am merely one man, not an army, Lady Anne. Warn your sister not to depend on Uffham's attendance."

"I believe you could make my brother do anything you wished, Mr. de Vere."

He was politely blank. “That would hardly augur well for the duchy, my lady.”

My lady, my lady. He did it deliberately to slide to the minion level. She reached out and touched his arm. “Come to Lady Welsford’s on your own, Mr. de Vere.”

Uffham was at the door. “Come on, de Vere!”

De Vere looked at her for a moment, then he slipped away from her touch and obeyed Uffham.

Thirteen

Anne hissed in pure annoyance, both at him and at herself for weakening close to begging. Why couldn't she ignore the wretched man's existence? After all, marrying him would be nearly as bad as marrying a highwayman met on the road.

The theater was emptying, leaving orange peel and stray forgotten items, curdled smells and dead candle smoke. Workers were moving into the pit to sweep and tidy for tomorrow's production of the adventure. It hadn't been real. It should not affect her.

Tris waited with her staff in hand. She took it and left the box with him. "Caroline will be frantic with impatience," she said.

"I told her to go on, that you would need more time."

Did that refer to her limp or had he noticed her preoccupation with de Vere? She was relieved not to have to rush, however, and they worked their way out at the tail end of the chattering box audience. Everyone seemed pleased with the play, excited and a little shocked.

People enjoy being excited and shocked, she realized, and wondered if de Vere knew that and did it deliberately. Hadn't he mentioned the experiment with electricity? He did it, however, like an actor in a play. When the curtain dropped it was over, and the audience was supposed to know that.

Outside the theater, carriages were queuing to pick up ladies and gentlemen, and hackneys hovered nearby. Tris summoned one of them and helped her in.

"I've never been in a hackney before," she said.

"What a sheltered life you've led."

"I know."

He settled beside her and the plain carriage jolted off. "You'll note an absence of good springs, but the seats appear to have been washed and the straw on the floor is fresh. Pining for adventures and highwaymen, Mouse?"

She pulled a face at him. "No."

"Good. I fear Rosalinde is in for a hard life."

The thought, *But a merry one*, popped into her head. "You don't believe in gallant highwaymen?"

"Not at all."

She decided it was time to turn the tables and tease him. "Perhaps the gentleman doth protest too much. In French, Corbeau means both crow and raven, and didn't you recently buy an estate near Buntingford? That's Le Corbeau's territory.

He actually gaped. "Are you suggesting that *I'm* playing the high toby?"

"Are you saying it's mere coincidence?"

"That, or a very peculiar sense of humor. Dammit, I'll cage the rascal and find out what this is all about."

"You'll have to catch him first, and he seems to be a clever bird."

His face settled to that dangerous look. "So am I, Mouse, so am I."

A shiver slid across her shoulders, because of other matters entirely. "Tris, why were you behaving so ferociously with poor de Vere?"

"Poor de Vere? You might as well say 'poor Le Corbeau.' "

"Come now. You are worlds apart, but you were fencing with him as if he were your equal."

"I have to spar with someone. It grows so boring on this chilly elevation."

Anne sighed. "Why, Tris? You weren't snarling at any of the other men we talked to."

His lids lowered, making it hard to read his expression in the light of the dim tallow lamp. Eventually he said, "De Vere is more dangerous than any of the other men we talked to."

"Dangerous? To you?"

"To you, Mouse."

She sucked in a breath. "He wouldn't dare." After a moment she added, "He's not interested in me."

"Oh, yes he is."

Despite her will, her heart began a patter of excitement. "What makes you think that?"

"Male instinct." He took her hand. "Caroline mentioned that he was at Benning Hall when your sister was confined."

"Well, damn her."

"Tut, tut."

Anne knew she'd revealed too much. "I spent the evening gaming with him, Uffham, and Benning. But that's the extent of my wickedness," she lied.

"I wonder."

"He's avoided me ever since! Look at tonight. Is he here, pursuing me? No, he's in the green room with Uffham, the enchanting Mrs. Hardcastle, and a bevy of other theater beauties!"

She squeezed her eyes shut and tried to pretend that she hadn't let such telling comments escape. Having done so she might as well go on. This was Tris, after all, closer than any of her real brothers.

She met his thoughtful eyes. "He kissed me. No. We kissed. I haven't been able to entirely put it out of my mind."

"Was it your first kiss?"

"No. Yes. Like that, it was."

She thought she heard a hiss of breath. "I'll kill him."

"No!" She tightened her hold on his hand. "I asked him, Tris. I persuaded him. He did nothing I did not want."

"Do you want him, then? I'll get him for you if you do."

"Oh, Lord," she laughed. "Are you my hunting dog, to be sent out to bring back my chosen dinner? You know I'd never want a husband who came that way."

She considered Tris, in many ways her oldest and best friend who would do almost anything to help her. "He said I was discouraging. Do you think I am?" Reluctantly, she added, "Do you think I've discouraged him?"

"Sweetheart, I don't think a cannon ball would discourage de Vere from something he truly wants."

It was gentle, almost pitying.

Oh, God. Pity.

She swallowed and stiffened her spine. "Then I must get over it, mustn't I?" She looked at him, this fine, handsome man alone with her for a little while. "Would you kiss me, Tris? As he did? A strange thing to ask, I know, but we aren't brother and sister. And I can be sure you won't make too much of it."

After a moment, he asked, "Why?"

It would be revealing again, but there was no help for it. "I need to know if it's the kiss or the man."

He drew her into his arms, but slowly. "I'm not sure if I can do this right with you, Mouse, but come, let me try to kiss you better."

His lips were warm and soft on hers, his body hard and strong. She relaxed. It was certainly not unpleasant. She pressed a little closer and opened her mouth. . . .

Then she drew back. "It's not working, is it?"

In the dim light, she saw his rueful smile. "No."

She rested against him. "What am I going to do? What if it's only like that with him?"

"It won't be. I'm too like a brother, and you're too like a sister to me. But there will be other men."

"There have to be. I am resolved to find Mr. Mouse this season."

"Lord Mouse, at least, love."

She laughed, and he stroked her back as if she were the mouse's enemy, a cat. It was wonderfully comforting, but not the tiniest bit arousing.

How strange this all was.

Finding a quiet corner in the crowded, noisy green room, Race fought the temptation to worry about Anne Peckworth.

He should never have encouraged Uffham to come up to London for Anne's grand entrance at the theater, but he'd had to know how she was. He'd thought that seeing her in triumph, seeing her secure in her proper place in her world, attended by suitable aristocratic gentlemen, would enable him to get on with his life.

It hadn't worked.

When she'd appeared in that theater box, he'd seen only terror. But then she'd relaxed, and even flirted with her handsome escort. Uffham had identified him as the new Duke of St. Raven. An eligible *parti par excellence* and an old family friend.

That had stung, he admitted it, but he knew he had no hope there, so he'd been happy for her. He'd thought his mission over until he'd remembered that Anne had not wanted a life on the social stage.

Was she being pressured into a grand match by her family? Uffham was little use there, though he'd given a sketchy history of the duke's interaction with the Peckworth family.

Perhaps being duchess to an old friend would be to Anne's taste, but he'd had to know more. When the command came down from Lady Welsford, it hadn't been hard to get Uffham to obey. He seemed terrified of all his sisters. Race could probably have dragged him to Lady Welsford's party, but enough was enough.

For now at least.

Anne was safe. He was a good judge of men, and St. Raven would protect her as securely as he would himself. But did their temperaments suit? The duke was more of an eagle than a raven, and in some ways Anne was a mouse.

Meddling, meddling.

It went beyond tidying loose ends now, though. He cared for Anne Peckworth beyond sense, but more than that, he accepted his responsibility. She was out in the world, vulnerable, in part because of his interference in her life. He had to see her safe.

"Race! How lovely to see you again!"

He pulled himself out of his thoughts to greet Blanche Hardcastle, to pay homage to her outstretched hands, and then to shake hands with Major Hal Beaumont by her side. He'd met them both in Melton, when Con had taken him to Lord Arden's hunting lodge. He'd felt close to Blanche then, perhaps because they were both outsiders in that aristocratic enclave.

In fact there was a strangely familiar pattern in their love lives. Beaumont wanted to marry Blanche, but Blanche insisted that it was unsuitable because she was a butcher's daughter who'd worked her way up in her profession by any means available. She'd be his mistress but nothing more.

Of course, Anne Peckworth was not trying to persuade him into marriage, and there was no possibility of an unblessed union.

"Isn't it time you made an honest man of him?" he said to Blanche, teasing.

"Don't you start! I grant you did well interfering with Con, but find someone else to exercise your restlessness on now, sir." Perhaps he glanced at Uffham, because she lowered her voice. "You think you can work miracles there?"

"The greater the task, the greater the achievement . . . But no. Poor man, I'm using him."

"Ah," said Beaumont, who was no fool. "Lady Anne. She certainly set everyone talking tonight. No sign of a broken heart?"

"None. The Rogues can cease fretting."

"Then why," asked Blanche, who was no fool either, "are you so attached to Lord Uffham?"

"I'm barnacle to his bottom, dear lady," Race said, and refused their laughing demands for an explanation.

Fourteen

Anne woke the next morning feeling unaccountably depressed. And the sun was even shining!

No, not unaccountably. She had to accept that she was depressed by Race de Vere's lack of pursuit. She'd spent the hours of Caroline's successful party waiting and hoping for his arrival. She could hardly remember the various men who'd paid flattering court to her.

Tris might say that de Vere was interested, but she saw no sign of it, and as Tris had also said, mere unsuitability would not deter a man like Race de Vere.

He *was* unsuitable, though. Drifting asleep, her mind had wandered into storylines better fitted to a play. He was a lord in disguise, engaged in some secret work for the government. Or in a wager. He would challenge her to marry the poor man and then reveal himself to be worthy of her in every way. . . .

In daylight she laughed at such folly. In society everyone who was anyone knew everyone.

At Caroline's party she'd spoken to three military men who knew him, one quite well. The fact that they all thought highly of him didn't help. The fact that they all, in one way or another, described him as a madman proved that they knew what they were talking about.

She'd mentioned him to Lord Kimbleholt, who was from Derbyshire. "De Vere?" Kimbleholt had said. "There are no de Veres, certainly not in Derbyshire, Lady Anne." It was a large county, but it didn't augur well.

Major d'Arraby, the one who'd claimed to know de Vere well, had said that there was a rumor that his family came from trade and had assumed the name. Surely that couldn't be true. There was no trace of the shop about de Vere, and he had been an officer.

But then, so had Captain Crump. In wartime, many men rose from simple beginnings.

De Vere was a Mr. Nobody of Nowhere. There was no hope.

Where there's life, there's hope. She imagined him marching off like Jeremy Goodman to make his fame and fortune. Or better, doing such noble service that he received a title. After all, she *had* money, so that was not the issue. Sitting up in bed, chin on hands, she decided that Rosalinde had been wrong to reject that solution.

She shook her head. It was a play! Plays didn't have to make sense, but reality did. The reality was that marriage to Racecombe de Vere would outrage her friends and family and make her a laughingstock. And besides, the man had sense enough to not be courting her at all!

She forced her mind to the eligible men, but not even a fanciful imagination could turn any of the ones she'd met last night into her heart's choice. The pick of the aristocracy had flirted with her, and her heart hadn't missed a beat.

It was enough to turn a lady to laudanum, and now here she was still on country time, awake too early, before Hetty had even brought her washing water.

She straightened and stretched. Enough of this. Last night had been only the first step. She had weeks left and couldn't have met all the eligible men yet. And perhaps some would improve on acquaintance.

She decided that she had better be orderly about her search, however. She climbed out of bed and found her journal. She opened it to a blank page, checked the pen on her desk, and began a neat annotated list of the eligible men she had met, including their virtues and limitations.

She did not include Race de Vere.

By the time Caroline wandered in, yawning, tousled, and looking, Anne couldn't help thinking, well loved, Anne had her love life in order, on paper at least.

"What's that?" Caroline asked, peering over her shoulder. "A list? Really, Anne."

"How else am I supposed to go about this?"

"So who is your favorite at the moment?"

Anne picked a name. "Lord Alderton. His sister and I are friends."

"A consideration," Caroline agreed, lukewarm. She closed the book. "You are too impatient. Simply enjoy yourself and love will come."

Love? At the moment Anne would be content with someone she could tolerate. She put her pen back in the holder, and her book back in a drawer. "So, what are our plans for today?"

Caroline yawned again. "Visits, the park. The Fortescue ball unless you wish otherwise."

"I loathe the thought of all of it, but I will suffer in order to be married."

Caroline laughed and wandered off to dress.

The day progressed according to plan. The round of visits went better than Anne expected. Everyone was talking about the play, which was a great improvement on the usual dull conversation spiced only by malicious gossip.

In keeping with her new resolution not to hide her skills, she rode Monmouth in the park, wearing her smart gray habit with military frogging, a shako-style hat on her head. She was soon surrounded by an escort of horsemen, and was glad that Monmouth stood at fifteen and a half hands. She'd seen ladies dwarfed by their escorts, and she was determined never to be ridiculous.

She overheard Lord Michael Norton say he was hurrying home to get his horse so as to be able to accompany the "fair Lady Anne," and managed not to laugh. It confirmed her belief that the life of the ton was an absurdity.

She was enjoying it, however. In fact, she was slightly shocked at how much she was enjoying all this male attention. Did all the sorry bystanders in society secretly long to be at the center, so secretly that they did not even know it themselves?

At the same time she was aware that this enjoyment

was temporary. To live much of her time on this stage, acting in this trivial play, was not to her taste at all.

Yes, she thought, listening to Major d'Arraby on her right talk about himself at length, that was the London season—a weeks-long amateur theatrical, put on at great expense.

If she was constantly alert for Uffham—and his favorite companion—walking on stage, that was her folly to hide.

At nine o' clock, in a blue-spangled evening gown, she left with Tris, Caroline, and Welsford for the ball. When she arrived, the admirers swarmed in even greater numbers, male and female.

Caroline found a moment to whisper, "You are all the rage, as I predicted. Everyone wants to be seen with you."

Anne was tempted to swing her staff to clear some space around herself, but Tris neatly dispersed her admirers and led her into the ballroom. That was a relief, but it also presented a problem.

"You're scaring all my suitors away."

"If they're worthy of you, they'll brave my frown. But don't worry. I'll have to dance, and that will leave you open to attack."

"A very pleasant way to put it, I'm sure." She couldn't help noticing the avid female eyes fixed on him. "It's quite a sacrifice for you to come here, isn't it?"

"I can handle the bitches on the hunt."

"Tris!"

He smiled. "Technical term, my dear. And in hunting, bitch is an honorary name."

They were approached then by Lord Tewkesbury, his hopeful sister, Miss Raile, on his arm. He was a handsome man and smooth, very smooth. It didn't appeal, but she supposed that over a lifetime smooth would be better than rough. He was quite a wit and had her laughing.

Then Tris said, "Gads, a rat just ran over my foot!"

Miss Raile screeched and raised her skirts. They all looked down at the innocent polished floor. People nearby turned to look.

"Damned pests are everywhere," Tris said, raising his quizzing glass to eye Miss Raile's lower legs. Sadly, they were sticklike, which was not helped by horizontally striped stockings. "It's all right, Miss Raile. I don't *think* it ran up your skirts."

The lady's eyes went wide, and she made her brother take her in search of the ladies' room for a thorough check.

Anne made herself match Tris's straight face. "Wretch. Is he, though? A rat?"

"Definitely. Drink, women, and gambling."

"Ah, well, I don't think I would care for him anyway. He likes this fashionable life too much."

"Not a candidate for Lord Mouse of the Countryside?"

"Don't sneer. There has to be such a man somewhere."

Tris sat out the first dance with her, but after that he had to do his duty and bring stars to the eyes and magical hope to the breasts of some of the ladies. Anne was promptly swarmed.

She was tempted to cross every man present off her list simply for taking part in this folly. Scanning the mass of smiles, she caught sight of Alderton holding back. He was somewhat shy. She smiled brilliantly at him and held out her hand. He went pink, but he came to sit beside her, so she could wave the others away.

"Not surprising you created such a furor, my dear Lady Anne. You look like the stars in heaven."

A pretty sentiment, but she had no idea what it meant. She gave him the sort of smile a lady was supposed to give to a gentleman who paid her flowery compliments and then settled to well-practiced conversation.

They talked of the music, which was excellent, and the gracious ballroom, which few London houses could boast of. They admired the floral decorations and some of the more interesting fashions. It was, in other words, just like the other balls she had attended over the years.

After the set was over, another gentleman took his place. In fact two this time, one at either side. Smiling, listening—it had not struck her before how happy most men were simply to be listened to, how uninterested in anything a woman had to say—she made mental notes for her list.

She must marry a man who listened as much as he talked, and who treated her words with the attention they deserved. That ruled out d'Arraby, even though he was handsome, eldest son of a viscount, and rode well.

After three sets of dances, she knew that her husband must not be fond of this life. A week or two a year if he insisted, but beyond that it was a quiet country life for her. And the ban included Bath, Brighton, and every other fashionable spot.

She mentally crossed off Lord Vane—an aptly named dandy—and Sir Pomfret de Court. Both men had shimmered with the pleasure of seeing and being seen.

She regretfully crossed off Sir Rupert Grange. He was not a peer, but he was member of an eminent family, and had a reputation for involvement with important social issues. She might like that.

However, within minutes she knew she could not live with a man who laughed like a donkey. The strange *hee-haw* sound he made after each witticism was making her laugh, which convinced him of his cleverness. In fact, his bons mots were quite witty, and he was an intelligent, responsible man, so it was all rather sad.

For a moment she thought of taking him on as a challenge and somehow training him to laugh differently, or in fact, not to laugh at his own jokes at all. She stamped on that notion. She could imagine nothing more foolish than to go into marriage as an act of charity.

Pity in reverse. Horrible.

Her husband must not have a dominating mother. She made that resolution when she was again ambushed by Lady Flawborough, Mr. Pitt-Meadowing in tow, trying to ensure that he took Anne into supper.

Pitt-Meadowing was an unlikely contender in any case. He had the bloodlines, but no fortune or likelihood of making one. He was a pure fortune hunter. There were plenty of those in the upper ranks of society, and she wanted no part of them. Her husband must have a purpose in life other than to spend her money. She gave Tris a warm smile when he rescued her.

He found them a table and went to gather some food for her—an honor that would make most ladies swoon. Sad, really, that they did not suit. She could only pray that he one day find the perfect wife. She had little hope of finding the perfect husband.

Then a stir made her glance to the door. She felt her eyes widen. There was Uffham with Miss Rolleston-Stowe on his arm. Race de Vere came behind with giggly Miss Cottesly, Diane Rolleston-Stowe's adoring bosom-bow, on his arm.

Lady Fortescue must be in alt. Two eligible ducal prospects at her ball. For her part, Anne felt as Frances must have when she soaked her chair—shocked and unable to act.

In fact Lady Fortescue looked as stunned as Anne felt. Perhaps she feared a full-scale hunt, bitches in cry. Anne bit her lip to prevent any hint of that thought escaping, but she could only watch as Uffham hailed her as if she was his savior, and hurried over.

"Come to see how you're doing," he said, seating his partner in one of the spare chairs and taking the other. He seemed to be sweating slightly. Miss Rolleston-Stowe did have a very hunting-hound look on her face.

There were only four chairs at the table. De Vere commandeered two from nearby and seated Miss Cottesly, who giggled.

He said, "Good evening, Lady Anne," but then went off to the buffet tables, presumably to collect food for all four. No wonder Uffham was so fond of him. The man was indispensable.

But not, she thought sternly, *to me.*

She saw Tris notice de Vere and exchange some comments. She wished she could hear what they were. Mere pleasantries, or some inquisition? Tris had, after all, said that de Vere was interested in her.

Despite will, despite sense, the sizzle of excitement had started. If she wasn't careful, she was going to make as much of a fool of herself over de Vere as the other two ladies were doing over Uffham.

Tris and de Vere turned from the tables together. De Vere seemed to have solved his logistical problem by finding a large platter and loading it with food and bringing along the plates. Anne had to laugh. He was outrageous, but ingenious.

It was only as he put his collection down that she realized that the two empty places at the table were to either side of her. Of course. Uffham was opposite, bracketed by his hounds.

Tris gave her a plate of carefully selected food and sat to her right. De Vere sat to her left and chose items from the platter for Miss Cottesly. Who giggled. A footman came by with the wine and filled their glasses.

Interestingly, Anne didn't feel the same challenge shooting through from the men to either side of her. Was Tris not worried, or was de Vere not interested?

De Vere ate a little pâté, then said, "It's a pleasure to see you again, Lady Anne."

She would be cool and rational. "We saw one another last night, Mr. de Vere."

"True, but it is still a pleasure to see you again."

As she tried to assess that, Uffham made a remark about Berkshire and horse racing, which was apparently where they had been after Portsmouth and yachting.

When Uffham and Tris started swapping horse stories, she said, "I hope the racing was enjoyable, Mr. de Vere."

"Tolerably so, Lady Anne. I—"

"Tolerably!" Uffham interrupted, helping himself to another lobster patty. "Won a fifty guinea purse racing against that big black stallion of Arden's!"

"I did have a horse," said de Vere mildly. Then he added, "and the stallion had to carry a rider. Fair's fair."

Anne almost choked on a crumb. She knew why Uffham liked to have him around.

"I let him ride my Trafalgar," Uffham said. "Rides lighter than I do, and it paid off."

"Cavalry, de Vere?" asked Tris.

"Yes, Your Grace."

"St. Raven, please. I didn't think Arden's Viking was beatable. Was he riding?"

"Came over from his place at Hartwell." Uffham summoned the footman for more wine. "Wife's almost in the straw. I knew Trafalgar had it in him to beat Viking, and by gad, we proved it." He raised his glass. "To Trafalgar!"

They all drank, but Tris added, "And to his rider."

Anne smiled her thanks to him, but at his fixed look she knew it wasn't wise. She didn't know what Tris would do if he thought she was seriously interested in de Vere. Have him abducted to the Antipodes, probably.

Uffham leaned to inspect the platter. "I say, de Vere, those lobster patties were dashed tasty. Go and find me a few more, that's a good fellow."

Anne longed for de Vere to tell Uffham to forage for himself, but he rose and went off, just like a good and faithful servant.

"I admire your staff, Lady Anne," said Diane Rolleston-Stowe. "I wish I had an excuse to carry one, too."

Anne looked at her. "Really?"

The blond beauty blushed. "A sprained ankle or such, I mean."

The creature was trying to make an impression that would help her in her hunt for Uffham, but this was a pathetic effort. "If you sprain your ankle, Miss Rolleston-Stowe, you'd be better advised to stay at home with a cold compress on it."

"Take that advice," Tris said, drawing all the fire of the big green eyes. What was the heir to a dukedom, when an actual duke spoke to her?

"Oh, I'm sure, Your Grace," she gasped. "So kind. Of course, I hope not to sprain my ankle at all."

"Not until after marriage, at least."

"No, Your Grace?"

Anne recognized the wicked glint in his eyes and wondered what was coming.

"It's cant for getting with child, Miss Rolleston-Stowe," Tris explained.

The poor lady went pink, and Anne pinched Tris under the table on the nearest spot. His thigh. Which meant there was hardly anything to pinch. She was sure it was the same with de Vere's thighs. . . .

She was going mad.

"I say, St. Raven," Uffham objected.

"I say, indeed," said Anne. "We ladies do not need to know such things."

"Yes, you do." Tris was not at all deterred. "Then people won't be able to play tricks on you with double meanings."

The two hounds giggled.

Giggling hounds. She *was* going to go mad.

Uffham was quite eclipsed by Tris, and in typical contrary manner, was looking peevish about it. "Where the hell's de Vere?" he demanded, disregarding good manners entirely.

Anne couldn't take any more of this. She rose, which meant Tris had to rise and leave with her.

In the corridor he said, "Are you all right?"

"Perfectly."

"Be honest. Is it de Vere?"

She looked him in the eye. "No. If I'm upset it's because I've realized that I absolutely have to marry. One day Uffham is going to be caught in the slavering jaws of one of those bitches, and I have no intention of being the quiet sister-in-law under her paw."

"Bravo! But don't make a foolish choice out of urgency, Mouse."

She suspected that he was warning her off de Vere, and of course, he was quite right. "I won't, I promise."

That day established a pattern for her life, a pattern that soon came to feel worse than a treadmill. Morning visits, the park, and one or two events in the evening. As usual, she enjoyed the theater, the lectures, and the musical soirées. However, too many of the events Caroline dragged her to were those designed for people to see and be seen. The same people, over and over.

They said the same things over and over, too, and yet they all seemed so pleased with themselves. It was indeed like a play—one that was repeated day after day, night after night. *The Daring Lady* was a great success, still running after three weeks. Did actors weary of their parts? Especially when the most exciting player left the theater.

Right after the Fortescue ball, Uffham had gone to a house party in Oxfordshire, taking his favorite companion with him.

Fifteen

Anne met de Vere again nearly two weeks later at the Swinamer ball.

She arrived in some distress, for she'd foolishly agreed to attend a rout first. She always avoided them because they involved nothing more than walking and standing, but it had presented a challenge, so she'd insisted. To make matters worse, she was too vain to wear her supportive shoe for evening events.

At the Swinamers', she went up the stairs with Caroline and Welsford, trying not to limp more than usual, greeted their hosts, and passed into the ballroom. Or rooms. The Swinamers had elected not to hire assembly rooms for this event but didn't really have a large enough house for the number of guests they had invited.

They'd cleared three linked rooms in their house to serve, but the rooms were already crowded and likely to become more so. Worse, Anne immediately noticed that there were an inadequate number of chairs.

She longed to claim one, but few were sitting yet and she didn't want to be so obvious. She stood, more grateful than usual for her staff, and let the men come to her.

Lord Alderton hurried over with flattering speed. His confidence was growing, and she really must consider him. He was pleasantly ordinary in looks, with soft brown hair and a long nose. He wasn't at all overwhelming, which she liked. He didn't excite her in any way, but she refused to be sad about that. Presumably that would come in time.

No other man eclipsed him.

She watched the chairs begin to fill. Eventually she

said, "Perhaps you could escort me to a chair, Alderton."

Pleased as a dog asked to perform a trick, he crooked his arm for her and led her tenderly to a group of empty chairs. "Which one would you like, Lady Anne?"

This seemed so silly she had to bite her lip, but she thanked him and settled in the middle one. Immediately, as if someone had rung a dinner bell, she was surrounded by men. They blocked her view of the dance floor, and in moments they had moved the chairs to either side of her and filled that space, too.

Panic struck for a moment, but then she pushed it aside. She wasn't going to be eaten by ravening dogs tonight, even if Marlowe's grinning teeth were right in front of her.

"Lord Marlowe," she said, "my foot is aching most terribly. Could you find me a footstool?"

He reared back like a horse at this unwelcome command, but went, as he must.

"Please," she said quickly to the men who were pushing in to fill the space, "don't block my view of the dance floor, gentlemen."

A small space was left, jealously guarded. Anne peered through it, looking for help. She wished Tris were here, but he disliked balls as much as Uffham, and for the same reason, so she'd not asked him. She couldn't see Caroline or Welsford.

Besides, she should be able to handle this on her own.

She hated to be such a center of attention, however. She knew everyone must be aware of the ridiculous scene, and all the young ladies must be grinding their teeth. She didn't even want most of these men!

Then Lord Osmunde, rotund heir to the Earl of Balbeckstone, threw himself prostrate on the floor and beseeched her to rest her foot on him.

Straight out, her foot would have to go on his ample bottom.

"Get up, Osmunde. Please!"

She looked around for help, and her eyes collided with the laughing ones of Race de Vere across the room. Heat surged into her face, but she had to bite her lip not to smile for simple pleasure.

He was here!

"Like Lord Raleigh, you know," Osmunde said.

She pulled her attention back. "He only laid his cloak over a puddle, Osmunde."

"There, see!" He leaped to his feet with admirable agility for someone of his size. "He should have laid his person. Doubtless have won a title for it, and then King James wouldn't have topped him, eh? Ancestor of mine on me mother's side."

Clearly he didn't feel at all ridiculous. How did people like him have such thick skins?

"Please, gentlemen, do not let me prevent you from dancing."

They didn't move. She prayed for the dance music to start. Presumably then Lady Swinamer would command some of them into duty. She glanced across the room again, but de Vere had disappeared.

Had he been a figment of her imagination?

Was she going mad?

Osmunde moved into her precious gap. "I would like to watch the dancing, sir."

He shuffled to the right. Other men shuffled around, trying not to lose place. In a moment, she was going to scream.

Race de Vere walked through the opening as if the men had parted just for him, went to one knee, and placed a cloth-wrapped object in front of her. It was exactly the right height for a footstool, but since this was de Vere, anything could be under the purple brocade.

"What is it?" she asked, heart thundering. As well as his presence, she was panicked by fear of being even more outrageous. Oh, for the days when she had faded into the wallpaper.

Still on one knee he met her eyes, a twinkle saying that he knew what she was thinking. "Quite safe, Lady Anne, and it won't get you into trouble."

Then he took her foot by the heel, thus by the shoe, thus not quite touching her skin, and placed it on the object. Tingles shot right up her leg to alarming effect.

The impromptu footstool was even padded. A cushion of some sort?

She didn't dare look to see how all the titled gentlemen around her were taking this interloper, but she tried to make light of it. "If I had a title to bestow, Mr. de Vere, you would have it."

"Fool," someone muttered as suggestion.

Anne extended her hand to de Vere. "Hero," she said.

"You honor me, my lady." He kissed her hand, but then he rose, still holding it. She tugged and could not break free. She should have known not to encourage the wretch.

"However," he said, "heroes have a high casualty rate. I would rather be your fool. As your fool I could sit at your feet and amuse you while these highborn gentlemen do their duty by young ladies who are able to dance."

As if on cue, the musicians signaled the first dance. He released her hand and suited action to words by subsiding, cross-legged, to the floor.

She bit her lip. The wretch was going to have her laughing out loud. When she was in control, she smiled around at her looming suitors. "Alas, sirs, he's correct. The music is starting, and you cannot ask me to be so selfish as to claim all your attention when other ladies wish to dance."

She was reinforced, thank heavens, by Lady Swinamer, who descended upon them, smile fixed. "My dear sirs, you must take turns sitting by Lady Anne and be kind to the other ladies." She seized two by the arms and dragged them away.

Fearing the same fate, the others followed, all jealously watching to see that no other stole a move by staying. De Vere obviously didn't count. As the lines formed for the dance Anne found herself alone for a little while, with only him, still sitting by her chair.

She fixed her gaze on the dancers. "Do please get up, Mr. de Vere. You make me feel like a figure of fun."

"You, Lady Anne?" But he rose, neatly rearranged the chairs to either side of her, then sat on her left. It was all done so smoothly and efficiently that she became breathless. And by now she was watching him.

Here was trouble again, and yet she couldn't be sorry.

It was as if someone had added a thousand candles to the chandeliers.

The other seats around were instantly taken, but she was glad to see deaf old Lady Leveson on her right side.

"What is supporting my foot?" Anne asked.

"Four of Sir John Swinamer's weightier tomes, covered by a cushion and a small curtain."

Anne's eyes widened and she shifted her foot to the floor. "Sir John's collection of ancient books is quite famous, you know."

"Is it?" But then his false shock turned to humor. "You are not abusing his Gutenberg and Caxton, dear lady, merely some volumes of decades-old sermons."

She put her foot back with relief, but still wondered what might happen if Lord Swinamer realized what was going on. He was famously proud and protective of his library.

"He has a first folio of Shakespeare, I believe," she said.

"You tempt me to go exploring again. . . ."

When the first dance of the set ended Anne emerged from an entrancing discussion of books. She blinked at de Vere, almost dazed. "I assume Uffham is here."

"Am I not a barnacle? Besides, they wouldn't admit me otherwise."

"Come, come, you are hardly such an outsider as that."

"Am I not?"

In fact, he was. "You are certainly a miracle worker to persuade Uffham to step into this lions' den."

His smile was quick and delightful. "Lady Swinamer's ball as a recreation of the Coliseum! The evening will be perfect if Miss Swinamer and Miss Rolleston-Stowe come to blows over Uffham. I think I will design a new sort of fan—with spikes at the end of the spokes."

She rapped him with her own unarmed fan, then wished she hadn't. It seemed shockingly intimate.

He clearly didn't think so. He was as relaxed as a happy cat. "In fact Uffham is here to give you moral support . . ."

She raised her brows and looked around.

". . . but at the moment is gathering his courage in the gaming room. Playing hazard, perhaps. We could join him there."

A connection shot between them. "I doubt they'd accept farthing points."

"I could bank you. I'm good for about fifty guineas at the moment."

"Your winnings at racing?"

He smiled. "Precisely."

Was that truly all he had in the world? The clothes she wore had cost more than that. It reminded her that he did not belong on her list of suitors, amusing and interesting though he was.

What did she know about him? He had admitted to being the oldest son, and he presumably had the de Vere blood somewhere on the family tree. Not the sort of man she was expected to marry, but not completely impossible.

As she indulged in these outrageous thoughts, she watched the dancing, enjoying the swirl and sway of it. Sometimes at home, at private parties, she danced the simpler measures. She knew she was inelegant, but she enjoyed it. Inelegant steps, inelegant marriage . . .

She glanced to her side. "Are you fixed in London long, Mr. de Vere?"

"Perhaps you should ask your brother."

"Nonsense. You will leave when it suits you. When will that be?"

"I am a creature of whim, remember. And a fool."

"I doubt that, too." Desperately, she added, "Will you not tell me something real about yourself?"

"I am no mystery."

"Yet you are here in poverty, almost a servant, while an oldest son. Is your rift with your father so unhealable?"

Then she wished it all unsaid. Something in his eyes suggested that her question stung.

He replied calmly, however. "Not at all. We have met and blood did not run. It is simply that my father has grand ambitions for his line which I do not share. I was not, and am not, a good and dutiful son."

"You surprise me," she said dryly. "What are his plans?"

But he shook his head. "I escaped into the army, and he's never forgiven me."

There were many questions she'd like answered, but it was clear he would tell her only what he chose. "How did you escape, then? He must have tried to stop you."

He relaxed, which was when she realized that he had been tense. Since the mention of being the oldest son. Why? What question had he feared? Her curiosity about Race de Vere was as dangerous as opium, but like an opium-eater, she could not resist.

"He tried, but too late. My ally was my uncle, Colonel Edward Racecombe." He shifted to turn to her, now seeming lightly amused. "I was army mad, and Uncle Edward persuaded my father that a visit to a barracks would cure me. He was recruiting at the time, and when he sailed for Portugal, he took me with him."

She stared at him. "Wasn't that illegal?"

"Highly, but the Horse Guards weren't eager to release a new recruit, and my father did not have the influence to force the matter."

She saw him weigh whether to tell her something or not, and prayed hard that no one interrupt. If he was hesitating, it must be of importance.

"My father, you see, won a lottery."

She gaped. "Truly? I've bought tickets sometimes for fun, but I've never known anyone who won."

His lips twitched. "Now, indirectly, you do. He decided to take his fortune and become a gentleman. He bought an estate, and a wife. But first," he added, and she sensed the important thing coming, "he changed his name."

"Not de Vere," she breathed.

"I told you the truth when I said I was a de Vere born of a de Vere, but he wasn't born a de Vere. Thus he had nothing to throw into the battle. No powerful relatives, no influential friends, and not even much money. By then it had been sunk into house, land, and the trappings of a gentleman. By the time he'd bludgeoned the officials to write to my uncle about it, I'd been serving for six months."

"What happened then?"

"I was summoned into the presence of Sir Arthur Wellesley and asked whether I wished to serve king and country or go home. The implication was clear that if I answered the latter, I deserved to be shot, but I didn't want it anyway. I'd flown the coop and on the whole was having a marvelous time. The last thing I wanted was to return to the cage."

Her heart warmed at the intimacy of the moment, the trust implied in what he was telling her, but then a chill trickled after.

Now she knew. There was no de Vere blood. He was not a gentleman in any way her circle would understand the term. He did not even have right to the name he carried. He was beyond the pale—and, she suspected, that was why he had told her all these things. Had her reaction to his reappearance, her fledgling hopes, been so obvious that he felt he must warn her off?

She swallowed and grasped their conversation as refuge. "All this at sixteen," she said, wafting her fan. "Without influence or money, it must have been hard."

"You will insist on trying to make a romance out of this, won't you? I had my uncle, don't forget, until he fell at Burgos. And my father began sending me a quarterly draft for a hundred guineas. If I was to be an officer, I was to do the *nouvelle* de Veres proud. I'm afraid he still doesn't fully realize what an unfortunate choice of name that was."

"Have you not considered reverting to the real one?"

He laughed. She wasn't quite sure why. "What is real?"

Not this. The current set of dances was ending. Their time was almost at an end.

"Is the Duke of St. Raven not here?" he asked.

"No. Why?"

"I would trust him to protect you from the ravening mass of asses."

Strictly in the manner of light flirtation, she asked, "Are you not going to, sir?"

"I don't have the firepower. Here comes Lord Marlowe, teeth and footstool to the fore."

She looked through the dancing couples, and there indeed was the heavy-muscled man, bearing a footstool. In moments he would have to see that she already had one of sorts.

De Vere slipped to one knee again and reversed his procedure, gently lifting her foot off the books and putting it on the floor. It occurred to her for the first time that he must finally have had a good look at her ugly, twisted foot.

She looked down and met his eyes, his serious eyes.

"If it wouldn't embarrass you, Anne, I would kiss it." Instead, he took her hand. "Pretend, if you will, that this is your poor foot."

His lips pressed, gentle and in some strange way healing. Ridiculous though it was, she felt that if Race de Vere could stroke and kiss her foot it would instantly straighten.

And he had called her Anne. . . .

Then he rose and walked away, his bundle borne before him like a holy relic. The cream of society parted before him, staring. Then they turned to stare at her.

Anne hated it, but she didn't hate what had just happened.

Now, however, she had Marlowe placing a proper footstool before her. She praised his resourcefulness, but that didn't prevent complaints about de Vere.

"Damned impudence. Who is he, anyway? De Vere? Pretentious upstart."

"He served excellently in the war, Lord Marlowe."

"By his own account, I suppose."

"Not at all. Many men have spoken well of him."

Marlowe frowned, but then said, "Come to think of it, saw him hunting this year. Good rider."

"Cavalry, I gather."

"Suppose so." He took possession of the chair to her right. "Saw him out on one of Cavanagh's horses one day. Almost bought the beast." He settled into hunting stories, and she could smile and nod and think her own thoughts.

She knew that in the Shires at hunting time a great

deal of horse trading went on. Men who wanted to sell their horses would sometimes hire excellent riders to ride them in a hunt to show them off to best advantage. Roughriders, they were called.

She supposed that was another way de Vere had been making money. It wasn't to his discredit, but it was worlds apart. Perhaps he gambled, as well. Tris hadn't known, but he might be discovering such things now. Perhaps he was even a libertine. He'd been free enough with his kisses.

Rats, mice, and farthings.

The dance ended, and Marlowe surrendered his place to young Lord Laverly who required rather more conversational assistance. Or at least, he expected clear agreement every few moments.

She agreed that the music was loud, the rooms crowded and far too hot. She sympathized on his headache. Then he asked for her favorite headache remedy.

When she confessed that she never had any, he sighed. "You are blessed with a sturdier constitution than I, Lady Anne."

He didn't look particularly frail, but now she noticed how pale and puffy he was.

"Perhaps you need more fresh air, Laverly. I find a brisk ride clears most complaints."

He shuddered. "But this weather. It has been so inclement. Sciatica, dear lady. Been a martyr to it all my life."

Since he couldn't be much older than she was, she didn't believe him. She could trump his complaint with her foot, which also ached in the damp and which truly had plagued her all her life, but he wasn't worth the bother. He'd probably claim a fatal disease just to win the hand.

Mentally, however, she was scribbling black lines through his name on her husband list. She couldn't bear a hypochondriac.

She knew he collected glass, so she ruthlessly switched the subject to that. Soon she was back into nodding and smiling as he lectured her on the mysteries of colored stemware.

That was when she saw that Race de Vere was dancing. Wonderfully. His army life must have included such things. Officers were expected to play their part at social events. It wasn't that he performed and posed as some dancers did, but simply that he was athletic, graceful, and clearly did not have to think about the steps. It was an eight, and as he wove his way through the ladies she watched each lose a bit of her heart to his flirtatious smile.

Then she noticed that one of the ladies in his eight was Phoebe Swinamer. In fact Miss Swinamer was his partner.

Now that was strange.

Phoebe Swinamer was a raving beauty with a high opinion of herself. It was well known that she intended to marry as high as possible, which was why she was still unwed. Not for lack of offers, but because none yet had been quite to her standard. She had also doubtless driven some away. She was so cold and self-centered that even the most dazzled earl, marquess, or duke had to notice eventually.

Anne smiled and murmured some response to Laverly, but mostly she watched Phoebe wind her way through the dance, completely aware of every graceful pose she struck. The beauty wore the blank smile of a china doll until she interacted with someone she thought important, whereupon her brilliant smile flashed out.

Every time she danced with de Vere, that smile shone.

At de Vere? Anne was sure that in Phoebe Swinamer's judgment he was less than a flea. Was his charm powerful enough to dazzle that ruthless mind?

Oh, Lord, she suddenly thought, Uffham!

De Vere was Pheobe's key to Uffham.

And Uffham was just possibly stupid enough to be caught in the trap.

". . . dropped dead right under me. Shattered my nerves."

"What?" Anne turned and stared at Lord Laverly.

"Barbary Wench."

"What?"

"Heart. No sign, of course. And now Dancing Girl has the scours."

She realized he had switched to talking about horses.

A more interesting subject to her, but she did not want to listen to a recitation of poor Dancing Girl's revolting symptoms. What was more, she needed to check on Uffham and talk to de Vere.

"Speaking of bowels . . . ," she most indelicately said, then rose to walk away. She couldn't help but delight in the shocked look on his face. This London season was going to drive her into lunacy.

Sixteen

Anne found the gaming room where mostly older people were seated at card tables. She realized then that, of course, no one was playing hazard. Dice games were technically illegal, and certainly improper. Gambling was illegal, but no one paid attention to that. Most people were playing whist for penny points. One table was playing brag, a much simpler game, and Uffham was there.

She went to stand by him. He looked up and smiled. "What ho the sister. Enjoying yourself?"

"It's a ball, Uffham, and I can't dance. I've just escaped a bore."

"Good for you. Want to play?"

The other men looked a little taken aback, and she was tempted to accept just to shock them. "No, thank you. You won't be dancing, then?"

The whites of his eyes showed. "I should think not. Only came to show the flag for you."

She didn't see how sitting in the card room was doing her any good, but she thanked him and went on her way sure that he was safe for a while. She'd confer with Caroline later and find a long-term strategy to avoid the Swinamer trap.

De Vere was the one who could do the most good, however, and she needed to alert him. She was surprised that he'd been drawn in so far as to dance with Miss Swinamer, but it was possible he'd been fooled. She was startlingly beautiful, with her glossy dark curls, perfect complexion, and large blue eyes. Last year she'd almost hooked Lord Arden, heir to the Duke of Belcraven, but he'd escaped.

A string twanged in the back of her head. Arden was one of the Rogues. She remembered, too, that Mrs. Hardcastle had been his mistress before his marriage.

All useless information since he was safely married. She did a quick mental review of the names Uffham had given her to be sure there were no lurking Rogues among her suitors. She would not be married out of pity.

Sir Stephen Ball. She knew him slightly, so he couldn't take her unawares. Major Beaumont, apparently current protector of Mrs. Hardcastle. Who else? A Simon St. Bride. For a moment she toyed with the idea of de Vere being St. Bride in disguise, but then she shook her head. People knew him, people who had known him for years, and besides, despite the occasional mystery, she was sure that he spoke the truth.

She was safe from Rogues, but for respite from the pests she went to the ladies' room. She tidied herself, chatting to a couple of women who were resting there, feet up. It didn't require a deformed foot for them to ache. When a flurry of ladies came in, she knew the set had ended. Now to find de Vere.

She went out to hunt, but didn't have to hunt at all. She almost ran into him in the corridor.

"I wanted to talk to you." It spilled out brashly, so she added, "About Uffham."

He crooked his arm for her. "Of course, Lady Anne. There is a problem?"

She put her hand on his arm, aware of how much even this restrained touch affected her. It was a strictly physical thing, but quite extraordinary. Shouldn't it mean something to him, too?

She had to find out.

"Not here." She smiled as if they spoke of the weather. "You mentioned a library. Is it nearby?"

He looked at her, and she saw wariness. She gave a light laugh. "My dear sir, I have no designs on your virtue!"

It was true. She wasn't planning to tear off his clothes.

She had to fight wild giggles at the thought as he led her along the corridor and around a bend to a set of quiet stairs to the ground floor. There, he opened a door, peeped in, and then widened it for her. She entered a book-filled room lit only by one well-shielded lamp.

Anne came to her senses. What on earth did she think she was doing? She knew young ladies who made an art of going apart with men at these events, but she'd never, ever done it before.

"We should leave the door open," she said.

"Most certainly." He was still by the door, in fact, distancing himself.

She fluttered her fan. "Come now, sir, you can't possibly think I will try to compromise you. What would be the point?"

His lips twitched. "None at all." He came a few steps closer. "So, Uffham?"

Pity take her, she'd been arch to protect her pride, and rude, as well. There was no point in apologizing, however. It was all true. He was a nobody, and they had no connection except Uffham.

"Phoebe Swinamer," she said.

"You're worried that Miss Swinamer is on Uffham's trail. Correct, of course, but I think I've distracted her for the moment."

She rolled her eyes. "Mr. de Vere, no matter how fascinating you are, you will not draw Phoebe Swinamer off the track of one of the only ducal prospects around."

He was unoffended. "True, but I argued St. Raven's case. I pointed out that he was already a duke, and that he had confided to me that he wanted to marry as soon as possible."

Anne stared at him. "Did he?"

"Of course not."

"He'll throttle you!"

His lips twitched. "Like all the rest, he'll have to catch me first. And I'm sure he can cope with the Swinamers of the world." He sobered. "Does it bother you?"

"Me? No, why?"

"I think you would suit."

"St. Raven and I? We certainly would not."

"Perhaps you need to open your mind to the idea, Lady Anne. He is not your brother. He's no blood relation at all."

He was advising her to marry another man!

But she thought she heard ambivalence, and she could not forget the way he had handled her foot, kissed her hand, and called her Anne.

Stealing time, she turned to look at the shelves. "Did you say there was a Gutenberg?"

"Yes, but it's locked in that case along with the other treasures."

She went to peer through metal-barred glass. "I'm not used to being locked out of such things."

"And I'm not used to being let in. We should return to the company."

She turned to study him. "Why do you keep hammering home the differences between us?"

His brows rose. "Isn't it more that they simply exist?"

Unable to resist, she limped toward him. "I don't know if they matter."

His face became a mask, a smiling handsome mask concealing everything. "You have only to ask anyone of your acquaintance."

"Perhaps I don't care."

"That my father was a carriage maker?"

She stopped dead. A *carriage maker?* She licked her lips. "Perhaps no one need know."

It was, of course, the wrong thing to say.

Pity. That was the emotion behind his slight smile. "It's the sort of thing to come out, particularly if society's curiosity is stirred."

That should settle it—she couldn't marry the son of a carriage maker—but being close to him, private and close, seemed to make such harsh realities evaporate. Her skin tingled, and the need to touch was almost overwhelming. She put her gloved left hand on his jacket, slid it up to his shoulder.

He captured it with his own, pulled it away. But he didn't let it go. Instead he kissed it.

If only she wasn't wearing gloves.

"What is this?" she whispered.

"Folly." But he let her hand drop, pushed shut the door, and pulled her into his arms.

The kiss was everything she remembered and more, swirling down and around her like heat and honey, satisfying places that had longed for this for weeks. The taste—his taste—was a feast for the starving. She lost her grip on her staff, but he caught it and propped it up against the wall.

When he drew her close again, she raised her hands to cradle his head the better to explore him with lips, with tongue, with every inch of her sizzling body.

His mouth, hotly, hungrily on hers.

His hands, pulling her harder and harder against his hard body.

She wanted more. She crushed against him urgently, achingly, longing to fuse with him in some impossible way. . . .

She only realized when he broke the kiss to suck in air that she'd driven him up against the door. Their eyes met. Were hers as dark and desperate as his?

Suddenly he reversed their positions, driving her hard against wood panels. He grasped her chin and held her for a brutal kiss.

Brutal?

Race?

But there was something different here. Her back hurt where an edge dug into her spine and his hot mouth attacked her, his tongue thrusting deep and hard.

Then she felt his hand on her thigh, on her skin there. He had her skirt up!

No! She tried to shake her head free, to escape, to scream for help.

His lips freed hers, but his hand replaced them, blocking sound. His other hand slid between her thighs.

"Not what you want?" asked this demonic stranger.

She shook her head desperately.

"Are you sure? You did entice me here, after all. . . ."

She could only shake her head and swallow tears.

He moved one hand but kept the other over her mouth. "Far be it from me to force a lady fair. A warning, though. If you scream you could cause me a great deal of trouble, but it's just possible that you'd end up married to me, and you don't want that, do you?"

Emphatically, she shook her head.

He took away his hand and stepped back, smiling.

Anne slapped him with all the strength she had. Then

she grabbed for her staff in order to hit him harder. He was there before her and moved it out of reach.

"You'd regret it later," he said, still smiling. "I'll leave it outside."

Then he left and she sagged back against the shelves, scrubbing at her wet face. *Oh, Lord, the paint.* There was no mirror here, but she had a handkerchief tucked away. She blotted her face as best she could, trying to swamp the turmoil of feelings that burned like lye.

Her hand still stung, but she was glad, so glad, that she'd hit him like that. It was tempting to tell Uffham or Tris, who'd thrash him properly, but guilt stayed her.

She had inveigled him in here, and it hadn't really been to talk about Uffham. Unacknowledged, she'd hoped for something, for kisses, and perhaps a little more than kisses. He had held back, and she had pushed.

Pushed him over the edge.

She knew the truth now, however. At bottom he was no gentleman. He'd said she should try out a husband's kisses before committing herself, and he was clearly right.

She sucked in some deep breaths and checked her hair and headdress by feel. All seemed fine. She opened the door and peeped out into the corridor. No one was about, but her staff, as promised, leaned against the wall. She grasped it, feeling complete again, glad all in all that he'd stopped her from murdering him with it.

A bubble of wild laughter threatened. That would be a ridiculous end to her ridiculous season.

She made her cumbersome way up the quiet stairs again, then realized that they brought her out on a bedroom corridor. Taking a risk, she opened a door and was rewarded by a deserted bedroom, and a mirror. When she saw herself she gave thanks that she had checked. Her eye color had smudged, and strands of hair were sticking out. As well scream to the world about what had happened.

There was half a jug of cold washing water, enough to repair her face, though it meant removing most of her false bloom. She did away with it entirely. What good had it done her so far?

She pinned up her hair and surveyed Lady Anne

Peckworth, more like her old self, but in fine feathers. Race de Vere had said something about flying high, and warned of the possibility of disaster.

Now she knew what he'd meant. Inside her growled a place that had enjoyed his fierce assault, that had slapped him because she'd enjoyed it more than was decent. A place that wanted to fling herself out of her lofty tower and try to fly.

But Icarus's fine feathers, she remembered, had melted in the heat, and Icarus had died.

Seventeen

Two days later Uffham came round to Caroline's in the pouring rain to complain that "damned de Vere" had left with hardly a by-your-leave to go heaven knows where, and what the devil was he to do without him? Life was so flat.

Looking at rain-drenched windows, Anne could only agree, but her life had been flat since de Vere's outrageous behavior. Now, apparently, he had truly walked off the stage.

"Perhaps he's gone home to Derbyshire," she suggested.

Uffham frowned. "Do you think so? Never mentioned it. I wouldn't have minded a trip to Derbyshire."

Who was the barnacle on whom? It would seem de Vere pulled men to him as well as women.

"If he's gone there, it will be on personal business," Caroline said. "He might not want a stranger present."

"You think he'll be back?"

"Why not? And I do hope so. He's excellent company."

Anne looked out at the rain knowing that he wouldn't return. She had to be glad of it. She was now free to apply herself wholeheartedly to choosing among more appropriate gentlemen. There had to be at least one who was tolerable.

Five men had already asked her if they could approach her father. She'd told them all that she wasn't ready to make a decision yet, but in truth they'd all been impossible.

Alderton had not yet asked, but she suspected that

she could have him any time she chose to encourage him. Not yet. Not yet. There had to be some man in her world who could stir a trace of the same excitement as de Vere, but her time was almost up. The season was almost over.

Perhaps her practice of riding in the park was hindering some prospects. Not everyone kept a riding horse in town and besides, riding in a group did not give an amorous gentleman many opportunities.

Moreover, her equestrian abilities had caused some other ladies to copy her. Poor Miss Cottesly had been thrown and received not the sprained ankle she'd wished for, but a nasty bang on the head.

Anne decided that as soon as the weather cleared she would drive instead. She'd be able to take gentlemen up with her and give them a fairer chance.

So she sent to Lea Park for her phaeton and matched grays, and when they arrived she tooled them into Hyde Park. She had to admit to enjoying the stares and even exclamations, and thanked Tris for pressing her to learn to drive so many years ago.

As if summoned by her thought, she saw Tris with a group of men. De Vere was not among them. Of course not. She groaned that the thought had even crossed her mind.

Tris smiled and summoned her to stop. When she obeyed, he climbed in.

"You're not driving," she said, setting off again.

"Why would I want to, though I do admire your team. Are they for sale?"

"Of course not."

"Pity. Glad to see you still have all your skills, though."

"Thank you. Not that there's much chance to show them here."

"Devil a bit. Managing not to lock wheels with the other carriages requires finesse. So, how's the assault? I hear that you nearly created a riot at the Swinamers' the other night."

"Nonsense, though the men behaved badly. It's pure competition with most of them, I swear it. I don't think more than half are seriously interested in marriage."

"Probably not. We're a terrible lot for wanting the other dog's bone. So, who leads the pack?"

Wearily, she said, "Alderton."

"There's a bit of the season left yet."

She supposed that summed it up.

She tried to resist but couldn't. "That de Vere has left Uffham, casting my poor brother into despair."

"He wasn't in despair last night, but then, he was in female company."

She glanced at him. "Do I want to know?"

"Probably, but I'm not about to tell you."

"Of course not. You were there, too."

"Precisely."

She growled at him. "I don't understand men."

"Good."

"How am I to make a rational choice if I don't understand what's going on?"

"Watch the road." When she obeyed he added, "Listen to your male relatives."

He ran through her most obvious suitors, tagging some as rats, mice, or farthings, but leaving over half acceptable, including Alderton. She longed to ask if he'd checked on de Vere, and if so what he'd found, but she had enough control to resist.

"Time for me to get down," he said. "A queue is forming."

Anne slowed her horses and saw that he was correct. A number of men were standing around obviously waiting to replace him.

"They look like children queuing for pony rides at a country fair," she murmured. "I'm tempted to charge them a penny each."

He laughed. "Charge Sir Pomfret de Court a farthing."

She surveyed the group. "I see. And Marlowe probably eats rats for breakfast."

"I can believe that."

"Good."

He swung down from the vehicle. "Step right up, gentlemen. Step right up! One ride a guinea, all to go to charity."

Anne was tempted to flick him with her long whip,

but she laughed and took the guinea offered by Sir Pomfret, and set off on another circuit of the park.

Race had cut free of Anne Peckworth and London and ridden south into Sussex, heading for sanctuary at Somerford Court. He was, after all, still technically employed as secretary to Con Somerford, Viscount Amleigh. He'd parted from Con over a month ago, forced to miss Con's wedding because of the need to make contact with Lady Anne before the news broke.

He wondered what Con would think of his recent work. He hoped he never heard the whole of it.

As it happened, he met his employer three miles from the Court, not far off the London Road. Con—dark-haired, handsome, and steady—was riding out of the lane to Mitchell's farm. Race ran a quick assessment and was pleased. The steadiness that had made Con an excellent officer was still there, but now it blended with an ease that spoke of a contented country gentleman and husband.

"The wanderer returns," Con said amiably.

Race drew Joker to a halt. "I left work undone."

"I tell you, young man, the work is never done."

Con turned his horse ambling toward home, and Race fell in beside him. "The burden of the married state aging you? If not, I'm only two years your junior."

Con smiled. "You don't act it, gadding about wherever you please. So, what have you been up to? 'Matters to attend to' isn't very informative."

"I've been tidying up Lady Anne Peckworth."

Con looked at him. "I don't recall her being particularly disordered. What have you done?"

That was the officer speaking. Race knew he was on tricky ground. "Nothing to her detriment. I left the lady well and in fine spirits." Best ignore the unfortunate parting.

"You'd be bound to say that. Both for your own sake and mine."

"Con, this is me, remember? If she'd slit her wrists, I'd tell you. She was taken aback by the news of your wedding, but not heartbroken. I'm sorry if that wounds your pride."

"No, of course not. I'm delighted." Con, however, still looked as if he didn't believe it.

"In fact, she has taken her place in society and is going about finding a husband more to her taste."

Con drew his horse to a stop. "Anne? Lady Anne Peckworth? The one with the limp?"

"Yes, the one with the damned limp. Lord, you sound as if she should be kept in a locked room!"

"Anything she wants to do, of course. It just doesn't sound like . . ." He frowned. "It's not her family, is it? Pressuring her?"

"Her younger sister is eager to marry, but that's the only pressure."

"Marianne? She's still in the schoolroom." But then he frowned. "How the devil did you find all this out? Even for you, it's a trick."

"Not at all. I simply ate toads for Uffham."

Con shook his head as if it were buzzing. "You've been fetching and carrying for Uffham? Is he still alive?"

Race laughed. "Very much so, but angry with me. I've come to hide."

"Angry? Why?"

"For leaving."

Con shook his head again, but in a wondering way, and put his horse to the walk again. "Does it not grow tedious?"

"What?"

"The way people become attached to you."

"You didn't throw a fit when I left you. I thank you for it."

"I've missed you."

The statement didn't burden because Race knew Con had many friends, both near to hand and scattered, and now had a beloved friend-for-life. It was perhaps why he and Con rubbed along so well.

"To be honest," Con said, "I didn't expect you back. Your work was done, wasn't it, when I married Susan?"

"I left some papers unordered."

"That was never your true work."

Race shrugged. He'd as good as admitted in Devon that he'd attached himself to Con to straighten out his life. Con had left the army in 1814 to take up his title, then returned for Waterloo. The battle had hit him hard, but it had been the death of fellow Rogue, Lord Darius Debenham, that had been the last straw. Since Con was a career soldier and Lord Darius a hasty volunteer, Con had felt that he should have kept his friend safe—though heaven knows, there was no way he could have done so.

Race had met Con again on a hunting field in the winter and worried about him, especially when Con had inherited the added burden of the Earldom of Wyvern. He'd attached himself—like a barnacle—in order to sort things out. Becoming the new earl's secretary had been a useful device. The irony was that he'd found his vocation.

"I need something useful to do and a place to think," he said. "One that puts few demands on me."

"Somerford Court should fit the bill. Now, tell me exactly what's happening with Anne. . . ."

Race gave thanks for Con and passed the rest of the ramble home with an edited account of Benning Hall and Anne's emergence in London.

Unpretentious and undemanding, Somerford Court did fit the bill, and so did Con and his family. Susan Amleigh, the remarkable woman blessed—or cursed—with angelic looks similar to his own, seemed delighted to see him again. Con's mother and sister were warm. He paid for dinner with amusing stories about London, none of them unkind, and felt as if he were relaxing for the first time in weeks.

Con observed Race over dinner. Normally he didn't bother lingering over brandy and tobacco, especially as he neither smoked a pipe nor took snuff. Tonight he decided to create more time with Race. He wanted to know what was going on. He sent a silent message to Susan. She caught it, of course, and led the ladies away.

The table covers were drawn, and port, brandy, snuff, and nuts left between them. When the door closed on the servants, he said, "Amusing as always, but there's no need to work so hard. Consider us family."

Race took a hazelnut and broke it neatly with the silver crackers. "I don't know how to behave with family."

"Then you need to go home and find out."

"I have been home."

Con stared at him. "I didn't know that. It went badly?"

Race ate the nut. He had not yet touched the ruby port in his glass. He rarely drank much. Con had learned that about him. He seemed a wild spirit, but Con had learned that he seldom stepped beyond his own control.

"My father has married again. I have a half brother and sister."

"Good God. And you didn't know?"

Race took a sip of wine. "I knew. Perhaps it is our plebian blood, but we are not the sort for high drama. My uncle insisted that I send him duty letters, and he wrote to tell me of important matters, such as my mother's death, and later his marriage and the children."

With Race it had always been hard to detect mood. "How do things stand now?"

The shrug was so slight Con felt it might even have been a flicker of candlelight. "Unsettled." He took another sip of port then seemed to contemplate the play of candlelight on crystal and ruby wine. "He loved me deeply. Too much. It hurt him when I ran away. It's natural to avoid hurt. Love's the devil, isn't it? But is it love if it's eight-tenths possession? He planned my life to suit his ambitions. I was to be the first true gentleman of his line."

"Then you should please him greatly."

Race shook his head. "I was to make all the right friends at school and at Oxford, then go to London. If possible, I was to marry a blue-blooded lady." He looked up, amused. "He's on his way to buying a title."

"Lord!"

Con meant it as a mild expletive, but Race said, "Precisely."

Con laughed. "There's nothing wrong with that, you know. My ancestor was a younger son who got a barony for clerking for the monarch, then my great-great grandfather upped it to a viscountcy by groveling to the first George."

"At least they were working for it rather than giving interest-free loans to important people. The main problem is, of course, that any title must come to me in time."

"You don't want it?"

"Not particularly." Interestingly, however, Race's lids lowered at that question, hiding something. "The problem arises because my half brother, little Tommy, is now the apple of my father's eye."

"How old is the child?" It was a pointless question, but it covered a moment where Con couldn't think what to say.

"Five. A most promising youngster. I don't think I mentioned that this time my father had the sense to marry a sturdy, practical lady—daughter of a prosperous farming family. She seems to be thriving on giving birth and creating a genuine home at Shapcott House."

"If your father gets a title, it has to come to you not to his second son. There's no way around it."

Race looked at him, and the hair stirred on Con's neck. "Not if I were to become illegitimate."

"What? That's not possible."

"It is, as it happens. I told you that my father changed his name, choosing the damnable de Vere. And then he wanted to puff off my mother's fine connections by giving me her family name as my Christian one. Positively pagan, if you ask me. The thing is, he had gone through no legal processes to change his name but he married as Thomas de Vere. And that, technically, makes his first marriage null and void."

"Good God. He's going to bastardize you?"

"He was well on the way to it until I went home." Race rose suddenly and walked away from the table. Deeply revealing for him. "I knew that it would be a bad idea to go there, but I felt I owed him that. I had no idea . . ."

He turned to face Con, but now from beyond the candlelight. "I think he'd persuaded himself that I was nothing to him any longer, but he's my father, and in his way was a good one. He always loved me more than I deserved. And now I have placed him on the horns of a painful dilemma."

Con rose, too, with outrage. "He still wants to bastardize you in favor of this other child?"

Race made an impatient movement of his hand. "In general principle, I don't mind. There's no one in my mother's family left to care, and I've long suspected that I can never live the life my father wants. Going back confirmed it. I'm not sure what I want to do, but it's not to be squire, or even lord, of a small estate in Derbyshire. Add to that, with my mother's death, my father's mercantile blood has resurged, and he's dabbling in mining, iron-foundry, even banking."

"You'd be good at banking."

"Not really. I don't have a scrap of interest in profit." He laughed. "I could spin that off into a really bad pun, but I'll spare you." He strolled back to the table, seeming relaxed again. "I can't imagine wanting any profession where being a bastard on a technicality would affect me, and I would be delighted to have my relationship with my father uncontaminated by our clashing interests and ambitions, but . . ."

"But?"

Race, however, shook his head. He picked up his glass and raised it. "To my brilliant but sinister future!"

A play on the bar sinister of heraldry, signifying bastardy.

Con drank, but asked, "Future doing what?"

"I rather liked being a secretary."

"Your father won't approve of that," Con said without thinking.

Race's eyes sparkled. "That's the beauty, isn't it? This way, he won't care."

Con put down his glass, thinking there was more to this than he'd immediately grasped. "You are certainly welcome to consider yourself my secretary for as long as it's convenient. But it's too lowly a position."

"That does rather depend on the rank of the employer, and how he treats the secretary. You treated me as a companion."

"True. Thinking of becoming Uffham's secretary, then?"

"Tallying his gaming debts? He has a while to go before he needs one of my caliber, and he's too tempting. I'm resolved to stop trying to fix people's lives."

Con was almost distracted by that, but resisted. He tried to think of a question that would be useful. "What is it you really want to do?" he asked. "Strange sort of question, isn't it? I was a second son, so I needed a profession, but I went into the army more on a whim than a plan. Once Fred died, my fate was settled. Like it or not, it's my role to manage my estates, take part in Parliament, be a magistrate, and generally meddle in the world around me. If I wanted to be a scientist or blacksmith, I'd have to fight centuries of tradition to do it. But what sort of work, day-to-day work, would you like to do?"

Race stared at the uninspired portrait of the second viscount. "I truly do enjoy paperwork, but I'm not sure I would once it became routine. How many employers are going to conveniently inherit chaotic estates as you did?"

"Few, please God."

"I found the discovery aspect of the Wyvern estate entrancing. So much to learn in those papers—about history, legend, local gossip, and national movements. About smuggling—and strange fertility beliefs."

Con laughed. His distant relative the mad earl of Wyvern had been obsessed with his own lack of fertility and had gathered bizarre objects from around the globe in a hunt for a cure.

"I might," Race said, "like to write books about the things learned when digging into forgotten papers. I'm not sure how that is done, but there must be a way."

"I doubt it makes much money."

"I seem able to live on very little." Race strolled to the door and opened it, thus signaling that the confidences were at an end.

Even so, Con said, "You'll need a decent income when you want to marry."

"I doubt I'll marry," Race said.

Later that night when Susan joined Con in bed, she asked, "So, what's wrong with him?"

He pulled her comfortably against him and gave a brief account of Race's situation.

"Do you think he truly doesn't mind being bastardized?" she asked, stroking his shoulder, his neck, his chest. She was a bastard herself, so knew something of it.

"It would be a nine day's wonder, but everyone would know it was a technicality. The de Vere name gives him more trouble, and he's learned to cope with that. Certainly a slightly irregular birth will be no problem if he finds a way to play with dusty records and write books."

"But?" she asked.

"But?" he repeated, mind drifting almost entirely to the magic her hands were creating, to the soft silk of her skin and the delicious, familiar smell of her.

"I'm sure there's something else on your mind," she whispered against his lips.

"I have a mind?" He slipped down to taste her breasts.

She chuckled softly. "About Race."

"You're pursuing this to torment me."

"Of course."

He stroked her nipple with his tongue, tormenting her in turn. "What was your question?"

He felt desire shudder through her and smiled, but she'd always been a strong-willed woman. "About Race. Something else is bothering you."

He kissed and gently sucked, considering the question only to stretch this moment out, to linger before plunging deep. "Ah, yes. There's something about the illegitimacy that does bother him. Something he fears to lose, perhaps. He's keeping it private and that is his right, but I think it might be a woman. . . ."

Any interest in that was evaporating, however, even as he spoke the words. He surrendered to mindless passion.

Eighteen

The day after Anne drove in the park, she opened the newspapers to find the story there, written so as to make her sound heartless and mercenary in a time of hardship. Anne had Welsford send a notice to the papers that the money was going to the fund for crippled veterans, but despite a clamor for it, she refused to drive out again. The attention was too unbearable. Instead, determined to be her unashamed self, she walked.

She drove to the park with Caroline in Welsford's carriage, but then they both descended and walked. No one could be driven to copy her, and she couldn't create some new stir. Moreover, surely some of her suitors would be turned away by how clumsy she looked, even with her staff. She was, after all, wearing her leather boots, the right one heavily built to support her foot.

Alas, her lack of grace didn't discourage many, and she was hindered by too many men around her. But then she remembered *The Daring Lady.* If Mrs. Hardcastle could control a whole audience of men, surely she could control a few. She assessed her selection and decided that it was time. She chose Alderton and sternly waved the others away. Reluctantly, they obeyed.

Her mother always said that if a woman turned her mind to it, she could fall in love with anyone. It was time to apply her mind to falling in love with the most appealing of her court. As Alderton talked and she nodded, she reminded herself of all his virtues.

He was titled, had a pleasant estate, and as a bonus, she was already friends with his sister. She knew through Harriet that he was a good and generous brother. Tris had not found any mice, rats, or farthings. Alderton had confessed to only wanting to spend a few weeks in London each year for essential Parliamentary matters, though he did like to spend a month or two in the Shires in hunting season.

The sad fact about that was that she saw it as a bonus. There was nothing wrong with the man, but he might as well be a plaster statue for all the impact he had on her. She could link arms with him without the tiniest frisson, and didn't even want to try a kiss. Would that change in time? Surely it would.

"I say, Alderton. Fair's fair. Time to give you a chance with the lovely Lady Welsford."

Anne hadn't paid any attention to Caroline's escort, but she turned to find that it was indeed burly Lord Marlowe, showing his teeth and phrasing his request in a way that made it impossible for Alderton to refuse.

What's more, Anne saw no sign that Alderton tried. She knew that Tris would not give up a desired lady in this situation. Nor would de Vere. She remembered Tris saying that even a cannonball wouldn't stop de Vere going after something he wanted.

She took Marlowe's arm and strolled on, smiling as he talked about hunting. She was unable, however, to prevent her mind leaping on the subject of de Vere like a starving dog on a lump of meat.

A strange idea had suddenly popped into her head. She and de Vere had been growing close that night at the Swinamer ball. Becoming friends, perhaps. They'd talked about books and libraries, and she'd made the surprising discovery that he was as interested and perhaps as knowledgeable as she. Then he'd talked so freely about himself.

That kiss in the library had started like the one in Benning's study—a blissful merging.

But all that night, he'd been telling her how unsuitable he was. Had that switch to violence, that crude invasion, been yet another calculated act, designed to disgust her forever? That might mean that the earlier part of the evening had been as wonderful for him as for her, but that he'd tried to protect her from it.

Such a conclusion was probably a sign of insanity,

but she couldn't quite dismiss it. Before she settled her mind on some other man, she must meet de Vere again. He'd disappeared, but she had no doubt that with her family's powers, and Tris's if need be, she could find him.

How did she do that without alerting anyone to her interest? Perhaps she could pretend an unpaid debt. . . .

For now, though, she had Marlowe looming beside her, all big shoulders, big bones, and big teeth, and obviously a serious suitor. She wished she could ask him why.

"I suppose you spend the winter in the Shires, Marlowe."

"Of course, Lady Anne. Though when married, I might break the habit a bit."

If married to him, she would make sure he went there from November to Easter!

"Such a shame that ladies cannot hunt there," she said, simply to upset him.

"They'd get in the way, though I admit that you ride well enough, Lady Anne, to perhaps be tolerable."

A meager compliment, but one she quite liked. She didn't want him to start being pleasant. A damp spot on her face was a relief. "Oh, dear. It's going to rain."

They instantly turned back toward the waiting carriage, but it was some distance, and the rain began to come down more heavily. Her frivolous parasol shielded her for a while, but then became soaked. Caroline and Alderton broke into a laughing run, clearly forgetting that Anne couldn't.

Marlowe tried to sweep her into his arms.

"Stop that!" Panicked, Anne swung at him with her staff. She got in more of a swing than she planned, and the amber knob clunked heavily against his head. His eyes crossed and he sat on the damp earth.

Despite the rain, everyone stopped to stare. Caroline had her hand over her mouth.

Anne dropped the staff and went to her knees, rubbing the lump in his hair. "Oh, Lord Marlowe, I'm so sorry! I don't know what came over me. Please say you're all right!"

The third time she'd hit a man!

He blinked at her and then suddenly grinned, showing

more teeth than ever. "Right as rain, dear lady, to have you playing the ministering angel. Don't worry about that little tap. I must have frightened you."

Others were there by then, including Caroline and Alderton, and they were helped to their feet. Marlowe was still grinning, and Anne realized that he was grinning at her. At her body.

She glanced down and saw that her flimsy muslin dress was sticking to her. So were most of the other ladies' dresses, but because she was small in the bosom she wore only the lightest corset. The shape of her breasts was clear, and her nipples were standing out. She dreaded to think what her legs looked like.

Marlowe licked his lips. Any moment he'd be drooling. . . .

Thank heavens that the carriage drew up beside them, the hood already raised, and she and Caroline could climb in and escape.

Anne collapsed back against the seat. "I hate London!"

"You do seem to have a way of stirring trouble," Caroline said, but Anne could see that she wanted to laugh.

"This is all your fault!"

"I have arranged it so that you have all the admirers you could want. Probably more after looking like that."

Anne covered her breasts with her hands.

"To end it, all you have to do is pick one."

"But I don't love any of them!"

"You know what mother says about that."

"I'm sure you had to work to fall in love with Welsford."

Caroline's wry face was acknowledgment of that hit. "Not Marlowe, I assume. He is a fine figure of a man."

Anne saw that she was serious. The taste for men was so very different. "Definitely not Marlowe. He's a libertine."

"Is he? I wonder how you know that. I suppose it's Alderton, then."

After a moment, Anne said, "Not yet."

"Not ever," Caroline stated. "Anne, you can't marry someone you feel so lukewarm about. The right man is out there somewhere."

"Where? I feel as if I've met every peer and his brother."

"You haven't, though. And there's no great hurry, after all."

Anne blew out a breath. There certainly wasn't, not if she wanted time to think more about de Vere, perhaps to find him again.

"I suppose not. I set a target of the end of the season, though, and I do so long to get back to Lea Park."

"That," Caroline said, "would be a totty-headed reason to marry anyone! There are still house parties, and Brighton, and any number of other occasions."

Treadmill, thought Anne, but she agreed.

They entered the house, still damp, to the news that Lord Welsford was entertaining the Duchess of Arran in the drawing room.

"Mama!" gasped Anne, covering her breasts again.

Caroline looked similarly schoolgirlish. "Let's tidy ourselves. Quickly!"

Caroline ran upstairs, and Anne followed as fast as she could. Both of them were ready to go down in record order, and Anne noticed that Caroline had little if any paint on. The Duchess of Arran was a warm and loving mother, but she'd always been a strict one, too.

They entered the drawing room to find not just their mother, but also Marianne sitting beside her beloved, injured hero, Captain Lord Percy Shreve. Marianne was almost as slender as Anne, but with a robust bloom and a reddish glint to her hair.

Anne could practically smell the orange blossom around them, but she was also shocked at Lord Percy's appearance. She'd last seen him as a vigorous, strapping young man. He must have lost at least a stone and his drawn face made him look years older.

He attempted to rise, and was urged back to his seat by everyone. Anne saw that he hunched slightly, favoring his left side and leg, and was clearly in pain. Marianne rose to adjust a cushion to support his arm, looking as if she felt every stab of agony herself.

Anne had only to marry to clear the way for Marianne to take care of him all the time.

Welsford escaped as the tea tray he'd ordered arrived.

"Your father wished to attend the last weeks of Parliament," said the duchess as Caroline sat to serve tea, looking as if she were taking a test. "We took the opportunity to bring dear Percy to see a new doctor recommended by Dr. Normanton. And Marianne needs new clothes."

Consolation, Anne thought, *for not being able to marry immediately.*

She was not happy about this development. She did not need her mother interfering in her affairs.

"We're not receiving, though," the duchess continued. "So tiresome, and not good for Percy."

Marianne patted Lord Percy's shoulder and hurried over to Caroline. "I'll help serve tea. Don't try to get up, Anne!"

Anne hadn't thought of it—a maid stood ready to help—but now she felt set apart as one of the cripples.

At least Caroline passed her test. The duchess took her cup, sipped, and then smiled. "Thank you, my dear. Just as I like it.

"So difficult," the duchess went on. "Marianne's clothes, I mean. She should have her season next year, but matters might fall out differently." She sent a long look at the sofa where Marianne was back to hovering over her love. Anne couldn't decide whether that look predicted a wedding or a funeral.

The duchess sighed. "She may as well have some of the wardrobe now. Caroline, you can advise me on the latest fashions."

"Of course, Mama."

"Is Uffham in town? I haven't seen him in an age."

"No, Mama. He's in Oxfordshire, I believe."

"And St. Raven?"

"I believe he left for his Hertfordshire house."

"Naughty of him not to have visited Lea Park since he returned from abroad," the duchess said, "but I'm sure London has its charms. Hertfordshire. A new estate?"

Anne remembered that her tongue was not crippled. "Apparently he bought it nearly a year ago, Mama, wanting something close to London as well as his Cornish properties."

"Very sensible. What is it called?"

Anne shared a look with Caroline. "Nun's Chase. I think he bought it for the name alone."

Her mother tutted, but with a twinkle in her eye. "I assume he is up to no good there. Not, I hope, an attempt to revive the Hell-Fire Club."

Anne had an alarmed vision of her mother's reaction if it was. She'd probably sweep down and put all the men on bread and water for a week.

"Is that de Vere still with Uffham?" the duchess asked, holding her cup in the air. The maid moved instantly to take it to Caroline to be refilled.

Anne drained hers and held it out, too, giving herself a few minutes breathing space. "You have met Mr. de Vere, Mama?"

"He has visited Lea Park with Uffham. He seemed a good influence on the dear boy, and I understand he was very helpful to Frances in her little emergency. Frances always could be impetuous."

Anne shared a look with Caroline. Apparently the duchess's daughters were expected to manage even childbirth in good order.

"He was," she said. "Useful. Especially in sobering up Benning."

"Pas devant la bonne, Anne," said the duchess. Such matters should not be spoken of before the maid. Anne was sure the servants knew all the shadier goings-on of their employers.

"We really should do something for that young man," the duchess went on. "I'm sure your father could find him a position—in a government department perhaps. He seems just the sort to move up brilliantly."

Anne didn't disagree about the brilliance, but her mother's plans stung all the same. He was viewed as a servant again.

But then, he was a carriage maker's son.

The duchess put down her cup. "I do hope dear St. Raven hasn't drawn away all the eligible gentlemen to his Nun's Chase. They are so easily distracted."

"I gather it's a small house, so it must be a small party."

"When they have a mind to it, dear, the gentlemen

can be happy sleeping ten to a room. So"—the duchess turned all barrels on Anne—"how are you enjoying yourself?"

Anne knew what that meant. "I'm sorry, Mama. I have not yet settled on a husband."

"Five offers, I understand."

"Not formal ones."

"None to your taste, dear?"

Anne thought of giving a complex answer, but she didn't want to raise anyone's hopes. "No."

"I don't mind, Mama," Marianne said, clutching Lord Percy's hand.

"This is nothing to do with you, dear. Anne, you know we would be delighted for you to live on with us at Lea Park. I'm sure in time you could bring your father and me gruel, and tuck blankets around our legs. However, I am not convinced that you want that life, despite your fondness for lurking in libraries. If you wish to be married, you must put your mind to it. It is not something to be approached halfheartedly. And sometimes," she added, "it is not wise to be too particular."

Anne was mortified by this public lecture, before a servant, even. Since her mother seemed to have forgotten the maid, Anne gestured for the stone-faced woman to go. She thought the woman sent her a flicker of sympathy as she left.

Lord Percy looked pained by more than his wounds, and her mother suddenly sported splashes of color in her cheeks. She had forgotten the maid. Anne couldn't remember ever taking command of a family situation like this, and it encouraged her to speak her mind.

"Caroline married for love, Mama. So did Frances. Marianne has stars in her eyes. Why must I settle for less?"

"As I understand it, you could *settle* for an earl, two viscounts, and a baronet of considerable wealth and lineage."

"Not all at once."

"Don't resort to flippancy, dear."

Startled at herself, Anne made herself calm down. "Then, in all seriousness, Mama, title is not the main point."

"Not the *main* point, dear, but you could hardly marry lower. Look at poor Claretta Tregallows." The duchess actually shuddered. "The man's family are fishmongers! Prosperous ones, I understand, but even so. It is extraordinary what sorts of people ended up as officers because of the trials of war."

"Captain Crump is generally admired, Duchess," Lord Percy said. "He is an excellent officer."

Anne liked him even more for that. She wished she could ask if he had an opinion of de Vere.

"The simple fact," said the duchess relentlessly, "is that by now you must have spent time with most of the eligible titled gentlemen, Anne. If your heart has not been touched, you may as well pick the most suitable." She shook her head. "Such a mistake to let you hide away for so long. These matters always become more difficult when a girl gets older. I'm sure if Claretta had married before she was twenty she would have made a more suitable choice."

Anne felt like a sulky schoolroom miss, and just as tongue-tied.

"What about St. Raven?" her mother demanded.

Anne jumped. "Heavens, no!"

"And why not?"

"He's like a brother, Mama."

"Nonsense. And didn't those Egyptians marry brother and sister? You should think about it."

"Him being the only eligible duke."

Her mother didn't so much as blink. "Precisely. Such a shame to let some other woman have him, especially as you always rubbed along so well." She rose. "Don't try to get up, Percy. In fact, why don't you and Marianne stay here while I attend to some errands." She swept out leaving the couple, Anne knew, as a living reproach to her.

In the Duchess of Arran's mind, all ladies should marry, marry young, and marry well. To do less was a sign of a weak will. Anne had no doubt that her mother had been eyeing Tris as a juicy target for years—not for Anne, but for Marianne. Now Marianne's heart had fixed elsewhere, her target had obviously changed.

Temptation flickered along her raw nerves. Marriage

would offer Tris escape from the hunt, and her escape from this predicament. It would indeed be comfortable. Was that so bad?

But then she thought of that attempted kiss and knew it wouldn't work. Even if they could bring the necessary passion into the business, their hearts would not be touched. She might have to marry for mere comfort, but she would not condemn Tris to that, too.

"Are you cold, Anne?" Caroline asked.

She must have shivered.

"Only in a daughterish manner."

Caroline grimaced in sympathy. "I thank heaven daily that I fell in love with an earl." Then she grinned at Lord Percy. "I'm sure you can't *help* being a younger son."

The man smiled, then winced, and Marianne cried, "Don't make him laugh!" She looked at Anne with great seriousness. "You are not to let our affairs hurry you, dearest. I know now how very important the deepest feelings are. You must not settle for less. And," she added with a bright smile, "Mama will be sure to let us marry soon, even if you haven't . . . chosen yet."

Anne knew, however, how every day must seem a day too long, and then, as they all chattered and gossiped a picture of Lord Percy's current situation emerged, innocently she was sure.

He was living with his mother at the Shreve dower house. The dowager Marchioness of Gravender was frantic over the state of her younger son and insisting on doing a great deal of the nursing herself.

Her fretting and weeping was hard on the invalid, but it was the treatments she insisted on that were worst. Poor Percy was being bled and even blistered on a regular basis, but didn't have the heart, or perhaps the strength, to refuse.

Bleeding and blistering did have their uses, but Anne couldn't imagine how they would help muscles and sinews that refused to heal. The problem seemed to be the large quantity of shrapnel driven into his body and the numerous operations to try to dig it out. Poor man. Having suffered a number of attempts to straighten her foot, she shuddered in sympathy.

The only way to free him was marriage and a move to a new home. Marianne's plan, though not spoken directly, seemed to involve a small house on the Lea Park estate, peace, rest, and the gentle attentions of Dr. Normanton.

When healed, Lord Percy wanted diplomatic work, and Marianne sparkled at the thought of traveling and living in many of the world's capitals. But would he survive to take up that future if things went on as they did now?

When Anne heard the duchess's carriage draw up, she went to intercept her mother in the hall. "Mama, do you not think that Marianne and Percy should be allowed to marry? They are young, but it seems very much a fixed thing, and truly, I would not mind."

"You're very kind, dear, but it will do them no harm to wait."

"It seems to be doing Percy a great deal of harm!"

"He needs resolution. A young man who cannot stand up to his mother might not make the best husband, you know."

Anne hadn't thought of that. "He's a loving son. Is that so bad?"

"No, dear, of course not."

"If I were to marry, there really would be no barrier to their union, would there?"

The duchess smiled. "No dear, unless dear Percy's health did not permit it."

There, it was clear. Quite likely her mother had accepted the inevitability of Marianne and Percy's marriage—assuming he survived. She was using it to force Anne, in particular to force Anne to marry Tris.

She met her mother's eyes in a way she could not remember doing before. "You have no fear that I will plunge into an unsuitable match in order to clear the way?"

"Of course not, dear. You have always done just as you ought."

The duchess returned to the others, but Anne took refuge in her bedroom, burning with anger. It was unfair. It was *wrong*!

It was, however, inescapable. Her mother had a will

of iron when it came to what she saw as her children's welfare. Her father, powerful as he was, left family matters to her mother. An appeal to him would not help.

It was some consolation, Anne decided, that her mother's dearest wish would never come true. She would not end up as the Duchess of St. Raven.

It would have to be Alderton.

He would make an acceptable husband, and at least she need not fear that he would try to bully her. He had been timid even when suggesting a visit to his estate. If nothing changed before Parliament ended and the fashionable throng dispersed, then she would take up his invitation and doubtless end up his wife.

Parliament completed its business and closed on July second. A few days later Anne traveled to Alderton's Wiltshire estate, with her mother as chaperon. The duchess was somewhat disgruntled.

Anne loved her mother and knew that she truly thought she was doing the right thing in pushing for the marriage with Tris. During the journey she tried to explain their feelings. She even mentioned, without the reason, their failed kiss.

"Nonsense," said the duchess. "I'm sure my feelings for your father have always been more comfortable than passionate, and it has worked out very well."

Anne wished she dared ask whether her mother thought passion ill-bred, but the answer was probably yes.

If passion was ill-bred, then the visit to Alderton Hall did not threaten good breeding. Anne tried very hard to picture herself there as happy wife and mother, but it was a formal house not helped by relentlessly overcast days.

Alderton Hall was new, the previous house having burned down thirty years before. It was elegant. It had been recently enhanced with all the latest conveniences, including a patent stove in the kitchen and two indoor water closets.

It was ruled, however, by Alderton's doting mother and grandmother, who were both permanently in residence. Both ladies were gratified to think that their son might marry a daughter of the Duke of Arran. Both were unhappy that said daughter was a cripple. Both clearly intended to continue to rule the roost.

Anne felt that she could perhaps fight one incumbent, but two?

The final straw in Anne's mind was that there were no family records older than thirty years. They had all gone up in flames.

Certainly Alderton's sister, Harriet, was as sweet and pleasant as ever, and she lived only four miles away. She was into her second pregnancy, however, and busy with her home and community. Anne suspected that they would only meet occasionally.

Alderton being Alderton, she managed to put off an outright declaration, and here her mother's plans came in useful. Once Anne gave her the hint, the duchess smoothly extricated them from Alderton Hall without unpleasantness, but with no commitment made.

Anne traveled back to London, relieved, but with her situation unimproved. She still wanted to marry, but now she didn't know where to turn.

"Why," Caroline declared when asked, "to Brighton, of course! Welsford and I are off there in a few days, and you must come. There will be different faces there and as well the whole atmosphere is different in Brighton. You will see!"

Nineteen

Anne had never been to Brighton. Summers had always been at Lea Park. After a few days in the Regent's summer playground, she was coming to the opinion that this had been a wise choice. She liked the country in the summer, and Brighton was a continuation of London society with an extra layer of frothy silliness on top.

Gambling, for pennies or guineas, was everywhere, and people seemed to feel obliged to stroll endlessly "taking the sea air," but in effect, meeting and being met. When not strolling, they were having picnics on just about any open space, or riding donkeys, or staging silly contests such as who could hop farthest.

She'd remarked to Caroline that she thought everyone in Brighton was bored. Her sister had been appalled, and Anne had accepted that Caroline did enjoy it, so perhaps most other people did, too. That only confirmed her suspicion that she was out of step with society in more ways than having a limp. The thought of all the enjoyably useful things she could be doing at home, such as charitable works, summer pleasures with old friends, and exploring the family documents, was almost a physical pain.

At times she became short-tempered, but it didn't seem to deter her admirers, old and new.

As Caroline had predicted, there were new faces in Brighton. Many of the officers of the local regiment had joined her court, a few seriously, and there were half-pay officers aplenty here. None of them seemed to have anything better to do than bother her every hour of the day.

She had to admit that there were some appealing men among them, at least on a superficial level. Dashing Captain Ralstone, for example, with the dark curls and laughing eyes, was very pleasant company. She wasn't sure she could or should take him seriously, however.

She began to suspect that her affairs had gone beyond courtship and become a kind of sport. Perhaps wagers were being laid. She asked Welsford, and he confirmed it, but refused to give details. "Anne, Anne, how very unsporting. It might affect your choice."

"I don't suppose the fox is interested in being sporting either, only in a safe covert. If there's anything about those wagers that might affect my choice, Welsford, then I want to know about it."

But he shook his head. "If there was anything dishonorable, you know I'd put a stop to it."

Thwarted, Anne wrote to both Uffham and Tris, insisting that they find out all the details and report to her. She dropped sealing wax on the letters and stamped her seal into it, acknowledging a coil of anxiety deep inside.

Her instinct to privacy was offended by wagers, but she wished she was more sure about the outcome than those placing bets. She might as well just roll the dice, which made her think of de Vere, which was not uncommon.

Damn the man. How dare he disappear off the face of the fashionable world?

No one had heard a word from him. His absence was made worse by how often it was remarked on. He might have been a nobody, but he had stamped an impression on the soft wax of the ton. He was remembered by ladies as a charmer, and by gentlemen as amusing. The term *madman* often came up, but always fondly.

There were other stories, too. He had helped Mrs. Hatley's son out of a disastrous entanglement, and extricated shamefaced Lieutenant Gore from a gaming hell before he'd lost all.

It would seem that he couldn't walk by anyone in trouble.

Including her?

Was that the explanation? That he'd arrived at Benning Hall with Uffham, assumed her to be broken-hearted, and set out to heal her? And then his attentions had interested her too much so that in the end he'd had to be cruel to be kind.

When she remembered driving him back against a door in frustrated passion she wanted to take laudanum and go to sleep forever.

It fit, it all fit, but then there was the memory of the way he'd handled her foot, the way he'd kissed her hand. *"Pretend, if you will, that this is your poor foot."*

Had he driven her away because she was a tiresome barnacle, sealed to him with pity, or simply because he believed himself too low for her happiness?

If the latter, wasn't it true?

She put her elbows on the desk and rested her chin in the cup of her hands. She was letting de Vere get in the way of a rational decision about her future, she knew she was. She must deal with the important question. If Race de Vere loved her, if he would like to marry her, was she willing to marry him, to be Lady Anne de Vere, horribly misaligned wife of a nobody?

In the end, she hadn't been able to resist investigating him. The Brighton libraries contained little detail about Derbyshire, but she had eventually found Shapcott Manor in a guide to Derbyshire. "A pleasant manor house in parkland, long home of the Racecombe family, but now owned by Thomas de Vere, Esquire."

That confirmed his story, but then she had never doubted that he told the truth. Fool that she was, she'd traced the few words in the book with her finger as if they were a living connection to the man who was never far from her thoughts.

When Caroline had hired an artist to do sketches of them both, Anne had asked the woman to execute a drawing of her hands. She still had it, but with no idea where to send it.

Perhaps, as she'd said to Uffham, he was in Derbyshire mending the breach with his father. If so, what did she do? Send him the picture? Write a letter like pathetic Miss Littleton? Hire a post chaise and dash up to Derbyshire?

She laughed. Everyone would think she was eloping.

She stopped laughing. If she wanted to marry de Vere, she'd probably have to elope. Her mother would lock her up rather than permit her to make a marriage like that.

Tris could probably find him. But then, if she asked Tris to do that, he'd know why, and he'd probably seek out de Vere in order to shoot him.

She could find him and flee abroad.

She sighed and stood. She was thinking like the heroine in a play instead of like a real and sensible woman. De Vere was impossible, and he was not here. She had no practical way of finding him, and if she could she didn't want to marry in a way that might cut her off from her home and family forever.

Would a truly passionate woman not care about such things? Then she clearly was not passionate.

She pulled out her list again and read the names through twice. There were additions, such as Ralstone.

Perhaps she should consider Ralstone. He had more in common with de Vere than any other of her suitors.

He was one of the half-pay officers—a cliché fortune hunter—but in fact he was heir to Lord Irlingham. A barony only, so even lower than Benning, but he would have a title one day. That should pacify her mother a little.

His family, however, was hard-put to keep up their dignity due to long extravagance and the folly of Lord Irlingham marrying twice and having twelve children, all healthy. There was little to start any of them in life, and nothing extra to support the heir in a suitable manner. She gathered that his father was also very healthy, so Ralstone's situation would not change in the near future.

But, as she'd often thought, money was not a significant factor in her choice.

Ralstone was a great favorite with all the ladies. Petty as it was, the idea of snatching up a man that other women wanted did have its appeal. He flirted beautifully, but could also talk sensibly if required. He seemed to think as he ought on all important subjects, and he had a way of looking at her across a room that implied he was lost in wonder.

Once that would have struck her as ridiculous. Now

she was at least willing to consider that he might be falling in love with her. Alderton clearly had, and Cedric Rolleston-Stowe had written tragic poetry after she'd cut his hopes short. She'd been as kind as she could to Ceddy, but she'd known she could never live with a man inclined to fly from alt to nadir in moments.

Ralstone?

She drew idle circles around his name.

There was something there. In worldly terms it would be a low match, but not impossible. She did enjoy his company. He was entertaining, considerate, and he even listened. He seemed to approve of many of her ideas, and could discuss politics and fashion with equal ease.

He was thinking of leaving the army, which was important to her. She had no taste for life as an army wife. He would need occupation, but her family could find that for him. A seat in Parliament, perhaps, or stewardship of one of her father's estates. Yes, that would be better. She did not want to spend much time in London.

In fact, on her money they could afford to lease a small country estate. One close to Lea Park, even, so she could have that and marriage, too.

There was a thought.

She decorated her circles with flowers.

Marrying a man without an estate of his own had distinct advantages. Quoyne House. It belonged to her father but was not part of the entailment. It sat just outside the walls of Lea Park. Near, but not too near . . .

Her mind was moving so quickly that she decided she needed a brisk ride to clear it. Not an amble in Brighton, but a gallop out on the downs. It was half past nine—too early for most of her suitors to be out of bed. She rang the bell and summoned her habit and Monmouth.

She kept to a sedate pace as she rode out of Brighton, one of Welsford's grooms behind, but when she reached the country road she speeded up. It was a cloudy day, but dry and fresh.

Monmouth stretched, showing how much he had longed for a good run. Anne felt as if she stretched, too, seeing Ralstone as a way to break free and get back to the country.

She could wish he wasn't quite so physical a man. It

was probably his strength and vigor that excited her, as riding a top quality horse excited her. Yet there were times when she wanted peace and a book or a box of papers. Would he allow her times like that?

She was spoiled. She hated the thought of a man allowing or not allowing anything.

Alderton would be easily managed. But he was so dull.

As she reined in on the downs to look down on the town and the sea beyond she couldn't help thinking that if she could mash Alderton and Ralstone into one person she would be close to her ideal.

What a strange state she had come to, to be trying to design her perfect husband. Laughing, she set Monmouth to the gallop and flew across the smooth downs, loving the thundering power beneath her and the fresh air against her skin—

"Halloo!"

She reined in a bit and glanced back to see a bunch of horsemen galloping toward her, Ralstone's scarlet coat to the fore. Her pestilential admirers had discovered her! Instinctively, she urged Monmouth to speed and raced to get away.

Hunting shouts echoed, and she looked for some escape. Her groom pounded alongside. "Lady Anne. Slow down, milady!"

He was Welsford's man, and didn't know her.

"They won't hurt you, milady!"

The infernal groom reached for her reins. She knocked his hand away with her crop, but began to rein in again. Fleeing like this would do no good, but she would not be *hunted*!

She drew Monmouth to a halt and turned him. Then as the group of grinning men slowed a mad urge took her.

She set her horse to speed again, right at them.

With startled exclamations, they broke apart and she flew through them and was off back toward Brighton, laughing with triumph.

It was a stupid thing to do. They chased her as if she truly were a fox, and when she had to slow to enter the town, they clustered around, exclaiming in admiration of her riding. By this evening she would be the gossip of all Brighton, and by tomorrow she would be in the papers. Again.

She glared at Captain Ralstone, riding grinning by her side, confident in his dashing good looks and charm.

His grin faded. "Did we alarm you, Lady Anne? Then I do sincerely apologize."

"You didn't *alarm* me, Captain Ralstone. It was only that I was enjoying the peace of the morning."

"It is the most precious time of the day, isn't it? And we invaded it."

His rueful expression, his understanding, melted her anger.

He reached to touch her hand. "It will not happen again, I promise you." Then, with a mischievous look he added, "If you were to summon my escort, I could make sure of it."

She found herself laughing and back in humor with him.

Why not? He would be a daring choice rather than a safe one, but why not be a daring lady?

She began to pay attention to Captain Ralstone, to truly let him woo her, but then Alderton arrived in Brighton, looking resolute.

Oh, dear. He was going to propose, and when he did she would have to say yes or burn that boat.

And then she learned that de Vere had been in Brighton just days before she had arrived.

She was with Caroline, Welsford, and a Major Trimball, strolling through a small charity fairground set up on the Steyne. They'd stopped to pay their pennies and try their hands at throwing balls into baskets when Miss Charnock, standing close by, said to her companion, "Do you remember that Mr. de Vere? He had the trick of this. Won three gifts for his fair companion before the stall holder refused him another go."

Caroline turned to them. "Racecombe de Vere? Has he been here recently?"

Anne was trying so hard not to show any reaction that she doubtless looked like a stuffed dummy.

Miss Charnock, a plain but pleasant lady, said, "Oh, yes, Lady Welsford. A week or so ago. My brother and

I met him at a large fair up on the downs." She introduced her brother, a man as plain and pleasant as herself. "Richard knows him quite well, don't you, Richard?"

"Has a mad streak, but a fine soldier," Major Charnock said.

"He was with the lovely Miss Trist," Miss Charnock said, "but I gather she has returned home to marry a neighbor, leaving many a broken heart."

Was de Vere's heart broken? Anne wanted to ask, alarmed by the sharp pain in her own. Instead, she said, "An heiress, I suppose."

"Oh no, Lady Anne, not at all. That was what made her so fascinating. A penniless beauty who looked set to steal a great catch. She was companion to the Deveril heiress, however. Now there was a fortune, and a scandal to go with it!"

"And she is snatched up, too," Major Charnock said, pretending suffering. "By a hawk, no less."

"What?" Anne was beginning to think that her wits had turned.

He smiled. "Major Hawkinville. A fine fellow who deserves good fortune and a pretty bride. Lives in these parts, too.

"Is Mr. de Vere still in Brighton?" Caroline asked, saving Anne from trying to find a way to ask without revealing anything. It would be hard when she was feeling slightly faint.

"I don't think so, Lady Welsford. I believe he was staying with the Vandeimens, though, if you wished to inquire. I assume you heard about Lord Darius Debenham?"

Anne listened as from a distance to discussion about the miraculous reappearance of the Duke of Yeovil's younger son who'd been assumed dead at Waterloo but had turned up alive though still suffering from his wounds. It had been the talk of England a week or more ago.

"Made his way from France," Major Charnock said, "and somehow turned up at the Vandeimen's house on Marine Parade. Remarkable!"

So remarkable that Anne wondered if de Vere had waved a magic wand. He had been here, right here, just days before she had arrived! And now, typically, he had melted into air again.

The Vandeimens. She didn't know them. She could find an excuse to call, however.

Oh, good heavens, she couldn't do a thing like that! It would be as bad as Lady Caroline Lamb invading Byron's rooms in hot pursuit. And anyway, de Vere couldn't be in Brighton anymore. Daily lists were produced of everyone present, of comings and goings. She could not have missed his name.

The Vandeimens would know where he'd gone. . . .

No. She would not be a bitch on the hunt.

Or a bitch in heat, she thought, remembering her appalling behavior. If the man was interested in her, he would have no difficulty in finding her.

And if he was nobly preventing her from taking a disastrous step?

What could she do about that? Kidnap and seduce him?

That evening at a musical soirée, Ralstone adroitly captured the seat beside her and amused her with a story about a donkey race on the downs that day. She made herself think about what a pleasant companion he could be.

Not as fascinating as de Vere, but not tedium.

Later, she agreed to a stroll in the lantern-lit gardens, to a pause in a discreet corner, and to a kiss. If she was considering him, she should follow de Vere's advice and try out his kisses.

Don't think about de Vere.

Ralstone was gentle at first, but when she didn't protest, he became more ardent. There was even, she thought, a little tingle from it. No sign that he might turn wild and grope her in unthinkable places, thank heavens.

Afterward he smiled at her with obvious optimism. "You encourage me to ask a special favor, Lady Anne."

"Yes?" she asked warily.

"The Regent has sent out invitations to all the military men in Brighton for a special assembly at the Pavilion on Friday. We are commanded to bring a lady, however, to represent 'the Britannia that we saved.' I quote."

She laughed with relief. "Are we to wear helmets and carry shields?"

"I don't think so. But you are to present your escort with a favor to wear."

"As in a medieval tournament? I hope he doesn't plan a joust."

"If he did," Ralstone said, capturing her free hand and pressing it to his chest, "I would be honored to fight under your colors."

It was overly dramatic, but she could grant this request at least. "Of course I will be your lady, Captain Ralstone. I am honored."

He carried her hand to his lips with such fervor that for a moment Anne worried that she had unwittingly agreed to marry him. But when he glanced at her, alerted by something, she smiled brilliantly and made herself relax.

When they returned to the soirée, she saw that Alderton was pouting. Her mental pen hovered over his name ready to strike him out, but then she made herself be sensible. In all ways that mattered, he would still be the wise choice, and if he was upset that she'd gone apart with Ralstone that was because he was in love with her.

She had made herself think about Alderton Hall. It had to be possible to move his mother and grandmother. There wasn't a dower house there at the moment, but one could be built. In a matter of months. They would still be in and out, she was sure, but they wouldn't be under the same roof.

She knew that if she was firm enough she could get Alderton to do anything she wanted, so he would adapt his house to her taste. He had an excellent stable, and it was good riding country.

Lastly, she had realized that she probably could take her papers with her to a new home. No one at Lea Park was interested in them. She could continue with her work.

Yes, life at Alderton Hall could in time be made much like life at Lea Park, and Alderton would be a much more comfortable husband than Ralstone.

She was not at all sure she could make Ralstone do as she wished.

She dismissed him and let Alderton take her for refreshments.

"A fellow like me don't have much chance when a man like Ralstone's in the field, does he?"

"Don't be foolish, Alderton. You have every advantage over him."

"Not with the ladies."

She gave him a playful look. "Are you suggesting that we ladies lack judgment?"

He opened his mouth once or twice, looking distressingly fishy. Then he laughed. "Oh, I see. I apologize. But a certain dash does catch the eye. Works the other way, too. Didn't really notice you until you spread your feathers this year, Anne."

It was, perhaps, tactless, but she rather liked his perception and his honesty. She'd much rather have that than perfect tact. Ralstone never said a wrong word.

They were in an anteroom that was deserted at the moment. She turned and put a hand on Alderton's shoulder. "Such honesty deserves a reward," she said, turning her face up to him.

The whites showed around his eyes, and she wondered if he would bolt. It was good, she told herself, that he was alarmed by an offered kiss. He was no libertine.

Did that make Ralstone a mouse or rat? She should get Tris's advice on that.

Thought was drowned by Alderton's mouth pressing hotly to hers, but only for the briefest second.

She blinked at him, but he had already moved back, out of reach. She supposed he was the wise one. Someone might come upon them here. That kiss hadn't been much to judge a man on, however, and had certainly not had any tingling effect.

Later in bed, like a person probing a sore tooth, she reviewed kissing de Vere, comparing and contrasting.

She hadn't shrunk from him. She grimaced at the dark ceiling. What point? He hadn't needed a kiss to shorten her breath, to make her toes curl, to make her smile for the simple pleasure of seeing him.

As Alderton had smiled at her? Did Alderton search

rooms for a glimpse of her, long for her, dream of her? . . .

Did Ralstone?

Her heart pattered as if a trap had closed.

Did she *love* Race de Vere?

Oh, no—she couldn't! This affliction was insanity, not love!

For some reason, however, she hardly slept that night, tossing between the sensible choice, the daring choice, and the impossible one.

When Alderton called two days later and asked her to drive out with him, she accepted without much thought. It was only as she sat beside him in his sensible gig that she noticed his set chin and pallor.

Oh, no! That kiss had been the encouragement he'd needed. He was going to pose the question, and she wasn't ready yet.

And yet, and yet, Alderton was the obvious choice. Ralstone was all flash and dash, and despite his charm, at heart he was selfish. She knew it. Alderton was not. He would give her all she desired.

De Vere was impossible. If he suddenly appeared before her and asked her to marry him, she would have to say no. There was no other rational response. She had to accept that.

As they drove along the Marine Parade, Anne looked out at the gray sea and turned her mind to falling in love with the Earl of Alderton. He was an excellent driver. That was a major point in his favor. He was well enough looking, titled, wealthy, kind, honorable, and he loved her.

What possible objection could she have?

She realized that her list of qualities seemed familiar. . . . Oh, no! They echoed what de Vere had said in Drury Lane about Captain Jeremy Goodman. Would Alderton hide under a coach and leave her to face a highwayman?

Idiotic question. It would never occur, and if it did, she was sure he would not. He would make her just the sort of husband she was supposed to have.

As they left Brighton in the direction of Hove, a pleasant tranquility settled on her agitated mind. She would marry him, and everything would all be as it should be. Her family would be delighted. No one could pity her choice. Marianne and Percy could wed. Perhaps in a double wedding.

As if to settle the matter, a bundle of rags and seaweed tumbled across the road, startling the horses. Alderton brought them under control without difficulty.

She complimented him on his driving, and he blushed with pleasure. She remarked encouragingly on his excellent stables at Alderton Hall, and he glowed. They chatted of yesterday's weather, and today's weather, and the forecast for tomorrow. They were in perfect harmony.

They kept on driving. When and where would he ask her? After all this, if he didn't, *she* might ask *him*!

Then he stopped the curricle at a quiet spot, and his tiger ran to the horse's heads. Anne waited to be assisted down, wishing her heart hadn't begun a mad pounding. She wasn't nervous. This was no great affair.

It would be the absolute limit to swoon, though.

If he behaved as she expected, then this would lead to kisses. To make matters easier, therefore, she left her staff behind, trusting entirely to his arm. He led her along a rough path to a place with an excellent view of the sea, but which was shielded slightly from the carriage by some bushes.

Had he scouted out this spot ahead of time?

Something about that struck her as ridiculous, and she fought nervous laughter. He hadn't planned for wind. Close to the sea, the breeze became brisk, whipping her skirt against her legs, making her clutch her bonnet.

He took his arm from hers and went to one knee on the earthen path. She couldn't help thinking that he would have a muddy stain on his knee. "Alderton, please . . ."

"I must speak." He swept off his hat and held it over his heart. "Dearest Anne, you must know how I feel. . . ."

He spun off into a speech he had clearly memorized and practiced. Anne hadn't the heart to cut him short, but now she truly felt as if she were on a stage, as if she might look aside and see a vast audience rather than the indifferent sea.

None of this seemed real.

None of what he was saying seemed real.

Was it really the dearest wish of his heart that they two be joined in connubial bliss? She supposed it must be, or he wouldn't be here on one knee spouting all this stuff.

Could he really promise her perfect happiness? . . .

He'd stopped speaking. He was waiting for her answer, beseechingly.

"Yes, of course I will."

Those were her lines. What else could she say?

He rose, tears of joy in his eyes. Tears stung her eyes, too. She wasn't sure they were joy, but she did feel relief. It was done. It was finally done, and her feet were set on the most solid, sensible, safe path.

"As soon as I have returned you to your sister's home, my dear, I will go to Lea Park to talk to your father. He can have no objection."

"No, I'm sure not." But he was holding out his arm to lead her back to the carriage.

"Shouldn't we kiss, Alderton? Properly."

He blushed. It was definitely a blush. "No need for that yet, my dear."

"Need? I would like you to kiss me."

He looked around as if seeking escape, but then he took her hand, leaned closer and pressed his lips to hers as tentatively as last night. Anne remembered de Vere recommending passionate kisses before commitment.

She moved forward, put her arms around him, and kissed him back. She felt him tense. When she opened her eyes, his were open, staring at her.

She moved back. "Alderton, do you not want to kiss me?"

He was red from his neck to his hair. "Of course, of course. But this is neither the time nor the place, Anne."

Anne supposed that there was some slight chance of someone passing on the road catching a glimpse of them. Months ago she would have been as excruciatingly aware of that as her husband-to-be. What had become of her?

She felt the heat in her own cheeks. "You are right. I'm sorry."

He tucked her hand into his arm. "Not at all, my

dear. A little warmth only increases my anticipation for our future."

That, she supposed, sounded promising. But as he helped her into the carriage and they turned back toward Brighton, Anne's feeling of accomplishment began to sink beneath a tide of unfulfillment. This didn't seem quite as it should be.

Middlethorpe had felt more passionate than this, and he hadn't proposed. She was sure that if he had, when she'd said yes, there would have been more . . . connection.

Alderton glanced at her, catching her eye and smiling. "I understand, Anne. At a time like this a lady can't be expected to chatter."

He turned his eyes forward again and began to whistle.

Anne wanted to press her fingers to her head. Though it didn't ache, it felt as if it ought to. Captain Ralstone had summoned more passion. And as for de Vere—!

"Don't go to Lea Park today," she said.

He looked at her. "Why ever not?"

She didn't know except that she needed more time to grow accustomed. Could she say that? Then she remembered. "Tonight is the military assembly. I've promised to attend with Captain Ralstone."

"You must decline, my dear. It is not suitable now you are engaged to marry me."

"It isn't that sort of event, Alderton. The officers are supposed to take a lady to symbolize Britannia. And I have given my word."

He frowned. It was close to a sulk. She remembered how she'd felt about his sulking.

"If you think it best," he said at last. "But that does not prevent me from traveling to Lea Park."

A flutter of panic began to build again. What had she done? She'd thought Alderton would be easy to manage, but no sooner had she said yes than he was sulking over not getting his own way.

She thought quickly. "If you wait a day, I can go with you, Alderton. We can receive my father's blessing together."

His stiffness melted into a smile. "A very suitable sentiment, my dear. By all means." He reached out and patted her hand. "I should not begrudge another man one evening with you, when soon you will be mine alone forever."

She smiled back, but something was wrong with this. On a stage, spoken by the right actor, those words would thrill. Here in this real world, they sounded like cell doors slamming shut.

Was she making a terrible mistake? Or was she simply letting the impossible get in the way of the sensible again?

Twenty

In mid-July, Race returned to Somerford Court from Crag Wyvern in Devon, where he'd been tying up a few more administrative loose ends. He knew it was weak to return. Lady Anne Peckworth was in Brighton, and he should avoid the vicinity entirely.

He was back because of a small item in a scandal sheet read by the Crag Wyvern housekeeper.

The *London Enquirer* had been lying open in the kitchen, and Anne's name had leaped out at him.

In fact it had said Lady Anne Pxxxxxxxx, but that had been enough to snare him. According to the paper, she had played fox to a bunch of military hounds on the downs near Brighton, creating great admiration by her brilliant equestrian talents. It went on to say that a large number of gentlemen were pursuing the beautiful young lady, both in and away from the field.

It sounded as if Anne was in trouble.

He'd visited Brighton with Con and Susan, staying with their friends the Vandeimens. It had been pleasant enough, but he had been impatient with the pointlessness of it. When the daily sheets had announced the imminent arrival of the Earl and Countess of Welsford and Lady Anne Peckworth, Con and Susan had decided to avoid embarrassment by leaving. Race had been happy to go with them.

He'd soon decided that six miles wasn't far enough for his weak willpower. He'd come up with reasons to return to Con's old estate in Devon and removed himself entirely.

He'd enjoyed another dip into the affairs of the late mad Earl of Wyvern, and it had given him the chance to take notes of some of the more interesting matters for a possible book, but all the same, it had been slightly flat, like ale that had stood too long in the jar.

Life felt slightly flat these days, and he knew why. It was the same reason a small item in a paper had drawn him back here. When he reached the place where the road to Somerford branched off the Brighton Road, he felt the tug. She was there. So close. Possibly in distress.

Was she in danger? Was she being harassed? Where was her family who should be taking care of her? Where was the Duke of St. Raven? Why hadn't he heard of her engagement to marry St. Raven, or some other suitable man?

He made himself continue on to Somerford. He'd find out what was going on from six miles away, and deal with it from six miles away, too.

He rode around to the Court stables, then entered the house from the back. The first person he encountered was Susan Amleigh in an apron, supervising the washing of the corridor walls.

"Race! My goodness, you startled me, turning up like that. All finished in Devon, then?"

"Yes, and it's pleasant to return to sanity."

For some reason that made her laugh. "Oh, Lord. If only you knew. Con!" she called. "Here's Race back admiring our sane world."

Con came out of his study, grinning, too, and Race knew instantly that something had changed. For the better.

"What's happened?"

Con insisted on Race going into his study with him, and on ordering ale for them both. Susan came along, still in her apron, clearly looking forward to the telling. Race was amused, but he was also delighted. Whatever it was, was good news.

When they both had tankards of ale, Con raised his. "To Lord Darius Debenham. We found him, Race. Alive! But that's the end of the tale."

"What?" But Race drank the toast, then went to shake

his friend's hand. He knew how much Lord Darius's assumed death at Waterloo had wounded Con. "But how on earth did this happen? Where has he been?"

What followed was a complex story of a French spy, a kidnapping, a death, and the elopement of Con's friend and neighbor Hawk Hawkinville with the Devil's Heiress. Race listened, shaking his head.

"A simpler story's been put out for public consumption," Con said, "but that's what really happened."

"And they call me wild! I'm put out to have missed all this."

"You're in time for the wedding, at least," Con said.

"What wedding?"

"Hawk and Clarissa. They never made it to Gretna, so they're doing it properly in Hawk in the Vale tomorrow."

Race encouraged Con to fill in the details of that adventure. Susan waved and went back to work.

Eventually Race said, "A grand affair. I wish I'd been part of it."

"More appealing than the Crag Wyvern paperwork? It must be growing dreary for you to be back so soon. You've been gone what? Ten days?"

"I've done all I need to there."

Con topped up Race's tankard. "I'm glad you're here for the wedding, since you missed ours."

"Speaking of which," Race said, hoping he sounded only curious, "what news of Lady Anne?"

"She's in Brighton still, but that's all. Why?"

"I read an item that suggested that she'd been chased on horseback on the downs."

"What?" Con looked at him as if he were mad. "I think the papers make up most of these things when it comes to the aristocracy."

"And I think they rarely need to. It was a scandal sheet, but it had the ring of truth."

"Dammit, what's her family thinking of?"

"Precisely my question."

Con looked at Race. "I know that look. You think I should get the meeting over with and make sure she's all right."

"You have to meet sooner or later, and as I said, I don't think she'll bite."

"Who knows what she'll do if she's charging all over the place on horseback? Armed with a fanciful staff, too, I gather."

"Not on horseback, I assume."

Con laughed. "All right, all right. I'll consider it. Van and Maria are coming in from Brighton for the wedding. They'll have the latest news."

Race didn't feel in the mood for a wedding, but he played his part. At least he didn't have to amuse the company. The couple did that themselves by dashing off to their home with unseemly haste.

Con laughed and toasted them, then he and Lord Vandeimen hosted the village party until nightfall. The Vandeimens hadn't mentioned Anne yet, and he was reluctant to raise the subject.

Race couldn't help noting that this event was even further proof that he had no hope with Anne. These men all had deep roots here, unlike his father at Shapcott. But then a scrap of gossip reminded him Hawkinville's father had been a man very like Race's—an outsider who had bought his way into a manor.

No, it wasn't the same. Hawkinville's father was blue-blooded. In fact he had now inherited a title of his own which would come to Hawkinville one day. It hardly mattered. The Hawkinvilles, like the true de Veres, could trace their line back to the Conquest, a far greater matter than a mere title.

Race thought his father a more thorough gentleman than Squire Hawkinville.

Hawk's father had charmed his way into both manor and fortune, then treated his wife shamefully. Race's father had bargained fortune for manor, and kept his part of the arrangement. He'd restored Shapcott Hall, and provided a life of elegance for his wife.

The world would not care about that. It was bloodlines not virtue that mattered.

There'd been times, many times, when he'd imagined persuading Anne into marriage and making her happy.

He suspected that he could do the first, but he doubted that he could do the second for a lifetime. He would be asking her to climb down from her gilded heaven to wade through the mud here below.

Nor would their marriage be attended by universal joy like this one. Her family would at best be disappointed, society would snigger, and her friends would drift away. What did he have to offer in return? No family, no home until he made one, no real name. He'd suffered the constant reaction to the name de Vere. Was he to ask her to become Lady Anne de Vere?

"Cheer up," Con said, slapping him on the back. "It's a wedding. Ah, I know your problem. You want to get married, too."

"Definitely not. I've my life to sort out."

"You haven't done it yet? Think of it as papers to be shuffled."

"Organized. Shuffling is the opposite."

"Ah, that must be why I never quite got the hang of it." Con was a bit tipsy. "So, have you decided what to do about your father?"

Race accepted more ale from a rosy-cheeked girl who blushed at his smile. "Oh, yes. I wrote to him from Devon to tell him to go ahead with the annulment."

Con shook his head but asked, "What now? Delighted as I am to have you around, I feel it's time for you to leave the nest."

Race laughed at that. "Yes, mama bird. I thought perhaps I would go to London and inquire about things like archives and libraries. There has to be an occupation there somewhere that would suit me."

Con pulled a face, but then he dug a card out of a pocket and scribbled something on the back. "If you need anything, look up Sir Stephen Ball. He's a friend of mine, and he probably knows a fair bit about that sort of thing."

Race looked at the address scribbled on the back and the words "All assistance."

"Thank you. A Rogue, I assume."

"I think you'll like him. In fact, if you wanted to continue in the secretary trade . . ."

"Doesn't he have one?"

"Probably. He's the sort to always have use for more. Always digging into something."

Race tucked the card away. "Susan was unwell this morning. Am I to wish you happy?"

Con blushed. Or perhaps it was just a glow. "Yes." He turned to look around at the happy village, and at his wife dancing and laughing. "It's a perfect world, isn't it?"

"Definitely," Race said. What else was there to say on the sun-kissed evening of a happy wedding day?

But then Con turned back to him. "You're right about Brighton and Lady Anne. But if I have to go to go there, you should come, too."

Race tensed. "You don't need me. I told you. She bears no grudge."

"If not to protect me, come for pleasure. The renovations on Vandeimen Hall are finished, so Van and Maria are giving up the Brighton house next week. They suggest we visit them for the last few days."

"I don't care for Brighton."

"I'd like you to come," Con said in the direct, honest way that he had. "It's been a crazy summer with very happy endings, and you've been part of much of it. This will be the end of many things, and the beginning of the rest of our lives." He put a hand on Race's shoulder. "I'd like you to come with us simply as a friend, Race, to tie up the last knot."

Race looked out at the merry, tipsy village and surrendered. Con was right. A stage of life was coming to an end.

"Put like that," he said, "how can I refuse?"

Three days later Race rode into Brighton with Con, alongside Susan in the carriage, amused as always by the elite in frivolous mood. One group on the promenade seemed to be playing blindman's buff, and others were bobbing along on small donkeys. A large sign promised a race between a Captain Philips and "Backward Barry," apparently over a mile, to be walked backward.

He couldn't stay here long, though. Normally he was the one using mischief to lighten the sober. Here he was tempted to either go too far or take to Methodism. He would spend a few days with his friends, check on Lady

Anne Peckworth from a safe distance, and then be on his way.

He caught himself scanning the Marine Parade for a glimpse of her, but a sudden flurry drew his attention to an approaching open carriage.

"The Regent," Con said, bowing when the genial fat man waved vaguely in their direction. "He declares that he doesn't want any formal fuss here, but would be very put out if ignored."

Race hadn't seen the poor man before. He was extremely fat, looked very uncomfortable in his fashionable garments, and despite the smile, rather sad. Vague ideas of improvement drifted into Race's head, and he hastily blocked them. He had no desire to take up Brummell's abandoned crown.

They drew up in front of the Vandeimens' bow-fronted house and were soon entering. Maria Vandeimen emerged from the front room declaring, "Welcome! We have such a treat for you!"

She was in her thirties and possessed of natural elegance, but at the moment her eyes sparkled with mischief.

"Race," Con said, stopping dead, "tell them not to take away the horses. We may need to leave."

Vandeimen, young, blond, and dashing, with a saber slash across his cheek, joined his wife. "Not at all. You won't want to miss this."

"What?"

"The Regent is holding a grand reception tonight for all the military officers in Brighton."

"Lord save us." Con pretended to head toward the door again, but was towed back by Susan and Race.

"The Regent will probably be in uniform," Con complained, as they dragged him into the drawing room, "and claiming again to have fought at Waterloo. Men only?"

Maria ordered tea. "Oh, no. You are all to have adoring ladies on your arms to symbolize Britannia, and you are to wear favors."

They all sat. "You have my sympathy, Van," Con said. "It has to be too late for us to get invitations."

"But would we leave you out of such a treat? We sent

immediately to say that two other gallant officers would be here."

"Traitor."

"Not at all. The implication is that any veteran officer present in Brighton who fails to show up will be viewed as malingering."

Con was still humorously complaining, but Susan poked him. "I've wanted a chance to see inside the Pavilion." Her attention turned to Maria. "What should I wear, and what favors should we make them wear? . . ."

In minutes, she and Maria had drifted off discussing fashion. Van instantly changed the refreshments from tea to ale, and the atmosphere made the subtle shift to masculine.

Race smiled sympathy at the other two. "I'm saved from this affair by not having a convenient lady."

A footman came in with the jug of ale and tankards. Van sent him away and poured himself. "Think again," he said, giving one to Race. "Maria's niece Natalie has just arrived to dabble her toes in social waters before a proper plunge next year. She's an excitable sixteen, and she, too, is desperate to get inside the Pavilion."

Race winced, then saw Van take it amiss, thinking he didn't want to bother with a mere girl.

"I have an unfortunate appeal to the young," he said quickly, trying, by limiting it to "the young," not to sound like an cockscomb. "I've been plunged into some embarrassing situations."

Van assessed it, then nodded. "We'll warn her, but she's very sensible about these things. Continental blood. She's the orphaned daughter of a relative of Maria's first husband."

Talk moved on to friends, horses, and sports, and Race could only hope that this Natalie was as sensible as her uncle thought.

He was thinking over another problem. He'd intended to lie low in Brighton. Last time he'd come here with Con, he hadn't attended society affairs. This reception might throw him into the same company as Anne, but it was impossible now to back out without giving offense.

It sounded as if the assembly would be a crush where

it would be easy to avoid her. In that case it could be useful—it would be an opportunity to gain a true impression of how she fared.

When Susan and Maria returned, they brought the young lady with them. Lord save him. She was plump, huge-eyed, almost bouncing with excitement, and rushed over to sit beside him on the sofa.

"I do thank you for escorting me, Captain de Vere! I can't wait to see the Pavilion. Do you think the Regent will pinch my cheek? They say he does that to all the young ladies."

"Not unless you learn to behave like a young lady," said Vandeimen. "Race, I make known to you Miss Natalie Florence. Natalie, Mr. de Vere. As he's sold out, the captain is inappropriate."

Unrepressed, Natalie dimpled and held out a hand. "Thank you again, Mr. de Vere."

Perhaps this would be all right. Her eyes were bright but met his directly, and only natural color flushed her cheeks. As a test, he took the pretty hand and kissed it.

Her eyes widened, and her full lips parted. He thought he'd made a mistake, but then she said, "Mr. de Vere, could you teach me all about flirtation?"

"No." It was a sharp response that sprang directly from Benning Hall. He immediately softened it. "Not *all*. But a little, perhaps, if Lord Vandeimen promises not to shoot me."

"I make no such promise."

Race let the girl's hand go. "Alas, my dear, you are too well guarded."

She gave a teasing pout, but the smile she sent Vandeimen showed she didn't take his threat seriously. Race did. He had no doubt that Vandeimen would eviscerate any man who harmed this charming girl. He himself would be next in line.

He was reassured about her, however, and even began to look forward to the evening. He gathered it would be her first true social event, so being her escort would certainly blow away any tedium. Tedium? With the possibility of meeting Anne Peckworth again?

If Anne was there, who would she be with? Not St. Raven, who was not a veteran. Would her escort be the man she had chosen? Race wondered what he would do if she was throwing herself away on a cad.

A tingle in his body was a warning. He'd felt this way sometimes before battle—when he'd expected something exciting, or dangerous. Or even disastrous.

Twenty-one

When the ladies came down in the evening, Race had no complaints about his partner. Natalie was no beauty—her hair was mousy, she was short, and he suspected that she'd always be plump. An enormous zest for life fizzed in her, however, and someone—presumably Maria Vandeimen—had excellent taste.

Natalie's stiff ivory silk gown was exactly right in its simplicity and severe cut, with only the most subtle trimming of deep blue to match her eyes. The bodice was low enough on her full breasts to be interesting while still being modest, and her jewels were delicately made of pearls and sapphire chips. Suitable yet unusual, and a reminder to the world that Natalie could be assumed to share some of her uncle's wealth—the uncle being Maria's first husband, Maurice Celestin.

People in society wore jewelry as a statement of their wealth, and people like Maria—born into one of the best families in England—knew the language in every subtle nuance.

From the deep recesses of his mind came the memory that his mother had only ever worn simple ornaments, even though his father had given her some lovely pieces. What had that meant?

Natalie came straight to him, dimples deep, with a knot of sapphire blue and white ribbons in her gloved hand. "For my hero!" she declared.

Laughing, he went on one knee before her so that she could pin it to his sleeve. He fought back a memory of kneeling like this before Anne when he provided that footstool. What would it be like if this were Anne and they were going to this event together?

Instantly the other ladies demanded the same from their gentlemen, and amid complaints, they complied.

They all set out in high spirits.

"With any luck," Vandeimen said, "the prince will be in some uniform of his own design, dripping with gold cord and glittering orders."

The Regent, however, was dressed in severe civilian evening dress, though his shirt collar was insanely high and stiff, making any movement of his head perilous. Race suspected that he was tight-corseted, as well. He looked red-faced and breathless.

This was the man who had once been called Prince Florizel because of his beauty, and who seemed never to have become at ease with himself. At fifty-six, he still was not true monarch, and his blind, demented father looked set to live forever.

Race took that as warning not to drift through his own life. For now, he settled to his duty for the night—to give Natalie a perfect evening.

It looked to be easy. She was enchanted by the Pavilion's Asian decorations and by the effect of massed, glittering uniforms and medals. Race was sure she'd rather be partnered by a serving officer than by a past one, but she was too well raised to show it.

Spirits were generally high despite inevitable thoughts of the missing. All these men had come to terms with loss—one had to or else go mad. There were the wounded, of course, as reminder. Scars, eye patches, empty sleeves, and the awkward gait of the wooden leg.

If Anne was here, perhaps she'd feel less peculiar. He kept constantly alert to avoid an accidental encounter. He hadn't seen her yet. Perhaps she wouldn't be here at all.

He forced relief over acute disappointment.

There were men who carried worse marks of the war than any here, Race knew. Those hideously scarred by burns or by a saber through the face. Those confined to their beds or a wheeled chair. Those destroyed in the mind.

They were the forgotten, the reminders of the truly dark side of war that civilians preferred to ignore. . . .

He shook off the mood and squired Natalie around. She behaved perfectly, but her excitement and delight were infectious, and she was soon everyone's darling. Heaven help the beau monde next year.

Many of the men flirted with her, men of all ages, but she took it in the playful spirit it was offered. As Vandeimen had said, she already had a touch of Continental sophistication. Race did notice a few subalterns who looked dazzled. No harm in that, but he'd keep a close eye on her.

Then, as he and Natalie rejoined Con and Susan, he saw Anne.

He noticed her by a flurry of excitement. Couples were moving toward a point like moths to a candle, and the candle was a lady carrying a tall staff decorated with a line of golden love knots. Her gown was pale silk, but shot through with gold. Straight and slender, Lady Anne Peckworth truly shone like a flame.

He fought through breathless bedazzlement to notice detail. This gown was not an older one smartened up. The lines were subtly dashing in the way only the very best mantua-maker could achieve, and the bodice was extremely brief, making her breasts seem fuller than they actually were. For a moment, he could imagine walking over and claiming some right to possess those breasts. . . .

He sucked in a breath and turned away, pretending that he knew what the hell Con and Susan were chatting about.

Insanity, need, and deep gnawing loss probably had him pale. Was he shaking? Natalie was chattering to Susan and no one seemed to notice anything wrong. Weeks ago, he had consciously surrendered any slight chance he'd had of claiming Anne Peckworth as his own. Since then it had seemed a minor ache.

Now it was like a lost limb, lost sight, lost life.

What had he done?

What had he done?

Sanity swooped back with beak and claw, and the buzz around became voices. He had done what he had done for her, not for himself, and now it was even more correct. She was queen of her world, able to take her pick of the best. It was all exactly as he'd wished.

He could look back at her now.

She wore a pearl collar on her elegant neck, but sparkles there spoke of diamonds, increasing the flame effect. More glittered in her headdress that he realized was vaguely reminiscent of Britannia's traditional helmet. And the staff, braced on the floor beside her, held at an angle, was actually Britannia's spear.

She'd come as Britain's warrior goddess, and her demeanor fit the part.

Bravo, Anne. Bravo.

"Who is that?" asked Natalie, wide-eyed.

"Lady Anne Peckworth, daughter of the Duke of Arran."

"She's beautiful."

And she was. Not just beautiful as he found her, but in everyone's eyes. Unlike the Regent, she had grown into herself, and that confidence along with all the skills available to her had created genuine, remarkable beauty.

Strangely he felt a pang of loss for the uneasy, uncertain lady he'd teased into brandy and hazard once, a long, long time ago, as distant as the battlefields of Spain.

She was smiling and chatting with the ladies and gentlemen around her, laughing at what was clearly a risqué touch of flirtation. She rapped one gentleman on the hand with her closed fan. No trace of shyness or nerves.

Then, another moth was drawn—the Regent. Among bows and curtsies he quickly raised Anne, and Race heard him say, "No, no, Lady Anne, do not strain your foot!"

"Good God."

Race glanced sideways at Con. "You see."

"I do. But, good God . . ."

"You don't approve?"

"I . . ." Con shook his head. "Of course, I'm delighted if she's happy, but . . . what has become of her?"

"You'd rather she was still the mouse?"

Con gave him a funny look, and Race knew his tone had been razor-sharp.

"Lady Anne," Race said calmly, "seems to have developed poise and confidence and to be very happy. Do not begrudge her that."

"You're right. I suppose we put people into roles and then expect them to stay there." As the Regent moved on, Con twitched at his cravat. "I had better go and speak to her."

"She won't bite."

"She might skewer me with that spear." But Con held his arm out to Susan. He glanced back at Race. "Are you coming?"

"You'll survive without an escort."

Con and Susan began to navigate their way across the crowded room. Casual observers would see nothing wrong, but Race knew they were both wound tight with nervousness, fearing that Anne would create a scene.

She wouldn't, Race knew, but he was fighting an urge to go with them, or to hurry ahead and warn her. Anne was skilled at hiding her reactions, but in a moment of surprise—?

It was all right. He saw no hint of discomfort or awkwardness when she first spotted Con. When they met, her smile seemed genuine, and she gave her hand to Susan without hesitation.

Some tension inside him relaxed.

Perhaps she would have followed this path anyway, but he'd like to think that his meddling at Benning Hall had played a small part in her blossoming. He'd like to think that his cruel treatment of her at the Swinamer ball had brought her here, too, blasting away any tendency to be distracted by him.

Who was she with tonight?

A man stood beside her, dashing and darkly handsome in his uniform, the knot of gold ribbons on his arm almost drowned by gold braid and frogging.

Who?

Good God, it was Dashing Jack.

Dashing Jack Ralstone, nicknamed for his reckless bravery in battle, but also for his reckless indulgence with women. A hero, he thought wryly, remembering Benning Hall, a worm of worry stirring. Was Dashing Jack simply her escort for tonight, or was there something more serious going on?

He checked on Natalie at his side, but she was happily chatting to three young couples not much older than she—subalterns and their ladies.

He pretended to be observing the crowded room, but in fact kept most of his attention on Anne and Ralstone. Con and Susan had moved on, and the crowd around Anne shifted as couples came and went. Race watched every nuance of her interactions with Ralstone. Not good. Her smile was too warm, and his was too confident.

Ralstone had been a good man to have around in battle, though he'd been inclined to dash off in reckless heroics. He'd been good company in an after-victory carouse, too, but Race had never felt inclined to call him friend.

He wasn't a drunkard, but he was much like Uffham about it—likely to slide into drink when he didn't have anything better to do. He wasn't a rake, but he was a womanizer. They came so easily to his charm and good looks, and he wasn't the sort to refuse a gift if pressed upon him.

Once or twice, he hadn't been so careful of the lady's reputation as he should have been. There'd been a couple of duels, but no one had been seriously injured. Wellington's opinion of duels was too well known.

He gambled, but not to excess. . . .

Good God, all that said was that Ralstone was a typical officer. Nearly everyone drank to excess sometimes, and enjoyed the thrill of dice and cards. What man rejected the offers of lovely ladies? Ralstone did at least have the kind of birth and family connections that wouldn't shame Anne. He had a title coming to him one day.

Enough. It was time he gave her credit for knowing her own mind. Which meant he'd better apply his mind to avoiding her.

He claimed Natalie and took her off to explore the lavish oriental decorations and meet new people. He watched with amusement as she finally became flustered by the obvious admiration of a redheaded ensign not much older than she. Young Armscote had been at Waterloo, however, and perhaps something of that lingered in his eyes. His partner was his sister, who clearly did not mind his wandering attention.

Race flirted mildly with the sister for a while, trying hard not to make an impression, and was relieved when another young couple joined the group, leaving him the outsider.

It left his mind vulnerable to Anne, however.

Would Ralstone be faithful? He was more rake than not. Some rakes changed when they married for love, but most? And was this love? That felt like a mean-spirited question, but some instinct was saying that Ralstone's happy glow was not love but triumph.

Of course, winning a bride like Anne would be a triumph. If he were in that position, he'd probably be crowing like a cock. But his crow would be love, not victory. . . .

Love?

He felt like bashing his head against one of the crimson walls. He couldn't be so stupid as to be in love with Lady Anne Peckworth!

Love. He noticed Natalie's bright eyes and Armscote's flushed cheeks and separated them before they fell into the same fate. Because of his distraction, he was probably too late. The best thing would be to find her another young officer and dilute the effect.

He should apply that advice to himself, but he couldn't imagine any other woman stirring his interest at the moment. He remembered saying to Con that he was unlikely to marry. He had to assume that all this would fade, that he'd change his mind one day, but at the moment . . .

At the moment he had the absurd temptation to seek Anne out and follow her like a puppy simply for the reward of being close.

He took Natalie for a turn in the lantern-lit gardens, hoping fresh air would blow away insanity. It was a pleasant relief from the heat and smells of the crowded Pavilion, but it did nothing for his brain.

He couldn't stand by and let Anne throw herself away on Ralstone. But what else could he do?

Alert Uffham?

He wasn't sure he had any influence with Uffham anymore. His rough break with the Peckworth family had seemed a good strategy at the time—remove temptation entirely—but now it was turning round to bite him.

And anyway, what could he say? That Ralstone was not entirely a sober, upright member of society? Neither was Uffham.

Neither, come to that, was he.

Quickly bored with gardens, Natalie asked that they return to the house to explore more chinoiserie. Anything to distract his mind. They went back inside, then, as they approached the end of the gallery, they came face-to-face with Anne on Ralstone's arm.

Twenty feet or more separated them, but now that people were all over the Pavilion, the crowd here was thin.

Her eyes widened, her lips parted, she paled, then flushed. With anger? No. He didn't want to think it, but he thought the anger had come a heartbeat after something else, something he'd thought he'd killed.

He did the only thing he could for her—he sent a message that he had no interest. He inclined his head and turned his attention to Natalie and a Chinese lantern over their heads. If he'd been with an older, more worldly-wise woman, he might have set up a blatant flirtation, perhaps even gone so far as a kiss, but he couldn't do that to Natalie.

He could only pray that Anne and Ralstone would go by without speaking. Anne wouldn't approach him, he was sure, but he'd served with Ralstone for a year at one time and a few months at another, and encountered him here and there all over the Peninsula. He might come over to talk.

In a mirror, he watched Anne and Ralstone move into the long room and past. Saw her glance toward him, caught her eyes in the reflection. Wide, blue, steady, and completely unreadable. Then she moved out of reflection like an actor moving off stage.

He led Natalie onward, toward the arch and the picture of the Chinaman there, painted on glass. Real and unreal. Solid and fragile. His head was buzzing again, but he would recover once they were safe.

But then the Regent swept in with his entourage and

chose them to speak to. Race's name gave the prince some problem.

"De Vere? De Vere? Thought there weren't any de Veres any more. Going to claim the Earldom of Oxford, then?" The prince was clearly worried that he'd been left in ignorance of something important.

Race gave the answer he used when he wanted to avoid complications. "Not at all, sir. A very minor branch, and—if you will forgive me—on the wrong side of the blanket."

"Oh, I see! And your home, sir?"

"Derbyshire, sir."

"Good, good. Grand place, Derbyshire. All those peaks . . ."

The prince went on to make some remarkably sensible comments about the war, and seemed to share all Race's disappointment at missing Waterloo.

He pinched Natalie's full cheeks, and Race feared she'd burst into giggles, but she managed to only beam at the prince, which pleased. Her honest delight at the Pavilion style pleased, too, so that the royal personage delayed to talk to her about his treasures.

By the time the prince bustled off to another couple, there was no sign of Anne. Race took Natalie off to explore the Pavilion in the opposite direction. This was going to be a strange hide-and-seek evening, but he thought he could manage it. After all, Anne must be as keen to avoid him as he was to avoid her.

Twenty-two

Anne laughed at some joke of Captain Ralstone's that she hadn't heard, trying desperately not to show that she was shaken.

Race de Vere was *here,* with no warning. She'd not seen his name in the daily list of arrivals, but then she realized she'd been so distracted all day that she hadn't even looked.

Even so, she felt betrayed.

And he'd had a pretty, glowing child on his arm. Who was she? How did he acquire this string of adoring ladies? And she was so young. Too young.

She was immediately shamed by her anger. Despite everything, she was jealous. Sharply jealous.

Have some pride, Anne!

She suggested to Ralstone that they join a group—safety in numbers—and concentrated on the conversation there. She fixed her entire consciousness on Ralstone as he told a lighthearted story about military life.

Why on earth did de Vere have to turn up now of all times, when she'd finally committed herself to Alderton? He must be fey! She felt almost fevered, unable to concentrate. She'd been that way all day, however.

Had she known without knowing that de Vere was here?

All day a conviction had been growing that she could not marry Alderton. She'd accepted him, which meant she was bound. To the best of her knowledge, no Peckworth lady had ever broken an announced engagement. On the other hand, nothing was announced yet, which meant she had a brief opportunity to retreat.

It was always possible that some fire, some passion would ignite between them after marriage, but doubt was filling her like cold water in a well. There'd been nothing, absolutely nothing in his kiss except discomfort and embarrassment. Imagine a life, an intimate life, like that.

And so, this evening, she had begun to turn to Ralstone. She had to marry. Apart from all the practical pressures, she was going to go mad if she had to play this game much longer. And here was a handsome, dashing hero whose tender kiss had made her toes curl. His family was acceptable, and if his fortune was small, that could be corrected.

As she'd moved through this evening on his arm, her assurance about it had calmed her soul. He had a wicked edge to him, yes, but she was willing to admit that she found it exciting. She didn't have Tris's assessment of him, but she would before she committed herself.

It was clear that the officers who'd served with him in the war thought him an excellent fellow, and there had even been a few anecdotes to his credit. He flirted and charmed with suspicious ease, but she couldn't really complain about that. His devotion to her seemed genuine.

She must have been encouraging Ralstone because he was becoming more attentive, more possessive by the moment. If she encouraged him a little bit more, he would propose.

She made a vague reply to a comment she hadn't heard, suppressing a desire to giggle. Was she really going to allow one gentleman to ask for her hand in marriage when she was already promised to another? What had become of perfectly behaved Lady Anne Peckworth?

And now de Vere was here, like a prickle down her neck and a quiver in her stomach.

He'd turned away, however, as soon as he'd seen her. Could anything be more clear than that? She'd wanted his place in her life cleared up, and now it was. She made herself focus entirely on the story Ralstone was telling to the group, to considerable laughter.

Perhaps it was her intense concentration, but she began to see that the anecdote was a little mean-spirited. The butt of his joke didn't deserve such treatment, and his laughter at his own story sounded brash.

As did everyone else's.

She remembered one aspect of marriage that she'd tried to keep in mind. She would end up friend to her husband's friends, part of his circle.

Who exactly were Ralstone's friends?

Oh, did it matter? He would have to accommodate to her friends and family, too.

They moved on toward another group. "Wasn't that Racecombe de Vere who bowed to you a while back, Lady Anne?" he asked.

Anne felt as if he must notice her start, but he seemed oblivious. "Yes," she managed to say. "He's a friend of my brother's. I hardly know him at all." *Stop babbling, Anne!* She calmed herself and asked, "You know him, Captain Ralstone?"

"We served together a time or two. Amusing company, but a dashed madman at times."

Anne knew she should leave it at that, change the subject, but her will crumpled. "In what way?" she asked, pausing as if to study an exquisite porcelain vase.

"Don't want to tell stories . . . ," Ralstone said, but then proved willing enough. "After all, it's nothing to his discredit. He was put in charge of a flogging one day and switched the whip for one made of ribbons."

Anne stared at him. "What? Why?"

Was de Vere truly mad? That might explain his strange behavior.

"We were under a Major Underwood at the time. A tyrant and getting worse. He'd have the men flogged for a missing button. Course, nothing anyone could do. Chain of command and all that."

"Yet Captain de Vere refused to carry out the punishment?"

Madness because of the risks, but a glorious sort of insanity, noble and just.

"Oh, he carried it out, but with the ribbons. Claimed there'd been nothing in the order about what the man should be flogged with. Old Underwood practically had an apoplexy and ordered de Vere flogged in the man's place. With the cat."

Anne felt as if her heart missed a number of beats. "He was *flogged*?"

"No, no, my dear lady. Of course not. The men set up a racket, and the commotion brought our colonel by. Ended up with Wellington involved. Equal blame laid on de Vere and Underwood, but Underwood was transferred to Irish duties. Poor bloody Irish." Then he colored charmingly. "Your pardon."

"No matter," Anne said, still fixed on the horrible idea. "Was Captain de Vere in danger of being flogged?"

In spirit, at least, he was a martyr.

But Captain Ralstone laughed. "Of course not, Lady Anne. Officers aren't punished in that way. Would erode the respect of the men, you see. That was why Wellington rid himself of Underwood."

The glowing light around de Vere's image faded. Mischief. That's what it had been. Typical mischief. No wonder, however, that he'd said it was touch and go in the army at times.

Another couple joined them, and Ralstone mentioned the incident with de Vere. It seemed to have made the rounds of the army. Colonel Emerson thought it amusing; Major Crispin, a mad piece of nonsense that could undermine authority.

Anne, however, settled on the result. De Vere had saved a man from an unjust flogging. She wanted to ask if these officers would have carried out the punishment as ordered, but she knew the answer. They all would. Including Ralstone.

"Captain de Vere suffered no consequences at all?" asked Mrs. Crispin.

"Only a terse public comment from Wellington that if de Vere ever disobeyed the letter and the spirit of an order of his he'd have him shot."

"So I should think," said Crispin.

Anne found that she had to speak. "Surely it shows Mr. de Vere in an admirable light."

The sudden silence showed how outrageous her objection was, but she no longer cared.

"Strange fellow, though," Ralstone said quickly. "Always had his men laughing, even as they waited for battle. Drove some of the other officers distracted. He called his men the Laughing Corpses, but they didn't seem to mind."

"Thank God I never had him under my command," said Crispin. "Sounds cracked in the nob to me."

Anne couldn't stop her response, though she tried to soften it with a smile. "If I were waiting to face the enemy, Major, I would rather do it laughing than quivering."

"Doubtless why we don't send petticoats to war, Lady Anne." With a stiff bow, he and his wife moved on.

Colonel Emerson said, "Never did have much sense of humor, old Crispin." Then he and his lady moved on, too.

"You are ardent in de Vere's defense, Lady Anne," Ralstone remarked. "He is important to you?"

Heat flooded her. She'd not thought of that in her instinctive support. She laughed. "Not at all! He is merely a friend of my brother's, and seems harmless enough."

It seemed so wrong to dismiss him like that, but what else could she say?

We drank brandy together, then kissed in a most improper way, and later I wished I had the wild folly to join him naked in a bed, or the even wilder folly to let him fondle and ruin me in a library during a ball. And, yes, I like his mischievousness and wit, and now I admire his courage and honor.

"Harmless?" Ralstone seemed to find that amusing, and she read beneath it the fact that de Vere had killed, as a soldier must. It shivered down her spine and through her nerves. She glanced around at smiling gentlemen realizing that all of them must have had days that ended with blood on their hands.

Her attention was caught by someone—a rather solid young woman in a bold blue gown and turban on the arm of a rugged officer.

"My goodness, it's Claretta!"

Ralstone followed her gaze. "Oh, Crump. Yes, he did very well for himself there, especially for a trade officer."

She wanted to poke him with her spear. "I must go and wish them well." As they crossed the room, she added, "She's cousin to my foster brother, the Duke of St. Raven."

"I'm sorry, Lady Anne. I didn't realize she was a connection of yours."

She wanted to tell him that wasn't the point, but they were already across the room. "Claretta. You're looking splendid, and it must be because of your fine husband."

"Anne!" Claretta hadn't magically become a beauty, but her bright smile and shining eyes made Anne suddenly feel that parts of the world were just as they should be.

Anne was introduced to Captain Crump, and she found him to be a no-nonsense man with a kind heart. His face was square, his brown hair cropped short, and his build could best be described as robust. She couldn't help feeling that he and Claretta would have very solid, robust children.

That reminded her to sneak a glance at Claretta's shape, but with her normally heavy build and a fussy gown it was impossible to tell. What did it matter anyway? They were happy.

She chatted to the couple, liking Captain Crump more all the time. His voice had a touch of Cockney to it, she thought, but it didn't matter. His words and manner were gentlemanly.

As Crump and Ralstone exchanged polite remarks, Anne said to Claretta, "Congratulations. He's wonderful."

Claretta smiled. "He is, isn't he? I hope you do as well, Anne. You should. You've become quite a beauty."

Anne felt like saying, *And what good has that done me?* but she simply smiled. "I hope you're not having any difficulties?"

"With people?" Claretta shrugged. "There are a few who turn up their noses. We don't care for them. We like a quiet life anyway. Of course, it might have been sticky if the parents were still alive, especially mother."

She pulled a face that made Anne smile.

"And I must say," Claretta added, "that Cornelia is being difficult. We never got along, though, and of course she married Tremaine. He might be an earl, but he's a pill. I think she's jealous."

Anne smothered outright laughter. It was all too true. In fact, it wasn't funny. It was a lesson about what could happen when a lady married for rank without considering the nature of her partner.

Was Claretta a lesson about the opposite? That the daring seizure of an unsuitable husband was worth it in the end?

"Spoiled for choice?" Claretta asked, and eyed Ralstone. "I like the look of that one."

"So do I," Anne said, and it was true. Ralstone was wonderful to look at.

"The betting seems to be on Alderton."

"He's a good man."

Claretta gave Anne a surprisingly shrewd look, as if she sensed Anne's ambivalence, but a burst of laughter distracted them both. Anne looked across the room and saw Race de Vere enter the room in the midst of a high-spirited group.

Enter fool, stage left. Yet he wasn't a fool except in the classic sense of the one who was allowed to prick the pride of a king.

The Laughing Corpses. If she were a soldier facing battle, she truly would prefer to be under his command. What's more, she'd rather face life laughing, too.

Their eyes met across the room for the briefest moment, and then he turned to his partner, the glowing young girl.

The cut again, and yet it wasn't. She knew it wasn't.

It was more like being accidentally kissed.

Had she given de Vere the impression earlier that *she* did not want to acknowledge *him*? After their last encounter, it wouldn't be surprising.

As conversation flowed around her, she thought back, tried to recreate that second of decision and reaction. She'd been so startled, she'd simply stared. Not even a smile. Oh, heavens, had it seemed she had been cutting him? It was, after all, for her to acknowledge him.

Then their eyes had met in the mirror. Such a strange moment, that, as if they were on two stages separated by glass. She knew now that she'd been searching for encouragement, for any hint that she could approach without embarrassing herself.

And all the time it had been her move to make. She was the lady, he the gentleman. She was the duke's daughter, he virtually her brother's servant.

It seemed that they had spoken through glass all along except for that one brief time in Benning's study when she had dared to reach, and the barrier had dissolved.

But no, it had disappeared again at the Swinamer ball. For a while. She must do something to dissolve that barrier again. She must, before she could consider marrying anyone else, be it Alderton, Ralstone, or any other man.

She must do it for herself, and for him, but also for the other men. How terrible to be married as second best.

And she must do it tonight before Race de Vere slipped out of her world again like a member of faery.

And if he wasn't being deliberately distant? If he wanted her?

He was still nobody.

Her family would still be appalled.

The ton would still snigger as they had over Claretta. . . .

It was as if glass shattered. She no longer cared.

She would be like Claretta. She would claim the man who could make the world glow for her.

When she looked again, however, Race had gone.

As soon as there was a break in the conversation, she said to Ralstone, "I do long to explore a little more." She took leave of their group and headed in the direction Race and his party must have taken.

How to find him in this place? And how to get time alone with him?

Ralstone put his hand over hers on his arm and squeezed her fingers. "Our minds are in accord, Lady Anne. I, too, would like some time alone together."

Oh, Lord. Not now. Not yet.

Twenty-three

"You are looking glorious tonight," Ralstone said softly, leaning so his lips brushed her ear. "So like a queen, I fear the Regent will try to steal you."

Idiocy. She twitched away. "He is already married. Or were you thinking I might become a royal mistress, Captain?"

He colored. "Of course not." But he moved closer again. "You know what I want you to become, Lady Anne."

He paused then, holding her left hand since her staff was in her right. She realized that they were in a short corridor that was deserted for the moment.

"Anne, you know I long to call you wife. Do I have reason to hope?"

His dark eyes were long-lashed and so very serious. She had encouraged him this far, she knew she had, and he deserved some kind of answer, but her heart was a thundering panic in her chest. First Alderton. Now this. What a mess she was making of things.

"I wouldn't be here with you, Captain Ralstone, if you didn't have hope."

His smile was beautifully rueful. "Jack. Can you not bring yourself to call me Jack?"

De Vere had asked her to call him Race.

She'd refused.

"In private, perhaps . . ."

His smile instantly radiated optimism. Confidence, even. "Then when may I speak to you in private, Anne?"

"It would be improper . . ."

He squeezed her hand. "I understand. You are so strong, so brave, that sometimes I forget that you are a delicately raised maiden. . . ."

Then he bowed reverently to kiss her hand.

Anne bit her lip on shocking laughter. What had Race said? That she shouldn't trust a man who bowed before her as if she were a saint. . . .

He lingered there, and she glanced around praying no one come upon them like this. Her prayer wasn't answered.

Race and his partner came around the corner. They stopped. Her eyes collided with his, no glass between them now.

His partner smiled in delight. Anne saw romantic visions dancing behind the big eyes and wanted to scream a warning. Then Race turned her, and they disappeared back the way they'd come.

Ralstone straightened, and in her dazed pity, she smiled brilliantly at him. He smiled brilliantly back, clearly thinking the delicately raised maiden was in the bag.

She, however, could only think of how to follow Race. No, how to get him alone.

Ralstone was saying something about a meeting. She made some reply, but hurried them in the direction Race had gone. She knew Ralstone was taking her behavior as maidenly embarrassment and felt cruel; but she could focus on only one thing.

Race.

She had to talk to him. She had to explain that the kiss had meant nothing. She had to find out what he felt.

She cruised the rooms with Ralstone until her foot began to ache, but caught no sight of her quarry. Had he already waved a magic wand and disappeared? She didn't think so. Absurd as it seemed, she felt his presence.

Impossible to have the meeting, though, with Ralstone by her side. Why hadn't she thought of that?

She had to get rid of him.

"I need the ladies' retiring room," she said with the hesitancy suitable for such a delicate subject.

Every inch the perfect escort, he discovered the location from a footman and escorted her down a corridor to an out-of-the-way spot. Of course, it was impossible for him to wait. Imagine the ladies having to pass a line of escorts on their way to the chamber pots!

"Perhaps you could wait for me in the central saloon, Captain Ralstone." Far enough away that he could not watch her emerge.

He bowed and left, and Anne went into the room blowing out a relieved breath. This wouldn't get rid of Race's companion, but it was halfway.

She didn't need to use the screened close-stools, so she sat to rest her foot. The spacious room contained perhaps a dozen ladies, some simply sitting as she was, some being tidied by the waiting maids. Of course, she knew everyone, and everyone knew her. Without reason, she felt sure that they all knew what she was up to.

All that was said, however, was praise of her costume and of her handsome escort.

Then she heard de Vere's name.

"Natalie's safe. Mr. de Vere's something of a devil with the ladies' hearts, but she's not ready for that sort of folly yet."

Anne saw that the speaker was Lady Vandeimen, who had been Maria Celestin, and before that had been Maria Dunpott-Ffyfe. She was talking to Lady Harlesdon, an older woman with a sour tongue.

"Girls are ready for folly from the day they get their front teeth, Maria. Be careful."

"I am, Clara, but I think it's good for them to cut those teeth on the dashing handsome ones. They're not so susceptible later."

Susceptible. The word pierced Anne like a pin piercing a bubble, and her mad confidence began to leak.

"De Vere does seem to have a fatal appeal for women," Maria Vandeimen was saying. "I don't know what it is. Perhaps that he appears to genuinely care. He has a very kind heart. Ah, Natalie, my dear. How are you enjoying yourself?"

Anne openly watched as the girl joined the older women, chattering of the wonders of the Pavilion as

Lady Vandeimen tidied her frothing curls. There was not one word about Race, so the fatal appeal had not struck there.

Anne found herself paralyzed by doubts, however. Was she simply another foolish woman to whom he'd been kind, who imagined herself special to him? Every instinct cried to retreat and protect her pride. To find Ralstone, to *engage* herself to Ralstone and show Race de Vere that he meant nothing to her.

To avoid that cruelest affliction—embarrassment.

But she had never been a coward, and she knew that if she didn't attempt to find out the truth, it would linger in her forever like a poison. And, she suddenly realized, if the girl was here, Race was free of her for a short while.

She grasped her spear and left the room, going down the corridor to reenter the more populated areas of the Pavilion. Where was Race likely to be?

Anywhere.

Ralstone was waiting in the saloon, so she could not go there, but she could wander everywhere else.

If only she could go quickly and unobtrusively around the place, but her foot made her slow, and her fame made her noticeable. And of course, everyone, from footmen to prince, wanted to be of assistance to the poor crippled lady.

She only prevented the Regent from sending for Ralstone by hinting for a personal tour of the room they were in. By the time that was finished she was sure Ralstone must appear in search of her, and that Race would be tied to his Natalie again.

Then, by miracle, he walked into the room—alone.

Before he could retreat, the Regent said, "Ah, sir! De Vere. It is de Vere, isn't it?" As Race bowed, the Regent continued, "I give you a rare treasure, sir, the hand of Lady Anne Peckworth."

Anne looked at Race and could see her own startlement in his face. Did he feel the same sharp longing?

The Regent tittered. "Just my little joke." But he placed Anne's hand on Race's arm, patting it. "Find her escort for her, there's a good man."

Then the prince was off to speak to someone else, and

Anne was, at last, alone with Racecombe de Vere. Alone in the wandering presence of dozens of other people.

Perhaps it was the desperation that had built in her over the past little while, but she was almost shaking. It certainly felt as if sparkles were dancing into her from the contact of her hand on his arm, and as if the air were suddenly thin.

Say something, Anne. Say something!

"I was surprised to see you here, Mr. de Vere."

Did it sound normal?

Heavens, did it sound as if she thought he shouldn't be here? As if he didn't deserve to be here?

She was staring ahead.

She couldn't look directly at him.

"Do we know where to look for Captain Ralstone, Lady Anne?"

Was he so anxious to be rid of her?

"I'm afraid not," she lied. "Do you not have a lady to care for, Mr. de Vere?"

"She has been recruited to play the harp."

"Shouldn't you be with her?"

"A devoted lieutenant is with her at the moment. I was definitely de trop."

She had to look at him and found him smiling.

"She's very good," he said.

I play the harp well, too. Thank heavens she didn't let the words out, but was he truly fond of the child? If Natalie was a relative of Lady Vandeimen's, it would be a brilliant match for him.

Not as brilliant a one as marrying *her*.

She had him by her side, and to herself, which she had wanted. What should she do? She could hardly say, *Is there a chance that you might marry me?*

"Perhaps if we stroll around, Mr. de Vere, I might encounter Captain Ralstone."

"By all means, Lady Anne, if it does not bother your foot."

"Not at all, especially with the staff."

"A charming new one. Do you have many?"

Was this all there was, this banal conversation? Surely not. He could hardly be expected to behave here as he had in the privacy of Benning's study, and he still might think her displeased with his company. They'd been forced together by royal command, she realized, and she still hadn't managed to smile at him.

Grasping her courage, she did just that. "I think I am able to enjoy my staffs as a result of our time together at Benning Hall, Mr. de Vere."

He seemed to study her, but she could not decipher it. Why did he have to be so hard to understand?

"I'm delighted if I was of service to you, my lady."

My lady. He was retreating behind subservience again. She would not let him go without settling matters.

"These rooms are very hot," she said. It was true, but merely being with him was making her hotter. "I cannot wield my fan, hold your arm, and use my staff at the same time."

She meant him to ply her fan for her, but he disconnected them and moved slightly apart. She opened her silk fan with a snap. "Perhaps we could step outside for a moment."

He stayed perfectly still, looking at her. "Why?"

She realized then that they were in that same short corridor that gave an illusion of privacy but could be invaded at any moment.

"For fresh air, sir." But she knew she had to address what he'd seen earlier. She waved her fan, long training preventing her from flapping it like a demented bird. "You came across me here earlier, Mr. de Vere. Did you, like me, think of a lesson in hand kissing at Benning Hall?"

"I thought mainly that Ralstone wasn't the man for you."

"Ah." She stilled her fan and looked over it. "And pray, who is the right man for me?"

Oh, dear heaven, she sounded intolerably arch, but might he be leading up to a proposal? She had her answer ready.

Yes. Against reason, against sanity, it would be yes, yes, yes!

His brows rose. "Provide me with a list of your suitors, my lady, and I will tick the suitable."

Her hand clenched on her spear so that the metal

bands bit through silk gloves. Retreating into coolness, she snapped her fan shut. "It is none of your business, sir."

"You seem to be making it my business, Lady Anne."

"Because you interfered in my life!"

He stepped closer and gripped her hand over the spear shaft. "Don't make a scene."

She almost said she would if she wanted to, which was madness. She wanted to jab him with the spear, which was perfectly reasonable, but impossible. Then a group strolled into the corridor, casting them a casual but interested glance. Had he heard their approach?

With a forced smile, she flexed her hand to shake off his, but he was already removing it.

"What a nest of misunderstandings we have, Mr. de Vere," she said lightly as the other party moved by and on. "It would not bother me if I never saw you again."

"I'm delighted to hear that, Lady Anne. I would not want to be a bother to a lady. But don't marry Ralstone."

She itched to murder him. "If I wish to, sir, I shall. And there is nothing you can do to stop me."

"I could tell Uffham certain things about him."

"What things?" If Ralstone was a scoundrel, where did that leave her? Stuck with Alderton. She realized then how very much she didn't want to marry Alderton.

"Duels, for a start. And women. I told you that a hero would not necessarily make a good husband. The Duke of St. Raven said the same thing, as I remember. Is he not one of your suitors, too?"

Tris? Her mind felt as tangled as neglected yarn. Simply to save face she said, "Of course."

Ralstone had killed men in duels? Over women?

Pride made her go on, "In fact, I am considering St. Raven's proposal now. So you don't have to concern yourself about Captain Ralstone. Speaking of which, I should find him."

She turned away, but he caught her arm. "Considering? Now you've found your feet in society, isn't marriage to St. Raven the ideal? He truly cares for you."

She summoned generations of pride to her tone. "You are impertinent, sir."

"Of course I am. It's my stock in trade. What are you going to do?"

She pulled sharply away from him. "It is none of your business. Approach me again, and I will hit you again, this time with intent to do serious injury!"

She turned and limped away, cursing the fact that she could not stalk, but giving thanks for the spear that lent her some dignity. Oh, God. Oh, God. If only she'd not sought out that horrible interview. He truly felt nothing for her except a strange meddlesome pity.

He wanted her to marry Tris, did he? If she'd been on the point of it, she might have backed away simply to thwart him. Now, however, she had to marry someone just to prove something to Race de Vere.

Ralstone.

Duels?

Alderton.

Cold kisses.

It had to be Ralstone, in part because Race de Vere had told her not to. At least there could be honest passion there. He'd doubtless fought duels to defend the honor of fair ladies, which was not such a bad thing. And she had responded to his kiss.

She passed by a pair of complacent china lovers that did not know the danger they were in. She could easily have swung her spear and smashed them into smithereens.

Twenty-four

Ralstone was dutifully waiting in the central saloon and came forward with flattering pleasure and relief. "I was worried about you, Anne."

"I encountered the Regent."

"Royalty must take precedence," he said with a smile. "Do you wish to sit and listen to the music?"

She saw the plump girl performing brilliantly on the harp. There was no reason to be jealous of the child, and yet at that moment Anne couldn't stand the sight of her.

"No. I need some fresh air."

He looked startled at her tone, but took her arm. "Come then, I know where we can go outside."

Soon they were in the lamplit garden. The night air was chilly after the heat inside, and Anne wished for a shawl. The cool seemed to go to her feet, too, and she hesitated about encouraging Ralstone here and now.

Tomorrow would be soon enough. It was time to start to behave properly. She could not possibly engage herself to one man while engaged to another. Tomorrow she would free herself from poor Alderton before picking up matters with Ralstone. She needed to get Tris's evaluation first, as well.

To deflect Ralstone now, she looked for a group to join. Lord and Lady Amleigh were with the Vandeimens and another couple. That would be safe and would prove to the Amleighs that she suffered not a trace of hurt.

Just as she was about to suggest joining them, Race de Vere came out of the Pavilion with his partner, and walked that way—to be greeted as a good friend.

Race and Amleigh?

The other gentleman was one-armed. She'd talked to him earlier. The name had seemed familiar. . . .

Major Beaumont. One of the Company of Rogues!

Her throat became so tight, she felt she should be wheezing.

Lord Amleigh—a Rogue.

Major Beaumont—a Rogue.

Race de Vere. Not a Rogue, but clearly a close friend of the group who seemed to regard her as their personal charity case. She hastily turned away and let Ralstone take her to another part of the gardens.

She'd always wondered what could have caused de Vere to spend so much time with Uffham, and now it was clear. It had been a way to get into circles he could not normally join. He'd been on a mission, sent by the Company of Rogues, to tidy up the unfortunate mess that was Lady Anne Peckworth.

Not by offering marriage. Heavens, no. Simply by shocking her out of her quiet ways and into society where she would marry and be off their collective conscience.

And tonight she had pursued him like a pathetic puppy begging for treats!

"Anne," Ralstone said, taking her hand.

She realized that he had led her into a quiet corner of the garden. Conversation and laughter was only a murmur—laughter at her?

"Are you ready to answer me, Anne? Don't keep me in suspense. Will you make me the happiest man in Christendom?"

Anne felt apart, apart from any semblance of reality. She wasn't even on a stage anymore, performing for a faceless crowd. It was as if she'd floated away to another dimension, one where she was alone.

She realized that she had been playing a part for weeks, secretly sure that at some point Race de Vere would return and reality would recommence.

"Anne?"

She looked at Captain Ralstone, positively delicious in his scarlet uniform, his dark eyes searching hers for hope. She could at least make someone happy.

"Yes," she said. "I will marry you." Deliberately she added, "Jack."

He took her hands and kissed them, raising them up to his mouth this time, and gazing into her eyes. "You have made me the happiest man in Christendom."

She almost pointed out that he was repeating himself, but it was time to begin a new role in the play of life—loving, tactful wife.

"When?" he asked.

Immediately, she wanted to say, but it would take a little time to manage, even with a license.

But then she remembered de Vere's threat to tell Uffham about women and duels. Was he going to snatch even this from her?

"I want to elope," she said.

Ralstone's delight turned to blank shock. "What? There's no need of that, love."

Unsuitable laughter tickled at her. This was all too like poor Jeremy in *The Daring Lady*! But now she'd thought of elopement she was as set on it as Rosalinde.

If they eloped, de Vere would have no chance to make mischief, and she would have no time to lose her nerve. What's more, there would be no question of this suitor being snared by a passing beauty.

She thought of Susan Amleigh. She was a fine looking woman, to be sure, especially enhanced by love and happiness, but her face was rather strong with a long nose and a square chin. She'd still swept Amleigh away. It would *not* happen again.

She looked Ralstone in the eye and lied. "My family doesn't approve of you. It will take forever to change their minds."

"Why? What stories have they heard? I can answer any accusation!"

"They have heard that you duel."

Guilt flashed over his face. "I confess it. But they were cases of the honor of ladies, Anne. I swear it."

She smiled. She'd known it must be so. "Would you fight for my honor, then?"

He pulled her into his arms. "Of course. I'd kill any man who offended you."

In a play, on a stage, it would be pure romance, and Anne indulged for a moment in the vicious pleasure of Ralstone killing de Vere. Reality was never far away, however, and reality threw up an alarming picture.

She pushed away from him. "If we elope, Uffham will pursue, and there'll be a duel, won't there?"

"I fear so, love. I'm no coward, but that would be scandal and disaster."

Reality locked around her again, and she sighed. "It was a foolish idea. I'm sure there will only be a little delay. A few questions of your commanding officers will doubtless appease my father."

He took her hands. "But delay will distress you, won't it? It is my task in life to save you from all distress. I would marry you here, now, tonight, if it were possible, Anne." He turned her left hand and pressed a kiss hotly into her palm.

This time it didn't stir the right response. She could hardly expect it after a night like tonight. To compensate, she pressed her hand against his lips.

He looked at her quickly. "You are passionate. I knew you must be under that cool exterior." He nipped at the base of her thumb, almost to the point of pain. "Let us elope then. Why wait when we know we are perfect for one another?"

"But Uffham—?"

That bite had sparked something in her. Something wicked, physical, hot. It reminded her of de Vere's attack, which had appalled her, but afterward had seemed so exciting. She was doing the right thing here, and she wouldn't let de Vere spoil it.

Ralstone pulled her to him and kissed her, kissed her as de Vere had kissed. His mouth commanded hers so that her senses swam. He was big, bigger than de Vere. Her head was stretched back and she felt powerless.

Was it thrilling or frightening?

One of her hands was at his nape, and she tightened her fingers in his hair, wondering if he would stop if she yanked on it.

He growled. It was a growl that resonated down in her own throat. This was certainly not like Alderton.

Alderton! Her eyes flew open and she saw stars above.

She was still engaged to marry Alderton, and was here sealing a pact with another man. At this rate she'd soon be kissing in the streets!

She pulled back and he freed her lips, smiling. "I've frightened you. I apologize, but I'm a passionate man, and you've been driving me wild for weeks. The thought that in days you could be mine forever . . ."

The look in his eyes turned her breathless. Yes. Once they were married, he would sear any other man from her mind.

"But what of Uffham? I cannot disappear and not be pursued, and I couldn't bear a duel."

"Well, in fact," he said, "I think we can do it."

In her mind it came out like a purr, a purr from a beast that had its dinner in its paws. But it was the way of men to hunt, and she had allowed herself to become the prize of the Marriage Mart. If he felt triumphant, it was not surprising.

"How?"

"You will visit my sister, Ellen, at Greenwich, love. She's married to a naval officer who is at sea, and would enjoy the company. Of course she won't have the chance. I will immediately take you on north."

Anne considered it, impressed by his keen mind. Better and better. She appreciated a fine mind.

"So I will arrive there in all propriety, in Welsford's coach, with Welsford's servants, and no one will know I have left. Will your sister not object?"

"Not when it means our happiness."

"It's very clever. But I will have to take my maid, and she will likely object."

"Is there no way to leave her behind?"

Anne assessed the problem, feeling more and more that this was a play she was planning, not her life. The plan could work, but she would still have to return to reality one day and break the shocking news.

She summoned up the picture of happy Claretta Crump and took the next step.

"How big is your sister's house?"

"Not very," he confessed. "I'm sure you know that there's little money in my family, and many to divide it amongst, and her husband, Yelland, has had little luck with prize money and such. But you will not actually be staying there, love."

Anne shook her head. "That doesn't matter, but it will be excuse to leave Hetty behind. I'm sure she won't mind a week to visit her family."

He brought her hands to his lips again, kissing the knuckles. "Then all is set, my love, my heart, my life, if you still wish it so."

"*Volo,*" she said, remembering the old Latin marriage vows.

"*Volo, utque*," he replied. I wish it, too.

It should not surprise her that he knew Latin, for he would have a normal gentleman's education, but it sealed their pact and soothed her nerves. He was large and physical and dashing, but he was a well-educated gentleman with a clever mind and a sensitive soul.

Despite flutters of panic, she went on tiptoe to kiss him. "We are going to be blissfully happy!"

He kissed her back. "My dearest, darling, Anne, we will. Your trust means more than I can say. And you *can* trust yourself to me. As of this moment, you are my treasured wife." He twisted off his signet ring. "I cannot give you a proper ring as yet, but keep this as testament to my devotion."

He pressed it warm into her hand, and lacking pockets in her slim evening gown, she popped it down her bodice. His eyes followed it and a sudden stillness in him dried her mouth.

Passion. It was what she wanted. The absolute commitment that passion implied.

Wiser to return to company now, however. "We really must go back inside. It would not do to raise suspicions. In fact, I think I should go home." She grasped an excuse she was coming to rely on far too much. "My foot, you know . . ."

He was concerned and careful as they returned to the Pavilion, and during the short carriage ride home. He made no attempt to use the privacy to kiss her again.

How wonderful it would be to be cherished and protected by a man like this.

Then she was chilled by a new problem. "Ralstone—Jack. What if we encounter people we know on the road? Even if I wear a veil, there's my limp. I'm not sure there is another young lady in England who walks as I do."

"Damnation. I don't suppose you can not limp for a step or two?"

"If I could, don't you think I would?"

He squeezed her hand again. "Yes, of course. Foolish of me. But you're right. That plays merry hell with our plan."

Anne would not give up now.

"What if I were to travel as an elderly widow? I could use a short cane and stoop a bit. With a mourning veil and dull clothes, no one would suspect. You could be my attentive son—no, grandson—escorting me to a funeral."

He pulled a face. "That takes the shine off it a bit, love." But then he smiled again. "Anything that gets us to our happy destination. And speaking of destinations, here we are at your sister's house."

He handed her down and escorted her into the house, taking farewell with a kiss on her hand. Looking into her eyes, he said, "Until tomorrow." Too quietly for the footman to hear, he added, "Granny."

She laughed as he left—and no one could feel hollow when laughing, could they?—then went to her room. The first thing she saw was a straw bonbon holder on her dressing table, and the pearl counter inside it.

There was no fire at this time of year so she crushed the straw in her hand, then opened a window and tossed both items out. Tomorrow she would be on her way north and soon Racecombe de Vere, upstart tradesman's son, would know that he and his advice meant nothing to her.

She tossed and turned that night, but it was entirely because tomorrow she would have to face Alderton and break his heart.

At the first acceptable moment she sent a note to him, then fiddled around the reception room awaiting his arrival. He arrived bearing flowers and a blissful smile. It was not a pleasant interview.

Eventually, fighting tears, she managed to convince him that there was no hope, that she thought of him as a brother. His tears escaped, and she found she wanted to cuddle and comfort him, indeed like a sister. Why hadn't she realized that earlier?

And why must that swoop back memories of the corridor outside Frances's bedroom. Of the midwife enveloping Frances inside, and de Vere's supportive embrace of her?

Soon, soon, Jack Ralstone would be her lifelong support. He would be as good as de Vere.

Better.

When Alderton finally left, Anne did let her tears fall, and she knew she was weeping for more than his pain. Unfortunately Caroline came in then.

"You're receiving early, Anne— Why, what is the matter?"

Anne let her sister draw her to the sofa. "Only Alderton," she lied. "I refused him. He cried, so I am crying in sympathy." She found her handkerchief and blew her nose. "It seemed the least I could do."

"Oh, poor Alderton. But indeed, he is a little dull for you."

Anne eyed her sister. "Would you have thought so a few weeks ago?"

"No. But you've changed."

"It's only costumes and paint."

"I don't think so. So, who is next in line? You have your pick."

Anne took the plunge. "I have promised to visit Captain Ralstone's sister in Greenwich. Today."

Caroline's eyes widened, but if she had objections she didn't speak them. "So it's to be Dashing Jack, is it? He'll certainly be more fun than most."

"Dashing Jack? Is that what they call him?" Was she making a terrible mistake?

"It's what some of the army men call him. Because he dashed into battle, I gather."

Anne's panic settled. "He intends to leave the army, of course." Had they actually discussed that? She couldn't remember. "It will be many years, God willing, before Jack inherits, so I was thinking that we could find an estate of our own, perhaps close to home."

Quoyne House.

Had she and Jack discussed that, either?

Caroline nodded. "You always were fond of Lea Park, weren't you? Do you think Ralstone will like to become a country squire, though?"

The hint of doubt was reasonable. Anne was sure they hadn't talked of all this. When had they had time?

"We could still have it as a country home. Perhaps he will take a seat in Parliament."

"Perhaps." Caroline cocked her head. "It seems very much a settled thing."

Anne swallowed. "I think it is."

Caroline leaned forward and kissed her. "Then I wish you very happy. And, of course, we will all tear the skin off him strip by strip if he causes you a moment of distress." She rose. "If you wish to leave today, I had better tell Welsford so he can arrange the carriage."

Anne sat for a moment after Caroline had left, absorbing the fact that Caroline thought her choice good but daring. *A Daring Lady,* she thought, biting her lip. If she encountered Le Corbeau on the way north she'd think she'd slipped out of reality entirely, even though they'd be passing through his territory. She wondered if Tris had found out if there was a connection between the name and his title.

Tris. She'd intended to check with him about rats, mice, and farthings. Too late now. She'd burned all her boats.

Ralstone would not be a placid husband, she knew that, but that was part of his appeal. He loved her and was an honorable, intelligent man. If she wasn't exactly in love with him yet, she would be once she set her mind to it.

She rose and went off to instruct Hetty as to what to pack for—ostensibly—a week in Greenwich. A significant advantage of Ralstone's quick-witted plan was that she could take a trunk rather than have to sneak away a few clothes. She thought carefully and added the pink sprig dress to wear for her wedding.

Two hours later, Anne left Brighton in Welsford's private chaise, Ralstone riding beside. She worked hard to take casual leave of Caroline, as if she really was returning unchanged in a week, but she was astonished that the truth wasn't written on her face.

Despite Welsford's excellent horses, and the prime changes his name commanded on the road, Anne had five hours of travel to think and rethink. She did her best to concentrate on a book she had purchased weeks ago and not had time to read—a history of Jeanne d'Arc in French. She was trying to gather a body of knowledge about women who had made their mark on their times. It was certainly a story to make her own fears seem insignificant. Even at the worst, no one was going to burn her at the stake.

They arrived at Ellen Yelland's small terraced house at three-thirty in the afternoon just as Jeanne had been handed over to the English for trial. Anne watched the Welsford carriage set off back to Brighton as if it were the Burgundian army leaving her in the hands of her enemies.

She shook her head. She had always been inclined to identify too much with the characters in books. She turned to greet Ellen Yelland, soon to be her sister.

Twenty-five

Race tried to put Lady Anne Peckworth out of his mind. He'd hurt her again, however, and he burned to try to slap some sort of apology or explanation over her wounds. It couldn't work. Perhaps if he gave her reason to hit him again, she'd feel better.

The morning after the military assembly, however, he couldn't resist trying to find out a few facts.

Maria Vandeimen was part of that world so it was easy to discover that the Duke of St. Raven had been disappointingly absent from the last weeks of the London season. He had hosted a gentlemen's house party at his Hertfordshire house and then traveled to his various estates, most of which were in the West Country.

Yet Anne had said he'd proposed.

Race risked a direct question. "I thought at one point that there would be a match between him and Lady Anne Peckworth. When I saw them in London they seemed very fond."

Lady Vandeimen was working effortlessly on a lovely piece of embroidery. "There was certainly talk, but it has come to nothing. She is here, and he is not."

"They might have an understanding."

Her brows rose. "Why make a mystery of it? And why encourage other suitors?" She took some tiny stitches then snipped off her thread. "The Earl of Alderton is making a complete cake of himself over her, and Captain Ralstone obviously has high hopes."

"She was with Ralstone last night. Not much of a match for the daughter of a duke."

She picked up another thread and squinted as she

threaded her needle. "His family is good enough, though strained by too many children, and he is the heir." She smiled at him, work paused for a moment. "I certainly cannot disapprove if she has chosen love rather than grandeur."

Race knew Maria had eloped with a foreign merchant for love when younger, then married a penniless young lord recently.

"How low could a woman like Lady Anne marry without inviting ridicule?" He knew Maria Vandeimen might see the meaning behind the question, but he also knew she would make no mention of it.

After a quick look she began her steady stitching again. "It is always a delicate question. For her to marry outside of the aristocracy would be startling, but if there was wealth or high renown . . ."

He watched her complete a charming violet as she continued.

"Generally speaking, a lady takes the rank and situation of her husband. A grand marriage raises her high, an inferior one sinks her low. It is assumed that she will be intimate with her husband's family and friends, and adjust her behavior to fit in with them. Of course, someone like Lady Anne, born to the highest station short of princess, nearly always marries beneath herself, and she will usually draw her husband into ducal circles to some extent, which is part of her value."

"So," he said, "marriage to St. Raven would be excellent, to Alderton comfortable, but to Ralstone a little déclassé."

She stilled her needle and looked at him. "And to you," she said gently, "very peculiar."

He laughed. "You don't know the half of it." After a moment's thought he told her. "My father was a carriage maker before he won the lottery and decided to be a gentleman."

Her brows rose, but she took it well. "An honorable profession, and a reasonable ambition, though hard to achieve."

"In fact, he's pretty well done it. I gather he'd always liked to think of bettering himself—education, good clothing, and such—and in the course of his trade he met many of the upper class. Once he had money, he moved far from his previous environment and bought a manor and a lady. I assume my mother completed the polish. He's more bluff country squire than elegant gentleman, but he doesn't embarrass himself. And he is a gentleman in every way that matters."

"I had the impression from Con that you were at odds."

"Only because he had ambitions for me that did not include the army. And, of course, that I would drive a saint to drink."

She laughed. "Then avoid saints. The world doesn't need to know this story."

"The world always knows these stories, especially when its curiosity is aroused. And, of course, there is his unfortunate choice of gentlemanly name."

"De Vere? Yes. It does raise instant curiosity."

"And suspicion. My father doesn't seem to notice, or perhaps he doesn't care, especially now he's married a farmer's daughter. Like should wed with like, don't you agree?"

She was embroidering again. "In general I do, but there are other like things than rank." She glanced up. "Despite your lineage, you fit in perfectly among aristocrats, Race, and I have to feel that you would be sadly out of place among the trades."

He laughed. "Absolutely. I haven't the steadiness for it, for a start." He rose, deciding not to burden her with the last twist in his reality. It was doubtless academic as far as Anne Peckworth was concerned.

She stopped her work and looked up. "Love and general suitability are more important than bloodlines, Race. I truly believe that. And if a match stirs talk, the world loses interest in time, especially if the union seems happy."

Race knew, however, that her first marriage, the marriage into trade, had not been happy.

He raised her hand and kissed it. "At least I can claim most worthy friends."

He left, accepting that any whimsical dreams of groveling to Anne and winning her were idiocy. Even if he could persuade her into marriage, he wouldn't wish it on her. He was objecting to Ralstone at least partly on grounds of rank, and Ralstone had him beat to flinders on that score.

On the other hand, Ralstone didn't feel like the right man for Anne. At the moment she appeared to be Queen of the World, but he knew that underneath still lay the quiet lady who did not believe in her attractions, who'd been hurt by two disappearing suitors, and then by himself.

She was perhaps driven by hurt pride, and also by a need to do the right thing—to please her family, to soothe everyone's anxieties. If she married unwisely, she would behave as Maria Vandeimen had. She would present a well-bred contentment to the world when she should really wrap her staff around her wretched husband's head.

Did Ralstone know and love the real Anne? Race had to answer that one question before he put this all behind him. His past acquaintance with Ralstone made a visit possible, and he hadn't ever known a man in love who didn't want to talk about the object of his affection.

He walked briskly to the post office, where it was easy to discover where Jack Ralstone had his lodging. Five minutes later, he knocked at the door of number ten, Charles Street, a narrow three-story house on a narrow street. It was opened by a narrow man with an apron over shirt and breeches. Race had the ridiculous image of the man being squeezed and stretched to fit the house.

"May I help you, sir?"

"I believe Captain Ralstone has rooms here?"

"Had, sir, had. He left this morning."

That struck Race as strange. "To take other rooms in town?"

"No, sir. He was leaving Brighton."

"Suddenly?"

"Indeed, sir." The man eased back. In moments he would try to shut the door.

"Back to Shropshire, I assume, on family business."

The suggestion of familiarity with Ralstone's affairs relaxed the landlord. "He did not say, sir."

"Not bad news, I hope."

Did this mean he'd proposed and been rejected? Or

had he gone to Lea Park to speak to Anne's father? Surely in that case he'd plan to return.

"Captain Ralstone was in excellent spirits, sir. Whistling, in fact." At that, the man seemed to decide that he had gone too far, and firmly shut the door.

Race didn't try to stop him. That well was drained, but he needed to find another. There were any number of explanations for Ralstone's behavior, including the simple one of running out of money. Brighton was expensive in the summer.

He stopped on the seafront, sucking in salty air, trying to let the brisk wind blow the dross from his mind so he could think. It was instinct, this panic beating in him, but his instinct was often right. There was nothing for it. He had to visit Anne to be sure.

He laughed, hoping she'd switched spear for staff. He'd take being beaten over being impaled.

When he inquired at the Welsfords' however, he was told that Lady Anne was unavailable. She might have instructed the servants to bar him at the door. As a last throw of the dice he asked for Lady Welsford. He was immediately admitted as far as a small, flower-filled reception room.

Anne truly wasn't here?

Had she left town with Ralstone? In that case, the only destination could be Lea Park to get her father's blessing on their union.

Too late, too late.

Not for himself, but for her.

Caro Welsford walked in, eyes brilliant with curiosity. She was what—nineteen?—but with lineage, training, and an understanding, loving husband, her poise grew day by day. Soon she would be one of the rulers of the polite world.

Different spheres.

"Mr. de Vere, I gather you wished to speak to Anne. I'm afraid she has left Brighton for a while."

"To return to Lea Park, no doubt, Lady Welsford."

She cocked her head, lips pursed. "No," she said at last. "She has gone to visit Captain Ralstone's sister in Greenwich."

"Greenwich?" he echoed, as if she'd said the moon.

It was an idiotic response, but he felt as he had once when a nearby cannonball had blown him off his feet.

"It is a perfectly respectable location, Mr. de Vere. Captain Ralstone's sister is apparently married to a naval officer."

Not quite so bad as Lea Park, but the same to all meaningful purposes.

"I assume this is a prelude to an announcement, Lady Welsford."

"I assume so too, Mr. de Vere." After a moment she added, "Do you think it wise?"

Did she have doubts, too? He respected her shrewdness and chose his words with care. "I'm sure Lady Anne has considered matters carefully, and that her family will advise her."

"Oh, indeed. But if she is set on it, she will doubtless have her way."

Was there really a double conversation going on here? Was she asking him to interfere?

"I know nothing particularly to Captain Ralstone's discredit, Lady Welsford. Just the sort of behavior forgivable to men at war."

"We are no longer at war, Mr. de Vere."

She *was* expecting something from him, but he had nothing to give. Anne had made her choice, and he had given as much warning as was reasonable.

He bowed. "When you see your sister again, Lady Welsford, please convey to her my best wishes for her future happiness."

"She will be back in a week. You will be able to speak to her then."

He smiled. "I don't think we're on speaking terms, and besides, I am leaving Brighton today."

"To go where?" she asked, with all the blunt arrogance of her blood—and even as if annoyed.

"Into the future, Lady Welsford." He bowed again and took his leave, but she stopped him near the door with a hand on his arm.

"You and Anne are at odds, it would seem."

"We have hardly been at evens, Lady Welsford."

Her brows snapped together, and if she'd lived in earlier times he could imagine her ordering him off to the dungeons. But then she smiled. "You have done well by my family, Mr. de Vere. If you ever require help that I or Welsford might be able to give, do not hesitate to approach us."

She was young and arrogant, but she had a strong core of wisdom and decency, and in that she reminded him of Anne. He took her hand and kissed it. Then he left the Peckworths forever.

Twenty-six

Anne paused in Greenwich only long enough for a light meal and for Ralstone to settle the details of the carriage he was hiring from the local inn to take them to London.

Anne was dismayed to find that she didn't immediately take to her future sister-in-law. Ellen Yelland had similar looks to her brother, but on her the dark eyes and hair seemed somewhat harsh. She was inclined to grovel to a duke's daughter, but also to make broad comments about marital bliss. She also whined about her straightened circumstances so much that Anne wondered if she was supposed to slip her a few guineas before she left.

Anne spent part of the time writing a letter to Caroline lightly describing her enjoyable stay in Greenwich. It felt truly deceitful, but she had to do it. Caro would expect some news. Ellen agreed to send it in two days.

Then she transformed herself into the elderly widow. She'd chosen to wear a dark gray traveling dress and Jack had found a black cloak, veiled bonnet, and a crook-necked cane. She hated to give up her staff, but she did it. She insisted on taking it with her, however, for later. It unscrewed in the middle, so could fit in her trunk.

Then, the elderly widow, she was ready to leave, to finally end all chance of going back. She did not let herself hesitate. Before leaving, however, she gave Jack two guineas and asked him to give them to his sister as if from himself, so it wouldn't seem like charity. She didn't begrudge the money, but it seemed a strange beginning to this adventure.

Then they were on their way. She leaned back in the well-worn carriage and made herself relax. It was done. She smiled at the handsome man beside her, the man who would soon be her husband. "Everything has gone so smoothly! You are a genius."

He smiled back. "But of course. I have managed to win you."

She blushed, as much from being alone with him as from the compliment. "But truly, your plan is so clever. No need to hurtle up the Great North Road afraid of pursuit, and instead of a few boxes or even a bundle, I have a trunkful of clothes with me, including an elegant dress for our wedding."

He took her black-gloved hand and kissed it. "Don't tell me what it will be. It's bad luck."

She tugged her hand free, teasing, "I don't think you should be doing that. Not to your ancient grandmother. Am I Mrs. Ralstone?"

"Not yet. But soon. Very soon. Mrs. Ralstone, mine to treasure. For now, however, I think perhaps you should be a great aunt. It is just possible we might meet someone who knows me, and who knows my grandmothers. Better to invent someone. You can be . . . Mrs. Crabworthy!"

She laughed, but then he dug in his pocket and produced a narrow gold band. He peeled off her left glove and slid it onto her finger.

"Should we?" she asked.

"My ancient great-aunt should have a wedding ring under her glove, my sweet."

"She could be a spinster."

"I admit, I like to see it there. It was my mother's."

Touched, perhaps to discomfort, Anne pulled on her glove again. "Are you sure this isn't unlucky?"

"We make our own luck, love, and now I am the luckiest man alive."

It was exactly the right thing to say. When would the little knot of anxiety inside her release and let her be completely happy? Perhaps not until Gretna.

He touched her chin. "Why the worry, love? Is it me? I won't embarrass you on the journey, ring or no. My word on it. It will be exactly as if you were my great-aunt."

"Should I slump into the corner and fall asleep snoring?"

He laughed. "If you wish."

"I'd rather talk." Anne realized that her hands were locked together and relaxed them. "We don't know a great deal about each other, do we?"

"Only that we love and will make each other happy."

His soothing comments were beginning to frustrate her.

"Tell me something. How did you end up in the army?"

He leaned back, long legs stretched as far as the coach allowed. "It was church, law, or the military, darling one, and I never fancied the navy. Better way to money, of course, during wartime, but I shouldn't like to drown."

"No thought of the church, I see."

His grin was answer enough.

"Did you enjoy army life?"

He shrugged. "At times. At others it is not something suitable for a lady's ears."

She took his hand. "But perhaps for a wife's ears? I would share your shadows, Jack."

He kissed her glove. "No need of that, my pet. There are no shadows anymore. I am home, and the most blessed of men."

There he went again, but really, she was the most difficult woman to please. The future was settled. The dice cast.

Crabs. A losing throw at dice.

Worthy of crabs . . .

"You do intend to sell out, don't you?" she asked.

"Of course, but it won't bring me much money. My promotion to captain was dead man's shoes. I didn't pay, so I don't get anything for it." He put on a leer. "I'm marrying you for your money, wench."

She laughed, delighted that he could joke about it. "So what will you want to do?"

"Rest, relax, enjoy myself." His lids lowered seductively. "Enjoy you, my bride. I think that will take all my time and energy."

She swallowed. "Did I mention Quoyne House?" Her voice seemed to squeak. She quickly described her plan. "It's a charming house, and not too large. Just four good bedrooms, and of course," she added, feeling absurdly awkward, "the nurseries. The farmland is excellent, but it has been leased out to a variety of tenants. I'm sure there will be improvements you can make."

"Perhaps after this your father won't give us the estate."

"I'm sure he will not be so angry as that."

But was she? She had never done anything so outrageous, nor had any of her brothers and sisters.

He squeezed her hand again. "If he kicks up about it, we can find some other home. You'll still have your portion."

"Yes, of course, but it will be all right."

"I hope so. I hope for your family's favor."

"They only need to see me happy." She didn't want to speak of it, but she must. "Because of my foot, you see, they have always fussed over me. They don't expect me to do anything grand, only be happy. I think they will like to have me living close to Lea Park, to see me nearly every day. They'll be checking up on you," she teased. "Caroline threatens to skin you alive if you upset me."

He seemed taken aback, so she hurried on, "Just teasing, love. Uffham is bound to marry one day, so our children will have cousins to play with."

He said nothing, still looking . . . dismayed?

"Don't you agree?" she prompted.

Instantly, he smiled. "Completely, my love. I am simply enjoying your enthusiasm."

"Do you not like the idea, Jack? If so, I'm not set on it." Despite a pang, she tried to make that true. "We could purchase some other estate. Perhaps," she added nobly, "one close to your family."

But he laughed at that. "Lord, no! An occasional visit will suffice there. I hope we'll jaunt to town now and then, though."

Compromise, compromise. "Of course. We will generally be able to use Arran House. It is kept ready for family year-round."

"How grand. But if you prefer the country, I won't drag you off to London to keep me company. In fact, if I'm going to be there by myself, it would probably be better to keep a small set of rooms."

Compromise. Compromise. "Perhaps you would like a seat in Parliament. My father has any number of them in his pocket."

"I'm sure he has, but politics, my angel? Good to serve one's country and all that, but I've been abroad at war so long I'm not sure I understand what's what."

Jack certainly wasn't marrying her for chance of preferment. Of course he wasn't. He loved her.

"It will all be as you wish, Jack."

"That's my girl. And I don't suppose you'd want to be a political hostess, living in London throughout every sitting of Parliament."

She smiled. "You know me well, don't you?"

A strange thought crept into her mind, however. She felt much the same about Jack as she had about Alderton. She'd rather like him to be away for long stretches of time.

That didn't seem the right thought to have on the way to her wedding, but married couples did not have to live in one another's pockets. Her mother rarely accompanied her father when he went to London for debates in the Lords or other matters of State. . . .

So many uncertainties and concerns. It would be the same if they were planning a wedding in a church. The problem here was that they were compressing it into days, even hours.

He smiled and tugged at her black bonnet ribbon, loosening it. "We can't have you worrying, sweetheart. I'm sure this is giving you a headache, and it's dashed ugly. You don't need a disguise in the coach."

In moments the mourning bonnet was off and tossed casually aside. She knew what he was up to now, and that flutter of panic started again, but it was time to get over it.

Yet hadn't he promised to treat her like an elderly relative? To free him of his promise, she smiled and touched his cheek. "A kiss would not embarrass or dishonor me, Jack. In fact, I would like it very much. And I do trust you not to go further than we ought."

"We are as good as married," he said, drawing her into his arms, pressing his lips to hers. Then, for the first time, his hand settled on her thigh, and through her dress, began to explore.

She thrust aside all thought of Race de Vere and surrendered to the inevitable.

Twenty-seven

Race took a coach to London. He'd find cheap lodging there and perhaps use his introduction to Sir Stephen Ball. What he needed was enthralling work to drive Anne out of his mind.

As London drew close, however, he found that he was not free yet. Somewhere along the way a memory had popped up in his mind.

Lisbon. An aristocratic colonel's daughter and a British diplomat. The young lady had accompanied the diplomat's mother to Cintra in the hills to escape the summer heat, but from there she'd run off with her lover. Her parents had not learned of it until she did not return a fortnight later. Too late by far to interfere. Ralstone had been in Lisbon then, too. Had he remembered it?

Impossible. Why would Anne do such a thing?

But then he remembered his threat to blacken Ralstone's name. Had that pushed her into disaster? He had to check to make sure that she was safe in Greenwich with the respectable sister.

He got off the coach at Brixton, leaving his bags to wait for him at the coaching inn in London. He managed to hire a horse, though it wasn't much of one, and arrived in Greenwich at just gone five. He stopped at the Ship, which seemed to be the only inn there. He didn't know the name or address of Jack Ralstone's sister, but assumed it would be easily found.

It was easier, and more disastrous, than he'd thought.

A mention of Ralstone's name to the innkeeper, a Mr. Birt, produced the information that Race had missed him. "Received bad news from his home, sir, and set off an hour or more ago with a grieving relative."

"His sister?"

"No, sir. An elderly lady."

"Who walks with difficulty?"

But the man shrugged. "I couldn't say, sir. My men took the coach to Mrs. Yelland's house to pick the lady up. They said she seemed old and frail, poor thing. Deaths hit them hard when their time is near, you know."

He rambled off into stories of people he'd known who succumbed soon after attending a funeral.

Race pretended to listen, weighing options.

It was possible that an elderly relative lived with Mrs. Yelland, and that Jack Ralstone had offered to escort her somewhere for a funeral. Possible, but damned unlikely. What better disguise for Anne than widow's weeds and age?

"Heading north, I assume," he said when he had the chance. "Captain Ralstone's home is in Shropshire. I'm heading north of London myself and might meet them on the road. Any idea what route they planned to take?"

The innkeeper eyed him, clearly wondering if there was trouble involved. Race did his best to look harmless, and it seemed to work.

"My coach took them as far as the Swan in London, sir. That's as far as I go, you see. You'll doubtless learn more of them there."

Race found that the fastest way from Greenwich to London was up the river when the tide was right. It was, and there was a boat leaving soon. Ralstone had left at half past four—Birt kept a log—and would have arrived in London in about an hour. Assuming he did not have to delay there for a suitable carriage and team, he might be assumed to stop for the night at Ware or Huntingdon when the sun began to set.

Mr. Birt poured them both ale as they waited for the boat, and happily speculated on all the possible routes north, along with the benefits and disadvantages of the various inns, and the effect of an elderly relative on speed and rest.

Race let part of his brain gather these details while

trying to come up with a plan. They had to be heading for Scotland, probably Gretna Green. North of London the main road split for a while. With luck, he'd get a clear direction at the Swan, but if the postilions had not returned there, or were on another run, he'd have to go blind, feeling his way.

Birt was probably right about them stopping at sunset. They would think themselves safe from pursuit so wouldn't need to push beyond reason.

What would they do when they stopped? Would Anne insist on propriety, on waiting for the wedding? Or would Ralstone want to secure his prize?

He looked at the ticking wall clock. Five-thirty. How was he going to catch them before nightfall? He didn't have the funds to hire a fast chaise, or even a decent horse. If he'd had his wits about him, or if he'd accepted that he'd have to check up on Anne, he could have borrowed from Con before leaving Brighton.

If they planned to anticipate the wedding, would they wait for nightfall? He knew how possible it was to make love in a carriage but it wasn't the way it should be for a woman's first time. It would be Anne's first time.

He saw the boat coming in and rose, interrupting Birt in midsentence. Something about Le Corbeau.

"That highwayman still plaguing people?" he asked, as he paid for the ale. He was down to a few guineas.

"No, sir, like I said. Caught him two days ago, they did!"

"Good news."

"That's to say," added Birt, walking with Race to the door, "they caught someone the magistrates swear is him. Pawning a ring taken from a lady not a week ago. But the man in question—a Frenchie, sir, so that fits—claims he won it at dice." Birt gave a face-twisting wink. "Have to see whether the crow still flies, won't we?"

Race spared a moment's pity for the Frenchman who could be just as he said. Feelings still ran high in England against the French, and the man could hang without real proof against him. That, at least, was no concern of his.

He arrived at the Swan With Two Necks in Lad Lane by hackney, just over an hour later, but in such a busy place it took time to find someone who remembered the officer escorting the elderly lady.

Race knew now that he should have checked Ralstone's sister's in case the grieving ancient was real and Anne was still there. Too late now. He was committed to this throw, and in his heart he knew he was right.

He talked the dispatch clerk into checking his log and found that the first set of horses had taken them to Enfield. He had the road, but no means of travel.

Then he remembered the card that Con had given him. Perhaps the gods would smile and Sir Stephen Ball would be in his Brooks Street rooms. As he went there he tried to plan for the worst, for catching up with Anne too late, after she was ruined.

She wouldn't be ruined unless the world knew about it. The disguise she was wearing helped there. If he returned her to Greenwich and then to her family, perhaps no one except him, her, Ralstone, and his sister need ever know. He'd make damn sure that Ralstone and his sister never spoke of it.

And what if she didn't want to be saved?

He'd do it anyway. If she insisted on marrying Dashing Jack, she could do it properly, from Lea Park, in virtue and orange blossom.

The porter at the door to the elegant gentleman's rooms was obviously not impressed by the dusty traveler. Race gave him the card to take up to Sir Stephen, trying to make new plans if the man was away. Most sane people spent summer away from the city.

In moments, however, Sir Stephen came down himself to take Race up to his rooms.

It was interesting how different the Rogues were. Solid, stable Con; mercurial Nicholas Delaney; and now this tall, vibrant man with the clever eyes and the quick brain. Race liked him immediately.

Ball's rooms were furnished with exquisite and expensive taste, but they had the feeling of not mattering. He probably lived so much in his mind that his surroundings were irrelevant, and yet some instinct saved him from the fusty disorder of the eccentric.

There was no time for further acquaintance, however. Race explained his situation, and within fifteen minutes, all was in hand. Ball sent a message to Con in case any assistance should be needed near Brighton—discretion was apparently taken for granted—and promised to make sure that Ralstone's sister was kept in line.

He'd sent a servant to the livery stable that had his patronage, and Race emerged from the house to find a superb bay gelding waiting for him, ready to fly.

Ball insisted on lending Race twenty guineas, some of it in small coins. "In case you need ready cash. You can repay me at your leisure."

Efficient and tactful.

At the last minute, with Race already mounted, Ball said, "A marriage between you and Lady Anne Peckworth will not be easy to arrange."

Efficient, perceptive, and frank.

"I don't think to marry her."

"The Rogues have an interest in her happiness."

"I know. Delaney asked me to look out for Lady Anne."

After a moment, Ball said, "I see. Good luck," and waved Race on his way.

Even though the new horse was ready to eat up the miles, it wasn't possible at first. London was too crowded. Once out of the city, however, he could let the horse stretch, and it proved to be as gallant and fast as he'd hoped. He made short work of the stage to Enfield, surely cutting a half hour off their lead. There he learned that they'd planned a change at Ware.

He pushed the horse on, being sure not to press him too hard, and made Ware by nine. With any luck they would have stopped here for the night.

The sun was down, however, when he reached the Saracen's Head, and the place was hectic with travelers who were stopping for the night. It took fifteen minutes and bribery before he found out that Ralstone had gone on nearly two hours earlier with no specified stopping place. Was he going to have to check every inn on the Great North Road?

"What of their postilions?" he asked. "Are they back yet?"

"Nay, sir. And likely they'll stay the night where they stopped, unless they get a late run."

Race suppressed curses. "What's the farthest they'd go?"

"Buntingford, likely, sir, though they might push on to Royston."

The man looked suspicious, so Race tossed him an explanation. "They're hurrying north to my grandfather's deathbed, but we received news that he's rallied and there's no need for haste. Hate to rattle my poor granny's bones, you know."

The man warmed. "I hope you find them, sir. I'm sure they must have stopped for the night by now."

Race was, too, and it gnawed at his gut. He swung back onto his horse, who was suitably named Horatio and seemed to be thoroughly enjoying the adventure. Race wished he could say the same.

Then the gods smiled.

As he was leaving the yard he had to pause to let a coach roll in, and the head ostler called out, "Here's Jim and Matt back, sir! They took your couple on from here."

Race turned to the two postilions. Their horses had been taken from the shafts, and new ones were being put in, with new postilions to ride and guide them.

The postilions were sitting on a bench to pull off the heavy boots that protected their right legs from crushing.

He went over. "I gather you took a couple north earlier, sirs."

They both looked up, and he saw the experienced glint of greed in their eyes. He produced two crowns this time. "An elderly lady who walks with a cane and a dark-haired military gentleman."

The crowns disappeared into pockets. "Buntingford, sir. Stopped for the night at the Black Bull. Now the Crown's the better place, sir, but the gentleman asked for the quieter house. On account of the grieving lady, you see. Though I 'as to say as the gentleman looked happy," the man added with a wink. "Likely money coming."

Race nodded. "Thank you. Can I expect any problems on the road?"

"Smooth as a lady's hand, sir, though the light'll be gone soon. We delivered 'em two hours ago. Stopped there for a meal, we did, then picked up the business coming back south."

Race mounted again, end in sight, knowing that this time he had to ride as fast as horse and road would allow.

He set off knowing all speed might not be enough. The light was going, and soon all good people would seek their beds.

Including Anne and Jack Ralstone.

Beds, or bed?

Twenty-eight

The clock struck ten as Race entered Buntingford. The main street was deserted, the inns lining it were quiet. He gave thanks that he didn't have to hunt through them. Lights glimmered in some windows, but there seemed no sign of lively activities apart from flambeaux burning by each inn's door. To Race, the flames gave night a hellish touch.

Too late, too late chimed ten drawn-out times, and he slowed the tired horse down to a walk. A few minutes now would not help, and the horse needed to start to cool down.

The Black Bull turned out to be one of the oldest inns, with crooked black timbers and small-paned windows. No lights showed except the flambeaux by the door and a glimmer from the stableyard arch to the right.

He dismounted and led his mount through the arch into a stableyard as old fashioned as the inn. Stables and coach-houses ran around it, but on his left wooden steps went up to a gallery in front of the inn's rooms. By the light of the lantern hanging up there he thought there were eight. All were dark and silent.

He burned to charge up the stairs, to burst through doors in search of Anne and Ralstone, but that would create the scandal he was trying to avert.

To Race's right, lines of light gleamed through a closed pair of shutters. He was about to knock on the door next to the shutters when it opened, and a wizened groom came out. "Stopping here, sir?"

"Yes."

The groom took the horse and unsaddled it. Race

took off the bridle, partly to get the necessary over so he could question the man, but also to give the sweating horse its due. He told Horatio how pleased he was with his service and praised his effort.

The groom carried the tack away and came back with a blanket and bridle, then began walking the horse around the yard.

Masking his urgency, Race kept pace. "I was delayed on the road. I was supposed to meet a friend here—a Captain Ralstone. Strapping, dashing sort of man with dark hair." Since he didn't know what story the couple were telling, he kept it vague. "Heading to a funeral . . ."

"He and his relative be here, sir, but in their beds no doubt."

Beds. Thank God.

"What rooms?" he asked, making it sound casual.

"Seven and eight, sir, and the private parlor in between." The groom sent him a suspicious look. He seemed a watchful sort. He'd certainly sound the alarm if Race tried to break in.

Perhaps there was no need. They'd taken separate rooms.

But then Race realized that they'd have to if Anne was pretending to be an ancient.

"Can someone take Captain Ralstone a message for me?"

"No one up but me, sir, and I's the stables to take care of. Anyway, they're in bed." He nodded toward the rooms above and indeed, all the windows were dark.

"I'll take a room beside them, then, to be sure to catch them in the morning before they leave. I assume you have the keys?"

The man still looked suspicious, but he said, "Aye, sir. Just wait while the horse cools."

Race approved of the priority but ground his teeth. He took the horse. "I'll walk him while you find the key."

For a moment it looked as if the man would refuse, but muttering, he went back into his room and returned with a key on a big ring.

Race took it. Number six. "I'll find my own way." He

slipped the man a sixpence, hoping it would mollify him without raising suspicion.

He didn't run up the stairs, but urgency pounded in him. Even up close, there was no sound from numbers seven or eight. He hadn't asked if there were other guests, but there were no sounds from any of the rooms.

In his haste, he couldn't seem to find the hole for the key. He steadied himself, inserted it, and turned it, opening the way to a dark room. Glancing back he saw the groom still walking the horse but watching him, as well.

Race went into the room, groped for the candle that stood waiting by the bed, and carried it out to light it from the tin lamp. Then he gave the groom a cheery wave before going into his room and shutting the door.

Leaning back against it, he sucked in a deep breath. He'd never felt this sick dread before, not even before the most harrowing battle.

He quickly assessed his room. A simple enough place, not that he cared. He was more interested in the fact that—God be praised—the rooms had adjoining doors. Common enough so that larger suites of rooms could be put together for families.

He went to press his ear to the door to room number seven.

Silence.

Did the room house Ralstone or Anne in righteous slumber, or the two of them together? If they were together, what did he do? Break in and drag them out of one another's arms? Perhaps Anne truly loved Ralstone. Perhaps Ralstone truly loved Anne. Perhaps they were entwined naked in the bed, supremely happy.

He sucked in a breath. Even so, this was not the way to go about it, and the elopement was his fault.

He sat on a bench and tugged off one muddy boot. Like an enemy in ambush, thoughts of Benning Hall attacked. . . .

Anne in that plain blue dress, the dull woolen shawl huddled around her, but looking more beautiful than she had at the Pavilion dressed in flame. If he'd been able to predict the future then, and been wise enough, he would have fled.

Her hair had been pulled back carelessly and pinned into a knot high on her head, leaving her untouched face to speak for itself. An ordinary face, but one that became extraordinary with every emotion. Lovely arched brows over lively eyes. Soft lips, as soft to kiss as they'd looked. A wicked sense of humor.

Despite everything, he grinned.

Barnacles and Derbyshire rams.

Poor Lady Anne, indeed. He yanked off the other boot. She was no such thing, and he wouldn't let her become it.

Slowly, Race drew the bolt on his side of the door, relieved to find that it was well-greased and silent. He lifted the latch, but it was too much to hope that Ralstone had conveniently unbolted it on his side.

Most old inn doors did not fit neatly, however, and this was no exception. A half-inch gap gave space to insert his knife.

This bolt, too, was well greased and made little noise as he eased it back, fraction by fraction. All the same, it wasn't a silent progress, and if anyone was awake in the room, he or she would have to notice.

Race's unruly sense of humor imagined Ralstone lying there watching the bolt draw back, waiting to see who the intruder was. Not even remotely funny. The man would surely have a pistol pointed.

The bolt was finally free.

Time to get shot.

He opened the door cautiously, praying it wouldn't squeak, preparing pacifying words. He felt inclined to murder, but above all he wanted to avoid scandal.

No fisticuffs. No shooting.

At least, not here.

The room was dark and silent. The only light was his own candle left beside his bed. He was suddenly sure that this room was empty, and it was like a sword in the gut.

They were together in the other bedroom.

Swallowing bile, he went back for his candle and then moved on to the next door. It was unbolted, of course, and led into the parlor. He walked around the plain dining table to the last door of this journey. No lock to hinder him. Nothing but his own reluctance to face the truth.

He pressed down the latch and went in. He heard the rhythmic breath of sleep. Holding still for a moment, he waited to see if either of them would be wakened by the light of his candle. When there was no sign of it, he went farther into the room.

The curtains around the heavy old bed were drawn to. A quick glance showed a valise on the floor and men's clothing thrown over a chair. Then he noticed two bottles and two glasses on a small table. Had Ralstone made Anne drunk in order to have his way with her?

To hell with this. He strode forward and dragged back the musty curtains with a rattle of rings.

Ralstone grunted something and turned away from the light.

Race just stood there.

Ralstone was alone in the bed.

For a moment he thought he must be mistaken. He peered for Anne on the far side, her slight form hidden in some way. But she wasn't there. He gently closed the curtains again, though clearly Ralstone was too drunk to care.

Relief almost staggered him. He should have known that Anne had too much sense and goodness to give herself to Ralstone before she was married.

But then, where the devil was she?

He went back to the other bedroom, though he was sure he couldn't have missed her. A small trunk with the initials AP in brass was full of a lady's clothing. He lifted an expensive Kashmir shawl that he remembered all too well. That distinctive perfume rose from it—a complex blend of flowers and spice, subtle, ladylike, discreet, but promising.

Anne.

He rose and looked around again. So where the devil was subtle, ladylike, discreet Lady Anne Peckworth?

On the white cloth on top of the chest of drawers lay a piece of white paper. Suddenly frightened, he went and picked it up. His candlelight glinted on something beneath. A plain gold ring.

Married already?

That crazy panic fled. The ring must have been part of their pretense—but why had she left it?

Why had she left?

What had Ralstone done?

Dreading the worst, he put down the candle and unfolded the note. He'd never seen Anne's writing before, but he would have known it was hers. Neat, small, but with interestingly generous loops.

Dear Captain Ralstone,

I am deeply sorry to have raised your expectations . . .

That's one way of putting it, Race thought grimly.

. . . but I find we would not suit. I ask you not to pursue me. I am quite safe.

Relief made him want to smash something. *Anne, Anne, you idiot! How can you be safe? Where have you run to?*

She'd eloped, devil take it, done heaven knew what with Ralstone here tonight, and then she primly decides they won't suit, and takes off into the night?

He'd wring her bloody elegant neck!

When he found her.

Before, pray heaven, she fell into even worse disaster.

He longed to drag Ralstone out of the bed and beat him to a pulp, but it would raise the house, and anyway, there wasn't time. Anne, pampered and protected Anne, crippled Anne, was out somewhere in the dark night, alone.

Thank heavens Le Corbeau was in jail. This was the heart of his country. Except perhaps the authorities had the wrong man. Race was sure the dashing thief was not as amiable and noble as portrayed on stage.

He went back to his room and pulled on his boots. Then he paused at the door.

What was he going to tell the overwatchful groom?

Where was he going to look?

What was Ralstone going to do in the morning?

Cursing every second wasted, Race went back into the

other room, careless of the noise his boots made. He picked up the note Anne had left, noticing now that it was engraved with a coat of arms. He shook his head and tore that part off.

Then he took out his pencil and added at the bottom,

Say what you must to explain your missing relative but protect the lady's name and bother her no longer. Any scandal will require satisfaction.

He wrote it in Greek characters, which any gentleman should be able to read, but no servant would. He didn't sign his name. Ralstone might even think it from Uffham, though not if he knew Uffham's hotheaded temperament.

Then he went back to his room and made himself think. Profit and loss, lists of numbers, indexes. Think of it like that.

Which way would she go? Was she on foot? How far could she walk, even with her staff?

Maps. He had his book of maps. He dug it out of his pocket and opened it to the page that covered this area. Despite his infuriation with her, Anne Peckworth wasn't a lunatic. If she'd set off from here, she had a place to go, and it would be closer than London.

With his finger he traced circles out from Buntingford. The map included side panels with details of local houses of significance. Aspenden Mount, Broadfield Manor, Widdiall Hall . . .

Hell's tits, for all he knew, any of these places could be owned by a friend or relative.

Then his finger stopped.

Nun's Chase.

The estate of the Duke of St. Raven, which had rapidly become famous as a desirable invitation for gentlemen who wanted liberal amusements. Anne was going *there*?

Even as he questioned it, he knew it was right. There was a bond between her and the duke that ensured her safety, even if she arrived in the middle of an orgy.

He hoped.

He stared at the dot on the map, wondering if in the

end all was going to work out. Was Anne already there, in St. Raven's arms, realizing that he was the ideal match after all? He had to wish for it, but he also had to make sure she'd made it there through countryside made disorderly by highwaymen, and by homeless vagrants and troublemaking Luddites.

Damn fool. He checked the mileage.

Three miles from Buntingford to Nun's Chase. Not far at all, but he didn't think Anne could walk that far, especially at night. She was probably sitting beside the road in tears.

He shoved the map book away and went out, locking the door behind him. He ran down the stairs to the coachyard and into the stall where the groom still worked, brushing down the slit-eyed, happy horse. The man looked at him, still brushing, not seeming surprised.

"I find I have to leave," Race said, holding out some coins. "This should pay for my room."

The man stopped brushing and took the coins. "I'm afraid I'll have to check your pockets, sir."

"O, thou good and faithful servant." Despite his urgency, Race waited as the man felt his pockets for stolen items.

The man stepped back. "No offense, sir."

"None taken." Race looked at his horse and asked, "Do you have another horse I can take?" For this mission, a cart horse would do. He was only riding at all to be able to carry Anne.

The man nodded and walked down the stable to stir a sleepy black. "He's been here a couple of days and could do with some work, sir. He's a bit of a temperament, so I haven't given him to the regular sort of rider, if you see what I mean."

He already had a saddle blanket on the horse and now added a saddle. The horse shook itself and looked around, ears pricking.

Wonderful. Race knew what 'a bit of temperament' meant. "Is he going to fight me?"

"Oh, no, sir—nothing like that. Not if you're firm with him."

Race gave the horse a look that he hoped conveyed that he could be very firm if required. He bridled the horse himself to make that clear, led the horse into the yard, and then mounted. If Anne was walking along the road to Nun's Chase, the rest should be easy.

Judging from matters thus far, however, he had little faith in any of this being easy. Least of all, now he came to think of it, not getting her staff wrapped around his head when he found her.

Twenty-nine

Anne paused, leaning on her staff and flexing her foot. She was close to tears, but they were as much of anger as of misery. Anger at Ralstone, but mostly at herself.

What a fool she was! She deserved everything that was going to happen to her. She probably deserved to end up married to Jack Ralstone, but she wouldn't. She would not pay for her stupidity with her life.

How far had she come?

How far to go?

She looked up at the moon and the stars, but if they could tell people where they were, she couldn't decode it.

The real question was, how far could she walk?

The signpost outside Buntingford had said three miles to Tris's place. That hadn't seemed so terrible a distance with the whole night to make it, but she'd overestimated her strength. Her cane had made walking easier, but it could help only so far, especially when the cloudy moonlight concealed ruts and dips.

Her ankle was feeling the strain, but her legs were positively aching. They were unused to continuous walking. Perhaps she should have come up with a way to hire a horse at the Black Bull, but she still couldn't imagine how to do it without creating a stir. Her one principal thought had been to make sure that no one ever knew that the old lady who'd arrived there with Captain Ralstone was in fact Lady Anne Peckworth.

Her legs hurt and even felt weak, and her spirits weren't helped by the eerieness of being out at night.

At first she'd found it liberating. She'd been alone—completely alone and unfettered—for the first time in her life. As she'd moved farther away from the civilization of Buntingford, however, every scurry of an animal, every hoot of an owl, had made her start.

She hadn't encountered anything dangerous except a startled badger that had snarled at her. She'd jabbed her staff at it, and it had slunk away. An owl had swooped overhead on whirring wings, but it hadn't been hunting her. She'd heard a fox bark and the squeal of an animal caught in some predatory jaws.

Not her. She had no reason to be afraid out here, but it was starkly clear in the depth of night that for some creatures death was just a jaw-snap away. And this was the territory of Le Corbeau. She'd not heard of him hurting anyone, but away from the theater she did not believe in gallant criminals. She didn't want to encounter him. But then she remembered that he, thank heavens, was in jail.

She looked at the winding road ahead—simply a gap between dark hedgerows. It lay empty and silent, as if she were the only person left in the world. That suggested safety, not danger.

On the other hand, it almost felt as if she had been transported out of human ken. Wasn't that what faery stories said? That people out at night could be bewitched by the faery folk, trapped for their amusement or forced to dance to death?

She shivered, and it was partly because of the chill breeze. She hadn't known how cold a summer night could grow, and though she was wearing her black cloak and bonnet, they didn't give much protection over the light summer dress she'd changed into for dinner with Ralstone.

At least she was wearing her boots.

She didn't like being out here. She didn't like it at all. If only she'd been able to stay at the inn, to demand a new room for herself and a chaise in the morning to carry her back to London, to her father's town mansion, where the servants were always ready. Back into the security of ducal power and privilege.

Might as well print the story in the papers. The inn

servants would know who she was, then, and what she had done. The story would be up and down the Great North Road with tomorrow's traffic.

In that situation, her family might want her to marry Ralstone, or Ralstone might find some way to persuade or compel her. She'd fled in terror that she might somehow end up married to him. For all the days of her life.

Tris would prevent that. Tris would do whatever was needed to get Ralstone out of her life, to prevent scandal, and return her to her family with no one else knowing. She had only to reach Nun's Chase before morning, before Jack emerged from his disgusting drunken stupor and took action.

Grimly, she set off again. Putting one foot in front of the other again and again, eventually she would arrive. She surely must have walked half the distance.

She should have *stolen* a horse. She'd thought of it, but a squint into the stables had shown a night groom there, very much awake and alert.

She stopped again, close to tears. She was going to have to sit down and rest, even though she feared that she might not be able to get started again. And she ached to sleep. She'd hardly slept last night for nerves, and not at all tonight. Tiredness weighed in her joints and scratched at her eyes.

She looked around, hoping to see some shelter, even a cow byre. Failing that, something to sit on other than the damp ground—a stile, a rock, a tree stump.

She could see only the dark hedge running along either side of the lane, with the occasional tree looming high out of it. Then she made out a gate ahead. That must go somewhere. Even if it only led into a field, she would be off the lane.

If Jack woke and came in search of her, he wouldn't find her. She'd thought him too drunk to stir, but what did she know of how he reacted to wine? She didn't know him at all.

That was the trouble.

She hadn't known him at all, and when he'd dropped his guard and begun to reveal his true self, she'd seen that she'd made a terrible mistake.

She forced herself into motion again, limping toward

the gate, leaning heavily on her staff. But when she got there, it was held shut by a rusty iron pin. She tried to force it out, but her hands were too tired, too chilled, perhaps too weak to move it.

Weak. That was what she was. Any notion of strength had been an illusion, like the belief of a fawned-upon lord that he was clever or handsome. She was a paltry, weak, stupid woman.

She leaned on the rough gate, looking into a field that was a complete mystery in the dark. After a moment, she rested her staff against it and draped her arms over it, letting the top bar take her weight. She might even be able to sleep this way, the hard bar digging into her chest. She let her head sink forward, closed her eyes . . .

She started, shuddered, and forced her eyes open. She couldn't go to sleep here! She made herself stand straight and take up her staff again.

Then she glimpsed a light.

Through another hedge to her left. A little, flickering light.

A farm. A cottage. Some sort of shelter. A place to rest in safety. She tried to judge route and distance, but the dark made orienting herself peculiarly difficult, as if the land around followed no pattern that she knew. If she continued along the road, however, there had to be a lane soon. A lane leading to that sanctuary.

She set the tip of her staff to the ground and pressed on. The hedge hid the light, but she held to the faith that she'd seen it, that a place was there, not far away.

She thought she saw a gap in the hedge but closer to, she saw only a stile. Would there be a stile on a lane leading to a house? Surely they'd want to drive a cart or gig down there sometimes. . . .

Then she heard a voice.

A man's quiet voice, then a laugh.

She froze. Was she that close to the house? But what were people doing up, laughing, at this time of night?

A figure nipped nimbly over the stile, swaying lantern in hand. She saw others behind him, carrying things.

Sticks. Axes. And their faces were darkened.

Her light, her precious light had been these men, and they were up to no good!

She froze, praying that in her black cloak and bonnet she might be invisible, but then the man with the lantern turned and stared right at her. "Someone's here," he hissed.

Her face. His face was visible even through the soot or dirt he'd smeared on it. Hers must be white as the full moon.

She couldn't run, so she had no choice but to wait, shivering with cold, weariness, and fear. She tightened her grasp on her staff, willing to use it if she had to.

The man with the lantern came over, boots crunching heavily on the road. His lantern was tin pierced with many holes, and though not very bright it blinded her to him so his voice came out of a void. "Who're you, then?"

Her tongue stuck in her mouth.

"Come on! What you doing out here, and who be with you?"

A solid country voice, and a solid sweaty smell with him, and fear. Frightened animals were the most dangerous.

"No one." She'd found her voice, though it was breathy. "I'm walking to a friend's house!"

"At midnight?"

Anne tried to imitate Hetty's country accent. "I have no money to pay for a room, so I must walk."

She sensed other men coming closer, dark shapes beyond the holes of the lantern. Then they began to spread out, to encircle her. Panic tightened her throat, and her heart was going to burst.

She couldn't step back, for she'd bump into those behind. She turned one way and then the other, trying to keep them in sight.

"Where's this friend live, then?"

Attack was the best form of defense. She stood as tall as she could, gripping her staff. "What business is it of yours? And what are *you* doing out at midnight?"

She could guess, but she hoped they didn't know that. She'd seen sticks and the glint of metal. Axes, perhaps.

Not poachers. They didn't go out in large groups.

These men were machine-breakers. They thought their living would be taken away by a new machine—a threshing machine perhaps—and were set on smashing it. They were risking their freedom and perhaps their lives to do it, and might murder a witness.

The men were silent except for the odd shuffle or rustle of clothes. She could smell them, though: unwashed wool on their bodies, onions and beer on their heavy breath, and something else. Something primitive, violent, and dangerous.

By day they were probably decent enough farm laborers, like the ones she greeted cheerfully at Lea Park—hardworking sons and fathers. But here, at night, they were menace, and her heart beat like a frightened bird.

She could say that she hadn't seen any of them clearly, that she wouldn't be able to point them out tomorrow, but would they believe her?

A hand grasped her staff just below hers. The lantern shifted so she saw his face. Long, suspicious, big crooked teeth. "This is a fancy stick for a wandering pauper."

Someone grabbed her cloak from behind. "Fancy cloak, too."

She fought to keep hold of her only weapon, trying to twitch out of the hold on her cloak. "I've fallen on hard times. The cloak was charity. Let me be!"

"Can't do that, luv. Who knows who you might run off to?"

She pulled fiercely at the staff. He let go suddenly so that she fell back onto her bottom, at their feet. They laughed.

She screamed, *"No!"* at the vague but potent threat that hovered over her.

Then she heard it, felt it through the earth. Hooves at the gallop.

"Soldiers!" a man cried, and they began to scatter, but the horses were already on them. On her. She fell to the ground, arms over her head.

Thunder of hooves in her ears and through her body. Confused yells and shouted orders.

"Hide!"

"Run!"

Then: "It's only one man. Get him!"

She peeped, and then sat up.

A huge dark horse was wheeling and kicking. Too

close! She rolled toward the hedge, hearing her straw bonnet crunch, then peered out again.

Men were fleeing, calling to others to run, but some had stopped to fight, long sticks and heavy blades catching the moonlight. The horse reared up over them, and they fell back. The magnificent rider brought the horse down and turned it. The horse kicked out behind with a force that could have shattered heads if the men weren't already backing away.

Horse and rider turned and charged, the rider hitting out with a weapon of some sort. Cavalry! Had the military come to her rescue?

It broke the rabble. The men scattered, rolling under hedges, fighting one another to get over the stile. . . .

She sat up and almost cheered, but then she realized this was disaster. She couldn't be found like this! Hastily she began to squeeze back farther into the shadow of the hedge, trying to find a way through it into the field.

Crack!

A pistol?

She stopped to see the horse riderless and rampaging.

One horse.

One rider.

Not the military.

And now her rescuer had been shot. She must help. . . .

To her shame she stayed frozen in her lair, afraid of being identified, afraid of being hurt.

She stayed there as the villains fled, their crashes and cries fading. The horse stamped and jerked. Wounded, too? She should help the poor horse. . . .

And then she heard a murmuring voice.

She shuddered, resting her head on her hands. The gallant man wasn't dead at least.

He might be wounded, though, and she must help him. Perhaps he need not know who she was. She crawled away from the hedge, amazed by how deeply she'd pushed herself. She had to tug her cloak free of one hawthorn spike after another, scratching her skin at times.

Surely no one would recognize Lady Anne Peckworth in this bedraggled creature.

By the time she could stand the horse was calmer, and she thought she saw six legs not four. The man was standing on the far side of the horse. Thank God. He didn't seem hurt at all.

She froze under a new thought.

Perhaps it was Le Corbeau.

If so she was grateful for his help, but all in all, she'd rather not meet him. Would he hear if she moved again? If she turned her back, would her black clothing make her invisible?

As her heart calmed, she made out the soothing murmur. "There, there, my fine brave fellow. I'll see to you."

Shot, no doubt. Poor creature. But there was nothing she could do for it, and perhaps the man would be so keen to get his horse to help that he wouldn't search for the lady he'd rescued.

All she had to do was keep very quiet.

Then the man spoke louder. "Anne?"

Her breath caught. Surely she knew that light, crisp voice.

"Anne? Where are you? Are you all right?"

It was as if a mighty hand had shaken the world and turned it upside down. Or had *she* been shot and blasted out of her wits?

The avenging Horseman of the Apocalypse was Race de Vere?

"Anne?"

The clear anxiety in his voice cut through her daze. She tugged herself free again from the hedge and limped into the moonlit road, picking up her staff. The dark horse still had six legs, but one pair of legs moved. Race ducked under the horse's neck and into view.

Hatless, slender in comparison to the bulk of the horse, not far from a time of violence, he seemed completely at his ease. It infuriated her.

"What on earth are you doing here?"

"As usual, Lady Anne, getting you out of trouble."

"As usual!" She shook her staff at him. "I am never in trouble."

He laughed.

"I'm not! Or at least," she amended, being a stickler

for justice, "I have not been before tonight. And this is all your fault."

That was unfair, and she expected him to say so. Instead, he said, "You're doubtless right."

It reminded her of things. "You're a Rogue. Or at least, a servant of Rogues."

"True."

"You went to Benning Hall to . . . to do something for the Rogues."

"True after a fashion." He turned his attention back to the horse. "That pistol ball creased his back, poor fellow. I need to get him to shelter and help."

She stared. Was that it? He charges in here, rescues her from some unspecified but terrible fate—single-handedly against dozens—and now his main concern was shelter for his horse? She approved, but it struck her as extremely strange.

"How did you come to be here?" she demanded.

"Magic," he said.

For a moment, out here in the unreality of the night, she considered whether it might be true. Then she sighed. "Can you ever talk sense?"

He glanced back. "I do so frequently—as when I told you not to marry Ralstone."

"I didn't."

There was a silent question in the air between them—had she acted as if married? That was one she wasn't ready to answer.

"Come on," he said. "The horse can doubtless carry your light weight as far as Nun's Chase."

She put a hand to her dazed head. Finding her battered bonnet there, she tore it off and flung it on the road. She was very tempted to stamp on it. "You cannot simply appear out of nowhere and not explain yourself!"

Race looked at her, and an explanation occurred.

"Oh, heavens. Do my family know? Have they sent you after me?"

"Why me, not Uffham? I followed an instinct and checked on you in Greenwich. Unless anyone else does the same thing, you are safe."

"Safe?" She started to laugh.

Then she was in his arms, as it had been that first time

at Benning Hall, strong, solid, comforting. He thought she was distraught and she was not, but she let him think it because this was where she wanted to be.

Suddenly everything was clear. This man, this hero, this rock—for all his mischievous ways—was the only one she could share her life with. And he could not be indifferent to her.

Why else was he here if he did not want her, at least a little bit? She knew, however, that he was trying to protect her, just as people had all her life. He wanted to wrap her in flannel and tuck her safely away in aristocratic splendor.

How was she going to get what she truly wanted?

She drew back a little, looking up at him. "You saved me."

The moon was behind him making his expression a mystery. "I shouldn't have needed to."

Undeterred by his stern tone, she said, "Thank you." She slid her arm around his neck and kissed him.

He resisted for a moment, then his arms tightened and his mouth sealed hers. She heard her staff clatter to the ground, then her other arm was around him so she could kiss him back as she wanted to, as she never quite had before, with no limit, with no thought of limit.

For the first time she let her hands take possession of him, of his shoulders, his skull, his jaw. Twisting, she slid one arm lower, to his back, then to his strong buttocks. . . .

He pulled back, pushed her at arm's length. "Anne, stop it."

"Why?"

"Don't be stupid."

"I've been stupid. I'm not anymore. I want you."

That wasn't quite so gracious as she'd intended, yet she felt his hands tighten under the power of it. Before she could amend it, he put his hands at her waist and lifted her into the saddle. The horse shifted for a moment, and she clutched the mane, but at a word from him, it settled.

What a remarkable feat of strength to lift her like that. It melted her even more. She would not let him go. He was hers. She reached down to tangle her fingers gently in his silvery hair. She wanted freedom to do this all her days.

He looked up, seeming exasperated if anything. "It's fear, relief, and battle aftermath, Anne. You'll have your wits back soon."

She just smiled. A month ago, a week ago, yesterday, she would have shriveled at that and fled. She had, in fact. It was all different now. A deep instinct told her that he wanted her in the same way that she wanted him. She had only to break the barriers that he thought came of honor.

She didn't underestimate the challenge. Men, good men, took those things so seriously. On the other hand, she didn't underestimate her own abilities when it came to a challenge.

He was clearly determined on getting her to Nun's Chase. Then, she suspected, he would disappear. One way or another, she would not allow that. Would Tris lock him up for her until he saw reason?

He picked up her staff and took the reins to lead the horse down the road. She'd rather stay here, but what argument could she make? She was racking her brain when fate solved her problem.

"Pleeze," said a laconic, French-accented voice, "stand and deliver."

Anne stared at the stile, and at the man now sitting on top of it, a pistol pointed at them. The tone might be lazy, but the pistol was not.

The man was dressed in black, with black mask, mustache and beard, and the broad-brimmed hat with the sweeping white plume.

"Le Corbeau?" she said. "I don't believe this!"

Perhaps this was all a crazy dream.

Thirty

The man inclined his head. *"A vôtre service, mademoiselle."* Eyes and pistol remained steady.

Anne wondered how Race was taking this and prayed that he not do anything dangerous. "If you are thinking of a duel, sir," she said to the highwayman, "I assure you that I am not interested."

Le Corbeau grinned. "You refer to zat absurd play, *minou.* I would not give up my way of life for a mere woman."

Kitten. He was calling her kitten? She preferred Mouse.

Race spoke at last. "What do you want?" His tone was chilly, as if he addressed a thoughtless child.

Le Corbeau dropped down from his perch, pistol steady all the time. Fifteen feet or so lay between them, so Anne didn't think there was much they could do. If she weren't seated sideways she might be able to charge the horse at the highwayman. It was clearly cavalry trained, but she wasn't. She didn't know how to make it fight. And, of course, it was injured.

It was all intolerably frustrating, and she was sure it was worse for Race. She didn't want him to take risks, however. She had such high hopes for their future.

"Your money or your life," the man said, but again as if amused by the trite line.

"I have about ten guineas," Race responded. "The lady has nothing."

"I doubt it. Perhaps I should search her."

Anne heard Race sigh. "As we're trading clichés, *monsieur*—over my dead body."

Anne shivered with dread, but also, she had to admit, with a thrill at the absolute challenge of it.

Le Corbeau seemed to study Race for a moment. "She is your wife?"

"No."

"Your lover?"

"No."

"Your beloved?"

"No."

Was it her imagination that Race hesitated before saying that? It could simply be the mounting tension she sensed in him.

She plunged into speech, in French. "You, sir, are supposed to be in jail."

"My poor simulacrum," he replied in the same language. "I never thought to win so well by losing a few trinkets at dice."

That answered one question. He really was French. She had been taught by a Frenchwoman and could detect no falseness in his fluency.

"If you are known to be still working these roads," she pointed out, "they will have to let him go free."

"It seems only fair."

"Very well. Let us assist you. Permit us to go on, and we will immediately report your activities to the magistrates."

"How kind. However, to have full effect, it is necessary that I steal something from you. No necklace, my pretty cat? No rings? Or did those you drove off before take them? I heard a shot."

Her jewelry was in her pocket beneath her gown. "They were frame-breakers, not thieves, and I'm a poor cast-off maidservant with only the clothes I stand up in."

For some reason he seemed to find that amusing, but he turned his attention to Race. "And you, my silent sir?"

"Oh, I'm nobody."

Anne was touched to discover that while Race's French was tolerable, his accent was atrocious.

"Does Mr. Nobody fight with the sword?" Le Corbeau asked.

"It has been known. I fear that you, sir, have been

sneaking into Drury Lane to watch your own adventures. Why the devil should I fence with you?"

"For your lady's honor."

A silky menace in it made Anne come alert. This was all so strange, so dreamlike, that she'd been treating it like a play. But it was real, the villain was real, and he might well have foul designs on her body. If Race fought him, one or other might die. She hiked up her skirts and swung her right leg over so she was astride.

"This is nonsense," she protested. "I have money. Take it!"

"Oh, I will," the highwayman said, eyeing her exposed legs with interest. "You doubtless have it tucked away next to your skin. Beneath your garter, perhaps, or between your breasts. . . ."

Mouth dry, she realized that she might have made things much, much worse.

In a swirl of movement, Race tossed the reins to her, and slapped the horse to make it run. She missed the reins so clutched the horse's mane as it careered away.

She screamed, "No!" She was going to fall without balance or stirrups, and she wasn't going to leave Race to face an armed man alone.

Perhaps the horse obeyed, or perhaps it was its wound, but it halted, shifting nervously beneath her. Muttering about highwaymen, heroes, and men in general, she grabbed the reins, settled herself in the staddle, and turned the horse back. A fight was going on. And there seemed to be three men involved!

"Sorry," she said to the horse. "Go!" She kicked as hard as she could and, praise heaven, some warrior instinct sent it hurtling back to the fray.

Anne saw the three men stop fighting to stare at her—three white faces, two masked, and all ludicrously alarmed. She hauled on the reins to stop the beast, but she'd obviously found one of its battle cues. It reared up, slashing out with its hooves. She clung to the mane, praying not to fall.

The men all rolled for cover, but she heard one laugh. She knew who that must be.

She brought the horse down, soothing it, wondering exactly where her bravado had brought them. She'd split the men, but was Race alone, or with one of the villains? Should she now ride on to safety or try to rescue her hero?

This daring lady business was not so easy as it seemed. She circled the horse, peering around. "Race?"

A movement. Before she could react, she was dragged off the saddle and over a broad shoulder. Struggling, screaming, she couldn't get free.

Then she was whirled to her feet, a gloved hand over her mouth. Race hurtled out of the shadows, but the man behind her said, "Don't."

Race stopped, but Anne saw a death-promise in his eyes, the sort made by a man who knew what it was to kill.

"Do not be rash, sir," Le Corbeau said from behind her, in English now, and wisely speaking very carefully, indeed. "As you know, I am not alone. My friend, he has two pistols and can stop you dead at any moment."

Anne tried to speak, to tell Race not to take any risks. All she could do was shake her head at him.

Race was focused on the man behind her. "You, sir, are a dead man."

"Perhaps. But at ze moment, you sir, are a man who must do exactly as I say, no? And what I say is, you walk. Over the stile, down ze path a little way, to a cottage."

"Why?"

"You do not take ze orders very well, do you?"

"It has been said." It was as if Race relaxed, but Anne wasn't fooled, and neither, she suspected, was the highwayman. She didn't know where the third man was now, but she didn't doubt that he was nearby and with pistols. They had no choice but to do as Le Corbeau said.

"You want a reason?" the highwayman asked. "Very well. Ze swords are in ze cottage."

"And if we fight and I win?"

"Zen you both go free."

"If I lose?"

"Zen you are both entirely at my disposal, but I promise you your lives. You have been a soldier, I tink. You know it is good to live to fight another day."

Race nodded, but Anne was glad she wasn't the focus of his wide, steady eyes. Perhaps they gave the highwayman pause, for time passed before he spoke again, and then it was to her.

"Do not scream, *minou*. It will do no good." He then removed his hand from her mouth, though he still had an arm around her, pressing her to his body. He was a tall man, not heavy, but all muscle.

"Should I have ridden away?" she asked Race. "I'm sorry. I couldn't do it."

He smiled. "I don't suppose I could have either." He picked up her staff from the road and gave it to her. "Let's go to this cottage and see the end of this. Don't worry. I won't let anyone hurt you."

He couldn't be sure of that, and yet she felt as if safety had been wrapped around her. She wanted this security all her life.

Le Corbeau let her go, and she limped to the stile. "I wish I could make sure no one hurts you."

Race smiled at that, shaking his head, then went nimbly over the stile and turned to help her. Le Corbeau's henchman was on that side, pistols at the ready, but Race acted as if he didn't exist. A glance back showed Le Corbeau behind, a pistol pointing at them.

Anne faced the man, trying for the same nonchalance that came so easily to Race. "Someone has to take care of the poor horse, sir."

"But of course, my grand lady. As soon as you are at ze cottage. I see you limp. I am sorry for it. Would you wish me to carry you?"

She gave a deliberately theatrical shudder, turned, and made her way inelegantly over the stile. At the far side, Race swung her into his arms. "You don't find my touch repulsive, I hope."

What to say to that? She contented herself with a simple "No" and made sure her staff was not in his way. Despite their situation, the feeling of being in his arms was magical.

The henchman turned to lead the way down the rough, shadowy lane. He kept glancing back, however, and Le Corbeau was behind. Up ahead Anne saw a flickering light, and this time it really was the lit window of a cottage.

The highwayman's lair.

Where Race would fence with Le Corbeau if she didn't think of some way to avoid it. To add to her problems, at some point tonight she had to win Race de Vere. Her arm was looped around his neck, and she let her hand cherish his strong shoulder.

"I'm sorry for dragging us into this mess," she murmured.

"It would have been wiser to stay safely in Brighton."

Anne surprised herself by digging her nails into him and making a growl of irritation in her throat.

"Little cat," he said, and she heard amusement. "Is that an improvement on Mouse?"

"I wasn't *purring*. I fled Brighton because you threatened to turn my family against Ralstone."

"Ah, yes, Ralstone. Perhaps you wish to be returned to him."

"No!" A moment later she wished she'd softened it.

"What did he do?" That cold murderous edge was unmistakable.

"Nothing. Stop sounding as if you want to kill someone."

"If you're going to go adventuring, Anne, you are going to run into violence and bloodshed. Get accustomed to it."

"Ralstone did nothing particularly offensive. He was merely himself."

After a moment, she felt laughter shake him. "What a sad epitaph. You, however, deserve to be spanked for leading the poor man on."

Anne didn't have to find a response to that justified accusation and outrageous suggestion. They had arrived at the cottage.

The darkness hid many flaws, but even so *ramshackle* was the word that came to mind. It was so old that the small windows had no glass, only vertical wooden bars to keep out intruders. The whole place tilted, and the henchman had to heave the door up to get it to open. He went into the dimly lit interior, and they followed.

Race stood her on the earthen floor, and Anne straightened her clothes, glancing around. This must be the main room of the cottage because it had a large hearth in the center wall. A rough door to one side which would lead into another simple room. There would be a space above under the roof, perhaps once used for sleeping, but if there were stairs, they were in the other room.

The light came from a pierced tin lantern similar to the one the Luddites had carried, and the smell of tallow mixed with a general smell of damp and rot.

She turned to face Le Corbeau. "A suitable hole for a rat," she said in French.

"Does it not occur to you to be a little careful of what you say to me, *minou*?"

"I will be polite if you promise to let us go."

"Do I collect slaves? Of course I will let you go." He put on a look of horror. "My God! You think I will murder you? No, no. Too messy by far."

"The swords," Race said in that cold, forbearing voice.

"Ah, yes—the swords."

Le Corbeau looked between them, the light glimmering on his face. It wasn't the face, however, so much as the mischievous smile that made Anne's breath catch.

She knew that smile.

Tris! Le Corbeau was Tris.

What on earth was he up to, and why was he playing this game with them? To punish her for being in this mess? She almost spoke, but then remembered. Once this adventure was over Race would disappear. She wasn't sure even Tris could stop him short of tying him up, and where would that get her?

His eyes met hers. He knew she knew. He was telling her to say nothing. Heart beating hard, she obeyed for the moment.

"I am afraid, my dear sir," he said to Race, "that our fight will have to wait a little while. For one thing, I must go out and rob someone or my poor substitute might hang. For another, we can hardly fence in the moonlight, no matter how romantic that might seem. Morning is the time for duels."

"Then let us go, for God's sake."

Race's tone made Anne chill with guilt. He still thought this for real and was afraid for her. She should tell him the truth, but she had the feeling that Tris was on her side and had some purpose. He was not stupid in his mischief and adventures.

"I fear you might raise the alarm, sir," Tris said, the French disguising his voice so well, "and increase the risk of my capture. I wish to bring about the release of the innocent man, but not at risk of my own neck."

"What, then, do you intend?"

"Merely to keep you securely here until morning, at which time we can play our little game."

Race was cold as stone. "I, sir, am not playing games. The lady will be missed. A search will be made."

"For a cast-off serving maid?"

Now Anne knew why Le Corbeau had found that funny. Damn Tris and his wayward sense of mischief. At heart, he and Race were two of a kind.

And she loved them both.

It couldn't come to violence and blood, could it? Anne knew, without doubt, that Race was poised to take any chance to kill their captors and get her away to safety.

She moved closer to him.

Race glanced at her and put an arm around her. "Don't worry. I won't let him hurt you."

"I know." That was the problem. She'd moved close so as to be able to stop him doing murder.

"Take off your clothes," Tris said in his heavily accented English.

"What?"

She and Race said it together, and she was probably the more shocked.

"What on earth—?"

But again, the look in Tris's eyes stopped her. "Not all your clothes," he said, lips twitching. "Your outer clothes. Zen you will be locked in ze upper room. I don't think you will find a way out in the next few hours, but if you do, perhaps running across the countryside in your underwear will make you hesitate."

"We're not doing it, Anne," Race said. "He has neither time nor inclination to make a struggle over it. I don't know what makes the madman tick, but this is a game to him, nothing more."

An accurate assessment, but Anne would quite like to get Race out of some of his clothing. Wicked though it was, compromising them both was the only way to capture this man, and less clothing would be a step in the right direction.

A few months ago such outrageous ideas would never have occurred to her, but now she was a daring lady who knew exactly what she wanted—to make love to Race here, tonight, so that he'd have to marry her.

And Tris was on her side?

Perhaps this was a dream, but if so, she would enjoy it.

With a loud *click*, Tris cocked his pistol. "If you do not take off your cloak, dress, and shoes, *minou,* I am going to shoot your so gallant escort. I will try to do it in a nonfatal spot, but I cannot guarantee it."

"If you shoot me," Race said, "I can hardly fence with you in the morning."

"As you have guessed, I am quite mad. The best ting to do is to humor me. I am also a man of my word. If you win ze duel in ze morning, you both go free."

Race looked at Anne, exasperated and apologetic. "I'm sorry. He clearly is mad, and thus there's no point reasoning with him. I'd willingly be shot to save you, but it's unlikely to do any good."

"Of course it isn't. Don't even think of it. As it happens, I'm quite well covered underneath."

She leaned her staff against the wall, untied her black cloak, and let it fall to reveal the cream muslin dress she'd put on for dinner with Ralstone. Ignoring Tris and his man—doubtless some poor innocent groom forced into this mayhem—she turned her back to Race. "You'll have to unbutton it for me."

She stood there, eyes closed, sucking in every scrap of pleasure from his fingers working at the row of small buttons down the back. From just that, from the elusive brush of his fingers against her spine, something wild and fevered stirred deep inside her.

Plots and motives began to fade beneath a sharp, animal need. How easy it would be to turn, to move into one of their blistering kisses, to go on from there this time. . . .

He parted her dress and untied the laces that gathered the waist beneath her breasts, then she felt, surely she felt, his knuckles brush comfortingly against her skin for a moment. She had to catch her breath before she turned, dress loose, to face all three men.

Perhaps it was a lifetime of servants, or perhaps just that she knew that underneath she was almost as well covered as in the gown, but she felt no embarrassment. In fact, she quite enjoyed the discomfort on their faces.

Serve Tris right!

She pulled out of the sleeves, and let the dress fall to the ground. Beneath, she wore a petticoat of white cotton which was little different to the dress except that it was sleeveless. Beneath that—she knew at least—she had a light corset over her shift and drawers.

Chill hit her bare arms but she didn't rub them. Race would probably risk death to put her cloak back on her.

"Now you, sir," Tris said. "Ungallant to leave ze lady so far ahead of you."

"You're a lunatic." But Race shed his jacket, waistcoat, and shirt. "Will that do?"

"Oh yes." She saw that Tris was having trouble staying serious. For her part, she was having trouble concentrating on anything but Race and the feelings his strength and his beautiful body stirred in her.

"Is that all?" she demanded, desperate now to get Race alone. Surely that was part of Tris's plan.

"Alas, *minou,* your footwear. If you are willing to run around the countryside in your petticoat, perhaps you will hesitate to do so barefoot."

"The lady has a crippled foot," Race said. "She needs her boots."

"Even so. Perhaps, sir, you would help her."

Anne saw Race was close to breaking point, ready to fight. She sat on one of the rough benches that were the only furniture. After a tense moment, Race turned his back on their captors and came to kneel before her.

His eyes met hers and she winced at the angry tension there.

"Don't fight them," she murmured. "This is nothing terrible."

"You're very brave."

She winced with guilt. "Not really."

He shook his head and undid her left half-boot. She

could take off her boots herself, but she had no objection to Race doing it for her, especially wickedly naked from the waist up. She couldn't resist. Pretending to need the balance, she put a hand on his broad shoulder.

So warm, so firm, so strong.

He glanced up, perhaps puzzled, perhaps wary, perhaps warning her of something. He made short work of her boot then began to unlace her right one. The heavy boot she wore on her crippled foot.

He'd handled her right foot before, at the Swinamer ball, but worry tugged at her. What did he really think about it? Would it repulse him when it came to intimacy?

He eased the half-boot off, then looked at her again, and this time she saw nothing but assurance in his expression. He traced with his fingers the awkward turn of her ankle and the crease in her sole. Then slowly, he raised her foot and kissed the instep.

Her hand on his shoulder tightened of its own accord, and she felt him become still. Did something ripple through him as it did through her, dizzying her, shooting aches into private places?

It did. She saw it in his eyes, but he rose, took off his own boots, and faced their captors. "Now what?"

It was the same forbearing tone that said that their captors were simpletons. Harmless, and mindless. Anne prayed that Tris wouldn't fall out of his role and shoot Race for pure impertinence.

She could shoot him for excessive willpower, but it did not truly daunt her. He was hers, and soon would be in all senses of the word. He had to be. She could not bear for it to be any other way.

Apparently unmoved, Tris gestured toward the door beside the hearth, where his henchman waited with the lantern. "Now you follow my friend upstairs. We secure you up zere, and you peacefully await the dawn. See, it is perfectly simple."

"So is death," promised Race, extending an arm to Anne.

Shaken by nerves and desire, she needed it, but she did her best to walk with dignity. In many ways it was more comfortable for her to walk without the corrective shoes, but her limp was worse. Race moved to carry her, but she stopped him.

"I prefer to walk."

A bit of sanity remained, and she wanted him to see her like this before she bound him to her. If he couldn't bear it, she would have to let him go. With another man she could hide her blemish, but not with Race. With him, reality had to be all or nothing.

Had Tris known that, too? Was it why he'd insisted on her being in her stocking feet? As she made her way awkwardly up narrow stairs, she prayed that Race never learn who Le Corbeau was. God knows what he would do.

The stairs emerged into an empty space beneath the roof with a small window at one end. This was not much of a prison unless Tris intended to chain them to the rafters.

The henchman put down the lantern, went to what looked like an end wall, did something, and opened a rough plank door. Perhaps in daylight it would be clearer, but there would never be much daylight here. A secret room, doubtless where Le Corbeau kept his loot.

Where Tris kept his loot? She remembered to puzzle over his role in this. He couldn't really be a highwayman. A resolute traveler might put a pistol ball in him one of these nights. Could she be wrong about his identity?

She peered at him, and even in the dim light, she was sure. She'd known his voice, too, once she'd recognized him. Though he was pitching his voice a little higher, it was still his. What on earth could he be up to?

She had no time to fret about his role now. They were ordered into the shadowy space beyond the door.

The distant lantern light showed some locked chests and a rough bed. A place for Le Corbeau to live for a day or two if hunted? Other than that, the room was just another attic space, the ceiling being the timber roof frame and the thatch beyond.

She suppressed a shudder, imagining spiders and even bigger invaders dropping down from that thatch in the night. Race put an arm around her. That instantly made everything wonderful, but could she really attempt to seduce him in such a place?

Thought of pests raised other worries.

She turned to where Tris and his man stood in the doorway. "Are there mice here? Or rats?"

Race drew her closer. "There are bound to be, Anne. Don't worry—"

But Tris said, "Not as far as I know."

He was telling her that he knew nothing to Race's discredit. Of course. He wouldn't be throwing them together like this if he did.

And he was. He was clearly arranging things to make it as easy as possible for her to capture her elusive beloved. It was close to miraculous, but she'd take a miracle.

She blew Tris a kiss and saw him fight a smile.

They were both mad, and this was wicked, but she was sure of her course. She knew in her heart that Race loved her as much as she loved him. Rank and fortune no longer mattered. This was her chance for a true treasure, and she would not let it slip by.

"I no longer play for farthing points," she said, and saw Tris understand her, and Race fail to do so. In fact Race looked as if he feared she was scared out of her wits.

Tris smiled and put the lantern just over the threshold. "I wish you all pleasure of the night, my friends, and a glorious tomorrow."

And then he closed the door.

Thirty-one

Despite what she knew, the closing door sent a shudder through Anne and she moved into Race's arms. She might be terrified if not for him. Once their bodies touched, however, desire pulsed back into her, making her body and Race's body the only things that mattered.

The sounds at the door seemed distant to her, the sounds of Tris or his man locking them in here.

She rubbed against Race, waiting for a kiss, but he gently moved away from her and went to check both door and tiny window.

Willpower, damn his eyes.

She considered the bed. Unpromising though it was, it was her target. She limped over to sit on it. The wooden frame seemed solid, and the only smell was a faint one from the wool blanket. In fact, it was quite a respectable bed for its surroundings, and when she felt the sheets, they were fine cotton.

She suppressed a smile. Of course. Tris would not contemplate sleeping in a coarse and grubby bed. Worry pricked at her again.

Had he really left to hold up a coach in order to prove that the poor man in jail was not Le Corbeau?

She made herself put it aside. There was nothing she could do about it now, whereas there was something she could do about her future. As she watched Race move around the small room, never looking at her, doubts stirred. She fought them down. She remembered the way they'd kissed on the road. She remembered the look in his eyes downstairs.

He was hers. She only had to break him.

The sagging mattress made sitting on the edge of the bed awkward, so she hitched herself up onto it and leaned back against the low wall. The roof angled up just above her head. She tried hard not to think about spiders in her hair.

This would be a lot easier, she was sure, in a gracious bedroom. But perhaps not. Race was going to resist, and their circumstances were weapons she could use.

He'd picked up the lantern and turned from the door with it in his hand. "Unfortunately, I can't see any way of getting out. I could try battering the door down with one of the chests, but it's very solid and securely fixed in some way. This cottage may look run down, but it's well maintained where it matters." He moved back into the center of the space. "We could set fire to the bed and hope they rescue us."

"Don't!"

He turned to her. "I'm sorry. Damnable army instincts. Assess the possibilities and hazards."

"The roll of the dice?" she suggested.

He laughed and put the lantern on one of the chests. Then he came over to sit on the bed by her side, but a foot away. "You're very brave."

"I don't feel brave." It was true, but her fear was nothing to do with highwaymen, and all to do with failing here. She moved closer. "Hold me, please."

She counted his hesitation in heartbeats, but then he met her and took her into his arms. "You're cold," he said, and drew her closer.

"You're warm," she breathed with relief.

She pressed as much of herself as possible against him, exploring the wonder of her naked arms against his naked chest. He did feel delightfully hotter than she was, and the firmness of him, his strength, his self, warmed parts deeper than her skin.

She rested her head on his shoulder, breathing in his spicy smell.

She felt him tense.

That was doubtless good.

"Thank God you're here with me," she whispered against his skin. "He might have captured me when I was by myself."

"Or the frame-breakers might have slit your throat. What crazy impulse took you out into the night?" His tone was cool, but he began to stroke her, comforting her.

Such pleasure, such power in his clever, soothing hands, burning through the fine lawn and silk of her underclothes. She breathed in the scent of him. She longed to turn her head and kiss him, kiss his throat, his chest, his muscular torso. . . .

He'd said something. She should reply. . . .

"Out into the night," she echoed, most of her mind on other things. "I had to. I couldn't be there with Ralstone in the morning. If anyone found out, I might have had to marry him."

"Wasn't that the idea?"

Her arm rested across him. She dared to move her fingers, to explore a little. "Not by then. If I'd stayed and refused to go on with him, he might have revealed my identity to force me."

"He still might."

"Without my presence, it's just his story." If she raised her head, would he kiss her?

She felt him nuzzle in her hair. "Anne, you left your monogrammed luggage behind."

She winced. "Oh."

She looked up to see rueful amusement in his eyes. "And a note on your crested note paper. I tore off the crest, but I couldn't do much about your luggage. I added a postscript to your note, however, that should make Ralstone keep it all quiet."

"And I felt so competent, so brave!" All her confidence, all her courage, fled into the gloom. She moved away from him. "I'm useless, aren't I? A spoiled duke's daughter. I can't do anything right—"

He captured her shoulders and made her meet his eyes. "Your bravery humbles me. For you, for Lady Anne Peckworth, to set off into the night, to face down wandering troublemakers, to face down a highwayman, took more courage than I possess."

"Or a foolish miscalculation of the danger involved."

Lantern light showed his smile. "That's usually the

way it is. Few heroes really know what they're letting themselves in for. If they did, they'd run away."

"I don't think so. I'm sure you knew what you risked when you had a man flogged with ribbons."

His smile disappeared. "Who told you that story?"

"Ralstone."

"A gossip, too, is he? It was no act of heroism."

"You were almost flogged yourself."

"Almost. There was no real danger."

"You couldn't have been sure of that."

She realized that they were back to arguing and a foot apart. She had a strong suspicion that he'd arranged it that way. What did she do now? She'd assumed that they would fall into mad passion as they had before, but she saw now that he had himself under tight control.

Very well, it was a challenge, like a game of chess against a masterly player. She was good at chess. On the other hand, she didn't underestimate Race's intelligence and willpower. In a strange twist on Tantalus, she was sure he would deny himself water when dying of thirst if he thought it was the right thing to do.

She settled back into his arms. He could hardly refuse to comfort the poor maiden in distress. "Explain how you came to be on that road to rescue me, and how it was not the action of a hero."

He leaned against the rough wall, but she was aware now of how he kept himself a little apart, a little restrained. What if she stroked? Kissed? It seemed shamelessly bold but she would need to be bold to win. . . .

"It's hardly heroic to drive off a handful of frightened farm laborers when I had a cavalry-trained mount burning to attack."

"What was your weapon?"

"A stick."

"Whereas they had blades and a pistol. You were almost shot."

"A miscalculation of the dangers." She heard the smile in his voice and smiled herself.

"I see. If you'd realized one of them was armed, you would have left me to my fate."

She felt his chuckle. "No, love, I couldn't have done that."

She noted the *love* and gathered it to herself as a precious gift. His arm shifted to settle more neatly at her waist, and his head came to rest against hers. With deep satisfaction, she thought she felt another kiss in her hair. She inhaled slowly, struggling not to show her response. Yet.

Race inhaled the scent of Anne, struggling with his body and his conscience. He hadn't followed her to trap her, and he couldn't let that happen. Not even if she was maddeningly bent on her own destruction. Safer by far to keep his distance, but he couldn't refuse to comfort her when she was frightened.

Her delicate perfume alone could undo him, especially now, mixed with a tang of earthy sweat that said she'd left the safety of her elevated sphere to fall to earth. His task was to return her to her cloud, but for this brief time she was here, below, and intimately in his arms.

Perhaps she'd regain her wits when she realized how much of her situation was his fault.

"I couldn't have abandoned you," he said, "because your situation was my fault. I threatened to warn your family about Ralstone simply to scare you off him. And instead," he added, "I scared you into his arms."

"Not scared," she protested, but then said, "Oh, I suppose I was. Scared of failure. But how did you find me? I thought Ralstone's plan was quite clever."

"He stole it from an ingenious couple in Portugal, and I remembered it."

Then he described his visit to Ralstone's lodging and what had followed. All the time, however, he fought the enchantment of her slender body so close to his, her bare arm across him, the awareness of all of her, so close, so warm, so vulnerable, so desirable. . . .

He knew—God, how he knew—that she wanted to give herself to him now. She had some romantic idea in her head, perhaps because of her situation with Ralstone, perhaps because she saw him as a gallant hero. As he'd told her, it was battle madness. He couldn't take advantage of it.

She shifted. Pressed closer.

Damnation.

"But how did you know which way I'd gone from Buntingford?" she asked, looking up, so her lips were only inches away.

"Map. Looked at the map." Dear Lord, he was degenerating to incoherence. He forced himself to make sense. "I knew you were too sensible to set off into the night without a destination. When I saw that Nun's Chase was in the area, I gambled on that."

"Do you gamble a lot?"

"Rarely."

"Good."

Were her lips closer? Had she moved, or had he?

Resist, he commanded, while his body, on its own, strove not to.

"Thank you," she murmured, only an inch away now.

"For rescuing you?"

"For crediting me with sense after such a nonsensical adventure."

"Not nonsensical. Goaded you. Into it."

In her move, she'd shifted a leg over his. His right hand had somehow ended up above her neckline, on her naked back. Her knee pressed against the erection he was fighting. Did the minx know what she was doing? Lady Anne? She couldn't possibly.

Resist. Resist.

He moved slightly, but she moved with him.

"Goaded me into eloping?" she asked, sliding her cool hand up his chest to his shoulder, then across his shoulder to his arm. A ripple of fire.

"No." He grabbed her hand and moved it but then couldn't think what to do with it. "Not elopement. Bad idea." She moved his hand—or did he?—to his lips. "Hades, Anne, stop it!"

He surged off the bed and put the width of the small room between them. His body ached, burned, for what she so idiotically offered.

He waited for the innocent "Stop what?" but this was Anne, not some lesser woman.

"I want you, Race."

He turned at bay to see her sitting on the bed, apparently composed, an angel in white, pale skin, pale hair, pale hands narrow in her lap. How could he long to do such earthy things to an angel?

How could he not?

"I don't know anything about this," she said, "but I think there are natural forces, aren't there? I know what I want, and it is to become one with you here, now, tonight."

"No—"

"Because," she overrode, "if I don't, tomorrow you will leave my life forever."

He was shaking as if with a fever. "It's the only sensible thing to do." He was arguing with himself as much as with her.

"It doesn't make sense to me, and you said I was sensible."

"Sometimes."

"Only when it suits you, apparently."

He laughed, loving her more, desiring her more by the second. "Anne, sweetheart—"

"Am I?"

He didn't ask the stupid question, but he didn't answer, either.

She cocked her head. "When . . . when Le Corbeau asked if I was your beloved, you hesitated. Am I, Race?"

So easy to say no.

Impossible, though, here in this moment.

He found some cool spot in his mind and drew control from it. "Yes. But it wouldn't last, Anne. You'd be cut off from your natural sphere like a fish out of water. Haven't you read myths about marriages between humans and fish? They never turn out well. Especially for the fish."

She laughed, a lovely chuckle that wove through the room and into his aching heart. "We're not so different as that! I don't have a serpent's tail to hide like Melusine, nor do you." She drew her knees up and wrapped her arms around them, resting her chin on top. "Explain to me exactly why our union is so unnatural."

"Your world will not accept me."

"Yes, they will."

"A pleasant myth, but a myth. I suppose your family

might be polite out of love of you, but it would never be the same."

"The same as what? I've lived my life quietly and will be happy to return to that. As you say, my family will accept you, and I'm sure some of my friends will positively approve."

Some tone in that suggested a special meaning, but he had no energy to pursue it. "I don't believe that you want to live as privately as that. Where are your new friends to come from?"

"Perhaps from your circle. The Rogues?"

"They're not my friends, except Amleigh. And my relationship there is secretary."

She sat up straighter. "You're Lord Amleigh's secretary?" At last he had surprised her. Perhaps she'd see reason.

"Now and then."

She chuckled again. "As you please. I see. I have to warn you, Race, that when it comes to marriage it will not be as you please."

There were a number of things he could say to that, all of them dangerous. Verbal battles with Anne Peckworth, he was realizing far too late, had been dangerous from the start.

"As it is," she said, "I have a plan for the future that deals with your concerns. Of course, you may dislike it as much as Ralstone did."

"Is that why you left? Because he didn't like your plan?"

He hoped to distract her, but he also needed to know what Ralstone had done to her. Had he seduced her? Raped her? He'd kill him, but it might also be an excuse to take what was offered here, to marry her in order to save her.

"I left because we talked over dinner, and I realized we had nothing in common."

After a moment, he said, "That's it? Don't you think you should have realized that earlier?"

"Of course I do." She spread her hands. "I don't know why I didn't see it. He wants a life within society, and I want a private one. He wants a large circle of friends, and I want a small one. He does not want to live in my family's pocket—though I'm sure he was hoping to live out of it." She sighed. "I think he has a trick of telling people what they want to hear."

He hadn't seen that, but she was right. "It's not surprising that you were taken in by it."

"But mortifying. I hope no one ever knows."

"They won't."

"He might boast of it."

"He won't."

He saw her look become startled. "Did you threaten to kill him?"

He gave thanks for this conversation, which was giving back some control over his body and his wits. "Not in so many words—but yes."

"And would you?"

He wasn't sure what the right answer to that was. Women could be strange about these things. He gave her the only gift he could: honesty.

"If it came to it, of course, but a duel would hardly avoid scandal. I think he'll see sense."

Her gaze was thoughtful. "You are alien in so many ways, Race, but not because of your lineage. It's your wild spark and your army career."

"There are many men with an army career behind them."

"But how many who flogged a man with ribbons?"

Race shook his head. "I wish you'd forget that bit of foolishness."

"Why? You saved a man from unjust punishment."

"Not so unjust. Greely was a sloppy malingerer."

"Then why?"

"I simply grew tired of the bloody nonsense."

"Literally bloody. But I have to point out, sir, that your language is becoming a little strong for a lady's company."

She was teasing, and he'd never felt less like teasing in his life. "You, my lady, are trying to get me naked into that bed. A little swearing hardly counts."

He'd hoped the attack would shock her into sense, but the ethereal angel said, "True," and shrugged the straps of her petticoat off her shoulders. Then she undid the waist tie, and shimmied out of it, rising to get it under her bottom.

The only way to stop her was to physically restrain her, and getting any closer to her was the last thing he should do.

Smiling at him, she tossed the cotton-and-lace garment aside with all the ease of a naughty dancer. A delicate cloud of her perfume danced across to torment him. She was still well covered, but the sight of a corset could drive any man wild, and her shift reached only to her calves.

Then she raised it and untied her right garter. He watched frozen as she rolled down her pale stocking, uncovering her slender leg and long, aristocratic foot. He stood there, held up by the wall behind, able only to breathe as she slowly removed the other stocking to uncover the foot that was turned and misshapen.

He'd seen twisted feet that were worse—he'd seen a child with the ankle turned at ninety degrees—but the slight turn was enough to mean that she would never walk gracefully, never run, never dance except far from public eyes.

Resistance broke. He went, knelt, and took her foot to cherish. He stroked it gently, feeling the misplaced joints, the unnatural seam in her sole.

Her hand gripped his. "Don't."

He looked up. "It is nothing to be ashamed of."

"You're going to make me cry."

He let her draw his hands away. "That's the last thing that I want, Anne. Believe that."

Holding his hands she said, "Then make love to me." With a wicked smile, she added, "Once you're my lover, I'll let you fondle my foot whenever you want."

He hid his face in her hands, laughing, but close to crying. "Anne, for pity's sake. Where did you learn to be so ruthless?"

Her fingers moved to flex against the side of his face, to move into his hair, shattering him. "I'm a duke's daughter. I'm used to having what I want. I come from a long line of people used to having what they want. And I want you."

He captured her hands and looked up at her, forced her to look at him. "But who do you want to be? Think, Anne. Do you want to be a laughable de Vere?"

"I don't mind."

He had to tell her all of it. Quickly, before he lost courage, he explained that his father was in the process of annulling his first marriage so that the son of his second marriage could carry on his glories. Then he told her that he'd agreed to the plan, thus willfully destroying hope of marriage to any high-born lady.

"So you see, I'm worse than nothing. I am not even a de Vere."

"Then take your mother's name. I don't mind."

"Racecombe Racecombe?"

She chuckled. "Such names have been known, but Race"—she cradled his face and looked into his eyes—"it truly doesn't matter. I thought it did, but it doesn't. Most of the people I care about won't care, and we will make our name one to be proud of, whatever it is. If you don't want de Vere, or Racecombe, what of your father's original name? Despite the annulment, he's not denying that he's your father. Will that suit you better?"

He suspected by now that it wouldn't dissuade her, but he tossed it like a challenge anyway. "You want to be Lady Anne Ramsbottom?"

She stared, and then she broke into giggles. "Ramsbottom!" She leaned forward into him, gasping, "Ram! Derbyshire Ram!" He had to move onto the bed to stop her from falling off.

She struggled out of giggles to cry, "Bottom! Barnacles!" and then collapsed again. And he caught it like virulent fever, laughing with her, kissing with her, on the bed with her, on her . . .

His whole body burning for her.

"On your head be it," he muttered, and surrendered.

She'd won! That was all Anne could think as she responded to the most ravishing kiss of her life. It flowed like their other passionate kisses, but now, here, beneath him, with her hands feasting on his bare back, it consumed her.

He suddenly reared up, kneeling over her. "Say stop, now."

A spasm of something that was almost fear collided with agonizing need. She managed to choke out, "Continue. Now."

Perhaps he was hesitating, regaining control. She sat up and locked her arms around him. *"Now,"* she repeated.

"Bloody aristocracy," he groaned, but she laughed. She had him. He would not fight her anymore.

"I love you," she said. "That's all that matters."

"Damned nonsense, but I love you, too." He cherished her face. "I'll make it my life's work to ensure that it doesn't matter, Anne. You've won, you've won. Perhaps I could let you go, but I can't let you go into the sort of disasters you seem to court."

"Me?" she asked innocently, and laughed at his groan.

His hands were fumbling behind with her corset laces, but they stilled. She braced for another fight, but he simply said, "Let's try to do this with a little grace."

He slid off the bed and helped her off, turned her, and tugged at her laces. Staring through the tiny window at a tree and hedge touched with silver moonshine, she inhaled victory like a perfume.

Some fear lingered. She did not underestimate the drama of the choice she had made or the struggles yet to come, but she knew that her decision was right. She knew they could make it right simply because of who they were.

He was still tugging, and she heard a muttered curse.

"Hetty knotted them," she said, fighting the giggles again. "This morning—yesterday morning. She has a special way of doing it so they won't slacken during the day."

"A modern chastity belt? Someone should tell her that a corset doesn't secure the essentials."

Thirty-two

There was a series of sharp tugs, and the corset went slack. She instinctively held it on at the front. "What did you do?"

"Penknife. Our captors didn't think to search me. Not that a penknife would get us out of here."

"It's as well I'm not intending to put it on again soon," she said, letting the corset fall to the ground and turning to him in just her shift and drawers. "I have no interest in escaping."

"There is a little matter of a duel in the morning."

She froze. She really should tell him the truth now. But she didn't dare interfere with this magical process. It could evaporate in her hands.

"Perhaps Le Corbeau will be caught."

She wasn't sure he was listening. His attention seemed fixed on her breasts. She looked down and saw her nipples pressing out the fine silk. She'd always thought her small breasts lacking, but they didn't feel lacking at the moment. They felt swollen and tingly, and the cloth tormented them with every breath she took.

He wasn't doing anything, and she didn't know what to do. In the end she let her hands do what they wanted to and cradled her own breasts, comforting them, pushing them up slightly. An invitation, she realized, and utterly shameless, but watching him, she couldn't regret it.

His hands replaced hers, resting on her ribs, raising her breasts, and his thumbs brushed her prominent nipples. An astonishing ripple of pleasure shot through her, and she grasped his arms for balance.

Still brushing her sensitive flesh, he kissed her again,

hot and wet, so she sighed and shuddered into his mouth. Her legs trembled and ached. Perhaps he knew. He stopped his pleasuring, picked her up, and placed her on the simple bed.

Then he undressed.

She watched as lantern light picked out slim hips and strong legs. Definitely worthy thighs.

His male member jutted, ready for her. A tremor struck her, part nervousness, part longing in her most private places. He was utterly beautiful, lean and graceful. She thought again of faery, but a faery warrior, mighty and brave.

Suddenly aware that she was still covered she sat up and stripped off her drawers, and then her last shield, her shift. But nerves struck, and she sat there with it clutched to cover herself.

He took it from her, and his expression eased away every trace of doubt. She could weep for happiness to be the woman Race de Vere looked at like that. Her heart pounded with love, with desire, and with a raw burning need to be his.

He straddled her legs and took the silk shift from her powerless hands. He flipped it behind her, then drew her to him with it like a bond. "Last chance, Anne. After this I will not let you escape. You will be mine forever as if we'd spoken the most binding vows in a cathedral. Think well."

She slid her hands up to his shoulders. "Think? Now? I've thought, Race. I've done too much thinking, much of it wrongheadedly. I know now. I know. Don't you?"

His kiss was his answer, and they fell back together onto the bed. His sure hands stroked and fondled her, and she touched and tasted wherever she wished. As always with him she knew she had only to trust and the lights would shine.

She ran her hand down his long back and found his taut buttock to squeeze as he sucked on her nipple, sending hot waves of pleasure rolling through her.

Rolling. Legs tangled, they rolled so she was half over him, stroking his flank, his belly, his springy curls and the hot promise there. Hot, hard, satiny, moving beneath her tentative touch.

She looked at him and saw his hungry eyes, his need, his patience. She slid back under him, loving to be under his naked strength. She spread her legs, aching, burning, and knowing what she wanted. "Come into me, Race. Now."

He laughed. "Yes, your ladyship."

She braced for some mighty force, but he took his weight and moved slowly despite the need she heard in his unsteady breaths. The brush against her burning flesh made her want to scream with impatience, but she waited, stroking his tense arm, trusting him.

Then slowly, smoothly he slid inside her, making her inhale with the astonishing sensation of stretching and fullness. Of completion.

Then she understood.

"You are the first," she said.

"I know. Come." With that he began to move, and her whole mind locked on to a rhythm as natural as breathing. As her hips caught the pattern and met with his, she knew that at last she'd found a dance that she could do.

He was touching her breasts again, making her arch. He kissed her again, then when his mouth slipped off hers, she kissed his shoulder, filled her mouth with his flesh, pressing him closer, demanding, demanding. If she'd had voice, she would have ordered him to do something, she knew not what. . . .

Then her body arched itself with a pleasure she'd never known existed. Again and again it rocked her, making her choke out incoherent things. She assembled enough control to say his name. It seemed important then to say it.

"Race."

"Anne."

She felt him shudder and knew that he'd been in a similar place, swept up in a similar pleasure. Together. Forever.

As her body came together again, heart thundering, nerves singing, she thought it was no wonder men enjoy this so much, and women, too. That people sometimes made complete fools of themselves over it.

He shifted, sliding out of her, and held her close, kissing her again. She kissed him back, a new sort of kiss for them. Slow, lazy, sated, delicious. How perfect this was, this complete union of skin, sweat, breath, and self.

Marriage, indeed.

"Race?" she said at last.

"Yes, love?"

She smiled. "I like that."

"What we just did?" He sounded amused.

"Yes, but you calling me love."

He kissed her cheek. "You could call me love, too."

"Haven't I?" She rolled to face him, to kiss him between sentences. "You are my love. My dear heart. My precious. My sweeting—"

He silenced her with a thorough kiss. "Enough." He climbed off the bed, pulled the blanket and sheet from under her, and covered her. Then he went to extinguish the guttering candle.

To be apart for a moment felt cold and empty, and when he slipped back into the bed she wrapped herself tightly around him. "You are mine now. Forever."

He nuzzled her. "And you are mine. Never doubt it. No changing your mind again tomorrow."

"Race!"

"You have been somewhat fickle, wench."

She bit her lip and told him about Alderton.

He shook with laughter. "Two engagements in two days! You never do things by half, do you love?"

"It's not the Peckworth way. But it was always you, Race. From Benning Hall."

"For me, too. That night in the corridor, I wanted to drag you into my bed."

"It might have saved a great deal of trouble if you had."

He slapped her bottom. "It would have caused disaster, and you know it." He rubbed the spot, that only stung a little. "We still have disaster on our hands, love. It's time for you to tell me your plan, the one that Ralstone didn't like."

She shifted to face him, though she could hardly see him in the shadows. "It doesn't matter. What life do you want?"

"I have no fixed point in the firmament, remember? It will be as you wish."

She growled. "You are not to be self-sacrificing about this. Tell me what your ideal life is."

His hand was still on her bottom, but now it flexed and played there, almost distracting her. "To replace Beau Brummell at the heart of society."

She heard the tease in it. "The Regent would doubtless be better for it. But?"

He shifted onto his back, drawing her half over his chest, hand still playing, sliding between her thighs, tickling a very sensitive spot.

"I became Amleigh's secretary for my own reasons but I enjoyed it. Or at least, I enjoyed the paperwork."

He slid his hand down to her knee and raised it, opening her against his hip. Her calf brushed hardness and her breath quickened. "You don't distract me so easily," she said.

"No?"

"No. Continue your explanation."

But her heart was pounding and a familiar ache built.

He sounded calm—and amused—as he went on. "I'd like to do more work with chaotic papers, but I'm not sure how to make a living at it. But even if there is such a way, it is hardly suitable for the husband of Lady Anne Whoever."

His other hand had found her private places, and moved in tiny, gentle, maddening circles.

"De Vere," she said, fighting not to gasp. "Lady Anne de Vere. People will become accustomed both to name and way of life. . . . *Race*!"

"Yes, love?"

Her breath came in gasps, her body clenched.

"You want something?" he whispered into her ear.

"You know what I want."

"To talk about our plans for our future . . ." His fingers slid into her, held her, as his thumb pressed.

"Wretch!"

He moved her onto her back and stroked between her thighs again. "I'm going to pleasure you, Anne. Let me."

His fingers slid inside her, his head lowered to her breasts. Anne clutched at him as hot waves built.

"What do I do? What should I do? Race?"

"Relax," he murmured. "Relax and fly."

So she surrendered and let her body move, let her mind dissolve, let her senses burn as she flew close to the sun. But survived. She buried her face in his chest as she came back to earth, not sure what to say after being played to a crescendo like a musical instrument.

"Do you not like that?" he asked.

She stirred to look where he was in the dark. "How could I not like it? It feels selfish, though."

"One of the curses of man is that we can't explode like that as often as a woman. A shame to deprive you of extra pleasure. But some time, if you want, you can do the same for me."

She smiled at the thought. "I want. I want a great many things." Her mind was back and clear. "I want our perfect happiness, and, Race, we are perfectly suited. You liked being a secretary, and my favorite way to spend time is among the chaotic papers at Lea Park!"

She expected the same delight, but he said, "I don't know about that. I hoped that you had just discovered an even better way—

She slapped his chest, shocked by the sting and the action. He laughed and retaliated with a kiss. "You're such a violent woman. Well, which is best? Paperwork or lovemaking?"

"One for night, one for day?"

"Sometimes I like to make love in daylight. Even outdoors . . ."

The idea sent a shiver of excitement through her. "There are always candles for night paperwork. Perhaps I can persuade my father to put in gas light in the library at Lea Park."

He ran his fingers through her hair and she felt his change of mood. "You're serious about this? You think you can be happy playing around in the Peckworth papers for the rest of your life?"

"I warn you, I don't play. I become lost in them."

"So do I." He moved so she was lightly in his arms. "So, what in particular are you engaged in?"

"Just women's papers."

Snuggled against him, skin to skin, she told him about the domestic papers and the picture they gave of the lives of the Peckworth women. Eventually she shared with him the last, most private part—her dream of writing a book based on them.

"Of course," she said, her hand circling his nipple, wondering if he found such things as pleasant as she did, "this won't interest you."

He caught her hand and sucked at her fingers. "Your teasing touch will always fascinate me. As for your papers, I'm enthralled already. I wonder how many other great houses have similarly neglected collections. . . ."

"You mean it."

"Oh, definitely. So, you want to live at Lea Park. If your father permits . . ."

She grasped her courage and told him the last bit. "Not actually at Lea Park. I was thinking of asking my father for a house as part of my dowry. Quoyne House. It's a simple manor house on the edge of Little Cawleigh, which lies just outside Lea Park. . . ."

He laughed. "I can imagine Ralstone balking at that, love, but it sounds like heaven to me. And if your family will accept me, I will be happy to be part of them. After all, I have no true family of my own."

"Your father can't be so unfeeling as that."

A silence made her think she'd intruded, but eventually he spoke. "He's not unfeeling, but I did abandon him, and for seven years I paid him little heed. What's more, I was never the son he wanted. He wanted one who would be a perfect gentleman, and also build the family both in grandeur and wealth."

"You are a perfect gentleman."

"With a strong undignified streak, you must admit."

"You have more dignity than Uffham!"

"Ah, and there you have a point that my father misses. He did too good a job of raising me to be one of the privileged set. I feel able to play fast and loose with the rules in the way he never could. But his main complaint is my lack of interest in achieving fame and fortune.

"Now my mother's dead, he's dabbling in trade again, making sure he can provide for his new wife and family, and making money to fund his title hunt. He dangled all kinds of opportunities in front of me, thinking they were bait. I only saw worms. He loves me, I'm sure, and in a way I love him, but we're mysteries to each other. I'm a Racecombe cuckoo in his Ramsbottom nest."

"Has he gone back to the Ramsbottom name?"

"Oh, no. He likes being a de Vere, but he made it legal before he married Sarah, so their children are completely legitimate. Little Tom will doubtless grow up to be just the sort of son he wants—the sort of aristocrat that England will need. One foot in tradition and the land, and the other in industry and new ideas."

"And you will truly be happy living quietly in the country spending large amounts of time among papers?"

He rolled over her. "Add in the frequent lovemaking and you have described my idea of heaven. . . . As you may have guessed, this poor male is ready for passion again."

She almost felt it was too much, that her nerve endings were too raw, but at first kiss resistance melted, and when he entered her it was the same, a natural fulfillment.

It was slow this time until the end, and she had more chance to know what was happening to her, to him. It was quieter for her, too, in the sweetest way, and she felt his wild explosion with delight. What a complex, fascinating mystery this all was.

She held him in her arms afterward, guarding him as he came back to earth.

"This is," she whispered, "perhaps almost as fascinating as a box of neglected household accounts. . . ."

"Almost?"

They settled together laughing, and tumbled into sleep.

Thirty-three

Anne woke when Race sat up. It was morning, and sunlight slanted in through the small window, gilding his lovely body. Warmth spiraled and tingled in her at the memory of what that body and her body had created in the night.

Birds sang, chirped, and complained, and a rustling in the thatch suggested other neighbors. She sat up, too, aware of aches in unusual places and of a deep, satisfied happiness.

She stroked the silken warmth of his back, full of wonderment that it was hers to do now as often as she wished. "What's the matter?"

He turned to her. "I think someone did something to the door."

Oh, Lord. Reality fell on her, and awareness that he still thought this morning would involve a duel with Le Corbeau. She had built heaven on a lie. She watched him get out of bed and walk splendidly naked to the partition wall to listen. She wanted him back in her arms, to touch him, stroke him, lick him, as she had in the night. She wanted reassurance that he would still be hers when he knew.

Perhaps he need never know.

He turned back, paused, and smiled at her. She could tell that he was thinking of her body exactly as she was thinking of his. Surely what they had created here could not easily change.

He came over and kissed her, one hand gentle on her face. "I love you, Anne."

She cradled his face in turn, delighted by the manly

mystery of stubble. "I love you, too. And we are, remarkable to say, perfectly matched."

"I think we are. But though I'd love to keep you naked in a bed for weeks, I think some covering wise before we venture out."

He found her crumpled shift and put it over her head. She wriggled into it, then scrambled off the bed to put on her petticoat and drawers. The corset was beyond hope, but she didn't really need it except to push her breasts up to fashionable heights.

By the time she was covered, he had his breeches on and was waiting by the door. There was a handle of sorts, and he pulled it. The door opened. They shared a wary look, then moved through it. The room beyond was empty.

She followed him down the narrow stairs to the deserted ground floor, heart fluttering with nerves and hope. If Tris kept away, perhaps she could get away with this.

In the main room, their outer clothes awaited them, neatly folded. A plain breakfast sat on one of the benches—a covered jug of ale with two wooden beakers, and a loaf of bread and a hunk of cheese in a covered pot.

"*En garde* against rats," Anne said.

"A very strange crow we have. I'd like to think I frightened him away, but I don't believe it."

While she put on her gown, he thoroughly searched the ground floor, but then shrugged and came to fasten her buttons. Such a lovely domestic intimacy, especially when he brushed her hair out of his way.

"It must be a mess," she said.

He dug in his jacket pocket and produced a comb. She would have taken it, but he sat her sideways on a bench and sat behind her to work it gently through her hair.

"It's like silk," he said, discovering some pins and handing them to her. "Am I hurting you?"

"No, you're an excellent lady's maid, sir."

"I intend to enjoy this sort of service often."

She smiled with delight and sat in silence as he worked, savoring the pleasure of his caring touch. Oh, if only there wasn't one small dishonesty between them. But even now she would not change it. She was sure that if he'd known the truth he would never have surrendered and made love to her.

"There," he said at last, and she felt him quickly plait her hair, then coil it. "A pin."

She passed them back, one by one, and soon her hair felt in good order. She turned to him. "Thank you." She took the comb and tamed his hair, but alas, it did not need nearly so much work.

When she'd finished, he pulled on his shirt and tucked it into his breeches, but he didn't bother with his waistcoat or jacket. He produced his knife, and hacked up the bread, then passed her a piece along with some of the cheese.

She poured them both ale. He took his and went to stand by one of the small windows to eat.

She sipped hers. "It's good."

"Good enough for a duke?" he asked.

It took a moment for it to sink in, then a shiver passed through her. She put down the mug, unable to read his expression. She could pretend innocence, but she knew that was the last thing she should do. Fear tightened her throat.

"When did you guess?"

He was leaning against the wall, unreadable. "When did you?"

Perhaps it had been right to hold back the truth before, but not now. "Last night."

He drank some of his ale, looking at her in a silent command to continue.

With a *humph*, she picked up her mug and drank. "You were being too noble! I knew you'd ride away as soon as you thought I was safe."

"I didn't have a healthy horse."

"Then you'd walk away! You would have, wouldn't you?"

He rested his mug against his lip, considering her. "Yes."

"And it wouldn't have been for the best, would it?"

After a moment he shook his head and came over to

sit near her. "Right or wrong, it would not be what I want. You should be a general, love. Or an orator. You could tie Sophocles in knots."

Tears pricked at her eyes, tears of relief. "I was so afraid you'd hate me."

"I would be an ungrateful fool to do that."

"I was going to tell you. What made you realize?"

"The unlocked door and the considerate breakfast. I have no faith in chivalrous highwaymen. Then I remembered that we are within a mile of Nun's Chase, and everything fell into place. I'm disappointed, though. I rather liked the man."

"Disappointed that he seems to be Le Corbeau?"

"Disgusted that he forced you to undress before himself and a servant. He'll pay for that."

She grabbed his arm. "No, Race! He may be the only friend we have."

"Friend? He arranged for me to compromise you."

"No. He arranged for me to compromise you."

After a moment, he burst out laughing. "Talk about alien people! I do not understand you, Anne Peckworth, or your sort. No care for the proprieties at all?"

She felt her face heat. "I am assuming that we'll marry soon."

"And if not," said a voice from the doorway, "there is still the matter of a duel."

Anne blushed even more at the sight of Tris, completely the Duke of St. Raven, and here she was with what she'd done in the night surely obvious.

Race rose to his feet and walked over. His fist connected with Tris's chin, staggering him. The threshold tripped the noble Duke of St. Raven, sending him sprawling into the dirt path outside.

Anne stood but was frozen in shock. Before she could do anything, Tris scrambled to his feet and charged Race. The two crashed to the floor of the cottage, wrestling like village boys.

Race's shirt ripped.

"Stop it!" she screamed.

They paid no attention. Tris slammed a fist at Race. Race caught it on his shoulder with a grunt, then somehow rolled them so he was on top with Tris grunting, facedown. Then Tris was on top, his hands at Race's throat.

Anne looked desperately for something to stop them. Oh, for a bucket of icy water!

Race broke the hold and used his joined fists to deliver a horrible blow that sent Tris crashing into the wall. The whole cottage shuddered. Race leaped after, but Tris tripped him, and they were rolling together on the floor like madmen.

Anne grabbed her staff but then couldn't bring herself to swing it at either of them. The amber knob could do serious damage.

She hissed with annoyance and then let herself sink to the floor in an apparent faint. She heard another grunt. A thud. A curse.

Was it not going to work?

But then silence fell.

Tris said, "Anne?"

A scrabbling sound, then Race grabbed her hand—she knew his touch. "Anne? Love?"

They deserved some panic. She let them fuss over her for a few moments before opening her eyes. "You are both," she said, "quite mad."

Hunkered down on either side of her, they jerked back.

She sat up and grabbed a battered hand of each. "What was that *about*?"

"He hit me," Tris said, hand becoming a fist.

"You forced Anne to undress, and in front of your servant."

Their renewed urge to fight rippled up both of her arms. She tightened her grip. "You are my only two friends. You can't kill each other."

"Oh," said Tris, "I'm sure one of us would survive."

She growled. "And what good would that do me? I don't want to marry *you*, but we probably need you to help us sort this out."

Race jumped to his feet, then winced. He sent Tris a dirty look but held a hand down to Anne. When she took it, he pulled her to her feet.

She laughed, and it was with delight. No one had ever

treated poor Lady Anne so casually. She was sure Tris would have tenderly lifted her, carried her to a bench, then fussed over her for an age. In fact, he was on his feet glowering at Race, presumably for the way he was treating her.

The noble Duke of St. Raven had a split lip.

Race wasn't untouched. She suspected that he was going to have a black eye, and from the wince she guessed Tris had managed to do other damage. When she thought of how much taller and heavier Tris was, she was astonished that it had been such an even match.

And impressed. And yes, the way Race had knocked Tris down thrilled a primitive part of herself, the part of womankind that had screamed with excitement at bloody jousts.

Race cocked his head at her. "You look like a cat with a bowl full of cream, *minou.*"

She blushed—but she grinned, too.

"Typical," Tris said, touching his lip. "Women always enjoy blood."

She covered her smile with her hand. "I'm sorry. But yes, it is rather thrilling."

Race picked her up and put her down on one of the benches. "This isn't a game. Let's see what we can do to get out of this mess without more bloodshed."

Tris sat with a wince of his own on the other bench. "You're planning to continue with the elopement?"

"No."

"No."

Anne and Race had spoken together, and she sent him a smile. He sat beside her, putting an arm around her as if it were the most natural thing in the world. As if they were country people in their cottage. As if they were a china shepherd and shepherdess.

She leaned comfortably against his shoulder. "Perhaps we could just live on here for the rest of our lives."

Race laughed. "Hardly."

She looked around and remembered that this little bit of heaven was in fact a cottage that should be torn down before it fell down.

"Hardly," she agreed. "So what are we going to do? Perhaps Tris is right and we should carry on to Gretna."

"Anne wants marriage in her home parish," Race said to Tris, "and to live at a place called Quoyne House. How do we arrange that?"

Tris's eyes widened a little. "It won't be easy. I think the family would accept an elopement as a fait accompli, but getting the duchess's agreement to a proper wedding will take time."

"After last night, we may not have time."

Anne straightened to look between them. "I don't mind society counting the months after our wedding."

"I do," Race said, "especially if the count stops at six or seven. I won't have you subject to that sort of gossip." Race was still looking at Tris. "You'd better know the facts." He quickly outlined his family history.

Tris's expression grew more stunned as Race spoke. When Race arrived at the matter of the approaching bastardy, Tris looked at Anne. "The duchess will lock you in a dungeon and throw away the key."

"We don't have a dungeon."

"She'll have one built specially. Mouse, you are attempting to marry the bastard son of a tradesman. Gretna's your only chance."

She looked at Race and saw bitter regret, saw that for her sake he'd like to wipe out last night.

"I regret nothing," she said. "*Nothing.* If my family cast me off, so be it. But they won't. Yes, my mother will probably try to prevent our marriage, but I come of age in October. And my father, though generally ruled by my mother in these things, won't agree to cutting me off. I know he won't."

"He won't," Tris agreed. "He's softheartedly devoted to all his children. Too softhearted, in Uffham's case."

Race looked between them. "But he won't overrule the duchess in the matter of marriage?"

"No," Tris said. "Or not quickly or easily."

"What if we tell them that we have anticipated marriage?"

Anne gulped at that, but if it was called for . . .

"Lord," Tris said. "I don't know. I don't know. The duke's old-fashioned enough to have you horsewhipped. Fond fathers tend to be twitchy about *husbands* having their wicked way with their daughters, never mind upstart lovers."

Race pressed both hands to his face, then he ran his fingers through his hair.

Anne watched, heart breaking. "It would have been better for you, wouldn't it, if we'd never met? If I'd not pursued you. If I'd not seduced you last night."

"Seduced?" Tris echoed.

Race lowered his hands. "She did. Remarkably well, too." The look he sent her held regret, but memory and passion burned beneath it.

He pulled her to him and kissed her. "I regret nothing either, love, though I doubtless should. I can only hope that you won't regret either. It looks as if it has to be Gretna." He turned to Tris. "I'll have to ask a loan."

"I have money," Anne said.

"Very well." To Tris he said, "We should probably avoid Buntingford. Where's the next best place to hire a chaise?"

"The Swan at Stevenage."

In a few crisp moments the men had everything settled. Tris would have her trunk collected at the Black Bull and brought here. Then they would be taken to Stevenage, where they could hire a chaise.

Race's valise was apparently waiting for him at the White Horse in London. Tris would have it sent north. If it didn't catch up with them on the road, it would arrive at Gretna not far behind.

"Send it to the Angel in Chesterfield," Race said.

Anne asked, "Why?"

He gave her a rueful smile. "If we can't be at instant peace with one family, we might as well try for the other one."

"Are you perhaps thinking that if I meet your father, I'll change my mind?"

He laughed. "I doubt it. The Peckworths seem as changeable as a rock. It simply feels appropriate. I owe my father information about this important point in my life, especially as it's likely to cause trouble."

"Very well, love. I look forward to meeting your family." She smiled at Tris, but then a thought struck. "You're not Le Corbeau, are you?"

"Am I not?"

"No. I remember now that at Drury Lane, you didn't know who he was. That wasn't acting. Nor later when I pointed out that crow and raven are the same in French."

He looked rueful, but said nothing.

"You were out last night to protect the real crow, weren't you? Who is it?"

"Never you mind. You have enough tangles to deal with as it is."

She pulled a face but knew he wouldn't tell her. Or not yet. "Did you actually hold someone up?" she asked.

He grinned. "Oh yes. And it was a remarkable amount of fun."

"What folly!"

"That, from you?"

Race stepped between them. "Perhaps, Your Grace, we could set our plan in motion?"

Tris looked as if he'd like to pick another fight, but he said, "I am, of course, yours to command." With an ironic bow, he left to do his part.

Thirty-four

It took two days to reach Shapcott Hall, but despite everything Anne felt they were two of the best days of her life. Race was hers, and at last she could discover this man who had become so central to her life, and reveal to him more of herself.

They talked, sharing details from their pasts, but also spinning off into philosophical debates. They didn't always agree, but they always ended up in harmony.

They played cards and read books. He taught her brag, and she won a fortune off him. They bought a copy of *Headlong Hall* at St. Ives and read it aloud to each other, but soon abandoned it as cumbersome. She read parts of *Jeanne d'Arc* to him, but he refused to offend her with his French accent.

They spent a delightful night at a small inn on the outskirts of Stamford. Anne had abandoned her disguise—she was ready to face anyone—but they passed themselves off, suppressing laughter, as Mr. and Mrs. Ramsbottom. She had no ring, but kept her gloves on in public.

The next evening, however, when their chaise drew up before Shapcott Hall, she wasn't sure she was ready to face Race's father. He could not approve of this.

They paid the postilions to stay and take them on the next day—and also so that they would have transport if Mr. de Vere fell into a rage and would not let them in the house.

When the door opened and a sturdy man in country clothes stepped out looking puzzled Anne knew that would not happen. The instant he saw Race—out of the carriage and about to help her down—something moved across the father's face, part love, part loss, and part exasperated worry.

She could almost see the words, *What now?*

She let Race set the tone. He gave her his arm and led her toward the waiting man. As they crossed the few yards of driveway, other people emerged from the simple stone manor house. A sensible looking brown-haired woman, belly swelling beneath an apron, moved to stand beside her husband, a toddler in her arms. A bright-eyed blond boy ran out to clutch his father's hand.

Then the lad shouted, "Race!" and rushed forward.

Race freed himself from Anne and caught the boy, swinging him up. "Tom, my grand lad! But you know, you shouldn't rush at a gentleman who's escorting a lady." He put the boy down. "Make your bow to Lady Anne Peckworth."

The boy did a fine bow and then looked at her. "Lady? Are you very grand, then?"

What to say to that? "I suppose I am."

Race's father had come over by then, and he put a hand on his younger son's shoulder. "Tommy, we're going to have to teach you better manners." It was said kindly, however, though the look he gave Anne was wary at best.

"Father, this is Lady Anne Peckworth, who is to be my wife. I wished to make you known to each other before we tie the knot. In Gretna Green."

Race sounded smooth, but Anne heard a slight gulp before the last bit.

Wanting to laugh for tenderness and nervousness, she held out her hand to Mr. de Vere. "I'm very pleased to meet you, sir, and I assure you this is entirely my fault."

"I doubt that." He took her hand and pressed it. "You're welcome here, my lady, but I think we'll have to sort this wedding business out in better form."

Race had been right in his assessment. His father was a gentleman in the true sense, even if his speech carried a slight touch of his origins. Anne felt she could like him, but would he like her, who was bringing more trouble to his house?

She met Race's stepmother, who seemed flustered and worried. The toddler, little Amy, hid her face shyly against her mother's neck. Then they entered the oaken hall of Race's home, and all went into a cozy parlor, where tea was ordered.

She couldn't help thinking how different this was from her experience in Greenwich, and not just because Shapcott Hall was a solid, comfortable house. This was a home, and a happy one, and she immediately liked all Race's family.

Sarah de Vere had rid herself of her apron when she thought no one was looking and was presiding over tea, obviously thinking it a test. The little girl had been taken away by a nursemaid, but the boy was still here, fidgeting between his father and Race, who had clearly acquired another admirer.

They talked idly of the weather and the roads, and even a bit about fashionable gossip. It was all terribly artificial, but Anne didn't know what to do for the best.

Then Sarah stood, picking up the tea tray herself. "Come along, Tommy. It's time for your lessons. You can talk to your brother later if he's willing."

"Will you play soldiers with me, Race?"

"If I hear a good account of your lessons."

The boy pulled a face, but he went, and the door shut. Anne's nerves tightened. This was the moment of truth, and it mattered. She knew it mattered to Race.

"Well, my boy," Race's father said. "I don't like this Gretna thing, not at all."

Race flashed Anne a look. "Nor do I, Father, but Lady Anne's family won't approve of the marriage. And," he added, "we must marry."

Mr. de Vere's eyes flicked over Anne. "In the family way?"

She knew she was pink, but she tried to be composed. "We don't know yet."

He shook his head. "It's a bad situation, Race. Very bad. I'm disappointed in you."

"It was all my fault," Anne interjected. "All! You must believe me, Mr. de Vere. I pursued your son. I seduced your son."

He looked at her, bushy brows high. "Then you deserve a good whipping, miss."

"Probably. Especially as I started out yesterday eloping with a different man. And the day before that I was engaged to yet another."

"Anne!" Race protested, but when she looked at him, he was laughing.

"Oh, Lord, sir, I'm sorry. I should never have brought this mess here. It truly isn't as wicked as it seems, and a great deal of it is my fault. I never meant to upset you with it. I simply thought you should know."

Mr. de Vere sat there with a solid hand on each thigh. "I never have understood you, Race, but I'm wise enough to know that. I think I'm wise enough to know that you two are head over heels in love, aren't you?"

Race looked at Anne and said, "Yes."

"Yes," she said back to him, smiling.

"Well, I know a bit about that now. The truth is that I was never in love with your mother. I married her for her property and position, and she married me for my money. We rubbed along well enough, and I always did right by her, but it wasn't love. With Sarah, though, it's a different matter. So I reckon you should wed. Will money make any difference?"

Anne saw Race stiffen. "You owe me nothing, sir."

"Rubbish. You left before we could talk things over. You know I would never have gone ahead with the annulment without your say so, and I never intended to disinherit you."

"Father, you owe me nothing. I willfully left here—and hurt you in the process."

Mr. de Vere pushed himself to his feet. "Rubbish! You were always a high-spirited lad, and I drove you away with my follies. I won't make the same mistake with Tommy, even if he ends up the only lad we have. But whatever the case, you are my son. I want you to have your share of what I have."

Race had risen, too, and was looking rather exasperated. "Father, I will do well enough."

"Doing what? As far as I can see you know no trade but soldiering."

Race's jaw tensed, but he said, "I've been a secretary, and I intend to be a sort of librarian."

His father's blood rose into his face. "A *secretary*! A *librarian*! Is this what I raised you for?" Before Race could speak, he went on, "And how do you plan to support a lady born on those piddling sorts of wages?"

Race said nothing, and the older man turned narrow eyes on Anne. "I suppose you have plenty of money of your own, don't you?"

Anne had to say something. "Yes, but Race won't be a fortune hunter."

"You're right. He won't. He'll have a respectable income of his own!"

"Father, you don't want to take money away from Tom and your new family."

"There's enough."

"With the annulment to push through, and a title to buy?"

"Aye, and half a dozen more!" It came out as a bellow that made Anne flinch, but then Race's father rubbed a hand over his face looking, if anything, embarrassed. "Fact is, Race, that I'm more involved in trade than I let you know. I didn't think you'd like it."

"All the same—"

"Be quiet! I'm trying to tell you something. There were so many opportunities during the war," Race's father said, as if trying to excuse a sin. "And so many needs, too. And a mess of mismanagement that I just couldn't bear. Once your mother passed away, God bless her, there was no one to mind if I dabbled in trade. Things are harder now, of course, but I saw it coming so matters aren't too bad. I'm warm, now. Very warm."

"Father, I don't mind what you do. And a few hundred a year will not sway Anne's parents. They want her to marry a title. In fact her mother wants her to marry the Duke of St. Raven."

"An old fogy?" Mr. de Vere asked her.

"Not at all, but not the man I want to marry."

He turned back to Race. "Whether it sways her family or not, I want you to have your portion. It's only right. In fact, I'll feel very badly if you don't take it."

"That's blackmail."

"That's the truth!"

"I won't take it."

"Damn your eyes, boy, I'm your *father.* I have a right to give you money if I damn well want to!"

He'd turned red, but he looked at Anne and went redder still. "My lady, I'm sorry. But he drives me to extremes at times, indeed he does."

She went to take his hands. "He does the same to me, sir. And please call me Anne. I would be honored to be treated as your daughter."

He smiled at her. "And I'll be honored to see you so. I know this bastardy business isn't helping things, though he won't mention it. Too late to back down now, alas. The documents are in the hands of the church courts. You see how it is, though, don't you, Anne? It's my selfish plan that has you in a pickle, and I have to do something to try to set it right."

"Father," Race interrupted. "Your plan is pure common sense. With respect, there is nothing I want less than to live here and help manage this estate or your businesses."

Anne made her decision. She turned to Race. "Your father's right. He needs to give you some money, and you should take it. For his sake, and because it will sweeten the pill a little for my parents."

He met her eyes, and she worried that he was angry, but then he sighed. "Very well. How much did you have in mind, Father?"

Mr. de Vere seemed to be doing calculations, but Anne wondered if they were more to do with what he thought Race would take than with what he could afford. "I thought five thousand a year," he said at last.

Anne and Race both stared at him.

"Out of the question," Race said. "You'll beggar yourself."

"Do you think me such a fool? It's a fifth of my income now, but I've every expectation of making more once these hard times are over."

"I refuse to take that much."

"All or nothing," growled his father.

Anne stumbled over to grab Race's arm before he threw the offer in his father's face. "Race, stop and think." To his father she said, "You swear that your income is twenty-five thousand a year?" Given the simple state in which he lived, she had doubts, too.

"On the Bible, give or take. Plague take me, I'm fond

of the boy, but I have my Sarah and the children—and many more to come God willing—to think of. I'd not beggar them to satisfy some guilt of mine!"

"This is ridiculous," Race said as if he'd been offered a flogging rather than a fortune. He looked at Anne. "You want this money?"

She reined in her temper. "I neither want nor need any money. But your father needs to give it to you, and yes, it will help with my parents. In fact," she added, doing a rapid assessment, "with this money on our side we can roll the dice—turn back and see if we can marry properly."

"Five thousand a year will outweigh my origins?"

"It will help."

He sucked in a breath and turned to his father. "Very well, sir. Thank you."

"And that hurt to say," his father grumbled. "Believe it or not, I was just such a stiff-rumped fool as you when I was young. Wait here."

He marched out of the room, and Anne and Race looked at each other in puzzlement.

"Is he going to pour it out in front of us in cash?" she asked.

Race relaxed. "I doubt it. Am I being a fool over this?"

She took him into her arms. "No, love."

He kissed her. "All right, I know you're right about the money, and it means yours can go for our children's future. I'm not sure about your gamble, though. Wouldn't it be safer to seal things at Gretna before facing your family? We could marry again in an English church once the dust settles."

"Yes, but Race, I don't want a Gretna wedding. The closer we came, the more I disliked the idea."

He kissed her. "Then we won't do it."

Race's father returned with a few boxes, which he put on a table. "Your mother's jewelry. The stuff, such as it is, that she got from her family—they'd sold the best of it—and her engagement ring. I buried her in her wedding band."

They went over to the table. "Won't Sarah want these?" Race asked.

"She has those she likes of what I gave your mother, but she doesn't think the Racecombe jewels should come to her." Mr. de Vere looked at Anne. "These mostly won't seem much to you, daughter, but there's the ring." He opened a box to reveal a large diamond in a lovely setting.

"My goodness."

"I was so cock-a-hoop that a lady born would accept me that I bought her the finest stone I could find. Once we were wed, though, she never wore it. She said simplicity was the true sign of breeding."

Anne privately thought that Race's mother sounded unpleasant. How much of the trouble between father and son was her fault? And whose fault was it that there was only one child? If Race had had brothers and sisters, she was sure matters would have gone much better.

She looked at Race. "If you want me to have it, I would be honored."

He took the ring out of the box. "I never knew this existed. It is beautiful and deserves to be worn."

He slid it onto her finger. It was a little loose, but not so it would fall off.

"You're well and truly committed now, sir," she teased. "What next?"

Race looked at her, then at his father. "We rest. Tomorrow we go south to hazard our future."

Anne enjoyed her evening at Shapcott Hall, and even helped Sarah bathe little Amy. Sarah was thirty-two and ill at ease at first, but soon they were like sisters. Like sisters, they laughed and complained about the men in their lives.

She watched Race play model soldiers with Tom. The lad sounded as if he'd be army-mad one day but his father didn't seem to be worried yet. He was probably right that it was a passing phase.

Later, the adults played whist, and she truly enjoyed their company.

After a nightcap, Race's father and Sarah went up to bed. Anne and Race had been assigned separate rooms, but tactfully no great attention was paid.

Anne wasn't sure what she wanted to do here. She was certainly surprised when Race took her up another flight of stairs to the attic.

"I have a surprise for you," he said, shining his lamp on a number of wooden boxes.

"What's in there?"

"The Racecombe records. No one's looked at them in at least two generations except to dump more boxes on top. Probably no one's looked at them at all after they were put up here."

Anne's mouth dried. "Oh, my. You are ruthless, aren't you, about binding me to you. I think I can bear to marry you, Mr. de Vere, if you promise me many trips back here to explore all this."

He chuckled and kissed her. "You understand me. I will use any weapon to hand."

When they went back downstairs, however, they went to their separate rooms by silent accord. This was his father's house, and it was how his father would want it to be.

Race's valise caught up with him the next morning before they left, which let him change his clothes.

"Where's the rest of your belongings?" his father asked.

"That's it, except for a horse still stabled at Somerford Court."

"That's it!" His father went off to his study and returned with a bundle of bank notes, thrusting them into his hand. "To tide you over. And get yourself some more clothes before you present yourself to the duke and duchess!"

Race pulled a face at the money, but then he put it in his pocket. "There's no time for that, Father, and you know it, and it wouldn't serve. I've been to Lea Park before. They know me as I am."

Mr. de Vere shook his head but waved them off with no further interference.

As they returned south they talked about sleeping arrangements on the road and decided to travel as Mr. and Miss Ramsbottom. There was a rightness to waiting till their wedding. Race wryly said it was like a knight fasting and praying on the night before a court battle.

He also said that the less risk of her being with child the better.

Anne had slept alone in a bed for years. Strange how unnatural it felt after two nights with Race.

As they passed through Hertfordshire, she sent a note to Tris at Nun's Chase alerting him to the new plan and asking him to go to Lea Park to be on hand in case of need. She prayed he was there to receive it. They might need all the help they could get.

Thirty-five

Anne arrived back in Brighton six days and a lifetime after leaving.

Caroline greeted them cheerfully, only expressing surprise that Anne had arrived in a hired chaise rather than sending for Welsford's coach. The situation was so strange that Anne didn't know quite how to open the truth.

She took off her glove to reveal the ring.

"Anne! It's lovely. Ralstone?" But then Caroline looked at Race, her eyes going wide. *"De Vere?"*

Welsford came downstairs smiling, but he caught the atmosphere and the situation quickly.

"The Duchess of Arran will be very displeased," he said. "A word with you, de Vere."

Anne watched Race go with Welsford into the back parlor, longing to go along to protect someone. She listened for blows or breaking furniture. . . .

Caroline linked arms and drew her into the front parlor. "Tell me everything!"

After a moment Anne surrendered and gave her the story she and Race had agreed on. She'd gone to Greenwich and discovered she and Ralstone didn't suit. Race had turned up to ask her to marry him, she'd realized he was her true love, and they had returned here before going to Lea Park.

It felt as if she was leaving out the most important part of her life, but it would be easier for Caroline and Welsford to support them if they didn't know about mayhem and wickedness.

She could hear nothing from the men. They couldn't have fallen into violence at least.

"I don't know how you could have been so confused about things," Caroline said. "With Welsford, I knew."

Anne pulled her mind back. "I knew, too, Caro. But I thought I couldn't marry Race, so I tried to marry other men. Mama is wrong. It isn't solely within our willpower. I know now I can't be happy with anyone else—nor can he. But there are problems."

"An understatement!"

"Other problems." Anne told Caroline about Mr. de Vere's origins and the plan to declare Race illegitimate.

Caroline slumped back in her chair in a pretend faint. "It's better than a play! *The Bastard Heir.*"

"And *The Daring Lady.* I know. But this is real, and I will have my way."

Race and Welsford returned then, not apparently bruised. Welsford was on their side, but not taking it lightly.

"The duchess acted as if *I* was aspiring slightly above my rights."

"That's because she wanted me to marry St. Raven," Caroline said. "It's an obsession of hers."

Anne nodded. "I've asked Tris to meet us at Lea Park. Perhaps he can persuade her that it's out of the question."

"Is there anything we can do to get the duke on our side?" Race asked.

Welsford thought about it. "Perhaps," he said. "Let's settle down and come up with a strategy."

Anne traveled in the chaise with Caroline. Welsford and Race rode alongside. Race had sent for his horse from Somerford Court, and Anne was touched to find that it was his favorite cavalry horse and getting on in years. Horse and man were clearly devoted.

"Joker?" she asked quizzically at a stop, stroking the bay gelding.

"He doesn't have a serious bone in his body. For more demanding moments, I asked St. Raven to get me that horse I rented from the Black Bull."

"Shouldn't you be riding it now, then?"

He smiled. "Probably, but the poor creature has already suffered in the cause. We're not in any hurry today as we head toward our fate." He led her back to the coach. "Onward to the last throw."

Anne's heart began to race as soon as they turned in through the gilded gates of Lea Park. She tried to concentrate on how lovely all the vistas were, on how much she'd always loved being here, but a strangling sort of panic was building.

Her parents couldn't completely prevent her marriage to Race. The days were surely past when daughters were locked up on bread and water and upstart intruders were whipped and thrown off a property.

She hoped.

She did remember one story of a young lady who had apparently been dragged off to Europe and kept in close confinement there to prevent an unsuitable marriage. Surely her parents wouldn't go so far.

They might if they felt they were saving her from disaster.

Welsford would be there.

Tris, she hoped, would be there.

Race would be there, but she wasn't sure how much he could do in this situation.

She looked to Caroline for encouragement, but she was looking rather pale, too.

They drew up under the porte cochere, and servants poured out to take care of luggage and horses. Anne climbed out, legs unsteady, hand clenched on her staff. She was glad of Race's arm as they walked into the west gallery and headed for the center of the house. He seemed completely steady, but he didn't have a joke for her. That was telling.

The first person they saw was Uffham.

He was crossing the hall, two hounds at his heels. "What-ho the sisters!" But then his tone turned frosty. "De Vere. What are you doing here?"

Race inclined his head. "Uffham. Good to see you again."

The duchess swept down the stairs. "Anne, Caroline,

Welsford. Not bad news, I hope?" As an afterthought she nodded at Race. "Mr. de Vere." Her expression cooled. "Come. Into the saloon."

Tris appeared at that moment. Anne sent a prayer of thanks, even if he did roll his eyes at her. As they all filed into the nearby room she resisted the urge to wring her gloved hands.

The duchess turned. "Now, what is going on?" Her gaze rested on Anne and Race, coldly.

Race said, "Your Grace. I have come to ask for Anne's hand in marriage."

Color flared in her mother's cheeks, but it was Uffham who stepped forward and said, "The devil you are!"

"Language, Uffham," snapped the duchess.

Tris moved to Uffham's side. "This is a matter for cool discussion, not dramatics."

"I'll give him dramatics," snarled Uffham, trying to shake off the hand Tris had clamped on his arm. His hounds started to bark.

"Uffham!" snapped the duchess. "Desist. And get rid of those dogs."

While the fuming Uffham obeyed, the duchess addressed Race.

"Mr. de Vere, what possible argument can you put forward in favor of your suit?"

"That I love him, Mama," Anne said, "and he loves me. I have tried to fall in love with a title, but I find I cannot. I certainly have no intention of marrying St. Raven."

"And I," said Tris, "have no intention of marrying Anne, fond though I am of her."

"Then you can marry Alderton," her mother said to her.

"It would be very unfair to him when I love another." Anne ruthlessly used her most powerful weapon. "I'm sorry, but my foot is paining me. I must sit."

Amid a flurry of concern, Race led her to a sofa. Her mother had little choice but to sit, too, and in moments everyone was settled. As she'd hoped, the tension did slacken, even when Uffham returned and sat glowering opposite her.

Anne realized that Welsford was no longer with them,

but that was part of their plan. He'd gone to talk to her father.

She sent up a prayer and peeled off her gloves.

Her mother stared. "You have accepted his ring, Anne?"

"Yes, Mama."

"Without consulting your father?"

"Yes, Mama."

"Is it paste?"

Anne kept her temper. "No, Mama." Time to try the most important throw. "Mr. de Vere is quite rich."

"Race!" said Uffham with a crack of laughter. "He's gammoned you well, Anne."

Anne could sense the tension pulsing out of Race beside her and knew he hated this kind of horse-trading as much as she did. But his voice was calm when he said, "My father is a wealthy man, Uffham, and he has settled five thousand pounds a year on me. The ring was my mother's, who is now dead."

Anne saw her mother's eyes narrow at the amount. It wasn't enormous, but it was respectable. But then she said, "You cannot *buy* a Peckworth, Mr. de Vere." Her cold eyes turned on Anne. "And didn't you travel to visit another gentleman's family? Captain Ralstone? A paltry match, but at least a family we know and a title in due course."

Anne swallowed. "I realized we did not suit, Mama. That was when I knew that Mr. de Vere was the man I *must* marry."

She saw her mother's eyes sharpen, but before she could speak the door opened and her father came in with Welsford.

They all rose.

"What's this, then? Strange goings-on." He frowned around the room, and Anne knew he was put out at being dragged into a messy situation. His decision could go either way, but they'd decided they had to try for his support.

He walked over to his wife. "Put me a chair here, someone."

Race moved another armed, upholstered chair beside her mother's. Her parents were going to look enthroned.

Her father nodded and sat. "Thank you, de Vere."

Was his acknowledgement a good sign? He wouldn't acknowledge a servant.

They all sat. It was like a court, either a royal one or a legal one.

"I assume Welsford has told you about this, Arran?" her mother said.

"Some of it. Whether it's all of it, I don't know. Anne, take off that ring until I give you permission to wear it."

Coloring, Anne obeyed. She passed it to Race, who smiled encouragement at her. He, she realized, had stayed standing. The prisoner in the dock.

"Good for you, Father," said Uffham. "We can't allow this."

"You were happy enough with de Vere's company, Uffham. You brought him here!"

"I bring my valet here. And my grooms."

"You don't bring them to the dinner table!" Anne exploded. "Don't be so insufferable. You *liked* Race."

"Behave with more respect," her father growled, perhaps to both of them. He looked at Race. "Mr. de Vere, I've seen you here apparently as purposeless as my son, and penniless to boot. You'd hardly expect me to give my precious daughter into the care of a man like that, would you?"

Anne wanted to leap to the defense, but she made herself leave it in Race's hands.

"Definitely not, Your Grace. However, may I argue that it was a furlough after seven years of war? Everyone, I think, is entitled to a holiday. And as I informed the duchess, I am no longer penniless. I can take care of Anne as well as you would like, and will do so."

"But what's your *purpose*, man?" her father demanded. "I detest idlers."

A silence settled that crept down Anne's spine like icy water.

"What purpose do any of the men in this room have, Your Grace?" Race asked at last. Anne wondered, hair rising, whether he'd glanced at Uffham. Her brother was turning red. "I could purchase an estate and take care of it. I will do so if it is a condition of your goodwill."

Anne watched her father's eyes narrow, and she

winced. Race was going to drive someone to violence again soon. It wasn't so much his words as his tone.

"You don't *want* to be a gentleman?" her father asked.

"I *am* a gentleman, sir. I have no particular interest in land management, however. My interests are scholarly."

"Scholarly!" guffawed Uffham. "You'll be telling us next you want to take holy orders!"

"Not at all. What I want to do is join Anne in the organization and study of documents here at Lea Park and in other places with a view to writing a book or books about history from the distaff angle."

Silence rang.

Uffham laughed again. "A fine ambition for a man!"

"Many men are scholars, Uffham. I have, I believe, done my manly duty."

Uffham shot to his feet. "I would have been in the army if my father had allowed it!"

"*I* went without my father's permission."

The duke raised his hand, which stopped Uffham from rushing across the room to throttle Race. After a blistering moment, he stalked out of the room, slamming the door behind him so the windows rattled.

Her father stared at de Vere, unreadable. "A general disregard for parental rights and authority, I see." But then he shook his head. "I sometimes wish I'd bought Uffham a pair of colors." He looked at Tris. "What are you doing here, St. Raven?"

Tris stood. "Witness for the defense, sir. Anne asked me to look into the men who were courting her. I'd have warned her off Ralstone if she'd given me the chance."

"Why?" Anne asked.

"He's careless with money and women, and he's been involved in duels."

"To defend a lady's honor."

"Is that what he said? He was defending himself against outraged husbands. Unfortunately he's a crack shot, so they suffered rather than him."

What a fool she'd been. "Thank heavens I changed my mind. You've checked up on Race, then?"

What had Tris discovered? She knew it couldn't be bad or he'd never have arranged that night together, but there could be something. They were going to have to tell her father about his father's origins and the bastardy, but they'd agreed to hold those things back until after they had his approval.

"De Vere's war record is excellent, sir," Tris said, "even if tinged with eccentricity. I think the field of war must be a reliable place to judge a man, and I found out nothing from his fellow officers to suggest that de Vere would not be a good husband."

With a slight smile he added, "My personal experience is that he is a man of courage and honor. I say, let them marry."

"This is not an election, St. Raven," said Anne's mother. "I have no doubt that Mr. de Vere is an admirable man. I have thought him so when he was here with Uffham. He was a good influence. None of that, however, makes him suitable as a husband for one of my daughters!"

"Then what does, Your Grace?" said Welsford, also rising. "Surely at the end it is the nature of the man not his rank that matters most to a mother's heart."

Anne gulped, watching her mother's frozen face.

"A girl who puts her mind to it can find a man who is both good and of similar rank, Welsford. Like should marry like!"

"But there are," said Race, "different qualities to consider. With respect, Duchess, Anne and I are like in all the ways that matter. I know you worry particularly about Anne because of her handicap. Perhaps you might consider that, with your blessing, we would choose to live close to Lea Park in order to pursue our work. You will be sure of her comfort and happiness."

Anne sucked in a breath. This was their last major throw.

"I have no estate," Race continued, "and no expectation of inheriting one. The income my father has settled on me is in lieu of my interest in his property. Anne has mentioned a place called Quoyne House."

"Quoyne House, eh?" said her father, looking at her. "Seems that you've thought about this quite a bit, Anne. I have to say that I'd like to have you close." Then he glared at Race. "You know what this means, sir. One moment of unhappiness, and I'll have your skin!"

"No, you wouldn't, sir." After a heart-stopping moment, he added, "I would have flayed myself first."

Anne saw her father's lips twitch and had trouble not whooping. They'd won. Surely they'd won!

"Arran!" her mother protested.

But her father cut her off. "You know our daughter, my dear. For all her sweetness and frailty, she has always had a mind of her own. Seems she's settled on this man, and he has a solid head on his shoulders. Better to let them wed and have her under our eye than have them running off somewhere."

"No daughter of mine would ever do such a thing," said the duchess with such fervor that Anne gave thanks that they'd changed their plans. Her parents would have accepted a clandestine marriage in the end, but they would have been terribly hurt.

She rose and went over to take her father's hand. "We have your blessing, Papa?"

He tried to glower, but it wasn't convincing. "Aye, you have your way as usual. I've not missed that fact over the years. De Vere!" he barked.

Race came over to stand beside her.

"You can give her the ring now."

Race slid the ring back on her finger and then raised her hand to kiss it—in the way of a man who knows how to please a woman.

Then he laughed. "Don't cry, Anne. Your father will skin me alive!"

She laughed with him, wiping away her tears. She kissed her father, and then her mother. The duchess was stiff for a moment, but then she hugged her back. "I only want the best for you all," she said.

"I know, Mama, and I love you for it. I will be happy with Race, though. And," she added, "in due course I will be here to wrap blankets around you and Papa and feed you gruel. You really cannot depend on Uffham marrying the right kind of wife for that."

The duchess laughed, but almost with despair. "Uffham, poor Uffham. I don't know what we are to do with him."

"As to that," said the duke, "Welsford pointed out that with de Vere in the family we might have a better chance of keeping him on sensible ground. Once he gets over his tiff, that is."

Anne saw Race cast Welsford a baleful look, but he didn't protest except to say, "I expect to spend most of my time quietly here with Anne, sir, but if I can help in any way, I will. Uffham is not unsound. He might benefit from employment. Perhaps a small estate of his own. . . ."

Anne made herself not react to that clever move. If Uffham had an estate of his own he'd be at Lea Park even less, and it might serve to make her brother grow up.

The room suddenly drifted into male and female. Anne said to her mother, "I would like to marry soon, Mama."

Her mother gave her a piercing look, so she hurried on, "So that Marianne can marry Percy. At the same time perhaps."

Her mother huffed out a breath. "Oh, I suppose so. He does seem to be coming along a little better. And there is always Eliza," she added, looking over at Tris.

Anne made a note to warn Tris. If he was wise, he would be married by the time Eliza left the schoolroom. And perhaps after all this the youngest Peckworth daughter would have an easier time of it.

Marianne was summoned and told, and promptly burst into torrents of tears. When she recovered, a wedding day two weeks away was settled on, and the duchess left to demand her secretary and start to make arrangements.

Race was taken away by her father for discussion of marriage settlements. This was the time they'd decided would be best for the final revelations, so Anne waited on tenterhooks, letting Caroline and Marianne chatter about wedding outfits and attendants.

It was still possible that her father would rescind his approval.

At last, however, Race appeared, smiling. She went to him. "It's all right?"

"Yes."

By silent accord, they escaped into the vastness of the great house, seeking privacy but propriety. They ended up on a window seat in the portrait gallery, chaperoned by ranks of Anne's haughty ancestors.

"Was he very angry?" she asked, drawn irresistibly against Race as she remembered being in a theater box at Drury Lane so very long ago.

This time they could kiss, but he eased away to say, "It was touch and go, but as you predicted, once committed, he didn't back down. I think he does truly like me, which helped."

Despite their decision to behave, his hands moved on her in the way that was already familiar, in the same way hers moved on him. Caring, marking, *mine.*

"And of course," he went on, eyes dark on hers, "part of the bargain is that I do my best to stop Uffham falling into serious folly while he grows up."

"He's the same age as you."

"And I might be as foolish as he is if I'd stayed at home. To keep my word, I'll have to spend more time away from here than I wish, love, but it will be as little as possible. Especially if you do that. . . ."

She had somehow ended up on his lap and was nibbling his ear, which she'd discovered had interesting effects on him.

He moved her back onto the window seat, capturing her hands, holding her away. "Pay attention. We're to have Quoyne for a wedding gift. Just the house. I said we had no interest in the tenant farms attached to it. I hope that's true."

"Perfectly true." She turned her hands and brought his scarred one to her lips, inhaling this precious new certainty. "We have heaven, don't we?"

"For all our days . . ."

She knew the same hunger rose in him as in her, but they had decided to wait. She stood and pulled him to his feet. "What now? We could go and look at Quoyne House. It's empty."

"Or you could show me your papers." His fingers wove with hers. "Papers or home? Home or papers?"

She couldn't stand it. "Or our other delight . . ."

"Wicked wench. No, we wait. Show me the library."

"Willpower!" she complained, but she guided him through her home to her special room. She found the key and opened the door. "With all my worldly papers, love, I thee endow."

Seen with objective eyes, it was a simple space, however, with one small window and lined with shelves and drawers. As with her naked body in the cottage attic, she had a moment's fear that this—her gossip and laundry lists—would be inadequate.

But he looked around with a grin. "I do so love an orderly woman."

She leaned back against some shelves, watching his delight with delight.

He trailed his fingers along a line of boxes, then took one down—an unlabeled one, one with papers yet to be read. It was exactly what she would have done.

He looked in it, and suddenly laughed with delight.

"I think my female ancestors are going to be competition," she said.

He glanced across at her, and the look in his eyes was all the contradiction she needed. "My laughter, love, was because of what's on top here. Come and see."

She limped over and took the faded, fly-spotted leaflet he handed her.

"A Warning to the Ladies and Gentlemen of this Fair Land of the Wicked Ruin that comes from the Game that Goes By The Name Hazard."

She laughed, too. "Wicked ruin, indeed."

"Speaking of Hazard . . ." He dug in his breeches' pocket, pulled something out, and put it in her hand—something small, thin, and hard.

Anne looked. It was an ivory gaming counter. "From Benning House? And I threw mine away! Along with the straw heart."

"The what?"

She realized that he couldn't know about that.

"That was before you came on stage." She blinked away tears, tears of happiness, tears of relief over what might have been.

"Let me tell you a tale," she said, taking his hand. "Once upon a time, long long ago, a princess was imprisoned behind walls of power, sadly weaving a heart out of straw. . . ."

Author's Note

I hope you have enjoyed the story of Race de Vere and Lady Anne. Most of Race's problem came from something that was a surprise to me. I gave him the name de Vere carelessly.

I knew the de Vere title had died out for lack of male heirs, but I hadn't realized that the situation was quite as sweeping as it was until enlightened by fellow author Margaret Evans Porter. (Thank you, Margaret.)

The de Vere name was ancient and important, and anyone bearing it legitimately would probably have a claim on the title of Earl of Oxford. In Regency England, anyone claiming to be a de Vere would be instantly suspect.

What a turn of the screw on my poor hero. I thought he was minor gentry, but when I probed into his name, I realized that it had to be worse than that. Once I realized that his father had won a lottery (I've always wanted to use a lottery in a book because they were very popular at the time), the legitimacy of Thomas de Vere's first marriage was in question.

All quite delicious, really!

Race first appeared in *The Dragon's Bride,* which is the story of Con Somerford and Susan Kerslake. The exciting events Race missed while in Devon occur in *The Devil's Heiress*. These books can all be read separately, but there are links. As you might have guessed, the next novel will be about the intriguing Duke of St. Raven. When he was off playing the highwayman that night, he had an interesting encounter.

As he says to a young lady in involuntary residence at Nun's Chase:

"It seems to be my night for knight errantry."
"You've found another damsel in distress?"
His lips twitched. "After a fashion."
"This house must be becoming rather crowded."
"Oh, I stashed her in one of my other residences. Now, your story, Miss Whoever-you-are."

I don't have a title for this yet, but look for it in early 2003.

As for the dice game Hazard, it is the precursor of the modern game of craps. I hope I gave you enough to understand the action in Hazard. If you wish to know more, please visit my Web site below, where I have posted more information and also some links.

Dice have other uses, and have often been used for divination—for fortune-telling. If you want a little fun, try the following, which I have adapted from a Victorian fortune-telling book.

The Daily Oracle: using one die for daily wisdom.

Roll the die fairly and read the oracle's advice for the day.

1. Be open. You will meet someone of significance.
2. An act of kindness will bring an unexpected reward.
3. Be wary. There is a trap laid before you.
4. Someone in your family needs you.
5. Do not speak hastily. If you do, you will rue it.
6. Guard yourself around the one who smiles the most.

I have more forms of divination by dice on my Web page.

Here is a list of my other novels in print. You should be able to get any of these at your favorite bookstore. If they do not have a book, they can order it for you at no extra cost.

An Arranged Marriage (Regency. Company of Rogues.)
An Unwilling Bride (Regency. Company of Rogues.)
Christmas Angel (Regency. Company of Rogues.)
Devilish (Georgian. The Mallorens.)
Forbidden Magic (Regency.)
Lord of Midnight (Medieval.)
Secrets of the Night (Georgian. The Mallorens.)
Something Wicked (Georgian. The Mallorens.)
The Devil's Heiress (Regency. Company of Rogues. The Georges.)
The Dragon's Bride (Regency. Company of Rogues. The Georges.)

The excellent news is that the two other Malloren books will be reissued this year. *My Lady Notorious* will be out in July 2002, and *Tempting Fortune* in December. Soon the whole series will be in print.

I enjoy hearing from my readers. You can e-mail me at jobev@poboxes.com, or mail me c/o The Rotrosen Agency, 318 East 51st Street, New York, NY 10022. I appreciate a SASE if you would like a reply. My Web site is: www.poboxes.com/jobev

Dear Reader:

I hope you've enjoyed reading this adventure of the Company of Rogues.

I love these men, and I've had fun writing about them over the past thirty years. (Yes, really! My first Rogues novel was the first book I ever finished. It just took a while to get it right and sell it.)

The adventure started for them when they were schoolboys at Harrow. Boys' schools were rough places in those days and an enterprising lad called Nicholas Delaney gathered a group for mutual support—one for all and all for one—forging a bond that lasted into adulthood.

They're a mixed bunch because Nicholas chose the outsiders, the unusual, and the ones who needed protection most. For example, we have Miles Cavanagh, an Irish rebel, and Lucien de Vaux, Marquess of Arden, haughty heir to a dukedom. Leander Knollis was the suave son of a diplomat, who scarcely knew England at all, and quiet Francis Haile, Viscount Middlethrope, arrived at school grieving his recently dead father. Despite their variety, the Rogues are consistent in honor. Whatever their natures, they serve their country in Parliament, on the battlefield, or by tending the land, because that's what heroes do.

For me as an author, their differences have been a joy, because each Rogue has fallen into a different kind of adventure. Or perhaps I should say, they have run into a different kind of woman, seemingly designed to test their limits. A tempestuous ward. A Regency-era feminist. A woman trained in the erotic arts. A poet's widow who's fed up with being seen as the perfect "angel bride." (Want to guess which Rogue above gets which?)

All things come to an end, however, and they are nearly all settled in matrimony. *The Rogue's Return*, on sale in March 2006, will be followed by Lord Darius Debenham's story in 2007, completing the series.

However, there will be books about friends and relatives, all in the same "world." The Company of Rogues series (including some spin-offs*) is as follows: *An Arranged Marriage* (Nicholas), *An Unwilling Bride* (Lucien), *Christmas Angel* (Leander), *Forbidden* (Francis), *Dangerous Joy* (Miles), *The Dragon's Bride* (Con), *The Devil's Heiress**, *Hazard**, *St. Raven**, *Skylark* (Stephen), *The Rogue's Return* (Simon).

I hope you enjoy them all.

All best wishes,
Jo

DON'T MISS THE OTHER
PASSIONATE HISTORICAL ROMANCES
IN JO BEVERLEY'S
COMPANY OF ROGUES SERIES

The Dragon's Bride

Con Somerford, the new Earl of Wyvern, arrives at his fortress on the cliffs of Devon to find a woman from his past waiting for him—pistol in hand. Once, he and Susan Kerslake shared a magic that was destroyed by youthful arrogance and innocence. Can time teach them both to surrender to the desire that comes along only once—or twice—in a lifetime?

"Vintage Jo Beverley. Fast pacing, strong characters, sensuality, and a poignant love story make this a tale to cherish time and time again."

—*Romantic Times* (Top Pick)

"For those who enjoy a Regency setting and an intelligent, sensual plot, *The Dragon's Bride* is a must read."

—*Affaire de Coeur*

The Devil's Heiress

Clarissa Greystone is called the Devil's Heiress. Burdened with the wealth of a man she despised, she is a fortune hunter's dream. And no one needs that fortune more than Major George Hawkinville. But how will he ignore the hunger in his heart when Clarissa boldly steps into his trap?

"[A] deftly woven tale of romantic intrigue. . . . Head and shoulders above the usual Regency fare, this novel's sensitive prose, charismatic characters, and expert plotting will keep readers enthralled from first page to last."
—*Publishers Weekly*

"With her talent for writing powerful love stories and masterful plotting, Ms. Beverley cleverly brings together this dynamic duo. Her latest captivating romance . . . is easily a 'keeper'!" —*Romantic Times* (Top Pick)

St. Raven

Cressida Mandeville agrees to Lord Crofton's vile proposal, but secretly she has other plans. She will trick the loathsome man, find her father's hidden wealth, and save the family from ruin. All goes well, until a daring highwayman, Tristan Tregallows, Duke of St. Raven, stops their carriage, whirls Cressida up onto his dark horse, and demands a kiss. When St. Raven discovers Cressida is on a quest, he knows he must become her partner and protector. But he doesn't expect the dangers to his heart.

"Beverley's delicious, well-crafted, and wickedly captivating romance is a surefire winner." —*Romantic Times*

"A well-crafted story and an ultimately very satisfying romance." —*The Romance Reader*

Skylark

Once she was Mrs. Hal Gardeyne, the darling Lady Skylark of London society, but now she's a terrified mother. Hal's death has made young Harry heir to her father-in-law's title and estates, and she fears Harry's uncle wants those prizes enough to commit murder. Then a mysterious letter that could change everything arrives. Is there a long-lost heir to the Caldford estate? Laura must uncover the answers even if it means turning to Sir Stephen Ball—a man whose heart she broke years before. Together, Stephen and Laura must discover the truth despite the dangerous obstacles in their path. Will they be able to overcome their enemies before the passion that has reignited between them sweeps them both away?

"Beverley is a master who sets the tone for a wickedly sensual romance." —*Romantic Times*

"The story is told with charm and wit, with narrative limited to the pertinent, and plenty of lively and meaningful dialogue." —Romance Reviews Today

COMING IN MARCH 2006

The Rogue's Return

After years living in the New World of Canada, Simon St. Bride is ready to return to aristocratic life in England. But his plans are delayed by a duel and a young woman he feels honor bound to marry, even though his family is unlikely to welcome her. And despite her seeming innocence, Jane Otterburn is hesitant to speak of her enigmatic past. Then treachery strikes their world. As Simon and Jane fight side by side against enemies and fate—on land and sea—he discovers a wife beyond price and a passion beyond measure. But will the truth about Jane tear their love asunder?

"Wickedly, wonderfully sensual and gloriously romantic."
—Mary Balogh

"A delicious...sensual delight."
—Teresa Medeiros

"One of romance's brightest and most dazzling stars."
—*Affaire de Coeur*